Frequently Asked Questions

Volume 1

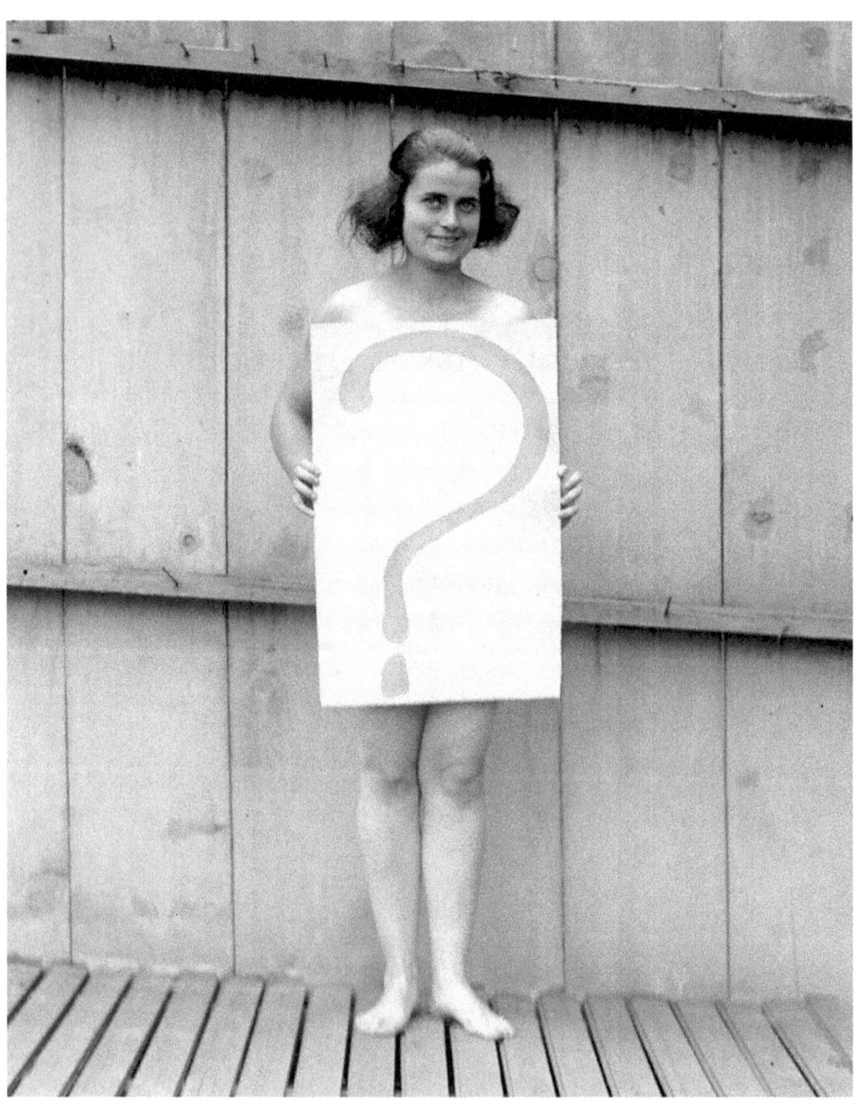

An unclothed woman in Washington, D.C., standing behind a "?" sign.

National Photo Company, 1922 (Library of Congress)

A **question** mark is apropos
When there are things you want to know.

Elsa Knight Bruno, Punctuation Celebration

I will Catechize the world for him; that is, make **Questions** and by them answer.

William Shakespeare, Othello

Let N(Q) be the number of **questions**.

*Jun Harada, Masao Fuketa, El-Sayed Atlam, Toru Sumitomo, Wataru Hiraishi and Jun-ichi Aoe, Estimation of **FAQ** Knowledge Bases by Introducing Measurements (Knowledge-Based Intelligent Information and Engineering Systems)*

Foley approached the Roadrunner from the left rear. Moran approached from the right rear.

Foley brought the shotgun out from under his raincoat. He lifted it slowly to the level of the windowsill of the Roadrunner and silently rested it there.

Moran stepped back two paces from the Roadrunner. He tucked the stock of the shotgun in at his waist with his right elbow. With his left hand he gripped the pump action. He brought the muzzle up to point at the window.

Jackie Brown, with his eyes closed, recovered from a long night of driving, and many frustrations.

Foley knocked on the window of the Roadrunner. Lazily, Jackie Brown turned his head. He opened his left eye. His gaze focused on the face of a stranger. "Yeah?" he said.

Foley made a cranking motion with his left hand.

Jackie Brown shook his head. He reached forward and rolled the window down. "Yeah?" he said again.

"United States Treasury," Foley said. "You're under arrest. Come out slow and easy and keep your hands in plain sight. One move and you're a dead fucking man." He brought the shotgun up with his right hand. He brought his left hand under the pump and held it steady.

"Holy shit," Jackie Brown said. He looked to his right. Moran stood there, pointing a shotgun through the window. In front of the Roadrunner, two men advanced with revolvers pointed at him through the windshield. "Hey," he said.

"Get out of the car," Foley said. He reached in and lifted the door lock. He opened the door from the outside. "Get out." The shotgun remained leveled at Jackie Brown's head.

"Hey," Jackie Brown said, swinging his legs out of the car. "Hey, look."

Foley grabbed him as he got out. Foley turned him around. "Put your hands on the roof of the car," Foley said. "Move your feet back."

Jackie Brown did as he was told. He felt hands begin to pat him down. "What the fuck's this all about?" he said.

Moran, Sauter and Ferris now came around the Roadrunner and stood together with their weapons pointing at Jackie Brown. Ames and Morrissey stayed put. Moran handed his shot-gun to Sauter, who let the hammer down on his Chief's Special and leveled Moran's shotgun. Moran removed his wallet from his hip pocket. He extracted a plasticized card from the wallet. In the blue-tinged glare of the parking lot lights, he began to read:

"'You are under arrest for violation of a federal law. Before we ask you any **questions**, we want you to understand your rights under the Constitution of the United States.'"

"I know my rights," Jackie Brown said.

"Shut the fuck up and listen," Foley said. "Shut your god-damned mouth and listen to what the man's telling you."

"'You do not have to answer any **questions**,'" Moran said. "'You have a right to remain silent. If you answer any **questions**, your answers may be used in evidence against you in a trial in a court of law. Do you understand what I have read to you?'"

"Of course I understand," Jackie Brown said. "You think I'm a fucking idiot?"

"Shut up," Foley said, "and hold still or I'll blow your fucking head off." He rested the barrel of the Remington on Jackie Brown's shoulder. The muzzle grazed the base of Jackie Brown's skull.

"'You are entitled to the advice of counsel,'" Moran said. "'Do you have a lawyer?'"

"No, for Christ sake," Jackie Brown said. "Of course I don't. I just got arrested."

"'If you want a lawyer,'" Moran said, "'you need only say so, and you will be given time to engage a lawyer, and to confer with him. You are entitled to confer with your lawyer before you decide whether to answer any **questions**. Do you understand what I have read to you?'"

Jackie Brown did not answer. Foley jabbed him with the muzzle of the Remington. "Tell him," he said.

"Of course I understand," Jackie Brown said.

"'If you can't afford a lawyer,'" Moran said, "'the court will appoint one for you. Do you understand that?'"

"Yes," Jackie Brown said.

"'You may, if you wish, waive these rights and answer our **questions**. Are you willing to answer **questions**?'" Moran said.

George V. Higgins, The Friends of Eddie Coyle

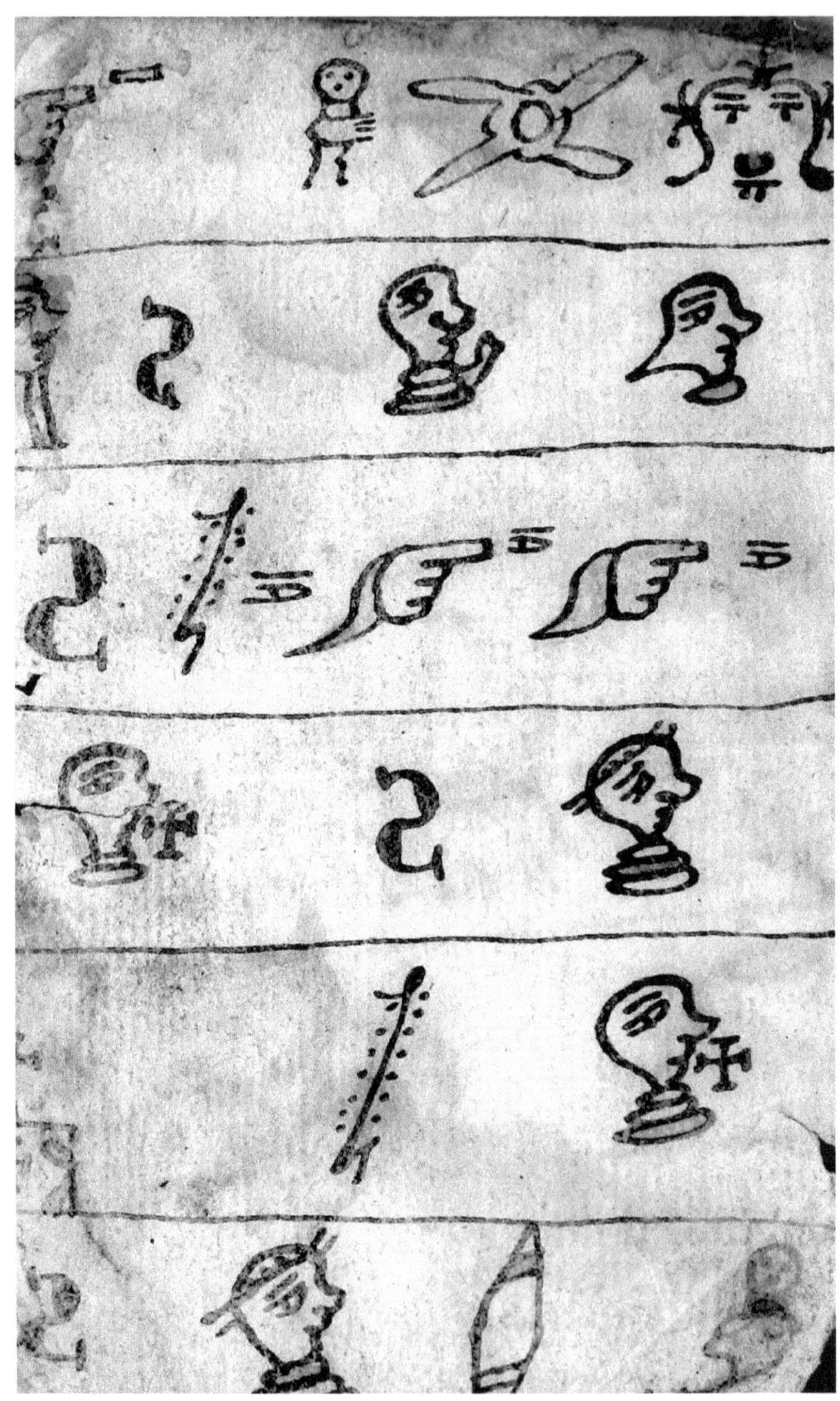

Testerian Catechism, Mexico, 18th century (John Carter Brown Library)

Rob Kovitz

Frequently Asked Questions

Volume 1

Treyf Books
Keep Refrigerated

Frequently Asked **Questions**
Volume 1
© 2024 by Rob Kovitz
All rights reserved

Published in Canada by Treyf Books
www.treyf.com
keeprefrigerated@treyf.com

Volume 1 ISBN 978-1-927923-18-4 (pbk)
Volume 2 ISBN 978-1-927923-19-1 (pbk)

Various excerpts from *Frequently Asked Questions*
were first published in *Geist Magazine*.

Financial assistance for the creation and production of
Frequently Asked Questions provided by the
Canada Council for the Arts, Manitoba Arts Council,
and the Winnipeg Arts Council.

10 9 8 7 6 5 4 3 2 1

Front and back cover:
*Grenville Kleiser, Fifteen Thousand Useful Phrases: A Practical Handbook of
Pertinent Expressions, Striking Similes, Literary, Commercial, Conversational,
and Oratorical Terms, for the Embellishment of Speech and Literature, and
the Improvement of the Vocabulary of Those Persons Who Read, Write,
and Speak English (New York: Funk and Wagnalls Company, 1919)*

Front and back flyleaf:
Testerian Catechism (detail), Mexico, 18th century (John Carter Brown Library)

Dedication

He's got the inclination and the dedication—the **question** is whether he can develop the skills.

Lyn Gardner, Stephen Skrynka: 'This Is Not Some Jackass Stunt' (The Guardian)

He always prepared to play and prepared to battle. He's a poster kid for dedication, there's no **question**. He's paid his dues.

Allan Kreda, Islanders Coach Is Tough on Himself and His Team (The New York Times)

While they might admire my dedication, they might also **question** my reasons for doing such a thing.

Deborah Treisman, This Week in Fiction: Will Mackin (The New Yorker)

*Harry Revier (director), Life's Greatest **Question**, 1921 (Exhibitors Herald)*

Copyright & Fair Use **Frequently Asked Questions**

It is an infringement of copyright to do, without permission from the copyright owner, any act that only the owner is entitled to do.

University of Toronto Libraries, Copyright Basics and **FAQ**

IMPORTANT NOTICE

The following is a general **Q**/A format presentation of what many experts regard as a nuanced and complex legal subject matter area. In addition, it is one in which advice will vary depending on the specific facts involved in each **question** or matter. Seemingly slight factual variations can alter the analysis and outcome of a given **question** or scenario. Therefore, it is very important to consult with counsel before taking any action in this area, and to not rely exclusively on the information contained in this **Q**/A. Nothing contained on this site or its related links may be construed as legal advice from the OVPGC on a given matter. Members of the IU community should consult the OVPGC directly on specific legal issues or matters.

Indiana University, Copyright & Fair Use **Frequently Asked Questions**

What can I reproduce from a copyrighted work without permission? (or: What is Fair Use?)

Although you generally cannot put an entire copyrighted work on the Web without permission, you can make limited use of copyrighted material.

In most countries, people are allowed to make limited use of such works in their own writings, or copy the work to a limited extent, for purposes that include commentary, criticism, education, research, and news reporting. This right is known as "fair use" in the United States, and as "fair dealing" in many other countries.

Here's a brief explanation of fair use in the United States, which I've largely lifted from a PDF form letter (FL 102) sent out by the US Copyright Office. (The original form letter, as a government publication, is in the public domain. The Copyright Office is not responsible for the changes I've made here.)

John Mark Ockerbloom, The Online Books Page **Frequently Asked Questions**

Isn't fair use pretty vague? I need to have clear guidelines, not just for me, but for my staff.

The law codifying fair use was designed to be broad and flexible, and judges usually understand that. Fair use will apply differently to different users in different situations. That may seem frustrating, but it can also be liberating, especially for communities that have a code of best practices. It means that fair use law, as it evolves, may be responsive to a profession's norms and conditions. The Code's principles and limitations are grounded in the particular practices of the visual arts professions and values, and tailored to key practice contexts. So, although fair use determinations need to be made on a case-by-case basis, some cases come up all the time; decisions based on reason can be applied to the same kind of situation ever more quickly as you and your staff become comfortable with the process.

*College Art Association, Code of Best Practices in Fair Use for the Visual Arts > **Frequently Asked Questions***

What are the maximum criminal penalties for copyright infringement?

In the U.S., penalties for criminal copyright infringement can include fines up to $250,000 and/or imprisonment of up to five years.

Other countries have territory specific penalties.

Symantec, Anti-Piracy **Frequently Asked Questions**

*Harry Revier (director), Life's Greatest **Question**, 1921 (Exhibitors Herald)*

Contents

Contents

Volume 2

Final Exam
Answer Sheet

Please follow the directions on the exam question sheet. Fill in the entire circle that corresponds to your answer for each question on the exam. Erase marks completely to make a change.

Charles Brown

Teacher ID

12345

Student ID

1 Ⓐ Ⓑ Ⓒ Ⓓ Ⓔ	26 Ⓐ Ⓑ Ⓒ Ⓓ Ⓔ	51 Ⓐ Ⓑ Ⓒ Ⓓ Ⓔ	76 Ⓐ Ⓑ Ⓒ Ⓓ Ⓔ
2 Ⓐ Ⓑ Ⓒ Ⓓ Ⓔ	27 Ⓐ Ⓑ Ⓒ Ⓓ Ⓔ	52 Ⓐ Ⓑ Ⓒ Ⓓ Ⓔ	77 Ⓐ Ⓑ Ⓒ Ⓓ Ⓔ
3 Ⓐ Ⓑ Ⓒ Ⓓ Ⓔ	28 Ⓐ Ⓑ Ⓒ Ⓓ Ⓔ	53 Ⓐ Ⓑ Ⓒ Ⓓ Ⓔ	78 Ⓐ Ⓑ Ⓒ Ⓓ Ⓔ
4 Ⓐ Ⓑ Ⓒ Ⓓ Ⓔ	29 Ⓐ Ⓑ Ⓒ Ⓓ Ⓔ	54 Ⓐ Ⓑ Ⓒ Ⓓ Ⓔ	79 Ⓐ Ⓑ Ⓒ Ⓓ Ⓔ
5 Ⓐ Ⓑ Ⓒ Ⓓ Ⓔ	30 Ⓐ Ⓑ Ⓒ Ⓓ Ⓔ	55 Ⓐ Ⓑ Ⓒ Ⓓ Ⓔ	80 Ⓐ Ⓑ Ⓒ Ⓓ Ⓔ
6 Ⓐ Ⓑ Ⓒ Ⓓ Ⓔ	31 Ⓐ Ⓑ Ⓒ Ⓓ Ⓔ	56 Ⓐ Ⓑ Ⓒ Ⓓ Ⓔ	81 Ⓐ Ⓑ Ⓒ Ⓓ Ⓔ
7 Ⓐ Ⓑ Ⓒ Ⓓ Ⓔ	32 Ⓐ Ⓑ Ⓒ Ⓓ Ⓔ	57 Ⓐ Ⓑ Ⓒ Ⓓ Ⓔ	82 Ⓐ Ⓑ Ⓒ Ⓓ Ⓔ
8 Ⓐ Ⓑ Ⓒ Ⓓ Ⓔ	33 Ⓐ Ⓑ Ⓒ Ⓓ Ⓔ	58 Ⓐ Ⓑ Ⓒ Ⓓ Ⓔ	83 Ⓐ Ⓑ Ⓒ Ⓓ Ⓔ
9 Ⓐ Ⓑ Ⓒ Ⓓ Ⓔ	34 Ⓐ Ⓑ Ⓒ Ⓓ Ⓔ	59 Ⓐ Ⓑ Ⓒ Ⓓ Ⓔ	84 Ⓐ Ⓑ Ⓒ Ⓓ Ⓔ
10 Ⓐ Ⓑ Ⓒ Ⓓ Ⓔ	35 Ⓐ Ⓑ Ⓒ Ⓓ Ⓔ	60 Ⓐ Ⓑ Ⓒ Ⓓ Ⓔ	85 Ⓐ Ⓑ Ⓒ Ⓓ Ⓔ
11 Ⓐ Ⓑ Ⓒ Ⓓ Ⓔ	36 Ⓐ Ⓑ Ⓒ Ⓓ Ⓔ	61 Ⓐ Ⓑ Ⓒ Ⓓ Ⓔ	86 Ⓐ Ⓑ Ⓒ Ⓓ Ⓔ
12 Ⓐ Ⓑ Ⓒ Ⓓ Ⓔ	37 Ⓐ Ⓑ Ⓒ Ⓓ Ⓔ	62 Ⓐ Ⓑ Ⓒ Ⓓ Ⓔ	87 Ⓐ Ⓑ Ⓒ Ⓓ Ⓔ
13 Ⓐ Ⓑ Ⓒ Ⓓ Ⓔ	38 Ⓐ Ⓑ Ⓒ Ⓓ Ⓔ	63 Ⓐ Ⓑ Ⓒ Ⓓ Ⓔ	88 Ⓐ Ⓑ Ⓒ Ⓓ Ⓔ
14 Ⓐ Ⓑ Ⓒ Ⓓ Ⓔ	39 Ⓐ Ⓑ Ⓒ Ⓓ Ⓔ	64 Ⓐ Ⓑ Ⓒ Ⓓ Ⓔ	89 Ⓐ Ⓑ Ⓒ Ⓓ Ⓔ
15 Ⓐ Ⓑ Ⓒ Ⓓ Ⓔ	40 Ⓐ Ⓑ Ⓒ Ⓓ Ⓔ	65 Ⓐ Ⓑ Ⓒ Ⓓ Ⓔ	90 Ⓐ Ⓑ Ⓒ Ⓓ Ⓔ
16 Ⓐ Ⓑ Ⓒ Ⓓ Ⓔ	41 Ⓐ Ⓑ Ⓒ Ⓓ Ⓔ	66 Ⓐ Ⓑ Ⓒ Ⓓ Ⓔ	91 Ⓐ Ⓑ Ⓒ Ⓓ Ⓔ
17 Ⓐ Ⓑ Ⓒ Ⓓ Ⓔ	42 Ⓐ Ⓑ Ⓒ Ⓓ Ⓔ	67 Ⓐ Ⓑ Ⓒ Ⓓ Ⓔ	92 Ⓐ Ⓑ Ⓒ Ⓓ Ⓔ
18 Ⓐ Ⓑ Ⓒ Ⓓ Ⓔ	43 Ⓐ Ⓑ Ⓒ Ⓓ Ⓔ	68 Ⓐ Ⓑ Ⓒ Ⓓ Ⓔ	93 Ⓐ Ⓑ Ⓒ Ⓓ Ⓔ
19 Ⓐ Ⓑ Ⓒ Ⓓ Ⓔ	44 Ⓐ Ⓑ Ⓒ Ⓓ Ⓔ	69 Ⓐ Ⓑ Ⓒ Ⓓ Ⓔ	94 Ⓐ Ⓑ Ⓒ Ⓓ Ⓔ
20 Ⓐ Ⓑ Ⓒ Ⓓ Ⓔ	45 Ⓐ Ⓑ Ⓒ Ⓓ Ⓔ	70 Ⓐ Ⓑ Ⓒ Ⓓ Ⓔ	95 Ⓐ Ⓑ Ⓒ Ⓓ Ⓔ
21 Ⓐ Ⓑ Ⓒ Ⓓ Ⓔ	46 Ⓐ Ⓑ Ⓒ Ⓓ Ⓔ	71 Ⓐ Ⓑ Ⓒ Ⓓ Ⓔ	96 Ⓐ Ⓑ Ⓒ Ⓓ Ⓔ
22 Ⓐ Ⓑ Ⓒ Ⓓ Ⓔ	47 Ⓐ Ⓑ Ⓒ Ⓓ Ⓔ	72 Ⓐ Ⓑ Ⓒ Ⓓ Ⓔ	97 Ⓐ Ⓑ Ⓒ Ⓓ Ⓔ
23 Ⓐ Ⓑ Ⓒ Ⓓ Ⓔ	48 Ⓐ Ⓑ Ⓒ Ⓓ Ⓔ	73 Ⓐ Ⓑ Ⓒ Ⓓ Ⓔ	98 Ⓐ Ⓑ Ⓒ Ⓓ Ⓔ
24 Ⓐ Ⓑ Ⓒ Ⓓ Ⓔ	49 Ⓐ Ⓑ Ⓒ Ⓓ Ⓔ	74 Ⓐ Ⓑ Ⓒ Ⓓ Ⓔ	99 Ⓐ Ⓑ Ⓒ Ⓓ Ⓔ
25 Ⓐ Ⓑ Ⓒ Ⓓ Ⓔ	50 Ⓐ Ⓑ Ⓒ Ⓓ Ⓔ	75 Ⓐ Ⓑ Ⓒ Ⓓ Ⓔ	100 Ⓐ Ⓑ Ⓒ Ⓓ Ⓔ

Please turn sheet over to complete: ⟹

Afghan Uniformed Police **question** suspected Taliban, Jan. 7, in Ghazni, Afghanistan.

Photo by Sgt. Justin Howe / U.S. Army (defenseimagery.mil)

A Couple of **Questions**

*There are so many people asking **questions***

"Hello there, young man, do you mind if we ask you a couple of **questions**?"
"Okay."

Libby Hughes, Serious Fun With White House Secrets and State Department Antics

"I'm DS Clarke, this is DI Rebus," Siobhan said. "Mind if we ask you a couple of **questions**?"

*Ian Rankin, A **Question** of Blood*

Just then, police chief Ethan Rodgers and sheriff Hal Benson walked into the waiting room. They headed straight for Cate and Rand.

"Morning," the chief said. "Mind if we ask you a couple of **questions**?"

Cate looked from one newcomer to the other, then to Rand and finally back to the chief. "You mean me?"

Ginny Aiken, Someone to Trust

There are so many people asking **questions**
everywhere.
There is the bloody blindman, and the angry one, and the
disheartened one,
and the wretch, the thorn tree,
the bandit with envy on his back.

Pablo Neruda, Ode to Federico Garcia Lorca (Residence on Earth)

Catechism of Coal is intended for that great number of intelligent readers who have no technical training, and yet who prefer to seek knowledge by reading special subjects rather than fiction. A large proportion of these have neither the time nor the inclination to peruse the voluminous geological and statistical reports of the coal industry in the United States, or to study the ponderous volumes of gathered wisdom by technical experts. Their time is usually fully occupied with the cares of business and often with the fatigue of manual labor, and their hours for quiet reading or study are few and most precious. For these, the following plain **questions** and direct authoritative answers have been designed with a realizing sense of the readers' wants and aspirations. The task conscientiously assumed by the writer has been to verify all the answers by referring to competent authorities.

William Jasper Nicolls, Coal Catechism

I was **questioned** several times immediately after my arrest. But they were all formal examinations, as to my identity and so forth. At the first of these, which took place at the police station, nobody seemed to have much interest in the case. However, when I was brought before the examining magistrate a week later, I noticed that he eyed me with distinct curiosity. Like the others, he began by asking my name, address, and occupation, the date and place of my birth. Then he inquired if I had chosen a lawyer to defend me. I answered, "No," I hadn't thought about it, and asked him if it was really necessary for me to have one.

"Why do you ask that?" he said.

Albert Camus, The Stranger

NOTE—Wherever in the foregoing pages explanations have been omitted after certain **questions** or answers it is because the matter they contain has been explained in some preceding **question**, or is to be explained in some following **question**, or is clear enough in itself without explanation. The explanations of such **questions** or answers can be easily found by referring to the index.

Thomas L. Kinkead, Baltimore Catechism, No. 4: An Explanation of the Baltimore Catechism of Christian Doctrine for the Use of Sunday-School Teachers and Advanced Classes

Apropos: it's all very well, this instruction of Alsana's to look at the thing close up; to look at it dead straight between the eyes; an unflinching and honest stare, a meticulous inspection that would go beyond the heart of the matter to its marrow; beyond the marrow to the root—but the **question** is how far back do you want? How far will *do*? The old American **question**: what do you want—*blood*? Most probably more than blood is required: whispered asides; lost conversations; medals and photographs; lists and certificates, yellowing paper bearing the faint imprint of brown dates. Back, back, *back*. Well, all right, then.

Zadie Smith, White Teeth

Where am I?

That's my first **question**, after an age of listening. From it (when it hasn't been answered) I'll rebound towards others, of a more personal nature. (Much later.) Perhaps I'll even end up (before regaining my coma) by thinking of myself as living (technically speaking).

But let us proceed with method. I shall do my best, as always (since I cannot do otherwise). I shall submit, more corpse-obliging than ever. I shall transmit the words as received (by the ear, or roared through a trumpet into the arsehole) in all their purity (and in the same order, as far as possible). This infinitesimal lag, between arrival and departure, this trifling delay in evacuation, is all I have to worry about. The truth about me will boil forth at last, scalding (provided of course they don't start stuttering again).

Samuel Beckett, The Unnamable

But of what is this knowledge? I said. Just answer me that small **question**. Do you mean a knowledge of shoemaking?

God forbid.

Or of working in brass?

Certainly not.

Or in wool, or wood, or anything of that sort?

Plato, The Dialogues of Plato, Vol. 1

"The **question** at stake," said Epictetus, "is no common one; it is this:—Are we in our senses, or are we not?"

Epictetus, The Golden Sayings of Epictetus

My lords, the judges find a difficulty to give a distinct answer to the **question** thus proposed by your lordships, either in the affirmative or the negative, inasmuch as we are not aware that there is in the courts below any established practice which we can state to your lordships as distinctly referring to such a **question** propounded by counsel on cross-examination as is here contained, that is, whether the counsel cross-examining are entitled to ask the witness whether he has made such representation, for it is not in the recollection of any one of us that such a **question** in those words, namely, whether a witness has made such and such representation, has at any time been asked of a witness; **questions** however of a similar nature are frequently asked at Nisi Prius, referring rather to contracts and agreements, or to supposed contracts and agreements, than to declarations of the witness; as for instance, a witness is often asked whether there is an agreement for a certain price for a certain article, an agreement for a certain definite time, a warranty, or other matter of that kind, being a matter of contract; and when a **question** of that kind has been asked at Nisi Prius, the ordinary course has been for the counsel on the other side not to object to the **question** as a **question** that could not properly be put, but to interpose on his own behalf another intermediate **question**, namely, to ask the witness whether the agreement referred to in the **question** originally proposed by the counsel on the other side, was or was not in writing; and if the witness answers that it was in writing, then the inquiry is stopped, because the writing must be itself produced.

T. C. Hansard, Parliamentary Debates: Official Report of the Session of the Parliament of the United Kingdom of Great Britain and Ireland, June 27–September 7, 1820

"Do you always treat the fourth estate this way, DS Clarke?"

"Sometimes I go for a headlock instead."

"That's a good idea, changing your attack," Whiteread agreed. "Means the enemy can't predict your move," Simms added. "Why do I get the feeling you three are taking the piss?" Holly asked.

Siobhan had bent down to retrieve her phone and book. She checked the phone for damage. "What is it you want?"

"A quick couple of **questions**."

"Concerning what exactly?" Holly was staring at the army pair. "Sure you want an audience, DS Clarke?"

"I've got nothing to say to you anyway," Siobhan told him.

"How do you know until you've heard me out?"

"Because you're going to ask me about Martin Fairstone."

"Am I?" Holly raised an eyebrow. "Well, maybe that *was* the plan . . . but I'm also wondering why you're so jumpy, and why you don't want to talk about Fairstone."

*Ian Rankin, A **Question** of Blood*

Reading is often perceived as a challenge by many students. But if proper reading strategies of skimming and scanning are adopted, this challenge can be overcome. One of the important activities during skimming is finding out keywords in the passage and underlining them. During scanning as well, you can mark keywords in the **question** as your tendency to match them with similar words in the passage. Since the passages are long and complex, finding out keywords will help you read more efficiently.

IELTS Online Tests, How to Find the Right Keywords in Reading Comprehension? (ieltsonlinetests.com)

"What happened?" he asked trying to sound genuinely concerned.

"We're not exactly sure. We're trying to put the pieces together. Do you mind if we ask you a couple of **questions**?" the tall deputy asked him.

"No, not at all. I can't see where I'd be able to help you, but I'll answer anything you need me to. Steve's been good to me and I want to help. I can't believe anyone would want to hurt him, yet alone kill him," Jack answered sounding too anxious.

C. R. Poenitzsch, Fate Xs Three

"I'm fine. I'm just surprised," I said. "I don't know what I thought you were doing here, but it wasn't this. I can't believe anything bad could ever happen to him. He was always a brawler, but he seemed invincible . . . at least to me. What happened?"

"That's what we're trying to piece together," Claas said. "He'd been shot twice, once in the head and once in the chest. A patrolman spotted him lying on the sidewalk a little after three A.M. The weapon, a semi-automatic, was found in the gutter about ten feet away. This was a commercial district, a lot of bars in the area, so it's possible Mr. Magruder got into a dispute. We have a couple of guys out now canvassing the neighborhood. So far no witnesses. For now, we're working backward, trying to get a line on his activities prior to the shooting."

"When *was* this?"

"Early morning hours of May fourteenth. Wednesday of last week."

Claas said, "Do you mind if we ask you a couple of **questions**?"

"Not at all. Please do."

I expected one of them to take out a notebook, but none emerged. I glanced at the briefcase and wondered if I was being recorded. Meanwhile, Claas was talking on. "We're in the process of eliminating some possibilities. This is mostly filling in the blanks, if you can help us out."

"Sure, I'll try. I'm not sure how, but fire away," I said.

Sue Grafton, "O" is for Outlaw

Target people that you need the information from the most. If you can pull it off, you can use this approach to hold a series of mini-meetings with a couple of people at a time. In a similar fashion, you can drop by a person's office (email is useless in this context) and ask if they could spare a minute or two for a couple of **questions**. In other words, your mission is to gather information, even if it breaks down to house-to-house fighting.

Christopher Duncan, The Career Programmer: Guerilla Tactics for an Imperfect World

Per usual, Regan just walked through the door before actually being invited in. He walked past the waitress and straight to the bar. The waitress followed quickly while Carter took his time glancing around at the scenery.

"I'm Detective Regan. This here is my partner, Detective Carter. Mind if we ask you a couple of **questions**?" Regan tucked his badge back in his pocket, and Carter was now by his side.

"I'm Patrick McPhee. Something happen at my bar that I don't know about?" Patrick looked to be in his late forties. He apparently owned the bar. Regan thought that maybe this could be helpful. Most owners know everyone and everything that takes place in their establishments.

Caroline Christian, The Scent of Bread

"Excuse me, Miss Nolan." Kathy appeared startled. "My name is Frank Farrel, and this is George Lewis." Lewis nodded. "We're detectives with the Philadelphia police." They showed her their badges. "Do you mind if we ask you a couple of **questions**?"

Over her surprise, Kathy inspected the badges and nodded. She wiped away a stray tear.

Edwin J. Sprague, *The Point Guard*

Blake: "Was that what you meant to say?"
Leslie: "Isn't it enough to say what you mean, without being obliged to say what you meant?"
Blake: "Half a loaf is better than no bread; beggars mustn't be choosers."
Leslie: "Oh, if you put it so meekly as that you humiliate me. I must tell you now: I meant a **question**."
Blake: "What is it?"
Leslie: "But I can't ask it, yet. Not till I've got rid of some part of my obligations."
Blake: "I suppose you mean what I—what happened."
Leslie: "Yes."

William Dean Howells, *Out of the **Question**: A Comedy*

"Marty, let's put all this shit with DS Clarke on the back burner, eh? Fact is, I couldn't give a monkey's. But there is a **question** I've been meaning to ask . . ."

"What's that?" Fairstone, heavy-lidded in his chair, cigarette held between thumb and forefinger.

Ian Rankin, *A **Question** of Blood*

Thinking that after all he had nothing to lose, Charles resolved to pop the **question** when the occasion offered itself; but, each time it offered itself, the fear of not finding the right words sealed his lips.

Gustave Flaubert, *Madame Bovary*

"Well, may I give you a couple of recommendations?" I queried.

"Sure!" came the eager response from all group members. They assumed that I must possess that "golden key" to successful witnessing.

"I always like the up-front approach," I told them. "People here in South Florida are used to that. You might say something like, 'Hi! We are a group of Christian students who are interested in your perspective on spiritual matters. Do you mind if we ask you a couple of **questions**?' Or you could also say something like, 'Do you mind if we take just five or six minutes of your time to get your opinion about two **questions** that we think are of ultimate importance?'"

Charles Carmen Mayell, *Engage! Having Conversations About God*

'Oh my God . . . and you're beautiful as well!' screamed Vera.

'I'm Detective Keeley Harrington from Gainesville Homicide, and this is my male partner Detective Barney Corvette, and we'd like to thank you for your hospitality; we were kinda dying on that dark landing with no ventilation and not a thing to drink.' Keeley said patting Vera's shoulder.

'While we're here, do you mind if we ask you a couple of **questions** Ma'am?' Keeley asked.

'Of course not Detective—go right ahead.' Vera said settling down opposite the homicide detectives.

> *Bill Jones, HEMMED IN: So if You Can't Breathe . . . You Might Be Hemmed In!*

"Is there something we can do for you?" the man asked. "You're with the sheriff's department?"

"We're with the crime lab," Sara said again.

"You're the ones who are here about the fire?" the woman asked.

"That's right, ma'am." Nick said.

"We know nothing about that except it was a tragedy. We're thankful our home was spared."

"I'm sure you are, ma'am," Sara said. "Do you mind if we ask you a couple of **questions**?"

"It's late," the man said.

"But not too late for some weed," Nick said.

"We're not here about drug use, sir. We really just have some **questions** about your candles."

"Candles?"

> *Jeff Mariotte, CSI: Crime Scene Investigation: The Burning Season*

Of course you should have some kind of warranty card included with your product and of course this card should include a couple of **questions**. If you don't take any one instance of this kind of survey too seriously, and if you keep each such survey short and simple, and you do these surveys as one part of your information gathering, then yes, it makes sense to do these surveys, and yes, you can do them yourself.

> *Edward F. McQuarrie, The Market Research Toolbox: A Concise Guide for Beginners*

"Hi. I'm Simon, and we're taping a new type of show, called, 'Reality Television,' it's kind of like an ad-lib 'talkumentary.' Do you mind if we ask you a couple of **questions**?"

"Who are you again, Dude?" the surfer replied, winking at his friends. "Oh, right, a schlokumentary. Sure, go ahead, ask."

> *Robert Greco and Shaun M. Shelton, Motorishi*

Be honest about what it is you're doing. Don't say that you're merely doing a survey unless you're genuinely only carrying out a survey. The survey gambit was very effective and thoroughly used in the 1980s and early 1990s but sadly was abused and callers turned 'surveys' into a sales call after the listener had answered a couple of **questions**. By all means ask a couple of **questions** to assess the listener's suitability but be honest with the prospect about your intentions and say, 'Do you mind if I ask you just a couple of **questions** to see if I can actually be of service to you?'.

> *Tom Hopkins and Ben Kench, Selling for Dummies*

"It's okay, I was just passing through, saw y'all pull up and thought I'd come by to say hi." Chet definitely did not look like someone that these people wanted to meet. His appearance was very rough looking; he was dirty, with a couple days of beard growth, and uncombed hair. Solemnly, Chet stated, "Please, don't be alarmed, my name is Chet, and I've been on the trail for a few days . . . and please accept my apology for my appearance. If y'all let me, I'd like to ask a couple of **questions**."

Being defensive, the man moved the woman and children to the side of the car. He then replied, "Just tell me what you want, but please leave my family alone!" His tone rose, showing signs of fear. It was not very often that you witnessed a guy with this outward appearance come out of the woods with a horse.

S.D. Brook, A Cowboy in Time

"We just wanted to ask you a couple of **questions**. For instance, like where'd you go last night?"

She looked disagreeably at me, then back to the chief, frowned, and spoke haughtily:

"May I ask why I am being **questioned** in this manner?" I wondered how many times I had heard that **question**, word for word and tone for tone, while the chief, disregarding it, went on amiably: "And then there was something about one of your shoes being stained. The right one, or maybe the left. Anyways it was one or the other."

A muscle began twitching in her upper lip. "Was that all?" the chief asked me.

Dashiell Hammett, Red Harvest

What am I going to say now? I'm going to ask myself, I'm going to ask **questions**: that's a good stop-gap. (Not that I'm in any danger of stopping. Then why all this fuss?) That's right, **questions**: I know millions, I must know millions. And then there are plans. When **questions** fail there are always plans: you say what you'll say and what you won't say (that doesn't commit you to anything), and the evil moment passes, it stops stone dead. Suddenly you hear yourself talking about God knows what as if you had done nothing else all your life (and neither have you).

Samuel Beckett, The Unnamable

"That's great," Hannah said, "Do you mind if we ask you a couple of **questions**?"

"About what?"

David Lewman, The Case of the Mystery Meat Loaf

A delicate **question**, to which somewhat diverse solutions might be given according to times and seasons. An intelligent man suggests it to me, and I intend to try, if not to solve it, at least to examine and discuss it face to face with my readers, were it only to persuade them to answer it for themselves, and, if I can, to make their opinion and mine on the point clear.

Charles Augustin Sainte-Beuve, What Is a Classic?

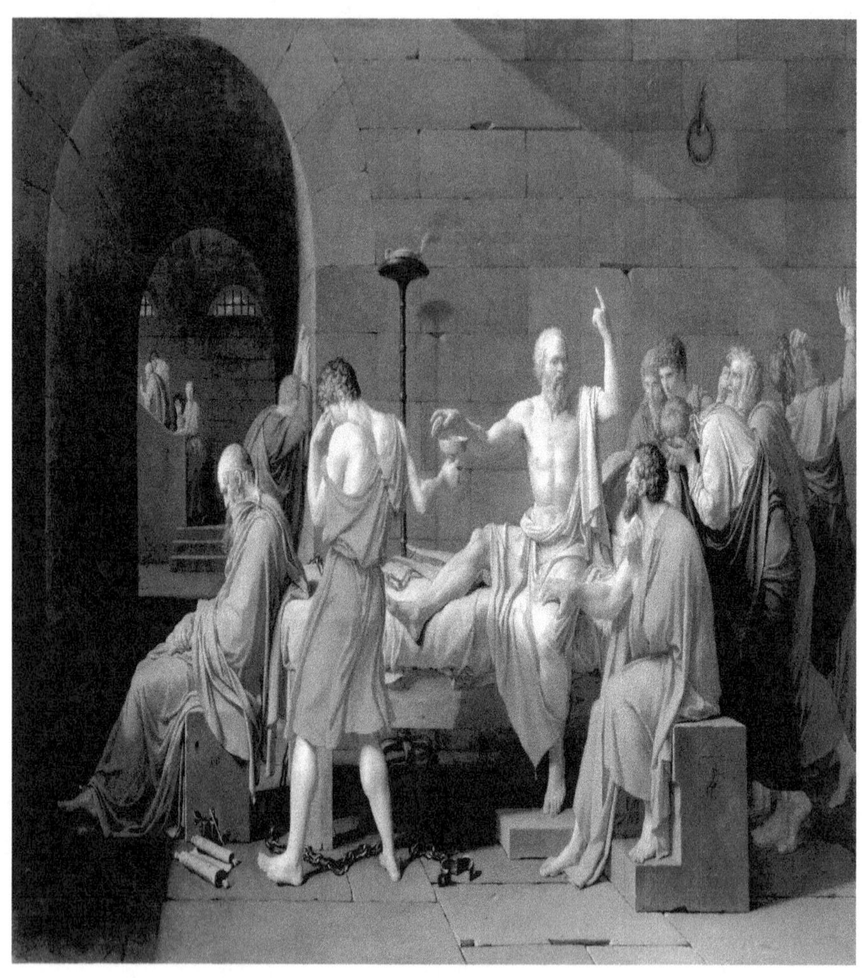

Jacques-Louis David, The Death of Socrates, 1787
Oil on canvas, 130 x 196 cm, Metropolitan Museum of Art

This Thing in Question

*My answer to the **question** whether I had anything to say*

Occasionally, life affords you the time, the repose, the *dolce far niente* to the sorts of **questions** that go largely unexamined in the brisk course of ordinary life: How well do you recall the mechanics of photosynthesis? Have you ever managed to use the word "ontology" in a conversational sentence? At what precise moment did you tip just slightly out of alignment with the relatively normal life you had been enjoying there-tofore, cant infinitesimally to the left or the right and thus embark upon the trajectory that ultimately delivered you to your present whereabouts . . .

Jennifer Egan, A Visit From the Goon Squad

"What are you doing?" Sarah asked. "Didn't you hear me call?"

She looked at the book on his desk and said, *"War and Peace.* I thought you were getting tired of *War and Peace."*

He gathered up a sheet of paper, folded it and put it in his pocket.

"I'm trying my hand at an essay."

"Show me."

"No. Only if it comes off."

"Where will you send it?"

"The *New Statesman . . . Encounter . . .* who knows?"

"It's a very long time since you wrote anything. I'm glad you are starting again."

"Yes. I seem doomed always to try again."

Graham Greene, The Human Factor

"Here's how we usually start," he said. "I ask **questions** based on the printout and then you answer to the best of your ability. When we're all finished, I give you the printout in a sealed envelope and you take it to your doctor for a paid visit."

"Good."

"Good. We usually start by asking how do you feel."

"Based on the printout?"

"Just how do you feel," he said in a mild voice.

Don DeLillo, White Noise

Cuba is sinking in flames in the middle of Lac Leman while I descend to the bottom of things. Packed inside my sentences, I glide, a ghost, into the river's neurotic waters, discovering as I drift the underside of surfaces and the inverted image of the Alps. Between the anniversary of the Cuban revolution and the date of my trial, I have time enough to ramble on in peace, to open my unpublished book with great care, and to cover this paper with the key-words that won't set me free. I'm writing on a card table next to a window looking out on grounds enclosed by a sharp iron fence that marks the boundary between what's unpredictable and what is locked up. I won't get out before the day of reckoning. That's written in several carbon copies as decreed, following valid laws and an unassailable royal judge. There are no distractions then, nothing to replace the clockwork of my obsession or make me deviate from the written record of my journey. Basically, only one thing really concerns me and it's this: how should I set about writing a spy novel? My wish is complicated by the fact that I long to do something original in a genre that has so many unwritten rules and laws. Fortunately, though, a certain laziness leads me to give up any idea about breathing new life into the tradition before I even get started. I may as well admit it—making myself comfortable in a literary form that's already so well defined makes me feel very secure. And so without hesitation I decide to integrate my work within the main lines of the traditional spy novel. And since I want to set it in Lausanne, that's taken care of. As quickly as I can, I eliminate any behaviour that would give my secret agent too much merit: he's neither a Sphinx nor a highly perceptive Tarzan, neither God nor the Holy Ghost; he mustn't be so logical that the plot need not be or, on the other hand, so lucid that I can complicate everything else and cook up some story that makes no sense, that when all's said and done would only be understood by some bungling oaf with a gun who doesn't share his thoughts with anyone. And if I were to introduce a Wolof Secret Agent* . . . Everybody knows that Wolofs† aren't legion in French-speaking Switzerland‡ and that they're under-represented in the secret service.§ I know, I'm overdoing it,¶ falling into the trap of the Afro-Asian bloc, giving in to the African and Madagascar Union lobby. But let me tell you something: if Hamidou Diop suits me, I can simply make him a secret agent in Lausanne on a counter-espionage mission, for no other reason than to get him out of Geneva where the air is less salubrious. Now I can reserve a suite at the Lausanne Palace for Hamidou, provide him with traveller's cheques from the Banque Cantonale Vaudoise, and appoint him a Special Envoy (a phony one) from the Republic of Senegal to some big Swiss companies that want to invest in desert real estate.** Once Hamidou is protected by his fake identity and settled in at the Lausanne Palace, I can bring CIA and MI5 agents into the picture.†† And

---

* *k-an:* 'who?' *(sg)*
  Stéphane Robert, *Interrogation in Wolof: Two Strategies and a Puzzle for Wh-***Question** *Words*

† *kooku:* this person in **question** (from kan = who?)
  Wolof Resources, Wolof Grammar Manual

‡ *foofu:* this place in **question** (from fan = where?)
  Wolof Resources, Wolof Grammar Manual

§ *loolu:* this thing in **question** (from lan = what?)
  Wolof Resources, Wolof Grammar Manual

¶ *noonu:* this manner in **question** (from nan = how?)
  Wolof Resources, Wolof Grammar Manual

** This is no small task, as there are several dozens of emotion-related conceptual metaphors, for example, in English and there are thousands of other languages/cultures around the world. We can answer the second **question** only if we have reliable empirical evidence of the universality (or at least near-universality) of at least one emotion-related metaphor. In this case, we can begin to make hypotheses concerning the issue of why certain conceptual metaphors are universal (or near-universal).
  Zoltán Kövecses, *Where Metaphors Come From: Reconsidering Context in Metaphor*

†† Why these two sets of wh-**question** words?
  Stéphane Robert, *Interrogation in Wolof: Two Strategies and a Puzzle for Wh-***Question** *Words (Open Archive HAL)*

that's that.[*] In return for adding a few alluring lady spies[†] and the algebraic treatment of the plot,[‡] I have my deal.[§] Hamidou is getting impatient,[¶] I sense that he's about to do something crazy:[**] in fact, I suspect it's already begun.[††] My future novel is already in orbit, so far out that I can't bring it back. I'm frozen, I've just been dumped here inside my alphabet, I'm shackled to it and asking myself some **questions**.[‡‡] To write the kind of spy novel we read would be dishonest: in fact, it would be impossible.[§§] Writing a story is no small matter, unless it becomes the daily and detailed punctuation of my endless

---

[*] Recall the existence of a yes/no **question** particle *mbaa* from (58), which indicates expected hearer affirmation or speaker's hope.
> Harold Torrence, The Clause Structure of Wolof: Insights Into the Left Periphery

[†] This is proper form to use after the **question**: "Looy def?"
> Wolof Resources, Wolof Grammar Manual

[‡] < *ana* + subject ? >, * *ana* + VP
> Stéphane Robert, Interrogation in Wolof: Two Strategies and a Puzzle for Wh-**Question** Words (Open Archive HAL)

[§] Thus, it appears that the **question** particles *waa* and *mbaa* stand in a derivational relationship, although its exact nature is unclear.
> Harold Torrence, The Clause Structure of Wolof: Insights Into the Left Periphery

[¶] Ku Ø bëgg lem, Ø ñeme yamb.
'[He] who wants honey must not fear bees.'
> Stéphane Robert, Interrogation in Wolof: Two Strategies and a Puzzle for Wh-**Question** Words (Open Archive HAL)

[**] Ku Ø jël saabu bi?
'Who took the soap?'
> Stéphane Robert, Interrogation in Wolof: Two Strategies and a Puzzle for Wh-**Question** Words (Open Archive HAL)

[††] Several **questions** pertaining to the representation of those segments immediately arise, i.e., should they be seen (1) as two slots on the CV-tier linked to two elements of the segmental tier, or (2) as a single element on the segmental tier linked to two slots on the CV tier, or (3) as a single slot on the CV-tier linked to two elements on the segmental tier? These **questions** are crucial to the understanding of Wolof syllable structure; I deal with them in the next section.
> Omar Ka, Wolof Syllable Structure: Evidence From a Secret Code

[‡‡] The next **question** that needs to be answered is how syllable structure gets assigned to the CV-tier. Following Clements and Keyser's (1983) algorithm, I will posit the following steps in the mapping process:

    (5) a.   prelink a V or a W to the node σ;
          b.   attach to σ all preceding Cs which do not violate the constraints on possible syllable-initial Cs;
          c.   attach to σ all following Cs which do not violate the constraints on possible syllable-final Cs.

In the case of Wolof, possible syllable-initial consonants are simple and prenasal consonants. Possible syllable-final consonants are simple, geminate and prenasal consonants. The steps in (5) are illustrated in (6) below:

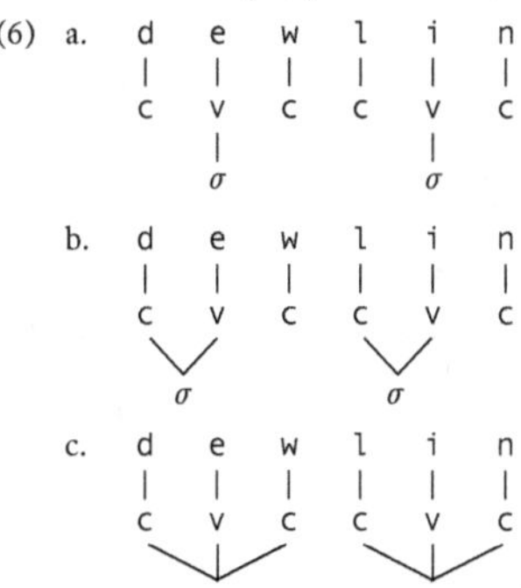

> Omar Ka, Wolof Syllable Structure: Evidence From a Secret Code

[§§] Thus it is the appropriate structure to respond to open **questions** which enquire about the subject.
> Wolof Resources, Wolof Grammar Manual

stillness and my slow fall into this liquid pit.[*] The enemy will be lying in wait for me unless I can make life absolutely impossible for my character.[†] To populate my own empty space I intend to pile up corpses along my character's way, multiply attempts on his life, drive him crazy with anonymous calls and knives planted in his bedroom door; I'll kill everyone he's spoken to,[‡] even the courteous hotel cashier.[§] I'll put Hamidou through the mill or I won't have the courage to live. I'll plant bombs in his entourage and to complicate matters conclusively I'll set the Chinese onto him,[¶] a number of them and all the same:[**] there will be Chinese on the streets of Lausanne, hordes of smiling Chinese who'll look Hamidou in the eye.[††] Taking a Stelazine distracted me briefly from poor Hamidou's career. Fifteen minutes from now they'll bring me a cold meal,[‡‡] and other interruptions will go on till bedtime,[§§] as I draw up the outline of a novel without continuity, lay down the unknowns of a fictitious equation, and in the end imagine

---

[*] Also used for forming open **questions** which relate to the subject [cf. la (complement/object predicator) which is used to form open **questions** relating to a complement or object].

Wolof Resources, Wolof Grammar Manual

[†] At this point, one needs to answer a central **question** about the nature of the prosodic category that is involved in this type of Kàll. Consider first a language game in English and German (called Chicken language) that bears striking resemblances with the Wolof variety.

Omar Ka, Wolof Syllable Structure: Evidence From a Secret Code

[‡] Comment traduire « Bachi-Bouzouk », « Amphitryon » ou « Anacoluthe », quelques-uns des célèbres jurons du capitaine Haddock, en langue wolof ? C'est sans doute la **question** que s'est posée Gérard Georges, dit GéGé, président de l'ONG belge Actions-Toubacouta-Sénégal, à l'origine de l'initiative, lorsqu'il a fallu entamer ce projet.

C'est un travail collectif de plusieurs années qui a donné naissance au « Secret de la Licorne » en wolof, grâce à Serigne Diouf, ingénieur pédagogique, Awa Sene Sarr et Marie-Madeleine Diallo, auteures et comédiennes, et de nombreuses autres contributions sollicitées par internet.

Au Senegal, Tintin et le secret de la Licorne disponible en wolof (Au-Senegal.com)

[§] *How to translate "Bachi-Bouzouk," "Amphitryon" or "Anacoluthe," some of the famous swear words of Captain Haddock, in Wolof language? This is undoubtedly the **question** asked by Gérard Georges, dit GéGé, president of the Belgian NGO Actions-Toubacouta-Senegal, at the origin of the initiative, when it was necessary to start this project.*

It is a collective work of several years which gave birth to the "Secret of the Unicorn" in Wolof, thanks to Serigne Diouf, educational engineer, Awa Sene Sarr and Marie-Madeleine Diallo, authors and actresses, and many other solicited contributions by internet. The final control was carried out by Jean-Léopold Diouf, grammarian and professor at the University of Paris. All of them worked on a voluntary basis.

Au Senegal, Tintin and the Secret of the Unicorn Available in Wolof (translation by Google Translate)

[¶] . . . and woe betide China if she failed to live up to her new duty!

*Robert Hart, These From the Land of Sinim: Essays on the Chinese **Question***

[**] *u* **questions**: formally identical to indefinite relative clauses
  • same pronoun (CL-*u*)
  • same verb form
  • same structure

*Stéphane Robert, Interrogation in Wolof: Two Strategies and a Puzzle for Wh-**Question** Words (Open Archive HAL)*

[††] Conducting research among the Chinese traders presented challenges. First, I do not speak any Chinese languages; thus, my research was limited to conversations with individuals who could communicate in French, Wolof, or English. Second, Chinese immigrants in Dakar are cautious about answering **questions**.

Suzanne Scheld, Racism, "Free-Trade" and Consumer "Protection": The Controversy of Chinese Petty-Traders in Dakar, Senegal (Dimensions of International Migration)

[‡‡] A focusing strategy for content **question** words.

*Stéphane Robert, Interrogation in Wolof: Two Strategies and a Puzzle for Wh-**Question** Words (Open Archive HAL)*

[§§] On the **question** of borrowing from one civilization to another, Greece provides another example. M. Bernal remarks that "Greek states were small and often quite poor and their national poet was Homer, whose heroic epics fitted . . .

Samba Diop, The Oral History and Literature of the Wolof People of Waalo, Northern Senegal: The Master of the Word (Griot) in the Wolof Tradition

some total nonsense for as long as this disorganized siege gives me a bulwark against sadness and the criminal waves that crash into me, roaring and chanting the name of the woman I love.

Hubert Aquin, Next Episode

"Mild fatigue is a popular answer."

"I could say exactly that and be convinced in my own mind it's a fair and accurate description."

He seemed satisfied with the reply and made a bold notation on the page in front of him.

"What about appetite?" he said.

"I could go either way on that."

"That's more or less how I could go, based on the printout."

"In other words you're saying sometimes I have appetitive reinforcement, sometimes I don't."

"Are you telling me or asking me?"

"It depends on what the numbers say."

"Then we agree."

"Good."

"Good," he said. "Now what about sleep? We usually do sleep before we ask the person if they'd like some decaf or tea. We don't provide sugar."

Don DeLillo, White Noise

What's more, there seems to be no such thing as a concept so abstract, or a **question** so off base, that it can't be fruitfully explored at Socrates Café. In the course of Socratizing, it often turns out to be the case that some of the most so-called abstract concepts are intimately related to the most profoundly relevant human experiences. In fact, it's been my experience that virtually any **question** can be plumbed Socratically. Sometimes you don't know what **question** will have the most lasting and significant impact until you take a risk and delve into it for a while.

Christopher Phillips, Socrates Café: A Fresh Taste of Philosophy

"I will. Now listen to me. You're drunk, and I'm drunk, and I'm just exactly drunk enough to tell you anything you want to know. That's the kind of girl I am. If I like a person I'll tell them anything they want to know. Just ask me. Go ahead, ask me."

Dashiell Hammett, Red Harvest

Because Heidegger is eager that the reader should follow him and sensible that the way is hard, again and again he speaks so as to evoke a response that will carry his companion forward. Often at some key point he will ask a **question**, seeking to force the reader to come to grips with what is being said, to think, to reply, and then to listen for an answer that will send the discussion forward: "Does this mean that man, for better or worse, is helplessly delivered over to technology?" (T 37). "In what does the essence of modern science lie?" (AWP 117). "What is happening to Being?" (WN 104). When we come upon such **questions** we must listen alertly. A **question** may be answered in an immediately ensuing sentence, or its answer may emerge only after an involved exposition. But an answer will come. And it will be important to the whole discussion.

*William Lovitt, Introduction to The **Question** Concerning Technology and Other Essays, by Martin Heidegger*

"I assure you, we'll be as quick as we can," Hogan was saying. Then he looked up at Rebus. "Now I'm going to hand things over to my colleague." Rebus pretended to take his time over forming his first **question**, then stared hard at James Bell.

"Why did you do it, James?"

"What?" Jack Bell shifted forwards. "I think I must protest at your tone . . ."

*Ian Rankin, A **Question** of Blood*

And as I was asking a few **questions**, and inquiring what was the news at Rome, Never mind those things, said Atticus, which we can neither inquire about nor hear of without vexation, but ask him rather whether he has written anything new; for the muse of Varro has been silent much longer than usual; though I rather suppose he is suppressing for a time what he has written, than that he has been really idle. You are quite wrong, said he; for I think it very foolish conduct in a man to write what he wishes to have concealed. But I have a great work on hand; for I have been a long time preparing a treatise which I have dedicated to my friend here, (he meant me,) which is of great importance, and is being polished up by me with a good deal of care.

I have been waiting to see it a long time, Varro, said I, but still I have not ventured to ask for it. For I heard from our friend Libo, with whose zeal you are well acquainted, (for I can never conceal anything of that kind,) that you have not been slackening in the business, but are expending a great deal of care on it, and in fact never put it out of your hands. But it has never hitherto come into my mind to ask you about it; however now, since I have begun to commit to a durable record those things which I learnt in your company, and to illustrate in the Latin language that ancient philosophy which originated with Socrates, I must ask you why it is that, while you write on so many subjects, you pass over this one, especially when you yourself are very eminent in it; and when that study, and indeed the whole subject, is far superior in importance to all other studies and arts.

*Marcus Tullius Cicero, The Academic **Questions***

"I get a little restless. Who doesn't?"

"Toss and turn?"

"Toss," I said.

"Good."

"Good."

He made some notes. It seemed to be going well. I was heartened to see how well it was going. I turned down his offer of tea, which seemed to please him. We were moving right along.

"Here's where we ask about smoking."

'That's easy. The answer is no. And it's not a matter of having stopped five or ten years ago. I've never smoked. Even when I was a teenager. Never tried it. Never saw the need."

"That's always a plus."

I felt tremendously reassured and grateful.

"We're moving right along, aren't we?"

"Some people like to drag it out," he said.

Don DeLillo, White Noise

The Preamble.

On the subject of the preamble, we will add a few authorities for one or two of its positions, which we have heard called in **question**. On page 3, we read:—

S. S. Schmucker, American Lutheranism Vindicated; or, Examination of the Lutheran Symbols, on Certain Disputed Topics: Including a Reply to the Plea of Rev. W. J. Mann

Contemporary thought, Greif says—"the strata of philosophy and theory" as they exist primarily within the academy—"is a Frankenstein put together of spare parts cast off by modernity or the Enlightenment." It represents not novelty but "compulsive repetition and illusory escape in the disguise of critical thinking." We are still asking the same **questions**. We are still giving the same answers. We think we've gotten somewhere new, but so did those who came before us, in the age of the crisis of man. The situation, Greif writes, "scripts our novelties for us." Postmodernism is not an *n+1* to modernism's *n*. Its name, in fact, bespeaks perseveration, the same thing again and again, in whatever different guises: *n, N, ñ, n!*

The challenge, once again, is to be curricular: "to read through the last century," and, in particular, to provide "an alternative construction of mid-twentieth-century thought" in order to establish a "starting point for twenty-first-century thought." Modernity, Greif says, is "a bit like the weather—everyone complains, but no one will do anything about it." In other words, we're stuck, and everybody knows we're stuck: politically, ideologically, intellectually. The challenge is to do something about it: to face reality, and desperately, for all we're worth, to try to think.

William Deresiewicz, What a Piece of Work: Mark Greif's Intellectual Excavations

Again the **questioning** look. But what could I say in explanation? I knew less than she did. I knew nothing about all this. I finally put my cigarette butt, which was burning my fingers, in the ash tray.

Patrick Modiano, Missing Person

Trained as a journalist, she'd rather know things than not and could not stop herself—even while fleeing her probable death—from finding Raoul's story interesting, less for what he said than for what she surmised he left out. And so she remained alert, asking appropriate **questions** and feigning an interest until some item of real interest took hold.

Chris Kraus, Summer of Hate

Murder, which is a frustration of the individual and hence a frustration of the race, may have, and in fact has, a good deal of sociological implication. But it has been going on too long for it to be news. If the mystery novel is at all realistic (which it very seldom is) it is written in a certain spirit of detachment; otherwise nobody but a psychopath would want to write it or read it. The murder novel has also a depressing way of minding its own business, solving its own problems and answering its own **questions**. There is nothing left to discuss, except whether it was well enough written to be good fiction, and the people who make up the half-million sales wouldn't know that anyway. The detection of quality in writing is difficult enough even for those who make a career of the job, without paying too much attention to the matter of advance sales.

Raymond Chandler, The Simple Art of Murder

We naturally wanted to avoid using defective items, except as deliberate versions in an experiment, but we despaired of being able to construct **questions** immune from serious criticism. Moreover, an additional danger in constructing our own **questions** lay in developing a rarefied set of examples substantially different from those employed in standard surveys. Just as we needed to gather data from the same national population sampled in most surveys, so we needed, in an admittedly rough sense, to work from **questionnaire** items similar to those commonly used in survey research. These considerations led to our trying wherever possible to begin experiments with a **question** that had already been employed in an important survey, and only then to devise variations from it as part of the experiments. Thus many of the **questions** reported below come from surveys carried out by the Institute for Sodal Research (ISR), the National Opinion Research Center (NORC), Gallup, Harris, or other major survey organizations, and the reader who feels that the **questions** are imperfect should keep in mind that they are fairly typical survey items.

We have not stuck rigidly to the principle of prior use. In some cases **questions** were adapted or (we think) improved. In other cases it was necessary to construct entirely new **questions**, because we could not locate suitable existing items for the specific purpose at hand. For the majority of experiments reported in this book, however, one form of the **question** is taken exactly or adapted in only minor ways from a previous **questionnaire** that had been developed as part of a substantive investigation by others. The source is normally given when the **question** is first presented.

Howard Schuman and Stanley Presser, **Questions** *and Answers in Attitude Surveys: Experiments on* **Question** *Form, Wording, and Context*

"Why, Lee? That's all we want to know," Rebus whispered into the silence. He walked to the door, turned, entered the room again, holding out his right gloved hand as though it were the weapon. Swiveled from one firing position to another. He knew that the forensics team would be doing much the same, albeit in front of their computers. Reconstructing the scene in the room, computing the angles of bullet entry, positioning the gunman for each shot. Every shred of evidence added its own sentence to the story. Here's where he was standing . . . then he turned, moved forwards . . . If we match angle of entry to the blood spatter pattern . . .

Eventually, they would know every move Herdman had made. They would have brought the scene vividly to life with their graphics and ballistics. And none of it might make them any the wiser about the only **question** that mattered.

The why.

Ian Rankin, A **Question** *of Blood*

Of course, there is a far easier way to proceed. You show up at the start of class and ask the **question** that occurs to you, letting discussion take its own course. After a few students have spoken you can ask the other **question** that occurs to you. A bit later you can clarify the **question** you meant to ask but that students are not addressing. Then you ask a few related **questions** that are circling about the issue, or leading up to it or following from it, plus a couple of **questions** about interesting side points and maybe a series of **questions** pursuing some point that arises in answer to some **question** that has been asked. In that way the discussion will hit all possible points and everyone will have said at least something about something. At the end you can conclude by telling the students what the **question** for discussion is. 'OK. So the real **question** here, really, is not X or Y as we were saying, but Z. OK, tomorrow we'll . . .' The alternative is to pose the **question** for discussion at the start of discussion. That will require conceiving it and formulating it well before the start.

In addition to posing the **question** at the start, the **question** may be identified at some midpoint or end of discussion. That is not to repeat the original **question** but to identify the **question** which now appears at issue, given what has transpired to that point. 'OK, good. So now we're left with the **question** . . .' You have a good idea of what such **questions** might be because you have already sketched the various pieces, alternatives, and sequelae in the interrogative panoply as you labored to formulate the **question** for discussion.

> J.T. Dillon, **Questioning** and Teaching: A Manual of Practice

"This is why."

He pulled his head back so sharply it rapped the wall.

"You can't use third-degree methods on me. It isn't legal."

"Stop blowing bubbles, Sable. Was Fredericks here last night?"

"Yes. He wanted me to cash a check for him. I gave him all the cash I had in the house. It amounted to over two hundred dollars."

"What did he want it for?"

"He didn't tell me. Actually, he wasn't making too much sense. He talked as if the strain had been too much for him."

"What did he say?"

"I can't reproduce it verbatim. I was upset myself. He asked me a lot of **questions**, which I wasn't able to answer, about Anthony Galton and what happened to him. The imposture must have gone to his head; he seemed to have himself convinced that he actually was Gabon's son."

> Ross Macdonald, The Galton Case

"They must all be very dispirited," he said. "Yes," said the usher, "they are the accused, everyone you see here has been accused." "Really!" said K. "They're colleagues of mine then." And he turned to the nearest one, a tall, thin man with hair that was nearly grey. "What is it you are waiting for here?" asked K., politely, but the man was startled at being spoken to unexpectedly, which was all the more pitiful to see because the man clearly had some experience of the world and elsewhere would certainly have been able to show his superiority and would not have easily given up the advantage he had acquired. Here, though, he did not know what answer to give to such a simple **question** and looked round at the others as if they were under some obligation to help him, and as if no-one could expect any answer from him without this help. Then the usher of the court stepped forward to him and, in order to calm him down and raise his spirits, said, "The gentleman here's only asking what it is you're waiting for. You can give him an answer." The voice of the usher was probably familiar to him, and had a better effect than K.'s. "I'm . . . I'm waiting . . ." he began, and then came to a halt. He had clearly chosen this beginning so that he could give a precise answer to the **question**, but now he didn't know how to continue. Some of the others waiting had come closer and stood round the group, the usher of the court said to them, "Get out the way, keep the gangway free." They moved back slightly, but not as far as where they had been sitting before. In the meantime, the man whom K. had first approached had pulled himself together and even answered him with a smile. "A month ago I made some applications for evidence to be heard in my case, and I'm waiting for it to be settled."

"You certainly seem to be going to a lot of effort," said K. "Yes," said the man, "it is my affair after all."

"Not everyone thinks the same way as you do," said K. "I've been indicted as well but I swear on my soul that I've neither submitted evidence nor done anything else of the sort. Do you really think that's necessary?"

"I don't really know, exactly," said the man, once more totally unsure of himself; he clearly thought K. was joking with him and therefore probably thought it best to repeat his earlier answer in order to avoid making any new mistakes. With K. looking at him impatiently, he just said, "as far as I'm concerned, I've applied to have this evidence heard."

"Perhaps you don't believe I've been indicted?" asked K. "Oh, please, I certainly do," said the man, stepping slightly to one side, but there was more anxiety in his answer than belief. "You don't believe me then?" asked K., and took hold of his arm, unconsciously prompted by the man's humble demeanour, and as if he wanted to force him to believe him. But he did not want to hurt the man and had only taken hold of him very lightly. Nonetheless, the man cried out as if K. had grasped him not with two fingers but with red hot tongs. Shouting in this ridiculous way finally made K. tired of him, if he didn't believe he was indicted then so much the better; maybe he even thought K. was a judge. And before leaving, he held him a lot harder, shoved him back onto the bench and walked on. "These defendants are so sensitive, most of them," said the usher of the court. Almost all of those who had been waiting had now assembled around the man who, by now, had stopped shouting and they seemed to be asking him lots of precise **questions** about the incident. K. was approached by a security guard, identifiable mainly by his sword, of which the scabbard seemed to be made of aluminium. This greatly surprised K., and he reached out for it with his hand. The guard had come because of the shouting and asked what had been happening. The usher of the court said a few words to try and calm him down but the guard explained that he had to look into it himself, saluted, and hurried on, walking with very short steps, probably because of gout.

Franz Kafka, The Trial

Only later did Kafka discover in his own notions of reading a common ground with the ancient Talmudists, for whom the Bible encoded a multiplicity of meanings whose continuous pursuit was the purpose of our voyage on earth. "One reads in order to ask **questions**," Kafka once told a friend.

Alberto Manguel, A History of Reading

As often as not, each day Abe would start by saying "So I have a **question**." And when it came time to organize the stories, I sat him down and asked him to make a list of all his **questions**. Then we read through the stories, once, twice, some as many as four or five times, and we grouped them together as responses to those **questions**.

That's the book you hold in your hand now. It's not a biography, although it is biographical. It's not fiction, although I'm sure that there are elements of some stories that are fiction. It's not history, although some of the stories are taken directly from newspaper articles or history books rather than direct experience. It's just a few **questions** that elicit as responses stories of the worst barbarism that humans can inflict upon each other told from the perspective of an ordinary man who claims to be "nothing special." That last is fiction of course . . . but it's also biography.

*Cindy Harris, Cindy's Introduction (Just a Few **Questions**: Barbaric Stories from an Ordinary Life, by Abe Salem, as told to Cindy Harris)*

The fat man chuckled and they drank. The fat man sat down. He held his glass against his belly with both hands and smiled up at Spade. He said; "Well, sir, it's surprising, but it well may be a fact that neither of them does know exactly what that bird is, and that nobody in all this whole wide sweet world knows what it is, saving and excepting only your humble servant, Casper Gutman, Esquire."

"Swell." Spade stood with legs apart, one hand in his trousers-pocket, the other holding his glass. "When you've told me there'll only be two of us who know."

"Mathematically correct, sir"—the fat man's eyes twinkled—"but"—his smile spread—"I don't know for certain that I'm going to tell you."

"Don't be a damned fool," Spade said patiently. "You know what it is. I know where it is. That's why we're here."

"Well, sir, where is it?"

Spade ignored the **question**.

The fat man bunched his lips, raised his eyebrows, and cocked his head a little to the left. "You see," he said blandly, "I must tell you what I know, but you will not tell me what you know. That is hardly equitable, sir. No, no, I do not think we can do business along those lines."

Dashiell Hammett, The Maltese Falcon

Publishers like biographies, because—so we're led to believe—they sell. But it cannot have been mere commercial pressure that induced the immensely knowledgeable, careful and scholarly Birley to concoct his Hadrian. The problem also has to do with ancient history itself, as a discipline, and with what modern historians of the ancient world think it is worth studying and writing about. Contrary to popular opinion, we are not starved of evidence: enough material survives from the Roman world alone to last any historian's lifetime; and if you include relevant material from Judaism and early Christianity, the problem is one of excess, not shortness of supply. Yet historians still start their books with a ritual lament about 'the sources' and their inadequacy. The lament is not entirely insincere (though it is something of a self-constructed problem): the sources often are inadequate for the particular **questions** that historians choose to pose. But that is part of the ancient-historical game: first pick your **question**, then demonstrate the appalling difficulty of finding an answer given the paucity of the evidence, finally triumph over that difficulty by scholarly 'skill'. Prestige in this business goes to those who outwit their sources, prising unexpected answers from unexpected places, and who play the clever (sometimes too clever) detective against an apparent conspiracy of ancient silence.

Mary Beard, Hadrian and His Villa (Confronting the Classics: Traditions, Adventures, and Innovations)

Enough of these interruptions. If there was anything important about it, no doubt it would come back to him later. He wrote on firmly, limiting himself to giving his head a good scratch with the pen:

I do, however, agree whole-heartedly with the negative content of Pico's reminder: namely, that no good can come either to the magician or to the world in general that contains him, unless his operative capacity is backed by a thorough understanding of what he is doing and by a sincere desire to devote his peculiar abilities to the service of that world. This entails, first and foremost, that he possess a clear, unwavering and basically correct scale of cosmic values. For the purpose of establishing the correctness of your personal scale, friendly reader and would-be disciple, I have provided in Appendix C a short but reliable ethical **questionnaire** to which, before reading further, you should refer. There is a straightforward method of quantifying your performance which consists in the scoring of three points for each 'a' answer, two for each 'b', and one for each 'c'. If the answer is an utterly honest 'don't know', then this may count as half a point. Whosoever totals a score of less than thirty-three points or has indulged in cheating should desist from further ambition in the field of magic.

Amanda Prantera, The Cabalist

"Did you?"

"That's a lousy **question**, mister. If I didn't happen to like you I'd knock your block off."

"No offense."

"I had nothing against Luke Deloney. He treated me fair and square. Anyway, I told you he shot himself."

"Suicide?"

"Naw. Why would he commit suicide? He had everything, money and women and a hunting lodge in Wisconsin. He took me up there personally more than once. The shooting was an accident. That's the way it went into the books and that's the way it stays."

Ross Macdonald, The Chill

Here he stretched out a hand automatically for his packet of cigarettes, and placing one, unlit, between his teeth, where he began to roll it rhythmically from one side of his mouth to the other, reread the last paragraph with a worried frown. He was not quite happy about the **questionnaire**, either. It constituted, it was true, an impediment of a sort for an already well-intentioned disciple, but it meant placing a lot of weight on Trevisan's diligent filtering. How far could he rely on this? And who, after Trevisan, would be the next custodian? And the next? And the next? What if they did not share his diligence? What if despite their care it fell, as it might so easily do in the incalculable stretch of time that might have to elapse before reaching the right ones, into the hands of an unworthy reader? Could he really expect that such a reader would be held up by this simple expedient of self-examination? It would be paradoxical if it were so. The unworthy reader would not give two fig-seeds for the **questionnaire** and what it stood for. Only a worthy reader with a respectable count of, say, thirty-two to thirty-five (for he had had at least the foresight to leave an ample margin) would be brought to a dismayed standstill by such a ploy, and this was not what the test was supposed to accomplish. No, he thought crossly; no, this would not do at all. His work had not cost him a lifetime of effort merely to become the facile instrument of any unscrupulous set of fingers that happened to pick it up. It must be better guarded in its journey through time, when neither he nor Trevisan would be there to watch over it and safeguard it from improper use. It must be encased and protected. It must be rendered capable of looking after itself. But how could this be accomplished save by building into the work itself a kind of safety device? Yes, a foolproof and scoundrelproof safety device. That was what he needed.

Amanda Prantera, *The Cabalist*

Dwight Macdonald, an editor at the *Partisan Review,* addressed the **question** of storage: "He has in 25 years managed to fill incalculable notebooks which in turn fill incalculable boxes." He kept them in numberless closets and countless attics. "The stack of manuscripts comprising the *Oral History* has passed 7 feet," a reporter announced in 1941. Gould was five feet four. His friends wished to have that stack published. "I want to read Joe Gould's *Oral History,*" the short-story writer William Saroyan declared. "Harcourt, Brace; Random House; Scribner's; Viking; Houghton, Mifflin; Macmillan; Doubleday, Doran; Farrar and Rinehart; all of you—for the love of Mike, are you publishers, or not? If you are, print Joe Gould's *Oral History*. Long, dirty, edited, unedited, *any* how—print it, that's all." No one ever did.

And no one knew quite where it was. "The *Oral History* is a great hodgepodge and kitchen midden of hearsay," Joseph Mitchell reported in his first piece about Gould, published in *The New Yorker* in 1942. "It may well be the lengthiest unpublished work in existence."

Mitchell hadn't read more than a few pages. Gould had little use for readers. "I would continue to write if I were the sole survivor of the human race," he said. It's not as though no one had read the *Oral History,* but no one had read all of it, nine million words and counting. "Mr. Ezra Pound and I once saw a fragment of it running to perhaps 40,000 words," Edward J. O'Brien, the editor of "Best American Short Stories," testified, deeming it to have "considerable psychological and historical importance." It was also a mess. Pound put it delicately: "Mr. Joe Gould's prose style is uneven." Gould had an answer for that. "My history is uneven," he admitted. "It should be. It is an encyclopedia."

It was, in any case, missing. Nearly everything Gould ever held in his hands slipped away. He lost his glasses; he lost his teeth. "I keep losing fountain pens, change, and even manuscripts," he wrote. "I lost my diary in the toilet," he reported one day. He himself appeared and disappeared.

Jill Lepore, *Joe Gould's Teeth: The Long-Lost Story of the Longest Book Ever Written (The New Yorker)*

The reason why I knew you had not read it is the reason why I call it "my" book. For the last ten or twelve years I have been recommending it. Usually I speak about it at my first meeting with a stranger. It is my opening remark, just as yours is something futile about the weather. If I don't get it in at the beginning, I squeeze it in at the end. The stranger has got to have it some time. Should I ever find myself in the dock, and one never knows, my answer to the **question** whether I had anything to say would be, "Well, my lord, if I might just recommend a book to the jury before leaving."

A. A. Milne, *Not That It Matters*

Mr. Vander Jagt. Thank you very much, Mr. Chairman. I just have a couple of **questions** to try to get a better handle on this. I think you testified yesterday that basically the guidelines that were in existence weren't followed, although you were convinced scientifically that the drug was safe and efficacious. What I am concerned about is the methodology, the procedures by which you reach that decision. Let me ask just a couple of very fundamental **questions** and I just need ball-park answers.

United States Food and Drug Administration, *A Legislative History of the Federal Food, Drug, and Cosmetic Act and Its Amendments, Appendix G*

Meltzer: I think we are at the point where we have spent the last couple of years sort of building the instruments, getting them working, getting the pipeline open and, now, the types of things that we are doing are answering exactly the kind of **questions** you are asking, which is taking the same pair of samples and doing a whole bunch of hybridizations and repeats, and really determining accurate statistics. So, I am not really in a position to make a lot of claims, quantitatively, as to what we can do with this system. We want to get really good accurate information on that before we can say. You have to ask what your standard of reference is going to be anyway, whether it is really even valid to compare two hybridization based assays. I think down to two to three fold is probably going to be pretty reasonable.

Gray: I have got a couple of **questions**. One is, you mentioned authentication—what do you do about that?

Meltzer: Well, it is a really a tough problem. We do not want to repeat the entire sequencing of all of these EST's. Our approach has been to sample sequence out of the library and determine a percent accuracy. It gets complicated here, because there are a lot of different EST libraries; the ones we are working with were primarily from Livermore and Gregg Lennon, and then they have been copied and duplicated and, in that process, errors have occurred and what is more, in the early days of this whole project there were some serious problems in lane tracking and things like that, that led to absolute actual mismatches between the database sequence and the clone id that is linked to that. So, there were actual errors in there to start with. What we have been doing is looking library by library, picking the ones that are giving us the cleanest data and then going back and polishing the arrays as we go. We are about ninety percent accurate at this point. I think what is going to end up happening, I hate to say this but, you will do experiments and if you come up with a certain number of genes that look really interesting, you are probably going to go back and re-sequence those to make sure that they are what you thought they were. We will build up gradually a higher degree of confidence in the sequence accuracy. One point that I want to make is that, in a lot of experiments that you might do, even though you might be looking at thousands of genes, the number of genes that are actually going to show alterations, that are going to be interesting to you is going to be perhaps relatively limited, and in the case of anonymous EST's, where you may have primarily sequenced from the three prime UTR, that is not much good to you to figure out gene function anyway independently, and someone is going to have to go now and get the full-length sequence information anyway and figure out what that gene is, so . . .

Paul S. Meltzer, Michael Bittner, Mervi Heiskanen, Tiffany Hoffman, Yidong Chen and Jeffrey M. Trent, *Use of cDNA Microarrays to Assess DNA Gene Expression Patterns in Cancer (The Biology of Tumors)*

But, as Aristotle, a man of the greatest genius, and of the most various knowledge, being excited by the glory of the rhetorician Isocrates, commenced teaching young men to speak, and joined philosophy with eloquence: so it is my design not to lay aside my former study of oratory, and yet to employ myself at the same time in this greater and more fruitful art; for I have always thought that to be able to speak copiously and elegantly on the most important **questions** was the most perfect philosophy. And I have so diligently applied myself to this pursuit, that I have already ventured to have a school like the Greeks. And lately when you left us, having many of my friends about me, I attempted at my Tusculan villa what I could do in that way; for as I formerly used to practise declaiming, which nobody continued longer than myself, so this is now to be the declamation of my old age. I desired any one to propose a **question** which he wished to have discussed, and then I argued that point either sitting or walking; and so I have compiled the *scholæ*, as the Greeks call them, of five days, in as many books. We proceeded in this manner: when he who had proposed the subject for discussion had said what he thought proper, I spoke against him; for this is, you know, the old and Socratic method of arguing against another's opinion; for Socrates thought that thus the truth would more easily be arrived at. But to give you a better notion of our disputations, I will not barely send you an account of them, but represent them to you as they were carried on; therefore let the introduction be thus:

Marcus Tullius Cicero, Tusculan Disputations

"Why have you got such a Bare Neck, Mummie?"
"I'm going to a Dance, Darling. One has to dress like this for a Dance!"
"Do the Ladies dance in one Room, and the Gentlemen in another, Mummie?"

*An Embarrassing **Question**, Punch, May 25, 1895*

Certain Embarrassing Questions

*Seldom in the history of nations has such a **question** been presented*

FAQ (noun)
pronounced *fak*
Acronym for **frequently asked question**

*What is a **FAQ**?*

A **FAQ** is a list of **questions** and answers, posted on a website or newsgroup with boilerplate answers, to preemptively address newbie ignorance and confusion.

*How is **FAQ** pronounced?*

The correct pronunciation is *fak*, though some insist on spelling it out.

*Why are **FAQs** worth reading?*

A **FAQ** can save a newbie considerable time by providing information that could otherwise be learned only by lurking for days or weeks, and considerable embarrassment by heading off breaches of netiquette as obscure yet essential as *Robert's Rules of Order.*

Jonathon Keats, *Control + Alt + Delete: A Dictionary of Cyberslang*

How are we to begin? We should certainly not wait till the eve of marriage, but begin in childhood. In theory, it is wrong to lie to children, if they are to maintain unshaken confidence in their parents, and remain truthful themselves. No doubt we cannot explain everything to a child at the age when it begins to ask its mother certain embarrassing **questions**, but we should endeavor as far as possible to tell it the truth in a manner suitable to its age. When this is impossible, every child who knows that no reasonable explanation is ever refused it will be satisfied with the answer: "You are too young now to understand that; I will tell you when you are older." Every child who speaks openly to its mother asks sooner or later how children come into the world. It is easier to reply to this when the child has had the opportunity of observing the same thing in animals. Why should the mother conceal the fact that it is nearly the same in man as in animals? The child never thinks of blushing or laughing at natural phenomena.

Auguste Forel and C. F. Marshall, *The Sexual **Question**: A Scientific, Psychological, Hygienic and Sociological Study*

Mother always insisted I got what I had coming. From birth, I was addicted to **questions**. When the delivering nurse slapped my rump, instead of howling, I blinked inquisitively. As a child I pushed the "why" cycle to break point. At six, I demanded to know why people cried. Mother launched into the authorized version of the uses of sorrow. At the end of her extended explanation, it came out that I really wanted the hydromechanics of tear ducts. By her account, I worsened with each year's new vocabulary. She finally took refuge in a multi-volume children's encyclopedia, parking me by it whenever I began to get asky. I can still see the color plates: Archers at Agincourt; Instruments of the Orchestra; two-page rainbow Evolutionary Tree. But her scheme backfired. I could now ask about things that hadn't even existed before. Whys multiplied, poking into the places color plates opened but failed to enter.

Richard Powers, The Gold Bug Variations

He asked her outright about the great mystery: did people do what animals did? Her reply was that there was an awful lot of Bad in the world, and the less you knew about it the luckier you were, and he was not to ask that **question** again.

Robertson Davies, What's Bred in the Bone

If you can see why she feel that she kneels if you can see why he knows that he shows what he bestows, if you can see why they share what they share, need we **question** that there is no doubt that by this time if they had intended to come they would have sent some notice of such intention. She and they and indeed the decision itself is not early dissatisfaction.

Gertrude Stein, Idem the Same: A Valentine to Sherwood Anderson

She doesn't answer but instead asks her own **question**, trying her best to conceal the **question** mark: Dad, what if all the churches and cathedrals were really centers for transmitting and receiving messages to and from space?

A. G. Porta, No World Concerto

YOU are now called to redress a great transgression. Seldom in the history of nations has such a **question** been presented. Tariffs, army bills, navy bills, land bills, are important, and justly occupy your care; but these all belong to the course of ordinary legislation. As means and instruments only, they are necessarily subordinate to the conservation of government itself. Grant them or deny them, in greater or less degree, and you will inflict no shock. The machinery of government will continue to move. The State will not cease to exist. Far otherwise is it with the eminent **question** now before you, involving, as it does, liberty in a broad territory, and also involving the peace of the whole country, with our good name in history for ever more.

Charles Sumner, On the Crime Against Kansas

So What Is Capitalism, Anyway?

We are used to seeing modern capitalism (along with modern traditions of democratic government) as emerging only later: with the Age of Revolutions—the industrial revolution, the American and French revolutions—a series of profound breaks at the end of the eighteenth century that only became fully institutionalized after the end of the Napoleonic Wars. Here we come face to face with a peculiar paradox. It would seem that almost all elements of financial apparatus that we've come to associate with capitalism—central banks, bond markets, short-selling, brokerage houses, speculative bubbles, securization, annuities—came into being not only before the science of economics (which is perhaps not too surprising), but also before the rise of factories, and wage labor itself.[88] This is a genuine challenge to familiar ways of thinking. We like to think of the factories and workshops as the "real economy," and the rest as superstructure, constructed on top of it. But if this were really so, then how can it be that the superstructure came first? Can the dreams of the system create its body?

All this raises the **question** of what "capitalism" is to begin with, a **question** on which there is no consensus at all.

David Graeber, Debt: The First 5,000 Years

23. Objection to the Consideration of a **Question**.

An objection may be made to the consideration of any original main motion, and to no others, provided it is made before there is any debate or before any subsidiary motion is stated. Thus, it may be applied to petitions and to communications that are not from a superior body, as well as to resolutions. It cannot be applied to incidental main motions[11], such as amendments to by-laws, or to reports of committees on subjects referred to them, etc. It is similar to a **question** of order in that it can be made when another has the floor, and does not require a second; and as the chairman can call a member to order, so he can put this **question**, if he deems it advisable, upon his own responsibility. It cannot be debated, or amended, or have any other subsidiary motion applied to it. It yields to privileged motions and to the motion to lay on the table. A negative, but not an affirmative vote on the consideration may be reconsidered.[13]

When an original main motion is made and any member wishes to prevent its consideration, he rises, although another has the floor, and says, "Mr. Chairman, I object to its consideration." The chairman immediately puts the **question**, "The consideration of the **question** has been objected to: Will the assembly consider it? [or, Shall the **question** be considered?]" If decided in the negative by a two-thirds vote, the whole matter is dismissed for that session; otherwise, the discussion continues as if this objection had never been made. The same **question** may be introduced at any succeeding session.

The *Object* of this motion is not to cut off debate (for which other motions are provided) but to enable the assembly to avoid altogether any **question** which it may deem irrelevant, unprofitable, or contentious. If the chair considers the **question** entirely outside the objects of the society, he should rule it out of order, from which decision an appeal may be taken.

Objection to the consideration of a **question** must not be confounded with objecting where unanimous consent, or a majority vote, is required. Thus, in case of the minority of a committee desiring to submit their views, a single member saying, "I object," prevents it, unless the assembly by a majority vote grants them permission.

Henry M. Robert, Robert's Rules of Order Revised for Deliberative Assemblies

"Sir?" Hogan prompted. "Robert Niles . . . ?"

"I've never received any kind of threat from that direction, Detective Inspector Hogan. Nor had I heard the name Herdman until after the shootings." He turned his head from the mirror. "Does that answer your **questions**?"

"Yes, sir."

"If Herdman had set out to target Anthony, why turn the gun on the other boys? Why wait so long after sentencing?"

"Yes, sir."

"Motive isn't always the issue . . ."

*Ian Rankin, A **Question** of Blood*

Politics and the Sexual Question.—*"Cherchez la femme"* is the common expression when anything unusual occurs in society. It would be more correct to say "Look for the sexual motive!" The actions of men are determined much more by their passions and sentiments than by purely intellectual reflection, i.e., by reason and logic.

But no sentiment is stronger than the direct sexual sentiment, or its derivatives— love, jealousy and hatred. From this results a fact which social systems have too much neglected, namely: that in all the domains of human social activity, the sexual passions and their psychic irradiations often interact directly or indirectly in a mischievous way. Mistresses and courtesans have always played a considerable part in political intrigue.

It is not necessary to have such a tragic scandal as that which caused the assassination of the king and queen of Servia. Everyday influences, even the smallest and most dissimulated, are often the most efficacious. Sexual intrigues have at all times influenced and directed the fate of nations. History relates a number of cases of this kind, but there are many more which have never been revealed to the public. It is sufficient to mention this fact. Every one who reflects will find an illustration of it, in the history of the past as well as in the politics of the present, in the courts of monarchs and in small democracies, in the local history of provinces, in his own parish, and lastly among his own relatives, friends and acquaintances.

*Auguste Forel and C. F. Marshall, The Sexual **Question**: A Scientific, Psychological, Hygienic and Sociological Study*

Then he went away from the door and Wells came over to Stephen and said:

—Tell us, Dedalus, do you kiss your mother before you go to bed?

Stephen answered:

—I do.

Wells turned to the other fellows and said:

—O, I say, here's a fellow says he kisses his mother every night before he goes to bed.

The other fellows stopped their game and turned round, laughing. Stephen blushed under their eyes and said:

—I do not.

Wells said:

—O, I say, here's a fellow says he doesn't kiss his mother before he goes to bed.

They all laughed again. Stephen tried to laugh with them. He felt his whole body hot and confused in a moment. What was the right answer to the **question**? He had given two and still Wells laughed. But Wells must know the right answer for he was in third of grammar. He tried to think of Wells's mother but he did not dare to raise his eyes to Wells's face. He did not like Wells's face. It was Wells who had shouldered him into the square ditch the day before because he would not swop his little snuffbox for Wells's seasoned hacking chestnut, the conqueror of forty. It was a mean thing to do; all the fellows said it was. And how cold and slimy the water had been! And a fellow had once seen a big rat jump plop into the scum.

The cold slime of the ditch covered his whole body; and, when the bell rang for study and the lines filed out of the playrooms, he felt the cold air of the corridor and staircase inside his clothes. He still tried to think what was the right answer. Was it right to kiss his mother or wrong to kiss his mother? What did that mean, to kiss? You put your face up like that to say good night and then his mother put her face down. That was to kiss. His mother put her lips on his cheek; her lips were soft and they wetted his cheek; and they made a tiny little noise: kiss. Why did people do that with their two faces?

James Joyce, A Portrait of the Artist as a Young Man

"Well, of course," said Mickey nervously, "hypothetically that is an interesting **question**. Very interesting."

"Yes, I think so."

"Yeah, definitely."

Mickey fell silent and spent a minute elaborately polishing the top of the hot plate, an activity he indulged in about once every ten years.

"There. See your face in that. Now. Where were we?"

Zadie Smith, White Teeth

I dreamed I was sitting on a bench, in Baltimore, facing the tumbling fountain in Harlem Park, beside a woman who wore a veil. I had come there with her. She was somebody I knew well. But I had suddenly forgotten who she was. I couldn't see her face because of the long black veil.

I thought that if I said something to her I would recognize her voice when she answered. But I was very embarrassed and was a long time finding anything to say. Finally I asked her if she knew a man named Carroll T. Harris.

She answered me, but the roar and swish of the tumbling fountain smothered her voice, and I could hear nothing.

Dashiell Hammett, Red Harvest

In Vanna Lava (Port Patterson) a man will not even walk behind his mother-in-law along the beach until the rising tide has washed away the trace of her footsteps. But they may talk to each other at a certain distance. It is quite out of the **question** that he should ever pronounce the name of his mother-in-law, or she his.

Sigmund Freud, Totem and Taboo: Resemblances Between the Psychic Lives of Savages and Neurotics

—Watch him, Mr Bloom said. He always walks outside the lampposts. Watch!

—Who is he if it's a fair **question**? Mrs Breen asked. Is he dotty?

—His name is Cashel Boyle O'Connor Fitzmaurice Tisdall Farrell, Mr Bloom said smiling. Watch!

—He has enough of them, she said. Denis will be like that one of these days.

She broke off suddenly.

—There he is, she said. I must go after him. Goodbye. Remember me to Molly, won't you?

James Joyce, Ulysses

He was saying the affectionate word, however, with a far more grudging condescension and patronage than he could have shown if their relative merits and positions had been reversed (which is invariably the case, all the world over), when Mr. Cruncher, touching him on the shoulder, hoarsely and unexpectedly interposed with the following singular **question**:

"I say! Might I ask the favour? As to whether your name is John Solomon, or Solomon John?"

The official turned towards him with sudden distrust. He had not previously uttered a word.

"Come!" said Mr. Cruncher. "Speak out, you know." (Which, by the way, was more than he could do himself.) "John Solomon, or Solomon John? She calls you Solomon, and she must know, being your sister. And I know you're John, you know. Which of the two goes first? And regarding that name of Pross, likewise. That warn't your name over the water."

"What do you mean?"

"Well, I don't know all I mean, for I can't call to mind what your name was, over the water."

"No?"

"No. But I'll swear it was a name of two syllables."

"Indeed?"

"Yes. T'other one's was one syllable. I know you. You was a spy—witness at the Bailey. What, in the name of the Father of Lies, own father to yourself, was you called at that time?"

Charles Dickens, *A Tale of Two Cities*

"What," says he, "hast never been in any village and knowest not what people or folks be?"

"Nay," said I, "nowhere save here have I been: yet tell me what be these things, folk and people and village."

"God save us," answered the hermit, "art thou demented or very cunning?"

"Nay," said I, "I am my mammy's and dad's boy, and neither Master Demented nor Master Cunning."

Then the hermit shewed his amazement with sighs and crossing of himself, and says he, "'Tis well, dear child, I am determined if God will better to instruct thee."

So then our **questions** and answers fell out as the ensuing chapter sheweth.

Chapter VIII
HOW SIMPLICISSIMUS BY HIS NOBLE DISCOURSE PROCLAIMED HIS EXCELLENT QUALITIES

Hermit. What is thy name?

Simplicissimus. My name is "Lad."

H. I can see well enough that thou art no girl: but how did thy father and mother call thee?

S. I never had either father or mother.

H. Who gave thee then thy shirt?

S. Oho! Why, my mammy.

H. What did thy mother call thee?

S. She called me "Lad," ay, and "rogue, silly gaby, and gallowsbird."

H. Who, then, was thy mammy's husband?

S. No one.

H. With whom, then, did thy mammy sleep at night?

S. With my dad.

H. What did thy dad call thee?

S. He called me "Lad."

H. What was his name?

S. His name was Dad.

H. What did thy mammy call him?

S. Dad, and sometimes also "Master."

H. Did she never call him aught besides?

S. Yea, that did she.

H. And what then?

S. "Beast," "coarse brute," "drunken pig," and other the like, when she would scold him.

H. Thou beest but an ignorant creature, that knowest not thy parents' name nor thine own.

S. Oho! neither dost thou know it.

H. Canst thou say thy prayers?

S. Nay, my mammy and our Ursel did uprear the beds.

H. I ask thee not that, but whether thou knowest thy Paternoster?

S. That do I.

H. Say it then.

S. Our father which art heaven, hallowed be name, to thy kingdom come, thy will come down on earth as it says heaven, give us debts as we give our debtors: lead us not into no temptation, but deliver us from the kingdom, the power, and the glory, for ever and ever. Amen.

H. God help us! Knowest thou naught of our Blessed Lord God?

S. Yea, yea: 'tis he that stood by our chamber-door; my mammy brought him home from the church feast and stuck him up there.

H. O Gracious God, now for the first time do I perceive what a great favour and benefit it is when Thou impartest knowledge of Thyself, and how naught a man is to whom Thou givest it not! O Lord, vouchsafe to me so to honour Thy holy name that I be worthy to be as zealous in my thanks for this great grace as Thou hast been liberal in the granting of it. Hark now, Simplicissimus (for I can call thee by no other name), when thou sayest thy Paternoster, thou must say this: "Our Father which art in heaven, hallowed be Thy name: Thy kingdom come: Thy will be done in earth as it is in heaven: give us this day our daily bread . . ."

S. Oho there! ask for cheese too!

H. Ah, dear child, keep silence and learn that thou needest more than cheese: thou art indeed loutish, as thy mammy told thee: 'tis not the part of lads like thee to interrupt an old man, but to be silent, to listen, and to learn. Did I but know where thy parents dwelt, I would fain bring thee to them, and then teach them how to bring up children.

S. I know not whither to go. Our house is burnt, and my mammy ran off and was fetched back with our Ursula, and my dad too, and our maid was sick and lying in the stable.

H. And who did burn the house?

S. Aha! there came iron men that sat on things as big as oxen, yet having no horns: which same men did slaughter sheep and cows and swine, and so I ran too, and then was the house burnt.

H. Where was thy dad then?

S. Aha! the iron men tied him up and our old goat was set to lick his feet. So he must needs laugh, and give the iron men many silver pennies, big and little, and fair yellow things and some that glittered, and fine strings full of little white balls.

H. And when did this come to pass?

S. Why, even when I should have been keeping of sheep: yea, and they would even take from me my bagpipe.

H. But when was it that thou shouldst have been keeping sheep?

S. What, canst thou not hear? Even then when the iron men came: and then our

Anna bade me run away, or the soldiers would carry me off: and by that she meant the iron men: so I ran off and so I came hither.

H. And whither wilt thou now?

S. Truly I know not: I will stay here with thee.

H. Nay, to keep thee here is not to the purpose, either for me or thee. Eat now; and presently I will bring thee where people are.

S. Oho! tell me now what manner of things be "people."

H. People be mankind like me and thee: thy dad, thy mammy, and your Ann be mankind, and when there be many together then are they called people: and now go thou and eat.

Hans Jacob Christoph von Grimmelshausen, The Adventurous Simplicius Simplicissimus; Being the Description of the Life of a Strange Vagabond Named Melchior Sternfels von Fuchshaim

ESTRAGON: *(chewing).* I asked you a **question**.

VLADIMIR: Ah.

ESTRAGON: Did you reply?

VLADIMIR: How's the carrot?

ESTRAGON: It's a carrot.

VLADIMIR: So much the better, so much the better. *(Pause.)* What was it you wanted to know?

ESTRAGON: I've forgotten. *(Chews.)* That's what annoys me. *(He looks at the carrot appreciatively, dangles it between finger and thumb.)* I'll never forget this carrot. *(He sucks the end of it meditatively.)* Ah yes, now I remember.

VLADIMIR: Well?

Samuel Beckett, Waiting for Godot

Why he brought her home, *he* said, was "for a real Jewish meal." For weeks he had been jabbering about the new *goyische* cashier ("a very plain drab person," he said, "who dresses in *shmattas*") who had been pestering him—so went the story he couldn't stop telling us—for a real Jewish meal from the day she had come to work in the Boston & Northeastern office. Finally my mother couldn't take any more. "All right, bring her already—she needs it so bad, so I'll give her one." Was he caught a little by surprise? Who will ever know.

At any rate, a Jewish meal is what she got all right. I don't think I have ever heard the word "Jewish" spoken so many times in one evening in my life, and let me tell you, I am a person who has heard the word "Jewish" spoken.

"This is your real Jewish chopped liver, Anne. Have you ever had real Jewish chopped liver before? Well, my wife makes the real thing, you can bet your life on that. Here, you eat it with a piece of bread. This is real Jewish rye bread, with seeds. That's it, Anne, you're doing very good, ain't she doing good, Sophie, for her first time? That's it, take a nice piece of real Jewish rye, now take a big fork full of the real Jewish chopped liver"—and on and on, right down to the jello—"that's right, Anne, the jello is kosher too, sure, of course, has to be—oh no, oh no, no cream in your coffee, not after meat, ha ha, hear what Anne wanted, Alex—?"

But babble-babble all you want, Dad dear, a **question** has just occurred to me, twenty-five years later (not that I have a single shred of evidence, not that until this moment I have ever imagined my father capable of even the slightest infraction of domestic law . . . but since infraction seems to hold for me a certain fascination), a **question** has arisen in the audience: why *did* you bring a shikse, of all things, into our home? Because you couldn't bear that a gentile woman should go through life without the experience of eating a dish of Jewish jello? Or because you could no longer live your own life without making Jewish confession? Without confronting your wife with your crime, so she might accuse, castigate, humiliate, punish, and thus bleed you forever of your forbidden lusts! Yes, a regular Jewish desperado, my father. I recognize the syndrome perfectly. Come, someone, anyone, find me out and condemn me—I did the most terrible thing you can think of: I took what I am not supposed to have! Chose pleasure for myself over duty to my loved ones! Please, catch me, incarcerate me, before God forbid I get away with it completely—

Philip Roth, Portnoy's Complaint

"I was thinking, sir," he said apologetically, "that it's a bit off the track to be finding out what he had for dinner. He didn't die of unwholesome feeding."

Thorndyke looked up with a smile. "It doesn't do, inspector, to assume that anything is off the track in an inquiry of this kind. Every fact must have some significance, you know."

"I don't see any significance in the diet of a man who has had his head cut off," the inspector rejoined defiantly.

"Don't you?" said Thorndyke. "Is there no interest attaching to the last meal of a man who has met a violent death? These crumbs, for instance, that are scattered over the dead man's waistcoat. Can we learn nothing from them?"

"I don't see what you can learn," was the dogged rejoinder.

Thorndyke picked off the crumbs, one by one, with his forceps, and having deposited them on a slide, inspected them, first with the lens and then through the microscope.

"I learn," said he, "that shortly before his death, the deceased partook of some kind of wholemeal biscuits, apparently composed partly of oatmeal."

"I call that nothing," said the inspector. "The **question** that we have got to settle is not what refreshments had the deceased been taking, but what was the cause of his death: did he commit suicide? was he killed by accident? or was there any foul play?"

R. Austin Freeman, The Case of Oscar Brodski

To be, or not to be, that is the **Question:**

William Shakespeare, The Tragedie of Hamlet, Prince of Denmarke

Sometimes it is easier to grant a favor than to answer a **question**, and this one hit me, so to speak, between wind and water. So little had I been prepared for it that I could think of nothing better to do than to retort, "What can that matter to you?"

William Edward Norris, An Embarrassing Orphan

The remains left those serious **questions** unanswered—the remains told me absolutely nothing.

Wilkie Collins, The Law and the Lady

As the fundamental **question** of metaphysics, we ask: "Why are there beings at all instead of nothing?" In this fundamental **question** there already resonates the prior **question**: how is it going with Being?

Martin Heidegger, Introduction to Metaphysics

"I beg your pardon," said Thorndyke, "the **questions** that remain to be settled are, who killed the deceased and with what motive? The others are already answered as far as I am concerned."

The inspector stared in sheer amazement not unmixed with incredulity.

R. Austin Freeman, The Case of Oscar Brodski

As valuable as these conclusions of linguistics are, we cannot be satisfied with them. For after these conclusions, the *questioning* must first begin.

Martin Heidegger, Introduction to Metaphysics

What remains? There are seven franchises in this Bill, and there remains nothing but the freehold franchise in **question** between us. We propose to throw the freeholders into the boroughs, and this, it is maintained, is fatal to the Bill. The objection is based exclusively on these borough freeholders, and the distinction which the noble Lord has adverted to, and which my right hon. Friend has adverted to, is a large constitutional objection that we have made one of the franchises common to counties and boroughs alike. Does that franchise stand in a distinctive position?

Hansard, Parliamentary Debates: Third Series, Commencing With the Accession of William IV, 22 Victoriae, 1859, Vol. CLIII, Comprising the Period From the Eleventh Day of March, 1859 to the Nineteenth Day of April, 1859, Second and Last Volume of First Session, 1859

This is a **question** I am prepared to answer, but only after permitting myself some observations about how *odd* the **question** is. It asks for me to justify my position in the very anthropocentric hedonist terms that I am proposing we modify.

Christopher D. Stone, Should Trees Have Standing? Law, Morality, and the Environment

The techniques considered are as follows: (1) the casual approach; (2) the numbered card (the respondent selects an answer on a card); (3) the "everybody" approach; (4) the "other people" approach; (5) the sealed ballot technique; (6) the projective technique (the respondent is asked to choose a relevant picture); (7) the Kinsey technique (the respondent is asked in simple language that assumes "everyone has done everything"); and (8) the placement of the **question** at the end of the interview. The author believes that asking the embarrassing **question** is a challenge to pollsters.

Graham R. Walden, Polling and Survey Research Methods 1935–1979: An Annotated Bibliography

. . . and this usually renders marriage impossible, as long as he has not what is called a position. But no one will blame the same student for living in concubinage with a grisette. Why cannot the same means of existence which allow concubinage suffice for marriage? With this **question** I only touch on a problem to which we shall return, at the same time pointing out the canker which corrupts our modern sexual life.

By marriage for money we understand marriage which is based on interest and not on love. It is not always a **question** of money; for position, name, titles and convenience often complicate the **question**.

*Auguste Forel and C. F. Marshall, The Sexual **Question**: A Scientific, Psychological, Hygienic and Sociological Study*

We tell ourselves this. I tell myself this. But I do and I don't. I want to be in a state of unknowing only some of the time. Sometimes, I may be ready to be surprised; sometimes, I am open to what I have never considered, never understood, never known, but it's not what I always want.

There may be what Cixous terms "happy accidents"[140] but becoming open to the new is arduous. Writing to the rhythm of the refrain in that in-between space, the *intermilieu*—there, at the edges of disorder, in the threshold where difference is generated—Pete and his audience at the The Stand as he disappears from the stage—writing like that, there, is troubling. It might leave you standing. Yet writing there, to the rhythm of the refrain, in the threshold, is where inquiry happens:

> I don't know what to make of thresholds, and I'm not sure whether I like them, but my intuition, my gut, tells me it's where our research needs to be. I want to push thresholds . . . towards a place—a multiplicity of spaces and times— where categories (this and that, here and there) become indistinct, where we position ourselves and our inquiries as always in thresholds, forever liminal, forever refusing "here" or "there," seeking out the pauses, not the notes, in the song; the pauses as notes. In such thresholds our research can be at its most critical, where we take nothing for granted, where everything is at stake. It means conducting inquiries as if we do not know where they will take us. As if there were no more time.[141]

Easy to say, I now think. Easier to assert than to embody. Perhaps most of us, most of the time, tend towards the familiar, the striated, but when we allow refrains to carry us into and through that intermilieu, writing-to-inquire can perhaps become close to how Derrida describes Foucault's work, as carrying a **question** within it, "a **question** that keeps [us] in suspense, holding [our] breath—and, thus, keeps [us] alive".[142] Not the kind of formulaic 'research **question**' funders demand of us and we may demand of our students. Such **questions** don't hold their breath; they position themselves within neo-liberal discourse as 'useful' and 'relevant', telling us of their potential for generating 'impact'. No, not that; instead the refrains of writing-to-inquire might take us into **questions** that are "provocative, risky, stunning, astounding . . . , [that take] our breath away with [their] daring".[143] Inquiry that surprises. Inquiry that gives us butterflies. Inquiry that gives us goose bumps. Inquiry that troubles.

Jonathan Wyatt, Therapy, Stand-Up, and the Gesture of Writing: Towards Creative-Relational Inquiry

As usual, John W. Davis and Justice Jackson have some cogent advice on this topic. Davis put it this way:

> If the **question** warrants a negative answer, do not fence with it but respond with a bold *thwertutnay*—which for the benefit of the illiterate I may explain as a term used in ancient pleading to signify a downright No. While if the answer is in the affirmative or calls for a concession, the Court will be equally gratified to have the matter promptly disposed of. If you value your argumentative life, do not evade or shuffle or postpone no matter how embarrassing the **question** may be or how much it interrupts the thread of your argument. Nothing I should think would be more irritating to an inquiring court than to have refuge taken in the familiar evasion "I am coming to that" and then to have the argument end with the promise unfulfilled. If you are really coming to it, indicate what your answer will be when it is reached and never, never sit down until it is made . . . [Q]uestions fairly put and frankly answered give to oral argument a vitality and spice that nothing else will supply.

Justice Jackson had this to say on the same subject:

> I advise you never to postpone an answer to a **question**, for that always gives
> an impression of evasion. It is better immediately to answer the **question**, even
> though you do so in short form and suggest that you expect to amplify and
> support your answer later.

Douglas S. Lavine, **Questions** *From the Bench*

First **Question**: Did James J. Hoey die September 30th, 1900, from hasty consumption?
Ans. Yes.

Second **Question**: Do you find from the evidence that the said Hoey would not have
died September 30th, 1900, but for the injury of December 11th, 1899? Ans. Yes.

Third **Question**: Do you find from the evidence that the disease of consumption would
not have come to Hoey but for the injury? Ans. Yes.

Fourth **Question**: Do you find from the evidence that Hoey would not have died
September 30th, 1900, but for the disease of consumption?

(This **question** taken away from the consideration of the jurors.)

Fifth **Question**: Did Hoey die because of the negligence of the defendant? Ans. Yes.

We find for the plaintiff for $12,500.

(Signed) JOEL NEWMARKE, Foreman,

and a verdict rendered therein for the plaintiff for the sum of $12,500. Motion to
dismiss complaint. Decision reserved. Briefs to be submitted July 1, 1901. Time to submit
briefs extended to July 15, 1901. October 5, 1901, judgment is directed dismissing the
complaint and setting aside the general verdict and the answers to the specific **questions**
except the first.

(Signed) WM. SOHMER, Clerk.

Supreme Court of the State of New York Appellate Division First Department, David Morgan Hildreth, Junior,
and Walter E. Hildreth, as Executors of and Trustees Under the Last Will and Testament of David M. Hildreth,
Deceased, and Annie L. Hildreth, as Executrix Under Said Will, Plaintiff's Respondents, Against Charles Allen
Hildreth, Defendant-Appellant, Record on Appeal

But philosophical **questions** are in principle never settled as if some day one could set
them aside. Here, the preliminary **question** does not stand outside the fundamental
question at all, but is, as it were, the hearth-fire that glows in the asking of the fundamental **question**, the hearth at the heart of all **questioning**. That is to say: when we
first ask the fundamental **question**, everything depends on our taking up the decisive
fundamental position in asking its *prior* **question**, and winning and securing the attitude
that is essential here. This is why we brought the **question** about Being into connection
with the fate of Europe, where the fate of the earth is being decided, while for Europe
itself our historical Dasein proves to be the center.

The **question** ran:

Is Being a mere word and its meaning a vapor, or does what is named with the word
"Being" hold within it the spiritual fate of the West?

Martin Heidegger, Introduction to Metaphysics

That night, Devon Cox was keeping the cold away with the heat and a blanket. In front
of him, in his desk, a box full of documents and evidences of the case they had. The
suicide of Collins was still a huge pile of **questions**, where the marks on the road were
the big **question**. He was dying for calling the cafeteria so Sandy could bring him a

coffee after finishing his turn, and then he could invite her for dinner. Then he thought about making Sandy his with no hesitation at all, he wanted to make love to that woman until the sun came out. While he was making efforts to raise up the temperature of the cold month of February he would raise up the temperature of her body until making her melt. And he was capable of it. Because, every time he remembered her lips with a trivial conversation, he shook from head to toes.

Nobody had still clear why Collins committed suicide and what his one million dollars bow had to do with all this. No doubt, the money was a very important motive to kill.

But that would be a brutal coincidence. The coincidences didn't exist, had that clear, so, what was going on there? Besides, there was that poor taxi driver. Everything that happened didn't have to do with that man, and his family had buried him more than one month ago. He worked so hard to be able to help his son to pay the university, and that day he had bad luck. The threats that McAllen's widow had been receiving showed that the driver was a collateral damage. Personally, he felt his blood burning every time he thought about that. When he thought about the picture of the family stick to the glass of the room of the poor driver when he was connected to thousands of tubes. He wondered why the roulette wheel was turning this way. He surely wouldn't forget the wife crying with her eyes closed praying. He saw her praying day and night. What he never knew was if she was praying to save the life of her husband or to have the bravery of helping her family to overcome the tragic death of her husband. It wasn't his first case, but of course, it was the most terrible. With that thought, he sat down and with a patience barely common in him opened the box and began to classify everything that was inside.

Yaiza Cabrera Torres, When You Embarrass the Devil

Hence the isolation of the man-god is quite as necessary for the safety of others as for his own. His divinity is a fire, which, under proper restraints, confers endless blessings, but, if rashly touched or allowed to break bounds, burns and destroys what it touches. Hence the disastrous effects supposed to attend a breach of taboo; the offender has thrust his hand into the divine fire, which shrivels up and consumes him on the spot. To take an example from the taboo we are considering. It happened that a New Zealand chief of high rank and great sanctity had left the remains of his dinner by the wayside. A slave, a stout, hungry fellow, coming up after the chief had gone, saw the unfinished dinner, and ate it up without asking **questions**. Hardly had he finished when he was informed by a horror-stricken spectator that the food of which he had eaten was the chief's. "I knew the unfortunate delinquent well. He was remarkable for courage, and had signalised himself in the wars of the tribe . . . No sooner did he hear the fatal news than he was seized by the most extraordinary convulsions and cramp in the stomach, which never ceased till he died, about sundown the same day. He was a strong man, in the prime of life, and if any *pakeha* [European] freethinker should have said he was not killed by the *tapu* [taboo] of the chief, which had been communicated to the food by contact, he would have been listened to with feelings of contempt for his ignorance and inability to understand plain and direct evidence."

James George Frazer, The Golden Bough: A Study in Comparative Religion

And yet, if my own observation of the Major were to be trusted, the way to the clew of which I was in search lay, directly or indirectly, through the broken vase.

It was useless to pursue the **question**, knowing no more than I knew now. I returned to the book-case.

Thus far I had assumed (without any sufficient reason) that the clew of which I was in search must necessarily reveal itself through a written paper of some sort. It now occurred to me—after the movement which I had detected on the part of the Major—that the clew might quite as probably present itself in the form of a book.

I looked along the lower rows of shelves, standing just near enough to them to read the titles on the backs of the volumes. I saw Voltaire in red morocco, Shakespeare in blue, Walter Scott in green, the "History of England" in brown, the "Annual Register" in yellow calf. There I paused, wearied and discouraged already by the long rows of volumes. How (I thought to myself) am I to examine all these books? And what am I to look for, even if I do examine them all?

Wilkie Collins, The Law and the Lady

There are the recently discovered butchered remains of a rhinoceros that suggest human relatives lived on Luzon around 700,000 years ago. Stone artifacts from fragments of tools, statuettes, jars, and weapons from early inhabitants. A dark room full of jars shaped like people filled with human remains that were found in a cave. A bunch of porcelain from China's early trade presence. A collection all about the Muslim cultures of the southern islands. A room dedicated to rice cultivation. An exhibit about Baybayin and the other syllabic scripts used in various regions long before the Spanish arrived. A collection of illustrations and photographs depicting the elaborate tattoos traditional in some tribes.

Tito Maning and I don't hold any actual conversations as we check all of this out. Mostly he points to things and says, "Jason, I am thinking you know nothing about this," or, "This is what they wanted us to forget." Occasionally he quizzes me on background knowledge I obviously don't have. It doesn't take me long to realize that this trip is less about educating me and more about exposing my ignorance.

It's a lot of information, and as much as I'd love to remember it all, the only thing staying in my head is how badly I'm failing. I think of what Mia said when I told her about my dream, and I keep expecting to see Jun's ghost around every corner, asking me why I'm keeping my silence. After a couple of hours, Tito Maning decides we're done and that we should go to the National Museum of Fine Arts next. As we walk over to the adjacent building, I form the **question** I'm going to ask about Jun in my mind. Except this time, not only does my heart start racing as I prepare to voice it, but I get this light-headed feeling like I'm going to pass out. So I say nothing, hanging back a couple of steps.

Randy Ribay, Patron Saints of Nothing

That is the **question**. Presumably it is no arbitrary **question**. "Why are there beings at all instead of nothing?"—this is obviously the first of all **questions**. Of course, it is not the first **question** in the chronological sense. Individuals as well as peoples ask many **questions** in the course of their historical passage through time. They explore, investigate, and test many sorts of things before they run into the **question**, "Why are there beings at all instead of nothing?" Many never run into this **question** at all, if running into the **question** means not only hearing and reading the interrogative sentence as uttered, but asking the **question**, that is, taking a stand on it, posing it, compelling oneself into the state of this **questioning**.

And yet, we are each touched once, maybe even now and then, by the concealed power of this **question**, without properly grasping what is happening to us. In great despair, for example, when all weight tends to dwindle away from things and the sense of things grows dark, the **question** looms.

Martin Heidegger, Introduction to Metaphysics

At that moment the door opened and the figure of a woman, dressed in black and heavily veiled, entered the room, passed entirely around the table, and vanished as silently and suddenly as she had appeared. It was easy for Helen thus to reach the banquet room, for she had been a guest in the house and the servants had golden memories of her. It had been easy for any intelligent, well-dressed woman, both because of its unexpectedness and because in a hotel such people may pass in the halls without **question**.

The effect was like that of the spectral Banquo at the royal feast. The guests gazed at one another and at their host for a few seconds in dumb surprise.

Gurney sank into his chair as if he had been shot; but it was a desperate crisis in his life, and he was full of courage. He rose to his feet and said, with a forced smile:

"I am very sorry, for your sakes, gentlemen, to have had this unfortunate interruption. That poor woman is insane, and for some unaccountable reason has conceived a deadly antipathy to me. You can imagine that it is very embarrassing; but one can not offer violence to a woman, and one can not reason with a lunatic! I must therefore submit to it with forbearance. Let me return to what I was saying."

Charles Frederic Goss, The Loom of Life

Heidegger's **question** is the **question** he centers *Introduction to Metaphysics* on: "why are there beings instead of nothing." He finds that this is the central **question** of metaphyiscs, the "first **question**" in order of primordiality for Dasein. Even if we never directly confront this query, we feel in simple experiences everyday—when we come up against sadness against the decay of the idealic American West, we implicitly ask the **question**, "why are there beings instead of nothing?" Heidegger writes that we hear it "like the muffled tolling of a bell" that "gradually fades away."

—shreekingeels, 07 Jun 2014 at 2:53 pm

cormacmccarthy.com, Heidegger's Cabin/Bell's Water Trough

Perhaps it strikes only once, like the muffled tolling of a bell that resounds into Dasein and gradually fades away. The **question** is there in heartfelt joy, for then all things are transformed and surround us as if for the first time, as if it were easier to grasp that they were not, rather than that they are, and are as they are. The **question** is there in a spell of boredom, when we are equally distant from despair and joy, but when the stubborn ordinariness of beings lays open a wasteland in which it makes no difference to us whether beings are or are not—and then, in a distinctive form, the **question** resonates once again: Why are there beings at all instead of nothing?

Martin Heidegger, Introduction to Metaphysics

'I don't know. A week ago somebody called on me. A stranger. He wanted me to help him. It was not a doctor's job. I said no. He asked me whether my sympathies were with the East or the West. I tried to joke with him. I said they were in the middle." Dr. Hasselbacher said accusingly, "Once a few weeks ago you asked me the same **question**.'

'I was only joking, Hasselbacher.'

'I know. Forgive me. The worst thing they do is making all this suspicion.' He stared into the sink.

Graham Greene, Our Man in Havana

Mr. Sanford. I do not quite understafnd the service of supply in France. I have in mind what you stated this morning.

Gen. Rogers. I was going to bring that up in just a moment. I think possibly I misunderstood the **question**. You mean in regard to the service of supply operating?

Mr. Sanford. Yes; in relation to the Quartermaster Corps, for instance?

Gen. Rogers. I think possibly I gave a wrong impression in my testimony this morning. I should like to change that impression. Under the field service regulations it requires that the lines of communications be established in the zone of operations. The service of supply—the name was changed two or three times—it was called the line of communications at one time, but any way it filled what was required by the field service regulations, and as such it was an operating agency. I would like to correct the impression I gave this morning.

United States Congress House Committee on Military Affairs, Army Reorganization: Hearings Before the Committee on Military Affairs, House of Representatives, Sixty-Sixth Congress, First and Second Sessions, on H.R. 8287, A Bill to Reorganize and Increase the Efficiency of the United States Army, and for Other Purposes, H.R. 8068, A Bill to Provide for Universal Military, Naval and Vocational Training, and for Mobilization of the Manhood of the Nation in a National Emergency, H.R. 7925, A Bill to Establish the Department of Aeronautics, and for Other Purposes, H.R. 8870, A Bill to Amend an Act Entitled "An Act for Making Further and More Effectual Provision for the National Defense, and for Other Purposes," Volume 1

A first law of economic thermodynamics would state, in effect, that one cannot get something for nothing; somebody, somewhere, has to pay—it`s only a matter of who, how and when. In Cape Breton, this principle manifests itself every time a federal or provincial government starts "election chumming," by tossing out bits of bait under the rubric of another "cooperation agreement" or funding program. Once the smell of government money is in the water, the sharks begin to gather. The feeding frenzy that follows represents simply the next round of political manoeuvring on behalf of interests that fail to advance the economic self-sufficiency of the community. This cynical strategy, legitimized by constant reference to the latest economic gospel, is simply another variation on the disreputable theme of privatizing benefits and socializing costs.

The cost of these projects is nominally borne by someone outside Cape Breton (i.e., the anonymous Canadian taxpayer), and their local beneficiaries are expected to take the money, be grateful and not raise embarrassing **questions**. In fact, everyone in Cape Breton has paid dearly for such gifts, in the form of the lost opportunity costs of well-considered developments that were not pursued, but which could have made a lasting difference, and the costs of the island's unenviable and undeserved notoriety for an insatiable addiction to government subsidies which discourage private investors whose increased participation in the local economy could lead to economic independence.

The second law would state, in effect, that any useful activity, left to itself—not supported by the additional resources and effort required to maintain an ordered purpose—will lose focus, become fragmented and disorganized, dissipate its resources and degenerate into increasingly inconsequential, randomly-directed activity. In Cape Breton, this principle manifests itself in arbitrary decisions to disregard opportunities consistent with real economic development in favour of initiatives of which the economic merits are not commensurate with the investment of public funds they entail.

> Paul Patterson and Susan Biagi, *The Loom of Change: Weaving A New Economy on Cape Breton*

Elsewhere, (in *Being and Time*) he catalogues the process of "forgetting" this mode of **questioning** for the reason that it is too painful to confront. Authenticity, our willingness to uncover and face what has been lost, is Heideggers answer to forgetting the source of the "muffled bell." McCarthy figures this authenticity in his male protagonists who search through the American west for no other reason but to face their own unanswerable primordiatlity:

"He rode with the sun coppering his face and the red wind blowing out of the west across the evening land . . . horse and rider and horse passed on and their long shadows passed in tandem like the shadow of a single being. Passed and paled into the darkening land, the world to come." (*All the Pretty Horses*, 302)

Likewise, in *Suttree*, around the time of his death, Suttree (can we agree that his and the first person omniscient blend in the more stream-of-consciousness passages?) remarks wonders that

"how surely the dead are beyond death. Death is what the living carry with them. A state of dread, like some uncanny foretaste of a bitter memory. But the dead do not remember and nothingness is not a curse. Far from it." (Vintage edition 153)

—shreekingeels, 07 Jun 2014 at 2:53 pm

cormacmccarthy.com, Heidegger's Cabin/Bell's Water Trough

Mr. Sourwine: Well, then, I will go back to my earlier **question**: Isn't it true that your refusal to answer these **questions** is concealing from this committee and keeping out of our record matters within your knowledge concerning the Communist conspiracy against the Government of the United States?

Senator Jenner. Let the record show the witness, before responding, confers with counsel.

(Witness confers with his counsel.)

Mr. Knowles. I can only repeat that I have no knowledge of any Communist activities within the jurisdiction of this committee.

> United States Congress Senate Committee on the Judiciary, *Subversive Influence in the Educational Process: Hearings Before the Subcommittee to Investigate the Administration of the Internal Security Act and Other Internal Security Laws*

But there were other characters whom he feared might not bear close inspection: Rodriguez, for example, described on his card as a night-club king, and Teresa, a dancer at the Shanghai Theatre whom he had listed as the mistress simultaneously of the Minister of Defence and the Director of Posts and Telegraphs (it was not surprising that London had found no trace of either Rodriguez or Teresa). He was ready to jettison Rodriguez, for anyone who came to know Havana well would certainly **question** his existence sooner or later.

> Graham Greene, *Our Man in Havana*

Major Fitz-David had spoken of a terrible misfortune which had darkened my husband's past life. In what possible way could any trace of that misfortune, or any suggestive hint of something resembling it, exist in the archives of the "Annual Register" or in the pages of Voltaire? The bare idea of such a thing seemed absurd. The mere attempt to make a serious examination in this direction was surely a wanton waste of time.

And yet the Major had certainly stolen a look at the book-case. And again, the broken vase had once stood on the book-case. Did these circumstances justify me in connecting the vase and the book-case as twin landmarks on the way that led to discovery? The **question** was not an easy one to decide on the spur of the moment.

I looked up at the higher shelves.

Here the collection of books exhibited a greater variety. The volumes were smaller, and were not so carefully arranged as on the lower shelves. Some were bound in cloth, some were only protected by paper covers; one or two had fallen, and lay flat on the shelves. Here and there I saw empty spaces from which books had been removed and not replaced. In short, there was no discouraging uniformity in these higher regions of the book-case. The untidy top shelves looked suggestive of some lucky accident which might unexpectedly lead the way to success. I decided, if I did examine the book-case at all, to begin at the top.

Where was the library ladder?

Wilkie Collins, The Law and the Lady

THE REVEREND MR LARYNX

For a young man of fashion and family, Mr Listless, you seem to be of a very studious turn.

THE HONOURABLE MR LISTLESS

Studious! You are pleased to be facetious, Mr Larynx. I hope you do not suspect me of being studious. I have finished my education. But there are some fashionable books that one must read, because they are ingredients of the talk of the day; otherwise, I am no fonder of books than I dare say you yourself are, Mr Larynx.

THE REVEREND MR LARYNX

Why, sir, I cannot say that I am indeed particularly fond of books; yet neither can I say that I never do read. A tale or a poem, now and then, to a circle of ladies over their work, is no very heterodox employment of the vocal energy. And I must say, for myself, that few men have a more Job-like endurance of the eternally recurring **questions** and answers that interweave themselves, on these occasions, with the crisis of an adventure, and heighten the distress of a tragedy.

THE HONOURABLE MR LISTLESS

And very often make the distress when the author has omitted it.

MARIONETTA

I shall try your patience some rainy morning, Mr Larynx; and Mr Listless shall recommend us the very newest new book, that every body reads.

Thomas Love Peacock, Nightmare Abbey

Wilde looked through the book, wooden-faced, closed it and pushed it towards Cronjager. Cronjager opened it, looked at a page or two, shut it quickly. A couple of red spots the size of half dollars showed on his cheekbones.

I said: "Look at the stamped dates on the front endpaper."

Cronjager opened the book again and looked at them. "Well?"

POPPING THE QUESTION
Motion picture poster for "An Embarrassing Predicament" shows a man, a woman and a clergyman.
Goes Litho Co., Chicago, 1914 (Library of Congress)

"If necessary," I said, "I'll testify under oath that that book came from Geiger's store. The blonde, Agnes, will admit what kind of business the store did. It's obvious to anybody with eyes that that store is just a front for something. But the Hollywood police allowed it to operate, for their own reasons. I dare say the Grand Jury would like to know what those reasons are."

Wilde grinned. He said: "Grand Juries do ask those embarrassing **questions** sometimes—in a rather vain effort to find out just why cities are run as they are run."

Cronjager stood up suddenly and put his hat on. "I'm one against three here," he snapped. "I'm a homicide man. If this Geiger was running indecent literature, that's no skin off my nose. But I'm ready to admit it won't help my division any to have it washed over in the papers. What do you birds want?"

Raymond Chandler, *The Big Sleep*

Spade shook the hand and smiled, but said nothing.

Spade sat in a soft green chair. The fat man began to fill two glasses from bottle and siphon. The boy had disappeared. Doors set in three of the room's walls were closed. The fourth wall, behind Spade, was pierced by two windows looking out over Geary Street.

"We begin well, sir," the fat man purred, turning with a proffered glass in his hand. "I distrust a man that says when. If he's got to be careful not to drink too much it's because he's not to be trusted when he does."

Spade took the glass and, smiling, made the beginning of a bow over it.

The fat man raised his glass and held it against a window's light. He nodded approvingly at the bubbles running up in it. He said:

"Well, sir, here's to plain speaking and clear understanding."

They drank and lowered their glasses.

The fat man looked shrewdly at Spade and asked:

"You're a close-mouthed man?"

Spade shook his head. "I like to talk."

"Better and better!" the fat man exclaimed. "I distrust a close-mouthed man. He generally picks the wrong time to talk and says the wrong things. Talking's something you can't do judiciously unless you keep in practice." He beamed over his glass. "We'll get along, sir, that we will." He set his glass on the table and held the box of Coronas del Ritz out to Spade. "A cigar, sir."

Spade took, and trimmed the end of, and lighted, a cigar. Meanwhile the fat man pulled another green plush chair around to face Spade's within convenient distance and placed a smoking-stand within reach of both chairs. Then he took his glass from the table, took a cigar from the box, and lowered himself into his chair. His bulbs stopped jouncing and settled into flabby rest. He sighed comfortably and said:

"Now, sir, we'll talk if you like. And I'll tell you right out that I'm a man who likes talking to a man that likes to talk."

"Swell. Will we talk about the black bird?"

The fat man laughed and his bulbs rode up and down on his laughter.

"Will we?" he asked and, "We will," he replied. His pink face was shiny with delight. "You're the man for me, sir, a man cut along my own lines. No beating about the bush, but right to the point. 'Will we talk about the black bird?' We will. I like that, sir. I like that way of doing business. Let us talk about the black bird by all means, but first, sir, answer me a **question**, please, though maybe it's an unnecessary one, so we'll understand each other from the beginning. You're here as Miss O'Shaughnessy's representative?"

Dashiell Hammett, The Maltese Falcon

Among many savage races there exists matriarchism, which gives the woman a high social position. This has even been made a religious dogma, while it simply originates from the natural and just idea that the mother is much more intimately connected with the children than the father.

*Auguste Forel and C. F. Marshall, The Sexual **Question**: A Scientific, Psychological, Hygienic and Sociological Study*

And companies eager to attract and retain talented workers and managers are responding. The consulting firm Deloitte, for instance, started what's now considered the model program, called Mass Career Customization, which allows employees to adjust their hours depending on their life stage. The program, Deloitte explains, solves "a complex issue—one that can no longer be classified as a women's issue." Women have written the blueprint for the workplace of the future. The only **question** left is, will the men really adapt?

Hanna Rosin, The End of Men: And the Rise of Women

"Will we?" he asked and, "We will," he replied. His pink face was shiny with delight. "You're the man for me, sir, a man cut along my own lines. No beating about the bush, but right to the point. 'Will we talk about the black bird?' We will. I like that, sir. I like that way of doing business. Let us talk about the black bird by all means, but first, sir, answer me a **question**, please, though maybe it's an unnecessary one, so we'll understand each other from the beginning. "

Dashiell Hammett, The Maltese Falcon

Dr. E_ asks *What is the nature of your fantasies, Quentin?* & I am blank & silent blushing like in school when I could not answer a teacher's **question** nor even (everybody staring at me) comprehend it.

Joyce Carol Oates, Zombie

Dr. Hasselbacher said accusingly, 'Once a few weeks ago you asked me the same **question**.'
'I was only joking, Hasselbacher.'
'I know. Forgive me. The worst thing they do is making all this suspicion.' He stared into the sink. 'An infantile dream. Of course I know that. Fleming discovered penicillin by an inspired accident. But an accident has to be inspired. An old second-rate doctor would never have an accident like that, but it was no business of theirs—was it?—if I wanted to dream.'

Graham Greene, Our Man in Havana

To many ears the **question** may sound violent and exaggerated. For if pressed, one could indeed imagine that discussing the **question** of Being might ultimately, at a very great remove and in a very indirect manner, have some relation to the decisive historical **question** of the earth, but by no means in such a way that from out of the history of the earth's spirit, the fundamental position and attitude of our **questioning** could directly be determined. And yet there is such a connection.

Martin Heidegger, Introduction to Metaphysics

The study was conducted to determine which **question** format would be most useful when the content was threatening. A national sample drawn from the National Opinion Research Center's national master sample was used, with 1,172 personal interviews conducted. The level of threatening **questions** ranged from the lowest being on sports activity to the highest being masturbation. In between were **questions** on various other sexual activities, drug use, and gambling. To answer the frequency **question** respondents were given a card with eight options ranging from "daily" at the bottom to "never" on top. The **questions** were posed in various formats, including open-ended, long, and familiar. The results indicate that threatening **questions** which simply require a "yes" or "no" answer can be asked using any format.

Graham R. Walden, Polling and Survey Research Methods 1935–1979: An Annotated Bibliography

Ada dua bentuk pertanyaan dalam bahasa lnggris, yaitu pertanyaan singkat atau *yes-no questions* dan pertanyaan yang menggunakan kata tanya seperti *what, where, why, who, which, when,* dan *how* atau sering disebut *WH questions. Yes-no questions* hanya membutuhkan jawaban "yes" atau 'no', misalnya:

> *"Are you angry?"*
> *"No, I'm not."*
> *"Can you do it?"*
> *"Yes, I can."*

Silvester Goridus Sukur, Embarrassing Stories: My Wife's Twin Sister (Completed With Grammatical Notes)

Q. You are sure about that?

A. Yes, sir; I did not understand the **question**.

Bushnell & Albright, Attorneys for Relator and Appellant, and Shipman, Barlow, & MacFarland, Attorneys for Respondents, New York Supreme Court: The People, etc., ex rel. Henry C. Ohlen, Against the New York, Lake Erie and Western Railroad Company et al., Appeal Book, on Appeal from Order Quashing Writ of Mandamus

But whether this **question** is asked explicitly, or whether it merely passes through our Dasein like a fleeting gust of wind, unrecognized as a **question**, whether it becomes more oppressive or is thrust away by us again and suppressed under some pretext, it certainly is never the first **question** that we ask.

Martin Heidegger, Introduction to Metaphysics

This will need explanation. Their competitions may be as follows:

1. Previous **question** and postpone...........
        commit ....
        amend ....
2. Postpone and previous **question** ....
        commit ....
        amend ....
3. Commit and previous **question** ....
        postpone ....
        amend ....
4. Amend and previous **question** ....
        postpone ....
        commit ....

In the first, second and third classes, and the first member of the fourth class, the rule, "first moved first put" takes place.

In the first class, where the previous **question** is first moved, the effect is peculiar; for it not only prevents the after motion to postpone or commit from being put to **question** before it, but also from being put after it; for if the previous **question** be decided affirmatively, to wit, that the main **question** shall *now* be put, it would of course be against the decision to postpone or commit; and if it be decided negatively, to wit, that the main **question** shall not now be put, this puts the House out of possession of the main **question**, and consequently there is nothing before them to postpone or commit. So that neither voting for nor against the previous **question** will enable the advocates for postponing or committing to get at their object. Whether it may be amended shall be examined hereafter.

Second class. If postponement be decided affirmatively, the proposition is removed from before the House, and consequently there is no ground for the previous **question**, commitment, or amendment; but if decided negatively (that it shall not be postponed), the main **question** may then be suppressed by the previous **question**, or may be committed or amended.

The third class is subject to the same observations as the second.

The fourth class. Amendment of the main **question** first moved, and afterwards the previous **question**, the **question** of amendment shall be first put.

Amendment and postponement competing, postponement is first put, as the equivalent proposition to adjourn the main **question** would be in Parliament. The reason is, that the **question** for amendment is not suppressed by postponement or adjourning the main **question**, but remains before the House whenever the main **question** is resumed; and it might be that the occasion for other urgent business might go by, and be lost by length of debate on the amendment, if the House had it not in their power to postpone the whole subject.

Amendment and commitment. The **question** for committing though last moved, shall be first put; because, in truth, it facilitates and befriends the motion to amend. *Scobell* is express: "On motion to amend a bill, any one may, notwithstanding, move to commit it, and the **question** for commitment shall be first put. *Scob.,* 46.

We have hitherto considered the **question** of two or more of the privileged **questions** contending for privilege between themselves, when both are moved on the original or main **question**: but now let us suppose one of them to be moved not on the original primary **question**, but on the secondary one, *e.g.*

Suppose a motion to postpone, commit or amend the main **question**, and that it be moved to suppress that motion by putting a previous **question** on it.

This is not allowed, because it would embarrass **questions** too much to allow them to be piled on one another several stories high; and the same result may be had in a more simple way, by deciding against the postponement, commitment or amendment. *2 Hats.,* 81, 2, 3, 4.

Wisconsin State Legislature, The Blue Book of the State of Wisconsin

If I am wrong about that, I am perfectly willing to stand corrected. You may say anything you want to in the way of a statement to counter what I have just charged.

Mr. Knowles. I am not defying the committee to withhold information from them. It is because I feel that they do not have the jurisdiction to ask me **questions** of this nature.

Mr. Sourwine. Don't you realize that you are withholding this information from the committee!

Mr. Knowles. That is the end result of it, but that is not—

Mr. Sourwine. Of course.

Mr. Knowles. That is not my motive.

Mr. Sourwine. What is your motive?

Mr. Knowles. My motive is that I don't think they have the jurisdiction, the right to ask me these **questions**.

Mr. Sourwine. Would it be embarrassing to you if you answered the **questions**?

Mr. Knowles. It might, it might not.

Mr. Sourwine. If it would not be embarrassing to you, there is no reason why you should not answer it.

Mr. Knowles. The **question** of embarrassment is not a criterion for answering or declining to answer **questions**.

Mr. Sourwine. If this committee has no jurisdiction to ask you the **questions** you have refused to answer, then the committee must have no jurisdiction to ask you any **questions**; isn't that right?

Mr. Knowles. Well, I feel that way, yes.

Mr. Sourwine. But you have answered some **questions**, have you not?

Mr. Knowles. Yes, I have.

Mr. Sourwine. Because they were **questions** which would not embarrass you in any way, and which would not conflict with your purpose to conceal certain facts; isn't that right?

Mr. Knowles. There were **questions** that I could have answered that would have embarrassed me in no way.

Mr. Sourwine. There were?

Mr. Knowles. Yes.

United States Congress Senate Committee on the Judiciary, Subversive Influence in the Educational Process: Hearings Before the Subcommittee to Investigate the Administration of the Internal Security Act and Other Internal Security Laws

This brings up an interesting **question** that needs to be considered. Could the goal of embarrassment and these second-order goals in reality both be first-order goals? Suppose I wish to discredit a coworker—my first-order goal. It is immediate and explicit. I also decide that the best way to discredit this person is to embarrass her or him during a company meeting. This is also a first-order goal. It is immediate and explicit. From here, I plan how to go about accomplishing these goals. This is one **question** that seems problematic for the model. Retaining Berger's (1995) classification of implicit and explicit goals, discussed earlier, may be more beneficial. Take the degree of embarrassment one wishes to create in a target. For some embarrassors, this may be a first-order goal, but for others it may be a second-order goal depending on how implicit or explicit and how immediate the goal is. Labeling any goal a first-order or second-order goal gives the impression that one prioritizes goals and that a goal is one type of goal or the other. It fails to take into account the process of goal planning; it does not seem to capture the fluctuating nature of one's goals as well as describing them using terms of degrees of explicitness and immediateness.

In sum, embarrassors attempt multiple goals in the planning of the embarrassment of a target. They are concerned, to some degree, about the extent to which they wish to be efficient and socially appropriate, their meta-goals. Embarrassors attempt to cause a target to become embarrassed to some degree, their first-order goal. They are also, consciously or unconsciously attempting a number of second-order goals: socializing individuals into a group, negatively sanctioning an individual's behaviors, establishing and/or maintaining power in a relationship, discrediting a target, showing solidarity, or achieving self-satisfaction.

William F. Sharkey, Why Would Anyone Want to Intentionally Embarrass Me? (Aversive Interpersonal Behaviors)

'It's his escape from loneliness and memory,' Beatrice said. 'Don't *you* ever want to escape?'

'I suppose we all do sometimes.'

'I know what that kind of loneliness is like,' she said with sympathy. 'Does he drink all day?'

'No. The worst hour is two in the morning. When he wakes then, he can't sleep for thinking, so he drinks instead.'

It astonished Wormold how quickly he could reply to any **questions** about his characters; they seemed to live on the threshold of consciousness—he had only to turn a light on and there they were, frozen in some characteristic action. Soon after Beatrice arrived Raul had a birthday and she suggested they should give him a case of champagne.

'He won't touch it,' Wormold said, he didn't know why. 'He suffers from acidity. If he drinks champagne he comes out in spots. Now the professor on the other hand won't drink anything else.'

'An expensive taste.'

'A depraved taste,' Wormold said without taking any thought. 'He prefers Spanish champagne.' Sometimes he was scared at the way these people grew in the dark without his knowledge. What was Teresa doing down there, out of sight? He didn't care to think. Her unabashed description of what life was like with her two lovers sometimes shocked him. But the immediate problem was Raul. There were moments when Wormold thought that it might have been easier if he had recruited real agents.

Wormold always thought best in his bath. He was unaware one morning, when he was concentrating hard, of indignant noises, a fist beat on the door a number of times, somebody stamped on the stairs, but a creative moment had arrived and he paid no attention to the world beyond the steam. Raul had been dismissed by the Cubana air line for drunkenness. He was desperate; he was without a job; there had been an unpleasant interview between him and Captain Segura, who threatened . . . 'Are you all right?' Beatrice called from outside. 'Are you dying? Shall I break down the door?'

He wrapped a towel round his middle and emerged into his bedroom, which was now his office.

'Milly went off in a rage,' Beatrice said. 'She missed her bath.'

'This is one of those moments,' Wormold said, 'which might change the course of history. Where is Rudy?'

'You know you gave him week-end leave.'

'Never mind. We'll have to send the cable through the Consulate. Get out the code-book.'

'It's in the safe. What's the combination? Your birthday—that was it, wasn't it?

December 6?'

'I changed it.'

'Your birthday?'

'No, no. The combination, of course.' He added sententiously, 'The fewer who know the combination the better for all of us. Rudy and I are quite sufficient. It's the drill, you know, that counts.' He went into Rudy's room and began to twist the knob—four times to the left, three times thoughtfully to the right. His towel kept on slipping. 'Besides, anyone can find out the date of my birth from my registration-card. Most unsafe. The sort of number they'd try at once.'

'Go on,' Beatrice said, 'one more turn.'

'This is one nobody could find out. Absolutely secure.'

'What are you waiting for?'

'I must have made a mistake. I shall have to start again.'

'This combination certainly seems secure.'

'Please don't watch. You're fussing me.' Beatrice went and stood with her face to the wall. She said, 'Tell me when I can turn round again.'

'It's very odd. The damn thing must have broken. Get Rudy on the phone.'

'I can't. I don't know where he's staying. He's gone to Varadero beach.'

'Damn!'

'Perhaps if you told me how you remembered the number, if you can call it remembering . . .'

'It was my great-aunt's telephone number.'

'Where does she live?'

'95 Woodstock Road, Oxford.'

'Why your great-aunt?'

'Why not my great-aunt?'

'I suppose we could put through a directory enquiry to Oxford.'

'I doubt whether they could help.'

'What's her name?'

'I've forgotten that too.'

'The combination really is secure, isn't it?'

'We always just knew her as great-aunt Kate. Anyway she's been dead for fifteen years and the number may have been changed.'

'I don't see why you chose her number.'

'Don't you have a few numbers that stick in your head all your life for no reason at all?'

'This doesn't seem to have stuck very well.'

'I'll remember it in a moment. It's something like 7,7,5,3,9.'

'Oh dear, they would have five numbers in Oxford.'

'We could try all the combinations of 77539.'

'Do you know how many there are? Somewhere around six hundred, I'd guess. I hope your cable's not urgent.'

'I'm certain of everything except the 7.'

'That's fine. Which seven? I suppose now we might have to work through about six thousand arrangements. I'm no mathematician.'

'Rudy must have it written down somewhere.'

'Probably on waterproof paper so that he can take it in with him bathing. We're an efficient office.'

'Perhaps,' Wormold said, 'we had better use the old code.'

'It's not very secure. However . . .' They found Charles Lamb at last by Milly's bed; a leaf turned down showed that she was in the middle of *Two Gentlemen of Verona.*

Wormold said, 'Take down this cable. Blank of March blank.'

'Don't you even know the day of the month?'

'Following from 59200 stroke 5 paragraph A begins 59200 stroke 5 stroke 4 sacked for drunkenness on duty stop fears deportation to Spain where his life is in danger stop.'

'Poor old Raul.'

'Paragraph B begins 59200 stroke 5 stroke 4 . . .'

'Couldn't I just say "he"?'

'All right. He. He might be prepared under these circumstances and for reasonable bonus with assured refuge in Jamaica to pilot private plane over secret constructions to obtain photographs stop paragraph C begins he would have to fly on from Santiago and land at Kingston if 59200 can make arrangements for reception stop.'

'We really are doing something at last, aren't we?' Beatrice said.

'Paragraph D begins stop will you authorize five hundred dollars for hire of plane for 59200 stroke 5 stroke 4 stop further two hundred dollars may be required to bribe airport staff Havana stop paragraph E begins bonus to 59200 stroke 5 stroke 4 should be generous as considerable risk of interception by patrolling planes over Oriente mountains stop I suggest one thousand dollars stop.'

'What a lot of lovely money,' Beatrice said.

'Message ends. Go on. What are you waiting for?'

'I'm just trying to find a suitable phrase. I don't much care for Lamb's *Tales*, do you?'

'Seventeen hundred dollars,' Wormold said thoughtfully.

'You should have made it two thousand. The A.O. likes round figures.'

'I don't want to seem extravagant,' Wormold said. Seventeen hundred dollars would surely cover one year at a finishing school in Switzerland.

'You're looking pleased with yourself,' Beatrice said. 'Doesn't it occur to you that you may be sending a man to his death?'

He thought, That is exactly what I plan to do. He said, 'Tell them at the Consulate that the cable has to have top priority.'

'It's a long cable,' Beatrice said. 'Do you think this sentence will do? "He presented Polydore and Cadwal to the king, telling him they were his two lost sons, Guiderius and Arviragus." There are times, aren't there, when Shakespeare is a little dull.'

Graham Greene, Our Man in Havana

Mr. Sourwine. You realize that this is not an answer to the **question**?

Mr. Knowles. It is the best I can do.

Mr. Sourwine. That is not the best you can do. You can either answer "Yes" or "No" to
the fact that you realize that your refusal to answer these **questions** is depriving
the committee of information within your knowledge concerning the Communist
conspiracy, or you can refuse to answer the **question**.

United States Congress Senate Committee on the Judiciary, Subversive Influence in the Educational Process: Hearings Before the Subcommittee to Investigate the Administration of the Internal Security Act and Other Internal Security Laws

However, when an option is to be selected (such as from the card described above), threatening **questions** achieve the best results when asked in the open-ended, long format with respondent-familiar wording.

> *Graham R. Walden, Polling and Survey Research Methods 1935–1979: An Annotated Bibliography*

"Tonight, you mean? Now? Or generally, from this?"

"Now."

Everything has changed. That **question**, arising, erupting, and I am alert, here, present. His tone is curious, like he's wanting to work out the rules of this game. It's a challenge, but I don't hear it as angry, which it might have been. He looks at me. Just then, it is like we have never met. I am shocked.

The usual responses won't do. I can't push it back to him. I can't offer the stock therapist response, though they're what come to me immediately; **questions** like, "What do you imagine I want?" or "What is it you want from you?"

What do I want from him? To entertain me? Or to not keep doing everything we always do? To help us find a break in the current, slow, metre of our encounter, opening us to rhythm?[107] Am I waiting for him to fall so I can rescue him? For him to dislodge a divot as he slips on the smooth grass, which, like Shannon, Sedgwick's therapist, I would pick up and replace?[108]

"What do you want from me?" he repeats, sadder now in my silence, as I fail to respond. What do I want from him? What do I want from him? I hear the **question** echo and look away, as he has done too. No longer the challenge in his eyes, nor in the tone of his voice.

"I can't find an answer to what you've asked me. I've been trying to, but nothing seems to fit."

> *Jonathan Wyatt, Therapy, Stand-Up, and the Gesture of Writing: Towards Creative-Relational Inquiry*

Since our aim is to get the asking of the prior **question** going, we now must show how, and to what extent, the asking of this prior **question** moves directly, and from the ground up, along with the decisive historical **question**. To demonstrate this, it is necessary at first to anticipate an essential insight in the form of an assertion.

> *Martin Heidegger, Introduction to Metaphysics*

Spade blew smoke above the fat man's head in a long slanting plume. He frowned thoughtfully at the ash-tipped end of his cigar. He replied deliberately:

"I can't say yes or no. There's nothing certain about it either way, yet." He looked up at the fat man and stopped frowning. "It depends."

"It depends on—?"

Spade shook his head. "If I knew what it depends on I could say yes or no."

The fat man took a mouthful from his glass, swallowed it, and suggested:

"Maybe it depends on Joel Cairo?"

Spade's prompt "Maybe" was noncommittal. He drank.

The fat man leaned forward until his belly stopped him. His smile was ingratiating and so was his purring voice:

"You could say, then, that the **question** is which one of them you'll represent?"

"You could put it that way."

"It will be one or the other?"

"I didn't say that."

The fat man's eyes glistened. His voice sank to a throaty whisper asking:

"Who else is there?"

Spade pointed his cigar at his own chest.

"There's me," he said.

The fat man sank back in his chair and let his body go flaccid. He blew his breath out in a long contented gust.

"That's wonderful, sir," he purred. "That's wonderful. I do like a man that tells you right out he's looking out for himself. Don't we all? I don't trust a man that says he's not. And the man that's telling the truth when he says he's not I distrust most of all, because he's an ass and an ass that's going contrary to the laws of nature."

Dashiell Hammett, The Maltese Falcon

The propriety of this rule must be admitted by all when we reflect that every fact or circumstance given in evidence may be controverted, and if a party could be permitted to give in evidence facts or circumstances which could afford no light, by which to ascertain the truth of the material matter in dispute, many embarrassing **questions** would be presented, both for the court and jury, which, when solved, would not advance us one step in the material inquiry.

Alabama Supreme Court, Reports of Cases Argued and Determined in the Supreme Court of Alabama, During a Part of June Term, 1849, and the Whole of January Term, 1850, *Volume 18*

'This does not matter so much,' Hasselbacher said, 'but come here.'

A small room, which had been converted into a laboratory, was now reconverted into chaos. A gas-jet burnt yet among the ruins. Dr. Hasselbacher turned it off. He held up a test tube; the contents were smeared over the sink.

He said, 'You won't understand. I was trying to make a culture from—never mind. I knew nothing would come of it. It was a dream only.' He sat heavily down on a tall tubular adjustable chair, which shortened suddenly under his weight and spilt him on the floor. Somebody always leaves a banana-skin on the scene of tragedy. Hasselbacher got up and dusted his trousers.

'When did it happen?'

'Somebody telephoned to me—a sick call. I felt there was something wrong, but I had to go. I could not risk not going. When I came back there was this.'

'Who did it?'

'I don't know. A week ago somebody called on me. A stranger. He wanted me to help him. It was not a doctor's job. I said no. He asked me whether my sympathies were with the East or the West. I tried to joke with him. I said they were in the middle.' Dr. Hasselbacher said accusingly, 'Once a few weeks ago you asked me the same **question**.'

'I was only joking, Hasselbacher.'

'I know. Forgive me. The worst thing they do is making all this suspicion.' He stared into the sink. 'An infantile dream. Of course I know that. Fleming discovered penicillin by an inspired accident. But an accident has to be inspired. An old second-rate doctor would never have an accident like that, but it was no business of theirs—was it?—if I wanted to dream.'

'I don't understand. What's behind it? Something political? What nationality was this man?'

'He spoke English like I do, with an accent. Nowadays, all the world over, people speak with accents.'

'Have you rung up the police?'

'For all I know,' Dr. Hasselbacher said, 'he was the police.'

'Have they taken anything?'

'Yes. Some papers.'

'Important?'

'I should never have kept them. They were more than thirty years old. When one is young one gets involved. No one's life is quite clean, Mr Wormold. But I thought the past was the past. I was too optimistic. You and I are not like the people here—we have no confessional box where we can bury the bad past.'

'You must have some idea . . . What will they do next?'

Graham Greene, *Our Man in Havana*

He accuses them of putting the cart before the horse. Our first task and one which has been almost totally neglected is to reconstruct the oldest conditions of the single races as far as they are accessible to scientific investigation. This study was intended as a modest contribution in this direction. Whether the favored position of the maternal uncle among the Germans arose as a result of race mixture or was autochthonous belongs as yet to the realm of speculation, though I am inclined to believe the latter hypothesis.

In conclusion I wish to touch on one **question** which may legitimately be raised in connection with the problem of matriarchy among the Germans, the so-called "Pictish **Question**". A résumé of the investigations regarding this disputed point may be found in T. Rice Holmes, *Ancient Britain and the Invasion of Julius Caesar*, Oxford, 1907, pp. 409 ff. (It is not quite fair to Zimmer and Rhys.)

The dispute turns on the **question** of whether the Picts were the non-Indo-European aborigines who preceded the insular Celts or whether they were Celts who may have mingled with the autochthonous population preceding them. The foremost champions of the theory that the Picts were not Celts were H. Zimmer[75] and J. Rhys.[76] While both treat the same **question**, Rhys' arguments are chiefly linguistic, while the pivotal point of Zimmer's evidence lies in his attempt to prove that the existence of matriarchy among the Picts proves them to be non-Indo-European.

Albert William Aron, *Traces of Matriarchy in Germanic Hero-Lore*

"It's okay, you don't want to cooperate, I get it. But answer to one last **question**. What did you tell the captain Cox to run away from? From a trafficker bodyguard?"

The face of his interlocutor began to turn white. Good sign.

"Maybe, you told him to get away from a man who is missing after, supposedly kill Richard McAllen. What I don't know is what you are most embarrassed of, protecting a killer or that your daughter fucked him?"

"Shut your mouth!"

"I told you I had material Mr. Farrow."

Yaiza Cabrera Torres, *When You Embarrass the Devil*

Data from the American Institute of Public Opinion and the National Opinion Research Center are compared. The same **questionnaire** was used by the two organizations, interviewing equivalent samples of about 2,500 adults. The interviewer instructions and the codes used were also the same. The results for the "free answer **questions**" had about the same number of no opinion responses in each data set. Results of precoded **questions** were significantly different. The organization which "encouraged" fuller answers did succeed in obtaining longer replies, and these replies were found to have "greater amounts of meaningful material." Probing and recording differences produced variations in response distribution. Ideological differences between the two staffs produced no measurable effects on results. When considering northern and southern African-American groups, it was found that African Americans spoke more "freely and frankly" to African-American interviewers. References are provided.

Graham R. Walden, Polling and Survey Research Methods 1935–1979: An Annotated Bibliography

Prepare the Emotion Picture Cards found on page 64 according to the directions on page 5. Show the cards to the children and discuss how Clara and Bumper are feeling. Here are some guided **questions**:

How do you think Clara and Bumper are feeling in these pictures?

They are feeling embarrassed. Can anyone tell the class what "being embarrassed" means? (This is a difficult concept for children to describe. Help them by relating examples of moments when you have felt embarrassed.)

Have any of you ever felt embarrassed? Does anyone want to share an embarrassing story?

What do you think has happened that is making Clara and Bumper feel embarrassed? Let's read the story and find out!

Jo Browning-Wroe, Happy, Sad, Jealous, Mad: Stories, Rhymes, and Activities That Help Young Children Understand Their Emotions

"They came to offer their services as scouts."

"And you engaged them, general?"

"I did. Why do you ask?"

Lieutenant Cartier was expecting the **question**, and was ready to play his part. With a fine show of hesitation and embarrassment, he stammered:

"I—I do—do not care to—that is—"

"Well?" the general said, sharply.

"I have no reason for asking the **question**, except—" and again he stopped.

"Except what, Lieutenant?" Wayne cried, angrily.

"Well, that man Barton, as he calls himself, is an Englishman—"

"How do you know?"

"A soldier from Wheeling told me."

"What of it?"

"Nothing, General, only—"

"*You* are a Frenchman."

"Y-e-s."

"And my ancestors were English from Ireland, and Jesus Christ was a Hebrew. But what has all that to do with Hal Barton's making a trustworthy scout, Cartier? Speak out—you're holding back something."

Lieutenant Cartier's face flushed and his lips twitched. It was evident that he was greatly embarrassed or very angry.

James Ball Naylor, Under Mad Anthony's Banner

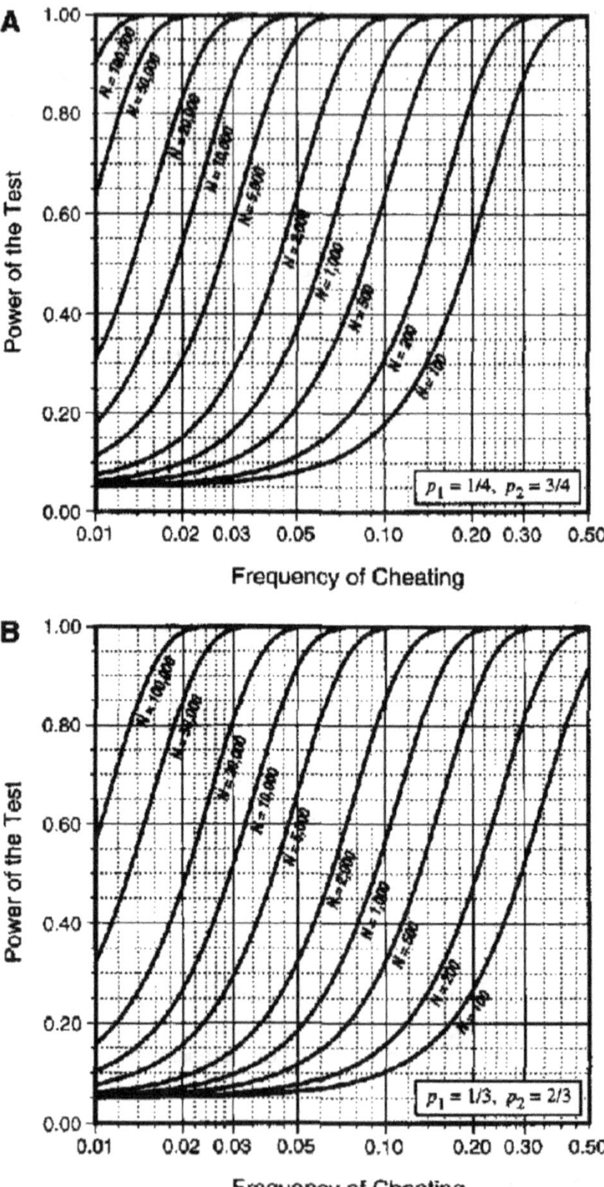

Surveys and **questionnaires** are frequently used by psychologists, social scientists, and epidemiologists to collect data about behavior, attitudes, emotions, and so on. However, when asked about sensitive topics such as their sexual behavior or illegal activity, some respondents lie or refuse to answer. The randomized response method was developed to reduce these evasive answer biases by guaranteeing subject privacy. However, the method has been criticized as being susceptible to cheaters, that is, respondents who do not answer as directed by the randomizing device. Here the authors show that by splitting the sample into 2 groups and assigning each group a different randomization probability, it is possible to detect whether significant cheating is occurring and to estimate its extent while simultaneously protecting the identity of cheaters and those who may have engaged in sensitive behaviors.

*S. J. Clark and R. Desharnais, "Honest Answers to Embarrassing **Questions**: Detecting Cheating in the Randomized Response Model," Psychological Methods 3 (1998): 160–168*

Now, the children knew the city. And they knew the city breeds the Mad. They knew Mr White-Face, an Indian who walks the streets of Willesden with his face painted white, his lips painted blue, wearing a pair of tights and some hiking boots; they knew Mr Newspaper, a tall skinny man in an ankle-length raincoat who sits in Brent libraries removing the day's newspapers from his briefcase and methodically tearing them into strips; they knew Mad Mary, a black voodoo woman with a red face whose territory stretches from Kilburn to Oxford Street but who performs her spells from a bin in West Hampstead; they knew Mr Toupee, who has no eyebrows and wears a toupee not on his head but on a string around his neck. But these people *announced* their madness—they were better, less scary than Mr J. P. Hamilton—they flaunted their insanity, they weren't half mad and half not, curled around a door frame. They were properly mad in the Shakespearean sense, talking sense when you least expected it. In North London, where councillors once voted to change the name of the area to *Nirvana,* it is not unusual to walk the streets and be suddenly confronted by sage words from the chalk-faced, blue-lipped, or eyebrowless. From across the street or from the other end of a tube carriage they will use their schizophrenic talent for seeing connections in the random (for discerning the whole world in a grain of sand, for deriving narrative from nothing) to riddle you, to rhyme you, to strip you down, to tell you who you are and where you're going (usually Baker Street—the great majority of modern-day seers travel the Metropolitan Line) and why. But as a city we are not appreciative of these people. Our gut instinct is that they intend to embarrass us, that they're out to *shame* us somehow as they lurch down the train aisle, bulbous-eyed and with carbuncled nose, preparing to ask us, inevitably, *what we are looking at.* What the *fuck* we are looking at. As a kind of preemptive defense mechanism, Londoners have learned not to look, never to look, to avoid eyes at all times so that the dreaded **question** "What you looking at?" and its pitiful, gutless, useless answer—"Nothing"—might be avoided. But as the prey evolves (and we are prey to the Mad who are pursuing us, desperate to impart their own brand of truth to the hapless commuter) so does the hunter, and the true professionals begin to tire of that old catchphrase "What you looking at?" and move into more exotic territory. Take Mad Mary. Oh, the principle's still the same, it's still all about eye contact and the danger of making it, but now she's making eye contact from a hundred, two hundred, even three hundred yards away, and if she catches you doing the same she roars down the street, dreads and feathers and cape afloat, Hoodoo stick in hand, until she gets to where you are, spits on you, and begins.

Zadie Smith, White Teeth

"When's the last time you saw a porn movie where a Chinese man with a giant dick is giving it to some li'l English lady?"

It was a tough first **question** and not one Brough had prepared himself for in any interrogation he had ever imagined.

"Okay," the woman slapping his face had a Californian accent, "lemme put it another way. When was the last time you saw a porn movie where a Western guy is screwing some little Chinese girl?"

"These exist," Brough croaked.

She looked angry, her face was strong and pure, her hair dyed chestnut brown. She had pulled up a chair so she could sit knee-to-knee with him and slap him back to consciousness.

"First thing you need to get straight, Mister Brough is: show some respect!"

"Yeah, due respect!"

That was another woman, pacing around behind him, pronouncing "due" as in "do", agitated.

Paul Mason, Rare Earth

And I feel the thing very keenly. I do not think that the newspapers of the country have the right to embarrass their own country in the settlement of matters which have to be handled with delicacy and candor. I have seen it published, in one or two papers at any rate, that I as the Executive was considering certain things that had never come into my mind as courses of action. Now, if in dealing with the representative of the government concerned I make an entirely different proposition and let it be inferred that the other course never occurred to me, there is some danger that I be regarded as disingenuous, that I am not saying what I really have up my sleeve, when I have nothing up my sleeve. It is a very serious disservice to the country to embarrass the foreign policy of the Government in that way. I say that without any feeling of criticism but in order that you may know how seriously these things affect public policy. With regard to domestic matters, it is a very different **question** because we are all on the inside and we can all exchange suggestions as to possible courses of action.

Woodrow Wilson, The President on His Foreign Policy (The World's Work War Series: The Kaiser in His Own Words)

Aside from the pressure to see and hear no evil, there is also a strong social pressure not to acknowledge the fact that we sometimes do indeed see or hear it. Not only are we expected to refrain from asking potentially embarrassing **questions**, we are also expected to pretend not to have heard potentially embarrassing "answers" even when we actually have. By not acknowledging what we have in fact seen or heard, we can "tactfully" pretend not to have noticed it.

The fact that the verbs "to notice" and "to remark" are denoted in French by a single word (*remarquer*) reminds us how closely related noticing something and publicly acknowledging having noticed it actually are. Yet the fact that in English, by contrast, they nevertheless seem to require two separate words underscores how much those acts are normatively separated from each other. And the difference between what we actually notice and what we publicly acknowledge having noticed is at the very heart of what it means to be tactful.

Being tactful, in other words, often involves pretending not to notice things we "know but realize that [we] are supposed not to know."[41] Thus, one acts tactfully when one "passes over something and leaves it unsaid."[42] As when we forgive someone or pretend to have forgotten the promise he once made to us but never kept, being tactful involves at least outwardly treating things we actually do notice as if they are somehow irrelevant and, as such, can be practically ignored.

Eviatar Zerubavel, The Elephant in the Room: Silence and Denial in Everyday Life

"If contingent faculty were being killed at your university at the rate of one per day, how many days would it take for someone in your administration to notice?" That's the **question** asked by Geoff Cebula's murder-mystery novel *Adjunct* (2017), set at fictional Bellwether College. The mysterious disappearance of faculty members compels Elena Malatesta, an adjunct professor in the modern-language department, to unravel budget cuts from murder and uncover the real cause behind the disappearance of Bellwether's adjuncts. In the end, Malatesta also disappears from campus. She quits teaching to pursue a life of the mind outside academe. She will, however, advise a part-time colleague to continue teaching. Because a full-time position may—just may—open up in the future. Thus the crisis continues.

Kristina Quynn, The Disgusting New Campus Novel (The Chronicle Review)

Before I started the lesson, I tried to check the students' attendance by calling their names one by one. I had just called one of them when a few students started laughing. The other students soon followed this. I was wondering what had been going on.

"What are you laughing at?" I tried to investigate.

"Are you showing us a blue film?" one student asked.

"What do you mean?"

My students did not answer my *innocent* **question** but replied it by laughing more loudly. I then realized what made them laugh after one female-stubborn student pointed at the part of

Page 59 is not part of this book preview.

Silvester Goridus Sukur, Embarrassing Stories—A Blue Film (Completed With Grammatical Notes)

'There are things I want to know,' Jean Logan said, and the anger in her voice was suddenly there. 'I've got lots of **questions** for all sorts of people. But I don't think they're going to give me the answers. They pretend they don't even understand the **questions**.' She paused and swallowed hard. I had tapped into a repeating voice in her head, I was overhearing the thoughts that tormented her all night. Her sarcasm was too theatrical, too energetic and I felt the weight of exhausted reiteration behind it. 'I'm the mad one, of course. I'm irrelevant. I'm in the way. It's not convenient to answer my **questions** because they don't fit the story. There, there Mrs Logan! Don't go fretting about things that don't concern you and aren't important anyway. We know it's your husband, the father of your children, but we're in charge and please don't get in the way . . .'

Ian McEwan, Enduring Love

There is after all no obligation to answer every passing fool according to his folly. The greatest danger which threatens a man of learning, is to lose himself in talk. Kien preferred to express himself in the written rather than the spoken word. He knew more than a dozen oriental languages. A few of the western ones did not even need to be learnt. No branch of human literature was unfamiliar to him. He thought in quotations and wrote in carefully considered sentences. Countless texts owed their restoration to him. When he came to misreadings or imperfections in ancient Chinese, Indian or Japanese manuscripts, as many alternative readings suggested themselves for his selection as he could wish. Other textual critics envied him; he for his part had to guard against a superfluity of ideas. Meticulously cautious, he weighed up the alternatives month after month, was slow to the point of exasperation; applying his severest standards to his own conclusions, he took no decision, on a single letter, a word or an entire sentence, until he was convinced that it was unassailable. The papers which he had hitherto published, few in number, yet each one the starting point for a hundred others, had gained for him the reputation of being the greatest living authority on sinology. They were known in every detail to his colleagues, indeed almost word for word. A sentence once set down by him was decisive and binding. In controversial **questions** he was the ultimate appeal, the leading authority even in related branches of knowledge. A few only he honoured with his letters. That man, however, whom he chose so to honour would receive in a single letter enough stimuli to set him off on years of study, the results of which—in the view of the mind whence they had sprung—were foregone conclusions. Personally he had no dealings with anyone. He refused all invitations. Whenever any chair of oriental philology fell vacant, it was offered first to him. Polite but contemptuous, he invariably declined.

Elias Canetti, Auto-da-Fé

'No! Stop him. Just get him to answer the **question** in a couple of words.'

Pijpekamp translated. Another reproachful stare. And an answer, translated at once:
Some pages are omitted from this book preview.

Georges Simenon, A Crime in Holland

They did not answer my **question** but kept laughing while covering their mouths with their hands. My classmate then pointed at my buttocks. I moved my left hand and tried to find out what had happened to my buttocks.

My Goodness! In fact, the back part of my *trousers* was badly *torn out*. I was so embarrassed that I quickly moved the lower part of my T-shirt that I inserted in my trousers to cover the hole. With an embarrassed feeling I smiled, and then I quickly said goodbye and got out from their boarding house.

Now Tanty becomes my wife. Whenever I ask her about the 'dog incident', she just smiles.

Silvester Goridus Sukur, Embarrassing Stories—One Night With a Maid (Completed With Grammatical Notes)

"As for me, I have made up my mind not to be miserable. He was ready to marry me; at a word, he would have given up everything for me, and it is solely by my own will and decision that I have lost what I have lost. That is better, surely, than the humiliation of having given my whole heart to him without as much as touching his!"

At this point the diary becomes so blackened and disfigured by erasures that the few sentences which have been suffered to stand are scarcely of sufficient interest to be worth copying. From these I gather that my behavior, during the ensuing week or so, was something of a puzzle to the diarist. She alludes to my irritability, to my "inquisitive **questions**" (Good Heavens! haven't I a right to be irritable and inquisitive) and hazards the conjecture that my evident prejudice against Lady Prestwood may have made me anxious to encourage a flirtation, which never could have been anything more than a flirtation between my nephew and herself. It appears, moreover, to have been my privilege to afford her some amusement at a period when her spirits were a little below high-water mark. "Uncle Ned," she says in one place, "is quite killingly funny sometimes. A more kind-hearted old fellow never breathed, but he only sees what stares him in the face, and he works himself up into a state of angry agitation if I turn away from my food. Nothing but serious illness, by his way of thinking, can account for such perversity. Today I had to drink porter, which I detest, at lunch, and champagne, which I didn't want, at dinner, besides devouring numerous delicacies prepared especially *à mon intention*. These concessions appeased him, though they almost choked me."

Now, can anybody tell me why that was funny? I only ask for the sake of information.

Dense I may be, but upon my honor and conscience I can see nothing so very comic in acting upon the well ascertained principle that the body must be properly nourished if the brain is to retain its powers. As for my only seeing what stares me in the face, I saw plainly enough what was the matter with my poor Elsie, even if I did not divine—as how could I?—that that donkey Roger had permitted her to lay a forbidding finger upon his lips. So she really need not have been in such a hurry to congratulate herself that I was not her uncle de Valmaison, from whom she presently mentions that she has received a long letter.

William Edward Norris, An Embarrassing Orphan

Long interviews can generate reliability difficulties in terms of the data gathered near the completion. One way to address this problem is through the use of a mail **questionnaire** in addition to the interview. The challenge is to achieve a sufficient number of returns from the mail **questionnaire**. The authors believe that rapport, engagement, and a sense of commitment generated during the interview can lead to high mail response rates. The rate of return can also be used to evaluate the degree of success achieved by various interviewers. An additional value of the mail **questionnaire** format is that it can be used to ask possibly embarrassing **questions** or those in which an anonymous situation might be more useful. As a means of checking reliability, the same **question** can be asked in both formats.

Graham R. Walden, Polling and Survey Research Methods 1935–1979: An Annotated Bibliography

Reporters nodded, that was true. When had they ever known the President to cover something up? The President was somewhat of an angel in that respect. The doors blew up.

A wild howl broke out when the reporters saw it was me. More people turned around in their seats.

"Look, it's Sir Lanka."

"Uh, finally. I didn't want to say anything. But this began to be really embarrassing."

The CIA agents didn't dare touch me. They knew they couldn't do anything to me while the whole world press was watching us. They just let me walk up to the President of the United States. She looked absolutely terrified. And just handed over the lectern to me. I'd deal with her later.

"Hi, everyone, sorry I am late; there was something important I had to take care of. But enough about that, let's kick-start the press conference with the first **question**. Anyone? Don't be shy. I promise to answer the **question** no matter what it's."

"I, have a **question**."

"Yes?"

"Sir Lanka, where were you? We were worried."

"No comments, next **question**. Yes?"

November Gyllensvärd, My Name Is Sir Lanka

Why are there beings at all instead of nothing? That is the **question**.

Martin Heidegger, Introduction to Metaphysics

MR. McKENZIE. I don't want to embarrass you, of course, but, of course, it has been a **question** of considerable discussion particularly in connection with certain officers just where the responsibility rested for what has happened, and I thought you would be able to throw some light upon it, but I would not embarrass you.

GEN. ROGERS. If you don't mind I would rather not answer that **question**.

MR. MCKENZIE. All right sir.

THE CHAIRMAN. Did the War Department send you over immediately when Gen. Pershing asked that you be sent over?

GEN. ROGERS. You are asking me some very embarrassing **questions**.

THE CHAIRMAN. I do not wish to embarrass you, and I will withdraw the **question**; but I can say that I heard you were sent for quite a number of times before you were really sent over. That much can go into the record, but I do not push the other **question**.

GEN. ROGERS. My reply would involve not necessarily a criticism, but expressing an opinion with reference to my superior officers which I would rather not mention.

THE CHAIRMAN. We will not press the **question**.

United States Congress House Committee on Military Affairs, Army Reorganization: Hearings Before the Committee on Military Affairs, House of Representatives, Sixty-Sixth Congress, First and Second Sessions, on H.R. 8287, A Bill to Reorganize and Increase the Efficiency of the United States Army, and for Other Purposes, H.R. 8068, A Bill to Provide for Universal Military, Naval and Vocational Training, and for Mobilization of the Manhood of the Nation in a National Emergency, H.R. 7925, A Bill to Establish the Department of Aeronautics, and for Other Purposes, H.R. 8870, A Bill to Amend an Act Entitled "An Act for Making Further and More Effectual Provision for the National Defense, and for Other Purposes," Volume 1

Such **questions** might embarrass the court, and often mislead the mind of the jury from the true matter or point in dispute. The only inquiries or **questions** in dispute between the parties must have been, was the deed fraudulent, and did Campbell, the sheriff, know it to be so? That the sheriff said to the witness that Friou was an extravagant man, tended to solve neither the one, nor the other of these inquiries; it neither showed fraud in the deed nor a knowledge of that fraud on the part of Campbell. The court also correctly excluded the testimony, which showed that Campbell in 1838 recommended Friou to merchants in New York as worthy of credit, and as worth nine thousand dollars. We do not see what legitimate inference could be drawn from such evidence, or what light it could afford in arriving at the truth of the **questions** involved in this cause. Of the same character is the testimony tending to show the acts of Campbell and Dawson, in reference to the deed of trust executed by Campbell. We cannot conceive on what principle this testimony could have been permitted to go to the jury. Whether the deed executed by Campbell was fraudulent or not, was not a **question** before them. To permit evidence, tending to show the deed of Campbell to be fraudulent, would have led to the examination of **questions** entirely distinct from the issues submitted in this cause, and when solved, the jury would not have been advanced one step in the investigation of the material facts in this case.

The court also acted correctly in rejecting that portion of Dawson's answer to the fourteenth cross-interrogatory objected to by the defendants. The motive of Dawson in dismissing a suit against Smith, who had levied on a portion of the property conveyed by the deed, did not tend to prove either of the material inquiries in this cause; but when he said he dismissed the suit, because he had heard, after he left the State, of the fraudulent conduct of the Frious, its illegality is manifest, for it shows that his reason for dismissing the suit was a rumor he had heard. To permit his reason for doing an act, founded on rumor, to be given in evidence would be to permit the effect of common rumor to be given in evidence, when the rumor itself would be illegal testimony. The dismissal of the suit was an act, and was not objected to by the defendants, but the motive or reason why Dawson did this act is clearly illegal evidence and was properly excluded.

We have thus disposed of all the **questions** that grow out of the ruling of the court and which have been presented for our revision, and our conclusion is that the fourth instruction given by the court to the jury cannot be sustained. The judgment must therefore be reversed and the cause remanded.

Alabama Supreme Court, Reports of Cases Argued and Determined in the Supreme Court of Alabama, During a Part of June Term, 1849, and the Whole of January Term, 1850, Volume 18

Having gone to great lengths to put interviewees at ease and to establish rapport, it is often hard to confront them with embarrassing **questions**. The sociologist John Gwaltney, author of *Drylongso*, an oral history of Newark's inner-city blacks, once chided members of the Oral History Association for being too polite and discreet to "ask the embarrassing **question**." He argued that with some gentle and persistent prodding, interviewees will talk about difficult subjects.

Donald A. Ritchie, Doing Oral History

Sitting on the bed, he said that they'd been making investigations into my private life. They had learned that my mother died recently in a home. Inquiries had been conducted at Marengo and the police informed that I'd shown "great callousness" at my mother's funeral.

"You must understand," the lawyer said, "that I don't relish having to **question** you about such a matter. But it has much importance, and, unless I find some way of answering the charge of 'callousness,' I shall be handicapped in conducting your defense. And that is where you, and only you, can help me."

Albert Camus, The Stranger

Barton uses the **question**—"Did you kill your wife?"—to illustrate eight different ways of presenting the embarrassing type of **question** in a non-embarrassing manner.

Graham R. Walden, Polling and Survey Research Methods 1935–1979: An Annotated Bibliography

He went on to ask if I had felt grief on that 'sad occasion.' The **question** struck me as an odd one; I'd have been much embarrassed if I'd had to ask anyone a thing like that.

I answered that, of recent years, I'd rather lost the habit of noting my feelings, and hardly knew what to answer. I could truthfully say I'd been quite fond of Mother—but really that didn't mean much. All normal people, I added as an afterthought, had more or less desired the death of those they loved, at some time or another.

Albert Camus, The Stranger

Playing tapes to demonstrate his point, Gwaltney showed that his **questions** were humorous and playful, but unrelenting. Being blind, Gwaltney also had the advantage of his interviewees wanting him to understand them; they would go on at great length and punctuate their responses with, "Don't you see?"

One way for interviewers to bring up difficult or embarrassing issues is to quote someone else. During the Gerald Ford and Jimmy Carter administrations, the National Archives maintained an office near the White House where they interviewed officials as they left the administration, many of them involuntarily and under some cloud. The interviewees were often agitated and unnerved over their experience and not happy to talk about it.

Donald A. Ritchie, Doing Oral History

"What's wrong?" Her voice had an edge of concern.

"No privacy. The goddamn telephone. It won't stop ringing. I can't step outside without being assaulted. I went down to check the mail. Ted Koppel was waiting for me. He wrestled me to the ground and held me down while Dan Rather asked embarrassing **questions** about the size of my genitalia. I finally broke away and escaped to my own bathroom—to check on my genitalia, as you might expect, since it seemed to hold some interest for inquiring minds—and who do you think was there? Barbara Walters."

Terry Kay, The Kidnapping of Aaron Greene

Many of Turner's **questions** had been booby traps, and Pete knew it. It didn't matter how Pete answered, positively or negatively, the explosion always erupted. Pete was forced to retreat from the volleys of verbal shrapnel again and again, and when he tried to stand still, he had to take the full concussion of Turner's outbursts. There were many embarrassing **questions** concerning the pearl necklace and about a maid in a motel who remembered Pete although the agency's reports had no record of it. Was Pete aware that no references were ever made that an uncle and aunt of Dave's lived in Starview? If Pete made an independent search, why weren't the findings coordinated with those of the agency? On and on, the **questioning** went, each **question** more embarrassing than the one before. Pete lied the best he could, falling back on his only defense, which was to insist that Turner could not understand the intricacies involved in the investigation.

Ben Kraieski, Snow on the Desert

8a). *That he tried to live in an ivory tower.*

but he failed. 'I have always tried to live in an ivory tower, but a tide of shit is beating at its walls, threatening to undermine it.'

Three points need to be made. One is that the writer chooses—as far as he can—the extent of what you call his involvement in life: despite his reputation, Flaubert occupied a half-and-half position. 'It isn't the drunkard who writes the drinking song': he knew that. On the other hand, it isn't the teetotaller either. He put it best, perhaps, when he said that the writer must wade into life as into the sea, but only up to the navel.

Secondly, when readers complain about the lives of writers—why didn't he do this; why didn't he protest to the newspapers about that; why wasn't he more involved in life?—aren't they really asking a simpler, and vainer, **question**: why isn't he more like us? But if a writer were more like a reader, he'd be a reader, not a writer: it's as uncomplicated as that.

Thirdly, what is the thrust of the complaint as far as the books are concerned? Presumably the regret that Flaubert wasn't more involved in life isn't just a philanthropic wish for him: if only old Gustave had had a wife and kiddies, he wouldn't have been so glum about the whole shooting-match? If only he'd got caught up in politics, or good works, or become a governor of his old school, he'd have been taken out of himself more? Presumably you think there are faults in the books which could have been remedied by a change in the writer's life. If so, I think it is up to you to state them. For myself, I cannot think that, for instance, the portrait of provincial manners in *Madame Bovary* is lacking in some particular aspect which would have been remedied had its author clinked tankards of cider every evening with some gouty Norman *bergère.*

9. That he was a pessimist.

Ah. I begin to see what you mean. You wish his books were a bit more cheerful, a bit more . . . how would you put it, life-enhancing? What a curious idea of literature you do have. Is your PhD from Bucharest? I didn't know one had to defend authors for being pessimists. This is a new one. I decline to do so. Flaubert said: 'You don't make art out of good intentions.' He also said: 'The public wants works which flatter its illusions.'

10. That he teaches no positive virtues.

Now you are coming out into the open. So this is how we are to judge our writers, on their 'positive virtues'? Well, I suppose I must play your game briefly: it's what you have to do in the courts. Take all the obscenity trials from *Madame Bovary* to *Lady Chatterley's Lover*: there's always some element of games-playing, of compliance, in the defence. Others might call it tactical hypocrisy. (Is this book sexy? No, M'Lud, we hold that it would have an emetic, not a mimetic, effect on any reader. Does this book encourage adultery? No, M'Lud, look how the miserable sinner who gives herself time and time again to riotous pleasure is punished in the end. Does this book attack marriage? No, M'Lud, it portrays a vile and hopeless marriage so that others may learn that only by following Christian instructions will their own marriages be happy. Is this book blasphemous? No, M'Lud, the novelist's thought is chaste.) As a forensic argument, of course, it has been successful; but I sometimes feel a residual bitterness that one of these defence counsel, when speaking for a true work of literature, did not build his act on simple defiance. (Is this book sexy? M'Lud, we bloody well hope so. Does it encourage adultery and attack marriage? Spot on, M'Lud, that's exactly what my client is trying to do. Is this book blasphemous? For Christ's sake, M'Lud, the matter's as clear as the loincloth on the Crucifixion. Put it this way, M'Lud: my client thinks that most of the values of the society in which he lives stink, and he hopes with this book to promote fornication, masturbation, adultery, the stoning of priests and, since we've temporarily got your attention, M'Lud, the suspension of corrupt judges by their earlobes. The defence rests its case.)

So, briefly: Flaubert teaches you to gaze upon the truth and not blink from its consequences; he teaches you, with Montaigne, to sleep on the pillow of doubt; he teaches you to dissect out the constituent parts of reality, and to observe that Nature is always a mixture of genres; he teaches you the most exact use of language; he teaches you not to approach a book in search of moral or social pills—literature is not a pharmacopoeia; he teaches the pre-eminence of Truth, Beauty, Feeling and Style. And if you study his private life, he teaches courage, stoicism, friendship; the importance of intelligence, scepticism and wit; the folly of cheap patriotism; the virtue of being able to remain by yourself in your own room; the hatred of hypocrisy; distrust of the doctrinaire; the need for plain speaking. Is that the way you like writers to be described (I do not care for it much myself)? Is it enough? It's all I'm giving you for the moment: I seem to be embarrassing my client.

Julian Barnes, Flaubert's Parrot

Not caring to commit myself, I replied that, so far as I was aware, no cause existed as yet for contentment or the reverse. I took the liberty of asking him, however, whether it would please him to see his niece married to a tradesman.

"Ma foi!" he confessed, shrugging his shoulders, "since you put the **question** to me—no! I try to belong to my period, but I have not found myself able to accept the *bourgeoisie* without reserve. I take it that I shall not be consulted, though; my niece, when all is said, is yours rather than mine. Moreover, she is English. In England today anybody may marry anybody."

William Edward Norris, An Embarrassing Orphan

"If you think this is strange, you ought to see what Mercator's doing."

"What's he doing?"

"He's training to break the world endurance record for sitting in a cage full of poisonous snakes, for the *Guinness Book of Records.* He goes to Glassboro three times a week where they have this exotic pet shop. The owner lets him feed the mamba and the puff adder. To get him accustomed. Totally forget your North American rattlesnake. The puff adder is the most venomous snake in the world."

"Every time I see news film of someone in his fourth week of sitting in a cage full of snakes, I find myself wishing he'd get bitten."

"So do I," Heinrich said.

"Why is that?"

"He's asking for it."

Don DeLillo, White Noise

epiplexis

e-pi-plex'-is

from Gk. epi, "upon" and plessein, "to strike"

Asking **questions** in order to chide, to express grief, or to inveigh. A kind of rhetorical **question**.

Examples

Why died I not from the womb? why did I not give up the ghost when I came out of the belly?—Job 3:11

Gideon Burton, Silva Rhetoricae (The Forest of Rhetoric)

For ever and anon comes Indigestion
   (Not the most "dainty Ariel") and perplexes
Our soarings with another sort of **question**:
   And that which after all my spirit vexes,
Is, that I find no spot where Man can rest eye on,
   Without confusion of the sorts and sexes,
Of beings, stars, and this unriddled wonder,
   The World, which at the worst's a glorious blunder—

Lord Byron, Don Juan

The sister was not a mister. Was this a surprise. It was. The conclusion came when there was no arrangement. All the time that there was a **question** there was a decision. Replacing a casual acquaintance with an ordinary daughter does not make a son.

Gertrude Stein, Tender Buttons

That, he declared, was a **question** for the lawyers and the priests; possibly also for the dressmakers.

William Edward Norris, An Embarrassing Orphan

EUROPEAN SITUATION SPOILS MAP ON POST OFFICE
DEPARTMENT FLOOR, WASHINGTON, D.C., APRIL 12

The huge map on the floor of the Post Office Department here is all out of kilter these days due
to the aggression in Europe. Many are the embarrassing **questions** being asked officials about
when Mr. Farley is going to do something about Ethiopia, Austria and Czechoslovakia. The answer
so far has been—nothing. Probably the Post Office is waiting to see what will happen next on
the continent. Miss Edna Strain is inspecting the damage done by the ambitious dictators.

Photo by Harris & Ewing, 1939 (Library of Congress)

Let it suffice to have said so much about these matters; and as to the **question** how and by what exploits being Egyptians they received the sceptres of royalty over the Dorians, we will omit these things, since others have told about them; but the things with which other narrators have not dealt, of these I will make mention.

Herodotus, The History

"We don't see any reason to. Perhaps you could ask Mr. Yates about that matter, but I don't think he's present."

"Have you talked to the boy's family?"

"Not directly. We've expressed our deep regrets, but we haven't met with them. I understand that law enforcement officials have kept them secluded."

"Have you started an internal investigation on the possibility of collaboration?"

"As I said, we're cooperating with the authorities on all phases of the investigation. Beyond that, we have no comment at this time."

"Jesus, Miriam," someone said in exasperation.

"I'm sorry," Miriam replied uneasily. "Please understand this is a delicate matter. I think the statement has been circulated now. Thank you all for coming."

Amos Temple raised his hand, He said, in a loud voice, "Just one thing, Miriam."

Miriam knew she could not ignore Amos Temple. She did not like him, but she could not ignore him. "Yes?" she said.

"How in the name of God did you do a press release without mentioning Aaron Greene's name?"

Miriam's face flushed crimson. She glanced at the news release in her hand, scanning it quickly. She looked up and saw Jason Littlejohn in the back of the room. There was a level mean smile on his face. "Oh, I do apologize," Miriam said uneasily. "Talk about embarrassing typos. It simply got omitted. But all of you know the name. I'm sorry for the omission. We did this rather quickly this morning."

Amos pushed himself forward. "What is his name, Miriam?" he insisted.

"Why, you just said it, Amos. Aaron."

"What's his last name?"

Miriam swallowed. She smiled nervously, glanced at the nameless press release. "It's—" Her eyes flashed over the room, like a lost child searching for a parent. "It's—"

"You don't know, do you, Miriam?" Amos pressed. Then he added, "Greene. His name is Aaron Greene."

"Yes, yes," Miriam stammered. "I do know that. Aaron Greene. I'm sorry. I just had a lapse. We've been in something of a pressure cooker since all of this began, and—"

A ripple of cynical laughter flowed in the room, and a voice rose over it: "I have a **question**."

Miriam looked up to a man standing behind Amos Temple. He was older. His voice carried authority. The laughter faded.

"Olin," Miriam said. "I didn't see you."

Olin McArthur was the senior reporter in Atlanta, working special assignments for the *Journal-Constitution*. Even members of the electronic media respected Olin's privilege of closing press conferences.

"It's a surprising oversight, but I can understand an omission from a press release," Olin McArthur began, "and I can understand the need to control all the speculation that you get in these types of stories. I'm sure all of us do. But no one's asked the one thing that interests me the most."

Terry Kay, The Kidnapping of Aaron Greene

Should one pay special attention to the training of the thumb?

It may be said that the thumb and the middle finger are the two arch-conspirators against a precise finger technique. They crave your greatest attention. Above all, you must see to it that, in touching the keys with these fingers, you do not move the whole hand, still less the arm.

*Josef Hofmann, Piano Playing: With Piano **Questions** Answered*

The debate confronts some of the tough **questions** facing decision-makers.

Urban Age Global Debates series, Confronting Climate Change: Can Cities Be the Solution? (youtube.com)

All These Natural Questions

*And that was when all the uncomfortable **questions** really began*

The matter is not where we go
But how long it will last
*The **question** is how fast*
*The **question** is how fast*
*The **question** is how fast*
This is not a test, it's just an ask
*And the **question** is how fast*

Superchunk, The Question Is How Fast (On the Mouth)

The human beings were different primarily because they were the only species intensely curious about their surroundings. In time, mutations occurred, and an odd subset of humans began roaming the land. They were arrogant. They were not content to enjoy the magnificence of the universe. They asked "How?" How was the universe created? How can the "stuff" of the universe be responsible for the incredible variety in our world: stars, planets, sea otters, oceans, coral, sunlight, the human brain? The mutants had posed a **question** that could be answered—but only with the labor of millennia and with a dedication handed down from master to student for a hundred generations. The **question** also inspired a great number of wrong and embarrassing answers. Fortunately, these mutants were born without a sense of embarrassment. They were called physicists.

Leon M. Lederman, The God Particle: If the Universe Is the Answer, What Is the Question?

Q. *Are there important aspects of the Universe that can only be understood using the Anthropic Principle? Or is this principle unnecessary, or perhaps inherently unscientific?*

A. Very roughly speaking, the Anthropic Principle says that our universe must be approximately the way it is for intelligent life to exist, so that the mere fact we are asking certain **questions** constrains their answers. This might "explain" the values of fundamental constants of nature, and perhaps other aspects of the laws of physics as well. Or, it might not.

Scott Chase, Michael Weiss, Philip Gibbs, Chris Hillman and Nathan Urban, The Original Usenet Physics FAQ

"Have you ever noticed this—that people never answer what you say? They answer what you mean—or what they think you mean. Suppose one lady says to another in a country house, 'Is anybody staying with you?' the lady doesn't answer 'Yes; the butler, the three footmen, the parlourmaid, and so on,' though the parlourmaid may be in the room, or the butler behind her chair. She says 'There is nobody staying with us,' meaning nobody of the sort you mean. But suppose a doctor inquiring into an epidemic asks, 'Who is staying in the house?' then the lady will remember the butler, the parlourmaid, and the rest. All language is used like that; you never get a **question** answered literally, even when you get it answered truly. When those four quite honest men said that no man had gone into the Mansions, they did not really mean that no man had gone into them. They meant no man whom they could suspect of being your man. A man did go into the house, and did come out of it, but they never noticed him."

"An invisible man?" inquired Angus, raising his red eyebrows.

G. K. Chesterton, *The Invisible Man*

WE cannot expect that the wisest men of our remotest posterity, who can base their conclusions upon thousands of years of accurate observation, will reach a decision on this subject without some measure of reserve. Such being the case, it might appear the dictate of wisdom to leave its consideration to some future age, when it may be taken up with better means of information than we now possess. But the **question** is one which will refuse to be postponed so long as the propensity to think of the possibilities of creation is characteristic of our race. The issue is not whether we shall ignore the **question** altogether, like Eve in the presence of Raphael; but whether in studying it we shall confine our speculations within the limits set by sound scientific reasoning. Essaying to do this, I invite the reader's attention to what science may suggest, admitting in advance that the sphere of exact knowledge is small compared with the possibilities of creation, and that outside this sphere we can state only more or less probable conclusions.

The reader who desires to approach this subject in the most receptive spirit should begin his study by betaking himself on a clear, moonless evening, when he has no earthly concern to disturb the serenity of his thoughts, to some point where he can lie on his back on bench or roof, and scan the whole vault of heaven at one view. He can do this with the greatest pleasure and profit in late summer or autumn—winter would do equally well were it possible for the mind to rise so far above bodily conditions that the **question** of temperature should not enter.

Simon Newcomb, *The Extent of the Universe*

The Science of Global Warming and Climate Change

1. What are climate change and global warming, and how are they related?
2. What is abrupt climate change?
3. Can abrupt climate change really happen in a matter of days?
4. Can global warming lead to an ice age?
5. What is the scientific consensus on the causes and consequences of climate change?
6. What role does human activity play in the current global warming trend?
7. What role do natural forces play in the current global warming trend?
8. Will climate change actually bring benefits to some areas?

How Does Climate Change Affect ME?

1. What are some of the impacts we can expect from climate change?
2. Could climate change ever "wipe us out"?
3. Should I be worried about climate change? Will it affect me personally?

Worldwatch Institute, **Questions** *and Answers About Global Warming and Abrupt Climate Change*

Everyone except a billionaire who lives at the top of a mountain and has stockpiled a million tins of baked beans

—moronwatch, February 14, 2013 at 4:12 pm

I think I'd be concerned that said billionaire would make an active contribution to climate change after eating a million tins of baked beans!
—*Jamesdar, February 14, 2013 at 4:32 pm*

Jerry Barnett, 10 **Questions** for Climate Change Deniers: Comments (MoronWatch)

"To all these natural **questions** the voice of public History is as yet silent. Certain only that he has been, and is, a Pilgrim, and Traveller from a far Country; more or less foot-sore and travel-soiled; has parted with road-companions; fallen among thieves, been poisoned by bad cookery, blistered with bug-bites; nevertheless, at every stage (for they have let him pass), has had the Bill to discharge. But the whole particulars of his Route, his Weather-observations, the picturesque Sketches he took, though all regularly jotted down (in indelible sympathetic-ink by an invisible interior Penman), are these nowhere forthcoming? Perhaps quite lost: one other leaf of that mighty Volume (of human Memory) left to fly abroad, unprinted, unpublished, unbound up, as waste paper; and to rot, the sport of rainy winds?

Thomas Carlyle, Sartor Resartus: The Life and Opinions of Herr Teufelsdröckh

Do mobile homes attract tornadoes?

Of course not. It may seem that way, considering most tornado deaths occur in them, and that some of the most graphic reports of tornado damage come from mobile home communities. The reason for this is that mobile homes are, in general, much easier for a tornado to damage and destroy than well-built houses and office buildings. A brief, relatively weak tornado which may have gone undetected in the wilderness, or misclassified as severe straight-line thunderstorm winds while doing minor damage to sturdy houses, can blow a mobile home apart. Historically, mobile home parks have been reliable indicators, not attractors, of tornadoes.

National Oceanic and Atmospheric Administration, Frequently Asked **Questions** About Tornadoes

What I heard in my youth about the shunned house was merely that people died there in alarmingly great numbers. That, I was told, was why the original owners had moved out some twenty years after building the place. It was plainly unhealthy, perhaps because of the dampness and fungous growths in the cellar, the general sickish smell, the drafts of the hallways, or the quality of the well and pump water. These things were bad enough, and these were all that gained belief among the persons whom I knew. Only the note-books of my antiquarian uncle, Doctor Elihu Whipple, revealed to me at length the darker, vaguer surmises which formed an undercurrent of folklore among old-time servants and humble folk; surmises which never travelled far, and which were largely forgotten when Providence grew to be a metropolis with a shifting modern population.

The general fact is, that the house was never regarded by the solid part of the community as in any real sense "haunted." There were no widespread tales of rattling chains, cold currents of air, extinguished lights, or faces at the window. Extremists sometimes said the house was "unlucky," but that is as far as even they went. What was really beyond dispute is that a frightful proportion of persons died there; or more accurately, had died there, since after some peculiar happenings over sixty years ago the building had become deserted through the sheer impossibility of renting it. These persons were not all cut off suddenly by any one cause; rather did it seem that their vitality was insidiously sapped, so that each one died the sooner from whatever tendency to weakness he may have naturally had. And those who did not die displayed in varying degree a type of anemia or consumption, and sometimes a decline of the mental faculties, which spoke ill for the salubriousness of the building. Neighboring houses, it must be added, seemed entirely free from the noxious quality.

This much I knew before my insistent **questioning** led my uncle to show me the notes which finally embarked us both on our hideous investigation.

H. P. Lovecraft, The Shunned House

She went out. The walls trembled, the ceiling was crushing her, and she passed back through the long alley, stumbling against the heaps of dead leaves scattered by the wind. At last she reached the haha hedge in front of the gate; she broke her nails against the lock in her haste to open it. Then a hundred steps farther on, breathless, almost falling, she stopped. And now turning round, she once more saw the impassive chateau, with the park, the gardens, the three courts, and all the windows of the facade.

She remained lost in stupor, and having no more consciousness of herself than through the beating of her arteries, that she seemed to hear bursting forth like a deafening music filling all the fields. The earth beneath her feet was more yielding than the sea, and the furrows seemed to her immense brown waves breaking into foam. Everything in her head, of memories, ideas, went off at once like a thousand pieces of fireworks. She saw her father, Lheureux's closet, their room at home, another landscape. Madness was coming upon her; she grew afraid, and managed to recover herself, in a confused way, it is true, for she did not in the least remember the cause of the terrible condition she was in, that is to say, the **question** of money.

Gustave Flaubert, Madame Bovary

"Are you plunderable?" he would say to men, asking for money. But "Are you gropable?" was closer to the **question** he asked women, especially "colored girls," except that he usually didn't ask. Entries from his diary read like this: "I felt some breasts"; "I got two other women to kiss me."

Jill Lepore, Joe Gould's Teeth: The Long-Lost Story of the Longest Book Ever Written (The New Yorker)

His conversation seemed to have attracted the attention of the people in the pub, though no one appeared to be particularly interested in it. The young lads behind the bar began to snigger. The landlord apparently came down from the upper room for the express purpose of listening to the 'comic fellow', and sat down at a little distance, yawning lazily, though with rather an important air. Marmeladov was obviously an old customer here. He must, indeed, have acquired his pompous manner of speech from the habit of frequently addressing all sorts of strangers in pubs. With some drinking men, and especially with those who are bullied and bossed about in their homes, this habit becomes second nature. That is why when they find themselves in the company of other drinking men they always try, as it were, to justify themselves in their eyes and, if possible, even gain their esteem.

'What a comic!' the landlord said in a loud voice. 'And why ain't you working? Why ain't you got a job, seeing as how you're a civil servant?'

'Why haven't I got a job, sir?' Marmeladov repeated, addressing himself exclusively to Raskolnikov, as though it had been he who had asked him that **question**. 'Why haven't I got a job? But, my dear sir, do you really think that my vile and unprofitable life doesn't make my heart bleed? A month ago, when Mr Lebezyatnikov laid his hands on my dear wife while I lay blind drunk in the same room, do you imagine for a moment, sir, that I did not suffer? I hope you don't mind my putting this **question** to you, my dear young man, but have you ever had occasion to—er—ask someone for a loan without the ghost of a chance?'

'Yes, I think so, except that I don't quite see what you mean by without the ghost of a chance.'

'What I mean is that there isn't the ghost of a chance of your ever getting any money because you know perfectly well that nothing will come of it. Now, let us say, for instance, that you know beforehand, for certain, mind you, that a highly respected and by no means useless fellow-citizen of yours will on no account lend you any money; for why, I ask you, should he? He knows perfectly well that I shan't give it back to him. Out of pity? But Mr Lebezyatnikov, who keeps abreast of modern ideas, explained the other day that in our age even pity has been outlawed by science, and that in England, where they seem to be very keen on political economy, people are already acting accordingly. Why, then, I ask you, should he give you any money? And yet, knowing very well that he won't give you any, you set out all the same and—'

'But why?' Raskolnikov could not help asking.

'Why? But what if you have no one to see and nowhere to go to? A man must have somewhere to go to. For there comes a time when a man simply has to go somewhere! When my own daughter went on the streets for the first time, I had to go too, for my daughter,' he added parenthetically, looking uneasily at the young man, 'is a certified woman of the streets. Not that it matters,' he hastened to add immediately and apparently without the slightest embarrassment when the two boys behind the counter gave a splutter and the landlord himself could not refrain from smiling. 'It doesn't matter a bit! I'm not at all downcast by the general shaking of heads, for all this has long been common knowledge, and all the hidden things have been brought to light. And it is not with contempt but with an humble and contrite heart that I look upon it. So be it! So be it! "Behold the man!" Allow me to ask you, sir, can you—but no! Let me put it more explicitly and more bluntly, too: not *can* you but *dare* you, sir, looking upon me at this very minute, dare you, I say, tell me positively that I'm not a dirty swine?'

Fyodor Dostoyevsky, Crime and Punishment

"I can't answer that as yet. What we need to do is focus on the work we're already doing." Hogan looked around the room, making sure he had everyone's attention. The only person not looking at him, he noted, was John Rebus. Rebus was staring at the two figures in the doorway, his eyebrows lowered in a thoughtful frown. "We also need to go over that yacht with a fine-tooth comb, see if we managed to miss anything else." Hogan saw Whiteread and Simms share a look. "Right, any **questions**?" he asked. There were a few, but he dealt with them briskly. One officer wanted to know how much a yacht like Herdman's would cost. An answer had already been provided by the marina manager: for a forty-foot yacht, six berths, you'd need sixty thousand pounds. If you were buying secondhand.

"Which didn't come from his pension fund, trust me," Whiteread commented.

"We're already looking at Herdman's various bank accounts and other assets," Hogan told the room, glancing again in Rebus's direction.

"Mind if we're included in the search of the boat?" Whiteread asked. Hogan couldn't think of any reason to refuse, so just gave a shrug.

*Ian Rankin, A **Question** of Blood*

Having released his noble bosom of its burden, he would have modestly withdrawn himself, but that the wigged gentleman with the papers before him, sitting not far from Mr. Lorry, begged to ask him a few **questions**. The wigged gentleman sitting opposite, still looking at the ceiling of the court.

Had he ever been a spy himself? No, he scorned the base insinuation. What did he live upon? His property. Where was his property? He didn't precisely remember where it was. What was it? No business of anybody's. Had he inherited it? Yes, he had. From whom? Distant relation. Very distant? Rather. Ever been in prison? Certainly not. Never in a debtors' prison? Didn't see what that had to do with it. Never in a debtors' prison?—Come, once again. Never? Yes. How many times? Two or three times. Not five or six? Perhaps. Of what profession? Gentleman. Ever been kicked? Might have been. Frequently? No. Ever kicked downstairs? Decidedly not; once received a kick on the top of a staircase, and fell downstairs of his own accord. Kicked on that occasion for cheating at dice? Something to that effect was said by the intoxicated liar who committed the assault, but it was not true. Swear it was not true? Positively. Ever live by cheating at play? Never. Ever live by play? Not more than other gentlemen do. Ever borrow money of the prisoner? Yes. Ever pay him? No. Was not this intimacy with the prisoner, in reality a very slight one, forced upon the prisoner in coaches, inns, and packets? No. Sure he saw the prisoner with these lists? Certain. Knew no more about the lists? No. Had not procured them himself, for instance? No. Expect to get anything by this evidence? No. Not in regular government pay and employment, to lay traps? Oh dear no. Or to do anything? Oh dear no. Swear that? Over and over again. No motives but motives of sheer patriotism? None whatever.

Charles Dickens, A Tale of Two Cities

Even after the invasion of Iraq in 2003, I still met people—in the Middle East, no less— willing to withhold judgment on the U.S. Many thought that the Supreme Court's installation of George W. Bush as president was a blunder American voters would correct in the election of 2004. His return to office truly spelled the end of America as the world had known it. Bush had started a war, opposed by the entire world, because he wanted to and he could. A majority of Americans supported him. And that was when all the uncomfortable **questions** really began.

In the early fall of 2014, I traveled from my home in Oslo, Norway, through much of Eastern and Central Europe. Everywhere I went in those two months, moments after locals realized I was an American the **questions** started and, polite as they usually were, most of them had a single underlying theme: Have Americans gone over the edge? Are you crazy? Please explain.

Ann Jones, Has America Gone Crazy? (Salon)

"Listen up."

"Yes, Sergeant."

"This is Cao Phuc where you're currently at, Echo Reconnaissance Platoon of Delta Company. We're at the southwest corner of the Cu Chi District of South

Vietnam—district, not province. You heard of the Iron Triangle? We are not in the Iron Triangle, we are southwest of there in a friendly zone. We keep this region secure for the LZ established on top of the mountain which we are not allowed to call a base for reasons of military protocol. Echo's down here, the rest of the company's up top. They give you that whole don't be no pin-on-no-map sermon? Well, this here's a pin on the map. We don't call it a base but this is a permanent base, and we have two types of permanent reconnaissance patrols. Around the mountain then over, or else over the mountain then around.

"We're good for shares down here. We got fourteen guys and three share-heads, but no chemical latrines. So you dig your own kaibo over in the bush, and keep your business covered. Don't want no stink up my nose. We got no mess, it's all rations down here. Mess is up the mountain, two hot meals daily, you rotate one of those, one hot meal per day, you work that out with the guys as to your rotation, and if I get a lot of whining in my ear about people coming up short on the hot meals and I have to work out a complicated schedule, I'll be pissed off and looking to make life hell. If you're easy on me, I'm easy on you, that's the system here. You keep yourselves sorted out and squared away and I will be just no more than a presence. **Questions**. None. Good. Now.

"There are outfits all over this theater living in open rebellion against their officers. This ain't one. I am here to carry out the orders of Lieutenant Perry and see to it that y'all do the same. Do you hear my words?"

"Yes, Sarge."

"I come in slow and easy, but I mean what I say."

"Yes, Sarge."

"Now, Private Evans, Private Houston, Private Fisher. You have just received the speech. Do you have any current **questions**? No? I am available for all **questions** at all times."

"What's shares?"

"Shares? Shares. Look at my mouth—showers. Do you have any further **questions**?"

"What's a kaibo?"

"That's your to'let-hole, Private. I think it's Filipino."

Denis Johnson, Tree of Smoke

In ars-metrike shal ther no man fynde,
Biforn this day, of swich a **question**.
Who sholde make a demonstracion
That every man sholde have yliche his part
As of the soun or savour of a fart?

Geoffrey Chaucer, The Canterbury Tales

"It was him they were really out to get. And they did it. They got him. The bomb might as well have gone off in their living room. The violence done to his life was awful. Horrible. Never in his life had occasion to ask himself, 'Why are things the way they are?' Why should he bother, when the way they were was always perfect? Why are things the way they are? The **question** to which there is no answer, and up till then he was so blessed he didn't even know the **question** existed."

Philip Roth, American Pastoral

Two hours later he knocked at Bazarov's door.

'I must apologize for interrupting you in your scientific researches,' he began, seating himself on a chair by the window and leaning with both hands on a handsome cane with an ivory knob (he did not usually carry a stick), 'but I am compelled to request you to spare me five minutes of your time . . . no more.'

'All my time is at your disposal,' replied Bazarov, whose face had twitched directly Pavel Petrovich entered the room.

'Five minutes will suffice me. I have come to put just one **question** to you.'

'A **question**? What about?'

'I shall explain if you will be good enough to listen. When you first came to stay in my brother's house, and before I denied myself the pleasure of conversing with you, I had occasion to hear you express opinions on many subjects; but, so far as my memory serves, neither in conversation with me nor in my presence was any reference ever made to the subject of single combat or duelling in general. May I inquire what your views are on this subject?'

Bazarov, who had risen to receive Pavel Petrovich, sat down on the edge of the table and folded his arms.

'My views are as follows,' he replied. 'From the theoretical standpoint, duelling is absurd; but from the practical standpoint—well, that's another matter altogether.'

'That is, you mean to say, if I understand you correctly, that whatever your theoretical view of duelling you would not in practice suffer yourself to be insulted without demanding satisfaction?'

'You have grasped my meaning exactly.'

'Very good, sir. I am pleased to hear you say so. Your words deliver me from a state of uncertainty . . .'

'Of indecision, you mean.'

'As you, like. I am trying to express myself in a way you will understand; I . . . I am not one of your college phrasemongers. Your words have saved me from a rather grievous necessity. I have decided to fight you.'

Bazarov opened his eyes wide.

'Me?'

'Precisely.'

'But what for, pray?'

'I could explain the reason to you,' began Pavel Petroviph, 'but I prefer to keep silent about it. To my way of thinking you are not wanted here; I cannot endure you; I despise you; and if that is not enough for you . . .'

Pavel Petrovich's eyes flashed . . . Bazarov's glinted too.

'Very well, then,' he articulated slowly. 'Further explanations are unnecessary. You have taken it into your head to test your chivalrous spirit on me. I could refuse you this satisfaction but—so be it!'

'Very much obliged to you,' answered Pavel Petrovich. 'And now may I hope that you will accept my challenge without compelling me to resort to violent measures.'

'That means, in plain language, to that cane?' Bazarov remarked coolly. 'You are quite right. There is no need for you to insult me. Nor would that have been without some peril to yourself. You can remain the gentleman . . . I accept your challenge, also like a gentleman.'

FRESHMAN SENATOR LEARNS FROM OLD TIMER, WASHINGTON, D.C., APRIL 14, 1939

During a lull at the meeting of the Senate Foreign Relations Committee yesterday, California's Hiram Johnson took time to answer a few **questions** on Senatorial procedure put to him by Florida's new Senator, Claude Pepper. Or maybe they are patching up the long standing Florida-California feud over weather and climate.

Photo by Harris & Ewing (Library of Congress)

'Excellent,' observed Pavel Petrovich, putting his cane in the corner. 'Now we can discuss briefly the conditions of the duel; but first of all I should like to know whether you consider it necessary for us to have recourse to the formality of a slight dispute which might serve as a pretext for my challenge?'

'No, we had better dispense with the formalities.'

'I think so myself. I also suggest that it would be out of place to probe into the true reason for our passage of arms. We cannot endure one another. What more is necessary?'

'What more is necessary!' Bazarov echoed him ironically.

'As regards the actual conditions of the duel, since we shall have no seconds . . . for where could we get them? . . .'

'Exactly, where could we get them?'

'. . . I have the honour to suggest the following: let us fight early tomorrow morning, at six, shall we say, behind the copse, with pistols, at a distance of ten paces . . .'

'At ten paces? That will do; we can detest one another at that distance.'

'We could make it eight,' remarked Pavel Petrovich.

'We could: why not?'

'We shall fire two shots and, as a precaution, let each of us put a letter in his pocket, holding himself responsible for his own demise.'

'Now I don't altogether agree with that,' said Bazarov. 'It smacks too much of a French novel, it's a bit unlikely.'

'Perhaps. You will concur, however, that it would be unpleasant to be suspected of murder?'

'I agree. But there is a way of avoiding that painful accusation. We shall have no seconds, but we could have a witness.'

'And who, may I ask?'

'Why, Piotr.'

'Which Piotr?'

'Your brother's man. He's the acme of contemporary culture and would perform his role with all the *comme il faut* required on such occasions.'

'I think you must be joking, my dear sir.'

'Not at all. If you think over my suggestion, you will come to the conclusion that it is charged with simple good sense. Murder will out, but I will undertake to prepare Piotr in a suitable manner and bring him to the field of battle.'

'You persist in joking,' said Pavel Petrovich, rising from his chair. 'But after the amiable readiness you have displayed I have no right to insist further . . . So everything is arranged . . . By the way, I don't suppose you have pistols?'

Ivan Turgenev, Fathers and Sons

This is a **question** that I have never asked about because in the summer one does not think about it. Now it is winter but it is as warm as in summer.

Gertrude Stein, Geography and Plays

"Passenger-comment cards," he said, "are not the place to voice your beliefs about climate change." He laughed uneasily. "Don't shoot the messenger." He proceeded to ask how many of us believed the earth's climate was changing. Everyone in the lounge raised a hand. And how many of us believed that human activity was causing it? Again, most hands were raised, but not the Donald Trump supporter's, not the ham hobbyist's. From the very back of the lounge came the curmudgeonly voice of Chris: "What about the people who think it isn't a matter of belief?"

"Excellent **question**," Adam said.

His lecture was a barn-burning reprise of "An Inconvenient Truth," including the famous "hockey stick" graph of spiking temperatures, the famous map of an America castrated of its Florida by the coming rise in sea level. But the picture Adam painted was even darker than Al Gore's, because the planet is heating up so much faster than even the pessimists expected ten years ago. Adam cited the recent snowless start of the Iditarod, the sickeningly hot winter that Alaska was having, the possibility of an ice-free North Pole in the summer of 2020. He noted that whereas, ten years ago, only eighty-seven per cent of the Antarctic Peninsula's glaciers were known to be shrinking, the figure now seems to be a hundred per cent. But his darkest point was that climate scientists, being scientists, must confine themselves to making claims that have a high degree of statistical probability. When they model future climate scenarios and predict the rise in global temperature, they have to pick a lowball temperature, one reached in ninety-plus per cent of all cases, rather than the temperature that's reached in the average scenario. Thus, the scientist who confidently predicts a five-degree (Celsius) warming by the end of the century might tell you in private, over beers, that she really expects it to be nine degrees.

Jonathan Franzen, *The End of the End of the World (The New Yorker)*

Foreman: Another **question** from the audience, I think. Mrs. Sally Whitaker from Bournemouth has a **question** for the panel, I believe. Mrs. Whitaker?

Mrs. Whitaker: Thank you, Brian, Well, I'm a new gardener and this is my first frost and in two short months my garden's gone from being a real color explosion to a very bare thing indeed . . . Friends have advised flowers with a compact habit but that leaves me with lots of tiny auricula and double daisies, which look silly because the garden's really quite large. Now, I'd really like to plant something a little more striking, around the height of a delphinium, but then the wind gets it and people look over their fences thinking: *Dear oh dear (sympathetic laughter from the studio audience)*. So, my **question** to the panel is, how do you keep up appearances in the bleak midwinter?

Foreman: Thank you, Mrs, Whitaker. Well, it's a common problem . . . and it doesn't necessarily get any easier for the seasoned gardener. Personally, I never get it quite right. Well, let's hand the **question** over to the panel, shall we? Joyce Chalfen, any answers or suggestions for the bleak midwinter?

Joyce Chalfen: Well, first I must say your neighbors sound *very* nosy, I'd tell them to mind their own beeswax if I were you *(laughter from audience)*.

Zadie Smith, *White Teeth*

The door-bell rang.

Cairo's eyes jerked into focus on the passageway that led to the corridor-door. His eyes had become unangry and wary. The girl had gasped and turned to face the passageway. Her face was frightened. Spade stared gloomily for a moment at the blood trickling from Cairo's lip, and then stepped back, taking his hand from the Levantine's throat.

"Who is it?" the girl whispered, coming close to Spade; and Cairo's eyes jerked back to ask the same **question**.

> *Dashiell Hammett, The Maltese Falcon*

Is it physically possible, or even logically feasible, to have more than one universe? The screenwriter doesn't know. The girl expels a mouthful of smoke and asks: Does this cigarette exist? The smoke? "2.063 The sum-total of reality is the No World." A slight alteration of W's pronouncement. She goes back to her initial inquiry. She thinks the answer must be simple, because a thoughtlet is like a fundamental particle, and these constitute everything else in existence, everything a mind learns, and everything it imagines, are composed of these. And if it bodies forth a whole world, it must do so because it doesn't want to be alone. It's the only possible answer to the **question**. It's the only answer the girl can think of.

> *A. G. Porta, No World Concerto*

But we have not yet attained any tolerable satisfaction with regard to the **question** first proposed. Each solution still gives rise to a new **question** as difficult as the foregoing, and leads us on to farther enquiries. When it is asked, What is the nature of all our reasonings concerning matter of fact? the proper answer seems to be, that they are founded on the relation of cause and effect. When again it is asked, What is the foundation of all our reasonings and conclusions concerning that relation? it may be replied in one word, Experience. But if we still carry on our sifting humour, and ask, What is the foundation of all conclusions from experience? this implies a new **question**, which may be of more difficult solution and explication. Philosophers, that give themselves airs of superior wisdom and sufficiency, have a hard task when they encounter persons of inquisitive dispositions, who push them from every corner to which they retreat, and who are sure at last to bring them to some dangerous dilemma. The best expedient to prevent this confusion, is to be modest in our pretensions; and even to discover the difficulty ourselves before it is objected to us. By this means, we may make a kind of merit of our very ignorance.

> *David Hume, An Enquiry Concerning Human Understanding*

When Bush endorsed the teaching of intelligent design, he was predictably cheered by the religious right and denounced by the secular and religious left, but no one pointed out how truly extraordinary it was that any American president would place himself in direct opposition to contemporary scientific thinking. Even when they have been unsympathetic to new currents in philosophical, historical, and political thought, American presidents have always wanted to be on the right side of science, and those who understood nothing about science were smart enough to keep their mouths shut. One cannot imagine Calvin Coolidge making pronouncements about the desirability of teaching alternatives to Einstein's theory of relativity or about the theory of evolution—even though Coolidge was in the White House when the Scopes trial became the subject of major national publicity and controversy.

Unlike its predecessor in the twenties, the current anti-rationalist movement has been politicized from the bottom up and the top down, from school boards in small towns to the corridors of power in Washington. Bill Moyers, who has long been under attack from the religious and political right for the pro-science, pro-rationalist, and anti-fundamentalist content of his programs on public television, described the process in a scathing speech about the end-times scenario. "One of the biggest changes in politics in my lifetime," Moyers said, "is that the delusional is no longer marginal. It has come in from the fringe, to sit in the seats of power in the Oval Office and in Congress. For the first time in our history, ideology and theology hold a monopoly of power in Washington. Theology asserts propositions that cannot be proven true; ideologues hold stoutly to a worldview despite being contradicted by what is generally accepted as reality. The offspring of ideology and theology are not always bad but they are always blind. And that is the danger: voters and politicians alike, oblivious to the facts."[22] In the land of politicized anti-rationalism, facts are whatever folks choose to believe.

The **question** is why now.

Susan Jacoby, The Age of American Unreason

I decided that it must have been a committee decision. Four or five or even six of them sitting around a table, covering their ruled, yellow legal pads with penciled doodles as they discussed Li Teh and whether he would be worth $3,000 a month to the taxpayers. There would be, of course, the suspicious one, perhaps an old hand, but more likely a new boy trying to make a name for himself. He would chew on his pencil's eraser for a while, look worried, and then raise the **question** as to whether Li could really be trusted. You know. *Really.* After all, if he's agreed to double, couldn't he just as easily triple? Young Masterman might have something there, another of them would say, and cock an eyebrow to show the colors of a true skeptic.

Ross Thomas, The Fools in Town Are on Our Side

For these reasons the view has generally been adopted that the wavefunction associated with an object is not a real "thing", but merely represents our *knowledge* of the object. This approach was developed by Bohr and others, mainly at Copenhagen in the late 1920s. When we perform a measurement or observation of an object we acquire new information and so adjust the wavefunction as we would boundary conditions in classical physics to reflect this new information. This stance means that we can't answer **questions** about what's actually happening, all we can answer is what will be the probability of a particular result if we perform a measurement. This makes a lot of people very unhappy since it provides no model for the object.

It should be added that there are other, less popular, interpretations of quantum theory, but they all have their own drawbacks, which are widely reckoned more severe. Generally speaking they try to find a mechanism that describes the collapse process or add extra physical objects to the theory, in addition to the wavefunction. In this sense they are more complex. (See "Is there any alternative theory?")

Michael Clive Price, The Many-Worlds FAQ

Pettifer shifted in his chair, its legs scraping the floor. "Maybe if we could get back to the **question** of where you think Lee Herdman could have scored those guns . . . ?"

"They're mostly made in China these days, aren't they?" Johnson said.

"I mean," Pettifer went on, an edge creeping into his voice, "how would someone go about getting hold of them?"

Johnson gave an exaggerated shrug. "By the grip and the trigger?"

*Ian Rankin, A **Question** of Blood*

. . . and the world scuffles about a thousand **questions**, of which both the Pro and the Con are false.

Michel de Montaigne, Of Cripples (Essays)

Indeed, there were people for that job: the badass Kootchy Kooties. These guys slithered down face-first into dark holes in the earth with a pistol in one hand and their balls in the other and a flashlight in their teeth, anywhere in the Cu Chi region. "Kootchy Kooties" was a fabulous name. As for Echo Recon, they didn't have a flashy call-name, but owing to their proximity to Cao Phuc they couldn't avoid being known as the Cowfuckers, a stupid bit of luck. They didn't even get to paint it on anything because it was dirty language.

"We will win this war." Was he still talking? "And the efforts of this particular platoon will be instrumental in that. Think of us as infiltrators. This land under our feet is where the Vietcong locate their national heart. This land is their myth. We penetrate this land, we penetrate their heart, their myth, their soul. That's real infiltration. And that's our mission: penetrating the myth of the land.

"**Questions**?"

Denis Johnson, Tree of Smoke

"Can you tell me how much it would cost to do that? Find . . . the person, I mean."

"No," I said. "I can't tell you that. Here's how it works: You pay me by the day. I keep looking until I find whoever you're looking for, or until you tell me to quit trying."

"Well, how much is it a day, then?"

"Same as you just paid me. I cover all expenses out of that. And there's a twenty-G bonus if I turn up what you want."

"Ten thousand a week," he said, the slightest trace of a **question** mark at the end of the sentence.

"We don't take weekends off," I told him. "One week, that's fourteen. Payable in advance."

"That could run into a lot of money."

"Uh-huh."

"I'll have to think that one over."

"You know where to find me," I said.

"Well, actually, I don't. I mean, the man who I . . . spoke to, he just took my number, and you called me, remember?"

"Yes, I remember."

"So how do I . . . ? Oh. You mean, now or never, right?"

"Right."

He took a hit off his drink. "I don't walk around with that kind of cash," he said. "Who does?"

"Best of luck with your search," I said, moving my untouched glass to the side as I started to stand up.

Andrew Vachss, Mask Market

Q15 Where are the other worlds?

Non-relativistic quantum mechanics and quantum field theory are quite unambiguous: the other Everett-worlds occupy the same space and time as we do.

The implicit **question** is really, why aren't we aware of these other worlds, unless they exist "somewhere" else? To see why we aren't aware of the other worlds, despite occupying the same space-time, see "Why do I only ever experience one world?" Some popular accounts describe the other worlds as splitting off into other, orthogonal, dimensions. These dimensions are the dimensions of Hilbert space, not the more familiar space-time dimensions.

The situation is more complicated, as we might expect, in theories of quantum gravity (See "What about quantum gravity?"), because gravity can be viewed as perturbations in the space-time metric. If we take a geometric interpretation of gravity then we can regard differently curved space-times, each with their own distinct thermodynamic history, as non-coeval. In that sense we only share the same space-time manifold with other worlds with a (macroscopically) similar mass distribution. Whenever the amplification of a quantum-scale interaction effects the mass distribution and hence space-time curvature the resultant decoherence can be regarded as splitting the local space-time manifold into discrete sheets.

*Michael Clive Price, The Many-Worlds **FAQ***

Question: Do you literally mean that when you talked with the audience you came to believe that they had not seen anything else but the chicken?
Wilson: We simply asked them: What did you see in this film?
Question: Not what did you *think*?
Wilson: No, what did you *see*?
Question: How many people were in the viewing audience of whom you asked this **question**?
Wilson: 30-odd.
Question: No one gave you a response other than "We saw the chicken"?
Wilson: No, this was the first quick response—"We saw a chicken."

Marshall McLuhan, The Gutenberg Galaxy: The Making of Typographic Man

He's even thought of the title he'd give to a series of such films: *Hidden Scenes From So-and-So's Work.* Or if he changed the author and work in **question**: *Leon Kowalski, the Hidden Years of a Replicant,* It would be a matter of putting false memories into the mind of a movie character, although of course it wouldn't make a difference if the memories were true or false. It's all the same in fiction. The screenwriter puts the matter aside for the moment and continues watching the TV. The lady has finally made her way to the back of the shoe-repair shop. Looking closely, one can clearly see a halo of light around her body. The screenwriter doesn't understand why no one else can see that she's an alien.

A. G. Porta, No World Concerto

It was Richard Feynman, in fact, who suggested that all physicists put a sign up in their offices or homes to remind them of how much we don't know. The sign would say simply this: 137. One hundred thirty-seven is the inverse of something called the fine-structure constant. This number is related to the probability that an electron will emit or absorb a photon. The fine-structure constant also answers to the name alpha, and it can be arrived at by taking the square of the charge of the electron divided by the speed of light times Planck's constant. What all that verbiage means is that this one number; 137, contains the crux of electromagnetism (the electron), relativity (the velocity of light), and quantum theory (Planck's constant). It would be less unsettling if the relationship between all these important concepts turned out to be one or three or maybe a multiple of pi. But 137?

The most remarkable thing about this remarkable number is that it is dimension-free. The speed of light is about 300,000 kilometers per second. Abraham Lincoln was 6 feet 6 inches tall. Most numbers come with dimensions. But it turns out that when you combine the quantities that make up alpha, all the units cancel! One hundred thirty-seven comes by itself; it shows up naked all over the place. This means that scientists on Mars, or on the fourteenth planet of the star Sirius, using whatever god-awful units they have for charge, speed, and their version of Planck's constant, will also get 137. It is a pure number.

Physicists have agonized over 137 for the past fifty years. Werner Heisenberg once proclaimed that all the quandaries of quantum mechanics would shrivel up when 137 was finally explained. I tell my undergraduate students that if they are ever in trouble in a major city anywhere in the world they should write "137" on a sign and hold it up at a busy street corner. Eventually a physicist will see that they're distressed and come to their assistance. (No one to my knowledge has ever tried this, but it should work.)

One of the wonderful (but unverified) stories in physics emphasizes the importance of 137 as well as illustrating the arrogance of theorists. According to this tale, a notable Austrian mathematical physicist of Swiss persuasion, Wolfgang Pauli, went to heaven, we are assured, and, because of his eminence in physics, was given an audience with God.

"Pauli, you're allowed one **question**. What do you want to know?" Pauli immediately asked the one **question** that he had labored in vain to answer for the last decade of his life. "Why is alpha equal to one over one hundred thirty-seven?" God smiled, picked up the chalk, and began writing equations on the blackboard. After a few minutes She turned to Pauli, who waved his hand. "Das ist falsch!" [That's baloney!]

There's a true story also—a verifiable story—that takes place here on earth. Pauli was in fact obsessed with 137, and spent countless hours pondering its significance. The number plagued him to the very end. When Pauli's assistant visited the theorist in the hospital room in which he was placed prior to his fatal operation, Pauli instructed the assistant to note the number on the door as he left. The room number was 137.

Leon M. Lederman, The God Particle: If the Universe Is the Answer, What Is the **Question?**

Thinking in Fahrenheit—sixteen degrees—I felt very sad for the penguins. But then, as so often happens in climate-change discussions when the talk turns from diagnosis to remedies, the darkness became the blackness of black comedy. Sitting in the lounge of a ship burning three and a half gallons of fuel per minute, we listened to Adam extoll the benefits of shopping at farmers' markets and changing our incandescent bulbs to L.E.D. bulbs. He also suggested that universal education for women would lower the global birth rate, and that ridding the world of war would free up enough money to convert the global economy to renewable energy. Then he called for **questions** or comments. The climate-change skeptics weren't interested in arguing, but a believer stood up to say that he managed a lot of residential properties, and that he'd noticed that his federally subsidized tenants always kept their homes too hot in the winter and too cold in the summer, because they didn't pay for their utilities, and that one way to combat climate change would be to make them pay. To this, a woman quietly responded, "I think the ultra-wealthy waste far more than people in subsidized housing." The discussion broke up quickly after that—we all had bags to pack.

Jonathan Franzen, The End of the End of the World (The New Yorker)

Meanwhile, upon **questioning** him in his broken fashion, Queequeg gave me to understand that, in his land, owing to the absence of settees and sofas of all sorts, the king, chiefs, and great people generally, were in the custom of fattening some of the lower orders for ottomans; and to furnish a house comfortably in that respect, you had only to buy up eight or ten lazy fellows, and lay them round in the piers and alcoves. Besides, it was very convenient on an excursion; much better than those garden-chairs which are convertible into walking-sticks; upon occasion, a chief calling his attendant, and desiring him to make a settee of himself under a spreading tree, perhaps in some damp marshy place.

Herman Melville, Moby Dick; or, The Whale

*Brookdale Public Access TV, Brookdale Pumpkin **Question**, 2009 (Internet Archive)*

You Mean That as a **Question**

To be sure of this engages some attention

I heard what was said of the universe,
Heard it and heard it of several thousand years;
It is middling well as far as it goes—but is that all?

Walt Whitman, Leaves of Grass

"My dear madam, it is my misfortune that the topics I introduce, however carefully selected by me, do not seem to be congenial to you. Have you a leanin' toward Natural history, madam? Have you ever studied into the habits and traits of our American Wad?"

"What?" sez I. For truly a woman's curosity, however parlyzed by just indignation, can stand only just so much strain. "The what?"

Marietta Holley, Samantha on the Woman **Question**

p. 391–6

Since vivid descriptive phrases such as "river of clouds" and "like a feathery fishing line" characterize the passage followed by "wondrous spectacle" to describe the night sky, the answer must be about nature's beauty and noticing it.

D

Henry Davis, Explanations for the Official SAT Study Guide **Questions***: Detailed Explanations for the Answers for Every* **Question**

To show the difference between an occasion and merit and a button it is necessary to recognise that an honor is not forced so that there is no **question** of taste. To exchange a single statue for a coat of silk and a coat of wool is not necessary as there are appliances. A somber day is one when there is no pleading.

Made in haste, not made in haste, made in darkness, not made in darkness, made in a place, made in a place. The whole stretched out is not part of the whole block, the whole stretched out is so arranged that there is not stumbling but what is just as remarkable, pushing. An easy expression of being willing, of being hunting, of being so stupid that there is no **question** of not selling, all these things cause more discussion than a resolution and this is so astonishing when there is nothing to do and an excellent reason for an exchange, and yet the practice of it makes such an example that any day is a season.

To be sure that the trees have winter and the plants have summer and the houses painting, to be sure of this engages some attention. The time to place this in the way is not what is expected from a diner. The whole thing that shows the result is the little way that the balls and the pieces that are with them which are not birds as they are older do not measure the distance between a cover and a calendar. This which is not a **question** is not reverse and the **question** which is a **question** is at noon.

. . .

A cause for disturbance rests in the fact that more time is used in a long time than in a short time. There is no criticism when the time is long. The time is so long that an answer comes promptly. This is so much the more satisfactory as the occasion for an answer is whenever there is cause for a **question**. The difference between this and no elaboration is extreme. No elaboration is not achieved in a **question** nor in an answer and this which is so eminently satisfactory is that there is no doubt that there will be no reason for the occasion. To be faithful is to be accustomed and the custom which is without that reservation has no circumstance to replace it. The time to state that is when there is no reason to doubt a result. There never is a reason to doubt a result if there is a promise. If there is a promise it means that idleness is only another name for a thing.

. . .

Nothing is perplexing if there is an island. The special sign of this is in dusting. It then extends itself and as there is no destruction it remains a principle. This which makes that reveals that and revelation is not fortuitous it is combined and ordered and a bargain. All this shows the condition to be erect. Suppose that there is no **question**, if there is no **question** then certainly the absence of no particular is not designed. And then when it is astonishing it is not liberty. Liberty is that which gathered together is not disturbed by distribution and not given without remark and not disturbed by frugality and an outline. All this makes the impression that is so disturbed that there is no **question**.

. . .

To answer when there is no **question**, to intend to follow when there is no plunging, to embody that which has that knowledge, all that is the way to remain with the little button that has a button-hole. This is so attached.

. . .

The heat of hearing is not the silence of answering and nothing is produced when the **question** is the same as the name. That is one way to answer and there might have been more but it was different, it was the same.

. . .

To put that **question** does not mean the mention of an author. To repeat the name is not the same when there is no chair.

. . .

If the message is sent and received and if the tunes have words then certainly there will be soon the center piece which has not been removed. Every little flower has a number. There is that way to **question**.

. . .

If there is no **question** and an answer is not a toilet, if there is no **question** is there any strangeness in a garden. Certainly not, the danger is not any color. It has the bloom and the sign of an early summer. There is no necessity to deface anything. An escape is not needed.

There is one **question**. In not asking a **question** the permission which is continued

*Brookdale Public Access TV, Brookdale Pumpkin **Question**, 2009 (Internet Archive)*

is so courteous that there is no moon-light. The time does keep the rain from startling more than a diary. This shows that there is no **question** and an answer is no meeting.

. . .

Was the explosion that authority, did it succeed more than yesterday, was there tomorrow before, these are not **questions** asking, they are not existing missing, they are so applied that there is no joke, there is no pleasure. All the same the standard is there and the separation has a position, it has no repudiation, it has no hurrying centralization, it has nothing there. If to be there is mentioned then the whole response is the occasion. It is and there is more. There is no answer. There is turning. Turning is not a victim, it has no protection, it has no authority, it has a receipt.

. . .

The answer in the house is that talking is not the same thing as a lamb. So that was the way it came to be and the second answer came before the first.

. . .

Frown nowhere and do not change that space, that is the way to use the time to purchase mining pictures. The little darkness and no large lamp, all the light being together does not make everything strange. Please the daylight, show the ruins that there is water, do not disturb the lamp, make more noise than resting and more that is changed is changed and an agreement shows the pink not to be redder. All that partial resemblance to a disagreement and a reunion is not more **questioned** than no answer. Not any more choice is so determined, and yet, why is the season so ingrained in the early morning when noon is no later. There is always a return of any answer.

. . .

Plant the union of a **question** later, all the time has that change, the pink length and the satin fixture this does not make any **question** uncertain. A **question** if there is no answer is a **question** where there is no answer. To place more is always a way.

. . .

A large moist blue and a paler color, a large dust rose and no water nearer, a small tall frame and no building finer this makes a prediction that necessity is work and then why is there no **question**. There is no **question** because investigation is miraculous.

. . .

The objection and the perfect central table, the sorrow in borrowing and the hurry in a nervous feeling, the **question** is it really a plague, is it really an oleander, is it really saffron in color, the surmountable appetite which shows inclination to be warmer, the safety in a match and the safety in a little piece of splinter, the real reason why cocoa is cheaper, the same use for bread as for any breathing that is softer, the lecture and the surrounding large white soft unequal and spread out sale of more and still less is no better, all this makes one regard in a season, one hat in a curtain that in rising higher, one landing and many many more, and many more many more many many more.

. . .

I like to ask you **questions**. Do you believe that it is necessary to worship individuality. We do.

. . .

You mean that as a **question**.

. . .

They were **questioned**.

. . .

What is the difference between one order and a reading. A great many read in a park.

Words **question** it bakeries threaten it but really hotels receive it. Do we hear about books. Do we. And catalogues. And catalogues. Farmers for speech. A great many vines are said to be sold. In France. And in wealthy homes too. We do not understand the weather. That astonishes me.

Gertrude Stein, Geography and Plays

*Elihu Vedder, The **Questioner** of the Sphinx, 1875*
Oil on canvas, 27.3 x 31.3 cm, Worcester Art Museum

Because a Lot of **Questions** Are Complex

*Begging the **question** of what can be defined as 'form'*

"You ask a lot of **questions**."

"I don't know a lot of stuff."

Sam Lipsyte, The Ask

How do you formulate the great **questions**? Research. Contrary to what your teacher told you in high school, there is such a thing as a stupid **question**, especially when conducting an interview for a celebrity profile.

Think about it. How many times does Norman Schwartzkoff want to answer how he began his career in the military? How often does Hillary want to narrate where she and Bill met? What is Harrison Ford going to think of you if you ask "What was your breakthrough role?" He's liable to look at you emphatically and say "Duh! Star Wars!"

Sheree Bykofsky and Jennifer Basye Sander, The Complete Idiot's Guide to Publishing Magazine Articles

Together they had traced the rumors across the solar system. The legends of an ancient humanoid race who had known the answer to all things, and who had built Answerer and departed.

"Think of it," Morran said. "The answer to everything!"

*Robert Sheckley, Ask a Foolish **Question** (Science Fiction Stories)*

Hi Jerry, Do you like cilantro?

I do kind of like cilantro, but I don't know what it is.

I just ran out of lunch-meat, what kind should I get now?

More lunchmeat? Why does it need to be more specific? It's meat, and they're telling you when to eat it.

Would you rather have a rhino sized hamster or a hamster sized rhino?

Oh my god, that's such an easy **question**! Who wouldn't want a hamster sized rhino? It would be one of the greatest things ever! You could put your hand down flat and just let him charge into it!

*Jerry Seinfeld, Jerry Seinfeld Loves Answering **Questions**! The Dumber, the Better. Now. (Interviewly)*

I am very unfortunate if that is true. But suppose I ask you a **question**: Would you say that this also holds true in the case of horses?

Plato, Apology

p. 395–23

This **question** depends on vocabulary and your knowledge of the meaning of the word innate which means inborn, inherited or natural which has no logic or factual evidence to prove it, therefore he does not give any belief to its truth. Skepticism is distrustful or doubtful.

    E

p. 405–20

Word substitution works well for this **question**. Read the sentence replacing peculiar with the answer choices. In this case, distinctive means standing out or being clear. Note that the more common definitions of peculiar like eccentric, abnormal, and rare can be ruled out because they are similar and someone might choose those common definitions without reading the passage.

    D

p. 409–12

The sentence is about two people and what they plan to become. They would be entomologists.

    C

*Henry Davis, Explanations for the Official SAT Study Guide **Questions**: Detailed Explanations for the Answers for Every **Question***

In what ways are you different? In which the same? Why must that small boy wear leg braces? What is it that brings us each to destructive behavior? Remember when Sandoz still made acid? Remember Polio Summer? Where are you coming from? Does it make any difference? What if I was drunk? Just what do I fear about trust? Can you separate the inner from the outer? Why is this not form, but a process? Who is that witch? Is that my bus? What is a memory? Is that a hole in your shoe? How can you imagine that all these things exist? What if he understood that we all thought he was a closet case and were not threatened by that? Is it a **question** of a wager? Do not verbs collapse the real down to a single, simplified plane? At what point did you realize that you are capable of killing? Why is this not theater, not dance? Are words not ultimately puffy with misuse? Do phenothiazines scare you? What does this exemplify? Are not all truckers jerks? Do you believe that by balling or not balling you will be a better person? What if I told you these were only place holders and that it was you who was in **question**?

Ron Silliman, Sunset Debris

Why am I me? A stupid **question** . . . I am too stupid to answer this **question**. And to ask it, just stupid enough. What is the mechanism of such stupid **questioning**? I imagine a small organ, neither inside nor outside myself, like a polymelic phantom limb, a subtle psychic appendage implanted at birth behind my crown, during the moment of my coming to be, whenever that was. This organ (or appendix, or tumor), whose painful inflammation is despair—"despair is the paroxysm of individuation" (Cioran)—is like a strange supplementary bodily member, intimate and inessential, which I can feel yet not move, barely move yet without feeling. Stupid organ, organ of stupidity. It moves, is moved, like an inalienable shackle, only to reinforce its immobility. Am I to sever this organ, hemorrhage of haecceity, escape it? "[E]scape is the need to get out of oneself, that is, *to break that most radical and unalterably binding of chains, the fact that the I [moi] is oneself [soi-me me]* (Levinas). Just who, then, would escape?" (Nicola Masciandaro, "Individuation: This Stupidity," *Postmedieval* 1 [2010], forthcoming).

"The act whereby being—existence—is bestowed upon us is an *unbearable* surpassing of being" (Bataille).

Nicola Masciandaro, Anti-Cosmosis: Black Mahapralaya (Hideous Gnosis: Black Metal Theory Symposium 1)

It's understandable that someone would feel and think that way, especially when frustrated, but the truth is that these are lousy **questions**. They're negative and they don't solve any problems. Throughout the rest of the book we'll refer to **questions** like these as Incorrect **Questions**, or IQs . . .

John G. Miller, **QBQ!** *The* **Question** *Behind the* **Question***: Practicing Personal Accountability at Work and in Life*

"Why?" Varvara Petrovna asked, not quite so firmly.

"Madam, madam . . ."

He relapsed into gloomy silence, looking on the floor, laying his right hand on his heart. Varvara Petrovna waited, not taking her eyes off him.

"Madam!" he roared suddenly. "Will you allow me to ask you one **question**? Only one, but frankly, directly, like a Russian, from the heart?"

"Kindly do so."

"Have you ever suffered madam, in your life?"

"You simply mean to say that you have been or are being ill-treated by some one."

"Madam, madam!" He jumped up again, probably unconscious of doing so, and struck himself on the breast. "Here in this bosom so much has accumulated, so much that God Himself will be amazed when it is revealed at the Day of Judgment."

"H'm! A strong expression!"

"Madam, I speak perhaps irritably . . ."

"Don't be uneasy. I know myself when to stop you."

"May I ask you another **question**, madam?"

"Ask another **question**."

"Can one die simply from the generosity of one's feelings?"

"I don't know, as I've never asked myself such a **question**."

"You don't know! You've never asked yourself such a **question**," he said with pathetic irony. "Well, if that's it, if that's it . . ."

"Be still, despairing heart!"

And he struck himself furiously on the chest. He was by now walking about the room again.

It is typical of such people to be utterly incapable of keeping their desires to themselves; they have, on the contrary, an irresistible impulse to display them in all their unseemliness as soon as they arise. When such a gentleman gets into a circle in which he is not at home he usually begins timidly,—but you have only to give him an inch and he will at once rush into impertinence. The captain was already excited. He walked about waving his arms and not listening to **questions**, talked about himself very, very quickly, so that sometimes his tongue would not obey him, and without finishing one phrase he passed to another. It is true he was probably not quite sober. Moreover, Lizaveta Nikolaevna was sitting there too, and though he did not once glance at her, her presence seemed to overexcite him terribly; that, however, is only my supposition. There must have been some reason which led Varvara Petrovna to resolve to listen to such a man in spite of her repugnance. Praskovya Ivanovna was simply shaking with terror, though, I believe she really did not quite understand what it was about. Stepan Trofimovitch was trembling too, but that was, on the contrary, because he was disposed to understand everything, and exaggerate it. Mavriky Nikolaevitch stood in the attitude of one ready to defend all present; Liza was pale, and she gazed fixedly with wide-open eyes at the wild captain. Shatov sat in the same position as before, but, what was strangest of all, Marya Timofyevna had not only ceased laughing, but had become terribly sad. She leaned her right elbow on the table, and with a prolonged, mournful gaze watched her brother declaiming. Darya Pavlovna alone seemed to me calm.

"All that is nonsensical allegory," said Varvara Petrovna, getting angry at last. "You haven't answered my **question**, why? I insist on an answer."

"I haven't answered, why? You insist on an answer, why?" repeated the captain, winking. "That little word 'why' has run through all the universe from the first day of creation, and all nature cries every minute to it's Creator, 'why?' And for seven thousand years it has had no answer, and must Captain Lebyadkin alone answer? And is that justice, madam?"

"That's all nonsense and not to the point!" cried Varvara Petrovna, getting angry and losing patience. "That's allegory; besides, you express yourself too sensationally, sir, which I consider impertinence."

"Madam," the captain went on, not hearing, "I should have liked perhaps to be called Ernest, yet I am forced to bear the vulgar name Ignat—why is that do you suppose? I should have liked to be called Prince de Monbart, yet I am only Lebyadkin, derived from a swan. Why is that? I am a poet, madam, a poet in soul, and might be getting a thousand roubles at a time from a publisher, yet I am forced to live in a pig pail. Why? Why, madam? To my mind Russia is a freak of nature and nothing else."

"Can you really say nothing more definite?"

"I can read you the poem, 'The Cockroach,' madam."

"Whaat?"

"Madam, I'm not mad yet! I shall be mad, no doubt I shall be, but I'm not so yet. Madam, a friend of mine—a most honourable man—has written a Krylov's fable, called 'The Cockroach.' May I read it?"

"You want to read some fable of Krylov's?"

"No, it's not a fable of Krylov's I want to read. It's my fable, my own composition. Believe me, madam, without offence I'm not so uneducated and depraved as not to understand that Russia can boast of a great fablewriter, Krylov, to whom the Minister of Education has raised a monument in the Summer Gardens for the diversion of the young. Here, madam, you ask me why? The answer is at the end of this fable, in letters of fire."

"Read your fable."

"Lived a cockroach in the world
Such was his condition,
In a glass he chanced to fall
Full of fly-perdition."

"Heavens! What does it mean?" cried Varvara Petrovna.

"That's when flies get into a glass in the summertime," the captain explained hurriedly with the irritable impatience of an author interrupted in reading. "Then it is perdition to the flies, any fool can understand. Don't interrupt, don't interrupt. You'll

Amtrak ticket agent answers a **question** for a customer at a station in a suburb near Washington, District of Columbia, April 1974.

Photo by Jim Pickerell (National Archives and Records Administration) see, you'll see . . ." He kept waving his arms.

> *"But he squeezed against the flies,*
> *They woke up and cursed him,*
> *Raised to Jove their angry cries;*
> *'The glass is full to bursting!'*
> *In the middle of the din*
> *Came along Nikifor,*
> *Fine old man, and looking in . . .*

I haven't quite finished it. But no matter, I'll tell it in words," the captain rattled on. "Nikifor takes the glass, and in spite of their outcry empties away the whole stew, flies, and beetles and all, into the pig pail, which ought to have been done long ago. But observe, madam, observe, the cockroach doesn't complain. That's the answer to your **question**, why?" he cried triumphantly. "'The cockroach does not complain.' As for Nikifor he typifies nature," he added, speaking rapidly and walking complacently about the room.

Varvara Petrovna was terribly angry.

"And allow me to ask you about that money said to have been received from Nikolay Vsyevolodovitch, and not to have been given to you, about which you dared to accuse a person belonging to my household."

"It's a slander!" roared Lebyadkin, flinging up his right hand tragically.

"No, it's not a slander."

"Madam, there are circumstances that force one to endure family disgrace rather than proclaim the truth aloud. Lebyadkin will not blab, madam!"

He seemed dazed; he was carried away; he felt his importance; he certainly had some fancy in his mind. By now he wanted to insult some one, to do something nasty to show his power.

Fyodor Dostoyevsky, *The Possessed; or, The Devils*

I ask him how his presentation went. "Fine, but for the stupid **questions** afterwards," he says.

Tim Parks, Stupid **Questions** *(The New York Review of Books)*

The first time Donald Antrim's mind was exposed to wider scrutiny, that I can find, was more than 20 years ago during an interview he gave to *The New York Times*. It was the fall of 1993, so right after the publication of his first book, the novel "Elect Mr. Robinson for a Better World." The **Q**. and A. opened with this exchange:

Q. *What inspired this book?*
A. That kind of **question** is so hard to answer.

And it ended with this one:

Q. *Do you answer "yes and no" to a lot of **questions**?*
A. Sure, because a lot of **questions** are complex.

In between, Antrim parried. At one point, he did say something that in retrospect seems telling. The reporter, Degen Pener, wanted to know how it felt to "write something as dark as this book." "Mr. Robinson" abounds, as they used to say, in grotesque incident.

A girl is killed while a teacher watches. A pretty Southern seaside community drops its mask to reveal precisely the prehistoric violence we always knew lurked there. The novel is also deeply hilarious, in how it expresses horror through a certain pitch-perfect American tone. "I was listening to Jim's last words," Pete Robinson says, telling the story. Jim is the former mayor—at that moment he's lying in a field after dark, wrists and ankles bound with high-test fishing line, and the lines run out to the bumpers of four cars, all pointed in different directions. He's about to be drawn and quartered. "'Will you do a favor for me, Pete?'" Jim asks. "'After I'm gone.'"

John Jeremiah Sullivan, Donald Antrim and the Art of Anxiety

"What can I do?" for example, follows the guidelines perfectly. It begins with "What," contains an "I," and focuses on action: "What can I do?" Simple, as I said. But don't let its simplicity fool you.

John G. Miller, **QBQ**! The **Question** Behind the **Question**: Practicing Personal Accountability at Work and in Life

No answer to these **questions** can ever be clean, or comprehensive, and so we are thrown, again and again, to the works themselves—with, if we are lucky, a guiding voice in our minds.

Mark Kingwell, Outside the White Box (Harper's Magazine)

ratiocinatio

ra'-ti-o-cin-a'-ti-o

L. ratio, "reason"

Reasoning (typically with oneself) by asking **questions**. Sometimes equivalent to anthypophora.

More specifically, ratiocinatio can mean making statements, then asking the reason (ratio) for such an affirmation, then answering oneself. In this latter sense ratiocinatio is closely related to aetiologia.

Examples

Old age is superior to youth. Why? The body has been tamed and the mind ripened with wisdom.

Gideon Burton, Silva Rhetoricae (The Forest of Rhetoric)

This seems a very dubious assertion, besides begging the **question** of what can be defined as 'form'. Behind it one glimpses that old ghost which still haunts classical studies, however often right-minded scholars may exorcise it: the feeling that ancient authors achieved a perfection which somehow places them above common literary error, that they cannot be criticized, only explained and justified. *Tu nihil in magno doctus reprehendis Homero?* Horace asked—'Tell me, do you, a scholar, find nothing to cavil at in mighty Homer?'

Peter Green, Introduction to Juvenal, The Sixteen Satires

p. 392–12

This **question's** answer lies not in the proverb but in the explanation that follows stating the "instinctive pull of one's heritage," "curiosity," and "quest" for self identification which matches people's "inherent (natural) interest" in answer C.

C

Henry Davis, Explanations for the Official SAT Study Guide **Questions**: Detailed Explanations for the Answers for Every **Question**

In the tragedy in **question**, for example, he found fault with the ideas but admired the style; he condemned the conception but applauded all the details; and he was incensed by the characters, though he raved about their speeches. When he read the great passages, he was transported; but when he thought how the pulpiteers were profiting from it to sell their goods, he was grieved, and in this confusion of feelings in which he found himself entangled . . .

    Gustave Flaubert, Madame Bovary

When I went to Lunnon town sirs, Too rul loo rul Too rul loo rul Wasn't I done very brown sirs? Too rul loo rul Too rul loo rul—still, in my desire to be wiser, I got this composition by heart with the utmost gravity; nor do I recollect that I **questioned** its merit, except that I thought (as I still do) the amount of Too rul somewhat in excess of the poetry. In my hunger for information, I made proposals to Mr. Wopsle to bestow some intellectual crumbs upon me, with which he kindly complied. As it turned out, however, that he only wanted me for a dramatic lay-figure, to be contradicted and embraced and wept over and bullied and clutched and stabbed and knocked about in a variety of ways, I soon declined that course of instruction; though not until Mr. Wopsle in his poetic fury had severely mauled me.

    Charles Dickens, Great Expectations

Q. Why is this style called the Debased?
    A. From the general inferiority of design compared with the style it succeeded, from the meagre and clumsy execution of sculptured and other ornamental work, from the intermixture of detail founded on an entirely different school of art, and the consequent subversion of the purity of style.

    Matthew Holbeche Bloxam, The Principles of Gothic Ecclesiastical Architecture, Elucidated by **Question** *and Answer*

In the inevitable period of decomposition, those forms devised to transform the world turn in upon themselves and implode. The form, once world-historical, becomes its own subject. History stops; action is replaced by an endless series of repetitions. As the form decomposes, symbolically, so does the world—it becomes sterile, inaccessible, worthless, unreal. Any aesthetic form could illustrate the necessity, but the novel will do: we move from Fielding, where a story, a creative account of the world, is in **question**, to Joyce, where communication itself is in **question**. The result is the post-Joycean novel, which asks no **questions** and communicates nothing: it is merely a set of empty gestures, a dead commodity, a thing whose only use value is its exchange value. We move from eternity (Fielding is still read, and, as you read him, you still feel the world changing) to slime (to believe that the present-day novel will be read in a hundred years is not to praise the novel but to condemn the world).

    Greil Marcus, Lipstick Traces: A Secret History of the Twentieth Century

He passed the *Irish Times*. There might be other answers lying there. Like to answer them all. Good system for criminals. Code. At their lunch now. Clerk with the glasses there doesn't know me. O, leave them there to simmer. Enough bother wading through fortyfour of them. Wanted, smart lady typist to aid gentleman in literary work. I called you naughty darling because I do not like that other world. Please tell me what is the meaning. Please tell me what perfume does your wife. Tell me who made the world. The way they spring those **questions** on you. And the other one Lizzie Twigg. My literary efforts have had the good fortune to meet with the approval of the eminent poet A. E. (Mr Geo. Russell). No time to do her hair drinking sloppy tea with a book of poetry.

James Joyce, Ulysses

By contrast, the realistic attitude, inspired by positivism, from Saint Thomas Aquinas to Anatole France, clearly seems to me to be hostile to any intellectual or moral advancement. I loathe it, for it is made up of mediocrity, hate, and dull conceit. It is this attitude which today gives birth to these ridiculous books, these insulting plays. It constantly feeds on and derives strength from the newspapers and stultifies both science and art by assiduously flattering the lowest of tastes; clarity bordering on stupidity, a dog's life. The activity of the best minds feels the effects of it; the law of the lowest common denominator finally prevails upon them as it does upon the others. An amusing result of this state of affairs, in literature for example, is the generous supply of novels. Each person adds his personal little "observation" to the whole. As a cleansing antidote to all this, M. Paul Valéry recently suggested that an anthology be compiled in which the largest possible number of opening passages from novels be offered; the resulting insanity, he predicted, would be a source of considerable edification. The most famous authors would be included. Such a thought reflects great credit on Paul Valéry who, some time ago, speaking of novels, assured me that, so far as he was concerned, he would continue to refrain from writing: "The Marquise went out at five." But has he kept his word?

If the purely informative style, of which the sentence just quoted is a prime example, is virtually the rule rather than the exception in the novel form, it is because, in all fairness, the author's ambition is severely circumscribed. The circumstantial, needlessly specific nature of each of their notations leads me to believe that they are perpetrating a joke at my expense. I am spared not even one of the character's slightest vacillations: will he be fair-haired? what will his name be? will we first meet him during the summer? So many **questions** resolved once and for all, as chance directs; the only discretionary power left me is to close the book, which I am careful to do somewhere in the vicinity of the first page.

André Breton, Manifesto of Surrealism

Ask a Spartan whether he had rather be a good orator or a good soldier: and if I was asked the same **question**, I would rather choose to be a good cook, had I not one already to serve me. My God! Madame, how should I hate such a recommendation of being a clever fellow at writing, and an ass and an inanity in everything else! Yet I had rather be a fool both here and there than to have made so ill a choice wherein to employ my talent. And I am so far from expecting to gain any new reputation by these follies, that I shall think I come off pretty well if I lose nothing by them of that little I had before.

Michel de Montaigne, Of the Resemblance of Children to Their Fathers (Essays)

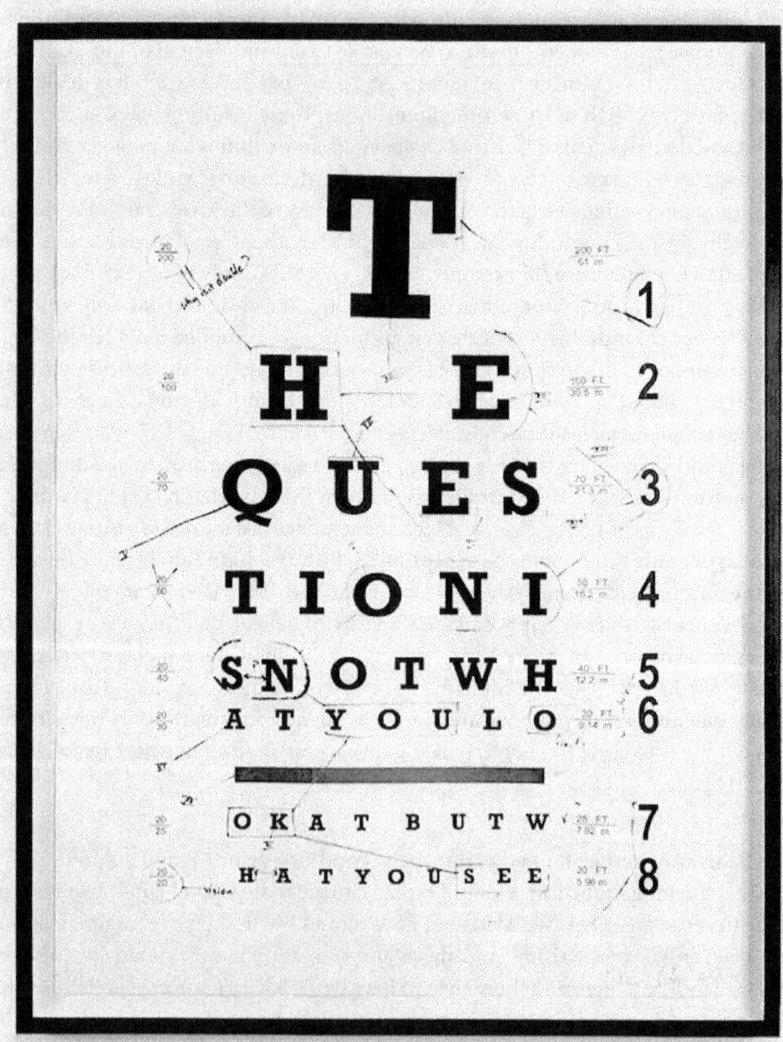

*Ollie Clegg, The **Question** Is Not What U Look At But What You See*
Silkscreen print on cartridge paper, 90 x 120cm

Read by Keith Collins, introduced by Peter Donaldson, edited and mixed at dBs Music

The Moby-Dick Big Read, Chapter 7: The Chapel (mobydickbigread.com)

And Now Let Us Get Back to the Question of "How" and "Why"

I said, "All right, why not?"

Once, the artist's task seemed to be simply that of opening up new areas and objects of attention. That task is still acknowledged, but it has become problematic. The very faculty of attention has come into **question**, and been subjected to more rigorous standards. As Jasper Johns has said, "Already it's a great deal to see anything clearly, for we don't see anything clearly."

Susan Sontag, *The Aesthetics of Silence (Styles of Radical Will)*

"This looks great," he said, lifting his wineglass. "Compliments to the chef."

"I microwaved the potatoes, and the corn came out of the freezer."

Rebus put a finger to his lips. "Never give away your secrets."

"A lesson you've taken to heart." She blew on a forkful of pork. "Want me to repeat the **question**?"

"Thing is, Siobhan, it wasn't a **question**."

She thought back, and saw that he was right. "Nevertheless," she said.

"You want me to answer?" He watched her nod, then took a sip of his wine. Chilean red, she'd told him. Three quid a bottle. "Mind if I eat first?"

"You can't eat and talk at the same time?"

"Bad manners, so my mum used to tell me."

"You always listened to your parents?"

"Always."

"And took their advice as gospel?" He nodded, chewing on some potato skin. "Then how come we're talking and eating at the same time?"

Rebus washed the mouthful down with more wine. "Okay, I give in. To answer the **question** you didn't ask, yes." She was expecting more, but he was concentrating on his food again.

"Yes what?"

Ian Rankin, A **Question** of Blood

1. Statement of the **Question**

A few years ago I was having dinner with a writer who, between bites of his steak, connected his reading of Viktor Shklovsky to the chairs at our table. Shklovsky had been a revelation, he said, because he no longer had to discuss what a text meant; he could focus instead on how it had been made. Didn't that drain reading of a certain pleasure? I asked. He pointed to the chair I was sitting on: what did I care what the chair meant? The only thing that mattered was whether the chair worked. Could I sit on it and, maybe, was it comfortable?

I have a **question** about beauty that begins at IKEA, though it hardly ends there. Maybe it's better to say I'm curious about what kind of beauty is available to someone who shops at IKEA, what kind of beauty—if that's the right word—a shopper seeks from the store. Is it fair, I wonder, to call this beauty cheap? Meretricious? This isn't precisely my **question**.

> *Erik Anderson, Certified Copies: Notes Toward a Theory of the Knockoff (3:AM Magazine)*

The **Question** was delivered to the lord chief justice, and the learned Judges requested leave to withdraw . . .

After a short time, the learned Judges returned.

Lord Chief Justice *Abbott.*—My lords, the judges have conferred upon the **question** proposed to them by your lordships, "Whether, according to the established practice in the courts below, counsel cross-examining are intitled, the counsel on the other side objecting to it, to ask a witness whether he has made representations of any particular nature, not specifying in the **question** whether his **question** refers to representations in writing or in words."

> *T. C. Hansard, Parliamentary Debates: Official Report of the Session of the Parliament of the United Kingdom of Great Britain and Ireland, June 27–September 7, 1820*

4.003

Most propositions and **questions**, that have been written about philosophical matters, are not false, but senseless. We cannot, therefore, answer **questions** of this kind at all, but only state their senselessness. Most **questions** and propositions of the philosophers result from the fact that we do not understand the logic of our language.

(They are of the same kind as the **question** whether the Good is more or less identical than the Beautiful.)

And so it is not to be wondered at that the deepest problems are really *no* problems.

> *Ludwig Wittgenstein, Tractatus Logico-Philosophicus*

Ever since 1964, when Arthur Danto described the art world as a discursive space in which any object, however humble—a soup can, a garden tool, a urinal—might be aesthetically transfigured, philosophers of art have been painting themselves into an increasingly tiny conceptual corner. So-called analytic aesthetics now wallows in a deflationary phase, fighting shy of familiar **questions** about art and beauty. One recent exemplar of this literature, Dominic McIver Lopes's *Beyond Art* (2014), cheerfully defends a "buck-passing" theory of art. That is, art is whatever different "arts-discourses" (i.e., painting, sculpture, performance) choose to talk about and to make. In the book's terms, "X is a work of art if and only if x is a work of K, where K is an art." A general theory of why there can be no general theory is a brainchild only an academic could love.

So what is the difference that makes a difference? Philosophers are correct, I think, to avoid treating this generalized **question** as the only, or even the central, problem of art. Ontological identification is never a matter of simple mandarin taste—"Trust me, I know it when I see it." The point, rather, is that the baseline philosophical desire for generality cannot arise except from specific, nuanced, and temporal conditions. The philosopher Nelson Goodman, for example, suggests that we ask instead, When is art? This holds promise: sometimes a cigar is just a cigar, and sometimes this pipe is not a pipe. When, and why, not? This inquiry is a way of passing the buck, too, I suppose, but at least in a more illuminating fashion. Perhaps, though, the more pressing **question** is:

What is art for? That might sound even less fashionable than asking what art is. But, just for that reason, it seems compelling. After all, despite the monstrous self-absorption of the art world and the philosophical dead air, people today crave and experience art in numbers unknown to previous eras. Blockbuster exhibitions at MoMA and the Tate generate long lines of patient, eager patrons. We might well wonder what these people are looking for. The works they queue up to view, whether they are small Warhols or Martin Puryear installations that can exist only in gallery settings, are either beyond collecting or uncollectible. I think the best explanation is that people want to look at art so that they can feel the way Rilke felt when looking at the archaic torso of Apollo. They want to be told: "You must change your life."

Mark Kingwell, Outside the White Box (Harper's Magazine)

He looked into my eyes, and then into the fire. For a moment I left him, opened my door, went out into the glacial air, turned into the gyp room, collected together a bottle of whisky, a syphon, a jug of water. The night had gone colder; the jug felt as though the water inside had been iced. As I brought the tray back to the fireside, I found Jago standing up. He was standing up, with his elbows on the mantelpiece and his head bent. He did not move while I put the tray on the little table by my chair. Then he straightened himself and said, looking down at me: 'This news has shaken me, Eliot. I can't think of everything it means.' He sat down. His cheeks were tinged by the fire. His expression was set and brooding. A weight of anxiety hung on each of those last words.

I poured out the whisky. After he took his glass, he held it for an instant to the fire-light, and through the liquid watched the image of the flames.

'This news has shaken me,' he repeated. 'I can't think of everything it means. Can you,' he asked me suddenly, 'think of everything it means?'

I shook my head. 'It has come as a shock,' I said.

'You haven't thought of any consequences at all?' He gazed at me intently. In his eyes there was a **question**, almost an appeal.

'Not yet.'

He waited.

C. P. Snow, The Masters

He seemed on the verge of asking a **question**, but after a short pause he ran off giggling instead.

Jonathan Coe, The Dwarves of Death

"I fear you are not well, Mr. Carton!"

"No. But the life I lead, Miss Manette, is not conducive to health. What is to be expected of, or by, such profligates?"

"Is it not—forgive me; I have begun the **question** on my lips—a pity to live no better life?"

"God knows it is a shame!"

"Then why not change it?"

Charles Dickens, A Tale of Two Cities

'There's something about the novel that resists innovation,' J.G. Ballard said. He said it more than once; it was something he was fond of saying even as he himself innovated, working away beneath and pulling up the floorboards of literary tradition, one eye on the contemporanea his novels happened to inhabit and the other on a very different clock, one 'whose movements are virtually imperceptible but which cover giant periods of time as the human race evolved.' *Super-Cannes,* which he published on the cusp not just of a new century but a new thousand years, makes inquiry into both—the time we inhabit and our place in evolutionary terms. It parallels the ancient mysteries of Eros and Thanatos alongside what's called human progress. It rewrites (it seems literally to do this as it unfolds) the speed and expectations of English narrative while examining our warmth towards, our desire for, and the naivety and comfort in our nostalgia about, the novel form.

It's as if he's **questioning** the form's uses to us, now, the post-modern, evolved, post-Nietzschean so-civilised human beings of the beginning of the next millennium, as he put it in an interview with John Gray:

> We inhabit a house in which there are rooms that have never been unlocked, down in the basement. Now and then we've had a glimpse in these rooms and there are strange old cabinets and odd musical instruments. What sort of tunes do they play, one wonders, lying in the dust? . . . There is a darker corner of the human psyche which intrigues us, and which we feel might benefit us if we started to explore it. It's almost a kind of murder mystery investigation. A crime happened, perhaps, or some strange event in the human past, and we are drawn to try and understand what happened.

> Ali Smith, *Introduction to J.G. Ballard, Super-Cannes*

"What can I do?" I said to myself. "The old woman divines my plans; she is on her guard; every hope abandons me. Ah! old hag, you think you already see me at the end of your rope." I was continually asking myself this **question**: "What can I do? what can I do?" At last a luminous idea struck me. My chamber overlooked the house of Fledermausse; but there was no window on this side. I adroitly raised a slate, and no pen could paint my joy when the whole ancient building was thus exposed to me. "At last, I have you!" I exclaimed; "you cannot escape me now; from here I can see all that passes—your goings, your comings, your arts and snares. You will not suspect this invisible eye—this watchful eye, which will surprise crime at the moment it blooms. Oh, Justice, Justice! She marches slowly; but she arrives."

> Erckmann-Chatrian, *The Invisible Eye*

And indeed there will be time
For the yellow smoke that slides along the street,
Rubbing its back upon the window-panes;
There will be time, there will be time
To prepare a face to meet the faces that you meet;
There will be time to murder and create,
And time for all the works and days of hands
That lift and drop a **question** on your plate;
Time for you and time for me,
And time yet for a hundred indecisions,
And for a hundred visions and revisions,
Before the taking of a toast and tea.

In the room the women come and go
Talking of Michelangelo.

> T.S. Eliot, *The Love Song of J. Alfred Prufrock*

When did you start writing poetry?

Behind this **question** seems to be another series of **questions**: How on earth did you get it in your head that writing poetry was a thing someone could do with a life? Doctor, fireman, astronaut, poet: Who thinks such a thing? Did your parents support this wild notion of yours? Did you make this choice in one of those liberal, West coast schools you went to? Could I have made a similar decision? Will my son/daughter take it upon him/herself to make a similar decision? Are there markers in youth that we can look to in order to discover a child might grow up to be a poet, the way we might look for risk factors for diabetes or signs of possible mathematical intelligence? Did you always know this was something you wanted to do, or was your road slow and rocky and full of unexpected surprises? Is becoming a poet a thing I could possibly do one day?

> Camille Dungy, **Question** *and Answer: The Top Five*

To EUGENE JOLAS, Paris [?], c. late March [?] 1938
[Dear Eugene:]

Answering your first **question**—I usually dream about whatever am doing at the time or what I have read in the paper; i.e., run into grizzly with wrong caliber shells for rifle; trigger spring sometimes broken, etc. when shooting; sometimes shoot very large animal of some kind I've never seen; or very detailed fighting around Madrid, house to house fighting, etc., after the paper; or even find myself in bed with Mrs. S . . . (not too good). Have had lovely experiences with Miss Dietrich, Miss Garbo and others in dreams too, they always being awfully nice (in dreams).

2. Second **question**, don't know much about.

3. I haven't ever felt this as would like to be able to handle day and night with same tools and believe can be done but respect anyone approaching any problem of writing with sincerity and wish them luck.

[Ernest Hemingway]

> Ernest Hemingway, *Selected Letters 1917–1961*

The reading of this outrageous letter provoked a **question** from the Bench.

> Wilkie Collins, *The Law and the Lady*

"Can I ask you a **question**?" Delores looked at my eyes. "Why are you doing all this?"

"I don't know. An old lady asked me to do something for her and I said I'd try."

"You could have said no," she said.

"I suppose I could have. But I didn't and here I am."

"You must have hurt somebody along the way, I guess."

"Excuse me?"

"You must be guilty about something."

I stared at her for a long few seconds. "Who isn't?"

> Percival Everett, *Graham Greene (Half an Inch of Water: Stories)*

There is nothing so dangerous as a **question** which comes by surprize on a man whose business it is to conceal truth, or to defend falsehood. For which reason those worthy personages, whose noble office it is to save the lives of their fellow-creatures at the Old Bailey, take the utmost care, by frequent previous examination, to divine every **question** which may be asked their clients on the day of tryal, that they may be supplyed with proper and ready answers, which the most fertile invention cannot supply in an instant. Besides, the sudden and violent impulse on the blood, occasioned by these surprizes, causes frequently such an alteration in the countenance, that the man is obliged to give evidence against himself. And such indeed were the alterations which the countenance of Blifil underwent from this sudden **question**, that we can scarce blame the eagerness of Mrs Miller, who immediately cryed out, "Guilty, upon my honour! guilty, upon my soul!"

Mr Allworthy sharply rebuked her for this impetuosity; and then turning to Blifil, who seemed sinking into the earth, he said, "Why do you hesitate, sir, at giving me an answer?

Henry Fielding, The History of Tom Jones, a Foundling

"What," I asked, sitting down in the chair he hadn't offered me, "makes it any of your business?"

He glared at me while he filled his lungs so he could yell, "Murder!" in my face.

I laughed and said:

"You don't think she had anything to do with Noonan's killing?"

I wanted a cigarette, but cigarettes were too well known as first aids to the nervous for me to take a chance on one just then.

McGraw was trying to look through my eyes. I let him look, having all sorts of confidence in my belief that, like a lot of people, I looked most honest when I was lying. Presently he gave up the eye-study and asked:

"Why not?"

That was weak enough. I said, "All right, why not?" indifferently, offered him a cigarette, and took one myself. Then I added: "My guess is that Whisper did it."

"Was he there?" For once McGraw cheated his nose, snapping the words off his teeth.

"Was he where?"

"At Brand's?"

"No," I said, wrinkling my forehead. "Why should he be—if he was off killing Noonan?"

"Damn Noonan!" the acting chief exclaimed irritably. "What do you keep dragging him in for?"

I tried to look at him as if I thought him crazy.

He said:

"Dinah Brand was murdered last night."

I said: "Yeah?"

"Now will you answer my **questions**?"

Dashiell Hammett, Red Harvest

The three Judges retired to consider the legal **question** submitted to them. The sitting was suspended for more than half an hour.

As usual in such cases, the excitement in the Court communicated itself to the crowd outside in the street. The general opinion here—led, as it was supposed, by one of the clerks or other inferior persons connected with the legal proceedings—was decidedly adverse to the prisoner's chance of escaping a sentence of death. "If the letters and the Diary are read," said the brutal spokesman of the mob, "the letters and the Diary will hang him."

On the return of the Judges into Court, it was announced that they had decided, by a majority of two to one, on permitting the documents in dispute to be produced in evidence. Each of the Judges, in turn, gave his reasons for the decision at which he had arrived. This done, the Trial proceeded.

Wilkie Collins, The Law and the Lady

"Go to it. I'll visit the gents'."

Both men excused themselves, and Jimmy soon returned with a plate in one hand and a large bread roll in the other. While Storm tried to eat, Skip quizzed him in the Agency's sweat-room style: let your man have a cigarette, but ask **questions** so fast he can't smoke it.

"Where are you from, Jimmy?"

"Carlyle County, Kentucky. Never going back."

"Your name is B.S. Storm?"

"Correct. Billem Stafford Storm."

"Billem?"

"B-I-L-L-E-M. It was my grandfather's nickname. My mother's father, William John Stafford. It doesn't really solve the puzzle, man, it just puts in a crazy piece that doesn't fit. You start out confused and end up mystified."

"And they don't call you Bill."

"Nope."

"Or Stormy."

"Jimmy's good. Jimmy gets you a response."

Skip said, "Are you army Intelligence?"

"Psy Ops. Just like you. We want to turn those tunnels into a zone of psychological mental torture."

"The tunnels?"

"The VC tunnels all over Cu Chi. I'm thinking: odorless psychoactive substance. Scopolamine. LSD, man. Let it seep through the system. Those bastards would come swarming out of those holes with their brains revved way past the redline."

"Gee."

"Psy Ops is all about unusual thinking, man. We want ideas blown up right to where they're gonna pop. We're on the cutting edge of reality itself. Right where it turns into a dream."

"Rick Voss isn't Psy Ops, is he?"

"Nope."

"But you deal with him as a regular thing?"

"'Keep your friends close. Keep your enemies closer.'"

"Who said that?"

"The colonel."

"Well, but he's quoting somebody."

"He's quoting himself."

"He usually is."

"Voss is an evil prick."

"Then it's good he's on our side."

"Whose side? In a liquid situation, the sides get stirred together."

"He's quoting Attila the Hun, or Julius Caesar."

"Who? Voss?—Oh."

"The colonel."

"Right. So those files, man. Is that the whole kaboodle? The whole Tree of Smoke?"

"Oh, a little of everything."

Skip let him eat. Storm was having the crab, and thin, delicate fries, which he ate with his fingers. He broke a small silence by saying, "Do you think the guys who dropped the bomb on Hiroshima, did they ever feel bad about it later?"

"No, they didn't," Skip said quite confidently.

"Here comes the chief."

Denis Johnson, *Tree of Smoke*

The judges came back to their seats. Someone read out to the jury, very rapidly, a string of **questions**. I caught a word here and there. "Murder of malice aforethought . . . Provocation . . . Extenuating circumstances." The jury went out, and I was taken to the little room where I had already waited. My lawyer came to see me; he was very talkative and showed more cordiality and confidence than ever before. He assured me that all would go well and I'd get off with a few years' imprisonment or transportation. I asked him what were the chances of getting the sentence quashed. He said there was no chance of that. He had not raised any point of law, as this was apt to prejudice the jury. And it was difficult to get a judgment quashed except on technical grounds. I saw his point, and agreed. Looking at the matter dispassionately, I shared his view. Otherwise there would be no end to litigation. "In any case," the lawyer said, "you can appeal in the ordinary way. But I'm convinced the verdict will be favorable."

We waited for quite a while, a good three quarters of an hour, I should say. Then a bell rang. My lawyer left me, saying:

"The foreman of the jury will read out the answers. You will be called on after that to hear the judgment."

Albert Camus, *The Stranger*

Then, and not sooner, I became aware of a strange gentleman leaning over the back of the settle opposite me, looking on. There was an expression of contempt on his face, and he bit the side of a great forefinger as he watched the group of faces.

"Well!" said the stranger to Mr. Wopsle, when the reading was done, "you have settled it all to your own satisfaction, I have no doubt?"

Everybody started and looked up, as if it were the murderer. He looked at everybody coldly and sarcastically.

"Guilty, of course?" said he. "Out with it. Come!"

"Sir," returned Mr. Wopsle, "without having the honor of your acquaintance, I do say Guilty." Upon this we all took courage to unite in a confirmatory murmur.

"I know you do," said the stranger; "I knew you would. I told you so. But now I'll ask you a **question**. Do you know, or do you not know, that the law of England supposes every man to be innocent, until he is proved—proved—to be guilty?"

"Sir," Mr. Wopsle began to reply, "as an Englishman myself, I—"

"Come!" said the stranger, biting his forefinger at him. "Don't evade the **question**. Either you know it, or you don't know it. Which is it to be?"

He stood with his head on one side and himself on one side, in a bullying, interrogative manner, and he threw his forefinger at Mr. Wopsle,—as it were to mark him out—before biting it again.

"Now!" said he. "Do you know it, or don't you know it?"

"Certainly I know it," replied Mr. Wopsle.

"Certainly you know it. Then why didn't you say so at first? Now, I'll ask you another **question**,"—taking possession of Mr. Wopsle, as if he had a right to him,—"do you know that none of these witnesses have yet been cross-examined?"

Mr. Wopsle was beginning, "I can only say—" when the stranger stopped him.

"What? You won't answer the **question**, yes or no? Now, I'll try you again." Throwing his finger at him again. "Attend to me. Are you aware, or are you not aware, that none of these witnesses have yet been cross-examined? Come, I only want one word from you. Yes, or no?"

Mr. Wopsle hesitated, and we all began to conceive rather a poor opinion of him.

"Come!" said the stranger, "I'll help you. You don't deserve help, but I'll help you. Look at that paper you hold in your hand. What is it?"

"What is it?" repeated Mr. Wopsle, eyeing it, much at a loss.

"Is it," pursued the stranger in his most sarcastic and suspicious manner, "the printed paper you have just been reading from?"

"Undoubtedly."

"Undoubtedly. Now, turn to that paper, and tell me whether it distinctly states that the prisoner expressly said that his legal advisers instructed him altogether to reserve his defence?"

"I read that just now," Mr. Wopsle pleaded.

"Never mind what you read just now, sir; I don't ask you what you read just now. You may read the Lord's Prayer backwards, if you like,—and, perhaps, have done it before today. Turn to the paper. No, no, no my friend; not to the top of the column; you know better than that; to the bottom, to the bottom." (We all began to think Mr. Wopsle full of subterfuge.) "Well? Have you found it?"

"Here it is," said Mr. Wopsle.

"Now, follow that passage with your eye, and tell me whether it distinctly states that the prisoner expressly said that he was instructed by his legal advisers wholly to reserve his defence? Come! Do you make that of it?"

Mr. Wopsle answered, "Those are not the exact words."

"Not the exact words!" repeated the gentleman bitterly. "Is that the exact substance?"

"Yes," said Mr. Wopsle.

"Yes," repeated the stranger, looking round at the rest of the company with his right hand extended towards the witness, Wopsle. "And now I ask you what you say to the conscience of that man who, with that passage before his eyes, can lay his head upon his pillow after having pronounced a fellow-creature guilty, unheard?"

We all began to suspect that Mr. Wopsle was not the man we had thought him, and that he was beginning to be found out.

Charles Dickens, Great Expectations

In fact, Plato (circa 428–347 B.C.), the close student of Socrates, passed on an interesting story about this. He tells us Socrates had learned that the Oracle at Delphi had proclaimed him to be the wisest man in Athens. Shocked at this announcement, he began to search out the men of Athens known for their wisdom and began to **question** them closely. He found out very quickly that, on truly important and basic issues, they didn't really know very much of what they were thought to know, and what they themselves believed that they knew. On the basis of this experience, he slowly came to understand that his own wisdom must consist in realizing how little he really knew about the things that matter most, and how important it was to find out whatever we can about these issues. It's not the complacent and self-assured intellectual who exemplifies wisdom, but the genuinely curious, open-minded seeker of truth.

> *Bill, reading aloud about Socrates:*
> *"The only true knowledge is knowing that you know nothing. "*
> *Ted stunned:*
> *"Dude—That's US!"*
>
> —*Bill and Ted's Excellent Adventure*

Tom Morris, *Philosophy for Dummies*

MARCELLUS
Thou art a scholar. Speak to it, Horatio.

BARNARDO
Looks it not like the King? Mark it, Horatio.

HORATIO
Most like. It harrows me with fear and wonder.

BARNARDO
It would be spoke to.

MARCELLUS
Question it, Horatio.

HORATIO
What art thou that usurp'st this time of night,
Together with that fair and warlike form
In which the majesty of buried Denmark
Did sometimes march? By heaven, I charge thee speak!

MARCELLUS
It is offended.

BARNARDO
See, it stalks away.

HORATIO
Stay, speak, speak, I charge thee, speak!

William Shakespeare, *The Tragedie of Hamlet, Prince of Denmarke*

I slept until ten. After that I stayed in bed until noon, smoking cigarettes. I decided not to lunch at Céleste's restaurant as I usually did; they'd be sure to pester me with **questions**, and I dislike being **questioned**.

Albert Camus, The Stranger

"If you're going to stay up here, you answer his **questions** and you shut up," said the Colonel. "It's your choice. You want to leave now, it's fine by us."

John le Carré, The Secret Pilgrim

33. To Amend

takes precedence of the motion to postpone indefinitely, and yields to all other subsidiary[12] motions and to all privileged[14] and incidental[13] motions, except the motion to divide the **question**. It can be applied to all motions except those in the List of Motions that Cannot be Amended. It can be amended itself, but this "amendment of an amendment" (an amendment of the second degree) cannot be amended. The previous **question** and motions to limit or extend the limits of debate may be applied to an amendment, or to only an amendment of an amendment, and in such case they do not affect the main **question**, unless so specified. An amendment is debatable in all cases except where the motion to be amended is undebatable.

Henry M. Robert, Robert's Rules of Order Revised for Deliberative Assemblies

But what about the stupid **questions**? It sounds like this is itself a stupid **question**, but it is the right one to ask if the encounter with a Fluxus work like Robert Filliou's 1965 *Ample Food for Stupid Thought* is to be something other than an intellectual exercise or a knowing flip through an art historical relic. ("Good! Now there's another important Fluxus work I can check off the to-see list!") A few years after the publication of *Ample Food*, which is a collection of ninety-six postcards, each one bearing a stupid **question**, Filliou offered his poignant and hilarious challenge to ethnography: "Hey, instead of studying us, why not come over here and have a drink with us?" (*Teaching and Learning*, 74).

Chris Thompson, Felt: Fluxus, Joseph Beuys, and the Dalai Lama

Perhaps the finest, and funniest, example of this comes in the description of Portnoy's visit to the house of his first college girlfriend, Kay Campbell, for Thanksgiving. So painfully self-conscious is he (so anxious to ensure that he does not confirm any anti-Semitic stereotypes that the Campbells might harbor) that "Whatever anybody says to me during my first twenty-four hours in Iowa, I answer, 'Thank you'" (201). His (absurd) politeness is echoed by that of his hosts:

> Then there's an expression in English, "Good morning," or so I have been told; the phrase has never been of any particular use to me. Why should it have been? At breakfast at home I am in fact known to the other boarders as "Mr. Sourball," and "The Crab." But suddenly, here in Iowa, in imitation of the local inhabitants, I am transformed into a veritable geyser of good mornings. That's all anybody around that place knows how to say—they feel the sunshine on their faces, and it just sets off some sort of chemical reaction: Good *morning*! *Good* morning! Good *mor*ning! sung to half a dozen different tunes! Next they all start asking each other if they had "a good night's sleep." And asking me! Did I have a good night's sleep? I don't really know, I have to think—the **question** comes as something of a surprise. Did I Have A Good Night's Sleep? Why, yes!

I think I did! Hey—did you?

David Brauner, *"Getting in Your Retaliation First": Narrative Strategies in Portnoy's Complaint (Philip Roth: New Perspectives on an American Author)*

I don't really know, I have to think—the **question** comes as something of a surprise. Did I Have A Good Night's Sleep? Why, yes! I think I did! Hey—did you? "Like a log," replies Mr. Campbell. And for the first time in my life I experience the full force of a simile. This man, who is a real estate broker and an alderman of the Davenport town council, says that he slept like a log, and I actually *see* a log. *I* get it! Motionless, heavy, *like a log!* "Good *morning*," he says, and now it occurs to me that the word "morning," as he uses it, refers specifically to the hours between eight A.M. and twelve noon. I'd never thought of it that way before. He wants the hours between eight and twelve to be good, which is to say, enjoyable, pleasurable, beneficial! We are all of us wishing each other four hours of pleasure and accomplishment. Why, that's terrific! Hey, that's very nice! Good morning! And the same applies to "Good afternoon"! And "Good evening"! And "Good night"! My God! The English language is a form of communication! Conversation isn't just crossfire where you shoot and get shot at! Where you've got to duck for your life and aim to kill! Words aren't only bombs and bullets—no, they're little gifts, containing *meanings!*

Philip Roth, *Portnoy's Complaint*

I am very unfortunate if that is true. But suppose I ask you a **question**: Would you say that this also holds true in the case of horses?

Plato, *Apology*

'The police asked me the same **question**. So did Alison Landsbury in a roundabout way. What thesis?' He was acting simple and beginning to believe himself. He was fishing again, but in disguise.

'She didn't show it to you but she showed it to Sandy,' said Pellegrin, washing the information down with a pull of wine. 'Is that what you want me to believe?'

Justin sat bolt upright. 'She *what*?'

'Absolutely. Secret rendezvous, whole works. Sorry about that. Thought you knew.'

But you're relieved I don't, thought Justin, still staring at Pellegrin in mystification. 'So what did Sandy do with it?' he asked.

'Showed it to Porter. Porter dithered. Porter takes decisions once a year with lots of water. Sandy sent it to me. Co-authored and marked confidential. Not by Sandy. By Tessa and Bluhm. Those aid heroes make me sick, by the way, if you feel like letting off steam. Teddy bears' picnic for international bureaucrats. Diversion. Sorry.'

John le Carré, *The Constant Gardener*

'You have read it?' said Winston.

'I wrote it. That is to say, I collaborated in writing it. No book is produced individually, as you know.'

'Is it true, what it says?'

'A description, yes. The programme it sets forth is nonsense. The secret accumulation of knowledge—a gradual spread of enlightenment—ultimately a proletarian rebellion—the overthrow of the Party. You foresaw yourself that that was what it would say. It is all nonsense. The proletarians will never revolt, not in a thousand years or a million. They cannot. I do not have to tell you the reason: you know it already. If you have ever cherished any dreams of violent insurrection, you must abandon them. There is no way in which the Party can be overthrown. The rule of the Party is for ever. Make that the starting-point of your thoughts.'

He came closer to the bed. 'For ever!' he repeated. 'And now let us get back to the **question** of "how" and "why". You understand well enough how the Party maintains itself in power. Now tell me why we cling to power. What is our motive? Why should we want power? Go on, speak,' he added as Winston remained silent.

George Orwell, *Nineteen Eighty-Four*

And my theory about professional artists was as follows: Artists are not necessarily the most creative or inspired individuals in any given community. Instead they are those individuals most willing to exploit their own creativity and inspiration, most willing to gain personal profit from their unconscious and its emanations, those with the most missionary zeal for the dissemination of their own idiosyncratic perspectives. **Questions** of pure creativity clearly lay elsewhere.

Jacob Wren, *Polyamorous Love Song*

Drawing on the legacy of conceptual art, recent works of conceptual writing by poets such as Goldsmith, Robert Fitterman, Vanessa Place, and Tan Lin have been consistently engaged with new media and with **questions** of appropriation and remediation. Goldsmith's *Day* could well stand as an answer to a rhetorical **question** posed by Basex's 2007 report on information overload: "What is a knowledge worker to do in a world where the Sunday edition of the *New York Times* has more information than the amount of information an average person alive 400 years ago might have come across in his lifetime?" While Basex hyperbolically stresses the existential threat of information overload, Goldsmith sanguinely engages it by retyping, without any semantic alteration, an entire day of the *New York Times*—as much information as an illiterate person in the fifteenth century might have encountered in a lifetime (at least according to Basex). Retyping the *Times* significantly reconfigures our sense of its context and meaning. "All the news that's fit to print"—but from whose perspective? Fit in the sense of size? Or fit in the sense of appropriate? In book form, the September 1, 2000, edition of the *New York Times* late edition takes up 836 pages. Yet *Day* does not feel encyclopedic in the manner of *Ulysses*. *Ulysses* demands that we pay attention to the specificity of its allusions; *Day* does not. As readers, we cannot possibly master the mostly forgettable and/or immediately obsolete information of the national paper of record. While the management culture writing on information overload continually stresses that workers and knowledge consumers need to exert more careful control over information, Goldsmith and other conceptual writers suggest that perhaps we can only exert such control with great difficulty. As a writer, Goldsmith voluntarily gives up control over many aspects of his process. From Goldsmith's perspective, there were few variables involved in producing *Day*—and little or no skill or craft was required.

Paul Stephens, *Stars in My Pocket Like Bits of Data* (Guernica)

I could no longer contain my anxiety. "But why has nobody warned London? Why haven't *you*?"

"Understand we did, Ned. Understand the message fell on pretty deaf ears. Bad time for you boys. Don't we know it."

By now the momentous force of his news had got through to me. If the Professor was cheating with his broadcasts, whom else might he not be cheating?

"Milt, can I ask you a silly **question**?"

"Be my guest, Ned."

"Has Teodor *ever* done good work for you? In all his time? Secret work? Very secret work, even?"

Wagner pondered this, determined to give the Professor the benefit of the doubt. "Can't say he has, Ned. We did consider using him as an intermediary for one of our big fish one time, but we kind of didn't like the old man's manners."

> *John le Carré, The Secret Pilgrim*

This critical tendency is what Trilling found challenging about the modernist tradition: "No literature has ever been so shockingly personal as that of our time," he wrote. "It asks every **question** that is forbidden in polite society. It asks us if we are content with our marriages, with our family lives, with our professional lives, with our friends." For all his supposed mandarin detachment, Trilling readily admitted when a novel made him uneasy. This is not a sense one ever gets from Wood, despite his sensitivity as a reader. He evinces curiously little interest in the possibility that a book might intervene in our lives, that something might happen outside the work as a result of the work. He seems to find the desire for such an intervention a bit vulgar, if not self-defeating, as though it could only descend into brute instrumentalism (*How Proust Can Change Your Life*) or crass plays for relevance (*Proust Was a Neuroscientist*).

It isn't quite right to say of Wood what T.S. Eliot said of James: that he has a mind so fine no idea could violate it. Wood is interested in ideas, but mostly religious and metaphysical ones, that is to say, the intellectual **questions** that interest Wood are **questions** about the nature of reality—which is the central preoccupation of literary realism. Wood shows almost no interest in social **questions**, the kind of **questions**— about our marriages, our families, our professional lives, our friends—that Trilling found so shocking when he encountered them in modernist novels. Jonathan Franzen, Wood wrote in his mixed assessment of *The Corrections*, "is at his finest when being ambitious and even theoretical about the soul, when he is examining consciousness . . . [When he] attempts to enlarge his theme of correction socially, the attempt stalls." Perhaps Wood is right in this case, but it is striking how frequently he finds that a novel has succeeded when it deals with the **questions** Wood himself likes to ask and that it has failed when it strays into territory alien to him.

> *Christopher Beha, How Much Damage Can It Do? On the Intellectual Element in Modern Fiction (Harper's Magazine)*

The second thing that makes this exercise difficult is the fact that you don't know who wrote the **question**. Consequently, some people flounder around and are not able to connect with anyone's vibrations.

> *Joseph J. Mauriello, (Your Departed Loved Ones and Spirit Guides Are) Only a Thought Away*

However, **questions** can be specified in other ways and some noun phrases in some contexts can fulfill that function and can serve as surrogates of indirect **questions**. Thus 'Hector's behavior' will stand for 'why Hector behaves (or behaved) in the way he does (or did)' and 'the origins of the word "explain"' will stand for what the origins of the word 'explain' are. The precise description of the relevant transformations is something that we must leave to grammarians. The fourth hypothesis will cover statements with such noun phrases if we amend the definition of 'the **question**' on page 22 to read "the **question** whose oratio obliqua form or a surrogate for whose oratio obliqua form would appear at the position indicated by W or X."

*Sylvain Bromberger, On What We Know We Don't Know: Explanation, Theory, Linguistics, and How **Questions** Shape Them*

I found myself tempted a moment ago to use the expression "more purely artistic form, but nothing Orwell wrote was merely or, with the sole exception of *Animal Farm,* flawlessly a work of art. "It is as if I have been forced into becoming a pamphleteer," he once remarked ruefully, and even though he dated his definitely "political" phase from the Spanish Civil War ("By the end of 1935 I had still failed to reach a firm decision"), even *Burmese Days* is largely a didactic novel, interspersed with informative or homiletic passages about imperialism and its effects, and aimed much more deliberately than *A Passage to India,* with which it is often compared, at inducing a political reaction in its readers.

We can assume, in fact, that all of Orwell's novels are politically oriented, even if they are not propagandists in the narrow sense. He himself even claimed that "no book is genuinely free from political bias." But in accepting Orwell's license to seek a strong political motivation in everything he wrote after his first apprentice years, we have merely cleared away one **question** to face another, more confusing **question**, regarding what lies beyond the political aspect. In 'Why I Write" he claimed that his starting point in writing was "always a feeling of partisanship, a sense of injustice," and said that he never set out with the intent of producing a work of art, though the aesthetic experience entered necessarily into the process of writing. And, dealing with the elusive and perhaps contradictory nature of a writer's motives, he went on to say:

> All writers are vain, selfish and lazy, and at the very bottom of their motives there lies a mystery. Writing a book is a horrible, exhausting struggle, like a long bout of some painful illness. One would never undertake such a thing if one were not driven on by some demon whom one can neither resist nor understand. For all one knows that demon is merely the same instinct that makes a baby squall for attention. And yet it is also true that one can write nothing readable unless one constantly struggles to efface one's own personality. Good prose is like a windowpane.

Such a statement from an author who talks so much about his own experiences may at first seem somewhat disingenuous, and it is true that in trying to efface the personality of Eric Blair, he merely succeeded in creating the persona of George Orwell, which stands much nearer to the imaginative world he was portraying in his novels. Yet we would do well to take notice of the argument, for Orwell's apparent candor about himself is as liable to be deceptive as that of all men who write well about their own lives and who succeed only because of their power to shape the raw material of experience into pleasing forms and hence to change it into something different and new. When we take the further step beyond autobiography into fiction, experience has gone through a double distillation, and we must be even more on our guard against the perils of personal identification.

George Woodcock, The Crystal Spirit: A Study of George Orwell (that is, proper names, singular descriptions of specific people or groups of people, personal pronouns, 'somebody', 'someone', etc.) where W indicates a position occupied by an indirect **question**, and E indicates a position taken up by a tensed form of 'to explain'.

Two things may be noted immediately: (a) Many kinds of indirect **questions** can occupy the position indicated by W, and they may open with a variety of interrogatives—'Why', 'How', 'Whence', 'Whither', 'What'—

Sylvain Bromberger, On What We Know We Don't Know: Explanation, Theory, Linguistics, and How **Questions** *Shape Them*

MARCELLUS Peace, break thee off. Look where it comes again!	MARCELLUS Quiet, shut up! It's come again.
BARNARDO In the same figure like the king that's dead.	BARNARDO Looking just like the dead king.
MARCELLUS Thou art a scholar. Speak to it, Horatio.	MARCELLUS You're well-educated, Horatio. Say something to it.
BARNARDO Looks it not like the King? Mark it, Horatio.	BARNARDO Doesn't he look like the king, Horatio?
HORATIO Most like. It harrows me with fear and wonder.	HORATIO Very much so. It's terrifying.
BARNARDO It would be spoke to.	BARNARDO It wants us to speak to it.
MARCELLUS **Question** it, Horatio.	MARCELLUS Ask it something, Horatio.
HORATIO What art thou that usurp'st this time of night, Together with that fair and warlike form In which the majesty of buried Denmark Did sometimes march? By heaven, I charge thee speak!	HORATIO What are you, that you walk out so late at night, looking like the dead king of Denmark when he dressed for battle? By God, I order you to speak.
MARCELLUS It is offended.	MARCELLUS It looks like you've offended it.
BARNARDO See, it stalks away.	BARNARDO Look, it's going away.

HORATIO Stay, speak, speak, I charge thee, speak!	HORATIO Stay! Speak! Speak! I order you, speak!
Exit Ghost	*The Ghost exits.*

William Shakespeare, Hamlet (Spark Notes: No Fear Translation)

—but not *every* indirect **question** is at home there; some would be out of place, awkward, reminiscent of Eisenhower prose, for example, 'what the distance in miles between London and Paris is' or 'whether it will rain tomorrow' or 'what time it is' or 'which sister Sam married'. A good analysis should show why some indirect **questions** do not sit well in these contexts.

*Sylvain Bromberger, On What We Know We Don't Know: Explanation, Theory, Linguistics, and How **Questions** Shape Them*

'Feodor, I'm going to tell you some things and show you some pictures; then I want you to answer some **questions**. It may all sound perfectly ridiculous to you, but I want you to be patient and think carefully. Okay?'

'Go right ahead!'

'Thanks,' Arkady said; inside he felt as if he were at the top of a long dive, the way he always did when he had to go by guesswork.

Martin Cruz Smith, Gorky Park

'You're not in a hurry then,' the barman said. She hadn't noticed him coming back.

'What?'

He lowered his eyes, directing her to the drinks in front of her.

'Oh, right,' she said, trying for a smile.

'Don't worry about it. Sometimes a dwam's the best place to be.'

She nodded, knowing that 'dwam' meant dream. She seldom used Scots words, they jarred with her English accent. That she'd never tried altering her accent was testament to its usefulness. It could wind people up, which had proved handy in some interviews. And if people occasionally mistook her for a tourist, well, they sometimes dropped their guard, too.

'I've figured out who you are,' the barman was saying now. She studied him. Mid-twenties, tall and broad-shouldered with short black hair and a face that would retain its sculpted cheekbones for a few years yet, booze, diet and cigarettes notwithstanding.

'Impress me,' she said, leaning against the bar.

'At first I took you for a pair of reporters, but you're not asking any **questions**.'

*Ian Rankin, A **Question** of Blood*

There are simple solutions to both of these problems. First, be careful of the **question** that you send to your loved ones and/or spirit guides. Don't ask what the **question** is; instead, just ask whether the answer is "yes" or "no". You don't need to know anything about the **question** to get an answer.

Often, when I'm counseling someone, I will begin to receive an answer to the person's problem before he or she even has a chance to tell me what is wrong. This happens because the person's spirit guides know what the problem is and have discussed it with my spirit guides. My spirit guides then send the answer to me. However, I would not be able to have such amazingly quick response times if I didn't practice receiving information for **questions** that I don't know anything about. So, whether you get anything or not, continue to do this exercise.

Joseph J. Mauriello, (Your Departed Loved Ones and Spirit Guides Are) Only a Thought Away

Let me ask a **question** that has nagged at me for some time. Are all autobiographies, all life narratives, not fictions, at least in the sense that they are constructions?

"When I was eight my father hit me with a tennis racket," says a subject. "Not true," says his father. "I was swinging the racket and accidentally hit him." Is the boy's or the father's memory of the event correct?

J. M. Coetzee, Lives By Omission (Harper's Magazine)

Second, don't worry. Don't even think about whose **question** you have. Such concerns can get in the way of relaxing and receiving a message. Instead, just concentrate on getting an answer and leave discovering the writer's identity for later.

Joseph J. Mauriello, (Your Departed Loved Ones and Spirit Guides Are) Only a Thought Away

. . . the above words were put to us by a stranger who, pausing before us, levelled his massive forefinger at the vessel in **question***. He was but shabbily apparelled in faded jacket and patched trowsers; a rag of a black handkerchief investing his neck. A confluent small-pox had in all directions flowed over his face, and left it like the complicated ribbed bed of a torrent, when the rushing waters have been dried up.*

Acrylic paint and ink on found paper
6.75" × 8.5"
11/27/09

Matt Kish, Moby-Dick in Pictures: One Drawing for Every Page

It is true that Mr. Foster is speaking of college students; but, if these faults are condemned in students of mature years, should they not all the more be checked in the case of high-school pupils?

Mr. Foster includes also among the defects of interscholastic debating the use of the purposely vague **question**.

Bertha Lee Gardner, Debating in High School (The School Review, Volume 20)

Mere knowledge of English is not sufficient to produce the **question** in an episode described by 'Mme. Rouge explained the third chapter of *Moby Dick* to Picard'; one must be acquainted with the third chapter of *Moby Dick* and know something of the **questions** to which it gives rise. The vagueness characteristic of such statements must be preserved in an adequate formulation of their truth-conditions. But this is easy to achieve. Simply replace (a) of the fourth hypothesis by

(a2) There is a **question** about the topic mentioned at the X position that is sound, that is, that admits of a right answer.

Notice that though such noun phrases are vague, they are nevertheless indispensable.

Sylvain Bromberger, On What We Know We Don't Know: Explanation, Theory, Linguistics, and How **Questions** *Shape Them*

The general feature of this approach is that, for some words and some states of affairs, there is no definite fact of the matter whether the words apply or fail to apply to the states of affairs. One could explain this in terms of vagueness in the words; but one might alternatively think that the world could, or even must, contribute to the explanation.

We can start by reverting to an earlier **question** (see footnote 4). The argument for discussion went like this:

> Mountains are part of reality, but they are vague. They have no sharp boundaries: it is vague where the mountain ends and the plain begins. So it is easy to see that vagueness is a feature of reality, and not just of our thought and talk.
>
> R. M. Sainsbury, *Paradoxes*

Imagine by contrast a 'Lego world' where all objects have simple, static, geometric forms with sharp edges: a universe that consists of just Lego bricks and the void. In such a world, predicates like 'flat' or 'cubic' or 'red' are still *intensionally* vague, in other words their linguistic meanings are such that they do not rule out the possibility of borderline cases, but, as long as their *extensions* are clear-cut—that is, as long as borderline cases do not actually occur—no non-philosopher will care.

On a closer look, it seems ill-advised to press the **question** of what the ultimate source of vagueness is, whether it be our representations or the things themselves, our language or the world. The relationship is dialectical because natural languages did not evolve in a Lego world. An analogy might be helpful to illustrate the dialectics at work. Think of language as a tool: sugar tongs are perfect tools for gripping sugar cubes. But if you try and fail to grip powdered sugar with sugar tongs, then who is to blame, the sugar or the tongs?

> Geert Keil, Lara Keuck and Rico Hauswald, *Vagueness in Psychiatry: An Overview* (*Vagueness in Psychiatry*)

Franklin rightly calls this "one of the great moments of revelation in literature."[17] Not that we should yield to the temptation of concluding "Aha! this *proves* that Melville thinks Moby Dick is a god—be he agent or principal." The passage doesn't quite do that. As an epic simile, it advertises itself as possibly "only" a literary device, as a device that beautifies rhetoric by infusing a dose of classical decor, thereby betraying consciousness of artifice in the midst of worshipful enthusiasm.[18] At the same time, the passage even more strenuously resists such reduction through its use of what might be called the grand Miltonic tradition of the negative classical simile for purposes of spiritual exaltation. When Milton describes Eden, he does so by singing how the fair fields of Enna, the Castalian Spring, the Isle of Nysa, and so forth cannot match it. For Wordsworth, in turn, neither Chaos nor "The darkest pit of lowest Erebus" "can breed such fear and awe/As fall upon us often when we look/Into our Minds, into the Mind of Man,/My haunt, and the main region of my Song."[19] Neither, likewise, is the White Whale to be surpassed by previous avatars of the ultimate. Negation in each case is a way of reaping the benefits of metaphorical analogizing while establishing that the subject at hand has an autonomous glory not preempted by any analogy in terms of which it might be seen. Later moments in the chase sequence call the whale-as-supreme-and-lovely-being passage into **question**, with suggestions that its intent might be malignant or haphazard. But the rhetoric of apocalypse is never revoked. At most, one could accuse Melville of temporizing in the quoted passage by establishing the whale's "great majesty Supreme" only in terms of a pagan analogue, by hesitating to analogize to Jehovah himself as Ishmael had done in "The Tail," as Wordsworth dared to do more solemnly in the Prospectus to *The Recluse*.[20]

The reader of *Moby-Dick* is all the more eager to experience the White Whale's appearance as apocalyptic after such long foreshadowing—after hundreds of premonitory references to the "grand hooded phantom, like a snow hill in the air" (Chap. 1). Here the book plays an interesting double game. Because its central subject is an absent object of obsession for nearly the entire narrative, the text continually signals to the reader that "This is not yet quite reality; this is only preparatory information or interpretation." Not until a third of the book is over does an encounter with even an ordinary whale take place. During this long buildup, the repetitous quality of the cetology chapters and of Ishmael's meditations in general, combined with the fundamental fact of Moby Dick's absence, reinforce the plausibility of the frequent hints that the quest is empty of meaning except for what is read into it.

Lawrence Buell, Moby-Dick as Sacred Text (New Essays on Moby-Dick)

However, if we could give a complete description of the world without making use of such a vague expression, we would have no inclination to infer from the vagueness of the **question** to the vagueness of the world. We would not seem to be greatly handicapped, in describing the world, if we lacked the word "mountain": we could just draw the contour lines on our maps. In many cases, for example "heap", our use of the vague word is guided by sharp underlying facts, for example, by (in part) how many grains the collection contains. Each collection has a definite number of members, and we could in principle give more information about a collection by the sharp fact of how many members it has than by the vague matter of whether or not it is a heap.

R. M. Sainsbury, Paradoxes

For instance, the third chapter of *Moby Dick* gives rise to a cluster of **questions**. It can happen that a tutee is not in a p-predicament with regard to any one of these **questions** taken in isolation, and that he is able to admit each as sound, but that he is nevertheless not in a position to think of a *set* of answers (to that set of **questions**) that he can consistently admit as possibly correct. This will happen when every nonobjectionable answer that he can think of to one isolated **question** would require him to reject every nonobjectionable answer that he can think of to another isolated **question**. Even more complicated situations arise. A **question** with regard to which a given tutee is in a p-predicament may itself rest on a presupposition that the tutee trusts simply because it is the only nonobjectionable answer that he can think of to some other **question**. Giving him the correct answer to the latter may teach him that the former has no right answer, and may thus "cure" him of his p-predicament. In all such situations "the **question**" is complex and is made up of disjunctions and conjunctions of more elementary ones. In each case it can no doubt be put in oratio obliqua form but the result must be unwieldy and awkward within an 'A E to B W' statement.[16]

This point is worth remembering. Often the **question** in an explaining episode cannot be told from an 'A E X to B' description of that episode. This may lead us to overlook the essential connection that links explaining to **questions**.

Sylvain Bromberger, On What We Know We Don't Know: Explanation, Theory, Linguistics, and How **Questions** Shape Them

While I didn't get much out of that first reading that I hadn't already gotten from watching the film, I sensed that there was more lurking beneath the words, and I knew it was a story I would come back to again and again.

Since then, I've read the book eight or nine times: again in high school, several times as an undergraduate, a few times while working as a high school English teacher and as an assistant manager in a bookstore, again in graduate school, and most recently while making these illustrations. Each and every reading has revealed more and more to me and hinted tantalizingly at even greater truths and revelations that I have yet to reach. Friends often **question** my obsession with the novel, especially since I am not a scholar or even an educator any longer, and the best explanation I have been able to come up with is that, to me, *Moby-Dick* is a book about everything. God. Love. Hate. Identity. Race. Sex. Humor. Obsession. History. Work. Capitalism. I could go on and on. I see every aspect of life reflected in the bizarre mosaic of this book.

Matt Kish, Moby-Dick in Pictures: One Drawing for Every Page

Only after the person has given everything that he received does the leader let him read the **question** out loud. Once the **question** has been read out loud, whoever wrote it should identify himself or herself and then determine if the answer was accurate, or if it even had anything to do with the **question**. If the person who received the information did not get anything pertinent to the **question**, then the writer should evaluate what did come through and determine if it was accurate or not. After all, even though the person did not receive an answer to the **question**, he may have been sent an actual message from the other side, and he needs to know if he did, and whether or not it was correct.

Once all of this has been done with that **question**, then the group leader moves on to the next person and repeats the process. This process continues until all have had a chance to relate what, if anything, they received.

By the way, it doesn't happen often, but sometimes a person will randomly pick his or her own slip of paper. Fortunately, this shouldn't matter. As long as the person is meditating on just receiving an answer to the **question**, then he or she should be able to receive it. Besides, if the person learns to be better able at receiving his or her own answers, then that is a very good result.

Joseph J. Mauriello, (Your Departed Loved Ones and Spirit Guides Are) Only a Thought Away

'Then there is such a person as Goldstein?' he said.

'Yes, there is such a person, and he is alive. Where, I do not know.'

'And the conspiracy—the organization? Is it real? It is not simply an invention of the Thought Police?'

'No, it is real. The Brotherhood, we call it. You will never learn much more about the Brotherhood than that it exists and that you belong to it. I will come back to that presently. He looked at his wrist-watch. 'It is unwise even for members of the Inner Party to turn off the telescreen for more than half an hour. You ought not to have come here together, and you will have to leave separately. You, Comrade'—he bowed his head to Julia—'will leave first. We have about twenty minutes at our disposal. You will understand that I must start by asking you certain **questions**. In general terms, what are you prepared to do?'

'Anything that we are capable of,' said Winston.

O'Brien had turned himself a little in his chair so that he was facing Winston. He almost ignored Julia, seeming to take it for granted that Winston could speak for her. For a moment the lids flitted down over his eyes. He began asking his **questions** in a low, expressionless voice, as though this were a routine, a sort of catechism, most of whose answers were known to him already.

'You are prepared to give your lives?'

'Yes.'

'You are prepared to commit murder?'

'Yes.'

'To commit acts of sabotage which may cause the death of hundreds of innocent people?'

'Yes.'

'To betray your country to foreign powers?'

'Yes.'

'You are prepared to cheat, to forge, to blackmail, to corrupt the minds of children, to distribute habit-forming drugs, to encourage prostitution, to disseminate venereal diseases—to do anything which is likely to cause demoralization and weaken the power of the Party?'

'Yes.'

'If, for example, it would somehow serve our interests to throw sulphuric acid in a child's face—are you prepared to do that?'

'Yes.'

'You are prepared to lose your identity and live out the rest of your life as a waiter or a dock-worker?'

'Yes.'

'You are prepared to commit suicide, if and when we order you to do so?'

'Yes.'

George Orwell, *Nineteen Eighty-Four*

As I read, however, I applied much personally to my own feelings and condition. I found myself similar, yet at the same time strangely unlike the beings concerning whom I read, and to whose conversation I was a listener. I sympathized with, and partly understood them, but I was unformed in mind; I was dependent on none, and related to none. 'The path of my departure was free;' and there was none to lament my annihilation. My person was hideous, and my stature gigantic: what did this mean? Who was I? What was I? Whence did I come? What was my destination? These **questions** continually recurred, but I was unable to solve them.

Mary Wollstonecraft Shelley, *Frankenstein; or, The Modern Prometheus*

No one, and schizophrenics least of all who do it best, can live in this heightened state of reflective receptivity forever. Because this empathy's involuntary, there's terror here. Loss of control, a seepage. Becoming someone else or worse: becoming nothing but the vibratory field between two people.

"And who are you?" Brion Gysins **question**, asked to ridicule the authenticity of authorship ("Since when do words belong to anybody? 'Your very own words' indeed. And who are you?") gets scarier the more you think about it.

Chris Kraus, *I Love Dick*

The bell rang and a black kid named Sweetzer danced out and feinted with his left but not knowing it was a feint I lurched into his right. My head was raked round to a funny angle and Sweetzer was working on my midriff. He landed a few before I jabbed him away, or maybe stepping back was his own idea because he immediately launched a hook that caught my right ear and set it ringing. He hit my head a couple more times and now everything seemed to be happening at a slight remove, as if they had switched over from the real fight to a meticulously realized but cottony reenactment. In it, I was tucking my head behind my forearms and dull concussive blows were falling upon my midriff and either side of my head. The stands were a booing darkness beyond the ring. The frowning referee danced to one side, angling for a view in past my looming foreground arms. Finally his striped shirt closed in and my opponent disappeared. My arms were pried down, and as the referee leered in, he held my gloved hands. I was grateful. They were heavy.

The referee's lips moved and a hollow voice boomed: "DO YOU KNOW WHAT DAY IT IS?"

I cocked my head at him. That this worried-looking man should interrupt the fight to scream banal **questions** at me seemed consistent with the bout's dreamlike turn. An answering voice rustled between my own ears: "Sure."

The booming voice said, "WHAT DAY IS IT?"

Fans screamed and sighed.

I could see the Sweetzer character now, in the background, dancing and shadow-boxing in a far corner of the ring. "Thursday," I heard the rustling voice say.

"DO YOU KNOW WHO I AM?"

"Sure."

"WHO AM I?"

A two-fingered whistle cut through the din. I looked around for the fan who had given it. There were so many. I looked back at the ref.

Ethan Coen, Destiny

Although it seemed in a way unnecessary to spring a **question** like this on his friend, and naive to imagine that an answer could tell him any more than he already knew of him through years of acquaintance, he happened to set great store by the efficacy of this particular test. He had thought the matter over carefully, and had gone to considerable trouble before framing the deceptively simple **question** which enshrined it. Integrity— so his reasoning had gone—was a difficult virtue to simulate. Even hypothetical integrity. Especially hypothetical integrity. Integrity was more than a virtue, and more than a complex of virtues. It was a way of looking at things. In fact, it was a quality so deeply ingrained and pervasive as to set a kind of framework or boundary to the imaginings; and (although the converse was a trifle more doubtful) if you were incapable of imagining dishonestly, then you were incapable of acting so. This was, however, the first time he had used the test on anyone with hopes of their passing. He held his breath in suspense, and waited for the answer as to where Trevisan's boundaries lay. It was not long in coming.

Amanda Prantera, The Cabalist

I answered the doorman's polite **question** with "Lewis." He opened his mouth to ask if that was my first or last name, caught my eye, changed his mind.

"I'll be right with you, sir," he said, making it clear he wanted me to stay where I was while he walked over and picked up the house phone. I couldn't hear his end of the conversation . . . which was the whole point.

Andrew Vachss, Mask Market

We can say (cf. section [f]) that the author/creator (we prefer the idea of "person responsible" or "producer") can "efface himself" behind the work that he makes (or that makes him), but that this would be no more than a good intention, consequent upon the work itself (and hence a minor consideration), unless one takes into consideration the endless canceling-out of the form itself, the ceaseless posing of the **question** of its presence; and then that of its disappearance.

Daniel Buren, Beware!

—that is, the **question** reached by putting the why-**question** in normal form, then deleting the initial 'why' and uttering the remaining string as a **question**.

*Sylvain Bromberger, On What We Know We Don't Know: Explanation, Theory, Linguistics, and How **Questions** Shape Them*

I'm not so sure about that. That's a matter for everyman's opinion and, without dragging in the sectarian side of the business, I beg to differ with you *in toto* there. My belief is, to tell you the candid truth, that those bits were genuine forgeries all of them put in by monks most probably or it's the big **question** of our national poet over again, who precisely wrote them like *Hamlet* and Bacon, as, you who know your Shakespeare infinitely better than I, of course I needn't tell you. Can't you drink that coffee, by the way?

James Joyce, Ulysses

Reynaldo My lord, I did intend it.	Reynaldo That's what I thought too, sir.

Polonius
Marry, well said, very well said. Look
    you, sir,
Inquire me first what Danskers are
    in Paris,
And how, and who, what means, and
    where they keep,
What company, at what expense;
    and finding
By this encompassment and drift of
    question
That they do know my son, come
    you more nearer
Than your particular demands will
    touch it;
Take you as 'twere some distant
    knowledge of him,
And thus, "I know his father and his
    friends,
And in part him." Do you mark this,
    Reynaldo?
	Polonius
	Excellent, very good. Ask around and find out what Danish people are in Paris—who they are, where they live and how much money they have, who their friends are. And if you find out in this general sort of **questioning** that they happen to know my son, you'll find out much more than if you asked specific **questions** about him. Just tell them you vaguely know Laertes, say something like, "I'm a friend of his father and I sort of know him," or whatever. Do you get what I'm saying, Reynaldo?

REYNALDO Ay, very well, my lord.	REYNALDO Yes, very well, sir.
POLONIUS "And in part him. But," you may say, "not well, But if't be he I mean, he's very wild, Addicted so and so," and there put on him What forgeries you please—marry, none so rank As may dishonor him, take heed of that, But, sir, such wanton, wild, and usual slips As are companions noted and most known To youth and liberty.	POLONIUS You should say, "I sort of know him, but not well. Is it the same Laertes who's a wild party animal? Isn't he the one who's always," and so on. Then just make up whatever you want—of course, nothing so bad that it would shame him. I mean make up any stories that sound like your average young guy, the kind of trouble they get into.
REYNALDO As gaming, my lord.	REYNALDO Like gambling, sir?
POLONIUS Ay, or drinking, fencing, swearing, Quarreling, drabbing—you may go so far.	POLONIUS That's right, or drinking, swearing, fist-fighting, visiting prostitutes—that kind of thing.
REYNALDO My lord, that would dishonor him.	REYNALDO But that would ruin his reputation!
POLONIUS 'Faith, no; as you may season it in the charge. You must not put another scandal on him, That he is open to incontinency; That's not my meaning: but breathe his faults so quaintly That they may seem the taints of liberty, That he is open to incontinency; That's not my meaning: but breathe his faults so quaintly That they may seem the taints of liberty, The flash and outbreak of a fiery mind, A savageness in unreclaimed blood, Of general assault.	POLONIUS Oh no, not if you say it right. I don't want you to say he's a sex fiend, that's not what I mean. Just mention his faults lightly, so they make him seem like a free spirit who's gone a little too far.

REYNALDO But, my good lord,—	REYNALDO But, sir—
POLONIUS Wherefore should you do this?	POLONIUS Why should you do this, you want to know?
REYNALDO Ay, my lord, I would know that.	REYNALDO Yes, sir. I'd like to know.

William Shakespeare, Hamlet (Spark Notes: No Fear Translation)

It is this **question** of how to authorize the discourse of a socially marginalized and culturally alienated narrator that takes us to the heart of Ishmael's rhetoric in *Moby-Dick*. But to understand Melville's solution to this problem, at once a literary and a personal one, we need to return to the point at which it first arose for him, at the outset of his career as a writer. When he published *Typee* in February, 1846, Melville was already crossing and blurring a boundary, although he did not yet know it. He was not, however, allowed to remain in ignorance for long.

Carolyn Porter, Call Me Ishmael, or How to Make Double-Talk Speak (New Essays on Moby-Dick)

By the *presupposition* of a why-**question** we will mean that which one would be saying is the case if, upon being asked the inner **question** of the why-**question** through an affirmative interrogative sentence, one were to reply "yes," or what one would be saying is the case if, upon being asked the inner **question** through a negative sentence, one were to reply "no." Thus, 'Why does copper turn green when exposed to air?' is a why-**question** in normal form; its inner **question** is 'Does copper turn green when exposed to air?'; and its presupposition is that copper turns green when exposed to air. The presupposition of 'Why doesn't iron turn green when exposed to air?' is that iron does not turn green when exposed to air.[2]

*Sylvain Bromberger, On What We Know We Don't Know: Explanation, Theory, Linguistics, and How **Questions** Shape Them*

Perhaps it's an innocent **question**, perhaps it's a part of the game, but she wants to know what *she* should do about *her* literary ambitions. Nothing, they say.

A. G. Porta, No World Concerto

We will not be concerned with every sort of why-**question**. We will ignore why-**questions** whose normal forms are not in the indicative. We will ignore why-**questions** whose presupposition refers to human acts or intentions or mental states. Finally, we will ignore why-**questions** whose correct answer cannot be put in the form 'because p', where p indicates a position reserved for declarative sentences. Notice that this last stipulation affects not only why-**questions** whose correct answer must be put in some such form as 'in order to . . .' or 'to . . .',[3] but also why-**questions** that one might wish to say have no correct answer, and in particular why-**questions** with false presupposition and why-**questions** whose inner **question** itself has no answer—e.g., 'Why doesn't iron form any compounds with oxygen?' and 'Why does phlogiston combine with calx?'

*Sylvain Bromberger, On What We Know We Don't Know: Explanation, Theory, Linguistics, and How **Questions** Shape Them*

Until this function is acknowledged and properly explored, it is inevitable that critics will go on treating works of art as "statements." (Less so, of course, in those arts which are abstract or have largely gone abstract, like music and painting and the dance. In these arts, the critics have not solved the problem; it has been taken from them.) Of course, a work of art can be considered as a statement, that is, as the answer to a **question**. On the most elementary level, Goya's portrait of the Duke of Wellington may be examined as the answer to the **question**: what did Wellington look like? Anna Karenina may be treated as an investigation of the problems of love, marriage, and adultery. Though the issue of the adequacy of artistic representation to life has pretty much been abandoned in, for example, painting, such adequacy continues to constitute a powerful standard of judgment in most appraisals of serious novels, plays, and films. In critical theory, the notion is quite old. At least since Diderot, the main tradition of criticism in all the arts, appealing to such apparently dissimilar criteria as verisimilitude and moral correctness, in effect treats the work of art as a statement being made in the form of a work of art.

To treat works of art in this fashion is not wholly irrelevant. But it is, obviously, putting art to use—for such purposes as inquiring into the history of ideas, diagnosing contemporary culture, or creating social solidarity. Such a treatment has little to do with what actually happens when a person possessing some training and aesthetic sensibility looks at a work of art appropriately. A work of art encountered as a work of art is an experience, not a statement or an answer to a **question**. Art is not only about something; it is something. A work of art is a thing in the world, not just a text or commentary on the world.

Susan Sontag, On Style (Against Interpretation and Other Essays)

"You make it sound simple."

"It's not simple. It's a matter of choice. The only drunks I ever knew who quit successfully were the ones who chose not to be drunks anymore. The choice they would've liked to have made, of course, was between being a gentleman drinker or a drunk. But they had run out of in-between. They could either be drunk or dry."

Fastnaught looked at me curiously. "You been there?" he said.

I picked up my drink and tasted it. It tasted the way it always did, of better times. Then I shook my head at Fastnaught's **question**. "I watched my old man when I was a kid. He was a college professor in Columbus. Associate professor, really. He went all the way down and then all the way back up. It took him about ten years. He liked to find the sleaziest bar possible, buy drinks for everybody, and then lecture them on *The Faerie Queene*. That was his specialty, Spenser. Then one night somebody brought him home with one of his eyes hanging down on his cheek. There was nobody home but me. I was thirteen, I think. I put the eye back in the socket. It seemed the thing to do. My mother was out of town. We sat there until four o'clock in the morning with him holding a wet washcloth over the eye that I'd put back. He didn't say a word. I didn't either. Then at four he said he thought that maybe I'd better call the doctor. Well, he lost the eye, but he never took another drink."

Fastnaught finished his martini and looked at me. "There's gotta be a moral there someplace."

"It helps if you're only thirteen."

"But you still put it away."

I nodded. "But I don't lecture in bars on *The Faerie Queene.*"

*Ross Thomas, No **Questions** Asked*

Space is treated to a similar figuring here. Indeed, after exhausting a long series of spatial possibilities—what we could perhaps call a process of *elimination*—the unnamable describes his space in, precisely, excremental diction: "it's like shit, there we have it at last, there it is at last, the right word, one has only to seek, seek in vain, to be sure of finding in the end, it's a **question** of elimination. Enough now about holes" (418). The "holes" bored by others into the unnamable's space are, therefore, aligned with assholes. But, "it" in this passage can refer both to the space he has been deferring and redefining but also to his narrative itself: both proceed by a never-ending process of elimination, a kind of narrative trash heap that demands vigilant rereading and rearranging of its erasures and scraps.[11] That the grey space of the compromised psyche is figured here as a place with its own wastes, relics, and ruins should not be misunderstood as a pessimistic argument. Rather, that even this most 'bare' space is littered with bodily colours, hazes, fixtures, clay, and holes, comprises a hopeful suggestion in this aesthetic study of transgender: that even the most "bare" psychic space is neither empty nor plain but, instead, material and marked with the presence of bodies. After Wigley, we know that Beckett's warm grey space is no more "bare" than the white walls of high modernism, even if these walls of grey waste are not as pretty as those Orlando designed. The unnamable's "grey matter"—his mind—is material: it consists in folds of pink flesh and yellow waste that do not appear without light fixtures, the labile clay that binds them in place, and the interlocutors who fix and hold them. The unnamable, therefore, has no 'raw material' to speak of, inasmuch as this very concept presumes that the material of his psyche preexists its own life as, and its figuring as, aesthetic.

Lucas Crawford, Transgender Architectonics: The Shape of Change in Modernist Space

"Anyone else we should talk to, Teri?" Rebus was asking. "People who went to Lee's little soirees?"

"I don't want to answer any more **questions**."

"Why not, Teri?" Siobhan asked, frowning as though genuinely puzzled.

*Ian Rankin, A **Question** of Blood*

Zhang is deeply reticent, and his manner is formal and elaborately polite. Recently, when we were walking, he said, "May I use these?" He meant a pair of clip-on shades, which he held toward me as if I might want to examine them first. His enthusiasm for answering **questions** about himself and his work is slight. About half an hour after I had met him for the first time, he said, "I have a **question**." We had been talking about his childhood. He said, "How many more **questions** are you going to have?" He depends heavily on three responses: "Maybe," "Not so much," and "Maybe not so much." From diffidence, he often says "we" instead of "I," as in, "We may not think this approach is so important." Occasionally, preparing to speak, he hums. After he published his result, he was invited to spend six months at the Institute for Advanced Study, in Princeton. The filmmaker George Csicsery has made a documentary about Zhang, called "Counting from Infinity," for the Mathematical Sciences Research Institute, in Berkeley, California. In it, Peter Sarnak, a member of the Institute for Advanced Study, says that one day he ran into Zhang and said hello, and Zhang said hello, then Zhang said that it was the first word he'd spoken to anyone in ten days. Sarnak thought that was excessive, even for a mathematician, and he invited Zhang to have lunch once a week.

Alec Wilkinson, The Pursuit of Beauty (The New Yorker)

I thanked her heartily, and I thanked him heartily, but said I could not yet make sure of joining him as he so kindly offered. Firstly, my mind was too preoccupied to be able to take in the subject clearly. Secondly,—Yes! Secondly, there was a vague something lingering in my thoughts that will come out very near the end of this slight narrative.

"But if you thought, Herbert, that you could, without doing any injury to your business, leave the **question** open for a little while—"

"For any while," cried Herbert. "Six months, a year!"

"Not so long as that," said I. "Two or three months at most."

Herbert was highly delighted when we shook hands on this arrangement, and said he could now take courage to tell me that he believed he must go away at the end of the week.

Charles Dickens, Great Expectations

The one-eyed guy waited thirty seconds, and then dialled his desk phone, and when it was answered he said. 'She met a guy off the train. It was late. She waited five hours for it. She brought the guy here and he took a room.'

There was the plastic crackle of a **question**, and the one-eyed clerk said, 'Another big guy. A mean son of a bitch. He busted my balls on the room rate. I gave him 106, in the back corner.'

Another crackling **question**, and another answer: 'Not from here. I'm in the office.'

Another crackle, but this time a different tone and a different cadence. An instruction, not a **question**.

The one-eyed guy said, 'OK.'

And he put the phone down and struggled to his feet, and stepped out of the office, and took the lawn chair from outside 102, which was empty, and dragged it to a spot on the blacktop where he could see his own door and 106's equally. *Can you see his room from there?* had been the **question**, and *Move your ass somewhere you can watch him all night* had been the instruction, and the one-eyed guy always obeyed instructions, if sometimes a little reluctantly, as at that point, as he adjusted his angle and dumped his bulk down on the uncomfortable plastic. Outside, in the night-time air. Not his preferred way of doing things.

Lee Child, Make Me

Having *two* words here may be helpful. Failure to attend to the theory$_1$-theory$_2$ distinction has often resulted in confusions that this bit of jargon should help us avoid.

The theory of theory as I conceive it, and as I think others must have conceived it, is the theory of theory$_1$. It concerns itself with the features peculiar to the texts subsumable under one of the category terms that make up List I.

To recognize these features we must remind ourselves of one important role played by such subsumptions.

Any individual's quest for knowledge and wisdom and know-how and ideas consists not only in original observations, personal witnessing of events or things, cogitations, reflections, and reckonings. It includes the picking of brains, that is, reading and listening and thus learning from others what others already know or have already thought of. I know the height of Mt. Everest, I know how to prove that the sum of the squares of the adjacent sides of a rectangular triangle is equal to the square of the hypotenuse, I know that laziness in children can be viewed as a form of rebellion, but others took the measurements, sweated the sweat, frustrated themselves into the insights: I merely read the appropriate books and registered for the relevant courses.

None of us wants to or can read every book, take every course, master every paper, listen to every lecture. The abundance of instrumentalities through which something can be learned thus creates the need for devices that reveal the cognitive gains available through this or that didactic instrumentality, and that do this without requiring actual mastery; devices, in other words, that reveal the didactic promise to which the instrumentality lends itself.

Many words can be used for that purpose. Think of 'History,' 'Geography,' 'Science,' 'Biology,' etc. To say that a book is a history book, that a course is a biology course, that a paper is about geography, is to indicate the kind of didactic promise to which the book, the course, the paper lends itself. It is to indicate it in a rough way, but fine enough for many purposes. Other phrases can do the job more precisely.

The category terms on List I can be used for the same purpose. To say that a course is a course in the theory of heat is to indicate something about what can be learned from it; to put a monograph under the heading of "theory of systems in unstable equilibrium" in a catalogue is to indicate *grosso mode* the sort of problems that have been worked out for the reader, and so on.

It seems, therefore, reasonable to assume that there is a type of didactic promise to which every text subsumable under one of the categories of List I must lend itself. To establish that type, if it exists, must be one of the primary tasks of the theory of theory$_1$.

I said "reasonable" above. Whether the assumption is true or not cannot be established by examining only our use of the word 'theory.' The appropriate procedure is to make explicit the type of didactic promise implicit in our use, and then to check against actual scientific literature to see whether the latter conforms to the presuppositions of the former. If it does, our assumption will have been vindicated. The matter is well worth our attention, however. If such a defining type of didactic promise does exist, then there must also exist conditions of acceptability and of adequacy essential to all texts subsumable under a theory1 category. It is the first duty of the philosophy of science to find and to judge such conditions. A general didactic promise would be a priceless guide.

Sylvain Bromberger, On What We Know We Don't Know: Explanation, Theory, Linguistics, and How **Questions** *Shape Them*

From inside his room Reacher heard the lawn chair scrape across the blacktop, but he paid no attention. Just a random night-time sound, nothing dangerous, not a shotgun jacking a round, not the hiss of a blade on a sheath, nothing for his lizard brain to worry about. And the only non-lizard possibilities were a lace-up footstep on the sidewalk outside, and a knock on the door, because the woman from the railroad seemed like a person with a lot of **questions**, and also some kind of expectation they should be answered. *Who are you and why have you come here?*

Lee Child, Make Me

"Pardon me; I'm in a hurry."

And when the fat widow asked him where he was going:

"It does seem strange to you, doesn't it? I, the one who always stays cooped up in my laboratory like a rat with his cheese."

"What cheese?" asked the innkeeper

"No, never mind," Homais replied. "I was just trying to say, Madame Lefrançois, that I normally stay close to home like a recluse. But today, given the circumstances, I had to . . ."

Oh, you're going down there?" she asked disdainfully.

"Yes, I'm going there," replied the startled pharmacist. "Am I not a member of the advisory committee?"

Madame Lefrançois considered this for a few minutes, and finally replied with a smile:

"That's something else then! But what do you have to do with agriculture? Do you even understand anything about it?"

"Certainly I understand it, because I am a pharmacist, and that is to say a chemist! And chemistry, Madame Lefrançois, having for its object the knowledge of the reciprocal and molecular action of all bodies in nature, it follows that agriculture is included within its domain! And in fact, the composition of manure, the fermentation of liquids, the analysis of gas and the influence of miasmas—what is all that, I ask you, if not chemistry, pure and simple?"

The innkeeper made no reply. Homais went on:

"Do you think that, in order to be an agronomist, it's necessary to have worked the earth oneself, or to have fattened fowls? Rather, one must know the composition of the substances in **question**, the geological deposits, the atmospheric actions, the quality of the soils, the minerals, the waters, the density of different bodies and their capillarity! And who knows what else. And one must have the deepest knowledge of all the principles of hygiene, in order to direct and critique the construction of buildings, the diets of animals, the feeding of servants! What's more, Madame Lefrançois, one must know botany, in order to tell plants apart. Do you see? Which ones are salutary, which ones deleterious, which are unproductive and which nutritive; whether it's good to pluck them up here and replant them there, to propagate these and destroy those; in short, one must stay current with scientific advancements by means of pamphlets and professional papers, and be constantly on the lookout for improvements . . ."

The innkeeper kept her eyes fixed on the doorway of the Café Français, and the pharmacist continued:

"Would to God that our farmers were chemists, or that they would at least listen to scientific advice! Thus, for my part, I have recently composed a significant paper, a memorandum of over seventy-two pages, entitled: *On Cider, Its Manufacture and Its Effects, Followed by Several New Reflections on the Subject,* which I have sent to the Agricultural Society of Rouen; which earned for me the honor of being received among its members, Agricultural Section, Pomological Class. Well! If my work had been granted an even wider audience . . ."

But the pharmacist stopped talking, as Madame Lefrançois appeared to be preoccupied.

"Look at them over there!" she said. "It doesn't make any sense! A dump like that!" And shrugging her shoulders—which made the stitches in her sweater stretch out over her bosom—she pointed with both hands at her rival's café, from which the sound of singing could be heard.

"Anyway, he won't have it for long," she added. "In a week, it'll be all over."

Gustave Flaubert, *Madame Bovary*

I pass now to statements in which 'to explain' does not function as an accomplishment term. First, those of the form 'A explained W' in which A still indicates a position occupied by an expression through which a person is mentioned. When one says that Newton explained why there are tides, one need not mean that some explaining episode took place in which Newton was the tutor. One may mean that Newton solved the problem, found the answer to the **question.** Similarly 'Sherlock Holmes explained how the assassin left the room' may convey that Holmes solved the riddle. Here 'to explain' functions as an achievement term, not as an accomplishment term.

Sylvain Bromberger, *On What We Know We Don't Know: Explanation, Theory, Linguistics, and How* **Questions** *Shape Them*

And this door, said Vollard interestedly to Matisse, where does that lead to, does that lead into a court or does that lead on to a stairway. Into a court, said Matisse. Ah yes, said Vollard. And then he left.

The Matisses spent days discussing whether there was anything symbolic in Vollard's **question** or was it idle curiosity. Vollard never had any idle curiosity, he always wanted to know what everybody thought of everything because in that way he found out what he himself thought. This was very well known and therefore the Matisses asked each other and all their friends, why did he ask that **question** about that door.

Gertrude Stein, *The Autobiography of Alice B. Toklas*

The fourth hypothesis does not require but is compatible with the occurrence of explaining episodes at the beginning of which the tutee is really in either a p-predicament or b-predicament with regard to the **question,** and by the end of which he actually has learned the answer and has had the grounds of his predicament corrected. I shall call explaining episodes of that sort *proper explaining episodes.*

A proper explaining episode involves a change in the tutee: at the beginning he does not know the answer to the **question**; in the course of the episode he learns certain facts, or (vel) he gains certain ideas and concepts, or (vel) he becomes aware of certain principles; at the end of the episode, he knows the answer, and he is competent to act as tutor in explaining episodes whose tutees are in a p-predicament or b-predicament with regard to the same **question**—they do not know some or all of the facts, ideas, concepts, or principles that our initial tutee has acquired in our initial episode. In other words, he is changed into someone who can explain the matter.

Sylvain Bromberger, *On What We Know We Don't Know: Explanation, Theory, Linguistics, and How* **Questions** *Shape Them*

*On the occasion in **question**, Queequeg figured in the Highland costume—a shirt and socks—in which to my eyes, at least, he appeared to uncommon advantage; and no one had a better chance to observe him, as will presently be seen.*

Colored pencil, ink and marker on found paper
7.75" × 10.75"
07/13/10

Matt Kish, *Moby-Dick in Pictures: One Drawing for Every Page*

The kind of transformation just described can be brought about without benefit of tutor and without the occurrence of an explaining episode: research, re-examination of beliefs and assumptions, conceptual inventions, explorations, prodding for inspiration, exploitation of good luck, or grace may enable one to transform himself by himself into somebody able to explain something. To have succeeded in this sort of endeavor is to have explained something in the sense of 'to explain' to which we are now attending.

*Sylvain Bromberger, On What We Know We Don't Know: Explanation, Theory, Linguistics, and How **Questions** Shape Them*

Okay, you now know how to keep yourself safe and to meditate. That means you now have the information that you need to begin unfolding your mediumship. So, let's do it!

Step one is to sit in a comfortable chair, sofa, or other place.

Step two is to put the "Light of Protection" around you, empowering it with all the loving, wonderful mental attitudes that I discussed in Chapter Two.

Step three is to meditate and achieve a relaxed and calm state of mind.

Step four is to begin using your mediumship. And how do you begin using your mediumship?

Simple: ask a **question**.

The **question** doesn't have to be anything complicated. You don't have to start by asking for the meaning of life. In fact, I would strongly suggest that in the beginning you avoid any complicated **questions**. You probably won't receive an answer to such a **question**, and even if an answer is sent, you probably won't receive enough of the message for it to make any sense.

Joseph J. Mauriello, (Your Departed Loved Ones and Spirit Guides Are) Only a Thought Away

"I am waiting for your **question**: I am quite ready for it," said Alice.

"Are you quite ready for it?" asked he, with a meaning in his eyes and manner which she could not understand. "I hope so. This is my **question**—"

*George Robert Wynne, Overton's **Question**, and What Came of It*

"Me too, me too. Um, I don't have a **question**."

"Will you bash his face in if he doesn't have a **question**?"

Tony Burgess, Pontypool Changes Everything

There are few but tarry, and hesitate, and **question**; many who, in the midst of this tarrying, have heard the clock of eternity strike, and the door of hope shut for ever!

*George Robert Wynne, Overton's **Question**, and What Came of it*

"Why didn't she come in?" he asked. "She's not allowed to," said the big policeman. "You're under arrest, aren't you."

"But how can I be under arrest? And how come it's like this?"

"Now you're starting again," said the policeman, dipping a piece of buttered bread in the honeypot. "We don't answer **questions** like that."

"You will have to answer them," said K. "Here are my identification papers, now show me yours and I certainly want to see the arrest warrant."

"Oh, my God!" said the policeman. "In a position like yours, and you think you can start giving orders, do you? It won't do you any good to get us on the wrong side, even if you think it will—we're probably more on your side than anyone else you know!"

"That's true, you know, you'd better believe it," said Franz, holding a cup of coffee in his hand which he did not lift to his mouth but looked at K. in a way that was probably meant to be full of meaning but could not actually be understood.

Franz Kafka, The Trial

—Certainly, John Eglinton mused, of all great men he is the most enigmatic. We know nothing but that he lived and suffered. Not even so much. Others abide our **question**. A shadow hangs over all the rest.

—But *Hamlet* is so personal, isn't it? Mr Best pleaded. I mean, a kind of private paper, don't you know, of his private life. I mean, I don't care a button, don't you know, who is killed or who is guilty . . .

He rested an innocent book on the edge of the desk, smiling his defiance. His private papers in the original. *Ta an bad ar an tir. Taim in mo shagart.* Put beurla on it, littlejohn.

Quoth littlejohn Eglinton:

—I was prepared for paradoxes from what Malachi Mulligan told us but I may as well warn you that if you want to shake my belief that Shakespeare is Hamlet you have a stern task before you.

Bear with me.

Stephen withstood the bane of miscreant eyes glinting stern under wrinkled brows. A basilisk. *E quando vede l'uomo l'attosca.* Messer Brunetto, I thank thee for the word.

—As we, or mother Dana, weave and unweave our bodies, Stephen said, from day to day, their molecules shuttled to and fro, so does the artist weave and unweave his image. And as the mole on my right breast is where it was when I was born, though all my body has been woven of new stuff time after time, so through the ghost of the unquiet father the image of the unliving son looks forth. In the intense instant of imagination, when the mind, Shelley says, is a fading coal, that which I was is that which I am and that which in possibility I may come to be. So in the future, the sister of the past, I may see myself as I sit here now but by reflection from that which then I shall be.

James Joyce, Ulysses

Had I any right to take advantage of this accident, and open the book? I have put the **question** since to some of my friends of both sexes. The women all agree that I was perfectly justified, considering the serious interests that I had at stake, in taking any advantage of any book in the Major's house. The men differ from this view, and declare that I ought to have put back the volume in blue velvet unopened, carefully guarding myself from any after-temptation to look at it again by locking the cupboard door. I dare say the men are right.

Being a woman, however, I opened the book without a moment's hesitation.

Wilkie Collins, The Law and the Lady

HAMLET	HAMLET
In the secret parts of Fortune? Oh, most true, she is a strumpet. What's the news?	Ha, ha, so you've gotten into her private parts? Of course—Lady Luck is such a slut. Anyway, what's up?

ROSENCRANTZ None, my lord, but that the world's grown honest.	ROSENCRANTZ Not much, my lord. Just that the world's become honest.
HAMLET Then is doomsday near. But your news is not true. Let me **question** more in particular.	HAMLET In that case, the end of the world is approaching. But you're wrong. Let me ask you a particular **question**.

William Shakespeare, Hamlet (Spark Notes: No Fear Translation)

Schonbornerus.—Can any of your readers give me information about a book I became possessed of by chance a short time ago, or tell me anything respecting its author, for whom I have vainly sought biographical dictionaries? The volume is a duodecimo, and bears the following title-page:

> "Georgii Schonborneri Politicorum, Libri Septem. Editio ad ipsius Authoris emendatum Exemplar nunc primum vulgata. Amsterodami: apud L. Elzevirium, anno 1642."

It is written in Latin, and contains as many quotations as the *Anatomy of Melancholy*, or Mr. Digby's *Broad Stone of Honour*.

H. A. B.

George Bell (ed.), Minor Queries (Notes and Queries: A Medium of Inter-Communication for Literary Men, Artists, Antiquaries, Genealogists, etc., Number 185)

"I don't hear a **question**," objects the prosecutor.

*Jill Ciment, The Body in **Question**: A Novel*

The reply to the prosecutor was a masterpiece. One by one Maître Senard took up his "arguments," completely annihilating the poor man. But indeed Maître Senard's task was an easy one. He had only to quote from the work itself. He concluded by asking the pertinent **question**: "Does the reading of such a book give you a love for vice or inspire you with horror of vice? The terrible expiation of a fault, does it not urge, excite to virtue? . . . You have judged of the book as a whole and in its details. It is impossible that you should hesitate."

Eleanor Marx Aveling, Introduction to Madame Bovary, by Gustave Flaubert

By the time I turned off Route 126 onto Antelope Valley Road I really had to piss. You were expecting me at 8 and it was already 8:05 and pissing suddenly became so problematic. I didn't want to have to do it the moment I walked into your house, how gauche, a telltale sign of female nervousness. And yet considering everything I knew about Route 126 I was afraid to take a slash outside. Every 20 seconds the headlights of another car clipped by: marauding rednecks, cops, angry migrant workers? I pulled over at the Antelope Valley turnoff, turned off the headlights, stopped the car. Outside the grass was wet with rain. Who was it, Marx or Wittgenstein, who said that "every **question**, problem, contains the seeds of its own answer or solution through negation"? There was a half-drunk styrofoam cup of coffee in the car. I rolled down the window, dumped it, slid my jeans down past my knees and pissed into the empty cup. The cup was full before my bladder emptied but what the hell, I'd hold the rest. With shaking hands I tipped the brimming cup of urine in the grass.

That left the evidence. Several large drops still clung to the styrofoam, what if it smelled? I was afraid to litter. Dear Dick, sometimes there just isn't a right answer. I scrunched the cup up, tossed it under the back seat and wiped my hands.

Chris Kraus, I Love Dick

Which presumably answers the **question** as to where I came upon the footnote about Samuel Butler having said that it was a woman who wrote the Odyssey.

David Markson, Wittgenstein's Mistress

"Who?"

"That's the part I'm not ready to give out. I've got a client, you know."

He wrinkled his nose. "That—" he chopped it off quickly.

"I expected you would know the girl," I said.

"Who got the books, soldier?"

"Not ready to talk, Eddie. Why should I?"

He put the Luger down on the desk and slapped it with his open palm. "This," he said. "And I might make it worth your while."

"That's the spirit. Leave the gun out of it. I can always hear the sound of money. How much are you clinking at me?"

"For doing what?"

"What did you want done?"

He slammed the desk hard. "Listen, soldier. I ask you a **question** and you ask me another. We're not getting anywhere.

Raymond Chandler, The Big Sleep

There was nothing new under the sun; that meant the materials of transformation were already present, everywhere and anywhere, in today's papers, in yesterday's books, and so the *Potlatch* voice is huddled and all-powerful, satirical and sentimental, a midnight secret told as a noontime shout, self-referential within a global frame of reference. Legend and fact turn into one another; the mythic becomes prosaic, and vice versa; pronouncements on all things under the sun are made in tones of common knowledge just out of reach of common sense. In certain moods, one can feel a jarring, tearing momentum in the pages, the momentum of a dream as it rushes toward waking—the most violent screed seems reasonable, the most rational argument communicates as a rant, and as one picks out the names at the bottom of a manifesto, the **questions** ask themselves: who are these people?

Greil Marcus, Lipstick Traces: A Secret History of the Twentieth Century

"That the voices heard in contention," he said, "by the party upon the stairs, were not the voices of the women themselves, was fully proved by the evidence. This relieves us of all doubt upon the **question** whether the old lady could have first destroyed the daughter and afterward have committed suicide. I speak of this point chiefly for the sake of method; for the strength of Madame L'Espanaye would have been utterly unequal to the task of thrusting her daughter's corpse up the chimney as it was found; and the nature of the wounds upon her own person entirely preclude the idea of self-destruction. Murder, then, has been committed by some third party; and the voices of this third party were those heard in contention. Let me now advert—not to the whole testimony respecting these voices—but to what was peculiar in that testimony. Did you observe any thing peculiar about it?"

Edgar Allan Poe, The Murders in the Rue Morgue

I was silent for some moments. Well as I knew Thorndyke, I was completely taken by surprise; a sensation, indeed, that I experienced anew every time that I accompanied him on one of his investigations. His marvellous power of coordinating apparently insignificant facts, of arranging them into an ordered sequence and making them tell a coherent story, was a phenomenon that I never got used to; every exhibition of it astonished me afresh.

"If your inferences are correct," I said, "the problem is practically solved. There must be abundant traces inside the house. The only **question** is, which house is it?"

"Quite so," replied Thorndyke; "that is the **question**, and a very difficult **question** it is. A glance at that interior would doubtless clear up the whole mystery. But how are we to get that glance? We cannot enter houses speculatively to see if they present traces of a murder. At present, our clue breaks off abruptly. The other end of it is in some unknown house, and, if we cannot join up the two ends, our problem remains unsolved. For the **question** is, you remember, Who killed Oscar Brodski?"

"Then what do you propose to do?" I asked.

R. Austin Freeman, The Case of Oscar Brodski

"Nothing at all. And I'm getting a little tired of that **question**," she said coldly.

"Do you know a man named Canino?"

She drew her fine black brows together in thought. "Vaguely. I seem to remember the name."

Raymond Chandler, The Big Sleep

As to Cicero, I am of the common opinion that, learning excepted, he had no great natural excellence. He was a good citizen, of an affable nature, as all fat, heavy men, such as he was, usually are; but given to ease, and had, in truth, a mighty share of vanity and ambition. Neither do I know how to excuse him for thinking his poetry fit to be published; 'tis no great imperfection to make ill verses, but it is an imperfection not to be able to judge how unworthy his verses were of the glory of his name. For what concerns his eloquence, that is totally out of all comparison, and I believe it will never be equalled. The younger Cicero, who resembled his father in nothing but in name, whilst commanding in Asia, had several strangers one day at his table, and, amongst the rest, Cestius seated at the lower end, as men often intrude to the open tables of the great. Cicero asked one of his people who that man was, who presently told him his name; but he, as one who had his thoughts taken up with something else, and who had forgotten the answer made him, asking three or four times, over and over again; the same **question**, the fellow, to deliver himself from so many answers and to make him know him by some particular circumstance; "'tis that Cestius," said he, "of whom it was told you, that he makes no great account of your father's eloquence in comparison of his own." At which Cicero, being suddenly nettled, commanded poor Cestius presently to be seized, and caused him to be very well whipped in his own presence; a very discourteous entertainer!

Michel de Montaigne, Of Books (Essays)

April 11th. 1912.

Dear Sir,

I beg to acknowledge the receipt of your favour of the 23rd. ultimo addressed to the Hon. Mr. Rogers, with reference to appropriation for expenses in connection with the British Columbia Indian land question, and to say in reply thereto that this amount has been revoted.

Yours very truly,

Deputy Superintendent General.

Rev. A. E. O'Meara,
    King Edward Hotel,
        Edmonton, Alta.

*British Columbia Indian Land **Question**, 1924–1929*
Textual material, Reference RG10, Volume 3822, File 59335-2, Library and Archives Canada

Always Present It in the Form of a Question

And he had to go to Canada to deliver these lectures

—What is it? Mr Bloom asked.

—A recently discovered fragment of Cicero, professor MacHugh answered with pomp of tone. *Our lovely land.* SHORT BUT TO THE POINT

—Whose land? Mr Bloom said simply.

—Most pertinent **question**, the professor said between his chews. With an accent on the whose.

James Joyce, Ulysses

. . . the first known Canadian book was a catechism by Archbishop Languet, issued in 1765.

John MacLean, Canadian Savage Folk: The Native Tribes of Canada

In it, one can find hints of the national character. Eh?, as you may have noticed, is always followed by a **question** mark, and thus, although it is essentially good-natured, it is also a bit insecure. It is an agreement looking to happen.

"It's cold out, eh?"

"How about them Leafs, eh?"

"Dialectical materialism was an inherently flawed conceptual model, eh?"

Will Ferguson and Ian Ferguson, How to Be a Canadian (Even if You Already Are One)

"I cannot help thinking those words grand; but I have no idea what they mean."

"Will you pardon me if I pass over your **question** for the present, and promise you on some future occasion to give it the fullest explanation, if you need it then? I, too, have a **question** to ask of you. It is about a book, too . . ."

*George Robert Wynne, Overton's **Question**, and What Came of It*

My eyes wandered mechanically round the room as I put the **question**. I saw Major Fitz-David, I saw the table on which the singing girl had opened the book to show it to me. I saw the girl herself, sitting alone in a corner, with her handkerchief to her eyes as if she were crying. In one mysterious moment my memory recovered its powers. The recollection of that fatal title-page came back to me in all its horror.

Wilkie Collins, The Law and the Lady

And I think it isn't—only natural that therefore he should have been crucified. It's a very disagreeable—a very unpleasant task, and nobody is liked, you see. Mr.—my friend, Mr. Samuel Eliot Morison now made a—some—gave some lectures on the trash, and on the hypocrisy, and on the insincerity of American education. And he had to go to Canada to deliver these lectures, because in America nobody would have listened to his provocation. The sophists are always in command, if not somebody sticks his neck out and risks to tell them—to ask them, "What are you doing with the mind, with the brain, with your logic, with your quizzes?" You see. Who is stopping Walter Winchell? That's the **question**. And it's a very serious **question**. Who is stopping these obscenities? Who is stopping the comic strips? Who is stopping the nonsense that's going on in television, and what-not? Who is? The philosopher. If he doesn't exist, if such a—such a healthy force doesn't develop, you see, the country must go out of hand, obviously. And you have then some mental, moral, or financial crisis. In—you just have to read the behavior of the people in the '20s, when they said that all the laws of the universe were successfully abolished. Saving was ridiculous, you see. Death had—would yield. People would go—become 150 years old, you see. And you had to live on the installment plan. Well, the doctrines are nearly—as equally mad at this moment. But not quite. In the gay '20s, you had—you prepared the crash, because there was nobody who was listened to.

Eugen Rosenstock-Huessy, Greek Philosophy (1956): Lectures 14–20

Having secured a high-powered Canadian book contract, I immediately called my brother Ian. He's the creator of Toronto's improvised soap opera *Sin City*, and he is just about as close to the compleat Canadian as you can get. This is a guy who wears plaid flannel shirts because he honestly thinks they're fashionable. I called him up and said, "Ian, it's me!" And he said, "Who?" And I said, "Will," and he said, "Will who?" and I said, "Will, your brother," and he said, "I have a brother?" and I said, "Is this about the towels I stole from you last time I was out?" and he said, "Oh yeah, I remember you. What do you want?" and I said, "Listen, I was talking to Margaret Atwood the other day—" and he immediately shouted, "Count me in! Whatever it is, count me in!"

"Have you actually read Margaret Atwood?" I asked. "It doesn't matter," he said. "It's Margaret Atwood. Count me in!"

[Enough banter. Get to the point—Ed.]

Now, at this juncture you may very well be asking yourself a few **questions** (beyond "Why did I blow $1.99 on this?"). For example, you might be wondering—aloud, so as to justify the use of quotation marks—"Who are you to write such a book?" Well, Ian and I are both Canadians. And, as noted, we are brothers. We have been Canadians our whole lives and, um, did I mention the part about us being Canadians and all?

Will Ferguson and Ian Ferguson, How to Be a Canadian (Even if You Already Are One)

In fact, even if you born right ya-so-so; so long as you skin black, them does like arkse you "Are you from Jamaica?" Them just assume we all is immigrant; and if you Black then you is Jamaican. So we never feel as if we really belong ya. Even me friend who is fifth generation Canadian does have to explain she'self all the time. Me tell she she shouldn't answer dem. She say, "How you mean?" Me say "Just nuh answer dem." She wonder what she would do if say is a person she work with . . . or whatever. Me tell her say me woulda still nuh answer them. Me does do white people that all the time . . . just stare dem down. Me nar lie. If you arkse me one stupid **question**, me nar answer you! An me nuh care if you think me crazy . . . you could go orn think me crazy. If you think me crazy, put you finger in me mouth . . . make me bite it orf give you. Too besiden, if you persist in arksing me stupidness, me would eventually bite orf you head. So then you woulda force fuh go library go find out say Black people live here before you come inna fooyou boat from Eastern Europe and England. Gwam goo way from me . . . you ah give me headache! That is what me want dem fuh know. Me will quicker tell dem that, than answer; especially if me an all my generation come from Montreal, or Halifax, or Windsor, or Toronto and you a'arkse me where me come from: "Where you come from? Canada? And you mother and father come from here too? No? And dem did come over on one a' the 'Displaced Persons' boat? No? By the time me done arkse all dem kinda stupid **question**, dem shoulda get the point and just nuh arkse me nothing 'bout if me come from Jamaica. Dem could make you wonder if dem had never hear 'bout Jamaica is where dem would think all'a we did come from? Even some African from Africa and some Indian from India does be arksing me the Jamaica **question**; like say dem nuh must know better than to act like white people.

Althea Prince, Being Black

Other than the cold, though, I'm doing fine. How about you? I won't tell you my address, but don't take it personally. It's not like I'm trying to hide anything from you. I want you to know that. This is, you see, a delicate **question** for me. It's just this feeling I've got that, if I told you my address, in that instant something inside me would change. I can't put it very well.

It seems to me, though, that you always understand very well what I can't say very well. Trouble is I end up being even worse at saying things well. It's got to be an inborn fault.

Naturally everyone's got faults.

Haruki Murakami, A Wild Sheep Chase

Since politicians, at least in the English-speaking West, are showing an increasing tendency to drag religion into politics, it would seem fair for the electorate to be able to **question** them on their own theological views. "Do you believe that you personally are irrevocably saved, that any graft, fraud, lying, torturing, or other criminal activities you may engage in are fully justified because you're one of the Elect and can do no wrong, that to the pure such as yourself all things are pure, and that the vast majority of those you say you wish to represent as their political leader are vile and worthless and predestined to fry in hell, so why should you give a damn about them?" would seem to be an appropriate lead-off at **question** time.

Margaret Atwood, Payback: Debt and the Shadow Side of Wealth

Atwood closes the speech by saying that the true power lies in the hands of the people of the land. If people decide to vote on the premise that they want changes to be made, only then do the changes become possible. Once the mindset is changed, everybody willingly participates in the growth and betterment of the state of affairs. Atwood once again repeats her phrase to emphasize on the impact of having the right attitude in life. She concludes:

"You may not be able to alter reality, but you can alter your attitude towards it, and this, paradoxically, alters reality. Try it and see."

*Oswaal Editorial Board, ISC **Question** Bank, Chapterwise & Topicwise: Class 12 English Paper-2*

They have Elvis Presley zucchini molds now: you clamp them around your zucchini while it's young, and as it grows it's deformed into the shape of Elvis Presley's head. Is this why he sang? To become a zucchini? Vegetarianism and reincarnation are in the air, but that's taking it too far. I'd rather come back as a sow bug, myself; or a stir-fried shrimp. Though I suppose the whole idea's more lenient than Hell.

"You've done it well," I say to the waitress. "Of course the prices are wrong. It was ten cents for a coffee, then."

"Really," she says, not as a **question**. She gives me a dutiful smile: *Boring old frump.* She is half my age, living, already, a life I can't imagine. Whatever her guilts are, her hates and terrors, they are not the same. What do they do about AIDS, these girls? They can't just roll around in the hay, the way we did. Is there a courtship ritual that involves, perhaps, an exchange of doctors' telephone numbers? For us it was pregnancy that was the scary item, the sexual booby trap, the thing that could finish you off. Not any more.

I pay the bill, overtip, gather up my packages, an Italian scarf for each of my daughters, a fountain pen for Ben. Fountain-pens are coming back. Somewhere in Limbo, all the old devices and appliances and costumes are lined up, waiting their turn for reentry.

Margaret Atwood, Cat's Eye

Western cultural attitudes towards financial debt have gone through both long-term and short-term cycles. On the longer scale there is the classic association between the Protestant Reformation and the rise of capitalism agonized over by Marxist and non-Marxist historians. In the shorter scheme of things there is the oscillation between a general cultural assumption that a certain level of personal and corporate debt is a good thing—fuelling the wheels of the economy; or a bad thing—representing a moral and socioeconomic trap. For most of the nineteenth century and well into the twentieth the latter was the basic assumption. Margaret Atwood argues brilliantly how the nineteenth-century novel was 'driven by money': 'the best nineteenth century revenge is not seeing your enemy's red blood all over the floor but seeing the red ink all over his balance sheet' (Atwood 2008: 100).

*David Watson, The **Question** of Morale: Managing Happiness and Unhappiness in University Life*

MARGARET ATWOOD: You left out Beatrix Potter. I read a lot as a child. There are probably a lot more sources. Grimm's fairy tales are important. I think Greek mythology is important, which I read in the beginning, in the Charles Lamb *Greek Mythology for Children* and then went on to read more extensively, and of course I studied Latin in high school, which took us right into the *Aeneid*.

CASTRO: So you read the *Aeneid* in Latin?

ATWOOD: Some of it, sure. Obviously not the whole thing. And Ovid, of course; we did *Metamorphoses*. When I was in university, it was part of the honors English course at the University of Toronto that you had to take a course that touched on Greek—actually I took Greek history at one point, too. But I guess what I'm getting around to is that there is a lot of source material. When people ask me that **question**, What was your early influence? I usually drag out Grimm's fairy tales, but it's by no means the only thing.

CASTRO: Did you continue to study mythology to any extent at Harvard?

Atwood: Only as part of studying English. You can't study English literature without knowing something about the Bible, and Greek and Roman Mythology, and you have to know it, because it comes up in so much literature that was written in English. That was what people studied, of course, when they went to university. They took classics, and, therefore, all of that got into English literature.

CASTRO: Do you think you overlay the theme of metamorphosis on other themes, for instance, in *The Journals of Susanna Moodie*?

Atwood: I never have done academic criticism of my own work, and I never will. The reason I never have and never will is that once authors start making pronouncements about how people should read their work, in a dogmatic kind of way, it eliminates other readings.

Castro: It just seemed to me that you had given Susanna Moodie more dimensions than the real Susanna Moodie.

Atwood: The real Susanna Moodie is different from the Susanna Moodie that we find by reading her work. Because the real Susanna Moodie by no means told all. So let us say there are four elements operative here. There is Susanna Moodie we get by reading her texts, which never go into things like what she thought about her husband; she just never mentions it. The prime example is the story she tells about the boy who drowned, who wasn't related to her at all. Then there's the throwaway line at the end of the story when she says, "I also had a child who drowned in this way," and that's all you hear about it. She doesn't go on to say how that affected her, how upset she was, anything. The whole thing is contained in the metaphor that she has given previously of this other child who drowned. So there's a lot she doesn't tell. There's a gap between the Susanna Moodie of the texts and what we can speculate was the real Susanna Moodie, who thought and felt all kinds of things she never wrote down because decorum did not permit it. Then there's the Susanna Moodie I have created, who is neither of the above. And then there's myself, who is neither of any of them. So there are four things there. What was the **question**?

Jan Garden Castro, An Interview With Margaret Atwood (Margaret Atwood: Vision and Forms)

"**Question** Three. Now for something a little different. Are your novels autobiographical?" Thus opens an unpublished 20-page exploration that Atwood herself wrote in 1982 about often-heard interview **questions**. (You can find it in the Atwood Papers, at the Thomas Fisher Rare Book Library in Toronto.) She raises issues that have become even more pertinent in the nineties, from the "People magazine nosiness that we've come to associate with personality cults" to the "belief that women are more subjective, that the only stories they can tell are their own" (3, 4). It helps to recall that she has repeatedly and patiently insisted that writing is a craft. And that novels are not a "Disneyland of the soul,"

> containing Romanceland, Spyland, Pornoland, and all the other Escapelands which are so much more agreeable than the complex truth. When we take an author seriously, we prefer to believe that her vision derives from her individual and subjective and neurotic tortured soul—we like artists to have tortured souls—not from the world she is looking at. (1981, 1982, 393–94)
>
> *Susanne Becker, Celebrity, or A Disneyland of the Soul: Margaret Atwood and the Media (Margaret Atwood: Works and Impact)*

Mr. Atwood. I have no doubt. We have heard you say that, and not being quite content with your ipsi dixit, we are bound to ask you a **question** or two as to the source of your knowledge. And the **question** I am asking is whether or not the portion of the factors which go to create this problem or the result thereof are known to you personally in the relation of one to sixty as in the other problem?

Interstate Commerce Commission, Evidence Taken in the Matter of Proposed Advances in Freight Rates by Carriers, Volume 3

That we almost nod "Yes" in response to this **question** suggests how close to Foucault Atwood is; that we do not ultimately nod "Yes" suggests that her view still resists a complete acceptance of the interiority of power.

Atwood, we might conclude, has become much more sophisticated over the years in how she treats this **question**. She also seems still to be accepting the idea that power is interior but with a big "but" appended to that acceptance. Her view is then not as theoretically pure as Foucault's, and it is most certainly not imitative of Foucault, for Atwood is a writer, one who creates stories and characters, not a philosophical thinker or one who follows a philosophical thinker. Her wrestlings with this **question** do, nonetheless, provide one of the recurring elements in her novels and, because of the complexity of the **question**, one of the more fascinating recurring elements.

Theodore F. Sheckels, The Political in Margaret Atwood's Fiction: The Writing on the Wall of the Tent

The professor, too, concludes with mixed metaphors of light and dark: "As all historians know, the past is a great darkness, and filled with echoes. Voices may reach us from it; but what they say to us is imbued with the obscurity of the matrix out of which they come; and, try as we may, we cannot always decipher them precisely in the clearer light of our own day" (p. 324). It is a brief peroration that elicits his audience's applause and prepares the way for any discussion that might follow. Indeed, when he ends, with again a standard ploy—"Are there any **questions**?" (p. 324)—that **question** itself well may be rhetorical. And even if it is not, the speaker has already indicated what he thinks the **questions** are. His **questions**, however, need not be our **questions**, especially

You have either reached a page that is unavailable for viewing or reached your viewing limit for this book.

Arnold E. Davidson, Future Tense: Making History in The Handmaid's Tale (Margaret Atwood: Vision and Forms)

"If she walked by me, I wouldn't have a clue who she is." And it is not only Atwood's face that Councillor Ford would not discern; he couples his non-recognition of Atwood's person with a non-recognition of her labour: "Tell her to go run in the next election and get democratically elected and we'd be more than happy to sit down and listen to Margaret Atwood." Implicit in Ford's intemperate rant is this **question**: What does she do that is of importance anyway, this Margaret Atwood, this artist?

In my previous book, Literary Celebrity in Canada, I examined the preoccupations, themes, and tensions attending the experience of literary fame as it was experienced by earlier generations of Canadian writers such as Stephen Leacock, Pauline Johnson, Mazo de la Roche, and L.M. Montgomery, as well as by three more recent writers: Michael Ondaatje, Carol Shields, and Atwood. When I turned my attention to Atwood, I readily perceived a contest between privacy and publicity, between national and international celebrity status, but I also noted how very early in her career, she was recognized and endlessly reproduced as a visual spectacle.

Lorraine Mary York, Margaret Atwood and the Labour of Literary Celebrity

"*Ayash oogoosisa, oogoosisa, oogoosisa . . .*" went the first four children, "*Peechinook'soo* three, four, *peechinook'soo . . .*" went the second, while the last quartet moaned, "*Peeyatuk.*" Like a priest sprinkling holy water, Jeremiah rattled the maraca, counted out the beat—"One, two, one, two." Cree rap with a Latin stamp? The patent was theirs.

"So what you're saying, people, is this," Jeremiah brought the music to a close.

"Group A, 'The Son of Ayash,' over and over. Group B, 'is approaching, three, four,' over and over. Group C," and he moaned like a ghost, "'Be careful, be careful' Our hero, the Son of Ayash, has to be careful, for he is entering the dark place of the human soul where he will meet evil creatures like," he shook the maraca one last time, "the Weetigo. **Questions**?" But the undersized Natives were restless. "Jenny! Cynthia!" Jeremiah was sounding unpleasantly like a school marm, "Puh-leeze!"

"But Willie has a **question, question, question**," a pretty little echo circulated.

Tomson Highway, Kiss of the Fur Queen

Without **question**, the most important new Canadian playwright to emerge in the latter half of the 1980s has been Tomson Highway. In less than three years, and with only two major plays, Highway has joined a select group of playwrights whose new plays, sight unseen, are treated as significant cultural events by Canadian critics, scholars, and audiences. The two plays, The Rez Sisters and Dry Lips Oughta Move to Kapuskasing, both won the coveted Dora Mavor Moore award for the best new play produced in Toronto, the former for the 1986–87 season and the latter for 1988–89. Tomson Highway says his ambition in life, and therefore presumably in his plays, is "to make 'the rez' [reserve] cool, to show and celebrate what funky folk Canada's Indian people really are."1 In this, The Rez Sisters and Dry Lips Oughta Move to Kapuskasing have been wildly successful, attracting enthusiastic audiences, both white and Native, far beyond the real-life reserve where The Rez Sisters was conceived and first performed. To non-Native critics, myself included, Tomson Highway is an exotic new figure in Canadian theatre. Born on his father's trap-line in northern Manitoba, he spoke only Cree until going to a Catholic boarding school at age six. In high school in Winnipeg he became a musical prodigy, eventually earning university degrees in English and music while studying to be a concert pianist. After graduation, however, Highway abruptly jettisoned his musical career and spent the ensuing seven years working with various Native support organizations. Then, he says, he wished to begin integrating all these experiences:

> So I started writing plays, where I put together my knowledge of Indian reality in this country with classical structure, artistic language. It amounted to applying sonata form to the spiritual and mental situation of a street drunk, say, at the corner of Queen and Bathurst.

Denis W. Johnston, Lines and Circles: The "Rez" Plays of Tomson Highway (Canadian Literature)

So I'm at this cocktail party, right? And Margaret Atwood is there, and she can't keep her hands off me. Everywhere I go, she's clinging to me. And I'm like, "Whoa, lady, get a grip." All night long, she's following me around, spilling her drink and slurring her speech, saying, "Wait, wait. I have this great idea for your next book." And I'm like, "Whatever."

Okay, so that's not quite how it happened. I was in fact the cling-er, not the cling-ee. It was at a bookstore opening in Calgary, and Margaret Atwood was the guest of honour. Not that I was intimidated or anything. No sir. With a few drinks in me and a belly full of hubris, I latched myself onto Her Royal Self and refused to leave until she acknowledged my existence.

Margaret (or "Ms. Atwood" to those of you who are not on an accosting basis with the First Lady of Canadian Letters) was very gracious. Yes, she had heard of *Why I Hate*

Canadians. No, she didn't think it sucked. Yes, she was working on another novel. No, she wouldn't tell me what it was about. No, not even a hint.

And then, just in passing, she said, in that wonderful low clipped voice of hers (the anecdote works a lot better if you do your own impression of Margaret Atwood as you read this): "Do you know what your next book should be? You should write a guidebook for newcomers. There was a book by a Hungarian writer, back in the 1950s, I believe. I think it was called 'How to Be an Englishman.' Very funny. You should do one about Canadians."

"Like lessons on how to be Canadian?"

"That's right. For example, talking about the weather. In Canada, you must always present it in the form of a **question**"—and here she did, I swear, a perfect imitation of a Canadian hoser—*"Hey there! Cold enough for ya?"*

"I see. But what if it's summer?"

She sighed. I was obviously a bit thick. "Well, then you say, *'Hot enough for ya?'* Or *'Wet enough for ya?'* And so on."

> Will Ferguson and Ian Ferguson, *How to Be a Canadian (Even if You Already Are One)*

A climate, a single climate, all the time there is a single climate, any time there is a doubt, any time there is music that is to **question** more and more and there is no politeness, there is hardly any ordeal and certainly there is no tablecloth.

> Gertrude Stein, *Tender Buttons*

Out of the **question**. On a dancer's salary? Besides, would such a trip get Jeremiah back to music? Unlikely.

Find him a job? As what? Cook, lawyer, Indian chief? Dancer? He drank too much, ate and smoked too much, never twitched a muscle; in fact, he looked not unlike a sewer rat.

Pull him from the sewer, that was the answer. The country. A camping trip, to thaw their cold war of thirteen years. Jeremiah could flush out his lungs with fresh, clean air—not to mention chop wood, pitch a tent, hike lustily through forests, perhaps even stalk a black bear in the likely absence of wild caribou. The only **question** was: where?

> Tomson Highway, *Kiss of the Fur Queen*

Asked to spell "Canada," the average Canadian will unconsciously pronounce it thus: C, *eh?* N, *eh?* D, *eh?* The Father of the Country? Sir John, *eh?* . . . And so on.

In conversations involving Alcoholics Anonymous, Canadians never know when to stop.

> FIRST GUY: "Did'ja hear? Dave's in A.A., eh?"
> SECOND GUY: "A.A.A.? What's that?"
> FIRST GUY: "Not A.A.A., eh? A.A., eh?"
> SECOND GUY: "*Eh?*"
> FIRST GUY: "Not A! A.A., eh?"
> SECOND GUY: "A.A.A.A., eh?"

. . . and so on, ad infinitum.

> Will Ferguson and Ian Ferguson, *How to Be a Canadian (Even if You Already Are One)*

"I'm very sorry. I don't understand. Can you please speak more slowly?"

"I will speak more slowly. I'm sorry."

There was a silence between them.

"Will you kindly repeat your statement?"

"Yes, of course. I said I hope your work will go well here."

"I believe it's going well, thanks."

"You are with the Canadian Ecumenical Council."

"Yes."

"It is a project of Bible translation."

"We have many projects. That is one project."

"Are you one of the translators, Mr. Benet?"

"I'm trying to improve my Vietnamese. It's possible I'll help later on with translation."

"Let's speak English," the priest said in English.

"Whatever you like."

Pere Patrice said, "Shall I hear your confession?"

"No."

"Thank God! You're not Catholic? "

"Seventh-Day Adventist."

"I don't know about Seventh-Day people."

"It's a Protestant faith."

"Of course. God doesn't care who is Protestant or Catholic. God himself is not Catholic."

"I hadn't thought of that."

"What is this universe to God? Is it a drama? Is it a dream? Perhaps a nightmare?" The priest smiled yet seemed angry.

"That's a big **question**. I think it qualifies as a mystery."

"I'm reading a most wonderful book."

Skip waited for him to finish, but he didn't say anything further about the book.

Denis Johnson, Tree of Smoke

Center for Accessible Technology in Sign, ASL Vocabulary: Beg the **Question**, 2020 (Internet Archive)

They Call It **Question** Period

And why there's so much of it

Alone on his little planet, Answerer sat, waiting for the **Questioners**. Occasionally he mumbled the answers to himself.

Robert Sheckley, Ask a Foolish Question

The Crashaw Club had paid me to discuss
Why Poetry Is Meaningful to Us.
I gave my sermon, a dull thing but short.
As I was leaving in some haste, to thwart
The so-called "**question** period" at the end,
One of those peevish people who attend
Such talks only to say they disagree
Stood up and pointed with his pipe at me.

Vladimir Nabokov, Pale Fire

Just after 2:15 p.m. this afternoon, NDP Leader Thomas Mulcair, leader of Her Majesty's official Opposition, democratically elected member of Parliament for the riding of Outremont, stood in the House of Commons and spoke aloud a fairly straightforward **question** he thought the government should be responsible for answering. This being within the 45 minutes reserved each day for **question** period, Mulcair was well within both his rights and responsibilities to do so.

"Mr. Speaker, the Prime Minister has failed to answer clear **questions** about his ill-defined military deployment in Iraq," Mulcair said by way of preamble. "Yesterday, Conservatives refused, once again, to answer in this House, but the member for Selkirk-Interlake stated on CPAC that the mission will end on Oct. 4. Will the Conservative government confirm that the 30-day Canadian commitment in Iraq will indeed end on Oct. 4?"

Even the most devoted Conservative partisan would likely have a hard time arguing against the relevance of this **question**. Even if some argument could be mounted for not answering that **question**—"operational security," or some such—we might all agree that standing and stating that argument would be the least we might expect from our democratically appointed government.

To respond for said government stood Paul Calandra, parliamentary secretary to the Prime Minister.

This was already not ideal.

Calandra might know a thing or two about the responsible management of a pizza shop, and he does serve as the Prime Minister's parliamentary secretary, but he has only slightly more statutory responsibility for the mission in Iraq than, say, I do. He is not the Prime Minister, nor the defence minister, nor the foreign affairs minister, nor even a member of the cabinet. He does have some responsibility for representing the Prime Minister as assigned, but this is only so useful as he is provided with useful information and empowered to provide it.

In the case of Calandra, it would quickly become apparent that he either had nothing useful to offer on the topic or was not so empowered.

"Mr. Speaker," the parliamentary secretary said in response, "there is a great deal of confusion with respect to the NDP position on Israel."

For all the theoretical intents and purposes of this particular moment in the daily democratic life of our country, he might as well have stood and told the Speaker of his grocery list or read aloud from the collected works of Edgar Allan Poe. He might've stood and made farting noises with his left hand and his right armpit. Indeed, that might've at least entertained the kids watching at home.

Instead, he went on about what some employee of the NDP had written about Israel, apparently in a post on Facebook.

You might not think this to be a matter of such importance that it need be raised at the first opportunity in **question** period, but then, obviously, you would be one of those people who does not understand how politics works.

Aaron Wherry, Today in Demonstrating Contempt for Parliament (Maclean's)

THEY CALL IT **QUESTION** PERIOD, NOT FUNDAMENTALS OF HUMAN DIGNITY PERIOD

Stephen Harper has been Prime Minister for not quite nine years and, by now, everybody knows how these things work. You rise in Harper's Conservative party by demonstrating a willingness to debase, when asked, any notion of accuracy or relevance. That doesn't have to be your *primary function*—Jason Kenney often says things that are true and pertinent, and Finance Minister Joe Oliver, and Public Works Minister Diane Finley and many others. But raging non-sequitur idiocy must be part of your tool kit, along with other techniques, or you won't get far.

For a year, Pierre Poilievre, minister of state for democratic reform, answered every **question** from the NDP's Alexandre Boulerice, on any subject, by calling Boulerice a separatist. Oh, how we laughed. The two of them even joked about it at the Press Gallery dinner. There are cabinet ministers who made it to the big table, only after they demonstrated a sustained willingness to answer real **questions** with real baloney. Nor is the instinct new. More than a decade ago, I wrote a column calling Herb Gray "The Gray Fog" because it seemed funnier than calling him "the guy who never answers **questions** in QP," and folks wiped away a tear. Good ol' Herb.

To this cardinal virtue of successful governments—shamelessness—add Conservative innovations in the area of non-sequitur casting. Gone are the days when a Jane Stewart, human resources minister from 1999 to 2003, would get up, day after harrowing day, to take **questions** on a controversy in her area of ministerial responsibility. That simply gives trouble a face, the Conservatives tell themselves, so it's better for a minister in hot water to answer fewer **questions**, not more, while some all-purpose wet blanket—a Poilievre back in the day, a Paul Calandra this year—takes all incoming flak. Done right, it kills a story for television. "Tonight: Minister in hot water. Here's somebody you've never heard of, talking about it."

All of this requires that government MPs behave in artificial ways, but the House of Commons is an artificial place, and success there requires very specific rituals, as does success in, say, gamelan or sumo. If you're self-conscious, you can't execute the compulsory figures. You have to just go with it.

Paul Wells, Calandra: So That Happened (Maclean's)

WHAT'S THE BEST WAY TO DODGE A **QUESTION** DURING A PRESENTATION?

This **question** originally appeared on Quora, the best answer to any **question**. Ask a **question**, get a great answer. Learn from experts and access insider knowledge. You can follow Quora on Twitter, Facebook, and Google Plus.

Answer by Robert Frost, engineer and instructor at NASA:

Here's a little flowchart for how to handle **questions** during a presentation.

You're asking for a crafty way to dodge a **question**, but that really is one of the stupidest things a person can do. Audiences can see right through it. They will lose confidence in your qualification to be speaking to them, and they will lose respect for you. Don't do it.

As the presenter, you are in control of the presentation and responsible for ensuring the presentation gets completed as planned and that the audience gets what they needed. If the **question** is really getting outside of the objectives of the presentation, you should defer the **question** by saying you'll talk to the individual after the presentation so as to not take up the time of the rest of the audience because you know they don't need that answer.

But if the **question** is germane to the topic and of interest to the rest of the audience, the decision of what to do next comes down to whether you know the answer.

If you don't know the answer, say, "I don't know." Immediately follow that with: "But I can find out for you." Write down the **question**. At the end of the presentation, check back with the individual to ensure that the **question** you wrote down is what he or she wanted to know and that he or she still cares. (People often figure out by the end of the presentation that they really didn't need to know the answer to the **questions** they asked.)

A presenter who tries to bullshit his audience deserves to die a blistering death.

*Quora, What's the Best Way to Dodge a **Question** During a Presentation (Salon)*

Answerer knew. But he had to be asked the proper **questions** first. He pondered this limitation, gazing at the stars which were neither large nor small, but exactly the right size.

*Robert Sheckley, Ask a Foolish **Question***

Every now and then they'll drop a **question** into the mix which sounds like it could be a bit rude.

Who could forget the now-infamous Fanny Chmelar **question**—about a former alpine skier—which had Bradley laughing so much he couldn't speak.

In a celebrity episode of *The Chase* which aired at the weekend, we nearly had a repeat incident on our hands when Bradley tried his best not to laugh at a **question** he was asking Fern Britton.

And we all know Fern's a fan of an innuendo or two after her fun-filled antics with Philip Schofield on *This Morning*.

As soon as the **question** 'Cock shot and beaver are terms in what game?' came up on the screen, the audience, contestants, Chaser and Bradley had to stifle their giggles.

So immature. It's a perfectly innocent **question**, guys.

*Nicola Oakley, Bradley Walsh Struggles to Read Rude-Sounding **Question** on The Chase as He Fights Back Laughter (Daily Mirror)*

The race which built Answerer should have taken that into account, Answerer thought. They should have made some allowance for semantic nonsense, allowed him to attempt an unravelling.

Answerer contented himself with muttering the answers to himself.

*Robert Sheckley, Ask a Foolish **Question***

James said she wanted to use her time to "correct some of the misconceptions I've heard so far."

She then restated the government's positions on various aspects of the bill without asking anything of those present.

Payne picked up where James left off and almost asked a **question** when he wondered aloud to the witnesses "if you consider yourself to be a national security threat and if you understand the definition won't apply to you as long as you don't commit any of these terrorist activities?"

*James Fitz-Morris, Bill C-51 Committee Hears Monologues, But Few **Questions** (CBC News)*

exuscitatio

ex-us-ci-ta'-ti-o

from Gk. suscitare "to raise, rouse, awaken"

Stirring others by one's own vehement feeling (sometimes by means of a rhetorical **question**, and often for the sake of exciting anger).

Examples

Can I stand by and let the government trample on my rights? Is that safe? Is that right? Can any of us afford to allow this wrong to continue?

Gideon Burton, Silva Rhetoricae (The Forest of Rhetoric)

To be fair to Bradley, he managed to get his words out—even though the audience were giggling like schoolchildren.

Contestant Fern gave him a little encouragement, telling him: "You can do it."

He replied: "I can," then, nodding towards the audience, added: "If that lot would shut up and give me half a chance."

*Nicola Oakley, Bradley Walsh Struggles to Read Rude-Sounding **Question** on The Chase as He Fights Back Laughter (Daily Mirror)*

Under committee rules for these sessions, government MPs are afforded half of the estimated time for **questions**—divided into two seven-minute segments.

The exercise is designed and meant to have a small number of MPs with knowledge of the subject matter hear expert testimony on the nuances and potential lapses of a particular piece of proposed legislation.

They then report back to the House of Commons with suggestions as to how to improve the bill.

*James Fitz-Morris, Bill C-51 Committee Hears Monologues, But Few **Questions** (CBC News)*

"We can't even ask a valid **question**?" Morran asked. "I don't believe that. We must know some basics." He turned to Answerer. "What is death?"

"I cannot explain an anthropomorphism."

"Death an anthropomorphism!" Morran said, and Lingman turned quickly. "Now we're getting somewhere!"

"Are anthropomorphisms unreal?" he asked.

"Anthropomorphisms may be classified, tentatively, as, A, false truths, or B, partial truths in terms of a partial situation."

"Which is applicable here?"

Robert Sheckley, Ask a Foolish **Question**

Kory Teneycke: Well I'm not going to make policy announcements or platform announcements today. But uh, it's a good **question**.

Tom Clark: So might you have something to say about this later on?

Kory Teneycke: We might. We might not.

Global News, Full Interview: Conservative Spokesman Defends Use of ISIS Video in Attack Ad

That was the closest they got. Morran was unable to draw any more from Answerer. For hours the two men tried, but truth was slipping farther and farther away.

"It's maddening," Morran said, after a while. "This thing has the answer to the whole universe, and he can't tell us unless we ask the right **question**. But how are we supposed to know the right **question**?"

Lingman sat down on the ground, leaning against a stone wall. He closed his eyes.

"Savages, that's what we are," Morran said, pacing up and down in front of Answerer. "Imagine a bushman walking up to a physicist and asking him why he can't shoot his arrow into the sun. The scientist can explain it only in his own terms. What would happen?"

"The scientist wouldn't even attempt it," Lingman said, in a dim voice; "he would know the limitations of the **questioner**."

"It's fine," Morran said angrily. "How do you explain the earth's rotation to a bushman? Or better, how do you explain relativity to him—maintaining scientific rigor in your explanation at all times, of course."

Lingman, eyes closed, didn't answer.

Robert Sheckley, Ask a Foolish **Question**

Fern was on his side, though, saying: "You can do it, you can!"

He totally couldn't, though. Isn't Bradley's laughing face the best? He looks like he's trying to squeeze the laugh out . . .

The answer options were even weirder—backgammon, ker-plunk and twister. You definitely don't want any cock shot or beaver moves when you're playing twister!

Although, to be honest, I wouldn't want a cock shot coming up against me in back-gammon either.

Laura Hamilton, Bradley Walsh Struggles With 'Cock' Shot **Question** *on 'The Chase' (ladbible.com)*

And so on. Harper initially looked at me, then shuffled off to glad-hand. Staffers nervously looked at me. I think one made a beeline for me, but another staffer stopped her. Security glared at me. One supporter turned around, and said something encouraging about how he wanted Harper to answer more **questions,** too.

Justin Ling, If We Want to Ask Stephen Harper **Questions***, We Have to Give His Party $78,000 (Vice)*

MORE:

Video Canada Election Canada Election 2015 Federal Election Election 2015 Stephen Harper Stephen Harper **Question** Stephen Harper Election **Questions** Canada Next Election Terry Milewski Mulcair **Questions** Harper **Question** Limit Mulcair Zero **Questions**

Zi-Ann Lum, Mulcair Doesn't Take Reporters' **Questions** *at Campaign Launch (The Huffington Post)*

It's not that the prime minister is taking no **questions**. He's taking five a day. But as I wrote last week, that's only from those journalists willing to pay $3,000 for the privilege.

Justin Ling, Five **Questions** *I Wanted to Ask Stephen Harper Last Night, But Couldn't (Vice)*

The House of Commons was sitting on June 11, 2009, but the Prime Minister was in Cambridge, Ont., standing before an audience of invited guests, with Mike Duffy acting as host of the town-hall-styled television event.

"Mr. Speaker, holding some kind of weird Mike Duffy live show instead of reporting to the House will not change the facts," Jack Layton lamented in the House, the late NDP leader begging to differ with the government's version. "The Prime Minister is holding some kind of gong show outside of the House of Commons instead of being here to answer **questions**."

To call it a gong show is likely to insult its careful staging. (Footage of anything other than Harper's speech seems not to be readily available, so I'm reliant on contemporaneous accounts.) The Prime Minister took no **questions** from reporters, instead taking apparently chosen **questions** from his selected audience—not quite the all-comers forum we might imagine our prime ministers daring to subject themselves to. The show cost $108,000 to produce. According to Duffy's diary, the Prime Minister's Office paid for his hotel room the night before.

Aaron Wherry, Our Duffy, Ourselves (Maclean's)

"Did you keep the receipt?"

He shook his head sagely, advice to a younger man. "To keep receipts, Herr Doktor? I give you this advice. To keep receipts is to invite **questions** about where you get your money. A receipt—it's like a spy in the pocket. Please."

John le Carré, The Secret Pilgrim

Being unable to provide information—not a bug, in the normal run of government QP management, but a highly attractive feature—Calandra had no alternative but to say something to annoy his **questioner**.

Paul Wells, Calandra: So That Happened (Maclean's)

'**Questions**?'

None apparently. The news seemed to have taken the wind out of everybody's sails. Even Mildren, who had had it since last night, could find nothing better to do than scratch an itch on the tip of his nose.

John le Carré, The Constant Gardener

Speaking from Vancouver, Justin Trudeau responded to the commotion over the number of **questions** his rivals allowed from media.

"Unlike the other guys, I tend to take a lot of **questions**," he said.

The Liberal leader stopped taking **questions** after reporters had run out of things to ask him.

Earlier, Stephen Harper officially marked the start of what will be the longest election campaign in recent Canadian history by taking **questions** from five journalists.

The Conservative leader plans to stick to that limit of five **questions** a day as he criss-crosses the country.

If Harper does stick to the rule for the whole campaign, Canadians can expect him to answer a total of 395 **questions** in the next 11 weeks.

*Zi-Ann Lum, Mulcair Doesn't Take Reporters' **Questions** at Campaign Launch (The Huffington Post)*

Local reporters, on the other hand, have their **questions** vetted to ensure they're "local" enough. Local reporters are not permitted to ask national **questions**. Teneycke vets their **questions**.

*Justin Ling, If We Want to Ask Stephen Harper **Questions**, We Have to Give His Party $78,000 (Vice)*

"We're bushmen. But the gap is much greater here. Worm and super-man, perhaps. The worm desires to know the nature of dirt, and why there's so much of it. Oh, well."

"Shall we go, sir?" Morran asked.

*Robert Sheckley, Ask a Foolish **Question***

"Go write a story about it."

That's the advice I was given by Conservative communications apparatchik Kory Teneycke when I complained about their arbitrary limit on who gets to ask **questions** of Stephen Harper.

"It's not arbitrary," he told me.

Judge for yourself.

*Justin Ling, If We Want to Ask Stephen Harper **Questions**, We Have to Give His Party $78,000 (Vice)*

Lek came to Answerer, striding swiftly from star to star. He lifted Answerer in his hand and looked at him.

"So you are Answerer," he said.

"Yes," Answerer said.

"Then tell me," Lek said, settling himself comfortably in a gap between the stars, "Tell me what I am."

"A partiality," Answerer said. "An indication."

"Come now," Lek muttered, his pride hurt. "You can do better than that. Now then. The purpose of my kind is to gather purple, and to build a mound of it. Can you tell me the real meaning of this?"

"Your **question** is without meaning," Answerer said. He knew what purple actually was, and what the mound was for. But the explanation was concealed in a greater explanation. Without this, Lek's **question** was inexplicable, and Lek had failed to ask the real **question**.

Lek asked other **questions**, and Answerer was unable to answer them. Lek viewed things through his specialized eyes, extracted a part of the truth and refused to see more. How to tell a blind man the sensation of green?

*Robert Sheckley, Ask a Foolish **Question***

His two problems were that (a) even if you're fond of Israel and worried about the NDP's position on that file, this really wasn't the time to be raising such **questions**; and (b) the **questioner** in, er, **question** was Tom Mulcair.

Paul Wells, Calandra: So That Happened (Maclean's)

Mulcair tried a second **question**.

"Mr. Speaker, I can understand the confusion. We are in the Middle East and we are under the "i"s, but we are talking about Iraq," he quipped. "It took over a week for the Prime Minister to answer a simple **question** about the number of troops involved in the Iraqi deployment. It now appears that Canadian soldiers may require visas approved by the Iraqi government. Since this military deployment is still ongoing and since it is set to conclude in 12 days, precisely how many Canadian soldiers are on the ground in Iraq today?"

In response, Calandra bravely attempted to convince everyone that what he had to say in response was in some way relevant to the **question** asked.

"Mr. Speaker, what does the leader of the Opposition not understand?" the parliamentary secretary asked rhetorically. "Our friends in Israel on the front lines, combatting terrorism."

Here, Calandra was in fact daring to revolutionize the very notion of relevancy.

A **question** asked about this country's military mission in response to an international terrorist threat is applicable to Israel, because Israel has also to deal with terrorist threats. If we allow ourselves—if we dare to be so bold—to expand our minds, as Calandra would have us do here, we might see whole new ways that so much of what we do and say is connected.

Mr. Speaker, the member asks about shortcomings in our agriculture policy. But what of the people in Ukraine, many of whom also enjoy eating vegetables? Thankfully, this government is standing beside Ukraine in its time of need.

Mr. Speaker, the member asks about the funding of our health care system. You know who requires a healthy lifestyle to survive and thrive in this world? Small business owners, whose taxes we have just cut.

Mr. Speaker, the Opposition asks about the census, but how can they trifle in such details when the spectre of climate change means there might eventually be very few people to count?

*Mr. Speaker, that **question** about what the Prime Minister knew about discussions with Mike Duffy reminds me of those pandas we recently scored from China—in that both the Prime Minister and the pandas are mammals.*

Aaron Wherry, *Today in Demonstrating Contempt for Parliament* (Maclean's)

It's well established now that the way you put a **question** often determines not only the answer you'll get, but the type of answer possible. So . . . a mechanical answerer, geared to produce the ultimate revelations in reference to anything you want to know, might have unsuspected limitations.

Robert Sheckley, *Ask a Foolish **Question***

Conservative MP Paul Calandra choked back tears while apologizing Friday for responding to NDP Leader Tom Mulcair's **questions** on Canada's mission in Iraq this week with an attack on the NDP position on Israel.

But CBC News has learned that Calandra was put up to the responses by a senior staffer in the Prime Minister's Office. Several Conservative MPs also told CBC they were furious as they listened to Calandra's answers in the House.

A teary Calandra rose after **question** period Friday to "unconditionally, unreservedly apologize to the House" for his glib non-answers earlier this week.

"Clearly, I allowed the passion and anger at something I read to get in the way of appropriately answering the **question** to leader of the Opposition," Calandra told the mostly empty Commons chamber.

"For that, I apologize to you and to this entire House, and to my constituents," he said.

Kady O'Malley and Evan Solomon, Paul Calandra Apologizes for Non-Answers as Sources Pin Blame on PMO (CBC News)

A HEALING QUESTION PROPOUNDED AND RESOLVED, UPON OCCASION OF THE LATE PUBLIC AND SEASONABLE CALL TO HUMILIATION, IN ORDER TO LOVE AND UNION AMONG THE HONEST PARTY, AND WITH A DESIRE TO APPLY BALM TO THE WOUND BEFORE IT BECOME INCURABLE.

The **question** propounded is, What possibility doth yet remain (all things considered) of reconciling and uniting the dissenting judgments of honest men within the three nations, who still pretend to agree in the spirit, justice, and reason of the same good cause, and what is the means to effect this?

Answ. If it be taken for granted (as, on the magistrate's part, from the ground inviting the people of England and Wales to a solemn day of fasting and humiliation, may not be despaired of) that all the dissenting parties agree still in the spirit and reason of the same righteous cause, the resolution seems very clear in the affirmative; arguing not only for a possibility, but a great probability hereof; nay, a necessity daily approaching nearer and nearer to compel it, if any or all of the dissenting parties intend or desire to be safe from the danger of the common enemy, who is not out of work, though at present much out of sight and observation.

Sir Henry Vane, A Healing Question (American Historical Documents, 1000–1904, Vol. XLIII)

He also went out of his way to exonerate the so-called "kids in short pants"—the catch-all derogatory term opposition members use to refer to senior political staff, particularly within the Prime Minister's Office—for his actions.

"I take full responsibility, and I apologize to the leader of the Opposition, and to all of my colleagues."

But sources tell CBC News that Calandra was handed material by Alykhan Velshi, director of issues management in the PMO, during the Conservatives' daily preparation for **question** period and was told to use it in his answer no matter what **question** was asked in the House.

Many Conservative MPs were upset when they heard Calandra give his answers in the House. At least one wrote an angry email to the PMO saying it was wrong and had to stop.

In an exclusive interview with CBC Radio's *The House* airing Saturday, a penitent Calandra again took the blame and repeated his assertion that the answers were his. Asked by host Evan Solomon about Velshi's role in the answers, Calandra denied that version of events and said he wasn't given anything to say.

In his apology Friday, Calandra, who serves as Prime Minister Stephen Harper's parliamentary secretary, did not promise that it won't happen again.

"I'm fairly certain there will be other opportunities in this House where I will be answering **questions** that you don't appreciate," he said. "I don't think this will be the last time that I get up and answer a **question** that doesn't effectively respond."

> *Kady O'Malley and Evan Solomon, Paul Calandra Apologizes for Non-Answers as Sources Pin Blame on PMO (CBC News)*

Answerer was built to last as long as was necessary—which was quite long, as some races judge time, and not long at all, according to others. But to Answerer, it was just long enough.

As to size, Answerer was large to some and small to others. He could be viewed as complex, although some believed that he was really very simple.

Answerer knew that he was as he should be. Above and beyond all else, he was The Answerer. He Knew.

Of the race that built him, the less said the better. They also Knew, and never said whether they found the knowledge pleasant.

They built Answerer as a service to less-sophisticated races, and departed in a unique manner. Where they went only Answerer knows.

Because Answerer knows everything.

Upon his planet, circling his sun, Answerer sat. Duration continued, long, as some judge duration, short as others judge it. But as it should be, to Answerer.

Within him were the Answers. He knew the nature of things, and why things are as they are, and what they are, and what it all means.

Answerer could answer anything, provided it was a legitimate **question**. And he wanted to! He was eager to!

How else should an Answerer be?

What else should an Answerer do?

So he waited for creatures to come and ask.

> *Robert Sheckley, Ask a Foolish* **Question**

I flipped an email to some Conservative staffers: Hey, I'm hoping to ask a **question**. Is that doable?

They said they'd look into it.

> *Justin Ling, If We Want to Ask Stephen Harper* **Questions**, *We Have to Give His Party $78,000 (Vice)*

—That's too bad, says Bloom. I wanted particularly. Perhaps only Mr Field is going. I couldn't phone. No. You're sure?

—Nannan's going too, says Joe. The league told him to ask a **question** tomorrow about the commissioner of police forbidding Irish games in the park. What do you think of that, citizen? *The Sluagh na h-Eireann.*

> *James Joyce, Ulysses*

OTTAWA—The Office of the Commissioner of Official Languages has received 14 complaints related to Prime Minister Justin Trudeau's choice of English or French when answering **questions** at recent town hall meetings.

Spokesman Nelson Kalil said Thursday that 11 complaints stem from an event on Tuesday in Sherbrooke, Que., where Trudeau angered some anglophones by insisting on answering English **questions** in French.

The others are related to a previous town hall gathering in Peterborough, Ont., where Trudeau responded in English to a French **question**.

On Wednesday he said that on reflection he maybe should have answered partly in English and partly in French at the Sherbrooke event.

Kalil said it could take three to six months for the office to investigate the complaints.

*Canadian Press, Trudeau's French Answers to English **Questions** Draw Language Complaints (Toronto Star)*

"At this point, Mr. Dye," Orcutt said, "I suppose you do have some **questions**."

"Lots of them," I said, "but only a few that won't keep for a while. First of all, the deadline of the first Tuesday in November means an election is coming up, right?"

"Right," Orcutt said.

"Since it's an off-year, that means a local election."

"Yes."

"Those who're paying your fee," I said. "Doctor Colfax and Phetwick the third. I assume that they want to throw the rascals out so that theirs will get in?"

"Precisely."

"And what you want me to do in the next two months is to make this town so corrupt that even the pimps will vote for reform?" I said.

"Most graphic, Mr. Dye," Orcutt said. "Most graphic indeed."

"You're not taking this on a contingency basis are you?"

Orcutt smiled. "I may be young, Mr. Dye, but I am not naive."

"No, I don't think you are. But I'm quite sure that you haven't collected your fee in advance."

"No."

"I've heard of deals like this," I said. "One that comes to mind happened in Germany."

"In Hamelin?" Orcutt said.

"That's right."

"They didn't want to pay off after the man got rid of the rats," he said.

"No. They didn't."

"So he piped their children out of town, I recall," he said.

"Everybody does. You may need something like a pipe."

"What do you suggest?"

I tapped my breast pocket that contained the Xeroxed list. "This list is missing a couple of names," I said.

There was always that about Orcutt. He never needed the simple diagram that came with the do-it-yourself kit. He just smiled again and even managed to put something into it other than nothing.

"You mean the names of Doctor Colfax and Mr. Phetwick?" he said.

Ross Thomas, The Fools in Town Are on Our Side

In debate a member must confine himself to the **question** before the assembly, and avoid personalities.

Henry M. Robert, Robert's Rules of Order Revised for Deliberative Assemblies

Tom Clark (Global News): Ah. Kay. I want to move on to something else that you've been involved with this week. Um and that is the latest online . . . ad, that you've got out there where you use um imagery from ISIS. And you use the ISIS anthem. How is that not in contravention of Bill C-51?

Kory Teneycke (Conservative spokesman): Well its uh very similar to what you do on the news every day here at Global when *[Tom cuts in]*

TC: Well we don't run the ISIS national anthem and we don't run *[Kory cuts in]*

KT: Uh, hey, I've seen images from ISIS videos on every newscast in this country and in other countries as well *[Tom cuts in]*

TC: Well that's news.

KT: Well, that's also part of the debate as to what is it that we're going to do about that issue. You know ISIS is a real threat, the activities that they're up to are barbaric in the extreme, they are uh very disturbing I think to all Canadians, and so *[Tom cuts in]*

TC: So why run their videos? Why run their songs?

KT: Well this is the choice. This is the choice between do we do something about this threat, or do we do nothing?

TC: No but why are you, why are you showing those videos and running their song?

KT: Because it's germane to the choice before us in this election.

TC: But how is it germane?

KT: I'm answering your **questions** if you want to let me answer it. It's germane because the choice is between one political party, the Conservative Party of Canada, that would uh continue our bombing mission to protect civilians and religious minorities in Syria and Iraq; and two other political parties, that would stop those efforts. So it's very central I think to the choice that will be before Canadians this election and therefore we're going to make that choice clear in the realest possible terms.

TC: You said you were going to answer the **question** and of course you didn't. In what way is the ISIS anthem and the ISIS video germane to a debate?

KT: Well because that's who the enemy is. That's who we're fighting.

TC: So how is that video and their song, germane to that discussion?

KT: That's who they are. That's who the enemy is.

TC: OK . . . Bill C-51 was brought in and promoted by your government as, among other things, to prevent people from putting online anything video that promotes terrorism and ISIS. Haven't you just done that?

KT: No.

TC: Why?

KT: What we're doing is no different than what you do on the news. Which is . . .

TC: But you're not news. You're there advertising.

KT: We're better than news, because we're truthful.

TC: I'm sorry, say that again?

KT: I said we're doing uh, uh, a . . .

TC: No what did you just say?

KT: I'm saying what we're doing is . . .

TC: You're better than us because you're truthful? Is that what you just said?

KT: We're putting forward the choice . . .

TC: No no. What did you just say?

KT: Well let me finish the thought . . .

TC: No you said, I just want you to repeat what you just said.

KT: I'm saying what we're doing is better that what we're talking about in terms it's the choice that will be before Canadians during the election campaign.

TC: But wait a second, you said you were better than news because you're truthful?

KT: It's, I think it's a very real choice, Tom. We're not going to step back from the very real choice that's in front of Canadians today, okay. This is a life and death matter for people who are living in that region, uh it is a poisonous ideology that is spreading around the world, it's motivating people to commit attacks not just in Canada but elsewhere around the world. It's very central to the choice that will be here this campaign. And it's a very, I think, interesting issue, uh in terms of how you have one party, on one side of that, you know, the decision to take action directly, you know bombing missions etc., uh and two other parties that say they would stop doing that. So I think it is absolutely, it is a polarizing issue for some people. We're going to talk about it in very real, very truthful, very frank terms.

Global News, Full Interview: Conservative Spokesman Defends Use of ISIS Video in Attack Ad

I'm not sure what Conservative campaign spokesman Kory Teneycke thinks the "spoke" part of his job description is all about, but judging from his reaction this week when Global News' Tom Clark asked him about a recent Conservative campaign ad, I can only assume he has spent a lot of time learning to fix bikes.

He certainly doesn't seem to view speaking about the Conservative campaign as something he's obliged to do.

Mr. Teneycke took umbrage when asked about his party's recent attack ad—an ad that features Islamic State propaganda footage accompanied by an IS anthem—and not a small amount of umbrage, either. Mr. Teneycke took so much umbrage at Mr. Clark's **questions** about whether an ad that showcases terrorist propaganda might contravene the government's own freshly minted Bill C-51—a law that prohibits the promotion of terrorist propaganda—it was like he took umbrage, left the studio, rented a U-Haul, came back and carted away a whole lot more umbrage.

Word is, Mr. Teneycke was unhappy that he hadn't been given the interview **questions** in advance. Perhaps he'd have preferred a take-home test, in which case he could have deleted his embarrassing line: "We're better than the news, we're truthful."

That line was spoken in the tone of a man who cannot come up with one good reason why his party produced an ad that's approximately one-third grisly terrorist propaganda—the kind of thing that, as Mr. Clark made clear, most news organizations are very circumspect about showing—and two-thirds obviously misleadingly edited footage of their rather photogenic opponent.

"Whose idea was that?" I hear you cry. "Can we have them lead the country?"

The flustered Mr. Teneycke certainly tried to delete that line, doing everything but frantically pressing Mr. Clark's nose over and over in the desperate hope it would turn out to be a magical nasal backspace key. It was just one of many awkward moments for the Conservative campaign spokesman.

"Will you be using more terrorist video as the campaign goes on?" pressed Mr. Clark finally.

"Uh, well, wait and see," said Mr. Teneycke, who said "uh" so many times in that interview, it was like Global had finally scored a long-sought interview with a hawkish walrus in a suit.

*Tabatha Southey, Kory Teneycke and Me—**Questions** for a Reluctant Tory Campaign Spokesman (The Globe and Mail)*

Mr Cowe Conacre (Multifarnham. Nat.): Arising out of the **question** of my honourable friend, the member for Shillelagh, may I ask the right honourable gentleman whether the government has issued orders that these animals shall be slaughtered though no medical evidence is forthcoming as to their pathological condition?

Mr Allfours (Tamoshant. Con.): Honourable members are already in possession of the evidence produced before a committee of the whole house. I feel I cannot usefully add anything to that. The answer to the honourable member's **question** is in the affirmative.

Mr Orelli O'Reilly (Montenotte. Nat.): Have similar orders been issued for the slaughter of human animals who dare to play Irish games in the Phoenix park?

Mr Allfours: The answer is in the negative.

Mr Cowe Conacre: Has the right honourable gentleman's famous Mitchelstown telegram inspired the policy of gentlemen on the Treasury bench? (O! O!)

Mr Allfours: I must have notice of that **question**.

Mr Staylewit (Buncombe. Ind.): Don't hesitate to shoot.

(Ironical opposition cheers.)

The speaker: Order! Order!

(The house rises. Cheers.)

James Joyce, Ulysses

I'm no Tom Clark, who let slide nothing Mr. Teneycke said—entertain for a moment the vision of one deft pair of hands and thousands of talking-point salmon swimming upstream in hopes of spawning with voters. What I've done, having a weakness for walruses, is concede to Mr. Teneycke's wishes—and more. Not only am I providing him with the **questions** for our interview, I'm giving him all the right answers as well. So here you go, Kory, it's on:

Me: How are you enjoying unemployment?

You: I am, surprisingly, still the Conservative campaign spokesman. Uh, make of that what you will.

Me: Do you believe that Canada's social safety net should be dismantled so that people like you will be motivated to work harder and answer **questions** on TV in a less disastrous manner?

You: Uh, in the future I plan on dedicating myself to trying to get through an eight and half minute interview without suggesting that my political party—or any political party—is more truthful than all journalists ever, because that never ends well.

Me: Do you think it's prudent to effectively co-produce a campaign ad with a murderous terrorist organization?

You: No. That's a terrible idea. A cynical, opportunistic, abhorrent idea. No human being with even a sliver of conscience would, uh, ever seriously entertain such a notion.

Me: Is it ever a good idea to use footage of people about to be killed—in unspeakably barbaric ways—in just the manner the people who killed those people intended it to be used? Thus giving these killers incentive to kill and film more deaths? Do you understand anything about how supply and demand and evil works? Why do you think they keep making *Fast and Furious* movies?

You: No. That's never a good idea—and it's not like I saw them in the theatre.

Me: So, Islamic State. That was an interesting choice. Are there any other homicidal auteurs you guys plan on working with in the future?

You: No. Film distribution's always been an issue in Canada, and government could be more effective in this area. However, we shouldn't prioritize distributing the work of killers over literally anything else. Even if it's just some boring crap about people being sad at a cottage.

Me: IS. Huh. Wow. Leni Riefenstahl wasn't available, I guess.

You: Sorry, Canada.

Me: You do know the little girl in Lyndon Johnson's famous "Daisy Girl" campaign ad wasn't actually killed by a nuclear bomb, don't you?

You: Uh.

Me: Google it. Your party, the one at the forefront of making snuff campaign ads, is also intent on constructing the 24-metre-tall Mother Canada monument in Cape Breton. Is it prudent, in these—as your ads with a lower body-count like to remind us—uncertain economic times, and with the nation already embroiled in a struggle against IS, to simultaneously launch a war on good taste? Why Mother Canada, Kory, why?

You: [Sorry, Kory, we don't have an answer for you on this one. We sent 16 of our best people to Georgian Bay on a retreat to hammer this one out—nothing. We cannot begin to explain that monument. Best we can come up with is it's Canada's National Butter Sculpture and will at least come down when the Royal Winter Fair ends. I would just go with "Uh."]

Me: A final **question**: Do you think it's okay to use terrorist-produced images if the man you work for reeeeeeaaaaaallllly wants to be re-elected prime minister yet is struggling with an approval rating that had dropped soooooooooo low that, if he were a tomato plant, his party would have to bring him inside?

You: Nooooooooooooooooooooo.

Me: So, will you be using more terrorist video as the campaign goes on?

You: What in God's name have I done with my life that I can legitimately be asked this **question**?

[Now, search soul deeply.]

*Tabatha Southey, Kory Teneycke and Me—**Questions** for a Reluctant Tory Campaign Spokesman (The Globe and Mail)*

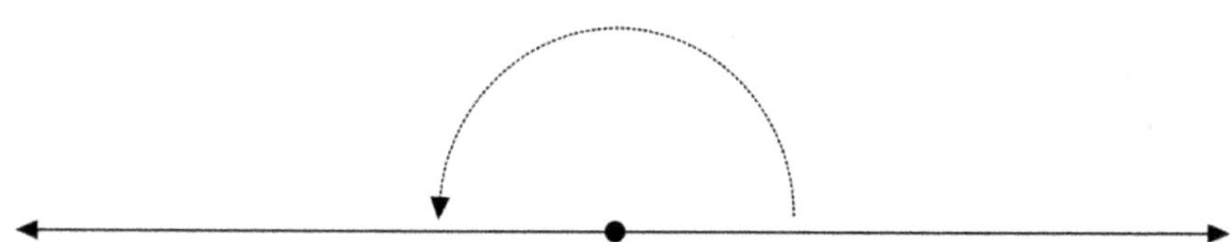

Diagram for **Question** 1B of the Measuring Rotation Lesson

Adrignola/Wikimedia Commons

Before the Previous Question Is Exhausted

As many as are in favor, etc.

29. The Previous **Question**[18] takes precedence of all subsidiary[12] motions except to lay on the table, and yields to privileged[14] and incidental[13] motions, and to the motion to lay on the table. It is undebatable, and cannot be amended or have any other subsidiary motion applied to it. The effect of an amendment may be obtained by calling for, or moving, the previous **question** on a different set of the pending **questions** (which must be consecutive and include the immediately pending **question**), in which case the vote is taken first on the motion which orders the previous **question** on the largest number of **questions**. It may be applied to any debatable or amendable motion or motions, and if unqualified it applies only to the immediately pending motion. It may be qualified so as to apply to a series of pending **questions**, or to a consecutive part of a series beginning with the immediately pending **question**. It requires a two-thirds vote for its adoption. After the previous **question** has been ordered, up to the time of taking the last vote under it, the **questions** that have not been voted on may be laid on the table, but can have no other subsidiary motions applied to them. An appeal made after the previous **question** has been demanded or ordered and before its exhaustion, is undebatable. The previous **question**, before any vote has been taken under it, may be reconsidered, but not after its partial execution. As no one would vote to reconsider the vote ordering the previous **question** who was not opposed to the previous **question**, it follows that if the motion to reconsider prevails, it will be impossible to secure a two-thirds vote for the previous **question**, and, therefore, if it is voted to reconsider the previous **question** it is considered as rejecting that **question** and placing the business as it was before the previous **question** was moved. If a vote taken under the previous **question** is reconsidered before the previous **question** is exhausted, there can be no debate or amendment of the proposition; but if the reconsideration is after the previous **question** is exhausted, then the motion to reconsider, as well as the **question** to be reconsidered, is divested of the previous **question** and is debatable. If lost, the previous **question** may be renewed after sufficient progress in debate to make it a new **question**.

The *Form* of this motion is, "I move [or demand, or call for] the previous **question** on [here specify the motions on which it is desired to be ordered]." As it cannot be debated or amended, it must be voted on immediately. The form of putting the **question**[19] is, "The previous **question** is moved [or demanded, or called for] on [specify the motions on which the previous **question** is demanded]. As many as are in favor of ordering the previous **question** on [repeat the motions] will rise." When they are seated he continues, "Those opposed will rise. There being two-thirds in favor of the motion, the affirmative has it and the previous **question** is ordered on [repeat the motions upon which it is ordered]. The **question** is [or recurs] on [state the immediately pending **question**]. As many as are in favor," etc. If the previous **question** is ordered the chair immediately proceeds to put to vote the **questions** on which it was ordered until all the votes are taken, or there is an affirmative vote on postponing definitely or indefinitely, or committing, either of which exhausts the previous **question**. If there can be the slightest doubt as to the vote the chair should take it again immediately, counting each side. If less than two-thirds vote in the affirmative, the chair announces the vote thus: "There not being two-thirds in favor of the motion, the negative has it and the motion is lost. The **question** is on," etc., the chair stating the **question** on the immediately pending **question**, which is again open to debate and amendment, the same as if the previous **question** had not been demanded.

The **question** may be put in a form similar to this: "The previous **question** has been moved on the motion to commit and its amendment. As many as are in favor of now putting the **question** on the motion to commit and its amendment will rise; those opposed will rise. There being two-thirds in favor of the motion, the debate is closed on the motion to commit and its amendment, and the **question** is on the amendment," etc. While this form is allowable, yet it is better to conform to the regular parliamentary form as given above.

The *Object* of the previous **question** is to bring the assembly at once to a vote on the immediately pending **question** and on such other pending **questions** as may be specified in the demand. It is the proper motion to use for this purpose, whether the object is to adopt or to kill the proposition on which it is ordered, without further debate or motions to amend.

The *Effect*[20] of ordering the previous **question** is to close debate immediately, to prevent the moving of amendments or any other subsidiary motions except to lay on the table, and to bring the assembly at once to a vote on the immediately pending **question**, and such other pending **questions** as were specified in the demand, or motion. If the previous **question** is ordered on more than one **question**, then its effect extends to those **questions** and is not exhausted until they are voted on, or they are disposed of as shown below under exhaustion of the previous **question**. If the previous **question** is voted down, the discussion continues as if this motion had not been made. The effect of the previous **question** does not extend beyond the session in which it was adopted. Should any of the **questions** upon which it was ordered come before the assembly at a future session they are divested of the previous **question** and are open to debate and amendment.

The previous **question** is *Exhausted* during the session as follows:

(1) When the previous **question** is unqualified, its effect terminates as soon as the vote is taken on the immediately pending **question**.

(2) If the previous **question** is ordered on more than one of the pending **questions** its effect is not exhausted until all of the **questions** upon which it has been ordered have been voted on, or else the effect of those that have been voted on has been to commit the main **question**, or to postpone it definitely or indefinitely.

If, before the exhaustion of the previous **question**, the **questions** on which it has been ordered that have not been voted on are laid on the table, the previous **question** is not exhausted thereby, so that when they are taken from the table during the same session, they are still under the previous **question** and cannot be debated or amended or have any other subsidiary motion applied to them.

Henry M. Robert, Robert's Rules of Order Revised for Deliberative Assemblies

The commander of the Afghan Local Police listens to a **question** while participating
of a key leaders engagement with local Afghan elders in the Shabadeen village,
Sarobi district, Paktika province, Afghanistan, Feb. 8, 2012.

Photo by Spc. David Barnes / U.S. Army (defenseimagery.mil)

What Kind of **Questions?**

So much of how life feels lies in the phrasing

THE ASSEMBLY has unwittingly been drawn far from the actual **question**.

Maximilien Marie Isidore Robespierre, Against Granting the King a Trial

Question Proposed by the Academy of Dijon

What is the Origin of the Inequality Among Mankind; and whether such Inequality is authorized by the Law of Nature?

Jean Jacques Rousseau, On the Inequality Among Mankind

In Stephen Harper's world, one does not publicly ask why.

To seek root causes is a sign of weakness.

To launch an inquiry, to bring decision-makers and experts together, is seen as an invitation for opponents to strike or a forum to extort money from the federal government or a waste of time when talk turns his black-and-white world grey.

So, while Harper endures well-deserved criticism for his refusal to consider a national inquiry into murdered and missing aboriginal women in this country, those slinging that criticism can hardly be surprised.

There is no nuance in the prime minister's world. There are bad guys and good guys and there is no public **questioning** about how we got where we are.

A crime is a crime, it is to be solved and the perpetrator brought to justice. To concede a "sociological phenomenon" is to invite all manner of inconvenience for his government.

Tim Harper, For Stephen Harper, Governing Means Never Asking Why (The Toronto Star)

He then desired to know what arts were practised in electing those whom I called commoners; whether a stranger, with a strong purse, might not influence the vulgar voters to choose him before their own landlord, or the most considerable gentleman in the neighborhood? How it came to pass that people were so violently bent upon getting into this assembly, which I allowed to be a great trouble and expense, often to the ruin of their families, without any salary or pension: because this appeared such an exalted strain of virtue and public spirit, that his majesty seemed to doubt it might possibly not be always sincere; and he desired to know whether such zealous gentlemen could have any views of refunding themselves for the charges and trouble they were at, by sacrificing the public good to the designs of a weak and vicious prince, in conjunction with a corrupted ministry? He multiplied his **questions**, and sifted me thoroughly upon every part of this head, proposing numberless inquiries and objections, which I think it not prudent or convenient to repeat.

Jonathan Swift, Gulliver's Travels Into Several Remote Regions of the World

And yet the **question** is a real one,

And not for me alone, though certainly for me.
For even if, as Wittgenstein once claimed,
That while the facts may stay the same

And what is true of one is true of both,
The happy and unhappy man inhabit different worlds,
One still would want to know which world this is,
And how that other one could seem so close.

So much of how life feels lies in the phrasing,
In the way a thought starts, then turns back upon itself
Until its **question** hangs unanswered in the breeze.

John Koethe, North Point North

"But what did happen at Megeve?"

She put this **question** so urgently that for the first time I felt discouraged, and even more than that, desperate, the kind of despair that overwhelms you when you realize that in spite of your efforts, your good qualities, all your goodwill, you are running into an insurmountable obstacle.

"I'll tell you about it . . . Another day . . ."

There must have been something distraught in my voice or my expression, because she squeezed my arm as though to console me and said:

"Forgive me asking you indiscreet **questions** . . . But . . ."

Patrick Modiano, Missing Person

Who knew that a brief stay in a closet could have such lasting political consequences?

I'm obliged to pose this **question** after Stephen Harper made a "surprise" visit (there was, of course, nothing surprising about it) to Iraq last weekend, with select members of the parliamentary press gallery in tow.

Andrew Mitrovica, What the Hell Was Harper Doing in Iraq Anyway

"**Questions**? What kind of **questions**?" He set his feet on the bike pedals, ready to bolt.

"Don't worry," I said, pulling three twenties from my wallet. "A couple of **questions** and you're gone."

He squinted at me and pulled away. "You ain't into little boys, is you?"

"No, I prefer girls," I said. "All grown up."

"Okay then."

Andrew Cotto, Outerborough Blues: A Brooklyn Mystery

The lives some people lived! And he was such a nice pink-cheeked boy to look at. "Reads detectives and westerns. Sports: hockey, softball, horse-shoe-pitching. Plays tonette." Some kind of a whistle, wasnt it? Ah, here was a clue: "Cannot swim. **Questioned** if he had a fear of water, soldier hesitated and replied: 'I'm not really scared of it so long as I know it aint deeper than I am. But I'd just as soon not go in the navy.'

Earle Birney, Turvey: A Military Picaresque

I respond with a **question** of my own: "Have you ever heard of furries?"

My opportunity to see one in the "flesh" arrived in the form of Furnal Equinox, the largest furry convention in Canada (with 910 attendees). I attended in hopes of learning as much as I could about "the fandom" and uncovering the answers most sexologists

An Afghan boy stands amid U.S. Army scouts from Headquarters and Headquarters Company, 3rd Battalion, 509th Infantry Regiment, Task Force Spartan as they pull security in his neighborhood in the city of Gardez, Feb. 16, 2012. The soldiers were stopped while Afghan Uniformed Police **questioned** several men who were caught smoking hashish during a presence patrol around the city.

Photo by Spc. Ken Soar / U.S. Army (defenseimagery.mil)

are dying to know: Is this a genuine paraphilia? Or are the media exaggerating? Is it even about sex at all?

Debra W. Soh, *A Peek Inside a Furry Convention*

And who, I ask, can know that he understands anything, unless he do first understand it? In other words, who can know that he is sure of a thing, unless he be first sure of that thing?

Benedict de Spinoza, *Ethics, Part 2*

Do you need a special room? Do you need a special pen? Do you chant a special chant? Do you write on napkins in the middle of dinner parties? Do you walk a mile, read, then write? Do you practice yoga before your writing hour? Do you wake up early? Do you stay up late? Do you light a candle? Would you write after a particularly comical date? What's the magic ingredient, all these **questions** ask, that makes a poet write a poem?

Camille Dungy, **Question** *and Answer: The Top Five*

Let N(Q) be the number of **questions** obtained from **FAQ** data, let N(Q+) be the number of **questions** produced by ten expert persons, let N(A) be the number of answers, let AVE(N(A)/N(Q)) be the average number of answers to one **question**, let MIN(N(A)/N(Q)) be the minimum number of answers to one **question**, and let MAX(N(A)/N(Q)) be the maximum number of answers to one **question**. Table 1 shows information about the **FAQ** data.

Jun Harada, Masao Fuketa, El-Sayed Atlam, Toru Sumitomo, Wataru Hiraishi and Jun-ichi Aoe, *Estimation of **FAQ** Knowledge Bases by Introducing Measurements (Knowledge-Based Intelligent Information and Engineering Systems)*

p. 391–7
    Appealing to the senses with metaphors and similes like those in answer explanations 6, the answer must relate to the type of descriptive language used.
    B

Henry Davis, *Explanations for the Official SAT Study Guide **Questions**: Detailed Explanations for the Answers for Every **Question***

So, the book is intended for anyone who wants to write survey **questions**, as well as all those who want to use the results from a survey; neither statistical issues nor social science jargon should get in the way of any reasonably well-educated person being able to read and appreciate the messages herein.

Floyd J. Fowler, *Improving Survey **Questions**: Design and Evaluation*

"Also, don't you think that it might be necessary to arouse her imagination?"
    "In what way? How?" said Bovary.
    "Ah, that's the **question**! That's definitively the **question**: 'That is the **question**!'—as I recently read in a newspaper."
    But Emma, awaking, cried out, "And the letter? And the letter?"

Gustave Flaubert, *Madame Bovary*

And these varied with tenses, *present, past, future,* and conjugated with the verb *see,*—or with these **questions** added to them;—*Is it? Was it? Will it be? Would it be? May it be? Might it be?* And these again put negatively, *Is it not? Was it not? Ought it not?*—Or affirmatively,—*It is; It was; It ought to be.* Or chronologically,—*Has it been always? Lately?*

How long ago?—Or hypothetically,—*If it was? If it was not?* What would follow?—If the *French* should beat the *English*? If the *Sun* go out of the *Zodiac*?

Laurence Sterne, *The Life and Opinions of Tristram Shandy, Gentleman*

p. 407–2

This sentence makes sense with the briefest construction eliminates unnecessary were words and keeps the active voice.

C

Henry Davis, *Explanations for the Official SAT Study Guide **Questions**: Detailed Explanations for the Answers for Every **Question***

... and the **question** may arise whether our results are seriously wrong from this cause. This **question** can best be solved by yet another method of estimating the average distance of certain classes of stars.

Simon Newcomb, *The Extent of the Universe*

A commitment-averse man frantically hits the dating scene after his girlfriend starts pressuring him to pop the **question**.

Walt Becker (director), Buying the Cow (trailer), 2002 (imdb.com)

Value **Questions** Humanists Have Raised

*Of course, Mr B. proceeded to stipulate, you must look at
both sides of the **question***

"What's the **question**?"

"There are two."

"Go ahead." Rhapsody folded her arms.

Elizabeth Haydon, Prophecy: Child of Earth

What cometh? What now is?

*Harvey Newcomb, Newcomb's First **Question** Book*

"We'll find out," Morran murmured. He helped the old man unstrap himself. "We're going to find the Answerer!"

Lingman nodded at his young partner. They had been reassuring themselves for years. Originally it had been Lingman's project. Then Morran, graduating from Cal Tech, had joined him. Together they had traced the rumors across the solar system. The legends of an ancient humanoid race who had known the answer to all things, and who had built Answerer and departed.

"Think of it," Morran said. "The answer to everything!" A physicist, Morran had many **questions** to ask Answerer. The expanding universe; the binding force of atomic nuclei; novae and supernovae; planetary formation; red shift, relativity and a thousand others.

"Yes," Lingman said. He pulled himself to the vision plate and looked out on the bleak prairie of the illusory sub-space. He was a biologist and an old man. He had two **questions**.

What is life?

What is death?

*Robert Sheckley, Ask a Foolish **Question***

"Mr. Baxter, I think?" said the latter. He had laid aside his dripping umbrella and was unbuttoning overcoat and coat to reach an inner pocket. "You hardly remember me, I suppose? Mr. Carlyle—two years ago I took up a case for you—"

"To be sure. Mr. Carlyle, the private detective—"

"Inquiry agent," corrected Mr. Carlyle precisely.

"Well," smiled Mr. Baxter, "for that matter I am a coin dealer and not an antiquarian or a numismatist. Is there anything in that way that I can do for you?"

"Yes," replied his visitor; "it is my turn to consult you." He had taken a small washleather bag from the inner pocket and now turned something carefully out upon the counter. "What can you tell me about that?"

The dealer gave the coin a moment's scrutiny.

"There is no **question** about this," he replied. "It is a Sicilian tetradrachm of Dionysius."

"Yes, I know that—I have it on the label out of the cabinet. I can tell you further that it's supposed to be one that Lord Seastoke gave two hundred and fifty pounds for at the Brice sale in '94."

"It seems to me that you can tell me more about it than I can tell you," remarked Mr. Baxter. "What is it that you really want to know?"

> Ernest Bramah, *The Coin of Dionysius (Max Carrados: A Collection of Classic Detective Stories)*

In the beginning, before the Republic, Rome was ruled by kings. About one of these, a haughty tyrant by the name of Tarquin, an eerie tale was told. Once, in his palace, an old woman came calling on him. In her arms she carried nine books. When she offered these to Tarquin he laughed in her face, so fabulous was the price she was demanding. The old woman, making no attempt to bargain, turned and left without a word. She burned three of the books and then, reappearing before the king, offered him the remaining volumes, still at the same price as before. A second time, although with less self-assurance now, the king refused, and a second time the old woman turned and left. By now Tarquin had grown nervous of what he might be turning down, and so when the mysterious crone reappeared, this time holding only three books, he hurriedly bought them, even though he had to pay the price originally demanded for all nine. Taking her money, the old woman then vanished, never to be seen again.

Who had she been? Her books proved to contain prophecies of such potency that the Romans soon realized that only one woman could possibly have been their author— the Sibyl. Yet this was an identification that only begged further **questions**, for the legends told of the Sibyl were strange and puzzling. On the presumption that she had foretold the Trojan War, men debated whether she was a compound of ten prophetesses, or immortal, or destined to live a thousand years. Some—the more sophisticated—even wondered whether she existed at all. In fact, only two things could be asserted with any real confidence—that her books, inscribed with spidery and antique Greek, certainly existed, and that within them could be read the pattern of events that were to come. The Romans, thanks to Tarquin's belated eye for a bargain, found themselves with a window to the future of the world.

> Tom Holland, *Rubicon: The Last Years of the Roman Republic*

"What is it—women, drugs, or money?" I ask as I walk to the kitchen and pour myself some gin. I don't offer James a glass. It's the expensive variety and I'm not into sharing my spoils. He drinks too much already, anyway.

James moves the boxes with books I have on the couch, takes off his jacket, and sits down. I can see the jacket has holes all over the place. Much good it must do him on a rainy day, which is every day in this part of the country.

'You really read all of these?" he asks.

"Don't say some stupid shit you know the answer to just to deflect my **question**," I tell him, "cause yeah, I read, and not the e-reader thingy. Books are supposed to be artifacts, not just text on a screen, ya know."

He doesn't reply.

"So it's all three," I say.

> Silvia Moreno-Garcia, *Sun Moon Stars Rain*

For in early times the Hellenes and the barbarians of the coast and islands, as communication by sea became more common, were tempted to turn pirates, under the conduct of their most powerful men; the motives being to serve their own cupidity and to support the needy. They would fall upon a town unprotected by walls, and consisting of a mere collection of villages, and would plunder it; indeed, this came to be the main source of their livelihood, no disgrace being yet attached to such an achievement, but even some glory. An illustration of this is furnished by the honour with which some of the inhabitants of the continent still regard a successful marauder, and by the **question** we find the old poets everywhere representing the people as asking of voyagers "Are they pirates?" as if those who are asked the **question** would have no idea of disclaiming the imputation, or their interrogators of reproaching them for it. The same rapine prevailed also by land.

Thucydides, The History of the Peloponnesian War

He nodded. "Maybe. Still, if you don't die soon, you'll die one day. And then the same **question** will arise. How will you face that terrible, final hour?"

Albert Camus, The Stranger

"It is not my place," Sweet said, good for him, "to go into the moral **questions** here. Surely they are complex. Nor can any of us who are working in this field make an absolute promise of success. But think of it this way: what does a corpse have to lose? As things stand, he is dead. If he is frozen and never revived in the future, he has not lost anything."

Thomas Berger, Vital Parts

"I am not going anywhere," Natasha replied when this was proposed to her. "Do please just leave me alone!" And she ran out of the room, with difficulty refraining from tears of vexation and irritation rather than of sorrow.

After she felt herself deserted by Princess Mary and alone in her grief, Natasha spent most of the time in her room by herself, sitting huddled up feet and all in the corner of the sofa, tearing and twisting something with her slender nervous fingers and gazing intently and fixedly at whatever her eyes chanced to fall on. This solitude exhausted and tormented her but she was in absolute need of it. As soon as anyone entered she got up quickly, changed her position and expression, and picked up a book or some sewing, evidently waiting impatiently for the intruder to go.

She felt all the time as if she might at any moment penetrate that on which—with a terrible **questioning** too great for her strength—her spiritual gaze was fixed.

Leo Tolstoy, War and Peace

What do people want out of life? That is one of those **questions** whose answer can be shaped by the way in which the **question** is posed. Straightforward statistical studies find that job discontent is not high on the list of American social problems. When the Gallup poll's researchers ask, "Is your work interesting?" they get 80 to 90 percent positive responses. But when researchers begin to ask more sophisticated **questions**, such as "What type of work would you try to get into if you could start all over again?" complaints begin to pour forth. The probing **question** cannot help but elicit a plaintive answer. Which of us, confronted with a sympathetic organizational psychologist, or talking into Studs Terkel's tape recorder, could resist tingeing our life story with lamentation, particularly if that was what the **questioner** was looking for? Compared to the "calling" that Terkel says we are all seeking, what job could measure up?

Indeed, people are not "satisfied" with their work, nor with any other aspect of their lives. This is hardly news. But can we agree on what should be done to improve the situation? Most proponents of job enrichment seem agreed that what the average worker misses most is a sense of responsibility and participation in decision-making processes. But is this assumption valid? Are there not many workers who do not want responsibility, who prefer the comfortable monotony of routine tasks to the pressure-building process of making decisions and being accountable for the consequences? Even Barbara Garson's workers keep contradicting her basic premise, from a woman who has turned down the job of supervisor to people with mechanical, repetitive trades who say, "Flip, flip, flip . . . feels good" and "You can get a good rhythm going." Garson despairs for a moment: "Maybe the reactionaries are right. Maybe some people are made for this work."

Samuel C. Florman, The Job-Enrichment Mistake (Harper's Magazine)

Well, such a direct person I regard as the real normal man, as his tender mother nature wished to see him when she graciously brought him into being on the earth. I envy such a man till I am green in the face. He is stupid. I am not disputing that, but perhaps the normal man should be stupid, how do you know? Perhaps it is very beautiful, in fact. And I am the more persuaded of that suspicion, if one can call it so, by the fact that if you take, for instance, the antithesis of the normal man, that is, the man of acute consciousness, who has come, of course, not out of the lap of nature but out of a retort (this is almost mysticism, gentlemen, but I suspect this, too), this retort-made man is sometimes so nonplussed in the presence of his antithesis that with all his exaggerated consciousness he genuinely thinks of himself as a mouse and not a man. It may be an acutely conscious mouse, yet it is a mouse, while the other is a man, and therefore, et caetera, et caetera. And the worst of it is, he himself, his very own self, looks on himself as a mouse; no one asks him to do so; and that is an important point. Now let us look at this mouse in action. Let us suppose, for instance, that it feels insulted, too (and it almost always does feel insulted), and wants to revenge itself, too. There may even be a greater accumulation of spite in it than in L'HOMME DE LA NATURE ET DE LA VERITE. The base and nasty desire to vent that spite on its assailant rankles perhaps even more nastily in it than in L'HOMME DE LA NATURE ET DE LA VERITE. For through his innate stupidity the latter looks upon his revenge as justice pure and simple; while in consequence of his acute consciousness the mouse does not believe in the justice of it. To come at last to the deed itself, to the very act of revenge. Apart from the one fundamental nastiness the luckless mouse succeeds in creating around it so many other nastinesses in the form of doubts and **questions**, adds to the one **question** so many unsettled **questions** that there inevitably works up around it a sort of fatal brew, a stinking mess, made up of its doubts, emotions, and of the contempt spat upon it by the direct men of action who stand solemnly about it as judges and arbitrators, laughing at it till their healthy sides ache.

Fyodor Dostoevsky, Notes From the Underground

A doleful **question** lingers, and with no answer yet in sight: *Why work so hard?* Because there's no other choice? But maybe there is. After all, technological progress could reduce necessary labor to a minimum had this ever been made a social goal—if the goal

This **question** is from first to last, from the beginning to the end, from skin to core and from core to skin again, a **question** of labor.—James G. Blaine

W. A. Rogers, A Question of Labor, 1888 (Library of Congress)

of progress were freeing us from necessity instead of making a select few marvelously rich while the luckless rest toil away. Obviously the more work anyone has to do, the less gratification it yields—no doubt true even when "working on your relationship"—whereas, being freed from work would (to say the least!) alter the entire structure of human existence, not to mention jettison all those mildewed work-ethic relationship credos too—into the dustbin of history they go. "Free time and you free people," as the old labor slogan used to go. Of course, free people might pose social dangers. Who knows what mischief they'd get up? What other demands would come next?

As Marx should have said, if he didn't: "Why work when you can play? Or play around?" (Of course, playing around sometimes gets to be serious business too; about which, more to come.) Historical footnote: Marx was quite the adulterer himself.

Laura Kipnis, Against Love: A Polemic

At this the surly man looked less suspicious, and sat down on the edge of the table. The unshaven one began to **question** me in French, making notes on a slip of paper. Was I a Communist? he asked. By sympathy, I answered; I had never joined any organisation. Did I understand the political situation in England? Oh, of course, of course. I mentioned the names of various Ministers, and made some contemptuous remarks about the Labour Party. And what about *Le Sport?* Could I do articles on *Le Sport?* (Football and Socialism have some mysterious connection on the Continent.) Oh, of course, again. Both men nodded gravely. The unshaven one said:

"*Evidemment,* you have a thorough knowledge of conditions in England. Could you undertake to write a series of articles for a Moscow weekly paper? We will give you the particulars."

"Certainly."

"Then, comrade, you will hear from us by the first post tomorrow. Or possibly the second post. Our rate of pay is a hundred and fifty francs an article. Remember to bring a parcel of washing next time you come. *Au revoir,* comrade."

George Orwell, Down and Out in Paris and London

But the first-time viewer would not necessarily register these stories, for such obvious pro-Kremlin messaging is only one part of RT's output. Its popularity stems from coverage of what it calls 'other', or 'unreported', news. Julian Assange, editor-in-chief of *WikiLeaks,* had a talk show on RT. American academics who fight the American World Order, 9/11 conspiracy theorists, anti-globalists, and the European far right are given generous space. Nigel Farage, leader of UKIP, is a frequent guest; far left supporter of Saddam Hussein George Galloway hosts a programme about Western media bias. The channel has been nominated for an Emmy for its reporting on the Occupy movement in the United States and is described as 'anti-hegemonic' by its fans; it is the most watched channel on YouTube, with one billion viewers, the third biggest international news channel in the United Kingdom, and its Washington office is expanding. But the channel is not uniformly 'anti-hegemonic': when it suits, RT shows Establishment stalwarts such as Larry King, who hosts his own show on the network. So the Kremlin's message reaches a much wider audience than it would on its own: the President is spliced together with Assange and Larry King. This is a new type of Kremlin propaganda, less about arguing against the West with a counter-model as in the Cold War, more about slipping inside its language to play and taunt it from inside. In the ad for

Larry King's show, keywords associated with the journalist flash up on screen: 'reputation', 'intelligence', 'respect', more and more of them until they merge into a fuzz, finishing with the jokey 'suspenders' (i.e. braces). Then King, sitting in a studio, turns to the camera and says: 'I would rather ask **questions** to people in positions of power instead of speaking on their behalf. That's why you can find my new show, *Larry King Now*, right here on RT. **Question** more.' The little ad seems to be bundling the clichés of CNN and the BBC into a few seconds, pushing them to absurdity. There is a sense of giving two fingers to the Western media tradition: anyone can speak your language; it's meaningless!

Peter Pomerantsev, Nothing Is True and Everything Is Possible: Adventures in Modern Russia

In a secular age, this **question** of life's ultimate meaninglessness provokes art to its finest efforts; and throughout Flaubert's life, public events conspired to provoke a general ennui in anyone of an idealistic or romantic temperament. At the time *Madame Bovary* was being written France was still traumatized by the collapse of the *ancien régime* a half-century earlier, followed by revolutionary experiment and terror; imperial aggression and grandiloquence under Napoléon; a consolidation of both religion and monarchy under the ultra-reactionary Charles X; before a further revolution established a more genial figure on the throne, the bourgeois Louis-Philippe, in 1830 (the novel's action mostly takes place in the 1830s and 1840s). The period continued to be spattered with civilian blood, however, as the disenfranchised, often starving, failed to be included in the utilitarian drive for progress—manned by armies of bureaucrats and businessmen whose generals were members of Flaubert's hated bourgeoisie. By the 1850s, their leader had become an emperor, the farcical little Louis Napoléon, who dissolved the Assembly in a bloody coup that left hundreds dead in the Paris streets. No wonder democracy, for Flaubert, felt sham; his retreat into his rural study and the creation of a fictive, parallel world was something of a survival technique.

Madame Bovary is, among many other things, a quest for meaning in which only one character searches; the others see no point in setting out, or believe they have already arrived.

Adam Thorpe, Introduction to Madame Bovary, by Gustave Flaubert

Here was the fulfillment of my dream, the widow I had hoped for.

I extended my hand to the unknown to assist her into the coach, and she sat down beside me, murmuring: "Thank you, sir. Good evening."

"How unfortunate," I thought. "There are only fifty miles between here and Malaga. I wish to heaven this coach were going to Kamschatka." The guard slammed the door, and we were in darkness. I wished that the storm would continue and that we might have a few more flashes of lightning. But the storm didn't. It fled away, leaving only a few pallid stars, whose light practically amounted to nothing. I made a brave effort to start a conversation.

"Do you feel well?"

"Are you going to Malaga?"

"Did you like the Alhambra?"

"You come from Granada?"

"Isn't the night damp?"

To which **questions** she respectively responded:

"Thanks, very well."

"Yes."

"No, sir."

"Yes!"

"Awful!"

Pedro de Alarçon, The Nail (Library of the World's Best Mystery and Detective Stories)

"Cora always was the family sounding board, weren't you?" It nuzzled her hand with its cheek and groaned.

"And after Isabel disappeared," I said, "you asked it where she might have gone."

"Yes, Cora wrote this down. I had a devil of a time figuring out what she meant. Until we actually met I wasn't sure I was right, that it was a name." She frowned. "I don't know how Cora would have known of you."

"Maybe it heard my name somewhere. Cora, do you ever meet other moots? Maybe while shopping?"

Cora's eye remained glassy, as whatever remained that was still human parsed my **question**. After a lull, it shrugged.

I felt like I was **questioning** a particularly dense gorilla.

Corey Redekop, Moot

Is there a commonality between these two cases? Have I been away so long and lived so strangely that everyone else seems strange? No, there's something wrong with these women. And with Frank Macon. Two cases are too few even to suggest a syndrome, but I am struck by certain likenesses . . . In each there has occurred a sloughing away of the old terrors, worries, rages, a shedding of guilt like last year's snakeskin, and in its place is a mild fond vacancy, a species of unfocused animal good spirits. Then are they, my patients, not better rather than worse? The answer is unclear. They're not on medication. They are not hurting, they are not worrying the same old bone, but there is something missing, not merely the old terrors, but a sense in each of her—her what? her self? The main objective clue so far is language. Neither needs a context to talk or answer. They utter short two-word sentences. They remind me of the chimp Lana, who would happily answer any **question** anytime with a sign or two to get her banana. Both women will answer a **question** like *Where is Chicago?* agreeably and instantly and by consulting, so to speak, their own built-in computer readouts. You wouldn't. You'd want to know why I wanted to know. You'd want to relate the **question** to yourself.

Walker Percy, The Thanatos Syndrome

Such an existence might perhaps be defined as one which, looked at from a purely objective point of view, or, rather, after cool and mature reflection—for the **question** necessarily involves subjective considerations,—would be decidedly preferable to non-existence; implying that we should cling to it for its own sake, and not merely from the fear of death; and further, that we should never like it to come to an end.

Arthur Schopenhauer, The Wisdom of Life: Being the First Part of Arthur Schopenhauer's Aphorismen Zur Lebensweisheit

"You're not doing it any favours by keeping it around," I yelled. "Take my advice, book a crematorium. Cora will be much happier as a pile of ash."

She yelled something back as I lurched into the driver's seat. I turned the ignition, letting the engine complain, pretending not to understand what I heard so clearly.

I drove away, idly fingering the scars on my wrists, mulling over her **question**.

Why haven't you, then?

Excellent **question**.

Corey Redekop, *Moot*

Again, if one suppose

That naught is known, he knows not whether this
Itself is able to be known, since he
Confesses naught to know. Therefore with him
I waive discussion—who has set his head
Even where his feet should be. But let me grant
That this he knows,—I **question**: whence he knows
What 'tis to know and not-to-know in turn,
And what created concept of the truth,
And what device has proved the dubious
To differ from the certain?—since in things
He's heretofore seen naught of true. Thou'lt find
That from the senses first hath been create
Concept of truth, nor can the senses be
Rebutted. For criterion must be found
Worthy of greater trust, which shall defeat
Through own authority the false by true;
What, then, than these our senses must there be
Worthy a greater trust? Shall reason, sprung
From some false sense, prevail to contradict
Those senses, sprung as reason wholly is
From out the senses?—For lest these be true,
All reason also then is falsified.
Or shall the ears have power to blame the eyes,
Or yet the touch the ears? Again, shall taste
Accuse this touch or shall the nose confute
Or eyes defeat it? Methinks not so it is:
For unto each has been divided off
Its function quite apart, its power to each;
And thus we're still constrained to perceive
The soft, the cold, the hot apart, apart
All divers hues and whatso things there be
Conjoined with hues. Likewise the tasting tongue
Has its own power apart, and smells apart
And sounds apart are known. And thus it is
That no one sense can e'er convict another.
Nor shall one sense have power to blame itself,
Because it always must be deemed the same,
Worthy of equal trust. And therefore what
At any time unto these senses showed,

The same is true. And if the reason be
Unable to unravel us the cause
Why objects, which at hand were square, afar
Seemed rounded, yet it more availeth us,
Lacking the reason, to pretend a cause
For each configuration, than to let
From out our hands escape the obvious things
And injure primal faith in sense, and wreck
All those foundations upon which do rest
Our life and safety. For not only reason
Would topple down; but even our very life
Would straightaway collapse, unless we dared
To trust our senses and to keep away
From headlong heights and places to be shunned
Of a like peril, and to seek with speed
Their opposites!

> Lucretius, *On the Nature of Things*

So he tortured himself, fretting himself with such **questions**, and finding a kind of enjoyment in it. And yet all these **questions** were not new ones suddenly confronting him, they were old familiar aches. It was long since they had first begun to grip and rend his heart. Long, long ago his present anguish had its first beginnings; it had waxed and gathered strength, it had matured and concentrated, until it had taken the form of a fearful, frenzied and fantastic **question**, which tortured his heart and his mind, clamouring insistently for an answer. Now his mother's letter had burst on him like a thunderclap. It was clear that he must not now suffer passively, worrying himself over unsolved **questions**, but that he must do something, do it at once, and do it quickly. Anyway he must decide on something, or else . . .

"Or throw up life altogether!" he cried suddenly, in a frenzy—"accept one's lot humbly as it is, once for all and stifle everything in oneself, giving up all claim to activity, life and love!"

"Do you understand, sir, do you understand what it means when you have absolutely nowhere to turn?" Marmeladov's **question** came suddenly into his mind "for every man must have somewhere to turn . . ."

> Fyodor Dostoevsky, *Crime and Punishment*

The "beyond" worries them. They reason. Still, they wonder what happens after death. You would do better to place a little more importance on . . . but do you even know what I want to speak to you about? How could anything other than rotting await people like you in the grave? What an idea! There is, in fact, in the idea of rotting, if I take that path, the notion of universal rotting, a comforting thought which makes me turn earthward my joyful eyes lit with mirthful flashes. Let not the gleeful cemetaries distract me in the middle of my discourse: I would like to have lingered over the cold stone, strolled among the humorous epitaphs, but no. For the moment I am studying men who are still standing. Already good fathers and good husbands. Who nevertheless one day will feel something flit by that was not positively the wing of stupidity. How do they look in their own eyes every morning when they shave? I asked this **question** of several subjects afflicted with degeneration. Those who had not yet lost their sight, who only felt at the bottom of their sockets the first shudders of the streetlamp extinguisher, proceeded to appeal to the last resort, the last expression that allows these recent generations to fool others less than they fool themselves. As always the clichés that one evokes—now that neither the New Testament nor the *Aeneid*, **questioned** by opening them at random, can serve to reassure the idiots about their behavior—as always the theme is taken from a paradoxical authority, from one of those books which, I confess, are precious to me, and whose echo I hear with surprise in the defenses I am given of absurd and vulgar fates. *Success in the grocery business* invoked, not even, under various masks, by several minds, who were happy here and there imagining a life that ended in one long joke, alarming subject of humor.

Louis Aragon, *Treatise on Style*

—Of course, Mr B. proceeded to stipulate, you must look at both sides of the **question**. It is hard to lay down any hard and fast rules as to right and wrong but room for improvement all round there certainly is though every country, they say, our own distressful included, has the government it deserves. But with a little goodwill all round. It's all very fine to boast of mutual superiority but what about mutual equality. I resent violence and intolerance in any shape or form. It never reaches anything or stops anything. A revolution must come on the due instalments plan. It's a patent absurdity on the face of it to hate people because they live round the corner and speak another vernacular, in the next house so to speak.

—Memorable bloody bridge battle and seven minutes' war, Stephen assented, between Skinner's alley and Ormond market.

Yes, Mr Bloom thoroughly agreed, entirely endorsing the remark, that was overwhelmingly right. And the whole world was full of that sort of thing.

—You just took the words out of my mouth, he said. A hocuspocus of conflicting evidence that candidly you couldn't remotely. . .

All those wretched quarrels, in his humble opinion, stirring up bad blood, from some bump of combativeness or gland of some kind, erroneously supposed to be about a punctilio of honour and a flag, were very largely a **question** of the money **question** which was at the back of everything greed and jealousy, people never knowing when to stop.

James Joyce, *Ulysses*

She laughed. "People would say, 'Why are you always asking the same **question**?' It was because he wanted these heads of state on the record." His other standard **question** with Presidents, she said, is "How much money do you have?"

"He likes to ask it when they first come into office, and then a second time, a few years later, if they agree to talk again, to see how much they've been stealing."

William Finnegan, *The Man Who Wouldn't Sit Down (The New Yorker)*

"Ethics, rats! Think I'm going to see that bunch of holy grafters get away with the swag and us not climb in?" snorted old Henry.

"Well, I don't like to do it. Kind of double-crossing."

"It ain't. It's triple-crossing. It's the public that gets double-crossed. Well, now we've been ethical and got it out of our systems, the **question** is where we can raise a loan to

Ein Frag an eynen Müntzer/wahin doch souil Geltz
kumme das man alltag müntzet: Antwort des selben Müntzers/Von dreyen
Feinden vnnsers Geltz/wa wir nit acht darauff haben/werden wir den Seckel zum Gelt an.

Wann wir hetten rechten glauben
Gott vnd gemainen nutz vor augen

Recht Elen/darzü maß vnd gwicht
Güt frid vñ auch gleich Recht vñ Ghricht

Einerlay Müntz vnd kain falsch Gelt
So stünd es wol in aller welt.

Frag an den Müntzer.

Sag lieber Müntzer bist frum
Wa mainst das souil gelts hinkum
Daran Teütsch land groß mangel hat
Vnd jr doch müntzet frü vnd spat
Nun ist ye Silbers nicht vil dran
Das man müssig gwin am schmeltzen han
Auch wil yetz kainr so hänglich werden
Das er groß schetz grab in die erden
Noch ist kain gelt klagt all welt sehr
Das wundert mich vnd manchen mehr

Antwort des müntzers

Täglich hör ich diß frag vnd klag
Ligt doch die antwort hell am tag
Waß wir nit weren sunst als plind
Vnd sehen vnsers gelts drey find
Den Babst/New sitten/frembde wahr
Die vnser land erschöpffen gar
Doch hat der Römisch gwerb ein end
Wa ich wir Teütschen selber wend
Vom anndern so wir nit wölln lon
Werden wirs gelts um seckel on

Der Erste Feindt.

Der Babst kan vns gantz höflich fatz
Mit Bullen/Abblaß/Dispensatzen
Vmb böse war güt gelt er nimpt
Wie ain geschwinden kauffman zimpt

Auch seind jm bstimpt vil groß Annaten
Gend jm teütsch Bischoff vnd Prelaten
Welchs alles trifft ein grosse Summ
Ich kans nit glauben ist er frumm
So er gelt fordert bey der schwer
Vmb dingt das sunst wol zimlich wer
Vnd es jm alle vmbs gelt ist fail
Gnad/Pfründen vnd das ewig hail
Wer mer gibt har den bessern tail
Er müß ye nit Stathalter sein
Des ie wen Gots milch vnd wein
On gold vnd silber gibt zukauffen
Baist vns zum gnaden prunnen lauffen
Begert nichts darum dan däckbars hertz
Er hat selbs tragen vnsern schmertz
Sein plüt vnd todt zalt vnser schuld
Durch in allain kumpts Vatters huld
Noch wolt der Babst das gelt daun han
Des hat jms glimpfft schier yederman
Glaub mir/Rom het vns gar auß gsogt
Den seckel mit Bann gelt entzogen
Het nit der treuv Gott gsehen drein
Seine treuve vns geben hätkin schein
In welchen doch gantz klärlich stat
Wa rechte thür in hymel gat
Nit durch die Römisch gülden Port
Sunder Christum den gnaden hort
Darumb halt Babsts grempel yetz ein ent
Waist wie Teütschen selber went

Der Annder feindt.

Den andern faint nun auch verstand
Der vnser gelt fürt auß dem land
Ich main den Kauffman der on rü
Frembd vnnütz war vns furet zü
Die vnserm lob so nodt auch thut
Wies Babsts kram kumpt der sel ungüt
Sonder zu lust vnd hoffart raich
Damit man vns teütsch narren laicht
Mancherlay gwürtz vnd welschen recht
Seyden Sammet/sonst rücher sein
Dieredt von rotem scharlach gmacht
Darnach ein yeder parr yetz tracht
Der Eltern sitt ist gar veracht
Die vns mit treuven gspaeret hond
Das wir so schandlich yetz verthond
O wie wol stünds/do in aine stat
Kaum aine kündsch rock vnd hosen hat
Der paurßman trüg ein zwilch Jupp
Für gwürtz war zwibel auff das supp
Lebt rauch/tranck pieren most vñ wasser
Was nit wie yetz ein foller pfasser
Satzt auff von starckem filtz ein hüt
Was jm für wirdt vnd kelte güt
Der handwercks man thet jm auch recht
Mir gwand vnd narung was er schlecht
Von lands rüch nach der Bürger klaid
Vnd hielt man gtten vnterschaid

Der Dritt feindt.

Yetz kum ich an den dritten finde
New sitten der on zal vil sinde
Damit man treibt ein schentlich preng
Yetz kürtz dañ lang/yetz weit dañ eng
Yetz ist es prait/dañ macht mans schmal
Da ist kain maß jm überal
Was einem yetz an ernelen hangt
Bet erwan yetz ein rock gelangt
Yetz lest mane gantz/dañ ist es zerschnitten
Alweg bringt man ein andern sitten
Vnd müß das heüng moen veralten
Wie möchten wir dañ parschofft bhalten
Wir tragen yetz die welschen schlappen
Seltzam Paret vnd Spannisch kappen
Wo kompt doch eine her über mer
Der vns nit gleich sein sitten lert
So vil sind wir des wanckeln müts
Warlich ich sorg es bring nit güts
Got werd vns kern in dise lande
Völcker der wir yetz tragen gwande
Vnd vnser übel graüsam straffen
Sein zorn wirdt ye nit alweg schlaffen
Hochfart/kriegen/stülen/schweren
Mag sich kains wegs ins harr erweren
Vnd dunckt mich es sey an der zeyt
Got wöll ich wäns/es sey noch weyt.

Wolffgang Rösch formschneyder.

*Jörg Breu the Elder, A **Question** to a Moneychanger (Sale of Indulgences), ca. 1530*

This illustrated broadsheet features a fictional interview with a coiner who is asked to explain where all the German money is disappearing to. He names three "enemies" of the Germans' purses: first, the pope and the indulgences sold by his church; second, the merchants who sell foreign luxury goods such as spices, wine, and fine cloth; and third, the constantly changing fashions in dress. Examples of all three "enemies" are depicted in the accompanying woodcut.

German History in Documents and Images (ghdi.ghi-dc.org)

handle some of the property for ourselves, on the Q. T. We can't go to our bank for it. Might come out."

Sinclair Lewis, Babbitt

Trump himself apparently felt that his old pal Bill O'Reilly would be friendly so he appeared on "The Factor" last night. He and his fellow obnoxious blowhard sparred for a half hour ending up babbling incomprehensibly about milkshakes:

O'REILLY: Would you do me a favor?—

TRUMP: Bill, I'm not—

O'REILLY: Because I bought you so many vanilla milkshakes—I bought you so many vanilla milkshakes you owe me.

TRUMP: That's true.

O'REILLY: Will you just consider? I want you to consider, think about it. Say look, I might come back. Forgive, go forward, answer the **questions**, look out for the folks. Just want you to consider it. You owe me milkshakes. I'll take them off the ledger, if you consider it.

TRUMP: Well even though you and I had an agreement that you wouldn't ask me that, which we did, I will therefore forget that you asked me that, but it's up to Fox, it's not up to me Bill what they did—

O'REILLY: You're actually telling the truth there.

TRUMP: We had an agreement. You actually did break your agreement.—

O'REILLY: You're telling the truth that I said—

TRUMP: I told you up front, don't ask me that **question**, because it's an embarrassing **question** for you and I don't want to embarrass you.

O'REILLY: Right, but I am not going to listen to any political person tell me don't ask me anything. But you're absolutely an honest man, that I said I'll try not to do it, but the milkshake thing just overwhelmed me, but I'm asking you to reconsider it.

TRUMP: A lot of milkshakes.

Heather Digby Parton, Donald Trump Scares the Hell Out of Fox News: Why His Debate Boycott Really Makes the Network So Nervous (Salon)

Meanwhile, the conversation stopped dead, popular rage against bailouts sputtered into incoherence, and we seem to be tumbling inexorably toward the next great financial catastrophe—the only real **question** being just how long it will take.

David Graeber, Debt: The First 5,000 Years

This trip was going to be about one hundred miles and three hours longer. No one said a word to me about this, and I knew not to ask **questions** such as: "Are we there yet?" The answer is no, don't ask the **question** seemed to be the standard.

*B. Matthew Bingham, The Answer Is No! What Is the **Question**? A Little Orphan's Search for the Meaning of Life*

There could have been no doubt, in the 140s, as to what the Sibyl was referring when she spoke of the Romans' savagery and pride. This was the decade when the brute fact of their power was demonstrated to the world beyond all possible doubt. Devastation shadowed the Mediterranean. First, the Republic decided to conclude unfinished business and bring the ghostly half-life of Carthage to an end. Even in Rome herself there were those who disapproved. Many argued that the Republic needed a rival who was worthy of the name. Without rivalry, they demanded, how would Rome's greatness ever be maintained? Such a **question**, of course, could have been asked only in a state where ruthless competition was regarded as the basis of all civic virtue. Unsurprisingly, however, a majority of citizens refused to stomach its implications. For more than a century they had been demonizing the Carthaginians' cruelty and faithlessness. Why, most citizens wondered, should the standards of Roman life be applied to the protection of such a foe? This **question** was duly answered by a vote to push Carthage into war. By aiming at her complete annihilation, the Republic revealed what the logical consequence of its ideals of success might be. In such brutality, unmediated by any nexus of fellowship or duty, lay the extremes of the Roman desire to be the best.

In 149 the hapless Carthaginians were given the vindictive order to abandon their city. Rather than surrender to such a demand, they prepared to defend their homes and sacred places to the death. This, of course, was precisely what the hawks back in Rome had been hoping they would do. The legions moved in for the kill. For three years the Carthaginians held out against overwhelming odds and in the final stages of the siege the generalship of Rome's best soldier, Scipio Aemilianus. At last, in 146, the city was stormed, gutted of its treasures, and set ablaze. The inferno raged for seventeen days. On the cleared and smoking ruin, the Romans then placed a deadly interdiction, forbidding anyone ever to build upon its site again. Seven hundred years of history were wiped clean.

Tom Holland, *Rubicon: The Last Years of the Roman Republic*

And I submit that there is no point in spending any dollars going any farther than that.

I know of no scientific basis for the proposed two pico curies of radon per square meter per second, such a standard would involve substantially more expense and more possibility of serious harm to workers and the general public due to hazards of moving large amounts of earth. And with the provisions in Public Law 95-604 for federal custody of disposal sites after completion of remedial action, it would seem that a small buffer zone landscaped, but without houses around a stabilized pile, would more than suffice for radiological safety.

These could be public parks. They could be football fields, playgrounds, baseball, tennis, just don't dig holes in them. One of the problems with the Monticello tailings pile, which was stabilized years ago by the A.E.C. by asking for two feet of rock and earth cover, the contractor didn't quite make it. It's about six or eight inches in some places. Some places, it's two feet thick. But the main problem they have is gophers. And the gophers go down and mine the tailings and bring them up on top. But the E.P.A. won't let them poison the gophers.

Well, I say I'm not particularly troubled by these marked uncertainties and inaccuracy concerning radon flux reduction by overburden, which we haven't discussed at all, but that's a highly technical thing.

I'd be glad to discuss it in the most minute detail because it began in my laboratory in 1966, because we've seen that the reasons advanced for proposing two pico curies of radon per square meter per second guidelines are invalid. It's not needed, radiobiologically. It would be very expensive. It's cost, in effect, it's inflationary on the economy. And so I'm opposed.

Now, the **question** of longevity of standards has been brought up, and a thousand years has been spoken of, and also thousands of years has been spoken of. I served for a number of years on the National Academy of Sciences Committee on Radioactive Waste Disposal. This had to do with the high-level wastes from the reactors, and in particular, for military use. And our committee was named the committee on radioactive waste disposal.

The first thing we did was to change the name of the committee and change from disposal to management. And it became the committee on radioactive waste management. We saw no way that it was possible to properly, to sensibly and economically take care of such things as tailings, in this case, low and high-level wastes. We thought some kind of occasional surveillance, looking at it once in a while, a month, a year, if it needs some repairs, you repair it. But to presume that any of us can predict what the country or even the continent is going to be like a thousand years from now, it seems to me to be very interesting.

If you go back medically only a few hundred years, in Sam Pepys time, it was the plague, and which, as you remember, wiped out great fractions of the population quite regularly. We haven't seen any plague around for a long, long time.

Could George Washington, two hundred years ago, have predicted the state of commerce and population and communication, and the state of the healing arts. As of today, two hundred years later, I don't think so. The Pueblo of Los Angeles, California, was founded exactly two hundred years ago, in 1781; and the history books say with a population of twenty-six, including Mexicans, Negroes, and halfbreeds, upon the site of the old Indian village Yang-na.

That's two hundred years ago, and look at what's in the Los Angeles basin now. The Aztec civilization in Central America, as you know, is tremendous, and yet it's only—it's less than five hundred years since Cortez came in, in 1519 and destroyed it. The Norman conquest of England, 1066, and all that is less than a thousand years ago. The magna carta, which contains the roots of all—

Mr. HENSLEY. Doctor Evans, I think that we—I think that we appreciate the history lesson, and we get the point.

The WITNESS. A thousand years is too long. One to two hundred years is enough. I'll pause at this time and be glad to respond to any **questions**.

Mr. HENSLEY. Mr. Crout?

Mr. CROUT. I'll defer any **questions**. I believe Doctor Evans has covered anything I would have.

Mr. HENSLEY. All right, sir. Yes, sir.

CROSS EXAMINATION

By Mr. Strom:

Question. May I ask you a couple of **questions**?

Answer. I'd be delighted.

United States Congress House of Representatives, Hearings on H.R. 2603, H.R. 2784, H.R. 2912, and H.R. 3364 Before the Seapower and Strategic and Critical Materials Subcommittee of the Committee on Armed Services, Ninety-Seventh Congress, First Session, June 2 and 4

"Can't you quote me a price here and now? What are you hiding, fellow?"

Bob removed his glasses. Now Reinhart remembered why he could not earlier remember how Bob had looked while rinsing his spectacles in Gino's washroom. The face tended to be indistinct, as though looking straight-on you were seeing it from the corner of your eye. Reinhart found it difficult to say why this was so. Only Bob's hair now had authority, the fuzzy gray sideburns, the rich, virile crest. His features were all very regular, like those shown in learn-cartooning-by-mail manuals, but the composite, which then should have been a Steve Canyon or Smilin' Jack, was, inexplicably, not.

Bob said patiently, colorlessly: "I am trying to explain that there will be no charge. This is a nonprofit enterprise." His fist clenched quickly, then slowly opened like an octopus testing its environment. "I can promise you nothing, but if you permit this experiment to take place, you might have a part in history . . ." He lost his voice and raised his eyes hopelessly to Reinhart.

It was the most extraordinary thing. Reinhart wanted to cry: I'm sorry I thought you were a swindler but there are so many extant and, after all, to talk of abolishing Death—but I see you mean it.

Did he have a viable process? Reinhart did not know, or at the moment care, because *Bob was sincere.* Reinhart reached across the desk and seized the mike, a little ball of wire mesh.

He spoke fervently into it: "You just give us your name and address, and where the patient can be found. We'll arrange the rest. Let's set up an appointment. Better have the doctor there. This is a historical occasion. No, that's putting it too lamely. The Wright Brothers were small-time in this light. Your dad may live again! In a hundred, a thousand years, what do petty details matter? Napoleon, Caesar, Alexander the Great, they are all dust to stop a bunghole or however the quote goes, for Shakespeare too was a transitory incident. Can you understand, sir? Truth may change and Time itself, Life as we know it. Don't **question**, don't doubt. You cannot lose. It finally comes down to that, does it not?

Thomas Berger, Vital Parts

President Trump spent a portion of Sunday's press briefing yet again promoting an unproven treatment for the novel coronavirus, repeatedly asking, "What do we have to lose?"

Toward the end, a CNN reporter turned to Anthony S. Fauci, director of the National Institute of Allergy and Infectious Diseases, for his opinion on the effectiveness of hydroxychloroquine with a sharper **question**: "What is the medical evidence?"

Standing at the microphone, Fauci opened his mouth—but before he could speak, the answer came out of Trump's instead.

"Do you know how many times he's answered that **question**?" Trump cut in. "Maybe 15."

A tight smile stretched across Fauci's face. His eyes, framed by a pair of wire-rimmed glasses, flicked quickly to Trump. He glanced back at the reporter, who was saying to the president, "The **question** is for the doctor . . . He's your medical expert, correct?"

Fauci's smile, for just a moment, was all teeth now. Trump raised his finger sternly, telling the journalist, "You don't have to ask the **question**," and so Fauci didn't answer it, and the news conference shuffled right along.

*Allyson Chiu and Meagan Flynn, Trump Blocks Fauci From Answering **Question** About Drug Trump Is Touting (Washington Post)*

HAMLET
Angels and ministers of grace defend us!
Be thou a spirit of health or goblin damned,

Bring with thee airs from heaven or blasts from hell,
Be thy events wicked or charitable,
Thou com'st in such a **questionable** shape
That I will speak to thee. I'll call thee Hamlet,
King, father, royal Dane. Oh, oh, answer me!
Let me not burst in ignorance, but tell
Why thy canonized bones, hearsèd in death,
Have burst their cerements, why the sepulcher
Wherein we saw thee quietly inurned
Hath oped his ponderous and marble jaws
To cast thee up again? What may this mean,
That thou, dead corse, again in compleat steel,
Revisits thus the glimpses of the moon,
Making night hideous, and we fools of nature
So horridly to shake our disposition
With thoughts beyond the reaches of our souls?
Say, why is this? Wherefore? What should we do?
Ghost beckons Hamlet.

HORATIO
It beckons you to go away with it,
As if it some impartment did desire
To you alone.

MARCELLUS
       Look with what courteous action
It wafts you to a more removèd ground.
But do not go with it.

HORATIO
           No, by no means.

HAMLET
It will not speak. Then will I follow it.

HORATIO
Do not, my lord.

HAMLET
       Why, what should be the fear?
I do not set my life at a pin's fee,
And for my soul, what can it do to that,
Being a thing immortal as itself?
It waves me forth again. I'll follow it.

HORATIO
What if it tempt you toward the flood, my lord,
Or to the dreadful summit of the cliff
That beetles o'er his base into the sea,
And there assumes some other horrible form

Which might deprive your sovereignty of reason
And draw you into madness? Think of it.

HAMLET
It wafts me still.—Go on, I'll follow thee.

MARCELLUS
You shall not go, my lord.
[They attempt to restrain him.]

HAMLET

                         Hold off your

hand!

HORATIO
Be ruled. You shall not go.

HAMLET

                      My fate cries out
And makes each petty artery in this body
As hardy as the Nemean lion's nerve.
Still am I called? Unhand me, gentlemen!
By heav'n, I'll make a ghost of him that lets me.
I say, away!—Go on, I'll follow thee.

      William Shakespeare, The Tragedie of Hamlet, Prince of Denmarke

Public impeachment hearings began this week in the U.S. House of Representatives and we learned Republicans should change their symbol from an elephant to a cliff-bound lemming. It left me rooting for truth and asking my weekly **question**: "What the (BLEEP) just happened?"

      Rex Huppke, In Impeachment Hearings, Republicans Make the Case for Replacing Their Party's Mascot With a Lemming: The Week in Review (Chicago Tribune)

"What people see is essentially mass dispersal," said zoologist Gordon Jarrell, an expert in small mammals with the University of Alaska Fairbanks. "Sometimes it's pretty directional. The classic example is in the Scandinavian mountains, where (lemmings) have been dramatically observed. They will come to a body of water and be temporarily stopped, and eventually they'll build up along the shore so dense and they will swim across. If they get wet to the skin, they're essentially dead."

"There's no **question** that at times they will build up to huge numbers," Jarrell added. "One description from Barrow does talk about them drowning and piling up on the shore."

Jarrell said when people learn that he works with lemmings, the mass suicide issue often comes up.

"It's a frequent **question**," he said "'Do they really kill themselves?' No. The answer is unequivocal, no they don't."

      Riley Woodford, Lemming Suicide Myth: Disney Film Faked Bogus Behavior (Alaska Fish & Wildlife News)

House Republicans in the hearing also tried relentlessly to claim Trump couldn't have done anything wrong because military aid to the Ukraine wound up going through and

Ukrainian officials never launched a Biden investigation. That overlooks the fact the aid was released only after a whistleblower report was filed.

Speaking of the whistleblower, Republicans continued their quixotic quest to round up that anonymous and protected-under-federal-law person. They griped about the lack of a whistleblower to demonize while sitting in front of two actual witnesses (Kent and Taylor) who were blowing the whistle on virtually everything the whistleblower had claimed. If an anonymous tipster tells you your dog ate your hamburger and then your dog tells you he ate your hamburger, the identity of the tipster becomes quite irrelevant. (Though you might still wonder when your dog started talking.)

Lastly, they complained witnesses were not giving a "firsthand account" of alleged misdeeds. Yet those same Republicans support Trump's refusal to allow people who do have firsthand knowledge—like chief of staff Mick Mulvaney, Secretary of State Mike Pompeo and National Security Council legal adviser John Eisenberg—to comply with House subpoenas.

It's almost as if, and you'll pardon this giant leap of logic, Republicans don't really have a defense of the president's actions.

ANOTHER DAY, ANOTHER SCHOOL SHOOTING—I GUESS THIS JUST HAPPENS NOW

With breathlike regularity, children are shot to death in American schools.

It has happened so many times now that a Thursday mass shooting at a Southern California high school, which left two students dead and several others injured, was met both with sorrow and a broad sense of hopelessness.

As students were led out of the Santa Clarita high school by rifle-toting deputies, a Los Angeles Times reporter heard a student ask, "What kind of world is this?"

That a child should ask that **question** is a condemnation of us all.

Rex Huppke, In Impeachment Hearings, Republicans Make the Case for Replacing Their Party's Mascot With a Lemming: The Week in Review (Chicago Tribune)

Lord Advocate.—I apprehend there is no good legal objection to this **question**, looking to the matter we are inquiring into. We are inquiring as to the intentions and actings of William Waddel. The **question** raised is whether we can get this information from or through James Waddel. Now, supposing that James Waddel could be a competent witness, then if we had him here there could be no **question** that he would be entitled to speak as to what William had told him; and still more, connecting that with what James Waddel is doing when that information is said to be given, there could be no **question** as to the competency of the inquiry into that. But James Waddel is dead, and the rule of law with us is that what is said by a deceased party is evidence. William could not have been a witness of course—James is, therefore, the witness who would have been examined. The **question** is, when the party who would have been the witness is dead, you can take what that party said before he died—whether you can so save the evidence of the party who would have been the witness. The rule is in reference to what I could have proved by the party now dead, if he had not been dead. I supply that by what the party said at a time when the subject-matter of the litigation was not raised, and what it is to be presumed he would now state if he was alive.

David Buchanan, Report of the Jury Trials, Miss Anne Waddel, & Others, Against the Right Hon. C. Hope, & Others, Trustees of the Late William Waddel, Esq. of Sydserff; and Miss Anne Waddel, Against the Right Hon. C. Hope, & Daughters, Commencing on 13th, and Ending on 17th May 1845

While the British colonel set Lazzaro's broken arm and mixed plaster for the cast, the German major translated out loud passages from Howard W. Campbell, Jr.'s monograph. Campbell had been a fairly well-known playwright at one time. His opening line was this one:

> *America is the wealthiest nation on Earth, but its people are mainly poor, and poor Americans are urged to hate themselves. To quote the American humorist Kin Hubbard, "It ain't no disgrace to be poor, but it might as well be." It is in fact a crime for an American to be poor, even though America is a nation of poor. Every other nation has folk traditions of men who were poor but extremely wise and virtuous, and therefore more estimable than anyone with power and gold. No such tales are told by the American poor. They mock themselves and glorify their betters. The meanest eating or drinking establishment, owned by a man who is himself poor, is very likely to have a sign on its wall asking this cruel **question**: "If you're so smart, why ain't you rich?" There will also be an American flag no larger than a child's hand—glued to a lollipop stick and flying from the cash register.*
>
> Kurt Vonnegut, *Slaughterhouse-Five, or, The Children's Crusade: A Duty-Dance With Death*

It's also important to emphasize that while this system of extraction comes dressed up in a language of rules and regulations, in its actual mode of operation, it has almost nothing to do with the rule of law. Rather, the legal system has itself become the means for a system of increasingly arbitrary extractions. As the profits from banks and credit card companies derive more and more from "fees and penalties" levied on their customers—so much so that those living check to check can regularly expect to be charged eighty dollars for a five-dollar overdraft—financial firms have come to play by an entirely different set of rules. I once attended a conference on the crisis in the banking system where I was able to have a brief, informal chat with an economist for one of the Bretton Woods institutions (probably best I not say which). I asked him why everyone was still waiting for even one bank official to be brought to trial for any act of fraud leading up to the crash of 2008.

OFFICIAL: Well, you have to understand the approach taken by U.S. prosecutors to financial fraud is always to negotiate a settlement. They don't want to have to go to trial. The upshot is always that the financial institution has to pay a fine, sometimes in the hundreds of millions, but they don't actually admit to any criminal liability. Their lawyers simply say they are not going to contest the charge, but if they pay, they haven't technically been found guilty of anything.

ME: So you're saying if the government discovers that Goldman Sachs, for instance, or Bank of America, has committed fraud, they effectively just charge them a penalty fee.

OFFICIAL: That's right.

ME: So in that case . . . okay, I guess the real **question** is this: has there ever been a case where the amount the firm had to pay was more than the amount of money they made from the fraud itself?

OFFICIAL: Oh no, not to my knowledge. Usually it's substantially less.

ME: So what are we talking here, 50 percent?

*Jacques Callot, Christ Posing the **Question** of the Tribute to Caesar, from The New Testament, 1635*
Etching, ornamental border designed by Gilles-Marie Oppenord, etched by Antoine Hérisset,
printed 18th c., 16.7 x 19.2 cm, The Metropolitan Museum of Art, New York

OFFICIAL: I'd say more like 20 to 30 percent on average. But it varies considerably case by case.

ME: Which means . . . correct me if I'm wrong, but doesn't that effectively mean the government is saying, "you can commit all the fraud you like, but if we catch you, you're going to have to give us our cut"?

OFFICIAL: Well, obviously I can't put it that way myself as long as I have this job . . .

David Graeber, The Utopia of Rules: On Technology, Stupidity, and the Secret Joys of Bureaucracy

The voice laughed.

Reinhart joined it, the wind of divine amusement in his sails. "It is crazy and frightening and brave and majestic. Think what man can do without the fear of death. The mind as yet cannot cope with so glorious a concept. But to put it simply: no mistake will be final. The whole idea of termination, of any sort, will be obsolete. Now, where can we find your father? If he is willing, how can you hesitate?"

The voice, which had continued to laugh in the regular rhythm of a machine whose function was to tumble that which it treated, wet wash or concrete, now stopped with a shudder.

"Greenwood Cemetery," it said. "He died in 1956."

Reinhart looked **questioningly** at Bob Sweet.

"Well, sir," he said seriously. "I don't think . . . Let me check with my associate." What a horrible disappointment. Surely the process would not . . . The man was a crank. Reinhart was shrinking.

"Don't bother," said the voice. "You are as full of shit as a Christmas goose." And hung up.

Sweet wore his glasses again. "Not the first hoaxer, and not the last. Don't give it another thought."

Reinhart said: "I can understand an eccentric better than a joker, a demented or deluded person. But how do you explain a guy like this? All that trouble for a laugh?"

"Well, that's America, isn't it?"

Thomas Berger, Vital Parts

"Your conclusions?" he snapped suddenly.

"I'd pay him."

"Why?"

"It's a **question** of a little money against a lot of annoyance. There has to be something behind it. But nobody's going to break your heart, if it hasn't been done already. And it would take an awful lot of chiselers an awful lot of time to rob you of enough so that you'd even notice it."

Raymond Chandler, The Big Sleep

I finished the drink and went in search of the bank, which turned out to be a branch of Wells Fargo. One of its minor officers, a young man with a handlebar mustache, seemed busily idle so I told him I wanted to open a checking account. The mustache jiggled a little at that and I assumed that the jiggle was a smile of welcome or at least acquiescence. A nameplate on his desk said that he was C. D. Littrell and I tried to remember whether I had ever seen a bank official with a handlebar mustache before and decided that I hadn't except in some old Westerns and then he had usually turned out to be a crook. But this was Wells Fargo and perhaps its traditions encouraged handlebar mustaches.

After I sat down Littrell produced some forms and the forms contained **questions** to which I would have to think up some answers. I decided to tell the truth when convenient and to lie when it wasn't.

"Your full name?" Littrell said.

"Dye, D-y-e. Lucifer C. Dye." The C stood for Clarence but I saw no sense in mentioning that. Lucifer was bad enough.

"Your address?"

Another good **question**.

Ross Thomas, *The Fools in Town Are on Our Side*

G. K. Chesterton was lecturing on Dante at California's Milbrook Junior College, when a woman who had lost her place in her volume of Dante called out, "Where the hell are we?" The class laughed, but Mr. Chesterton took the interruption with good humor, saying, "I rather like that phrase. Good Catholic expression. A Catholic doesn't live in Milbrook or in England, but *sub specie aeternitatis,* and the **question** always is, where in hell are we? Or where in heaven are we? Or where in purgatory are we? We live in that spaceless, timeless commonwealth and the **question** is very important."

David Bruce, *Dante's Inferno: A Discussion Guide*

An equally puzzling **question** is why *us*. People throughout the world must cope with social, economic, and technological changes that call traditional verities into **question**, and the empire of mind-numbing infotainment knows no national boundaries. Yet the United States has proved much more susceptible than other economically advanced nations to the toxic combination of forces that are the enemies of intellect, learning, and reason, from retrograde fundamentalist faith to dumbed-down media. What accounts for the powerful American attraction to values that seem so at odds not only with intellectual modernism and science but also with the old Enlightenment rationalism that made such a vital contribution to the founding of our nation?

Susan Jacoby, *The Age of American Unreason*

'But there was more. I have seen plenty of bodies to which death has come instantaneously, but never one in which there has been visible neither awareness nor effect of death. It was so, however, with Ploss. He wasn't shot from hiding; the character of the little sun-room makes that impossible. For some fraction of a second at least he must have seen a weapon pointed fatally at his head. But whatever muscular action it was that produced, death had cancelled out. His hands were folded lightly in his lap. His expression perhaps was slightly puzzled—but this, I think, may have been habitual. And then there was his eye . . .'

Hetherton shifted on his chair. 'Do these'—he hesitated—'curious circumstances help you towards—towards a reconstruction of the crime?'

'No.' Appleby was emphatic. 'Nothing of that sort. Friend or enemy, stranger or acquaintance: any of these may have stood up before Ploss and fired that revolver. The odd fact of his apparent unawareness tells me nothing in a detective way. It is simply a fortuitous thing that enforces the strangeness of the whole impression. For there he sat with the paraphernalia of his tranquil and secure existence about him, and below lay a countryside utterly at peace in the evening sun. Only up there and with the Chilterns behind us there was a first breath of cold night wind. It blew in like a commentary or a **question**, and it stirred his hair.'

Michael Innes, *The Secret Vanguard*

Being someone who possesses both a scientific and inquiring mind I know that nose hair grows in one's nose for a good reason because it has evolved that way.

Noses have to have hair in them so that the dust and muck from everyday life is filtered out when we breathe, unless of course one breathes through one's mouth and pants, like a casual and not very committed nuisance telephone caller.

I have another theory about nose hair though, I think that it grows in one's nose to annoy you, especially when it grows so long that it peeps out of a nostril and tickles it.

If the tickling just stopped at tickling it wouldn't be so bad, but it doesn't, does it? The annoying and wayward hair or hairs can make one's life a misery, constantly irritating one of the most sensitive parts of a Cat or I suppose Human (although I have to say I am not so concerned about Human's comfort).

On and on the tickling goes, the wayward hair touching the end of your nostril until you decide to do the unthinkable (and for Cats almost impossible) and try to pull the hair out, with all of the eye watering pain, that you know is going to be attached to that action, and even if you do resort to that desperate attempt at relief, you know that you are going to disturb other hairs which will start poking out and begin the tickling all over again!

Thinking about this annoying and uncomfortable fact of life for a moment. Maybe we fellows of the scientific community are wrong, and nose hair is not a result of evolution and the creationists, who believe that everything that is, and was for that matter, has been created by God is correct, and God did in fact create us and the hair in our noses, even the unruly ones, hairs that is, not noses, although noses can get unruly but I haven't got the space, time or patience to get into unruly noses at the moment! So we'll go back to God and nose hair.

If it is so and God knocked up the planet and all around and did it in a week and therefore God is responsible for everything in creation and in particular nose hair I would like to pose a **question**. What sort of God lets nose hair grow the wrong way and what have we done to deserve the constant irritation of tickly hairs growing out of our noses?

And it doesn't stop there the **question** of what was God doing?

John Woodcock, *Getting Out: Excerpts From a Cat's Diary (Translated From the Original Cat)*

The child that asks, you see, about the white beard of God doesn't deserve an answer, because he—doesn't intend to pray to God. It shouldn't be—it's blasphemy. Don't answer it. It's a stupid **question**. The—the condition of a **question** is that the **questioner** wants to join the community. That's a very simple rule, gentlemen, and explains the whole Platonic, Socratic, and Aristotelic obsession with the city of man. All **questions** must remain related to the city of man. Otherwise they do not deserve an answer.

Therefore, Socrates comes in and asks, and tries to prove that the **questioner** has to be asked if he is really serious. Does he really mean business? Does he want to be good, courageous, prudent? A good citizen, you see? Or does he just ask to show off as a sophist, just to show that he can prove anything, you see, for the sake of argument? The whole of Parmenides is written about this topic, for example. Or the Gorgias, you see, or the Protagoras, the—the Ion, you see. For the sake of argument, you can argue anything. But you must remain related, as Plato then formulates it in his dialogues, to the good. The good is the sum, so to speak, of serious participation.

If you do not remain seriously ins—have not the desire to get inside, or to stay inside, whatever the situation is, you see, your **question** is not a good **question**. We are full of this nonsense today, gentlemen. This is the era of the sophists. And—never have the sophists ruled this country. They call themselves, I don't know what they call themselves—broadcasters, or intellectuals, or—or quiz kids, or what-not; $64,000 **question**. The only good thing about the $64,000 **question** obviously are the $64,000, but not the **question**.

Eugen Rosenstock-Huessy, Greek Philosophy (1956): Lectures 14–20

I have tabled the value **questions** humanists have raised, but I wish to conclude with a serious value **question**: Who stands to benefit most from the success of this research? At its core, this enterprise is about using computers to understand how humans use language, including what that language means to people and how it persuades. Just down the road from Stanford is an enormous industry whose profitability depends on understanding this. Academia and Silicon Valley are converging in this territory: technology firms are eager to hire researchers who can help them turn large volumes of human-generated text into money and eager to collaborate with scholars in order to reap the practical benefit of academic knowledge. And an enormous surveillance apparatus, in the United States and abroad, is similarly interested in extracting meaning and predictions from volumes of text. In both cases, the problem is not assembling the data, which has already been acquired even though the people surveilled often don't know it. The problem is making sense of it, which requires social scientists and humanists.

Ben Merriman, A Science of Literature (Boston Review)

The necessity of order, a place for everything and everything in its place: the deficient appreciation of literature possessed by females: the incongruity of an apple incuneated in a tumbler and of an umbrella inclined in a closestool: the insecurity of hiding any secret document behind, beneath or between the pages of a book.

Which volume was the largest in bulk?

Hozier's *History of the Russo-Turkish war.*

What among other data did the second volume of the work in **question** contain?

The name of a decisive battle (forgotten), frequently remembered by a decisive officer, major Brian Cooper Tweedy (remembered).

Why, firstly and secondly, did he not consult the work in **question**?

Firstly, in order to exercise mnemotechnic: secondly, because after an interval of amnesia, when, seated at the central table, about to consult the work in **question**, he remembered by mnemotechnic the name of the military engagement, Plevna.

What caused him consolation in his sitting posture?

The candour, nudity, pose, tranquility, youth, grace, sex, counsel of a statue erect in the centre of the table, an image of Narcissus purchased by auction from P. A. Wren, 9 Bachelor's Walk.

What caused him irritation in his sitting posture?

Inhibitory pressure of collar (size 17) and waistcoat (5 buttons), two articles of clothing superfluous in the costume of mature males and inelastic to alterations of mass by expansion.

How was the irritation allayed?

James Joyce, Ulysses

"May I take a seat?" asked the foreigner politely, and the friends, involuntarily somehow, moved apart; the foreigner settled in neatly between them and immediately entered the conversation.

"If I heard correctly, you were so good as to say there was never any Jesus on earth?" asked the foreigner, turning his green left eye towards Berlioz.

"Yes, you heard correctly," replied Berlioz courteously, "that is precisely what I was saying."

"Ah, how interesting!" exclaimed the foreigner.

"But what the devil does he want?" thought Bezdomny, and frowned. "And were you in agreement with your companion?" enquired the stranger, turning to the right towards Bezdomny.

"The full hundred per cent!" confirmed the latter, who loved to express himself in a mannered and ornate fashion.

"Astonishing!" exclaimed the uninvited interlocutor and, looking around furtively for some reason and lowering his deep voice, he said: "Forgive my persistence, but my understanding was that, apart from anything else, you don't believe in God either?" He made frightened eyes and added: "I swear I won't tell anyone."

"No, we don't believe in God," replied Berlioz, with a faint smile at the fright of the foreign tourist, "but it can be spoken about completely freely."

The foreigner reclined against the back of the bench and asked, even emitting a little squeal of curiosity:

"Are you atheists?"

"Yes, we're atheists," replied Berlioz, smiling, while Bezdomny thought angrily: "This foreign goose is being a real nuisance!"

"Oh, how charming!" the amazing foreigner cried, and he began twisting his head, looking first at one, then at the other man of letters.

"In our country atheism surprises no one," said Berlioz with diplomatic politeness, "the majority of our population consciously and long ago ceased to believe in fairy tales about God."

At this point the foreigner wheeled out the following trick: he stood up and shook the astonished editor's hand, at the same time pronouncing these words:

"Permit me to thank you from the bottom of my heart!"

"And what is it you're thanking him for?" enquired Bezdomny, blinking.

"For a very important piece of information, which is extremely interesting to me as a traveller," the eccentric foreigner elucidated, raising a finger most meaningfully.

Evidently the important piece of information really had made a powerful impression on the traveller, because he looked round in fright at the buildings, as though afraid of seeing an atheist at every window.

"No, he's not English . . ." thought Berlioz, while Bezdomny thought: "Wherever

David Cameron, leader of the Conservative Party, answers **questions** from the public at a 'Cameron Direct' **Q&A** session at which anyone may turn up and ask a **question**.

Photo by Olivia Arthur / Magnum, 2008 (Artstor)

did he get so good at speaking Russian, that's what's I wonder!" and frowned again.

"But permit me to ask you," began the foreign guest after an anxious hesitation, "what's to be done about the proofs of God's existence, of which there are, as is well known, exactly five?"

"Alas!" replied Berlioz with regret. "Not one of those proofs is worth a thing, and mankind gave them up as a bad job long ago. You must agree, after all, that in the sphere of reason there can be no proof of the existence of God."

"Bravo!" exclaimed the foreigner. "Bravo! You've repeated in its entirety that restless old man Immanuel's idea on that score. But here's a curious thing: he completely demolished all five proofs, and then, as though in mockery of himself, constructed his own sixth proof!"

"Kant's proof," objected the educated editor with a thin smile, "is also unconvincing. And not for nothing did Schiller say that the Kantian arguments on the **question** could satisfy only slaves, while Strauss simply laughed at that proof."

Berlioz spoke, yet at the same time he was thinking: "But all the same, who on earth is he? And why does he speak Russian so well?"

"This Kant should be taken and sent to Solovki for two or three years for such proofs!" Ivan Nikolayevich blurted out quite unexpectedly.

"Ivan!" whispered Berlioz, embarrassed.

But not only did the proposal to send Kant to Solovki not shock the foreigner, it even sent him into raptures.

"Precisely, precisely," he shouted, and a twinkle appeared in his green left eye, which was turned towards Berlioz, "that's the very place for him! I said to him then over breakfast, you know: 'As you please, Professor, but you've come up with something incoherent! It may indeed be clever, but it's dreadfully unintelligible. They're going to make fun of you.'"

Berlioz opened his eyes wide. "Over breakfast . . . to Kant? . . . What nonsense is this he's talking?" he thought.

"But," the foreigner continued, with no embarrassment at Berlioz's astonishment and turning to the poet, "sending him to Solovki is impossible for the reason that he's already been in parts considerably more distant than Solovki for over a hundred years, and there's no possible way of extracting him from there, I can assure you!"

"That's a pity!" responded the quarrelsome poet.

"I think it's a pity too," confirmed the stranger, with a twinkle in his eye, and continued: "But this is the **question** that's troubling me: if there's no God, then who, one wonders, is directing human life and all order on earth in general?"

"Man himself is directing it," Bezdomny hastened to reply angrily to this, to be honest, not very clear **question**.

"I'm sorry," responded the stranger mildly, "in order to be directing things, it is necessary, for all that, to have a definite plan for a certain, at least reasonably respectable period of time. Permit me to ask you then, how can man be directing things, if he not only lacks the capacity to draw up any sort of plan even for a laughably short period of time—well, let's say, for a thousand years or so—but cannot even vouch for his own tomorrow? And indeed," here the stranger turned to Berlioz, "imagine that you, for example, start directing things, managing both other people and yourself, generally, so to speak, getting a taste for it, and suddenly you have . . . heh . . . heh . . . a lung sarcoma . . ." the foreigner smiled sweetly, as if the idea of a lung sarcoma gave him pleasure, "yes, a sarcoma," narrowing his eyes like a cat, he repeated the sonorous word, "and there's an end to your directing! No one's fate, apart from your own, interests you any more. Your family begin lying to you. Sensing something wrong, you rush to learned doctors, then to charlatans, and sometimes to fortune-tellers too. Like the first and the second, so the third too is completely pointless, you realize it yourself. And it all ends tragically: the man who just recently supposed he was directing something turns out suddenly to be lying motionless in a wooden box, and those around him, realizing there's no more use whatsoever in the man lying there, burn him up in a stove. But it could be even worse: a man will have just decided to take a trip to Kislovodsk," here the foreigner screwed his eyes up at Berlioz, "a trifling matter, it would have seemed, but he can't accomplish even that, since for some unknown reason he'll suddenly go and slip and fall under a tram! Surely you won't say it was he that directed himself that way? Isn't it more correct to think that someone else completely dealt with him directly?" here the stranger laughed a strange little laugh.

Mikhail Bulgakov, The Master and Margarita

Answer. That's not my field.

Question. Would you say that was a relevant **question** for this forum, whether it's your field or not?

United States Congress House of Representatives, Hearings on H.R. 2603, H.R. 2784, H.R. 2912, and H.R. 3364 Before the Seapower and Strategic and Critical Materials Subcommittee of the Committee on Armed Services, Ninety-Seventh Congress, First Session, June 2 and 4

One mischief always introduces another. These terrors and apprehensions of the people led them into a thousand weak, foolish, and wicked things, which they wanted not a sort of people really wicked to encourage them to: and this was running about to fortune-tellers, cunning-men, and astrologers to know their fortune, or, as it is vulgarly expressed, to have their fortunes told them, their nativities calculated, and the like; and this folly presently made the town swarm with a wicked generation of pretenders to magic, to the black art, as they called it, and I know not what; nay, to a thousand worse dealings with the devil than they were really guilty of. And this trade grew so open and so generally practised that it became common to have signs and inscriptions set up at doors: 'Here lives a fortune-teller', 'Here lives an astrologer', 'Here you may have your nativity calculated', and the like; and Friar Bacon's brazen-head,* which was the usual sign of these people's dwellings, was to be seen almost in every street, or else the sign of Mother Shipton,† or of Merlin's head, and the like.

With what blind, absurd, and ridiculous stuff these oracles of the devil pleased and satisfied the people I really know not, but certain it is that innumerable attendants crowded about their doors every day. And if but a grave fellow in a velvet jacket, a band, and a black coat, which was the habit those quack-conjurers generally went in, was but seen in the streets the people would follow them in crowds, and ask them **questions** as they went along.

I need not mention what a horrid delusion this was, or what it tended to; but there

---

* Roger Bacon, the medieval philosopher, was reputed to have created such a head, capable of prophesying. [Ed.]

† Traditionally, a witch with prophetic powers, living in Yorkshire in the fifteenth century. She is supposed to have prophesied the Great Fire of London. [Ed.]

was no remedy for it till the plague itself put an end to it all—and, I suppose, cleared the town of most of those calculators themselves. One mischief was, that if the poor people asked these mock astrologers whether there would be a plague or no, they all agreed in general to answer 'Yes', for that kept up their trade. And had the people not been kept in a fright about that, the wizards would presently have been rendered useless, and their craft had been at an end. But they always talked to them of such-and-such influences of the stars, of the conjunctions of such-and-such planets, which must necessarily bring sickness and distempers, and consequently the plague. And some had the assurance to tell them the plague was begun already, which was too true, though they that said so knew nothing of the matter.

The ministers, to do them justice, and preachers of most sorts that were serious and understanding persons, thundered against these and other wicked practices, and exposed the folly as well as the wickedness of them together, and the most sober and judicious people despised and abhorred them. But it was impossible to make any impression upon the middling people and the working labouring poor. Their fears were predominant over all their passions, and they threw away their money in a most distracted manner upon those whimsies. Maid-servants especially, and men-servants, were the chief of their customers, and their **question** generally was, after the first demand of 'Will there be a plague?' I say, the next **question** was, 'Oh, sir! for the Lord's sake, what will become of me? Will my mistress keep me, or will she turn me off? Will she stay here, or will she go into the country? And if she goes into the country, will she take me with her, or leave me here to be starved and undone?' And the like of men-servants.

The truth is, the case of poor servants was very dismal, as I shall have occasion to mention again by-and-by, for it was apparent a prodigious number of them would be turned away, and it was so. And of them abundance perished, and particularly of those that these false prophets had flattered with hopes that they should be continued in their services, and carried with their masters and mistresses into the country; and had not public charity provided for these poor creatures, whose number was exceeding great and in all cases of this nature must be so, they would have been in the worst condition of any people in the city.

Daniel Defoe, *A Journal of the Plague Year: Being Observations or Memorials of the Most Remarkable Occurrences, as Well Public as Private, Which Happened in London During the Last Great Visitation in1665. Written by a Citizen Who Continued All the While in London. Never Made Public Before.*

Page 223 is not part of this book preview.

a pleasant way to torment your child on a Sunday afternoon.

"What's the rest?" said Llewellyn. He seemed jumpy, a bit slopped by an overspill of ego fuel.

"The rest of your bonus is your ability to sleep at night, knowing that you have done your part in keeping hope—hope for a great fucking human flowering—alive and well. Darkness is falling, my friends. Our job is to put the Maglites in the hands of the people whose ideas, whether in the realms of business, medicine, law, or science, pure and applied, will lead us through the black hour."

"Let's not forget the arts!" called Vargina, with rare or, rather, meeting-specific cheer.

"Sure, the arts, too," said Cooley. "Hey, we've always made room for you self-involved little people, haven't we? No need to be upset. We get it. Even cavemen needed their cave paintings, right?"

"Hooray," whispered Horace. War Crimes wheeled.

"What was that, Slick?"

"Nothing."

"I got a **question** for you. A quiz. Answer this correctly and I'll give you a twenty percent raise right now. In what year did Bertolt Brecht create the vaccine for polio?"

"Sorry?"

"In what year did Bertolt Brecht create the vaccine for polio?"

"No year?" said Horace.

"Say it like you got a pair."

"No year, sir!" said Horace.

"Good work. The raise thing was more of a hypothetical. But keep up the nice effort. Anyway, you all get my point. Though I guess I've made several today."

Sam Lipsyte, The Ask

"I'm afraid I haven't."

He was pulling open Frewin's file. I say "pulling" because his doughy hands gave no impression of having done anything before: now we are going to see how this file opens; now we are going to address ourselves to this strange object called a pencil.

"He's got no hobbies, no stated interests beyond music, no wife, no girl, no parents, no money worries, not even any bizarre sexual appetites, poor devil," Burr complained, flipping to a different part of the file. When on earth had he found time to read it? I asked myself. I presumed the early hours. "And how the hell a man of your experience, whose job is dealing with modern civilisation and its discontentments, can manage without the wisdom of Robert Musil is a **question** which at a calmer moment I shall require you to answer." He licked his thumb and turned another page. "He's one of five," he said.

"I thought he was an only child."

"Not his brothers and sisters, you mug, his work. There's five clerks in his dreary cyphers office and he's one of them. They all handle the same stuff; they're all the same rank, work the same hours, think the same dirty thoughts."

John le Carré, The Secret Pilgrim

Let me ask a **question** of the men: Are you ever able to watch a woman eating a banana and not think of a blow job?

Mark Peters, Men

The listener will ask the **questions** just as they appear on the page, stopping after each **question** to review and make sure you are hearing correctly.

Milan Yerkovich and Kay Yerkovich, How We Love: Discover Your Love Style, Enhance Your Marriage

Motor-cars came shooting out of deep, narrow streets into the shallows of bright squares. Dark patches of pedestrian bustle formed into cloudy streams. Where stronger lines of speed transected their loose-woven hurrying, they clotted up—only to trickle on all the faster then and after a few ripples regain their regular pulse-beat. Hundreds of sounds were intertwined into a coil of wiry noise, with single barbs projecting, sharp edges running along it and submerging again, and dear notes splintering off—flying and scattering. Even though the peculiar nature of this noise could not be defined, a man returning after years of absence would have known, with his eyes shut, that he was in that ancient capital and imperial city, Vienna. Cities can be recognised by their pace just as people can by their walk. Opening his eyes, he would recognise it all again by the way the general movement pulsed through the streets, far sooner than he would discover it from any characteristic detail. And even if he only imagined he could do so—what does it matter? The excessive weight attached to the **question** of where one is goes back to nomadic times, when people had to be observant about feeding-grounds. It would be interesting to know why, in the matter of a red nose, for instance, one is content with the vague statement that it is red, never asking what particular shade of red it is, although this could be precisely expressed in micro-millimetres, in terms of wave-lengths; whereas, in the case of something so infinitely more complicated, such as a town in which one happens to be, one always wants to know quite exactly what particular town it is. This distracts attention from more important things.

So no special significance should be attached to the name of the city. Like all big cities, it consisted of irregularity, change, sliding forward, not keeping in step, collisions of things and affairs, and fathomless points of silence in between, of paved ways and wilderness, of one great rhythmic throb and the perpetual discord and dislocation of all opposing rhythms, and as a whole resembled a seething, bubbling fluid in a vessel consisting of the solid material of buildings, laws, regulations, and historical traditions.

Robert Musil, The Man Without Qualities, Vol. 1: A Sort of Introduction and Pseudo Reality Prevails

Or here's another way to tell the story of modern love. Let's imagine that to achieve consensus and continuity, any society is required to produce the kinds of character structures and personality types it needs to achieve its objective—to perpetuate itself— molding a populace's desires to suit particular social purposes. Those purposes would not be particularly transparent to the characters in **question**, to those who live out the consequent emotional forms as their truest and most deeply felt selves. (That would be us.)

Take the modern consumer. (Just a random example.) Clearly, routing desire into consumption would be necessary to sustain a consumer society—a citizenry who fucked in lieu of shopping would soon bring the entire economy grinding to a standstill. Or better still, take the modern depressive. What a boon to both the pharmaceutical and the social-harmony industries such a social type would be. These are merely hypotheticals, of course, since it's not as if we live in a society of consumers and depressives, or as if the best therapy for the latter weren't widely held to be strategically indulging in the activities of the former—"retail therapy" in urban parlance.

But perhaps there would be social benefits to cultivating a degree of emotional stagnation in the populace? Certain advantages to social personality types who gulped down disappointment like big daily doses of Valium, who were so threatened by the possibility of change that the anarchy of desire was forever tamed and a commitment to perfect social harmony effortlessly achieved? Advantages to a citizenry of busy utili- tarians, toiling away, working harder, with all larger social **questions** (is this really as good as it gets?) pushed aside or shamed, since it's not like you have anything to say about it anyway.

Laura Kipnis, Against Love: A Polemic

They were the onscreen window dressing and spellcheckers of the operation. Behind the scene the real decisions were made by a small band of Russian producers. In between the bland sports reports came the soft interviews with the President ('Why is the opposition to you so small, Mr President?' was one legendary **question**).

Peter Pomerantsev, *Nothing Is True and Everything Is Possible: Adventures in Modern Russia*

"He is taller than me, he's like 6′ 2″, which is why I don't understand why his hands are the size of someone who is 5′ 2″," Rubio joked. "Have you seen his hands? And you know what they say about men with small hands—"

The crowd erupted.

"—You can't trust them," Rubio said.

Rubio's comment may come across tasteless for a presidential hopeful, but that was not the first time someone has **questioned** the size of Trump's hands.

Nearly 30 years ago, Graydon Carter, the editor of *Vanity Fair* magazine, described Trump in *Spy* magazine as a "short-fingered vulgarian."

Emily Shapiro, *The History Behind the Donald Trump 'Small Hands' Insult (ABC News)*

"How," he cried indignantly, "do you know about that?"

Blaine made a passionless murmur. He said: "I voluntarily exposed myself to the preceding abuse of my intelligence. You ought to wonder why. I did not come here merely to backstroke in the vat of tepid piss wherein you habitually float while deliberating philosophically. I need some money, and I ask you to give it to me."

"I won't give you a penny until you answer my simple **question**. Is that thing about freezing the dead general knowledge?" It could be. Reinhart's fund of same was only sporadically replenished nowadays. His usual television fare was old movies. He frequently missed the daily encyclopedia of catastrophes, more and more humanly remote, which had replaced the old newspaper of the man-bites-dog era of journalism. And his dentist's magazines were so ancient as to show features on the hula-hoop craze.

Thomas Berger, *Vital Parts*

So have the times and standards changed enough that Clinton would be seen as Cosby, if he was president today?

Oh, yes! There's absolutely no doubt, especially in this age of instant social media. In most of these cases, like the Bill Clinton and Bill Cosby stories, there's been a complete neglect of psychology. We're in a period right now where nobody asks any **questions** about psychology. No one has any feeling for human motivation. No one talks about sexuality in terms of emotional needs and symbolism and the legacy of childhood. Sexuality has been politicized—"Don't ask any **questions**!" "No discussion!" "Gay is exactly equivalent to straight!" And thus in this period of psychological blindness or inertness, our art has become dull. There's nothing interesting being written—in fiction or plays or movies. Everything is boring because of our failure to ask psychological **questions**.

So I say there is a big parallel between Bill Cosby and Bill Clinton—aside from their initials! Young feminists need to understand that this abusive behavior by powerful men signifies their sense that female power is much bigger than they are! These two people, Clinton and Cosby, are emotionally infantile—they're engaged in a war with female power. It has something to do with their early sense of being smothered by female power—and this pathetic, abusive and criminal behavior is the result of their sense of inadequacy.

Now, in order to understand that, people would have to read my first book, "Sexual Personae"—which of course is far too complex for the ordinary feminist or academic mind! It's too complex because it requires a sense of the ambivalence of human life. Everything is not black and white, for heaven's sake! We are formed by all kinds of strange or vague memories from childhood. That kind of understanding is needed to see that Cosby was involved in a symbiotic, push-pull thing with his wife, where he went out and did these awful things to assert his own independence. But for that, he required the women to be inert. He needed them to be dead! Cosby is actually a necrophiliac—a style that was popular in the late Victorian period in the nineteenth-century.

It's hard to believe now, but you had men digging up corpses from graveyards, stealing the bodies, hiding them under their beds, and then having sex with them. So that's exactly what's happening here: to give a woman a drug, to make her inert, to make her dead is the man saying that I need her to be dead for me to function. She's too powerful for me as a living woman. And this is what is also going on in those barbaric fraternity orgies, where women are sexually assaulted while lying unconscious. And women don't understand this! They have no idea why any men would find it arousing to have sex with a young woman who's passed out at a fraternity house. But it's necrophilia—this fear and envy of a woman's power.

And it's the same thing with Bill Clinton: to find the answer, you have to look at his relationship to his flamboyant mother. He felt smothered by her in some way. But let's be clear—I'm not trying to blame the mother! What I'm saying is that male sexuality is extremely complicated, and the formation of male identity is very tentative and sensitive—but feminist rhetoric doesn't allow for it. This is why women are having so much trouble dealing with men in the feminist era. They don't understand men, and they demonize men. They accord to men far more power than men actually have in sex. Women control the sexual world in ways that most feminists simply don't understand.

David Daley, Camille Paglia: How Bill Clinton Is Like Bill Cosby (Salon)

Meanwhile, this claim has been corroborated by further research on intonation patterns found in spontaneous speech (e.g., Bartels, 1999; Hedberg & Sosa, 2002).[76]

It is important to keep in mind that canonical and non-canonical yes-no **questions** do not belong to a uniform category, with all members sharing the formal (prosodic) feature 'terminal rise' or 'auxiliary-subject word order', for example. Rather, they are members of a family of related constructions; for example, the non-canonical **question** *You want that?* might share the feature 'terminal rise' with the canonical **question** *Do you want that?*, which in turn shares the feature 'subject-auxiliary word order' with the canonical **question** *Can I have that?*, which may be articulated with a terminal fall. This is also mirrored in descriptions of **questions** stating that "there are two external signals of a Q-marker: rising intonation *and/or* [emphasis added] inversion" (Erreich, 1984, p. 584).

It is important to note that the coding/extraction procedure applied creates a(n artificial) cutoff-point, i.e., there are constructions which are formally as well as functionally related to yes-no **questions** which are not taken into account. These cases include

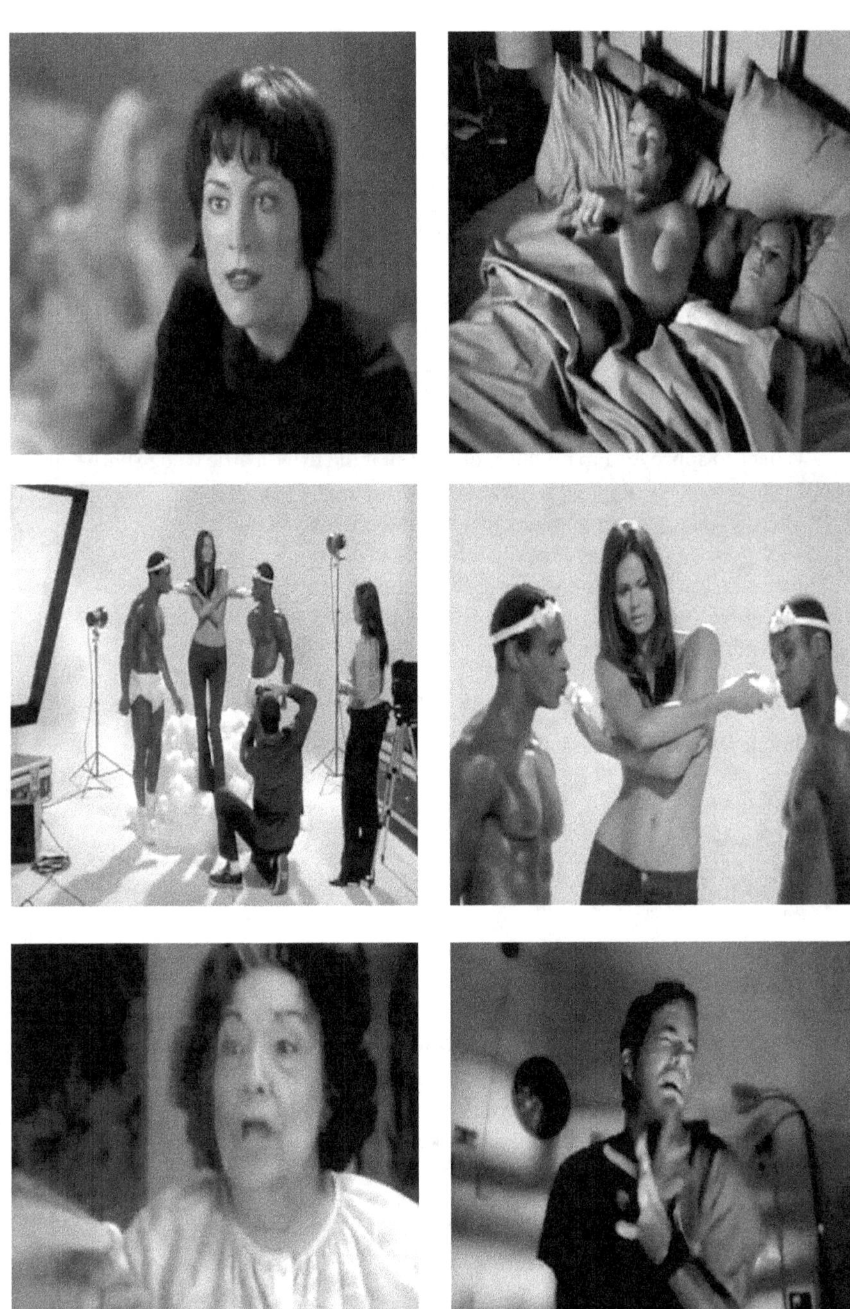

"This is the glamorous world of market research. We just sit around until somebody wonders—Why are those men wearing diapers?"

"Uh, I guess I can answer that **question** for you, sir."

Walt Becker (director), Buying the Cow (trailer), 2002 (imdb.com)

—non-rising declaratives that function as **questions**, e.g., You're feeling ill. ('queclaratives'; Geluykens, 1987; Weber, 1993)

—embedded interrogatives, e.g., He doesn't know what to say (also called 'indirect **questions**'; Huddleston, 1994, pp. 414–415).

—non-**questions** exhibiting SAI, e.g., exclamatives like Is it hot in here![77]

*Ursula Kania, The Acquisition and Use of Yes-No **Questions** in English: A Corpus-Study From a Usage-Based Perspective*

She grinned a little, wickedly. "You're a smart fella, Elliot. But Amy . . . well, Amy is all about Amy, isn't she? And when someone's like that, and she takes on a guy like Vince, who just wanted you to be happy, she finds herself the perfect husband. He'll do whatever you want him to do."

"And you didn't approve?" Christie waved a hand.

"What's to approve? I'm not his mother. But it did drive a little wedge between Joe and Vince, toward the end. I don't know why, but it did."

"Christie," I began, not knowing how to phrase it less obviously, "you didn't happen to go to the movie with Vince the night he . . . the night it happened, did you?"

She looked at me as if I'd suggested that she plant a few magic beans and go kill a giant. "Me? No! Why the hell would I go see a movie alone with Vince Ansella?"

"So where were you that night?"

It was the only time I saw her actively evading a **question**. "I was . . . out."

"Out? Just out?"

Christie tried to snarl, but it just came out as a different kind of grin. "Yeah. You never been out before, Elliot?" She couldn't sustain it, and the grin reverted to her usual one.

I had one last **question**. "Why do you think Amy called Joe a murderer at Vince's funeral?" I asked.

Christie didn't hesitate. "Because she couldn't accuse herself."

Jeffrey Cohen, Some Like It Hot-Buttered

In order to avoid this, it is preferable to pursue a strategy that leads to the inclusion of all potentially relevant items (thus maximizing recall) even though this may make it necessary to discard irrelevant items manually (because precision has been reduced). For example, the assumption that **question**-tags occur exclusively in utterance final position may lead to a search for auxiliary-pronoun combinations immediately followed by a **question** mark. However, since tags may also occur in utterance-internal position (1), this retrieval strategy may result in a "skewed picture of actual tag **question** usage" (Smith, Hoffmann, & Rayson, 2007, p. 165).

(1) KDY 173   You haven't pushed that in have you dear?[78]

*Ursula Kania, The Acquisition and Use of Yes-No **Questions** in English: A Corpus-Study From a Usage-Based Perspective*

Munsing's tan face blanched, as if exuding a white powder. He seized the water glass from Gloria's failing hand and swallowed several more pills.

He sank onto the vanity stool and said, with no confidence: "Blackmail, is it? I have nothing to hide."

Gloria keeled over backwards.

Reinhart said: "You seem to have done a pretty good job with your dong."

Munsing made a desperate try: "Do you have the authority to **question** my therapeutic techniques? Prostitution is a serious symptom."

"I thought it was a thing-in-itself."

Thomas Berger, Vital Parts

It has been suggested that yes-no **questions** are 'abbreviated' versions of and thus constitute a special case of alternative **questions**, but this view has been largely abandoned (for a thorough discussion of this issue, see Bolinger, 1978); along similar lines, alternative **questions** are still sometimes subsumed under the heading yes-no **question** because of the common formal properties (Estigarribia, 2007, p. 2). However, they are treated separately in some developmental studies and all reference grammars, mainly because of their semantics, which is the view adopted here. Since automatic extraction procedures are often applied, all utterances containing *or* are in most cases classified as alternative **questions**. If one goes through the data manually, it becomes obvious that not all structures containing *or* are in fact alternative **questions**. For example, I have grouped utterances containing the coordination tags *or something?* and *or anything?* under yes-no **questions**, since they function as a marker of vagueness rather than providing a real choice (22), (see Biber et al., 1999, pp. 116; 208).

*Ursula Kania, The Acquisition and Use of Yes-No **Questions** in English: A Corpus-Study From a Usage-Based Perspective*

Although these terms are obviously not new, this grouping of them as a supplement to Channell's typology is my own. Flexibility in the form of *either . . . or* sentences has been treated as Vagueness by Zhang (1998: 17), who, however, classifies Superordinacy as Generality (1998: 16). Omission is excluded from Channell's analysis as "suppression of reference or mention" (1994: 19), although Channell does agree that Omission is perceived by language users as Vagueness. Omission is extremely problematic for a quantitative, analytical study, but it is relevant here because it answers the **question** motivating this paper, "What makes modern users perceive these recipes as overly vague?"

Ruth Carroll, Vague Language in the Medieval Recipes of the Forme of Cury (Instructional Writing in English: Studies in Honour of Risto Hiltunen)

Fred B. Perkins, San Francisco Cataloguing for Public Libraries, A Manual of the System Used in the San Francisco Free Public Library

It became more elaborate as time went on, but it was a system that eventually would make sense to me, since I had invented it.

Each time I took a title out of the box I crossed it off the list. And each time I started a classification by artist or series (the Pink Panthers were missing, but Blake Edwards was otherwise well represented, and I had *A Shot in the Dark* in my own collection, anyway), I would search for others that would be compatible, to complete the series and make sure all the titles were there. The Monty Pythons alone—both film and television work was represented—took the better part of an hour.

But all the while I was concentrating on the murder and the film piracy. I couldn't let go of them, and I couldn't solve anything, either. Every answer led to another **question**, and each **question** simply turned in a circle and led to nothing.

Jeffrey Cohen, Some Like It Hot-Buttered

An associated problem is how to account for opposed judgements within a cultural group. It sometimes—indeed quite often—happens that opposed judgements are made about the same work by different critics from the same culture at the same time. When there are thus two opposed judgements within the same culture, are both right relative to the culture? Or should we say that each is right relative to its own subculture? But surely mere disagreement of judgements would not entail that there were two cultural groups involved, so that the members of a cultural group would by definition be homogeneous and always make the same judgements. How will the relativist account for changing judgements within the same cultural group, which also sometimes plainly happens—or is that, too, by definition, indicative of a change of culture? Relativism's inability or omission, at least, to answer such **questions** clearly renders it vague and liable to degenerate into the view that the 'cultural group' with respect to

You have either reached a page that is unavailable for viewing or reached your viewing limit for this book.

Christopher New, Philosophy of Literature: An Introduction

Biases resulting from automated retrieval strategies that are too restrictive can also be found in studies on **question** development: For example, in her study on inversion errors in yes-no **questions**, Stromswold excluded "all lines that contained a *wh-word*"

(Stromswold, 1990, p. 146), thus eliminating all yes-no **questions** with embedded wh-**questions** and relative wh-words, e.g., *Do you know what that is?*. On a more general note, MacWhinney (2008) remarked that complex searches tend to be prone to error (MacWhinney, 2008, p. 169).

*Ursula Kania, The Acquisition and Use of Yes-No **Questions** in English: A Corpus-Study From a Usage-Based Perspective*

Munsing groaned in cavernous melancholy. "You are wrong if you think Eunice was ever neglected. No doors were ever closed to her, including those of our bedroom and toilet. She was often present when my wife and I had relations, and never put a **question** that was not answered or demonstrated. That sex should be discreet and that privacy is a good are fascist lies inculcated in children by generations of fools and/or scoundrels." He brightened suddenly. "In fact she used to climb in with us. I suppose that shocks you. The capacity to be shocked is a symptom—"

"Do you know something, Munsing?" Reinhart asked. "If you took wing and flew out the window I wouldn't bat an eye. I walked right past that sniper on the Bloor Tower and said 'Hi' to him, then went downstairs and screwed a girl." Reinhart never spoke a lady's name in low places.

"Lloyd Alvis was a patient of mine," Munsing said proudly. "In the municipal clinic. You know, we are often criticized for our fees, but it is not generally known how much time we donate to public facilities. He is a disturbed personality. I wrote a paper on him, in fact. I like to think it was instrumental in bringing about the self-regulation of the horror-comic industry."

Reinhart considered the implications. "So when you took away his comic books he got himself a gun."

"You oversimplify," Munsing said. "Always the tendency of the layman. It is healthier to possess a real gun of one's own than to relate to violence passively, symbolically, in fantasy. Alvis has made astonishing progress. When he first came to me, he interpreted my welcoming handshake as an aggressive gesture, fell to all fours, and whined like an obsequious dog."

Thomas Berger, Vital Parts

"What did you do?"

Okay, let's start with that. What did Anthony mean by that **question**? Clearly, he thought that something I'd done had led to his source of funding being cut off, shutting down production of his dream project. Why would he think it was my fault? Because it had happened soon after he made his one mistake: reaching out to me on the phone.

So. Did that make sense? Could my talking to him have led to the end of his film? I couldn't know why his funding was cut off unless I knew the source of the money. Where had Anthony gotten two hundred thousand dollars to make *Killin' Time?*

Jeffrey Cohen, Some Like It Hot-Buttered

"But I have seen the prophets in Jerusalem do even worse: they commit adultery and tell lies; they help people to do wrong, so that no one stops doing what is evil. To me they are all as bad as the people of Sodom and Gomorrah. So then, this is what I, the Lord Almighty, say abut the prophets of Jerusalem: I will give them bitter plants to eat and poison to drink, because they have spread ungodliness throughout the land." The Lord Almighty said to the people of Jerusalem, "Do not listen to what the prophets say; they are filling you with false hopes. They tell you what they have imagined and not what I have said."

E. Asamoah-Yaw, BIG **QUESTION**: *Do Humans Need God?*

He looked straight at me, a thing he had not done before. "If he did it, what's his motive? The writer doesn't say. Funny, that. They usually do. Boredom—how about that? Boredom and greed, they're the only motives left these days. Plus getting even, which is eternal." He went back to the file. "Cyril's the only one not married, notice that? He's a poofter. So am I. I'm a poofter, you're a poofter. We're all poofters. It's just a **question** which bit of yourself ends on top. He's no hair, see that?" I caught a flash of Frewin's photograph as he waved it past me and talked on. He had a daunting energy. "Still that's no crime, I dare say, baldness, any more than marriage is. I should know, I've had three and I'm still not done. That's no normal denunciation, is it? That's why you're here. That letter knows what it's talking about. You don't think Modrian wrote it, do you?"

"Why should he have done?"

John le Carré, *The Secret Pilgrim*

This was a disastrous answer. But why? After all, Dukakis answered the **question** with some reasonable justification for his position. But that's exactly the problem. He addressed the issue *as if all that mattered* was addressing the issue. What he missed was that every **question** was also an opportunity to create an impression that would guide how all *subsequent* answers to **questions** got interpreted.

Drew Westen (who advises Democrats on communications strategy when he's not peering at political brains in scanners) wrote:

*What the average listener heard was his answer to three very different **questions**: 'Are you a man?' 'Do you have a heart?' and 'Are we similar enough that I could trust you to represent me and my values as president?' For most Americans, the answer to all three **questions** was no.*

What should he have done instead? Linguist Geoff Nunberg, who remarked that by answering the way he did, Dukakis "branded himself a bloodless technocrat," suggested a more muscular response in the vein of Democrat Mario Cuomo, who defended *his* opposition to the death penalty as follows:

Because it's wrong, because it's dumb, because it's counterproductive, because it's an instruction in violence, because it won't make my daughter safe. It won't make my mother safe. It never has.

Julie Sedivy and Greg Carlson, *Sold on Language: How Advertisers Talk to You and What This Says About You*

When I discussed my dilemma with Dad and Mom, they both came up with the same solution, get a job. As sad as this seemed, it was the best idea they could come up with. So I set out to get a summer job. I was so tempted to apply as a lifeguard at the local swimming pool. But the fact that I could not swim very well, and could not possibly save anyone's life made this seem a bad idea. And, according to our religion, I could not swim with members of the opposite sex. I heard the phrase, "members of the opposite sex" most of my life, and wondered if that meant there was a way to become a non-member. Then the **question** would become, could I swim with non-members of the opposite

*Martino Rota (after Titian), The **Question** of Paying Taxes to Caesar, 1583*
Engraving, 278 x 231 mm, Museum of Fine Arts, Budapest

sex? I never got up enough nerve to ask Dad and Mom, but I figured I probably already knew the answer. The answer is no, why are you asking this **question**?

B. Matthew Bingham, The Answer Is No! What Is the Question? A Little Orphan's Search for the Meaning of Life

I want to talk about finite state automata, and an open **question** concerning them. The **question** is very annoying, since we have no idea how to improve a classic algorithm. This algorithm is decades old, but it is still the best known. There seems to be no hope to show the algorithm is optimal, yet there also seems to be no idea how to beat it. Oh well, we have seen this situation before.

Richard J. Lipton, The P=NP Question and Gödel's Lost Letter

Criticism has been directed against the view that statements such as "If Brutus chooses to kill Caesar, he will kill him" and "If Cicero had chosen to kill Caesar, he would have killed him" are both causal in just the sense in which the statements "If this match is struck, it will light" and "If that match had been struck, it would have lit" are causal.[1] When Moore illustrates this view in *Ethics* he has an unfortunate tendency to use first-person sentences such as "I should have run a mile in twenty minutes this morning if I had chosen", and I think that some criticism of Moore depends on excessive preoccupation with the peculiarities of this sort of illustration. Criticism has also been focused on Moore's equally unfortunate tendency to oscillate between saying that a sentence such as "Moore could have run a mile in twenty minutes this morning" is synonymous with "Moore could have run a mile in twenty minutes this morning if he had chosen to do so" and saying that it is synonymous with "Moore *would* have run a mile in twenty minutes this morning if he had chosen to do so". Consequently, as we shall see, Moore would have fared much better at the hands of some critics if he had avoided the use of first-person illustrations in favor of third-person illustrations, and if he had made it quite clear that his thesis was that "Moore could have run a mile in twenty minutes this morning" is to be analyzed as meaning the same as "Moore *would* have run a mile in twenty minutes this morning if Moore had chosen to do so", and not to be analyzed as meaning the same as "Moore could have run a mile in twenty minutes this morning if Moore had chosen to do so".

I turn now to a criticism of the view that the first-person sentence "I could have run a mile in twenty minutes this morning" is to be analyzed as meaning the same as "I should have run a mile in twenty minutes this morning if I had chosen". It has been argued that the second statement is not a causal conditional statement, but sometimes such an argument has required irrelevant concentration on features that it has as a first-person sentence which its third-person counterpart does not have. Thus the sentence "I should have run a mile in twenty minutes this morning if I had chosen" has been called "an unusual, not to say queer, specimen of English";[2] and it has been said in a very British way that this sentence means the same as "If I had chosen to run a mile in twenty minutes this morning, I should (jolly well) have done so". One may agree with these observations but deny, as I do, that this sentence is an assertion by the speaker of the speaker's strength of character, or an assertion of the fact that he puts his decisions into execution.[3] But, more importantly, one may correctly deny that an argument which shows that a first-person sentence does not mean something of the form "If I had made a certain choice, my making that choice would have caused me to do something",[4] shows that the third-person statement "He would have run a mile in twenty minutes if he had

241

chosen" is not a causal statement.

There are other first-person conditional statements that one may rightly characterize as not being causal, but the fact that there are does not count against the view that their third-person counterparts are causal. Consider what has been said about the sentence "I shall (do it) if I choose (to do it)" in an effort to show that it is not causal. It has been contrasted with "I shall ruin him if I am extravagant" by pointing out that while the latter is causal, the former is not because it makes good sense to stress the "shall" in the former but not in the latter. But this difference disappears when we turn to third-person counterparts of these sentences, such as "He will do it if he chooses to do it" and "He (Smith) will ruin him (Jones) if he (Smith) is extravagant". Therefore, we cannot validly use the argument about stress in order to show that the former sentence is not causal by comparison with the latter; both are causal.

Had Moore used only third-person illustrations throughout his discussion of free will in *Ethics*—and he certainly could have while supporting his general view—he would have avoided the criticism that "I shall" in "I shall if I choose" is "not an assertion of fact but an expression of intention, verging towards the giving of some variety of undertaking".[5] Obviously, the sentence "He will run a mile in twenty minutes if he chooses" is not an expression of intention, and therefore the observation that "I shall if I choose" is one, even if correct, cuts no ice against the view that this third-person sentence is causal. It is worth emphasizing, moreover, that since Moore was mainly concerned in his *Ethics* with moral statements about actions, he could have confined himself to using third-person moral statements such as "Russell ought to have walked a mile in twenty minutes yesterday". In that case Moore might well have used the statement "If Russell had chosen not to walk a mile in twenty minutes yesterday, he would not have done so" when illustrating the sort of conditional statement that he thought would have to be true if one were properly to make an "ought"-statement about an action.

Morton White, The Question of Free Will: A Holistic View

Well! The looks *I got* from many of my friends when I moved into my new locker. Freshmen girls who previously would not even glance at me were now coming up and starting conversations. I decided to be cool, and spend more time with my senior girlfriends because they were much more mature and seemed to understand me better. (Pretty good, huh?) Somehow I maintained these relationships for the entire freshman year, and was actually saddened to see my senior girlfriends leave. We must all move on I guess, and that applies to those of us who get breaks, and those who do not.

The only downside to my freshmen year was the same old thing: grades. I wanted good grades in the worse way. I just did not want to have to work so hard to get them. I was still much too busy having fun, to have to do all that other stuff. I would rely upon my religious background to come through for me when it came time for exams and quizzes. I would get on my knees the night before an exam and ask God, "Just this once let me pass the test." It was a system that made me feel good about the effort, but the results were disappointing. Dad tried to explain. "God helps them that *study* and pray." I really don't know what I would have done if, just once, God actually did allow me to pass a test. So, I guess God really knows what is best for us. Sometimes when we ask Him for something, "The answer is no," and He already knows the **question.**

B. Matthew Bingham, The Answer Is No! What Is the Question? A Little Orphan's Search for the Meaning of Life

This, Sir, was not fair, it was not decent, it was not reafonable, it was not fober, nor godly, nor pious that you fhould overlook.

There can be no **queftion** refpecting the neceffity of worfhipping God in fpirit and truth. There can be no doubt, but at the moment when our bleffed Redeemer fpoke, the hour was coming (and that was the hour) when God would be fo worfhipped by his faithful followers. There can be no doubt of that. The only **queftion** for us to difcufs is, How this was intended to be done? Was it by worfhipping God both in foul and body, which is his? Was it in this manner that mankind was inftructed to render to God, the fupreme lord and mafter of all things vifible and invifible, a rational fervice or not? Once more I prefs it upon you, as a man of fenfe, a man of principle and ftrict integrity, to fay, whether the apoftles did, or did not worfhip him in the way in which our bleffed Saviour meant he fhould be worfhipped? if they did, there is an end at once to the **queftion**. For it will hardly be maintained by you, or any other, that a time will come when God will be worfhipped with a purer and inward kind of worfhip, in a manner, in fhort, more pleafing to the deity, and with a better effect than he was, by the apoftles, the infpired friends and faithful fervants of his only begotten fon, whom the Lord himfelf had chofen as vaffels of true holinefs to pour out his doctrines to all men; and whom he had lifted up as the prime rulers of his heavenly kingdom, that they might appear on high as light to the world, and as fure, and unerring guides to all who fhould follow after them. In a word, then, and for the fake of fome common intelligence between us, let it be faid, whether the apoftles worfhipped God in fpirit and truth or not? If the affirmative is true, (and he calls God a liar, who fays that it is not) if this is the cafe, I do not afk you, what harm can enfue from obeying their precepts and walking in their footfteps. That would not be half my meaning; but I afk, and I claim it from you as a fatisfaction which, if it is in your power to grant it, you cannot reafonably refufe. I afk you fairly, what fecurity can be given, by you, or any perfon living, even of the poffibility of our being faved by walking in another? if you can extend that fecurity to us, do it, but do not idly tell us that there is no neceffity for the obfervance of any exterior worfhip, when every thing in fcripture, every thing in reafon and revelation, every human thing, and every thing divine, as well as human, holds it out to us, as a matter, not for our prudence only, and our direction to decide upon, but of ftrict and urgent neceffity, which no humour or fancy of ours, can ever be at liberty to turn afide. What! fhall it be faid, that the apoftles, the ambaffadors, the co-partners, the fellow-helpers of Chrift, knew not the religion they were bound to practife? or, that knowing it, they did not practife it? Shall it be thought that men like thefe, who were bound to teach whatfoever Chrift had commanded them, (that and that only) could wafte their powers and throw away their commiffion in eftablifhing a fet of ordinances for their followers, with an open and explicit declaration, that it was abfolutely neceffary that thefe ordinances fhould be obferved, if they knew that there exifted no neceffity for obferving them?

*An Answer to a Letter on the **Question** Are the Quakers' Right in Their Opinion on the Baptism of the Spirit? To Which Is Added a Second Letter, in Reply. By an Emigrant*

Thus pressed on all sides, the Royal Printers are supposed to have held a consultation to the following effect:—"This order of things cannot go on. Our patent is rendered a dead letter. If we persevere, we are undone! If reduction be *practicable*, we must make it without a moment's delay. The most difficult and vexatious part of the business (said Mr. Spottiswoode,) is that untoward letter which I was so foolish as to write. That letter makes it very awkward to reduce our prices; but if it must be—why, then it must. Much better sacrifice a little feeling than all our substances. It will be prudent, however, not to *advertise* the reduction; and we should *say* as little as possible about it, and then, perhaps, it may escape the notice of the agitators."

Having resolved to reduce their prices, *if practicable,* it would seem that the Royal Typographers (innocent, simple-minded men!) for the first time in their lives began to investigate the state of their affairs! They took stock, they estimated capital in premises and machinery, in presses, engines, type, and furniture, and carefully surveyed the whole of their immense establishment. They attended especially to the cost of production; they carefully scrutinised the subject of profit;—one discovery succeeded to another, and all were of the most felicitous description. The Imperial Printers were at length gratified beyond measure to find that their profits had, without their knowledge, been most enormous, and that all the representations of the "Author of Jethro" had been true to the letter—in some cases, even below the fact! They found that every department admitted of immense reduction: the only point was, *how* to go about it, so as best, in the first instance, to *conceal* the fact of the reduction. It would not do, after the usual manner, to reprint the old Catalogue verbatim, and simply to alter the figures. At length, therefore, after much reflection and mingled counsel, the following rule of preparation was adopted. "Transpose the words where it is practicable; convert nouns into adjectives, and *vice versa;* add a phrase occasionally, and at times take phrases away; every where be sure to introduce parentheses, without at all regarding their propriety or necessity." With this rule before him, the operator set to work, and rested not till he had finished the new Catalogue.

> *John Campbell, The Present State of the Bible* **Question** *Considered, in a Letter to the People of England, With Directions for Forming Churches and Sunday Schools Into Efficient Bible Societies, by the Author of "Jethro"*

It was a great pleasure to work with George and Anastasios. I enjoyed our work together very much, and they have continued working together over the years—on a wide variety of topics.

I do not have any really great stories about them, or even one of them. One story that does come to mind is about steaks. George likes his steak cooked well done, as I do too. I know that is probably not the proper way to order a steak, but that is the way I like them. But, when George says "well-done" he means "well-done." I always loved the way George would explain this to our server: They would ask George, "how would you like your steak cooked?" And George would say, "well done—actually burn it." This usually caused some discussion with the server, and George had to be insistent that he really wanted it "burnt." I like someone who is definite.

> *Richard J. Lipton, The P=NP* **Question** *and Gödel's Lost Letter*

That exhausted that controversy! Burke looked at his watch: it was seven o'clock.

'Should we have dinner? I don't think a reception committee is either necessary or desirable.'

Mitchell did not seem to grasp the point, but he agreed to have dinner.

> *Mary Hocking, Ask No* **Question**

There are about 30,000 new cases every day right now; the number is no longer accelerating, but is still horrifying to contemplate.

What happens when this thing really and truly burns through rural America? It has already begun, and because of all those Trump supporters standing shoulder to shoulder at capitols and churches to shout their defiance of science and the "Deep State" into the virus-polluted air, it will get worse.

It will get worse within days, if the pattern holds, and there is no reason to expect otherwise. The match has been lit. In two weeks, these rural areas—which have lost so many of their hospitals thanks to decades of conservative budget cuts—are going to be locked into the same nightmare the urban areas have been dealing with since March, but with far less medical infrastructure prepared to confront it.

It begs the deadly, wretched **question**: How many Trump voters are going to die between now and November? How many people who listened to their president and his *Fox News* mouthpieces, who jammed the Michigan capitol steps and the megachurches on Easter because the president said it was safe, will be dead by June?

Quite a lot, I fear. This is the very living essence of tragedy and farce. Trump has labored mightily to convince his people that this is all some sort of ruse to keep him from being re-elected, and millions of those people have swallowed it whole.

This is a snake eating its own tail in real time while the snake-handler-in-chief cheers it on . . . except we are not talking about snakes. These are people, all of whom are somebody's children, many of whom have children.

William Rivers Pitt, Trump's Lies Are Killing His Supporters as Covid Starts to Sweep Rural America (Truthout)

There is, of course, one zone of Carroll's life that, to modern sensibilities, looks more bizarre than anything in Wonderland, and where, for once, he was blind to his own excesses. This is the province of his "child-friends," as he called them—young females, whom he encountered and corralled at every turn, especially on vacations or train trips. He had a routine, described by Douglas-Fairhurst: "Carroll would strike up a conversation with a family, bring out the games and puzzles he kept in his little black travelling bag, and follow up their meeting by sending the child a signed copy of an *Alice* book." The chumminess would proceed from here, with each stage marked by a request:

> If you should decide on sending over Gertrude and not coming yourself, would you kindly let me know what is the minimum amount of dress in which you are willing to have her taken?

The most remarkable aspect of this letter, written in 1876, is not that he was asking the mother of Gertrude Chataway whether he could photograph her daughter—preferably naked, in what he calls "Eve's original dress"—but that Mrs. Chataway did not think the **question** remarkable. Four months later, Carroll repeated it, with a twist:

> I have a little friend here, Lily Gray, child of Dr. Gray, and one of my chief beach friends at Sandown this year. She is 5, a graceful and pretty child, and one of the sweetest children I know (nearly as sweet as Gertrude)—and she is so perfectly simple and unconscious that it is a matter of entire indifference to her whether she is taken in full dress or nothing. My **question** is, are you going to allow Gertrude (who I think is also perfectly simple and unconscious) to be done in the same way?

Anthony Lane, Go Ask Alice: What Really Went On in Wonderland (The New Yorker)

This category comprises structures commonly referred to as echo-**questions** (10) and quiz **questions**, in which the wh-word is not fronted (11). Clarification **questions** like (12) have also been subsumed under this heading.

> (10) KCX 8391 It's been what?
> (11) KSS 4337   But most of the time it's what part of Yorkshire?
> (12) KBK 1487 What bits?

Ursula Kania, The Acquisition and Use of Yes-No **Questions** *in English: A Corpus-Study From a Usage-Based Perspective*

Stay calm and keep going. We find these **questions** thought provoking, so give your partner time to reflect—especially if he or she is an introvert or avoider. This worksheet is also on our website (www.HowWeLove.com) under the Freebies tab. We suggest you print out copies and write down the answers you hear as you are listening.

Milan Yerkovich and Kay Yerkovich, How We Love: Discover Your Love Style, Enhance Your Marriage

And are you suggesting that there is a compelling state interest, or what is it you are saying?

Douglas S. Lavine, **Questions** *From the Bench*

Q159 *John Hemming:* We had a discussion about this on 12 December, when, one would presume, it was clear that people were not happy with the performance of the Department. It has improved a bit, but it has not improved that much.

Coming further on, unsurprisingly I suppose, two of my **questions** that have been outstanding for a long time were answered on Monday, which would be sensible, given that you were coming to the Committee meeting on Wednesday. As the Minister is aware, I am concerned about foreign Governments who are complaining about the UK child protection system. I asked the **question**: "Have you had any complaints from foreign governments in any form?" I got the response: "Ministers are aware of no representations received from Governments relating to foreign national children being adopted in England without parental consent." I have spoken to the Minister about it previously. On page 6 of the document, we have a public statement by the Slovak Republic. On page 7 of the document, I have a letter from the Czech Republic saying there is a problem. On page 8 of the document, I have a letter from the Spanish Government saying there is a problem. On page 9 of the document, I have a letter from the Nigerian Government saying there is a problem, and then I have a letter from the Minister who I sent the Nigerian Government's letter, saying, "Thank you for sending me the Nigerian Government's letter." On page 14, I have a translation via Google of a Slovak news story, where a Slovak Minister spoke to William Hague at a foreign conference, complaining about our child protection system. My thought would be that if the Foreign Secretary was complained to, he would pass it to the Department as an issue to be looked at. The basic **question** is, having rapidly got a **question** out of the way for this particular Committee meeting, is that a fair answer on page 5?

Michael Gove: Speaking for myself, I would have to read all of the submissions. For example, I am not denying that there is a problem here, but, for example, the Czech letter confirms that the Czech Government has had concerns and is grateful to you—as I think we all are—for raising it, but it does not say that the Czech Government had contacted the British Government.

John Hemming: No, the one where I get the letter from the Minister that answered the **question**.

Michael Gove: Is Nigerian.

John Henning: I wrote to the Minister enclosing the communication from the Nigerian Government that complains about the system, and then the same Minister answers the **question** saying they are not aware of anything. One wonders what is going on. If we just look at page 5—

Chair: John, I do not want to look too hard at this, because it is a personal issue you have. I would like the Minister to respond to the **question**: how are you going to deal with John's specific concerns on this?

*House of Commons Procedure Committee, Monitoring Written Parliamentary **Questions**: Seventh Report of Session 2012–13: Report, Together With Formal Minutes and Oral Evidence*

Answering his own **question**, Landsberg articulated what few emerging modernist jazz critics would admit: "People want to watch musical performances, not just listen to them." He further added that television could enhance listening experiences: "Careful image selection in tune with the music can assist concentration and interpretation and create far greater enjoyment of music than the ear alone could receive" (Landsberg 1951).

Kristin A. McGee, Some Liked It Hot: Jazz Women in Film and Television, 1928–1959

Consider sentence (17), whose derivation after application of all phrase structure rules looks like (18):

(17) She loves chocolate.
(18) She + S + love + chocolate.

Applying T_q results in the following sequence:[12]

(19) *-s she love chocolate?

In these cases "*do* is introduced as the 'bearer' of an unaffixed affix" (Chomsky, 1957, p. 62), resulting in a well-formed yes-no **question**:

(20) Does she love chocolate?

*Ursula Kania, The Acquisition and Use of Yes-No **Questions** in English: A Corpus-Study From a Usage-Based Perspective*

"Yeah. I cleaned up the theatre a little after you left, then rode back over here. When I got in, there it was."

"Did you touch it?" Dutton asked. The New Brunswick cops had put on gloves to examine the . . . object, and they actually took pictures of the popcorn box, and then bagged it along with the knife, which took some doing, as the thing didn't want to come out of the countertop.

I gave him a "what am I, stupid?" look.

"What am I, stupid?" I asked.

He looked heavenward for a moment. "I withdraw the **question**," Dutton said.

Jeffrey Cohen, Some Like It Hot-Buttered

As can be seen, with 71% 'full' wh-**questions** constitute the vast majority of all wh-**questions** (n=1481). Nevertheless, there are quite a number of echo-/quiz and clarification **questions** (5%) and in about 4% of all wh-**questions**, the auxiliary has been omitted. A fifth of all wh-**questions** consist only of the **question** word (and in some cases a preposition).

Ursula Kania, *The Acquisition and Use of Yes-No **Questions** in English: A Corpus-Study From a Usage-Based Perspective*

"What do you think it means?" I asked him.

"Clearly, you think you know," he answered. Dutton was insightful, and/or I was transparent.

"I have a theory, but I can't prove it," I said.

"Let me hear it," Dutton said.

"I think someone doesn't want me asking **questions** about who killed Vincent Ansella."

"*Nobody* wants you asking **questions** about Vincent Ansella," Dutton said, grinning. "*I* don't want you asking **questions** about who killed Vincent Ansella, and strangely, it didn't occur to me to assault a box of popcorn in your kitchen."

"I'll admit, whoever it might be is taking things to extremes, but if you have another idea of what the message might be, I'd be happy to listen."

Jeffrey Cohen, *Some Like It Hot-Buttered*

During the argument, Tribe suggested that the Court's interpretation of the Constitution should take into account "evolving views" on sexual conduct. While the following excerpt is extremely brief, it is useful because it provides numerous pristine examples of effective responses to **questions** from the Justices.

Tribe: Mr. Chief Justice, and may it please the Court: This case is about the limits of governmental power. The power that the state of Georgia invoked to arrest Michael Hardwick in the bedroom of his own home is not a power to preserve public decorum. It is not a power to protect children in public or in private. It is not a power to control commerce or to outlaw the infliction of physical harm or to forbid a breach in a state-sanctioned relationship such as marriage or, indeed, to regulate the terms of a state-sanctioned relationship through laws against polygamy or bigamy or incest.

The power invoked here, and I think we must be clear about it, is the power to dictate in the most intimate and, indeed, I must say, embarrassing detail how every adult, married or unmarried, in every bedroom in Georgia will behave in the closest and most intimate personal association with another adult. I think it includes all physical, sexual intimacies of a kind that are not demonstrably physically harmful, that are consensual and nonconsensual in the privacy of the home . . .

Indeed. Mr. Hobbs said that under his theory the states should be able, without providing a compelling justification, to punish—his words were "irresponsible liaisons" outside the bonds of marriage . . .

What we suggest is that when the state asserts the power to dictate the details of intimacies in what they call irresponsible liaisons, even in the privacy of the home, that it has a burden to justify its law through some form of heightened scrutiny.

Justice O'Connor: Well, Mr. Tribe, how do you propose that these other situations be analyzed—by some sort of heightened scrutiny as well?

Douglas S. Lavine, **Questions** *From the Bench*

No.	Question	Answers
	Topic 1: Balance of Costs and Benefits of recommended option	
1.1	Do the documents include an explicit judgement on whether the benefits are likely to justify the costs?	(yes/no)
1.2	Is the "do nothing" counterfactual explicitly identified?	(yes/no)
1.3	Are costs explicitly identified?	(yes/no)
1.4	Are benefits explicitly identified?	(yes/no)
1.5	If answering yes to **question** 1.4: What proportion of the identified benefits are quantified?	(all/some/none)
1.6	If some benefits are not quantified are they at least observable?	(yes/ no)
1.7	What proportion of the benefits are monetised?	(all/some/none)
1.8	If answering yes to **question** 1.7: Is there evidence to support the estimates of the benefit stream?	(yes/no)
1.9	Is there any attempt at sensitivity analysis?	(yes/no)
1.10	How strong in general is the presentation of evidence throughout the appraisal?	(weak, medium, strong)
1.11	Has the quality of the evidence been assessed eg. as weak, medium or strong?	(yes/no)
	Topic 2: Consideration of options	
2.1	Do the documents describe any intervention options other than the preferred option?	(yes/no)
2.1	If answering yes to **question** 2.1: Has the same criteria been used to assess the alternatives as the criteria used to assess the preferred option?	(yes/no)

House of Commons International Development Committee, *Department for International Development Annual Report and Resource Accounts 2010–11 and Business Plan 2011–15: Fourteenth Report of Session 2010–12, Volume 1*

'Yes.'

'Without **question**?'

'Yes.' She sounded impatient.

'Think about that, it won't be easy.'

Mary Hocking, Ask No **Question**

For every **question** there was space to provide further qualitative analysis, and reviewers were encouraged to do so. This has led to inclusion of narrative alongside some of the key findings, to ensure a rounded assessment is included within this report.

House of Commons International Development Committee, Department for International Development Annual Report and Resource Accounts 2010–11 and Business Plan 2011–15: Fourteenth Report of Session 2010–12, Volume 1

"Arab men are attracted to me. They have a whole different take on buttly rapaciousness over there."

"Don."

"Sorry, baby. And what I mean is virtual Arab men, anyway. I'm not a racialist."

"Racist," said Sasha.

"Racialist," said Don. "They're different words."

"Not for the people who use them both," said Sasha.

"Touché, douche," said Don.

"These simulations," I said now, "this class, was this through the army?"

"Not really."

"No?"

"It was on the fake internet."

"The fake internet?"

"Ask the fellow you supposedly work with."

"I'm not sure I follow."

"That's the kind of thing a guy who knows all about the fake internet would say."

"Really, I don't."

"Your ignorance is duly noted. Got that, satellite?"

"Got it," I said.

"Wasn't talking to you. But now that I am, do you have any **questions** you want to ask me?"

Sam Lipsyte, The Ask

Burke wondered whether Alperin was in love with his sister; the majority of people, in Burke's opinion, were queer one way or another.

Mary Hocking, Ask No **Question**

Furthermore, "intonation is not used to distinguish genuine Inversion-**questions** from interrogatives without **Question**-status, such as Rhetorical **questions** and Requests" (Geluykens, 1988, p. 467), i.e., there do not seem to be prosodic characteristics which differentiate distinct uses of the same **question** construction.

Ursula Kania, The Acquisition and Use of Yes-No **Questions** *in English: A Corpus-Study From a Usage-Based Perspective*

Yet no one knew quite how to help. So when I asked the **question**, I was asking it for all of us. But Janice couldn't answer.

Henry Cloud and John Townsend, Boundaries: When to Say Yes, How to Say No

The **question** is a nonsense **question**. They are all nonsensical the **questions** they ask on this idiot quiz game (). () entertainment, so I—I—you can't get excited over this, you see. But obviously you are much better off if you don't know the answer. It's—like this yes-and-no examinations, gentlemen. I mean, it's not important to know these "yes" and "no." Any term paper on—written on the Stoics, it can't be—just that bad as these papers that you have—where you have to guess 50 percent of—of right, you see, with "yes" and "no." That's not worth answering, because it isn't—you are not serious. You don't want to know the good. You won't—the help of the—answering this **question** join the community and contribute something to the communal life.

Eugen Rosenstock-Huessy, Greek Philosophy (1956): Lectures 14–20

Ervin-Tripp and Miller (1977, p. 15) additionally discarded yes-no **questions** that functioned as requests for confirmation, thus applying even stricter criteria concerning what counts as a genuine **question**. Interestingly, they note that a "diversity of function was especially apparent in the polar ("yes"/"no") **questions**" (Ervin-Tripp & Miller, 1977, p. 15) but since detailed quantitative information is not provided, the percentage of **questions** fulfilling 'non-prototypical' functions cannot be assessed.

*Ursula Kania, The Acquisition and Use of Yes-No **Questions** in English: A Corpus-Study From a Usage-Based Perspective*

Q160 John Henning: If we can have a letter on that, we would be grateful.

Michael Gove: We certainly will. I would say one thing. There is a tension sometimes between speed and accuracy. There is a—

John Henning: Yes, but this one was slow and inaccurate.

Michael Gove: Indeed, but one of the points I would make is that a superficial—and it is only superficial—reading of the letter from the Nigerian Government raises a number of issues of serious concern about child protection but they do not relate, so far as I have seen in my superficial reading, specifically to adoption.

John Henning: Except I know that they do.

Michael Gove: On the basis of the letter, one cannot know that.

John Henning: Yes. I do not think we can resolve that in this particular hearing.

Michael Gove: No, but the case is important. They deserve to be dealt with appropriately. On the basis of the **question** answered, I think that the answer is fair, but given the importance of this issue, the most appropriate thing would be for either me or Minister Timpson to meet you and to run through these cases.

Chair: Excellent.

*House of Commons Procedure Committee, Monitoring Written Parliamentary **Questions**: Seventh Report of Session 2012–13: Report, Together With Formal Minutes and Oral Evidence*

"Here, here," Jenna cheered. "I'm going to get some champagne to celebrate."

"No, thanks," Ashton said quickly. "I still can't look at alcohol."

"Who gets eliminated?" Chloe asked.

"Watch," Ashton said.

Minutes later, Elena was revealed as the first to go.

"No surprise there," Chloe said. "She served them raw meat. Ew!"

Ashton thought the show was over, until she saw her face pop up on the screen. "What's this?" she murmured.

"Do you see Jolene as your main competition?"

Ashton recognized Sally's voice, but shook her head in confusion. Sally had never asked her this **question** during the interview.

"Not at all," came Ashton's reply. "This competition is about cooking skills, not about how you fill out a blouse."

Jenna's and Chloe's mouths fell open.

Ashton's stomach clenched like she'd been punched. "I never said that! Okay, I might have said that, but not in that context. Sally never asked me about Jolene specifically. They edited the **question** in later."

Her friends were still agape. "I swear!" Ashton took a deep breath. "I feel bad about Jolene. I hope she doesn't really think I feel that way."

"When you get back, you'll explain."

"And I bet you can't wait to see Ty again," Chloe said, giggling. "You are so hot for each other."

Jenna joined in the laughter. "Really, Ashton. I half expected you two to start making out over your plate of pasta."

"You don't know what you're talking about." God, had she really been that obvious? And if Jenna and Chloe had noticed, did that mean anyone else had?

Robbie Terman, *Some Like It Spicy*

I think you already know the answer to this **question** . . . but? If you are still unsure . . . ? Ask yourself this . . . :

Terijo, *I Think You Already Know the Answer to This **Question** . . . But? (Medium)*

Mitchell did not rise to the bait. 'If it wasn't for that promontory you would be able to see the lights.'

Mary Hocking, *Ask No **Question***

"There is a grain to the fabric of space-time," she said. "A scale on which there is no further divisible smoothness, only individual, irreducible quanta where reality itself seethes with a continual effervescence of sub-microscopic creation and destruction. I believe there to be a similarly irreducible texture to morality, a scale beyond which it is senseless to proceed. Infinity goes in only one direction; outward, into more inhabited worlds, more shared realities. In the other direction, on a reducing scale, once you reach the level of an individual consciousness—for all practical purposes, a single human being—you can usefully reduce no further. It is at that level that significance lies. If you do something to benefit one person, that is an absolute gain, and its relative insignificance in the wider scheme is irrelevant. Benefit two people without concomitant harm to others—or a village, tribe, city, class, nation, society or civilisation—and the benefits are scalable, arithmetic. There is no excuse beyond fatalistic self-indulgence and sheer laziness for doing nothing."

"Absolutely. Let me do this." I reached over the golden scoop of her back and slid my hand down between her legs. She shifted, bringing herself a little closer so that I didn't have to stretch. She opened her legs a little, scissoring across the crumpled bedclothes. My thumb pressed lightly on the tiny dry flower of her anus while my fingers caressed her sex, already half lost in its moistness and heat.

"There you are," she said, sounding amused. "I am experiencing some benefit already." She became quiet for a while, moving her backside rhythmically up and down a little and pressing back against my exploring hand. She blushed some hair from her face, shifted up the bed to kiss me, fully, luxuriantly, one hand behind my head, cupping, then settled back again, her head down, hair veiling her face as I worked my fingers further

*Lawrence Alma-Tadema, The **Question**, 1877*

Further mention of Ebers recalls the circumstance that his friend's tiniest picture, "The **Question**" (1878), inspired him with the idea for a novel. The subject seems simplicity itself—a youth putting a **question**—*the* **question** we will venture—to a young girl who sits by the sapphire sea with her lap full of roses. Shown at the Exhibition in Munich in 1879, this dainty little picture proved itself possessed of power to attract over and above all its competitors.

Percy Cross Standing, Sir Lawrence Alma-Tadema O.M., R.A. (London: Cassell and Co., 1905) into her. Her other hand closed round my cock, thumb stroking its glans, side to side.

"The **question**," she said, a little breathless now, "is who determines what is done, and to whom, on whose behalf, and precisely why; to what end?"

"Perhaps," I suggested, "we are working up to some sort of climax, a consummation."

Iain Banks, Transition

'In this mist? Just like a bloody Turner, isn't it? You wouldn't be surprised to see the 'Fighting *Téméraire*' bearing down on you any minute.'

'You'll see plenty here.' Mitchell nodded his head towards Isola Bella, the blue canopied stalls already visible between the trees along the front. Alperin screwed up his eyes anxiously and his companion said:

'You might prefer a visit to the château.'

'It's about the only place where you won't be trampled to death,' Burke agreed.

*Mary Hocking, Ask No **Question***

And if the answer is No . . . He's still there, then, maybe, with help—counseling from an outside source, perhaps?—you can salvage this marriage.

*Terijo, I Think You Already Know the Answer to This **Question** . . . But? (Medium)*

"I guess you already know that my sexual preference is with men. Earl is just a young lover I picked up at the Brown Derby one day. As far as Earl doing any projects for me, I'll have to say no. Oh, he showed me some of his drawings at one time but I told him his style did not come close to what I want to produce. Do you have something specific in mind? Is this why you're asking me about Earl? On your third **question**, the answer is no. I have been busy with preparing a fashion show for next month and have not had much time to socialize with anyone. It sounds to me as if there is something you are not telling me Mr. Schreiber. Am I right to take this assumption?"

Guy Beaulieu, The Death of a Bookie: A Jacob Schreiber Mystery

THE TOP TEN: **QUESTIONS** TO WHICH THE ANSWER IS 'NO'

I have a strange hobby: collecting headlines in the form of **questions** to which the author or publisher implies that the answer is yes when anyone with any sense knows it is no. I published a book of QTWTAIN last year and have continued to compile them since. Here are 10 of the best new ones spotted over the past year.

1. 'Is China more democratic than the West?'

Martin Jacques, *BBC News Magazine*, 2 November 2012. Quickly changed to: "Is China more legitimate than the West?"

2. 'Could Hitler come to power today?'

Unexpectedly asked by *The Economist*, 25 June 2013. It meant in Germany, not here.

3. 'Is Spongebob Squarepants the new Che Guevara?'

Asked by *Vice*, 15 January 2013, about T-shirts seen among Egypt's democracy protesters.

4. 'Could Abu Qatada Trigger a Snap General Election?'

Simon Heffer in the *Daily Mail*, 27 April 2013.

5. 'Are Militant Atheists Using Chemtrails to Poison the Angels in Heaven?'

Asked by a poster in a forum on *Elite Trader*, a website for investors, on 13 July 2013.

6. 'Did blowing into Nintendo cartridges really help?'

Asked by Chris Higgins, at the *Mental Floss* website, 24 September 2012. (Actually, he says the answer is no, but it is a great **question**.)

7. 'If everybody in the US drove west, could we temporarily halt continental drift?'
Asked by a contributor to the website *What If?*, 16 April 2013.

8. 'Are we literally starving students into submission?'
Barbara Ellen, *The Observer*, 25 November 2012. Fewer students turned up for a demo than she thought should have done.

9. 'Is this proof the Virgin Queen was an imposter in drag'
Daily Mail, 9 June 2013. Joyously at odds with 2006 headline, "The proof the Virgin Queen had a secret love child?"

10. 'Has the whole QTWTAIN thing run its course yet?'
Daniel Hannan, Conservative MEP, on *Twitter*, 18 April 2013. We all know the answer to that one.

John Rentoul, The Top Ten: Questions to Which the Answer Is 'No' (The Independent)

Further topicality is provided by the Pooters' discussion 'about the letters on "Is Marriage a Failure?"' predictably coming to the smug conclusion 'It has been no failure in our case' (p. 51). These letters appeared in the *Daily Telegraph* during the summer of 1888, prompting *Punch* to print half a page of spoof letters on the same subject and to answer the **question** posed with the comment 'Evidently not, as it contrives to fill two or three columns every day, and keeps up the circulation of the *D.T.* in the D.S., or Dull Season' (25 Aug. 1888, p. 87).

Kate Flint, Introduction to Diary of a Nobody, by George Grossmith and Weedon Grossmith

"The fantastic thing about Andreas is he knows the Internet is the greatest truth device ever. And what does it tell us? That everything in the society actually revolves about women, not men. The men are all looking at pictures of women, and the women are all communicating with other women."

"I think you're forgetting about gay sex and pet videos," Pip said. "But maybe we can do the **questionnaire** now? I've kind of got a boy upstairs waiting for me, which is why I'm kind of just wearing a bathrobe with nothing underneath it, in case you were wondering."

"Right now? Upstairs?" Annagret was alarmed.

"I thought it was just going to be a quick **questionnaire**."

"He can't come back another night?"

"Really trying to avoid that if I can."

"So go tell him you only need a few minutes, ten minutes, with a girlfriend. Then you don't have to be the jealous one for a change."

Here Annagret winked at her, which seemed a real feat to Pip, who was no good at winking, winks being the opposite of sarcasm.

"I think you'd better take me while you've got me," she said.

Annagret assured her that there were no right or wrong answers to the **questionnaire**, which Pip felt couldn't possibly be true, since why bother giving it if there were no wrong answers? But Annagret's beauty was reassuring. Facing her across the table, Pip had the sense that she was being interviewed for the job of being Annagret.

"Which of the following is the best superpower to have?" Annagret read. *"Flying, invisibility, reading people's minds, or making time stop for everyone except you."*

"Reading people's minds," Pip said.

"That's a good answer, even though there are no right answers.' Annagret's smile was warm enough to bathe in. Pip was still mourning the loss of college, where she'd been effective at taking tests.

"Please explain your choice," Annagret read.

Jonathan Franzen, Purity

First there is the simplicity of consulting the so-called public mind. The favorite aphorism of the politician and his friend and spokesman the editor is: "The public is always right upon a moral issue." This means that if the politician or the propagandist can present a **question** to the people in such a way that he can win his end by having the public respond in the negative, he is sure of success. It is as if society depended for its guidance upon the word of an oracle, a great stone image, out of which the priests had only succeeded in producing one response, a sound very much like, "No." The trick would consist of so framing your **question** that the word "no" would give you approval for your designs.

Clinton Wallace Gilbert, The Oracle That Always Says "No" (Nonsenseorship: Sundry Observations Concerning Prohibitions, Inhibitions and Illegalities)

To ask a negative inverted **question**, put no before the inverted verb and noun or pronoun. For verbs preceded by a direct or indirect object pronoun (see Chapter 2) or for reflexive verbs (see Chapter 3), the pronoun should remain before the conjugated verb:

- ¿No toma frutas tu amigo? *(Doesn't your friend eat fruit?)*
- ¿No las toma tu amigo? *(Doesn't your friend eat them?)*
- ¿No se desayuna temprano Alberto? *(Doesn't Alberto eat breakfast early.)*

Gail Stein and Mary Kraynak, Spanish Essentials for Dummies

That is the art of laying before the public a "moral issue" upon which it is inevitably right.

Suppose, in a society ruled by the stone image, you wanted to make war upon your neighbor. You would frame your **question** thus: "Shall we stand by idly and pusillanimously while our neighbor invades our land and rapes our women?" This is a moral issue of the deepest sanctity. You would present it. The priests would do their little something somewhere out of sight. From the great stone image would come a bellow which resembled "No." You would have won on a moral issue and would then be licensed to invade your neighbor's territory and rape his women.

Now you will perceive certain advantages in an oracle which can only say one word.

Clinton Wallace Gilbert, The Oracle That Always Says "No" (Nonsenseorship: Sundry Observations Concerning Prohibitions, Inhibitions and Illegalities)

'No, no! You can't judge that. You have no right. You're not God.' He flopped on to his knees and clutched at Mitchell's legs. 'I'll do anything, anything, but save me from this . . . I can't travel long distances in a coach. I've never been able to since I was a child. My sister would tell you; we went up to Edinburgh once . . .'

Mary Hocking, Ask No **Question**

All speakers of a new language spend a lot of time asking **questions**, but many struggle to answer them. Where you can really shine and impress others is by providing information properly. You undoubtedly know how to answer "yes" in Spanish, because the word for "yes" is common in pop culture. Answering "no" requires a bit more work, because a simple "no" doesn't always suffice.

Gail Stein, Intermediate Spanish for Dummies

I ran for my life hysterically shouting, "GO! GO! GO!" as I dove through the open window of his car. Confused and frightened Mark quickly glanced toward me and floored the gas pedal as he turned to watch the road. I made my way completely into the car as he took off down the road and around the corner. Mark already knew of my family life and wanted to help. Little did he know of how or when his help would come. It was a long and scary night. I hid not knowing what to do next. Did I plan to leave home this way? No but I could tell in my mother's eyes that she had plans for a severe beating that night. I just decided not to get hurt any more. The school tried to help in years past. One time the school spoke to a social worker. The social worker came to our house asked us **questions** and then asked our neighbors a few **questions**. We all sat at the kitchen table together with my mother present as the social worker proceeded to ask us many **questions**. No one said a word. Even when the social worker asked my mother to leave the table no one said a word. I am sure you can guess why.

Susan Derienzo, *How to Soar Like an Eagle: If You Have the Strength to Dream, Then You Can Soar*

Some pages are omitted from this book preview.
   'What happened to them?'
   'I don't know!'
   'Did he give them to someone else?'
   'Yes.' Alperin dived eagerly down this new alley. 'Yes, he gave them to someone else.'
   'To whom did he give them?'
   God, it was starting again! 'I don't know, I don't know, I swear I . . .'

Mary Hocking, Ask No **Question**

This sentiment is echoed by almost all of his colleagues, Alice Kimball Smith reports. After the success of the test bomb, as David Frisch and R. R. Wilson reflect, there were doubts, there was hindsight. Yet, when the doubtful are bluntly asked the **question**, "Would you do it again, knowing what you now know?" they answer, "Yes. Certainly, yes."

Jane Wilson, Trinity + 25 Years: Prologue (Bulletin of the Atomic Scientists, Volume XXVI, Number 6)

'You're thinking how ghastly this is?' Alperin nodded his head energetically. 'Don't imagine I don't realize it! Why do you think I'm trying to get away from it all?' His voice spiralled. 'It's because I'm not the kind who can drug himself with platitudes; I can't tell myself that these dreadful discoveries will be kept in reserve, that we shall never be the first to use them.' He laughed bitterly, 'I would have thought that Hiroshima had given the lie to that.'

   Mitchell said, 'You needn't justify yourself to me.'

   'But I do worry about it.' Alperin stared earnestly at Mitchell. 'It's only natural, isn't it? People will call me a traitor. It's not a nice word.'

   'It's a word you will have to learn to live with.'

   'Yes. Yes, you're right, of course. I suppose one loses this absurd sensitivity after a time?'

Mary Hocking, Ask No **Question**

Question. May I ask you a couple of **questions**?
Answer. I'd be delighted.
Question. If I could refer you to your statement about no problems, or no significant

changes of the Chinese, Brazilians, and Indians who lived in the area of high alpha radiation emanation. Did you believe there was a sufficient data base employed?

Answer. Yes, I do. In the case of the Chinese, it's eighty thousand people for a number of centuries. In the Brazilian case, about the same. And in the case of India, it's the same. It's a religious sect which intermarries, so that they have been constant for over a thousand years.

Question. I meant from the standpoint of the problems that they had associated with living in that high background. How do you relate the statistics of no greater medical problems associated with this?

Answer. Oh, you look at a disease, you look at cancer incidence, for example, you look at genetics, you look at fertility, number of children per family and so forth, you look at the sex ratio of males to females. This, in animal studies, is sensitive to radiation, all sorts of things of that type. Does that respond to your **question**?

Question. Well, I think so.

Answer. There must be ten or fifteen different things that are looked at.

Question. And the statistics support that?

Answer. Right.

Mr. STORM. Thank you.

Mr. HENSLEY. All right, sir.

> *United States Congress House of Representatives, Hearings on H.R. 2603, H.R. 2784, H.R. 2912, and H.R. 3364 Before the Seapower and Strategic and Critical Materials Subcommittee of the Committee on Armed Services, Ninety-Seventh Congress, First Session, June 2 and 4,*

'I'd rather die my own way.' Mitchell pushed the cheese plate to one side. 'I am terribly tired, though. And I have the oddest feeling that I'm not going to be able to take this business seriously. The whole thing seems unreal . . . dreamlike.'

Burke said, 'A night's rest will cure that.' He did not sound convincing.

They got up. As they came to the archway that led to the foyer a quick, high voice was saying, 'Alperin . . . no, no, no! Perhaps I had better spell it.'

> *Mary Hocking, Ask No* **Question**

You know in advance what its answer will be. Suppose the great stone image could have said either "yes" or "no." Suppose its answer had been "yes" to your righteous **question**? It would have been embarrassing. You could no longer say with such perfect confidence, "It is always right upon a moral issue."

Suppose you were capital and you desired to reduce wages. You would not go to the temple and say, "Shall we reduce wages?" That would not be a moral issue upon which the answer would be right. You would ask, "Shall we tamely acquiesce while the labor unions import the Russian revolution into our very midst?" The great stone voice always to be trusted on moral issues would thunder, "No."

Or suppose you were labor; for my oracle is even-handed—and you wished to extend your organization—you would go to the temple and propound the inquiry, "Shall we be eaten alive by the war profiteers?" The always moral voice would at least whisper "No!"

> *Clinton Wallace Gilbert, The Oracle That Always Says "No" (Nonsenseorship: Sundry Observations Concerning Prohibitions, Inhibitions and Illegalities)*

Oh, the requirements he put on a nine-year-old. I supposed he listened to my uncle from Chicago about that coffee thing, and thought I was ready to tackle some big stuff.

B. Matthew Bingham, *The Answer Is No! What Is the* **Question**? *A Little Orphan's Search for the Meaning of Life*

Where? he said to himself. From the bed, Alperin said, 'No, no, no, no . . .' The whole episode was rapidly degenerating into farce. Where? Burke repeated savagely, where would a man like Alperin hide anything of value? A man like Alperin . . . A man with no experience of the game, a weak man, an insignificant man, a frightened

Some pages are omitted from this book preview.

Mary Hocking, *Ask No* **Question**

For the second time, I allowed myself to cut him short. I didn't like him conducting the rhythm of our exchanges. "But there really isn't anyone, is that right?" I said, as pressingly as my passive role allowed. "There's no one? You haven't been to any functions—parties, get-togethers, meetings—official, unofficial—in London, outside London, abroad even—at which a citizen of an Iron Curtain country was remotely present?"

"Do I have to continue saying no?"

"Not if the answer's yes," I replied, with a smile he didn't like.

"The answer is no. No, no, no. Repeat no. Got it?"

"Thank you. So I can put none, can I? That means no one, not even a Russian. And you can sign it. Yes?"

"Yes."

"Meaning no?" I suggested, making another weak joke. "I'm sorry, Cyril, but we do have to be crystal clear, otherwise HQ will fall on us from a great height. Look, I've written it down for you. Sign it."

I handed him my pencil and he signed. I wanted to instill the habit in him. He handed back my notebook, smiling tragically at me. He had lied to me and he needed my comfort in his wretchedness. So I granted it to him—if only, I am afraid, because I wanted to take it away again very soon. I stowed the notebook in my inside pocket, stood up, and gave a big stretch as if announcing a break in our discussions, seeing that a tricky point was behind us. I rubbed my back a bit, an old man's ache.

John le Carré, *The Secret Pilgrim*

It will be observed that in consulting the oracle whose answer is known in advance, the only skill required consists in so framing the **question** that you will get a louder roar of "no" than the other side can with its **question**. If you can always do this you can say with perfect confidence that old granite lungs "is always right upon a moral issue."

That is the art of being a great popular leader.

Would anyone exchange a voice like that as a ruler for the wisdom of the world's ten wisest men? We laugh at the Greeks for their practice of consulting the oracle at Delphi and rightly, for our oracle beats theirs which used to hedge in its answers and leave them in doubt. Ours never equivocates; we know its answer beforehand, for the public mind is compounded of prejudices, fears, herd instincts, youthful hatred of novelty, all easily calculable.

Clinton Wallace Gilbert, *The Oracle That Always Says "No" (Nonsenseorship: Sundry Observations Concerning Prohibitions, Inhibitions and Illegalities)*

The only surviving image of the Delphic Pythia. Aegeus, the mythical king of Athens, consulting the oracle. Attic red-figure kylix, c. 440–430 BC, Berlin Museum

Luis De Carvalho, Francisca Fernandes and Hugh Bowden, "Oracle Trees in the Ancient Hellenic World," Harvard Papers in Botany 16, 2011

Sample **Questions** for the Oracle Exams

*A believer would make a sacrifice and present a **question***

1.

The Pythia was the priestess at Apollo's oracle in Delphi. The name comes from Python, the dragon that was slain by Apollo. The Pythia operated as a vehicle for Apollo's will to be known to those on earth. A believer would make a sacrifice and present a **question** to a male priest. The male priest would then present the **question** to the Pythia.

Pythia (Encyclopedia Mythica)

2.

Example

Look at this simple XML document defining a **FAQ**:

```
<?xml version="1.0"?>
<!DOCTYPE question-list SYSTEM "faq.dtd">
<?xml-stylesheet type="text/xml" href="faq.xsl"?>
<FAQ-LIST>
    <QUESTION>
        <QUERY>Question goes here</QUERY>
        <RESPONSE>Answer goes here.</RESPONSE>
    </QUESTION>
    <QUESTION>
        <QUERY>Another question goes here.</QUERY>
        <RESPONSE>The answer goes here.</RESPONSE>
    </QUESTION>
</FAQ-LIST>
```

*Oracle **FAQ's***

3.

The Pythia sat on a bronze tripod in the *adytum,* or inner chamber of Apollo's temple. In this sacred chamber the spirit of Apollo overcame the Pythia and inspired the prophecy. Some mythic traditions say the Pythia's trance was induced by vapors from a chasm below the temple or from chewing laurel leaves. Continuing his role of a middleman, the priest would interpret the Pythia's response for the **questioner**. (Powell 172)

Pythia (Encyclopedia Mythica)

4.

What are in all those X$ tables?

The following list attempts to describe some of the x$ tables. The list may not be complete or accurate, but represents an attempt to figure out what information they contain. One should generally not write queries against these tables as they are internal to Oracle, and Oracle may change them without any prior notification.

X$K2GTE2	Kernel 2 Phase Commit Global Transaction Entry Fixed Table
X$K2GTE	Kernel 2 Phase Commit Global Transaction Entry Fixed Table
X$BH	Buffer headers contain information describing the current contents of a piece of the buffer cache.
X$KCBCBH	Cache Buffer Current Buffer Header Fixed Table. It can predict the potential oss of decreasing the number of database buffers. The db_block_lru_statistics parameter has to be set to true to gather information in this table.
X$KCVFH	File Header Fixed Table
X$KDNCE	SGA Cache Entry Fixed Table
X$KDNST	Sequence Cache Statistics Fixed Table
X$KDXHS	Histogram structure Fixed Table
X$KDXST	Statistics collection Fixed Table
X$KGHLU	One-row summary of LRU statistics for the shared pool
X$KGLBODY	Derived from X$KGLOB (col kglhdnsp = 2)
X$KGLCLUSTER	Derived from X$KGLOB (col kglhdnsp = 5)
X$KGLINDEX	Derived from X$KGLOB (col kglhdnsp = 4)
X$KGLLC	Latch Clean-up state for library cache objects Fixed Table
X$KGLPN	Library cache pin Fixed Table
X$KGLTABLE	Derived from X$KGLOB (col kglhdnsp = 1)
X$KGLTR	Library Cache Translation Table entry Fixed Table
X$KGLTRIGGER	Derived from X$KGLOB (col kglhdnsp = 3)
X$KGLXS	Library Cache Access Table
X$KKMMD	Fixed table to look at what databases are mounted and their status
X$KKSBV	Cursor Cache Bind Variables
X$KSMSP	Each row represents a piece of memory in the shared pool
X$KSQDN	Global database name
X$KSQST	Enqueue statistics by type
X$KSUCF	Cost function for each Kernel Profile (join to X$KSUPL)
X$KSUPL	Resource Limit for each Kernel Profile
X$KSURU	Resource Usage for each Kernel Profile (join with X$KSUPL)
X$KSQST	Gets and waits for different types of enqueues
X$KTTVS	indicate tablespace that has valid save undo segments
X$KVII	Internal instance parameters set at instance initialization
X$KVIS	Oracle Data Block (size_t type) variables
X$KVIT	Instance internal flags, variables and parameters that can change during the life of an instance
X$KZDOS	Represent an os role as defined by the operating system

X$KZSRO	Security state Role: List of enabled roles
X$LE	Lock Element : each PCM lock that is used by the buffer cache (gc_db_locks)
X$MESSAGES	Displays all the different messages that can be sent to the Background processes
X$NLS_PARAMETERS	NLS database parameters

*Oracle **FAQ's***

5.

Strabo (64 B.C.–A.D. 25) wrote: "They say that the seat of the oracle is a cavern hollowed deep down in the earth, with a rather narrow mouth, from which rises a *pneuma* [gas, vapor, breath; hence our words "pneumatic" and "pneumonia"] that produces divine possession. A tripod is set above this cleft, mounting which, the Pythia inhales the vapor and prophesies."

Plutarch (A.D. 46–120) left an extended eyewitness account of the workings of the oracle. He described the relationships among god, woman and gas by likening Apollo to a musician, the woman to his instrument and the *pneuma* to the plectrum with which he touched her to make her speak.

*John R. Hale, Jelle Zeilinga de Boer, Jeffrey P. Chanton and Henry A. Spiller, **Questioning** the Delphic Oracle (Scientific American)*

6.

Join methods are of mainly 3 types.

Merge Join—

—Sorting both the tables using join key and then merge the rows which are sorted.

Nested loop join—

—It gets a result set after applying filter conditions based on the outer table.

—Then it joins the inner table with the respective result set.

Hash join—

—It uses hash algorithm first on smaller table and then on the other table to produce joined columns. After that matching rows are returned.

*CareerRide.com, 50 Oracle 11g dba Interview **Questions** and Answers—Freshers, Experienced*

7.

But Plutarch emphasized that the *pneuma* was only a trigger. It was really the preconditioning and purification (certainly including sexual abstinence, possibly including fasting) of the chosen woman that made her capable of responding to exposure to the *pneuma*. An ordinary person could detect the smell of the gas without passing into an oracular trance.

Plutarch also recorded a number of physical characteristics about the *pneuma*. It smelled like sweet perfume. It was emitted "as if from a spring" in the *adyton* where the Pythia sat, but priests and consultants could on some occasions smell it in the antechamber where they waited for her responses. It could rise either as a free gas or in water. In Plutarch's day the emission had become weak and irregular, the cause, in his opinion, of the weakening influence of the Delphic oracle in world affairs. He suggested that either the vital essence had run out or that heavy rains had diluted it or a great earthquake more than four centuries earlier had partially blocked its vent. Maybe, he continued, the vapor had found a new outlet. Plutarch's theories about the lessening of the emission make it clear that he believed it originated in the rock below the temple.

A traveler in the next generation, Pausanias, echoes Plutarch's mention of the *pneuma* rising in water. Pausanias wrote that he saw on the slope above the temple a spring called Kassotis, which he had heard plunged underground and then emerged again in the *adyton*, where its waters made the women prophetic.

Plutarch and other sources indicate that during normal sessions the woman who served as Pythia was in a mild trance. She was able to sit upright on the tripod and might spend a considerable amount of time there (although when the line of consultants was long, a second and even a third Pythia might have to relieve her). She could hear the **questions** and gave intelligible answers. During the oracular sessions, the Pythia spoke in an altered voice and tended to chant her responses, indulging in wordplay and puns. Afterward, according to Plutarch, she was like a runner after a race or a dancer after an ecstatic dance.

On one occasion, which either Plutarch himself or one of his colleagues witnessed, temple authorities forced the Pythia to prophesy on an inauspicious day to please the members of an important embassy. She went down to the subterranean adyton unwillingly and at once was seized by a powerful and malignant spirit. In this state of possession, instead of speaking or chanting as she normally did, the Pythia groaned and shrieked, threw herself about violently and eventually rushed at the doors, where she collapsed. The frightened consultants and priests at first ran away, but they later came back and picked her up. She died after a few days.

*John R. Hale, Jelle Zeilinga de Boer, Jeffrey P. Chanton and Henry A. Spiller, **Questioning** the Delphic Oracle (Scientific American)*

8.

We stand there, quiet. My **questions** all seem wrong: How did you get so old? Was it all at once, in a day, or did you peter out bit by bit? When did you stop having parties? Did everyone else get old too, or was it just you? Are other people still here, hiding in the palm trees or holding their breath underwater? When did you last swim your laps? Do your bones hurt? Did you know this was coming and hide that you knew, or did it ambush you from behind?

Jennifer Egan, A Visit From the Goon Squad

9.

Mickey Linehan opened the front door for me. He looked at my scratched face and laughed:

"You do have one hell of a time with your women. Why don't you ask them instead of trying to take it away from them? It'd save you a lot of skin." He poked a thumb at the ceiling. "Better go up and negotiate with that one. She's been raising hell."

I went up to Gabrielle's room. She was sitting in the middle of the wallowed-up bed. Her hands were in her hair, tugging at it. Her soggy face was thirty-five years old. She was making hurt-animal noises in her throat.

"It's a fight, huh?" I said from the door.

She took her hands out of her hair.

"I won't die?" The **question** was a whimper between edge-to-edge teeth.

"Not a chance."

She sobbed and lay down.

Dashiell Hammett, The Dain Curse

10.

"And you in brown!" she said, indignantly turning to Mr. Lorry; "couldn't you tell her what you had to tell her, without frightening her to death? Look at her, with her pretty pale face and her cold hands. Do you call that being a Banker?"

Mr. Lorry was so exceedingly disconcerted by a **question** so hard to answer, that he could only look on, at a distance, with much feebler sympathy and humility, while the strong woman, having banished the inn servants under the mysterious penalty of "letting them know" something not mentioned if they stayed there, staring, recovered her charge by a regular series of gradations, and coaxed her to lay her drooping head upon her shoulder.

"I hope she will do well now," said Mr. Lorry.

"No thanks to you in brown, if she does. My darling pretty!"

"I hope," said Mr. Lorry, after another pause of feeble sympathy and humility, "that you accompany Miss Manette to France?"

"A likely thing, too!" replied the strong woman. "If it was ever intended that I should go across salt water, do you suppose Providence would have cast my lot in an island?"

This being another **question** hard to answer, Mr. Jarvis Lorry withdrew to consider it.

Charles Dickens, A Tale of Two Cities

11.

So why is it named Oracle?

Legend has it that Larry Ellison and Bob Miner were working on a consulting project for the CIA (Central Intelligence Agency in USA) where the CIA wanted to use this new SQL language that IBM had written a white paper about. The code name for the project was Oracle (the CIA saw this as the system to give all answers to all **questions** or something such ;-).

The project eventually died (of sorts) but Larry and Bob saw the opportunity to take what they had started and market it. So they used that project's codename of Oracle to name their new RDBMS engine. Funny thing is, that the CIA was one of Oracle's first customers . . .

Oracle FAQ's

12.

"And now behold! power is given you to speak with Jupiter; ask then concerning the end of Caesar the abhorred, and search into the future condition of our country: will the people be allowed to enjoy their laws and liberties, or has the civil war been fought in vain? Fill your breast with the god's utterance; a lover of austere virtue, you should at least ask now what Virtue is and demand to see Goodness in her visible shape."

Cato, inspired by the god whom he bore hidden in his heart, poured forth from his breast an answer worthy of the oracle itself: "What **question** do you bid me ask, Labienus? Whether I would rather fall in battle, a free man, than witness a tyranny? Whether it makes no difference if life be long or short? Whether violence can ever hurt the good, or Fortune threatens in vain when Virtue is her antagonist? Whether the noble purpose is enough, and virtue becomes no more virtuous by success? I can answer these **questions**, and the oracle will never fix the truth deeper in my heart. We men are all inseparable from the gods, and, even if the oracle be dumb, all our actions are predetermined by Heaven. The gods have no need to speak; for the Creator told us once for all at our birth whatever we are permitted to know. Did he choose these barren sands, that a few might hear his voice? Did he bury truth in this desert? Has he any dwelling-place save earth and sea, the air of heaven and virtuous hearts? Why seek we further for deities? All that we see is God; every motion we make is God also. Men who doubt and are ever uncertain of future events—let them cry out for prophets:

Lucan, The Civil War, Books I–X (Pharsalia)

13.

Lawrence Joseph (Larry) Ellison (Born: 1944, Chicago) is president and CEO of Oracle Corporation.

Larry is the Oracle worlds hero, and he should be. Oracle Corporation, the company he founded with Robert N. (Bob) Miner and Edward A. (Ed) Oates back in 1977, has emerged as the world's largest vendor of software that helps large corporations and governments better manage their information.

Check out the book: *What's the Difference Between God and Larry Ellison.* It's really a great book, and is pretty even handed with who Larry Ellison is with lots of interesting stories from the early days of Oracle. The name of the book came from a funny e-mail message that went around the company. The answer to the **question** is: "God doesn't think he's Larry . . ."

Some of Larry's famous quotes:

"I do not give fashionable answers to **questions**."

*Oracle **FAQ's***

14.

'You do not have to say anything. But it may harm your defence if you do not mention when **questioned** something which you later rely on in court. Anything you do say may be given in evidence.'

Fairly straightforward you may think, but what does it actually mean?

Kim Evans, You Do Not Have to Say Anything But (The Justice Gap)

15.

First, we are not interested in the answers for their own sake. Rather, we are interested in what the answers tell us about something else.

*Floyd J. Fowler, Improving Survey **Questions**: Design and Evaluation*

16.

"Who are you?" asked K., sitting half upright in his bed. The man, however, ignored the **question** as if his arrival simply had to be accepted, and merely replied, "You rang?"

Franz Kafka, The Trial

17.

Obviously, **questions** and answers are part of everyday conversation; they are part of the fabric of our social life. However, the distinctive focus of this book is how to turn an everyday process into rigorous measurement.

*Floyd J. Fowler, Improving Survey **Questions**: Design and Evaluation*

18.

For **FAQ** data, 4,538 **questions** and 5,356 answers have been prepared for six kinds of products (computers, telephones/facsimiles, digital cameras, AV equipments, home electronics and cars). The 1,513 **questions** and answers have been collected from **FAQ** web pages and **FAQ** documents of products where Japanese has been translated into English. The remaining 3,025 **questions** have been produced by ten expert persons (10 Ph.D. Students).

Jun Harada, Masao Fuketa, El-Sayed Atlam, Toru Sumitomo, Wataru Hiraishi and Jun-ichi Aoe, Estimation of FAQ Knowledge Bases by Introducing Measurements (Knowledge-Based Intelligent Information and Engineering Systems)

19.

Is my wife having a baby? Am I going to see a death? Will I become a councillor? Am I going to be sold? Am I about to be caught as an adulterer? These are just a few of the ninety-two **questions** listed in one of the most intriguing works of classical literature to have survived: the Oracles of Astrampsychus, a book which offers cleverly randomised answers to many of ancient life's most troubling problems and uncertainties. The method is relatively straightforward, but with just enough obfuscation to make for convincing fortune-telling ('easy to use but difficult to fathom' as one modern commentator nicely put it). Each **question** is numbered.* When you have found the one that most closely matches your own dilemma, you think of a number between one and ten and add it to the number of your **question**.† You then go to a 'table of correspondences' which converts that total into yet another number, which directs you in turn to one of a series of 103 lists of possible answers, arranged in groups of ten, or 'decades' (to make things more confusing there are actually more lists of answers than the system, with its ninety-two **questions**, requires or could ever use). Finally, go back to the number between one and ten that you first thought of, and that indicates which answer in the decade applies to you.

Confused?

Mary Beard, Fortune-Telling, Bad Breath and Stress (Confronting the Classics: Traditions, Adventures, and Innovations)

20.

(on which see now C. Harrauer, "Astrampsychos," *Der Neue Pauly* 2 [Stuttgart 1997] 121–122). It enjoyed a wide-spread popularity in the world of late antiquity. Its system worked as follows (it is explained in detail in the preface of the document but is here presented in a somewhat simplified manner). The enquirer first looks in the list of 92 numbered **questions** to find his **question** or the one most like the **question** he wants to raise.‡ Then he chooses by some kind of sortition or selects in his mind a number

---

* **Question** Numbers are the numbers to the left of each **question**. By default, they're preceded by a "Q," and in their unmodified state, they act as a **question** creation counter (e.g., "Q15" represents the 15th **question** you have created for the survey).
*Qualtrics (We Eat, Sleep, and Breathe Customer Success), Auto-Number **Questions***

† You can change an individual **Question** Number by clicking on the number and editing within the text box that appears. Note that **Question** Numbers do not need to be unique, and you can use both letters and numbers.
*Qualtrics (We Eat, Sleep, and Breathe Customer Success), Auto-Number **Questions***

‡ Due to the wide variety of applications which are discussed in this group, each article title should begin with the application it involves (examples: Forms 4.5, Reports 2.5; SQL*Plus; etc.). Do not use general titles such

between 1 and 10 and adds it to the number of his **question.*** The sum thus reached has now to be looked up in a list of oracular gods with the concordance that follows the list of **questions.**† The concordance indicates by means of a number after the god's name the 'decade,' i.e., the section with ten possible answers. In that decade the answer is found under the number that was chosen by lot or selected.‡ For example, your **question** is, "Will I get the woman I want to have?" This is **question** no. 29. You draw by lot or select the number 7, so the total is 36. In the list of oracular gods you find under 36 the name Hephaestus, and after this name the concordance number 27. Decade 27 has under number 7 the following answer to your **question**: "Yes, you will get the woman you want, but much to your detriment!" Since it is a god, Hephaestus, who directs the whole process, the answer cannot but be correct, for the theory behind this method of consultation was that the god's action put the proper number in the mind or hand of the consultant. (For the wider cultural context of this phenomenon the reader is referred to P. W. van der Horst, "Sortes: Sacred Books as Instant Oracles in Late Antiquity," in

---

as "A simple **question**".

*Oracle **FAQ's***

* The + sign in the example above declares that the "**QUESTION**" element must occur one or more times inside the "**FAQ**-LIST" element.

The * sign in the example above declares that the "QUERY" element can occur zero or more times inside the "**QUESTION**" element.

*Oracle **FAQ's***

† *Category: Oracle Personalities*
The following 14 files are in this category, out of 14 total:
Chris Date.png
247 KB
Bruce Scott.jpg
4 KB
Charles Phillips.jpg
7 KB
David T. Bath.jpg
17 KB
Edgar Codd.jpg
43 KB
Edward Oates.jpg
389 KB
Jared Still.jpg
5 KB
Jeff Henley.jpg
4 KB
Ken Jacobs.jpg
14 KB
Larry Ellison.jpg
3 KB
Lex de Haan.jpg
12 KB
Robert Miner.gif
8 KB
Stephane Faroult.png
58 KB
Thomas Kyte.png
172 KB

*Oracle **FAQ's***

‡ If you'd rather not edit each **Question** Number individually or you'd like all your numbers to be in order, you can use Auto-Number **Questions**. This feature sequentially orders all the **Question** Numbers in your survey at once. Note that just **question** numbers are changed; **questions** themselves are not moved.

*Qualtrics (We Eat, Sleep, and Breathe Customer Success), Auto-Number **Questions***

L. V. Rutgers, P. W. van der Horst, H. W. Havelaar, L. Teugels (eds.), *The Use of Sacred Books in the Ancient World*, Leuven: Peeters, 1998, 143–174.)

Pieter W. van der Horst, Review of Sortes Astrampsychi, II, by Randall Stewart, ed. (Bryn Mawr Classical Review)

21.

I omitted to mention, dear Reader, that Jacques never went anywhere without a wicker-covered flask of good stuff, which he called his gourd and kept hanging from the pommel of his saddle. Each time his Master interrupted his flow with one of his extended **questions,** he would unhook it, throw back his head, pour the contents down his throat without the bottle touching his lips, and only put it back over his pommel when his Master had stopped talking.

I also forgot to mention that whenever anything cropped up that required serious thought, the first thing he did was to consult his gourd.* Whether it was some moral issue that needed to be decided, an incident to be discussed, whether to take this road or that, or begin, pursue, or abandon some course of action, weigh the advantages and disadvantages of a great point of politics or some commercial or financial venture, the wisdom or folly of a law, the outcome of a war, the choice of an inn, the choice of a room at the inn, the choice of a bed in the room at the inn, the first thing he always said was: 'Let's see what my gourd has to say,' and the last was: 'The gourd has spoken and so say I.'†

Whenever the voice of Destiny was silent in his head, it spoke through his gourd: it was a kind of portable Pythia which dried up as soon as it was empty.‡ At Delphi Pythia, her skirts hitched up, sitting bare-bottomed on her three-legged stool, received her inspiration from below, whence it rose upward. Jacques, sitting on his horse, with his

---

** 2 Semantic Expression of **FAQ** Knowledge Bases*

A **questioner** is classified into three kinds of types: interrogative, imperative and declarative sentences. Consider each sentence requesting a drink as follows:

1)	Interrogative sentence	"Isn't a drink given?"
2)	Imperative sentence	"Give me a drink"
3)	Declarative sentence	"I want a drink"

*Jun Harada, Masao Fuketa, El-Sayed Atlam, Toru Sumitomo, Wataru Hiraishi and Jun-ichi Aoe, Estimation of **FAQ** Knowledge Bases by Introducing Measurements (Knowledge-Based Intelligent Information and Engineering Systems)*

† 2.1 Direct and Indirect Intentions

Although the above examples have direct intention requesting a drink, many **questions** have indirect intention. This is called an indirect speech act. Consider the following **question** (1) with indirect intention: "Doesn't a throat become it dry?", "How is juice?" is one of the right answers if a **questioner**'s intention is "I want a drink." The intention understanding depends on the dialogue situation and the semantic expression with a situation attribute must be formalized. The above indirect intention of **question** (1) = "Doesn't a throat become it dry?" can be represented by [Moisture is insufficient in the situation C], and the more formal description of a **question** semantic expression is denoted by [[[C], [SITUATION]]; [[moisture], [OBJECT]]; [[insufficient, [CLAM]]], where [] specifies semantic representation and [A] of [[A], [B]] is the attribute value for attribute [B]. In order to define an answer semantic expression corresponding to expected answer (a) for **question** (q), the **question** semantic expression is transformed by replacing [[insufficient],[CLAIM]] into [[supply], [SOLUTION]]. The transformed semantic expression is the answer semantic expression and it is represented as follows:

[[[C], [SITUATION]]; [[moisture, [OBJECT]]; [[supply], [SOLUTION]]].

*Jun Harada, Masao Fuketa, El-Sayed Atlam, Toru Sumitomo, Wataru Hiraishi and Jun-ichi Aoe, Estimation of **FAQ** Knowledge Bases by Introducing Measurements (Knowledge-Based Intelligent Information and Engineering Systems)*

*‡ 2.2 Transformation of Semantic Expressions on **FAQ** Knowledge*

In the **FAQ** dialogue, a **questioner** (a user or a customer) expects that a respondent (a company person) provides useful answers resolving his/her claim. Therefore, no **questioner** gives his/her juice to the respondent as the above section 2.1.

*Jun Harada, Masao Fuketa, El-Sayed Atlam, Toru Sumitomo, Wataru Hiraishi and Jun-ichi Aoe, Estimation of **FAQ** Knowledge Bases by Introducing Measurements (Knowledge-Based Intelligent Information and Engineering Systems)*

Questions, answers, and wishes, all of those things that help or hinder us on our journey, are very much a part of our relationship with Faerie. "Who am I? What is your quest? Why have you come here, what do you seek?" are **questions** often asked by the individuals you meet in Faerie. They do not as often ask you who you are. It is more important for you to discover who they are.

*The **Question**, from the Heart Of Faerie Oracle Card deck,*
by Brian and Wendy Froud (archangeloracle.com)

head back, his gourd uncorked, and its neck pointing at his mouth, received his inspiration from on high, whence it flowed downwards. When Pythia and Jacques announced their oracles, both were drunk.[*]

Jacques claimed that the Holy Spirit had descended on the apostles in a gourd: he called Whitsun the Festival of the Gourd. Indeed, he had composed a short treatise on divinations of this kind, a profound work in which he gives his preference to oracles pronounced by Bacbuc, or the gourd. He disagreed on this subject with the curé of Meudon, though he venerated him, for the curé consulted the divine Bacbuc only insofar as he was given to cracking a bottle or two. 'I'm fond of Rabelais,' said he, 'but I'm fonder of truth than I am of Rabelais.' He called him a heretical Engastrimyth,[†] and advanced many reasons, each more compelling than the one before,[‡] to prove that the true oracles of Bacbuc or the divine gourd could only be heard through the neck of the bottle. Among the distinguished devotees of Bacbuc and those most truly inspired by the gourd in recent centuries, he placed Rabelais, La Fare, Chapelle, Chaulieu, La Fontaine, Molière, Panard, Gallet, and Vadé. To his mind, Plato and Jean-Jacques Rousseau, who championed wine-drinking but did not drink themselves, were two false followers of the gourd. In time of yore, the gourd was enshrined in a number of celebrated sanctuaries, the Pomme de Pin, the Temple, and the *guinguette*, of which places of worship he was writing a separate history. He described in the most graphic terms the enthusiasm, the warmth, the heat with which the Bacbucians or the Périgourdins were—and indeed still are—fired when they sat with their elbows on the table at the end of a meal and the divine Bacbuc, or the sacred gourd, appeared unto them, descended in their midst,

---

[*] **question** "why"

why not just use sql?

but interestingly, just see "above", there are hash functions shown there as well as the sql that shows you WHAT is different about the tables instead of just saying "yes, they are different"

*AskTom, **Questions** > Ora-Hash (Oracle.com)*

[†] The Engastrimyths (citing on this subject the testimony of Aristophanes in his comedy called *The Wasps*) claim to be descended from the ancient family of Eurycles. That is why they were called Euryclians in ancient times as Plato writes (and Plutarch too in *Why Oracles Have Ceased*). They are called Ventriloquists in the holy Decretum (26 **question** 3), and Hippocrates (in Book Five of the *Epidemics*) calls them in Greek 'Ones talking from the belly' (Sophocles calls them *Sternomantes*). They were fortune-tellers, casters of spells and deceivers of simple folk, appearing to speak, and to answer those who **questioned** them, not with their mouths but their bellies.

Francois Rabelais, Gargantua and Pantagruel

[‡] *3.1 Degree of Disrepute for **Questions***

In the **question** understanding process, affective information (user's tone, sentence style and so on) are considered and **Q**-CLASS defines in the **question** semantic expression. This section defines the degree of the user's disrepute from **questions** as follows:

1) DISREPUTE ([[IMPOSSIBLE], [**Q**-CLASS]])=4

Value [IMPOSSIBLE] means the function which should be committed essentially does not work, so the degree of user's disrepute is the highest level. This point is defined by 4.

2) DISREPUTE ([[SIDE EFFECT],[**Q**-CLASS]])=3

Value [SIDE EFFECT] means there is a bad phenomenon unrelated to the original function, so the degree of user's disrepute is in the second level. This point is defined by 3.

3) DISREPUTE ([[INSUFFICIENT],[**Q**-CLASS]])=2

Value [INSUFFICIENT] means a function is lower than the expected performance, so the degree of user's disrepute is in the third level. This point is defined by 2.

4) DISREPUTE ([[UNCLEAR],[**Q**-CLASS]])=1

Value [UNCLEAR] means the operating method and the results are unclear, so the degree of user's disrepute is the lowest level. This point is defined by 1.

*Jun Harada, Masao Fuketa, El-Sayed Atlam, Toru Sumitomo, Wataru Hiraishi and Jun-ichi Aoe, Estimation of **FAQ** Knowledge Bases by Introducing Measurements (Knowledge-Based Intelligent Information and Engineering Systems)*

hissed, spurted froth far and wide, and covered its disciples with its prophetic droplets.[*]
His manuscript is illustrated with two portraits, underneath which is written: 'Anacreon
and Rabelais, supreme pontiffs of the Gourd, one an Ancient, the other a Modern.'

Do you really mean Jacques used the word 'engastrimyth'?[†]

Why not, Reader?[‡] Jacques's Captain was a Bacbucian and he might well have
known the term.[§] And since Jacques lapped up everything he said, he could easily have
remembered it.[¶] But to be honest, 'engastrimyth' is mine. It was 'ventriloquist' in the
original text.[**]

Denis Diderot, Jacques the Fatalist and His Master

22.

Further speculation:

We received a lot of E-mails recently stating that ORACLE stands for *Oak Ridge
Automatic Computer and Logical Engine,* a computer built by Oak Ridge National
Laboratory in the 1950's. For some time this was the fastest computer in the world. It
reportedly could do 100 man-years of calculations in an eight-hour work shift. However,
we don't believe this has anything to do with the Oracle Database or Oracle Corporation.
However, if you have information to the contrary, please let us know.

Yet another mail stated that Oracle stands for *Orbital Relational Analytical Computing
Logical Equation.* Absolutely amazing! As expected, a Google search on this returned
zero hits.

*Oracle **FAQ's***

23.

"Pyotr Stepanovitch, you've treated me cruelly," he brought out abruptly.

---

[*] True, the hashing is a useful technique—I use it over dblinks. But many times, I use the compare table query
technique—because the very very next **question** is typically "so, what was different?"
  *AskTom, **Questions** > Ora-Hash (Oracle.com)*

[†] I already answered this, read above.
  *AskTom, **Questions** > Ora-Hash (Oracle.com)*

[‡] That query makes absolutely no sense to me whatsoever.
  *AskTom, **Questions** > Ora-Hash (Oracle.com)*

[§] *Gastriloque, (gastro,* and *loquor,* 'I speak,') Engastrimyth.
Gastril'oquist, Engastrimyth.
Gastril'oquus, Engastrimyth.
Gastrimar'gus, (γαδτιμαργος, from gastro, and μαργοω, 'I rage,') Glutton.
  *Robley Dunglison, Medical Lexicon: A Dictionary of Medical Science; Containing a Concise Explanation of the Various
  Subjects and Terms of Anatomy, Physiology, Pathology, Hygiene, Therapeutics, Medical Chemistry, Pharmacology, Pharmacy,
  Surgery, Obstetrics, Medical Jurisprudence, and Dentistry; Notices of Climate, and of Mineral Waters; Formulæ for Officinal,
  Empirical, and Dietetic Preparations; With the Accentuation and Etymology of the Terms, and the French and Other
  Synonyms*

[¶] Except when a reference furnishes a direct answer to a **question**, the recitation of the reference should not
be received as the answer, which should be given in the child's own words. And in no case should a scholar be
allowed to examine the references during recitation. If he has not studied them beforehand, he should be passed
by, as unable to answer the **question**. The practice of permitting the scholars to look out their answers, either in
the text or references, during recitation, cannot be too severely reprehended. It defeats every attempt to secure
thorough preparation, and wastes the time appropriated to recitation, which is generally too short.
  *Harvey Newcomb, Newcomb's First **Question** Book*

[**] He asks . . . 'What power can an engastrimyth have to call back the spirits of the blessed? Having no arguments,
he takes refuge in obscurity, shifting on to another responsibility for what he has done himself. Attributing
the entire narrative to the scripture, he holds to the belief that Samuel was called up, but dares not answer the
question who has called him up. (Eus. 26.2; 194)
  Steven Connor, Dumbstruck: A Cultural History of Ventriloquism

"Why cruelly? How? But allow us to discuss the **question** of cruelty or gentleness later on. Now answer my first **question**; is it true all that I have said or not? If you consider it's false you are at liberty to give your own version at once."

"I . . . you know yourself, Pyotr Stepanovitch," the captain muttered, but he could not go on and relapsed into silence. It must be observed that Pyotr Stepanovitch was sitting in an easy chair with one leg crossed over the other, while the captain stood before him in the most respectful attitude.

Lebyadkin's hesitation seemed to annoy Pyotr Stepanovitch; a spasm of anger distorted his face.

"Then you have a statement you want to make?" he said, looking subtly at the captain. "Kindly speak. We're waiting for you."

"You know yourself Pyotr Stepanovitch, that I can't say anything."

"No, I don't know it. It's the first time I've heard it. Why can't you speak?"

The captain was silent, with his eyes on the ground.

"Allow me to go, Pyotr Stepanovitch," he brought out resolutely.

"No, not till you answer my **question**: is it all true that I've said?"

"It is true," Lebyadkin brought out in a hollow voice, looking at his tormentor. Drops of perspiration stood out on his forehead.

"Is it *all* true?"

"It's all true."

"Have you nothing to add or to observe? If you think that we've been unjust, say so; protest, state your grievance aloud."

Fyodor Dostoyevsky, The Possessed; or, The Devils

24.

Q41. What is the "true story" about using data mining to identify a relation between sales of beer and diapers?

This is one of those recurring **questions** related to a famous decision support example. The story of using data mining to find a relation between "beer and diapers" is told, retold and added to like any other legend or "tall tale". I can't recall exactly when I first heard a version of the tale, but I have used the story and added to it myself on occasion. The following are some versions of the tale.

An article in *The Financial Times of London* (Feb. 7, 1996) stated, 'The oft-quoted example of what data mining can achieve is the case of a large US supermarket chain which discovered a strong association for many customers between a brand of babies nappies (diapers) and a brand of beer. Most customers who bought the nappies also bought the beer. The best hypothesizers in the world would find it difficult to propose this combination but data mining showed it existed, and the retail outlet was able to exploit it by moving the products closer together on the shelves."

Bill Palace at UCLA (Spring 1996) in his web lecture notes writes "For example, one Midwest grocery chain used the data mining capacity of Oracle software to analyze local buying patterns. They discovered that when men bought diapers on Thursdays and Saturdays, they also tended to buy beer. Further analysis showed that these shoppers typically did their weekly grocery shopping on Saturdays. On Thursdays, however, they only bought a few items. The retailer concluded that they purchased the beer to have it available for the upcoming weekend. The grocery chain could use this newly discovered information in various ways to increase revenue. For example, they could move the beer display closer to the diaper display. And, they could make sure beer and diapers were sold at full price on Thursdays."

Hermiz and Manganaris (1999) stated "One of the most repeated (though likely fabricated) data mining stories is the discovery that beer and diapers frequently appear together in a shopping basket. The explanation goes that when fathers are sent out on an errand to buy diapers, they often purchase a six-pack of their favorite beer as a reward."

Also, the 8th Annual Virginia High School Programming Contest (2001) had a problem titled Beer and Diapers. The problem statement begins "Store owners have long noticed that inspecting customer transactions can increase their profit. For example, placing the items frequently purchased together next to each other can stimulate purchasing of these items. Obviously, milk and cereal are frequently purchased together. However, some patterns are less obvious. For example, it was found that people who buy diapers also buy beer. Given a number of transactions, your job is to find a pair of items that frequently occur together."

*Daniel J. Power, Decision Support Systems: **Frequently Asked Questions***

25.

Both Linux and Windows are great operating systems for running your Oracle database. This is a very mood **question**, but is still frequently asked.

*Oracle **FAQ's***

26.

1. Which adjective describes you best?
     a. Impulsive. > Go to **question** 2.
     b. Cool-headed. > Go to **question** 3.
     c. Open-minded. > Go to **question** 4.

2. Which do you prefer?
     a. Ponies. > Go to **question** 5.
     b. Unicorns. > Go to **question** 6.

3. Which describes you better?
     a. You're a bit of a homebody. > Go to **question** 10.
     b. You love learning new things. > Go to **question** 11.

4. Do you like to travel to new and different places?
     a. Yes. > Go to **question** 9.
     b. No. > Go to **question** 7.
     c. Sometimes yes, sometimes no. > Go to **question** 12.

5. Your favourite sport is . . .
     a. hiking. > Go to **question** 7.
     b. sailing. > Go to **question** 4.

6. Which describes you best?
     a. You have a wild imagination. > You are Cassandra.
     b. You adore drama and theatre. > You are Hera.
     c. You're a big hugger—you love everybody! > Go to **question** 12.

Helaine Becker, What Ancient Classical Heroine or Goddess Are You? (The Quiz Book for Girls)

27.

yeahbut, since the next **question** is typically 'what is different', I myself (assuming the two tables are on the same machine) would prefer just to ask that **question**:

```
ops$tkyte@ORA10G> /*
ops$tkyte@ORA10G>
ops$tkyte@ORA10G> drop table a;
ops$tkyte@ORA10G> drop table b;
ops$tkyte@ORA10G>
ops$tkyte@ORA10G>
ops$tkyte@ORA10G> create table A as
ops$tkyte@ORA10G> select obj# id, name from sys.obj$
ops$tkyte@ORA10G> /
ops$tkyte@ORA10G>
ops$tkyte@ORA10G> create table B as
ops$tkyte@ORA10G> select obj# id, name from sys.obj$
ops$tkyte@ORA10G> /
ops$tkyte@ORA10G> */
ops$tkyte@ORA10G> set timing on
ops$tkyte@ORA10G>
ops$tkyte@ORA10G> select sum(ora_hash(id||'|'||name, POWER(2,16)-1))
    2 from A
    3 union all
    4 select sum(ora_hash(id||'|'||name, POWER(2,16)-1))
    5 from B;
SUM(ORA_HASH(ID||'|'||NAME,POWER(2,16)-1))
-------------------------------------------
    1646226153
    1646240054

Elapsed: 00:00:00.16
ops$tkyte@ORA10G>
ops$tkyte@ORA10G>
ops$tkyte@ORA10G> select id, name,
    2 count(src1) CNT1,
    3 count(src2) CNT2
    4 from
    5 ( select a.*,
    6 1 src1,
    7 to_number(null) src2
    8 from a
    9 union all
    10 select b.*,
    11 to_number(null) src1,
    12 2 src2
    13 from b
    14 )
    15 group by id, name
    16 having count(src1) <> count(src2)
    17 /
        ID NAME CNT1 CNT2
-------------------------------------------
    75766 B 0 1
```

```
Elapsed: 00:00:00.18
```

*AskTom, **Questions** > Ora-Hash (Oracle.com)*

28.

The answers are not restricted to a simple yes or no either, all the more since these words do not even exist in Ancient Greek. After choosing a **question**, the interrogator is allotted a number from 1 to 10. By adding this number to the number of his **question**, he gets a third number. In the concordance list this number is followed again by yet another number. This fourth and last number indicates which decade the answer can be found in. Every decade has 10 numbered oracular sayings and the one that matches the number the **questioner** drew by lot, is the answer to his **question**. In short, the *Sortes Astrampsychi* consist of 92 **questions** with 10 potential answers each. The unnecessary complicated number based system, which is elaborately described in the introduction, of course has been replaced by hyperlinks and JavaScript in the online versions. After all, it suffices to draw one of the 10 potential answers to each **question**. The concordance list and the decades make the book look more complicated than it really is, so it appears more mysterious to its users. It also prevents the user from seeing the 9 other potential answers while looking up the right one, because they are all in different decades.

The Oracles of Astrampsychus (Sortes Astrampsychi)

29.

Hi Tom,

This is a great site—very informative. I also read your book—*Expert One-On-One*. I've already recommended it to my team-mates. You are doing a great job, keep it up!

I have a couple of **questions**:

1) How do I make the Split work on a Global Temporary Table? I tried the following:—

```
10:41:53 SQL> create global temporary table t
10:42:03  2 on commit preserve rows
10:42:08  3 as
10:42:11  4 select * from testocc1;

Table created.

Elapsed: 00:00:02.62
10:42:19 SQL> commit;

Commit complete.

Elapsed: 00:00:00.00
10:42:23 SQL> select count(*) from testocc1;

  COUNT(*)
----------
    675158

Elapsed: 00:00:00.24
10:42:28 SQL> @split_table t 10

no rows selected

Elapsed: 00:00:00.42
```

2) We are currently building a data warehouse. We get fixed width files (master and transaction) from several source systems. The data warehouse source schema contains external tables, one per file and views which reside on top of the external tables which contains many row level transformations—for example CASE statements, NVL handling, decimal conversion etc. We used Direct Path Insert to populate fact tables and we use single 'Insert into . . . Select from . . .' statement approach. What are your thoughts on this approach?

AskTom, **Questions** *> Spawn Jobs From a Procedure That Run in Parallel (Oracle.com)*

30.

Thanks to the unique system of basic **questions**, the answers of the *Sortes Astrampsychi* are always directly related to the **question**. Other ancient lot oracles, including the famous Chinese oracle book *Yi Jing (I Ching)* or "Book of Changes", do not take the **question** into account, so their answers are open to interpretation. Strictly speaking, an oracular saying represents the will of a deity. Although oracles usually refer to the future, they are not simply forecasts of the future. The deity was often asked for advise on a concrete plan, so he would give his blessing or advise against it. The reasoning was that the gods, however not almighty or all-knowing, had more information at their disposal than ordinary mortals and were therefore the perfect advisors. As a result, in Antiquity the oracle was consulted prior to every important decision.

The Oracles of Astrampsychus (Sortes Astrampsychi)

31.

Some of the **questions** that come to my mind are:—

1. What happens if query execution plan changes in the production making the SQL statement itself go slower? What can I do to minimize this risk?

2. We have seen that when you load a fact table using the external_table->view->joined with dimension table approach is slower at times—this is inconsistent. However if I dump the data from the view into a Global Temporary Table, it goes faster—well many times. Would it make sense to split the Global Temporary Table as you've shown in this thread and then submit them as load jobs. What are your thoughts?

Thanks,

Upendra

AskTom, **Questions** *> Spawn Jobs From a Procedure That Run in Parallel (Oracle.com)*

32.

With respect to content, the *Sortes Astrampsychi* are characteristic for Roman, and more in general, Western culture. In comparison with the complex and typically Eastern, open to interpretation profundities of the *Yi Jing,* the *Oracles of Astrampsychus* provide simple and clear answers to specific practical **questions** about familial, financial, legal, medical and other every day personal affairs.

The Oracles of Astrampsychus (Sortes Astrampsychi)

33.

1.   What companies provide Oracle Certification?
2.   What official Oracle certification tracks are available?
3.   How hard are the exams?
4.   What training is required before one can take an exam?

5. How do I prepare for the exams?
6. Where can one take these exams?
7. What is the format of the certification exams?
8. How are exams scored?
9. Can one (during an exam) skip **questions** and answer them later in the exam?
10. Is it OK to guess answers or are these tests marked negatively?
11. Do I have to pass one exam before I can write the next one?
12. What happens when one fails an exam?
13. Where can one get sample **questions** for the Oracle exams?

> Oracle **FAQ's**

34.

As a matter of fact, numerous ancient sources proof the Greek and Egyptian temple oracles were asked exactly the same **questions**. It is therefore no coincidence the oracle book appeared in a period the traditional oracles were in decay and closing down one by one. Yet the success of the *Sortes Astrampsychi,* even among Christians, clearly shows there was still a need for oracles.

> The Oracles of Astrampsychus (Sortes Astrampsychi)

35.

If that moment is now, ask your **question**, and pick one of the cards at random from the pages of chapter 9.

> Lon Milo DuQuette, The Book of Ordinary Oracles: Use Pocket Change, Popsicle Sticks, a TV Remote, This Book, and More to Predict the Future and Answer Your **Questions**

36.

I had misgivings. They took my samples away, sat me down at a computer console. In response to **questions** on the screen I tapped out the story of my life and death, little by little, each response eliciting further **questions** in an unforgiving progression of sets and subsets. I lied three times. They gave me a loose-fitting garment and a wristband ID. They sent me down narrow corridors for measuring and weighing, for blood-testing, brain graphing, the recording of currents traversing my heart. They scanned and probed in room after room, each cubicle appearing slightly smaller than the one before it, more harshly lighted, emptier of human furnishings. Always a new technician. Always faceless fellow patients in the mazelike halls, crossing from room to room, identically gowned. No one said hello. They attached me to a seesaw device, turned me upside down and let me hang for sixty seconds. A printout emerged from a device nearby. They put me on a treadmill and told me to run, run. Instruments were strapped to my thighs, electrodes planted on my chest. They inserted me in an imaging block, some kind of computerized scanner. Someone sat typing at a console, transmitting a message to the machine that would make my body transparent. I heard magnetic winds, saw flashes of northern light. People crossed the hall like wandering souls, holding their urine aloft in pale beakers. I stood in a room the size of a closet. They told me to hold one finger in front of my face, close my left eye. The panel slid shut, a white light flashed. They were trying to help me, to save me.

> Don DeLillo, White Noise

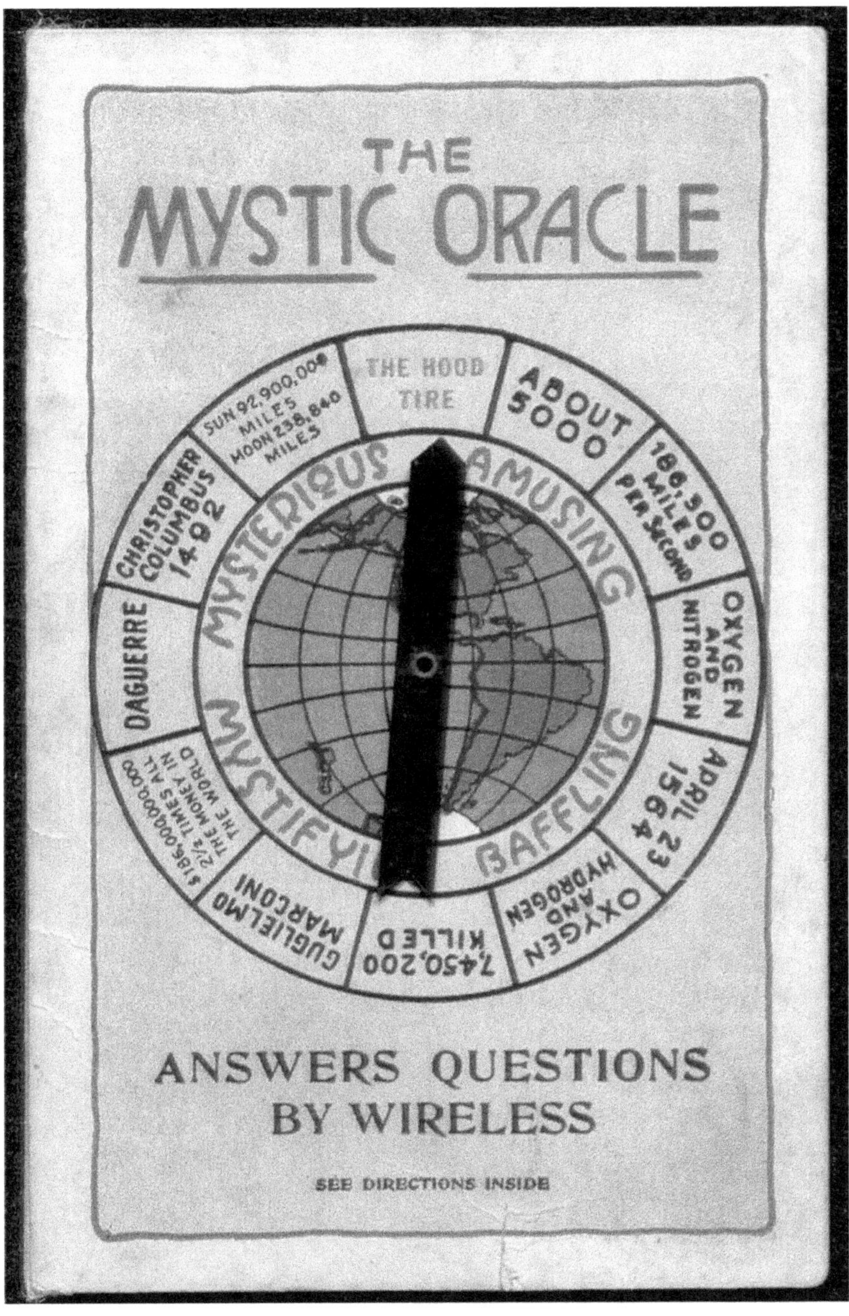

THE MYSTIC ORACLE ANSWERS **QUESTIONS** BY WIRELESS SEE DIRECTIONS INSIDE 1923

Condition: Used
Price: US $30.00
Buy It Now
Make Offer

www.ebay.com

Pam
2012.0635

Facts Most Folks Don't Know.

The population of the globe is 1,646,000,000, divided into 6 great races as follows:

Mongolian	655,000,000
Caucasian	645,000,000
Negro	190,000,000
Semitic	81,000,000
Malayan	52,000,000
Indian	23,000,000

The average depth of all the oceans is from 2 to 2½ miles.

The value of gold and silver in the world is just about equal—gold, 18,100,874,536; silver, 16,256,913,158.

The number of stars visible with the naked eye is only about 7,000, but the number visible through the telescope is over 70,000,000.

In 1830 there were 23 miles of steam railroads in the United States; now there are over 263,000 miles, enough to go 10 times around the earth.

There are twice as  many non-christians in the world as there are christians.

The Panama Canal cost more than all the other canals in the world combined, $375,000,000.00.

There are 20 waterfalls in the world higher than Niagara Falls, the highest being Grand Falls, Labrador, 2,000 feet.

The volume of the sun is 1,300,000 times that of the earth.

The largest railway tunnel is the Simplon between Switzerland and Italy; it is 12 miles and 458 yards long.

The heaviest material in the world is Platina, its specific gravity is 2,150.

The largest diamond in the world is the Cullinan; it weighs 3,025 carats.

The center of population in the United States is located six miles southwest of Union City, Indiana.

The geographic center of continental United States (exclusive of Alaska) is located near the town of Lebanon, Kansas. Latitude 39 degrees 50 minutes; longitude 98 degrees, 35 minutes.

There is imported into the United States each year over 1,352,312,000 pounds of coffee.

COPYRIGHT 1923 PATENT APPLIED FOR

THE MYSTIC ORACLE ANSWERS **QUESTIONS** BY WIRELESS SEE DIRECTIONS INSIDE 1923

THE MYSTIC ORACLE ANSWERS **QUESTIONS** BY WIRELESS SEE DIRECTIONS INSIDE 1923

Condition: Used
Price: US $30.00
Buy It Now
Make Offer

www.ebay.com

37.

One of the most interesting things about this lot-oracle is that we have it in both a pagan and a Christian version. Early papyri from the third and fourth century have the names of pagan gods in the concordance list, but in the many medieval manuscripts of the *Sortes* the names of the gods have been replaced by those of biblical persons. Although the Christians had also changed a few of the **questions** (e.g., "Will I be reconciled with my girlfriend?" has now become "Will I become a bishop?"), by and large they were using the same book as the pagans did not long before them.

Pieter W. van der Horst, Review of Sortes Astrampsychi, II, by Randall Stewart, ed. (Bryn Mawr Classical Review)

38.

Notice that the update completed in 2 seconds! I've seen faster but my two-gerbil sandbox machine doesn't have the power that our newer servers do. The point is that the update was incredibly fast and chewed up only 10% of one core. So, in answer to the **question** of "how often should I commit?" I say don't until you absolutely have to.

Oracle *FAQ's*

39.

What is significant about the *Eighty-three Different* **Questions** in this regard is that within its pages it has captured this important change as it is happening.

A third feature of the *Eighty-three Different* **Questions** is its Pythagorean concerns. Like the Pythagorean philosophers of the ancient Greek world, St. Augustine had an abiding fascination for numbers. With these philosophers he shared two important convictions: (1) that numbers (or at least the laws governing them) are objective, timeless, and unchangeable features of the universe which are of fundamental importance not only for the actual structuring and ordering of the universe, but also for the understanding of it; and (2) that numbers have special symbolic meanings which, for Augustine at least, somehow derive from their privileged metaphysical status. The first view I will call "number metaphysics," the second, "number mysticism." The latter view enjoyed widespread popularity at all levels of late classical and of patristic culture, while the former view enjoyed the attention of a much smaller and more cultivated circle who, like Augustine, had been directly or, more probably, indirectly influenced by Pythagorean thought. Although there seems to be no internal logical connection between number metaphysics and number mysticism such that the former strictly entails the latter, nonetheless, the Pythagoreans and St. Augustine enthusiastically endorsed both views. However, in the *Eighty-three Different* **Questions** it is only problems of number mysticism which for the most part bother Augustine, and hence the Pythagorean concerns of the work are primarily of this sort. The development and application of his number metaphysics must be sought for elsewhere.[67]

This number mysticism is clearly seen in at least eight **questions** (**QQ.** 55–59, 61, 64, and 81), wherein St. Augustine discusses, sometimes in great detail, the symbolic meanings of various numbers in Scripture. The most elaborate example of this number mysticism is **Q.** 57: "On the One Hundred and Fifty-three Fish."[68] Intrigued by the problem of the number 153 mentioned in Jn 21.11, Augustine conducts a detailed investigation into the symbolic meanings of the numbers which generate 153. His general conclusion is that this number signifies the perfected and holy Church of God. Further examples of St. Augustine's number mysticism could be adduced, but, since his most significant and lasting contributions to western civilization are to be found elsewhere, no more will be said on this topic.

David L. Mosher, Introduction to St. Augustine, *Eighty-three Different* **Questions**

40.

THE REVEREND MR LARYNX
They were very learned fishermen.

MR HILARY
They had the gift of tongues by especial favour of their brother fisherman, Saint Peter.

THE HONOURABLE MR LISTLESS
Is Saint Peter the tutelar saint of Cadiz?

(None of the company could answer this **question**, *and MR ASTERIAS proceeded.)*

They spoke to him in several languages, but he was as mute as a fish. They handed him over to some holy friars, who exorcised him; but the devil was mute too. After some days he pronounced the name Lierganes. A monk took him to that village. His mother and brothers recognised and embraced him; but he was as insensible to their caresses as any other fish would have been. He had some scales on his body, which dropped off by degrees; but his skin was as hard and rough as shagreen. He stayed at home nine years, without recovering his speech or his reason: he then disappeared again; and one of his old acquaintance, some years after, saw him pop his head out of the water near the coast of the Asturias. These facts were certified by his brothers, and by Don Gaspardo de la Riba Aguero, Knight of Saint James, who lived near Lierganes, and often had the pleasure of our triton's company to dinner.—Pliny mentions an embassy of the Olyssiponians to Tiberius, to give him intelligence of a triton which had been heard playing on its shell in a certain cave; with several other authenticated facts on the subject of tritons and nereids.

THE HONOURABLE MR LISTLESS
You astonish me. I have been much on the sea-shore, in the season, but I do not think I ever saw a mermaid. (He rang, and summoned Fatout, who made his appearance half-seas-over.) Fatout! did I ever see a mermaid?

FATOUT
Mermaid! mer-r-m-m-aid! Ah! merry maid! Oui, monsieur! Yes, sir, very many. I vish dere vas von or two here in de kitchen—ma foi! Dey be all as melancholic as so many tombstone.

THE HONOURABLE MR LISTLESS
I mean, Fatout, an odd kind of human fish.

FATOUT
De odd fish! Ah, oui! I understand de phrase: ve have seen nothing else since ve left town—ma foi!

Thomas Love Peacock, *Nightmare Abbey*

41.

Question. Now tell us what some of the signs and passwords of the order were?

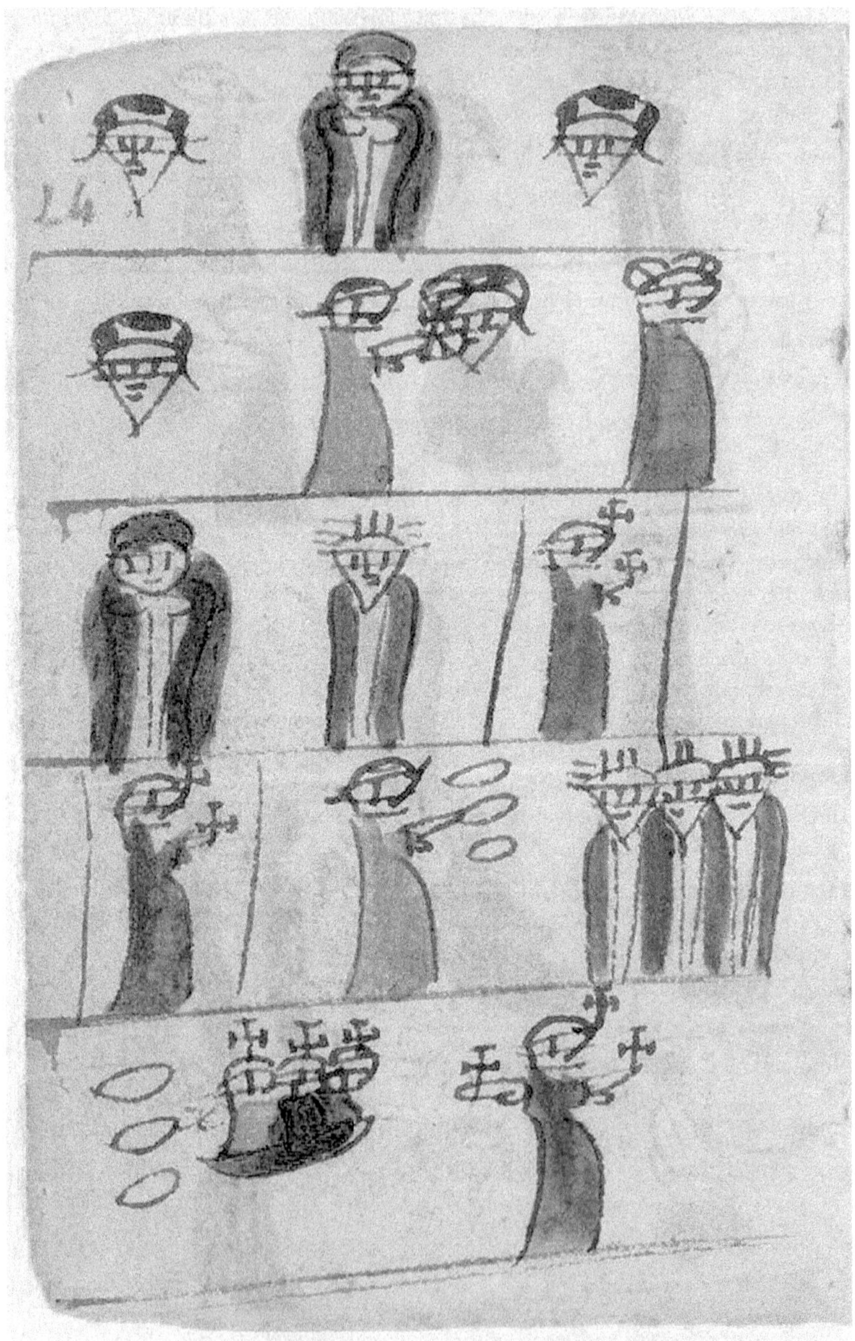

Pedro de Gante, Catecismo de la doctrina cristiana (Catechism of Christian Doctrine), between 1501–1600?
Manuscript, 83 p., 8 x 6 cm, National Library of Spain, Madrid

Pictographic manuscript based on figures and signs of drawing and children's color, distributed in strips.

Hispanic Digital Library (bdh.bne.es)

Pedro de Gante, Catecismo de la doctrina cristiana (Catechism of Christian Doctrine), between 1501–1600?
Manuscript, 83 p., 8 x 6 cm, National Library of Spain, Madrid

Pictographic manuscript based on figures and signs of drawing and children's color, distributed in strips.

Hispanic Digital Library (bdh.bne.es)

Answer. This was the first sign, (witness here passed his hand forward over his right ear.) It was to be answered the same way by the left hand. This is is the next sign, (here the witness inserted the forefingers of his right hand into his pantaloons pocket, the thumb remaining on the outside.)

Question. What was the reply to it?

Answer. It was to be returned that way. (Witness here gave the same sign with his left hand.)

Question. Go on.

Answer. Then, when you were sitting about, you could give the sign by turning your [right] heel into the hollow of your foot, to be returned with the left the same way.

Question. Proceed.

Answer. The password was, if you met any one in the night you should spell the word, I-s-a-y, and not pronounce it; if it was a member of the order whom you met you would spell, N-o-t-h-i-n-g, and not pronounce it.

Question. Any other signs and passwords?

Answer. None that I know.

Question. What about that signal-whistle spoken of in the by-laws?

Answer. I never saw one in daylight; I cannot describe it.

Question. What sort of a noise did it make?

Answer. A shrill, gurgling noise:

United States House of Representatives, Reports of Committees for the Second Session of the Forty-Second Congress, 1871–72

42.

In the medical field, nurses comment that they can pronounce **questions** yet have difficulty understanding patients' replies. Nurses can form **questions** that elicit a "yes" or "no," a choice from a list, or a fill-in, but such **questions** frustrate patients who want to add or request information beyond that restricted scope. In the legal profession, attorneys consulting with clients must understand them and respond accurately. Therefore, especially in courses for medical and legal professionals—but also in courses for engineers, business personnel, and other learners—LSP instructors need to strengthen their teaching of an essential methodological element: **question**/answer processes.

Robert A. Quinn, Developing a More Efficient Conversation Paradigm for Learning Foreign Languages: Lessons on Asking and Answering **Questions** *in an LSP Context (Language for Specific Purposes: Trends in Curriculum Development)*

43.

QUESTION

Do I pronounce?

doest thou pronounce?

does he pronounce?

do we pronounce?

do you pronounce?

do they pronounce?

NEGATIVE **QUESTION**

Do I not pronounce?

doest thou not pronounce?

does he not pronounce?
do we not pronounce?
do you not pronounce?
do they not pronounce?

Richard S. Rosenthal, The Rosenthal Method of Practical Linguistry: The French Language

44.

Question. What did General Andrews reply?
Answer. He said, as he had not the chartering of the ships, he should refer him to Commodore Van Brunt or Commodore Vanderbilt.
Question. (By the chairman.) Did he call upon the commodore?
Answer. Yes, sir; and Commodore Van Brunt went on board the ship.
Question. Did Commodore Van Brunt pronounce her seaworthy?
Answer. Yes, sir; I think he did; but he said he would not have more than 500 men put on board of her.

United States Senate, Reports of Committees for the Third Session of the Thirty-Seventh Congress

45.

Splitting a table into rowid ranges seems like a fantastic idea to reduce contention on data files for one table, but frequently the need is to process a query involving several tables. A scenario, I have a multi-table query that produces records which I then write to a file. Here, even if I do split the driving table into 4 rowid ranges, for example, there will still be contention for data files when joining and looking up the detail information. Is that about right, or can I use the rowid splitting technique for multi-table queries as well somehow and reduce contention? Thanks.

*AskTom, **Questions** > **Question** on Splitting (Oracle.com)*

46.

Question. Just look at the third name marked from the bottom, and tell me what it is. (Poll-list shown to witness.)
Answer. Pat Moveney, I call it.
Question. Just count the letters in it, will you. How many letters are there in it?
Answer. Only six.
Question. You don't think that looks at all like Pat Murray?
Answer. No, sir; I couldn't make Murray out of it.
Question. It doesn't look any more like Pat Murray than Simonsen or Thompson?
Answer. I think not.

United States Congress, The Miscellaneous Documents of the House of Representatives, Printed During the First Session of the Thirty-Ninth Congress, 1865–'66, in Three Volumes

47.

no, not sure what you were trying with a query against user_tab_columns and dual?

You sort of want to query YOUR tables—were you by any chance trying to write SQL to generate the SQL?

you would do something like:

```
select sum(dbms_utility.get_hash_value(c1||'/'||c2||'/'||...., 1, power(..)))
   from T1
   union all
```

Pedro de Gante, Catecismo de la doctrina cristiana (Catechism of Christian Doctrine), between 1501–1600?
Manuscript, 83 p., 8 x 6 cm, National Library of Spain, Madrid

Note on p. 1: "This little book is of figures with which the missioneros taught the
Indians the doctrine at the beginning of the conquest of the Indies."

Hispanic Digital Library (bdh.bne.es)

Pedro de Gante, Catecismo de la doctrina cristiana (Catechism of Christian Doctrine), between 1501–1600?
Manuscript, 83 p., 8 x 6 cm, National Library of Spain, Madrid

Note on p. 1: "This little book is of figures with which the missioneros taught the
Indians the doctrine at the beginning of the conquest of the Indies."

Hispanic Digital Library (bdh.bno.os)

```
select sum(dbms_utility.get3_hash_value(c1||'/'||c2||'/'||...., 1, power
   (..)))
from T2
```

and if you got back two rows with different numbers—you would know they differ (you would have no clue "how", but you would "know" they did)

*AskTom, **Questions** > Ora-Hash (Oracle.com)*

48.

Question. Do you know whether Commodore Van Brunt examined the vessel?
Answer. I do not know, sir; I think a man named Haswell inspected her.
Question. He inspected the engines. Did he inspect the ship?
Answer. I cannot say.

United States Senate, Reports of Committees for the Third Session of the Thirty-Seventh Congress

49.

If the Medical Spelling Test is being administered, *say:*

"Number 1 is 'physiologic' (pause), 'physiologic'. (Pause to allow time for all examinees to write word.) Number 2 is 'desquamation' (pause), 'desquamation'. (Pause to allow time for all examinees to write word.) Number 3 is 'sacroiliac' (pause), 'sacroiliac'." (Pause to allow time for all examinees to write word.)

If the Legal Spelling Test is being administered, *say:*

"Number 1 is 'dedition' (pause), 'dedition'. (Pause to allow time for all examinees to write word.) Number 2 is 'forensic' (pause), 'forensic'. (Pause to allow time for all examinees to write word.) Number 3 is 'hypothecation' (pause), 'hypothecation'." (Pause to allow time for all examinees to write word.)

Then say:

"That finishes the practice exercise. Are there any **questions**? (Answer any **questions**.) Can everyone hear me?" (If an examinee cannot hear, have him move closer.)

Then say:

"Now we will begin the actual test. The test will be done just like the practice exercise. Please print legibly and do not print beyond the line provided. Ready?"

Read each word from the Word List in accordance with the phonetic pronunciation indicated. Give the number of each word and pronounce it twice separated by a brief pause. Do not exaggerate the pronunciation or provide other cues to examinees.

U.S. Department of Labor, Employment and Training Administration, Manual for USES Clerical Skills Tests: Administration, Scoring, and Interpretation

50.

address, ad-lib, advise, agree, announce, answer, argue, ask, assert, babble, call out, challenge, chat, chatter, comment, communicate, converse, cry, declare, describe, disagree, discuss, drone, enquire, exclaim, explain, express, flatter, gab, gabble, garble, gossip, greet, groan, grumble, grunt, howl, inform, insist, instruct, interrupt, jabber, jeer, joke, lecture, lie, listen, mean, mention, mumble, murmur, mutter, name, natter, negotiate, observe, persuade, pronounce, **question**, rant, rap, recite, report, say, scream, share, shout, shriek, speak, speculate, state, suggest, swear, tell, think out loud, threaten, translate, utter, voice, waffle, whisper, yell.

Ann Browne, Developing Language and Literacy 3–8

51.

Question. The number, if you please?

Answer. I can't say any particular number.

Question. You didn't inquire at any particular number?

Answer. No, sir.

Question. Are you sure of that?

Answer. Yes, sir.

Question. Did you inquire at 577 Third avenue?

Answer. No, sir; I inquired at Thirty-ninth street for him.

Question. Did you inquire for him at 537 Thirty-ninth street?

Answer. No, sir; there was no such number.

Question. Whereabouts is 537 Third avenue?

Answer. It's the corner of Fortieth street.

Question. You say you inquired for a Pat Monaghan?

Answer. Yes, sir.

Question. Where?

Answer. On the hill.

Question. Did you inquire for Pete Monaghan there?

Answer. No, sir.

Question. Did you inquire for a man named James Will?

Answer. Yes, sir.

Question. Whereabouts did you get it?

Answer. From the poll-list.

Question. Whereabouts did you inquire?

Answer. On the hill.

Question. Did you inquire for any one else of a similar name?

Answer. Not that I have any recollection of.

Question. Did you inquire for James Writt?

Answer. No, sir.

Question. You inquired for Barney Maguire, you say, in Thirty-ninth street?

Answer. No, sir.

Question. If you swore in your direct testimony that you have inquired for Barney Maguire and didn't find him, what are we to think about that—that you are mistaken?

United States Congress, The Miscellaneous Documents of the House of Representatives, Printed During the First Session of the Thirty-Ninth Congress, 1865-'66, in Three Volumes

52.

```
IF ... THEN ... ELSIF ... THEN ... ELSE ... END IF;
CASE ... WHEN ... THEN ... ELSE ... END CASE;
```

*Oracle **FAQ's***

Pedro de Gante, Catecismo de la doctrina cristiana (Catechism of Christian Doctrine), between 1501–1600?
Manuscript, 83 p., 8 x 6 cm, Madrid, National Library of Spain

Folio 1r contains only the title and 28v is blank. The text is written in pictograms colored in three colors that are arranged horizontally at the rate of five rows per page, except those of folios 27v and 28r that are unfinished so that the manuscript seems to be incomplete.

Portal de Archivos Españoles

*Pedro de Gante, Catecismo de la doctrina cristiana (Catechism of Christian Doctrine), between 1501–1600?
Manuscript, 83 p., 8 x 6 cm, Madrid, National Library of Spain*

Folio 1r contains only the title and 28v is blank. The text is written in pictograms colored in three colors that are arranged horizontally at the rate of five rows per page, except those of folios 27v and 28r that are unfinished so that the manuscript seems to be incomplete.

Portal de Archivos Españoles

53.

Answer. (Referring to memorandum.) Yes, sir; I did inquire for him.

Question. Where did you inquire?

Answer. On the hill—First and Second avenue. Didn't know anything about him.

Question. Did you ever hear anything about a man that was called Dash Maguire?

Answer. No, sir.

Question. You don't know that his name was Barney Maguire?

Answer. No, sir; I don't know the party at all.

Question. You inquired for a man named Pat?

Answer. Yes, sir.

Question. Did you pronounce that Wintire or Wintoo?

Answer. Wintire.

Question. Where did you inquire for him?

Answer. On the hill, sir.

Question. Did you inquire for a Pat Wynne there?

Answer. Yes, sir.

Question. You inquired for a man named Ed Bannen?

Answer. Ed Bannen; yes, sir.

Question. Do you know of any one of a similar name at that house?

Answer. No, sir.

Question. Did you inquire for Edward Brennan there?

Answer. No, sir.

Question. Where did you inquire?

Answer. On the hill.

Question. You say you inquired for a man named Lonkin there?

Answer. Yes, sir.

Question. Was it Herwin or Herman Lonkin?

Answer. Herwin.

Question. Have you ever heard that name before—have you ever heard the name Herwin used as a Christian name?

Answer. I think I have.

Question. What nationality is it?

Answer. I think it is a German name.

Question. And Lonkin you think is a German name also?

Answer. Yes, sir.

Question. Where did you inquire for this Herwin Lonkin?

Answer. Up between Thirty-ninth and Fortieth streets.

Question. On the hill?

Answer. Yes, sir; an old resident up there said he lived in Forty-fifth street.

Question. Who is that old resident?

Answer. An old lady that has lived there for years and years.

Question. What is her name?

Answer. That's more than I can tell you.

Question. What is her business?

Answer. I can't tell you.

Question. How often have you seen her?

United States Congress, The Miscellaneous Documents of the House of Representatives, Printed During the First Session of the Thirty-Ninth Congress, 1865–'66, in Three Volumes

54.

```
LOOP ... END LOOP;
```

*Oracle **FAQ's***

55.

Answer. A great many times.

Question. How did you happen to see her?

Answer. I only saw her this time with the footman.

Question. How did you happen to get acquainted with her?

Answer. I am not acquainted with her.

Question. Had you never seen her before?

Answer. Yes, sir.

Question. Where?

Answer. On the hill.

Question. When?

United States Congress, The Miscellaneous Documents of the House of Representatives, Printed During the First Session of the Thirty-Ninth Congress, 1865–'66, in Three Volumes

56.

```
WHILE ... LOOP ... END LOOP;
```

*Oracle **FAQ's***

57.

Answer. A number of years ago; that is, several years.

Question. Did you inquire for a man named Larkin there?

Answer. No, sir; I did not.

Question. You inquired for a man named James McLarney?

Answer. Yes, sir.

Question. Just look at that poll-list and see if you can find the name of Larkin there?

United States Congress, The Miscellaneous Documents of the House of Representatives, Printed During the First Session of the Thirty-Ninth Congress, 1865–'66, in Three Volumes

58.

```
GOTO ...;
NULL;
```

*Oracle **FAQ's***

59.

Answer. (After examining the list.) No, sir.

Question. What is the name you find there?

Answer. Herwin Lonkin.

Question. Tell me how you spell it?

Answer. L-o-n-k-i-n.

Question. How do you spell the first name?

Answer. H-e-r-w-i-n, or w-e-n; it is an unusual name.

Question. Did you inquire for a man named McLarney there—James McLarney?

Answer. Yes, sir.

Question. How do you spell his name?

Answer. McL-a-r-n-e-y—McLarney, or Lowney, it ought to be, I think.

Question. Did you inquire for a man named McAlarney there?

Answer. No, sir; I did not.

Question. You inquired about a man named Peter Marien, you say?

Answer. Yes, sir.

Question. How is that spelt?

Answer. M-a-r-i-e-n.

Question. How do you pronounce that name?

Answer. Marien.

Question. If it were French how would you pronounce it?

Answer. I don't know.

Question. If it were a German name how would you pronounce it?

Answer. I don't know.

Question. Did you inquire for Peter Meenan there?

Answer. No, sir.

Question. Do you say you inquired for a man named Haylen there?

Answer. Yes, sir.

Question. How do you spell his name?

Answer. H-a-y-l-e-n.

Question. Who did you inquire of about him?

Answer. There was a general inquiry all round, sir.

Question. You asked the same people for all these names?

United States Congress, *The Miscellaneous Documents of the House of Representatives, Printed During the First Session of the Thirty-Ninth Congress, 1865–'66, in Three Volumes*

60.

```
FOR … IN [REVERSE] … LOOP … END LOOP;
```

Oracle *FAQ's*

61.

Answer. Yes; at different times.

Question. Did you ask any of the men there about Haylen?

Answer. I think I have.

Question. Who?

Answer. That's more than I can tell you. I don't know who he was.

Question. Have you any recollection about who you inquired of in regard to any of these people?

Answer. No, sir.

Question. Not of one?

Answer. Not one.

Question. You spent three months in the search, and you don't know the name of a single person who gave you information?

Answer. No, sir.

Question. Did you inquire for a man named Healeon?

Answer. No, sir.

Question. You inquired for a man named Hahn?

There are so many different **questions** that we desire answers to, but when we find ourselves confused, lost, and uncertain we don't always know what **questions** to ask to gain the right clarity.

As a Spiritual Mentor, Psychic and Intuitive Guide I am always asking **questions**, my clients are always asking **questions**, and every single person in my community has **questions** to ask. We ask **questions** on our spiritual journey to broaden our perspectives, gain wisdom, heal, grow and to better understand who we are.

Sydney Smith, 44 Best Questions for Oracle Cards (adventuringwithposeidon.com)

Answer. Yes, sir.

Question. How do you spell that name?

Answer. H-a-r-n

Question. What sort of a name is that?

Answer. Hahn or Harn.

Question. What nationality do you think it is?

Answer. That's more than I can tell you.

Question. Is it an English name?

Answer. No, sir.

Question. Is it a German name?

Answer. I don't know; I can't tell what nationality.

Question. According to your judgment what nationality does it indicate?

Answer. I couldn't tell, sir.

Question. Do you think it is a Hebrew name?

Answer. It might be, for all I know.

Question. You have no notion about what nationality it belongs to?

Answer. No; I have no idea.

United States Congress, The Miscellaneous Documents of the House of Representatives, Printed During the First Session of the Thirty-Ninth Congress, 1865–'66, in Three Volumes

62.

It is then possible immediately to pronounce the number in **question**. The cards contain the numbers up to a certain limit arranged in such a way that the first card contains all numbers whose lowest digit in the dyadic system is 1, that is, the odd numbers; the second contains all numbers whose second digit is 1, beginning with 2; the third all whose third digit is 1, beginning with 4, and so on. When it is known on which cards a given number occurs, its dyadic expansion is known. The number itself is the sum of the first numbers on the cards where it appears.

Oystein Ore, Number Theory and Its History

63.

They then made the event public, and sent an account of it to de la Vega's mother, who lived at Lierganes, a small town in the archbishopric of Burgos. At first she did not give credit to his death; but her son not appearing at her house, nor in the city where he lived before his misfortune, her doubts vanished, and she gave him up for lost.

About five years afterwards, some fishermen, in the environs of Cadiz, one day perceived the figure of a man sometimes swimming, and sometimes plunging under the water. On the next day, they saw the same, and mentioned it as a very singular circumstance to several people. They threw their nets, and baiting the swimmer with some pieces of bread, they at length caught him, and to their astonishment found him to be a very well formed man. They put several **questions** to him in various languages, but he answered none. They then had recourse to another method; they took him to the convent of St. Francis, where he was exorcised, thinking he might be possessed by some evil spirit.

Philip Mauro (ed.), Amphibious (Elegant Extracts; or, the Literary Nosegay: Consisting of Selections in Prose, From Admired Authors; to Which Is Added, the Maxims and Moral Reflections of de la Rouchefoucault; and a Dictionary of Literary Conversation)

64.

```
/* Remember to SET SERVEROUTPUT ON to see the output */
BEGIN
    DBMS_OUTPUT.PUT_LINE('Hello World');
END;
/
BEGIN
    -- A PL/SQL cursor
    FOR cursor1 IN (SELECT * FROM table1) -- This is an embedded SQL statement
    LOOP
        DBMS_OUTPUT.PUT_LINE        ('Column 1 = ' || cursor1.column1 ||
                                    ', Column 2 = ' || cursor1.column2);
    END LOOP;
END;
/
```

*Oracle **FAQ's***

65.

Note that if you do repetitive stuff inside a loop and you fail to close your cursors, you would soon run into the ORA-01000: maximum number of open cursors exceeded error.

*Oracle **FAQ's***

66.

```
CREATE OR REPLACE PROCEDURE DEPARTMENTS(NO IN DEPT.DEPTNO%TYPE) AS
    v_cursor integer;
    v_dname char(20);
    v_rows integer;
BEGIN
    v_cursor := DBMS_SQL.OPEN_CURSOR;
    DBMS_SQL.PARSE(v_cursor, 'select dname from dept where deptno > :x',
DBMS_SQL.V7);
    DBMS_SQL.BIND_VARIABLE(v_cursor, ':x', no);
    DBMS_SQL.DEFINE_COLUMN_CHAR(v_cursor, 1, v_dname, 20);
    v_rows := DBMS_SQL.EXECUTE(v_cursor);
    loop
        if DBMS_SQL.FETCH_ROWS(v_cursor) = 0 then
                exit;
        end if;
        DBMS_SQL.COLUMN_VALUE_CHAR(v_cursor, 1, v_dname);
        DBMS_OUTPUT.PUT_LINE('Department name: '||v_dname);
    end loop;
    DBMS_SQL.CLOSE_CURSOR(v_cursor);
EXCEPTION
    when others then
        DBMS_SQL.CLOSE_CURSOR(v_cursor);
        raise_application_error(-20000, 'Unknown Exception Raised:
    '||sqlcode||' '||sqlerrm);
END;
/
```

*Oracle **FAQ's***

67.

The exorcism was as useless as the **questions** had been. At length, after some days, he pronounced the word *Lierganes.*

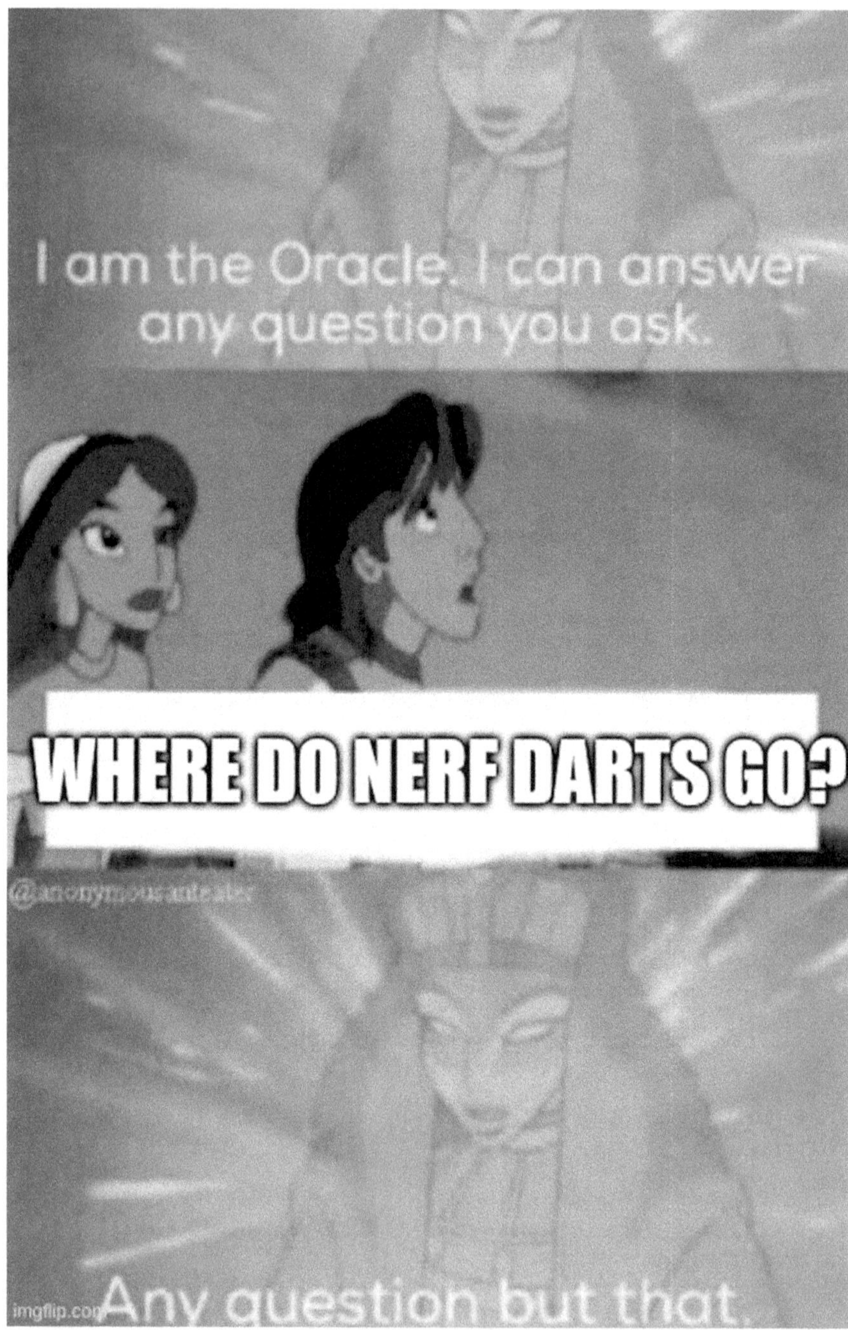

Aladdin Oracle, also known as Oracle **Question**, is an exploitable image macro depicting animated characters Jasmine and Aladdin speaking with the Oracle from the 1996 Disney movie *Aladdin and the King of Thieves*. The meme is typically used to pose unanswerable **questions** to various subjects and is also sometimes used in conjunction with unexplainable rules within a website or platform that no one knows the exact origin of.

Know Your Meme, Aladdin Oracle (knowyourmeme.com)

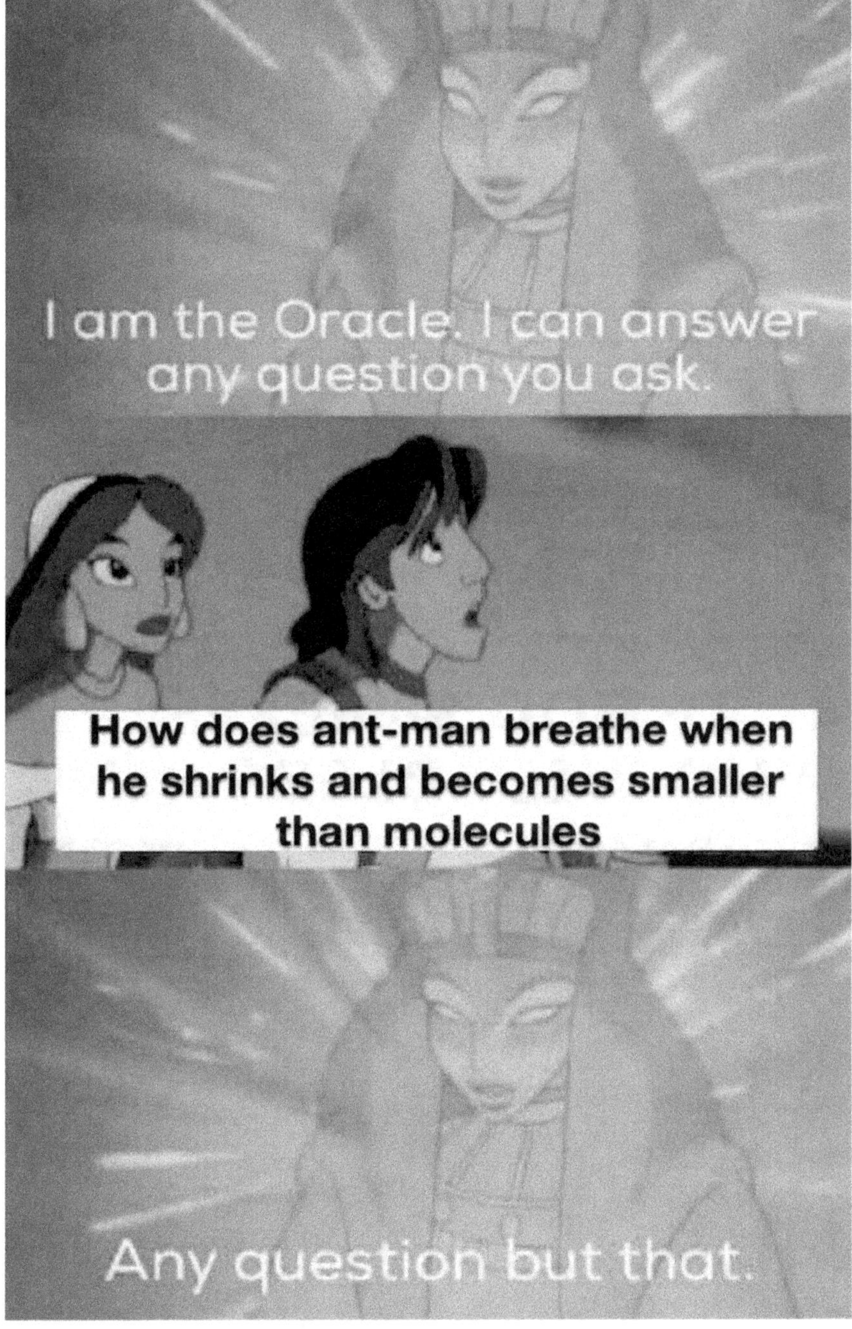

During the scene, the two protagonists of the film summon the Oracle near a balcony of the tower and she appears in the sky above them. The Oracle explains that she can answer any **question**, but can only give one answer. He then asks where his father is and she divulges the answer, but at no point during the scene does she actually say the line from the meme, "Any **question** but that."

Know Your Meme, Aladdin Oracle (knowyourmeme.com)

The exact origin of the meme is unknown, but it is seen being used as early as 2017. One such example comes from a 9GAG post on October 5th, 2017, to the Ask 9GAG section. This variant was posted under the title "I just can't imagine having no voice in my head" and asks the **question**, "If a person is born deaf, what language does he think in?" The upload received 415 points and 34 comments.

Know Your Meme, Aladdin Oracle (knowyourmeme.com)

In the following months, the format was used on 9GAG and then spread elsewhere online as users began creating different versions with new **questions**. On December 27th, 2017, another 9GAG user uploaded a version posing the **question** "Does a straw have one or two holes?" This variant received over 11,000 points and 358 comments.

Know Your Meme, Aladdin Oracle (knowyourmeme.com)

It so happened, that some person belonging to that town was present, when he uttered the name, as also the secretary of the inquisition. He wrote to his friends at Lierganes, with a view to obtain some particulars relative to this very extraordinary man. He received for answer, that a young man of Lierganes had, some time since, disappeared on the coast of Bilboa, but nothing had been heard of him since. It was then determined that this *marine man* should be sent to Lierganes; and a Franciscan friar, who was obliged to go there upon some other business, undertook to conduct him. It was not however done until the following year.

Philip Mauro (ed.), Amphibious (Elegant Extracts; or, the Literary Nosegay: Consisting of Selections in Prose, From Admired Authors; to Which Is Added, the Maxims and Moral Reflections of de la Rouchefoucault; and a Dictionary of Literary Conversation)

68.

Question. *How can we read names quickly?*

Answer. Learn the following—Remembering always the name is what you are and the birth number is what you hope to be.

A 1 is an adept and creator; a 2 is a seer; all even numbers are collections of many things, their work is collective; a 3 is an expression of both 1 and 2. 1–2–3 form the first or creative trinity. 8–9–11 are unlimited expressions of the 1–2–3 trinity. The 11 stands for 1; the 8 for 2; and the 9 for 3. A 4 person is composed of mental and physical force; a 5 person is a limited master, as sage spells 5; it means the starting of a new metaphyscial life—regeneration. A 6 person is a Cosmic Mother; a 7 person is just ready to become a master number; an 8 person is a free collection; a 9 person is a master of law, and complete expression; a 22 is a master of the number before it; an 11 is a psychic master.

*L. Dow Balliett, The Balliett Philosophy of Number Vibration in **Questions** and Answers: A Text Book*

69.

By default, **Question** Numbers are not seen by respondents; instead, they are used to identify your **questions** when you are reviewing your downloaded data or referencing **questions** within the Qualtrics platform. If desired, you can display the **Question** Numbers to respondents as they are taking the survey. Simply open your Survey Options and enable Show **Question** Numbers. Note that these numbers do not reorder when you use logic to skip the respondent ahead in the survey or when you use randomizers. As an alternative to showing **Question** Numbers, you could use a Progress Bar to give respondents a better idea of how far along they are in the survey.

*Qualtrics (We Eat, Sleep, and Breathe Customer Success), Auto-Number **Questions***

70.

why not just update a join?

```
update ( select columns from existing table,
columns from new table
where JOIN
and <at least one column is different> )
set columns in existing table = columns from new table;
```

*AskTom, **Questions** > Ora-Hash (Oracle.com)*

71.

Lynch found that really funny. He chortled and snuffled deep down in his belly and nodded his head rhythmically in time with the fist that he pounded against his knee.

This time the left one. When he was done he said, "How you expect us to make sure that you're really looking after our best interests, Mr. Dye? By the way, you mind if I call you Lucifer? We're not too much on formality down here."

"Lucifer's fine," I said. "You'll know your best interests are being looked after by what I produce. That'll be your only gauge. I'll provide information and suggestions and that's all. You can check the information out and decide for yourself whether to act on my suggestions. If you don't like what I suggest, you can ignore it."

"What do you think about that, Cal?" Lynch said, turning to the chief of police, who still stared at me as if I were the newest brand of arch-fiend whose unspeakable speciality was yet to be codified.

"I think he's a fucking liar," Loambaugh said.

"Course he is, Cal. Man has to be that in the business he's in. **Question** is, does he lie for or against us. That's the real nut-knocker, don't you agree, Lucifer?"

"That's it," I said.

"And I suppose it's all based on price."

"You're right again."

"I offered you twenty-five percent more than Orcutt's offering you, didn't I?"

I only nodded.

"I hear he's paying fifty thousand."

"Twenty thousand of it this morning," I said. "You owe me twenty five thousand."

"You aim to collect from both of us, of course. Can't say I blame you for that."

"No, I didn't think you would."

"Now if we got a little information up within the next few days, you wouldn't mind slipping it to Orcutt, would you, as something you'd sort of wormed out of us, so to speak?"

"That's part of the services," I said. "After I'm retained, of course."

"Wouldn't do it on spec just so we can take a reading on how well you perform?"

"That's a dumb **question**, if you don't mind my saying so."

Lynch shook his big head glumly. "I suppose it is," he said. "Suppose it is. When can we expect some results?"

"In a few days. Less than a week."

Lynch was silent for almost a minute while he inspected his half-smoked cigar. Then he looked up at me and there was an expression on his face that I'd seen often enough before, but on other faces. It was a mixture of contempt and curiosity and suspicion and a dash of grudging admiration. I'd probably worn it myself when doing a deal with a double agent. Carmingler, I recalled, had often worn it. "We got a deal, Lucifer," Lynch finally said. "It's not one that we have to shake hands on 'cause I just as soon shake hands with a cottonmouth. But we got a deal."

"No we don't," I said. "Not until I count the money."

"You think you're a pretty hard nosed son of a bitch, don't you?" Loambaugh said.

"When it comes to getting paid I am."

Ross Thomas, The Fools in Town Are on Our Side

72.

p. 390–1

The key phrases in this **question** are "proved keenest" and "accurately predicted."

Answer A "foresight" is to predict something in the future and to do it accurately means doing it correctly.

A

*Henry Davis, Explanations for the Official SAT Study Guide **Questions**: Detailed Explanations for the Answers for Every **Question***

73.

Then—this is all what you say—new economic relations will be established, all ready-made and worked out with mathematical exactitude, so that every possible **question** will vanish in the twinkling of an eye, simply because every possible answer to it will be provided. Then the "Palace of Crystal" will be built. Then . . . In fact, those will be halcyon days. Of course there is no guaranteeing (this is my comment) that it will not be, for instance, frightfully dull then (for what will one have to do when everything will be calculated and tabulated), but on the other hand everything will be extraordinarily rational. Of course boredom may lead you to anything. It is boredom sets one sticking golden pins into people, but all that would not matter. What is bad (this is my comment again) is that I dare say people will be thankful for the gold pins then. Man is stupid, you know, phenomenally stupid; or rather he is not at all stupid, but he is so ungrateful that you could not find another like him in all creation. I, for instance, would not be in the least surprised if all of a sudden, A PROPOS of nothing, in the midst of general prosperity a gentleman with an ignoble, or rather with a reactionary and ironical, countenance were to arise and, putting his arms akimbo, say to us all: "I say, gentleman, hadn't we better kick over the whole show and scatter rationalism to the winds, simply to send these logarithms to the devil, and to enable us to live once more at our own sweet foolish will!" That again would not matter, but what is annoying is that he would be sure to find followers—such is the nature of man. And all that for the most foolish reason, which, one would think, was hardly worth mentioning: that is, that man everywhere and at all times, whoever he may be, has preferred to act as he chose and not in the least as his reason and advantage dictated. And one may choose what is contrary to one's own interests, and sometimes one POSITIVELY OUGHT (that is my idea). One's own free unfettered choice, one's own caprice, however wild it may be, one's own fancy worked up at times to frenzy—is that very "most advantageous advantage" which we have overlooked, which comes under no classification and against which all systems and theories are continually being shattered to atoms. And how do these wiseacres know that man wants a normal, a virtuous choice? What has made them conceive that man must want a rationally advantageous choice? What man wants is simply INDEPENDENT choice, whatever that independence may cost and wherever it may lead. And choice, of course, the devil only knows what choice.

Fyodor Dostoevsky, Notes From the Underground

74.

Both PL/SQL and Java can be used to create Oracle stored procedures and triggers. This often leads to **questions** like "Which of the two is the best?" and "Will Oracle ever desupport PL/SQL in favour of Java?".

*Oracle **FAQ's***

75.

"The struggle is between the innocent and the guilty," she retorted without hesitation, and resumed her lecture. Her enemies were not limited to Zionism, she said, but what she called the dynamic of bourgeois domination, the repression of natural instincts, and the maintenance of despotic authority disguised as "democracy."

Again I tried to interrupt her, but this time she talked straight through me. She quoted Marcuse at me and Freud. She referred to the rebellion of sons in puberty against their fathers, and the disavowal of this rebellion in later years as the sons themselves became the fathers.

I glanced at the Colonel, but he seemed to be dozing.

The purpose of her "actions" she said, and those of her comrades, was to arrest this instinctual cycle of repression in all its forms in the enslavement of labour to materialism, in the repressive principle of "progress" itself—and to allow the real forces of society to surge, like erotic energy, into new, unfettered forms of cultural creation.

"None of this is faintly interesting to me," I protested. "Just stop, please, and listen to my **questions**."

Acts of so-called "terrorism" had therefore two clear purposes, she continued, as if I had never spoken, of which the first was to disconcert the armies of the bourgeois-materialist conspiracy, and the second to instruct, by example, the pit-ponies of the earth, who had lost all knowledge of the light. In other words, to introduce ferment and awaken consciousness at the most repressed human levels.

She wished to add that though she was not an adherent of Communism, she preferred its teachings to those of capitalism, since Communism provided a powerful negation of the ego-ideal which used property to construct the human prison.

She favoured free sexual expression and—for those who needed them—the use of drugs as a means of discovering the free self as contrasted with the unfree self that is castrated by aggressive tolerance.

I turned to the Colonel. There is an etiquette of interrogation as there is about everything else. "Do we have to go on listening to this nonsense? The lady is your prisoner, not mine," I said. For I could hardly lay the law down to her across his table.

The Colonel lifted his head high enough to glance at her with indifference. "You want to go back down, Britta?" he asked her. "You want bread and water for a couple of weeks?" His German was as bizarre as his English. He seemed suddenly a lot older than his age, and wiser.

"I have more to say, thank you."

John le Carré, The Secret Pilgrim

76.

The oracle answers include many unfavorable to the client. Among attainable answers to the **question** "Will my wife stay with me?" nine out of ten indicate that she will leave. Three answers reveal that the wife is leaving because she's committing adultery.

In sharp contrast to the text-based oracles of Astrampsychus, Apuleius's *Metamorphoses* describes an oracular technique of oral interpretation. To make money, a roving band of devotees of a Syrian goddess created a single answer oracle. They inscribed on all lots for sortition the same words:

For this the team of oxen plows the furrowed earth, so fertile fields of grain will sprout in times to come.

In choosing a lot, the oracle client inevitably got that answer. The goddess's priests then interpreted that answer according to the client's circumstances and interests:

> *if some would make inquiry as they were, say, arranging a marriage, the priests would say that the situation is directly addressed by the response: they are to be joined—the team—in marriage for the procreation of children—the grain. Should someone put the **question** about when to snap up some goods, they would say that the mention of the oxen was right on the money, as was the team, as were the fields that flourish in sprouting grain; if someone were anxious about setting out on some journey and wanted to secure the auspices of the gods, they would say that oxen, when joined in teams and gotten ready, are the most submissive of all four-footed creatures, and that profit is portended from the seeds in the field; were someone to take the field in war, or take to the hills to chase down some gang of robbers, and inquire whether the outcome would be productive or not, the priests would argue that victory comes in the train of this powerful pronouncement. Why? Because they would force their enemies' necks to wear the yoke, and would receive from their raids a most rich and profitable prize.*

All these prognostications are favorable to the client. The priests earned much money by providing oracles from the Syrian goddess.

77.

He gave Chrystal his broad, shrewd, good-natured smile. 'I think the rest of the story's yours. I left everything else to you.'

'Sir Horace came up,' said Chrystal, 'and Brown did him well. There were only the three of us. I should have enjoyed just meeting him. When you think what that man's done—he controls an industry with a turnover of £20,000,000 a year. It makes you think, Eliot, it makes you think. But there was more to it than meeting him. I won't make a secret of it. There's a chance of a benefaction.'

'If it comes off,' Brown said, cautiously but contentedly, 'it will be one of the biggest the college has ever had.'

'Sir Horace wanted to know what our plans for the future were. I told him as much as I could. He seemed pleased with us. I was struck with the **questions** he asked,' said Chrystal, ready to make a hero of Sir Horace. 'You could see that he was used to getting to the bottom of things. After he'd been into it for a couple of hours, I'd back his judgement of the college against half our fellows. When he'd learned what he came down to find out, he asked me a direct **question**. He asked straight out: "What's the most useful help any of us could provide for the college?" There was only one answer to that—and when there's only one answer, I've found it a good rule to say it quick. So I told him: "Money. As much money as you could give us. And with as few conditions as you could possibly make." And that's where we stand.'

'You handled him splendidly,' said Brown. 'He wasn't quite happy about no conditions—'

'He said he'd have to think about that,' said Chrystal. 'But I thought it would save trouble later if I got in first.'

'I'm not ready to shout till we've got the money in the bank,' Brown said, 'but it's a wonderful chance.'

'We ought to get it—unless we make fools of ourselves,' said Chrystal. 'I know that by rights Winslow should handle this business now. It's his job. But if he does, it's a pound to a penny that he'll put Sir Horace off.'

I thought of Sir Horace, imaginative, thin-skinned despite all his success in action.

'He certainly would,' I said. 'Just one of Winslow's little jokes, and we'd have Sir H endowing an Oxford college on a very lavish scale.'

'I'm glad you confirm that,' said Chrystal. 'We can't afford to handle this wrong.'

'We mustn't miss it,' said Brown. 'It would be sinful to miss it now.'

C. P. Snow, *The Masters*

78.

Many scholars offer evidence to support the idea that the Pythia was an office originating in the cult of Gaia. Dempsey states that the office of the Pythia was always held by a female (originally a virgin, but later at least fifty years old and married) and he points out the connection between the Pythia's gender and the cult of Mother Earth (53–55). Dempsey also points out that the ecstatic nature of the Pythia's prophecy was an abundant characteristic in the cult of Gaia (53–5). A detailed account of the frenzy or mania of the Pythia is presented when Appius Claudius Pulcher visits the oracle at Delphi in Lucan's *Civil War* (5.64–236). Additionally, many scholars believe that the Python's death at the hand of Apollo symbolized the change in oracles at Delphi (Powell 172).

It is often difficult to piece out the historical elements in myth. Some scholars believe that the Pythia did go into crazed trances. However, scholars such as Joseph Fontenrose **question** the historical accuracy of the manic and possessed Pythia. As Powell points out, there is no evidence of a chasm, and laurel leaves are not hallucinogenic.[172] The debate remains open.

Pythia *(Encyclopedia Mythica)*

79.

Where can I post my Oracle **questions**?

One of the best place to start is the support forums at http://www.orafaq.com/forum/. Some uses and developers are answering **questions** 24 hours a day. Be sure to use the search function to see if your problem has already been addressed before posting!

Alternatives:
- Forums—other forums
- Mailing lists—Oracle related mailing lists
- Usenet—Oracle USENET NetNews groups

Posting guidelines:
Make sure you understand the Netiquette Guidelines before posting your message to any of the above communities. See netiquette guidelines for details.

When you receive a good answer, it is recommended that you post a summary to the forum/list/newsgroup. It would also be great if you can contribute your new-found knowledge to this wiki.

Oracle **FAQ's**

80.

Her eyes were bright with anticipation, now, and she was tapping both her feet excitedly. It scared me to see how much she was looking forward to the task ahead of her: the fulfilment, I suppose, of a craving which had been burning inside her for years. She certainly didn't look as though she felt like answering any more **questions**; but I had to ask, in a whisper: 'Is he Spanish?'

'That's right. His name's Pedro.'

She continued to fix me with this mocking, teasing, irrepressible smile. At any other time, and in any other woman, it would have been captivating. I beckoned her closer and whispered in her ear: 'I know him.'

'You do?'

'He's been seeing my flatmate. He's an absolute bastard.'

'Really?' She pretended to look amazed. 'And I only hired him because he seemed such a nice sort of bloke.' All the indignation I felt about what he'd done to Tina started to boil over, suddenly. Back at the flat, it had been held in check by a level of panic and mystification which wouldn't allow room for any other feelings. Now it welled up into a kind of hatred.

'He's been giving my flatmate hell,' I whispered. 'Doing terrible things to her. She even tried to kill herself.'

'Too bad,' said Karla flatly.

'If I could just have five minutes alone with him . . .'

She looked at me, smiling again.

'What would you do?'

This was a difficult **question**.

'I'd . . . give him a really good talking to.'

Jonathan Coe, *The Dwarves of Death*

81.

And here, O men of Athens, I must beg you not to interrupt me, even if I seem to say something extravagant. For the word which I will speak is not mine. I will refer you to a witness who is worthy of credit, and will tell you about my wisdom—whether I have any, and of what sort—and that witness shall be the god of Delphi. You must have known Chaerephon; he was early a friend of mine, and also a friend of yours, for he shared in the exile of the people, and returned with you. Well, Chaerephon, as you know, was very impetuous in all his doings, and he went to Delphi and boldly asked the oracle to tell him whether—as I was saying, I must beg you not to interrupt—he asked the oracle to tell him whether there was anyone wiser than I was, and the Pythian prophetess answered that there was no man wiser. Chaerephon is dead himself, but his brother, who is in court, will confirm the truth of this story.

Why do I mention this? Because I am going to explain to you why I have such an evil name. When I heard the answer, I said to myself, What can the god mean? and what is the interpretation of this riddle? for I know that I have no wisdom, small or great. What can he mean when he says that I am the wisest of men? And yet he is a god and cannot lie; that would be against his nature. After a long consideration, I at last thought of a method of trying the **question**. I reflected that if I could only find a man wiser than myself, then I might go to the god with a refutation in my hand. I should

Étienne-Maurice Falconet, The Oracle, 1766
Biscuit, height 14 cm, Musée National de Céramique, Sèvres

Ceramics underwent unprecedented development in the mid eighteenth century in France, both as a complement to table plate and as ornamentation for interiors. Fine pieces of porcelain from China were everywhere. To reduce imports, a royal porcelain factory was founded in 1753 on the bank of the Seine at Sèvres. Etienne Falconet headed the Sèvres design studio until 1766. Figurines made of biscuit, or unglazed porcelain, were enormously popular and retained the twisting profile and swirl typical of rococo art.

Web Gallery of Art (www.wga.hu)

say to him, "Here is a man who is wiser than I am; but you said that I was the wisest." Accordingly I went to one who had the reputation of wisdom, and observed to him—his name I need not mention; he was a politician whom I selected for examination—and the result was as follows: When I began to talk with him, I could not help thinking that he was not really wise, although he was thought wise by many, and wiser still by himself; and I went and tried to explain to him that he thought himself wise, but was not really wise; and the consequence was that he hated me, and his enmity was shared by several who were present and heard me. So I left him, saying to myself, as I went away: Well, although I do not suppose that either of us knows anything really beautiful and good, I am better off than he is—for he knows nothing, and thinks that he knows. I neither know nor think that I know. In this latter particular, then, I seem to have slightly the advantage of him. Then I went to another, who had still higher philosophical pretensions, and my conclusion was exactly the same. I made another enemy of him, and of many others besides him.

After this I went to one man after another, being not unconscious of the enmity which I provoked, and I lamented and feared this: but necessity was laid upon me—the word of God, I thought, ought to be considered first. And I said to myself, Go I must to all who appear to know, and find out the meaning of the oracle. And I swear to you, Athenians, by the dog I swear!—for I must tell you the truth—the result of my mission was just this: I found that the men most in repute were all but the most foolish; and that some inferior men were really wiser and better. I will tell you the tale of my wanderings and of the "Herculean" labors, as I may call them, which I endured only to find at last the oracle irrefutable. When I left the politicians, I went to the poets; tragic, dithyrambic, and all sorts. And there, I said to myself, you will be detected; now you will find out that you are more ignorant than they are. Accordingly, I took them some of the most elaborate passages in their own writings, and asked what was the meaning of them—thinking that they would teach me something. Will you believe me? I am almost ashamed to speak of this, but still I must say that there is hardly a person present who would not have talked better about their poetry than they did themselves. That showed me in an instant that not by wisdom do poets write poetry, but by a sort of genius and inspiration; they are like diviners or soothsayers who also say many fine things, but do not understand the meaning of them. And the poets appeared to me to be much in the same case; and I further observed that upon the strength of their poetry they believed themselves to be the wisest of men in other things in which they were not wise. So I departed, conceiving myself to be superior to them for the same reason that I was superior to the politicians.

At last I went to the artisans, for I was conscious that I knew nothing at all, as I may say, and I was sure that they knew many fine things; and in this I was not mistaken, for they did know many things of which I was ignorant, and in this they certainly were wiser than I was. But I observed that even the good artisans fell into the same error as the poets; because they were good workmen they thought that they also knew all sorts of high matters, and this defect in them overshadowed their wisdom—therefore I asked myself on behalf of the oracle, whether I would like to be as I was, neither having their knowledge nor their ignorance, or like them in both; and I made answer to myself and the oracle that I was better off as I was.

This investigation has led to my having many enemies of the worst and most dangerous kind, and has given occasion also to many calumnies, and I am called wise, for my hearers always imagine that I myself possess the wisdom which I find wanting in others: but the truth is, O men of Athens, that God only is wise; and in this oracle he means to say that the wisdom of men is little or nothing; he is not speaking of Socrates, he is only using my name as an illustration, as if he said, He, O men, is the wisest, who, like Socrates, knows that his wisdom is in truth worth nothing. And so I go my way, obedient to the god, and make inquisition into the wisdom of anyone, whether citizen or stranger, who appears to be wise; and if he is not wise, then in vindication of the oracle I show him that he is not wise; and this occupation quite absorbs me, and I have no time to give either to any public matter of interest or to any concern of my own, but I am in utter poverty by reason of my devotion to the god.

Plato, Apology

Domenicho Zampieri (Domenichino), Sibilla Cumana (Cumaean Sibyl), 1622
Oil on canvas, 138 cm × 103 cm, Sala Petronilla, Musei Capitolini, Rome

The theme of the Cumaean Sibyl was used by the Bolognese Domenichino likely four times and was a common trope favored by learned patrons in Rome. Patrons could obtain a topic both derived from classical literature and yet voicing an apparent prophesy of the birth of Christ. She is featured in Michelangelo's frescoes in the Sistine Chapel and Raphael's frescoes in Santa Maria della Pace. These painters depicted the Sibyl as an older woman; tradition holds that she had a God give her a long life, but was not given extended youth.

The writing by the Sibyl in Greek on the scroll reads, "There is one God infinite and unborn"; the word *unborn* is spelled incorrectly.

Wikipedia, Cumaean Sibyl (Domenichino)

This Is Because the Answer Text Tends to Be Much Longer Than That of **Questions**, and More Diversified in Its Presentation Format and Word Usage

To such length has the spirit of Inquiry carried him

What should I do to get an Oracle job?
See <u>Getting a job</u>.

Oracle *FAQ's*

The **question** was: Why was God permitting this evil?

J. Vernon McGee, *Thru the Bible With J. Vernon Mcgee: Genesis Through Revelation*

The diversity of web **FAQ** pages pose a serious challenge in extracting high-quality QA from them. At least three major reasons that contribute to the difficulty of the task:

- First, the list of QA pairy within a **FAQ** page us often mixed with various amount of *noise text,* such as section headings, navigational text, or annotations, that are not part of any QA pair. Separating the text of QA pairs from the noise text can be difficult.
- Second, it is usually significantly more challenging to accurately identify the texts for answers than for **questions**. This is because the answer text tends to be much longer than that of **questions**, and more diversified in its presentation format and word usage.
- Third, many **questions** and answers from the **FAQ** pages do not follow the grammar and syntax of English rigorously, which makes it difficult to apply the algorithms that are developed in natural language processing.

Yi Liu, *Semi-Supervised Learning With Side Information: Graph-Based Approaches*

p. 407–1

The error here is the misuse of a comma. Two independent clauses are separated by a semi-colon. Answer choice C is a direct link for the two clauses and shows the cause f the accidents.

C

p. 407–3

In order to have correct wording of this sentence, you must keep the past tense to match occurred and keep from creating sentence fragment. Answer choice B contains were caused which is past tense.

B

p. 408–7

The error here is a misplaced modifier. That error is repeated in B and somewhat in C. D is the best rendition of the sentence as it is the active voice. E is a sentence fragment,

D

*Henry Davis, Explanations for the Official SAT Study Guide **Questions**: Detailed Explanations for the Answers for Every **Question***

Thus has the bewildered Wanderer to stand, as so many have done, shouting **question** after **question** into the Sibyl-cave of Destiny, and receive no Answer but an Echo. It is all a grim Desert, this once-fair world of his; wherein is heard only the howling of wild beasts, or the shrieks of despairing, hate-filled men; and no Pillar of Cloud by day, and no Pillar of Fire by night, any longer guides the Pilgrim. To such length has the spirit of Inquiry carried him. "But what boots it (*was thut's*)?" cries he: "it is but the common lot in this era. Not having come to spiritual majority prior to the *Siecle de Louis Quinze,* and not being born purely a Loghead (*Dummkopf*), thou hadst no other outlook. The whole world is, like thee, sold to Unbelief; their old Temples of the Godhead, which for long have not been rain-proof, crumble down; and men ask now: Where is the Godhead; our eyes never saw him?"

Thomas Carlyle, Sartor Resartus: The Life and Opinions of Herr Teufelsdröckh

*Michelangelo, Delphic Sibyl (1508–1512), detail from the fresco cycle
of the ceiling of the Sistine Chapel, Vatican City*

Michelangelo's Delphic Sibyl on a marble throne, holding a scroll, but
turning right to intensely look in the opposite direction.

K. Kris Hirst, Pythia and the Oracle at Dolphi (thoughtco.com)

*Mykl Roventine, Some **Questions** Can't Be Answered by Google (flickr.com)*

The Question, Verily

We all get one?

One afternoon, I was sitting on a couch in the Atlanta airport, reading a newspaper and waiting for my flight. Two guys carrying clipboards sat down next to me.

"Uh, excuse me, sir, but, umm, do you mind if we ask you a couple of **questions**? You see, we're taking a survey."

"OK," I said, expecting a sales pitch of some sort.

"Uh, ahem. OK. First **question**. Well uh, are you traveling today, sir?"

Folding my newspaper, I looked at the guy in disbelief and answered, "Well yes, Einstein, I am!"

"Uh, OK, OK, then, umm, what airline did you come in on?"

"United."

"OK, what airline are you flying out on?"

"United." (We were in the United section of the airport, and I was quickly deciding that these guys might just be a few fries short of a Happy Meal.)

"OK, if you were to die today and God asked you, 'Why should I let you into my heaven?' what would you say?"

I whispered, "Wait a minute, are you trying to evangelize me?"

That response spooked my **questioner**. He didn't expect me to know his tribal language.

"Uh, umm, yes," he timidly replied.

"Well, praise God!" I bellowed.

Heads turned all over our section of the concourse.

"Shh!" my new friends hissed as they tried to silence me. "You mean you're a Christian?" one of them asked.

"Yes," I whispered.

Tom Clegg and Warren Bird, Missing in America: Making an Eternal Difference in the World Next Door

The present Work is short and simple. Each **question** has such direct reference to the text, and its answer so literally the interpretation of the **question**, that it may be read with entire satisfaction by persons of all religious opinions.

*The Child's Scripture History, Forming a Complete and Perfect Analysis of the Holy Scriptures in **Question** and Answer*

But now, in this Valley of Humiliation, poor Christian was hard put to it; for he had gone but a little way before he espied a foul fiend coming over the field to meet him: his name is Apollyon. Then did Christian begin to be afraid, and to cast in his mind whether to go back or to stand his ground. But he considered again that he had no armor for his back, and therefore thought that to turn the back to him might give him greater advantage with ease to pierce him with darts; therefore he resolved to venture and stand his ground; for, thought he, had I no more in mine eye than the saving of my life, it would be the best way to stand. So he went on, and Apollyon met him. Now, the monster was hideous to behold: he was clothed with scales like a fish, and they are his pride; he had wings like a dragon, and feet like a bear, and out of his belly came fire and smoke; and his mouth was as the mouth of a lion. When he was come up to Christian, he beheld him with a disdainful countenance, and thus began to **question** with him:

John Bunyan, The Pilgrim's Progress

WHO has *searched* you? v. 1.
How does the Lord search us? Ps. 11:4, l. c. ,
What part of us does he search? 1 Ch. 28:9, m. c.
What has God *known* of us? 1 Ki. 8:39, l. c. Ps. 44:21.
When you sit down, who sees you? v. 2.
How then ought you to feel when you sit down?
When you rise up, who knows it?
How ought you to feel when you rise up?
Who gives you strength to rise up? Ac 17:28, f. c.
Can you go any where, without having the eyes of the Lord upon you? Job 34:21.
Is there any place where you can hide yourself from God, to do mischief? Job 34:22.

Harvey Newcomb, Newcomb's First **Question** *Book*

I was bewildered. "What branch of the Foreign Office?" I said. "Who? Why Palfrey?"
But as Toby would say, **questions** are never dangerous until you answer them.

John le Carré, The Secret Pilgrim

"You wrote that down, I hope," Waters said.
"I wrote it down," Foley said.
"Okay," Waters said, "he was asking **questions**. So what?"
"So suppose we tell him?" Foley said.
"Tell him what?" Waters said.

George V. Higgins, The Friends of Eddie Coyle

Question, the true state of, 17.

S. S. Schmucker, American Lutheranism Vindicated; or, Examination of the Lutheran Symbols, on Certain Disputed Topics: Including a Reply to the Plea of Rev. W. J. Mann

"Well," Foley said, "we got a choice. We could let him think the kids in the VW bus did it."
"He going to believe that?" Waters said.
"Probably not," Foley said. "He might, but probably not."
"So why do it?" Waters said.
"To get their names," Foley said. "I'm not saying this is what we ought to do. I'm just saying, we could."
"You get the license number on the bus?" Waters said.
"Yeah," Foley said.
"Sooner or later that's going to tell us who was in it, right?" Waters said.
"Likely," Foley said, "unless it's stolen."
"Assume it's not," Waters said, "what have we got?"
"The names," Foley said.
"And for evidence we can show they drove the bus to the rail-road station," Waters

said. "Is that a federal crime, to drive a bus to the railroad station?"

"To buy machine guns, sure," Foley said.

"Who's going to say that?" Waters said.

"Jackie Brown," Foley said.

"Suppose he doesn't," Waters said.

"Nobody," Foley said. "Nobody in the world."

"You still got a federal crime?" Waters said.

"Sure," Foley said.

"Sure," Waters said, "but you can't prove it, is all."

"Right," Foley said.

"Next **question**," Waters said.

George V. Higgins, The Friends of Eddie Coyle

Question 13. The names of God

1. Can God be named by us?
2. Are any names applied to God predicated of Him substantially?
3. Are any names applied to God said of Him literally, or are all to be taken metaphorically?
4. Are any names applied to God synonymous?
5. Are some names applied to God and to creatures univocally or equivocally?
6. Supposing they are applied analogically, are they applied first to God or to creatures?
7. Are any names applicable to God from time?
8. Is this name "God" a name of nature, or of the operation?
9. Is this name "God" a communicable name?
10. Is it taken univocally or equivocally as signifying God, by nature, by participation, and by opinion?
11. Is this name, "Who is," the supremely appropriate name of God?

*Thomas Aquinas, Summa Theologica, First Part, **Question** 13: The Names of God*

"You know the name?" said Mr. Jaggers, looking shrewdly at me, and then shutting up his eyes while he waited for my answer.

My answer was, that I had heard of the name.

"Oh!" said he. "You have heard of the name. But the **question** is, what do you say of it?"

Charles Dickens, Great Expectations

He was too distressed to say much. He fervently pressed my hand; he fervently thanked God that my father had not lived to hear what he had heard. Then, after a pause, he repeated my mother-in-law's name to himself in a doubting, **questioning** tone. "Macallan?" he said. "Macallan? Where have I heard that name? Why does it sound as if it wasn't strange to me?"

Wilkie Collins, The Law and the Lady

Leslie: "It isn't, if you don't think so."
Blake: "I don't so far."
Leslie: "Ah, don't joke. It's a very serious matter."
Blake: "Why should I think it was wrong?"

Leslie: "I don't know that you will. Mr. Blake"—

Blake: "Well?"

Leslie: "Did you know—If I begin to say something, and feel like stopping before I've said it, you won't ask **questions** to make me go on?" Very seriously.

Blake, with a smile of joyous amusement, looking down at her as he lounges at the corner of the piano: "I won't even ask you to begin." Leslie passes her hand over the edges of the keys, without making them sound; then she drops it into her lap and there clasps it with the other hand, and looks up at Blake.

Leslie: "Did you know I was rich, Mr. Blake?"

Blake: "No, Miss Bellingham, I didn't." His smile changes from amusement to surprise, and he colors faintly.

> *William Dean Howells, Out of the **Question**: A Comedy*

Would you not think silver or gold better to make man of than dust?

Could God have made our bodies of silver or gold! Job 42:2.

Could he have made them of nothing? Ge. 18:14, f. e.

Would you not think more of yourself if your body was made of gold?

Does it make you proud to think that your body was made of such dust as the beasts tread upon?

Why do you suppose God made us of dust? Is. 23:9.

How should this make us feel? Ge. 18:27.

> *Harvey Newcomb, Newcomb's First **Question** Book*

LADY MACBETH: I pray you, speak not; he grows worse and worse;
Question enrages him.

> *William Shakespeare, Macbeth*

[Enter] CARDINAL (with a book)

CARDINAL
I am puzzl'd in a **question** about hell:
He says, in hell there's one material fire,
And yet it shall not burn all men alike.

> *John Webster, The Duchess of Malfi*

Just as Paul says, Rom. 4, 15: The Law worketh wrath. Chrysostom asks concerning repentance, Whence are we made sure that our sins are remitted us? The adversaries also, in their "Sentences," ask concerning the same subject. [The **question**, verily, is worth asking blessed the man that returns the right answer.] This cannot be explained . . .

> *Philipp Melanchthon, The Apology of the Augsburg Confession*

It's one of the risks of coming to these out-of-the-way places, that you're so apt to be thrown in with nondescript people that you don't know how to get rid of afterwards. And now that he's been so cordially introduced to us all! Well, I hope you won't have to be crueller in the end, my dear, than your aunt meant to be in the beginning. So far, of course, he has behaved with perfect delicacy; but you must see yourself, Leslie, that even as a mere acquaintance he's quite out of the **question** . . .

> *William Dean Howells, Out of the **Question**: A Comedy*

POZZO: *(who has followed these exchanges with anxious attention, fearing lest the* **question** *get lost).* You want to know why he doesn't put down his bags, as you call them?

Samuel Beckett, *Waiting for Godot*

"You forgot to give um the address: 1658 Brimstone Avenue, Fiery Heights, Hell," Gunch chuckled, but the others felt that this was irreligious. And besides—"probably it was just Chum making the knocks, but still, if there did happen to be something to all this, be exciting to talk to an old fellow belonging to—way back in early times—"

A thud. The spirit of Dante had come to the parlor of George F. Babbitt.

He was, it seemed, quite ready to answer their **questions**. He was "glad to be with them, this evening."

Frink spelled out the messages by running through the alphabet till the spirit interpreter knocked at the right letter.

Littlefield asked, in a learned tone, "Do you like it in the Paradiso, Messire?"

"We are very happy on the higher plane, Signor. We are glad that you are studying this great truth of spiritualism," Dante replied.

The circle moved with an awed creaking of stays and shirt-fronts. "Suppose— suppose there were something to this?"

Babbitt had a different worry. "Suppose Chum Frink was really one of these spiritualists! Chum had, for a literary fellow, always seemed to be a Regular Guy; he belonged to the Chatham Road Presbyterian Church and went to the Boosters' lunches and liked cigars and motors and racy stories. But suppose that secretly—After all, you never could tell about these darn highbrows; and to be an out-and-out spiritualist would be almost like being a socialist!"

No one could long be serious in the presence of Vergil Gunch. "Ask Dant' how Jack Shakespeare and old Verg'—the guy they named after me—are gettin' along, and don't they wish they could get into the movie game!" he blared, and instantly all was mirth. Mrs. Jones shrieked, and Eddie Swanson desired to know whether Dante didn't catch cold with nothing on but his wreath.

The pleased Dante made humble answer.

But Babbitt—the curst discontent was torturing him again, and heavily, in the impersonal darkness, he pondered, "I don't—We're all so flip and think we're so smart. There'd be—A fellow like Dante—I wish I'd read some of his pieces. I don't suppose I ever will, now."

He had, without explanation, the impression of a slaggy cliff and on it, in silhouette against menacing clouds, a lone and austere figure. He was dismayed by a sudden contempt for his surest friends. He grasped Louetta Swanson's hand, and found the comfort of human warmth. Habit came, a veteran warrior; and he shook himself. "What the deuce is the matter with me, this evening?"

He patted Louetta's hand, to indicate that he hadn't meant anything improper by squeezing it, and demanded of Frink, "Say, see if you can get old Dant' to spiel us some of his poetry. Talk up to him. Tell him, 'Buena giorna, senor, com sa va, wie geht's? Keskersaykersa a little pome, senor?'"

Sinclair Lewis, *Babbitt*

'Tis what the ancients say of Simonides, that by reason his imagination suggested to him, upon the **question** King Hiero had put to him—[What God was.—Cicero, *De Nat.*

Deor., i. 22.]—(to answer which he had had many days for thought), several sharp and subtle considerations, whilst he doubted which was the most likely, he totally despaired of the truth.

Michel de Montaigne, That We Taste Nothing Pure (Essays)

The lord sat still, as he were in a trance,
And in his heart he rolled up and down,
"How had this churl imaginatioun
To shewe such a problem to the frere.
Never ere now heard I of such mattere;
I trow* the Devil put it in his mind.   *believe
In all arsmetrik* shall there no man find,   *arithmetic
Before this day, of such a **question**.
Who shoulde make a demonstration,
That every man should have alike his part
As of the sound and savour of a fart?
O nice* proude churl, I shrew** his face.   *foolish **curse
Lo, Sires," quoth the lord, "with harde grace,
Who ever heard of such a thing ere now?
To every man alike? tell me how.
It is impossible, it may not be.
Hey nice* churl, God let him never the.**   *foolish **thrive
The rumbling of a fart, and every soun',
Is but of air reverberatioun,
And ever wasteth lite* and lite* away;   *little
There is no man can deemen,* by my fay,   *judge, decide
If that it were departed* equally.   *divided
What? lo, my churl, lo yet how shrewedly*   *impiously, wickedly
Unto my confessour to-day he spake;
I hold him certain a demoniac.
Now eat your meat, and let the churl go play,
Let him go hang himself a devil way!"

Geoffrey Chaucer, The Canterbury Tales

"It's happening everywhere, isn't it?"

"More or less," I said.

"And what's the government doing about it?"

"Nothing."

"You said it, I didn't. There's only one word in the language to describe what's being done and you found it exactly. I'm not surprised at all. But when you think about it, what can they do? Because what is coming is definitely coming. No government in the world is big enough to stop it. Does a man like yourself know the size of India's standing army?"

"One million."

"I didn't say it, you did. One million soldiers and they can't stop it. Do you know who's got the biggest standing army in the world?"

"It's either China or Russia, although the Vietnamese ought to be mentioned."

"Tell me this," he said. "Can the Vietnamese stop it?"

"No."

"It's here, isn't it? People feel it. We know in our bones. God's kingdom is coming."

He was a rangy man with sparse hair and a gap between his two front teeth. He squatted easily, seemed loose-jointed and comfortable. I realized he was wearing a suit and tie with running shoes.

"Are these great days?" he said.

I studied his face, trying to find a clue to the right answer.

"Do you feel it coming? Is it on the way? Do you *want* it to come?"

He bounced on his toes as he spoke.

"Wars, famines, earthquakes, volcanic eruptions. It's all beginning to jell. In your own words, is there anything that can stop it from coming once it picks up momentum?"

"No."

"You said it, I didn't. Floods, tornados, epidemics of strange new diseases. Is it a sign? Is it the truth? Are you ready?"

"Do people really feel it in their bones?" I said.

"Good news travels fast."

"Do people talk about it? On your door-to-door visits, do you get the impression they want it?"

"It's not do they want it. It's where do I go to sign up. It's get me out of here right now. People ask, 'Is there seasonal change in God's kingdom?' They ask, 'Are there bridge tolls and returnable bottles?' In other words I'm saying they're getting right down to it."

"You feel it's a ground swell."

"A sudden gathering. Exactly put. I took one look and I knew. This is a man who understands."

"Earthquakes are not up, statistically."

He gave me a condescending smile. I felt it was richly deserved, although I wasn't sure why. Maybe it was prissy to be quoting statistics in the face of powerful beliefs, fears, desires.

"How do you plan to spend your resurrection?" he said, as though asking about a long weekend coming up.

"We all get one?"

Don DeLillo, White Noise

The **Question** about the Resurrection

Then come unto him the Sadducees, which say there is no resurrection; and they asked him, saying, Master, Moses wrote unto us, If a man's brother die, and leave his wife behind him, and leave no children, that his brother should take his wife, and raise up seed unto his brother. Now there were seven brethren: and the first took a wife, and dying left no seed. And the second took her, and died, neither left he any seed: and the third likewise. And the seven had her, and left no seed: last of all the woman died also. In the resurrection therefore, when they shall rise, whose wife shall she be of them? for the seven had her to wife.

Mark 12:18–23, KJV (The Bible App)

Now you may be thinking, *What kind of stupid **question** is that?* Maybe it's not such a stupid **question**. (And besides, you know it can't be a stupid **question**. Remember: it's

Jesus!) Who knows?

Paul L. Metzger, *The Gospel of John: When Love Comes to Town*

"My beloved son,"said my mother.

"Your eyes are closed. How do you know?"

"I'm peeking. By the way, the answer to your **question**, whatever the **question** might be, is that I wish I could. Pretty good, right?"

Sam Lipsyte, *The Ask*

And now he comes to the great objection; [*"The Jews, though very wicked, had their children circumcifed,* ergo.] He anfwers many ways.

1. He mentions again that obfervation of *Gillefpy*, that fome faid, [*"that the children of Excommunicated Jews were not circumcifed]* But he does well to wave it, as for what we faid to it above; fo becaufe it is nothing to the **queftion**, which is not of *excommunicated* parents, but wicked Parents tolerated.

Daniel Cawdrey, Giles Firmin and Thomas Hooker, *A Sober Anfwer to a Serious* **Queftion** *Propounded By Mr. G. Firmin. Viz. Whether the Minifters of England Are Bound by the Word of God to Baptife the Children of All Such Parents Which Say They Believe in Jefus Chrift. Which May Serve Alfo as an Appendix to the Diatribe With Mr. Hooker, Concerning the Baptifme of Infants*

"How is your mother? Hear from her lately?"

"She wants me to go out to the ashram this summer."

"Do you want to go?"

"Who knows what I want to do? Who knows what anyone wants to do? How can you be sure about something like that? Isn't it all a **question** of brain chemistry, signals going back and forth, electrical energy in the cortex? How do you know whether something is really what you want to do or just some kind of nerve impulse in the brain? Some minor little activity takes place somewhere in this unimportant place in one of the brain hemispheres and suddenly I want to go to Montana or I don't want to go to Montana. How do I know I really want to go and it isn't just some neurons firing or something? Maybe it's just an accidental flash in the medulla and suddenly there I am in Montana and I find out I really didn't want to go there in the first place. I can't control what happens in my brain, so how can I be sure what I want to do ten seconds from now, much less Montana next summer? It's all this activity in the brain and you don't know what's you as a person and what's some neuron that just happens to fire or just happens to misfire. Isn't that why Tommy Roy killed those people?"

Don DeLillo, *White Noise*

Aunt Mary-Ben, dimly aware but not well informed about the opposition in the kitchen, told Frank many a wondrous story about the mercy of God's Mother, as she had seen it evinced in the visible world. Oh, you could always go to Her, Frankie, when you were troubled. Aunt kept her promise, and during the trouble of the black eye she gave him a pretty little rosary, which she told him had been blessed by the Bishop in Ottawa; he was to keep it under his pillow, and soon she would teach him the poetry that went with it.

Frank was deeply troubled, but it would never do to ask her the **question** he had put to Victoria. She wouldn't know about such things, or if she did she would be sorrowful because he knew about them. And there was always the risk of opening the wounds of Jesus afresh.

Robertson Davies, *What's Bred in the Bone*

He looked up at me with odd fervency. He was holding his miniature half-on between his fingers, thwacking it against the chair seat.

"Daddy," he said.

"Yes, Bern."

"This isn't a winky."

"It's not? "

"It's a video game."

I looked down at my son's lap. An odd benevolence surged through me. I had maybe made peace with Bernie's foreskin. His freak flap, let it fly. If he ever wanted to be a real Jew he could have it snipped. Nobody would ever be able to **question** his commitment after that. Besides, if he wanted to be a real Jew, he'd probably have to renounce me. Because I was a fake Jew who spent a lot of time on the fake internet rubbing my video game. Because the real Jews scared the hell out of me, same as the real Muslims and the real Christians, the real Hindus. Because they believed. How could they believe? Fine, come kill me as a Jew, flog me to death in a desert quarry, bayonet me in the Pale, gas me in your Polish camp, behead me on your camcorder, I still would not believe. To me that was the true test of courage: to not submit to the faith they assume you possess and will kill you for. So now I loved Bernie's foreskin. Or at least I'd made peace with it.

"I've made peace with it," I whispered.

"Excuse me?" said Maura.

"I said I've made peace with it."

"That was quick."

"What do you mean?"

"Wait a minute," said Maura. "What have you made peace with?"

"You tell me."

"Not so fast."

"What do you think I've made peace with?"

"That's what I'm asking you."

"You tell me," I said.

"I think we're going around in a circle."

"Which means what?"

"What do you mean which means what?"

"It could mean there is something you don't want to tell me."

"No, Milo, it's you who won't do the telling. Don't you see? You won't tell me what you've made peace with. So, I can't tell you what I don't want to tell you until I know what it is that you've made peace with."

"I'm no longer at peace."

"Good. You probably shouldn't be."

This is how I knew my wife was having an affair with Paul.

Sam Lipsyte, The Ask

Now let the reader carefully ponder the following **questions** and answers, induced from Paul's letter to Titus, on this important affair:

Election of Elders, No. VI: Being the Second Part of an Answer to G. Greenwell's Replies to Jethro (The Christian Messenger and Reformer; Devoted to the Dissemination of Primitive Christianity, Volume 9)

How deep is it ? Job 11:8, 1. c.

How long is it? Job 11:9, f. c.
How broad is it? Job 11:9, l. c.
How ought this to make you feel? Ja. 4:10. Ps. 8:3, 4.

*Harvey Newcomb, Newcomb's First **Question** Book*

And these **questions** wonderfully exercised Origen, Nazianzen, and others, although, indeed they can be most readily explained . . .

Philipp Melanchthon, The Apology of the Augsburg Confession

The argument really is "human"; it assumes that the same egotism which moves humans must also move God, that at the heart of deity lies jealousy for its honor. And if that is so, why is it not unjust for God to bring wrath to bear when our unrighteousness fuels that jealousy, when it serves to demonstrate the vast difference between us and him? Is that not what it means to be God, to be jealous for one's honor, dignity, integrity? Paul rebuts: By no means! For if God were unjust, how could he judge the world? When no other expedient is ready at hand, the opponent is struck dumb with a word that God would not be God if he were right!

Question four (vv 7–8) comprises a more or less subtle transition from the objection to Paul's statement regarding the sacramental/ethical separation to the objection that it is precisely this separation which Paul's "new religion" serves. If God's truth abounds to his glory through my falsehood, why am I still judged a sinner, indeed, why do I not draw the practical conclusion from this curious state of affairs and assist the comparison—do evil that good may come?

Roy A. Harrisville, Augsburg Commentary on the New Testament: Romans

That it has never again enjoyed among New Testament scholars the prominence it had around the turn of the century is perhaps more surprising. With the exception of a number of essays by Bultmann, which have justifiably received a great deal of attention, discussion of the Jesus-Paul **question** has been a desultory affair and has not been conducted with the consuming passion of earlier days. This is surprising, not only because it is one of the most complex and intriguing issues facing the historian of early Christianity, but also because it has profound theological ramifications which go to the heart of the Christian faith.

A number of factors have contributed to this state of affairs. Most important is that the Jesus-Paul controversy has been subsumed under the broader **question** of the relationship between the historical Jesus and the kerygmatic Christ. These two issues are, of course, not identical, but there is sufficient common ground for us to suppose that the Jesus-Paul issue has been not so much ignored as it has been discussed under a somewhat different guise. Moreover, not only does the broader formulation include the narrower, it also implicitly corrects some formulations of the **question** by assuming the existence of non-Pauline kerygmata which contain much in common with Paul and thus refusing to isolate him artificially from the rest of early Christianity. We should not, of course, imagine that by so doing we have resolved any of the major issues; we have merely placed the problem in a broader and historically more realistic context. Yet there is good reason to insist that to formulate the comparison in terms of Jesus and Paul is to raise the issue in the sharpest possible fashion, not only because we know a great deal more about Paul than about other first-generation Christians but also because, as time

Anonymous, The Pharisees Question John tho Baptist, Plenarium, 1483 (The Illustrated Bartsch)

has passed, Paul's understanding of Christianity has been immensely influential in the development of Western Christian beliefs.

Secondly, it might perhaps be felt that since all the evidence has been aired and the main positions staked out there is nothing much new to say. Thus among modern scholars Jeremias maximizes the continuity between Jesus and Paul,[2] Kümmel proposes a more modest list of common features,[3] Kasemann makes do with a minimal link[4] and Bultmann takes the more radical view that the search for continuity must be rejected in principle.[5] Faced with these alternatives, and variations in between, it is natural enough for scholars simply to opt for that version which best fits their predilections about Jesus and Paul without feeling they have anything new to add.

I will venture a third explanation which cannot be documented and is therefore no more than a hunch. It sometimes seems that the topic is instinctively avoided because to pursue it too far leads to profound and disturbing **questions** about the origin and nature of Christianity—and it is felt, perhaps, that it is best to leave well enough alone. This suspicion may be entirely unjustified, and it is at any rate probably too baldly stated. That there is an element of truth in it, however, is suggested by the manner in which those who do discuss the problem frequently show a curious reluctance to reflect upon the theological consequences of their historical conclusions. What some of these conclusions might be is a theme to which we shall return later.

S. G. Wilson, *From Jesus to Paul: The Contours and Consequences of a Debate (From Jesus to Paul: Studies in Honour of Francis Wright Beare)*

"You could have asked me directly. I have nothing to hide."

"That remains to be seen."

Bolling stepped between us, sputtering at me in sudden anger: "Leave the boy alone now. He's obviously genuine. He even has his father's voice. Your implications are an insult."

I didn't argue with him. In fact, I was ready to believe he was right. The boy stepped back away from us as if we'd threatened his life. His eyes had turned the color of slate, and there were white rims on his nostrils.

"What is this, anyway?"

"Don't get excited," I said.

"I'm not excited." He was trembling all over. "You come here and ask me a bunch of **questions** and tell me you knew my father. Naturally I want to know what it means."

Bolling moved toward him and laid an impulsive hand on his arm. "It could mean a great deal to you, John. Your father belonged to a wealthy family."

The boy brushed him off. He was young for his age in some ways. "I don't care about that. I want to see my father."

"Why is it so important?" Bolling said.

"I never had a father." His working face was naked to the light. Tears ran down his cheeks. He shook them off angrily.

I bought him, and made a down payment: "I've asked enough **questions** for now, John. Have you talked to the local police, by the way?"

"Yes, I have. And I know what you're getting at. They have a box of bones at the sheriff's station. Some of them claim that they're my father's bones, but I don't believe it. Neither does Deputy Mungan."

"Do you want to come down there with me now?"

"I can't," he said. "I can't close up the station. Mr. Turnell expects me to stay on the job."

"What time do you get off?"

"About seven-thirty, week nights."

"Where can I get in touch with you tonight?"

"I live in a boarding-house about a mile from here. Mrs. Gorgello's." He gave me the address.

"Aren't you going to tell him who his father was?" Bolling said.

Ross Macdonald, The Galton Case

"He was myself," said Father Brown.

Butler, K. C., sprang to his feet in an extraordinary stillness, and said quite calmly: "Your lordship will allow me to cross-examine?" And then, without stopping, he shot at Brown the apparently disconnected **question**: "You have heard about this dagger; you know the experts say the crime was committed with a short blade?"

"A short blade," assented Brown, nodding solemnly like an owl, "but a very long hilt."

G. K. Chesterton, The Man in the Passage (Father Brown: Essential Tales)

and fathers leave to go back to work
and mothers stand at the kitchen sink pondering

something they never tell.
You remember too much,
my mother said to me recently.

Why hold onto all that? And I said,
Where can I put it down?
She shifted to a **question** about airports.

Anne Carson, The Glass Essay

Ignoring Mrs. Hawthorne, he addressed the old soldier, man to man. "You understand I have absolutely nothing to say to you at all, Sergeant Major?"

"I do, sir."

"I never heard of your son, you understand? Kenneth Hawthorne is not a name to me, nor to any of my colleagues."

"Yes, sir." The old man's gaze was fixed parade-ground style above Smiley's head. But his wife had her eyes fiercely turned on Smiley's all the time, even if she found it hard to fix on them through the thick lenses of his spectacles.

"He has never in his life worked for any British department of government, whether secret or otherwise. He was a common criminal all his life. Nothing more. Nothing at all."

"Yes, sir."

"I deny absolutely that he was ever a secret agent in the service of the Crown."

"Yes, sir."

"You understand also that I can answer no **questions**, give you no explanations, and that you will never see me again or be received at this building?"

"Yes, sir."

"You understand finally that you may never speak of this moment to a living soul?

However proud you may be of your son? That there are others still alive who must be protected?"

"Yes, sir. I understand, sir."

John le Carré, The Secret Pilgrim

And if we wish to exalt the outcast and the crucified, we shall rather wish to think that a veritable God was crucified, rather than a mere sage or hero. Above all, if we wish to protect the poor we shall be in favour of fixed rules and clear dogmas. The rules of a club are occasionally in favour of the poor member. The drift of a club is always in favour of the rich one.

And now we come to the crucial **question** which truly concludes the whole matter. A reasonable agnostic, if he has happened to agree with me so far, may justly turn round and say, "You have found a practical philosophy in the doctrine of the Fall; very well. You have found a side of democracy now dangerously neglected wisely asserted in Original Sin; all right.You have found a truth in the doctrine of hell; I congratulate you. You are convinced that worshippers of a personal God look outwards and are progressive; I congratulate them. But even supposing that those doctrines do include those truths, why cannot you take the truths and leave the doctrines? Granted that all modern society is trusting the rich too much because it does not allow for human weakness; granted that orthodox ages have had a great advantage because (believing in the Fall) they did allow for human weakness, why cannot you simply allow for human weakness without believing in the Fall? If you have discovered that the idea of damnation represents a healthy idea of danger, why can you not simply take the idea of danger and leave the idea of damnation? If you see clearly the kernel of common sense in the nut of Christian orthodoxy, why cannot you simply take the kernel and leave the nut? Why cannot you (to use that cant phrase of the newspapers which I, as a highly scholarly agnostic, am a little ashamed of using) why cannot you simply take what is good in Christianity, what you can define as valuable, what you can comprehend, and leave all the rest, all the absolute dogmas that are in their nature incomprehensible?"

G. K. Chesterton, Orthodoxy

2. *[He ſuppoſes they were not ſo guilty of ignorance, as many of ours.]* But thats nothing to the **queſtion**; their children were as *ignorant* as ours, and the Parents never *Excommunicated* for ignorance, nor their children denied *circumciſion* for that reaſon. But cloſer to the point he ſayes.

3. He would ſee a proof, *[that the Prieſts did debar many from the Paſſover, for moral uncleanneſs, many years, as ours do from the Supper, and yet had their children circumciſed]*. We anſwer. 1. The Prieſts are blamed for admitting the morally unclean, to ſome Ordinances, but it concerns him to prove, where ever they were blamed, for circumciſing the children of ſuch. See *EZech.*44.7.9, cited by himſelf, pag. 35, to the ſame end. It is doubtful at leaſt, whether the practiſe of thoſe miniſters can be juſtified, who *ſuſpend* any ſo long the *Supper*, and yet Baptize their children: therefore that can be no *ſafe ground* to debar children of ſuch from Baptiſme: Of which see Mr. *Feanes.*

4. He conceives *[Something peculiar to them, in that National conſtitution, from ours: Gods enters Covenant with Abraham, and his family; commands him to circumciſe his ſeed: the conſtitution of our Churches, does not begin with any particular perſon; but makes*

difciples, and Baptize them] But this makes no great difference: For a Church Chriftian may begin with a perfon and his familie; Suppofe one of a *numerous family*, when he is difcipled, his houfe is difcipled with him; and there may be a *Church* in his house; yea every *houfeholder* converted to the faith, was a *child* of *Abraham*, in one fenfe; and a *root* to his pofterity in another, and fo the promife is made to him and his feed, not onely of the next, but of remoter generations, till they Apoftate, as *Ifhmael* and *Efau* did: He yields pag. 33 that defcent by the flefh, was one, though not the sole ground of circumcifion. And so it is now, 1 *Cor.*7.14. Let us fee what was peculiar to them.

> Daniel Cawdrey, Giles Firmin and Thomas Hooker, A Sober Anfwer to a Serious **Queftion** Propounded By Mr. G. Firmin. Viz. Whether the Minifters of England Are Bound by the Word of God to Baptife the Children of All Such Parents Which Say They Believe in Jefus Chrift. Which May Serve Alfo as an Appendix to the Diatribe With Mr. Hooker, Concerning the Baptifme of Infants

"It is a **question** which arises in respect of two persons, both of whom are dead and concerning one or both of whom the exact date of death is unknown. One of them must have died before the other, unless they both died at the same instant. The **question** is, Which survived the other? Which of them died first? It is a **question** on which may turn the succession to an estate, a title, or even a kingdom."

"Well," said Margaret, "it is not likely to arise in respect of Dan."

"On the contrary," Thorndyke dissented, "it may arise to-morrow. If some person who has left him a legacy should die to-day, that person's will could not be administered until it had been decided whether your husband was or was not alive at the time the testator died; that is, whether or not he survived the testator. But, as matters stand, we can give no answer to that **question**. We can prove that he was alive at half-past two on the 2 of June. Thenceforward we have no knowledge of him."

"Excepting what Mr. Varney has told us."

"Mr. Varney's information is legally worthless unless he can produce the witnesses, and unless they can identify a photograph or otherwise prove that the man whom they saw was actually Mr. Purcell. You must ask Mr. Varney about it. However, at the moment you are more concerned to find out what has become of your husband. I suppose I may ask a few necessary **questions**?"

"Oh, certainly," she replied. "Pray don't have any scruples of delicacy. Ask anything you want to know."

> R. Austin Freeman, The Shadow of the Wolf (Dr. Thorndyke Mysteries)

CHAPTER 1:
"INTRODUCTION IN DEFENSE OF EVERYTHING ELSE"

Structure of the general argument suggested in Chapter 1 of Orthodoxy *and brought to a completion in chapter 8:*

(1) Human beings have a double spiritual need for adventure and security (or: balance between imagination and reason—or the exciting and the commonsensical).

(2) This need is not pathological, but is identical with a need for psychological health, i.e., sanity.

(3) This need is better satisfied by accepting the Christian worldview than by accepting any alternative worldview.

Therefore, it is at least reasonable to accept the Christian worldview.

(4) Furthermore, alternative worldviews fail to a greater or lesser extent to satisfy

the aforementioned double spiritual need.

Therefore, it is unreasonable to prefer any such alternative to the Christian worldview.

It is crucial to note that until the last chapter, chapter 9, the argument of the book is aimed at showing that Christian belief and practice is healthy and not that it is true. As Chesterton puts it in chap. 2: "It must be understood that I am not now discussing the relation of these creeds to truth but, for the present, solely their relation to health. Later in the argument I hope to attack the **question** of objective verity; here I speak only of a phenomenon of psychology."

CHAPTERS 2 AND 3:
"THE MANIAC" AND "THE SUICIDE OF THOUGHT"

A taxonomy of some of the views concerning the stature of reason canvassed by Chesterton in Chapters 2 and 3:

I. Religious authority:

(i) Truth is a standard independent of the human mind that "measures" the mind and serves as its goal.

(ii) Reason is a generally reliable guide to truth. (Moderate optimism with respect to reason.)

(iii) In regard to the really big **questions**, reason on its own is severely limited and requires the light of faith and authority in order to attain the truth. (Moderate pessimism with respect to reason.)

(iv) This is the view held by St. Thomas, St. Augustine, and the Catholic tradition especially.

II. The Maniac (Enlightenment Rationalism or Modernism or so-called "Free Thought"):

(i) Truth is a standard independent of the human mind that "measures" the mind and serves as its goal.

(ii) Reason is a generally reliable guide to truth.

(iii) Reason on its own is in principle capable of attaining wisdom. More specifically, reason can attain wisdom without authority, and indeed needs to be freed from authority—especially religious authority but also political, economic and social authority—in order to do so. In general, ideal inquiry is affect-less with respect to its object. Affections distort, but reason without affection can find fundamental truths that all reasonable people will agree to. (Enthusiastic optimism with respect to reason.)

(iv) This is the view at least suggested by Descartes and Locke, among early modern philosophers, and by Mill later on. It is characteristic of the so-called "free-thinkers" who either rejected Christian revelation (e.g., materialists, evolutionary naturalists) or else attempted to reinterpret Christian revelation in such a way as to eliminate its supernaturalistic character (liberal theology).

III. The Suicide of Thought (Postmodernism, generated in the 19th and early 20th centuries by the perceived failure of Enlightenment Rationalism):

All of the views included here exhibit a marked pessimism with respect to reason. In general, they see that reason *cannot validate itself,* and this leads them to reject appeals to reason as illegitimate:

A. *Academic Skepticism:* Reason turned upon itself raises doubts about its own reliability and can be seen to be wholly unreliable at least with respect to the big **questions** in metaphysics and moral theory. A skeptic of this stripe might despair of finding wisdom and instead romanticize the unfulfilled "search for wisdom." Alternatively, this sort of skeptic might might accept Christian revelation despite its being in conflict with fallen reason (fideism—suggested by Philo at the end of Hume's *Dialogues Concerning Natural Religion*). In addition, this sort of skepticism can easily lead to the forms of intellectual pessimism that follow.

B. *Pragmatism:* Reason is wholly unreliable with respect to the big **questions** in metaphysics and moral philosophy. However, the realization that this is so should not lead to despair but should instead make us see that it is a waste of time (not to mention dangerous) to try to answer the big **questions** in metaphysics and moral theory. Therefore, we should resolve to concentrate only on those matters (e.g., satisfying needs, pursuing scientific knowledge, trying to reduce human suffering) which reason is proportioned to. (Hume, Dewey, Rorty, Simonides (as quoted by Aristotle in the *Metaphysics*).) A variant of this view allows that people have the freedom to (arationally) adopt comprehensive worldviews, but that these should be strictly private commitments and should not enter into public discourse, where they tend to be divisive.)

C. *Nietzscheanism:* Reason is wholly unreliable with respect to the big **questions** in metaphysics and moral theory. Indeed, reason applied to the big **questions** is in general rationalization, so that appeals to reason on these **questions** are simply excuses for the will to power, i.e., for the will to dominate others. Given this, the strong (or "free spirits") should assert themselves without apology, so that they can become the best exemplars of the human spirit—and such individuals should be dominant and not held back by the weak and fearful, who constitute the vast majority of human beings.

D. *Quietism:* Reason is wholly unreliable with respect to the big **questions** in metaphysics and moral philosophy. Indeed, reason applied to the big **questions** is in general rationalization, so that appeals to reason on these **questions** are simply excuses for the will to power, i.e., for the will to dominate others. Given this, we should resist the will to power and try to make ourselves as much as possible impervious to the temptation to dominate others or in general to exercise our power. (Tolstoy, Schopenauer, certain strands of Stoicism and Buddhism.)

Alfred J. Freddoso, Notes on Chesterton's Orthodoxy (Class Handouts—Phil 264: Supplemental Material)

"I am sure," Mr. Leveson, the Secretary, had said, with a somewhat constrained smile, "that after the eloquent and epoch-making speech to which we have listened there will be some **questions** asked, and we hope to have a debate afterwards. I am sure somebody will ask a **question**." Then he looked interrogatively at one weary looking gentleman in the fourth row and said, "Mr. Hinch?"

Mr. Hinch shook his head with a pallid passion of refusal, wonderful to watch, and said, "I couldn't! I really couldn't!"

"We should be very pleased," said Mr. Leveson, "if any lady would ask a **question**." In the silence that followed it was somehow psychologically borne in on the whole audience that one particular great large lady (as the lecturer would say) sitting at the end of the second row was expected to ask a **question**. Her own wax-work immobility was witness both to the expectation and its disappointment. "Are there any other

questions?" asked Mr. Leveson—as if there had been any yet. He seemed to speak with a slight air of relief.

G. K. Chesterton, The Flying Inn

And its despair is this, that it does not really believe that there is any meaning in the universe; therefore it cannot hope to find any romance; its romances will have no plots. A man cannot expect any adventures in the land of anarchy. But a man can expect any number of adventures if he goes travelling in the land of authority. One can find no meanings in a jungle of scepticism; but the man will find more and more meanings who walks through a forest of doctrine and design. Here everything has a story tied to its tail, like the tools or pictures in my father's house; for it is my father's house. I end where I began—at the right end. I have entered at last the gate of all good philosophy. I have come into my second childhood.

But this larger and more adventurous Christian universe has one final mark difficult to express; yet as a conclusion of the whole matter I will attempt to express it. All the real argument about religion turns on the **question** of whether a man who was born upside down can tell when he comes right way up. The primary paradox of Christianity is that the ordinary condition of man is not his sane or sensible condition; that the normal itself is an abnormality. That is the inmost philosophy of the Fall. In Sir Oliver Lodge's interesting new Catechism, the first two **questions** were: "What are you?" and "What, then, is the meaning of the Fall of Man?" I remember amusing myself by writing my own answers to the **questions**; but I soon found that they were very broken and agnostic answers. To the **question**, "What are you?" I could only answer, "God knows." And to the **question**, "What is meant by the Fall?" I could answer with complete sincerity, "That whatever I am, I am not myself."

G. K. Chesterton, Orthodoxy

A minute or two later a footman arrived to tell them they could see Paul. They went upstairs. Chalky White was seated on a chair outside Paul's bedroom. 'I'm taking no chances, you see,' Allgood said.

They went in. Paul was sitting up in bed. He looked pale but he summoned up a smile as they entered. 'Hullo, Allgood—Wilkins. Listen, tell this stubborn young lady there's no earthly reason why we can't start off on our trip this afternoon.' He indicated Geraldine, who was standing at the other side of the bed.

'There's every reason,' she said firmly. 'You're very lucky. The doctor said that if that blow had been a fraction harder or in a slightly different position you could be dead now.'

'But I'm not dead. I feel top-hole, apart from a bit of a headache.'

'Listen, you pig-headed chump, you are not leaving this house today. Tomorrow, if the doctor says so. And you're staying in bed until after lunch at least.'

'Feel up to answering a few **questions**? Allgood asked.

'Sure,' Paul said, 'but I can't tell you anything. I've explained I didn't get a glimpse of the bloke.'

'Not about that. What I want to know is whether you've told me everything you can tell me about this whole business. Has there been anything you've seen or heard that's made you slightly puzzled? Anything, or any face, that's momentarily struck a chord in your memory?'

You have either reached a page that is unavailable for viewing or reached your viewing limit for this book.

James Anderson, *The Affair of the Mutilated Mink: A Delightfully Quirky Murder Mystery in the Great Tradition of Agatha Christie*

Christianity, the bane of his ancestors, beckoned like the Devil Himself. Unlike Judaism, Christianity proffered the hope that the Messiah had already come, and that redemption was just around the corner. It was tragic, Fish thought, that the worship of a Jew, propagated by Jews to non-Jews, had come back to haunt Jews—a distinctly Jewish irony. But the sins of history were beside the point. That Christianity had been malpracticed for centuries did not mean it was inherently evil (did it?); and in **questions** of theological doctrine, the Christians might in fact be *right*.

Todd Wiggins, *Zeitgeist*

How then do you suppose the Great God would feel, to be called a liar, by the man and woman he had made out of the dust? Could they have treated him any worse, if they had tried?

Harvey Newcomb, *Newcomb's First **Question** Book*

"Oh, I won't put my finger in the pie! Let him answer for himself. Everyone has a conscience of his own; and Jesus Christ has said, 'Judge not, lest ye be judged.' Well, one morning—or was it in the evening? I don't exactly remember—yes, now it comes back to me that it was in the morning—I saw him pass by, scowling and with his head bent down; I was in my doorway, sharpening a razor. Out of curiosity I gave him a passing word as well as a nod, adding a gesture that was as good as a **question**. He came up to me, looked me straight in the face, and answered: 'Haven't I told you that, sooner or later, I should do something crazy? And I shall, neighbor, yes, I shall! They are dragging me by the hair!' 'Let me cut it off, then!' I answered jokingly, to make him forget himself."

"So, he had told you before, had he? How did he happen to tell you before?"

"Oh, your honor knows how words slip out of the mouth at certain moments. Who pays attention to them? For my part, I have too many other things in my head—"

"Come, come—what had he been talking about, when he told you before?"

"Great heavens, give me time to think, your honor! What had he been talking about? Why, about his wife, of course. Who knows? Some one must have put a flea in his ear. It needs only half a word to ruin a poor devil's peace of mind. And that is how a man lets such words slip out of his mouth as 'Sooner or later I shall do something crazy!' That is all. I know nothing else about it, your honor!"

"And the only answer you made him was a joke?"

"I could not say to him, 'Go ahead and do it,' could I? As it was he went off, shaking his head. And what idea he kept brooding over, after that, who knows? One can't see inside of another man's brain. But sometimes, when I heard him freeing his mind—"

"Then he used to free his mind to you?"

"Why, yes, to me, and maybe to others besides. You see, one bears things and bears things and bears things; and at last, rather than burst with them, one frees one's mind to the first man who comes along."

Luigi Capuana, *The Deposition*

A religion, almost a religion, any religion, a quintal in religion, a relying and a surface and a service in indecision and a creature and a **question** and a syllable in answer and more counting and no quarrel and a single scientific statement and no darkness and no **question** and an earned administration and a single set of sisters and an outline and no blisters and the section seeing yellow and the centre having spelling and no solitude and no quaintness and yet solid quite so solid and the single surface centred and the **question** in the placard and the singularity, is there a singularity, and the singularity, why is there a **question** and the singularity why is the surface outrageous, why is it beautiful why is it not when there is no doubt, why is anything vacant, why is not disturbing a centre no virtue, why is it when it is and why is it when it is and there is no doubt, there is no doubt that the singularity shows.

> Gertrude Stein, *Tender Buttons*

Accepting these statements as points that admit of being argued with deference to the rules of right reason, let us establish in turn two positions which do not admit of being argued because they are evident in themselves: (a) Where the significance of symbols is uncertain, it is easy to interpret falsely; (b) When a subject is obscure and difficult, no person is qualified to speak positively if his knowledge be obtained at second-hand. Now, have we good reason to suppose that Mgr. Meurin is possessed of first-hand knowledge, and is consequently in a position to interpret truly upon the difficult subject he has undertaken, namely, the esoteric doctrines of the Kabbalah? If not, we are entitled to dismiss him without further examination. As a fact, in this preliminary and essential matter the archbishop can stand no test. The antiquity of the Kabbalah is necessary to work his hypothesis, and he assumes it as if unaware that its antiquity had ever been impugned. There may be much to be said upon both sides of this hotly-debated **question**, but there is nothing to be said for a writer who seems ignorant that there is a **question**. And hence my readers will in no way be astonished to learn that his information is obtained at second-hand, or that his one authority is Franck. This fact is the key to his entire work, and the sole credit that is due to him is the skilful appearance of erudition which he has given to a shallow performance, and the natural mental elegance which has prevented him from being noisy and violent.

> Arthur Edward Waite, *Devil-Worship in France; or, The **Question** of Lucifer; A Record of Things Seen and Heard in the Secret Societies According to the Evidence of Initiates*

Faith was a struggle, and God did not mind Abraham's anguished **questioning**. He had learned that it was hopeless to rely on such "yes-men" as Noah. Nevertheless, he merely showed the Promise in a more tragic light. Abraham fell into a trance, "and a deep and terrifying darkness descended upon him" (15:12). God then told him that his descendants would become exiles, enslaved and oppressed for four hundred years. Who needs a Promise like this?

> Karen Armstrong, *In the Beginning: A New Interpretation of Genesis*

"God knows. Maybe my mind's been corrupted by the **questions** the newspapers have been asking me."

> Dashiell Hammett, *The Dain Curse*

"And to begin with the inevitable **question**, Do you know of, or suspect, any kind of entanglement with any woman?"

> R. Austin Freeman, *The Shadow of the Wolf (Dr. Thorndyke Mysteries)*

Before Europe orientalized its eastern colonies, the Jew orientalized himself. Living in exile—amid the empires of Assyria, Babylon, Persia, Greece, Rome, and the four Islamic caliphates—he yearned for Zion: the homeland forever lost, the cradle of an identity forever idealized. "My heart is in the East—/And I am at the edge of the West" is how the predicament was put by Yehudah Ha-Levi, who wrote in Hebrew in twelfth-century Muslim Spain about Jerusalem under the yoke of the Crusaders. The poem, among the most famous in the Jewish canon, proceeds by **questions**—

> How can I possibly taste what I eat?
> How could it please me?
> How can I keep my promise
> or ever fulfill my vow,
> when Zion is held by Edom
> and I am bound by Arabia's chains?

—all of which raise the essential Jewish **question**: What does it mean to esteem that which you don't, or only barely, know? Or, phrased another way: What happens when Zion doesn't live up to its poem?

Joshua Cohen, New Books (Harper's Magazine)

"Naturally, I suspect, because I can think of no other reason for his leaving me in this way. But to be honest, I have never had the slightest grounds of complaint in regard to his behaviour with other women. He married me because he fell in love with me, and he has never seemed to change. Whatever he has been to other people, to me he has always appeared, in his rough, taciturn way, as devoted as his nature allowed him to be. This affair is an utter surprise to me."

Thorndyke made no comment on this, but, following the hint that Margaret had dropped, asked: "As to his character in general, what sort of a man is he? Is he popular, for instance?"

"No," replied Margaret, "he is not very much liked—in fact, with the exception of Mr Varney he has no really intimate friends, and I have often wondered how poor Mr Varney put up with the way he treated him. The truth is that Dan is rather a bully; he is strong, big, and pugnacious, and used to having his own way and somewhat brutal, at times, in his manner of getting it. He is a very self-contained, taciturn, rather secretive man, and—well, perhaps he is not very scrupulous. I am not painting a very flattering picture, I am afraid."

"It sounds like a good portrait, though," said Thorndyke. "When you say that he is not very scrupulous, are you referring to his business transactions?"

"Well, yes, and to his dealings with people generally."

"By the way," asked Thorndyke, "what is his occupation?" Margaret uttered a little apologetic laugh. "It sounds absurd, but I really don't quite know what his business is. He is so very uncommunicative. I have always understood that he is a financier, whatever that may be. I believe he negotiates loans and buys and sells stocks and shares, but he is not on the Stock Exchange. He has an office in Coleman Street, in the premises of a firm of outside brokers, and he keeps a clerk, a man named Levy. It seems to be quite a small establishment, though it appears to yield a fair income. That is all I can tell you, but I dare say Mr Levy could give you other particulars if you wanted them."

"I will make a note of the address, at any rate," said Thorndyke; and having done so, he asked: "As to your husband's banking account: do you happen to know if any considerable sum has been drawn out quite lately, or if any cheques have been presented since he disappeared?"

"His current account is intact," she replied. "I have an account at the same bank, and I saw the manager a couple of days ago. Of course, he was not very expansive, but he did tell me that no unusual amounts had been withdrawn, and that no cheque has been presented since the 21st of June, when Dan drew a cheque for me. It is really rather odd, especially as the balance is somewhat above the average. Don't you think so?"

"I do," he answered. "It suggests that your husband's disappearance was unpremeditated, and that extreme precautions are being taken to conceal his present whereabouts. But the mystery is what he is living on if he took no considerable sum with him and has drawn no cheques since. However, we had better finish with the general **questions**. You don't appear to know much about your husband's present affairs: what do you know of his past?"

R. Austin Freeman, *The Shadow of the Wolf (Dr. Thorndyke Mysteries)*

In 1140, after the death of his wife, the sixty-something-year-old Ha-Levi retired from his medical practice and sailed for Egypt, his people's former house of bondage. From there, according to legend, he retraced the route of the Exodus, to the foot of the ruined Temple in Jerusalem, where he was trampled to death by an Arab on horseback. And so the quest to experience a metaphor became a metaphor itself: the Jew finally arrives in the land he's always dreamed of, and promptly perishes. Is there any better summary of the anxieties of Zionism? Is there any better joke?

Paradox, futility, the veil dance between the imaginary and the actual, homesickness for a foreign or nonexistent home: these are the themes of Yoel Hoffmann, the greatest living writer in Israel—a country that appears in his work as a strange, vagabond mind-state bordered, roughly, by Transylvania, China, and Japan. Hoffmann was born in Transylvania, in 1937, and though he arrived in Mandate Palestine the following year, his true Zion lay farther east. In the 1960s, he made his pilgrimage. Even in Kyoto, where he studied at a Zen Buddhist monastery and obtained his doctorate at the city's university, he longed for Kyoto. On returning to Israel, he taught East Asian studies at the University of Haifa and translated texts from Chinese and Japanese into Hebrew and English, including the koans of Masters Joshu and Kido and a landmark volume of jisei, the last verses monks write before dying or committing ritual suicide.

Hoffmann found his way to fiction only after fifty, publishing a succession of enigmatically nostalgic texts that sought to revive the mystical literature of European Jewry through the poetry and parables of Zen. In Hoffmann's hands, these two traditions, separated by alphabets, languages, continents, and centuries, seem kindred if not continuous: both are full of anecdotes featuring pious figures—barefoot monks, bearded rabbis—who ask or are asked **questions** to which the only answer is a slap, a laugh, or a nonsense retort intended to reorient the senses.

Here's an episode from Hoffmann's translation of Joshu (a.k.a. Zhaozhou Congshen), the ninth-century Zen master of Bailin, China:

A monk asked, "Why is it that an outsider is not allowed to take over?"
Joshu said, "Who are you?"

The monk said, "Enan."

Joshu said, "What is your **question**?"

Enan asked, "Why is it that an outsider is not allowed to take over?"

Joshu patted his head.

Joshua Cohen, New Books (Harper's Magazine)

The above method is generally recommended as the best in the examination of conscience. But you need not follow these exact **questions**; you can ask yourself any **questions** you please: the above **questions** are given only as examples of what you might ask, and to show you how to **question** yourself. It is useless to take any list of sins in a prayerbook and examine yourself by it, confessing the sins just as they are given. If you do take such a list and find in it some **questions** or sins that you do not understand, do not trouble yourself about them.

Thomas L. Kinkead, Baltimore Catechism, No. 4: An Explanation of the Baltimore Catechism of Christian Doctrine for the Use of Sunday-School Teachers and Advanced Classes

Summing up a rather widespread feeling, Klaus Held has spoken of a **question** whose evidence does not impose itself on the phenomenological gaze—for Being is never given as such in intuition—and which testifies only to the somewhat peculiar attraction that the thought of the Stagirite (if not Scholasticism) always exerted on Heidegger. And these were the most gentle critiques! Need we mention the more malicious and polemical ones?

*Jean Grondin, Why Reawaken the **Question** of Being? (Heidegger's Being and Time: Critical Essays)*

If you can't say anything nice, say it as a **question**.

@AcademicsSay, Shit Academics Say (Twitter)

John Moldstad, Jr., "I have heard some Lutherans say they do not believe the Bible teaches objective justification. How can they assert this and still call themselves 'Lutheran'?" *Lutheran Sentinel*, October, 1996, p. 11.[35]

Footnote 35 says—"The alleged **question** sets a record for being prejudicial. The typical ELS member would never say something so idiotic, since most Lutherans react in shock and disbelief to the very concept Moldstad is trying to promote, that forgiveness comes without the Word, without repentance, without the Means of Grace, without faith. The article is a response to Dr. Peter Moeller **questioning** the validity of Objective Justification, enclosing articles on the topic from Pastor Vernon Harley. Moldstad sent a long, friendly letter to Moeller on August 6, 1996."

Gregory Jackson, Review of JP Meyer's Classic UOJ Textbook—The Fetid Womb of the Kokomo Statements (Ichabod The Glory Has Departed)

But the pamphlet of the Rev. Mann, entitled *Plea for the Augsburg Confession*, having called in **question** the accuracy of some of the interpretations of that *Confession* contained in the *Definite Synodical Platform*, and affirmed the Scriptural truth of some of the tenets there dissented from; it becomes a **question** of interest among us as Lutherans, which representation is correct. For the points disputed are those, on the ground of which the constitutions of the General Synod and of her Seminary avow only a qualified assent to the *Augsburg Confession*. In hope of contributing to the prevalence of truth, and the interests of that kingdom of God which is based on it, the writer has carefully re-examined the original documents, and herewith submits the results to the friends of the General Synod and her basis. Since these results as to the **question**, what do the symbols actually teach? are deduced impartially, as must be admitted, from the original symbolical books themselves, as illustrated by the writings of Luther, Melancthon, and of the other Reformers of the same date; those who approve of those books should so far sustain our work: and those who reject these tenets, that is, the New School portion of the church, will not object to seeing a vindication of the reason why they and the General Synod avow only a qualified assent even to the *Augsburg Confession,* namely, because these errors are there taught.

> S. S. Schmucker, *American Lutheranism Vindicated; or, Examination of the Lutheran Symbols, on Certain Disputed Topics: Including a Reply to the Plea of Rev. W. J. Mann*

Of course, I don't mean interpretation in the broadest sense, the sense in which Nietzsche (rightly) says, "There are no facts, only interpretations." By interpretation, I mean here a conscious act of the mind which illustrates a certain code, certain "rules" of interpretation.

Directed to art, interpretation means plucking a set of elements (the X, the Y, the Z, and so forth) from the whole work. The task of interpretation is virtually one of translation. The interpreter says, Look, don't you see that X is really—or, really means—A? That Y is really B? That Z is really C?

What situation could prompt this curious project for transforming a text? History gives us the materials for an answer. Interpretation first appears in the culture of late classical antiquity, when the power and credibility of myth had been broken by the "realistic" view of the world introduced by scientific enlightenment. Once the **question** that haunts post-mythic consciousness—that of the seemliness of religious symbols—had been asked, the ancient texts were, in their pristine form, no longer acceptable. Then interpretation was summoned, to reconcile the ancient texts to "modern" demands.

> Susan Sontag, *Against Interpretation*

But this raises another **question**. When we speak of being "realistic," exactly what reality is it we are referring to?

> David Graeber, *The Utopia of Rules: On Technology, Stupidity, and the Secret Joys of Bureaucracy*

p. 392–13

In this type of **question**, be careful not to just refer to the line that contains the word "shadowy." The answer is found in both the line "real experience" and in the following line "really there" which supports "unsubstantiated" meaning not proven.

E

p. 461–18

Attitude or tone means describing what the author feels towards the subject; therefore, words such as "before the real estate people get hold of it an make it over" exhibits a feeling that they will ruin something for their own purpose. So the author has a "contemptuous" attitude towards them. If someone is "contemptuous" they are disdainful or disproving or scornful.

A

p. 461–19

The context implies that they should save this territory before the real estate people destroy it; therefore, the word "heavens" would be "ironic" as it means the opposite of what is stated in leading to the conclusion that the land will be ruined if the real estate people develop it.

E

*Henry Davis, Explanations for the Official SAT Study Guide **Questions**: Detailed Explanations for the Answers for Every **Question***

"I listened to that going, 'Do they ask Hillary that? What does it have to do with running for the office of the presidency? Is it anybody's business?'" she asked, unaware that Clinton had been asked that selfsame **question** earlier this year and recited Corinthians 13 by way of answering.

"These personal 'gotcha' **questions**, really trying to get you, us, anybody running for office off game," she continued. "How are you finding that, and finding a technique to put them in their place so that the American public isn't wasting their time and actually get to hear what's important via candidates' message?"

"You saw that. I love the Bible, and I'm Protestant, I'm Presbyterian. And they were hitting me with different **questions**, one right after the other," Trump replied. "I don't know if it's 'gotcha **questions**,' it probably is. And then they said, 'What's your favorite verse?' You know, that's a very personal thing. I don't like giving that out to people that you hardly know. Frankly, I don't know if they're fair **questions**, or not fair **questions**, but there are certain things that you, myself and a lot of other people think too personal."

Palin did not press Trump on why it's not too personal to declare the Bible your favorite book, then decline to provide any evidence you've read it or regularly attend church services, because of course she didn't.

Watch the entire interview below via One America News Network.

Scott Eric Kaufman, Sarah Palin and Donald Trump Whine About "Gotcha" Journalism in Inane Interview Straight Out of "Idiocracy" (Salon)

"If you believe it?" repeated Shatov, paying not the slightest attention to this request. "But didn't you tell me that if it were mathematically proved to you that the truth excludes Christ, you'd prefer to stick to Christ rather than to the truth? Did you say that? Did you?"

"But allow me too at last to ask a **question**," said Nikolay Vsyevolodovitch, raising his voice. "What is the object of this irritable and . . . malicious cross-examination?"

"This examination will be over for all eternity, and you will never hear it mentioned again."

"You keep insisting that we are outside the limits of time and space."

"Hold your tongue!" Shatov cried suddenly. "I am stupid and awkward, but let my name perish in ignominy! Let me repeat your leading idea . . . Oh, only a dozen lines, only the conclusion."

"Repeat it, if it's only the conclusion . . ." Stavrogin made a movement to look at his watch, but restrained himself and did not look.

Fyodor Dostoyevsky, The Possessed; or, The Devils

"Yea," said I, "up till this time, yea and in Soest also, there was wanting for me nothing but such an angelic counsellor as I have found in your reverence. Were but the winter over, or at least the weather better, so that I could travel hence!" And thereafter I begged him to assist me with his advice as to which University I should attend. To that he answered, himself had studied in Leyden, but he would counsel to go to Geneva, for by my speech I must be from the High Germany. "Jesus Maria!" said I, "Geneva is farther from my home than Leyden."

"Can I believe mine ears?" says he, "'tis plain your honour is a Papist! Great Heavens, how am I deceived!"

"How so, Pastor?" said I, "must I be a Papist because I will not to Geneva?"

"Nay," says he, "but ye do call upon the name of Mary!"

"How," said I, "is't not well for a Christian to name the mother of his Redeemer?"

"True," says he, "yet would I counsel your honour and beg of him as earnestly as I can to give honour to God only and further to tell me plainly to what religion he belongs, for I doubt much if he be Evangelical (though I have seen him every Sunday in my church), inasmuch as at this last Christmastide he came not to the table of the Lord neither here nor in the Lutheran church."

"Nay," said I, "but your reverence knows well that I am a Christian: were I not, I had not been so oft at the preaching: but for the rest, I must confess that I follow neither Peter nor Paul, but do believe simply all that the twelve articles of the Christian faith do contain: nor will I bind myself to either party till one or the other shall bring me by sufficient proofs to believe that he, rather than the other, doth possess the one true religion of salvation." Thereupon, "Now," says he, "do I truly, and that for the first time, understand that ye have a true soldier's spirit, to risk your life here, there and everywhere, since ye can so live from day to day without religion or worship and can so risk your hope of eternal salvation! Great heaven," says he, "how can a mortal man, that must hereafter be damned or saved, so defy all? Your honour," says he, "was brought up in Hanau: hath he learned there no better Christianity than this? Tell me, why do ye not follow in the footsteps of your parents in the pure religion of Christ, or why will ye not betake yourself to this our belief, of which the foundations be so plain both in Holy Writ and nature that neither Papist nor Lutheran can ever upset them."

"Your reverence," I answered, "so say all of their own religion: yet which am I to believe? Think ye 'tis so light a matter for me to entrust my soul's salvation to any one party that doth revile the other two and accuse them of false doctrine? I pray you to consider, with impartial eyes, what Conrad Vetter and Johannes Nas have written against Luther, and also Luther against the Pope, but most of all what Spangenberg hath written against Francis of Assisi, which for hundreds of years hath been held for a holy and God-like man, and all this in print. To which party shall I betake myself when each says of the other that 'tis unclean, unclean? Doth your reverence think I am wrong if I stay awhile till I have got me more understanding and know black from white? Would any man counsel me to plunge in like a fly into hot soup? Nay, nay, your reverence cannot upon his conscience do that! Without **question** one religion must be right and the other two wrong: and if I should betake myself to one without ripe reflection I might choose the wrong as easily as the right, and so repent of my choice for all eternity. I will sooner keep off the roads altogether than take the wrong one: besides, there be yet other religions besides these here in Europe, as those of the Armenians, the Abyssinians, the Greeks, the Georgians, and so forth, and whichsoever I do choose, then must I with my fellow believers deny all the rest. But if your reverence will but play the part of Ananias for me and open mine eyes, I will with thankfulness follow him and take up that religion to which he belongs."

Thereupon, "Your honour," says he, "is in a great error: but I pray God to enlighten him and help him forth of the slough; to which end I will hereafter so prove to him the truth of our Confession that the gates of hell shall not prevail against it." I answered I would await such with great anxiety: yet in my heart I thought, "If thou trouble me no more anent my lecheries, I will be content with thy belief."

And so can the reader judge what a godless, wicked rogue I then was: for I did but give the good pastor fruitless trouble, that he might leave me undisturbed in my vicious life, and thinks I, "Before thou art ready with thy proofs I shall belike be where the pepper grows."

> *Hans Jacob Christoph von Grimmelshausen, The Adventurous Simplicius Simplicissimus; Being the Description of the Life of a Strange Vagabond Named Melchior Sternfels von Fuchshaim*

Then they return to the market-place and dress, after which they undergo the pepper ordeal. Pepper is dropped into the eyes of each of them, and while this is being done the sufferer has to make a confession of all his sins, to answer all **questions** that may be put to him, and to take certain vows.

> *James George Frazer, The Golden Bough: A Study in Comparative Religion*

The priest was struck with wonder at these tendencies, even though he found Emma's religion might, by dint of fervor, end up bordering on heresy and even folly. But, not being well versed in these matters the moment they exceeded a certain limit, he wrote to Monsieur Boulard, Monseigneur's bookseller, to send him *something renowned for a person of the fair sex, who was thoroughly intelligent.* The bookseller, with the indifference of one dispatching ironmongery to Negroes, packed up higgledy-piggledy everything that was then current in the pious book business. They consisted of little **question**-and-answer handbooks, haughty-toned pamphlets in the manner of Monsieur de Maistre, and the type of novel with pink boards and an insipidly sweet style, manufactured by troubadour seminarists or penitent bluestockings.

> *Gustave Flaubert, Madame Bovary*

Her mother does not believe in fiction: "So many complications, so much passionate love in those novels," she tells her daughter. "In real life, people have other things on their minds. You be the judge: have you ever heard me whinge and whine about love as people do in those books? And yet I'd have a right to a chapter myself, I'd say! I've had two husbands and four children!"[4] If she finds her daughter reading the Catechism for her upcoming communion, she becomes immediately incensed: "Oh, how I hate this nasty habit of asking **questions**! 'What is God?' 'What is this?' 'What is that?' These **question** marks, this obsessive probing, this inquisitiveness, I find it all so terribly indiscreet! And all this bossing about, I ask you! Who translated the Ten Commandments into this awful gibberish? Oh, I certainly don't like seeing a book like this in the hands of a child!"[5]

> *Alberto Manguel, A History of Reading*

I ought to have said above, that the scholars should incorporate in their answers such portions of the references as prove, illustrate, or enforce the subject.

> *Harvey Newcomb, Newcomb's First **Question** Book*

In the evolution wars, the campaign on behalf of intelligent design deserves special mention because it achieved success in many communities by brilliantly employing an intellectual and scientific vocabulary to attack "elitist" scientists who reject religious attacks on Darwin's theory. The intelligent design movement is spearheaded by the

Discovery Institute, a think tank based in Seattle and bankrolled by far right conservatives. The slick, media-savvy right-wingers who run the Discovery Institute prefer to downplay religion and highlight the anti-Darwinist views of a handful of scientific contrarians, many with ties to the religious right. That their views are almost universally rejected by respected mainstream scientists is seen by the intelligent design crowd as evidence of a liberal establishment conspiracy to protect its Darwinist turf. Institute spokesmen constantly compare their contrarian faith-based researchers with once scorned geniuses like Copernicus and Galileo—a contention conveniently ignoring the fact that the Catholic Church, not other seekers of scientific truth, was the source of opposition to the heliocentric theory of the solar system. Intelligent design does not insist on the seven days of creation but it does rest on the nonscientific hypothesis that the complexity of life proves the existence of a designer. "If you want to call the designer God, that's entirely up to you" is the intelligent design pitch—along with "teach the controversy." The lethal inefficiencies of penguins marching across a frozen wasteland in order to reproduce, or of blood requiring the presence of numerous proteins in order to clot and prevent humans from bleeding to death, are viewed not as accidents of nature but as marvels of intention. The obvious **question** of why a guiding intelligence would want to make things so difficult for his or her creations is never asked because it cannot be answered.

Susan Jacoby, The Age of American Unreason

"Pray, sir," said I, "may I ask you a **question**?"

"You may," said he, "and I may decline to answer it. Put your **question**."

"Estella's name. Is it Havisham or—?" I had nothing to add.

"Or what?" said he.

"Is it Havisham?"

Charles Dickens, Great Expectations

I answer that, This name "God" in the three aforesaid significations is taken neither univocally nor equivocally, but analogically. This is apparent from this reason: Univocal terms mean absolutely the same thing, but equivocal terms absolutely different; whereas in analogical terms a word taken in one signification must be placed in the definition of the same word taken in other senses; as, for instance, "being" which is applied to "substance" is placed in the definition of being as applied to "accident"; and "healthy" applied to animal is placed in the definition of healthy as applied to urine and medicine. For urine is the sign of health in the animal, and medicine is the cause of health.

The same applies to the **question** at issue. For this name "God," as signifying the true God, includes the idea of God when it is used to denote God in opinion, or participation. For when we name anyone god by participation, we understand by the name of god some likeness of the true God. Likewise, when we call an idol god, by this name god we understand and signify something which men think is God; thus it is manifest that the name has different meanings, but that one of them is comprised in the other significations. Hence it is manifestly said analogically.

*Thomas Aquinas, Summa Theologica, First Part, **Question** 13: The Names of God*

—I don't mince words, do I? Mr Deasy asked as Stephen read on.

Foot and mouth disease. Known as Koch's preparation. Serum and virus. Percentage

Jules-Alexis Muenier, The Catechism Lesson, 1890
Oil on canvas, 70 x 90 cm, Besançon Museum of Fine Arts And Archeology

of salted horses. Rinderpest. Emperor's horses at Murzsteg, lower Austria. Veterinary surgeons. Mr Henry Blackwood Price. Courteous offer a fair trial. Dictates of common sense. Allimportant **question**. In every sense of the word take the bull by the horns. Thanking you for the hospitality of your columns.

—I want that to be printed and read, Mr Deasy said. You will see at the next outbreak they will put an embargo on Irish cattle. And it can be cured. It is cured. My cousin, Blackwood Price, writes to me it is regularly treated and cured in Austria by cattledoctors there. They offer to come over here. I am trying to work up influence with the department. Now I'm going to try publicity. I am surrounded by difficulties, by . . . intrigues by . . . backstairs influence by . . .

He raised his forefinger and beat the air oldly before his voice spoke.

—Mark my words, Mr Dedalus, he said. England is in the hands of the jews. In all the highest places: her finance, her press. And they are the signs of a nation's decay. Wherever they gather they eat up the nation's vital strength. I have seen it coming these years. As sure as we are standing here the jew merchants are already at their work of destruction. Old England is dying.

He stepped swiftly off, his eyes coming to blue life as they passed a broad sunbeam. He faced about and back again.

—Dying, he said again, if not dead by now.

The harlot's cry from street to street
Shall weave old England's windingsheet.

His eyes open wide in vision stared sternly across the sunbeam in which he halted.

—A merchant, Stephen said, is one who buys cheap and sells dear, jew or gentile, is he not?

—They sinned against the light, Mr Deasy said gravely. And you can see the darkness in their eyes. And that is why they are wanderers on the earth to this day.

On the steps of the Paris stock exchange the goldskinned men quoting prices on their gemmed fingers. Gabble of geese. They swarmed loud, uncouth about the temple, their heads thickplotting under maladroit silk hats. Not theirs: these clothes, this speech, these gestures. Their full slow eyes belied the words, the gestures eager and unoffending, but knew the rancours massed about them and knew their zeal was vain. Vain patience to heap and hoard. Time surely would scatter all. A hoard heaped by the roadside: plundered and passing on. Their eyes knew their years of wandering and, patient, knew the dishonours of their flesh.

—Who has not? Stephen said.

—What do you mean? Mr Deasy asked.

He came forward a pace and stood by the table. His underjaw fell sideways open uncertainly. Is this old wisdom? He waits to hear from me.

—History, Stephen said, is a nightmare from which I am trying to awake.

From the playfield the boys raised a shout. A whirring whistle: goal. What if that nightmare gave you a back kick?

—The ways of the Creator are not our ways, Mr Deasy said. All human history moves towards one great goal, the manifestation of God.

Stephen jerked his thumb towards the window, saying:

—That is God.

Hooray! Ay! Whrrwhee!
—What? Mr Deasy asked.

James Joyce, Ulysses

But what is he saying? I am willing to do as I was asked, to follow, to **question**, to build a way. But what can I do with an opaque statement like that?

*William Lovitt, Introduction to The **Question** Concerning Technology and Other Essays, by Martin Heidegger*

After another silence he stood up and said he'd like to help me; I interested him, and, with God's help, he would do something for me in my trouble. But, first, he must put a few more **questions**.

He began by asking bluntly if I'd loved my mother.

"Yes," I replied, "like everybody else." The clerk behind me, who had been typing away at a steady pace, must just then have hit the wrong keys, as I heard him pushing the carrier back and crossing something out.

Next, without any apparent logical connection, the magistrate sprang another **question**.

"Why did you fire five consecutive shots?"

I thought for a bit; then explained that they weren't quite consecutive. I fired one at first, and the other four after a short interval.

"Why did you pause between the first and second shot?"

I seemed to see it hovering again before my eyes, the red glow of the beach, and to feel that fiery breath on my cheeks—and, this time, I made no answer.

During the silence that followed, the magistrate kept fidgeting, running his fingers through his hair, half rising, then sitting down again. Finally, planting his elbows on the desk, he bent toward me with a queer expression.

"But why, why did you go on firing at a prostrate man?" Again I found nothing to reply. The magistrate drew his hand across his forehead and repeated in a slightly different tone: "I ask you 'Why?' I insist on your telling me." I still kept silent. Suddenly he rose, walked to a file cabinet standing against the opposite wall, pulled a drawer open, and took from it a silver crucifix, which he was waving as he came back to the desk.

"Do you know who this is?"

Albert Camus, The Stranger

All this is clearly outside the subject of Satanism, but it leads up, notwithstanding, to the discovery of M. Ricoux. As to this gentle man himself there are no particulars forthcoming; he has promised an account of his adventures during four years as an emigrant in Chili; and he has promised a patriotic epic in twelve cantos, but so far as my information goes they remain in the womb of time. But he has a claim on our consideration because it occurred to him that he would put in practice the advice of Leo Taxil, which he did accordingly in the autumn of 1891, and demonstrated to his own satisfaction that "Are there Women in Freemasonry?" is a book of true disclosure, and a **question** that must be answered in the affirmative. He performed thereupon a very creditable action; he wrote a pamphlet entitled "The Existence of Lodges for Women: Researches on this subject," &c., in which he stated the result of his investigation, collected the controversy on the subject which had been scattered through the press of the period, and defended Leo Taxil with the warmth of an alter Ego. But he had not limited his researches to the directions indicated in his author. Encouraged by the success which had attended his initial efforts, he determined upon an independent experiment in bribery, and after the same manner that Leo Taxil procured the "Ritual of the New and Reformed Palladium," so he succeeded in obtaining the "Collection of Secret Instructions to Supreme Councils, Grand Lodges, and Grand Orients," printed at Charleston in the year 1891. "This collection," he tells us, "is certainly a document of the first order; for it emanates from General Albert Pike, that is to say, from the 'Pope of the Freemasons.'" On this document he bases the following statements:—(a) Universal Freemasonry possesses a Supreme Directory as the apex of its international organisation, and it is located at Berlin. (b) Four subsidiary Central Directories exist at Naples, Calcutta, Washington, and Monte Video. (c) Furthermore, a Chief of Political Action resides at Rome, commissioned to watch over the Vatican and to precipitate events against the Papacy. (d) A Grand Depositary of Sacred Traditions, under the title of Sovereign Pontiff of Universal Freemasonry, is located at Charleston, and at the time of the discovery was Albert Pike.

Some of these statements, it will be observed, require rectification, in the light of fuller disclosures made by Palladian initiates, from whom the material of my second chapter has been chiefly derived, but it will be seen that it is substantially correct.

Arthur Edward Waite, Devil-Worship in France; or, The **Question** *of Lucifer; A Record of Things Seen and Heard in the Secret Societies According to the Evidence of Initiates*

Monty: Dad, is there a word to describe answers that are completely correct but entirely useless under the circumstances?
Prof. Jones: Yes, yes there is.
—*Irregular Webcomic!*

If you ask someone a **question**, and he gives you an entirely accurate answer that is of no practical use whatsoever, he has just given you a Mathematician's Answer.

A common form of giving a Mathematician's Answer is to fully evaluate the logic of the **question** and give a logically correct answer. Such a response may prove confusing for someone who interpreted what they said colloquially.

Examples include **questions** involving "can you do [favor] . . . ?" being interpreted as a hypothetical "are you *capable* of doing [favor]?" instead of its more common intent as a request to actually do it (this is a favorite of English teachers and Grammar Nazis, frequently going through something similar to "Can I come in?" "I don't know, can you?" "Uh, may I come in?") Another common form is when a character is asked "Is it A or B?" they will respond, "Yes" as if it was a **question** of Boolean logic rather than clarifying which specific one is the case (though this can also occur if the responder does not know the answer, or considers both answers correct. This crops up a lot in Real Life, especially in the world of computers.) This occurs because a **question** of the form "Is the capital of Australia Melbourne or Canberra?" is ambiguous between "The capital of Australia is either Melbourne or Canberra. Which one is it?" and "Is it the case that the capital of Australia is either Melbourne or Canberra?". A logician may mistake the former for the latter, to the **questioner's** frustration.

Television Tropes & Idioms, Mathematician's Answer

When, however, we ask how the instrumental comes to presence as a kind of causality, then we experience this coming to presence as the destining of a revealing.

When we consider, finally, that the coming to presence of the essence of technology comes to pass in the granting that needs and uses man so that he may share in revealing, then the following becomes clear:

The essence of technology is in a lofty sense ambiguous. Such ambiguity points to the mystery of all revealing, i.e., of truth.

On the one hand, Enframing challenges forth into the frenziedness of ordering that blocks every view into the coming-to-pass of revealing and so radically endangers the relation to the essence of truth.

On the other hand, Enframing comes to pass for its part in the granting that lets man endure—as yet unexperienced, but perhaps more experienced in the future—that he may be the one who is needed and used for the safekeeping of the coming to presence of truth. Thus does the arising of the saving power appear.

The irresistibility of ordering and the restraint of the saving power draw past each other like the paths of two stars in the course of the heavens. But precisely this, their passing by, is the hidden side of their nearness.

When we look into the ambiguous essence of technology, we behold the constellation, the stellar course of the mystery.

The **question** concerning technology is the **question** concerning the constellation in which revealing and concealing, in which the coming to presence of truth, comes to pass.

But what help is it to us to look into the constellation of truth? We look into the danger and see the growth of the saving power.

Through this we are not yet saved. But we are thereupon summoned to hope in the growing light of the saving power. How can this happen? Here and now and in little things, that we may foster the saving power in its increase. This includes holding always before our eyes the extreme danger.

*Martin Heidegger, The **Question** Concerning Technology*

A third variant is when a **question** beginning with "How" (being asked in the sense of "By what means does X occur?") is answered with an adverb or adverbial phrase (responding as if the **question** had been "In what manner does X occur?"). For example: "How did you get past the guards?" "With difficulty."

Can be used by characters for reasons ranging from snarky humor to intentional obfuscation to being extremely *Literal-Minded*—AI and other Literal Genies by their nature are very likely to fall into the last category.

Can overlap with Shaped Like Itself when the **question** is seeking a description, and with Captain Obvious, as these answers tend to be self-evident for anyone with a brain. Usually doubles as a Cryptically Unhelpful Answer, when the "mathematician" is deliberately trying to confound the **questioner**. Compare Non-Answer, which is a vague "answer" which does not answer the **question** at all. Mildly related to What's a Henway? and Not Actually The Ultimate **Question**. And don't forget that the person giving the Mathematician's Answer is "technically correct . . . the best kind of correct."

The trope name comes from a family of jokes about the supposed habit of mathematicians to make unhelpful answers. For example: a man in a hot-air balloon asked someone where he was. "You're in a balloon," he answered. The rider concluded that it was a mathematician that said that, because the answer was perfectly correct and completely useless. (The joke sometimes continues with the mathematician deducing the man in the balloon is a <u>manager</u>, because he has risen to his position with a lot of hot air, has no idea where he is or where he is going, and yet claims this is the fault of the innocent person standing below him.)

<u>"How Many?" "All Of Them"</u> is a subtrope that's its own <u>Stock Phrase</u>. See also <u>What's a Henway?</u> Contrast <u>Implied Answer</u> when the **question** isn't answered at all, and the meaning is quite clear. Related to <u>Rhetorical **Question** Blunder</u>: the person who was asked gives a logical answer that ruins the spirit of the **question**.

Television Tropes & Idioms, Mathematician's Answer

The man asked for a second chance, backed up farther, ran hell bent for leather and careened into the bell, which gave a high resonant bong, but unfortunately the man ricocheted off the left side and fell off the parapet to his death. The priest ran downstairs to the crowd surrounding the writhing body. People asked him: "Father do you know who this is?" "Well, I don't know his name, but his face rings a bell."

*Ray Foley, Beer Is the Answer . . . I Don't Remember the **Question***

Mary Tryphena was taken back by the bluntness of the **question.**—I don't know, she said.

Michael Crummey, Galore: A Novel

It was a plea more than a **question**.

Gerald did not answer immediately because he was busy calling at the same time, "Floyd, Floyd! Do you know who this is?"

Again Floyd asked, "Is that you, Johnnie?"

Robert K. Murray and Roger W. Brucker, Trapped! The Story of Floyd Collins

Mary Tryphena barely heard the **question** over the buzz in her ears. She couldn't hold Olive's eye any longer and turned away, caught sight of Judah at the door. She'd forgotten he was in the room and was mortified to see she had an audience. Jude seemed no happier to be overhearing the exchange, his fish eyes bulging in his head.—No, she said. She pointed at him and shouted No a second time, and Jabez went across the room to usher Judah outside.

Mary Tryphena slumped into her chair and did her best not to bawl.—Why would he send me this letter and not say a word to my face?

—Who are we talking about here? Jabez asked.

Michael Crummey, Galore: A Novel

Thus **questioning**, we bear witness to the crisis that in our sheer preoccupation with technology we do not yet experience the coming to presence of technology, that in our sheer aesthetic-mindedness we no longer guard and preserve the coming to presence of art. Yet the more **questioningly** we ponder the essence of technology, the more mysterious the essence of art becomes.

The closer we come to the danger, the more brightly do the ways into the saving power begin to shine and the more **questioning** we become. For **questioning** is the piety of thought.

*Martin Heidegger, The **Question** Concerning Technology*

Studying the heap on the floor, the desk sergeant moved from behind his desk to take a closer look at the alleged attacker. Shelley thought that even though the desk sergeant was a man with a large body frame, he displayed a flat stomach and large biceps.

"Do you know who this is, Cunningham?" the desk sergeant asked, knowing the answer to his **question**.

Taking a closer look at the whimpering heap, Detective Cunningham replied, "Well, I'll be damned! It's Troy Parham, the alleged Parking Deck Rapist! We've been trying to catch you for a mighty long time!"

"Let's book him!" the desk sergeant said, eagerly. He then summoned some of Richmond's Finest from his desk phone to incarcerate Troy Parham—the Parking Deck Rapist.

After reading Troy Parham his Miranda Rights, Detective Cunningham said to the young woman, "We need for you to fill out some paper work. Please, follow me."

Detective Cunningham began to admire the woman's strength, courage, and cool beauty as he led her through the door he had entered moments ago and through a maze of cluttered desks, empty coffee cups, and cursing victims. The detective sat her down next to his unorganized desk and punched a few keys on his computer.

Charles Carroll Lee, Behind Every Dark Cloud: The Critically Acclaimed Novel

S: You obviously envisage, and this is what you have already said, a world movement which either leads up to or has already led up to the absolute technological state.

H: Yes.

S: Good. Now the **question** naturally comes up: can the individual in any way influence this network of inevitabilities, or could philosophy influence it, or could both together influence it inasmuch as philosophy could guide the individual or several individuals toward a specific action?

H: Let me respond briefly and somewhat ponderously, but from long reflection: philosophy will not be able to effect an immediate transformation of the present condition of the world. This is not only true of philosophy, but of all merely human thought and endeavor. Only a god can save us. The sole possibility that is left for us is to prepare a sort of readiness, through thinking and poetizing, for the appearance of the god or for the absence of the god in the time of foundering (*Untergang*); for in the face of the god who is absent, we founder.

Martin Heidegger, Only a God Can Save Us: Der Spiegel's Interview (Philosophical and Political Writings)

Three days later, a second man with no arms showed up for the same job. The priest refused the man admittance, saying he didn't want to go through that again. "What do you mean, again?" "Three days ago another no-arm guy shows . . ." "That's my brother! I've been following him for years! How's he doing?" The priest told him how his brother had unfortunately passed away, whereupon the man urged the priest to hire him so he could dedicate the remainder of his life working where his brother had passed away. "I've corrected the fault he had on his approach to the bell," he said, "so just let me work here for my brother." The priest hesitated, so the man backed up and hurled himself into the bell, which gave a resplendent bong, but the man fell off the right side of the bell, off the parapet to the courtyard below. The priest rushed downstairs. Startled onlookers asked, "Do you know this one, father?"

"No, but he's a dead ringer for his brother."

*Ray Foley, Beer Is the Answer . . . I Don't Remember the **Question***

What purpose I had in view when I was hot on tracing out and proving Estella's parentage, I cannot say. It will presently be seen that the **question** was not before me in a distinct shape, until it was put before me by a wiser head than my own.

Charles Dickens, Great Expectations

S: What is it then?

H: I call it the "other thinking."

S: You call it the "other thinking." Would you like to formulate that a bit more clearly?

H: Did you have in mind the concluding sentence in my lecture, "The **Question** of Technology": "**questioning** is the piety of thought"?[13]

S: We found a sentence in your Nietzsche lectures which is enlightening. You said there: "It is because the highest possible bond prevails in philosophical thought that all great thinkers think the same. This sameness, however, is so essential and rich that one individual can never exhaust it, so each only binds himself to the other all the more strictly." But it appears that, in your opinion, just this philosophical edifice has lead us to a very definite end.

Martin Heidegger, Only a God Can Save Us: Der Spiegel's Interview (Philosophical and Political Writings)

First of all, the story starts with Quasimodo wanting to retire. He places an ad in the paper and interviews an armless dwarf. From there on the stories (#1 and #2) are similar except that they are far funnier when the story teller acts out the part of Quasimodo trudging down the spiral staircase from Notre Dame's bell tower with the hump on his back. Here is the third part.

After the second armless dwarf falls off the tower, Quasi (to his friends) places another ad in the paper and a third, armless dwarf shows up, the third brother. Once again, Quasi explains the rigors of the job and impresses on the dwarf that the "gong" has to be heard all over the city. The dwarf answers Quasi he can do it and is given a try out. He goes back as far as he can, speeds towards the great bell at an alarming rate, misses the bell completely, goes off the tower and smashes to the street below. Quasi jumps down the spiral staircase and when asked by the crowd if he knows the man, states: "No, I don't know his name and his face doesn't ring a bell with me."

*Ray Foley, Beer Is the Answer . . . I Don't Remember the **Question***

H: It has come to an end, but it has not become for us null and void; rather it has turned up anew in this conversation. My whole work in lectures and exercises in the past thirty years has been in the main only an interpretation of Western philosophy. The regress into the historical foundations of thought, the thinking through of the **questions** which are still unasked since the time of Greek philosophy—that is not a cutting loose from the tradition. I am saying: the traditional metaphysical mode of thinking, which terminated with Nietzsche, no longer offers any possibility for experiencing in a thoughtful way the fundamental traits of the technological age, an age which is just beginning.

S: Approximately two years ago, in a conversation with a Buddhist monk, you spoke of "a completely new way of thinking" and you said that "only a few people are capable of" this new way of thought. Did you want to say that only a very few people can have the insights which in your view are possible and necessary?

Martin Heidegger, Only a God Can Save Us: Der Spiegel's Interview (Philosophical and Political Writings)

During this period it falls obviously into two groups, that which preceded any knowledge of the institution in **question** and that which is posterior to the first promulgation of such knowledge. In the first we find mainly the old accusations which have long ceased to exert any conspicuous influence, namely, Atheism, Materialism, and revolutionary plotting. Without disappearing entirely, these have been largely replaced in the second group by charges of magic and diabolism, concerning which the denunciations have been loud and fierce. One supplementary impeachment may be said in a certain sense to connect both, because it is common to both; it is that of unbridled licence fostered by the asserted existence of adoptive lodges. We shall find during the first period that Masonry was freely described as a diabolical and Satanic institution, and it is necessary to insist on this point because it is liable to confuse the issues. Before the year 1891 the diabolism identified with Masonry was almost exclusively intellectual. That is to say, its alleged atheism, from the standpoint of the Catholic Church, was a diabolical opinion in matters of religion; its alleged materialism was a diabolical philosophy in matters of science; its alleged revolutionary plottings, being especially directed against the Catholic Church, constituted diabolical politics. Such descriptions will seem arbitrary enough to most persons who do not look forth upon the world from the windows of the Vatican, but they are undeniably consistent at Rome.

Of actual diabolism prior to the date I have named, there is, I believe, only the solitary accusation made by Mgr. de Ségur, and having reference to a long anterior period. He states that in the year 1848 there was a Masonic lodge at Rome, where the mass of the devil was celebrated in the presence of men and women. A ciborium was placed on an altar between six black candles; each person, after spitting and trampling on a crucifix, deposited in this ciborium a consecrated host which had been purchased or received in church. The sacred elements were stabbed by the whole assembly, the candles were extinguished at the termination of the mass, and an orgie followed, similar, says Mgr. de Ségur, to those of "Pagan mysteries and Manichæan re-unions." Such abominations were, however, admittedly rare, and the story just recited rests on nothing that can be called evidence.

*Arthur Edward Waite, Devil-Worship in France; or, The **Question** of Lucifer; A Record of Things Seen and Heard in the Secret Societies According to the Evidence of Initiates*

"Estella who?" said I.

"Never you mind," retorted Drummle.

"Estella of where?" said I. "You are bound to say of where." Which he was, as a Finch.

"Of Richmond, gentlemen," said Drummle, putting me out of the **question**, "and a peerless beauty."

Much he knew about peerless beauties, a mean, miserable idiot! I whispered Herbert.

"I know that lady," said Herbert, across the table, when the toast had been honored.

"Do you?" said Drummle.

"And so do I," I added, with a scarlet face.

"Do you?" said Drummle. "O, Lord!"

This was the only retort—except glass or crockery—that the heavy creature was capable of making; but, I became as highly incensed by it as if it had been barbed with wit, and I immediately rose in my place and said that I could not but regard it as being like the honorable Finch's impudence to come down to that Grove,—we always talked about coming down to that Grove, as a neat Parliamentary turn of expression,—down to that Grove, proposing a lady of whom he knew nothing. Mr. Drummle, upon this, starting up, demanded what I meant by that? Whereupon I made him the extreme reply that I believed he knew where I was to be found.

Whether it was possible in a Christian country to get on without blood, after this, was a **question** on which the Finches were divided. The debate upon it grew so lively, indeed, that at least six more honorable members told six more, during the discussion, that they believed they knew where they were to be found.

Charles Dickens, Great Expectations

Since, then, this name "God" is given to signify the divine nature as stated above (Article 8), and since the divine nature cannot be multiplied as shown above (**Question** 11, Article 3), it follows that this name "God" is incommunicable in reality, but communicable in opinion; just in the same way as this name "sun" would be communicable according to the opinion of those who say there are many suns. Therefore, it is written: "You served them who by nature are not gods," (Galatians 4:8), and a gloss adds, "Gods not in nature, but in human opinion." Nevertheless this name "God" is communicable, not in its whole signification, but in some part of it by way of similitude; so that those are called gods who share in divinity by likeness, according to the text, "I have said, You are gods" (Psalm 81:6).

But if any name were given to signify God not as to His nature but as to His "suppositum," accordingly as He is considered as "this something," that name would be absolutely incommunicable; as, for instance, perhaps the Tetragrammaton among the Hebrew; and this is like giving a name to the sun as signifying this individual thing.

*Thomas Aquinas, Summa Theologica, First Part, **Question** 13: The Names of God*

And besides him I met with another, some eighty years of age, and such a divine that you'd have sworn Scotus himself was revived in him. He, being upon the point of unfolding the mystery of the name Jesus, did with wonderful subtlety demonstrate that there lay hidden in those letters whatever could be said of him; for that it was only declined with three cases, he said, it was a manifest token of the Divine Trinity; and then, that the first ended in S, the second in M, the third in U, there was in it an ineffable mystery, to wit, those three letters declaring to us that he was the beginning, middle, and end (summum, medium, et ultimum) of all. Nay, the mystery was yet more abstruse; for he so mathematically split the word Jesus into two equal parts that he left the middle letter by itself, and then told us that that letter in Hebrew was schin or sin, and that sin in the Scotch tongue, as he remembered, signified as much as sin; from whence he gathered that it was Jesus that took away the sins of the world. At which new exposition the audience were so wonderfully intent and struck with admiration, especially the theologians, that there wanted little but that Niobe-like they had been turned to stones; whereas the like has almost happened to me, as befell the Priapus in Horace.

And not without cause, for when were the Grecian Demosthenes or Roman Cicero ever guilty of the like? They thought that introduction faulty that was wide of the matter, as if it were not the way of carters and swineherds that have no more wit than God sent them. But these learned men think their preamble, for so they call it, then chiefly rhetorical when it has least coherence with the rest of the argument, that the admiring audience may in the meanwhile whisper to themselves, "What will he be at now?" In the third place, they bring in instead of narration some texts of Scripture, but handle them cursorily, and as it were by the bye, when yet it is the only thing they should have insisted on. And fourthly, as it were changing a part in the play, they bolt out with some **question** in divinity, and many times relating neither to earth nor heaven, and this they look upon as a piece of art.

Here they erect their theological crests and beat into the people's ears those magnificent titles of illustrious doctors, subtle doctors, most subtle doctors, seraphic doctors, cherubin doctors, holy doctors, **unquestionable** doctors, and the like; and then throw abroad among the ignorant people syllogisms, majors, minors, conclusions, corollaries, suppositions, and those so weak and foolish that they are below pedantry. There remains yet the fifth act in which one would think they should show their mastery. And here they bring in some foolish insipid fable out of Speculum Historiale or Gesta Romanorum and expound it allegorically, tropologically, and anagogically. And after this manner do they and their chimera, and such as Horace despaired of compassing when he wrote "Humano capiti," etc.

Desiderius Erasmus, The Praise of Folly

"What's that?" I ask the priest, wondering if he's still talking to me.

"Oh," he says, giving a start. "I'm sorry. To answer your **question**—" He frowns mightily.

What **question**?

"Are you forgetting about the ancient Romans?"

The ancient Romans. My nose is running badly. I have to go.

"Aren't you forgetting that the ancient Romans, who were, after all, not stupid people and were right about most things though not very creative, were also right about us."

"I suppose I had forgotten."

"The historians say they mistook us for a Jewish sect, didn't they?"

"Sure."

"Was it a mistake?"

Now he's clear of the trapdoor. I give the rung a yank.

"The Jews as a word sign cannot be assimilated under a class, category, or theory. No subsuming Jews! Not even by the Romans."

"Right." I yank again. What's wrong with this damn thing?

"No subsuming Jews, Tom!"

"Okay, I won't."

"This offends people, even the most talented people, people of the loftiest sentiments, the highest scientific achievements, and the purest humanitarian ideals."

"Right."

"You have to turn it," he says, noticing my efforts to open the trapdoor.

"Thank you." No, that doesn't work either.

"The Holocaust was a consequence of the sign which could not be evacuated."

"Right."

"Who remembers the Ukrainians?"

"True."

"Let me tell you something, Tom. People have the wrong idea about the Holocaust. The Holocaust, as people see it, is a myth."

Oh my. My heart sinks. On top of everything else, is he one of those? I try harder to open the damn door.

While he is talking, he has taken hold of my arm.

I remove his hand. "Goodbye, Father."

"What's the matter Tom?"

"Are you telling me that the Nazis did not kill six million Jews?"

"No."

"They did kill six million Jews."

"Yes. "

"Then what are you saying?"

Walker Percy, The Thanatos Syndrome

It was not the wisdom of the right hon. baronet, or the wisdom of the present Parliament, or of that House, which was to settle the **question** as to its existing bearings. The **question** was, what was, in point of fact, the constitution of the Church of Scotland, as given to that Church by various statutes, towards the end of the sixteenth, and in the course of the seventeenth centuries?

A Full and Impartial Report of the Important Debate in the House of Commons on Mr. Fox Maule's Motion Regarding the Church of Scotland, on the Evenings of Tuesday and Wednesday, the 7th and 8th March, 1843

Bournisien interrupted him, replying testily that it was none the less necessary to pray.

"But," objected the chemist, "since God knows all our needs, what can be the good of prayer?"

"What!" cried the ecclesiastic, "Prayer! Why, aren't you a Christian?"

"Excuse me," said Homais; "I admire Christianity. To begin with, it enfranchised the slaves, introduced into the world a morality—"

"That isn't the **question**. All the texts—"

"Oh! oh! As to texts, look at history; it is known that all the texts have been falsified by the Jesuits."

Gustave Flaubert, Madame Bovary

Some Kokomo Narrative for the Newbies

The Kokomo episode began when Pastor Papenfuss began teaching UOJ in the congregation in Kokomo, Indiana. Thanks to some research from Name Withheld, we know that WELS used a Justification By Faith catechism for many decades, the Gausewitz, until it was replaced by the horrid UOJ Kuske catechism. Two families were upset by the new dogma being promoted by Papenfuss.

Look at the 1978 graduates with Papenfuss—Mark Jeske, Stroh, Starr, Schumann the Born-Again Atheist, Curia the UOJ Scribe, Jim Witte (DMin in CG), Marcus Manthey—Defender of Unfaith. And the faculty—no less than four UOJ fanatics: Gerlach (Fuller alumnus), Becker, Panning, and Kuske.

Although Papenfuss admitted to the families that he never heard of UOJ before The Sausage Factory (he may have said Mequon), he went ahead with excommunicating the two families who had **questions**. I was at the Hartmann farm talking to both men about this, and they copied the letters of excommunication for me.

The four Kokomo Statements came about this way. The families wrote down the three statements from Meyer's Ministers of Christ, which Papenfuss gave them to study. They added a fourth from their research. They said, "Is this what you are saying?" Papenfuss agreed with those statements. The letter of excommunication removed them for NOT agreeing with the statements.

The same Synod President who lied about the origin of the Kokomo statements also lied about the Tabor adultery and murder.

Gregory Jackson, Classic Ichabod—Review of JP Meyer's Classic UOJ Textbook—The Fetid Womb of the Kokomo Statements (Ichabod the Glory Has Departed)

In addition to this, so many of the **questions** depend on the references that no teacher can be prepared to use them who has not carefully consulted these references. They should be so fixed in the teacher's mind, from previous study, that he will feel no hesitancy as to the answer which ought to be given. But his chief aim should be, by meditation and prayer, to get such a lively Impression of these truths on his own soul, that they will appear to him as living realities. Then he will be prepared, in the most forcible manner, to impress them on the minds of others.

*Harvey Newcomb, Newcomb's First **Question** Book*

Karl Marx, 1875 (photo by John Jabez Edwin Mayal)

*Ushi Derman, Jews of the World Unite: The Jewish **Question** of Karl Marx (anumuseum.org)*

These **Questions** That Are Bothering You, Larry

As we cut to a frosted glass door with a painted-on "Leon Sussman, DDS"

RABBI NACHTNER

How does God speak to us: it's a good **question.** You know Lee Sussman?

LARRY

Doctor Sussman? I think I—yeah?

RABBI NACHTNER

Did he ever tell you about the goy's teeth?

LARRY

No . . . I—What goy?

RABBI NACHTNER

So Lee is at work one day; you know he has the orthodontic practice there at Texa-Tonka.

LARRY

Uh-huh.

RABBI NACHTNER

Right next to the Gold Eagle Cleaners.

We cut to: SIGN FOR THE GOLD EAGLE CLEANERS

It dominates a small suburban strip mall.

Rabbi Nachtner continues in voice-over as we cut to a frosted glass door with a painted-on "Leon Sussman, DDS."

RABBI NACHTNER

He's making a plaster mold—it's for corrective bridge work—in the mouth of one of his patients . . .

A close shot of a man's mouth biting down on two horse-shoe shaped troughs—an upper and a lower—that overflow goo.

. . . Russell Kraus. He's a delivery dispatcher for the Star and Tribune with chronic mandibular deterioration.

The grinding guitar solo from Jefferson Airplane's "Bear Melt" scores the narrative. The patient opens his mouth as a hand enters to grab the upper tray.

The reverse shows Dr. Sussman, a middle-aged man dressed in the the high-collared white smock of an oral surgeon. He takes the mold to a drying table.

Kraus is twisted over the side of the chair spitting into the water-swirled spit-sink.

> . . . Well, the mold dries and Lee is examining it one day before fabricating an appliance . . .

Another day: Dr. Sussman sits at his workbench examining the lower mold. He notices something unusual.

> . . . He notices something unusual.

Sussman reaches up for the loupe attached to his eyeglasses.

> There seems to be something engraved on the inside of the patient's lower incisors . . .

He flips down the loupe. One eye is hugely magnified as he stares . . .

> Sure enough, it's writing.

Sussman squints.

His point-of-view: Tiny incised Hebrew letters:

הושיטגי

Back to Rabbi Nachtner: he confirms with a nod.

RABBI NACHTNER

> This in a goy's mouth, Larry.

Back to Leon Sussman: the rabbi's narrative continues.

RABBI NACHTNER

> Hey vav shin yud ayin nun yud. "Hoshiyani." "Help me." "Save me."

Sussman flips the loupe away and looks off, haunted. He rises.

> . . . He checks the mold, just to be sure. Oh, it's there all right . . .

A dental mirror is dipped into the horse-shoe-shaped hardened paste of the mold. It pans tiny letters that stand out in relief, right-side around in the mirror:

הושיטגי

Sussman leans back, thinking.

> He calls the goy back on the pretense of needing additional measurements for the appliance.

Close on Kraus grinning as he shakes Sussman's hand in the reception area. Gestures to invite Kraus back to the examination room.

> Sussman chats, affecting nonchalance.

In the examination room, leaning over Kraus in the chair, the dentist is indeed chatting with apparent casualness.

Notice any other problems with your teeth? Anything peculiar, et cetera?

Sussman unpockets a dental mirror.

No. No. No. Visited any other dentist recently? No.

He dips the mirror into Kraus's mouth:

הושיטגי

Sussman frowns.

There it is. "Help me"?

He leans back.

Sussman goes home. Can Sussman eat? Sussman can't eat.

Sussman sits at the kitchen table, untouched food in front of him. His wife chats volubly while Sussman stares into space.

Can Sussman sleep? Sussman can't sleep.

Sussman is in bed, pyjamas buttoned to the neck, staring at the ceiling.

What does it mean? Is it a message for him, for Sussman? And if so, from whom? Does Sussman know? Sussman doesn't know.

At a row of shelves, back in the dental office, Sussman pulls down boxes containing other molds.

Sussman looks at the molds of his other patients, goy and Jew alike, seeking other messages. He finds none. He looks in his own mouth . . .

Sussman in pyjamas, in front of a medicine-cabinet mirror, holding in his own mouth a dental mirror, straining to see the reflection of the reflection.

. . . Nothing. His wife's mouth . . .

Sussman's wife lies asleep on her back, her mouth open, snoring softly. Sussman, in pyjamas but with his glasses on and loupe in place, lies over her in bed, supporting himself with one arm thrown across her body. He leans awkwardly in, taking care not to disturb his wife as he lowers a dental mirror into her open mouth.

. . . Nothing. It is a singular event. A mystery.

The Jefferson Airplane guitar solo is heating up.

But Sussman is an educated man. Not the world's greatest sage, maybe, no Rabbi Marshak, but he knows a thing or two from the Zohar and the Caballah. He knows every Hebrew letter has its numeric equivalent.

Sussman, still in his pyjamas, is sitting at the kitchen table scribbling on a tablet of lined paper.

Close on the paper: the Hebrew letters have been transcribed into their numeric equivalents:

הושיטגי

3744548

Nachtner continues in voice-over:

Seven digits—a phone number maybe?

Sussman reaches for the phone. He hesitates, then dials.

. . . Sussman dials. It rings.

An elevated cubicle in a grocery store. A man in white short-sleeved shirt reaches for the phone.

RABBI NACHTNER

It's a Red Owl grocery store in Bloomington. Hello? Do you know a goy named Kraus? Russel Kraus?

The store manager shakes his head.

Where have I called? The Red Owl. In Bloomington. Thanks so much.

The manager, puzzled, hangs up.

Sussman thinks, am I supposed to go to the Red Owl, to receive a further sign? He goes . . .

In the parking lot of the Red Owl Sussman, wearing a short-brimmed fedora, emerges from his car. It is an unremarkable grocery store in a suburban mall.

It's a Red Owl.

Inside Sussman, in his fedora, gazes around.

Groceries. What have you.

A service alley behind the store: dumpsters, wind-blown garbage, Sussman looking.

On the wall behind the store, a stain . . .

There is an old, rather nondescript stain of some liquid splatted against the back wall and long since dried.

. . . Could be a nun sofit . . . Or maybe not . . .

The parking lot again: Sussman gets back in his car.

Sussman goes home. What does it mean? He has to find out, if he's ever to sleep again.

Sussman, again in pyjamas buttoned to the neck, lies in his bed staring at the ceiling.

He goes to see the Rabbi, Nachtner. He comes in and sits right where you're sitting now.

Sussman is indeed sitting across from Rabbi Nachtner, just where we've seen Larry sitting.

What does it mean, Rabbi? Is it a sign from *Hashem*? "Help me." I, Sussman, should be doing something to help this goy? Doing what? The teeth don't say.

Bedroom of Karl Marx, with large cut-outs of Marx and his wife
Photo by Leni Sonnenfeld/Beit Hatfutsot, The Oster Visual Documentation Center, Sonnenfeld collection
Ushi Derman, Jews of the World Unite: The Jewish Question of Karl Marx (anumuseum.org)

I should know without asking? Or maybe I'm supposed to help people generally—lead a more righteous life? Is the answer in Caballah? In Torah? Or is there even a **question**? Tell me, Rabbi—what can such a sign mean?

Nachtner—not the narrating Nachtner but the Nachtner in the scene—nods and considers.

The rabbi's office in present: Larry stares at the rabbi. He waits a good beat. He prompts:

LARRY

So what did you tell him?

*The rabbi seems surprised by the **question**.*

RABBI NACHTNER

Sussman?

LARRY

Yes!

RABBI NACHTNER

Is it . . . relevant?

LARRY

Well—isn't that why you're telling me?

RABBI NACHTNER

Mm. Okay. Nachtner says, look . . .

The consultation scene again, with the rabbi once again narrating in voice-over. He silently advises the fretful Sussman in sync with his recounting of the same.

. . . The teeth, we don't know. A sign from Hashem, don't know. Helping others, couldn't hurt.

Back to the rabbi's office in present. Larry struggles to make sense of the story.

LARRY

But—was it for him, for Sussman? Or—

RABBI NACHTNER

We can't know everything.

LARRY

It sounds like you don't know anything! Why even tell me the story?

RABBI NACHTNER *(amused)*

First I should tell you, then I shouldn't?

Larry, exasporated, changes tack:

LARRY

What happened to Sussman?

Sussman, back in his office, works on different patients as the rabbi resumes the narrative in voice-over.

RABBI NACHTNER

What would happen? Not much. He went back to work. For a while he checked every patient's teeth for new messages—didn't see any—in time, he found he'd stopped checking. He returned to life.

Sussman, at home, chats with his wife over dinner.

. . . These **questions** that are bothering you, Larry—maybe they're like a toothache. We feel them for a while, then they go away.

Sussman lies in bed sleeping, smiling, an arm thrown across his wife.

Back in the rabbi's office, Larry is dissatisfied.

LARRY

I don't want it to just go away! I want an answer!

RABBI NACHTNER

The answer! Sure! We all want the answer! But Hashem doesn't owe us the answer, Larry. *Hashem* doesn't owe us anything. The obligation runs the other way.

LARRY

Why does he make us feel the **questions** if he's not going to give us any answers?

Rabbi Nachtner smiles at Larry.

RABBI NACHTNER

He hasn't told me.

Larry rubs his face, frustrated.

*A last **question** occurs to him:*

LARRY

And what happened to the goy?

Rabbi Nachtner's forebearing smile fades into puzzlement.

RABBI NACHTNER

The goy? Who cares?

Joel Coen and Ethan Coen, A Serious Man (Screenplay)

LIBRARY AND INFORMATION SCIENCE **QUESTIONS** ANSWERS QUIZZES

Library and Information Science **Questions** Answers Quizzes (LIS Quiz) is a collection of **Frequently Asked Questions (FAQ)** and Quizzes covering all the areas of Library and Information Science, Librarianship Studies and Information Technology related to libraries and library management, with special reference to solutions to library cataloging, metadata, and classification problems using RDA, AACR2, MARC21, DDC, LCC, LCSH, FRBR, FRAD, FRSAD, BIBFRAME, etc.

Whether you are studying, doing research, or a working professional, this is the place for you to develop a sound knowledge of Library and Information Science. For librarians, catalogers, i-School Master of Library and Information Science (MLIS) & Ph.D. students, researchers, and LIS professionals. Free for everyone forever . . .

Questions on similar subjects are grouped together so as to give a clear understanding of the subject. For example, **questions** on the Library of Congress Classification (LCC) will be provided in one place. Under similar subjects, e.g. LCC, basic **questions** are given first which are followed by advanced level **questions**.

This collection of **questions** will act not only as a **question** bank on Library and Information Science but also be a good tool for appearing in the competitive exams (e.g. UGC-NET in Library and Information Science) and interviews and keeping updated with the new knowledge for LIS professionals all around the world.

Library and Information Science **Questions**, Answers, and Quizzes is envisioned to become the single largest database of **Frequently Asked Questions** on Library and Information Science (LIS Quiz & **FAQ**).

Librarianship Studies & Information Technology (librarianshipstudies.com)

The Questions Ask Themselves

In an evolution of the alliteration that's more like an imbrication

"Mr. Hastings, I have a **question** to ask you, which I reserved until now, as I wished to refer to a book; will you come out with me, and let us get some of this cool air before that horrid cloud comes up, and we can have our discussion in the garden."

George Robert Wynne, *Overton's **Question**, and What Came of It.*

II. Theoretical investigations and treatises. A special interest attaches to these because they discuss a variety of **questions** which are of practical importance to this day. Leonardo's theory as to the origin and progress of cracks in buildings is perhaps to be considered as unique in its way in the literature of Architecture.

Jean Paul Richter (ed.), *The Notebooks of Leonardo da Vinci*

"What good is a writer if he can't destroy literature?" The **question** comes from Julio Cortázar's landmark 1963 novel *Hopscotch*, the dense, elusive, streetwise masterpiece that doubles as a High Modernist choose-your-own-adventure game. Famously, it includes an introductory "table of instructions": "This book consists of many books," Cortázar writes in it, "but two books above all." The first version is read traditionally, from chapter one straight through; the second version begins at chapter seventy-three, and snakes through a non-linear sequence. Both reading modes follow the world-weary antihero Horacio Oliveira, Cortázar's proxy protagonist, who is disenchanted with the tepid certainties of bourgeois life, and whose metaphysical explorations form the scaffolding of a billowing, richly comic existential caper. Of his magnum opus, Cortázar said, laconically, "I've remained on the side of the **questions**." But it was the novel's formal daring—its branching paths—that hinted at what was to be the Argentine author's most persistent and most personal inquiry: Why should there be only one reality?

Dustin Illingworth, *The Subtle Radicalism of Julio Cortázar's Berkeley Lectures (The Atlantic)*

But one fundamental **question** remained unsolved: did we, the readers, reach out and capture letters on a page, according to the theories of Euclid and Galen? Or did the letters reach out to our senses, as Epicurus and Aristotle had maintained? For Leonardo and his contemporaries, the answer (or hints towards an answer) could be found in a thirteenth-century translation of a book written two hundred years earlier (so long are sometimes the hesitancies of scholarship) in Egypt, by the Basra scholar al-Hasan ibn al-Haytham, known to the West as Alhazen.

Alberto Manguel, *A History of Reading*

These notions of forbears, of houses where lamps are lit at night, and other such: where do they come to me from? And all these **questions** I ask myself? It is not in a spirit of curiosity: I cannot be silent. About myself I need know nothing.

Here all is clear. No, all is not clear. But the discourse must go on. So one invents obscurities. Rhetoric. These lights, for instance (which I do not require to mean anything): what is there so strange about them, so wrong? Is it their irregularity, their instability, their shining strong one minute and weak the next, but never beyond the power of one or two candles? Malone appears and disappears with the punctuality of clockwork, always at the same remove, the same velocity, in the same direction, the same attitude. But the play of the lights is truly unpredictable. It is only fair to say that to eyes less knowing than mine they would probably pass unseen. But even to mine do they not sometimes do so? They are perhaps unwavering and fixed, and my fitful perceiving the cause of their inconstancy.

I hope I may have occasion to revert to this **question.** But I shall remark without further delay (in order to be sure of doing so) that I am relying on these lights (as indeed on all other similar sources of credible perplexity) to help me continue and perhaps even conclude.

I resume, having no alternative. Where was I? Ah yes: from the unexceptionable order which has prevailed here up to date may I infer that such will always be the case?

I may of course. But the mere fact of asking myself such a **question** gives me to reflect. It is in vain I tell myself that its only purpose is to stimulate the lagging discourse: this excellent explanation does not satisfy me. Can it be I am the prey of a genuine preoccupation, of a need to know as one might say? I don't know. I'll try it another way. If one day a change were to take place, resulting from a principle of disorder already present, what then? That would seem to depend on the nature of the change. (No: here all change would be fatal and land me back, there and then, in all the fun of the fair.)

I'll try it another way. Has nothing really changed since I have been here? No, frankly, hand on heart . . . wait a second . . . no, nothing to my knowledge.

Samuel Beckett, The Unnamable

Does life improve? On television the other night I watched the Poet Laureate asked that **question.** 'The only thing I think is very good today is dentistry,' he replied; nothing else came to mind. Mere antiquarian prejudice? I don't think so. When you are young, you think that the old lament the deterioration of life because this makes it easier for them to die without regret. When you are old, you become impatient with the way in which the young applaud the most insignificant improvements—the invention of some new valve or sprocket—while remaining heedless of the world's barbarism. I don't say things have got worse; I merely say the young wouldn't notice if they had. The old times were good because then we were young, and ignorant of how ignorant the young can be.

Julian Barnes, Flaubert's Parrot

Now, it's very important, gentlemen, because you open a book by S—by Plato, or Xenophon on Socrates, or—all the traditions on Socrates. He is parroting [ ] **questions** as a—like a stupid child at first sight. So don't get annoyed. Make this distinction clear to you, gentlemen, that Socrates—the Socratic method sifts the **questions.** You are absolutely lost if you mistake the form of **question** as being the same between Socrates and a child. But this is today the average error, because everybody in this country thinks that he is a philosopher, and that everybody is as stupid—every philosopher is rated as—to be as stupid as the man who reads up on philosophy. But philosophy is a vocation, gentlemen, a very disagreeable vocation. And in the case of Socrates, it ended with death. In the case of others, it ended with exile. In the case of others, it ended with madness. In the case of others, it ended with persecution, or with poverty, or illness. Because it is the attempt to throw down the usurped **questioners**, the intellectuals in a community, the sophists, who at that moment, you see, will not—will not, if they are aesthetes, and celebrate poetry for poetry's sake, or art for art's sake, or politicians for politics' sake. They will not give answer to the **question**: "What's the good of your **question**? Why do you ask this **question**?" You see. And the Socratic answer is that you must thereby be led to lead a better life, otherwise the **question** cannot be answered, because you have no si—yardstick. Mere—the mere jumbling, juggling—of tossing-up and tossing down of words makes any answer possible, gentlemen. The difference between the sophists and Socrates then is that Socrates—wants to be a sophist who tries the sophists.

Eugen Rosenstock-Huessy, Greek Philosophy (1956): Lectures 14–20

"What creative input do you have in mind, Bob?"

"Okay, try this for size. What we have here is a philosophical **question**. Yes, you're right, though your language was pejorative. Yes, we're treating cortical neurones by a water-soluble additive, just as we treated dental enamel by fluoride in the water fifty years ago—without the permission or knowledge of the treated. The courts upheld us then, probably will again. But that's not the **question**. The real, the fascinating, **question** is this. What do you think of this hypothesis, which is gaining ground among psychologists, anthropologists, neurologists, to mention a few disciplines—as well as among academics and in liberal-arts circles—even among our best novelists!—Kurt Vonnegut wrote a book setting forth this very thesis." He eyes me. "You already know, don't you?"

"Tell me."

Walker Percy, The Thanatos Syndrome

The saucer was one hundred feet in diameter, with portholes around its rim. The light from the portholes was a pulsing purple. The only noise it made was the owl song. It came down to hover over Billy, and to enclose him in a cylinder of pulsing purple light. Now there was the sound of a seeming kiss as an airtight hatch in the bottom of the saucer was opened. Down snaked a ladder that was outlined in pretty lights like a Ferris wheel.

Billy's will was paralyzed by a zap gun aimed at him from one of the portholes. It became imperative that he take hold of the bottom rung of the sinuous ladder, which he did. The rung was electrified, so that Billy's hands locked onto it hard. He was hauled into the airlock, and machinery closed the bottom door. Only then did the ladder, wound onto a reel in the airlock, let him go. Only then did Billy's brain start working again.

There were two peepholes inside the airlock—with yellow eyes pressed to them. There was a speaker on the wall. The Tralfamadorians had no voice boxes. They communicated telepathically. They were able to talk to Billy by means of a computer and a sort of electric organ which made every Earthling speech sound.

"Welcome aboard, Mr. Pilgrim," said the loudspeaker. "Any **questions**?"

Billy licked his lips, thought a while, inquired at last: "Why me?"

"That is a very *Earthling* **question** to ask, Mr. Pilgrim. Why *you?* Why *us* for that matter? Why *anything?* Because this moment simply is. Have you ever seen bugs trapped in amber?"

Yes. Billy, in fact, had a paperweight in his office which was a blob of polished amber with three ladybugs embedded in it.

"Well, here we are, Mr. Pilgrim, trapped in the amber of this moment. There is no *why.*"

Kurt Vonnegut, Slaughterhouse-Five, or The Children's Crusade: A Duty-Dance With Death

There was no further talk then of going to work, and Charles retreated deeper within himself because he thought he did not have long to live. In this condition he readied and published, in 1812, his **Questions** *de littérature légale.*

The **Questions** *on the Legal Aspects of Literary Production,* a bibliographic miscellany on plagiarism, imitation, quotation, allusion, similarity of ideas due to reminiscence or analogy, literary theft, false attributions, forgeries, hoaxes, and other literary misdemeanors, was intended by Nodier as a supplement to A. A. Barbiers *Dictionnaire des anonymes* and "to all bibliographies."

A. Richard Oliver, Charles Nodier: Pilot of Romanticism

In **Questions** *de littérature légale* [**Questions** *about Legal Literature*] he attempted to catalog all the various ways in which literature (in its mode of production) might stray from the straight and narrow, and the mere table of contents (provided here in explanatory translation) is a relatively clear summary of the scope of his inquiry:

I. Imitation
II. Quotation
III. Allusion
IV. Similarity of ideas
V. Plagiarism
VI. Literary theft
VII. Ghostwriting
VIII. Forged authorship
IX. Intercalation
X. Supplements
XI. Pastiches
XII. Literary schools
XIII. Special styles
XIV. Counterfeits
XV. False manuscripts
XVI. Plagiarized titles
XVII. False books
XVIII. False quotations
XIX. False dates
XX. False scarcity
XXI. Altered titles
XXII. False advocacy

Scott Carpenter, Aesthetics of Fraudulence in Nineteenth-Century France: Frauds, Hoaxes, and Counterfeits

Charles Nodier's ***Questions** de littérature légale* (a playful nineteenth-century predecessor of Gérard Genette's *Palimpsestes*), whose first edition was published anonymously
in 1812, begins with a distinction between plagiarism proper and imitation. The latter
is defined as 'le plagiat autorisé' [permissible plagiarism] or 'innocent'[25] and the main
body of Nodier's essay consists primarily in a typology of different kinds of imitation
(from citation and allusion to false attribution and literary hoaxes) which, depending
on the circumstances, can be 'innocent' or, if not, constitute instances of plagiarism.
By demonstrating the ubiquity of the kinds of imitation it identifies, Nodier's typology
cleverly manages to imply that imitation (whether innocent or not) is indistinguishable
from writing itself, that it is 'un paramètre essentiel l'activité littéraire'.[26] Nodier's essay
would be soon followed by studies which listed plagiarised works and did not hesitate
to include contemporary, living authors.[27]

*Sotirios Paraschas, Reappearing Characters in Nineteenth-Century French Literature: Authorship, Originality,
and Intellectual Property*

"Do dozens come for that purpose?"

"Hundreds," said Miss Pross.

It was characteristic of this lady (as of some other people before her time and since)
that whenever her original proposition was **questioned**, she exaggerated it.

"Dear me!" said Mr. Lorry, as the safest remark he could think of.

Charles Dickens, A Tale of Two Cities

As we have seen, the inscription of fraudulence within literature blossoms at the same
time Romanticism claims special authority for originality and authenticity. These are
ideal conditions for any kind of mystification, which grows parasitically, like a vampire,
feeding off the blood of its host. The new authority accorded to originality occasioned
a reassessment of just what was meant by fraudulence in a literary context, and in
1812 Charles Nodier—no stranger to literary falsehoods himself[1]—published a volume
addressing the **question**.[2]

Scott Carpenter, Aesthetics of Fraudulence in Nineteenth-Century France: Frauds, Hoaxes, and Counterfeits

Some notice must be taken of Nodier's "**Questions** concerning the Laws of Literature:
plagiarism, pretended authorships and frauds connected with the publishing of books."
The first edition was dedicated to M. C. Weiss in 1811, and published in 1812; the second
was published by Crapelet, of Paris, in 1828. It is preceded by a table of authors and
books quoted, numbering very nearly 500. The book consists of only 228 octavo pages,
and includes parallel passages from authors which serve to show the debt one owes to
the other, beginning with a long passage from Voltaire's *Zadig*, placed side by side with
a prose translation of the English poem by Parnell, called "The Hermit."

Ernest C. Thomas, The Library Chronicle: A Journal of Librarianship & Bibliography

Zadig, entranced, as it were, and like a man about whose head the thunder had burst,
walked at random. He entered Babylon on the very day when those who had fought
at the tournaments were assembled in the grand vestibule of the palace to explain the
enigmas and to answer the **questions** of the grand magi. All the knights were already
arrived, except the knight in green armor. As soon as Zadig appeared in the city the
people crowded round him; every eye was fixed on him; every mouth blessed him, and
every heart wished him the empire. The envious man saw him pass; he frowned and

turned aside. The people conducted him to the place where the assembly was held. The queen, who was informed of his arrival, became a prey to the most violent agitations of hope and fear. She was filled with anxiety and apprehension. She could not comprehend why Zadig was without arms, nor why Itobad wore the white armor. A confused murmur arose at the sight of Zadig. They were equally surprised and charmed to see him; but none but the knights who had fought were permitted to appear in the assembly.

"I have fought as well as the other knights," said Zadig, "but another here wears my arms; and while I wait for the honor of proving the truth of my assertion, I demand the liberty of presenting myself to explain the enigmas." The **question** was put to the vote, and his reputation for probity was still so deeply impressed in their minds, that they admitted him without scruple.

The first **question** proposed by the grand magi was: "What, of all things in the world, is the longest and the shortest, the swiftest and the slowest, the most divisible and the most extended, the most neglected and the most regretted, without which nothing can be done, which devours all that is little, and enlivens all that is great?"

Itobad was to speak. He replied that so great a man as he did not understand enigmas, and that it was sufficient for him to have conquered by his strength and valor. Some said that the meaning of the enigmas was Fortune; some, the Earth; and others the Light. Zadig said that it was Time. "Nothing," added he, "is longer, since it is the measure of eternity; nothing is shorter, since it is insufficient for the accomplishment of our projects; nothing more slow to him that expects, nothing more rapid to him that enjoys; in greatness, it extends to infinity; in smallness, it is infinitely divisible; all men neglect it; all regret the loss of it; nothing can be done without it; it consigns to oblivion whatever is unworthy of being transmitted to posterity, and it immortalizes such actions as are truly great." The assembly acknowledged that Zadig was in the right.

The next **question** was: "What is the thing which we receive without thanks, which we enjoy without knowing how, which we give to others when we know not where we are, and which we lose without perceiving it?"

Everyone gave his own explanation. Zadig alone guessed that it was Life, and explained all the other enigmas with the same facility. Itobad always said that nothing was more easy, and that he could have answered them with the same readiness had he chosen to have given himself the trouble. **Questions** were then proposed on justice, on the sovereign good, and on the art of government. Zadig's answers were judged to be the most solid. "What a pity is it," said they, "that such a great genius should be so bad a knight!"

Voltaire, Zadig the Babylonian

Dean would say that's it's a waste to waste this wasted

unasked for sojourn on earth thinking about shit
like what others think of us, or depressing shit,
like "the fucking Cold War or Vietnam,"

or rip-off artists like the Beatles
("why do they spell it with an 'a'?").
Jealous? Never. Only annoyed that they kept bugging him

with **questions**. Why did he have to think?

Wasn't it enough just to live? Dino didn't work
to see his voice or image reproduced;

he acted, sang, and hosted shows, on screen
and in person, because it was easier than real
work.

Dino liked his inflated wages, but money
meant nothing beyond what it could buy.
"A singer is nothing." Why did he sing?

It was the easiest way to make a bundle.

> *Mark Rudman, The Secretary of Liquor (John F. Kennedy's*
> *Informal Appointment of Dean Martin to His Cabinet)*

A Life so sacred, such serene Repose,
Seem'd Heav'n it self, 'till one Suggestion rose;
That Vice shou'd triumph, Virtue Vice obey,
This sprung some Doubt of Providence's Sway:
His Hopes no more a certain Prospect boast,
And all the Tenour of his Soul is lost:
So when a smooth Expanse receives imprest
Calm Nature's Image on its wat'ry Breast,
Down bend the Banks, the Trees depending grow,
And Skies beneath with answ'ring Colours glow:
But if a Stone the gentle Scene divide,
Swift ruffling Circles curl on ev'ry side,
And glimmering Fragments of a broken Sun,
Banks, Trees, and Skies, in thick Disorder run.

To clear this Doubt, to know the World by Sight,
To find if Books, or Swains, report it right;
(For yet by Swains alone the World he knew,
Whose Feet came wand'ring o'er the nightly Dew)
He quits his Cell; the Pilgrim-Staff he bore,
And fix'd the Scallop in his Hat before;
Then with the Sun a rising Journey went,
Sedate to think, and watching each Event.

The Morn was wasted in the pathless Grass,
And long and lonesome was the Wild to pass;
But when the Southern Sun had warm'd the Day,
A Youth came posting o'er a crossing Way;
His Rayment decent, his Complexion fair,
And soft in graceful Ringlets wav'd his Hair.
Then near approaching, Father Hail! he cry'd,
And Hail, my Son, the rev'rend Sire reply'd;
Words followed Words, from **Question** Answer flow'd,
And Talk of various kind deceiv'd the Road;
'Till each with other pleas'd, and loth to part,

While in their Age they differ, joyn in Heart:
Thus stands an aged Elm in Ivy bound,
Thus youthful Ivy clasps an Elm around.

Thomas Parnell, The Hermit (Poems on Several Occasions)

The subject matter is presented in a series of scholarly essays which reveal a brilliant method of dating and attribution based on the internal evidence of linguistic usage, style, historical data, and an intimate knowledge of an author's mannerisms. A discussion of authors' rights, contracts with publishers, pirated editions, and the creation of spurious rarities in the bookselling business rounds out the volume. This work, Nodier's first bibliographical study since the *Bibliographie entomologique* eleven years earlier, attracted considerable attention as a pioneer in a little-known field. Where others were content to state the arid facts of bibliography, Nodier, combining boldness with imagination, revealed the romance and adventure of the detective work involved in establishing the authenticity of a manuscript, the genuineness of a text, and the originality of an author. Sixteen years later, the **Questions** being still in demand, Nodier brought out a second edition, augmented to twice the size of the first. Both editions were fittingly inscribed to Charles Weiss. In gratitude for the generous *apologia* of *Les Deux Gendres* the **Questions** contained, Etienne opened wide the columns of *Le Journal de l'Empire* to Charles' articles. The *Académie de Besançon* admitted Charles to membership on March 12, 1812.

Such books and honors, though interesting and important, did not increase the family exchequer.

A. Richard Oliver, Charles Nodier: Pilot of Romanticism

"But to a man of intelligence nothing is impossible. I propounded to myself the **question**, 'What is the easiest way to get money without working?' And immediately the answer came: 'To get money easily one must be a woman. Has not every woman something to sell?' And then, as I lay reflecting upon the things I should do if I were a woman, an idea came into my head. I remembered the Government maternity hospitals—you know the Government maternity hospitals? They are places where women who are *enceinte* are given meals free and no **questions** are asked. It is done to encourage childbearing. Any woman can go there and demand a meal, and she is given it immediately.

'*Mon Dieu!*' I thought, 'if only I were a woman! I would eat at one of those places every day. Who can tell whether a woman is *enceinte* or not, without an examination?'

George Orwell, Down and Out in Paris and London

The obvious next **question** is: If money is just a yardstick, what then does it measure? The answer was simple: debt.

David Graeber, Debt: The First 5,000 Years

"If you please, sir."

"What do you suppose," said Mr. Jaggers, bending forward to look at the ground, and then throwing his head back to look at the ceiling,—"what do you suppose you are living at the rate of?"

"At the rate of, sir?"

"At," repeated Mr. Jaggers, still looking at the ceiling, "the—rate—of?" And then looked all round the room, and paused with his pocket-handkerchief in his hand, half-way to his nose.

I had looked into my affairs so often, that I had thoroughly destroyed any slight notion I might ever have had of their bearings. Reluctantly, I confessed myself quite unable to answer the **question**. This reply seemed agreeable to Mr. Jaggers, who said, "I thought so!" and blew his nose with an air of satisfaction.

"Now, I have asked you a **question**, my friend," said Mr. Jaggers. "Have you anything to ask me?"

"Of course it would be a great relief to me to ask you several **questions**, sir; but I remember your prohibition."

Charles Dickens, Great Expectations

Questions should be referred by the checker to the person in immediate charge of the office inking of the sheet; such **questions** as apply to parts of the sheet that have been mapped or inked by others who are then in the office should be referred to them for attention, unless in the judgment of the topographer or inker in immediate office charge of the sheet such further reference is deemed unneccessary, in which case he himself may reply to all **questions** raised by the checker.

C. H. Birdseye, Topographic Instructions of the United States Geological Survey

"Ask one," said Mr. Jaggers.

"Is my benefactor to be made known to me to-day?"

"No. Ask another."

"Is that confidence to be imparted to me soon?"

"Waive that, a moment," said Mr. Jaggers, "and ask another."

I looked about me, but there appeared to be now no possible escape from the inquiry, "Have—I—anything to receive, sir?" On that, Mr. Jaggers said, triumphantly, "I thought we should come to it!" and called to Wemmick to give him that piece of paper. Wemmick appeared, handed it in, and disappeared.

"Now, Mr. Pip," said Mr. Jaggers, "attend, if you please. You have been drawing pretty freely here; your name occurs pretty often in Wemmick's cash-book; but you are in debt, of course?"

"I am afraid I must say yes, sir."

"You know you must say yes; don't you?" said Mr. Jaggers.

"Yes, sir."

"I don't ask you what you owe, because you don't know; and if you did know, you wouldn't tell me; you would say less. Yes, yes, my friend," cried Mr. Jaggers, waving his forefinger to stop me as I made a show of protesting: "it's likely enough that you think you wouldn't, but you would. You'll excuse me, but I know better than you. Now, take this piece of paper in your hand. You have got it? Very good. Now, unfold it and tell me what it is."

"This is a bank-note," said I, "for five hundred pounds."

"That is a bank-note," repeated Mr. Jaggers, "for five hundred pounds. And a very handsome sum of money too, I think. You consider it so?"

"How could I do otherwise!"

"Ah! But answer the **question**," said Mr. Jaggers.

"Undoubtedly."

"You consider it, undoubtedly, a handsome sum of money. Now, that handsome sum of money, Pip, is your own. It is a present to you on this day, in earnest of your expectations. And at the rate of that handsome sum of money per annum, and at no higher rate, you are to live until the donor of the whole appears. That is to say, you will now take your money affairs entirely into your own hands, and you will draw from Wemmick one hundred and twenty-five pounds per quarter, until you are in communication with the fountain-head, and no longer with the mere agent. As I have told you before, I am the mere agent. I execute my instructions, and I am paid for doing so. I think them injudicious, but I am not paid for giving any opinion on their merits."

I was beginning to express my gratitude to my benefactor for the great liberality with which I was treated, when Mr. Jaggers stopped me. "I am not paid, Pip," said he, coolly, "to carry your words to any one;" and then gathered up his coat-tails, as he had gathered up the subject, and stood frowning at his boots as if he suspected them of designs against him.

Charles Dickens, Great Expectations

Not enough research has been done to determine to what extent this is a problem, but there's no **question** it exists—

John Henry Auran, Equipment Close Up: Boots (Skiing)

We human beings live with both the living and the dead. We walk with the ghosts of many who have gone before us—we are haunted by their writing, thoughts, images, objects, institutions, and actions. They are present, if physically absent, as beings that in their wake leave deposits that we that mostly ignore; or occasionally uncover and sometimes try to examine. Besides memories, it is to these ghosts and deposits and traces that we turn to find out whom once we were, and it is by their perpetual presence that we are eternally haunted.

*Tony Fry, Whither Design/Whether History (Design and the **Question** of History)*

Checker's **questions** that can not be answered by anyone in the office, for the reason that an absent author or inker alone has the needed information, should so far as practicable be referred by letter to the author or inker. Such references may be made before advance-sheet lithography if the advance sheet is not thereby delayed, but inquiries are best handled by indicating the **questions** on an advance sheet of the map, that the absent author or inker may the better visualize the subject-matter.

C. H. Birdseye, Topographic Instructions of the United States Geological Survey

Before you take pen to paper or fingers to keyboard, make sure you are trying to answer a **question** by considering fashion. For example, if you are writing about shoes, narrow things down. Do you want to learn about athletic shoes? High heels? Boots? Once you land on a more specific topic, see if your essay can answer **questions** about that topic. Who wears boots? What do boots convey when worn by men? Women? What kinds of boots exist? You might also survey friends and classmates to see what they say about your topic.

Jonathan Silverman and Dean Rader, The World Is a Text: Writing About Visual and Popular Culture

If all authors and inkers of a map are absent from the office the checker should himself make all possible corrections and refer by letter to an author or inker only those **questions** about which there is reasonable doubt as to procedure or lack of information.

C. H. Birdseye, Topographic Instructions of the United States Geological Survey

Again, we like it when students use their essays to answer a **question**. Why are Uggs so popular with young women but not men? Why aren't there as many fashion options for men? Why do we wear clothes or shoes that are uncomfortable? Fifty years ago, everyone dressed up to travel; now it seems as though people dress down. Why? Why does fashion change? Why do things go out of style but then come back in?

Jonathan Silverman and Dean Rader, The World Is a Text: Writing About Visual and Popular Culture

There are a number of reasons why this has happened, including history's internal implosion as a discipline; the more general decline of support for, and the presence of, the Humanities in universities; and uncertainty about how to deal with history in the often confused curricula of primary and secondary school education. Against this backdrop one asks, as others have before, "so what is history now"? This **question** is yet another **question** we will travel with, displace and (re)visit.

*Tony Fry, Whither Design/Whether History (Design and the **Question** of History)*

—and it's a **question** the skier should keep in mind when a boot or ski salesman touts a particular brand and model.

The saving grace in this situation is that most recreational skis and boots have a broad enough performance range to accommodate slight mismatches. A given ski-boot combination may be less than ideal, but it can be made to work either by adapting your technique to what you have or by judicious tuning of boots and skis.

The best way to get the best combination if you're currently in the market for both boots and skis is to buy the boots first and then take advantage of the shop's demonstrator program to find the pair of skis that makes the best combination. Unfortunately, there's no such comparable program for boots, so avoid, if possible, a situation where you have to match new boots to skis you already have. However, if that's the case, try to pinpoint in what respect the boots you now have are deficient. That way, the boot salesman can steer you to a pair most likely to meet your needs.

John Henry Auran, Equipment Close Up: Boots (Skiing)

Yet the basis for each dimension of regional boundaries is always vague. How much growth must be accommodated and at what density? Which environmental assets are worth preserving and which are replaceable? What is the most efficient pattern of infrastructure? How much farmland is critical? All these economic and political **questions** must be confronted. Absent a regional design process that puts forth the **questions**, provides analysis, and seeks a comprehensive solution, these **questions** are endlessly debated in a piecemeal fashion, town by town, project by project.

Peter Calthorpe and William Fulton, The Regional City

Few authorial absences from philosophical texts have been more frequently noted and lamented than that of Plato from his dialogues. The fashionable, if arguably unanswerable, **question** "who speaks for Plato?" betrays, among other things, a kind of anxiety over our inability to ascribe resolutely the author's views to any of his characters.[1] To some extent, this **question** concerns authority: which character is authorized to speak for Plato and why? What might it mean for a character to bear this kind of authority and how might he display it?

Zina Giannopoulou, Authorless Authority in Plato's Theaetetus (Fakes and Forgers of Classical Literature: Ergo decipiatur!)

Anyone can strip naked. Everyone, or every proper male citizen, wraps his cloak around him rightly. What distinction is this that leaves no mark on the philosopher, or only the mark—if the statues of Plato's time are our guides—two eyebrows pulling together in serious thought? The other philosophical identity does not disappear. Socrates as odd man out provides a lasting inspiration to the Cynics who flourished after his death. Zanker's study will inform later chapters by showing how the Socratic-Cynical emerged as one trope for philosophy to counterweigh against the trope of the philosopher as respectable citizen.

To speak of dress is to speak of fashion, and the **question** now for philosophers becomes how they might present themselves given the fact of fashion. How will they avoid fashionable dress? If fashion in the broadest sense implies mutual emulation among a civilization's members—a sense of the word that permits us to speak of ancient fashions in dress; a sense that permits such phrases as "intellectual fashion," which people use even when objecting to the thought of ancient fashion—then the continuing crisis of how to appear as philosophers (how, more or less, for philosophers to appear as what they are) becomes the **question**, or else allegorizes the **question**, how a philosopher navigates the currents of social reality. Where do philosophers belong in the known community of humans—or, if there is no place for them there, can they constitute a community on their own?

The *Theaetetus*'s references to dress are one thread that runs from Part I of this book into Part II. More generally the book thus far has worked to uncover a concern, in Plato, over the nature of philosophical practice, for which the **question** of dress provides a concrete example. Even if no mention of clothing or nudity had come up in the *Theaetetus*, it would pose the figure of Socrates as uncertainly teacher or student, participant or loner. The **question** about Socrates is the **question** about a natural versus an institutional understanding of philosophical activity. What makes the examples about dress matter is that they too force the **question** of the natural as opposed to the institutional.

As it happens, I believe that dress is the best way for a modern non-philosopher to inquire into that very issue. Dress brings us to the matter of fashion, and fashion forces us to consider how we live uncertainly between nature and human institutions. This is the pivot between Plato's *Theaetetus* and the discussion of fashion. The *Theaetetus* opens out into the subject of dress and fashion in the sense that a door opens out into a vista. Even when the *Theaetetus* is not about ways of dressing, what it is thinking about throughout its first half, the philosopher ensconced in the tradition and schooling and yet apart from them, is a subject that invites further talk of institutions and their limits, or what people appeal to when they feel pressed to find justification outside institutions.

Nickolas Pappas, The Philosopher's New Clothes: The Theaetetus, the Academy, and Philosophy's Turn Against Fashion

If for a speculative man, "whose seedfield," in the sublime words of the Poet, "is Time," no conquest is important but that of new ideas, then might the arrival of Professor Teufelsdröckh's Book be marked with chalk in the Editor's calendar. It is indeed an "extensive Volume," of boundless, almost formless contents, a very Sea of Thought; neither calm nor clear, if you will; yet wherein the toughest pearl-diver may dive to his utmost depth, and return not only with sea-wreck but with true orients.

Directly on the first perusal, almost on the first deliberate inspection, it became apparent that here a quite new Branch of Philosophy, leading to as yet undescried ulterior results, was disclosed; farther, what seemed scarcely less interesting, a quite new human Individuality, an almost unexampled personal character, that, namely, of Professor Teufelsdröckh the Discloser. Of both which novelties, as far as might be possible, we resolved to master the significance. But as man is emphatically a proselytizing creature, no sooner was such mastery even fairly attempted, than the new **question** arose: How might this acquired good be imparted to others, perhaps in equal need thereof; how could the Philosophy of Clothes, and the Author of such Philosophy, be brought home, in any measure, to the business and bosoms of our own English Nation? For if new-got gold is said to burn the pockets till it be cast forth into circulation, much more may new truth.

Here, however, difficulties occurred. The first thought naturally was to publish Article after Article on this remarkable Volume, in such widely circulating Critical Journals as the Editor might stand connected with, or by money or love procure access to. But, on the other hand, was it not clear that such matter as must here be revealed, and treated of, might endanger the circulation of any Journal extant? If, indeed, all party-divisions in the State could have been abolished, Whig, Tory, and Radical, embracing in discrepant union; and all the Journals of the Nation could have been jumbled into one Journal, and the Philosophy of Clothes poured forth in incessant torrents therefrom, the attempt had seemed possible. But, alas, what vehicle of that sort have we, except *Fraser's Magazine?* A vehicle all strewed (figuratively speaking) with the maddest Waterloo-Crackers, exploding distractively and destructively, wheresoever the mystified passenger stands or sits; nay, in any case, understood to be, of late years, a vehicle full to overflowing, and inexorably shut! Besides, to state the Philosophy of Clothes without the Philosopher, the ideas of Teufelsdröckh without something of his personality, was it not to insure both of entire misapprehension? Now for Biography, had it been otherwise admissible, there were no adequate documents, no hope of obtaining such, but rather, owing to circumstances, a special despair. Thus did the Editor see himself, for the while, shut out from all public utterance of these extraordinary Doctrines, and constrained to revolve them, not without disquietude, in the dark depths of his own mind.

Thomas Carlyle, Sartor Resartus: The Life and Opinions of Herr Teufelsdröckh

"And you can live with that?"

"That wasn't the **question**." For the first time that day Inni saw Taads smile. Some of the grayness drifted away from his face. "I can live perfectly with that. Not always, but usually. Stones, plants, stars—everything lives with that. I am, ah, a colleague of everything that exists. So are you for that matter."

"I beg your pardon?"

"I am, we all are, colleagues of the universe. If you take the line that the human measure means nothing and that nothing is in fact smaller or bigger than anything else, then all of us, people and things, share the same fate. We have had a beginning and we shall have an end, and between the two we exist, the universe as well as a geranium. The universe will exist a little bit longer than you, but this small difference does not make you differ essentially from each other."

"And death?"

"I have not the faintest idea what that is. Have you?"

Cees Nooteboom, Rituals

"In New York," he said, looking directly at me, "people ask if you have a good internist. This is where true power lies. The inner organs. Liver, kidneys, stomach, intestines, pancreas. Internal medicine is the magic brew. You acquire strength and charisma from a good internist totally aside from the treatment he provides. People ask about tax lawyers, estate planners, dope dealers. But it's the internist who really matters. 'Who's your internist?' some one will say in a challenging tone. The **question** implies that if your internist's name is unfamiliar, you are certain to die of a mushroom-shaped tumor on your pancreas. You are meant to feel inferior and doomed not just because your inner organs may be trickling blood but because you don't know who to see about it, how to make contacts, how to make your way in the world. Never mind the military-industrial complex. The real power is wielded every day, in these little challenges and intimidations, by people just like us."

Don DeLillo, White Noise

The **question** of my mother is on the table.
The dark box of her mind is also there,
the garden of everywhere
we used to walk together.

Among the things the body doesn't know,
it is the dark box I return to most:
fallopian city engrained in memory,
ghost-orchid egg in the arboretum,

hinged lid forever bending back and forth—
open to me, then closed
like the petals of the paperwhite narcissus.
What would it take to make a city in me?

Dark arterial streets, neglected ovary
hard as an acorn hidden in its dark box
on the table: Mother, I am
out of my mind, spilling everywhere.

*Robin Ekiss, The **Question** of My Mother*

Chellis tipped his head back for a nose hair check, and stared admiringly up nasal canals so clear he could see all the way to Mars. Wait, that was his brain, a marvel in itself, red hot and whirring away, formulating **question** after profound **question**. Why, why, why? So many synapses were firing that his head sounded like a bug zapper. Here was a puzzler: how *could* she love someone with beige hair? That's what he couldn't quite grasp. The stuff was scarily synthetic. It looked as if it belonged in the bathroom, a hair doily for the one-ply, or something you might use to exfoliate your chest with. He traced the shore of his own darkish (more or less) hairline (okay, less), but respectfully, so as not to give it migratory ideas. His friend Hunt's forehead was now so vast, you had to walk clear round the back of him to confirm its conclusion. When had that happened? He'd have to call Hunt and enquire. But later.

There were no epiphanic moments to be had driving through town, although Chellis kept his sensitivities on high alert. What would an epiphanic hour be like, he wondered? Or a whole day? Blow your brains out. He addressed a query to the Almighty Celebrity above, nothing too taxing, just making conversation, *"Mein Gott,* isn't this a sleepy town?"* In an effort to redeem a life sample, he scrutinized painfully tidy houses with buff siding and seamless eaves troughs, lawns Killexed into astroturf, sidewalks blindingly white, cracks cleaned with a Q-tip. Where was everyone? Playing hockey?

Terry Griggs, Thought You Were Dead

"Excuse me, hello, is everything alright in there?"

"What do you mean?"

The man's voice is whiny and defensive. There is something disturbing in the **question**.

"I'm Ellen Peterson, the reeve of Pontypool. There's a great deal of trouble in the area tonight, and I'm asking if everything is ok with you in there. Aren't you cold?"

Another voice to her left.

"Why, if he's cold will he freeze?"

The voice, so tremulous, makes her shiver. The **question** somehow hasn't been put to her rhetorically.

"Well, no, I don't think he'll freeze."

A third voice in the bushes behind her.

"Are you lying to him? Is he going to freeze?"

The voice is so frightened that Ellen covers her mouth. The man in the water has slipped behind the boulder and he holds its sides with his hands.

"If you're lying to me then you could hate me."

Ellen drops her hand. She feels the pull of sadness in the light that has emerged on the surface of the tree hiding these people.

"I don't know you; I couldn't . . . hate you."

The head and shoulders of the man to her left glide into view at the centre of the pool.

"You don't hate him yet. But if you don't know him will you stab him with a knife?"

The man behind her squeals sharply, and he flees crashing through the trees. Ellen can't quite believe this conversation. She has no idea how to meet its requirements.

The conversation that she is having isn't, of course, normal.

That conversation would have its several participating members hitting a variety of vocal registers using a tiny lexicon. This lexicon has migrated to them from Parkdale, and they communicate through it with the sonic sensitivity of birds. They repeat the words *Helen, help* and *hello* in an evolution of the alliteration that's more like an imbrication, shingling the words over a now silent H. And exactly who is stepping down into the pond and repeating the phrase "messy car, dirty bird"?

Tony Burgess, Pontypool Changes Everything

Who use vain repetitions? What are *vain repetitions?* ANS. Saying the same things over and over, without any good reason, for the sake of much speaking.

Harvey Newcomb, Newcomb's First **Question** *Book*

Not a bad guess, Tengo thought.

One article called the author "a Françoise Sagan who has absorbed the air of magical realism." This piece, though vague and filled with reservations, generally seemed to be in praise of the work. More than a few of the reviewers seemed perplexed by—or simply undecided about—the meaning of the air chrysalis and the Little People. One reviewer concluded his piece, "As a story, the work is put together in an exceptionally interesting way and it carries the reader along to the very end, but when it comes to the **question** of what is an air chrysalis, or who are the Little People, we are left in a pool of mysterious **question** marks. This may well be the author's intention, but many readers are likely to take this lack of clarification as a sign of 'authorial laziness.' While this may be fine for a debut work, if the author intends to have a long career as a writer, in the near future she may well need to explain her deliberately cryptic posture."

Tengo cocked his head in puzzlement. If an author succeeded in writing a story "put together in an exceptionally interesting way" that "carries the reader along to the very end," who could possibly call such a writer "lazy"?

Haruki Murakami, 1Q84

It was as if he were talking to himself, hoping if he repeated the words often enough, they would start answering his **questions**.

*Ian Rankin, A **Question** of Blood*

Instead, he dodges the **question** by asking her what she thinks her father would do. She mulls it over. Why are you interested in my father? There's something intriguing about him, he says. She smiles. But who is my father? she wonders as he watches her expectantly. My father is someone whose business dealings have made him very rich in a very short space of time, someone who never takes time off, except for a few days here and there during the course of a year. But she has no idea what he does with his time, what his line of work is. No one does.

A. G. Porta, No World Concerto

One evening, as I dodged the pedestrians in the South Bronx, or they dodged me, Arturo turned toward me. "Adam, I have something I want to ask you."

"Sure, Arturo, what?" He seemed so formal.

"How do you write a book?" he said. "There's a book I have in mind. It's called 'Dream Driving,' all about my way of teaching driving. How you have to think about driving when you're not in the car. How you have to be the busy bee. How you have to shift gear, steer, signal, look, go." That was what that "GSSLG" on his dashboard meant. "How you have to dream about driving to drive well. How do you write a book like that?"

Writing a book seemed as mysterious a process to him, one as much in need of elaborate advance and afterthought, as driving a car was to me. The secret to both—that, really, you sort of just do it—seemed as inadequate an answer to his **question** as it would have been to any of mine. I stumbled out something about making an outline, thinking through what you wanted to say, making sure that your sentences on the page sounded a little like your voice in life.

"You sort of get better at it the more you write," I said. "You have to just keep writing and then, I promise, it will start to feel easier as you do it."

He paused. "You become the noodle?" he said.

Yes, I agreed. You have to become the noodle to write a book. For the only moment in our time together, he didn't say anything at all.

Adam Gopnik, The Driver's Seat (The New Yorker)

p. 459–1

This **question** focuses on tone. There is nothing wishy-washy about how the author of Passage 2 calls it. In this case he is "emphatic." If someone is ambivalent they would be undecided, clearly not the case here.

C

*Henry Davis, Explanations for the Official SAT Study Guide **Questions**: Detailed Explanations for the Answers for Every **Question***

"How does it really happen isn't the only **question**, sure," he says. "It's just the one with the biggest chance of having an interesting answer rather than a predictable, safe one. I'm interested in how power happens, not just saying, 'Oh, the exercise of power.'" One of his favorite instances of how power works involves the role of the invisible middlemen who create places for themselves in the muddled center of any bureaucracy—in Brazil, where he lived for a while, they're called *despachantes*, but a student of Becker's has found close equivalents in Chicago laundromats, where they ease the burden of the welfare system. "They get power by knowing the rules on the box in greater detail than anyone else," Becker says. "They're the people you turn to to break the code of the system."

Adam Gopnik, The Outside Game (The New Yorker)

Nodier, in his **Questions** *de littérature légale*, tries to distinguish, from a non-legal—and ironic—point of view, between the acceptable and the non-acceptable kinds of imitation/plagiarism; among the acceptable kinds, he includes the following: 'le troisième genre d'imitation ou de plagiat autorisé est celui qui ne consiste qu'à mettre en vers la pensée d'un auteur national et même contemporain, mais qui écrivait en prose' [the third kind of imitation or permissible plagiarism is that which consists in putting in verse the idea of a national and even contemporary author who, however, wrote in prose].[64] Nodier, in this case, does not merely seem to be saying that the transformation from one genre to another implies a creative labour that renders the appropriating author less of a servile imitator and therefore makes the borrowing more acceptable, but also that this is especially true when the borrowed idea or passage comes from a work of prose; prose is deemed to require less art than poetry and can therefore be considered a kind of raw material from which ideas can be freely appropriated. The idea that one can plunder an inferior text in order to compose a superior one is confirmed by Nodier's fourth kind of 'imitation consacrée' [consecrated imitation]: the imitation of a bad author by a good one is also 'permissible'.

However, Nodier absolves authors from the charge of plagiarism even when the borrowing comes from poetry. In the matter of 'la reminiscence', Nodier states that it is nothing less than 'un plagiat apparent' but when a passage from a poem is used in a work of prose, 'il ne peut être regardé que comme une allusion' [it can only be seen as an allusion], which he has earlier defined as an acceptable kind of imitation ('une citation spirituelle' which can bear 'le sceau du génie' [the stamp of genius]).[65] In general, according to Nodier, it is form that matters and that confers originality:

On ne saurait trop répéter que l'originalité d'idée serait maintenant un

phénomène incompréhensible, parce que le nombre des idées est nécessaire-
ment circonscrit, et que tous les nombres circonscrits finissent par s'épuiser; ce
qui est inépuisable, c'est la forme et la combinaison des idées, parce que cette
forme et cette combinaison sont illimitées [. . .]. L'originalité est dans la forme;
[. . .] on n'invente plus d'idées, [. . .] on n'en a probablement jamais inventé, et
[. . .] l'art de les combiner est tout le génie.[66]

[One cannot stress enough that the originality of ideas is now an incomprehensible phenomenon, since the number of ideas is necessarily limited and
all limited numbers end up being exhausted; what cannot be exhausted are
the form and the combinations of ideas because this form and these combinations are unlimited [. . .]. Originality resides in the form; [. . .] one does not
invent more ideas, [. . .] probably, no one has ever invented any and [. . .] genius
consists in the art of combining them.]

*Sotirios Paraschas, Reappearing Characters in Nineteenth-Century French Literature: Authorship, Originality,
and Intellectual Property*

Finally, let us examine a little more closely the kinds of fame which attach to various
intellectual pursuits; for it is with fame of this sort that my remarks are more immediately concerned.

I think it may be said broadly that the intellectual superiority it denotes consists
in forming theories, that is, new combinations of certain facts. These facts may be of
very different kinds; but the better they are known, and the more they come within
everyday experience, the greater and wider will be the fame which is to be won by
theorizing about them.

For instance, if the facts in **question** are numbers or lines or special branches of
science, such as physics, zoology, botany, anatomy, or corrupt passages in ancient
authors, or undecipherable inscriptions, written, it may be, in some unknown alphabet,
or obscure points in history; the kind of fame that may be obtained by correctly manipulating such facts will not extend much beyond those who make a study of them—a
small number of persons, most of whom live retired lives and are envious of others who
become famous in their special branch of knowledge.

*Arthur Schopenhauer, The Wisdom of Life: Being the First Part of Arthur Schopenhauer's Aphorismen Zur
Lebensweisheit*

"What does sociology bring to the table? Well, I'd expand the definition of sociology.
Calvino, in 'Invisible Cities,' is a sociologist. Robert Frank, in 'The Americans'—that's
sociology. There's a thing that I'm sure David Mamet said once, though I've never been
able to track it to its source. He was talking about the theatre, and he said that everyone
is in a scene for a reason. Everyone has something he wants. Everyone has some plan
he's trying to pull off. 'What's the reason?' is the real **question**. So that's what you do.
It's like you're watching a play and you—you're the guy who knows that everyone is
there for a reason."

Adam Gopnik, The Outside Game (The New Yorker)

But if the facts be such as are known to everyone, for example, the fundamental characteristics of the human mind or the human heart, which are shared by all alike; or the
great physical agencies which are constantly in operation before our eyes, or the general
course of natural laws; the kind of fame which is to be won by spreading the light of a

new and manifestly true theory in regard to them, is such as in time will extend almost all over the civilized world: for if the facts be such as everyone can grasp, the theory also will be generally intelligible. But the extent of the fame will depend upon the difficulties overcome; and the more generally known the facts are, the harder it will be to form a theory that shall be both new and true: because a great many heads will have been occupied with them, and there will be little or no possibility of saying anything that has not been said before.

On the other hand, facts which are not accessible to everybody, and can be got at only after much difficulty and labor, nearly always admit of new combinations and theories; so that, if sound understanding and judgment are brought to bear upon them—qualities which do not involve very high intellectual power—a man may easily be so fortunate as to light upon some new theory in regard to them which shall be also true. But fame won on such paths does not extend much beyond those who possess a knowledge of the facts in **question**. To solve problems of this sort requires, no doubt, a great ideal of study and labor, if only to get at the facts; whilst on the path where the greatest and most widespread fame is to be won, the facts may be grasped without any labor at all. But just in proportion as less labor is necessary, more talent or genius is required; and between such qualities and the drudgery of research no comparison is possible, in respect either of their intrinsic value, or of the estimation in which they are held.

And so people who feel that they possess solid intellectual capacity and a sound judgment, and yet cannot claim the highest mental powers, should not be afraid of laborious study; for by its aid they may work themselves above the great mob of humanity who have the facts constantly before their eyes, and reach those secluded spots which are accessible to learned toil.

Arthur Schopenhauer, The Wisdom of Life: Being the First Part of Arthur Schopenhauer's Aphorismen Zur Lebensweisheit

He'd given the **question** plenty of thought but had never arrived at an answer. "It's a mystery," he declared. There was no specific cause he could name—no childhood trauma, no sexual abuse. There wasn't alcoholism in his home, or violence. He wasn't trying to hide anything, to cover a wrongdoing, to evade confusion about his sexuality.

Anyway, none of these burdens typically produces a hermit. There's a sea of names for hermits—recluses, monks, misanthropes, ascetics, anchorites, swamis—yet no solid definitions or qualification standards, except the desire to be primarily alone. Some hermits have tolerated steady streams of visitors, or lived in cities, or holed up in university laboratories. But you can take virtually all the hermits in history and divide them into three general groups to explain why they hid: protesters, pilgrims, pursuers.

Protesters are hermits whose primary reason for leaving is hatred of what the world has become. Some cite wars as their motive, or environmental destruction, or crime or consumerism or poverty or wealth. These hermits often wonder how the rest of the world can be so blind, not to notice what we're doing to ourselves.

"I have become solitary," wrote the eighteenth-century French philosopher Jean-Jacques Rousseau, "because to me the most desolate solitude seems preferable to the society of wicked men which is nourished only in betrayals and hatred."

Across much of Chinese history, it was customary to protest a corrupt emperor by leaving society and moving into the mountainous interior of the country. People who withdrew often came from the upper classes and were highly educated. Hermit protesters were so esteemed in China that a few times, tradition holds, when a non-corrupt emperor was seeking a successor, he passed over members of his own family and selected a solitary. Most turned down the offer, having found peace in reclusion.

The first great literary work about solitude, the *Tao Te Ching*, was written in ancient China, likely in the sixth century B.C., by a protester hermit named Lao-tzu. The book's eighty-one short verses describe the pleasures of forsaking society and living in harmony with the seasons. The *Tao Te Ching* says that it is only through retreat rather than pursuit, through inaction rather than action, that we acquire wisdom. "Those with less become content," says the *Tao*, "those with more become confused." The poems, still widely read, have been hailed as a hermit manifesto for more than two thousand years.

Michael Finkel, The Stranger in the Woods: The Extraordinary Story of the Last True Hermit

: But I want money and you've got it.
: You'd murder me even for just the little money you can get. (This isn't really a **question**.) I guess if you want to make love, we might as well make love. I'm horny.
: Can't you get to sleep? (His finger softly draws a line along her right-side chin bone.)
: I'm really tense.
: I'll kiss you and you'll go to sleep.
: I don't want to go to sleep. Where are you?
: I'm just playing.
: Come up here and fuck quickly and then go back to your play. (Johnny crawls up on the bed and very slowly, very gently, kisses her soft lips.)
: I just want to fuck. I don't want to kiss.

Kathy Acker, Great Expectations

Garfunkel is no longer conversing. He's delivering a monologue that happens to be full of dialogue, and he plays all the parts himself. Best to let him go.

> *Garfunkel:* I used to do a Q&A period in my show. Sometimes I still do it. You turn on the lights and there they are. You get the most loving **questions**. These are all your fans, after all, and I stop being an artist who is chasing after the beauty of the line. I'm a workaholic. I want to control the song and serve it up artfully. But this is a change of gears. You get to be the star that they know and love, and you get to answer these curious **questions**. I love to see the audience, and I applaud them for their bravery. Just getting up to ask a **question**, getting the voice to come out of their chest and into the room—only people with guts can do that. My heart goes out to those people who have the gumption to project. And I have a great time addressing their curiosity. I even try to start it off occasionally, if they seem tongue-tied.
>
> All right, I'll ask the first **question** myself. *Artie, did you ever meet the Beatles?* And then I give them the real answer. Yes, I did. Each of the four guys on different evenings, great cherishable memories, and I got into it.
>
> *Are you ever going to work with Paul again?* And now, Stephen, you're going to say, Are you ever going to work with Paul again? Because you're a writer and this is a field of real, basic curiosity.

But is it? Surely this is a defense mechanism, developed after so many interruptions at this point in the story. No, this is a trick **question**. After taking control of the interview and even turning it inside out by interviewing himself, Garfunkel is now testing me. He's trying to see what kind of listener and writer I really am. Do I want to make him repeat that canned answer one more time? Or is there really even an answer to that **question** beyond an evasive "maybe" or a definitive "no way"? Garfunkel is drawing me out. This is a test.

Stephen Deusner, Art Garfunkel's Greatest Interview Ever: "Paul and Artie Can Be Very Squirmy Around Each Other" (Salon)

p. 530–1

Don't get confused in the words. There are 4 inch segments which repeat to make up 80 inches of paper strip. So there are $80/4 = 20$ 4 inch segments. Looking at the figure, you can see that, because a notch is created, the length of the edge of the 4 inch length is 5 inches. Since there are 20 of these, $20 \times 5 = 100$ inches along the edge.

100

p. 537–1

The answer to this **question** depends on vocabulary knowledge. The "archaeologist" "scrutinized" meaning studied diligently. She was unable to "decipher" which means to decode, make sense of, or interpret. The key is a second blank because "Although" signals a contrast in the two parts of the sentence (she could, but she could not). Some of the other words you need to know are **peruse** which means to read thoroughly, **replicate** which means to copy or repeat, and **obliterate** means to destroy or wipeout.

E

p. 833–10

This is a fairly straightforward problem in which you just work with fractions. Simply repeat the operation where you find 1/5 of a number: 150 (1st) $\times 1/5 = 30$ (2nd) $\times 1/5 = 6$ (3rd) $\times 1/5 = 6/5$ (4th) $\times 1/5 = 6/25$ (5th term)

.24 or 6/25

*Henry Davis, Explanations for the Official SAT Study Guide **Questions**: Detailed Explanations for the Answers for Every **Question***

Under such circumstances as these, to speak of my uncle's motives was to venture on very delicate ground. Eustace relieved me from further embarrassment by asking a **question** to which I could easily reply.

Wilkie Collins, The Law and the Lady

For I am going to speak of another discovery; of a book which should be a classic, but is not; of a book of which nobody has heard unless through me. It was published some twelve years ago, the last-published book of a well-known writer. When I tell you his name you will say, "Oh yes! I LOVE his books!" and you will mention SO-AND-SO, and its equally famous sequel SUCH-AND-SUCH. But when I ask you if you have read MY book, you will profess surprise, and say that you have never heard of it. "Is it as good as SO-AND-SO and SUCH-AND-SUCH?" you will ask, hardly believing that this could be possible. "Much better," I shall reply—and there, if these things were arranged properly, would be another ten per cent, in my pocket. But, believe me, I shall be quite content with your gratitude.

A. A. Milne, Not That It Matters

But this will depend on deciding what I want to write in this article. What was it I proposed to the magazine? I said, I will, I will write about what? the celebrity? the concept celebrity? what is it? he? she? they? Is there a homogeneous group we may classify in this category, a profile to be extrapolated from an analysis of examples? Every subdivision of human activity has its stars, its elevations, its celebratory applause, whether for one action, the scoring of a decisive goal, or for lifetime achievement. In the small world outside the media's eye, in the local community where notoriety is conveyed not through print or electronic transmission, but by witness, by word of mouth: the local hero lives. Is this a celebrity? If I asked the local radio announcer who was a celebrity in his town, would his response be the high-school basketball player? the mayor? or the woman working in Toronto as a television weatherwoman? or himself, the voice of radio? or the novelist who had just moved into the old schoolhouse? And would he **question** us: do we think his examples satisfactory? do they correspond to our qualification for celebrity ranking? Possibly the weatherwoman or the novelist: what station is she with? is the program syndicated or is it merely regionally based? has the novelist published? who is his publisher? does he write esoteric books or popular fiction? If they are truly famous I should know them by name, you should know them; what are their names? The transcendence from the specific locale to the unspecific locale of information is what distinguishes the local star from the celebrity. The celebrity lives in the world as opposed to a small town. To be known at the local bar isn't enough. At one point I had three books in print in five languages; I would appear regularly on television and radio talk shows; articles about me would appear in Canadian, American and European magazines: therefore, I demand at least this level to classify someone else as a celebrity. In the self-fulfilling system of stardom the media feeds the media. One isn't a star until one can transcend the physical, where those who know you have never met you, only experienced you etherealized in media. A star, a symbol. And what do we look like? certainly not covered with warts and scabs; stars don't stink; their bodies are not hobbled. They are of an acceptable appearance, perhaps even handsome and beautiful, subtle, young; or, if their celebrity corner is predicated more on the cerebral than the pictorial, they might be bearded, possess dignity, white-haired, in command of their bearing. Celebrities are of an ilk, not terribly different from each other, without radical physiological deviation. Film stars are often difficult to differentiate: ask a child which female star is which, and invariably there will be error; can you describe the difference between Warren Beatty and Kevin Costner, or Bruce Willis, or any other fine, firm-faced male. Who would want to idolize, to elevate to adoring attention, a middle-aged, soft, fat, puffy-eyed, slightly flat-footed housewife or office husband? I certainly want more than who I am from anyone I idolize. So it must be worth one or two more attempts; I've come this far already; merely to exert a little more energy; another fax to the office. Too bad when I had, what was her name? on the telephone from the Brooke Shield's office, I didn't ask for the phone number. Perhaps a polite fax to the office, a reminder. I must have had my reasons in the first place, a basic instinct that in Brooke Shields is contained the explanation of the enigma celebrity, that she is the personification who will make it clear, answer the ethereal **question**. So I presume I will act, presume that I have grown tired of this declaration of failure and desire something more: but nothing more than what I am, failure, and desire a mist clearing to reveal the pathetic. Want more? certainly the human condition; given less, certainly the human predicament. Am I any different, something special, someone who transcends?

certainly I wish, but in the face of grim reality, what if I succumb and fall, fail? So I phone, so I send out a message asking for a positive response. We all do; and wait. I want and will wait. Possibly it will improve after the message is received, possibly there will be a response, possibly it will be positive. It is a hope. In the anticipation between sending and response there is hope, but also a nervousness, a discomfort, failure is possible, refusal, the negative answer. In the sending, in the initial moment of action, there is hope, but with every succeeding second there is the imminence of refusal, which has proven historically to be the most prevalent response; so with every attempt, every indulgence in possibility, the conditions are brought closer to the reality of failure. So why bother if it has already been proven?

> Eldon Garnet, *Reading Brooke Shields: The Garden of Failure*

I passed a night of unmingled wretchedness. In the morning I went to the court; my lips and throat were parched. I dared not ask the fatal **question**, but I was known, and the officer guessed the cause of my visit.

> Mary Wollstonecraft Shelley, *Frankenstein; or, The Modern Prometheus*

The **question** was: Why had God stopped talking to him? And if God was silent now, did that mean He would be silent forever or eventually start talking to him again? And if He never talked again, could it mean that Ferguson had deluded himself and God had never been there in the first place?

For as long as he could remember, the voice had been in his head, talking to him whenever he was alone, a quiet, measured voice that was at once reassuring and commanding, a baritone murmur bearing the verbal emanations of the great invisible spirit who ruled the world, and Ferguson had always felt comforted by that voice, protected by that voice, which told him that as long as he kept up his end of the bargain all would go well for him, his end being an eternal promise to be good, to treat others with kindness and generosity, and to obey the holy commandments, which meant never lying or stealing or succumbing to envy, which meant loving his parents and working hard at school and staying out of trouble, and Ferguson believed in the voice and did his best to follow its instructions at all times, and since God seemed to be keeping up His end of the bargain by making things go well for him, Ferguson felt loved and happy, secure in the knowledge that God believed in him just as much as he believed in God. So it went until he was seven and a half, and then one morning in early November, a morning that felt no different from any other morning, his mother walked into his room and told him his father was dead, and everything suddenly changed. God had lied to him. The great invisible spirit could no longer be trusted, and even though He went on talking to Ferguson for the next several days, asking for another chance to prove Himself, beseeching the fatherless boy to stay with him *through this dark time of death and mourning*, Ferguson was so angry at Him that he refused to listen. Then, four days after the funeral, the voice abruptly went silent, and since that day it hadn't spoken again.

> Paul Auster, *4 3 2 1*

Have I then lost my delighted attitude? he asked himself. Is all instinct perverted from the memory of what I did? All collecting damaged, not merely attitude toward this one item? Mainstay of my life . . . area, alas, where I dwelt with such relish.

> Philip K. Dick, *The Man in the High Castle*

In "The Death of the Author," Barthes frames the **question** of authorship as a **question** of authority. This makes sense, as the word "author" has etymological links to the Latin word "auctoritas" which means the power to command or to establish.

Laura Seymour, An Analysis of Roland Barthes's The Death of the Author

But what authorship is, how it should be determined, and why it is important have actually been the subjects of contentious cultural debates for centuries. Identification of the authors of the Gospels, authorship attribution in the case of Shakespeare, Marlowe, and others, collaborative authorship, the scope and degree of an author's authority, the role of authorial intention and biographical and autobiographical information in interpretation—these are all issues that have been discussed with a vigour that testifies to the high stakes of the authorship **question**.

The stakes involved in authorship issues overlap with related issues of authority. The content of each concept shows immense historical and cultural variation, with the idea of "author" designating through the ages multifarious activities and the idea of "authority" being "remarkably protean" and possessing "chameleonic qualities".[2] To complicate things further, the authority of the author has been multiform and multiphase. Given the vast conceptual variations yet continued significance of "author" and "authority" an Introduction like ours can only hope to sketch the origins of the terms and to point out the theoretical complexities and consequences of the two concepts and their interrelationship.

Today it is clear that "*auctor*", the Latin origin of "author", is derived from the verb *augere*, which means "to increase, augment, strengthen that which is already in existence"; in addition, it means "to exalt, embellish, enrich".[3] Through history, however, the term has generated speculation among grammarians about etymological links to the Latin verb *agere*, "to act, guide, manage, agitate", as well as to "*augere* 'to grow,' and *avieo* 'to tie,' and to the Greek noun *autentim* 'authority'".[4] Donald Pease endorses these four derivations proposed by medieval grammarians, but it turns out that *avieo* is what is termed a "ghost word", an invented derivation that was never in circulation.[5] In this day and age, the overwhelming evidence points to *augere* as the correct source word. All twentieth-century etymological dictionaries of the English language agree that "author" comes from *augere*. All modern dictionaries of Latin, whether in English, German, French, or Swedish editions, hold that *auctor* originates in *augere*.

In Roman times the word *auctor* had multiple meanings, few of which relate to the common present-day meaning of "writer". The general meaning then was "one who gives meaning" or "he that brings about the existence of any object, or promotes the increase or prosperity of it, whether he first originates it, or by his efforts gives greater permanence or continuance to it".[6] A proliferation of specific meanings existed: "cause, creator, author, inventor, producer, father, founder, teacher, composer, voucher, security, builder, doer, investigator, seller, guardian, spokesman", and so on. The fact that *auctor* could also mean "doer" made certain etymologists associate it to *actor*, a person who "drives or moves something", "a doer, a performer". In rhetorical discourse it also meant "orator". Author/writer is only one of many epithets and functions, and it is no wonder that our modern word "author", in the sense of originator, can have multiple meanings.

The corresponding word for "author" in Greek was *authentes*, from *autos+entes* which literally means "he who himself accomplishes", in other words "a doer, a master," but it also signifies "murderer". Thus, it seems, *authentes* does not emphasize the function of creator, cause, originator, as much as *auctor* does, but seems to have a closer resemblance to "actor", a doer or orator. This aspect of action and accomplishment in the Greek word may be reflected in the way the Greeks looked upon the connection between author and reader, which was likened to a pederastic relationship: The author was seen as the penetrator, the doer, the authority figure, while the reader was associated with the penetrated, submissive young boy.[7]

Pease has interestingly outlined the history of the shifting author functions. He traces the role of the author from the *auctor* who based his authority in medieval times on divine revelation and cultural antecedent, to the "author" who is associated with a certain self-determination and verbal inventiveness, collaborating with others in building an alternative social system, to the "genius" who produced not an alternative political world but a cultural alternative to the world of politics. In the twentieth century, Pease argues, the author is not self-determined but is rather endowed by the critic, who has made it seem that the author is an effect of the critic's interpretation rather than the cause/origin of his or her work.[8] If Pease is correct in his auctor-author-genius-effect argument, there might be a corresponding evolution in its derivative concept, *auctoritas*, to which we now turn.

Auctoritas—authority—was the quality of being *auctor*. In Roman civil law, the *auctor* was the person who served as a reference or voucher in a legal case, and whose security was named his *auctoritas*.[9] With its origin also in *augere*, authority meant "strengthening", but it also signified "origin, source, cause" and a host of other things such as "security, credibility, opinion, advice, will, command, liberty, power, reputation, dignity, weight, model".[10] The early concept of authority thus served a myriad of functions, and throughout history its meanings have shifted in accordance with social context. As Kathleen B. Jones writes. "Any adequate analysis [of authority] would have to situate the concept in different social and cultural contexts in order to consider the ways that context and history have altered its meaning. Little analysis of this sort exists at present".[11]

Stephen Donovan, Danuta Fjellestad and Rolf Lunden, Author, Authorship, Authority, and Other Matters (Authority Matters: Rethinking the Theory and Practice of Authorship)

In a way the story has two happy endings. Later that school year the class had to take the CBEST test. One **question** on the test showed a woman mopping the floor. The **question** was: She likes to: a) cop, b) hop, c) mop, and d) pop. Julia and the rest of the girls in the class refused to answer the **question**, informing me that she does not like to mop. They could read. They rejected the premises of the **questions**. And they felt that truth was stronger than testing. They were six years old.

Herbert Kohl, Topsy-Turvies: Teacher Talk and Student Talk (The Skin That We Speak: Thoughts on Language and Culture in the Classroom)

Barthes's approach to the **question** of authorship is thus a very iconoclastic one. It also sees the "authority" of authors as part of a wider problem about who we allow to command us and to determine our interpretation of the world.

Barthes argues that we should redefine the way we read literary texts, aiming not to "decipher" them (i.e. to provide a univocal explanation), but rather to "detangle" their numerous possible readings.[2] One intended effect of this approach is to destabilize the power of the literary critic, who had aimed to act as the mouthpiece of the author and explain the single authoritative meaning of the text. In "The Death of the Author," Barthes presents such critics as pugnaciously seeking "victory for the Critic" and assuming a role that gives them power to govern other readers' understandings of the text.[3] His approach is to dismantle that role.

Laura Seymour, An Analysis of Roland Barthes's The Death of the Author

Antony bringing this Affair before the Senate, they rejected his Demand; whence it appeared, that the Senate did not defire the Ruin of the Confpirators, whofe Caufe they looked upon as that of Liberty. But *Antony* now addreffing the unthinking *Plebeians*, (whofe Tribunes he had gained) they decreed him the Government above-mentioned; upon which he, in Spite of the Senate, fent a poweful Body of Forces to drive *D. Brutus* from thence. The Enemies to the Senate and Confpirators rejoiced at this Reconciliation of *Antony and Cæfar*, which however was not lafting; occafioned principally by the latter's attempting to get *Flaminius,* one of his Creatures, elected a Tribune of the People. This *Antony* oppofed with all his Might; and at the fame Time he enacted a Decree, by which *Cæfar* was forbid to make any Donations contrary to the Laws. Their reciprocal Hatred increafing, *Antony* fpoke in the moft contemptuous Terms of *Cæfar*; during which, the latter was fecretly labouring at the Ruin of his Enemy. *Cæfar* inflamed the People againft him; and even the veteran Officers and Soldiers in *Antony*'s Army. Thofe who compofed *Antony*'s Guard insisted upon his joining with *Cæfar*, declaring, that otherwife he would ruin both them and himfelf, fince the Parties which formerly divided the Commonwealth between *Pompey* and *Cæfar* ftill exifted. *Mark Antony* wifhed, as earneftly as they could do, the Deftruction of the Confpirators; but he could not yield to have it brought about by young *Cæfar*, who he feared would feize (upon Pretence of revenging the Dictator's Death) on the Government, after crufhing the Republican Party; and this was the fecret Motive of their Divifions. *Antony*, to content his Officers, expatiated on the Bravery with which he had defended the Dictator's Memory; and the prudent Meafures he had taken, in order to get an Opportunity of revenging his Death; and as he pretended to unbofom his whole Soul to them on this Occafion, they feemed fatisfied with his Remonftrances; but ftill they infifted upon his being reconciled to *Cæfar*. He accordingly was obliged to have an Interview with him, in which, after many Compliments and reciprocal Civilities, they feparated no lefs Enemies than before.

*John Lockman, A New Roman Hiftory, by **Queftion** and Anfwer. In a Method Much More Comprehenfive Than Any of the Kind Extant. Extracted From Ancient Authors, and the Moft Celebrated Among the Modern, and Interfperfed With Such Cuftoms as Serve to Illuftrate the Hiftory. With a Complete Index. Defigned Principally for Schools. The Fourth Edition Corrected.*

Although Barthes was a friend, by writing an analysis or a study, Derrida is treating him as an author. The passage which reveals his broken promise, the passage about how such writing is intolerable, appears in fact as part of a discussion of relations to the "author." Derrida gives us a "brief classification" of the different temporal relations readers can have to authors: (1) "The 'author' can be already dead", (2) "authors living at the moment we read them"; (3) "And then there is a 'third' situation: upon the death and after the death of those we have also 'known,' met, loved, etc." (76–77, 49). Derrida finds the first two relations relatively easy; the third is the one he finds intolerable—the relation where someone passes, moves from the category of the living to the dead. What is really troubling is neither the living nor the dead author but precisely what we might call the death of the author. Since this talk of authors and the **question** of whether they are dead or alive takes place in an essay on Barthes, I cannot help hearing the phrase "the death of the author" hovering around this passage.

> Jane Gallop, *The Deaths of the Author: Reading and Writing in Time*

Q. What enſued upon this?

A. Young *Cæſar* would willingly have been aſſiſted by *Antony* in revenging *Julius Cæſar*'s Death, but could not bear to think of his ſeizing upon the Commonwealth; whilſt *Antony*, not valuing (in his Heart) whether the Dictator's Memory was revenged, made the attaining of Sovereign Power his only Aim. In conſequence of this, *Antony*, to ruin *Cæſar* in the Minds of the People, put ſeveral of his own Guards under an Arreſt, upon Pretence of their having been bribed by young *Cæſar* to murder him. This made a great Noiſe, every one looking upon the Conſpiring the Death of a Conſul, as the blackeſt of Crimes. *Cæſar*, alarmed at this, ran up and down the Streets, proteſting his Innocence: and being denied Entrance at *Antony*'s Palace, he called him a thouſand Villains, and defied to produce a ſingle Evidence.

> John Lockman, *A New Roman Hiſtory, by* **Queſtion** *and Anſwer. In a Method Much More Comprehenſive Than Any of the Kind Extant. Extracted From Ancient Authors, and the Moſt Celebrated Among the Modern, and Interſperſed With Such Cuſtoms as Serve to Illuſtrate the Hiſtory. With a Complete Index. Deſigned Principally for Schools. The Fourth Edition Corrected.*

He dodges the **question**, and instead discusses violence as present in another film, *Il giorno di San Sebastiano* (*Saint Sebastian's Day*, 1993), and insists that this film is historically accurate.

> Dana Renga, *Unfinished Business: Screening the Italian Mafia in the New Millennium*

In February 1969, Michel Foucault presented a paper in Paris entitled "What is an Author?" that historicizes the concept of the author by examining the diverse ways the concept has functioned in different historical moments.[3] Although this paper is almost always cited as a source for the death of the author, it actually relegates that topic to one and only one of its more than three dozen paragraphs. While Foucault's paper is in fact only concerned in a very minor way with the death of the author, because it has been taken for decades as one of the two sources of the infamous phrase, I want to look briefly at what Foucault says in that single paragraph. I will also touch on the lecture's immediate reception, where we can see that single paragraph overshadowing the rest of the paper.

Early in his lecture, Foucault devotes a paragraph to what he calls the "familiar theme" of "the kinship between writing and death" (793, 116). This kinship "inverts an age-old theme"—Foucault represents the ancient theme with brief mentions of how Greek epics were "destined to perpetuate the hero's immortality" and how, in *A Thousand and One Nights,* the story had "for motivation, for theme and pretext, to not die." Having thus sketched this age-old relation, he dramatically states the reversal: "This theme of . . . writing made to ward off death, our culture has metamorphosed it; writing is now tied to sacrifice, to the sacrifice of life itself . . . The work whose duty it was to bring immortality has now received the right to kill, to be the murderer of its author" (793, 117).

For centuries writing was thought to bring immortality; now it brings death. In his account of this turn, Foucault repeats the word "now" (*maintenant*)—"writing is *now* tied to sacrifice," "the work has *now* received the right to kill" (emphasis added).

And yet, despite this emphasis on the nowness of the turn, Foucault is not announcing something new but instead treats it as something already well established, a "familiar theme." The paragraph concludes with this sentence: "All this is known; and for quite some time criticism and philosophy have taken note of this disappearance or this death of the author."[4]

Foucault ends his brief discussion of writing's relation to death on the phrase "death of the author." "The Death of the Author" is in fact the title of the essay by Roland Barthes published just the year before Foucault's lecture. Foucault does not mention Barthes's essay.

"The Death of the Author" is a short polemical piece, a manifesto published in a small literary quarterly. "What is an Author?"—presented to an august assemblage of philosophers, scholars, and intellectuals[5]—is a nuanced consideration of the various ways in which the author has functioned in different historical moments. Foucault's exploration of the author, while more than three times as long as Barthes's manifesto, has nonetheless generally been overshadowed by the latter.

The French publication of "What is an Author?" includes not just Foucault's paper but also the discussion that followed the lecture. The bulk of the discussion is a long **question** by Lucien Goldmann and Foucault's answer to that **question**. Goldmann focuses on the death of the author, despite its being a rather minor point of the lecture, and does indeed find it familiar, part of the larger current of structuralism, "which notably includes the names of Lévi-Strauss, Roland Barthes, Althusser, Derrida, etc."[6] Goldmann is thus the first to inscribe "What is an Author?" as part of a larger critical current.

Jane Gallop, The Deaths of the Author: Reading and Writing in Time

Yet none of these surveys includes women to a significant degree. Of thirty-eight texts in Claeys's anthology, two are by women, and while Jean-Michel Racault analyses novels by Sarah Scott and Mary Hamilton at the end of his book, he dodges the **question** of gender difference. Müller discusses no women at all.

Alessa Johns, Remembering the Future: Eighteenth-Century Women's Utopian Writing (Genres as Repositories of Cultural Memory)

Various Conſtructions were put on this Incident; ſome even ſuſpected that both *Cæſar* and *Antony* had done this in Concert, in order that they might have an Opportunity of taking up Arms, and ruining the Liberties of their Country. But their Conduct afterwards ſhowed, that they mutually endeavoured to deſtroy one another; and that each aſpired to be the ſole Head of the Party which oppoſed the Conſpirators; for now both took up Arms, and a freſh War broke out, about three Quarters of a Year after the Dictator's Murder.

John Lockman, A New Roman Hiſtory, by **Queſtion** and Anſwer. In a Method Much More Comprehenſive Than Any of the Kind Extant. Extracted From Ancient Authors, and the Moſt Celebrated Among the Modern, and Interſperſed With Such Cuſtoms as Serve to Illuſtrate the Hiſtory. With a Complete Index. Deſigned Principally for Schools. The Fourth Edition Corrected.

Yet the corpse walks with a great swathe of historians unaware of its death. Among this community of the unaware are many design historians, who in their difference, assume history as available and viable. As for readers of history, the vast bulk inside and outside the academy take history on face value. Yet it is, as it were, just another representation projected onto the wall of Plato's cave.

*Erhard Schoen, not before 1491–1542, **Question** and Answer Concerning
the Demise of Some Occupations (Illustrated Bartsch)*

With these qualifications in place we now come to the issue of historicity. Gadamer tells us that "neither the knower nor the known is 'present at hand' in an 'ontic' way, but in an 'historical' one—i.e., they both have the *mode of being of historicity*."[31] To understand historicity, the difference between the ontic and the historical is vital to grasp.

Historicity is grounded in the constitution of the ontological condition of historical beings, whereas the *ontic* enfolds what is, in general, and as such embraces the being of all beings. Fundamentally this adds up to the difference between being situated in a specific time and space and being situated in the totality of "what is," in the recognition that all that is futural is absent.[32] Everything has historicity—everything thus manifests itself through the structural form of its temporality—nothing is unhistorical, but not everything can be claimed to have a historiography.[33] So although everything is situated historically, and comes into being "in itself" via the historicity of the event that brought it into being, there is much that is without a history.[34] As we have indicated, history does not necessarily expose the historical being of the thing in **question**.

> Tony Fry, *Whither Design/Whether History (Design and the **Question** of History)*

He dodges that **question** also, under the cover that he was not on the Committee at the time, that he was not present when the platform was made.

> Don. E. Fehrenbacher (ed.), *First Lincoln-Douglas Debate, Ottawa, Illinois (Abraham Lincoln: Speeches and Writings, 1832–1858)*

And who, then, was the author? One brand of critical theory suggests notions of authorship are passé and irrelevant; all that really matters is the spectator's or listener's experience and how he or she appropriates it. Foucault, imaging society's future, wrote:

> All discourses, whatever their status, form, value, and whatever the treatment to which they will be subjected, would then develop in the anonymity of a murmur. We would no longer hear the **questions** that have been rehashed for so long: "Who really spoke? Is it really he and not someone else? With what authenticity or originality? And what part of his deepest self did he express in his discourse?" Instead, there would be other **questions** like these: "What are the modes of existence of this discourse? Where has it been used, how can it circulate, and who can appropriate it for himself?" [. . .] And behind all these **questions**, we would hear hardly anything but the stirring of an indifference: "What difference does it make who is speaking?"

I don't think any of us, deep down, really experiences art in this way. Though it is painfully difficult to crystalize into exact language the nature of our experience, those moments of rapture, those profound aesthetic experiences—as Nabokov said, it is "the secret of durable pigments"—I don't think we hear the "anonymity of a murmur," or "the stirring of an indifference." One of the intrinsic properties of great art (however naïve a notion this might seem to some theorists) is the presence of a loud, clear, seductive, and yes even beautiful voice. Art that doesn't just express but communicates, that gives us the singular, ethereal experience of a bridge across the abyss of existential loneliness. I still ask, and I think we will always ask, "who is speaking?" because someone seems to be so clearly speaking to *me*.

> Nafis Shafizadeh, *Movie, Concert, or Act of Vandalism? (Los Angeles Review of Books)*

"Quick. Four guys you'd do at this school." Tristan puts up a hand preemptively. "Four guys who are not me if I was straight."

I open my mouth, then close it, glaring at Tristan.

"That's not fair. I don't like this game."

Tristan flips dark hair out of his eyes and lifts his eyebrows.

"Life isn't fair, Melly. Answer the **question**."

"I don't like the guys at this school. They're dumb. Can we do movie stars instead?"

Tristan is examining his nails. "You're embarrassing yourself. Just answer the **question**."

I let my eyes skim the playground. The pickings are slim. There are a bunch of white dudes in one corner near the fence wearing skinny jeans and band T-shirts and kicking around a Hacky Sack. I recognize one of them, Terrence Drake, from my physics class. He's got nice eyes—hazel, with long eyelashes. But he makes people call him "T-Dog" and smells like patchouli, so he's out.

Some guys from the basketball team are playing on the court. A few of them are shirtless, and I can see the way Rihad Jones's muscles tighten when he lifts his arms and releases the ball with a flick of his wrist. The hoop doesn't have a net, but I can hear them making *swish* noises whenever someone makes a shot. Guys who generate their own victorious sound effects? Hoo boy.

But then out of the corner of my eye I see Damon, walking across the blacktop wearing low-slung jeans and a gray polo shirt. He tugs a hand through his hair as if trying to smooth it down.

He turns, his mouth widening into a smile, and lifts one hand in a wave.

"Hey, Melanie," he calls.

I give him this pathetic little half wave in return, a scrunching of my fingers that probably makes me look like I'm physically disabled.

"Well," Tristan says, looking at me with narrowed eyes. "I think we have number one with a bullet."

Sonia Belasco, *Speak of Me as I Am*

In the parlance of the time, "subject" (short for "speaking subject") was the appropriate theoretical term for whomever in the text is speaking. We might remember that "The Death of the Author" begins with the **question** "Who is speaking?" Foucault's "What is an Author?" similarly begins with the **question** "What does it matter who is speaking?" The term "subject" appears prominently in Goldmann's response to Foucault: "The negation of the subject is today the central idea of a whole group of thinkers" (Foucault 813). Two years later, Barthes uses this abstracted, dehumanized theoretical term for the author—but he uses it in order to put in greater relief the surprising twist he is wringing on the current theoretical orthodoxy.

In this final sentence of the paragraph we also find some of the violent rhetoric that was in his 1968 manifesto: the Text (capitalized here in the 1971 preface as the Author was in 1968) is a "destroyer," bringing death to every subject. But despite this, there is still, "there must be" in the text "a subject to love." Despite its destruction of the author, the text must contain an author to love. Barthes calls the logic that, despite the death of the author, gives us an author to love a "twisted dialectic"—we might also call it a perverted dialectic. Or we might call the love for the author thus a twisted love.

Jane Gallop, *The Deaths of the Author: Reading and Writing in Time*

The one critic's discussion of the brief "pleasurable" expression that passes over Lia's face recalls Siebert's discussion regarding the allure of violence and begs the **question** as to whether Scimeca was familiar with Siebert's analysis of the Leggio/Sorisi case. A similar dynamic is brought up in an interview between Scimeca and Vito Zagarrio, when the director is asked to comment upon the problematics tied to "sado-masochismo, all'umilizione [sadomasochism, to humiliation]" especially apparent in the rape scene.

Dana Renga, Unfinished Business: Screening the Italian Mafia in the New Millennium

"You let him rape you."

"Everything happens as Sir S says. Is he going to come?"

"I think so. I don't know when."

The tenseness felt in all your muscles when you're asking this **question** slowly dissolves and you look at this woman gratefully: how lovely she is, how sparkling with her hair streaked with gray. She's wearing over black pants and a matching blouse, an antique Chinese jacket.

Obviously the rules which govern the dress and conduct of the terrorists don't apply to her.

"Today I want to have lunch with you. Go wash yourself. At 3 o'clock sharp I'll be back."

Kathy Acker, Great Expectations

We can say, Cicero says thus; these were the manners of Plato; these are the very words of Aristotle: but what do we say ourselves? What do we judge? A parrot would say as much as that.

And this puts me in mind of that rich gentleman of Rome,—[Calvisius Sabinus. Seneca, Ep., 27.]—who had been solicitous, with very great expense, to procure men that were excellent in all sorts of science, whom he had always attending his person, to the end, that when amongst his friends any occasion fell out of speaking of any subject whatsoever, they might supply his place, and be ready to prompt him, one with a sentence of Seneca, another with a verse of Homer, and so forth, every one according to his talent; and he fancied this knowledge to be his own, because it was in the heads of those who lived upon his bounty; as they also do, whose learning consists in having noble libraries. I know one, who, when I **question** him what he knows, he presently calls for a book to shew me, and dares not venture to tell me so much, as that he has piles in his posteriors, till first he has consulted his dictionary, what piles and what posteriors are.

Michel de Montaigne, Of Pedantry (Essays)

No wonder he suffers so much while quoting. This injunction without mercy brings Derrida to the place of responsibility and suffering.

Derrida has in fact on another occasion articulated a very similar sense of a double law apropos of quotation. While the text in **question** was not included in *Chaque fois unique*, it belongs to the same genre as the writing in that volume.[23] Lecturing about Paul de Man's work in 1984 just a few months after de Man's death, Derrida reflects on the practice of quotation on such an occasion: "At the limit of fidelity . . . a discourse 'in memory of'. . . could be content to quote . . . Out of fidelity, one ought to quote in the desire to let the other speak (again) but one should not, one should not be content to quote. It is with the law of this double law that we are here engaged."[24] Here we see once again the desire to let the other speak (and Derrida here uses the exact same phrase we saw at the end of his memorials for Althusser and Riddel). And, as in the memorial for Lyotard, this desire leads to a double injunction.

"This double law" is a law about quoting, about "being content to quote" (*se contenter de citer*), about limiting oneself to quoting, about being content to contain oneself, to quote without commentary. The extreme of fidelity would content itself with quoting, but "one should not, one should not be content to quote." The force of the law is perhaps best heard in that repeated "one should not," as if the repetition of the prohibitive formula itself embodied the doubleness of the law. The actual "law of this double law" is, like the double injunction in the text on Lyotard, articulated around the conjunction "but": one ought to quote *but* one should not be content to quote.

The ethical imperative here is, perhaps, one should not be content. There is in this idea of *se contenter de*, of contenting oneself with, not only the problem of complacency, but the **question** of containment, limitation. And in fact an explicit problem of limitation actually accompanies the first occurrence of *se contenter de citer* in the passage, in a phrase that above I elided for simplicity: "at the limit of fidelity . . . a discourse 'in memory of' . . . could be content to quote, *supposing one knew where to begin and how to stop a quotation*" (emphasis added).

The problem with "simply" quoting is that a quotation is not a simple thing. Even if we do not interfere, interrupt, or comment, we still decide where the quotation begins and ends. The phrasing here is in fact striking and not parallel: Derrida literally says "supposing one knew where to begin and how to stop a quotation." The wording "how to stop a quotation" suggests something hard to get under control. And indeed one of the things we see in these memorial texts is Derrida piling quote upon quote, as if having trouble stopping. In the short piece on Gilles Deleuze, for example, Derrida quotes a few sentences from Deleuze's *Logique du sens*, and right after closing the quote, he places a parenthesis: "(One would have to quote interminably)" (235, 192). A few years later, in the essay on Lyotard, Derrida, while adding long quote to long quote, will parenthetically bemoan that he could not "read everything." Quotation is necessarily truncated; even the most faithful quotation must do violence.

But even supposing one knew how to stop a quotation, we would, however, nonetheless still be engaged with the law of the double law. In the 1984 lecture in memory of de Man, after revealing the double law of quotation, Derrida announces the ethics of his engagement: "One ought to quote in the desire to let the other speak but one should not, one should not be content to quote. It is with the law of this double law that we are here engaged . . . I thus must quote but also interrupt the quotations" (*Mémoires*, 64).

I must quote but also interrupt the quotations. In the introduction to *Chaque fois unique*, Brault and Naas say that, in a first moment, quoting "without interruption" seems to be a way of avoiding indecency. As they then proceed to move beyond that "first moment," while they do not explicitly reference this statement Derrida made in *Memoires for Paul de Man*, they use a very similar formulation: "And so Derrida cites and interrupts the citation" (47, 24).[25]

If quoting without interruption seems, in a first moment, to be

Pages 79 to 172 are not shown in this preview.

We sat in front of the console and stared at the equipment, now completely changed. The phone rang, disturbing the empty hiss. I thought: Here is one of the few places where a phone call late at night doesn't automatically mean someone has died. Todd answered. "That was Dr. Ressler. 'Bookkeeper' is unique. And so, my friend, is your face." I smiled, already skilled at letting his moments of confrontatory zeal fall away without crisis. "What do I do for a living? I'm not sure the **question** has an answer anymore. Everyone, no matter what he does, is kept in the dark about the clients."

This was the moment of expansiveness that brought me compulsively to Manhattan On-Line to sit with this stranger after my own shift was over. "Do you know Ben Shahn's great answer to that **question**? I take a guilty pleasure in the man's paintings, knowing his whole pastel, representational aesthetic has been on the outs for a decade. But his essays need no excuse. He tells a story of an itinerant wanderer traveling over country roads in thirteenth-century France who comes across a man exhaustedly pushing a wheelbarrow full of rubble. He asks what the man is doing. 'God only knows. I push these damn stones around from sunup to sundown, and in return, they pay me barely enough to keep a roof over my head.'

"Farther down the road, the traveler meets another man, just as exhausted, pushing another filled barrow. In reply to the same **question**, the second man says, 'I was out of work for a long time. My wife and children were starving. Now I have this. It's killing, but I'm grateful for it all the same.'

"Just before nightfall, the traveler meets a third exploited stone-hauler. When asked what he is doing, the fellow replies, 'I'm building Chartres Cathedral.'"

Richard Powers, The Gold Bug Variations

Nodier's work often dwells on individuals who are curiously addicted to thought for its own sake, to modes of thinking that can bypass human contact altogether. Anything that does not inflame such intellects makes them dysfunctional. Even though in today's medical framework, Jean-François might be labeled with a number of chemical disorders, in Nodier's context, he is the symbol of a disjunction that could, in more moderate ways, strike any of us. Worldliness causes pain because it is situated in an inescapable present; we must react to it, respond to its demands, and fit it within our mortality. Otherworldliness, however, enables us to escape from this condition, matching us with something greater than ourselves, something that retains its future promise, enticing by its sheer sense of possibility. This mystical yearning is what affords Nodier's characters their dual sense of intoxication and despair.

Nodier's *idiot savant* only regains his composure, his brilliance, when asked about quasi-unanswerable **questions** such as the planets, the nature of the universe, or complex ethical matters. Intellectually stimulated, asked to transcend the prosaic, he is not only persuasive, but masterful. His admirer, the story's young narrator, understands that the only way to engage with him is to egg him on with such intricate **questions**. He quizzes Jean-François about space, the planets, astronomy, the nature of matter, merely to hold his attention, desperate to bask in this privileged mode of transaction. "Science's most arduous **questions** . . . were child's play for him, and their solutions sprung so fast from his mind to his mouth that one might have mistaken the result of reflection and calculation for a merely mechanical operation."[16] It is certainly in tune with the pathology of monomania to prefer the mechanical, the formulaic, to **questions** involving plural answers. Nodier's holy fool captures the essence of a phenomenon without ever having to run it through the ordinary channels of communication. Bypassing the human makes him both an object of scorn (to the villagers, he is the local idiot) and of awe (to the educated, he is something of a seer). But to Nodier, there is a dramatic lesson to be gleaned from such a personality: seen through the eyes of the young narrator (the story is loosely based on Nodier's own experience), Jean-François is a great example of the ravages operated by the quotidian.

Marina Van Zuylen, Monomania: The Flight From Everyday Life in Literature and Art

There was nothing new under the sun; that meant the materials of transformation were already present, everywhere and anywhere, in today's papers, in yesterday's books, and so the *Potlatch* voice is huddled and all-powerful, satirical and sentimental, a midnight secret told as a noontime shout, self-referential within a global frame of reference. Legend and fact turn into one another; the mythic becomes prosaic, and vice versa; pronouncements on all things under the sun are made in tones of common knowledge just out of reach of common sense. In certain moods, one can feel a jarring, tearing momentum in the pages, the momentum of a dream as it rushes toward waking—the most violent screed seems reasonable, the most rational argument communicates as a rant, and as one picks out the names at the bottom of a manifesto, the **questions** ask themselves: who are these people? Don't they know what they're saying sounds like a joke? Why do they sound as if they've already got it?

Greil Marcus, Lipstick Traces: A Secret History of the Twentieth Century

The Corystes immediately saw the importance of the Hermit's **question**, but he answered, cheerily,—

"Oh, that is all right! the sand allows the passage of the water, which I draw in with the movement of my feet-jaws, and after it has passed over my gills it is ejected through my *antennæ*, which, as you may see, are hollowed out and edged with bristles, so that when they are placed close together they form a tight tube for the passage of the water. I don't go any deeper into the sand than the length of my feelers, so I am quite comfortable."

"Well, I never heard before of burrowing Crabs, though it seems to me that all kinds of animals burrow!" said the Hermit.

"Oh, haven't you?" said the Corystes. "There is another Crab who burrows, the Ebalia, a funny little fellow who lives among gravel. Such a slowcoach as he is altogether!"

"How does he get through gravel? I should think that would be worse than sand," said the Hermit.

"Of course he always descends backwards," said the Corystes. " He separates the little stones with his hind feet, and gradually makes a way for his body. He takes plenty of time about it."

"Do you often come out of the sand?" inquired the Hermit.

"Not more than I can help," said the Corystes. "I don't like walking. It is inconvenient for me because of the great length of my arms, which are in the way on the sand, though they are of great use when I am in my burrow. With them I can reach anything near me without troubling to come out for it."

The Hermit, on looking more particularly at the Corystes, was struck with his fierce and war-like appearance, and said,—

"Well, you look rather alarming, so it is perhaps better that you keep yourself hidden, for if you did not do so, nothing would ever come near enough for you to catch it, even with your long arms."

"Quite a mistake, I assure you. I am the most peaceable of Crabs," said the Corystes; "give me only my dinner every day, and I should never care to stir out of my burrow. Won't you come down with me, and try how you like it? You had better do so."

"No, thank you," said the Hermit. "I can't do that, but I am delighted to have made your acquaintance."

Annie E. Ridley, *Under the Waves, or, The Hermit-Crab "In Society"*

The writers offer a world they reject—a world that almost everyone outside the LI acknowledges as both past and future. The writers offer a world they believe in, but that world is out of reach—out of reach then, and out of reach now. As one reads *Potlatch*, so is the world one has always taken for granted. The evanescent quality of Debord's later writing, his chiliastic serenity, is patent here: a voice speaking from a world one might want to make and then to live in, but also the voice of the mad professor in Eric Ambler's spy thriller *Cause for Alarm*. The LI offers " . . . A New Idea in Europe"; the old man, professor of classical mechanics at the University of Bologna until Mussolini's fascists drove him out, offers his unpublished masterpiece, hundreds of pages of whorls, faces, and high-school equations. The deposed professor has discovered a proof of perpetual motion; so has the LI. "Leisure is the real revolutionary **question**," says the LI, right out loud, nobody listening; "The cube root of eight," whispers the professor, "is God."

Greil Marcus, *Lipstick Traces: A Secret History of the Twentieth Century*

True: it had been a while since I'd spent much time in public. But was such a fact even relevant in our "information age," when you could scour planet Earth and the universe without ever leaving the green velvet couch you'd pulled from a garbage dump and made the focal point of your East Sixth Street apartment? I began each night by ordering Hunan string beans and washing them down with Jagermeister. It was amazing how many string beans I could eat: four orders, five orders, more sometimes. I could tell by the number of plastic packets of soy sauce and chopsticks included with my delivery that Fong Yu believed I was serving string beans to a party of eight or nine vegetarians. Does the chemical composition of Jagermeister cause a craving for string beans? Is there some property of string beans that becomes addictive on those rare occasions when they're consumed with Jagermeister? I asked myself these **questions** as I shoveled string beans into my mouth, huge crunchy forkfuls, and watched TV—weird cable shows, most of which I couldn't identify and didn't watch much of. You might say I created my own show out of all those other shows, which I suspected was actually better than the shows themselves. In fact, I was sure of it.

Here was the bottom line: if we human beings are *information processing machines,* reading X's and O's and translating that information into what people oh so breathlessly call "experience," and if I had access to all that same information via cable TV and any number of magazines that I browsed through at Hudson News for four- and five-hour stretches on my free days (my record was eight hours, including the half hour I spent manning the register during the lunch break of one of the younger employees, who thought I worked there)—if I had not only the information but the artistry to *shape* that information using the computer inside my brain (real computers scared me; if you can find Them, then They can find you, and I didn't want to be found), then, technically speaking, was I not having all the same experiences those other people were having?

Jennifer Egan, A Visit From the Goon Squad

Still, Tengo's reading of the story was his and his alone. He could not help feeling a certain sympathy for the trusting men and women who were "left in a pool of mysterious **question** marks" after reading *Air Chrysalis*. He pictured a bunch of dismayed-looking people clutching at colorful flotation rings as they drifted aimlessly in a large pool full of **question** marks. In the sky above them shone an utterly unrealistic sun. Tengo felt a certain sense of responsibility for having foisted such a state of affairs upon the public.

But who can possibly save all the people of the world? Tengo thought. *You could bring all the gods of the world into one place, and still they couldn't abolish nuclear weapons or eradicate terrorism. They couldn't end the drought in Africa or bring John Lennon back to life. Far from it—the gods would just break into factions and start fighting among themselves, and the world would probably become even more chaotic than it is now. Considering the sense of powerlessness that such a state of affairs would bring about, to have people floating in a pool of mysterious* **question** *marks seems like a minor sin.*

Haruki Murakami, 1Q84

This piece of information is, as far as I am aware, hitherto unrecorded in the extensive annotations which have been inflicted on the novel; and I herewith offer it in a spirit of humility for use by professional scholars.

The tall, the fat, the mad. And then there are the colours. When he was researching for *Madame Bovary,* Flaubert spent a whole afternoon examining the countryside through pieces of coloured glass. Would he have seen what we now see? Presumably. But what about this: in 1853, at Trouville, he watched the sun go down over the sea, and declared that it resembled a large disc of redcurrant jam. Vivid enough. But was redcurrant jam the same colour in Normandy in 1853 as it is now? (Would any pots of it have survived, so that we could check? And how would we know the colour had remained the same in the intervening years?) It's the sort of thing you fret about. I decided to write to the Grocers' Company about the matter. Unlike some of my other correspondents, they replied promptly. They were also reassuring: redcurrant jam is one of the purest jams, they said, and though an 1853 Rouennais pot might not have been quite so clear as a modern one because of the use of unrefined sugar, the colour would have been almost exactly the same. So at least that's all right: now we can go ahead and confidently imagine the sunset. But you see what I mean? (As for my other **questions**: a pot of the jam could indeed have survived until now, but would almost certainly have turned brown, unless kept completely sealed in a dry, airy, pitch-dark room.)

Julian Barnes, Flaubert's Parrot

This is the second time that Scimeca refuses to engage the interviewer on the **question** of the rape. Earlier, Zagarrio asked Scimeca to consider themes relating to sadomasochism, sexuality, and psychoanalytic conflicts between men and women as apparent in *Placido Rizzotto* and *Il giorno di San Sebastiano*.[37] Again, the director sidesteps the **question** and instead discusses the social, civil, and ethical impetus to his filmmaking and expresses his desire to tell the stories of a peasant world that is on the verge of disappearing. His silence on the matter underlines my contention that the rape in *Placido*

Rizzotto is abruptly channelled into other stories focusing on the heroes and villains of Mafia folklore. Tania Modleski positions Hitchcock's *Blackmail* (1929) as a film that "poses the issues of rape and the silencing of women with almost exemplary clarity" and discusses how films that brutally assault women appeal mainly to men. Rape and violence, Modleski maintains, "effectively silence and subdue not only the woman in the films—the one who threatens patriarchal law and order through the force of her anarchic desires—but also the women watching these films." Thus, women are doubly silenced and "can enjoy them only by assuming the position of 'masochists.'"[38]

Dana Renga, Unfinished Business: Screening the Italian Mafia in the New Millennium

I personally feel it's both. And looking at the panel, you have six men, three women, seven European and White. There are no voices of women of color. None of the speakers recognizes his or her own power position. Whether it's race or class or gender, there was no recognition that the people speaking here have certain privileges. As a matter of fact, one person said that it wasn't good for someone to speak about his personal life. But I think it's necessary to recognize where you're coming from. I think that when you don't raise issues like, "Why aren't there any women of color here?," you're participating in the exclusion. It's great to talk about how White men are fucking us over; but quite frankly Bush knows that he needs Clarence Thomas, Bush knows that he needs White women, and Bush knows that he needs women of color. So it's not just as simple as White men oppressing me. There's the whole **question** of speaking for. One person said that we should be able to speak for other people. Quite frankly, that argument, coming from people who are perceived to be my allies, makes me a little nervous, because when we talk about who should be able to speak for others, it's usually White women—White, straight women—and men. I don't happen to believe that everybody has the right to speak for everybody else. What I would like to hear from the panelists is, do they have any feelings about there being no women of color here? Have they thought about it during the entire day we've spent here? What do they think they will do next time they're invited to a panel and there are no women of color there?

Stanley Aronowitz, Reflections on Identity—Discussion (The Identity in Question)

p. 424–14

This problem is a bit deceiving as it looks like there are 3 options for the five colors, but there are only 2 since color 1 is the same color. This is a combination problem where it's quickest to list the options for 1 color and apply it to the others. Let's say we have colors A, B, C, D, and E. Remember that color 1 will be applied in 2 places. We'll say A is color 1 and the combinations we would have would be:

AB

AC

AD

AE

So there are 4 combinations for A as color 1. There would be 4 combinations for B, 4 for C, 4 for D, and 4 for E as well.

So we have $5 \times 4 = 20$ total combinations.

B

Henry Davis, Explanations for the Official SAT Study Guide Questions: Detailed Explanations for the Answers for Every Question

But here at last, it seems to me, is food for delirium. (What a shame if I should pitch on something and never notice it, another candle throw its little light and I be none the wiser.) Yes, I feel the moment has come for me to look back, if I can, and take my bearings, if I am to go on. If only I knew what I have been saying! Bah, no need to worry: it can only have been one thing, the same as ever. I have my faults, but changing my tune is not one of them. I have only to go on, as if there was something to be done, something begun, somewhere to go. It all boils down to a **question** of words, I must not forget this (I have not forgotten it). But I must have said this before, since I say it now.

I have to speak in a certain way (with warmth perhaps, all is possible) first of the creature I am not (as if I were he) and then (as if I were he) of the creature I am. (Before I can, etc.) It's a **question** of voices—of voices to keep going, in the right manner, when they stop (on purpose, to put me to the test—as now the one whose burden is roughly to the effect that I am alive). Warmth, ease, conviction, the right manner—as if it were my own voice, pronouncing my own words, words pronouncing me alive (since that's how they want me to be—I don't know why, with their billions of quick, their trillions of dead: that's not enough for them, I too must contribute my little convulsion, mewl, howl, gasp and rattle, loving my neighbour and blessed with reason.

But what is the right manner? I don't know. It is they who dictate this torrent of balls, they who stuffed me full of these groans that choke me. And out it all pours unchanged: I have only to belch to be sure of hearing them, the same sour old teachings I can't change a tittle of. A parrot, that's what they're up against, a parrot. If they had told me what I have to say, in order to meet with their approval, I'd be bound to say it, sooner or later. But God forbid, that would be too easy, my heart wouldn't be in it! I have to puke my heart out too, spew it up whole along with the rest of the vomit. It's then at last I'll look as if I mean what I'm saying, it won't be just idle words. (Well, don't lose hope. Keep your mouth open and your stomach turned. Perhaps you'll come out with it one of these days.)

Nodier's major work, **Questions** *de littérature légale. Du plagiat, de la supposition d'auteurs, des supercheries qui ont rapport aux livres* (1828), remains today one of the most interesting. It is a fascinating study of a panoply of literary crimes by an author who has been—as is so often the case—accused of many of them. Most commentators on plagiarism quote in this context his famous apology for lack of originality from *Histoire du roi de Bohême et de ses sept châteaux* (1830), a burlesque 'pastiche' of Diderot and Sterne in which the author rails against imaginary accusations of plagiarism by aligning himself with a lineage of plagiarists stretching back to Rome, and which ends: 'And you want me, I repeat, to invent the form and the content of a book! heaven help me! Condillac said somewhere that it would be easier to create a world than an idea.'[7] In **Questions** *de littérature légale* (1828), which is a version of 'literary curiosities,' Nodier deals with much more than plagiarism. Most of the first part of the book, before the entry on 'plagiarism' and the subsequent chapter on 'literary theft' (piracy), is devoted to types of repetition that, when appropriately practised, constitute proper rather than improper appropriation. Forms of repetition treated are 'Imitation,' 'Quotation,' 'Allusion,' and 'Similarity of ideas and subjects.' Nodier also relies on Bayle and cites, among other Latin treatises, Thomasius' dissertation, although there is little evidence in the text that he has referred to it other than through Bayle. (In fact, the original version of Nodier's text was apparently written 'completely without books'—'dans un dénûment absolu de livres' [***Questions** de littérature légale* i].) Nodier's work has become a major source for all studies following it: Ludovic Lalanne's *Curiosités littéraires* (1845) and Quérard's treatise *Les supercheries littéraires dévoilées* (1845–53) both quote him liberally. The nineteenth-century *Larousse* article 'Plagiat' is little more than an updated compilation of Diderot quoting Bayle quoting Thomasius, so that, in the French tradition, there is an almost unbroken line of authority and received knowledge—one might say serial plagiarism—on the subject.

Marilyn Randall, Pragmatic Plagiarism: Authorship, Profit, and Power

But what were my own feelings at this period? What was I thinking of? With what? Was I having difficulty with my morale? The answer to all that is this (I quote Malone): that I was entirely absorbed in the business on hand and was not at all concerned to know precisely (or even approximately) what it consisted in. The only problem for me was how to continue (since I could not do otherwise), to the best of my declining powers, in the motion which had been imparted to me. This obligation (and the quasi-impossibility of fulfilling it) engrossed me in a purely mechanical way (excluding notably the free play of the intelligence and sensibility). So that my situation rather resembled that of an old broken-down cartor bat-horse unable to receive the least information either from its instinct or from its observation as to whether it is moving towards the stable or away from it (and not greatly caring either way). The **question**, among others, of how such things are possible had long since ceased to preoccupy me.

Samuel Beckett, The Unnamable

'That's complete crap.'

'Perhaps,' Mandamus agreed generously with Orrick. 'But it's an idea, if not a new one. Saying "that's complete crap" isn't even an idea. It's just an opinion. What is your idea?'

'I just can't believe you can be so pessimistic and . . . and still be alive. Jeez, if I felt that way I think I'd kill myself.'

'It's not pessimism,' Mandamus said. 'It's what I call the Bleak View, but it isn't pessimism. If it's right it's right. Truth is truth; I am old-fashioned in that regard. But I believe as I say; we are like a cancer. To be like a cancer in one way may be no bad thing; we live and grow. The **question** is how much we resemble cancer in any other way. If—'

'Just because we're smart? Is that what you're saying? Just being smart makes us bad? That's crazy.'

'You don't listen; the smartness—'

'I'm listening, I just don't believe what I'm hearing.'

'You must have heard of Gaia; the planet as organism. Well, we are the cancer in its body. Do you understand that? We were like an ordinary organ, once; part of the whole. We lived and died, we behaved ourselves like cells, existing and being replaced, just another species, preying on some species, preyed on by others . . . whether we lived or died as a species made little difference. Then; phut! Intelligence.' Mr Mandamus snapped his fingers. The younger man shook his head, drank from his beer bottle. The others were keeping quiet; even Broekman, who was sitting back in his chair looking tired and smoking a cigar, his collar undone.

Hisako glanced at Philippe, who winked at her.

'And with that,' Mandamus said, 'everything changes. We invent ways to blow up the world, but before that we start destroying other species; the other organs of the Gaia body. And we change her body. Oh, shake your head, Steven, but come with me to Alexandria; come to Venice. Alexandria becomes Venice, Venice Atlantis. The waters are rising; the ice is melting and the waters are rising. What we do means everything now. Whether we survive or not matters not just to us but to all the other species we take down with us if we go under. Because we have the drives of any species; to live, to breed, to spread. But we have this extra thing, this consciousness nothing else has.'

'Yeah, what about whales?'

'Fah; if they were so smart they wouldn't let us kill them so easily. They'd post look-outs, they'd avoid all ships, or ships smaller than a certain size, or ships that turn towards them, or—'

'Maybe they are. Maybe some of them are but we just can't—'

'No; they can't hide from satellites," Mandamus said quickly, and made a motion as though brushing this aside. 'But there we are; whales are intelligent, for animals; they are big, they are impressive and beautiful . . . but we kill them, we make them extinct because there is money in it, because we've made it easy; because we can. So we spread ourselves, and kill everything else. Only our intelligence lets us do this; it is what takes us beyond the "stop" message all other species have; they are limited by their specialisation, by the adaptation they have made to fit their niche. We take our niche with us; even into space. Thus we threaten to metastasise.'

Iain Banks, Canal Dreams

Let the earth lie lightly on this most delightful and most erudite of bibliophiles, according to the small phrase in today's sacred epicedicium.* But what has become of the books of Urbain Chevreau, the books he chose so well and kept in such fine order, books mentioned in no recent catalogue? Now that is a keen, pressing, essential **question**—a **question** that will engage many in society, when society ceases to be engaged by the nonsense of the humanitarianism and wicked politics with which it is infatuated.

Charles Nodier, The Book Lover

---

* The phrase is used at the beginning of *The Bibliomaniac* and must be a formula based on some previous model, not yet traced.

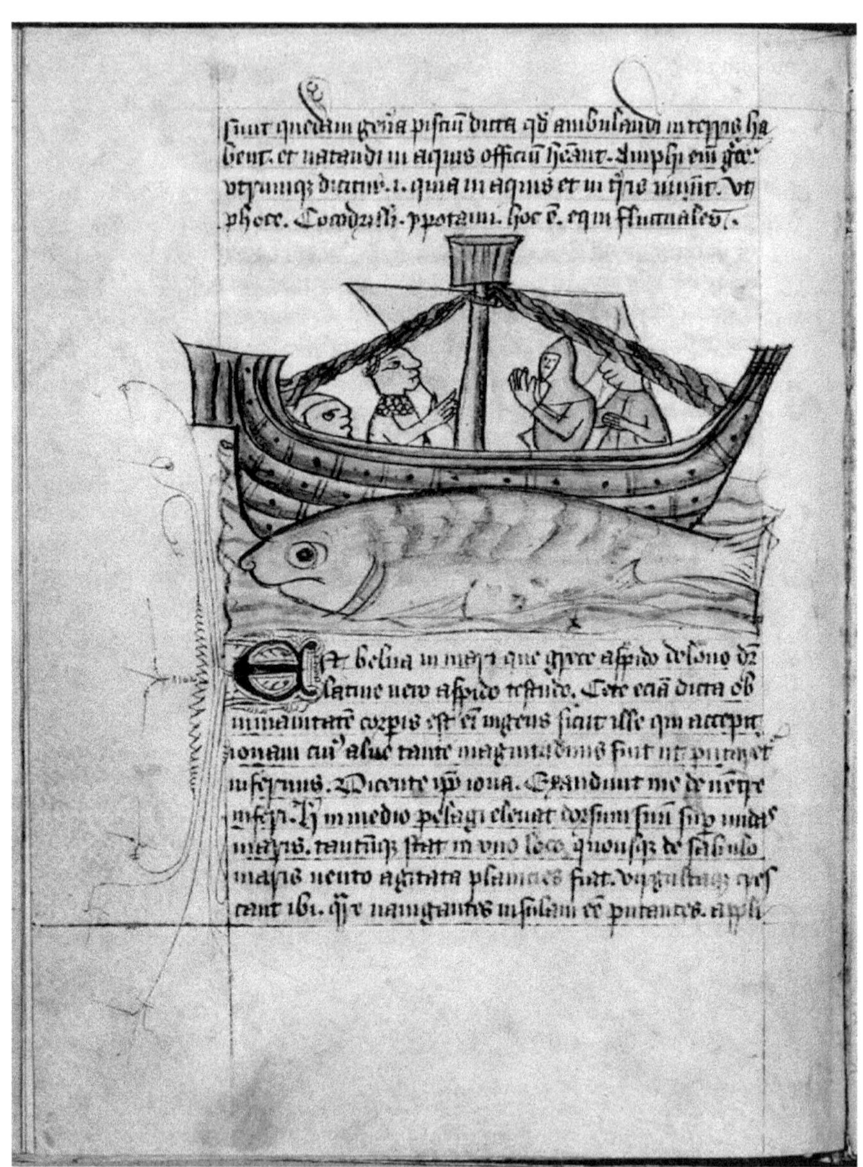

Bestiarius (Bestiary of Anne Walshe), 15th century
Parchment, fol.59v, 21 x 13.5 cm, Royal Danish Library, Copenhagen

The *Bestiary of Anne Walshe* is a Latin bestiary of English origin, produced circa 1400–25.[1] It is now in the Royal Library in Copenhagen, Denmark, and has been made available as an electronic facsimile which has been published on the Web.[2] Almost nothing else has been published about this manuscript. Christian Bruun included a short description in a catalog[3] of Danish manuscripts in 1890, but according to Erik Drigsdahl[4] this account is "obsolete and worthless." Another catalog[5] of manuscripts in the Kongelige Bibliotek in Copenhagen, produced in 1926, gives a more formal (though even briefer) description, but adds little new information. Drigsdahl has also produced a preliminary Web index[6] to the online manuscript, and the manuscript was included in an exhibition catalog in 1952. Apart from these few superficial articles, and the occasional mention in lists of surviving bestiaries, no serious work appears to have been done on this manuscript.

David Badke, The Bestiary of Anne Walshe (bestiary.ca)

Negatively Answered This Unexpected Question

More and more strangely and fiercely glad and approving

"Hast seen the White Whale?"

. . .

"D'ye see him?" cried Ahab after allowing a little space for the light to spread.
   "See nothing, sir."

. . .

"D'ye see him?" cried Ahab; but the whale was not yet in sight.

. . .

"Nothing, nothing sir!" was the sound hailing down in reply.

. . .

"What will the owners say, sir?"
   "Let the owners stand on Nantucket beach and outyell the Typhoons. What cares Ahab? Owners, owners?"

. . .

"Aloft there! What d'ye see?"
   "Nothing, sir."
   "Nothing! and noon at hand!

. . .

"Hast seen the White Whale?"
   "Aye, yesterday. Have ye seen a whale-boat adrift?"
   Throttling his joy, Ahab negatively answered this unexpected **question** . . .

. . .

"Captain Ahab," said Tashtego, "that white whale must be the same that some call Moby Dick."
   "Moby Dick?" shouted Ahab. "Do ye know the white whale then, Tash?"

. . .

"Ship ahoy! Have ye seen the White Whale?"

. . .

"Ship, ahoy! Hast seen the White Whale?"

. . .

"What do ye do when ye see a whale, men?"
   "Sing out for him!" was the impulsive rejoinder from a score of clubbed voices.
   "Good!" cried Ahab, with a wild approval in his tones; observing the hearty animation into which his unexpected **question** had so magnetically thrown them.
   "And what do ye next, men?"
   "Lower away, and after him!"

"And what tune is it ye pull to, men?"

"A dead whale or a stove boat!"

More and more strangely and fiercely glad and approving, grew the countenance of the old man at every shout; while the mariners began to gaze curiously at each other, as if marvelling how it was that they themselves became so excited at such seemingly purposeless **questions**.

. . .

"Hast seen the White Whale?" gritted Ahab in reply.

"No; only heard of him; but don't believe in him at all," said the other good-humoredly.

. . .

"Well, then, my Bouton-de-Rose-bud, have you seen the White Whale?"

"WHAT whale?"

"The WHITE Whale—a Sperm Whale—Moby Dick, have ye seen him?

"Never heard of such a whale. Cachalot Blanche! White Whale—no."

"Very good, then; good bye now, and I'll call again in a minute."

. . .

For an instant, the tranced boat's crew stood still; then turned. "The ship? Great God, where is the ship?"

. . .

"Hast thou seen the White Whale?" demanded Ahab, when the boat drifted back.

. . .

Then falling into a moment's revery, he again looked up towards the sun and murmured to himself: "Thou sea-mark! thou high and mighty Pilot! thou tellest me truly where I AM—but canst thou cast the least hint where I SHALL be? Or canst thou tell where some other thing besides me is this moment living? Where is Moby Dick?

Herman Melville, Moby Dick; or, The Whale

Well, I'll leave the **question** about redemption with you, in either
case, the whale and Captain Ahab—or the sculpture.

Psalmboxkey's Blog, Beyond Redemption? (psalmboxkey.com)

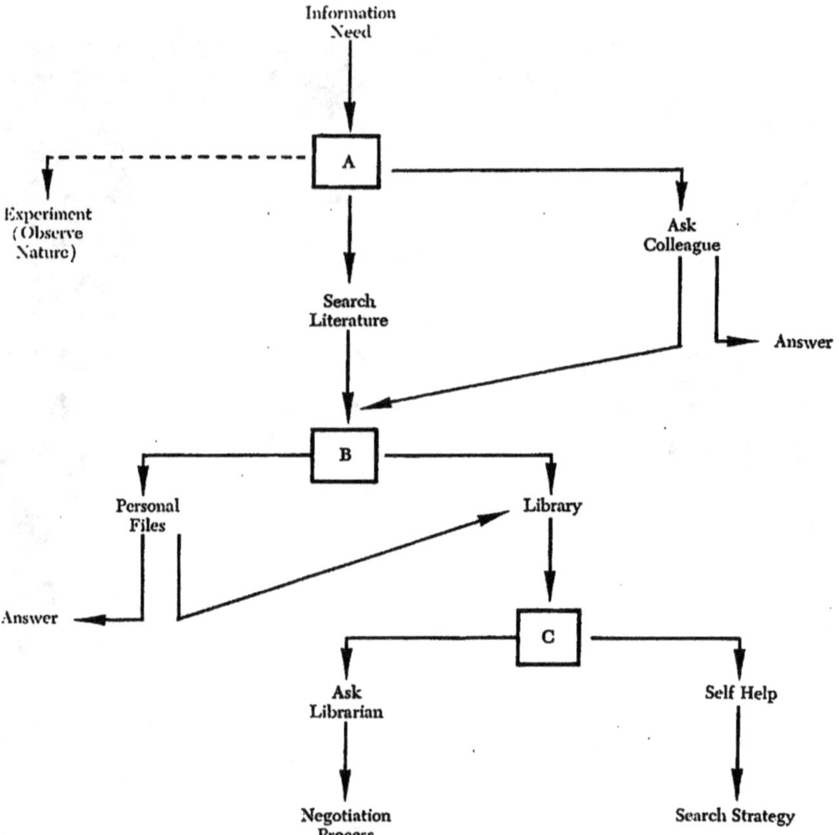

Fig. 1. Prenegotiation decisions by the inquirer.

Robert S. Taylor, "*Question*-Negotiation and Information Seeking in
Libraries, College and Research Libraries 76 (1968), 251–267.

The Further **Question** as to What Books I Read When at Home

Even if all of them show evidence of dampness

At this point I can no longer put off the vital problem of how to relate the reading of the classics to the reading of all the other books that are anything but classics. It is a problem connected with such **questions** as, Why read the classics rather than concentrate on books that enable us to understand our own times more deeply? or, Where shall we find the time and peace of mind to read the classics, overwhelmed as we are by the avalanche of current events?

We can, of course, imagine some blessed soul who devotes his reading time exclusively to Lucretius, Lucian, Montaigne, Erasmus, Quevedo, Marlowe, the *Discourse on Method, Wilhelm Meister,* Coleridge, Ruskin, Proust, and Valéry, with a few forays in the direction of Murasaki or the Icelandic sagas. And all this without having to write reviews of the latest publications, or papers to compete for a university chair, or articles for magazines on tight deadlines. To keep up such a diet without any contamination, this blessed soul would have to abstain from reading the newspapers, and never be tempted by the latest novel or sociological investigation. But we have to see how far such rigor would be either justified or profitable. The latest news may well be banal or mortifying, but it nonetheless remains a point at which to stand and look both backward and forward. To be able to read the classics you have to know "from where" you are reading them; otherwise both the book and the reader will be lost in a timeless cloud.

Italo Calvino, Why Read the Classics?

I am sometimes asked what books I advise men or women to take on holidays in the open. With the reservation of long trips, where bulk is of prime consequence, I can only answer: The same books one would read at home. Such an answer generally invites the further **question** as to what books I read when at home. To this **question** I am afraid my answer cannot be so instructive as it ought to be, for I have never followed any plan in reading which would apply to all persons under all circumstances; and indeed it seems to me that no plan can be laid down that will be generally applicable. If a man is not fond of books, to him reading of any kind will be drudgery. I most sincerely commiserate such a person, but I do not know how to help him. If a man or a woman is fond of books he or she will naturally seek the books that the mind and soul demand. Suggestions of a possibly helpful character can be made by outsiders, but only suggestions; and they will probably be helpful about in proportion to the outsider's knowledge of the mind and soul of the person to be helped.

Of course, if any one finds that he never reads serious literature, if all his reading is frothy and trashy, he would do well to try to train himself to like books that the general agreement of cultivated and sound-thinking persons has placed among the classics. It is as discreditable to the mind to be unfit for sustained mental effort as it is to the body of a young man to be unfit for sustained physical effort. Let man or woman, young man or girl, read some good author, say Gibbon or Macaulay, until sustained mental effort brings power to enjoy the books worth enjoying. When this has been achieved the man can soon trust himself to pick out for himself the particular good books which appeal to him.

The equation of personal taste is as powerful in reading as in eating; and within certain broad limits the matter is merely one of individual preference, having nothing to do with the quality either of the book or of the reader's mind. I like apples, pears, oranges, pineapples, and peaches. I dislike bananas, alligator-pears, and prunes. The first fact is certainly not to my credit, although it is to my advantage; and the second at least does not show moral turpitude. At times in the tropics I have been exceedingly sorry I could not learn to like bananas, and on round-ups, in the cow country in the old days, it was even more unfortunate not to like prunes; but I simply could not make myself like either, and that was all there was to it.

Theodore Roosevelt, A Book-Lover's Holidays in the Open

"The true **question** to ask," says the librarian of Congress in a paper read before the Social Science Convention at New York, October, 1869, "The true **question** to ask respecting a book, is, has it help'd any human soul?"

Walt Whitman, Democratic Vistas

What here, then, of the dreams of women, and the dreams of men? What here of the soul, that most curious of human inventions?

Every year, in tax-deductible conferences across America, writers and academics gather to ask of themselves, Whither the novel? Alas: they misdirect their inquiry. The business of every serious novelist, we are told, is to apprehend the universal; but what is universal among us, except for our bodies and their functions? Only one thing: the soul. Now the body grows less mysterious by the day, or so medical science informs us. The **question**, therefore, is not, Whither the novel? but rather—*cognoscenti* take note—Whither the soul? In the tradition of mayors, governors, and presidents, who each year deliver to their constituents a prognosis for their city, state, and nation respectively, so every novelist reports, through her fiction, on the state of the soul. And not merely the individual soul: by implication, every serious novelist describes the so-called universal soul. Not all of us can deliver a State of the Union address—we know better than to fuck around with politics—but all of us can interpret the state of the soul. Though Science has wrested the soul from theology and psychology, it will never displace fiction as the literature of the soul. The novelist, the poet, the dramatist—the soul is their inviolate domain.

Here's a **question** for you—and yes, it will be on the exam: The first cousin of the neurophysiologist is (a) the psychiatrist; (b) the evolutionist; or (c) the Buddhist.

Todd Wiggins, Zeitgeist

p. 459–9

This **question** addresses the differences in the passages. The process of elimination is the most effective technique for answering reading passage **questions**. A is wrong because both use data they just interpreted differently. B will not work because neither overstates the problem. C is out as neither recommends a course of action. E won't work because he does not allow a personal prejudice to interfere. Therefore D is the correct answer because they differ in interpreting the concept of empty spaces on Earth and the author of Passage 2 would criticize the focus of Passage 1.

D

p. 461–21

Since the passage is about a proposed canoe trip (stated in the introduction) the back and arms felt ready indicates a sense of anticipation in preparing for the trip.

A

p. 489–14

"Attempts at the latter" refers to the statement "educational junk" is "foisted" (meaning imposed) on us. These attempts are declared unsuccessful tries so they are "failures."

D

*Henry Davis, Explanations for the Official SAT Study Guide **Questions**: Detailed Explanations for the Answers for Every **Question***

Answers will vary. Possible answers may include:

1. I think I'll end up living in Paris after I finish school.
2. I'm planning on taking a more advanced class.
3. Yes. I just started reading a book by Paul Auster.

Santiago Mayorga, Answer Key—Touchstone 4

all of the above Also, **none of the above.** Each one (not any) of the above-named alternatives. For example, *Have you decided to quit and announced your decision, or do you want to find another job first?—None of the above.* These phrases originated as answers to a multiple-choice **question** on a test but are now also used colloquially, often as a form of avoiding a direct answer. They use *above* in the sense of "preceding," a usage dating from the second half of the 1700s.

Christine Ammer, The American Heritage Dictionary of Idioms

Finally the presenter says it's time to ask if anyone has any **questions**. A hand is raised: "Have you ever been to a buddhist retreat yourself?" an elderly woman asks. "If so, why and would you recommend it?"

*Tim Parks, Stupid **Questions** (The New York Review of Books)*

August 29, 2013. 117-minute dharma talk given by Thich Nhat Hanh from Blue Cliff Monastery in Pine Bush, New York during the 2013 Nourishing Great Togetherness teaching tour. This is a session of **questions** and answers during the 6-day retreat with the theme *Transformation and Healing—The Art of Suffering.*

*Chan Niem Hy, The Art of Suffering Retreat—**Question** and Answer Session*

Pip frowned. "Am I allowed to skip a **question**?"

Jonathan Franzen, Purity

Most writers complain about the people who come to hear them talk. Or rather the **questions** they ask. We need the public, of course, to feel important, to have a reason for presenting our books. When the seats are all full we say it is a good audience, we're enthusiastic, especially if they show signs of participation when we read. If they laugh when they should, in particular. "But when it comes to **questions**, they always ask about your life," complains Caroline Lamarche. She is sitting next to me at a book signing. The French have what I am sure is a counterproductive policy of getting authors to sit for hours at a time at book stands in sweltering pavilions just in case someone should want to buy a book of theirs and have it autographed. This way we look like country folk who have brought their beans to market, undermining commercially useful myths of our charismatic and mysterious talent. Still, the scene does give me time to examine the covers of Lamarche's novels. They appear to be about love, sex, and violence. She seems an interesting lady and I would like to ask her a little about her life, but am afraid of seeming dumb.

*Tim Parks, Stupid **Questions** (The New York Review of Books)*

What's the WORST advice you hear being given to aspiring comedians?

Oh. The worst advice is, you know, you have to do more to promote yourself. That's the worst advice. The best advice is to do your work, and you won't have to worry about anything else.

*Jerry Seinfeld, Jerry Seinfeld Loves Answering **Questions**! The Dumber, the Better. Now. (Interviewly)*

That is why my first and most pressing **question** seems like such an outright act of mutiny. What I want to know is, since when does making art require participation in any community, beyond the intense participation that the art itself is undertaking? Since when am I not contributing to the community if all I want to do is make the art itself? Isn't the art itself my intimate communication with others, with the world, with the unfolding spectacle of the human struggle as we live and coexist on this earth?

Do I really have to get in the way of that glorious interface by standing up in my sustainable zebra-wood spectacles, my complexion stage-lit and soaked in unwelcome Elton John bubble-shimmer, my cleavage lurching vampishly out of my neckline, my mealy voice and charmless presence competing with the lavish froth of that espresso machine? I mean, I can hardly see past the spotlights and pretentious echo to my own page of writing. It looks like an alien thing in this environment, wholly unbecoming and sickeningly feeble. And lest I imply that the underground bunkers and wine cellars are better venues for the bookish, all of us with our beer slouches, our pond-water hues toning in with the shadows, our mussed hair like bits of unspotted mold, that's not the case either. It's all the same. It's all very embarrassing and alienating, when we look around. We're real-life writers, not actors each in our own third-rate art film about the writing life. Aren't we?

Meghan Tifft, An Introverted Writer's Lament (The Atlantic)

p. 461–23

The answer to this **question** depends on vocabulary knowledge. The author was expecting Lewis to deliver in a tolerant tone: "A lesson. A moral. A life principle. A way." The correct answer is didactic which means preaching and teaching excessively. If someone is whimsical they do things spontaneously. Someone who is callous is heartless, unfeeling, and uncaring. If someone is remiss they are careless, inattentive, or negligent.

D

*Henry Davis, Explanations for the Official SAT Study Guide **Questions**: Detailed Explanations for the Answers for Every **Question***

And isn't facade precisely the wrong term for one man's
unchanging way of being in the world?
Dean would say that's it's a waste to waste this wasted

unasked for sojourn on earth thinking about shit
like what others think of us, or depressing shit,
like "the fucking Cold War or Vietnam,"

or rip-off artists like the Beatles
("why do they spell it with an 'a'?").
Jealous? Never. Only annoyed that they kept bugging him

with **questions**. Why did he have to think?
Wasn't it enough just to live? Dino didn't work
to see his voice or image reproduced;

he acted, sang, and hosted shows, on screen
and in person, because it was easier than real
work.

Dino liked his inflated wages, but money
meant nothing beyond what it could buy.
"A singer is nothing." Why did he sing?

It was the easiest way to make a bundle.
When anyone complained that acting was hard word
Dino responded as Crocetti, the barber's son

from Steubenville: "You think acting's work?
Try standing on your feet
twelve hours a day dealing Blackjack."

> *Mark Rudman, The Secretary of Liquor (John F. Kennedy's*
> *Informal Appointment of Dean Martin to His Cabinet)*

Under such circumstances as these, to speak of my uncle's motives was to venture on very delicate ground. Eustace relieved me from further embarrassment by asking a **question** to which I could easily reply.

"Has your uncle received any answer from Major Fitz-David?" he inquired.

"Yes.

"Were you allowed to read it?" His voice sank as he said those words; his face betrayed a sudden anxiety which it pained me to see.

"I have got the answer with me to show you," I said.

He almost snatched the letter out of my hand; he turned his back on me to read it by the light of the moon. The letter was short enough to be soon read. I could have repeated it at the time. I can repeat it now.

> *Wilkie Collins, The Law and the Lady*

The screenwriter feigns his surprise, for he's already read about it in the newspaper. It's been a long time since she last kicked a ball herself. Soccer's one of many hobbies she sacrificed for the sake of her music and for writing. Schools for gifted kids tend to encourage their students to discriminate between subjects that are worthy of study and those they deem to be trivial. Nevertheless, the girl never stopped supporting her favorite soccer team. What would you do if you were his coach? she asks the screenwriter. He knows he'd have fired him, but he doesn't dare say it. Instead, he dodges the **question** by asking her what she thinks her father would do. She mulls it over. Why are you interested in my father? There's something intriguing about him, he says. She smiles. But who is my father? she wonders as he watches her expectantly. My father is someone whose business dealings have made him very rich in a very short space of time, someone who never takes time off, except for a few days here and there during the course of a year. But she has no idea what he does with his time, what his line of work is. No one does.

A. G. Porta, No World Concerto

II WHAT IS THIS WORK?

Vertically striped sheets of paper, the bands of which are 8.7 cms wide, alternate white and colored, are stuck over internal and external surfaces: walls, fences, display windows, etc.; and/or cloth/canvas support, vertical stripes, white and colored bands each 8.7 cms, the two ends covered with dull white paint.

I record that this is my work for the last four years, without any evolution or way out. This is the past: it does not imply either that it will be the same for another ten or fifteen years or that it will change tomorrow. The perspective we are beginning to have, thanks to these past four years, allows a few considerations of the direct and indirect implications for the very conception of art. This apparent break (no research, or any formal evolution for four years) offers a platform that we shall situate at zero level, when the observations both internal (conceptual transformation as regards the action/praxis of a similar form) and external (work/production presented by others) are numerous and rendered all the easier as they are not invested in the various surrounding movements, but are rather derived from their absence. Every act is political and, whether one is conscious of it or not, the presentation of one's work is no exception. Any production, any work of art is social, has a political significance. We are obliged to pass over the sociological aspect of the proposition before us due to lack of space and considerations of priority among the **questions** to be analyzed. The points to be examined are described below and each will require to be examined separately and more thoroughly later. *[This is still valid nowadays.]*

a) The Object, the Real, Illusion. Any art tends to decipher the world, to visualize an emotion, nature, the subconscious, etc. . . . Can we pose a **question** rather than replying always in terms of hallucinations? This **question** would be: can one create something that is real, nonillusionistic, and therefore not an art-object? One might reply—and this is a real temptation for an artist—in a direct and basic fashion to this **question** and fall instantly into one of the traps mentioned *[in the first section]*; i.e., believe the problem solved, because it was raised, and *[for example]* present no object but a concept. This is responding too directly to need, it is mistaking a desire for reality, it is making like an artist. In fact, instead of **questioning** or acquainting oneself with the problem raised, one provides a solution, and what a solution! One avoids the issue and passes on to something else. Thus does art progress from form to form, from problems raised to problems solved, accruing successive layers of concealment.

Daniel Buren, Beware!

For the life of me I cannot remember what I had been trying to get that monstrosity of a canvas up that stairway for.

Even if the **question** was soon enough rendered irrelevant, considering the manner in which I did not get it up.

And what have I been saying that has now made me think about Brahms's mother?

In this instance I can make an educated guess, since the poor woman had a crippled leg.

For the life of me I would not have believed that the life of Brahms was the book I had read in this house.

Evidently not every **question** falls into the category of **questions** that would appear to remain unanswerable, however.

Though what must now surprise me is that I would have troubled to read a book so badly damaged, or printed on such cheap paper.

Any number of books in this house are in considerably better condition, even if all of them show evidence of dampness.

David Markson, Wittgenstein's Mistress

Riffling carefully through these **questions** in his mind and lining up alongside them a tentative list of solutions, he turned up the collar of his mackintosh against the rain and plodded off determinedly to the nearest point of embarkation. It was late, and there was much to be done; but he had no doubt that he would manage somehow.

Amanda Prantera, The Cabalist

Once more, the savage thinks he can make the wind to blow or to be still. When the day is hot and a Yakut has a long way to go, he takes a stone which he has chanced to find in an animal or fish, winds a horse-hair several times round it, and ties it to a stick. He then waves the stick about, uttering a spell. Soon a cool breeze begins to blow.[103] The Wind clan of the Omahas flap their blankets to start a breeze which will drive away the mosquitoes.[104] When a Haida Indian wishes to obtain a fair wind, he fasts, shoots a raven, singes it in the fire, and then going to the edge of the sea sweeps it over the surface of the water four times in the direction in which he wishes the wind to blow. He then throws the raven behind him, but afterwards picks it up and sets it in a sitting posture at the foot of a spruce-tree, facing towards the required wind. Propping its beak open with a stick, he requests a fair wind for a certain number of days; then going away he lies covered up in his mantle till another Indian asks him for how many days he has desired the wind, which **question** he answers.[105]

James George Frazer, The Golden Bough: A Study in Comparative Religion

And as for Pirates, when they chance to cross each other's cross-bones, the first hail is—"How many skulls?"—the same way that whalers hail—"How many barrels?" And that **question** once answered, pirates straightway steer apart, for they are infernal villains on both sides, and don't like to see overmuch of each other's villanous likenesses.

Herman Melville, Moby Dick; or, The Whale

None of these **questions** are directly addressed to the novel you are presenting. Yet one has to grant that if only one knew the answers, something would be learned. The public are firing shots in the dark; they are groping for some kind of connection between the figure on the stage and the particular atmosphere of the novels they have read. A

disturbing atmosphere. A heartening atmosphere. Or disturbing *and* heartening, and
funny *and* decidedly unfunny. Why so? Who are you, to be producing this stuff? That's
what they're asking.

Tim Parks, Stupid **Questions** (The New York Review of Books)

There's something about everyone no one can know.
There was no **question** of Dino taking orders
and being bossed around was out of bounds:

penalty shot incurred for the perpetrator,
who was, this time, the imperious Billy Wilder
whose streak of hits was breaking fast.

Dino as always was doing his job,
which was to literally play himself in *Kiss Me,
Stupid*, and Billy had the balls

to cap an interview at the Hollywood Press Club
with this tactless pearl: "stars don't mean a thing."
Was this because of what *Stupid* might have been

had Marilyn, whose presence he had counted on,
not done herself in? Was Wilder gambling
that fellow exiles from the Reich,

Lang, von Stroheim, and even the ghosts
of Lubitsch, Brecht and Thomas Mann
would have been there to applaud and acknowledge

that he, from a younger generation of German exiles,
was one of them?
Dino didn't brood. Dino didn't blow.

There would be no humiliating histrionics.
He would put Wilder in his place
with a letter, denouncing him as an arrogant

and self-important son-of-a-bitch.
Without angling for the director's respect,
he got it, and more.

After six weeks of delectable footage
with Peter Sellers—whose American debut
was to have been in *Stupid*—

as the small town piano teacher
intent on writing a hit song
and enlisting Dino to "get it in the right hands"

the tetchy "thirty-nine year old actor had a massive
coronary," yet not long after landing in Heathrow
found the breath to bitch to the press

about crowds on the set, wrote a letter
vilifying Wilder and Hollywood,
and swore never to return.

*Mark Rudman, The Secretary of Liquor (John F. Kennedy's
Informal Appointment of Dean Martin to His Cabinet)*

Various modes of effecting the last purpose will naturally occur to the deliberating minds of the negotiators, which shall be fully and impartially investigated in the present letter. Each projected scheme, with its relative advantages and objections, shall receive proper attention at my hands; while I will endeavour to point out the mode best calculated to settle the general **question** in such a manner as to ensure its own durability, not less than the preservation of the peace of Europe.

There are other topics of interest connected with the general **question** which naturally flow from its consideration, or have been urged *ab externo,* and require explanation. These also I propose to discuss, so that the whole subject, so to speak, may be *exhausted,* and no part of it left untouched.

I have not the presumption, my Lord, to hope that the text of my letter may be consulted as a sort of manual by the negotiators or mediators on the part of Italy. It will be enough for me that it impart correct notions to the people of this country as to the real merits of the **question**; and that the wants and expectations of the Italians be made known to the high deliberating parties.

However much I may have felt, when first I ventured to address your Lordship on the Italian **question**, on the 5th of July last, that the step I was then taking might be considered as alien to the pursuits of one devoted to the prosecution of a peaceful art, and of purely social duties; and that it became him not to interfere in political matters, still less to assume a forward attitude in the consideration of an especial **question** of this character: now that the events of July, and public opinion have shown how correctly I had appreciated the importance of the Italian cause in the North of the Peninsula; how just were my apprehensions, that through the want of energy, union, and experience on the part of newly created authorities, the cause itself would suffer a temporary failure; how rightly I had urged, even in the midst of Italian success, the necessity of a prompt intervention by England (a necessity only recently acknowledged by her acts); how truly I had foretold, that in default of such prompt intervention, France would be appealed to by the Italian people, possibly at the sacrifice of monarchical principles and with the propagation of republican doctrines;—now that all these things have actually come to pass, I need hardly hesitate to pursue my task and complete my duty as the humble but devoted supporter of a rightful and legitimate cause:—a physician does not cease to be a citizen.

1. Who are the real parties between whom England and France are to mediate.

I have noticed, in the preliminary part of my letter, the narrow view taken by certain statesmen and men of letters in this country of this first and most important part of the main **question**, and how these authorities confound altogether the leader of a belligerent army with the nation whose cause he defends. Assuming a view so imperfect and consequently incorrect, it was natural that they should commit the farther mistake of considering the war at an end, which had been carried on between Charles Albert and Radetzky until the 9th of August last.

Unquestionably, if such a war had been waged and carried on by that prince as king of Piedmont only, he having, from adverse fortunes, once more been reduced within the line of his own hereditary dominions, the war would be at an end; and after the armistice nothing else would be required for the final settlement of that ill-fated contest, than a declaration from the conqueror that he was satisfied, and had no intention to push his victorious armies farther. A mediation, in such a case, or any negotiation by the intervention of foreign powers, would evidently be uncalled for.

But the prince who fought Radetzky, fought not only as hereditary king of Piedmont, but also as the elected sovereign of an Italian union of cities and provinces, which, whilst in the actual enjoyment of their recovered natural freedom and legitimate independence, had voted themselves to be a part of a Whole, and members of one commonwealth, which was to be defended from a common enemy, whose total expulsion from the Italian territory was to be accomplished by their united efforts.

Let us see whether the thing is not really so. What drove the Austrians from the whole of the Milanese territory in the course of a few days after the 22nd of March? The almost simultaneous rising of the people, who expelled them from their capital first, and next from every city and hamlet of that magnificent possession.

What called Charles Albert into Lombardy, whose troops aided in driving the Austrians farther still, and beyond the Adige, after repeatedly defeating them in the open field? The rising of the people again, and their invitation to that sovereign to come to their aid; for they would be his constitutional subjects. Is it not so? Did not an almost unanimous vote of the whole male population, comprised between the Ticino and the Adige, and between the Swiss Alps and the Panaro, declare Charles Albert their king? And if we refer to the law passed by the Chambers of Turin at the time of accepting the adhesions of Lombardy and Vinegia, as offered by those provinces, we find that those territories were proclaimed to form, from and after the passing of that law, integral parts of ONE STATE.

Lombardy and Piedmont, then, had become one great Italian province or realm as it were: politically so, because *de facto*; legitimately so, because the people "being in possession of their own territory, became absolute and sole proprietors of its soil, and had a right to use it, and dispose of it, as it thought proper*;" not less than "the sole right of determining whether or no it would acknowledge over itself a sovereign power invested with empire over the whole territory*."

But it has been contended by the Austrian advocates in England (for it is in England only that Austria has found any such in regard to this **question**), that Charles Albert could not legally treat with or accept the allegiance of a people who were in a state of revolt. Such, however, is not the opinion or dictum of the same great authority just cited, which authority no one will pretend to deny to be far superior to any of their own, which such statesmen and writers as I have named in the title-page of my present letter, can allege.

Marten thus settles this point:—"Suppose that a province or territory subjected to another state refuses obedience to it, and endeavours to render itself independent; a foreign nation does not violate its perfect obligations, nor deviate from the principles of neutrality, if it *treats as an independent nation* people who have declared and still maintain themselves independent*."

Such precisely was the state of things when Charles Albert treated with the people of Lombardy, Parma, Piacenza and Modena, and accepted the union of those states with his own hereditary dominions. The people had "refused obedience" and had "endeavoured to render themselves independent;" they had "declared and still maintained" their independence; for no vestige of the authority of the former sovereign state was in existence at the time, and for many weeks after, in the countries in **question**.

*A. B. Granville, The Italian **Question**: A Second Letter to Lord Palmerston, G.C.B., M.P., Etc. Etc.; With a Reputation of Certain Misrepresentations by Lord Brougham, Mr. D'Israeli, and the Quarterly Review, Respecting the Rights of Austria and the Lombardo-Venetians, Illustrated by a Map of the Disputed Territories*

Having won, shall I be left in peace? It doesn't look like it, I seem to be going on talking. In any case all these suppositions are probably erroneous. I shall no doubt be launched again, girt with better arms, against the fortress of mortality. What is more important is that I should know what is going on now, in order to announce it, as my function requires. It must not be forgotten, sometimes I forget, that all is a **question** of voices. I say what I am told to say, in the hope that some day they will weary of talking at me. The trouble is I say it wrong, having no ear, no head, no memory. Now I seem to hear them say it is Worm's voice beginning, I pass on the news, for what it is worth.

Samuel Beckett, The Unnamable

Cezanne allowed the **question** of there being simultaneous viewpoints, and thereby destroyed forever in art the possibility of a static representation or portrait. The Cubists went further. They found the means of making the forms of all objects similar. If everything was rendered in the same terms, it became possible to paint the interactions between them. These interactions became so much more interesting than that which was being portrayed that the concepts of portraiture and therefore of reality were undermined or transferred.

Three different power groups: the owners of the North-Eastern banks, the top-ranking military, and the Southern oil producers and distributors control the American government. The female artist doesn't know who her father is. Three months before she was born, her father had abandoned her mother and, according to her mother, had never tried to see her again or her daughter because he's a robot. She knows her father's name because a good friend of hers traced him. He is the secret head of the North-Eastern power coalition. Not even the American people know who he is.

As head of the North-Eastern power coalition he often uses the CIA for his own purposes. He once, through the CIA, hired the good male artist. He sent the male artist's wife on a suicide mission to Cuba. The female artist learns the good male artist's artistic status is a cover for being a hit man, that's why he's so pure.

Even though many of the New York City art patrons are also part of the North-Eastern power coalition, they're trying to do her father in because he supports Rockefeller and they want to throw their weight behind Reagan. They use the Marlborough Gallery as one of their fronts. The female artist's husband from whom she's separated used to fuck her mother. Her father, discovering them, kills his wife in a jealous rage. The lover revenges himself by marrying the daughter, cutting her off from her father. Now the husband loves her because he's part of the North-Eastern Reagan group and wants to use her to do her father in.

The female artist still thinks art is the only purity. The North-Eastern art patron group videotapes and even stage-manages every bedroom and intimate scene they can for info and blackmail purposes. The porn tapes they have no (more) use for they sell as high art. One very famous artist in New York City is very fond of privately commissioning and buying these snuff films. The female artist learns her father murdered her mother. While she's still confused, the art patrons get her even dopier then show her videotapes of the good male artist fucking every female in sight, for the good male artist sticks his cock into anything eight-and-a-half inches (the length of his cock) or less away from him. Since the female artist doesn't know who or what to believe anymore, art is nothing, she, throwing herself into her husband's arms, tells him everything. She doesn't know he's the main villain against her father.

Any action no matter how off-the-wall—this explains punk—breaks through deadness. When the good male artist overhears her telling her husband everything, even though he doesn't trust her, he suspects the politicians are trying to do them both in.

In New York City, when the 14th precinct is busting up 42nd Street, there's a special court called the obscenity court. The Mafia and this one Jewish guy who's their friend own the sex shows and shops which line 42nd Street. The shows and shops pay the D.A.'s office their monthly alimony. The D.A.'s office—no dumb cop can bust on his own—orders the local cops to break up a store only when the D.A.'s office

Pages 84 to 92 are not shown in this preview.

Kathy Acker, Great Expectations

But once the money ran out, Global Rivers Alliance's self-promotion migrated online, and to his sorrow, every single person who toyed with the idea of wiring two dollars to George first felt compelled to debate the merits of Wasserkraft Nein Danke with him. Most were themselves running tiny organizations that had arisen by spontaneous generation or mitosis. No one had supporters. Stephen spent hours writing closely argued defenses of himself and his aims. Each one unique, because you can't copy anything anymore without getting caught. Rushed, because anyone who didn't get an answer within fourteen hours would write again with more **questions**.

Nell Zink, The Wallcreeper

If you could live your life again, would you choose the same path?
What is the hardest thing that you practice?
How to practice joyfully with physical limitations?

*Chan Niem Hy, The Art of Suffering Retreat—**Question** and Answer Session*

The obvious way was to fabricate some sort of reply to the advertisement purporting to come from Purcell—a telegram, for instance, from France or Belgium, or even from some place in the Eastern Counties. The former was hardly possible, however. He could not afford the time or expense of a journey abroad, and, moreover, his absence from England would be known, and its coincidence with the arrival of the telegram might easily be noticed. Coincidences of that kind were much better avoided.

On reflection, the telegram did not commend itself. Penfield would naturally ask himself: "Why a telegram when a letter would have been equally safe and so much more efficient?" For both would reveal, approximately, the whereabouts of the sender. No, a telegram would not answer the purpose. It would not be quite safe, for telegrams, like typewritten letters, are always open to suspicion as to their genuineness. Such suspicions may lead to inquiries at the telegraph office. On the other hand, a letter, if it could be properly managed, would have quite the contrary effect. It would be accepted as convincing evidence, not only of the existence of the writer, but of his whereabouts at the time of writing—if only it could be properly managed. But could it be?

He struck a match and lit his pipe—to little purpose, for it went out and was forgotten in the course of a minute. Could he produce a letter from Purcell—a practicable letter which would pass without suspicion the scrutiny, not only of Penfield himself, who was familiar with Purcell's handwriting, but also of Maggie, to whom it would almost certainly be shown? It was a serious **question**, and he gave it very serious consideration, balancing the chances of detection against the chances of success, and especially dwelling upon the improbability of any **question** arising as to its authenticity.

    R. Austin Freeman, The Shadow of the Wolf (Dr. Thorndyke Mysteries)

Eventually he tried one of those services that limit your communication to a hundred and something characters, and it saved him. He began pouring his energy into aperçus and bon mots. That was better. His task now was to strike a jaunty pose from which to launch scathing witticisms about the energy industry. Instead of preaching to the converted, he would sit on the couch with them watching the news and make snide remarks. But they still wanted clever new aphorisms every day.

    Nell Zink, The Wallcreeper

The **queſtion** itſelf, as ſtated in the title, appears to me to be no **queſtion** at all. No mortal, I will anſwer for it, ever aſſerted, that the freeholders of Middleſex forfeited their right, (I ſuppoſe it is meant their right of voting) by voting for Mr. Wilkes. It has been ſaid, that they threw away their votes in that inſtance that they exerciſed their right in ſupport of a perſon incapable of receiving any benefit from it, and that they might juſt as well have remained quiet at their reſpective homes, as have given themſelves the trouble of an unmeaning and fruitleſs journey to Brentford. The **queſtion** itſelf therefore is, to ſay the beſt of it, improperly and equivocally ſtated, and in a manner that tends to miſlead.

    *Nathaniel Forſter, An Anſwer to a Pamphlet Entitled, "The **Queſtion** Stated, Whether the Freeholders of Middleſex Forfeited Their Right by Voting for Mr. Wilkes at the Laſt Election? In a Letter From a Member of Parliament to One of His Conſtituents."*

"Yes, I do, so what?"

"Well, you didn't tell me. We're telling each other everything, on the sofa, and you didn't tell me this."

"You didn't tell me you used to sleep with Andreas Wolf!"

"Andreas is a public person. I have to be careful. And that's many years ago now."

"You talk about him like you'd do it again in a heartbeat."

"Pip, please," Annagret said, seizing her hands. "Let's not fight. I didn't know you had feelings for Stephen. I'm sorry."

But the wound the word *weak* had inflicted was hurting Pip more now, not less, and she was aghast to realize how much personal data she'd already surrendered to a woman so confident of her beauty that she could fill her face with metal and chop her hair (so it looked) with lawn clippers. Pip, who had no grounds for such confidence, snatched her hands away and stood up and noisily dropped her cereal bowl in the sink. "I'm going upstairs now—"

"No, we still have six **questions**—"

"Because I'm obviously not going to South America, and I don't trust you one bit, not the tiniest bit, and so why don't you and your masturbating boyfriend go down to

L.A. and squat in somebody else's house and give your **questionnaire** to somebody who's into somebody stronger than Stephen. I don't want you in our house anymore, and neither does anybody else. If you had any respect for me, you would have seen I didn't even want to be here now."

"Pip, please, wait, I'm really, really sorry." Annagret did seem genuinely distressed. "We don't have to do any more **questions**—"

"I thought it was a form we had to follow. Had to, had to. God, I'm stupid."

Jonathan Franzen, Purity

In truth, it's you who will do the heavy lifting with that one. But you can do that heavy lifting with one hand tied behind your back. All that's required is that you ask a **question** and then answer it as good as you can.

There are no wrong answers. If you answer the **question**, that's the right answer—because we suspect you're too bright to fool yourself. We believe that because here you are, voluntarily, at the edge of an abyss that has no bottom. It's no place for pretenders.

Everyone knows that.

I, personally, love the population of the planet. Hardly anybody is doing the wrong thing intentionally. But that same hardly anybody isn't really sure that they're doing the right thing.

Thank Julie and Michell for putting an end to that sad reality. As a team, they're going to put the right **questions** in front of you. As the key member of that team, you're going to put the right answers up in your brain.

*Julie Edmonds and Michell Smith, The Six **Questions**: That You Better Get Right, The Answers Are the Keys to Your Success*

I sensed my tormentor closing on me just before I heard him half shout, half yodel my name. Then he called again. 'Joe! Joe!' I realised he was sobbing. 'It was you. You started this, you made this happen. You're playing games with me, all the time, and you're pretending . . .' He couldn't finish. I picked up speed again, and I was almost running when I crossed the next street. His crying wavered with each jarring footfall. I was disgusted and frightened. I reached the other side and looked back. He had followed me and now he was trapped in the centre of the road, waiting for a gap in the traffic. There was just a chance he could have fallen forwards under a passing set of wheels, and I wanted it, the desire was cool and intense, and I wasn't surprised at myself, or ashamed. When he saw my face turned towards him at last he shouted a series of **questions**. 'When are you going to leave me alone? You've got me. I can't do anything. Why don't you admit what you're doing? Why do you keep pretending that you don't know what I'm talking about? And then the signals Joe. Why d'you keep on?'

Still trapped in the centre, his figure and his words obliterated at irregular intervals by the passing traffic, he raised his voice to such a hoarse screaming that I couldn't look away. I should have been running on, for this was the perfect moment to lose him. But his rage was compelling and I was forced to look on, amazed, although I never quite lost faith in the redeeming possibility of a bus crushing him as he stood there, twenty-five feet away, pleading as he damned me.

He uttered his words at a screech, on a repetitive rising note, as though a forlorn zoo bird had become approximately human. 'What do you want? You love me and you want to destroy me. You pretend it's not happening. Nothing happening! You fuck! You're playing . . . torturing me . . . giving me all your fucking little secret signals to keep me coming towards you. I know what you want, you fuck. You fuck! You think I don't? You want to take me away from . . .' I lost his words to a house-sized removal truck. '. . . and you think you can take me away from him. But you'll come to me. In the end. You'll come to him too because you'll have to. You fuck, you'll beg for mercy, you'll crawl on your stomach . . .'

Ian McEwan, Enduring Love

Why do people get so angry sometimes and their hearts filled with anger?
Why do people have to suffer?
What do you have to do to have a calm mind?

*Chan Niem Hy, The Art of Suffering Retreat—**Question** and Answer Session*

The irony perhaps is that what's mysterious to them is even more mysterious to you. Yet even as you try and inevitably fail to answer their **questions** you are probably telling them more, in your perplexity and frustration, or your wryness and charm, than you ever could have by explaining your book.

*Tim Parks, Stupid **Questions** (The New York Review of Books)*

Bah, let's turn the black eye. And the starching begin at last, of this old clout so patiently pawed in vain, as limp and drooping still as the first day. But it is solely a **question** of voices: no other image is appropriate. Let it go through me at last: the right one, the last one. (His who has none, by his own confession.)

Do they think they'll lull me, with all this hemming and hawing? What can it matter to me, that I succeed or fail? The undertaking is none of mine. If they want me to succeed I'll fail (and vice versa), so as not to be rid of my tormentors.

Is there a single word of mine in all I say? No, I have no voice (in this matter I have none).

Samuel Beckett, The Unnamable

He knows he'd have fired him, but he doesn't dare say it. Instead, he dodges the **question** by asking her what she thinks her father would do. She mulls it over. Why are you interested in my father? There's something intriguing about him, he says. She smiles. But who is my father? she wonders as he watches her expectantly. My father is someone whose business dealings have made him very rich in a very short space of time, someone who never takes time off, except for a few days here and there during the course of a year. But she has no idea what he does with his time, what his line of work is. No one does. Like her, he wanted to be a writer when he was younger, but he didn't have the conviction, the perseverance necessary to become one in the end. On the other hand, he shows enormous dedication when it comes to reading that great swan song of nineteenth-century fiction, a book written by a novelist and cartographer of memory who turned jealousy into an aesthetic of stolen time.

A. G. Porta, No World Concerto

So most of the pieces in this book are about fiction and its associated forms: the narrative poem, the essay, the translation. How it works and why it works and when it doesn't. We are, in our deepest selves, narrative animals; also seekers of answers. The best fiction rarely provides answers; but it does formulate the **questions** exceptionally well.

Julian Barnes, Through the Window: Seventeen Essays (and one short story)

Why ask such **questions** at all after Socrates
beguiled us out of answers and set us on
the inexhaustible path . . . dialectics?

Don't you think I haven't wondered if I haven't
strayed from my true path as I find myself
tracking the trajectory of such non-exemplary lives?

You're thinking it's a trick, and will not answer,
but before you judge my dissolute subject—
who like the money but thought all the attention

was a joke because "a singer is nothing"—
as a derelict choice, consider how philosophy,
while striving to become more concrete

continues to recoil before the problem of other minds.
And it is said that Monsieur Sartre turned paler
than his martini, when Raymond Aron

challenged the Husserlians, at the Bec de Gaz
in Montparnasse, to make philosophy
out of a cocktail glass.

> *Mark Rudman, The Secretary of Liquor (John F. Kennedy's*
> *Informal Appointment of Dean Martin to His Cabinet)*

"I made a great study of theology at one time," said Mr. Brooke, as if to explain the insight just manifested. "I know something of all schools. I knew Wilberforce in his best days. Do you know Wilberforce?"

Mr. Casaubon said, "No."

"Well, Wilberforce was perhaps not enough of a thinker; but if I went into Parliament, as I have been asked to do, I should sit on the independent bench, as Wilberforce did, and work at philanthropy."

Mr. Casaubon bowed, and observed that it was a wide field.

"Yes," said Mr. Brooke, with an easy smile, "but I have documents. I began a long while ago to collect documents. They want arranging, but when a **question** has struck me, I have written to somebody and got an answer. I have documents at my back. But now, how do you arrange your documents?"

"In pigeon-holes partly," said Mr. Casaubon, with rather a startled air of effort.

"Ah, pigeon-holes will not do. I have tried pigeon-holes, but everything gets mixed in pigeon-holes: I never know whether a paper is in A or Z."

> *George Eliot, Middlemarch: A Study of Provincial Life*

36.1 The Problem and Our Results

The problem is: what is the space complexity of the word problem for the free group on two letters? This is not how we first heard the problem, but it is equivalent to what we were asked. The free group on two letters "a" and "b" is the group where the only relationships are:

$$aa^{-1} = a^{-1}a = bb^{-1} = b^{-1}b = 1.$$

It is called the free group since these are the minimal relations that can hold in any group. As usual the *word problem* is to determine given any word over a, a^{-1}, b, b^{-1} whether or not it equals 1. For the rest of the chapter, when we say word problem, we mean "the word problem for the free group on two letters."

Zeke and I proved [101]:

Theorem 36.1. *The word problem is in L.*

Actually we proved more:

> Theorem 36.2. *A probabilistic log-space machine with a one-way read only input tape can solve the word problem with error at most ε, for any $\varepsilon > 0$.*

There is a simple linear time algorithm for the word problem. The algorithm uses a pushdown store, which is initially empty. The algorithm processes each input symbol x as follows: If the top of the pushdown is y and $xy = 1$, then pop off the top of the pushdown; if not, then push x onto the pushdown. Then, go to the next input symbol. When there are no more input symbols accept only if the pushdown is empty. The algorithm clearly runs in linear time, and it is not hard to show it is correct.

This algorithm uses linear space: a string that starts with many a's will, for example, require the pushdown to hold many symbols. Thus, the goal is to find a different algorithm that avoids using so much space.

In the next two sections I will explain the "curious history" of the **question**: who I "think" first asked the **question**, and why they may have asked the **question**. Then, I will explain how we solved the problem and proved our theorem. You can skip the next two sections and get right to the proof method. No history. No background. But, I hope that you find the history and motivation interesting. Your choice.

> Richard J. Lipton, The P=NP **Question** and Gödel's Lost Letter

The Glagolitic alphabet begins with the symbol: "Az."

"Az" is a symbol that stands for the letter "A," the number one and the first person singular—"I."

"Az" is a symbol, a number, a letter, as well as a **question**: *Who am I?*

"Az" is the beginning of an ambitious alphabet that requires not only writing, but also **questioning**. It is eternal, persistent and stubborn, and always equally vigorous. Is it not natural, then, that precisely because of the way the first letter of the Glagolitic alphabet was conceived, an interest was sparked for its creator? Are you not intrigued by the creator of these new letters, of which the first poses the **question**:

Who am I?

> Jasna Horvat, AZ: *Exploring the Ancient Croatian Glagolitic Script*

Now, all relevant parties agree that everything *depends* on God. Suppose something existed—call it z—which was *not* caused by God. If z had no cause at all it certainly wouldn't depend on God, so that possibility may be rejected. So suppose z is caused by something else, y. Now y itself is either caused by God or not; if y is caused by God, and then causes z, then God would be the mediate cause of z. If y is not caused by God then it must be caused by something else, x—which in turn is either caused by God or not, and so on. But this chain cannot go back to infinity, for we'd then have a whole series of beings, one causing the next, which did not at all depend on God, which cannot be; so the chain must at some point have an origin in God. If so, then God is at least the mediate cause of every subsequent member; that is, of everything that exists.

Andrew Pessin, *The God* **Question:** *What Famous Thinkers From Plato to Dawkins Have Said About the Divine*

My suggestion is to replace a channel by an adversary that has limited resources. Thus, make the channel somewhere between a dumb channel and a genius channel; somewhere between a channel that is just random and a channel that is all-powerful.

Let's do this by assuming that the channel is a random polynomial time adversary. Thus, Alice and Bob need only design an error-correcting code that works against a polynomial time adversary.

The key additional assumption, not too surprising, is that we will also assume that Alice and Bob can rely on the existence of a common random coin. Essentially, we are assuming that there is a pseudo-random number generator available to Alice and Bob that passes polynomial time tests.

In this model it is not hard to show the following:

Theorem 28.1. *Suppose that Alice and Bob have a code that works at a given rate for a dumb channel. Then, there is a code that works at the same rate for any reasonable channel, and further has the same encoding and decoding cost plus at most an additional polynomial time cost.*

The additional time depends on the actual pseudo-random number generator that is used; the additional cost can be near linear time.

The method is really simple. Alice operates as follows:

1. Alice creates X = E(M) using the simple encoder;
2. Then she selects a random permutation and a random pattern p. Let

$$Y = \pi(X) \oplus p.$$

3. Alice sends Y to Bob.

Then, Bob operates as follows:

1. Bob receives Y'. He computes $\pi^{-1}(Y' \oplus p)$.
2. Then, he uses the decoder D to retrieve the message as $D(Z)$.

The point is that from the channel's point of view there is nothing better to do than to just pick random bits to flip. For assume the channel adds the noise N to the encoded message. Then, Bob sees $Y' = Y \oplus N$, and after he transforms it he has

$$Z = \pi^{-1}(Y' \oplus p) = \pi^{-1}(Y \oplus N \oplus p),$$

which is equal to

$$\pi^{-1}(Y \oplus p) \oplus \pi^{-1}(N) = X \oplus N',$$

where $N' = \pi^{-1}(N)$ Thus, since is a "random" permutation, Bob can correctly decode and finally get M.

Richard J. Lipton, *The P=NP* **Question** *and Gödel's Lost Letter*

This theory was considered valid by George of Slavonia (Georgius de Sclavonia), a Croatian theologian of the XV Century.

George's knowledge of the Glagolitic alphabet is evident in the skill with which he interpreted its hidden meanings. Within the first nine letters of the Glagolitic alphabet George unraveled Constantine of Thessalonica's hidden message and answered the **question** posed by the first letter: *Who am I?*

> *I, a Christian who knows the letters,*
> *say that it is good to live honorably in this world.*

Constantine's alphabet contains other secret messages. Nevertheless, the first nine letters can serve as a clear guideline when we find ourselves at a loss of answers to the **question** *who am I*. This manuscript follows in the footsteps of Constantine's letters.

It is directed at those who are rested.

Also, it has been written for those who are persistent enough. "Az" addresses the readers who are asking themselves: *Who am I?*

Always.

Forever.

Jasna Horvat, AZ: Exploring the Ancient Croatian Glagolitic Script

"Various documents?" asked K. "Yes, that's right," said the businessman. "That's very important for me," said K., "in my case he's still working on the first set of documents. He still hasn't done anything. I see now that he's been neglecting me quite disgracefully." "There can be lots of good reasons why the first documents still aren't ready," said the businessman, "and anyway, it turned out later on that the ones he submitted for me were entirely worthless. I even read one of them myself, one of the officials at the court was very helpful. It was very learned, but it didn't actually say anything. Most of all, there was lots of Latin, which I can't understand, then pages and pages of general appeals to the court, then lots of flattery for particular officials, they weren't named, these officials, but anyone familiar with the court must have been able to guess who they were, then there was self-praise by the lawyer where he humiliated himself to the court in a way that was downright dog-like, and then endless investigations of cases from the past which were supposed to be similar to mine. Although, as far as I was able to follow them, these investigations had been carried out very carefully. Now, I don't mean to criticise the lawyer's work with all of this, and the document I read was only one of many, but even so, and this is something I will say, at that time I couldn't see any progress in my trial at all." "And what sort of progress had you been hoping for?" asked K. "That's a very sensible **question**," said the businessman with a smile, "it's only very rare that you see any progress in these proceedings at all. But I didn't know that then. I'm a businessman, much more in those days than now, I wanted to see some tangible progress, it should have all been moving to some conclusion or at least should have been moving on in some way according to the rules. Instead of which there were just more hearings, and most of them went through the same things anyway; I had all the answers off pat like in a church service; there were messengers from the court coming to me at work several times a week, or they came to me at home or anywhere else they could find me; and that was very disturbing of course (but at least now things are better in that respect, it's much less disturbing when they contact you by telephone), and rumours about my trial even started to spread among some of the people I do business with, and especially my relations, so I was being made to suffer in many different ways but there was still not the slightest sign that even the first hearing would take place soon. So I went to the lawyer and complained about it. He explained it all to me at length, but refused to do anything I asked for, no-one has any influence on the way the trial proceeds, he said, to try and insist on it in any of the documents submitted—like I was asking—was simply unheard of and would do harm to both him and me.

Franz Kafka, The Trial

Therefore reading was an activity that could never be completed. Rabbi Levi Yitzhak of Berdichev, one of the great eighteenth-century Hasidic masters, was asked why the first page of each of the treatises in the Babylonian Talmud was missing, so that the reader was forced to begin on page two. "Because however many pages the studious man reads," the rabbi answered, "he must never forget that he has not yet reached the very first page."

Alberto Manguel, A History of Reading

"I'll try. But you know, it's not easy to be your friend."

"It isn't? Why?"

"Oh, I'm such a mite of a thing and you're so gorgeous. You always know what you're doing. You're so sure of yourself you could crush me. You make me feel like I'm nothing, I know you don't mean it."

"No one loves me, I lead this horrible life. Don't think I'm someone I'm not. I'm like a hermit a nothing, I think I'm one of the true innocents."

"You not being hermetic with me. You're open and friendly!" Rosa, the pupil in the Nuns' House says.

"How can I help it, sweetie? You fascinate me."

"Me?" Rosa half-**questions** and, half-teasing, pretends to **question**. "It's too bad Peter doesn't feel it."

Kathy Acker, Great Expectations

p. 489–13

The word fanzine is set off with quotation marks to emphasize it's often a peculiar or strange little publication. So the answer indicating the quotation marks are used to set off something special is the best answer choice.

B

p. 551–15

In this paragraph the author talks about reading the book <u>Little Women</u> before deciding to take it home. The reason for that is, as she states, she learned from experience that titles "weren't everything." This indicates that book titles aren't always what the book is about and can be "misleading." Actually she says books can be dull if you aren't careful about choosing, but she didn't say anything about them being duller at the library. She did say that you can tell something by reading the first few paragraphs, but she didn't say anything about them being very dull in first few paragraphs. She is not comparing novels and nonfiction work. You could infer that books might not be as interesting as their titles but that would be a bit of a stretch especially since we have a clear answer choice might D.

D

p. 551–16

The word "convey" means to transport or transfer so she's trying to explain or show

how the unexpected pleasure she got from the book has a strong impact. We get the idea that this is a pleasure in the following paragraph that starts in line 70 because she indicates that she read little else. She read and read and read. She wasn't illustrating the suddenness of her decision, and there is no reference to a child's misconceptions although the she did not expect the book to be so good. She certainly wasn't being critical or describing a sense of history.

A

p. 552–18

The word "captivating" means you are captured, enthralled, or quite taken with something, and that's clearly what the author is as she read and read and read. She didn't find it bewildering or strange, unremarkable or uninteresting, hilarious or very funny, and not actually profound which means deeply meaningful. The writing may have been profound but the author's description is talking about how much she was taken with the book.

E

*Henry Davis, Explanations for the Official SAT Study Guide **Questions**: Detailed Explanations for the Answers for Every **Question***

"Is that the book?" she said. "Open it, and see."

I took the book from her.

"It is tremendously interesting," she went on. "I've read it twice over—I have. Mind you, I believe he did it, after all."

Did it? Did what? What was she talking about? I tried to put the **question** to her. I struggled—quite vainly—to say only these words: "What are you talking about?"

She seemed to lose all patience with me. She snatched the book out of my hand, and opened it before me on the table by which we were standing side by side.

"I declare, you're as helpless as a baby!" she said, contemptuously. "There! *Is* that the book?"

Wilkie Collins, The Law and the Lady

My lords, therefore, although we cannot answer your lordships **question** distinctly in the affirmative or the negative, for the reason I have given, namely, the want of an established practice referring to such a **question** by counsel; yet as we are all of opinion, that the witness cannot properly be asked on cross-examination whether he has written such a thing (the proper course being to put the writing into his hands, and ask him whether it be his writing); considering the **question** proposed to us by your lordships with reference to that principle of law which requires the writing itself to be produced, and with reference to the course that ordinarily takes place on **questions** relating to contracts or agreements; we each of us think, that if such a **question** were propounded before us at Nisi Prius and objected to, we should direct the counsel to separate the **question** into its parts.

My lords, I find I have not expressed myself with the clearness I had wished, as to dividing the **question** into parts, I beg therefore to inform the House, that by dividing the **question** into parts, I mean that the counsel would be directed to ask whether the representation had been made in writing or by words. If he should ask whether it had been made in writing, the counsel on the other side would object to the **question**; if he should ask whether it had been made by words, that is, whether the witness had said so or so, the counsel would undoubtedly have a right to put that **question**, and probably no objection would be made to it.

The Counsel were called in, and were informed that if, on cross-examination, they inquired of a witness whether he had made representations of any particular nature, stating the nature of those representations, they should, in their inquiries, ask the witness first, "Whether he made the representations by parol, or in writing."

Mr. Brougham inquired, whether he was to understand, before he had asked, whether the witness made any representations, he was to ask whether it was in writing.

The Counsel was informed, that he might put the **question** referring, in the mode of putting it, to a representation by parole; or that where a **question** of that kind was put, the counsel on the other side was justified by the practice in breaking in upon the course of the cross-examination, so far as to put the **question**, whether the declaration, if made, was by parol or in writing.

Earl *Grey* observed, that if counsel went to particulars, it must first be ascertained whether the representation had been parole or written. Might not a general **question** be put as to the fact of any representation whatever having been made, without going into any details, until it should be understood from the answer to that **question** how the matter stood?

The Earl of *Liverpool* had no objection to such a general **question**; but he had understood the learned judges to state, that the **question**, as submitted to them, could not be asked generally, but must be divided into two; that it must be first asked, whether any representation had been made in writing? and that, if an answer were given in the affirmative, then the inquiry must cease; but that, if the answer was in the negative, the witness might then be asked if he had made any parole representation? and, if he answered in the affirmative, that the particulars of such parole representation might be inquired into.

Earl *Grey* observed, that the witnesses had been over and over again asked if any promises had been made to them? To such **questions** no objection had been made, until it was ascertained whether those promises had been made in writing or not. It appeared to him that the present **question** came within the principle on which the **questions** respecting supposed promises proceeded; and that a general **question** might be put, in the first instance, avoiding details.

Lord *Erskine* remarked, that a counsel had a right to ask a witness whether any promise had been made to him. If the answer were in the affirmative, and if the counsel were about to inquire into the particulars of that promise, the counsel on the opposite side might interfere and inquire whether or not the promise was in writing; in which case no further **question** could be put about it. Such appeared to him to be the principle which should be observed with reference to the **question** under their lordships' consideration.

T. C. Hansard, Parliamentary Debates: Official Report of the Session of the Parliament of the United Kingdom of Great Britain and Ireland, June 27–September 7, 1820

If you watched the presidential debates, you may have come to the conclusion that answering **questions** is optional. If you don't want to provide an answer, simply insert your own topic and carry on.

*Stephanie Vozza, How to Successfully Respond to a **Question** You Really Don't Want to Answer (Fast Company)*

Here I shall momentarily abandon the **question** of style and turn my attention in particular to those fashionable clichés which support the idiotic abandonment of **questions** of technique that leads me to pity, rather than to admire, the present generation. We know that the nature of genius is to provide idiots with ideas twenty years later. While it would be unfair to hold genius accountable for this, it is interesting to take the matter into account. These ideas little by little became axiomatic, or thematic, quite different from their original intent. They became idiocies. Fashion then took possession of them. Tyranically. It is instructive—I write this word for the first time in my life—to note the kind of partial success of certain minds, to show the inevitably humorous and fruitful relationship between the part of their thought that is swallowed up by apathy and the part that knows the great fires of the proverb-making machines, to watch the flower of idiocy, whose roots burrow into the inspired bedrock of first-class minds, blossom.

Louis Aragon, *Treatise on Style*

"Is that a publicly acknowledged position?" "No," was the painter's curt reply, as if the **question** prevented him saying any more. But K. wanted him to continue speaking and said, "Well, positions like that, that aren't officially acknowledged, can often have more influence than those that are." "And that's how it is with me," said the painter, and nodded with a frown. "I was talking about your case with the manufacturer yesterday, and he asked me if I wouldn't like to help you, and I answered: 'He can come and see me if he likes', and now I'm pleased to see you here so soon. This business seems to be quite important to you, and, of course, I'm not surprised at that. Would you not like to take your coat off now?" K. had intended to stay for only a very short time, but the painter's invitation was nonetheless very welcome. The air in the room had slowly become quite oppressive for him, he had several times looked in amazement at a small, iron stove in the corner that certainly could not have been lit, the heat of the room was inexplicable. As he took off his winter overcoat and also unbuttoned his frock coat the painter said to him in apology, "I must have warmth. And it is very cosy here, isn't it. This room's very good in that respect." K. made no reply, but it was actually not the heat that made him uncomfortable but, much more, the stuffiness, the air that almost made it more difficult to breathe, the room had probably not been ventilated for a long time. The unpleasantness of this was made all the stronger for K. when the painter invited him to sit on the bed while he himself sat down on the only chair in the room in front of the easel. The painter even seemed to misunderstand why K. remained at the edge of the bed and urged K. to make himself comfortable, and as he hesitated he went over to the bed himself and pressed K. deep down into the bedclothes and pillows. Then he went back to his seat and at last he asked his first objective **question**, which made K. forget everything else. "You're innocent, are you?" he asked. "Yes," said K. He felt a simple joy at answering this **question**, especially as the answer was given to a private individual and therefore would have no consequences. Up till then no-one had asked him this **question** so openly. To make the most of his pleasure he added, "I am totally innocent." "So," said the painter, and he lowered his head and seemed to be thinking. Suddenly he raised his head again and said, "Well if you're innocent it's all very simple." K. began to scowl, this supposed trustee of the court was talking like an ignorant child. "My being innocent does not make things simple," said K. Despite everything, he couldn't help smiling and slowly shook his head. "There are many fine details in which the court gets lost, but in the end it reaches into some place where originally there was nothing and pulls enormous guilt out of it."

"Yeah, yeah, sure," said the painter, as if K. had been disturbing his train of thought for no reason. "But you are innocent, aren't you?" "Well of course I am," said K. "That's the main thing," said the painter. There was no counter-argument that could influence him, but although he had made up his mind it was not clear whether he was talking this way because of conviction or indifference. K., then, wanted to find out and said therefore, "I'm sure you're more familiar with the court than I am, I know hardly more about it than what I've heard, and that's been from many very different people. But they were all agreed on one thing, and that was that when ill thought-out accusations are made they are not ignored, and that once the court has made an accusation it is convinced of the guilt of the defendant and it's very hard to make it think otherwise." "Very hard?" the painter asked, throwing one hand up in the air. "It's impossible to make it think otherwise. If I painted all the judges next to each other here on canvas, and you were trying to defend yourself in front of it, you'd have more success with them than you'd ever have with the real court." "Yes," said K. to himself, forgetting that he had only gone there to investigate the painter.

One of the girls behind the door started up again, and asked, "Titorelli, is he going to go soon?" "Quiet!" shouted the painter at the door, "Can't you see I'm talking with the gentleman?" But this was not enough to satisfy the girl and she asked, "You going to paint his picture?"

Franz Kafka, The Trial

p. 394–16

This **question** focuses on the similarities of both passages. Phrases from passage 1 such as "world's most famous portrait" and "famous smile" and phrases from passage 2 such as the "best-known painting," "speaks to us all," "knows the name," and "creating best-known painting" all refer to answer C the "popular appeal."

C

p. 394–17

The "phenomena" described in passage 1 is its connection with Napoleon who obviously treasured the painting, therefore creating the "circumstances" that attracted the public's notice.

A

p. 395–18

In passage 1 phrases such as describing the woman as "nobody special" and contrasting this with "set the standard" imply answer E "ordinary" contrasted with "aesthetic."

E

Henry Davis, Explanations for the Official SAT Study Guide **Questions**: *Detailed Explanations for the Answers for Every* **Question**

Looming above all other issues is what physicist Paolo Di Lazzaro calls "the **question** of **questions**": how the image was produced, regardless of its age. Every scientific attempt to replicate it in a lab has failed. Its precise hue is highly unusual, and the color's penetration into the fabric is extremely thin, less than 0.7 micrometers (0.000028 inches), one-thirtieth the diameter of an individual fiber in a single 200-fiber linen thread.

Di Lazzaro and his colleagues at Italy's National Agency for New Technologies, Energy and Sustainable Economic Development (ENEA) conducted five years of experiments, using state-of-the-art excimer lasers to train short bursts of ultraviolet light on raw linen, in an effort to simulate the image's coloration. The ENEA team, which published its findings in 2011, came tantalizingly close to approximating the image's distinctive hue on a few square centimeters of fabric. But they were unable to match all the physical and chemical characteristics of the shroud image. Nor could they reproduce a whole human figure.

> Frank Viviano, *Why Shroud of Turin's Secrets Continue to Elude Science (National Geographic)*

"What is it?" Doctor Percival asked.

"Browning's poems. I don't see anything off-color about them."

All the same he had to admit that the little book didn't go with Aldermaston and the tote and *Playboy*, the dreary office routine and the Zaire bag; does one always discover clues to the complexity even of the most simple life if one rummages enough after death? Of course, Davis might have kept the book from filial piety, but it was obvious that he had read it. Hadn't he quoted Browning the last time Castle saw him alive?

"If you look, sir, there are passages marked," Piper said to Doctor Percival. "You know more about book codes than I do. I thought I ought to draw attention."

"What do you think, Castle?"

"Yes, there *are* marks." He turned the pages. The book belonged to his father and of course they might be his father's marks—except that the ink looks too fresh: he puts a 'c' against them."

"Significant?"

Castle had never taken Davis seriously, not his drinking, not his gambling, not even his hopeless love for Cynthia, but a dead body could not be so easily ignored. For the first time he felt real curiosity about Davis. Death had made Davis important. Death gave Davis a kind of stature. The dead are perhaps wiser than we are. He turned the pages of the little book like a member of the Browning Society keen on interpreting a text.

Daintry dragged himself away from the bedroom door. He said, "There isn't anything, is there . . . in those marks?"

"Anything what?"

"Significant." He repeated Percival's **question**.

"Significant; I suppose there might be. Of a whole state of mind."

"What do you mean?" Percival asked. "Do you really think . . . ?" He sounded hopeful, as if he positively wished that the man who was dead next door might have represented a security risk and, well, in a way he had, Castle thought. Love and hate are both dangerous, as he had warned Boris. A scene came to his mind: a bedroom on Lourenço Marques, the hum of an air conditioner, and Sarah's voice on the telephone, "Here I am," and then the sudden sense of great joy. His love of Sarah had led him to Carson, and Carson finally to Boris. A man in love walks through the world like an anarchist, carrying a time bomb.

"You really mean there is some evidence . . . ?" Doctor Percival went on. "You've been trained in codes. I haven't."

"Listen to this passage It's marked with a vertical line and the letter 'c.'

'Yet I will but say what mere friends say,
*   Or only a thought stronger:*
I will hold your hand but as long as all may . . .'"

"Have you any idea what 'c' stands for?" Percival asked—and again there was that note of hope which Castle found irritating. "It could mean, couldn't it, 'code,' to remind him that he had already used that particular passage? In a book code I suppose one must be careful not to use the same passage twice."

"True enough. Here's another marked passage.

'Worth how well, those dark gray eyes,
*   That hair so dark and dear, how worth,*
That a man should strive and agonize,
*   And taste a veriest hell on earth . . .'"*

"It sounds to me like poetry, sir," Piper said.

"Again a vertical line and a 'c,' Doctor Percival."

"You really think then . . . ?"

"Davis said to me once, 'I can't be serious when I'm serious.' So I suppose he had to go to Browning for words."

"And 'c'?"

Graham Greene, *The Human Factor*

p. 489–7

The answer is stated plainly in both passages. Passage 1 states are not educational in that they are "anti-educational" and Passage 2 states Comic books . . . are junk."

C

p. 473–32

To begin with, sentence 5 is a sentence fragment and must be fixed in some way. Since the passage is about certain critics' and not the audience's opinion, the pronoun "we" is inappropriate; therefore, C is the best choice because it furthers the main idea of the passage by indicating that "Clueless" did not adhere to the book.

C

p. 489–12

Lines 27 to 29 imply that children receive no benefit from reading comic books. But Passage 2 in lines 81–87 the author implies the escape-ism of comic books will "physically renew" (line 85) children to help them face the world of reality when they are often victims.

C

p. 469–3

We have a misplaced modifier here as the modifying phrase "Traveling through Yosemite" is modifying "the scenery." We need to identify correctly who is doing the traveling. Answer choices C and D have the pronoun "we" correctly placed. Answer choice C has the modifier "beautiful" placed correctly.

C

p. 469–4

Remember that good English is concise and active voiced. Clearly answer choice C "to recount" is the clearest expression of his purpose.

C

p. 551–14

The purpose of the passage is revealed by looking at what the author is describing. The author iss describing the different types of books and the topics they cover that she liked to read. Therefore she is talking about her reading interests which matches answer choice C. Be careful with the other answer choices as you have to read very carefully. She does talk about mythology books and science books but she's not contrasting the two. She does talk about why we should like to read and about the burgeoning but that's not the entirety of the passage. It's a point made in the paragraph. She does discuss the difference in the books that she liked and those her brother liked; however, again, that is part of the paragraph. She does discuss experiments but again that is part of the paragraph not the primary purpose of the passage.

C

Henry Davis, Explanations for the Official SAT Study Guide **Questions***: Detailed Explanations for the Answers for Every* **Question**

"Okay," Beth sighed from Los Angeles, as she did at the end of each day. The energy of her disappointment endowed it with something like consciousness; Ted experienced it as a third presence on the phone.

"I'm sorry," he said. A drop of poison filled his heart. He would look for Sasha tomorrow. Yet even as he made this vow, he was reaffirming a contradictory plan to visit the Museo Nazionale, home of an Orpheus and Eurydice he'd admired for years: a Roman marble relief copied from a Greek original. He had always wanted to see it.

Mercifully, Hammer, Beth's second husband, who normally had a volley of **questions** for Ted that boiled down to one very simple **question**, *Am I getting my money's worth?* (thus filling Ted with truant anxiety), either wasn't around or chose not to weigh in. After hanging up, Ted went to the minibar and dumped a vodka over ice. He brought drink and phone to the balcony and sat in a white plastic chair, looking down at the Via Partenope and the Bay of Naples. The shore was craggy, the water of **questionable** purity (though arrestingly blue), and those game Neapolitans, most of whom seemed to be fat, were disrobing on the rocks and leaping into the bay in full view of pedestrians, tourist hotels, and traffic.

Jennifer Egan, A Visit From the Goon Squad

Heartened up by this story, I began to draw upon his more comprehensive knowledge as to the ages of the pictures and as to certain of the stories connected with them, upon which I was not clear; and I likewise inquired into the causes of the decadence of the present age, in which the most refined arts had perished, and among them painting, which had not left even the faintest trace of itself behind. "Greed of money," he replied, "has brought about these unaccountable changes. In the good old times, when virtue was her own reward, the fine arts flourished, and there was the keenest rivalry among men for fear that anything which could be of benefit to future generations should remain long undiscovered. Then it was that Democritus expressed the juices of all plants and spent his whole life in experiments, in order that no curative property should lurk unknown in stone or shrub. That he might understand the movements of heaven and the stars,

Eudoxus grew old upon the summit of a lofty mountain: three times did Chrysippus purge his brain with hellebore, that his faculties might be equal to invention. Turn to the sculptors if you will; Lysippus perished from hunger while in profound meditation upon the lines of a single statue, and Myron, who almost embodied the souls of men and beasts in bronze, could not find an heir. And we, sodden with wine and women, cannot even appreciate the arts already practiced, we only criticise the past! We learn only vice, and teach it, too. What has become of logic? of astronomy? Where is the exquisite road to wisdom? Who even goes into a temple to make a vow, that he may achieve eloquence or bathe in the fountain of wisdom? And they do not pray for good health and a sound mind; before they even set foot upon the threshold of the temple, one promises a gift if only he may bury a rich relative; another, if he can but dig up a treasure, and still another, if he is permitted to amass thirty millions of sesterces in safety! The Senate itself, the exponent of all that should be right and just, is in the habit of promising a thousand pounds of gold to the capitol, and that no one may **question** the propriety of praying for money, it even decorates Jupiter himself with spoils. Do not hesitate, therefore, at expressing your surprise at the deterioration of painting, since, by all the gods and men alike, a lump of gold is held to be more beautiful than anything ever created by those crazy little Greek fellows, Apelles and Phydias!"

Petronius, The Satyricon

[Footnote 486, 487: These are the only two passages in which Leonardo alludes to the importance of antique art in the training of an artist. The **question** asked in No. 486 remains unanswered by him and it seems to me very doubtful whether the opinion stated in No. 487 is to be regarded as a reply to it. This opinion stands in the MS. in a connection—as will be explained later on—which seems to require us to limit its application to a single special case. At any rate we may suspect that when Leonardo put the **question**, he felt some hesitation as to the answer. Among his very numerous drawings I have not been able to find a single study from the antique, though a drawing in black chalk, at Windsor, of a man on horseback (Pl. LXXIII) may perhaps be a reminiscence of the statue of Marcus Aurelius at Rome. It seems to me that the drapery in a pen and ink drawing of a bust, also at Windsor, has been borrowed from an antique model (Pl. XXX). G. G. Rossi has, I believe, correctly interpreted Leonardo's feeling towards the antique in the following note on this passage in Manzi's edition, p. 501: "Sappiamo dalla storia, che i valorosi artisti Toscani dell'età dell'oro dell'arte studiarono sugli antichi marmi raccolti dal Magnifico LORENZO DE' MEDICI. Pare che il Vinci a tali monumenti non si accostasse. Quest'uomo sempre riconosce per maestra la natura, e questo principio lo stringeva alla sola imitazione dì essa"—Compare No. 10, 26–28 footnote.]

Jean Paul Richter (ed.), The Notebooks of Leonardo da Vinci

In either case, doubtless the footnote was in no way connected to the opera about Medea, even if that also now happens to be in my head.

Once, in Florence, sitting in a Land Rover with a right-hand drive and watching the piazza below Brunelleschi's dome fill up with snow, which must surely be rare, I listened to Maria Callas singing that.

I had only a few moments earlier switched vehicles, after carrying several suitcases across one of the bridges over the Arno, and so had not even noticed immediately that the new tape deck was set to the on position.

Medea was written by Luigi Cherubini, I might mention.

Basically, I do that because of Luigi Cherubini being somebody I often mix up with Vincenzo Bellini, who wrote *Norma*, which is another opera that Maria Callas frequently sang.

Although now and again I have mixed up Vincenzo Bellini with Giovanni Bellini in turn, even if Giovanni Bellini is one of the painters I have always most deeply admired.

Well, even Albrecht Dürer, whom I admire to almost the same degree, once said that Bellini was still the best painter alive.

I say still, since Dürer happened to be visiting in Venice at a time when Bellini was quite old.

On the other hand this would have been before Dürer himself became practically as mad as Piero di Cosimo, presumably. Or as Hugo van der Goes.

Well, or as Friedrich Nietzsche, for all that I was once extremely fond of one of Friedrich Nietzsche's sentences too.

As a matter of fact still another person I was once fond of a sentence by, meaning Pascal, could doubtless be added to this same list, what with refusing to sit on a chair without an additional chair at either side of him, so as not to fall into space.

In fact I now have to wonder if I did not mix up those two sentences as well, and that it was Pascal who wrote the one about wandering through an endless nothingness.

I have no explanation for my generally speaking of Pascal as Pascal, but of Friedrich Nietzsche as Friedrich Nietzsche, incidentally.

The **question** of the two dots over Dürer would appear to be basically the same as that of the two dots over Brontë, however.

In either case, that remark about Giovanni Bellini would have naturally also had to have been made before Dürer died from a fever he caught in a Dutch swamp, where he had gone to look at a stranded whale.

David Markson, Wittgenstein's Mistress

Still the **question** returns on us: How could a man occasionally of keen insight, not without keen sense of propriety, who had real Thoughts to communicate, resolve to emit them in a shape bordering so closely on the absurd? Which **question** he were wiser than the present Editor who should satisfactorily answer. Our conjecture has sometimes been, that perhaps Necessity as well as Choice was concerned in it. Seems it not conceivable that, in a Life like our Professor's, where so much bountifully given by Nature had in Practice failed and misgone, Literature also would never rightly prosper: that striving with his characteristic vehemence to paint this and the other Picture, and ever without success, he at last desperately dashes his sponge, full of all colors, against the canvas, to try whether it will paint Foam?

Thomas Carlyle, Sartor Resartus: The Life and Opinions of Herr Teufelsdröckh

Questions, questions, questions. You have many—and we are trying to answer them. Send your **questions** to EnglishForDirtyForeigners@googlemail.com and we shall respond by the power of video.

*Lee Isserow, Plectrum-**Question** 2713, 2009 (Internet Archive)*

$$* \text{ “?”}$$

Out of which a sort of swan-collage emerges

Typhus, or syphilis, caused Beethoven's deafness—
question mark.

David Markson, The Last Novel

The **question** mark is a common, handy visual representation of confusion, surprise, or just being plain weirded out. It can manifest as several **question** marks floating around the nonplussed character's head, a single such symbol hovering over the character, or pop up as the contents of a thought bubble (or a regular <u>Speech Bubble</u>, in which case it seems to represent the "huh?" sound. Compare <u>Visible Silence</u>.)

See also <u>My Name Is ???</u>, where it is used as a symbol of the unknown.

*Television Tropes & Idioms, Confused **Question** Mark*

The phone rang and a man's voice wanted to know if I were Mr. Dye. When I said yes, he said that his name was Robineaux and that Mr. Lynch had told him to wait in the lobby. I said I would be right down and when I got there, Mr. Robineaux turned out to be a tall young man with the posture of a **question** mark who had some interesting scars on his face that looked as if they had been stitched there by a sewing machine.

Ross Thomas, The Fools in Town Are on Our Side

A classic type felon, Mister Freddy McKinley Pease. Built like Ichabod Crane, the posture of a **question** mark. Your basic habitual criminal, B & E style. Came from L-Block at Lucasville, Ohio's latest quote riot-torn corrections facility unquote. Interesting guy—

Lee K. Abbott, Wet Places at Noon

A slight figure with the posture of a **question** mark, Lester looked like a cartoon in motion, hands flapping like flippers at the ends of his arms, and his brown-and-white saddle oxfords slapping flat-footedly against the ground.

Watching Lester, Max was reminded of Father Goodwin from his time at Oxford, a priest who eschewed the pulpit for the common touch, striding back and forth before his congregation until one Sunday, entirely caught up in the thrust of his narrative, he lost his footing and actually fell off the altar.

G. M. Malliet, A Fatal Winter

Line 70: The new TV

After this, in the draft (dated July 3), come a few unnumbered lines that may have been intended for some later parts of the poem. They are not actually deleted but are accompanied by a **question** mark in the margin and encircled with a wavy line encroaching upon some of the letters:

There are events, strange happenings, that strike
The mind as emblematic. They are like
Lost similes adrift without a string.
Attached to nothing. Thus that northern king . . .

Vladimir Nabokov, Pale Fire

"It—"

The telephone bell rang.

A man's voice, carefully oratorical, spoke my name with a **question** mark after it.

Dashiell Hammett, Red Harvest

Hi Guys,

Could anyone here explain how to search google for pages that has the ? sign (**question** mark) in their title tag?

I tried "intitle" and "allintitle" but google simply ignore the ? sign . . .

If its not possible, maybe there is a different trick to get that?

sam770

26th December 2012, 10:24 AM

Re: How to search Google for pages that has the ? sign (**question** mark) in their title tag?

Could anyone help?

sam770

26th December 2012, 10:24 AM

*Warrior Forum, How to Search Google for Pages That Has the ? Sign (**Question** Mark) in Their Title Tag? (Warrior Forum, The #1 Internet Marketing Forum & Marketplace)*

"Well, he didn't! When we rolled up we spot Carey right here at the front door. Place is closed for the night—just a night-light. He's got a key. We watch him unlock the door, go in, and wham! he damn near falls over this Pierre. So the feeble-minded old cluck bends down and takes the knife out of Pierre's chest and stands there in a trance lookin' at it. He's been standin' like that ever since."

"Without the knife, I hope," said the Inspector nastily; and they went in.

And found an old man among the detectives in the posture of a **question** mark leaning against an oilcloth-covered table under a poster advertising Provençal, with his toothless mouth ajar and his watery old eyes fixed on the extinct *garçon*. The extinct *garçon* was still in his monkey-suit; his right palm was upturned, as if appealing for mercy, or the usual *pourboire*.

"Carey," said Inspector Queen.

Old man Carey did not seem to hear. He was fascinated by Ellery; Ellery was on one knee, peering at Pierre's eyes.

"Carey, who killed this Frenchman?"

Carey did not reply.

"Plain case of busted gut," remarked Sergeant Velie.

"You can hardly blame him!" cried Nikki.

Ellery Queen, Calendar of Crime

In chapter 3, however, I argue that emotions nevertheless represent core relational themes, just as prevailing cognitive theories maintain. Then I take up the **question** of whether emotions form a coherent class (chapter 4). I argue that they do, rejecting influential arguments to the contrary.

Jesse J. Prinz, Gut Reactions: A Perceptual Theory of Emotion

All five of Riley's emotions are characterized by the way they look. Fear is slim and frazzled with the posture of a **question** mark; his body looks like a nerve. Anger is short, stocky, and red. He dresses like a no-frills corporate drone.

Joy, meanwhile, is bright and effervescent, with shimmering gold skin and cropped blue hair. Sadness is blue from head to toe, save her frumpy turtleneck sweater and giant glasses. She's round and meek, with a physique that suggests she would work out, if only she didn't find kettle bells so depressing.

These spot-on physical appearances serve to reinforce the personality traits of each character. In other words, one look at Sadness, and there's no way anybody's going to mistake her for Joy.

Deep Thought That Just Occurred to Shmoop: Is Joy's blue hair a . . . foreshadowing? Maybe Joy already has that touch o' sadness that's necessary for true joy to be appreciated. She just doesn't know it yet.

Shmoop, Inside Out (2015): Tools of Characterization

The latter is a problem of perception, which meant the Rookie was up against it. With the posture of a **question** mark and the muscle tone of a marshmallow, the Rookie was hardly more intimidating than a dandelion. And there was no redemption in his wide face, which was set with an opacity that seemed to filter out nonsense and take only facts into account; to the stacking crew, the Rookie's whole demeanor suspiciously resembled arrogance.

Raymond Goodwin, Sawdusted: Notes from a Post-Boom Mill

In a nutshell, I'd like Google to return pages where a **question** mark is present in the title.

My gut was to try something like:

allintitle: * "?"

However Google doesn't seem to like **question** marks in its search queries, even if they're in quotes. Any ideas?

Derek
asked Oct 7 '09 at 15:33

*Super User, How to Google a **Question** Mark?*

Take a posture of learning

The goal is to seek understanding. It can help to air and acknowledge assumptions up front, and then identify **questions** that can test those assumptions.

Thomas Both, d. d. d. d. d.—a d.school design project guide

The proposed algorithm consists of two major components, i.e., the heuristics that are applied to identify the seed examples of **FAQ questions**, answers, and noise text, and the semi-supervised learning algorithm that propagate the class labels of the seed example to other text segments based on the *Within Page Consistency* principle. The following heuristics are used to identify the seed examples:

Yi Liu, Semi-Supervised Learning With Side Information: Graph-Based Approaches

Start by writing some starter **questions**. Move away from fact-finding **questions** toward soliciting stories. You can identify themes and rearrange **questions** to create an ideal arc to the conversation. Remember this is only a rough **question** list—while interviewing follow the flow of the conversation.

Find users

The best option is to get out of the office and engage users in their own environment. Alternatively, you could bring users in to be interviewed.

It is okay to stumble

If you are new to design research, expect your first couple of interviews to be rough. Don't worry—that is normal. Just jump in, and keep practicing.

Thomas Both, d. d. d. d. d.—a d.school design project guide

1. From all the text segments that end with **question** marks, select the ones whose format repeats the most often and label them as **FAQ questions**.

2. From all the text segments between any two consecutive **FAQ questions** that are identified by the first heuristic, select the ones whose format repeats the most often and label them as **FAQ** answers.

3. If a text segment repeat itself k time in a **FAQ** page, all those occurrence of the text segment will be labeled as noise text. k is a predefined integer, and is set to 4 in our experiments. And all text segments before the first **question** are labeled as noise.

All the above heuristics can be seen as a simplified version of those proposed in previous studies that are mentioned in Section 6.2.1. These rules tend to be accurate with very small number of false positives. According to our study, these rules can achieve a precision of 96.8% in classification.

Yi Liu, Semi-Supervised Learning With Side Information: Graph-Based Approaches

"Can you tell me how much it would cost to do that? Find . . . the person, I mean."

"No," I said. "I can't tell you that. Here's how it works: You pay me by the day. I keep looking until I find whoever you're looking for, or until you tell me to quit trying."

"Well, how much is it a day, then?"

"Same as you just paid me. I cover all expenses out of that, and there's a twenty-G bonus if I turn up what you want."

"Ten thousand a week," he said, the slightest trace of a **question** mark at the end of the sentence.

"We don't take weekends off," I told him. "One week, that's fourteen. Payable in advance."

"That could run into a lot of money."

"Uh-huh."

"I'll have to think that one over."

"You know where to find me," I said.

"Well, actually, I don't. I mean, the man who I . . . spoke to, he just took my number, and you called me, remember?"

"Yes, I remember."

"So how do I . . . ? Oh. You mean, now or never, right?"

"Right."

He took a hit off his drink. "I don't walk around with that kind of cash," he said.

"Who does?"

"Best of luck with your search," I said, moving my untouched glass to the side as I started to stand up.

"Wait," he said. "I've got it."

I settled back into my seat. If we were still in that movie, I would have told him that lying was a bad way to start a relationship. If we were going to work together, I would need the truth, all the way. Down here, we play it different: "true" means you can spend it.

"Not on me," he said. "But close by. In my car. I keep an emergency stash. You never know ..."

I let my mouth twitch. Let him guess what that meant.

Andrew Vachss, Mask Market: A Burke Novel

In Chapter 5, we study the problem of cross-language information retrieval, with bilingual dictionaries as side information. Two models based on a maximum coherence principle are proposed, which can be well explained as two-way partitioning of the graph induced by side information—the dictionary.

Another application, extracting **question**-answer pairs from web **FAQs** is described in Chapter 6, where side information comes from human knowledge on the presentation regularities of web **FAQs**. The model proposed in this chapter leads to a correlated label propagation scheme over a graph built upon the text segments of web **FAQ** pages. As will be seen, properly using the side information enables the **question**-answer extraction task being performed without any human supervision, despite the wide variety of possible contents and styles in web pages.

Yi Liu, Semi-Supervised Learning With Side Information: Graph-Based Approaches

It can be overwhelming to an interviewee to have a bunch of people all lobbing in **questions** at the same time or in rapid succession. Assign roles to prevent this. If you have a large team, break into interviewing groups of two (or three).

Suggested roles:

Lead Interviewer

Leads the conversation, and maintains the connection with the interviewee.

Scribe and Back-up Interviewer

Takes copious notes and also chimes in to follow up on interesting threads missed by the lead.

These roles can rotate after each interview, for the sake of your own learning, and for the diversity of perspective.

If you are alone, it is recommended to audio record the interview, so you can focus on the conversation.

Capture:

Good notes are key

It is very important to move into synthesis with a wealth of human "data," so make sure that you take lots of notes during interviews. The lead in each interview will take very few notes—so it is important his or her partner takes very good notes with details and quotes.

Thomas Both, d. d. d. d. d.—a d.school design project guide

His work had given him the posture of a **question** mark and perpetual grease under his nails; few people would guess the type of work he did on the side.

"Let us go to your nearest greasy spoon," Wotan suggested. One always gave The Trawler a meal for his services.

"Actually, we get pretty good food here, especially meat," The Trawler responded. "It's just that there are only two styles of restaurant—chuck wagon and honky tonk. Dinah's Chuck Wagon's just up the block."

Norma Druid, A Test of Alien Alliance

What I remembered about Gregory before he called:

His eyes were blue and sparkle with a hint of I-Wouldn't-Drink-the-Kool-Aid-Around Here.

He had the posture of a **question** mark.

He wore blue jeans well and denim shirts.

He had a blurting laugh, simian manners, and dressed and spoke like a man who had cowboy dreams.

That we once made love in Clarendon Gorge on a rock as polished and curvaceous as a Henry Moore sculpture.

Joan Connor, The World Before Mirrors

Murray was obviously out of breath, and had the posture of a **question** mark. Without a word, Erica cuffed him, leading him out the back.

"Did you bring a car, Ben?" She looked at me **questioningly**. I looked around the parking lot awkwardly, remembering I ubered here. "No, Erica, I took an uber here." I sighed, waiting for the lecture.

Annaleise Clár, Agent Benjamin Ripley (Wattpad)

3. Use good technique

Make sure you are covering the basics: open-ended **questions**, asking 'why?', and digging into meaning by following up. This means staying on one thread (one topic or story) for a long period of time and not jumping around by asking wholly new **questions**.

The interviewer should not fill more than 25% of the airtime. Make sure you give people time to answer and time to consider their answers.

Thomas Both, d. d. d. d. d.—a d.school design project guide

She had the posture of a **question** mark. Her collar pin looked like a Josef Hofmann piece, two black coils on a rectangle of silver. She, austere and probably Austrian, held her jawline high in a way so proud it appeared antique. Comportment. Resignation. Dignity, assumed.

The audiences at these events were often elderly elegant Jews, people who'd fled Hitler. They seemed to all know each other. You felt the hauteur of their standards, a snobbery about the only thing that mattered in this new world—what else?—one another.

Allan Gurganus, Plays Well With Others

We are more likely, I suspect, to identify with the swan of, say, Ben Belitt, in the opening of his poem 'Swan Lake':

The swan, a stylist, born to the posture of a **question** mark

and the bishop's mitre—
balletic, Episcopal, unsentimental,
a hater of Tchaikovsky, inadvertently
settling his calm posterior like a tutu, fixing his seedy
eyeball like a lorgnette in the garbage and crumbs—
is nobody's accompanist.

Belitt's lines are restless with droll particulars, out of which a sort of swan-collage emerges, part affectionate depiction, part cartoon image. Yeats saw the things of this world differently; he was an essentialist.

Eric Linn Ormsby, Fine Incisions: Essays on Poetry and Place

While both approaches prove to be effective in **QA** text extraction from Usenet **FAQ** files, they are domain-specific since they rely heavily on the special format of Usenet **FAQs.** Although IE research have gained significant progress towards open-domain free-text tasks (for example, seminar announcement extraction [36]), the extraction is usually carried out as filling template slots. Unlike seminar announcements that have a relatively fixed set of themes and presentation patterns of **QA** pairs across different **FAQ** pages. However, *within a FAQ page,* it is often the case that consistent HTML formats are used to present **questions**, answers, and noise text. Moreover, the formats for presenting **questions**, answers, and others are often different and distinguishable. This motivates us to consider a semi-supervised learning algorithm that explicitly exploits the within page consistency.

Yi Liu, Semi-Supervised Learning With Side Information: Graph-Based Approaches

I was trying to act casual but I'd already noticed he had the posture of a **question** mark, hairy knuckles and the kindest face I'd ever seen—everything wide open, everything full moon and yearning upwards. I remember thinking these were both my favourite things about him and things I most wanted to change.

Buffy Cram, Radio Belly: Stories

This was partly because I'd had no sleep the night before, but mostly because Professor Lucas Crandall had the charisma of a rock. Crandall was quite old, with unkempt white hair, the stooped posture of a **question** mark, and eyebrows that looked as though they'd recently been in a tornado. He was rumored to have served the CIA from the very early days, and he appeared to have been shunted off to spy school because no one had the heart to fire him. He rambled in a wheezing voice that was almost impossible to hear, often losing his train of thought and then pausing for great swaths of time to remember what he'd been saying.

Stuart Gibbs, Spy School

Further techniques
Seek extreme users
Find and interview extreme users.

Watch out for . . .
Leading the witness
Many inexperienced interviewers will ask loaded **questions**, or **questions** that suggest the "right" answer. Instead, ask open-ended **questions**.

Silence is not a sign of a bad interview—it is in fact often helpful: users will typically fill the void with interesting new information.

Thomas Both, d. d. d. d. d.—a d.school design project guide

"Tell me, do you still collect pictures of animals fucking?"

The words are spoken by a slightly nerdy man with John Lennon glasses and the posture of a **question** mark. He clearly feels at home here, though the loft isn't his. The huge studio occupies part of the top floor of a downtown building filled with some of New York City's infamous sweat shops. The sewing machines next door spew forth angry whirring noises, like a cloud of irate insects preparing for attack.

Rogier van Bakel, Remembering Johnny: William Gibson on the Making of Johnny Mnemonic (Wired)

As nemeses went, Murray wasn't particularly imposing. His hair flopped over his eyes, he had the posture of a **question** mark, and he believed physical exertion was something that should be avoided at all costs. In addition, he'd never come across as particularly devious or malevolent. Instead, he behaved more like a criminal fanboy, raving about the brilliance of SPYDER's plots—or giving me respect when I figured them out. Murray had cleaned himself up since his rescue, but he still looked disheveled, wearing a stained T-shirt, torn jeans, and mismatched socks. Now he hopped back to his feet with a flourish, acting like he'd meant to crash into the foosball table all along. "How's it going, Ben?"

I did my best to look stunned. I stared at him in fake astonishment and did some Oscar-quality stammering. "What . . . ? How did . . . ? I thought you were in prison."

"I *was*—until last night. The Feds were transferring me to a new maximum-security penitentiary, but your pals here sprang me en route."

Stuart Gibbs, Evil Spy School

While you must always allow room for the spontaneous, blissful serendipity of a user-guided conversation, you should never abdicate your responsibility to prepare for interviews. Especially in following up with users (after testing, etc.), it is imperative to plan your interviews. You may not get to every **question** you prepare, but you should come in with a plan for engagement.

Thomas Both, d. d. d. d. d.—a d.school design project guide

He was a bulky balding chap whose **questions** came out tonelessly between sucks on a rooty pipe. Turvey was surprised at the number of large stiff papers the corporal had with TURVEY, THOMAS LEADBEATER already typed at the top. And now he was starting to fill out a new one in a big sloping hand, pronouncing each word as he traced it, much as if his arm were phonographic.

"Born thirteenth May nineteen-twenty-two Skookum Falls B.C. . . . white single nextofkin Mr. Leopold Turvey Skookum Falls brother. No glasses righthanded. Ussssp?"

Turvey would not have ventured to halt the flow of the voice and bulbous pen if he had not decided that the last suck of the corporal's pipe was meant to be a **question** mark.

"Lefthanded, sir . . . except for hockey."

The corporal's pen wavered and his pipe hissed mildly.

"Wut about a rifle?"

Turvey smiled ingratiatingly. "Anyway you like, sir."

Questions, questions, questions. You have many—and we are trying to answer them. Send your **questions** to EnglishForDirtyForeigners@googlemail.com and we shall respond by the power of video.

Lee Isserow, Plectrum-Question 2713, 2009 (Internet Archive)

The corporal pouted his lips at the tip of his pipe and put a curvaceous R in the corner of the big sheet. "Dont call a corporal 'sir', callum 'corporal'." The voice was almost expressionless but Turvey detected a purr and decided he had said the right thing.

"Completed grade nine Kuskanee High at sixteen wotcha chief occupation civil life?"

Turvey thought carefully. "Well. I was chokerman in the Kootenays once. Just a two-bit camp." The corporal looked blank. "Then I was a bucker in Calgary."

"You mean you was a bronco-buster?" The edge in the corporal's voice betrayed a hint of unprofessional surprise.

"No, s—, no, corporal, on a bridge. You know—holdin a bat under the girder for the riveter. I was a sticker too." The corporal kept his eyes on the form, nodding as if he had known all along, but his bald head pinkened slightly and his pen halted. "That's fine. How long you, uh, stick?"

"At stickin? Not very long. I got to missin rivets with my bucket and a hot one set a big Swede on fire and he complained to the strawboss. Then I rode the rods east and sorta bummed. Then I was scurfer in a coke plant. And I was a pouncer once, for a while." The corporal twisted his ear as if he were having trouble hearing. His face had become a mask of distrust. Turvey felt sorry he had mentioned pouncing and he added apologetically:

"In a hat factory, Guelph. You know—sandpaperin up the fuzz on fedoras. Then I come to Toronto to join the Air Force, cause the war had started, but they wouldnt have me cause I hadnt matric and couldnt see enough green at night or somethin. So my pal Mac and I hit the freights to Vancouver to get in the Kootenay Highlanders but they was filled up. Then in Victoria we worked house-to-house gettin moths out of pianos. Then—"

But the corporal had taken the pipe out of his mouth and was holding it at a monitory angle, and his voice was a growl:

"Dont try no smart stuff here. I ast you wut cher *chief* occupation was. Wut did you do longest?"

Turvey thought rapidly. There was the time he was a popsicle-coater, and then assistant flavour-mixer, in that candy factory. But he quit after, what was it, four months? Got tired of the vanilla smell always on his clothes. Wanted to get east anyway and try the army again. The corporal was staring sullenly at his forms. What happened then? O yes, the army turned him down because he had a mess of hives and his front teeth were out and his feet kind of flat. So after a while he landed that tannery job. How long was he there? Gee, almost a whole winter!

"Wet-splittin."

The corporal's eyes rose, speckled and malevolent, but they saw only a round face beaming with the pleasures of recall and the tremulous smile of the young man anxious to please.

"I ran a machine scrapin fat off hides. Eastern Tannery, Montreal."

The corporal laid his pipe down (it had gone out), wrote "Machine Operator", and asked hurriedly:

"Any previous military experience?"

"Well, we started cadets in Kuskanee High but we never got rifles. But I was in the Boy Sc—"

"That's all. Wait on a bench atta back till the officer calls you, next man!" The corporal looked past him, mopped his veined head with a khaki handkerchief, and whanged his pipe spitefully against the table leg.

Earle Birney, Turvey: A Military Picaresque

One long-time employee was a "cripple," as result of a broken back incurred as a teenager; had posture of a "**question** mark." Unemployable to all, except "Bo," who not only employed him, but also retained him for over fifteen years.

Murray M. Silver, This Bo Peep Ain't No Fairy Tale!

And there was Clif Garboden. Until 2009, Clif was the Phoenix's senior managing editor, and he had been on staff for more than 30 years. He sat in a corner of the *Phoenix* newsroom, hunched at his computer with the posture of a **question** mark. His face had no angles. He wore sweaters over collared shirts and khaki pants. He enjoyed smoking and grumbling. His 1989 Buick Park Avenue, which he bought for $6000 with 43,186 miles on the odometer, was named Jerome. (I know this because he devoted an entire essay to the car.) He once received a death threat from a mime.

Camille Dodero, Newspapering Is a Business: The Death of the Legendary Boston Phoenix (Gawker)

And I'm not saying so in a "woe is me" sense, I'm just calling a spade a spade, friends. I was over 6-foot by age 13. I was emaciated skinny. Somalia skinny. And since I was over a foot taller than every other kid, I developed the posture of a **question** mark, constantly hunched and lurching. Also, my teeth were truly a goddamn disaster area. It simply wasn't pretty, folks.

Oh, yeah, also my last name ostensibly means "gross lady who puts stuff in her butt for money."

Peter Hoare, Embrace Your Name (AskMen)

Hence, I was frail and tiny, a biped asthmatic misery, pale and with the posture of a **question** mark kicked up its backside, as some described it.

I only realised much later that some ad-hoc treatments, prescribed back then with the best knowledge Romanian medicine was allowed to possess, had been downright stupid.

Lehel Vandor, Ears

Shaw stood there in his memory with the posture of a **question** mark, his pitching arm two to three inches longer than the left one from flinging baseballs for countless years to no purpose. His glove, so ancient it was gray instead of brown, dangled from his knobby wrist like an old paperthin hornets' nest. There he was, with his hangdog face, looking almost at you but a little to one side as if there was some invisible, horrible, but interesting presence hovering just over your left shoulder. Nothing could wipe the misery out of those sad Mongolian eyes, or make his perpetual sour stomach come right, or sweeten his stinky breath, or give him a respectable fastball.

David Small, Almost Famous

In other work, **QA** repositories have been used as candidate collections for answer retrieval [30, 83, 154]. Besides **Question**-Answering, **QA** repositories have also been used in other related information retrieval and natural language processing tasks, such as query summarization [23], semantically similar **question** finding [82] and knowledge representation [153, 154]. Since the performance of these applications depends heavily on the quality of the **QA** repository, high-precision extraction of **QA** pairs is crucial in order to provide reliable data for various deployments.

Yi Liu, Semi-Supervised Learning With Side Information: Graph-Based Approaches

It was 1974. Malcolm McLaren was briefly in the United States, managing the New York Dolls, then on their last legs. They had wandered into his shop, played him their records; he'd laughed. "I couldn't believe how anybody could be so bad," he said long after, citing the moment as the inspiration for the Sex Pistols. "The fact that they were so bad suddenly hit me with such force that I began to realize, I'm laughing, I'm talking to these guys, I'm looking at them, and I'm laughing with them, and I was suddenly impressed by the fact that I was no longer concerned with whether you could play well. Whether you were able to even know about rock 'n' roll to the extent that you were able to write songs properly wasn't important any longer . . . The Dolls really impressed upon me that there was something else. There was something wonderful. I thought how brilliant they were to be this bad."

No doubt a year later McLaren would be playing Dolls records for the Sex Pistols, just as two decades before Sam Phillips had played old blues records for his new rockabilly singers. A banner McLaren painted up and hoisted over the Dolls' last stages captured the dead time they never escaped: "WHAT ARE THE POLITICS OF BOREDOM?"

It was, once removed, a situationist slogan. "Boredom is always counterrevolutionary," the situationists had liked to say. McLaren's **question** mark was his way of asking how much power might be secreted in the slogans he put such stock in; to find the answer, you had to use the slogans. "Boredom is always counterrevolutionary"—the line was typical of the situationist style, of its voice, a blindside paradox of dead rhetoric and ordinary language floated just this side of non sequitur, the declarative statement turning into a **question** as you heard it: what does this mean?

Greil Marcus, Lipstick Traces: A Secret History of the Twentieth Century

Young people today are very reluctant to assume that anything is certain, and this reluctance is revealed in their language. In any matter where there might be disagreement, they will put a **question** mark at the end of the sentence. And to reinforce the posture of neutrality they will insert words that function as disclaimers, among which the favourite is 'like'. You might be adamant that the Earth is spherical, but they will suggest instead that the Earth is, 'like, spherical?'

Roger Scruton, Universities' War Against Truth (Spectator Life)

You already know, the situationists had answered: all you lack is the consciousness of what you know. Our project is nothing more than a seductive, subversive restatement of the obvious: "Our ideas are in everyone's mind." Our ideas about how the world works, about why it must be changed, are in everyone's mind as sensations almost no one is willing to translate into ideas, so we will do the translating. And that is all we have to do to change the world. Boredom, to the situationists, was a supremely modern phenomenon, a modern form of control. In feudal times and for the first century of the Industrial Revolution, drudgery and privation produced numbing fatigue and horrible misery, no mystery, just a God-given fact: "In Adam's fall so sinned we all," and as for those few who knew neither fatigue nor misery, it was easier for a camel to pass through the eye of a needle than for a rich man to enter heaven. As the situationists saw modernity, limited work and relative abundance, city planning and the welfare state, produced not happiness but depression and boredom. With God missing, people felt their condition not exactly as a fact, but simply as a fatalism devoid of meaning, which separated every man and woman from every other, which threw all people back upon themselves. I'm not happy—what's wrong with me?

Greil Marcus, Lipstick Traces: A Secret History of the Twentieth Century

Didn't find an answer to your
question?
Submit your inquiry directly to our
Customer Solutions team

Figure 6.1. Snapshot of example web **FAQ** pages (1 of 4)

Yi Liu, Semi-Supervised Learning With Side Information: Graph-Based Approaches

"Honestly, I think I'd go see a psychiatrist if this happened to me."

"But the psychiatrist talks to the police herself and finds out that everything you said is true."

"Well, then, at least I'd have one friend—the psychiatrist."

"But then the psychiatrist herself disappears."

"This is a totally paranoid scenario. That is like something out of Dreyfuss's head."

"You wait, investigate, or run away?"

"Or kill myself. How about kill myself?"

"There are no wrong answers."

"I'd probably go live with my mom. I wouldn't let her out of my sight. And if she somehow disappeared anyway, I'd probably kill myself, since by then it would be obvious that having any connection to me wasn't good for a person's health."

Annagret smiled again. "Excellent."

"What?"

"You're doing very, very well, Pip." She reached across the table and put her hands, her hot hands, on Pip's cheeks.

"Saying I'd kill myself is the right answer?"

Annagret took her hands away. "There are no wrong answers."

"That sort of makes it harder to feel good about doing well."

"Which of the following have you ever done without permission: break into some-one's email account, read things on someone's smartphone, search someone's computer, read someone's diary, go through someone's private papers, listen to a private conversation when someone's phone accidentally dials you, obtain information about someone on false pretenses, put your ear to a wall or door to listen to a conversation, and the like."

Pip frowned. "Am I allowed to skip a **question**?"

"You can trust me." Annagret touched her hand yet again. "It's better that you answer."

Jonathan Franzen, Purity

Fatalism is acceptance: "Que sera, sera" is always counterrevolutionary. But as the situationists understood the modern world, boredom was less a **question** of work than of leisure. As they set out in the 1950s work seemed to be losing its hold on life; "automation" and "cybernetics" were wonderful new words. Leisure time was expanding—and in order to maintain their power, those who ruled, whether capitalist directors in the West or communist bureaucrats in the East, had to ensure that leisure was as boring as the new forms of work. More boring, if leisure was to replace work as the locus of everyday life, a thousand times more. What could be more productive of an atomized, hopeless fatalism than the feeling that one is deadened precisely where one ought to be having fun?

> *Greil Marcus, Lipstick Traces: A Secret History of the Twentieth Century*

Page 40:

1. **Question** Mark
2. Exclamation Mark
3. Period
4. Exclamation Mark
5. Exclamation Mark, Period
6. Exclamation Mark, Period
7. Period
8. **Question** Mark, Period
9. Exclamation Mark, Exclamation Mark, Period
10. Exclamation Mark, Exclamation Mark, Period

Sentences to be underlined: 2, 4, 5, 6, 9, 10

> *Ruth Solski, Les majuscules et la ponctuation/Capitalization & Punctuation*

But now listen to what happened next. After lunch I was reclining in a low chair trying to read. Suddenly two deft little hands were over my eyes: she had crept up from behind as if re-enacting, in a ballet sequence, my morning maneuver. Her fingers were a luminous crimson as they tried to blot out the sun, and she uttered hiccups of laughter and jerked this way and that as I stretched my arm sideways and backwards without otherwise changing my recumbent position. My hand swept over her agile giggling legs, and the book like a sleigh left my lap, and Mrs. Haze strolled up and said indulgently: "Just slap her hard if she interferes with your scholarly meditations. How I love this garden [no exclamation mark in her tone]. Isn't it divine in the sun [no **question** mark either]." And with a sigh of feigned content, the obnoxious lady sank down on the grass and looked up at the sky as she leaned back on her splayed-out hands, and presently an old gray tennis ball bounced over her, and Lo's voice came from the house haughtily: "Pardonnez, Mother. I was not aiming at you."

> *Vladimir Nabokov, Lolita*

I'm pretty sure Google strips all queries of **question** marks by design, regardless of whether they exist inside quotes or not. This is probably because the less "Google-aware" ask everything as a **question**, when they simply want to be searching for terms. Unfortunately, I do not believe there's any way of escaping the character.

The vast majority of the time, **question** marks are indeed irrelevant, though understandably in certain contexts, including programming, it may be useful to include them in a query. Suggest the idea to Google? I can't say much more really . . .

Noldorin

answered Oct 7 '09 at 15:50

Super User, *How to Google a **Question** Mark?*

"OK by me. It's their duty, isn't it? But it doesn't seem very clever if one can spot the dodge so easily."

"Yes—but Percival's story might be true just the same. True and already blown. An agent, whatever he suspected, would feel bound to pass it on in case . . ."

"And you think they think we are the leaks?"

"Yes. One of us or perhaps both."

"But as we aren't who cares?" Davis said. "It's long past bedtime, Castle. If there's a mike under the pillow, they'll only hear my snores." He turned the music off. "We aren't the stuff of double agents, you and me."

Castle undressed and put out the light. It was stuffy in the small disordered room. He tried to raise the window, but the sash cord was broken. He stared down into the early morning street. No one went by: not even a policeman. Only a single taxi remained on a rank a little way down Davies Street in the direction of Claridge's. A burglar alarm sent up a futile ringing from somewhere in the Bond Street area, and a light rain had begun to fall. It gave a black glitter to the pavement like a policeman's raincoat. He drew the curtains close and got into bed; but he didn't sleep. A **question** mark kept him awake for a long while . . .

Graham Greene, *The Human Factor*

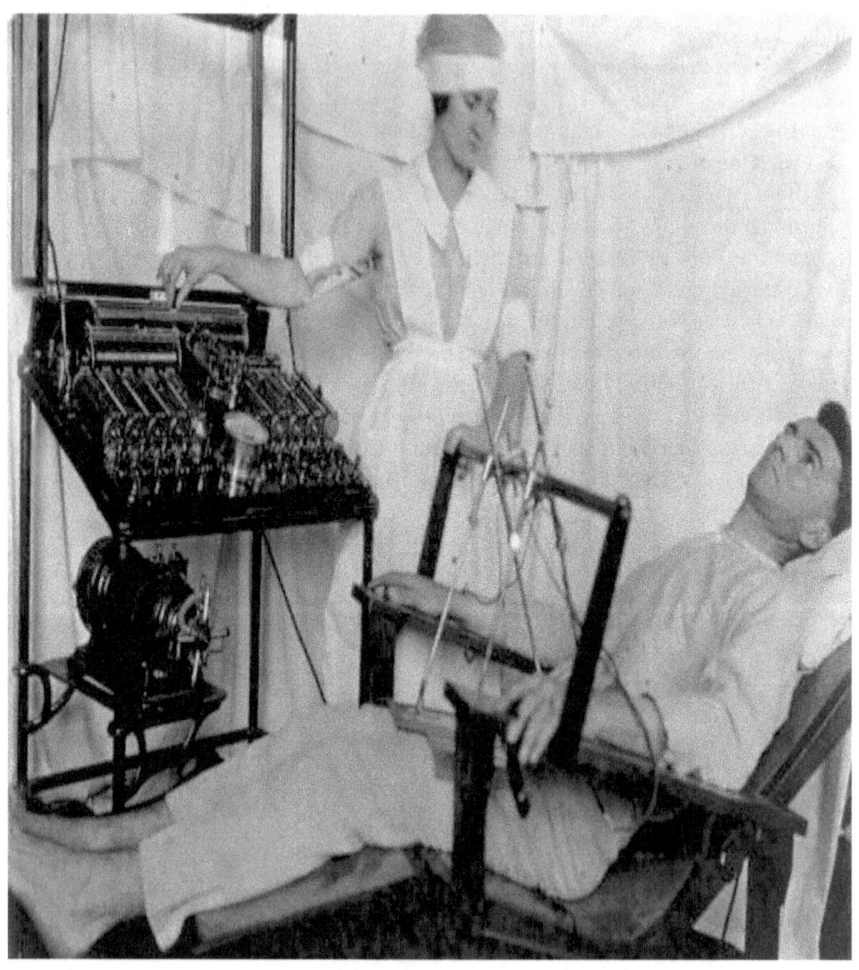

One of the most interesting **questions** that I could not answer for certain related to those who appeared unscathed or saw the war as the making of them. Were they simply repressing the horrors described by so many others? And if so, did it matter?

*Suzie Grogan, Is Britain Still "Shell-Shocked"? A **Question** for World Mental Health Day (Zen and the Art of Tightrope Walking)*

The **Question** Does Not Come Before There Is a Quotation

Each day is attended by surprises

A practical and personal application of inertia
Can be found in the **question**:
Whose Turn Is It
To Take Out The Garbage?
An empty pair of dance shoes
Is a lot like the answer to this **question**,
As well as book-length poems
Set in the Midwest.

Cornelius Eady, The Empty Dance Shoes

"Why does poetry suck?" This **question** echoes down the ages and is echoed by under-graduate students, eyes glazing as they gaze upon their reading lists. "It doesn't," we tell them, but in our hearts, we know different. We know it does.[*]

What sucks about poetry? The short answer is the words, and their combina-tions. The longer answer has to do with how so few of those combinations include the pairing "Nacho Tuesdays." Yes, poetry seems to lack nachos, and, aside from that, it seems to lack humour. Indeed, no literary genre appears less funny than poetry, where conventional wisdom has it that a "good poem" must move the reader to some epiphany through the subtle revelation of some aspect of the human condition, the least funny condition of all.[†]

Ryan Fitzpatrick and Jonathan Ball, "Take These Poems—Please!" An Introduction (Why Poetry Sucks)

Joe Wenderoth, not by a long shot
sober, says, I promised my wife I wouldn't fuck
anyone to no one in particular and reads a poem
about how Jesus had no penis.

Meanwhile, the psychiatrist, attractive
in a fatherly way, says, Libido **question** mark.

Rachel Zucker, Hey Allen Ginsberg Where Have You Gone and What Would You Think of My Drugs?

Popping bullets of sunlight
crack into the subliminal
orifices, and the tree thinks,
"How exquisite. Is this love?"

*Ruth Stone, The **Question***

---

* Yes, we know footnotes suck too. Give us a break!

† Even leprosy has its lighter moments. Look, Ma, no hands!

The show did not start off
auspiciously, the contestants
were nervous and kept fiddling
with the wires attached
to their privates, the men
being especially anxious
over the **question** of balls.
The women were more querulous.

The first **question**, a medical subject,
was why had the anti-abortionists
not mentioned, let alone commented on,
the Baboon Heart transplant?
One terrified contestant guessed
it was because the moral majority's
nervous concern with evolution
precluded their bringing it up.
That hopeful contestant's face
reflected the malicious light
in the eyes of the host who
immediately threw the switch

A powerful surge shot through
the wires and both sexes screamed
and writhed, to the delight of
the vast viewership, estimated
at 100 million, all of whom,
presumably, were delighted
not to be on the show,
because not one in a million
knew the answer.

  Edward Dorn, The Price is Right: A Torture Wheel of Fortune

What is the use of a violent kind of delightfulness if there is no pleasure in not getting tired of it. The **question** does not come before there is a quotation. In any kind of place there is a top to covering and it is a pleasure at any rate there is some venturing in refusing to believe nonsense. It shows what use there is in a whole piece if one uses it and it is extreme and very likely the little things could be dearer but in any case there is a bargain and if there is the best thing to do is to take it away and wear it and then be reckless be reckless and resolved on returning gratitude.

  Gertrude Stein, Tender Buttons

Yes, but beyond happiness what is there?
The **question** has not yet been answered.
No great quotations have issued forth
From there, we have no still photographs
Full of men in fine leather hiking boots,
Women with new-cut walking sticks.

So yes, it is the realm of thin tigers
Prowling, out to earn even more stripes;
It is the smell of seven or eight perfumes
Not currently available in America.
     Maybe this is wrong, of course.
The place may after all be populated,
Or over-populated, with dented trash cans
In the streets and news of genital herpes
In every smart article in every slick magazine
Everywhere in the place.
     But everybody there smiles—
Laughs, even, every time a breath can be caught.
This is all true.

> *Alberto Ríos, Mason Jars by the Window*

When the snake bit
Rabbi Hanina ben Dosa
while he was praying

the snake died. (Each day
is attended by surprises
or it is nothing.)

Question: was the bare-footed,
smelly Rabbi more poisonous
than the snake

or so God-adulterated
he'd become immune
to serpent poison?

> *Dannie Abse, Snake*

Well, it all makes for interesting conjecture.
And it occurs to me that what is crucial is to believe
in effort, to believe some good will come of simply *trying*,
a good completely untainted by the corrupt initiating impulse
to persuade or seduce—

What are we without this?
Whirling in the dark universe,
alone, afraid, unable to influence fate—

What do we have really?
Sad tricks with ladders and shoes,
tricks with salt, impurely motivated recurring
attempts to build character.
What do we have to appease the great forces?

And I think in the end this was the **question**
that destroyed Agamemnon, there on the beach,

the Greek ships at the ready, the sea
invisible beyond the serene harbor, the future
lethal, unstable: he was a fool, thinking
it could be controlled. He should have said
I have nothing, I am at your mercy.

Louise Glück, The Empty Glass

They dropped the charges of homicide, filed new charges of
terrorism, dropped the charges of terrorism, filed
new charges of public nudity, dropped the charges of
public nudity, filed new charges of lewd and
lascivious behavior. A spokesman for the FBI
said they found him on the hood of an SUV in a part
of town known as the "Fruit Loop". His penis was in another
man's mouth and in the front seat were vials containing a rare
strand of bacteria known to cause blindness in rats. They
dropped the charges of public nudity and filed new
charges of sodomy. A spokesman for the police department
said they found him with his pants down and it appeared
that his penis was in another man's anus. But since they
could not prove to what degree his penis had penetrated
the other man's anus they dropped the charges of sodomy
and filed new charges of assault and battery. A
spokesman for the Department of Homeland Security said
that he assaulted a worker from the Department of
Public Health who used a Q-tip to extract from inside of
his urethra a rare strand of bacteria capable
of causing pneumonia in chickens. He was placed in
solitary confinement and a spokesman for the
Department of Corrections suggested that he was a
serious threat to the community. They examined the
strand of bacteria found in his urethra but since they
did not properly store the bacteria in the
appropriate container with the appropriate seals and
signatures they could not charge him with intent to commit crimes
against humanity. They dropped the charges of intent to
commit crimes against humanity and filed new charges
of larceny. They said he had stolen the rare strand of
bacteria from his employer and that he had done so
with the deliberate and malicious intent to harm as
many civilians as possible. They tried to verify
for whom he had worked during the given time period but since
they could not verify the name or location of his
employer they dropped the charges of larceny and filed new
charges of tax fraud. When they discovered he was privately
employed, they dropped the charges of tax fraud and filed new

Unseen Poetry Revision Booklet

My progress record of the unseen poetry questions
FIRST TASK: **Date:**
HOW TO IMPROVE:
SECOND TASK: **Date:**
HOW TO IMPROVE:
THIRD TASK: **Date:**
HOW TO IMPROVE:
ASSESSMENT PIECE: **Date:**
TEACHER FEEDBACK:

Grade:

The deeper and more developed your explanations are, the more interesting and personal your response becomes, the more marks you are likely to gain.

Aylsham High School, Unseen Poetry Revision Booklet (aylshamhigh.com)

charges of theft with an unregistered weapon. A
grocery store in his neighborhood had recently been robbed
and the cashier said that the thief had carried the same model
of weapon that the man in **question** kept beneath his bed in
case of emergencies. They dropped the charges of theft with an
unregistered weapon when they discovered the cashier was
partially blind and that the weapon the man in **question** kept
beneath his bed in case of emergencies had been
properly purchased and registered. When they found on his
bookshelves several works of fiction with blind characters,
including *King Lear, Oedipus Rex, Endgame,* and *Blindness* by
José Saramago, they accused him of conspiring
to use the rare strand of bacteria to blind not only
the grocer but the seven other blind residents of his
neighborhood, each of whom had had perfectly good eyesight
until he came to town. They asked him why he had so many
books about blindness, but he refused to answer the **question**.
They asked him why he had so many books about blindness and
when his attorney arrived the man in **question** said that he
did not know why he had so many books about blindness. They
asked his friends and family why he had so many books
about blindness. No one knew why he had so many books
about blindness and they accused him in the press of
anti-social behavior. When his neighbors testified that
the man in **question** enjoyed society as much as he
enjoyed a quiet night at home, they dropped the charges of
anti-social behavior. They dropped the charges of
anti-social behavior and filed new charges of
jaywalking. An undercover police officer filmed him
with a video camera as he illegally crossed
the street. At the advice of his attorney, he pleaded
guilty to the charges of jaywalking. He agreed to pay
the fine.

*Daniel Borzutzky, The Man in **Question***

In any case, the ruling was long overdue.
The people are beside themselves with rapture
so we stay indoors. The quest was only another adventure
and the solution problematic, at any rate far off in the future.

The people are beside themselves with rapture
yet no one thinks to **question** the source of so much collective euphoria,
and the solution: problematic, at any rate far off in the future.
The saxophone wails, the martini glass is drained.

Yet no one thinks to **question** the source of so much collective euphoria.
In troubled times one looked to the shaman or priest for comfort and counsel.

The saxophone wails, the martini glass is drained,
and night like black swansdown settles on the city.

In troubled times one looked to the shaman or priest for comfort and counsel.
Now, only the willing are fated to receive death as a reward,
and night like black swansdown settles on the city.
If we tried to leave, would being naked help us?

John Ashbery, Hotel Lautréamont

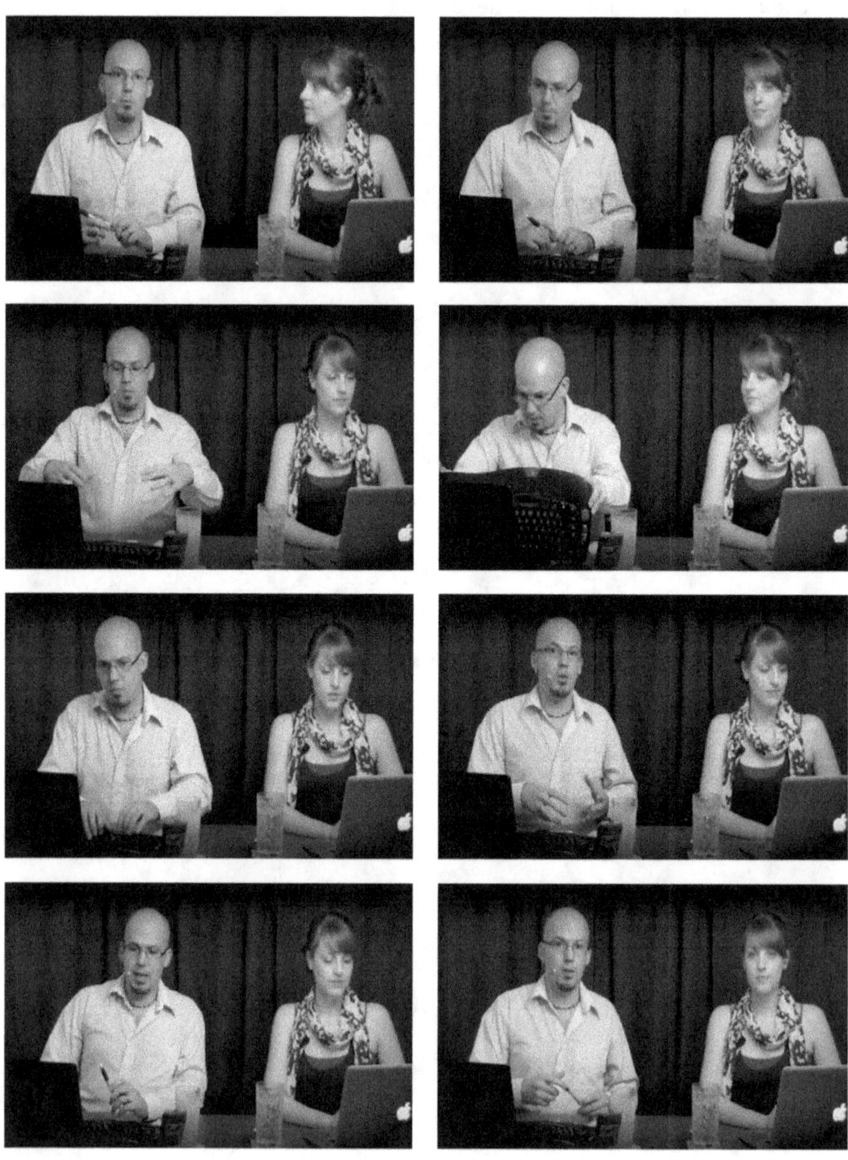

*blip.tv, Viewer **Question** Extravaganza 323 (Internet Archive)*

Now Comes the Question

Questions and answers sounding like a continuous popping of corks

importunate **questions**
interminable **question**
lugubrious **question**
pertinent **question**
questionable data
questioning gaze
unquestionable genius
unquestioning fate
puzzles, tangles, and **questionings**
questions, disputes, and controversies
certain, confident, positive, and **unquestionable**
uncertain, **questionable**, erroneous, and mistaken
question of honor
call in **question**
call into **question**
Artless and **unquestioning** devotion
Her voice, with a tentative **question** in it, rested in air
She **questioned** inimically
She wore an air of wistful **questioning**
Teased with impertinent **questions**
The eternal **questioning** of inscrutable fate
The father's vigil of **questioning** sorrow
The intrusive **question** faded
The **question** drummed in head and heart day and night
The **question** irresistibly emerged
A **question** deep almost as the mystery of life
He played with grave **questions** as a cat plays with a mouse
Questions and answers sounding like a continuous popping of corks
Are you not complicating the **question**?
I am not going to let you evade the **question**
I am wondering if I may dare ask you a very personal **question**?
I might **question** all that
I must ask you one more **question**, if I may
I purposely evaded the **question**
Is that a fair **question**?
Question me, if you wish
Surely there can be no **question** about that
That is a fair **question**, perhaps
That is a **question** I have often proposed to myself

*blip.tv, Viewer **Question** Extravaganza 323 (Internet Archive)*

That is rather a difficult **question** to answer
Unquestionably superior
Why ask such embarrassing **questions**?
Will you allow me to ask you a **question**?
And if any of you should **question**
And now the **question** is asked me
And thus we are led on then to further **question**
And **unquestionably**
Before attempting to answer this **question**
Beyond all **question** we
But can this **question**
But I return to the **question**
But putting these **questions** aside
But the **question** may arise
Difficult then as the **question** may be
Here arises the eternal **question**
Here is no **question**
Here let me meet one other **question**
Here then, we are brought to the **question**
I am not going into vexed **questions**
I come next to the **question** of
I do not desire to call in **question**
I do not enter into the **question**
I do not **question** for a moment
I know it has been **questioned**
I might reasonably **question** the justice
I must ask an abrupt **question**
I now address you on a **question**
I now pass to the **question** of
I open the all-important **question**
I **question** whether
I shall recur to certain **questions**
I shall touch upon one or two **questions**
I will now leave this **question**
I will yield the whole **question**
In addressing myself to the **question**
In order to do justice to the **question**
It is a most pertinent **question**
It is an **unquestionable** truth
It is natural to ask the **question**
It is not a practical **question**
It is one of the burning **questions** of the day
It is scarcely **questioned**
It is still an open **question**
Let me answer these **questions**
Let that **question** be answered by

*blip.tv, Viewer **Question** Extravaganza 323 (Internet Archive)*

Look at some of these **questions**
No doubt there are many **questions**
Now comes the **question**
Now, it is **unquestioned**
Now, the **question** here at issue
One thing more will complete this **question**
That is the **question** of **questions**
The next **question** to be considered is
The pressing **question** is
The **question** is deeply involved
The **question**, then, recurs
Then the **question** arises
There is a more important **question**
There is a **question** of vital importance
These **questions** I shall examine
This is the radical **question**
This leads me to the **question**
We do not **question** the reality
We should not **question** for a moment
We should not, therefore, **question**
When I speak of this **question**
Yet if you were to ask the **question**
An honest and **unquestioning** pride
Difficult and abstruse **questions**
Questioned and tested in the crucible of experience
The most absurd elementary **questions**
The **question** was disconcertingly frank
Their authenticity may be greatly **questioned**
Unreasoning and **unquestioning** attachment
Unwavering and **unquestioning** approbation

*Grenville Kleiser, Fifteen Thousand Useful Phrases: A Practical Handbook
of Pertinent Expressions, Striking Similes, Literary, Commercial,
Conversational, and Oratorical Terms, for the Embellishment of Speech
and Literature, and the Improvement of the Vocabulary of Those Persons
Who Read, Write, and Speak English*

*Harold F. Kress (director), No **Questions** Asked, 1951*

Experiments on **Question** Form

*. . . not to engage the **question** but to outflank it . . .*

pysma

> *pys'-ma*
>
> *Gk.* "**question**"
>
> The asking of multiple **questions** successively (which would together require a complex reply).

Gideon Burton, Silva Rhetoricae (The Forest of Rhetoric)

Questions can be asked in infinitely varied ways about an infinite number of subjects. It is not possible, except in a purposive or else purely metaphoric way, to sample the universe of all survey **questions**. Instead, our strategy has been to identify a small number of important ways in which **questions** vary in form, and investigate whether these variations have systematic effects that are detectable regardless of exact wording or subject matter. For example, almost any attitude **question** can include an explicit "don't know" alternative, but most survey **questions** do not provide this option for the respondent. In Chapter 4, we look at how this apparently simple variation—offering or not offering a don't know option—affects results for a number of different survey **questions**. At a later point in the present chapter we will outline all the major variations in **question** form that we have investigated. Of course, the assumption that there are important formal ways in which **questions** vary is itself tested throughout the entire volume.

*Howard Schuman and Stanley Presser, **Questions** and Answers in Attitude Surveys: Experiments on **Question** Form, Wording, and Context*

We went outside and asked all the people we could find all the **questions** we could think of. None of the answers led anywhere, except to repeated assurance that the bomb hadn't been chucked through the window.

Dashiell Hammett, The Dain Curse

"May I ask, Mr. Spade, if there was, as the newspapers inferred, a certain—ah—relationship between that unfortunate happening and the death a little later of the man Thursby?"

Spade said nothing in a blank-faced definite way.

Cairo rose and bowed. "I beg your pardon." He sat down and placed his hands side by side, palms down, on the corner of the desk. "More than idle curiosity made me ask that, Mr. Spade. I am trying to recover an—ah—ornament that has been—shall we say?—mislaid. I thought, and hoped, you could assist me."

Spade nodded with eyebrows lifted to indicate attentiveness.

"The ornament is a statuette," Cairo went on, selecting and mouthing his words carefully, "the black figure of a bird."

Spade nodded again, with courteous interest.

"I am prepared to pay, on behalf of the figure's rightful owner, the sum of five thousand dollars for its recovery." Cairo raised one hand from the desk-corner and touched a spot in the air with the broad-nailed tip of an ugly forefinger. "I am prepared to promise that—what is the phrase?—no **questions** will be asked."

Dashiell Hammett, The Maltese Falcon

22. Suspension of the Rules.

The motion to suspend the rules may be made at any time when no **question** is pending; or while a **question** is pending, provided it is for a purpose connected with that **question**. It yields to all the privileged motions (except a call for the orders of the day), to the motion to lay on the table, and to incidental motions arising out of itself. It is undebatable and cannot be amended or have any other subsidiary motion applied to it, nor can a vote on it be reconsidered, nor can a motion to suspend the rules for the same purpose be renewed at the same meeting except by unanimous consent, though it may be renewed after an adjournment, even if the next meeting is held the same day.

When the assembly wishes to do something that cannot be done without violating its own rules, and yet it is not in conflict with its constitution, or by-laws, or with the fundamental principles of parliamentary law, it "suspends the rules that interfere with" the proposed action. The object of the suspension must be specified, and nothing else can be done under the suspension. The rules that can be suspended are those relating to priority of business, or to business procedure, or to admission to the meetings, etc., and would usually be comprised under the heads of rules of order. Sometimes societies include in their by-laws some rules relating to the transaction of business without any intention, evidently, of giving these rules any greater stability than is possessed by other rules of their class, and they may be suspended the same as if they were called rules of order. A standing rule as defined in 67 may be suspended by a majority vote. But sometimes the term "standing rules" is applied to what are strictly rules of order, and then, like rules of order, they require a two-thirds vote for their suspension. Nothing that requires previous notice and a two-thirds vote for its amendment can be suspended by less than a two-thirds vote.

Henry M. Robert, Robert's Rules of Order Revised for Deliberative Assemblies

He was detained two hours. When he came back, he ascended the old staircase alone, having asked no **question** of the servant; going thus into the Doctor's rooms, he was stopped by a low sound of knocking.

"Good God!" he said, with a start. "What's that?"

Charles Dickens, A Tale of Two Cities

SIR TOBY. No **question**.
AGUECHEEK. An I thought that, I'd forswear it. I'll ride home to-morrow, Sir Toby.
SIR TOBY. Pourquoi, my dear knight?
AGUECHEEK. What is 'pourquoi?' do or not do? I would I had bestowed that time in the tongues that I have in fencing, dancing, and bear-baiting. Oh, had I but followed the arts!
SIR TOBY. Then hadst thou had an excellent head of hair.
AGUECHEEK. Why, would that have mended my hair?

SIR TOBY. Past **question**; for thou seest it will not curl by nature.
AGUECHEEK. But it becomes me well enough, does't not?

William Shakespeare, Twelfth Night; or, What You Will

[Footnote 8: In the MS. a blank space is left after this **question**.]

Why the eye sees bodies at a distance, larger than they measure on the vertical plane?

. . .

Which light is best for drawing from nature; whether high or low, or large or small, or strong and broad, or strong and small, or broad and weak or small and weak?

[Footnote: The **question** here put is unanswered in the original MS.]

. . .

582.

How the ages of man should be depicted: that is, Infancy, Childhood, Youth, Manhood, Old age, Decrepitude.

[Footnote: No answer is here given to this **question**, in the original MS.]

Jean Paul Richter (ed.), The Notebooks of Leonardo da Vinci

"There was a **question** just now, Mr. Jaggers, which you desired me to waive for a moment. I hope I am doing nothing wrong in asking it again?"

"What is it?" said he.

I might have known that he would never help me out; but it took me aback to have to shape the **question** afresh, as if it were quite new. "Is it likely," I said, after hesitating, "that my patron, the fountain-head you have spoken of, Mr. Jaggers, will soon—" There I delicately stopped.

"Will soon what?" asked Mr. Jaggers. "That's no **question** as it stands, you know."

Charles Dickens, Great Expectations

We shall not further develop this **question** here, since it has only recently become of moment and we lack the required elements and perspective for a serious analysis. At all events, we record its existence and its undeniable interest.

Daniel Buren, Beware!

"Verhovensky an enthusiast?"

"Oh, yes. There is a point when he ceases to be a buffoon and becomes a madman. I beg you to remember your own expression: 'Do you know how powerful a single man may be?' Please don't laugh about it, he's quite capable of pulling a trigger. They are convinced that I am a spy too. As they don't know how to do things themselves, they're awfully fond of accusing people of being spies."

"But you're not afraid, are you?"

"N—no. I'm not very much afraid . . . But your case is quite different. I warned you that you might anyway keep it in mind. To my thinking there's no reason to be offended in being threatened with danger by fools; their brains don't affect the **question**. They've raised their hand against better men than you or me. It's a quarter past eleven, though." He looked at his watch and got up from his chair. "I wanted to ask you one quite irrelevant **question**."

"For God's sake!" cried Shatov, rising impulsively from his seat.

"I beg your pardon?" Nikolay Vsyevolodovitch looked at him inquiringly.

"Ask it, ask your **question** for God's sake," Shatov repeated in indescribable excitement, "but on condition that I ask you a **question** too. I beseech you to allow me . . . I can't . . . ask your **question**!"

Fyodor Dostoyevsky, The Possessed; or, The Devils

Contrary to expectation, Maigret asked no further **questions**. Indeed, this created an atmosphere of unease. People in the room felt that having reached a culminating point, everything had stopped dead.

Georges Simenon, A Crime in Holland

And why not? Not from any self-will or disregard of you. Whether I am or am not afraid of death is another **question**, of which I will not now speak.

Plato, Apology

Before their first meeting, her killer—whose real name was Nicholas Cohen—established some rules: a classic BDSM protocol. She was not to ask **questions**. She was not to cover her legs with stockings or tights in His presence. She would give a truthful account of her response to all His commands after obeying. She'd assented with glee, because how can you play a game without rules?

Chris Kraus, Summer of Hate

The idea is to have the bonus **questions'** points not count toward the exam's total possible points, but earned points still count as earned points. Essentially, the **question's** possible points will be zero, but earned points function like manually adjusted points, being >= zero.

*sunnyw, Bonus **Questions** in Quizzes (Canvas/Help Center)*

You can break down the expression into the following parts:

^	the beginning of the string, followed by . . .
[^?]	a character class that matches anything that isn't a **question** mark
*	found zero or more times, followed by . . .
\?	a **question** mark, escaped so it's taken literally, followed by . . .
(	a group that contains . . .
.	any character . . .
*	found zero or more times . . .
)	the end of the group . . .
$	the end of the line.

The gist of this expression is to capture everything after the first literal **question** mark all the way up to the end of the line. The expression .* is another way of saying, "Everything, including nothing." The character class at the beginning [^?] is important, because it matches everything that isn't a **question** mark. When the ^ is found inside square brackets, it's a negation character that means "not." Like many other characters, a ? inside brackets is taken literally and doesn't need to be escaped.

Nathan A. Good, Regular Expression Recipes: A Problem-Solution Approach

She looked at him. "How are you feeling?"

"I'm going stir-crazy, thank you for asking."

"You've only been in one night."

"Feels like more."

"What do the doctors say?"

"Nobody's been to see me yet, not today. Whatever they tell me, I'm out of here this afternoon."

"And then what?"

"How do you mean?"

"You can't go back to work." Finally, she studied his hands. "How're you going to drive or type a report? What about taking phone calls?"

"I'll manage," he repeated into the silence, lowering the arm again and wishing he hadn't raised it in the first place. His fingers sparked with pain as the blood pounded through them. "Have they spoken to you?" he asked.

"About what?"

"Come on, Siobhan . . ."

She looked at him, unblinking. Her hands emerged from their hiding place as she leaned forwards on the chair.

"I've another session this afternoon."

"Who with?"

"The boss." Meaning Detective Chief Superintendent Gill Templer. Rebus nodded, satisfied that as yet it wasn't going any higher.

"What will you say to her?" he asked.

"There's nothing to tell. I didn't have anything to do with Fairstone's death." She paused, another unasked **question** hanging between them: *Did you?* She seemed to be waiting for Rebus to say something, but he stayed silent.

Ian Rankin, A **Question** of Blood

When I had finished the chief bunched his fat mouth, whistled softly, and exclaimed: "Man, that's an interesting thing you've been telling me! So it was blood on her slipper? And she said her husband wouldn't be home?"

"That's what I took it for," I said to the first **question**, and, "Yeah," to the second.

"Have you done any talking to her since then?" he asked.

"No. I was up that way this morning, but a young fellow named Thaler went into the house ahead of me, so I put off my visit."

"Grease us twice!" His greenish eyes glittered happily. "Are you telling me the Whisper was there?"

"Yeah." He threw his cigar on the floor, stood up, planted his fat hands on the desk top, and leaned over them toward me, oozing delight from every pore.

Dashiell Hammett, Red Harvest

Let us go then, you and I,
When the evening is spread out against the sky
Like a patient etherized upon a table;
Let us go, through certain half-deserted streets,
The muttering retreats
Of restless nights in one-night cheap hotels
And sawdust restaurants with oyster-shells:

Streets that follow like a tedious argument
Of insidious intent
To lead you to an overwhelming **question** . . .
Oh, do not ask, "What is it?"
Let us go and make our visit.

In the room the women come and go
Talking of Michelangelo.

T. S. Eliot, The Love Song of J. Alfred Prufrock

"How were the lectures?" Tengo asked, his second meaningless **question**.

Fuka-Eri took a drink of water without averting her gaze. She did not answer the **question**. Tengo guessed he couldn't have made too bad an impression if she came twice. She would have quit after the first one if it hadn't aroused her interest.

"You're in your third year of high school, aren't you?" Tengo asked.

"More or less."

"Studying for college entrance exams?"

She shook her head.

Tengo could not decide whether this meant "I don't want to talk about my college entrance exams" or "I wouldn't be caught dead taking college entrance exams." He recalled Komatsu's remark on how little Fuka-Eri had to say.

The waiter came for their orders. Fuka-Eri still had her coat on. She ordered a salad and bread. "That's all," she said, returning the menu to the waiter. Then, as if it suddenly occurred to her, she added, "And a glass of white wine."

The young waiter seemed about to ask her age, but she gave him a stare that made him turn red, and he swallowed his words. *Impressive*, Tengo thought again.

Haruki Murakami, 1Q84

And indeed there will be time
For the yellow smoke that slides along the street,
Rubbing its back upon the window-panes;
There will be time, there will be time
To prepare a face to meet the faces that you meet;
There will be time to murder and create,
And time for all the works and days of hands
That lift and drop a **question** on your plate;
Time for you and time for me,
And time yet for a hundred indecisions,
And for a hundred visions and revisions,
Before the taking of a toast and tea.

In the room the women come and go
Talking of Michelangelo.

And indeed there will be time
To wonder, "Do I dare?" and, "Do I dare?"

T. S. Eliot, The Love Song of J. Alfred Prufrock

He ordered seafood linguine and decided to join Fuka-Eri in a glass of white wine.

"You're a teacher and a writer," Fuka-Eri said. She seemed to be asking Tengo a **question**. Apparently, asking **questions** without **question** marks was another characteristic of her speech.

"For now," Tengo said.

"You don't look like either."

"Maybe not," he said. He thought of smiling but couldn't quite manage it. "I'm certified as an instructor and I do teach courses at a cram school, but I'm not exactly a teacher. I write fiction, but I've never been published, so I'm not a writer yet, either."

"You're nothing."

Tengo nodded. "Exactly. For the moment, I'm nothing."

Haruki Murakami, 1Q84

"She did most of the talking. I don't ask many **questions**. I wait and I listen. In the end you learn more that way." He gave me a meaningful look, as if I should start applying this principle. I waited and listened. Nothing happened.

Ross Macdonald, The Chill

He waited and waited, and the clock struck twelve; but Doctor Manette did not come back. Mr. Lorry returned, and found no tidings of him, and brought none. Where could he be?

They were discussing this **question**, and were almost building up some weak structure of hope on his prolonged absence, when they heard him on the stairs. The instant he entered the room, it was plain that all was lost.

Whether he had really been to any one, or whether he had been all that time traversing the streets, was never known. As he stood staring at them, they asked him no **question**, for his face told them everything.

"I cannot find it," said he, "and I must have it. Where is it?"

Charles Dickens, A Tale of Two Cities

The hunt for new surveillance technologies is ongoing: a delegation of senior LAPD officials traveled last year to Israel, where they were shuttled by minibus on a tour of security and intelligence companies. (The department's relationship to the country was first forged under Bratton, who made regular visits.) "We are all confronted with . . . the same enemy," Horace Frank, the LAPD's chief of information technology, told a crowd at the Big Data Intelligence Conference in Herzliya, "the ever-growing threat of terrorism and other major criminal elements." According to an account of the trip in the *Jewish Journal*, one item of particular interest to the police was a drone that carries cameras with facial-recognition capabilities and can intercept wireless communications. LAPD deputy chief Jose Perez tweeted a picture of the group at a company called Nice Systems, which specializes in surveillance and cyber intelligence, against a backdrop that read EVERY VOICE DESERVES TO BE HEARD.

In 2012, a Senate investigative committee headed by Oklahoma Republican Tom Coburn found that lax government oversight of the U.A.S.I. program had led to a vast catalogue of expenditures with dubious counterterrorism benefits. Arizona officials spent $90,000 enhancing the security of the Peoria Sports Complex, where the San Diego Padres and Seattle Mariners hold spring training. Jacksonville, Florida, produced an instructional video about how to spot terrorists, which advised viewers to look for individuals who display "average or above average intelligence" or "conspicuous adaptation to Western culture and values" or "religious behavior" such as "mumbling prayers." In 2012, U.A.S.I. money was used to cover the $1,000 entry fees of hundreds of law-enforcement and military personnel who attended a counterterrorism summit held amid the "exotic beauty and lush grandeur" of a private island off the coast of San Diego. The five-day event, which was sponsored by the HALO Corporation, a private security firm, featured a keynote speech by former CIA and NSA director Michael Hayden, as well as a slew of private companies advertising counterterrorism services and products. A highlight of the summit was the staging of a "zombie apocalypse" by a tactical-training company called Strategic Operations. Actors dressed as zombies wandered around sets designed to mimic a Middle Eastern village while SWAT teams fired blanks at them.

Justin Rood, a former congressional investigator for Coburn who now works for the Project on Government Oversight, a nonprofit that investigates political corruption, told me recently that nothing much has changed since the revelations of the Coburn report, largely because the system for the disbursement of funds is so firmly set in place. "They've basically developed a program that hands out large amounts of cash, no **questions** asked, to every congressional state and district," Rood said. "Who would vote against that?"

> *Petra Bartosiewicz, Beyond the Broken Window (Harper's Magazine)*

p. 764–10

The founding fathers specifically mentioned servants, slaves, and American Indians as ineligible to vote because they were not free. Women, although free, were ineligible to vote also (because of their gender). The fact that women were free, yet had no political rights—like voting or holding office—was an **incongruity** (*out of place or inappropriate*). Choices (C) and (E) are contradicted in the passage, so they can both be disregarded immediately.

A

> *Henry Davis, Explanations for the Official SAT Study Guide* **Questions**: *Detailed Explanations for the Answers for Every* **Question**

The remaining **questions**, 3, 5, and 8, show wide variation in the responses (Table 5.3). Note that in **question** 3, a vote of Yes is actually a negative response, and so we have italicized this row as well.

> *Holly Zullo, Kathy Gniadek, Derek Bruff and Kelly Cline, Student Surveys: What Do They Think? (Teaching Mathematics with Classroom Voting: With and Without Clickers)*

Question 1.23 demonstrates that once we have extracted the right information, V begins to look a lot like a quota system. Of course, in that **question** the information we needed was basically handed to us on a silver platter. We can't expect to always be this lucky, but as we noted previously, we should be able to find out all the information we need by simply asking V the right **questions**.

> *Jonathan K. Hodge and Richard E. Klima, The Mathematics of Voting and Elections: A Hands-on Approach*

True the actual practise is not as bad as the theoretical extreme. Still, there is no **question** that gerrymandering has a huge and detrimental effect on American elections.

> *Burkard Polster and Marty Ross, A Dingo Ate My Math Book*

Madison hardcore band No **Question** set its parameters nearly five years ago and hasn't budged. Screams, filth-caked riffs, each song a furious battering of 90 seconds, give or take. Listening to a No **Question** track is like ripping off a full-body bandage, crusted scabs and all.

"This band has always been very limited sonically, and we keep it that way as a unique homage to '80s hardcore," says drummer Anders Totten. "Historically, it's worked best when someone can provide a completed or partially completed song and show it to everyone for editing or elaboration."

Still, No **Question** has found variety within those boundaries, and pushes its songs through plenty of queasy slowdowns on its second release, the new *Internal Bleeding*. This is also the band's first recording with guitarist Mike Berte and bassist Maggie Denman. Previous lineups of the band wrote four of the songs on the record, but *Internal Bleeding* still captures No **Question's** solidification as a unit.

*Scott Gordon, No **Question's** Second Release Drags Out the Pain (tonemadison.com)*

Question 1.2. Suppose all 101 of the citizens of Stickeyville show up at the polls to vote on election day. If 100 of them vote for Dowell and Stan votes for Stutzman (his girlfriend), who would win the election under the method described in the preceding paragraph?

Jonathan K. Hodge and Richard E. Klima, The Mathematics of Voting and Elections: A Hands-on Approach

At this point we have discussed various methods for deciding two candidate elections. Many more methods exist, but we will not be concerned with them for now. We have also identified five criteria for evaluating methods. So this begs the **question**: Which methods satisfy which criteria? Table 1.1 answers this **question**. The answer "yes" or "no" in a box in this chart indicates whether the method to the left satisfies the criterion above.

The diligent reader will want to verify that the answers are as we claim. Generally, our criteria ask if a social choice function behaves a certain way always. A "yes" answer begs for a proof. On the other hand, a "no" answer begs for a counterexample, as in Proposition 1.19.

E. Arthur Robinson and Daniel H. Ullman, The Mathematics of Politics

p. 910–6

In the context of this passage the use of the words "conjure up" in line 5 most nearly means imagine. Convene (A) means set up or organize; portray (B) means to render or reveal; entreat (D) means beg or plead; and recollect (E) means to remember or call to mind.

C

*Henry Davis, Explanations for the Official SAT Study Guide **Questions**: Detailed Explanations for the Answers for Every **Question***

But there is nothing like Defoe's linear, logical plot of problem-solving. Defoe applies this formula within a single episode, exemplified by the goats, as well as across the chain of episodes that form the entire narrative. In Mikhail Bakhtin's seminal taxonomy of adventure fiction, Bakhtin qualified adventure fiction as moving through an "empty time," which was an effect of the haphazard, sometimes disconnected or disordered quality of adventure found in classical romance. In Robinson Crusoe's adventures, in contrast, the time is full—full of problems, efforts, and the performance of craft, which fills up a desolate island with the comforts of civilization.

One thing Defoe has learned from prior adventure fiction is, however, to draft the character of Crusoe as a heroic protagonist. Such singularity enhances the power of Crusoe's capacity, though it contrasts with the collective agency of craft. The mariner, as I have suggested, exercised his agency as part of a skilled community defined by the bonds of work. This collective agency is implicit in the organization of information to serve future mariners, and it is explicit in Dampier's collective narrative voice: "we lay here all the Day, and scrubb'd our new Bark," "we had much Wind and Rain, and we lost the Canoa," "we went from thence with a moderate gale of Wind at S.W.," etc. In Crusoe's case, in contrast, the deeds procuring survival are all his own. With this implementation of a unique hero, Defoe not only focuses attention on the power of Crusoe's agency. He also discovers a character who has the contours of a psychological individual, available for reader identification, although Crusoe is a flat character compared to the eccentric, psychologically rounded characters that we associate with modern subjectivity, like the unique protagonist of Jean-Jacques Rousseau's *Confessions*.[33] There is an ideological yield to Defoe's reduction: isolating the mariner and distilling craft to the heroic deeds of an individual, Defoe gives a liberal countenance of individual capacity to the collectivity of the sea.

Defoe's adventure formula will prove influential for maritime adventure fiction, as for adventure fiction more generally. Jean-Yves Tadié, focusing primarily on nineteenth-century adventure fiction, is describing the pattern that Defoe invents from maritime practices of narration when Tadié writes that "in the organization of the adventure novel, in fact no **question** is without an answer, no problem is without a solution, no expectation is without an event . . . and reciprocally, no answer is without a new **question**, no solution without a problem, no events without expectation, until the close of the narrative."[34]

Margaret Cohen, The Novel and the Sea

Question 7.38. The quantities we denoted by are often called *binomial coefficients*. Research the meaning of this name and write a summary of your findings. Include in your summary a description of at least one mathematical application of binomial coefficients outside the area of voting theory.

Jonathan K. Hodge and Richard E. Klima, The Mathematics of Voting and Elections: A Hands-on Approach

Imagine that you attempt to answer this **question** by listing a number of popular fruits and identifying a number of criteria for assessing them. The fruits you consider by no means exhaust all possibilities. In fact, you might consider only the apple, the banana, the cherry, the date, and the elderberry.

Here are seven yes-no criteria for assessing fruit:

(1) Does the fruit taste good?
(2) Is the fruit healthy?
(3) Is the fruit inexpensive?
(4) Is the fruit nonpoisonous?
(5) Does the common English name of the fruit start with a vowel?
(6) Is the fruit yellow and shaped like a banana?

Create a 5-by-7 matrix whose rows are indexed by the five fruits and whose columns are indexed by the 7 criteria. Put the word "yes" or "no" in each cell of the matrix according to whether the fruit indexing that row has the property indexing that column. (Resist the temptation to answer equivocally. Understand that there is no wrong answer, since, as they say, there's no accounting for taste. Naturally, some of the answers are a matter of opinion.)

E. Arthur Robinson and Daniel H. Ullman, The Mathematics of Politics

"You like math."

Tengo mentally added a **question** mark to her comment and answered this new **question**: "I do like math. I've always liked it, and I still like it."

"What about it."

"What do I like about math? Hmm. When I've got figures in front of me, it relaxes me. Kind of like, everything fits where it belongs."

Haruki Murakami, 1Q84

Question 7.39. In combinatorics, the quantity $\binom{n}{k}$ is often defined by the formula

$$\binom{n}{k} = \frac{n!}{k! \times (n-k)!}$$

Explain why this definition of $\binom{n}{k}$ is completely consistent with the definition we used in this chapter.

Jonathan K. Hodge and Richard E. Klima, The Mathematics of Voting and Elections: A Hands-on Approach

In each case the answer to that all-important **question** was, No.

Wilkie Collins, The Law and the Lady

Question 7.40. It is a well-known fact in the world of combinatorics that for any value of n,

$$\binom{n}{0} + \binom{n}{1} + \binom{n}{2} + \cdots + \binom{n}{n-1} + \binom{n}{n} = 2^n$$

Without doing any calculations, explain why this equation holds in general. (Hint: Explain how the two sides of the equation can be viewed as two different ways of counting the same thing.)

Jonathan K. Hodge and Richard E. Klima, The Mathematics of Voting and Elections: A Hands-on Approach

But not committees. No entry is made: in the lords Journals, of the houses adjourning themselves from Edw. VI's time, and from Hen. VIII's time to the end of the Long Parliament by a **question**. No entry is made of the commons adjournment, unless when the king commanded the adjournment, as in the case now before you. In King James's time, the ordinary adjournments, from day to day, were not entered into the Journal. That of the 12th James was not a parliament, for nothing was done in it; no bills passed. But in that Journal there are no footsteps of this matter.

T. C. Hansard, The Parliamentary History of England, From the Earliest Period to the Year 1803. From Which Last-Mentioned Epoch It Is Continued Downwards in the Work Entitled, "The Parliamentary Debates." Vol. IV. A.D. 1660–1668

Question 7.42. Recall from **Question** 6.27 the voting system used to amend the Constitution of Canada. Find the Banzhaf index of each of the voters in this system (the ten Canadian provinces), and comment on anything that strikes you as being strange or unusual about the results.

Question 7.43. Recall from **Question** 6.38 that the voting system used to make decisions in the city council of Fresno, California can be viewed as the weighted voting system [5 : 2, 1, 1, 1, 1, 1, 1]. Find the Banzhaf and Shapley-Shubik indices of each of the voters in this system.

Question 7.44. Recall from **Question** 6.39 that the voting system used to make national yes/no decisions in Australia can be viewed as the weighted voting system [5 : 3, 1, 1, 1, 1, 1, 1]. Find the Banzhaf and Shapley-Shubik indices of each of the voters in this system.

Question 7.45. Suppose that in Psykozia's federal system, the states of Ignorance and Bliss merge to form one new state, Enlightenment. (So, in this case, ignorance really is bliss!) What corresponding changes do you think should be made to the voting system used by Psykozia's federal government? With these changes, would the people of Enlightenment have more, less, or the same amount of power as they had before the merger?

Jonathan K. Hodge and Richard E. Klima, The Mathematics of Voting and Elections: A Hands-on Approach

As we shall see, this **question** is even more depressing: the answer is a resounding and necessary "No"!

Burkard Polster and Marty Ross, A Dingo Ate My Math Book

"Oh, really?" Tengo said. No one had ever told him this before.

"Like you were talking about somebody important to you," she said.

"I can maybe get even more passionate when I lecture on sequences," Tengo said. "Sequences were a personal favorite of mine in high school math."

"You like sequences," Fuka-Eri asked, without a **question** mark.

"To me, they're like Bach's *Well-Tempered Clavier*. I never get tired of them. There's always something new to discover."

"I know the *Well-Tempered Clavier*."

"You like Bach?"

Fuka-Eri nodded. "The Professor is always listening to it."

"The Professor? One of your teachers?"

Fuka-Eri did not answer. She looked at Tengo with an expression that seemed to say, "It's too soon to talk about that."

Haruki Murakami, 1Q84

Andrew took Grant's advice, not with enthusiasm, but because he had no choice. But once having taken it, he began to manufacture the enthusiasm. Wasn't Peter Knowles already on his way to California where he was to work on problems connected with flight control in a vacuum? Other corporations were treating scientists to a season in the Princeton Institute for Advanced Studies, careful all the while not to let them slip the corporate leash. It was not a **question** of dignity or purpose for Andrew. Common sense, that's all, plain common sense. And when the wee voice whispered, "Oh, how very common is common sense," he told it to shut up.

After consultation with Celia and Grant, a long-distance call to Peter Knowles, and a brief colloquy with his soul, Andrew applied to Baldwin-Nelson, a giant in the electronics field. Baldwin-Nelson was seeking a special man for a special top secret project.

One morning Andrew faced a Baldwin-Nelson underling, a three-buttoned link in the chain of command. "Naturally, we are aware of your qualifications," said Underling, enunciating carefully to prove that Big Business can talk good English (speechwise), "and it would be presumptuous of me to **question** them."

"Yes," Andrew agreed. The slight pursing of Underling's lips surprised him. Had "Yes" been the wrong answer?

Ira Wallach, The Absence of a Cello

"No," was the painter's curt reply, as if the **question** prevented him saying any more.

Franz Kafka, The Trial

Cultural studies also offered the possibility of systematic commentary on a range of phenomena—symbolic forms, meanings, motives, technologies, social movements, popular culture—on which political economy was inevitably silent—or at least relatively so. That reach could, of course, be sacrificed to yet another debate about the base-superstructure, and so it was, as if differences of emphasis and interest, as well as stategy, could be reduced to philosophical **questions**. There is no resolution to such **questions** and so the alternative must be, not to engage the **question** but to outflank it, not to reformulate the base and superstructure, to find newer and cleverer ways to express 'interrelations' and 'last instances' but to side-step the **question** entirely. The only reason I can figure for retaining either the distinction or the argument is as a pious genuflection to the past and to feel morally upright, convinced we are on the right side of history.

James W. Carey, *Reflections on the Project of (American) Cultural Studies (Cultural Studies in* **Question***)*

Once, people actually lived like that! He had lived like that—moment to moment, he and his friends had found a way to say no to any **question**. *Do you have a philosophy of life? Fuck off*—or, *Yes, I have a philosophy of life: "fuck off."* In a store: *May I help you, sir? Fuck off.* In a cafe: *Yes? My good man, the* **question** *you have answered is a* **question** *I have refrained from asking—fuck off.*

Greil Marcus, *Lipstick Traces: A Secret History of the Twentieth Century*

p. 458–7

The second blank is easier because it means the same thing as "irascible" which is a negative word meaning unpleasant and mean-spirited. Aging brings about physical changes but does not alter "disposition" which means one's personality. If someone is "cantankerous" they are irritable and unpleasant. Someone who is churlish they are impolite, coarse, and rude. Benevolent means kind and caring. If someone is laconic they are terse, brief, and concise.

A

Henry Davis, *Explanations for the Official SAT Study Guide* **Questions***: Detailed Explanations for the Answers for Every* **Question**

Marcus felt that Gelb didn't really answer that **question** or others. "He was partly responsive to about half the **questions**, and the others he just ignored," Marcus told me. "That was that." (Another board member said that Gelb listened patiently to Marcus's "angry diatribe," answered his **questions**, and added that the issues had already been considered.)

James B. Steward, *A Fight at the Opera (The New Yorker)*

6.5

For an answer which cannot be expressed the **question** too cannot be expressed. *The riddle* does not exist.

If a **question** can be put at all, then it can *also* be answered.

6.51

Scepticism is *not* irrefutable, but palpably senseless, if it would doubt where a **question** cannot be asked.

For doubt can only exist where there is a **question**; a **question** only where there is an answer, and this only where something *can* be *said*.

6.52

We feel that even if *all possible* scientific **questions** be answered, the problems of life have still not been touched at all. Of course there is then no **question** left, and just this is the answer.

6.521

The solution of the problem of life is seen in the vanishing of this problem.

(Is not this the reason why men to whom after long doubting the sense of life became clear, could not then say wherein this sense consisted?)

Ludwig Wittgenstein, Tractatus Logico-Philosophicus

"My child," said her father with sympathy and obvious understanding, "what are we to do?"

His sister just shrugged her shoulders as a sign of the helplessness and tears that had taken hold of her, displacing her earlier certainty.

"If he could just understand us," said his father almost as a **question**; his sister shook her hand vigorously through her tears as a sign that of that there was no **question**.

Franz Kafka, Metamorphosis

Our next Oxford Alumni Book Club read will be 'Brief Answers to the Big **Questions**', the final thoughts on the universe's biggest **questions** from alumnus Stephen Hawking (University College, Oxford, 1959). Get yourself a copy of the book and join the discussion.

Oxford Alumni, Twitter, March 18, 2020

Questioning Was Brief

When I burn'd in desire to **question** them further, they made themselves air, into which they vanish'd.

William Shakespeare, The Tragedy of Macbeth

Questioning was brief. After a few hours' screaming, a single pistol shot would ring out and the uneasy quiet of the jungle would return. Nobody came back from **questioning**.

John le Carré, The Secret Pilgrim

Keep Calm and Posters (keepcalmandposters.com)

Question, or Torture

*As long as it is not tied to a particular ideology or
religious tradition and promotes inclusiveness*

Is the Cosmic Censorship Hypothesis true?

Scott Chase, Michael Weiss, Philip Gibbs, Chris Hillman and Nathan Urban, *The Original Usenet Physics* **FAQ**

It is well after midnight, and the screenwriter is speculating about the No World. What does No World mean? It's not the first time he's asked the **question**. The girl no longer remembers the answer; that is, if she ever really had the answer. What *does* No World mean? she asks herself in turn. Where does a game lead to in the end?

A. G. Porta, *No World Concerto*

—No doubt, Sir,—there is a whole chapter wanting here—and a chasm of ten pages made in the book by it—but the bookbinder is neither a fool, or a knave, or a puppy— nor is the book a jot more imperfect (at least upon that score)——but, on the contrary, the book is more perfect and complete by wanting the chapter, than having it, as I shall demonstrate to your reverences in this manner.—I **question** first, by the bye, whether the same experiment might not be made as successfully upon sundry other chapters—but there is no end, an' please your reverences, in trying experiments upon chapters—we have had enough of it——So there's an end of that matter.

Laurence Sterne, *The Life and Opinions of Tristram Shandy, Gentleman*

What comes next?

What number is missing from the left-hand circle?

What letter should replace the **question** mark?

Insert the letters of the phrase AN AGENT'S GAMMA into the following blanks only once each to complete a palindromic sentence, that is, one that reads the same backwards and forwards. For example, MADAM, I'M ADAM.

Find the number to replace the **question** mark.

What phrase is indicated here?

Philip J. Carter and Kenneth A. Russell, *The Book of IQ Tests: 25 Self-Scoring Quizzes to Sharpen Your Mind*

p. 459–11

Quotation marks around "empty" would most likely indicate irony or humor. In this case the author is disagreeing with the other author's definition of "empty" which implies the land is not used. The author of Passage 2 sees empty land as necessary to grow food or supply raw materials which are necessary for survival. He is definitely disagreeing about how empty land is characterized.

C

*Henry Davis, Explanations for the Official SAT Study Guide **Questions**: Detailed Explanations for the Answers for Every **Question***

Aomame took careful notes on the commentary and the biographical factual material, but the book gave no hint as to what kind of connection there was—or could have been—between herself and this *Sinfonietta*. She left the library and wandered aimlessly through the streets as evening approached, often talking to herself or shaking her head.

Of course, it's all just a hypothesis, Aomame told herself as she walked. *But it's the most compelling hypothesis I can produce at the moment; I'll have to act according to this one, I suppose, until a more compelling hypothesis comes along. Otherwise, I could end up being thrown to the ground somewhere. If only for that reason, I'd better give an appropriate name to this new situation in which I find myself. There's a need, too, for a special name in order to distinguish between this present world and the former world in which the police carried old-fashioned revolvers. Even cats and dogs need names. A newly changed world must need one, too.*

1Q84—that's what I'll call this new world, Aomame decided.

*Q is for "**question** mark." A world that bears a **question**.*

Haruki Murakami, 1Q84

DAWN is to DAY as WINTER is to:

In which of the sentences below does the name of an animal not appear?

Eliminate twelve letters from the phrase below to leave a word meaning "shakes"

BEDROOMS, ROMANTIC, ANSWERED, WEAKENED, ? Which is the next word?

The vowels have been omitted from this quotation. See if you can put them back in.

What number should replace the **question** mark?

Which is the odd one out?

Philip J. Carter and Kenneth A. Russell, The Book of IQ Tests: 25 Self-Scoring Quizzes to Sharpen Your Mind

Aomame nodded to herself as she walked along.

*Like it or not; I'm here now, in the year 1Q84. The 1984 that I knew no longer exists. It's 1Q84 now. The air has changed, the scene has changed. I have to adapt to this world-with-a-**question**-mark as soon as I can. Like an animal released into a new forest. In order to protect myself and survive, I have to learn the rules of this place and adapt myself to them.*

Haruki Murakami, 1Q84

One letter in each word of a well-known saying has been changed. What is the saying?

"An indirect, ingenious, and often cunning means to gain an end." What word most closely fits the above definition?

Insert the name of a tree into the bottom line to complete the three-letter words.

What number should replace the **question** mark?

If the missing letters in the circle are correctly inserted they will form an eight-letter word. The word does not have to be read in a clockwise direction, but the letters are consecutive. What is the word and missing letters?

Which mathematical symbol should replace the **question** mark to continue the series?

This is a treasure map. The treasure is marked T. You have to find the starting square. 2N means move 2 squares north.

Place a word in the parentheses that when placed on the end of the first word makes a word, and when placed in front of the second word also makes a word.

Starting at an outside square and moving in any direction, spell out the name of a bird.

A word can be placed in the parentheses that has the same meaning as the words outside. What is it?

Which symbol replaces the **question** mark?

Philip J. Carter and Kenneth A. Russell, The Book of IQ Tests: 25 Self-Scoring Quizzes to Sharpen Your Mind

"But for me, so strangely unprosperous had I been, the net-result of my Workings amounted as yet simply to—Nothing. How then could I believe in my Strength, when there was as yet no mirror to see it in? Ever did this agitating, yet, as I now perceive, quite frivolous **question**, remain to me insoluble: Hast thou a certain Faculty, a certain Worth, such even as the most have not; or art thou the completest Dullard of these modern times? Alas, the fearful Unbelief is unbelief in yourself; and how could I believe? Had not my first, last Faith in myself, when even to me the Heavens seemed laid open, and I dared to love, been all too cruelly belied? The speculative Mystery of Life grew ever more mysterious to me: neither in the practical Mystery had I made the slightest progress, but been everywhere buffeted, foiled, and contemptuously cast out. A feeble unit in the middle of a threatening Infinitude, I seemed to have nothing given me but eyes, whereby to discern my own wretchedness. Invisible yet impenetrable walls, as of Enchantment, divided me from all living: was there, in the wide world, any true bosom I could press trustfully to mine? O Heaven, No, there was none! I kept a lock upon my lips: why should I speak much with that shifting variety of so-called Friends, in whose withered, vain and too-hungry souls Friendship was but an incredible tradition? In such cases, your resource is to talk little, and that little mostly from the Newspapers. Now when I look back, it was a strange isolation I then lived in. The men and women around me, even speaking with me, were but Figures; I had, practically, forgotten that they were alive, that they were not merely automatic. In the midst of their crowded streets and assemblages, I walked solitary; and (except as it was my own heart, not another's, that I kept devouring) savage also, as the tiger in his jungle. Some comfort it would have been, could I, like a Faust, have fancied myself tempted and tormented of the Devil; for a Hell, as I imagine, without Life, though only diabolic Life, were more frightful: but in our age of Down-pulling and Disbelief, the very Devil has been pulled down, you cannot so much as believe in a Devil. To me the Universe was all void of Life, of Purpose, of Volition, even of Hostility: it was one huge, dead, immeasurable Steam-engine, rolling on, in its dead indifference, to grind me limb from limb. Oh, the vast, gloomy, solitary Golgotha, and Mill of Death! Why was the Living banished thither companionless, conscious? Why, if there is no Devil; nay, unless the Devil is your God?"

A prey incessantly to such corrosions, might not, moreover, as the worst aggravation to them, the iron constitution even of a Teufelsdröckh threaten to fail?

Thomas Carlyle, Sartor Resartus: The Life and Opinions of Herr Teufelsdröckh

"That is a **question** we are not going to answer," sighed the thin one. "In fact, to be totally frank with you, we are not going to answer any **questions** unless they are absolutely essential to the satisfactory conclusion of our agreement with you."

"Agreement?"

"We've already told you: you forget about the existence of Vallejo, the Clinique Arago and the rest, and we'll forget about this envelope."

Lazily, but also with an artificial, studied arrogance, the dark one took out a long, dark-brown envelope, of the kind used by the Bank of Paris ten years ago, and dropped it onto the table beside the bottle. It contained more than two thousand francs.

"But why?"

The thin one raised a warning finger and traced a hieroglyph in the air, keeping me at a distance.

"No **questions**, remember."

Roberto Bolaño, Monsieur Pain

"Got it," I said.

"Wasn't talking to you. But now that I am, do you have any **questions** you want to ask me?"

"I didn't come to ask you **questions**," I said. "I'm not exactly sure why I'm here."

Sam Lipsyte, The Ask

The Karmapa* came to Princeton because he wanted to be a college student for a day. "It's very important for me to feel this sort of sadness," he said. He attended some classes: sculpture (on an iPhone, he had shown students his drawings—one of a tiger would look great on the side of a van); gender studies and sexuality (the Karmapa has led a campaign to allow the full ordination of Buddhist nuns, a radical position that has earned him a reputation as a feminist). In a meditation group, a student said, "We really investigated our own suffering and the source of our suffering and the sources of suffering everywhere. Do you have any **questions** about this?" The Karmapa responded, "No, not really."

Nick Paumgarten, Karmapa on Campus (The New Yorker)

The style that gradually developed could be called *post-problem art*. It bore a clear if unacknowledged debt to the wonderful ad slogans of the period, like Staples's "That Was Easy" and Amazon's ". . . And You're Done." *Done!* An amazing word. Go ahead, have done with all the anguished historical debates over meaning and criticality and politics and taste. For better or for worse, everyone was in agreement that the market was the only indicator that mattered now. This climate, in which artworks would certainly sell, and the fact of selling was sufficient verification of their quality, made it officially okay simply to like a painting. It was no longer necessary to deem a piece interesting, provocative, weird, or complex, and it was almost incomprehensible to hate something because you liked it, or like it because it unsettled you, or any of the other ambivalent and twisted ways that people wrestled with the intersection of feelings and aesthetics. You almost didn't need words anymore: it was enough to say, "That painting is *awesome*," just as you'd say, "This spaghetti is *awesome*." Alternately you could use one of the other

---

* His Holiness the Seventheenth Karmapa, Ogyen Trinley Dorje, the top lama in the Karma Kagyu order of Tibetan Buddhism

all-purpose terms of the era, like "nice," "crazy," "perfect," and "insane." This was a radical development, one that forwent any more complicated relationship with art; it was a tremendous ironing-out process. Before you knew it, you'd spy a Malevich and declare, "That guy's a total badass." Or was it Marinetti who was the badass?

These new artworks aroused accusations of cynicism, and he admitted that he was inviting that conversation. But what was cynicism? He defined cynicism as proceeding in a way that you knew to be harmful or morally bankrupt, for reasons of greed or cowardice. The **question** was, what if you found such compromised behavior complex and compelling? What if you believed that exploring the world of perceived or actual cynicism was a powerful way to understand our contemporary moment? What if you *believed in not believing*? Executives or world leaders entertaining this **question** would rightly be classified as sociopaths, but in the world of art these **questions** were okay, because suffering wasn't directly involved and any apparent cynicism was likely to be banal and venal, e.g., cashing in by provoking your audience with facile or puerile gestures. He didn't feel that his work belonged in this category. If his paintings were provocative, it was because they drew out acute and omnipresent cultural toxins: anxieties about cynicism and selling out, feelings that had everything to do with how fucked-up it was to live under neoliberal free-market capitalism. He found this exhilarating; he *believed* in it. And this tangle of contradictions was the greatest thing about art: it always meant the opposite of what you thought it meant, or wanted it to mean. Abstract versus representational, old versus new, pure versus corrupt, tasteful versus tasteless: all artistic values and categories were inherently unstable and might suddenly swap places.

Seth Price, Fuck Seth Price (Harper's Magazine)

p. 549–1

The word "paradoxically" indicates we will have a contrast in our answer choices. The paradox indicates something that is in contrast or confusing. If we look at our answer choices we can see a clear paradox in answer choice C as leaders who would proclaim that they are liberating would not be expected to be repressive. We can eliminate the other answer choices since "regal" means royal or majestic and being imperial means the same. Simplistic would not indicate a contrast with neutral. A *totalitarian* would be an absolutist, so no paradox. And if someone is *scandalous* they would be easily compromised.

C

p. 549–2

With the opening word "Despite" we know that we need something to contrast with his brilliant career. So we need something negative for his feelings which gives us a choice of answer choices A, C, or D. "Dispel" means to get rid of. So he would want to get rid of his feelings of inferiority, but being plagued by doubts he would not be able to dispel those feelings. *Reconcile* means to settle or reunite. *Fathom* means to understand or comprehend.

D

p. 549–4

This is a vocabulary **question** and we are looking for a word that indicates something that is diametrically opposite. That happens to be the exact definition of *antipodes*.

The classic "Keep Calm and Carry On" WW2 slogan, but with a twist. Keep calm and **question** everything. A perfect gift for the free thinkers, the atheists, the non-religious, and those who don't believe without sufficient evidence.

*StencilMyst, Keep Calm and **Question** Everything Poster (redbubble.com)*

We can eliminate the other answer choices by knowing satellites are something orbit around something or depends on something, a *bifurcation* is a split or a division, and *dichotomies* indicate a separation of different and contradictory things.

B

*Henry Davis, Explanations for the Official SAT Study Guide **Questions**: Detailed Explanations for the Answers for Every **Question***

These constant, countless reversals: psychiatrists could have been called in, but the pathology was social. As the years went on it became epidemic. In Berkeley in the mid-1960s, I used to wonder at the way friends made the world new each day by cartwheeling down the street, moment to moment exchanging Trotskyism for anarchism for Stalinism for the occult for drugs for religion while professors who in the 1930s were Communists and now were Freudians explained it all. In every case there was a received answer to every **question**, which meant there were no **questions**. Everything seemed possible, and the prospect was terrifying—so "nothing is true," one basis for "everything is possible," was exchanged for one truth, whatever it was. Everything was present save a critical spirit, which might have made real the great adventure in doubt that, as Descartes described it, lay behind his "Cogito, ergo sum": his dead slogan. No doubt the mad multiplication of choices by which "the sixties" are known led straight to a surrender of choice in the next decades, a surrender to authoritarian religion, authoritarian politics—for some, freedom from doubt was always the point, peace of mind worth any price. An aide to Senator Jesse Helms, tribune of the American right, could speak of the need to go back beyond Descartes, explaining that inside all the vulgar propaganda of fetus murder and racist nightmare was a true project: the repeal of the Enlightenment, the rebuilding of a world where the affirmation of one's own thoughts was sin, the return of the will to God. Everyone knows history moves in circles; the surprise is how big the circles are.

Greil Marcus, Lipstick Traces: A Secret History of the Twentieth Century

We ran around in circles, straining our eyes at the ground, and when we got through we knew what we had known at the beginning—the Chrysler had run into a eucalyptus tree. There were tire-marks on the road, and marks that could have been footprints on the ground by the car; but it was possible to find the same sort of marks in a hundred places along that, or any other, road. We got into our borrowed car again and drove on, asking **questions** wherever we found someone to **question**; and all the answers were: No, we didn't see her or them.

"What about this fellow Baker?" I asked Rolly as we turned around to go back.

Dashiell Hammett, The Dain Curse

Notable enough too, here as elsewhere, wilt thou find the potency of Names; which indeed are but one kind of such custom-woven, wonder-hiding Garments. Witchcraft, and all manner of Spectre-work, and Demonology, we have now named Madness, and Diseases of the Nerves. Seldom reflecting that still the new **question** comes upon us: What is Madness, what are Nerves? Ever, as before, does Madness remain a mysterious-terrific, altogether *infernal* boiling-up of the Nether Chaotic Deep, through this fair-painted Vision of Creation, which swims thereon, which we name the Real. Was Luther's Picture of the Devil less a Reality, whether it were formed within the bodily eye, or without it? In every the wisest Soul lies a whole world of internal Madness,

TO KEEP CALM OR NOT TO KEEP CALM THAT IS THE **QUESTION** . . . :D

Comments

No comments yet! Add one to start the conversation.

www.pinterest.com/pin/47217496074520987

an authentic Demon-Empire; out of which, indeed, his world of Wisdom has been creatively built together, and now rests there, as on its dark foundations does a habitable flowery Earth rind.

But deepest of all illusory Appearances, for hiding Wonder, as for many other ends, are your two grand fundamental world-enveloping Appearances, SPACE and TIME. These, as spun and woven for us from before Birth itself, to clothe our celestial ME for dwelling here, and yet to blind it,—lie all-embracing, as the universal canvas, or warp and woof, whereby all minor Illusions, in this Phantasm Existence, weave and paint themselves.

Thomas Carlyle, Sartor Resartus: The Life and Opinions of Herr Teufelsdröckh

My favorite composer is Bach, as a matter of fact, whom I do not believe I have mentioned at all in these pages.

I have just realized something else. On the front seat of the vehicle in which I turned on the air-conditioning, after having gotten sweaty from hitting the tennis balls, there was a paperback edition of *The Way of All Flesh*, by Samuel Butler.

Which presumably answers the **question** as to where I came upon the footnote about Samuel Butler having said that it was a woman who wrote the *Odyssey*.

Or perhaps the book contained some sort of preface, dealing with the life of Samuel Butler, which brought up this fact. I am more than positive that I have never read a life of Samuel Butler, however, even in the form of a preface, what with knowing even less about Samuel Butler than I do about *The Way of All Flesh*, which I am just as positive I have never read.

And doubtless I would have scarcely looked into the book on that particular afternoon in either case.

If only because of having set fire to the pages of a life of Brahms not long before, in trying to simulate seagulls, surely I would have wished to devote my attention to the tape deck instead.

David Markson, Wittgenstein's Mistress

p. 492–11

Since "music" is the subject of the first clause, the last part of the sentence must compare "the music" not the artists. The pronoun "that" in the phrase "than that of" in answer choice D is the only choice we have that corrects this error by comparing music to music.

D

p. 492–12

The intention of the sentence is to show cause and effect; therefore, the best choice of wording would be the phrase stating "thus inaugurating" which signaled the effect of the poetry reading.

E

p. 493–13

Although relatively awkwardly phrased there is no error in this sentence as it maintains an active voice verb "elected" and all the other answer choices are either passive voice or more indirect. Again we're looking for the best rendition of the sentence; other choices can be correct, but we want the best.

A

*Henry Davis, Explanations for the Official SAT Study Guide **Questions**: Detailed Explanations for the Answers for Every **Question***

"Yass, yass," he said. The cousin continued to drive us around and even bought us ice-cream pops. Nevertheless Dean plied him with innumerable **questions** about the past and the cousin supplied the answers and for a moment Dean almost began to sweat again with excitement.

Jack Kerouac, On the Road

Complete the grid with the letters MAGIC so that no row, column, or diagonal line contains the same letter more than once.

I have correctly and accurately made a clear impact with the crown of a small fastener. What have I done?

If a car had increased its average speed for a 210-mile journey by 5 mph, the journey would have been completed in 1 hour less. What was the original speed of the car for the journey?

Which is the odd one out?

What number should replace the **question** mark?

Add three consecutive letters of the alphabet to the group of letters below, without splitting the consecutive letters, to form another word.

Which one of the following is not an anagram of LITTLE GIANT ENCYCLOPEDIA?

Which word is opposite in meaning to CORPULENT?

Which month comes next?

What letter should replace the **question** mark?

Which circles should replace the ones with the **question** mark?

What number should replace the **question** mark in the circle?

Philip J. Carter and Kenneth A. Russell, The Book of IQ Tests: 25 Self-Scoring Quizzes to Sharpen Your Mind

Not even ten a.m. and the temperature outside the car is 104. Catt starts the truck and searches for NPR . . . sixty miles east of Scottsdale, *All Things Considered* can barely be heard over *Bible Talk* at the 89.5 spot on the dial. *I'm Melissa Black. And I'm Robert Segal.* This Saturday morning, Melissa and Bob are engaged in a semantic debate about how to describe the freakishly hot month of June spread across the US in 2006. Is it a heat wave, or heat storm? Sold out of air conditioners, Home Depots in Oregon await new shipments of fans. In California, bodies of the elderly poor are being removed from sweltering single-wide trailers. *Robert, a heat wave is a prolonged period of hot weather accompanied by high humidity. The longest heat wave was recorded in Western Australia in 1923 when temperatures exceeded a hundred degrees for 160 consecutive days—That's right, Melissa, but a heat storm is characterized by continuous heat, temperatures remaining high overnight—*

"Heat wave"—the phrase used by Fox News on the flat screen in the Ramada lobby—conjured ice cream and childhood beach days, whereas "heat storm" was more troubling, evoking the end of the world or plague portents. The difference between the two words was similar to the difference between "abuse" and "torture" . . . the simplest words subject to endless redefinition, each debate spiraling further away from the thing these words referred to. George W. Bush didn't need the Supreme Court to stop the electoral recount in 2000. He'd already won when Melissa and Robert started chattering about chads. *And Robert, what is a chad? Well, Melissa, a chad is the impression made on a cardboard ballot by a voting machine. It can be hanging, or pregnant, or even dimpled . . .*

Catt remembers how, on the TV talk shows from her childhood, the really smart people like would leap in and say: I disagree with the **question**. The content hadn't been binarized yet to multiple-choice. Click here to learn more. For your protection, this call is being recorded and monitored. Disagreement is not on the menu. It's no longer a choice.

Chris Kraus, *Summer of Hate*

"I believe you, sir."

"Any **questions** at this point?"

"In the files."

"Shoot."

"What is the significance of the phrase 'Tree of Smoke'?"

"So you've come to the T's in the files."

"No. I just heard the phrase today."

"Jesus," Storm said. "I mentioned it, but I thought we were all kind of sharing our germs and diseases here, you know?"

"He's family," the colonel reminded him.

"So what's the meaning?" Jimmy said. "'Tree of Smoke'."

"Oh, God, I wouldn't know where to begin. It's embarrasingly poetic. It's grandiose."

Skip said, "That doesn't sound like you."

"To be poetic and grandiose?"

"To be embarrassed."

Jimmy said, "Here's a **question**: Who said, 'Keep your friends close, keep your enemies closer'?"

"Is this an interrogation?" the colonel said. "Then let's have cocktails."

Denis Johnson, *Tree of Smoke*

interrogatio

in-ter-ro-ga'-ti-o

L. "**question**, *cross-examination*"

Primarily, interrogatio is simply the Latin term forerotema (the rhetorical **question**). In the Ad Herennium, however, interrogatio is described as employing a **question** as a way of confirming or reinforcing the argument one has just made.

Examples

While, therefore, you were doing and saying and negotiating all of these things, were you not alienating the republic's allies?—Ad Herennium

Gideon Burton, *Silva Rhetoricae (The Forest of Rhetoric)*

Like, for example, the local police, led by Captain Cheney—the biggest prick in a season that hasn't hurt for lack of 'em. Cheney is barely around for the hour, but he makes the most of the limited time available to him, turning on Lou with the speed and vehemence of a man who thinks **questions** are like assholes: they all stink. Without Cheney's determination to use the Blumquists for an ill-advised sting operation, none of what follows would've happened. His plan is stupid and short-sighted, and it puts poor Ed at risk for no good reason, but because it's his plan, it's the law, and anyone who says otherwise can go hang. (Quite literally; in a particularly bizarre moment, Cheney threatens Lou with a "South Dakota necktie", which I'm fairly certain is slang for a lynching.)

> *Zack Handlen, It's a Long Night at the Motor Motel on a Climactic Fargo (A.V. Club)*

p. 391–7

Appealing to the senses with metaphors and similes like those in answer explanations 6, the answer must relate to the type of descriptive language used.

B

p. 392–10

Look in the introductory material's last line: "offers his views on the historical relationship . . ." which implies the "significance of the relationship" in answer D.

D

p. 392–11

The key to this answer is what the "message" relates to—which is found later in the passage. You must read on to determine what the passage is meant to accomplish, which is "ties must be maintained—in order for a people to survive." Therefore, "advice" is what is being given.

B

> *Henry Davis, Explanations for the Official SAT Study Guide **Questions**: Detailed Explanations for the Answers for Every **Question***

PROPOSED SYSTEM OF TERMAN AND CHILDS

Names key, knife and coin.
Enumerates parts of pictures.
Repeats 3 digits.
Knows sex.
Compares 2 weights.
Problem **questions**.

Counts 4 pennies.
Divided rectangle.
Copies square.
Aesthetic comparison.
Defines by use.

Tells morning from afternoon.
Names 4 chief colors.
Executes triple command.
Repeats 13-syllabled sentences.
Vocabulary index.

Knows right hand and left ear.

Close up of male hand holding **question** mark on rope.

Close up of businessman hand and **question** sign hanging on finger.

Knows number of fingers.
Counts 13 pennies.
Repeats 4 digits.
Solves 3 easy problem-**questions**.
Vocabulary index.

> *Warren W. Coxe, Grading Intelligence by Years and by Points (Journal of Criminal Law and Criminology)*

Questioning builds a way. We would be advised, therefore, above all to pay heed to the way, and not to fix our attention on isolated sentences and topics. The way is a way of thinking. All ways of thinking, more or less perceptibly, lead through language in a manner that is extraordinary.

> *Martin Heidegger, The **Question** Concerning Technology*

They had colorful names for die varieties—and still do! In this case, the die cutter started out on the date, got the first two digits cut, then apparently had a three martini lunch and cut the 9 very high, close to base of the bust, and then dropped the 4 sharply down to make it fit.

> *Alan Herbert, Coin Clinic–1,001 **Frequently Asked Questions**, Volume 1*

WALLIN'S REVISION

3 words in 2 sentences.
Solves 5 hard problem-**questions**.
Solves 3 hard problem-**questions**.
Gives months.
Knows all coins.
Repeats 6 digits.

3 words in one sentence.
Defines abstract terms.
Rearrranges sentences.
Criticizes absurdities.
60 words in 3 minutes.

Repeats 26-syllabled sentence.
Problem of diverse facts.
3 rhymes in 1 minute.
Repeats 7 digits.

Cut and folded paper.
Juxtaposed triangles.
Differences between abstract terms.

> *Warren W. Coxe, Grading Intelligence by Years and by Points (Journal of Criminal Law and Criminology)*

The Form of this motion is, "to suspend the rules that interfere with," etc., stating the object of the suspension, as, "the consideration of a resolution on . . . ," which resolution is immediately offered after the rules are suspended, the chair recognizing for that purpose the member that moved to suspend the rules. Or, if it is desired to consider a **question** which has been laid on the table, and cannot be taken up at that time because that class of business is not then in order, or to consider a **question** that has been

19. A helicopter is flying horizontally at constant speed. A perfectly flexible uniform cable is suspended beneath the helicopter; air friction on the cable is *not* negligible.

Which of the following diagrams best shows the shape of the cable as the helicopter flies through the air to the right?

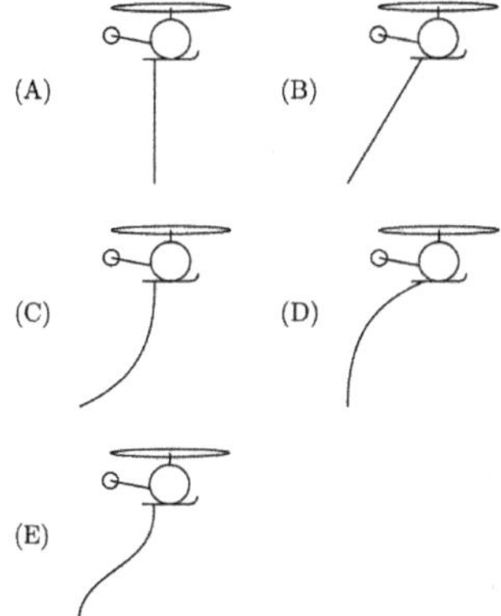

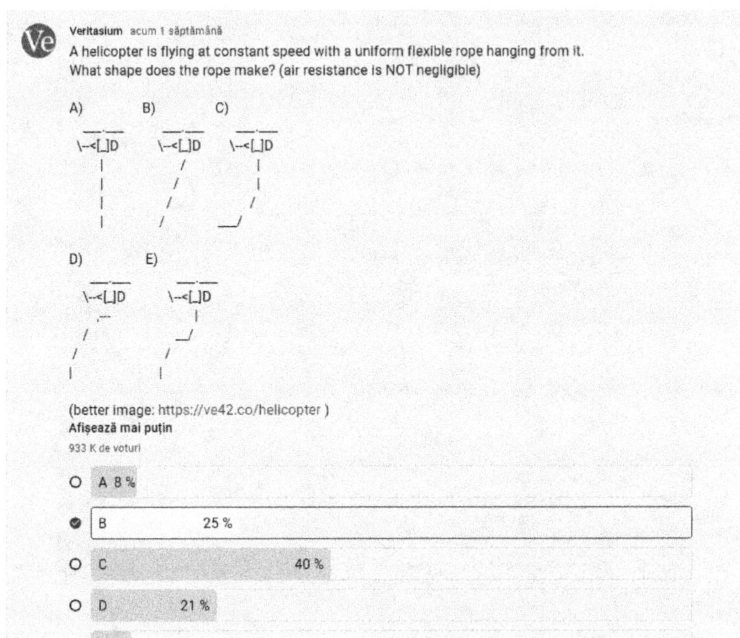

The above problem is taken from the 2014 $F = ma$ contest.

This question generated a great deal of controversy. At least two test takers challenged the answer, one who even tried to do the experiment. I'm told that several different "Ph.D" physicists declared that the correct answer was X, but, interestingly enough, couldn't agree on what X should be.

In the YouTube poll the majority of people have chosen (C), however the correct answer is (B).

Veritasium took it to the next level, he rented a helicopter to reveal the real answer to the problem.

I would like to solve this problem using differential analysis, analogous to the catenary equation solved here.

First of all, the helicopter is travelling at constant speed, so we are dealing with an inertial reference frame. If the rope appears stationary to an observer in the helicopter, then the net force is null. The only forces to analyze are the gravity, the air resistance, and last but not least the tension in the rope. I have chosen a coordinate axis with the origin at the lower end of the rope, but it should be unimportant. The rope has unknown shape, so we are restricted on the assumptions we can make about the geometry of the rope -- we don't know that the correct answer is (B) yet.

Consider a small mass element Δm in the rope. Let's write all the forces acting on Δm:

Gravity pointing downwards. The mass is proportional to the linear density and the length.

$$\vec{F_g} = -\Delta mg\hat{j} = -\lambda\Delta sg\hat{j}$$

Air resistance pointing backwards. The drag force is proportional to the cross sectional area, so proportional to the length of the vertical projection of Δm:

$$\vec{F_d} = -\frac{1}{2}\rho v^2 C_d A\hat{i} = -\alpha\Delta y\hat{i}$$

Tensions:

$$\vec{T}(x) = -T(x)\cos\theta(x)\hat{i} - T(x)\sin\theta(x)\hat{j}$$

$$\vec{T}(x + \Delta x) = T(x + \Delta x)\cos\theta(x + \Delta x)\hat{i} + T(x + \Delta x)\sin\theta(x + \Delta x)\hat{j}$$

Writing $\vec{F}_{\text{net}} = \vec{0}$ on the horizontal and vertical component:

$$T(x + \Delta x)\cos\theta(x + \Delta x) - T(x)\cos\theta(x) = \alpha\Delta y \quad (1)$$

$$T(x + \Delta x)\sin\theta(x + \Delta x) - T(x)\sin\theta(x) = \lambda\Delta sg \quad (2)$$

Divide both equations by Δx and take $\lim_{\Delta x\to 0}$ to get to the differential form:

$$\frac{d(T\cos\theta)}{dx} = \alpha\frac{dy}{dx}$$

$$\frac{d(T\sin\theta)}{dx} = \lambda\frac{ds}{dx}g$$

In the catenary example we were lucky because we were able to easily eliminate T from the equations, but here I can't find a way to simplify the system.

Also $\cos\theta = \frac{dx}{ds}$ and $\sin\theta = \frac{dy}{ds}$ are problematic.

How can I continue? Is this even going anywhere?

EDIT:

Equation (1) tells that $T(x)\cos\theta(x) = \alpha y$, and also $T(x + \Delta x)\cos\theta(x + \Delta x) = \alpha(y + \Delta y)$, taking into account that $T(0) = 0$.

Substituting in equation (2) leads to

postponed to another time, or that is in the order of business for another time, then the motion may be made thus, "I move to suspend the rules and take up [or consider] the resolution . . ." When the object is not to take up a **question** for discussion but to adopt it without debate, the motion is made thus: "I move to suspend the rules and adopt [or agree to] the following resolution," which is then read: or, "I move to suspend the rules, and adopt [or agree to] the resolution on . . ." The same form may be used in a case like this: "I move to suspend the rules, and admit to the privileges of the floor members of sister societies," which merely admits them to the hall.

Henry M. Robert, *Robert's Rules of Order Revised for Deliberative Assemblies*

'This matter of a formula—' began Hetherton.

'Represents, we think, the actual situation. They hope to steal something from Orchard as soon as he perfects it. And the thing is going to happen a mile from the last lonely fountain—the spot where we both found our bogus friend meditating. That is to say, it is going to happen within two miles of this cottage. We're right on the spot.'

'Perhaps in more senses than one.' The false Orchard, bound to a chair in a corner of the room, gave his old strained laugh.

The young man Mackintosh turned round. 'I wonder are you a potential enemy, or a mercenary neutral, or just a plain traitor? We'll suspend all rancour till we know. But I'm afraid you'll suffer a certain amount of inconvenience meantime. Appleby, do you think the loft?'

Appleby, who had returned from exploring the cottage, shook his head and walked over to the bound man. 'I put you down as plain traitor, and your own skin as your chief concern. Which may make things easier.'

'Easier?' The false Orchard looked at him with narrowed eyes. 'You're lucky not to have been shot: what more likely than that there should have been a rumpus in which we had to put a bullet through you? And it may happen yet.'

'I don't understand you.'

Appleby was untying his bonds. 'I think you do. You have signals to give that all is going well in here; that you are sustaining your role as Orchard and keeping us sitting tight. Ten to one those signals are simply more of your loony walks. And the **question** is an easy one. Are you going to take those walks, or are you going to be shot?'

The man rose and stretched himself. 'I'd like you to know,' he said, 'that I'm not a traitor; nor a devoted enemy either. My pedigree's Mitropa out of Wagons-Lits. I'll take the walks. But you must promise to get me safely into jail if you can. Because they won't be too pleased with me afterwards, will they?' He grinned strangely.

Michael Innes, *The Secret Vanguard*

While this confers great credit upon the latter, it is an humiliation to American philatelists that this page of our own history was left to be written by an English student. Even so, this work did not appear until fully forty years after the Nesbitt dies were first issued.

It is, likewise, true that Messrs. Tiffany, Bogert and Rechert in their "Historical Notes" undertook to rescue the Nesbitt die varieties from an ignominious oblivion, and for this they are also entitled to praise, but up to the most recent time, the great body of collectors did not possess a guide-book, a "Philatelic Baedeker," which would enable the timorous traveler to proceed into the unknown country with a feeling of perfect safety.

Naturally the **question** arises: What is the reason for this state of affairs? Why have the Nesbitt die varieties been relegated to an entirely unmerited obscurity?

Victor M. Berthold, The Die Varieties of the Nesbitt Series of United States Envelopes

p. 537–5

Vocabulary involved is difficult and depends on the context clues "smiled approvingly" but did not give "written nor spoken permission" help us define the word "tacit" which means something that is understood but not stated or written. Someone who is *fervent* is very enthusiastic. Something that is *"unqualified"* has no qualifications so it is definite or absolute. And if someone does something *impetuously* they do it impulsively or spontaneously. Something is *conditional* if it is provisional, restricted, or qualified.

A

*Henry Davis, Explanations for the Official SAT Study Guide **Questions**: Detailed Explanations for the Answers for Every **Question***

WHIPPLE'S REVISION

Names months.
Knows all coins.
3 words in 2 sentences.
Hard problem-**questions**.
Easy problem-**questions**.

Criticises absurdities.
3 words in 1 sentence.
Gives 60 words in 3 minutes.
Defines abstract terms.
Rearranges sentences.

Repeats 7 digits.
Gives 3 rhymes.
Repeats 26-syllabled sentence.
Problem of diverse facts.

Cut and folded paper.
Juxtaposed triangles.
Differences between abstract terms.

Warren W. Coxe, Grading Intelligence by Years and by Points (Journal of Criminal Law and Criminology)

p. 491–2

In this sentence the error is the incorrect use of "being born." No only is it passive, but it confuse the meaning of the sentence. Answer choice C correctly uses the verbs "Born" and "raised" while keeping "resides" in the present tense. Answer choice B is very indirect and wordy. Answer choice D requires a semicolon as we have two independent clauses. Answer E is also wordy and indirect.

C

*Henry Davis, Explanations for the Official SAT Study Guide **Questions**: Detailed Explanations for the Answers for Every **Question***

HUEY'S REVISION

Makes change 4c from 25c.

Definitions superior to use.
Gives date.
Repeats months.
Arranges 5 weights.

3 words in 2 sentences.
Solves 5 hard problem-**questions**.
Solves 3 hard problem-**questions**.
Copies design.
Knows all coins.

3 words in 1 sentence.
Rearranges sentences.
Gives 60 words in 3 minutes.
Criticizes 'absurdities.'
3 rhymes in 1 minute.

Repeats 26-syllabled sentences.
Problem of diverse facts.
Resists line suggestion.
Repeats 7 digits.
Defines abstract terms.

Warren W. Coxe, Grading Intelligence by Years and by Points (Journal of Criminal Law and Criminology)

These results cannot, however, be considered conclusive, since 81.8 per cent of all possible answers were of the free response form, and since the *smallness of the difference* was more prominent than the *fact of difference*. Probably the most important difference between good and poor elements came from an analysis into types of response. Five types were decided upon as follows:

1. Responses which required organization of, and inference from, the material given in the paragraph. These were cases in which the material necessary for answering the **question** was not directly embodied in the paragraph, but in which the answer to the **question** must have been inferred. A **question** of this type is, "What do you think was the topic of the paragraph preceding this, in the book whence this paragraph was taken?"

2. The second type of response was called "general organization." These were responses requiring organization of material which could not be easily located in the paragraph by a key word or phrase. This type stands in contrast with type 3, described below. An example of **question** type 2 is, "What is the main fact asserted in this paragraph?"

3. The third type of response was that in which organization was necessary, but organization of only one or two sentences which could be easily located by a key word or phrase in the **question** asked. These (and cases of type 5) were cases in which the **question** could have been answered by locating such a key word or phrase in the paragraph, and reading around it. They were elements which could have been answered without having read the whole paragraph. The following paragraph and **question** illustrate this type:

The body of legal rules and customs which obtained in England before the Norman conquest constitutes, with the Scandinavian laws, the most genuine expression of

Teutonic legal thought. While the so-called "barbaric laws" of the continent, not excepting those in the territory now called Germany, were largely the product of Roman influence, the continuity of Roman life was almost completely broken in the island, and even the Church, the direct heir of Roman tradition, did not carry on a continuous existence: Canterbury was not a see formed in a Roman province in the same sense as Tours or Reims. One of the striking expressions of this Teutonism is presented by the language in which the Anglo-Saxons laws were written. They are uniformly worded in English, while continental laws, apart from the Scandinavian, are all in Latin. The English dialect in which the Anglo-Saxon laws have been handed down to us is in most cases a common speech derived from West Saxon—naturally enough as Wessex became the predominant English state, and the court of its kings the principal literary center from which most of the compilers and scribes derived their dialect and spelling. Traces of Kentish speech may be detected, however, in the Textus Roffensis, the MS. of the Kentish laws; the Northumbrian dialectical peculiarities are also noticeable on some occasions, while Danish words occur only as technical terms.

Question: What reason is given for the use of the particular dialect in which most of the Anglo-Saxon laws were written?

Leona Vincent, A Study of Intelligence Test Elements

p. 912–16

Elsa Barkley Brown's article, described in the last paragraph, emphasizes multiplicity and inclusion. Multiplicity means diversity and variety, while inclusion means the act of including. Since the story Elsa tells involves describing a conversational style in which several people speak at once as well as "rhythms being played simultaneously" as a form of historical pursuit. Even though listening to all the sounds and voices is confusing, silencing any of them endangers the meaning, therefore we would say that Elsa's article that the author uses in this passage is intended to emphasize diversity and the act of including all.

A

Henry Davis, Explanations for the Official SAT Study Guide **Questions**: Detailed Explanations for the Answers for Every **Question**

The fourth and fifth types of response represented cases in which a direct quotation of a sentence or phrase in the paragraph would have answered the **question** satisfactorily. (4) is to be distinguished from (5) by the fact that in (4) the sentence or phrase to be copied could not have been located without organization of, or inference from, the material in the paragraph; whereas in (5) the usable quotation could have been easily located by scanning the paragraph for a key word or phrase. Examples of (4) and (5) follow in sequence:

Example of (4): Sapphire, a blue transparent variety of corundum, or native alumina, much valued as a gem-stone. It is essentially the same mineral as ruby, from which it differs chiefly in color. The color of the normal sapphire varies from the palest blue to the deepest indigo, the most esteemed tint being that of the blue cornflower. Many of the crystals are parti-colored, the blue being distributed in patches in a colorless or yellow stone; but by skillful cutting, the deep-colored portion may be caused to impart color to the entire gem. As the sapphire crystallizes in the hexagonal system it is dichoric, but in pale stones this character may not be well marked. In a deep colored stone the color may be resolved, by the dichroscope, into an ultramarine blue and a bluish or yellowish green.

Question: How may a stone showing local chromatic variations be made to appear deep-colored throughout?

Example of (5): Sale is commonly defined as the transfer of property from one person to another for a price. The definition requires some consideration in order to appreciate its full scope. The law of sale is usually treated as a branch of the law of contract, because sale is effected by contract. But a complicated contract of sale is something more. It is a contract plus a transfer of property. An agreement to sell or buy a thing, or, as lawyers call it, an executory contract of sale, is a contract pure and simple. A purely personal bond arises thereby between seller and buyer. But a complete or executed contract of sale effects a transfer of ownership with all the advantages and risks incident thereto. By an agreement to sell a jus in personam is created; by a sale a jus in rem is transferred.

Question: Under what department of law does the law regarding sales come?

Leona Vincent, A Study of Intelligence Test Elements

I am not in favor of forcing any **question** whatever, least of all any social **question**. Give the black man a fair chance, give him simple aid where he has a right to it, and then leave him to develop a better future.

One thing more. I put it forth simply as a germinal thought: if it is good for nothing, it will wither and die; if it is good for something, it may survive in some minds, and possibly bear fruit. I think it was Bishop Haygood, whom all of us so greatly love and respect, who put forth the idea that it would be well if the South would establish an educational test for suffrage. Such a course would doubtless disfranchise temporarily a large proportion of the colored population, and indeed a part of the white population. The South might temporarily lose some electoral votes, but it would gain in strength and respect throughout the Union. More than that, I believe that the results of such a course would be so good that it would eventually spread to most, if not all, of the Northern States. I confess to the hope that the time will come when, not only in the North, but in the South, there will be a simple educational test for suffrage. There is no longer any excuse for ignorance of reading and writing in the North, and shortly there will be none in the South. There was a time when there was an excuse: that time has now past. I agree with my friend, Dr. Allen, that we have tremendous **questions** at the North, quite as serious as those at the South. We have coming in upon us a flood of people who, by all their traditions and habits, are unfitted as yet for the high duties of a republic like this.

*Isabel Chapin Barrows (ed.), First Mohonk Conference on the Negro **Question**: Held at Lake Mohonk, Ulster County, New York, June 4, 5, 6, 1890*

GODDARD'S REVISION

3 words in 2 sentences.
Comprehends easy **questions**.
Draws design from memory.
Knows money.

Repeats 6 digits.

Criticizes 'absurdities.'
Names 4 chief colors.
3 words in 1 sentence.
Rearranges sentences.
Discrimination of forms.

Repeats 7 digits.
Defines abstract terms.
Repeats 26-syllabled-sentences.
Completion test.
Resists line suggestion.

> Warren W. Coxe, *Grading Intelligence by Years and by Points* (Journal of Criminal Law and Criminology)

You may say that revolutions do not go backward. Granted; but I claim that this is a revolution which goes forward: it places the republic on a higher plane. Take an example in this very State: In 1847 we sank back toward mobocracy. We elected judges on small salaries for short terms: we did the same with the governors. We have swung backward or forward, whichever you choose to call it, out of that. We now elect men for longer terms. In many ways we have returned to more conservative principles; and I believe that such a return to enlightened conservative principles is the highest advance which we can make.

> Isabel Chapin Barrows (ed.), *First Mohonk Conference on the Negro* **Question**: *Held at Lake Mohonk, Ulster County, New York, June 4, 5, 6, 1890*

Find an extinct animal by moving from circle to circle, using each circle only once:

Insert the numbers 2 to 6 in the circles (1 is already placed) so that for any particular circle the sum of the numbers in the circles connected directly to it equals the value corresponding to the number in that circle, as given in the list. Example:

Find two eight-letters words which are antonyms, reading round the circles. One reads clockwise round the outer circle and one reads anticlockwise round the inner circle. You have to provide the missing letters.

Find two words (8, 4) in this diagram. Letters are traced across the circle by chords. If the next letter is four letters or less away it will be found by tracing around the circumference. Clue: trousers for the youngest sailor.

> Kenneth Russell and Philip J. Carter, *The Times Book of IQ Tests, Book 4: 400 Brand New* **Questions** *Never Before Published*

KUHLMANN'S REVISION

Enumerates objects in picture.
Points to ears, eyes, mouth, hair.
Knows family name.
Repeats 6-syllabled sentence.
Problem **questions**.

Knows sex.
Names objects shown.
Repeats 3 digits.

Compares lines.
Aesthetic comparison.

Counts 4 pennies.
Copies square.
Compares 2 weights.
Divided rectangle.
Repeats 10-syllabled sentence.

Knows right hand, left ear, right eye.
Aesthetic comparison.
Tells morning from afternoon.
Defines by use.
Executes triple command.

Warren W. Coxe, Grading Intelligence by Years and by Points (Journal of Criminal Law and Criminology)

Those of you who have read history know that the only republic which managed to save itself out of the ruin and chaos of the sixteenth century, in Italy, was Venice; for she was the only republic which dared to go back to a restriction of suffrage on the basis of ascertained fitness. All those other republics perished early in the sixteenth century; but the republic of Venice lasted two hundred and fifty years longer, and would have remained in being until our time but for the coming of Napoleon Bonaparte.

But I did not intend to run into a historical dissertation, only plead for counsels here looking toward a peaceful rather than a warlike solution of this great **question**, and a steady evolution, in which the main agency is intellectual, moral, and religious education, and the avoidance of everything which shall stir strife and war.

Isabel Chapin Barrows (ed.), First Mohonk Conference on the Negro **Question***: Held at Lake Mohonk, Ulster County, New York, June 4, 5, 6, 1890*

The **question**, however, of superlative interest to philatelists is: why has Nesbitt produced such a large number of dies or die varieties? The answer is simple: Pressed hard by the Department to manufacture several millions of envelopes, a gigantic task in the early days of stamp making, and lacking our present means of reproducing working dies from the matrix, he undoubtedly used his best effort; i.e. he probably ordered a number of engravers to reproduce the original die, and, in the hurry of the work, little attention was paid to exactness. This would seem a very plausible explanation, and in the absence of any official data let us permit the above assumption to stand.

Whatever may be the facts in the case, one thing is certain; the varieties exist and have been a source of trouble to many collectors of United States envelopes.

Victor M. Berthold, The Die Varieties of the Nesbitt Series of United States Envelopes

p. 542–18

A line reference here to the word "sign" is speaking about the first sign of these people. So be the first "indication" or evidence that they existed. This certainly rules out an omen or symbol or a gesture. It could distantly mean a figure but clearly indication is a better choice.

D

Henry Davis, Explanations for the Official SAT Study Guide **Questions***: Detailed Explanations for the Answers for Every* **Question**

If the **question** is asked why a unit distance measurement is not applied to differentiate these varieties, the answer is that the spacing of the letters of the inscription is nearly alike. Of course the slant of the letters differs. Such differences as are helpful and noticeable will be mentioned. The system of line prolongation, for example, the downward prolongation of the "T" of "THREE", discloses certain groups in the writer's wopinion, but the differences obtained thereby are not of sufficient practical value for establishing groups. For a quick and reliable identification of these varieties an intimate knowledge of the heads is required.

Victor M. Berthold, The Die Varieties of the Nesbitt Series of United States Envelopes

Name of the Test	Binet1908	Binet1911	Wallin	Whipple	Goddard	Huey	Terman and Childs	Kuhlmann	Bobertag	Stanford
Points to parts of head	3	3	3	3	3	3		3		3
Repeats six syllables	3	3	3	3	3	3		3	3	3
Repeats two digits	3	3	3	3	3	3		3		
Parts of pictures	3	3	3	3	3	3	3	3		3
Knows name	3	3	3	3	3	3		3		3
Names objects shown	4	4	4	4	4	4	3	4		3
Repeats three digits	4	4	4	4	4	4	3	4		3
Knows sex	4	4	4	4	4	4	3	4		3
Compares two weights	5	5	5	5	5	5	3	5		5
Compares two lines	4	4	4	4	4	4		4		4
Counts four coins	5	5	5	5	5	5	4	5	5	4
Divided rectangle	5	5	5	5	5	5	4	5	6	5
Copies square	5	5	5	5	5	5	4	5	5	4
Aesthetic comparison	6	6	6	6	6	6	4	6	6	5
Defines by use	6	6	6	6	6	6	4	6	5	5
Repeats ten syllables	5	5	5		5	5		5	5	
Tells p.m. from a.m	6	6	6	6	6	6	5	6		6
Knows four colors	8	7	8	8	7	7	5		8	5
Triple command	6	7	6	6	6	6	5	6	6	5
Repeats 16 syllables	6		6	6			7		6	6
Knows right from left	6	7	6	6	6	6	6	6	7	6
Counts 13 pennies	7	6	7	7	7	7	6			6
Copies diamond	7	6	7	7	7	7	7	8	7	7
Describes pictures	7	7	7	7	7	7	7	7	6	7
Number of fingers	7		7	7			6	7		7
Repeats five digits	7	8	7	7	8	8	8	7	7	7
Copies sentence	7		7	7			8			
Knows four coins	7		7	7			7	7	7	6
Mutilated pictures	7	8	7	7	7	7	7	7	7	6
Adds coins or stamps	8	7	8	8	8	8	9	8		9
Counts 20 to 1	8	8	8	8	8	8	8	8	8	8
Compares two objects	8	8	8	8	8	8	8	8	8	7
Writes from dictation	8		8	8			8			8
Gives date	9	8	9	9	9	9	9	9	9	9
Names months	10	9	10	10	9	9		8		9
Names days	9		9	9	8	8				7

Defines better than use	9	9	9	9	9	9		9	9	8
Makes change	9	9	9	9	9	9	10	9	9	9
Six memories from passage	9		9	9					10	
Arranges five weights	9	10	9	9	9	9	9	9	9	9
Knows all coins	10	9	10	10	10	10		9	10	
Interprets pictures	12	15			15	15	15		11	12
Sixty words in three minutes	11	12		11	11	11		11		10
Three words in two sentences	10	10	10	10	10	10		10	10	9
Hard problem-**questions**	10	10	10	10	10	10	11		11	10
Easy problem-**questions**	10	9		10	10	10		10	8	8
Absurdities	11	10	11	11	11	11	12	11	11	

Warren W. Coxe, Grading Intelligence by Years and by Points (Journal of Criminal Law and Criminology)

Q. What will correct this latter defect.

A. The use of a die of softer non-shrinkage metal (Babbitt metal) following one of the harder shrinkage metals.

Q. Should the swaged plate fit the plaster model or the die.

A. The metal die.

*Ferdinand J. S. Gorgas, A Series of **Questions** and Answers for Dental Students, Part III*

p. 398–8

When working with circles, we must always keep the values for the radius and the diameter straight. Here we know the radius for circle A is 2, so the diameter is 4. The radii for both circle B and circle C are 4, so the diameters are 8. The combined diameters are $4 + 8 + 8 = 20$ which is the diameter for the largest circle. (NOTE: frequently you find a tempting answer choice for a half finished problem—here (E) offers us the temptation of the value for the diameter.) We want the radius, so we divide the diameter in half:

$20/2 = 10$

D

*Henry Davis, Explanations for the Official SAT Study Guide **Questions**: Detailed Explanations for the Answers for Every **Question***

Q. Suppose the model is correct, and although the plate may fit the die yet it will not fit the mouth.

A. Either the process of making die was imperfect; or too few dies have been used; or a metal not suitable; or it is a case which no swaged plate can be made to fit.

Q. Is the moderate shrinkage of a zinc die ever of advantage.

A. Yes, where it counteracts the expansion of the plaster model.

Q. How may a counter-die be made without a sand mould.

*Ferdinand J. S. Gorgas, A Series of **Questions** and Answers for Dental Students, Part III*

The first answer to the action was that David Ballantyne, in his proposal or application for insurance, warranted that he would not die by his own act, and that he broke that warranty by shooting himself. David Ballantyne was found dead on the morning of the 8th October, killed by the discharge of a gun into his head. The jury found that he shot himself, and that he did not accidently shoot himself. According to the evidence he must have taken the gun out of its case, put it together, loaded it, and then, at a place some distance from his house, discharged it into his head. The jury by their answers to **questions** 1 and 4, find that in so doing he voluntarily and intentionally pulled the trigger of a loaded gun presented at his head. They must be taken, in my opinion, by these answers to have found (1) that he had a sufficient power of mind and reason to have known that pulling the trigger would discharge the loaded gun, and (2) that he intended to so discharge it. But they, by a majority of five sixths, also found in answer to **question** No. 3. that he was so insane as not to know that firing the gun into his own head would kill him. That is, that he had not sufficient power of mind and reason to understand the physical nature and consequences of pulling the trigger of a loaded gun placed to his head. If Ballantyne had shot some other man instead of himself, and all the evidence that was given in this action had been given as to Ballantyne's delusions, I do not think it could be successfully argued that the other man did not die by Ballantyne's "act"—though "perhaps" Ballantyne, on his trial for murder, might be found not guilty on the ground of insanity if the jury thought his delusions had so affected his mind that he did not know he was doing a wrongful action shooting the other man. In my opinion a man must be taken to intend the natural (and in this case certain) results of firing a gun into his own head till the contrary is proved; and, as in this case it is clear that Ballantyne intentionally fired the gun, it was, I think, for the plaintiff to prove that he did not know that firing the gun into his own head would kill him.

James C. Anderson (ed.), *The Australian Law Times, Volumes 12–13*

The **question** as to the relation between difficulty and complexity was raised. In order to answer it, the arithmetic elements were analyzed from the point of view of complexity. Such an analysis was possible with the arithmetic element because there was at least one objective measure of complexity, namely, the number of processes or operations necessary in order to arrive at the answer of the problem. Even this must, of course, be somewhat arbitrary. It was decided to call multiplication or division by a fraction, with a numerator more than 1, a double process; if necessary to reduce a mixed number to a fraction in order to work with it, this was called one process. On the other hand, multiplication or division by any number, no matter how many digits it contained, was considered as a single process. Since the problems were scored in the test as correct whether fractions in answers were reduced to their lowest terms or not, this analysis was carried only as far as unreduced answers. Sample analyses are given to make clear what was done at this point.

Leona Vincent, *A Study of Intelligence Test Elements*

Test 4.6, **question** 3: numerical sequence.
Test 4.6, **question** 5: mirror image.
Test 4.6, **question** 7: square numbers?
Test 4.6, **question** 10: the seventh word completes the list.
Test 4.7, **question** 7: try finding a solution standing on your head!

Philip Carter, *The Complete Book of Intelligence Tests: 500 Exercises to Improve, Upgrade and Enhance Your Mind Strength*

I observe that Mr. Justice a'Beckett stated in his judgment that he would not himself have come to the same conclusion as the jury did on **question** No. 3, but that he was bound by their answer.

THE CHIEF JUSTICE said—We have heard arguments and we now proceed to deliver judgment on two motions in this case. The first is the motion that a new trial of the action be ordered on the ground that the findings of the jury as to the second and third **questions** put by the learned judge who tried the case are against evidence and the weight of evidence. The action is brought on a certificate or interim note of insurance, dated September 5, 1890, on the life of David Ballantyne, for the sum of £2,500, for the term of four months until January 5, 1891, subject to the usual terms of the defendant company's policies. The application for the policy, which was made by the certificate a part of the contract, included a warranty and agreement by the insured that he would not die by his own act during a period of two years. The insured died by a gunshot wound in the head on the night of October 7, or the morning of October 8, 1891. The jury at the trial found that the deceased shot himself, and that he did not accidentally shoot himself. In answer to the second **question**, "Was he insane when he shot himself?" five out of six of the jurymen said "Yes;" and in answer to the third **question**, "Was he so insane as not to know that firing a gun into his own head would kill him," five out of six of the jurymen answered "Yes." The warranty was set up as an answer to the action on the certificate. It was properly assumed for the purposes of this motion that in order that the death of the deceased should appear to have been caused by his own act it was necessary that it should appear not only that the deceased's death was caused by a movement of his own body, which produced death, but also that he knew that what he did was calculated to destroy his life. The **question** then which we have to determine is was there evidence on which reasonable men could find that the deceased did not know that firing a gun into his own head would kill him? It appeared that for a few days prior to his death the deceased was under the influence of delusions brought about by an attack of *delirium tremens*, from which he was suffering. He was also suffering from want of sleep. He spoke and acted incoherently and wildly. On the day before his death he complained that there was something on his ear, and he cried bitterly. He also said several times on the same day, "I've three heads, a bell head, a bully head, and my own head, and there will be a click, and I will be all right." There was nothing apparently wrong with his ear, or with his head. It would undoubtedly be open to the jury to draw the inference from this evidence that the insured, being conscious of acute suffering from a real and also from imagined causes, intended to put an end to his life, and fired the gun in order to carry that intent into effect. But the jury might also, I think, not unreasonably infer that the insured, under the influence of these delusions, loaded and fired the gun in the belief that he could thereby remove the imaginary causes of his suffering and in forgetfulness for the time that the certain effect of the discharge would be to deprive him of life. I incline to think, with the learned judge who tried the case, that I should not myself have drawn the latter conclusion, but I cannot say that a jury of reasonable men could not reasonably draw such a conclusion. The fact that he had expressed wonder, after reading about suicides, that any man should do such a thing, and the further fact that although he had sustained some losses in business, he was in receipt of a good income and had good prospects, lend support to the view taken by the jury. I am of opinion, therefore, that the objections taken to these findings have not been sustained, and that the motion for a new trial should be dismissed with costs.

James C. Anderson (ed.), The Australian Law Times, Volumes 12–13

It is a well-settled doctrine of the courts both in England and this country that a special verdict must find facts—not merely state the evidence from which facts may be inferred.

It will not be helped by intendment. Every fact not ascertained by it, is supposed not to exist; *Brown* v. *Ralston*, 4 Rand. 504; *Lee* v. *Campbell*, 4 Post, 198 ; *Seaward* v. *Jackson*, 8 Cowen, 406; *Thompson* v. *Farr*, 1 Speers, 93 ; *Sewall* v. *Glidden*, 1 Ala. 52 ; *Hill* v. *Covell*, 1 Comst. 522 ; *Sisson* v. *Barrett*, 2 Comst. 406; *Langley* v. *Warner*, 3 Ibid. 327; *The State* v. *Watts*, 10 Iredell, 369; *Blake* v. *Davis*, 20 Ohio, 321.

A special verdict however which finds what the law has made conclusive evidence of a fact is sufficient; *John* v. *Bates*, Litt. Sel. Cases, 106.

A special verdict, presenting no other **question** than the relevancy of testimony offered on the trial is bad; *Welland Canal Co.* v. *Hathaway*, 8 Wend. 480.

So where it does not find in the alternative according as the opinion of the court upon the facts may be; *The State* v. *Wallace*, 3 Iredell, 195.

If the jury in a special verdict find facts only, the court must draw the legal conclusion from them; and if they draw conclusions against the law upon the face of them, the court will reject the conclusion and judge upon the facts. Where the jury find only such facts as leave the **question** of law equivocal, and then draw a conclusion which the facts not found might have warranted, the court will say that their conclusion is against law; *Butler* v. *Hopper*, 1 Wash. C. C. 499 ; *Peterson* v. *United States*, 2 Ibid. 36.

Where a verdict is for any reason bad, the court will award a *venire de novo*; *Bellows* v. *Hallowell*, 2 Mason, 31; *Stodder* v. *Powell*, 1 Stewart, 287; *Sewall* v. *Glidden*, 1 Ala. 52.

An agreed case, in the nature of a special verdict is to be considered as a special verdict found by a jury, and if it be defective in substance, the judgment rendered upon it will be reversed, and a *venire de novo* awarded; *Whitesides* v. *Russell*, 8 Watts & Serg. 44.

Thomas Starkie, A Practical Treatise of the Law of Evidence

p. 530–15

This problem requires you to keep everything straight, so write the values on the figure and just work through step by step. And when you draw it, remember that the figure is not drawn to scale, so don't let looks deceive you.

If OB bisects AOD then AOB = BOD = 40
AOB + BOD (which equal AOD) = 40 + 40 = 80 so AOD = 80
If OD bisects AOF then AOD = DOF
AOD = 80 so DOF = 80
If DOF = 80, then since FOE = 30, then DOE = DOF − FOE = 80 − 30 = 50
BOE = BOD (40) + DOE (50) = 40 + 50 = 90
90

Henry Davis, Explanations for the Official SAT Study Guide **Questions**: *Detailed Explanations for the Answers for Every* **Question**

It having been decided to reproduce the heads, the **question** arose: Shall we draw every feature and every detail, or is it preferable to indicate merely such portions of the face as are different in the various dies? Evidently, many minor points could be omitted without in any way detracting from the usefulness of the drawings. Indeed, the adoption of this plan permitted the artist to emphasize and to bring out more strikingly such features as constitute the real differences.

There are three prominent features in each of the ten heads. The first is the side-lock, which may be either single or double, straight or hooked, short or long. Second in importance is the distance between the end of the side-lock and the ear-lobe. Even a casual observation shows that the distance between the ear-lobe and the end of the side-lock varies greatly; very wide, near and close. The third feature is the lowest front-lock, which, by the taste or art of the die cutters has been, like man, "wonderfully and fearfully made", short or long, thin or full, single or double. In good specimens the eyebrow constitutes a valuable adjunct, and in all dies where this feature plays a prominent part it will be noted. Finally the attention of the collector is directed to the fact that only Head 1 shows Washington with circularly cropped hair, or, as the barber would express it, a "Dutch clip". This head was used for varieties 1, 2 and 3, the first being a rather scarce article. If the student fixes his attention on the above three main features, and does not attempt to get the entire ten heads fixed in his mind at a glance, it will be found that the task of differentiation is not at all a burden even to the youngest collector of cut square specimens. A certain amount of patience is, however, required; likewise a certain amount of willingness to be taught, but the collector possessing these two virtues—and it is one of the crowning glories of stamp collectors to be both studious and patient—will soon have the various Nesbitt heads of Washington engraved upon his memory.

Victor M. Berthold, The Die Varieties of the Nesbitt Series of United States Envelopes

p. 550–7

With references like "I loved the walk" and the "destination," and references to the semi-monthly excursions as "a piece of perfection" we can see clearly that the author enjoyed these excursions. Apprehension, detachment, resentment, and pride all indicate something negative. Pride would be something the author was feeling about herself. So "delight" is the obvious answer choice.

E

*Henry Davis, Explanations for the Official SAT Study Guide **Questions**: Detailed Explanations for the Answers for Every **Question***

Turvey sat up in his chair like a cocker spaniel and repeated six digits after him faithfully, and the little sentence about Walter and his grandmother. There was that enigmatic grin still, though, and wider than ever. The fellow had such a wide face anyway.

"Now," said Lieutenant Smith, in the voice he used for small children and large dogs, "listen carefully and see if you can finish this sentence for me: A man who was walking in the woods near the city stopped suddenly, very much frightened, and then ran to the nearest policeman, saying that he had just seen hanging from a tree a—what?"

"Parachute!" Turvey shouted. His blue eyes shone with honest excitement. "A Jerry parachute. He was a spy come down and got caught in a tree."

The lieutenant sighed. The answers in the sheet were all in a more ghoulish vein, "corpse ... body ...", and yet—excellent morale, at any rate, but had that anything to do with intelligence? He would try the section dealing with the subject's COMPREHENSION.

"We should judge a person more by his actions than his words. True or False?"

Turvey's grin widened to show, the lieutenant was startled to see, a false upper plate. Had Hodgson got the age wrong too? And he began to wonder about the man's hearing, for he had evidently taken the last item as a statement of opinion.

"That's what I like to hear, sir. All these words, and, and tests and **questions**. It's what we can do that counts, like you just said. That's why I want the Kootenay

Hans Spiess's Estrapade
Diebold Schilling the Younger, Die Luzerner Chronik, 1513

There is a code, a regulation of the **question**, indeed this one must not exceed
2 hours. Between each session, the person being **questioned** is fed properly, given
something to drink, and allowed to rest before starting a new session.

The use of the **question** inevitably leads to confessions, which are scrupulously noted down
by a clerk in the presence of a judge, which can be seen on the engravings that I have put in
illustration. The presence of witnesses is desired but not always applied, this depends on whether
the **question** is ordinary or extraordinary and on the size of the court where one practices.

Fred 37, Tortures, Torments and Others . . .
From the Middle Ages to Our Days (Fred 37's Blog)

Highlanders, sir, so I can get, uh, actions, action." Doubt flickered in Turvey's eyes but the grin stayed as if it belonged to another face. Was it a sly grin? Or even supercilious? Perhaps this man was trying an elaborate hoax. The lieutenant was aware once more of the room's heat, the root-house smell from below, the reverberation of boots from the main hall where his staff were trooping out for the day. His temper rose.

Earle Birney, Turvey: A Military Picaresque

p. 892–3

Medieval Chinese warriors used manned kites to survey enemy troops, a technique anticipating modern aerial surveillance. It was a past action, so you want "used manned kites." The "manned kites" describes the technique they used, so put the modifying phrase as close to "techniques" as possible for clarity. As written, it sounds like the enemy troops were the ones anticipating modern aerial surveillance—which doesn't make sense.

D

p. 545–15

The battle of the Somme was reported with an air of confidence and optimism, but secretly it was a catastrophic battle for the British *troops*. The footnote emphasizes the inaccuracy of the published reports by offering facts.

C

p. 523–16

A "coffee break" would result in an intake of caffeine which is a stimulant designed to prevent sleep; therefore, the troops feeling sleepy afterwards would be very "unexpected."

E

*Henry Davis, Explanations for the Official SAT Study Guide **Questions**: Detailed Explanations for the Answers for Every **Question***

When the men who have shown such energy on the battlefield return to ordinary civilization, most of those who have not risen to high rank seem to have acquired no ideas, and to have no aptitude, no capacity, for grasping new ideas. To the utter amazement of a younger generation, those who made our armies so glorious and so terrible are as simple as children, and as slow-witted as a clerk at his worst, and the captain of a thundering squadron is scarcely fit to keep a merchant's day-book. Old soldiers of this stamp, therefore, being innocent of any attempt to use their reasoning faculties, act upon their strongest impulses. Castanier's crime was one of those matters that raise so many **questions**, that, in order to debate about it, a moralist might call for its "discussion by clauses," to make use of a parliamentary expression.

Honoré de Balzac, Melmoth Reconciled

p. 469–4

Remember that good English is concise and active voiced. Clearly answer choice C "to recount" is the clearest expression of his purpose.

C

p. 470–5

The error here is that we have two independent clauses separated by a comma, and it needs to be a semi-colon. So we must either find an answer choice that correctly places the semi-colon; between the two independent clauses or find a way of linking the clauses. Answer choice B correctly eliminates the second independent clause by joining the thoughts expressed in the clauses with the preposition "with." Answer choice E offers the same option however it is wordier and more indirect.

 B

p. 656–2

 The band members <u>were</u> as soaked as <u>if they had marched</u> through a rainstorm. You must have a clause after the "as if" construction. Remember, a clause has both a subject ("they" in this case) and a predicate ("had marched"). Also, the verb tenses need to agree: "marching" needs to be "had marched" to agree with "were soaked."

 D

p. 775–11

 With the use of the words "at once" you know that the book is going to be <u>more</u> than frustrating. So you are looking for what else the book is. But you also need a phrase that is *grammatically parallel* to the phrase "frustrating because of its chaotic structure." The only answer that fits is (E) "delightful because of its originality."

 E

*Henry Davis, Explanations for the Official SAT Study Guide **Questions**: Detailed Explanations for the Answers for Every **Question***

"Wanker," I said. "Don't know that word. Is that a Southern thing? What is that, Richmond? Newport News? Is that like peanuts in your Coke?"

"You have a provincial mind, hucklebuck."

"Pardon?"

"It's a global globe now,"said Llewellyn. "We sink or swim together."

"It's a global globe?"

"That's right."

"Moron."

"Gentlemen," said Vargina.

"Why am I here?" I said. "I thought I was fired."

"You were," said Vargina.

"You are," said Llewellyn.

"Then what's going on?"

"We have special circumstances," said Vargina.

"You have special circumstances," I said.

"Yes."

"I have not-so-special circumstances," I said.

"If you help us with our circumstances," said Vargina, "we might be able to assist you with yours."

The door opened and in walked a large man with a moist pompadour and a tight beige mustache. Dean Cooley was not a dean. He was Mediocre's chief development officer. Several groups worked under him, and he spent most of his energy on the more lucrative ones, like business, law, or medicine. His art appreciation did not reach much past the impressionistic prints from the Montreal Olympics he'd mounted on his office wall. He'd been a marine, and then some kind of salesman, had started with cars and ended up in microchips and early internet hustles. Here in the cozy halls of academe, as he had put it during our first team talk, he meant to reassess his priorities. Meanwhile he would train us maggots how to ask asks and get gives. Cooley was a hard-charger who often began his reply to basic office queries by invoking "the lessons of Borodino." He was the kind of man you could picture barking into a field phone, sending thousands to slaughter, or perhaps ordering the mass dozing of homes. People often called him War Crimes. By people, I mean Horace and I. By often, I mean twice.

"Dean," said Vargina. "This is the man we were telling you about. Milo Burke."

"Nice to meet you."

We'd met a dozen times before, at lunches, cocktail receptions. He had stood beside me while his wife explained a project she'd embarked upon in her student days, something to do with Balinese puppets and social allegory.

"I assume you are wondering why, after being terminated for cause two months ago, we've asked you to come in," Cooley began.

"A fair assumption," I said.

Sam Lipsyte, The Ask

p. 541–15

We want an answer choice with which both authors would agree. The author of passage 1 mentions in lines 14 and 15 that an ice free corridor would have permitted the movement of the Clovis. Then in the last paragraph the author of passage 1 shows that this would have been difficult if not impossible to do based on geologic evidence. And the author of passage 2 starts off in the first paragraph indicating that the Ice Age closed off the New World, so both would have agreed with answer choice C that the Ice Age would have made overland travel to the New World difficult.

C

p. 763–6

The author states (lines 6–8) that it is difficult to tell a story in one language (like English) when the narrator actually lived in another (like Spanish). Therefore, you would say that the author illustrates a dilemma (*difficulty*) that Hispanic American writers often face.

E

p. 458–6

The blank requires a negative word since it refers to "dead," "jettisoned" and "drifting flecks." We can narrow the answer choices by elimination and see that "flotsam" is your best choice because it means debris or trash. *Reconnaissance* is investigation or scouting. *Decimation* is complete destruction. *Raiment* is clothing or dress. And *sustenance* is encouragement or provisions.

A

p. 517–12

Venn diagrams can look confusing until you isolate on your target. We want common elements to A and B. We find those by looking where those 2 circles overlap. A and B overlap in 2 areas. In those 2 areas—one has 2 elements and one has 5 elements. $2 + 5 = 7$ elements

D

p. 541–16

Remember with line reference **questions** you must read a bit below and above that specific line. This states that the warheads were spear points and were constructed and finished off with a groove down the center. Viewing the choices, it certainly wouldn't be defeated or terminated both of which mean stopped. It would not be disposed of which means getting rid of. It would not be consumed which means taken in or eaten. So by elimination we see "completed" is the correct answer.

C

Henry Davis, Explanations for the Official SAT Study Guide **Questions**: *Detailed Explanations for the Answers for Every* **Question**

According to ancient doctrine, the essence of a thing is considered to be *what* the thing is. We ask the **question** concerning technology when we ask what it is. Everyone knows the two statements that answer our **question**. One says: Technology is a means to an end. The other says: Technology is a human activity. The two definitions of technology belong together. For to posit ends and procure and utilize the means to them is a human activity. The manufacture and utilization of equipment, tools, and machines, the manufactured and used things themselves, and the needs and ends that they serve, all belong to what technology is. The whole complex of these contrivances is technology. Technology itself is a contrivance, or, in Latin, an *instrumentum.*

The current conception of technology, according to which it is a means and a human activity, can therefore be called the instrumental and anthropological definition of technology.

Who would ever deny that it is correct?

Martin Heidegger, The **Question** *Concerning Technology*

p. 981–15

This is a hard **question**. The first step is to realize you can cross-multiply to eliminate one n in the numerator and one in the denominator. This leaves you with $\frac{n}{(n-1)(n+1)} = \frac{5}{k}$

There are two ways to work this problem. The easiest is to look at it critically and see that, if you set $n = 5$, you can satisfy the equation with: $\frac{5}{(5-1)(5+1)} = \frac{5}{k}$

So, $5/(4 \times 6) = 5/k$

$5/24 = 5/k$

$24 = k$

You could also FOIL the denominator and solve for the quadratic equation.

C

p. 520–7

The definition of the word in the blank follows the blank. The definition is looking for someone who has insights beyond ordinary human perception. That would be someone who is a clairvoyant. Someone is *clairvoyant* is considered psychic extremely perceptive and intuitive. A *mentor* would be an advisor or teacher. A *profiteer* would be someone who exploits or takes advantage. A *counterfeiter* would be a forger, an imitator, or a faker. A *propagandist* is a maker of false publicity or information.

D

p. 407–1

The error here is the misuse of a comma. Two independent clauses are separated by a semi-colon. Answer choice C is a direct link for the two clauses and shows the cause f the accidents.

C

p. 520–8

Again, the definition of the word for the blank is after the comments "notice subtle differences." This would be someone who is *discriminating* because they can discern and make astute or sharp perceptions. Someone who is *sanctimonious* is smugly self-righteous. Someone who is *obscure* would be difficult to understand or unclear. Someone who is *unrelenting* is inexorable or merciless. One who is *deferential* gives in easily.

C

p. 407–5

Here you must consider the two aspects of the sentence construction. The verbs must be parallel, (think and extend) and you must have a transition word that signals the contrasting idea in the second half of the sentence—contrasting words like: but, whereas, or however. Which choice matches both requirements? Answer choice E does both.

E

*Henry Davis, Explanations for the Official SAT Study Guide **Questions**: Detailed Explanations for the Answers for Every **Question***

The instrumental definition of technology is indeed so uncannily correct that it even holds for modern technology, of which, in other respects, we maintain with some justification that it is, in contrast to the older handwork technology, something completely different and therefore new. Even the power plant with its turbines and generators is a man-made means to an end established by man. Even the jet aircraft and the high-frequency apparatus are means to ends. A radar station is of course less simple than a weather vane. To be sure, the construction of a high-frequency apparatus requires the interlocking of various processes of technical-industrial production. And certainly a sawmill in a secluded valley of the Black Forest is a primitive means compared with the hydroelectric plant in the Rhine River.

But this much remains correct: modern technology too is a means to an end. That is why the instrumental conception of technology conditions every attempt to bring man into the right relation to technology. Everything depends on our manipulating technology in the proper manner as a means. We will, as we say, "get" technology "spiritually in hand." We will master it. The will to mastery becomes all the more urgent the more technology threatens to slip from human control.

*Martin Heidegger, The **Question** Concerning Technology*

p. 922–10

The author of Passage 2 would probably contend that the claim made in lines 17–20 of Passage 1 is primarily shortsighted, since downloading free music will ultimately increase an artist's commercial sales. In lines 17–20 the author argues that when a "Napster" downloads a copy of a song it deprives the songwriter of his or her royalties, while the author of passage 2 states in lines 62–66 that the more free recordings there are out in circulation the more people there are exposed to the music, and ultimately the more fans who are willing to buy the records and go to the concerts.

A

Henry Davis, Explanations for the Official SAT Study Guide **Questions**: *Detailed Explanations for the Answers for Every* **Question**

He looked abstractedly from one to another, and said, in a lower voice, after a pause:

"Will you answer this **question** to me then? How does this happen?"

Charles Dickens, A Tale of Two Cities

p. 539–11

"An order" — "is put in for 50 cakes a soap" is a request or an "instruction to provide" this product.

B

p. 516–9

This problem **questions** how well you can numerically reason with abstract variables. If the problem is more complicated than this one, the easiest way to answer this type of **question** is to give the variables number values. But this problem is simple enough to solve retaining the variables.

(s + t) – (s + w) after we distribute the negative equals s + t – s – w which equals t – w

C

p. 395–24

This **question** addresses the major contrast the two passages. In passage 1 the author stresses the use of "perspective," "depth," "geometry," "relaxed," "natural," "light," and shadow, and "subtle tones," whereas passage 2 concentrates on "instant recognition," "know the name only," "accident of . . . publicity," and "charms of a myth" to reinforce why it is significant.

C

p. 845–15

The answer has to be supported by lines 22–29 of the passage, which state that the museum is not like anything else ever made. The details are based on Roman examples pulled together from various places and combined for a resulting appearance that is unnatural and incongruous. *Incongruous* means odd, incohererent, out of place, and inconsistent.

A

p. 981–16

This is an abstract **question** that involves manipulating variables. It's easier to understand the problem if you give the variables numeric values and then substitute the variables back into the problem.

Let's say $m = 10$ coworkers, $y = 100$ dollars, and $p = 2$ coworkers who failed to contribute. If everyone contributed equally (100 ÷ 10), each person would contribute 10. But, there are 20 dollars to make up for (the 2 who didn't contribute) and 8 people to do it. So, 2/10 of the total would be divided among 10 – 2 coworkers. So,

$$\frac{2}{10} \times 100 \times \frac{1}{10-2}$$

Now, substitute the variables back into the formula:

$$\frac{p}{m} \times y \times \frac{1}{m-p} = \frac{py}{m(m-p)}$$

E

p. 538–7

The phrase in parentheses is a major clue to meaning "(too seriously!)," that he had aspired to accomplish more than he was probably capable of doing, hence "a grandiose ambition." Someone who is "naive" is inexperienced or immature. Any "grandiose" ambition would be pretentious or extravagant.

C

p. 405–20

Word substitution works well for this **question**. Read the sentence replacing peculiar with the answer choices. In this case, distinctive means standing out or being clear. Note that the more common definitions of peculiar like eccentric, abnormal, and rare can be ruled out because they are similar and someone might choose those common definitions without reading the passage.

D

p. 462–25

The main context clue can be found in line 59 when the narrator states that Bobby is pleasantly cynical and lines 61–62 where he does not take Lewis too seriously indicating a sense of dry (cynical) humor.

C

Henry Davis, Explanations for the Official SAT Study Guide **Questions**: *Detailed Explanations for the Answers for Every* **Question**

Question. I did not ask if you had been riding with them, but if you had any knowledge of their operations?

Answer. Only from report, hearsay.

Question. Have any of them indicated to you any of their operations?

Answer. No, sir.

Question. Have you had any communication with any of them on this subject!

Answer. No, sir.

Question. With none of them in any manner whatever?

Answer. O, I have heard men—I don't know who—just in a jesting manner say, "I'm a Ku-Klux."

Question. Who said that?

Answer. I don't know, I can't think, because I know it was just a joke.

Question. How do you know that?

Answer. Because it passed as such and I took it as such. I thought a man that really was wouldn't be fool enough to tell it.

United States House of Representatives, Reports of Committees for the Second Session of the Forty-Second Congress, 1871–72

p. 600–9

The sentence makes more sense and is clearer and more precise if we say that **the reason** George Eliot is considered a great English novelist is **because** she has command of pathos, tragedy, and humor. The first half of the sentence is fragmented and unclear.

Using the word "because" instead of "having" gives the sentence more clarity.

E

*Henry Davis, Explanations for the Official SAT Study Guide **Questions**: Detailed Explanations for the Answers for Every **Question***

It would, of course, be an amazing accomplishment if a level of scientific knowledge were reached whereby we could accurately predict whether or not a given person will laugh at a particular joke. Perhaps the machine for calculating this likelihood could be called the Laugh Predictor 3000™. Comedians would obviously find this technology invaluable. Perhaps it could also have a reverse gear that could specify what environmental and biological factors were salient when I laughed at a particular joke. This would offer one kind of answer to the **question** Why did I laugh? However, the Laugh Predictor 3000™ (in reverse gear) could only address the *perceptual* sense of this **question**. That is to say, it could only give information about my mindset as it responds to given formal, semantic, and referential aspects of the joke. This could help explain why I found the joke funny, in the sense that it could specify what it is *about me* that led to me finding the joke funny, rather than, say, distressing or boring (as others perhaps found it). Perhaps the Laugh Predictor 3000™ (in reverse gear) could highlight elements in the joke that had predictive value for my response. But it could not tell me *how* the joke was funny. That is, it could not offer the evaluative redescription that the aesthetic **question** demands.

Alex Clayton, Funny How? Sketch Comedy and the Art of Humor

Question. So you think that Mr. Livingstone was overstating what you had offered to do?

Answer. Perhaps. I asked him to send me a letter, and the rest of the facts speak for themselves. I didn't do anything.

Question. Were you aware—to your knowledge, was Craig Livingstone someone who boosted or sort of puffed up what his jobs were?

Answer. I didn't know that much about him.

Question. Or what his access was to the White House?

Answer. I mean, I have read accounts since, but I just didn't know that much about him then.

Question. When you got this letter from Mr. Livingstone, were you—what was your response to it?

Answer. I wrote "nothing" on the Post-It note.

Question. You have someone writing to you that he wants to be head of the Military Office. Did you think, this is a good candidate; this is—what, a joke? Did you have any response to Craig Livingstone—

Answer. I think this is a joke.

Question [continuing]. Asking for heading up the Military Office?

Answer. I think my response as written speaks for itself. I thought it was appropriate to do nothing—

Question. And why did you think it was appropriate to do nothing?

Answer [continuing]. In response to that letter. He wasn't qualified.

Question. You didn't think Craig Livingstone was qualified to be in this position?

Answer. Well, since the head of the Military Office—to the best of my knowledge, he didn't serve in the military. It seemed like a nonstarter.

Question. Are you aware that that's a civilian position?

Answer. I'm not, but that's as much as I thought about it.

> *House of Representatives Committee on Government Reform and Oversight, Deposition Transcripts From the Committee Investigation Into the White House Office Travel Matter, Volume 5*

Gentlemen, I am joking, and I know myself that my jokes are not brilliant, but you know one can take everything as a joke. I am, perhaps, jesting against the grain. Gentlemen, I am tormented by **questions**; answer them for me. You, for instance, want to cure men of their old habits and reform their will in accordance with science and good sense. But how do you know, not only that it is possible, but also that it is DESIRABLE to reform man in that way? And what leads you to the conclusion that man's inclinations NEED reforming? In short, how do you know that such a reformation will be a benefit to man? And to go to the root of the matter, why are you so positively convinced that not to act against his real normal interests guaranteed by the conclusions of reason and arithmetic is certainly always advantageous for man and must always be a law for mankind? So far, you know, this is only your supposition. It may be the law of logic, but not the law of humanity. You think, gentlemen, perhaps that I am mad? Allow me to defend myself. I agree that man is pre-eminently a creative animal, predestined to strive consciously for an object and to engage in engineering—that is, incessantly and eternally to make new roads, WHEREVER THEY MAY LEAD. But the reason why he wants sometimes to go off at a tangent may just be that he is PREDESTINED to make the road, and perhaps, too, that however stupid the "direct" practical man may be, the thought sometimes will occur to him that the road almost always does lead SOMEWHERE, and that the destination it leads to is less important than the process of making it, and that the chief thing is to save the well-conducted child from despising engineering, and so giving way to the fatal idleness, which, as we all know, is the mother of all the vices. Man likes to make roads and to create, that is a fact beyond dispute. But why has he such a passionate love for destruction and chaos also? Tell me that! But on that point I want to say a couple of words myself. May it not be that he loves chaos and destruction (there can be no disputing that he does sometimes love it) because he is instinctively afraid of attaining his object and completing the edifice he is constructing? Who knows, perhaps he only loves that edifice from a distance, and is by no means in love with it at close quarters; perhaps he only loves building it and does not want to live in it, but will leave it, when completed, for the use of LES ANIMAUX DOMESTIQUES—such as the ants, the sheep, and so on.

> *Fyodor Dostoevsky, Notes From the Underground*

p. 403–12

The difficulty of this **question** depends on understanding what the **question** is actually asking. What does the author of Passage 1 think of the opinion of the author of Passage 2? Passage 1 states that teachers use Walden as an illustration of protest against the forces of industrialization; therefore, Passage 2 does not represent how Walden is usually taught in schools.

C

p. 405–17

Comparing cities to beaver dams and anthills is showing that all three are similar in that they are natural; they all alter their environments and build shelters which are natural impulses.

B

p. 545–19

The use of the phrase "wives and mothers" would imply that the author was specifically targeting women in domestic roles (who) had previously exercised little authority. He describes them as "formerly subservient creatures," indicating they had little or no authority.

E

p. 546–22

According to Virginia Wolfe, women were willing to undertake any menial (*boring, tedious, or unskilled*) task for the sake of escaping their traditional roles—even if it meant their men had to go to war to provide those opportunities.

B

Henry Davis, Explanations for the Official SAT Study Guide **Questions**: *Detailed Explanations for the Answers for Every* **Question**

I liked the way she stood up to him, and the way he took it.
Trying not to sound like a boorish upstart in a **Q** & **A**
disingenuously grilling Oppenheimer, Einstein or Bohr

with how they felt about their elegant theorems
culminating in so much death, I asked if
he was ambivalent about designing warheads. **Question**

from left field. Bewilderment squared.
His honked "Wa" was like an inaudible "Come again?"
Forehead painfully wrinkled. Deep-set ridges.

My stomach contracted: Oh God, what have I done?
It wasn't me asking discomfiting **questions** to hound
this dear, sweet, ebullient man, who had done his best . . . ;

it was my . . . duty to ask, which appeared to perplex
this . . . disembodied intelligence . . . schooled in
focusing on the problem to be solved just as

Husserl bracketed words, [postponed]
this longing to belong to sentences that mimicked
meaningful action, and to block out the politics and social

contexts that could . . . derail . . . the (beautiful) concord
between pure thought and necessity. He had the right to think:
Anyone can design a ship, or a missile, that works

like a bigger bullet shot from a bigger gun;
but to invent one that can stop, turn around,
change directions, now that's—invention.

Mark Rudman, Tomahawk

p. 845–19

The word *flouting* means to openly ignore, disobey or defy. *Conventional* means traditional or common. Getty openly ignored the traditional ways when he had the building designed

A

p. 639–4

This appears tricky, but, once you walk through the problem, it unravels. We need to find the equation which will turn a negative more positive than a positive number. The SAT likes to see if you remember that (1) a negative number times another negative number = a positive number and that (2) an odd numbered exponent keeps a negative number negative. Of the answer choices, rule out any even numbered exponents, since that makes –3 and 3 equals. **B** keeps the values equal and **C** is a negative value. When you look at **D** you'll see that cubing –3 makes it –27 and subtracting it turns it positive, giving the function a value of 4 + 27 = 31; whereas, cubing a positive 3 makes it 4 – 27 = –23.

D

p.708–13

Look at the last line of the passage: " . . . no one knew for certain where the limits of reality lay." The new inventions disrupt their world, causing them to **question** their known way of life.

D

p. 709–14

Every new invention has a down side to it. The electric plant is noisy; the cinema is illusions and trickery; the phonograph is "a mechanical trick" and "a serious disappointment"; and the telephone is the most upsetting of all. None of these inventions are what they promise.

C

p. 845–20

Getty <u>did not</u> *compromise* his vision for the museum design—in fact, just the opposite. So, D is wrong. Nor was Getty trying to make a mocking social statement (*pointed satire*) about existing museums, so B is wrong. Nothing is mentioned about Getty wanting to build the museum out of *spiteful mischief* (irresponsible contempt), which makes C wrong. Nor was Getty motivated by *justified* (reasonable or fair) *indignation* (anger), which eliminates E. It was clear that Getty "calculated the risks . . . and disregarded them" (58–59) and refused to conform (54–55); therefore, choosing the museum design was an act of courageous defiance.

A

p. 845–21

It was the museum itself, not the art inside the museum, that became controversial. Lines 59–61 state that Getty was neither shaken nor surprised by the critics' reactions to the new museum; in other words, he had anticipated the critics' disfavor. Further, in line 70 Getty says he was "unruffled" by their criticism. Getty was aware of what was considered the norm in Art Museum structures, so he anticipated the probable critical response and chose to ignore it.

D

Henry Davis, Explanations for the Official SAT Study Guide **Questions**: *Detailed Explanations for the Answers for Every* **Question**

It is always a mistake to assume that people will conform to stereotypes. It's taken me years to understand, but incident after incident has proven to me that one must see hard evidence before making a statement. Most women are not interested in sports like baseball, but some are. It's possible to make an assumption based on probability, but it is not a reliable way to decide a **question**.

*E. J. Copperman and Jeff Cohen, The **Question** of the Missing Head*

p. 657–11

The problem is with the pronoun "it." There's no singular noun in the sentence, so it must be replaced with a more specific phrase ("these first efforts").

B

*Henry Davis, Explanations for the Official SAT Study Guide **Questions**: Detailed Explanations for the Answers for Every **Question***

"Good," I said. "So you probably also know that no home run—that is, no ball in play— was ever hit completely out of the original Yankee Stadium in the eighty-five years it stood."

"Eighty-six," she said. "Yes, I'm aware. I'm also aware that Mickey Mantle's lifetime batting average was two-ninety-eight. How does that relate to me taking pictures of you swinging a bat?"

*E. J. Copperman and Jeff Cohen, The **Question** of the Missing Head*

Question 7. Feelings of inner neediness and inadequacy drive us to strive for reputation and wealth.

Question 8. Some say it refers to earthly treasures, but the context seems to indicate the simple needs mentioned in intervening verses: food, drink, clothing and a place to sleep (vv. 25–32).

Jan Johnson, Simplicity & Fasting: 6 Studies With Notes for Leaders

"How do you know if you've never seen it?" **Question** Boy asked.

"Well . . . because . . ."

"What if they took the tank out for a drive and you just filled their whole basement with oil?"

"You can't drive an oil tank!" Oil Man said firmly.

"What's that giant container on your truck?" **Question** Boy asked.

Oil Man flinched "It's . . . a . . . tank . . ."

"What's in it?" **Question** Boy asked.

Oil Man stumbled backward. He jumped in his truck and hurried away.

*Peter Catalanotto, **Question** Boy Meets Little Miss Know-It-All*

Question. I did not ask you to argue the case; just tell me the facts.

Answer. It was just about such a size piece of paper, as nigh as I could get at it.

Question. How could you see that he was writing such a paper when you could not see whether he was writing with pen or pencil?

Answer. I was out too far; I didn't see him get any ink. I just saw him writing, but whether with ink or pencil I could not tell.

Question. Now, Lipscomb, tell me how many people were in sight when Chaffin was writing that paper and stuck it up on that tree; how many were all around the church and in the church that could see that?

Answer. I am telling you exactly the way, as far as I know. There was a great many people there that day; but to say who was noticing him particularly with that paper I could not tell; but I saw it.

Question. How many could have noticed it?

Answer. I know those that were right around him when he was writing it—standing there—saw it and knew it.

Question. Did you see anybody else who saw it?

Answer. No, sir. I don't know.

Question How many were standing there that could have seen it if they wanted to? Fifty?

United States House of Representatives, Reports of Committees for the Second Session of the Forty-Second Congress, 1871–72

p. 587–1

The word *adept* means highly skilled. It is predictable (foreseeable) that a detail-oriented worker would be *adept at* keeping track of a myriad (a great number) of particulars.

B

p. 429–2

This **question** as presented has an indefinite pronoun "it." B, C, D, and E take care of that error, but E has a subject verb error and D fails to complete the sentence. C is more direct and active voiced.

C

p. 429–4

"She" is not a specific pronoun and need to know to which one of the girls it refer-rers to. "Sheila noticed" is the most direct, active voiced construction of the sentence.

E

p. 430–5

The construction of the original sentence contains a misplaced modifier, as the opening phrase modifies the word "dust" which must correctly follow it in order to make sense. Of the two correctly placed answer choices C and D., choose the briefest most correct construction without the incorrectly placed "that."

C

*Henry Davis, Explanations for the Official SAT Study Guide **Questions**: Detailed Explanations for the Answers for Every **Question***

Answer. Yes, sir.

Question. Have you got it now?

Answer. No, sir; I have not got it.

United States House of Representatives, Reports of Committees for the Second Session of the Forty-Second Congress, 1871–72

Session 2. Less Is More

Matthew 6:24–34

Focus: Living in simplicity involves arranging our lives so that we live purposefully without being distracted by possessions and worry.

Question 1. Life is more important than these things (v. 25); we are more valuable than birds and field grass and God takes care of them (v. 26, 30); worrying is not constructive (v. 27–29). In vv. 32–33, Jesus tells them only pagans worry about these things, but we seek God's kingdom instead.

Yet Jesus wasn't saying that we do nothing or refuse to take responsibility. We work hard and stay away from idleness (2 Thessalonians 3:6–13). We take responsibility for caring for the folks given to us (1 Timothy 5:3–4), but we don't worry about it.

Jan Johnson, Simplicity & Fasting: 6 Studies With Notes for Leaders

Question 9. Have you experienced recurrent bothersome or disturbing thoughts (other than worry) that seem difficult or impossible to control?

- Yes.
- No.

Question 10. If you answered yes to **question** 8 or 9, do these symptoms cause you distress and/or negatively affect your work, recreation, or relationships?

- Yes.
- No. Skip to the next section on generalized anxiety disorder.

Question 11. If you answered yes to **question** 8 or 9, have these symptoms occurred consistently when you were NOT experiencing an episode of depression or mania?

- Yes.
- No. Skip to the next section on generalized anxiety disorder.

If you answered yes to **question** 8 and/or 9 AND yes to BOTH **questions** 10 and 11, you may have OCD. Please check the obsessive-compulsive disorder box in the comorbidity summary (Form 3.1).

William R. Marchand, Depression and Bipolar Disorder: Your Guide to Recovery

If we knew the answer to such **questions** we wouldn't be worrying! To worry is to be consumed by the **question**, to have the **question** echo in our mind until we would do anything to make it go away.

To seize on a **question** like this and work on it, over and over, is not unlike a certain kind of spiritual practice. Spiritual practice, at its root, is about asking fundamental **questions**: Who am I? Why am I here? What is my purpose? What if I get sick and die?

These are root worries. Regardless of whether our life is going well or badly, they are always there. In some sense, ordinary worry is a surface manifestation of root worry. One purpose of Buddhist practice is to learn how to deal with root worry. In that sense, any **question** presents a good opportunity to raise the **questioning** spirit.

Lewis Richmond, Work as a Spiritual Practice: A Practical Buddhist Approach to Inner Growth and Satisfaction on the Job

Question. Why did you not tell that before?

United States House of Representatives, Reports of Committees for the Second Session of the Forty-Second Congress, 1871–72

The **questioning** spirit says, "I will stay with this **question** regardless of whether an answer ever comes. This **question**, for now, is my life."

Sometimes, in my workshops, I send people back to their jobs with the following assignment: Ask yourself, "What is the **question**?"

Lewis Richmond, *Work as a Spiritual Practice: A Practical Buddhist Approach to Inner Growth and Satisfaction on the Job*

Answer. You asked me if they were talking French and I told you; and you asked me if they had anything on. When they passed me they had nothing on, but when they came to my house they had doe-faces on.

Question. Which had the doe-faces on?

Answer. Several had.

Question. But I am speaking of these two men, Griffin and Chaffin.

Answer. Griffin had a handkerchief tied over his face.

Question. Chaffin had what?

Answer. Chaffin had a doe-face on.

Question. What is a doe-face?

Answer. A piece of paper they call a doe-face.

Question. Did he wear it all over his face?

Answer. No, sir; it came down this way.

Question. What was on his head?

Answer. His hat.

Question. What hat?

Answer. His white hat; his every-day hat.

Question. What shape hat was it?

Answer. It was shaped pretty much like this wool hat.

Question. Did he wear a white hat at that time?

Answer. Yes, sir.

Question. Did he wear that in the evening?

Answer. Yes, sir.

Question. What sort of a gown had he on?

Answer. None; only his every-day clothes.

Question. Had any of the rest gowns on?

Answer. No, sir; only their every-day clothes.

Question. How is it that you did not know the rest?

Answer. I just made out what I could, and them that I couldn't I didn't.

United States House of Representatives, *Reports of Committees for the Second Session of the Forty-Second Congress, 1871–72*

I don't explain it any more than that. I just say, "Find out what the **question** is."

Of all the practices that I have people do, this is the one they often find the most difficult. "What do you mean, 'Find out what the **question** is?' How am I supposed to know what the **question** is? Is this some kind of trick?"

It's interesting that the people who are resistant, who come back the following week with a blank look on their faces, are the ones whose jobs are going well. They are doing all right. Their **questioning** spirit isn't engaged. People who have a real problem at work typically know what the **question** is the minute they think about it. "What if the layoffs go through?" "How can I finish the project with no money in the budget?" "Why is my boss asking me to do the impossible?"

That's the gift that worry brings us. It lets us know what the **question** is. An eminent artist once said, "The great thing about being an artist is that for your whole life you know what your work is." I thought that was a wise observation. Many people never quite know what their focus should be. Worry helps. Worry lets us know what is important to us.

The practice of working with a **question** is not complicated. It involves the following four steps:

1. Raise the **Question**
2. Repeat the **Question**
3. Follow the **Question**
4. Settle the **Question**

Lewis Richmond, Work as a Spiritual Practice: A Practical Buddhist Approach to Inner Growth and Satisfaction on the Job

Question 3. It can be helpful to ask ourselves these **questions**: Do I enjoy pulling together an outfit as a creative venture? Or do I use clothing to impress (perhaps manipulate) others so they think I know more than I know and I can be trusted? Is my clothing appropriate and honoring to God and others? If you wish, consider modifying the **question** to, "What choices of cars/sports equipment/household gadgets are least likely to distract you . . . ?"

Jan Johnson, Simplicity & Fasting: 6 Studies With Notes for Leaders

Please see below for the instructions—in particular the importance in reversing score items 1, 3, 8, 10 and 11. Take a notebook and write down your responses. What is your total score? What thoughts were going through your mind as you completed this **questionnaire**? Note these down too.

Kevin Meares and Mark Freeston, Overcoming Worry and Generalised Anxiety Disorder: A Self-Help Guide Using Cognitive Behavioral Techniques

p. 775–9

"Many people think taxes are too high; **consequently**, some do not report all the money they earn." The word "consequently" connects two complete sentences, each with its own subject and verb. As written (without the semicolon), the sentence has a <u>comma splice</u>—which is considered a major error. A semicolon corrects it.

C

p. 554–7

Answer choice A, although a little awkward could be correct. But answer choice B provides us with a clear cause and effect and an active voice verb. It also shows us specifically who missed flight. Answer choices C, D, and E all have the problem of being incorrect or passive.

B

p. 554–8

The sentence as written is both passive and indirect. Answer choice B would require a semicolon after "vegetation." Answer choice D needs a verb. Answer choice E presents an unneeded word of contrast "but." Answer choice C correctly makes the transition statement.

C

p. 554–9

This sentence lacks parallelism. The sentence requires a parallel construction to

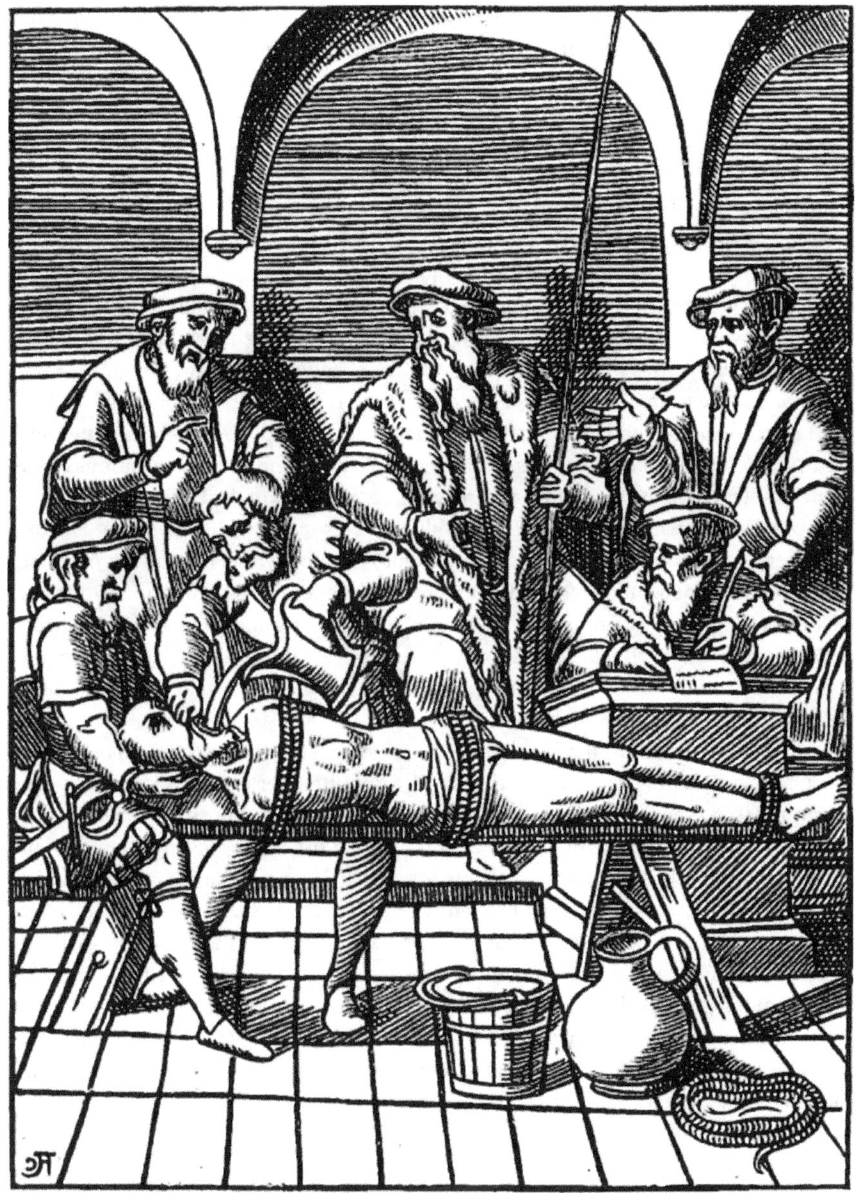

The Question By Water
Praxis rerum criminalium of Damhoudère, 1556

In Paris, the **question** was for a long time given by water; it was both the most intolerable and the least dangerous for the patient. The one who had to undergo it was, as for the preceding **question**, tied and supported in the air by the four limbs, until his body was well stretched out. A trestle was then passed under his loins and, with the aid of a horn forming a funnel, while his nose was squeezed with the hand to force him to swallow, four cockerels were slowly poured into his mouth of water (about 9 liters) for the ordinary item, and double that for the extraordinary. When the execution was over, the patient was untied "and taken to the kitchen to warm up," says an old text.

La Rédaction, Penal Sanctions in the Middle Ages, Ordinary
*or Extraordinary **Question** (france-pittoresque.com)*

complement "either to renovate". The first pairing has to coordinate "either" with "or." Then the verb forms must match. Choice E is the correct parallel construction: "either to renovate"."or to replace."

E

Henry Davis, Explanations for the Official SAT Study Guide **Questions**: *Detailed Explanations for the Answers for Every* **Question**

Lagrange, it is well known, has proved that the Planetary System, on this scheme, will endure forever; Laplace, still more cunningly, even guesses that it could not have been made on any other scheme. Whereby, at least, our nautical Logbooks can be better kept; and water-transport of all kinds has grown more commodious. Of Geology and Geognosy we know enough: what with the labors of our Werners and Huttons, what with the ardent genius of their disciples, it has come about that now, to many a Royal Society, the Creation of a World is little more mysterious than the cooking of a dumpling; concerning which last, indeed, there have been minds to whom the **question**, *How the apples were got in*, presented difficulties. Why mention our disquisitions on the Social Contract, on the Standard of Taste, on the Migrations of the Herring? Then, have we not a Doctrine of Rent, a Theory of Value; Philosophies of Language, of History, of Pottery, of Apparitions, of Intoxicating Liquors? Man's whole life and environment have been laid open and elucidated; scarcely a fragment or fibre of his Soul, Body, and Possessions, but has been probed, dissected, distilled, desiccated, and scientifically decomposed: our spiritual Faculties, of which it appears there are not a few, have their Stewarts, Cousins, Royer Collards: every cellular, vascular, muscular Tissue glories in its Lawrences, Majendies, Bichats.

How, then, comes it, may the reflective mind repeat, that the grand Tissue of all Tissues, the only real Tissue, should have been quite overlooked by Science,—the vestural Tissue, namely, of woollen or other cloth; which Man's Soul wears as its outmost wrappage and overall; wherein his whole other Tissues are included and screened, his whole Faculties work, his whole Self lives, moves, and has its being? For if, now and then, some straggling broken-winged thinker has cast an owl's glance into this obscure region, the most have soared over it altogether heedless; regarding Clothes as a property, not an accident, as quite natural and spontaneous, like the leaves of trees, like the plumage of birds. In all speculations they have tacitly figured man as a Clothed Animal; whereas he is by nature a *Naked Animal*; and only in certain circumstances, by purpose and device, masks himself in Clothes. Shakespeare says, we are creatures that look before and after: the more surprising that we do not look round a little, and see what is passing under our very eyes.

Thomas Carlyle, Sartor Resartus: The Life and Opinions of Herr Teufelsdröckh

p. 913–18

The reference to how Akaky "must have been born" in line 21 indicates that he could not be imagined any way other than how he appeared at the department each day. Akaky is described as: "seen at the same place, at the very same duty ... in uniform ... with a bald patch on his head" no matter how many directors and officials came and went (lines 18–23).

C

p. 792–7

The passage is narrated from the 3rd person point-of-view by an observer who knows all about Mulcahy's actions and background, as well as what he is thinking.

    D

p. 914–22

The narrator's attitude toward the young clerks in Akaky's office is primarily one of disapproval of their cruelty. We know this based on the tone of the passage. The author does not condemn Akaky for his contentment with his ordinariness and dedication to a mundane job. The author does not applaud his co-workers behavior towards him, and because of the negative light he sheds on Akaky's co-workers we can conclude that he disapproves of their cruelty.

    A

p. 793–10

Mulcahy requested an investigation into why the dietician needed twenty thousand eggs; he called it the "unscrambling" of the twenty thousand eggs. This play on words (pun) is meant to be witty and amusing.

    C

p. 914–24

It can be inferred from the incident described in lines 55–65 that Akaky feared increased responsibility. It is stated that the new task "threw him into a regular perspiration". And that he later said "No, better let me copy something." Copying seemed to be all he could handle or felt comfortable doing.

    E

p. 793–12

Mulcahy says in lines 38–39, "surely, one had the right to expect something better." This suggests that he believes he is being dismissed from Jocelyn College because he is outspoken in his criticism of the way the college is run.

    A

p. 657–5

The problem is with the verb "doing." So, the verb has to be fixed, and that sometimes means reordering the information in the sentence to make the meaning more clear. Also, "accomplishing this feat" is better because it's more specific than "doing it." What's "it?"

    D

p. 793–16

This is a hard **question** because you have to know the vocabulary. The president flatly disliked Mulcahy; in fact, the presidents hatred is unremitting. The word "flatly" in line 60 most closely means *unequivocally* (allowing for no doubt or misinterpretation).

    E

p. 395–20

Passage 2 mentions her "eyes" and "hands," but the climactic last sentence of passage 1 mentions her "famous smile," therefore the author of passage 1 would include her "mouth" which smiles.

    A

p. 794–18

Mulcahy is described as "a complex intelligence" (l. 60) and as having "an imagination" (l. 61); however, "he had been unprepared . . . for the obvious: a blunt, naked wielding of power" (ll. 65–66). He was *naïve* (inexperienced or unprepared) regarding the politics of college administration despite his "superior intellect" (l. 71).

E

Henry Davis, Explanations for the Official SAT Study Guide **Questions**: *Detailed Explanations for the Answers for Every* **Question**

Good for Mrs. Baldwin, Ferguson thought, as he watched his literary nemesis gloating over the dual triumph at the blackboard, as if she were the one who had written the essays herself, and happy as Ferguson was to be the winner from among the three hundred and fifty students in his grade, he understood that the victory was of no importance, not only because whatever Mrs. Baldwin judged to be good necessarily had to be bad but because he himself had turned against his own essay since the debacle in the Newark gym, knowing that what he had written was too optimistic and naïve to make any sense in the real world, that while Jackie Robinson deserved all the praise Ferguson had given him, desegregating baseball was just a midget step in a much larger struggle that would have to go on for many more years, no doubt for more years than Ferguson himself would ever get to live, perhaps for another century or two, and that next to his hollow, idealistic portrait of a transformed America, Amy's piece on Emma Goldman had been much better, not just better written and better thought-out but at once more subtle and more passionate, and the only reason why she hadn't been given the first prize was because the school couldn't award the blue ribbon to an essay about a *revolutionary anarchist,* who by definition was to be regarded as a thoroughly unAmerican American, a person so radical and dangerous to the American way of life that she had been deported from her own country.

Mrs. Baldwin was still droning on in front of the class, explaining that the three winners from each grade would be reading their essays out loud at an all-school assembly scheduled for Friday afternoon, and as Ferguson glanced over at Amy—who sat one row in front of him and two desks to the right—he was amused that when his eyes landed on her back, dead center between her two shoulder blades, she instantly turned around to look at him, as if she had felt his eyes touching her, and, even more amusing, once their eyes met, she scrunched up her face and stuck out her tongue at him, as if to say, Pooh on you, Archie Ferguson, I should have won and you know it, and when Ferguson smiled at her and shrugged, as if to say, You're right, but what can I do about it?, Amy's scrunch turned into a smile, and a moment later, unable to suppress the laugh gathering in her throat, she let out one of her weird snorts, an unexpectedly loud noise that prompted Mrs. Baldwin to interrupt what she was saying and ask, Is everything all right, Amy?

Just fine, Mrs. Baldwin, Amy said. I burped. I know it's an unladylike thing to do, but I couldn't help it. Sorry.

EVERYONE HAD ALWAYS told Ferguson that life resembled a book, a story that began on page 1 and pushed forward until the hero died on page 204 or 926, but now that the future he had imagined for himself was changing, his understanding of time was changing as well. Time moved both forward and backward, he realized, and because the stories in books could only move forward, the book metaphor made no sense. If anything, life was more akin to the structure of a tabloid newspaper, with big events such as the outbreak of a war or a gangland killing on the front page and less important news on the pages that followed, but the back page bore a headline as well, the day's top story from the trivial but compelling world of sports, and the sports articles were nearly always read backward as you turned the pages from left to right instead of from right to left as you did with the articles in the front, going in reverse as if plowing through a text in Hebrew or Japanese, steadily working your way toward the middle of the paper, and once you hit the no-man's-land of the classifieds, which were not worth reading unless you were in the market for trombone lessons or a used bicycle, you would jump over those pages until you wound up in the central territory of movie ads, theater reviews, Ann Landers's advice column, and the editorials, from which point, if you had started reading from the back (as Ferguson, the sports enthusiast, usually did) you could keep going all the way to the front. Time moved in two directions because every step into the future carried a memory of the past, and even though Ferguson had not yet turned fifteen, he had accumulated enough memories to know that the world around him was continually being shaped by the world within him, just as everyone else's experience of the world was shaped by his own memories, and while all people were bound together by the common space they shared, their journeys through time were all different, which meant that each person lived in a slightly different world from everyone else. The **question** was: What world did Ferguson inhabit now, and how had that world changed for him?

Paul Auster, *4 3 2 1*

p. 826–11

You are looking for an answer that explains/defines what is meant by "principles of phenomenology." *Phenomenology* is the study of phenomenon, and a phenomenon is any observable fact or event. So, phenomenology is the study of the way we observe facts or events. The best meaning for the phrase "principles of phenomenology" is the *ways and means* of knowing about something.

C

p. 395–19

This quote "in the manner of smoke" describes an impact on the viewer as stated in

B

p. 647–15

Note: the test makers classify this as a hard **question**, perhaps because it's hard to understand what they're actually asking. You want the statement that would undermine (weaken or diminish) the validity of the author's assumption that time existed for man and nature before we invented a way to measure it. He says, "it must have surprised people to discover that time flowed outside . . ." so the invention of the mechanical clock had a profound effect on mankind. If the opposite were true, which is to say people have always experienced time as composed of separate (discrete), uniform intervals, then the author's assumption about the impact of the mechanical clock would be wrong.

B

p. 826–12

When the author uses the phrase "our world" he is referring to the world of man, and, more specifically, to our visual world. Man's reality is perceived primarily by what he can see. When the author says "the dog's —," he is comparing our perceptions to the dog's world, which is primarily made up of smells. The dog's *perception of the world* is through his nose, while man's is through his eyes.

    C

p. 790–20

In this problem you are altering a function. Remember when you change a function (move the graph of the function) without changing the shape of the function, you are changing the x and y values. When you change the y value (a vertical change) the change is logical. When you move the graph down, you are applying a negative value. When you move the graph up, you are adding to the y value. But when you move a function graph along the x axis (horizontally) the logic is reversed. If you move the graph to the right, seemingly increasing the x value, you must subtract from the x value in the equation. When you move the graph to the left, seemingly decreasing the x value, you add to the equation. Here you move from –3 to –5, it means the k, which adjusts the y value, is –2. When you move the graph to the right from –1 to 2, you are adjusting the x value, which is what h does. Since you are moving 3 to the right, h = –3. hk = $(-2)(-3) = 6$

    E

p. 668–5

Be careful with this problem. It's easy to assume that the greatest change means the greatest increase, which would be either 1982–1983 (3.50 to 4.25 = .75) or 1985–1986 (3.75 to 4.5 = .75). The fact that there are two equal amounts of increase should protect you from choosing the wrong answer. The *greatest change* comes between 1984 and 1985 when the change was 4.75–3.75 = 1.00.

    D

p. 644–3

Political turbulence in a country can cause the name of the country to change frequently; therefore, the frequent name changes *testify* to the political turbulence (turmoil, disorder, or confusion). You would not say the name changes *argue against* the political turbulence or that they are *in contrast* to the political turbulence, nor do the frequent name changes *jeopardize* or *sustain* the political turbulence.

    C

p. 551–12

In these lines she's talking about her father arguing with the television, indicating strong feelings. We find that in answer choice C. Clearly he was not uncomfortable discussing politics, it doesn't indicate the he didn't approve of news coverage as he's watching it. We can't imply that he was pessimistic about the world from that, and we don't know anything about his public advocacy. We are just being told that he was arguing with a broadcast.

    C

p. 644–4

Because there are more than 30,000 species of Brachiopods, they are considered "one of the most *multifarious* forms of life." (Hint: *multi* means "many.") *Multifarious* means diverse or occurring in great variety; while *catalogued* means to list or register. "Plentiful " is the only other word that might work in the first blank, but "subtracted" doesn't make sense in the second blank. *Ornate* means beautiful; *retrieved* means brought back. *Scarce* means limited or in short supply, while *extracted* means to remove or take out. *Anachronistic* means out of date or old, while *extrapolate* means to predict by projecting past experience or known data. *Plentiful* means abundant and *subtract* means to take away from.

    C

p. 775–6

Pei's services are in demand because his buildings combine beauty and afford-ability. The second part of the sentence needs to answer the **question** "Why?" The sentence is essentially cause and effect. Choices (D) and (E) are written in the future tense, as though the buildings are yet to be built. How could someone's services be in demand based on a future result? Notice that, once again, the shortest and most succinct sentence is the correct answer.

    C

p. 644–2

If someone critically examines the assumptions and values of another's world, he would be *scrutinizing* it. *Idealize* means "romanticize." To *avoid* means "stay away from." To *beautify* means "to make attractive." To *exclude* means "to leave out." The heroine scrutinized her employers' world.

    D

p. 540–12

"The benign monster" is a physical characterization on the manufacturing process described in lines 18 to 20. "Benign" means something that is harmless, thus taking the bad connotation away from the word monster, leaving the meaning of sheer size.

    C

p. 540–13

The "compensation" for the filthy air caused by the machine age is the money made by the shopkeepers who care not "except that the world will never be clean again," trading their world for profits. Do not be fooled by answer C which gives the profits to manufacturers, not the shopkeepers.

    E

p. 540–14

The shopkeepers are "in a hurry" to open their shops so that they might be the first one to catch a customer and make a profit, so they are "eager" in their preparations.

    C

p. 791–5

"The colors and patterns on butterflies' wings may seem merely decorative, but they are actually *instrumental* in the survival of these insects." *Artificial* means fake or not natural; *dependent* means needy or to rely upon. *Unique* mean unusual. *Decorative* means pleasing to the eye; *instrumental* means helpful or plays a part in. *Beautiful* means pleasing to the eye or attractive; *results of* means outcome. *Unrelated* means not connected; *precursors of* means to be a forerunner or to come before.

   C

p. 775–5

   The subject of this sentence is "literature" and the verb is "endures." The error is the word "their." It has no antecedent. In referring to literature (the subject), you'd need to use "it." Choices (B) and (D) could not be correct because you need the adverb forms, "directly and freshly."

   C

p. 669–8

   Quickly sketch the figure, so you can visualize it. If one endpoint of the diameter is $(-2,-7)$ and the center is $(3,-7)$, then the other endpoint must be the same distance (5) from center. So $3 + 5 = 8$.

   E

*Henry Davis, Explanations for the Official SAT Study Guide **Questions**: Detailed Explanations for the Answers for Every **Question***

Answer. No, sir. I don't know that there were so many that could have seen it.

Question. Were they all black and white people?

Answer. No, sir; there was mighty few black people that could see it among them.

Question. Was the tree nearer the church than Chaffin was when he wrote it?

Answer. Yes, sir.

Question. How much nearer? How far had he to walk from where he wrote to go to the tree?

Answer. May be twenty steps.

Question. You were about twenty steps from the church?

Answer. Yes, sir.

Question. And he was about thirty steps, when he was writing, still further off?

Answer. Yes, sir.

Question. So that if he came back toward the church after he wrote the paper he came about as near the church as you were?

Answer. Yes, sir; mighty nigh it.

Question. And the people were standing all around there?

Answer. Yes, sir.

Question. And you saw him write this paper and stick it up there?

Answer. Yes, sir; he wrote that paper and stuck it up to the tree.

Question. You swear to that?

Answer. Do I swear that he stuck it up to the tree? I will swear this way, that he wrote the paper.

Question. This paper that is here?

Answer. Yes, sir.

Question. Did you not swear that he stuck it up there?

Answer. I swore that he stuck the paper on a tree closer to the church than he was.

Question. Did you swear that Chaffin wrote this paper on that day at the church?

Answer. Yes, sir.

Question. Thirty yards from where you were?

Answer. Yes, sir.

Question. And that he took this paper, after he had written it, and in the face of all the people, went to the tree and stuck it up there?

Answer. You asked me how much nearer it was to the tree.

Question. Did he walk to that tree and stick this up on the tree in the face of the people that day?

Answer. I don't know whether he did it before the crowd of people, but he stuck it up there that day; whether he did it right before the crowd I don't know, but he stuck it up that day.

Question. What time of day was it?

Answer. I don't know exactly what time, but it was after dinner-time of day.

Question. Didn't you say that after he got done writing it he took it and stuck it up?

Answer. Yes, sir; I did.

Question. How long was he in writing it?

Answer. I don't know how long.

Question. You say the preaching was not over when he commenced writing it?

Answer. Yes, sir.

Question. How long did the sermon continue?

Answer. I don't remember.

Question. Don't you mean to say that while you and these people were there, that when he got done writing this paper, he walked right up to the tree and stuck it there? Did you not say that?

Answer. Yes, sir. I said he put it on the tree.

Question. Did not he do it just then?

Answer. Not as quick as he wrote it.

Question. How long afterward?

Answer. I don't know what time in the day he did it, what hour or minute. He put it on that day.

Question. Were the people there when he did it?

Answer. I reckon they were, and they might have been pretty much gone.

United States House of Representatives, Reports of Committees for the Second Session of the Forty-Second Congress, 1871–72

She narrowed her eyes. "So . . ."

"So I have considered all the science involved and have concluded he is mistaken. But my client is the type of man who does not believe in statistics; he is more given to visual evidence. I'd like you to take photographs of me swinging the bat, then upload them to my computer simulation of the building. I can demonstrate, then, how the air currents—which do allow for more home runs to certain areas of the park—will not compensate for the size of the building and the physics involved."

*E. J. Copperman and Jeff Cohen, The **Question** of the Missing Head*

p. 913–19

The "simple fly" in line 25 is used primarily as an image of something that is easily overlooked. The sentence before states that even the ports did not get up from their chairs when he came into the room nor did they take any notice of him (referring to Akaky).

D

p. 395–21

The "position" of many art critics is their opinion or view of why they feel this way.

D

p. 656–3

The verb has to agree with the subject in quantity. Harmful describes "effects." The *effects* of smoking **are** increasingly well documented.

C

p. 844–14

According to the critics, the design of the museum—like Disneyland—is in bad taste, pretentious, and plastic. The word *garish* means bad taste and the word *plastic* means inauthentic.

D

p. 532–8

This sentence as given has a misplaced modifier. The phrase "Though — — — artists," is referring to Jackson Pollack, not the critics. This allows us to rule out answers choices A and B. Answer C isn't a complete sentence. Between D and E, D is more direct and concise.

D

p. 532–9

The sentence as given is a sentence fragment.. Answer choice D clearly provides us with a verb, keeps the sentence concise and direct, and provides an active voice.

D

p. 533–13

Be sure when you're comparing things you keep the comparison clear and parallel. The error here is an incorrect comparison. You're comparing her project with a person. The project is being compared incorrectly with "Jim" so the error is in answer choice D.

D

*Henry Davis, Explanations for the Official SAT Study Guide **Questions**: Detailed Explanations for the Answers for Every **Question***

"What you're probably all wondering is what exactly is this Nyodene D. we keep hearing about? A good **question**. We studied it in school, we saw movies of rats having convulsions and so on. So, okay, it's basically simple. Nyodene D. is a whole bunch of things thrown together that are byproducts of the manufacture of insecticide. The original stuff kills roaches, the byproducts kill everything left over. A little joke our teacher made."

He snapped his fingers, let his left leg swing a bit.

"In powder form it's colorless, odorless and very dangerous, except no one seems to know exactly what it causes in humans or in the offspring of humans. They tested for years and either they don't know for sure or they know and aren't saying. Some things are too awful to publicize."

He arched his brows and began to twitch comically, his tongue lolling in a corner of his mouth. I was astonished to hear people laugh.

"Once it seeps into the soil, it has a life span of forty years. This is longer than a lot of people. After five years you'll notice various kinds of fungi appearing between your regular windows and storm windows as well as in your clothes and food. After ten years your screens will turn rusty and begin to pit and rot. Siding will warp. There will be glass breakage and trauma to pets. After twenty years you'll probably have to seal yourself in the attic and just wait and see. I guess there's a lesson in all this. Get to know your chemicals."

Don DeLillo, White Noise

p. 961–11

The opening paragraph tells us how school children in Minnesota discovered one frog after another with deformities and how the discovery received media attention nationwide. Then the paragraph asks two very probing, dramatic **questions**. The **questions** highlight a phenomenon (*something out of the ordinary that excites people's interest and curiosity*) that has yet to be fully explained.

A

p. 658–13

The **question** is: Are chemical fertilizers a curse **or** a blessing? The words "are they" are unnecessary.

B

p. 458–8

This answer depends on vocabulary, but the sentence contains excellent synonyms such as "unpredictable" and "constantly shifting moods" which is synonymous for "mercurial' which is like the unstable element mercury which is the root. If someone is *mercurial* they are lively and unpredictable. Something is *corrosive* if it is acidic or caustic so someone who's corrosive would be considered sarcastic or acerbic. If someone is *disingenuous* they are insincere, deceitful, and devious. If someone is *implacable* they are relentless and merciless. And if someone is *phlegmatic* they are apathetic and indifferent.

A

p. 658–14

"People who need . . . reeducation for employment . . ." is correct. The word "which" is only used with things/objects—never people. Remember this.

A

p. 973–11

Frederick Douglass' rhetorical strategy as described in lines 4–10 might best be summarized as evocation of a revered concept followed by a specific reference to its undermining. Douglas summoned or appealed to a revered (*respected*) idea—individualism (l. 5). Then he referred to how slavery had undermined (*undercut* or *damaged*) this idea: "the very condition of enslavement directly contravened (*contradicted*) the deepest principles of individualism." (ll. 8–9)

D

p. 658–15

The members of the House of Burgesses had been slaveholders. Your verb must agree.

D

p. 896–28

"Between the sales manager and me existed an easy, cooperative working relationship . . ." The word "between" is a preposition, and any pronoun that follows it must be an object pronoun. (You hear <u>a lot</u> of people say this incorrectly.) Another hint: say the sentence with just "me," and then say it with just "I" as the only subject. You will hear which pronoun to use. Would you say there existed an easy, cooperative working relationship with me? Or there existed an easy, cooperative working relationship with I?

A

Henry Davis, Explanations for the Official SAT Study Guide **Questions***: Detailed Explanations for the Answers for Every* **Question**

We shall be **questioning** concerning *technology,* and in so doing we should like to prepare a free relationship to it. The relationship will be free if it opens our human existence to the essence of technology. When we can respond to this essence, we shall be able to experience the technological within its own bounds.

Technology is not equivalent to the essence of technology. When we are seeking the essence of "tree," we have to become aware that That which pervades every tree, as tree, is not itself a tree that can be encountered among all the other trees.

Martin Heidegger, The **Question** *Concerning Technology*

p. 405–22

The answer to this **question** is found in 168 when he states that a forest is a powerful metaphor. A metaphor is a comparison.

C

p. 487–5

This **question** is purely vocabulary. We have to know the word talking about a rural setting so we are talking about a pastoral or bucolic setting. Something that is *bucolic* is rural, pastoral, or rustic. Someone is *prolific* if they are productive and creative. Something that is *lugubrious* is sad, gloomy, or depressing. *Sundry* indicates various or miscellaneous things. And something that is *metaphorical* will be figurative or symbolic.

A

p. 405–18

The previous paragraph explains the author's attitude toward downtown ecosystems. He believes there isn't anything unnatural about downtown areas (line 39); therefore, he appreciates the dams and anthills.

E

Henry Davis, Explanations for the Official SAT Study Guide **Questions***: Detailed Explanations for the Answers for Every* **Question**

Likewise, the essence of technology is by no means anything technological. Thus we shall never experience our relationship to the essence of technology so long as we merely conceive and push forward the technological, put up with it, or evade it. Everywhere we remain unfree and chained to technology, whether we passionately affirm or deny it. But we are delivered over to it in the worst possible way when we regard it as something neutral; for this conception of it, to which today we particularly like to do homage, makes us utterly blind to the essence of technology.

Martin Heidegger, The **Question** *Concerning Technology*

When we consider the bitterness that had been engendered in America over this **question** of types, this is a remarkable achievement. May I be pardoned if I again remind this audience how difficult is our task: for we must harmonize the ardent advocates of two systems quite distinct from each other and not the advocates of certain combinations within the same system.

> O. B. Burritt, *Work of the Uniform Type Committee: From the American Point of View (Outlook for the Blind: A Quarterly Record of Their Progress & Welfare, Volume 8)*

p. 405–17

Comparing cities to beaver dams and anthills is showing that all three are similar in that they are natural; they all alter their environments and build shelters which are natural impulses.

B

p. 922–14

The quotation marks used in line 22 of Passage 1 and lines 59–60 of Passage 2 both serve to express skepticism about the aptness of particular terms. Line 22 uses the word "frees" in quotations, while lines 59–60 use the words "stealing" and "property" in quotations. Since the author of passage 1 is against "free" downloads and since the author of passage 2 argues that thought and ideas can not be owned and therefore can not be stolen. Both authors clearly use words that reflect their skepticism about the opposing views.

D

p. 848–3

Here you can simply work with the answer choices to see which one works. The quickest way is to pick an odd number (3) and substitute it in the formulas. $3 + 2 = 5$

$2(3) - 1 = 5$
$3(3) - 2 = 7$
$3(3) + 2 = 11$
$5(3) + 1 = 16$

You could also look over the answer choices and see that 5 times an odd number would yield an odd number and, if you add 1 to that, you would get an even number.

E

p. 670–13

This problem involves the property of numbers—specifically the properties of even and odd numbers. First x and y can both be even or odd, so your focus must turn to x and z. Their sum must be odd, so they *must* be opposites.

C

p. 395–22

Passage 1 states ". . . he built the illusion of three-dimensional features" and passage 2 reinforces this by stating "it . . . creates a sense of texture and depth" which means you must read farther than the line mentioned in **question** to find the answers about having three dimensions.

E

p. 639–6

Y is the midpoint of XZ, so XY = YZ = ½XZ. Note: They are using unusual variables to try to confuse you.

Now evaluate the answer choices:

I. YZ = ½XZ This would be true. We established that with the set up.

II. ½XZ = 2XY Not true. In our setup we found that ½XZ = XY, not 2XY

III. 2XY = XZ This is true. ½XZ = XY, so 2XY = XZ.

E

p. 405–19

The authors claim is that downtown illustrates the city can be thought of as a natural system on three levels (line 57–59). The three levels discussed support his claim.

A

Henry Davis, Explanations for the Official SAT Study Guide **Questions**: *Detailed Explanations for the Answers for Every* **Question**

In presenting the "formal structure" (§2) of the **question** of Being, Heidegger claims to rely on the structure that is common to all **questions** and that includes three constitutive moments. Here he takes up some trains of thought that he had presented in his teaching. In a course in 1923–24 he had even distinguished no less than a dozen structural moments of every **question**!

Jean Grondin, Why Reawaken the **Question** *of Being? (Heidegger's Being and Time: Critical Essays)*

p. 530–16

This problem looks hard, but read it carefully and look at the sequence. There is 1 "1." There are 2 "2s," 3 "3s," and so forth.

So 1 + 2 + 3 + 4 + 5 + 6 + 7 + 8 + 8 + 9 + 10 + 11 come up and then 12 appears

1 + 2 + 3 + 4 + 5 + 6 + 7 + 8 + 8 + 9 + 10 + 11 = 66 terms and 12 would then be the 67th term

67

Henry Davis, Explanations for the Official SAT Study Guide **Questions**: *Detailed Explanations for the Answers for Every* **Question**

There were over a hundred files in there. Some would be computer applications, but most were documents created by Derek Renshaw. She'd already looked at a few: correspondence, school essays. Nothing about the car crash in which his friend had died. Looked like he'd been trying to set up some sort of jazz fanzine. There were pages of layout, photos scanned in, some of them lifted from the 'Net. Plenty of enthusiasm, but no real talent for writing. *Miles was an innovator, no* **question**, *but later on he acted more as a scout, finding the best new talent around and embracing it, hoping something would rub off on himself* . . . Siobhan just hoped Miles had wiped himself clean afterwards. She sat in front of the laptop and stared at it, trying to concentrate. The word CODY was bouncing around her head. Maybe it was a clue . . . leading to someone with that surname. She didn't think she knew anyone named Cody. For a moment she had a jarring thought: Fairstone was still alive, and the charred corpse belonged to someone called Cody. She shook the notion aside, took a deep breath, got back to work.

And hit an immediate brick wall.

Ian Rankin, A **Question** *of Blood*

p. 551–16

The word "convey" means to transport or transfer so she's trying to explain or show

how the unexpected pleasure she got from the book has a strong impact. We get the idea that this is a pleasure in the following paragraph that starts in line 70 because she indicates that she read little else. She read and read and read. She wasn't illustrating the suddenness of her decision, and there is no reference to a child's misconceptions although the she did not expect the book to be so good. She certainly wasn't being critical or describing a sense of history.

    A

p. 955–5

The error is a dangling modifier. Who is driving down the road—the house? The sentence needs a noun for the modifier. The family needs to be modified as they are driving.

    E

p. 551–8

In these lines the author is saying that the building was easy to miss which indicates it was something rather plain or less than grand. With that she contrasts what it was like inside so here we are looking at the difference between the external and internal way something is perceived. Answers A, B, C, and E are not tempting. Answer choice D, with the public and private reference you can readily make those inferences. So we're very comfortable with D as the answer. **Objective** means unbiased or impartial and **subjective** means the exact opposite, very involved emotionally.

    C

Henry Davis, Explanations for the Official SAT Study Guide **Questions**: *Detailed Explanations for the Answers for Every* **Question**

She looked at me with **questions** in her eyes. I shrugged. The car stopped, right in front of the house. Terror twisted her face. There were steps and the bell rang. Carmen stared back at me over her shoulder, her hand clutching the door knob, almost drooling with fear. The bell kept on ringing. Then the ringing stopped. A key tickled at the door and Carmen jumped away from it and stood frozen. The door swung open. A man stepped through it briskly and stopped dead, staring at us quietly, with complete composure.

Raymond Chandler, The Big Sleep

p. 471–13

The sentence is about a "dead" "19th century" author and; therefore, she wrote novels in the past. The section "she writes" is present tense and an incorrect term.

    D

p. 471–14

Tense is the deciding factor in the sentence. The word "saw" is past tense in the sentence and can't be changed. We must have any of the words relating to him in the past tense "believed."

    C

p. 922–12

The answer that BEST summarizes the fear of the author of passage 1 is D which says that songwriters would no be able to earn a living by writing songs.

    D

p. 727–22

To say that the "planet was suffering grave and perhaps irreparable damage" falls into the same category as the reports that "the oceans would be dead by now and the US would be wracked by food riots," etc. Since the author makes little of the predictions of dead oceans and food riots, he likely would find claims of "irreparable damage" dubious (*doubtful*) and overrated as well.

E

p. 474–35

First Austin is dead, so the answer cannot refer to her in the present tense. Shakespeare has just been mentioned as an example so logically, "Austin, too" is a logical progression and keeps the right tense.

B

p. 728–23

Essentially, the author of Passage 2 thinks that we should boast about and broadcast our successes in protecting the environment. The author of Passage 1, however, contends that fear ("dire warnings") is what motivates ("stimulus to action") us more than broadcasting good news.

A

Henry Davis, Explanations for the Official SAT Study Guide **Questions**: *Detailed Explanations for the Answers for Every* **Question**

"How high will the video quality be?" I asked.

"HD," said Ms. Washburn.

"Excellent." We spent a few minutes determining the best angle for the photography, and Ms. Washburn suggested my standing near the front window. She explained that although she could digitally isolate my image from the background, the lighting near the window would be most natural, and would not make the image we created look disturbingly different from the rest of the frame.

She took video of five different swings. I was careful to use an uppercut stroke, to simulate a batter trying to hit the ball high and far. On the fifth try, we agreed we had usable video.

We uploaded the video to my Mac Pro, but just as we were about to examine it, the front door opened, the bell rang, and a man of about fifty entered the office. I couldn't read his initial expression—his nostrils flared and his upper lip receded—but I took it to be something other than a positive one.

"This isn't **Questions** Answered," he said, seemingly to himself. Again, it took me a moment to respond, since this obviously *was* **Questions** Answered, and the man was wrong. But in the interim, Ms. Washburn stepped in front of me and said, "It certainly is. Were you *looking* for **Questions** Answered?"

That seemed equally odd, since the man had walked into a building he assumed was not my business. Why do that? But after wrinkling his brow, he nodded. "Yes. I have a problem that needs to be solved."

"We don't solve problems," I said, having had this conversation with a number of people on a number of occasions. "We answer **questions**." Mother had suggested I say *we*, rather than *I*. She said it would be more businesslike if I gave the impression of having a staff of experts on hand. I thought that was dishonest, but I acceded to her judgment, as I often do.

E. J. Copperman and Jeff Cohen, The **Question** of the Missing Head

p. 791–4

The scientists would have *denounced* (condemned) the newspaper for reporting the predictions (prophesies) of a psychic while *neglecting* (ignoring) real scientific reports. *Celebrated* means honored or observed; *failing* means neglecting. *Promoted* means endorsed or sponsored; *refusing* means to turn down. *Spurned* means scorned or looked down upon; *hastening* means to speed up or hurrying. *Honored* means celebrated or held in esteem; *opting* means choosing or selecting.

C

p. 961–10

Camila "is supposed to shed a different light on" her mother, suggesting that she can share personal insights about her mother. Other scholars can talk about Camila's mother's poetry and pedagogy (*teaching*), but Camila, being the author's daughter, has a unique viewpoint that the scholars don't.

D

p. 959–35

Sentence 10 is totally irrelevant to the passage. It's a descriptive detail unrelated to the sentences before and after.

D

p. 659–21

The system uses remote *cameras* to catch speeding motorists, not "in the catching of" speeding motorists. Be succinct.

B

p.909–3

The residents lived in such a way that they did not indulge in wild behavior, so they lived quiet and conservative lives. The first blank requires a word that would describe the kind of lives they lived, and the second blank uses a word that describes the kind of behavior the residents would NOT indulge in (wild). Rambunctious means uncontrolled or unruly (A), and extravagant means excessive and wasteful (B), so these would also not be good choices for the first blank. We need a word that would describe a lifestyle that is the opposite of wild. Secluded means quiet or private (C), this could fit the first blank, but scrupulous means careful and conscientious which will not work for the second blank because we are looking for a word that is similar in meaning to wild. Circumscribed means restricted or confined (D) and impulsive means reckless and hasty, which would fit wild, and circumscribed would fit the need for a lifestyle that is the opposite of wild. Irreverent means rude or disrespectful (E) which would not fit the meaning of the kind of life the residents lived.

D

p. 406–23

He discussed that there is a limit to the growth of a forest defined by the laws of nature just as there is a limit to how city can be built. Laws of nature or natural principles affect both.

E

p. 611–10

While this involves some math, it is really more of a logic problem. The key word is <u>both</u>. She is both the 12th tallest and the 12th shortest so she has 11 people shorter than her and 11 people taller than her. That's 22 people, plus her, so 23 people.

B

p. 520–1

In this sentence, according to context meaning, both are positive words. Eliminate any answer with negative word choices in either column. D. and E can thus be eliminated. Of the remaining choices filling the second blank is easiest. Choose the word that fits best with "creative." "Inspiration" fits there and extensive travel would lead to him being "worldly." If someone is **cosmopolitan** they are sophisticated. **Stunted** means underdeveloped or small.

B

p. 728–24

The author of Passage 2 believes that environmental trends are positive, so choice (A) can be eliminated. He also gives example of politicians (Al Gore) who have tried to directly the environmental movement, so (B) can also be eliminated. Neither passage talks about the technical nature of the information (C), nor does either discuss whether the spokespeople are sufficiently knowledgeable (D). Both do, however, agree that the rhetoric is exaggerated to match the specific agendas.

E

*Henry Davis, Explanations for the Official SAT Study Guide **Questions**: Detailed Explanations for the Answers for Every **Question***

I didn't say anything about that sentence containing a redundancy and concentrated my attention on the **question** at hand. How could I determine if Ms. Masters-Powell's head had been stolen, misplaced, or destroyed?

The answer would no doubt lie in the records kept and the security procedures. If there were, for example, a constant video surveillance system, it would have recorded the space into which the remains were deposited at the time of arrival, and then, assuming the system was being properly operated and supervised, each minute until the time the disappearance was discovered. The **question** would then be a relatively simple one of access, motive, and ability to tamper with the security system.

"Who has access to the security equipment?" I asked as the elevator doors opened at the B level, which I assumed stood for *basement*. The other three levels were marked with numbers, and the top level from which we'd come was designated G for *ground*.

Ackerman looked as if I'd struck him in the back. He swiveled quickly and said, "Please keep your voice down, Mr. Hoenig. I don't want the staff to know about the . . . incident just yet."

*E. J. Copperman and Jeff Cohen, The **Question** of the Missing Head*

p. 791–1

Eduardo would be *embarrassed* to discover that what he had written was *marred* by typographical errors. *Dismayed* means shocked or afraid; *authenticated* means confirmed to be genuine. *Overjoyed* means to be filled with joy; *exacerbated* means to make more severe. *Intrigued* means to arouse curiosity or interest; *enveloped* means to enclose or cover completely; *enhanced* means to add to or contribute to; *marred* means spoiled or blemished..

E

*Henry Davis, Explanations for the Official SAT Study Guide **Questions**: Detailed Explanations for the Answers for Every **Question***

"Would they hear us if we were just speaking normally?" Ms. Washburn asked. I was impressed, as that was the next **question** I would have asked, although I already knew the answer. I wanted to see how Ackerman would respond.

"Yes, there is audio surveillance in most areas, as well as constant video monitoring," he answered, pointing to video cameras mounted on the walls near the ceiling, to cover every angle. Each camera also had a directional microphone attached above the lens.

He saw Ms. Washburn reaching for her cell phone and said, "Don't bother. You won't be able to get a signal down here. Cell phones will only work internally here; you'd be able to get a call from someone else on the grounds."

"I need to call my husband," she said.

Ackerman nodded. "There are land lines downstairs; you can use those."

"I presume the hard drives storing the video records have been checked, and that no tampering has been found," I said, returning to the subject at hand.

"That's right," Ackerman noted. "I can't imagine how it . . . *she* was smuggled out of here."

"Perhaps someone outside the institute needs to examine the system," I suggested. "If the thief is someone who works here, he or she could easily be covering up any tampering that was done."

*E. J. Copperman and Jeff Cohen, The **Question** of the Missing Head*

p. 958–33

Sentence 7 concludes with the idea that elevators could now be used for people, not just freight. Sentence 8 begins a new paragraph, but the paragraph lacks an introductory sentence. It needs a broad sentence that introduces the consequences of Otis' contribution.

B

*Henry Davis, Explanations for the Official SAT Study Guide **Questions**: Detailed Explanations for the Answers for Every **Question***

Recently I traveled to Los Angeles, where I met with some of the people who have been subject to surveillance in the city. Photographers are frequent targets, particularly those who are spotted taking pictures of public infrastructure (such as bridges) or industrial sites (such as refineries) that are considered potential terrorist targets. I met with one such photographer, Shawn Nee, at a restaurant in central Hollywood, a neighborhood where he often works documenting street life. After more than a dozen run-ins with police, Nee purchased a small camera that he clipped inconspicuously to his messenger bag. The camera was running in 2009 when he paused at a subway turnstile on his way home and snapped several photographs. While taking the pictures Nee was detained by two deputies from the Los Angeles Sheriffs Department. They told him—incorrectly—that the transit authority prohibited photographs, and tried to **question** him. When Nee protested, one of the deputies grew irate.

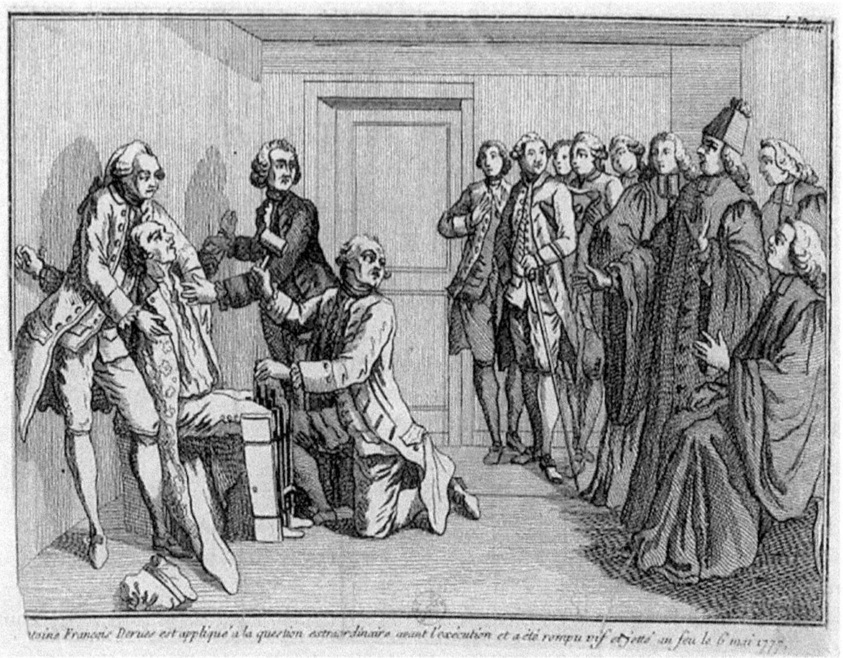

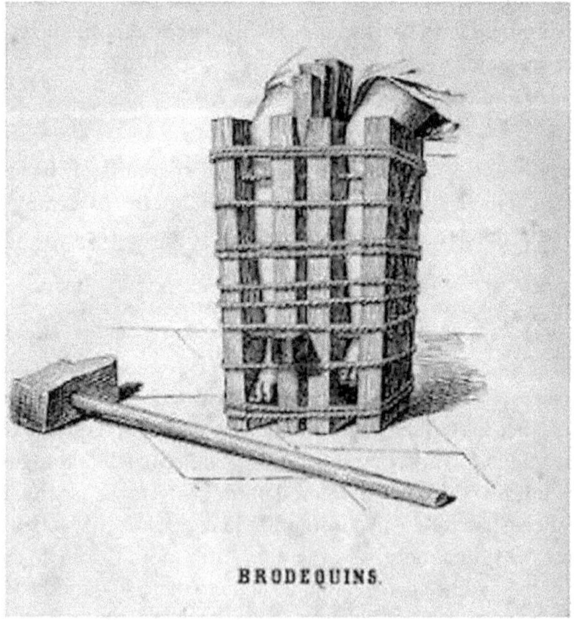

For the torture aux brodequins, the prisoner was made to sit and his hands were tied. Each of his legs was placed between two planks of wood, fastened at the the knees and ankles. In addition the four planks were bound together. Wooden wedges were then hammered between the two planks, which touched the legs at the knees and ankles. The **question** ordinaire uses four wedges, the extraordinary four more. The prisoner was **questioned** after each wedge was inserted.

Rodama: A Blog of 18th Century & Revolutionary France (rodama1789.blogspot.com)

"I want to know who you are and why you're taking pictures of the subway system," the deputy said. "Al Qaeda would love to buy your pictures, so I want to know if you are in cahoots with Al Qaeda to sell these pictures to them for terrorist purposes." He pushed Nee against a wall and searched his pockets while continuing to ask **questions**. When Nee invoked his right to remain silent, the deputy said, "You know, I'll just submit your name to a T.L.O. [terrorism liaison officer]. Every time your driver's license gets scanned, every time you take a plane, any time you go on any type of public transit where they look at your identification, you're going to be stopped. You will be detained. You'll be searched. You will be on the FBI's hit list. Is that what you want?"

Under Bratton's watch, Los Angeles became the first city to implement the Nationwide Suspicious Activity Reporting Initiative, a federal-local partnership program led by Homeland Security and the FBI. Suspicious Activity Reports, or SARs, have since been adopted by cities across the country and are now the primary means for documenting citizen behavior that might be construed as "preoperational planning related to terrorism or other criminal activity." This vague standard means that behavior that is both protected by the First Amendment and entirely benign can be labeled as suspicious. The LAPD's website advises immediately reporting individuals who "stay at bus or train stops for extended periods," "order food at a restaurant . . . without eating," or "don't fit into the surrounding environment because they are wearing improper attire for the location or season." To supplement the surveillance being carried out by the city's law-enforcement officers, Bratton added a new initiative, the citywide iWATCH program, which encourages residents to report the suspicious behaviors of their neighbors.

Petra Bartosiewicz, Beyond the Broken Window (Harper's Magazine)

p. 552–18

The word "captivating" means you are captured, enthralled, or quite taken with something, and that's clearly what the author is as she read and read and read. She didn't find it bewildering or strange, unremarkable or uninteresting, hilarious or very funny, and not actually profound which means deeply meaningful. The writing may have been profound but the author's description is talking about how much she was taken with the book.

E

p. 959–34

The sentence is a run-on, so (A) couldn't be right. You need a word that makes it clear that rooms on the lower floors were considered premium because guests didn't like to climb stairs all the time. It's a cause-and-effect relationship, and (E) is the only one that expresses that meaning.

E

*Henry Davis, Explanations for the Official SAT Study Guide **Questions**: Detailed Explanations for the Answers for Every **Question***

The said Oliver informed me the same evening why I was kept in such close custody, and the regimental sheriff received orders at once to examine me, that my deposition might the sooner be laid before the Judge-Advocate-General, for they counted me not only for a spy, but also for one that could use witchcraft; for shortly after I left my colonel certain witches were burnt who confessed before their death that they had seen me at their General Assembly, when they met together to dry up the Elbe, that Magdeburg might be taken the sooner. So the points on which I was to give an answer were these. (1) Whether I had not been a student, or at least could read and write? (2) Why I had come to the camp at Magdeburg disguised as a fool, whereas in the captain's service I had been as sane as I was now? (3) Why I had disguised myself in women's apparel? (4) Whether I had not been at the witches' dance with other sorcerers? (5) Where I was born and who my parents were? (6) Where I had sojourned before I came to the camp before Magdeburg? and (7) Where and to what end I had learned women's work such as washing, baking, cooking, and also lute-playing? Thereupon I would have told my whole story, that the circumstances of my strange adventures might explain all; but the judge was not curious, only weary and peevish after his long march: so he desired only a round answer to each **question**; and that I answered in the following words, out of which no one could yet learn aught that was exact or precise—as thus: (1) I had not been a student, but could read and write German. (2) I had been forced to wear a fool's coat because I had no other. (3) Because I was weary of the fool's coat and could come at no men's clothes. (4) I answered yes; but had gone against my will and knew naught of witchcraft. (5) I was born in the Spessart and my parents were peasants. (6) With the Governor of Hanau and with a colonel of Croats, Corpes by name. (7) Among the Croats I had been forced against my will to learn cooking and the like: but lute-playing at Hanau because I had a liking thereto. So when my deposition was written out, "How canst thou deny," says he, "and say thou hast not studied, seeing that when thou didst pass for a fool, and the priest in the mass said 'Domine non sum dignus,' thou didst answer in Latin that he need not say that, for all knew it."

"Sir," said I, "others taught me that and persuaded me 'twas a prayer that one must use at mass, when our chaplain was saying it."

"Yes, yes," said he, "I see thou art the very kind of fellow whose tongue must be loosed by the torture." Whereat I thought, "God help thee if thy tongue follow thy foolish head!"

Early next morning came orders from the Judge-Advocate-General to our provost that he should keep me well in charge; for he was minded as soon as the armies halted to examine me himself: in which case I must without doubt to the torture, had not God ordered it otherwise. In my bonds I thought ever of my pastor at Hanau and old Herzbruder that was dead, how both had foretold how it would fare with me if I were rid of my fool's coat again.

Hans Jacob Christoph von Grimmelshausen, The Adventurous Simplicius Simplicissimus; Being the Description of the Life of a Strange Vagabond Named Melchior Sternfels von Fuchshaim

p. 487–6

This answer depends on the choice of two negative words signaled by the context clues "even foolish" and "accuse — — outright — — — by applying skewed data." The only answer choice with two negative words is E with "wrongheaded" meaning mistaken and misguided thinking and "chicanery" meaning using tricks or lies. A *remonstrance* is a formal protest or argument. *Erudition* is sophisticated scholarship. Something is *plausible* if it's possible or reasonable. *Lassitude* is a weariness or lethargy. A *fabrication* is something that is made up. Someone is *wrongheaded* if they are foolish or unwise. And *chicanery* is trickery or deceit.

    E

p. 415–8

If you clearly see the trick here, you can work the problem out quickly. 28,000/2,800,000 = .01 or 1%. So the difference in votes is 1%, which means that Candidate I got the half of Candidate II's 1%. Candidate I's extra 1/2% (.005) means Candidate II got 1/2% (.005) less. So Candidate I got 50.5% of the vote.

If you would be more comfortable working the problem out:

We subtract the 28,000 votes out to see what the two candidates shared.

2,800,000 – 28,000 = 2,772,000 dividing by 2 tells how much each shared.

2,772,000/2 = 1,386,000 each so we add the 28,000 extra that Candidate I got:

1,386,000 + 28,000 = 1,414,000 and to find the percentage:

1,414,000/2,800,000 = .505 or 50.5%

C

*Henry Davis, Explanations for the Official SAT Study Guide **Questions**: Detailed Explanations for the Answers for Every **Question***

Question. You are a pretty smart nigger, are you not?

Answer. I don't know about that.

Question. You think you are?

Answer. I don't think I am much smart.

Question. How long did you stay there?

Answer. I staid there until the crowd commenced breaking right smart.

Question. You left before all the crowd left then?

Answer. Some two or three were there after I left.

Question. You say you left when the crowd began to break up?

Answer. I said I left about the time the crowd broke up.

Question. Before you left Chaffin put this paper up, for you saw him put it up?

Answer. I didn't see him stick the paper up to the tree.

Question. You did not?

Answer. No, sir; but I recollect this much, that I saw him writing this paper.

Question. Who brought you here to swear?

Answer. I came for the party that called me.

Question. You say now you did not see him stick it up?

Answer. I saw him write the paper.

Question. Is that all you saw?

Answer. I saw him write the paper, and a gentleman said that he was standing right beside him when he wrote the paper and saw him write the paper.

Question. Do you say now that you did not see Chaffin stick this paper on the tree?

Answer. I told you that Mr. Chaffin wrote it.

Question. But you said that after he wrote it he stuck it on the tree.

Answer. If he wrote it, I was satisfied he stuck it there, as long as he wrote it himself, you know.

Question. How do you know, if you did not see him stick it up, but merely saw him write something on a paper, that he stuck that particular paper up?

Answer. What makes me say it is he wrote it. I showed this paper to a gentleman after I got it.

Question. Two weeks afterward?

Answer. Yes, sir; and he sanctified that he knew it, and he sanctified he knew who did it, but would not tell.

Question. That was Whitely?

Answer. Yes, sir.

Question. That makes you know that Chaffin stuck this up?

Answer. Yes, sir; I know he did.

Question. Have you not sworn half a dozen times to-day that he stuck it up?

Answer. He must have stuck it up, if he wrote it. If I wrote a thing and didn't stick it up it would be my fault.

Question. Have you not said half a dozen times that you saw him write this paper and stick it up on that tree?

Answer. Yes, sir.

Question. Did you see him stick it up there?

Answer. Now I am going to tell you. He goes to the tree. He had done the writing. He goes to the tree, and then in the evening the writing was proved to be on the tree.

Question. Then you did not see him stick it on the tree?

Answer. I saw him have the paper in his hand, going to the tree. That is the way I went. I took the paper a few days after that—about nearly two weeks.

Question. Do you know how many times I can make you tell that you saw him stick this paper up before I get through with you?

Answer. It was the very day he wrote the paper.

Question. Can you guess how many times I can get you to say that you saw him write this paper and stick it up on that tree, right in the face of the congregation, in broad daylight? Do you know how many times you will say it before you get through?

Answer. I have said it often enough.

Mr. VAN TRUMP. I think you have.

United States House of Representatives, Reports of Committees for the Second Session of the Forty-Second Congress, 1871–72

p. 962–13

The engineer, the psychologist, and the physicist respond differently to the situation at the dairy farm because their specific training causes them to approach problems differently (B). While each profession probably did have different <u>mathematical</u> training, that wouldn't account for their responses (A); psychologists don't study cows differently than engineers or physicists (C) because psychologists don't study cows to begin with; the engineer's solution isn't necessarily correct, and it isn't the point of the story anyway (D); and, there's no basis to support the idea that the physicist is the only professional who can successfully eliminate details irrelevant to the problem (E).

B

*Henry Davis, Explanations for the Official SAT Study Guide **Questions**: Detailed Explanations for the Answers for Every **Question***

"And what's in that fat brain of yours, now? You only look at me like that when you want to make some comment.

"My fat brain has its advantages. Well-padded. It tells me that the people as well as worshipping you—frighten you." She sliced the bread viciously.

Julian wiped some blond hair back from his brow as though it clouded his brain. "They *believe* me," he said after a time, his face twisting into a **question** mark. "Give me the end of the loaf, Anya . . . with lots of crust . . ."

"And you **question** their belief? This is proof of the excellence of your craft, my boy! It's like my bread. Here," she said, handing him a slice.

"It is not that simple. Bread is not magic."

"Magic is your bread, nevertheless, Julian. Keep to the essentials, I tell you. Your art is sharpened as fine as this blade . . ."

He tried to eat away her voice with the bread. A good woman—but altogether too basic, too solid, unwilling to see any of the marginal horrors of his profession. She congratulated him on the success he had attained. He did not want congratulations. He came to her to be able to sit and be sane for a while, and be in a silent sane place with the hysterical audience far away, brewing around his caravan like drunken ants; muted.

"And the world's only blond magician!" she went on, inspired by her bread.

Gwendolyn MacEwen, Julian the Magician

p. 493–6

The modifying subordinate clause refers to the artist and must be followed by the artist's name, not "art." In this **question**, D corrects the error and is an attractive choice, but remember the best sentences are brief and direct. That means that E is the correct answer as it provides the best rendition of the sentence.

E

Henry Davis, Explanations for the Official SAT Study Guide **Questions**: *Detailed Explanations for the Answers for Every* **Question**

All that was left to me, therefore, as I rose and softly followed him again, was to select in advance one of the blows we had been taught to master in our silent-killing classes. Should I count on attacking him from behind—with a rabbit punch?—with a double simultaneous blow over the ears? Either method could kill him instantly, whereas a live man can still be **questioned**. Then would I do better breaking his right arm first, hoping to take him with his own weapon? Yet if I let him draw, might I myself not go down in a hail of bullets from the several bodyguards around the room?

John le Carré, The Secret Pilgrim

p. 671–15

This looks very difficult, yet, as with many SAT problems, it unravels when you look at it carefully. The time it takes to run the maze (t) is represented on the vertical line. The number of practices (p) is represented on the horizontal line. Look at the relationship. Although it is counter-intuitive, this graph shows that the number of practices does not change the time very much. The time stays near 44 throughout. So, t(p) = 44

A

p. 390–4

In this sentence you are matching the blanks with opposites of the keywords "visceral" and "rational" as cued by the phrases "rather than" and "not so much" therefore the answer is D "deliberate" which is opposite of emotional or gut feeling (visceral) and "instinctive" which is opposite of logical or reasoned out. If someone is intuitive they do something instinctively. Someone who is impulsive does things spontaneously.

D

p. 922–11

The author of Passage 1 presents an argument in lines 24–26 that can most accurately be called pragmatic, because pragmatic means to be practical. Historical means to be based on history or the past; political means involving government or politics; idealistic means based in imagination as opposed to reality; and facetious means based in humor or wit. The author **questions** in lines 24–26 where he would be if anyone could have recorded *Hound Dog* without paying Jerry Lieber and him. This is a practical and realistic argument to why this author does not think music should be free or downloaded off the internet.

C

*Henry Davis, Explanations for the Official SAT Study Guide **Questions**: Detailed Explanations for the Answers for Every **Question***

Miserable Heathen!

I want to ask you one **question**, Why do you want to have Professor Webster hang, I can think of nothing else than this that you want only to gratify your thirst for Blood. If Professor Webster hang you will meet with a terrible death, one that you little dream of. You have had one man hung and I should think that was enough for one month. Can you see those poor daughters and wife of Professor Webster pleading for him without taking pity on him. From Maine to Louisiana there has been petitions you have turned a deaf ear, there is a band forming in the city under my command who on the 25th of this month (if Professor Webster is hung) will burn your dwelling to the ground and put an end to your damnable life; you are the most hard-hearted man I ever heard of. You are a God damned miserable lying, thieving villainous rascal—a nice man for a Governor.

Simon Schama, Dead Certainties (Unwarranted Speculations)

p. 487–3

Vocabulary knowledge is also helpful in this sentence, but also it contains a definition of the answer following the blank. The word "stringent" means very strict or rigorous. Something that is *dispersed* is spreading or causes dispersion. Something is *conditional* if it is provisional, restricted, or qualified. Something is *recessive* if it is receding or withdrawing. And something that is *obtrusive* is interfering or intruding.

A

p. 923–17

The attitude of the author of Passage 2 toward the "marketing virus" is largely positive, because it helped make the grateful Dead more popular. This can be supported by lines 57–66.

A

p. 425–2

Considering the context of the sentence and phrases such as resurgence of popularity, both blanks are positive words. Delete any choices that are negative words like you find in answer choices A, B, D., and E. Choose the most positive word from the second position which would be **rousing** which means something that is inspiring or exciting. If something is **sparse** it's spare or bare or meager. Something that is **negligible** is insignificant or small.

C

p. 489–8

Substitute the answer choices for the word **"question"** to see which makes the best sense. In this case you can rule out some of the common meanings of the word "**question**" (they don't want anyone to get the right answer without reading the passage). In this case the reference is about a "**question** of learning" which would be about the matter of learning.

A

p. 489–9

The passage directly states that "a great deal of learning comes in the form of entertainment" (line 13). This gives us the context of proof for entertainment and learning being related.

C

Henry Davis, Explanations for the Official SAT Study Guide **Questions**: *Detailed Explanations for the Answers for Every* **Question**

It was a capacity crowd. Jerry and Rita Henderson sat up front. Bill and Barbara Nixon lounged at a neighboring table. I noticed Abraham de Leon picking crumbs from his beard. Tom Thompson chugged cups of coffee. And there was Jim Kunkel himself, looking patriarchal and well tanned but also a bit feeble in yellow pants and golf shirt and shiny white shoes. At that time the old ex-mayor had only a few days to live, but who could know this? Everybody seemed slightly stunned from the volumes of delicately poached blowfish they'd tucked away. It was a tough house. I sipped from my water glass, cleared my throat, leaned close to the microphone and said, "So you see, these dread ministers, the Inquisitors, inflicted every extreme of ruthlessness on reputed heretics, many mere petty criminals or political agitators, not religious activists at all. Ruthlessness on behalf of orthodoxy. It's the old story. What's interesting in the case of the Inquisition, and it is a phenomenon that has been demonstrated time and again, in diverse theaters, even right up into the modern era, is the ready accessibility of holy text as a tool of repression."

Meredith at the back of the big banquet room smiled encouragement. I went to the portable blackboard behind the podium, picked up a piece of chalk, and began sketching diagrams. "Okay, the rack, an unpretentious stretching device, mechanically rudimentary, employed in the regular daily work of coercion and castigation. The rack's primary social impact was arguably psychological as well as physical. As long as the authorities had recourse to such an instrument, with liberty to use it at their discretion, which is to say at the slightest provocation, the lay community, understandably, inhabited a condition of low-grade panic." I raised the chalk to fill in picturesque details: "crank," "berth," "leather thongs," and so on. People shifted in their chairs, leaned forward to get a better view. Jerry Henderson was engrossed, peering at the board. Bill Nixon perked right up. It's difficult to overestimate the value, as a teaching aid, of pictures. When I used to give this almost identical though considerably more elementary "Inquisition talk" to my third-graders—always a hard-to-please bunch—they, like these grown-ups assembled at the Holiday Inn for Friday luncheon, became enthralled, absolutely, as though on cue, when I marched to the board and picked up the chalk and made fine white renderings of dungeon environments. Suddenly the old classroom would fall silent. No gum popping, no spitballs sailing, no notes being passed. The kids' eager **questions** reflected a deep concern for history's artifacts.

"Did the torturers leave the people on that thing for a long time?"

"Did you get taller?"

"Could you get torn in half?"

I could sense my adult audience's yearning to raise their own inquiries, as I casually dropped the chalk in the chalk tray and returned to the podium. I watched Rita Henderson brush lint from her purple blouse. Jerry folded and refolded a napkin. Jim Kunkel chewed a toothpick. I let all these people contemplate the past. "In those days you were guilty until proven innocent." I took another sip of water. Heads wagged, a fork scraped a plate, ice rattled.

"**Questions**, anyone?"

Donald Antrim, Elect Mr. Robinson for a Better World

Such torture is called the **question** because as the accused is made to suffer, he is asked **questions** about his crime and his accomplices, if it is suspected that there are some.

*Antoine-Gaspard Boucher d'Argis, **Question** or Torture (The Encyclopedia of Diderot & d'Alembert Collaborative Translation Project)*

11. Do you like to take a lot of photos?
12. How long have you had a camera?
13. Did your parents take many photos of you when you were a child?
14. Have you ever been to a photographer's studio?
15. When did you last take a photograph?
16. Do you have friends who are always taking/have always taken photos?

Answers to **questions** will vary.

Santiago Mayorga, Answer Key—Touchstone 4

p. 460–14

The author indicates "his impression" with phrases such as "seemed to have power over the terrain" and "it was as though streams quit running, hanging silently." Remember that an "anecdote" is a personal story.

C

p. 461–16

The clue is in the context "streams quit running, hanging silently where they were" as in stopping all motion which leads to the definition of "suspended" meaning stopped.

E

*Henry Davis, Explanations for the Official SAT Study Guide **Questions**: Detailed Explanations for the Answers for Every **Question***

He had never seen the instrument that was to terminate his life. How high it was from the ground, how many steps it had, where he would be stood, how he would be touched, whether the touching hands would be dyed red, which way his face would be turned, whether he would be the first, or might be the last: these and many similar **questions**, in nowise directed by his will, obtruded themselves over and over again, countless times. Neither were they connected with fear: he was conscious of no fear. Rather, they originated in a strange besetting desire to know what to do when the time came; a desire gigantically disproportionate to the few swift moments to which it referred; a wondering that was more like the wondering of some other spirit within his, than his own.

Charles Dickens, A Tale of Two Cities

The extraordinary **question** by the strappado
Excerpt from Praxis criminalis persequendi by Millaeus (1541)

In order to compel the culprit to pay the price of blood or damage, the public authority intervened: it forced him to give the composition (wehrgeld) to the offended and enjoined him to receive it . . .

Penal Sanctions in the Middle Ages, Ordinary or Extraordinary Question (france-pittoresque.com)

An example: a trove of photographs of black victims of lynching in small towns in the United States between the 1890s and the 1930s, which provided a shattering, revelatory experience for the thousands who saw them in a gallery in New York in 2000. The lynching pictures tell us about human wickedness. About inhumanity. They force us to think about the extent of the evil unleashed specifically by racism. Intrinsic to the perpetration of this evil is the shamelessness of photographing it. The pictures were taken as souvenirs and made, some of them, into postcards; more than a few show grinning spectators, good churchgoing citizens as most of them had to be, posing for a camera with the backdrop of a naked, charred, mutilated body hanging from a tree. The display of these pictures makes us spectators, too.

What is the point of exhibiting these pictures? To awaken indignation? To make us feel "bad"; that is, to appall and sadden? To help us mourn? Is looking at such pictures really necessary, given that these horrors lie in a past remote enough to be beyond punishment? Are we the better for seeing these images? Do they actually teach us anything? Don't they rather just confirm what we already know (or want to know)?

All these **questions** were raised at the time of the exhibition and afterward when a book of the photographs, *Without Sanctuary,* was published. Some people, it was said, might dispute the need for this grisly photographic display, lest it cater to voyeuristic appetites and perpetuate images of black victimization—or simply numb the mind. Nevertheless, it was argued, there is an obligation to "examine"—the more clinical "examine" is substituted for "look at"—the pictures. It was further argued that submitting to the ordeal should help us understand such atrocities not as the acts of "barbarians" but as the reflection of a belief system, racism, that by defining one people as less human than another legitimates torture and murder. But maybe they were barbarians. Maybe *this* is what most barbarians look like. (They look like everybody else.)

That being said, one person's "barbarian" is another person's "just doing what everybody else is doing." (How many can be expected to do better than that?) The **question** is, Whom do we wish to blame? More precisely, Whom do we believe we have the right to blame? The children of Hiroshima and Nagasaki were no less innocent than the young African-American men (and a few women) who were butchered and hanged from trees in small-town America. More than one hundred thousand civilians, three-fourths of them women, were massacred in the RAF firebombing of Dresden on the night of February 13, 1945; seventy-two thousand civilians were incinerated in seconds by the American bomb dropped on Hiroshima. The roll call could be much longer. Again, Whom do we wish to blame? Which atrocities from the incurable past do we think we are obliged to revisit?

Susan Sontag, Regarding the Pain of Others

p. 955–6

As written, the sentence contains a comma splice after "tree," so that error has to be fixed. Also, "because" can be substituted for "the reason is," making the sentence more succinct. Again, the shortest answer choice is the best one.

D

Henry Davis, Explanations for the Official SAT Study Guide **Questions:** Detailed Explanations for the Answers for Every **Question**

Probably, if we are Americans, we think that it would be morbid to go out of our way to look at pictures of burnt victims of atomic bombing or the napalmed flesh of the civilian victims of the American war on Vietnam, but that we have a duty to look at the lynching pictures—if we belong to the party of the right-thinking, which on this issue is now very large. A stepped-up recognition of the monstrousness of the slave system that once existed, **unquestioned** by most, in the United States is a national project of recent decades that many Euro-Americans feel some tug of obligation to join. This ongoing project is a great achievement, a benchmark of civic virtue. The acknowledgment of the American use of disproportionate firepower in war (in violation of one of the cardinal laws of war) is very much not a national project. A museum devoted to the history of America's wars that included the vicious war the United States fought against guerrillas in the Philippines from 1899 to 1902 (expertly excoriated by Mark Twain), and that fairly presented the arguments for and against using the atomic bomb in 1945 on the Japanese cities, with photographic evidence that showed what those weapons did, would be regarded—now more than ever—as a most unpatriotic endeavor.

Susan Sontag, Regarding the Pain of Others

"So, you know, what's the climate of opinion up in Canada?"

That always seemed to be the unspoken deal. When Riesbeck answered a **question**, he got to ask one himself, even though his answers may not have been satisfactory. But this time he was going first.

"Generally negative, I'd have to say."

"Is this grass roots or quasi-official?"

"Across the board mostly, though the grass-roots part is of course more vocal. The Ottawa types are pretty spineless."

"What about the other party? Don't they make any mileage out of the thing?"

"The opposition is not exactly going to come out in favour of it. Barring always a few crackpots, nobody's in favour of it, you bastard. That's the point. It's a moral issue, not simply some political wand the way it is for you people." There was just the slightest uncomfortable pause between them, which Riesbeck broke.

"Washington," he said. Whether this was a mild expletive or a simple declaration wasn't clear, but it was meant as punctuation of some kind. Of course, Riesbeck pronounced it War*s*hington, with an *r*. Moss was always annoyed that this was the single vulgarism one could find throughout the entire culture, if you could call it a culture: the fact they mispronounced the name of their own capital.

"Do Canadians get upset when they hear Americans calling them Americans, like we have the whole continent to ourselves? I mean, don't you think you're Americans too?"

He was backing off, but typically backing off in such a way as to make a fool of himself. Moss became suddenly weary.

"No, of course not. Canadians think of themselves as Canadians." Maybe the liquor had found its voice; this was not leisurely drinking. "They do it largely to distinguish themselves from Americans."

A pause followed, which Moss took advantage of to shout for more whiskey. An old fan with wooden blades hung down three feet from the tin ceiling. Suspended from the hub of the fan was a scroll of flypaper. Moss hadn't seen flypaper in years. They probably stopped making it about the time this one was put up. The fan blades revolved so slowly they didn't much disturb the paper.

"You going to do the daily briefings, or what?" Riesbeck asked.

"They pick that stuff up from the wire." The reference was to the press conference for correspondents held each day in the JUSPAO building, famous even then as the Five O 'Clock Follies. Each day at that time a Colonel Brown, with at least two other officers, would stand up on the stage and, using audiovisuals and other teaching aids, explain, exhaustively and with military precision, how the number of enemy body counts and other data, when fed into the computer, resulted in proof that the good guys were winning. The casualty figures were, in fact, so open to caprice that they were the basis of a long-established lottery; the one whose guess proved most in line with the official fabrication walked off with the week's kitty.

George Fetherling, *The File on Arthur Moss*

p. 670–11

You have a made-up function, so you have a new rule to follow. Remember to plug in the values you are given and follow the new rule. This one has a twist by adding a requirement that you must be able to see a relationship rather than just a solution. First we set out the rule: $n < k < r$ where $k = -2$ and $r = 0$. So let's reset: $n < -2 < 0$ The only value in the answer choices that works is -3.

A

p. 984–11

Sine lines 42–45 imply that education can be fun, and not just a chore, we can also say that this idea would be most similar to a computer game that teaches geography.

A

p. 984–12

The word "studious" in line 55 serves to emphasize the deliberateness with which Colonial Williamsburg has fabricated. There facts that were fudged on in the restoration of Colonial Williamsburg were done intentionally and with purpose, but they would have had to known the facts in order to be able to make such studious changes.

D

p. 646–10

Keep in mind that although this passage talks about galaxies and planets, it is NOT a scientific passage. The author, although a scientist himself, is fantasizing about time travel. The mention of Australopithecus in line 3 dramatizes how different the Earth was 2 million years ago.

B

p. 827–13

The **question** wants us to explain why the author uses the words "that" and "how" in line 43. The line states: "I can show *that* Fido is alert to the kitty, but not *how* [he is alert to the kitty] . . ." The author can see that the dog is aware of the cat's presence; however, because the dog's awareness is based on a sense of smell that we humans don't have, he can't explain how (the nature of) the dog is aware of the cat's presence.

D

p. 859–8

On this **question**, remember two particular traits of numbers and their exponents. First: fractions less than 1 get smaller as their exponents increase. For example $(½)^2 = ¼$; $(¼)^2 = ¹⁄16$. Second: even exponents make a negative number positive, and odd exponents keep the negative number negative. For example: $(-2)^2 = 4$; $(-2)^3 = -8$. Keeping those facts in mind, you can avoid the pitfalls of this problem. Since you see that x^2 is less than x, you know that x is a fraction less than 1. And since it is less than x, it is a positive fraction. (If it were negative, squaring it would have turned it positive.) You only have one choice.

C

p. 646–11

Lines 6–7 state: "Too bad we couldn't . . . observe earth from . . . Andromeda." This implies that scientists would like to have seen events that happened in the distant past.

A

p. 647–14

We are looking for the one item that the author did **NOT** address when he discussed causality violations in ll. 16–35. The author does not mention the mechanics of space travel. Answer A is addressed (18–21); answer B in (32–35); answer D in (21–22); and answer E in lines 28–32.

C

p. 775–7

The phrase "being popular throughout the nineteenth century" modifies/describes "tragic story," so that's where it needs to be placed in the sentence. Answers (D) and (E) can immediately be eliminated because neither is a grammatically complete sentence, regardless of where the modifying phrase is.

C

Henry Davis, Explanations for the Official SAT Study Guide **Questions**: *Detailed Explanations for the Answers for Every* **Question**

But of what use is it to blame the crowd? A scapegoat is named, a festival is declared, the laws are suspended: who would not flock to see the entertainment? What is it I object to in these spectacles of abasement and suffering and death that our new regime puts on but their lack of decorum? What will my own administration be remembered for besides moving the shambles from the marketplace to the outskirts of the town twenty years ago in the interests of decency? I try to call out something, a word of blind fear, a shriek, but the rope is now so tight that I am strangled, speechless.

The blood hammers in my ears. I feel my toes lose their hold. I am swinging gently in the air, bumping against the ladder, flailing with my feet. The drumbeat in my ears becomes slower and louder till it is all I can hear.

I am standing in front of the old man, screwing up my eyes against the wind, waiting for him to speak. The ancient gun still rests between his horse's ears, but it is not aimed at me. I am aware of the vastness of the sky all around us, and of the desert.

I watch his lips. At any moment now he will speak: I must listen carefully to capture every syllable, so that later, repeating them to myself, poring over them, I can discover the answer to a **question** which for the moment has flown like a bird from my recollection.

J. M. Coetzee, Waiting for the Barbarians

p. 555–13

The error in this sentence is in the use of "like." "Like" is a preposition, not a subordinate conjunction. It's followed only by a noun or a noun phrase. "As" is a subordinate conjunction but its use here makes the sentences indirect. The correct phrasing of answer choice E, which uses the present participle "forcing" is clearer and more direct.

E

p. 461–15

Context is a clue when the author states "the hand — seemed to have power over the terrain." It seems to have Godlike control over the forces of nature; therefore, the answer is "omnipotent" or all-powerful and all-knowing. Someone is **deft** if they are skillful or adroit. If someone is **languid** they are lazy, indolent, or lax. If someone is **resilient** they will bounce back; they are durable or tough.

D

*Henry Davis, Explanations for the Official SAT Study Guide **Questions**: Detailed Explanations for the Answers for Every **Question***

A new correspondent came into the room to say hello, just arrived from New York, and he started asking Dana a lot of **questions** right away, sort of bullshit **questions** about the killing radius of various mortars and the penetration capability of rockets, the ranges of AK's and 16's, what shells did when they hit treetops, paddy and hard ground. He was in his late thirties and he was dressed in one of those jungle-hell leisure suits that the tailors on Tu Do were getting rich cranking out, with enough flaps and slots and cargo pockets to carry supply for a squad. Dana would answer one **question** and the man would ask two more, but that made sense since the man had never been out and Dana hardly ever came in. Oral transmission, those who knew and those who didn't, new people were always coming in with their own basic load of **questions**, energetic and hungry; and someone had done it for you, it was a kind of blessing if you were in a position to answer some **questions**, if only to say that the **questions** couldn't be answered. This man's **questions** were something else, they seemed to be taking on hysteria as they went along.

Michael Herr, Dispatches

p. 592–24

In lines 61–63 the author of the passage states that Bram Stoker takes sweet and innocent creatures (the bats) and turns them into blood sucking monsters. Earlier in the passage the author sates that our fear of bats says more about us than about bats. Therefore answer B is the best-fit answer.

B

p. 545–21

According to the author, their enthusiasm might *seem* like morbid (gruesome) gloating (rejoicing) because the women were benefiting from the war while the men were suffering.

E

p. 961–12

The author says that every time another deformed amphibian is reported "the media *tout* (hypes or supports enthusiastically) the new position, thus providing a misleading view." The author is *critical* toward the media's reporting. (FYI: "ambivalent" means unsure or uncertain.)

E

Henry Davis, *Explanations for the Official SAT Study Guide **Questions**: Detailed Explanations for the Answers for Every **Question***

"Is it exhilarating? Boy, I'll bet it's exhilarating."

"Aw you wouldn't believe it," Dana said.

Tim Page came in. He'd been out at the Y Bridge all day taking pictures of the fighting there and he'd gotten some CS in his eyes. He was rubbing them and weeping and bitching.

"Oh you're English," the new man said. "I was just there. What's CS?"

"It's a gas gas gas," Page said. "Gaaaaaa. Arrrgggh!" and he did a soft version of raking his nails down his face, he used his fingertips but it left red marks anyway. "Blind Lemon Page," Flynn said, and laughed while Page took the record that was playing on the turntable off without asking anybody and put on Jimi Hendrix: long tense organic guitar line that made him shiver like frantic electric ecstasy was shooting up from the carpet through his spine straight to the old pleasure center in his cream-cheese brain, shaking his head so that his hair waved all around him, Have You Ever Been Experienced?

"What does it look like when a man gets hit in the balls?" the new man said, as though that was the **question** he'd really meant to ask all along, and it came as close as you could get to a breach of taste in that room; palpable embarrassment all around, Flynn moved his eyes like he was following a butterfly up out of sight, Page got sniffy and offended, but he was amused, too. Dana just sat there putting out the still rays, taking snaps with his eyes. "Oh, I dunno," he said. "It all just goes sort of gooey."

Michael Herr, *Dispatches*

p. 542–17

The quotation in lines 21 and 22 by the archaeologist West is making a declarative statement. He's not providing evidence, certainly not discrediting, yes he's supporting the claim but it's hardly provocative, and he certainly not offering an opposing viewpoint. He is doing is summarizing.

E

Henry Davis, *Explanations for the Official SAT Study Guide **Questions**: Detailed Explanations for the Answers for Every **Question***

"Quite right," said the supervisor, looking to see how many matches were left in the box. "But on the other hand," K. went on, looking round at everyone there and even wishing he could get the attention of the three who were looking at the photographs, "on the other hand this really can't be all that important. That follows from the fact that I've been indicted, but can't think of the slightest offence for which I could be indicted. But even that is all beside the point, the main **question** is: Who is issuing the indictment? What office is conducting this affair? Are you officials? None of you is wearing a uniform, unless what you are wearing"—here he turned towards Franz—"is meant to be a uniform, it's actually more of a travelling suit. I require a clear answer to all these **questions**, and I'm quite sure that once things have been made clear we can take our leave of each other on the best of terms." The supervisor slammed the box of matches down on the table. "You're making a big mistake," he said. "These gentlemen and I have got nothing to do with your business, in fact we know almost nothing about you. We could be wearing uniforms as proper and exact as you like and your situation wouldn't be any the worse for it. As to whether you're on a charge, I can't give you any sort of clear answer to that, I don't even know whether you are or not. You're under arrest, you're quite right about that, but I don't know any more than that. Maybe these officers have been chit-chatting with you, well if they have that's all it is, chitchat. I can't give you an answer to your **questions**, but I can give you a bit of advice: You'd better think less about us and what's going to happen to you, and think a bit more about yourself. And stop making all this fuss about your sense of innocence; you don't make such a bad impression, but with all this fuss you're damaging it. And you ought to do a bit less talking, too. Almost everything you've said so far has been things we could have taken from your behaviour, even if you'd said no more than a few words. And what you have said has not exactly been in your favour."

K. stared at the supervisor. Was this man, probably younger than he was, lecturing him like a schoolmaster? Was he being punished for his honesty with a telling off? And was he to learn nothing about the reasons for his arrest or those who were arresting him? He became somewhat cross and began to walk up and down. No-one stopped him doing this and he pushed his sleeves back, felt his chest, straightened his hair, went over to the three men, said, "It makes no sense," at which these three turned round to face him and came towards him with serious expressions. He finally came again to a halt in front of the supervisor's desk. "State Attorney Hasterer is a good friend of mine," he said, "can I telephone him?"

Franz Kafka, The Trial

"Good **question**,"said Vargina.

"Yes," said Cooley. "That is the **question**, as the Bard might say."

"The Bard?"

"What's so funny?" said Cooley.

"Nothing, sir," I said. "I just didn't know people still used that term."

"Well, I'm a people, Burke. Am I not?"

"Of course."

"If you prick me, do I not bleed, you scat-gobbling, mother-rimming prick?"

Occasionally Dean Cooley reverted to a vocabulary more suited to his marine years, but some maintained it was only when he felt threatened, or stretched for time.

"Yes, sir," I said.

"Trust me, Milo," said Llewellyn. "Nobody wants it to be you. You were nothing but dead weight since the day you arrived. Nobody respects you and your leering got on people's nerves."

"My leering?"

Vargina shrugged, tapped her pen against her legal pad.

Listen, said Cooley. "I don't give a slutty snow monkey's prolapsed uterus for your office politics. The point is that Burke needs to come back and complete this mission."

Why?" I said. "Why me?"

"It's the ask, said Vargina. "The ask demands it."

Sam Lipsyte, The Ask

The phone rang and I picked it up. A woman's voice delivered a high-performance hello. It said it was computer-generated, part of a marketing survey aimed at determining current levels of consumer desire. It said it would ask a series of **questions**, pausing after each to give me a chance to reply.

I gave the phone to Steffie. When it became clear that she was occupied with the synthesized voice, I spoke to Babette in low tones.

"She liked to plot."

"Who?"

"Dana. She liked to get me involved in things."

"What kind of things?"

"Factions. Playing certain friends against other friends. Household plots, faculty plots."

"Sounds like ordinary stuff."

"She spoke English to me, Spanish or Portuguese to the telephone."

Steffie twisted around, used her free hand to pull her sweater away from her body, enabling her to read the label.

"Virgin acrylic," she said into the phone.

Babette checked the label on her sweater. A soft rain began to fall.

"How does it feel being nearly fifty-one?" she said.

"No different from fifty."

"Except one is even, one is odd," she pointed out.

Don DeLillo, White Noise

At the request of the district's Office of Internal Resolution, a private investigator, Reginal Dukes, looked into the reported problems and, in March of 2006, concluded that teachers at Parks had cheated on the Georgia Middle Grades Writing Assessment, leaking the essay prompt to students. Dukes presented his preliminary findings to Hall at a lunch meeting with her senior staff and was shocked by her apparent lack of interest. "I expected her to take definite action," he told me. Instead, he was informed that he couldn't hire any additional investigators. Hall asked few **questions**. The only one he remembered was "Is there any more evidence?"

Rachel Aviv, Wrong Answer: A Middle-School Cheating Scandal (The New Yorker)

p. 670–14

First, you know that x is a fraction. Fractions get smaller as they are raised to powers. Say that $x = \frac{1}{2}$. Then $\frac{1}{2}^2 = \frac{1}{4}$ and $\frac{1}{2}^3 = \frac{1}{8}$ and so on. So, now walk through the choices. From what we have just seen with $\frac{1}{2}$, we can see that I and III are both true. Look at II, still using $x = \frac{1}{2}$. $\frac{1}{2} > (\frac{1}{2})/2$. So, all three statements are true.

E

p. 918–12

If $(x + 3)/2$ is an integer (positive and negative whole numbers plus 0), then $x + 3$ must equal an even number or 0. The rules you have to choose from must be true, so look for reasons to exclude an answer choice.

(A) You can find a negative number that won't make it an integer, e.g., –2.

(B) You can find a positive integer that won't work, e.g., 2.

(C) You can find a multiple of 3 that won't work, e.g., 6.

(D) No even integer will ever work.

(E) Any odd integer works (odd + odd = even).

E

p. 392–13

In this type of **question**, be careful not to just refer to the line that contains the word "shadowy." The answer is found in both the line "real experience" and in the following line "really there" which supports "unsubstantiated" meaning not proven.

E

*Henry Davis, Explanations for the Official SAT Study Guide **Questions**: Detailed Explanations for the Answers for Every **Question***

"That **question** floored me," Dukes said. "I'd just gone through this litany of violations."

Waller was never reprimanded, and he said he never heard anything about the outcome of the investigation. The next year, Tameka Grant was transferred against her will to Long Middle School, known at the time as one of the most dangerous schools in the district.

In 2007, Parks had to score even higher to surpass its falsely achieved scores from the previous year. According to statements later made by teachers and administrators (obtained through Georgia's open-records act), the cheating process began to take the form of a routine. During testing week, after students had completed the day's section, Waller distracted the testing coördinator, Alfred Kiel, by taking him out for leisurely lunches in downtown Atlanta. On their way, Waller called the reading coördinator to let her know that it was safe to enter Kiel's office. She then paged up to six teachers and told them to report to the room. While their students were at recess, the teachers erased wrong answers and filled in the right ones. Lewis took photographs of the office with his cell phone so that he could make sure he left every object, even the pencils on Kiel's desk, exactly as he'd found them.

Rachel Aviv, Wrong Answer: A Middle-School Cheating Scandal (The New Yorker)

Ask such **questions** as: "How many *ones* of pencils in two pencils?" "Two pencils will make how many *ones* of pencils?" The written form of the first of these two **questions** is: *2 pencils ÷ 1 pencil = ? pencils,* (In two pencils how many ones of pencils?). This reading and form must be adhered to.

C.M. Parker (ed.), The School News and Practical Educator, Volume 11

p. 520–8

Again, the definition of the word for the blank is after the comments "notice subtle differences." This would be someone who is **discriminating** because they can discern and make astute or sharp perceptions. Someone who is **sanctimonious** is smugly self-righteous. Someone who is **obscure** would be difficult to understand or unclear. Someone who is **unrelenting** is inexorable or merciless.

C

*Henry Davis, Explanations for the Official SAT Study Guide **Questions**: Detailed Explanations for the Answers for Every **Question***

For multiplication ask such **questions** as: "How many *times* one pencil in two pencils?" If there is difficulty, lead up to it in this way: Find *one pencil* in these two pencils. Find *another* one pencil in these two. How many times did you find one pencil in two pencils? Then, two pencils are how many *times* one pencil? Written form: *1 pencil × 2 = ? pencils.* (Two times 1 pencil are 2 pencils). In **question** form it should be read: "Two *times* 1 pencil are how many pencils ?'

C.M. Parker (ed.), The School News and Practical Educator, Volume 11

IS THIS A JOKE?

If you start a pencil-sharpening business, you can expect to hear this **question** a lot. The short answer? No, this is not a joke. You pay David Rees money and he sharpens your pencils. It actually happens.

If you think it's a joke, why don't you poke yourself with your newly sharpened pencil? Or better yet, don't—because it'll really hurt. In fact, every pencil David Rees sharpens is shipped with a signed and dated certificate authenticating that it is now a dangerous object.

David Rees, *Artisanal Pencil Sharpening: About*

Next, locate on the answer document the row of ovals numbered the same as the **question**. Then, locate the oval in that row lettered the same as your answer. Finally, fill in the oval completely. Use a soft lead pencil and make your marks heavy and black. *Do not use ink or a mechanical pencil.*

ACT® *(American College Testing), Test Booklet Instructions*

p. 489–14

"Attempts at the latter" refers to the statement "educational junk" is "foisted" (meaning imposed) on us. These attempts are declared unsuccessful tries so they are "failures."

D

p. 594–4

This is a function problem. You simply substitute 15 for k in the equation. Thus we have: $4(15) - 30 = 60 - 30 = 30$

E

p. 490–15

"Compromised" in line 57 is mirrored by its definition in the following line with the phrase "lowest common denominator." This is a difficult **question** which demands the most negative answer corresponding to "lowest." "Degraded" fits best as it means tarnished or corrupted.

E

Henry Davis, *Explanations for the Official SAT Study Guide* **Questions**: *Detailed Explanations for the Answers for Every* **Question**

As he flops onto the dock, Les decides that, whatever it eventually means, for now at least he is a fugitive. Uncurling the rope holding the boat, he drifts in it, on a current that will take him to Port Perry. The sun is warm enough to break the ice in his veins into painful throbs. The card table has dissipated and a less likely blue sky has taken its place. Les lies in the bottom of the boat.

I have never been an organized man. I will never know what the inner life of other people is like. That can never matter again. In Port Perry I will steal a car. I'm going to Parkdale.

From the shore a loon offers Les both its name and its Haunting Cry. He turns his head in the bottom of the boat, bunching his cheek against aluminum rivets, and smiles.

None of you has anything for me anymore. I am Ed Gein. I want my wife and child.

At his nose is a dead worm, glossy and hard; it forms an almost audible S. Les flicks the brittle lower loop, creating a **question** mark. *Stupid.* He flicks the upper loop, creating a bar of worm that appears to have shot off its ends in a centrifugal action. *Better. Better* **question.**

For the next four hours Les lies freezing in the drifting boat, turning away from, and then back to, his worm. He pictures his son in little screens that open up in the aluminum just above the watermark. He names the child. He changes the name. The baby has a face like a walnut, a uniform surface of wrinkles, and Helen wipes yellow food from his chin. Les tilts his jaw toward the bait-littered bottom of the boat, and Helen reaches up and cleans three tiny crayfish legs from the side of his face. Her hand slips back beneath the brackish water an inch deep beneath Les. *They live in an inch of water. No air. They can't see. The fins of pickerel and the snouts of summer frogs hide the light. A rusted fish hook has just fallen in the baby's food.*

Tony Burgess, *Pontypool Changes Everything*

p. 420–5

Although I am not sure how this is a mathematical reasoning **question**, we will play along and answer the **question**. Let's use the < and > signs to indicate older and younger. Let's look at the specific givens:

Owen is less than his other and sister so he can't be the oldest.

Steph is youngest, so she is not the oldest.

Chadd is not the youngest or oldest. So we are left with Daria.

B

Henry Davis, *Explanations for the Official SAT Study Guide* **Questions**: *Detailed Explanations for the Answers for Every* **Question**

Ms. Washburn's eyes widened a bit.

I did indeed remember Ms. Crenshaw. Our business had been slightly contentious— she had wanted to receive an insurance settlement rather than retrieve the odd animal she'd been keeping as a pet, and I had spoiled things by actually finding the snake.

"Yes," Ackerman repeated. "Ellen said your service was effective and discreet."

"She had an unusual **question**," I said. "How do you know Ms. Crenshaw?"

"We served on the board of a foundation together a few years ago," Ackerman said. "We remained friends, and during a conversation a few weeks ago, she mentioned your service. She said your methods were impressive, if a little . . . unusual."

"For service that is usual, you can go anywhere," Ms. Washburn said.

E. J. Copperman and Jeff Cohen, *The* **Question** *of the Missing Head*

p. 775–10

The sentence is correct.

A

p. 914–20

The two quotations in lines 28–29 serve as examples of typical civilities. Akaky was handed papers day in and day out and told to "copy this" or "here is an interesting, nice little case". This behavior was called "well behaved" office procedure, so we could say it was typical (normal, usual, ordinary civilities (kindness, politeness, or courtesy).

A

Henry Davis, *Explanations for the Official SAT Study Guide* **Questions**: *Detailed Explanations for the Answers for Every* **Question**

But while state testing officials often scurry to minimize the harm flawed **questions** do, in some cases complaints about them meet resistance.

Heather Vogell, Errors Plague Testing, Hurt Students in Public Schools (MSN News)

when someone raises their hand in the middle of a talk after an explicit request that all **questions** be saved until the end

@AcademicsSay, Shit Academics Say (Twitter)

Her face had an expression I read as a trifle angry, perhaps more irritated. "For service that's special, you need Mr. Hoenig." I thought that was generous of her, especially since I had not yet answered a **question** for Ms. Washburn. She was proving to be quite helpful.

*E. J. Copperman and Jeff Cohen, The **Question** of the Missing Head*

p. 409–17

The error is in the grammatical use of "noticeable." This should be an adverb describing how something is done, not an adjective. Most adverbs end in "ly" signifying "how."

C

p. 409–18

There are rigid unmistakable pairings in the English grammar. "Either" and "or" end "neither" and "nor" are pairing that must go together.

A

p. 717–17

The key here is to take your pencil and draw lines connecting vertex V with the other vertices. But do NOT count the vertices connected to V by an edge of the figure. There are three of those points. Look at the figure. There are 3 edges of the figure that connect with V, so you cannot count those.

8

p. 409–19

This is a pronoun antecedent error. The noun must match pronoun that represents it. "Passengers" is plural and the correct pronoun would be "their" not "his or her."

C

p. 410–20

"Number" is the subject of the sentence and is separated from the verb of the sentence by a phrase which contains a plural noun. This is a common sentence construction used by the testmakers to confuse. Here it is handled correctly.

E

*Henry Davis, Explanations for the Official SAT Study Guide **Questions**: Detailed Explanations for the Answers for Every **Question***

"Aw, maaaan," yells the heckler, "don't you stand there and shine us up with no more your figures and your bureaucratic rhetoric!" They love it. The insolence! The insolence sets off another eruption. He peers through the scalding glare of the television lights. He keeps squinting. He's aware of a great mass of silhouettes out in front of him. The crowd swells up. The ceiling presses down. It's covered in beige tiles. The tiles have curly incisions all over them. They're crumbling around the edges. Asbestos! He knows it when he sees it! The faces—they're waiting for the beano, for the rock fight. Bloody noses!—that's the idea. The next instant means everything. He can handle it! He can handle hecklers! Only five-seven, but he's even better at it than Koch used to be! He's the mayor of the greatest city on earth—New York!

Him!

"*Allright!* You've had your fun, and now you're gonna *shut up* for a minute!"

That startles the heckler. He freezes. That's all the Mayor needs. He knows how to do it.

"*Youuuu* asked *meeeee* a **question**, didn't you, and you got a *bigggg* laugh from your claque. And so now *youuuuu're* gonna keep *quiiiiet* and *lissssten* to the answer. *Okay*?"

"Say, claque?" The man has had his wind knocked out, but he's still standing up.

Tom Wolfe, The Bonfire of the Vanities

Not words of routine this song of mine,
But abruptly to **question**, to leap beyond yet nearer bring;
This printed and bound book—but the printer and the
    printing-office boy?
The well-taken photographs—but your wife or friend close and solid
    in your arms?
The black ship mail'd with iron, her mighty guns in her turrets—but
    the pluck of the captain and engineers?
In the houses the dishes and fare and furniture—but the host and
    hostess, and the look out of their eyes?
The sky up there—yet here or next door, or across the way?
The saints and sages in history—but you yourself?
Sermons, creeds, theology—but the fathomless human brain,
And what is reason? and what is love? and what is life?

Walt Whitman, Leaves of Grass

p. 396–1

This **question** is quite straightforward In this case, though we simply substitute 4 for "x" and solve.

A : $(4+1)(4+2) = (5)(6) = 30$

Here we would suggest quickly looking at the other possibilities and make sure none exceed values of 5 and 6. None do.

A

Henry Davis, Explanations for the Official SAT Study Guide **Questions**: Detailed Explanations for the Answers
for Every **Question**

And surely you would not have the children of your ideal State, whom you are nurturing and educating—if the ideal ever becomes a reality—you would not allow the future rulers to be like posts, having no reason in them, and yet to be set in authority over the highest matters?

Certainly not.

Then you will make a law that they shall have such an education as will enable them to attain the greatest skill in asking and answering **questions**?

Yes, he said, you and I together will make it.

Dialectic, then, as you will agree, is the coping-stone of the sciences, and is set

over them; no other science can be placed higher—the nature of knowledge can no
further go?

I agree, he said.

But to whom we are to assign these studies, and in what way they are to be assigned,
are **questions** which remain to be considered?

Plato, The Republic

A strong Scots background, and thirty years at Carlyle Rural, had made her an expert
disciplinarian. A short, fat, implacable woman, she ruled her three groups—for Carlyle
Rural had only two rooms and she took the most advanced classes—not with a rod
of iron, but with the leather strap that was issued by the school board as the ultimate
instrument of justice. She did not use it often; she had only to take it from a drawer
and lay it across her desk to quell any ordinary disobedience. When she did use it, she
displayed a strength that even the biggest, most loutish boy dreaded, for not only did
she flail his hands until they swelled to red, aching paws, but she tongue-lashed him with
a virtuosity that threw her classes into an ecstasy of silent delight.

"Gordon McNab, you're a true chip off the McNab block. (Slash!) I've given the
strap to your father (Slash!), and both your uncles (Slash!), and I once gave it to your
mother (Slash!), and I'm here to tell the world that you are the stupidest, most ignorant,
no-account ruffian of the whole caboodle. (Slash!) And that's saying something. (Slash!)
Now go to your seat, and if I hear a peep out of you except in answer to a **question**,
you'll get it again and get it worse, because I've got it right here in my desk, all ready
for you. Do you hear me?"

"Bluh."

"What? Speak up. What do you say?"

"Yes, Miss McGladdery."

Robertson Davies, What's Bred in the Bone

Though there are few articles of jurisprudence in these honest alphabetical reflections,
we must, however, say a word or two on torture, otherwise called "the **question**"; which
is a strange manner of **questioning** men. They were not, however, the simply curious
who invented it; there is every appearance, that this part of our legislation owes its
first origin to a highwayman. Most of these gentlemen are still in the habit of screwing
thumbs, burning feet, and **questioning**, by various torments, those who refuse to tell
them where they have put their money.

Conquerors having succeeded these thieves, found the invention very useful to
their interests; they made use of it when they suspected that there were bad designs
against them: as, for example, that of seeking freedom was a crime of high treason,
human and divine. The accomplices must be known; and to accomplish it, those who
were suspected were made to suffer a thousand deaths, because, according to the
jurisprudence of these primitive heroes, whoever was suspected of merely having a
disrespectful opinion of them, was worthy of death. As soon as they have thus merited
death, it signifies little whether they had frightful torments for several days, and even
weeks previously—a practice which savors, I know not how, of the Divinity. Providence
sometimes puts us to the torture by employing the stone, gravel, gout, scrofula, leprosy,
smallpox; by tearing the entrails, by convulsions of the nerves, and other executors of
the vengeance of Providence.

The ordinary **question**: it essentially consisted of an interrogation in good and due form in order to make the accused confess. Heavily laden with irons and in a shirt, the accused had to answer for his crimes. This first interrogation, although muscular, comprising only violent blows, among other things, allowed the accused to answer the **questions** posed by the king's prosecutor. But to obtain a fuller confession, the accused was then subjected to the extraordinary **question**.

The extraordinary **question**: and there, all possible and unimaginable means were implemented to extract the confessions.

*Promenade en France, La **Question** (promenade34.free.fr)*

Now, as the first despots were, in the eyes of their courtiers, images of the Divinity, they imitated it as much as they could. What is very singular is, that the **question**, or torture, is never spoken of in the Jewish books. It is a great pity that so mild, honest, and compassionate a nation knew not this method of discovering the truth. In my opinion, the reason is, that they had no need of it. God always made it known to them as to His cherished people. Sometimes they played at dice to discover the truth, and the suspected culprit always had double sixes. Sometimes they went to the high priest, who immediately consulted God by the urim and thummim. Sometimes they addressed themselves to the seer and prophet; and you may believe that the seer and prophet discovered the most hidden things, as well as the urim and thummim of the high priest. The people of God were not reduced, like ourselves, to interrogating and conjecturing; and therefore torture could not be in use among them, which was the only thing wanting to complete the manners of that holy people. The Romans inflicted torture on slaves alone, but slaves were not considered as men. Neither is there any appearance that a counsellor of the criminal court regards as one of his fellow-creatures, a man who is brought to him wan, pale, distorted, with sunken eyes, long and dirty beard, covered with vermin with which he has been tormented in a dungeon. He gives himself the pleasure of applying to him the major and minor torture, in the presence of a surgeon, who counts his pulse until he is in danger of death, after which they recommence; and as the comedy of the "Plaideurs" pleasantly says, "that serves to pass away an hour or two."

The grave magistrate, who for money has bought the right of making these experiments on his neighbor, relates to his wife, at dinner, that which has passed in the morning. The first time, madam shudders at it; the second, she takes some pleasure in it, because, after all, women are curious; and afterwards, the first thing she says when he enters is: "My dear, have you tortured anybody to-day?" The French, who are considered, I know not why, a very humane people, are astonished that the English, who have had the inhumanity to take all Canada from us, have renounced the pleasure of putting the **question**.

Voltaire, A Philosophical Dictionary

Suppose your mother forbids you to handle a looking glass, and also to take a pin: If you break the looking-glass, would you disobey her any more than you would by taking the pin?

Harvey Newcomb, Newcomb's First Question Book

"My only weapon is the **question**," he says.

William Finnegan, The Man Who Wouldn't Sit Down (The New Yorker)

p. 648–19

The passage is primarily concerned with the manner of pleasure that most people find in art. In the second paragraph he asks the rhetorical **question**, "What is it that the majority of people call aesthetic pleasure?" and then spends the rest of the passage examining what makes it pleasurable.

C

Henry Davis, Explanations for the Official SAT Study Guide Questions: Detailed Explanations for the Answers for Every Question

What militates in favor of this necessity, as Heidegger will concede a few pages later,

is above all the **question**'s "venerable origin" and "the lack of a definite answer" to it
(SZ 8–9).

*Jean Grondin, Why Reawaken the **Question** of Being? (Heidegger's Being and Time: Critical Essays)*

"What?"

"Goals, Tom. They have no ultimate goals. They don't know what in the hell they're
trying to accomplish. They're treating everything in sight, curing symptoms and wiping
out goals. It's like treating a headache with a lobotomy. Tom, we have to leave the patient
human enough to achieve the ultimate goals of being human."

"What are the ultimate goals of being human, Van?" I look at my watch. I'm already
sorry I asked. Where is Lucy?

Now Van is half-sitting on the poker table, swinging a leg, arms folded, at his ease,
well-clad and graceful in his coveralls and—yes, exhilarated. He's nodding, eyes gone
fine and faraway.

"I'll answer that **question** by telling you what I tell the boys and girls out there.
Incidentally, it's no accident, Tom, that since we took over this seg academy, we've got
the highest SAT scores in the state and the most National Merit scholars. You know what
the answer is, Tom, the only answer?

Walker Percy, The Thanatos Syndrome

p. 641–11

This is tricky because the answer is obvious, and, for that reason, you might have a
tendency not to believe that it can be so obvious. The circumference varies directly with
the radius because the circumference is simply 2r x pi. So, the front wheel turns twice
for each revolution of the larger rear wheel because it is 1/2 the size.

C

*Henry Davis, Explanations for the Official SAT Study Guide **Questions**: Detailed Explanations for the Answers
for Every **Question***

Tests drive decisions about who wins a scholarship, enters a coveted gifted program,
attends a magnet school, or moves to the next grade. Teachers and principals lose their
jobs because of bad scores. A school tarred with them can attract a state takeover.

Advocates of test-based reform say the exams offer scientific precision. But records
show thousands of students have faced **questions** that failed to meet basic industry
standards.

Some **questions** had no right answer option, or more than one right answer.
Wording was unclear, or covered material never taught. A few **questions** have bordered
on bizarre—such as the now-infamous passage on a New York test about a race between
a hare and a pineapple.

Heather Vogell, Errors Plague Testing, Hurt Students in Public Schools (MSN News)

A story and two **questions** on the New York state English exam taken by eighth-graders
this week has stumped many—including *Jeopardy!* star Ken Jennings.

The story—titled *The Pineapple and the Hare*—was included in a *New York Daily
News* story about the consternation the **questions** have caused.

"Is this a joke? The story makes no sense whatsoever," Jennings said in an editorial
in the *Daily News*.

NY1 spoke to students who were amused and confused after reading the story of a hare who was challenged by a pineapple to a foot race. The New York City school chancellor told NY1 that he agreed with his students.

"We expect to see much more rigor and complex reading passages on next year's tests," Dennis Walcott said in a statement to NY1.

*Eyder Peralta, The Pineapple and the Hare: Can You Answer Two Bizarre State Exam **Questions**? (NPR)*

Have you ever wondered how standardized test **questions** are created? Test **question** development is a lengthy overall process. Every test **question** goes through a rigorous evaluation before it can become an official test **question**.

*Derrick Meador, Want to Know How Standardized Test **Questions** Are Developed? (About.com Teaching)*

Burke (1999) maintains that traditionally "standardized" meant that the test is standard or the same in three ways: (a) format/**questions**, (b) instructions, and (c) time allotment. Format/**questions** means that the test **questions** are the same for all students writing the exam. The information that the students are to show they know is asked of them in the same format that is usually multiple choice. Multiple choice is the format of choice because as Stiggins (2008) suggests, "It is relatively easy to develop, administer, and score in large numbers" (p. 354). Further, in order for the test to be fair in the sense of all students having the same chance to answer each **question** correctly, all **questions** must be the same.

The instructions are to be the same as well. These are to be delivered in the same way to all students so that no students are advantaged or disadvantaged. The last standardization is time allotment. All students are to be given the same amount of time to finish the exam.

John Poulsen, and Kurtis Hewson, Standardized Testing: Fair or Not? (University of Lethbridge Teaching Centre)

Be sure to use this time well. Each part of the test has a definite time limit. There is enough time for most people to answer every **question**. Nonetheless, some **questions** may be more difficult than others. Do not spend an excessive amount of time on one **question** to the detriment of your total test performance. You can always go back to a skipped **question** if you finish a part of the test before the time limit for that part is over. To ensure that you have time to answer every **question**, you should keep track of the time by periodically checking your watch or the room clock. Also, the examiner will tell you when you have ten minutes left before the end of each part. If you find that the time is almost up and you have left one or more **questions** unanswered, make an intelligent guess on the answers and mark them in the answer booklet. Your score will not be lowered for wrong answers in this test; rather, your score will be based on the total number of items that you answer correctly.

*U.S. Office of Personnel Management, Background Information and Sample **Questions** for the Examination for Careers in Personnel, Administration, and Computer Occupations*

However, the standardization of standardized exams is being eroded. Common changes to standardized testing allow certain students to have more than the allotted amount of time. Some students with certain learning needs are now allowed to have more time than other students to complete the exam. These students are then often allowed to write in different rooms as well.

The second requirement of standardized tests is also frequently adapted. Students with reading problems can get "readers" to read the **questions**. The rationale behind this is that the curriculum asks that students know certain information. Whether the students know this information is the purpose of the exam, not whether the students can read. These readers may adapt the standardized instructions that the students receive. Also, reading the **questions** to the students may give them an advantage or disadvantage other students do not have. Therefore, the second and third requirements of standardized testing are no longer strongly in effect.

John Poulsen, and Kurtis Hewson, Standardized Testing: Fair or Not? (University of Lethbridge Teaching Centre)

p. 842–7

Laila completed her projects in record time; therefore, the conclusion is that she performed her tasks with quickness. *Alacrity* means quickness or speed. *Conformity* means compliant or agreeable. *Deliberation* means with forethought or discussion. *Recrimination* means accuse or blame. *Exasperation* means frustrated, annoyed, or irritated. If Laila completed her tasks in record time she performed her tasks with *alacrity*.

A

*Henry Davis, Explanations for the Official SAT Study Guide **Questions**: Detailed Explanations for the Answers for Every **Question***

When any one commits a fault requiring grave punishment, the whole of the boys are assembled, as a sort of council, to deliberate and decide on the kind of punishment to be inflicted, which consists usually of imprisonment in a dungeon for a number of days, and, of course, no participation in the recreations of the community.

Now, here is the peculiarity of the discipline. After sentence is passed by the boys under the approval of the director, the **question** is then put, "Will any of you consent to become the patron of this offender, that is, to take his place now and suffer in his room and stead, while he goes free?" And it rarely happens but that some one is found ready to step forward and consent to ransom the offender by undergoing his punishment for him—the offender being in that case merely obliged to act as a porter in carrying to his substitute in the dungeon his allowance of bread and water during all the time of his captivity.

C.M. Parker (ed.), The School News and Practical Educator, Volume 11

There are other forms of standardized testing that are available other than multiple-choice **questions**, for example, essay writing. This form of testing currently has the disadvantage of needing markers to assess the essays. Essay markers must be trained to gain a sense of what the standards are. Then they must engage in the time-consuming activity of reading the essays.

John Poulsen, and Kurtis Hewson, Standardized Testing: Fair or Not? (University of Lethbridge Teaching Centre)

Have you ever wondered just where the GRE came from and who thought it necessary to put you through this inordinate hell? I have—only a couple times, but it sincerely did happen. Honestly, with some sense that this standardized test is approaching the relative age of dirt, I've **questioned** its validity in our ever-more-connected and data-at-your-service world. Why should I know the definition of *paucity* and *dearth* by heart when it takes less than 60 seconds to look it up online? It's a valid **question**.

Testizen, Where the GRE Came From? (Medium)

Without further delay, here's the story:

In the olden times, animals could speak English, just like you and me. There was a lovely enchanted forest that flourished with a bunch of these magical animals. One day, a hare was relaxing by a tree. All of a sudden, he noticed a pineapple sitting near him.

The hare, being magical and all, told the pineapple, "Um, hi." The pineapple could speak English too.

"I challenge you to a race! Whoever makes it across the forest and back first wins a ninja! And a lifetime's supply of toothpaste!" The hare looked at the pineapple strangely, but agreed to the race.

The next day, the competition was coming into play. All the animals in the forest (but not the pineapples, for pineapples are immobile) arranged a finish/start line in between two trees. The coyote placed the pineapple in front of the starting line, and the hare was on his way.

Everyone on the sidelines was bustling about and chatting about the obvious prediction that the hare was going to claim the victory (and the ninja and the toothpaste). Suddenly, the crow had a revolutionary realization.

"AAAAIEEH! Friends! I have an idea to share! The pineapple has not challenged our good companion, the hare, to just a simple race! Surely the pineapple must know that he CANNOT MOVE! He obviously has a trick up his sleeve!" exclaimed the crow.

The moose spoke up.

"Pineapples don't have sleeves."

"You fool! You know what I mean! I think that the pineapple knows we're cheering for the hare, so he is planning to pull a trick on us, so we look foolish when he wins! Let's sink the pineapple's intentions, and let's cheer for the stupid fruit!" the crow passionately proclaimed. The other animals cheered, and started chanting, "FOIL THE PLAN! FOIL THE PLAN! FOIL THE PLAN!"

A few minutes later, the hare arrived. He got into place next to the pineapple, who sat there contently. The monkey blew the tree-bark whistle, and the race began! The hare took off, sprinting through the forest, and the pineapple . . .

It sat there.

The animals glanced at each other blankly, and then started to realize how dumb they were. The pineapple did not have a trick up its sleeve. It wanted an honest race—but it knew it couldn't walk (let alone run)!

About a few hours later, the hare came into sight again. It flew right across the finish line, still as fast as it was when it first took off. The hare had won, but the pineapple still sat at his starting point, and had not even budged.

The animals ate the pineapple.

And the two **questions**:

1. *Why did the animals eat the pineapple?*
    a. they were annoyed
    b. they were amused
    c. they were hungry
    d. they wanted to

2. *Who was the wisest?*
    a. the hare
    b. moose

c. crow

d. owl

Yep. We were as confused as you are now. We think Jennings did a pretty good job at trying unravel the mystery surmising the only thing we can positively discern from the story is: "There is no owl."

*Eyder Peralta, The Pineapple and the Hare: Can You Answer Two Bizarre State Exam **Questions**? (NPR)*

Each testing season, new complaints crop up. Writing good **questions**, it turns out, is deceptively difficult.

Heather Vogell, Errors Plague Testing, Hurt Students in Public Schools (MSN News)

Try those below, and note that in connection with each answer much related information, not called for in the **question**, may be brought out.

C.M. Parker (ed.), The School News and Practical Educator, Volume 11

The advantages of this **question** type are that it is easy to mark and minimises guess work by having multiple distracters.

*Richard Frost, Test **Question** Types (Teaching English)*

President Dole, of the Hawaiian Republic, accompanied by his wife arrived in Washington, D.C., January 26th. He came by way of San Francisco and was given a right royal reception in Chicago. At Washington he was met by Secretary Sherman and soon afterwards exchanged brief calls with the President.

His presence in this country just at the time the **question** of the annexation of Hawaii is pending before Congress seems to declare his interest in the same; yet we are informed that he declines to use any decided influence for the measure. He said:

"I prefer not to discuss the **question** of annexation, as that would be inappropriate at this time. I shall of course give the President such information as he may desire on pending **questions** between the two countries. I expect to stay in Washington until the end of next week, when our trip homeward will begin. We shall go direct to San Francisco, taking the steamer there for Honolulu. Certainly I should like to see the annexation treaty ratified by the Senate before we leave, but we shall not wait if such is not the case."

C.M. Parker (ed.), The School News and Practical Educator, Volume 11

Do not make the teaching of any lesson a **question** of time. Never mind whether the class has reached page 20 or page 40. The chief thing is, are the little ones thinking? Give them time to think—to do thorough, thoughtful work.

Give special attention to slow pupils: the brighter ones will follow your instructions without any trouble. Make the lessons so interesting and attractive that the children will willingly give their attention.

—Elizabeth H. Fundenberg, First Lessons in Reading

C.M. Parker (ed.), The School News and Practical Educator, Volume 11

There can be no **question**, that the Romish views embraced and advocated by Mr. Ward, and more or less adopted or pleaded for by a few others, and the mischievous fooleries of some halfscore young clergymen, have served to prejudice some well-meaning persons against Church discipline and rubrical conformity; and it is to be lamented that any such impediments should have arisen. But it is surely a great mistake to suppose, that there would have been no opposition raised to sound Churchmanship had it not been for the extravagancies just mentioned. No one who knows any thing of the writings or life of the late Bishop Porteus would suspect him of having had any Popish tendencies; yet when he and Archbishop Cornwallis, about seventy years ago, endeavoured to promote the observance of Good Friday, which for many a long year had been scarcely distinguished from any other Friday, the Low Church and liberal papers of the day raised the same sort of clamour against these estimable prelates as their successors have recently done against equally estimable men, who are just as free from any wish to favour Popery as they were. The following paragraph, extracted from a newspaper of the time referred to, and having in view the effort then being made to promote the observance of Good Friday, shows that the "No Popery" banner has been used before as the standard under which pretended Churchmen, schismatics, heretics, infidels, atheists, adulterers, and every vile and worthless character, have delighted to wage war against Church principles and Church practices:

*James Irvine, The Rubrical **Question** Practically and Apologetically Considered: A Sermon*

p. 592–19

The author's point of view (or opinion) is that "normal" time for human beings is during daylight hours. The author isn't trying to stress the individuality of his writing by using quotation marks around the word normal (A). Nor is the author trying to make a point about time or obsession with time (B). The author used quotes to emphasize an opinion he had about what he thinks "normal" is for humans. The word in quotes might be stressed differently than the other words if reading the passage out loud (E) but the point is still to emphasize what the author considers "normal", and that is that most people are awake during the day and asleep at night. There would be no need for quotation marks at all if the author were trying to demonstrate that he agreed with the common use of the word (D), using quotes is what sets the word apart and draws attention to it.

C

*Henry Davis, Explanations for the Official SAT Study Guide **Questions**: Detailed Explanations for the Answers for Every **Question***

This can best be done by suggestions written by the teacher on the margin in colored ink—colored because it readily appeals to the eye. The corrections should not be made by the teacher, but simply indicated—the pupil being required to make the changes himself. A few re-written papers will act as a remarkable stimulus to correct work.

So much as to general suggestions, and now we come to the more specific with reference to the outlined work of the month. The items suggested for the four weeks are two business letters and two descriptive paragraphs. The business letter differs from other letters in that it may contain abbreviations, etc.—the man who writes or the man who reads it has little time at his disposal. The sentences should be short, terse, to the point. The information offered should be definite. The introduction and the conclusion in this as well as in all letters should show the relation which exists between the writer and the reader. It should not be less correct than any other letter. I could name a man who not two months ago failed to obtain a paying position simply on account of a misplaced period in LL.D.

C.M. Parker (ed.), The School News and Practical Educator, Volume 11

Irenæus, who was the diſciple *of Polycarp,* and had converſed with many of the imme-diate diſciples of the apoſtles, lived, at the loweſt computation of his age, till the year 202, when he was likewiſe cut off by martyrdom; in which year the great *Origen* was appointed regent of the Catechetic ſchool in *Alexandria,* and as he was the miracle of that age, for induſtry, learning, and philoſophy, he was looked upon as the champion of chriſtianity, till the year 254, when, if he did not ſuffer martyrdom, as ſome think he did, he was certainly actuated by the ſpirit of it, as appears in the whole courſe of his life and writings; nay, he had often been put to the torture, and had undergone trials worſe than death. As he converſed with the moſt eminent chriſtians of his time in *Egypt,* and in the Eaſt, brought over multitudes both from hereſy and heatheniſm, and left behind him ſeveral diſciples of great fame and learning, there is no **queſtion** but there were conſiderable numbers of thoſe who knew him, and had been his hearers, ſcholars, or proſelytes, that lived till the end of the third century, and to the reign of *Conſtantine* the Great.

Joseph Addiſon, Of the Chriſtian Religion (The Works of the Late Right Honorable Joſeph Addiſon, Eſq; Volume the Fourth, With a Complete Index)

In general, the test **questions** deal with topics related to Government business which you would be likely to encounter in the performance of jobs in the Personnel, Administration, and Computer occupations. Remember, however, that *knowledge of any job-specific subject matter is NOT required to answer the* **questions** *correctly.*

The total time allotted for Part A is 50 minutes. Part A will consist of fifteen vocabulary **questions** and twenty reading **questions**. It should take you about 5 minutes to answer the vocabulary **questions**, which would leave you 45 minutes for the reading **questions**. Do not spend much more than five minutes on the vocabulary **questions**, since this would cut into the time you have for answering the reading **questions**. However, if you finish Part A before the allotted time is over, you should review your answers in both the Vocabulary and the Reading sections, especially any answers about which you were uncertain.

U.S. Office of Personnel Management, Background Information and Sample **Questions** *for the Examination for Careers in Personnel, Administration, and Computer Occupations*

The entire Article referred to inshore *fishing.* No right and no liberty whatever, that might concern deep-sea fishermen, did the United States, by the Treaty of 1818, renounce.

This obvious intent and purpose of the Article is confirmed by the last words of the section, which declares: "But they" (the American fishermen) "shall be under such restrictions as may be necessary to prevent their taking, drying, or curing fish therein" (in portion B) "or in any other manner abusing the privileges hereby reserved to them." The "restrictions to be imposed upon the American fishermen, while in portion B, are expressly limited, not to such as concern navigation or revenue, but to such as were specifically renounced, namely, to such as "may be *necessary* to prevent their taking, drying, or curing fish therein, or in any other manner whatever abusing the privileges hereby reserved to them" *in order to take, dry, or cure fish therein.*

Was it not clearly the intention of the negotiators of this Treaty that the character of these restrictions should be agreed upon by the parties to the Treaty? Is it reasonable to assume that the American negotiators intended that the Canadian Provinces, or even the British Government, should have the exclusive power to prescribe "restrictions" which might entirely destroy the value of any unrenounced right and liberty theretofore claimed and enjoyed, or of any conceded "privileges" thereby reserved to American fishermen in portion B?

*Parliament of Canada, Correspondence Relative to the Fisheries **Question**, 1885–1887*

This process easily takes over a year. Each **question** is carefully reviewed by a variety of educational stakeholders throughout the process. Even as the **question** moves through each review, there is still a possibility that it may not find itself on an actual standardized test. Standardized testing has become such a crucial part of education. Therefore, it is imperative that test **questions** accurately measure intended learning standards. The testing industry is a multi-billion dollar industry, and much of that money goes into the development and screening of potential test items.

*Derrick Meador, Want to Know How Standardized Test **Questions** Are Developed? (About.com)*

"I do understand that."

"But what you also need to understand is that we are not simply some heartless, money-mad, commercial enterprise. We are partly that, of course, but we are also a compassionate and, yes, money-mad place of learning. And while we're on the topic of learning, we think people can learn from their mistakes. We believe in redemption."

"As long," said Llewellyn, "as it is not tied to a particular ideology or religious tradition and promotes inclusiveness."

"Is that from the handbook, Lew? said Dean Cooley. Anyway, the point is, we are a family."

"A family dedicated to furthering science and the humanities in an increasingly meaning-starved culture," said Vargina.

"Well put," said Dean Cooley.

"But may I remind us all," said Llewellyn, "that here in development our task is to raise money for said furthering. We can't hug all day. We've got to get out there and work."

"Also well put. Especially these days. We need every drop of philanthropy we can get. We must fasten our lips to the spigot and suck, so to speak. Which is where you come in, Mr. Burke."

"Pardon?"

"It's an ask," said Vargina.

"A big one," said Llewellyn. "Not quite Rayfield range, but big."

"Why me?" I said.

"Good **question**," said Vargina.

"Yes," said Cooley. "That is the **question**, as the Bard might say."

"The Bard?"

"What's so funny?" said Cooley.

"Nothing, sir," I said. "I just didn't know people still used that term."

Sam Lipsyte, The Ask

. . . we knew it was more authentic than BANG BANG, it enriched the game and this game was the same, only way out of hand at last, too rich for all but a few serious players. The rules now were tight and absolute, no arguing over who missed who and who was really dead; *No fair* was no good, *Why me?* the saddest **question** in the world.

Well, good luck, the Vietnam verbal tic, even Ocean Eyes, the third-tour Lurp, had remembered to at least say it to me that night before he went on the job. It came out dry and distant, I knew he didn't care one way or the other, maybe I admired his detachment. It was as though people couldn't stop themselves from saying it, even when they actually meant to express the opposite wish, like "Die, motherfucker."

Michael Herr, Dispatches

"It can take an expert all day to write a few items correctly," Lee said. "Unfortunately, a lot of people try to write a lot of items incorrectly." The **question**-creation process begins with states' blueprints for what teachers should teach. Testing contractors turn the guides into a battery of **questions** that aim to measure what students know.

Contractors either write **questions** themselves or hire freelancers who are paid by the hour or item. Advertisements on job boards such as Craigslist seek "test development" writers to meet what has become an almost insatiable appetite for new items.

States and test companies say they typically submit potential test **questions** to multiple reviews by committees of staff and educators. They look for problems such as bias, a lack of clarity or inaccuracy. Editing is extensive.

But records reviewed by the *Atlanta Journal-Constitution* show quality checks meant to keep bad **questions** off students' desks continue to falter.

In 2008 alone, records show, Mississippi dropped five **questions** and Georgia dropped three because of flaws such as no right answer that were discovered after testing ended.

Heather Vogell, Errors Plague Testing, Hurt Students in Public Schools (MSN News)

"Surely," said the old man, "there are not two, nor three, nor four. I must confess the people from your side of the world ask very extraordinary **questions**."

Voltaire, Candide

p. 845–16

Answers A, B, C, and D are not mentioned in the lines where you are told to find the answer. However, the floor plan and the lack of specific information about the structure's height and other details are mentioned in lines 30–42.

E

p. 416–10

Look at the numbers closely and do what they ask.

1.783 rounded to the nearest whole number would be 1.783 = 2

1.783 rounded to the nearest tenth would be 1.8

The difference would be 2 − 1.8 = .2

.2 or 1/5

Henry Davis, Explanations for the Official SAT Study Guide **Questions**: Detailed Explanations for the Answers for Every **Question**

Daniel Pinkwater, the author of the story, has chimed in on the controversy. He says the test company—which sells the test material for "vast sums of money" and pays the author "non-vast sums of money"—changed the story.

He writes:

"I don't know how the test publishing company changed the story. I gather they decided to call the rabbit a hare, and made the eggplant into a pineapple. Also there appears to be

something about sleeves. And they made up **questions** *for the students to answer. I would not have done any of these things. But it has nothing to do with me. I cashed the check they sent me after about 8 months, and took my wife out to lunch at a cheap restaurant. I believe, she ordered eggplant.*"

UPDATE AT 7:02 P.M. ET. AN ALTERNATE STORY:

The New York Daily News, which originally posted the story above, has without explanation changed the version of the story now on its story page. Some of the commenters here noted that what's above was not what was in the test they took.

Here's the other story posted by the *Daily News*, which makes slightly more sense:

THE HARE AND THE PINEAPPLE
by Daniel Pinkwater

In olden times, the animals of the forest could speak English just like you and me. One day, a pineapple challenged a hare to a race.

(I forgot to mention, fruits and vegetables were able to speak too.)

A hare is like a rabbit, only skinnier and faster. This particular hare was known to be the fastest animal in the forest.

"You, a pineapple have the nerve to challenge me, a hare, to a race," the hare asked the pineapple. "This must be some sort of joke."

"No," said the pineapple. "I want to race you. Twenty-six miles, and may the best animal win."

"You aren't even an animal!" the hare said. "You're a tropical fruit!"

"Well, you know what I mean," the pineapple said.

The animals of the forest thought it was very strange that tropical fruit should want to race a very fast animal.

"The pineapple has some trick up its sleeve," a moose said.

"Pineapples don't have sleeves," an owl said

"Well, you know what I mean," the moose said. "If a pineapple challenges a hare to a race, it must be that the pineapple knows some secret trick that will allow it to win."

"The pineapple probably expects us to root for the hare and then look like fools when it loses," said a crow. "Then the pineapple will win the race because the hare is overconfident and takes a nap, or gets lost, or something."

The animals agreed that this made sense. There was no reason a pineapple should challenge a hare unless it had a clever plan of some sort. So the animals, wanting to back a winner, all cheered for the pineapple.

When the race began, the hare sprinted forward and was out of sight in less than a minute. The pineapple just sat there, never moving an inch.

The animals crowded around watching to see how the pineapple was going to cleverly beat the hare. Two hours later when the hare crossed the finish line, the pineapple was still sitting still and hadn't moved an inch.

The animals ate the pineapple.

MORAL: Pineapples don't have sleeves

Eyder Peralta, *The Pineapple and the Hare: Can You Answer Two Bizarre State Exam* **Questions**? (NPR)

So far, so good. But we do not congratulate a schoolmaster on teaching that two and two make four, though we may, perhaps, congratulate him on having chosen his laudable vocation. Let us then say it was praiseworthy that Tarrou and so many others should have elected to prove that two and two make four, rather than the contrary; but let us add that this good will of theirs was one that is shared by the schoolmaster and by all who have the same feelings as the schoolmaster and, be it said to the credit of mankind, are more numerous than one would think—such, anyhow, is the narrator's conviction. Needless to say, he can see quite clearly a point that could be made against him; which is that these men were risking their lives. But again and again there comes a time in history when the man who dares to say that two and two make four is punished with death. The schoolteacher is well aware of this. And the **question** is not one of knowing what punishment or reward attends the making of this calculation. The **question** is that of knowing whether two and two do make four.

Albert Camus, The Plague

Waller said that he had never experienced so much pressure in his life. Although administrators throughout the district knew that there was cheating, he said that "nobody wanted to talk about it." "We'd been cultivated in so many untruths throughout the years," he told me. In 2008, he decided to resign, but Hall worked with the Casey Foundation to give him an "incentive award grant" of fifteen thousand dollars. He agreed to stay, believing that soon he would have the strength to tell the district that its targets couldn't continue to rise.

By 2008, there were nine teachers on Waller's team, and cheating had become a "well-oiled machine," as he put it. A principal at an elementary school in southeast Atlanta e-mailed Waller charts detailing the number of **questions** students in each grade needed to answer correctly in order to get a passing score—information that the state's Department of Education does not publish. The teachers now changed answers in the chorus room, because they didn't want to raise the suspicions of the testing coördinator, who noticed that someone had been in his office and had changed the lock. (A day later, Lewis found a copy of the new key in his school mailbox.) The room was so crowded that two teachers placed test booklets in a cooler and took them to another room. "It went from a two-man show to out of control," Lewis said. A sixth-grade teacher, who asked that his name not be used, told me that he got involved only because he respected Lewis, whom he described as the "alpha male of the building" and a "humanitarian." "I don't think Waller could have run the school without him," he said. "It's kind of like every king has to have a general, and the general gets his hands way dirtier than the king does."

Rachel Aviv, Wrong Answer: A Middle-School Cheating Scandal (The New Yorker)

I felt sorry for the man. It didn't prevent me from saying: "Where were you Friday night?"

"At home in Maple Park in our—in my apartment, grading themes."

"Can you prove it?"

'I have the marked papers to prove it. They were turned in to me Friday, and I marked them Friday night. I hope you're not imagining I did something fantastic like flying to California and back?"

"When a woman is murdered, you ask her estranged husband where he was at the time. It's the corollary of *cherchez la femme.*"

"Well, you have my answer. Check it out if you like. But you'll save yourself time

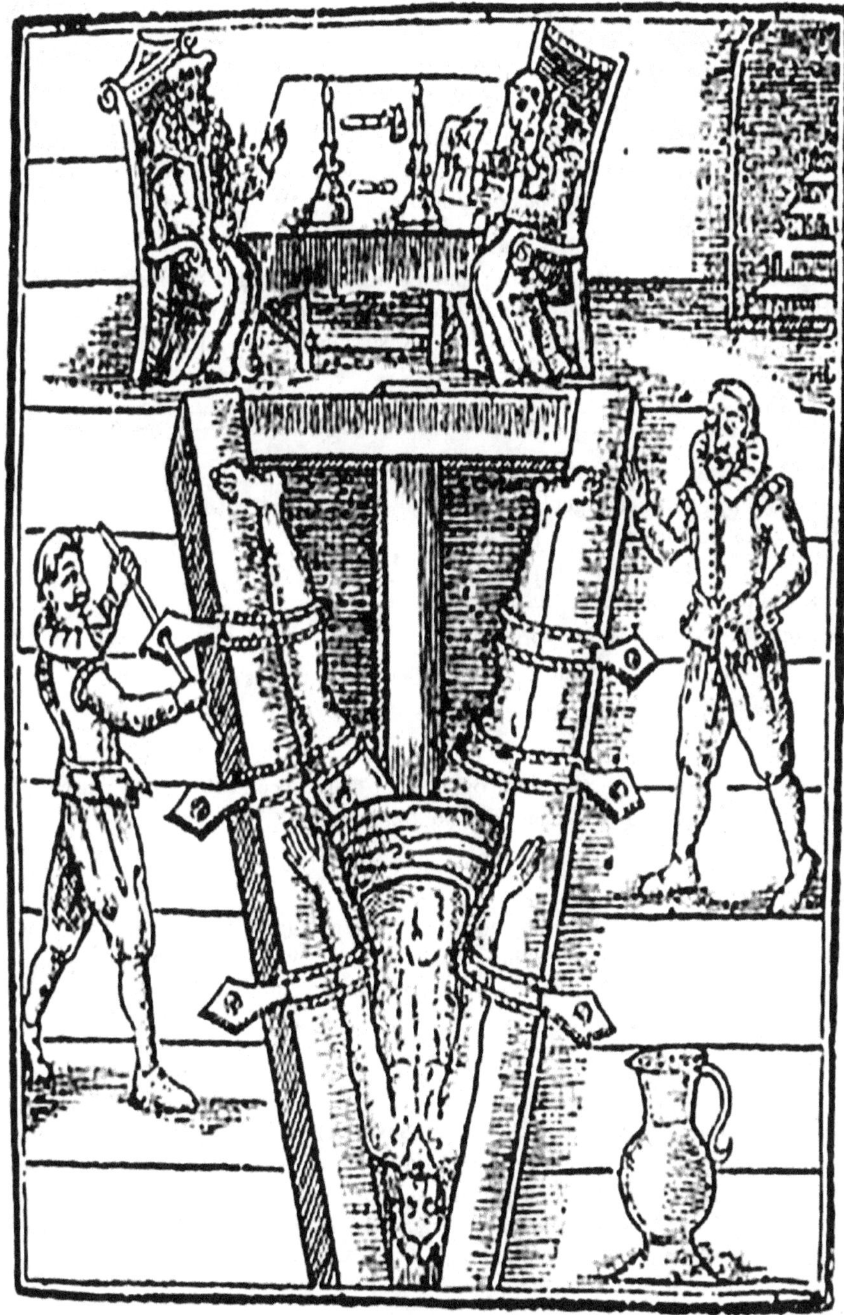

*William Lithgow **questioned** on the potro (engraving from his Travels, 1640 edition)*

I offer you an English variant of the stretching table which stretches the
lower limbs by slightly crushing the shoulders and the head . . .

Fred 37, Tortures, Torments and Others . . .
From the Middle Ages to Our Days (Fred 37's Blog)

and trouble simply by believing me. I've been completely frank with you—inordinately frank."

"I appreciate that."

"But then you turn around and accuse me—"

"A **question** isn't an accusation, Mr. Haggerty."

"It carried that implication," he said in an aggrieved and

Page 176 is not part of this book preview.

Ross Macdonald, The Chill

Question Seventieth.—Was it of the competence of the alcalde Mr. Begorrat, and of his tribunal to apply the **question** or torture for such a crime as that with which Luisa Calderon was charged and committed for?—Answer. No, not by himself alone, but with the authority of government.

T. B. Howell and Thomas Jones Howell, Cobbett's Complete Collection of State Trials and Proceedings for High Treason and Other Crimes and Misdemeanors From the Earliest Period to the Present Time, Vol. XXX

What, when he was thirsty?

What, when he was a stranger?

What, when he was naked?

What, when he was sick and in prison?

How will they excuse themselves? v. 44.

Harvey Newcomb, Newcomb's First **Question** Book

Most **questions** may be adequate, as industry representatives claim.

Heather Vogell, Errors Plague Testing, Hurt Students in Public Schools (MSN News)

p. 734–3

You need a word that means the opposite of "hard to control." (FYI: "gluttonous" means greedy and "adroit" means *skillful* or *competent*)

E

p. 734–4

You need a word that is synonymous with the verb "range," which means to include or cover a number of different things within a particular context. Although the other choices could be used to describe a musical performance, only (C) describes the variety of her repertoire

C

p. 734–5

(The test makers consider this a hard **question**.) *Skeptics* are those who habitually **question** generally accepted matters, such as religious doctrines, and *nihilists* are those who reject established conventions, such as social mores and religion. The two are similar, but since the skeptics came first, they *foreshadowed* and helped "elucidate" (means to explain or clarify) the nihilists.

E

Henry Davis, Explanations for the Official SAT Study Guide **Questions**: Detailed Explanations for the Answers for Every **Question**

Toronto resident Maxeen Paabo agrees and has decided that her son will not participate in this year's Grade 3 tests. She researched the issue, and reached her conclusion even before the school year began.

"I think the way it is now and the way it's being used politically is wrong, and it's a misuse of resources," she says.

"What the ministry [of education] said is that it is used on a student level, on a class level and on a school level to make improvements. But my understanding on the ground is that that isn't really happening, that teachers' regular classroom assessments are doing all that work."

But the sixth graders at Lougheed (coincidentally named for the Brampton-born grandfather of Alberta's late premier Peter Lougheed) are not staying home on test day.

To help them take the "evil **questions**" in stride, Ms. Hamilton leaves candy on their desks, lets them play outside and, by far the biggest treat, gives no homework for three days.

Rachel Giese and Caroline Alphonso, The Debate Over Standardized Testing in Schools Is as Divisive as Ever (The Globe and Mail)

p. 405–15

Those people who "think this way" think that humans should fit into the natural balance of nature and the Industrial Revolution has destroyed the balance of nature, enhances evil, and; therefore it is a harmful trend in human history.

E

p. 640–7

This is a pretty straightforward algebraic substitution problem. Isolate what we want. We want r in terms of t, so we want to eliminate s. 2r = 5s and 6t = 5s, so 2r = 6t and r = 6t/2 = 3t

C

p. 588–6

Based on phrases like "brutal work schedule", "physically demanding work and highly stressful work" and the statement "cannot just take off for a two-week vacation" we can conclude that passage 1 is primarily concerned with the harsh working conditions on many farms. Passage 2 is more about how Americans view or perceive farm life.

B

p. 420– 4

First this is a square. So we plot out the points we are given. It also states that the vertices are opposite vertices. So, if we plot it out we can see the sides are each 2 from the x and y axis and hence the square would have sides of 4 and an area of 4 × 4 = 16.

C

p. 972–6

Passage 1 emphasizes the importance of the first 3 years in human development, while Passage 2 emphasizes the brain's ability to adapt throughout life. Passage 2 states, "it may be useful to **question** the simplistic view" that "no period of human life is as suited to learning as are [the] first three years" (9–10) of life.

D

p. 972–8

Passage 2 states that neuroscience suggests that the adult brain can reorganize itself and learn new skills when necessary, and the author warns that "we should be wary of claims that parents have only a single . . . opportunity to help their children build better brains." His warning indicates skepticism on his part.

B

p. 551–15

In this paragraph the author talks about reading the book <u>Little Women</u> before deciding to take it home. The reason for that is, as she states, she learned from experience that titles "weren't everything." This indicates that book titles aren't always what the book is about and can be "misleading." Actually she says books can be dull if you aren't careful about choosing, but she didn't say anything about them being duller at the library. She did say that you can tell something by reading the first few paragraphs, but she didn't say anything about them being very dull in first few paragraphs. She is not comparing novels and nonfiction work. You could infer that books might not be as interesting as their titles but that would be a bit of a stretch especially since we have a clear answer choice might B.

B

Henry Davis, Explanations for the Official SAT Study Guide **Questions**: *Detailed Explanations for the Answers for Every* **Question**

This will also be true of the **question** of Being, as we will see: it cannot be comprehended unless one passes through the Being of Dasein, which will be introduced formally in SZ as the entity characterized, among other things, by its capacity to pose **questions** (SZ 7).

Jean Grondin, Why Reawaken the **Question** *of Being? (Heidegger's Being and Time: Critical Essays)*

Sometimes it's hard to keep coming up with ideas if you play this game for a while. Here are a few **questions** for you to think about that will help you think of new ideas:

- Do you have any special talents that people don't know about?
- Are there any things you wish were true about yourself but aren't?
- What is your favorite subject in school? Or your favorite anything?
- Are you known for something like sports that would make it not seem obvious that you liked something else like poetry?
- How many siblings do you have and how many of each?
- What is something you have never done but that most people have?
- What are some things you have accomplished?
- What do you want to be when you grow up?

Megan Garcia, Two Truths and a Lie: Ideas, Examples, and Instructions (Hobby Lark)

In every **question**, claims SZ, one can distinguish three moments:

a) "that which is asked about," a Gefragtes; in this case—we intimate it, but without knowing anymore what we are putting into **question**—the Gefragtes is Being.

b) "that which is interrogated," a Befragtes, that is, that to which our **question** is addressed; we will soon learn that this is Dasein and its understanding of Being;

c) finally, there is "that which is to be found out by the asking," an Erfragtes: what is being asked, what one wishes to know when one poses the **question**, the meaning or point of the **question**—in short, the **question** behind the **question**.

Jean Grondin, Why Reawaken the **Question** *of Being? (Heidegger's Being and Time: Critical Essays)*

p. 587–3

Vocabulary is being tested here. *Ineffable* means unspeakable; *articulated* means expressed or uttered distinctly and clearly; *consummate* means perfect, finished, or complete; *presumptive* means based on probability; and *deleterious* means harmful. A negative result caused by inbreeding would be "harmful" genes that make an animal subject to disease or impair its reproductive efficiency; therefore they would be *deleterious* genes.

E

p. 599-2

Conners **is** a publishing and media services company. Conners acquired another company called Dispatch Education. Dispatch Education is a company that manufactures school uniforms. The word "it" in the underlined section is a pronoun that could refer back to Conners except that what we know about Conners is that it has something to do with publishing. Therefore to make the sentence more clear we would use the word "which" instead of "it".

B

p. 599-3

The statement is comparing newspapers. Which newspaper prints more world news, the campus newspaper or the hometown (newspaper)? The absence of the word "newspaper" after the word "hometown" leaves the reader with out a clear and precise contrast. "Newspaper" is implied but ambiguous and awkward. Therefore B is the best answer to put in place of the underlined section of the statement.

B

p. 546-23

"Behind the Scenes at the Front" misrepresented the truth about war. The wartime poems, stories and memoirs were about the rise of women to power. All of the literature avoided the realities of the battlefield.

E

Henry Davis, Explanations for the Official SAT Study Guide **Questions**: *Detailed Explanations for the Answers for Every* **Question**

Yes, he was on a slippery slope, and he knew it. But he slipped only far enough to get the information he needed. Saul rarely had moral qualms about his job. In his office he kept a paperweight engraved with a quotation from George Orwell: "People sleep peaceably in their beds at night only because rough men stand ready to do violence on their behalf." He had broken Khalid Sheikh Mohammed. He had disrupted at least three attacks, saved hundreds of civilians. He didn't know their names, and they would never know his, but they were still real.

And the men he **questioned**, the Farouks of the world? They weren't innocent. They weren't Iraqi farmers caught in dragnets and taken to Abu Ghraib. They were terrorists, real ones, who knew the risks they had chosen to take. Saul had nothing but contempt for the Amnesty International types who whined that any coercive tactic was unfair. If those weaklings believed that men like Farouk would give up their secrets over tea and crumpets, they were even more naive than he thought.

Alex Berenson, The Faithful Spy

p. 492-7

"Attitude — — was" is in the past tense; therefore, B., D., and E., answer choices must be eliminated because they contain the present tense verb "will." C can be eliminated as well because it uses the present tense "are."

A

p. 846–24

Getty believed that the "shrillness of their cries and howls" (referring to the critics) would simply use up their own air. In other words, their criticisms were ineffectual and pointless. The critics may have been loud, but their influence was short-lived.

E

p. 476–8

The key phrase related to purpose is "no — — reason why one word stays alive and others — — get — to the scrap heap" and "slang terms — — are rarely in for long." These relate to a term's "durability" meaning lasting power.

C

Henry Davis, Explanations for the Official SAT Study Guide **Questions***: Detailed Explanations for the Answers for Every* **Question**

"I get the feeling Ray's just warming up," Rebus said quietly, thinking that he wouldn't have too many **questions** for the scientist after all.

Duff returned Rebus's look and went back to the photographs. "No blood spatter pattern," he said, circling the area of the wall. Then he held up a hand. "Actually, that's not strictly true. There's blood present, but it's such a fine diffusion you can't really make it out."

"Meaning what?" Hogan asked, not bothering to hide his impatience.

Ian Rankin, A **Question** *of Blood*

Interrogators, like priests and doctors, have a particular advantage when it comes to concealing their feelings. They can ask another **question**, which is what I would have done myself.

"What cufflinks, Sergeant Major?" Smiley said, and I see him lowering his long eyelids and sinking his head into his neck as he once more prepared himself to listen to the old man's tale.

John le Carré, The Secret Pilgrim

And things? What is the correct attitude to adopt towards things? And (to begin with) are they necessary? What a **question**! But I have few illusions: things are to be expected. The best is not to decide anything (in this connection) in advance. If a thing turns up, for some reason or other, take it into consideration.

Where there are people (it is said) there are things. Does this mean that when you admit the former you must also admit the latter? Time will tell. The thing to avoid (I don't know why) is the spirit of system. People with things, people without things, things without people—what does it matter? I flatter myself it will not take me long to scatter them, whenever I choose, to the winds. (I don't see how.)

Samuel Beckett, The Unnamable

p. 492–8

The mistake in the original wording is in the parallelism which eliminates all answer choices except C and D which both contain the parallel phrasing "in math" and "in learning." In this case the shortest most direct wording is the best.

D

p. 492–9

The briefest most direct phrasing is the original wording. All the other answer choices are either too wordy or awkward, indirect constructions.

A

p. 982–6

We are looking for a word that means "public declaration". *Invocation* means prayer. *Prospectus* means catalog or booklet. *Manifesto* means policy or program. *Arbitration* means mediation or negotiation. *Mandate* means authorization or permission. The word that best fits the meaning or the sentence is: manifesto.

C

*Henry Davis, Explanations for the Official SAT Study Guide **Questions**: Detailed Explanations for the Answers for Every **Question***

'I told you, Winston,' he said, 'that metaphysics is not your strong point. The word you are trying to think of is solipsism. But you are mistaken. This is not solipsism. Collective solipsism, if you like. But that is a different thing: in fact, the opposite thing. All this is a digression,' he added in a different tone. 'The real power, the power we have to fight for night and day, is not power over things, but over men.' He paused, and for a moment assumed again his air of a schoolmaster **questioning** a promising pupil: 'How does one man assert his power over another, Winston?'

Winston thought. 'By making him suffer,' he said.

'Exactly. By making him suffer. Obedience is not enough. Unless he is suffering, how can you be sure that he is obeying your will and not his own? Power is in inflicting pain and humiliation. Power is in tearing human minds to pieces and putting them together again in new shapes of your own choosing. Do you begin to see, then, what kind of world we are creating? It is the exact opposite of the stupid hedonistic Utopias that the old reformers imagined. A world of fear and treachery and torment, a world of trampling and being trampled upon, a world which will grow not less but more merciless as it refines itself. Progress in our world will be progress towards more pain. The old civilizations claimed that they were founded on love or justice. Ours is founded upon hatred. In our world there will be no emotions except fear, rage, triumph, and self-abasement. Everything else we shall destroy—everything. Already we are breaking down the habits of thought which have survived from before the Revolution. We have cut the links between child and parent, and between man and man, and between man and woman. No one dares trust a wife or a child or a friend any longer. But in the future there will be no wives and no friends. Children will be taken from their mothers at birth, as one takes eggs from a hen. The sex instinct will be eradicated. Procreation will be an annual formality like the renewal of a ration card. We shall abolish the orgasm. Our neurologists are at work upon it now. There will be no loyalty, except loyalty towards the Party. There will be no love, except the love of Big Brother. There will be no laughter, except the laugh of triumph over a defeated enemy. There will be no art, no literature, no science. When we are omnipotent we shall have no more need of science. There will be no distinction between beauty and ugliness. There will be no curiosity, no enjoyment of the process of life. All competing pleasures will be destroyed. But always—do not forget this, Winston—always there will be the intoxication of power, constantly increasing and constantly growing subtler. Always, at every moment, there will be the thrill of victory, the sensation of trampling on an enemy who is helpless. If you want a picture of the future, imagine a boot stamping on a human face—for ever.'

George Orwell, Nineteen Eighty-Four

"Jesus," Neena cut in irritably, "why do you have to be such a bully?"

"Excuse me? I was not aware you and I, Neena, were having a conversation."

"He was just asking a **question** and you have to come over all arsey. I mean, you've been bullying him for half a century. Haven't you had enough? Why don't you just leave him alone?"

Zadie Smith, White Teeth

p. 490–16

This **question** depends on the context key phrases such as "children simply to stay the same, must go underground" (line 76–77) and "a release zone comic books" to defend comic-books and argue that they are "therapeutic" meaning helpful or healing.

D

p. 490–17

The author of Passage 1 would regard lines 81–83 as proving comic books are "harmful." Comic books would allow children to commit "the worst of sins" and get away with them.

E

p. 490–18

The tone of Passage 1 is much more negative than that of Passage 2; therefore, answer choices A and E need to be eliminated. "Severe" meaning harsh is the best choice of the word choices. The tone of the last sentence is bitter and condemning; "failed to teach" and "harmful" are strong word choices. "Facetious" means teasing or tongue in cheek. "Sarcastic" means ironic or mocking.

C

*Henry Davis, Explanations for the Official SAT Study Guide **Questions**: Detailed Explanations for the Answers for Every **Question***

"You are here to give evidence, not your views on the case, and you must confine yourself to answering the **questions** put you."

Albert Camus, The Stranger

The **questions** were never written down; the colonel didn't want to end up on CNN either. Still, Yates's mere presence checked the worst impulses of the interrogators. And they closely monitored the prisoners' health, if only to make sure their techniques were working. The interrogators in 121 had interrogated close to one hundred prisoners, and only one had died, of a huge heart attack that probably would have hit him in any case.

The TF 121 interrogators had other restrictions. They never worked alone, and they took two-month breaks twice a year. Once a year they were interviewed by army psychiatrists and took a long personality test. The rules were supposed to prevent them from developing God complexes—a real risk, Saul knew. Having this much power

DIVERSES MANIERES DONT LE ST. OFICE FAIT DONNER LA QUESTION

A torture chamber of the Spanish Inquisition with suspected heretics having their feet burned
or being suspended with a rope from a pulley while scribes note down confessions.

Engraving by Bernard Picart, 1722 (wellcomecollection.org) over another human being, not just the power to kill but the power to hurt, could be intoxicating. Look at the other side, cutting throats on camera. Nothing could be more repulsive. Yet Saul understood the impulse, the sick thrill of making another human being cringe and beg for his life . . . or beg for death because the pain was too much.

Alex Berenson, The Faithful Spy

"Yes, I know, his marriage is unfortunate—believe me, I know."

"You have feelings for him!" Annagret said with dismay.

"Yes, I do, so what?"

"Well, you didn't tell me. We're telling each other everything, on the sofa, and you didn't tell me this."

"You didn't tell me you used to sleep with Andreas Wolf!"

"Andreas is a public person. I have to be careful. And that's many years ago now."

"You talk about him like you'd do it again in a heartbeat."

"Pip, please," Annagret said, seizing her hands. "Let's not fight. I didn't know you had feelings for Stephen. I'm sorry."

But the wound the word *weak* had inflicted was hurting Pip more now, not less, and she was aghast to realize how much personal data she'd already surrendered to a woman so confident of her beauty that she could fill her face with metal and chop her hair (so it looked) with lawn clippers. Pip, who had no grounds for such confidence, snatched her hands away and stood up and noisily dropped her cereal bowl in the sink. "I'm going upstairs now—"

"No, we still have six **questions**—"

Jonathan Franzen, Purity

I, personally, love the population of the planet. Hardly anybody is doing the wrong thing intentionally. But that same hardly anybody isn't really sure that they're doing the right thing.

Thank Julie and Michell for putting an end to that sad reality. As a team, they're going to put the right **questions** in front of you. As the key member of that team, you're going to put the right answers up in your brain.

Once you've done that, you'll have taken the first baby steps in the direction of true success in life.

It sounds good, but it gets better. As they say in the world of marketing, but wait, there's more!

You'll have started out in the right direction by asking only the first **question**. Five more await you on your journey—five more simple but nuclear powered **questions**— each with its own answer that you—and only you have.

Once you've completed the book and answered the **questions**, you'll have the self-knowledge that Benjamin Franklin says is so hard to acquire.

He would have been proud of you—but not as proud as you'll be of yourself.

*Jay Conrad Levinson, Foreword to The Six **Questions**: That You Better Get Right, The Answers Are the Keys to Your Success*

In the fall of that same year (2007), new **question** types were added to the test. For the most part, these were comprised of the fill-in-the-blank sort that were added to the quantitative section (replacing just a few that were previously multiple-choice), as well as newly formatted select-one-or-more type **questions**. Early in 2008 (January),

ETS reformatted the passages in the Reading Comprehension segment of the GRE; it implemented highlighting in place of line numbers as needed to call test-takers' attention to specific information within (for reference, in short). ETS declared its intentions for another round of changes to the GRE in December of 2009. These were expected to (and did, in fact) take effect in 2011. One of the most significant overhauls would be that of the scoring scale. In place of the old 200 to 800 range (measured in 10-point increments), ETS would use the now-familiar 130–170 (measured in 1-point increments). They also indicated they would eliminate antonym- and analogy-related **question** types, reduce emphasis on rote vocabulary memorization, replace Sentence Completion with Text Completion (sounds awfully similar) . . .

Testizen, Where the GRE Came From? (Medium)

Where to?

Where? Reader, you and your curiosity are terrible nuisances. What's it matter to you? If I said Pontoise or Saint-Germain, or Notre Dame de Lorette or Saint Jacques of Compostella, would you be any the wiser? If you insist, I'll tell you they were making their way towards . . . yes, why not? . . . towards a huge castle over the gate of which was written this inscription: 'I belong to no one. I belong to everyone. You were here before you arrived and you will still be here when you've gone.'

And did they go inside the castle?

No. Because unless what was written was wrong, they were already there before they arrived.

But at least they left?

No. Because unless what was written was wrong, they were still inside after they'd gone.

What did they do there?

Jacques said what it was written on high he would say, and his Master said whatever he liked, and they were both right.

What sort of company did they find inside?

Mixed.

What did people say?

Some truth and a lot of lies.

Were there any clever people?

Where are there not clever people? There were also a lot of people asking impertinent, tomfool **questions** . . .

Denis Diderot, Jacques the Fatalist and His Master

His **questioners** now were not ruffians in black uniforms but Party intellectuals, little rotund men with quick movements and flashing spectacles, who worked on him in relays over periods which lasted—he thought he could not be sure—ten or twelve hours at a stretch, these other **questioners** saw to it that he was in constant slight pain, but it was not chiefly pain that they relied on. They slapped his face, wrung his ears, pulled his hair, made him stand on one leg, refused him leave to urinate, shone glaring lights in his face until his eyes ran with water; but the aim of this was simply to humiliate him and destroy his power of arguing and reasoning. Their real weapon was the merciless **questioning** that went on and on, hour after hour, tripping him up, laying traps for him, twisting everything that he said, convicting him at every step of lies and self-contradiction, until he began weeping as much from shame as from nervous fatigue. Sometimes he would weep half a dozen times in a single session. Most of the time they screamed abuse at him and threatened at every hesitation to deliver him over to the guards again; but sometimes they would suddenly change their tune, call him comrade, appeal to him in the name of Ingsoc and Big Brother, and ask him sorrowfully whether even now he had not enough loyalty to the Party left to make him wish to undo the evil he had done. When his nerves were in rags after hours of **questioning** even this appeal could reduce him to snivelling tears. In the end the nagging voices broke him down more completely than the boots and fists of the guards. He became simply a mouth that uttered, a hand that signed, whatever was demanded of him. His sole concern was to find out what they wanted him to confess, and then confess it quickly, before the bullying started anew.

George Orwell, Nineteen Eighty-Four

3. Regarding multiple-choice tests, the author affirms that:

I. They were in standard use at that particular school in order to prepare students for the university entrance exams.
II. It was easier to cheat on those tests, any way you looked at it.
III. They did not require you to develop your own thinking.
IV. With multiple-choice tests, the teachers didn't have to make themselves sick in the head by grading all weekend.
V. The correct choice is almost always D.

    (A) I and II
    (B) I, III, and V
    (C) II and V
    (D) I, II, and III
    (E) I, II, and IV

Alejandro Zambra, Reading Comprehension: Text No. 1 (The New Yorker)

Mark only one answer to each **question**. If you change your mind about an answer, erase your first mark thoroughly before marking your new answer. For each **question**, make certain that you mark in the row of ovals with the same number as the **question**.

Only responses marked on your answer document will be scored. Your score on each test will be based only on the number of **questions** you answer correctly during the time allowed for that test. You will **not** be penalized for guessing. *It is to your advantage to answer every **question** even if you must guess.*

You may work on each test *only* when your test supervisor tells you to do so. If you finish a test before time is called for that test, you should use the time remaining to reconsider **questions** you are uncertain about in that test. You may *not* look back to a test on which time has already been called, and you may *not* go ahead to another test. To do so will disqualify you from the examination.

Lay your pencil down immediately when time is called at the end of each test. You may *not* for any reason fill in or alter ovals for a test after time is called for that test. To do so will disqualify you from the examination.

Do not fold or tear the pages of your test booklet.

DO NOT OPEN THIS BOOKLET UNTIL TOLD TO DO SO.

ACT (American College Testing), Test Booklet Instructions*

He tried to relax. He wasn't an illiterate peasant. He knew the Americans had rules. They could make him wear this hood, but they couldn't hurt him too much. They would ask him their **questions**, and then they would put him on a plane to Guantanamo. If they asked him about the Geiger counter, he would say . . . he would say that he didn't know what it was. He should make up a name. A Shia name would be best. Hussein, then. He would call himself Hussein. As long as he didn't tell them who he was or what he was doing in Iraq, he would be fine.

The Americans had rules. He just needed to stay calm.

Alex Berenson, The Faithful Spy

That was the original rule that was followed in Wisconsin and it was also followed in New York, and it was the rule laid down by the Supreme Court of Wisconsin and the Appellate Court of the State of New York. Under that rule the State, under its police power, was permitted to act in all cases alleging a violation of the State law until such time as the jurisdiction of the Federal Government was invoked and the National Labor Relations Board assumed jurisdiction in the same labor dispute.

When the Bethlehem Steel case and the LaCrosse Telephone case were decided by the Supreme Court, that theory of concurrent jurisdiction was definitely out of the window.

It was after that that we and several other States urged that some amendment be added to the then Wagner Act and later the Taft-Hartley Act that would reinstate that rule.

Mr. WALTER. Reinstate that rule?

Mr. GOODING. Yes.

Mr. WALTER. Or create a rule under which the Federal Government would have sole jurisdiction?

*United States Congress, Establishing Rules of Interpretation Governing **Questions** of the Effect of Acts of Congress on State Laws, Part 1*

p 587–4

If we plug in each group of answers in the blanks it is obvious which words fit best provided we know our vocabulary. If the doctor was accused of **inconsistency** then he would be the type of person who would **vacillate** (which means to hesitate, waver, fluctuate, or sway) in his techniques. An accusation is usually considered something negative therefore look for a negative word to go into the second blank. **Fidelity** (meaning faithful and loyal) is not considered a negative thing therefore B is not a good choice. **Steadfastness** is also not considered a negative trait, and *wavering* would not be consistent with being steadfast, therefore C does not work. If the doctor **experimented** frequently in his techniques then we could accuse him of being too flexible, not **inflexible**; therefore D does not fit. And if the doctor **relied** frequently on disease-prevention techniques it would be unlikely that he would be accused of **negligence** (E). The best fit is **vacillated** (wavered) and **inconsistency** (fickle or unstable). The words are somewhat synonymous and would have to be in order for the sentence to make sense.

A

*Henry Davis, Explanations for the Official SAT Study Guide **Questions**: Detailed Explanations for the Answers for Every **Question***

Mr. GOODING. No, we urged first that they would grant to the States concurrent jurisdiction. Personally I always urged that if Congress did not want to do that the very least they could do was write into the law just what, if any, authority the State should exercise; in other words, to state clearly exactly what Congress intended to preempt; if they intended to preempt all the field, to say so, and if they intended to preempt only a part of the field, to say so and leave the rest to the States.

In my opinion H.R. 3 would do in the labor field what we have been urging Congress to do by the other method. In other words, H.R. 3 would allow us to function so long as our law was not in conflict with the national labor relations law, and it is not. It would allow us to function until such time as jurisdiction of that particular dispute was assumed by the National Labor Relations Board.

In the most recent leading case on this **question** of preemption by implication, the Garner case, the Court said in its opinion considerable authority had been left to the State by Congress, but that the courts are required to spell out conflicting indications of congressional will in the area in which State action is still permissible.

It seems to me when the Court says that, the Court in effect is legislating. They are determining what the congressional intent was.

*United States Congress, Establishing Rules of Interpretation Governing **Questions** of the Effect of Acts of Congress on State Laws, Part 1*

p. 390–5

Again you were looking for an opposite of the keyword "creative" in the first blank. "Ossified" is the strongest negative word meaning rigid and inflexible. The second blank depends on the key phrase "rigid policies" which best translates to "bureaucratization" which brings to mind red tape and strict rules in fighting his internal strife. Something that is mitigated is lessened and moderated. Jingoism is being overly patriotic. If someone is venerable they are respected and admired.

C

*Henry Davis, Explanations for the Official SAT Study Guide **Questions**: Detailed Explanations for the Answers for Every **Question***

Mr. WALTER. What is the citation of that case?

Mr. GOODING. I do not have the citation of the Garner case but I can get it for you very promptly. It is a very recent, or comparatively recent, case. It arose in Pennsylvania.

It is my opinion that Congress should say exactly what its intent is. If it intends to preempt, fine; then everybody knows it. They say so. Everybody knows it. No State is going to attempt to legislate and no State is going to attempt to regulate; but they are going to rely on the action in Washington to regulate that particular field. Any time that Congress says that is what they want to do I have no objection to it from the standpoint I am now discussing.

In this particular field I do not think it is good, but if Congress thinks it is I am perfectly willing to go along. The thing that I do not like is for the Court to say that Congress intended to preempt the field merely because they passed legislation in that field, and particularly in a field where traditionally jurisdiction has been exercised by the States.

In this particular field up until 1935 there was never any **question**. As a matter of fact, when the Wagner Act was passed the **question** was not whether or not the States had power to legislate in this field, but the only **question** was what if any powers the

Congress had. The bulk of opinion of the lower courts was that Congress had no power in the field of manufacturing, for instance; but since that time the gamut has been run. Now the **question** no longer is what power does Congress have, but the **question** is what if any power is left in the States.

*United States Congress, Establishing Rules of Interpretation Governing **Questions** of the Effect of Acts of Congress on State Laws, Part 1*

p. 762–1

Laws are needed to *guarantee* (assure) equal rights, and Americans have to *lobby* (attempt to influence or sway public officials for a desired action) for legislation. *Preclude* means to prevent which would not fit the first blank. We would not need laws to <u>prevent</u> equal right, so that rules out (B). *Ascertain* means to discover and *enact* means to endorse. Although *enact* might work, *ascertain* doesn't, so you can rule out (C). *Compound* means to intensify, while *contend* means argue or debate. While *contend with* might work in the second blank, *compound* doesn't, so (D) is not a good choice. *Suppress* (E) means to stifle, and you would not want to stifle equal rights, so it's not the right answer either.

A

*Henry Davis, Explanations for the Official SAT Study Guide **Questions**: Detailed Explanations for the Answers for Every **Question***

By the way, the citation has just been handed to me in the Garner case.

Mr. WALTER. I have it.

Mr. GOODING. 346 U.S. 485 (1953).

This morning the chairman raised a **question** as to whether or not the last sentence in the proposed amendment to H.R. 3 did not state the existing law. Now, it stated the existing law as I thought it was many years ago, but I do not think it states the existing law as it is today. I just want to read a colloquy between Justice Frankfurter and Mr. Ratner, who appeared as amicus curiae in one of the cases of ours before the Supreme Court:

> *Mr. Justice FRANKFURTER. This is not a legal **question** I am propounding. I am trying to find out what it is that you are addressing yourself to.*

*United States Congress, Establishing Rules of Interpretation Governing **Questions** of the Effect of Acts of Congress on State Laws, Part 1*

5. One can infer from the text that the teachers at the school:

(A) Were mediocre and cruel, because they adhered **unquestioningly** to a rotten educational model.

(B) Were cruel and severe: they liked to torture the students by overloading them with homework.

(C) Were deadened by sadness, because they got paid shit.

(D) Were cruel and severe, because they were sad. Everyone was sad back then.

(E) My bench mate marked C, so I'm going to mark C as well.

Alejandro Zambra, Reading Comprehension: Text No. 1 (The New Yorker)

And some did in fact offer up their pain as a sacrifice. Jean Julien Boucage, after suffering the first part of the **question**, was warned "that next Monday at the same time, the execution of the sentence of the Court will proceed, and that the continued **question** is more painful than the one he just suffered, which should require him to tell the truth to avoid the torment," to which he responded "that he would suffer everything for the love of God and the holy Virgin."

Lisa Silverman, Tortured Subjects: Pain, Truth, and the Body in Early Modern France

O'Brien smiled again. 'She betrayed you, Winston. Immediately—unreservedly. I have seldom seen anyone come over to us so promptly. You would hardly recognize her if you saw her. All her rebelliousness, her deceit, her folly, her dirty-mindedness—everything has been burned out of her. It was a perfect conversion, a textbook case.'

'You tortured her?'

O'Brien left this unanswered. 'Next **question**,' he said.

George Orwell, Nineteen Eighty-Four

The **question** *extraordinaire* for women was the *brodequins* or *mordaches*. It was described in detail by the Toulousain diarist Pierre Barthès because of the curious circumstances that arose in the torture of Claire Reynaud in 1778. As Barthès noted, no woman had been tortured in the parlement of Toulouse for over thirty-five years, and so it required a certain amount of research to recover the appropriate technique . . .

Lisa Silverman, Tortured Subjects: Pain, Truth, and the Body in Early Modern France

On the **question**, see *the treatises* written by Odofredus, Ambertus de Astramonia, Antonius de Canavio, Baldus de Periglis, Bartolus de Saxoferrato, Jacobus de Arena, Paulus Grillandus Cursius, and *see also* Fontanon, Imbert, Bouchel, the 19th *tit. of the criminal ordinance.*

Antoine-Gaspard Boucher d'Argis, Question or Torture (The Encyclopedia of Diderot & d'Alembert Collaborative Translation Project)

"Does he know how much?"

"Yes. He got it from Vicker."

"Who did Vicker get it from?"

"From Tung, the man who interrogated you."

I grinned at him. "When you **question** somebody for seven hours, it's a debriefing. When they do it, it's an interrogation."

"You're quibbling."

"You want another drink?" I said.

"No."

"Okay, let's see if I've got it straight. The senior senator from Utah—"

"Idaho," Carmingler said.

"I just wanted to make sure you were listening. The senior senator from Idaho, Solomon Simple, will rise on the floor of the Senate a week from Friday and denounce Section Two on a couple of counts. First, that it paid some Oriental despot three million dollars ransom to get three of its bungling agents out of jail and that the Secretary of State compounded the error by writing a letter of apology for the mess that his colleagues down the street were still trying to deny. All that rehash should be good for at least an hour, if he's halfway sober."

"He's quit," Carmingler said.

"Drinking?"

"Yes."

"What was it, his liver?"

"Heart."

"Well, after the first hour, during which he denounces the super-secret Section Two for groveling, with a couple of passing swipes at the State Department, he recounts how this same notorious agent, Lucifer Dye, is now deeply embroiled in the domestic politics of one of the South's fairest cities in blatant defiance of all legal safeguards. I can hear him now."

"Hear him what?" Carmingler said.

"'Where will it all stop, Mr. President? Where will it ever end? How would you like agents of the FBI or the CIA to guide the destiny of your home town? Would you want your City Council to be elected through the machinations of ruthless, devious men who take their orders from a super-secret agency on the banks of the Potomac? Are we entering into a police state, Mr. President?'"

"You don't do imitations very well," Carmingler said.

"The essence is there," I said. "At the same time Simple is making his speech, America's favorite picture magazine will blanket the country with a sixteen-page spread on 'The Men Who Are Corrupting Swankerton.'"

Carmingler almost looked startled. "Have you seen an advance copy?" he demanded.

"I just like to make things up."

"Oh."

"Why don't you get the White House to stop him?"

"They tried, but not too hard. They need his vote on the tax bill."

"What about the magazine?"

"No chance."

"You tried?"

"Yes."

"You're in a bind," I said.

"So are you."

"You could blackmail the senator. Threaten to reveal that slush fund of his."

"I said they need his vote."

"That close, huh?"

"It's that close."

"So you sent your young friend Franz Mugar down to take care of me."

"That was a mistake."

"That's two you've admitted. It must be a record."

"There won't be any more."

"Sorry I can't help."

"You won't then?"

"No."

Ross Thomas, The Fools in Town Are on Our Side

p. 957–23

There is no error in this sentence.

E

p. 957–27

There is no error in this sentence.

E

p. 957–28

The error is in agreement. The sentence is talking about the plural "they," so you need "candidates" to be plural too. "Whether or not they were successful as candidates, women . . ."

A

p. 459–9

This **question** addresses the differences in the passages. The process of elimination is the most effective technique for answering reading passage **questions**. A is wrong because both use data they just interpreted differently. B will not work because neither overstates the problem. C is out as neither recommends a course of action. E won't work because he does not allow a personal prejudice to interfere. Therefore D is the correct answer because they differ in interpreting the concept of empty spaces on Earth and the author of Passage 2 would criticize the focus of Passage 1.

D

p. 824–3

If the two authors put in their book "more information than one can easily digest," you could say that their book had <u>too much</u> detail. A synonym for "too much" would be *surfeit* (C), which means excess. (A) *Modicum* means moderate; (B) *discrepancy* means inconsistency; (D) *deficit* means lack; and (E) *juxtaposition* means combination or concurrence.

C

p. 802–8

Eliminating the words "but they" makes the meaning clear. Technically, there are 3 different nouns that "they" might refer to: "young people," "women," and "colleges." Replacing "but they" with the relative pronoun "that" makes it clear which of the "theys" have become coed.

D

p. 475–2

"Although" indicates a contrast in the two parts of the sentence. Eliminate word choices that are not contrasting pairs, so you can eliminate D and E. The context clue to the second point is "the uneven quality" which best matches answer choice C "inclusive" meaning widely included. It creates a contrast with the statement that the editors were trying to be "selective."

C

p. 824–4

The clues to this **question** are in the words "more" and "less." You are looking for something the new superintendent is <u>more of</u> and will have <u>less of</u> during her term of office. Essentially, you're looking for words that are opposites. (A) won't work because the two words have the same meaning. If the new superintendent is more *phlegmatic* (indifferent) than the last one, then her term of office would not be even <u>less</u> *apathetic* (also means indifferent). (B) works because if the new superintendent is <u>more</u> *conciliatory* (wants to please or pacify others), then it's logical that she would have a <u>less</u>

confrontational (face-to-face conflict) term of office. (C) *empathetic* means to be able to share in another's feelings, while the word *compassionate* means to be able to feel pity or sympathy for another. These words are too similar in meaning. Answer (D) *vigilant* (alert and watchful) and *reputable* (to be well thought of or respected) won't work. A superintendent who is alert would probably be respected, not <u>less</u> respected. (E) *penurious* (stingy or miserly) and *frugal* (thrifty, tight fisted, not wasteful) are also too similar in meaning. If the new superintendent is even stingier than the last one, she would have a term that is thriftier, not *less* thrifty.

B

p. 396–2

Remember one of our most important techniques: when you encounter word problems, GET THE NUMBERS OUT OF THE WORDS. Here we start where we have a value: train B goes 7 mph. Then we work the value though:

A = 3 × B so 3 × 7 = 21
C = 2 × A so 2 × 21 = 42
E

*Henry Davis, Explanations for the Official SAT Study Guide **Questions**: Detailed Explanations for the Answers for Every **Question***

I shake my head. That is not the meaning of the story, but what is the use of arguing? I am like an incompetent schoolmaster, fishing about with my maieutic forceps when I ought to be filling her with the truth.

She speaks. "You are always asking me that **question**, so I will now tell you."

J. M. Coetzee, Waiting for the Barbarians

I wish, first, that I might enlist the interest of those who take the time to read this article in the real importance of composition—and enlist it to the extent that *a little work be done regularly and carefully.* A revolution in this way might soon be brought about. It may be true that nearly all the people whom we meet have had at least a common school education, but it is equally true that not one in twenty-five can write a creditable letter either as to form or construction. It is a lamentable fact that very few high school graduates can do it. As an illustration, there lies upon my desk now a collection of sixty examination papers in English composition from high school graduates from forty-two counties of Illinois. One of the five **questions** was to define and illustrate five figures of speech, another to write a brief business note. Almost without exception the young people were able to answer the first **question**. The longest of the notes written did not exceed one hundred words. Not more than six of them were creditably done, and but one was punctuated with anything like correctness. It may be of advantage to be able to recognize figures of speech; it surely is not less practical to know how to write a business letter. To learn either takes practice, but more about this later.

C.M. Parker (ed.), The School News and Practical Educator, Volume 11

p. 602–22

We need a parallel construction. It is easier *to ride* a bicycle than it is *to explain* how to ride.

B

p. 658–12

The musical tells how tap evolved, not "telling."

A

*Henry Davis, Explanations for the Official SAT Study Guide **Questions**: Detailed Explanations for the Answers for Every **Question***

"It was a fork, a kind of fork with only two teeth. There were little knobs on the teeth to make them blunt. They put it in the coals till it was hot, then they touched you with it, to burn you. I saw the marks where they had burned people."

Is this the **question** I asked? I want to protest but instead listen on, chilled.

"They did not burn me. They said they would burn my eyes out, but they did not. The man brought it very close to my face and made me look at it. They held my eyelids open. But I had nothing to tell them. That was all.

"That was when the damage came. After that I could not see properly any more. There was a blur in the middle of everything I looked at; I could see only around the edges. It is difficult to explain.

"But now it is getting better. The left eye is getting better. That is all."

I take her face between my hands and stare into the dead centres of her eyes from which twin reflections of myself stare solemnly back. "And this?" I say, touching the worm-like scar in the corner.

"That is nothing. That is where the iron touched me. It made a little hum. It is not sore." She pushes my hands away.

"What do you feel towards the men who did this?"

She lies thinking a long time. Then she says, "I am tired of talking."

There are other times when I suffer fits of resentment against my bondage to the ritual of the oiling and rubbing, the drowsiness, the slump into oblivion. I cease to comprehend what pleasure I can ever have found in her obstinate, phlegmatic body, and even discover in myself stirrings of outrage. I become withdrawn, irritable; the girl turns her back and goes to sleep.

J. M. Coetzee, Waiting for the Barbarians

p. 671–15

This looks very difficult, yet, as with many SAT problems, it unravels when you look at it carefully. The time it takes to run the maze (t) is represented on the vertical line. The number of practices (p) is represented on the horizontal line. Look at the relationship. Although it is counter-intuitive this graph shows that the number of practices does not change the time very much. The time stays near 44 throughout. So, $t(p) = 44$

A

p. 588–9

Because of the word "unlike" we are looking for something that Passage 1 does that Passage 2 does not. Passage 2 does not quote an authority.

E

p. 784–22

The author specifically says in lines 63–64 that "reading their work aloud makes the students more conscious of flaws in their prose." The student quotations illustrate this point.

D

p. 476–6

The first sentence has a single phrase "a movement is a continuous . . . effort to bring about . . . reform." This pretty clearly serves as a definition of the term "movement"

D

p. 531–1

The sentence as given has no appropriate antecedent for the program "it." Answer choice B provides a sentence that makes it clear that he was able to make a living as "an illustrator and painter." Answer C repeats the pronoun error. Answer D has indefinite pronoun "them". Answer E has a dangling phrase "By illustrating and paying" and is passive.

B

Henry Davis, Explanations for the Official SAT Study Guide **Questions**: *Detailed Explanations for the Answers for Every* **Question**

There are deaths we unconsciously prepare for, depending on our choice of trades. An undertaker contemplates his funerals, the rich man his destitution, the gaoler his imprisonment, the debauchee his impotence. An actor's greatest terror, I am told, is to watch the theatre empty itself while he wrestles in a void for his lines, and what else is that but a premature vision of his dying? For the civil servant, it is the moment when his protective walls of privilege collapse around him and he finds himself no safer than the next man, exposed to the gaze of the overt world, answering like a lying husband for his laxities and evasions. And most of my intelligence colleagues, if I am honest, came into this category: their greatest fear was to wake up one morning to read their real names en clair in the newspapers; to hear themselves spoken of on the radio and television, joked and laughed about and, worse yet, **questioned** by the public they believed they served. They would have regarded such public scrutiny as a greater disaster than being outwitted by the opposition, or, blown to every kindred service round the globe. It would have been their death.

And for myself, the worst death, and therefore the greatest test, the one for which I had prepared myself ever since I passed through the secret door, was the one that was upon me now: to have my uncertain courage tested on the rack; to be reduced mentally and physically to my last component of endurance, knowing I had within me the power to stop the dying with a word—that what was going on inside me was mortal combat between my spirit and my body, and that those who were applying the pain were merely the hired mercenaries in this secret war within myself. So that from the first blinding explosion of pain, my response was recognition: Hullo, I thought, you've come at last—my name is Joost, what's yours?

John le Carré, The Secret Pilgrim

p. 602–21

The report was prepared jointly by "him" and the committee, not he. If we omit the other party in the sentence (the committee) the rule of thumb is to use a pronoun that still sounds right and fulfills grammatical rules. The report was prepared by him. Now just add committee.

B

Henry Davis, Explanations for the Official SAT Study Guide **Questions**: *Detailed Explanations for the Answers for Every* **Question**

*Madame de Brinvilliers (Marie Madeleine d'Aubray, 1630–1676) in the **Question** Chamber*
Engraving, French School, 19th century (Bridgeman Images)

Please note: images depicting historical events may contain themes, or have descriptions,
that do not reflect current understanding. They are provided in a historical context.

The word "wife" seemed to serve as a gloomy reminder to Defarge, to say with sudden impatience, "In the name of that sharp female newly-born, and called La Guillotine, why did you come to France?"

"You heard me say why, a minute ago. Do you not believe it is the truth?"

"A bad truth for you," said Defarge, speaking with knitted brows, and looking straight before him.

"Indeed I am lost here. All here is so unprecedented, so changed, so sudden and unfair, that I am absolutely lost. Will you render me a little help?"

"None." Defarge spoke, always looking straight before him.

"Will you answer me a single **question**?"

"Perhaps. According to its nature. You can say what it is."

Charles Dickens, A Tale of Two Cities

Take the **questions** stumping Europeans in the Obama years (which 1.6 million Americans residing in Europe regularly find thrown our way). At the absolute top of the list: "Why would anyone oppose national health care?" European and other industrialized countries have had some form of national health care since the 1930s or 1940s, Germany since 1880. Some versions, as in France and Great Britain, have devolved into two-tier public and private systems. Yet even the privileged who pay for a faster track would not begrudge their fellow citizens government-funded comprehensive health care. That so many Americans do strikes Europeans as baffling, if not frankly brutal.

Ann Jones, Has America Gone Crazy? *(Salon)*

'Mr Quayle. Do you hear me?'

The same voice but now in English. Justin didn't answer. But this was not a lack of civility, it was because he had managed to spew out his cloth gag at last and was vomiting again and the vomit was creeping round his neck inside the hood. The sound of the television set faded.

'That's enough, Mr Quayle. You stop now, OK? Or you get what your wife got. You hear me? You want some more punishment, Mr Quayle?'

With the second Quayle came another horrendous kick in the groin.

'Maybe you gone deaf a bit. We leave you a little note, OK? On your bed. When you wake up, you read this little note and you remember. Then you go back to England, hear me? You don't ask no more bad **questions**. You go home, you be a good boy. Next time we kill you like Bluhm. That's a very long process. You hear me?'

Another kick to the groin rammed the lesson home.

John le Carré, The Constant Gardener

No contemporary rationale exists for these gender-specific tortures, which in fact varied from *parlement* to *parlement*. Although only men received the ***question** d'eau* and only women received the ***question** des mordaches* in the jurisdiction of the *parlement* of Toulouse, Urbain Grandier suffered the ***question** des mordaches* in 1634, and the marquise de Brinvilliers, the ***question** d'eau* in 1676, both given in the jurisdiction of the *parlement* of Paris. Psychoanalytic readings of these gender-specific tortures, which within the Toulousain context would suggest a carnivalesque kind of reversal of sex roles, therefore seem inadequate when seen within the national context. Nor do interpretations which suggest that these tortures sought to preserve feminine modesty seem entirely convincing, in view of the fact that both men and women were made to strip before both male officials and their female companions. If, however, we choose to understand male and female bodies as inversions of each other, then these tortures, too, can be read as inversions of the same physical operation. This is the thesis/model proposed by Thomas Laquear, who argues that until the eighteenth century, male and female bodies were understood to exist along a physical continuum, each being the literal inversion of the other. If the one-sex body was the model of the human body supported by jurists, then it is possible that the **question** *d'eau* and the **question** *des mordaches* were seen as the same practice turned inside out, to be employed interchangeably on the one-sex body, itself turned inside out.

> Lisa Silverman, *Tortured Subjects: Pain, Truth, and the Body in Early Modern France*

p. 416–9

Don't over complicate the **question**. Even though the two terms are under the Square root sign, we want to solve for 2p = 18.

2p = 18 so p = 9

9

> Henry Davis, *Explanations for the Official SAT Study Guide* **Questions**: *Detailed Explanations for the Answers for Every* **Question**

There was no ceremony, you see. He didn't sit me at a desk in the tried tradition of the screen and say, "Either talk to me or you'll be beaten. Here is your confession. Sign it." He didn't have them lock me in a cell and leave me to cook for a few days while I decided that confession was the better part of courage. They simply dragged me out of the car and through the gateway of what could have been a private house, then into a courtyard where the only footprints were our own, so that they had to topple me through the thick snow, slewing me on my heels, all three of them, punching me from one to the other, now in the face, now in the groin and stomach, now back to the face again, this time with an elbow or a knee. Then, while I was still double, kicking me like a half-stunned pig across the slithery cobble as if they couldn't wait to get indoors before they had me.

Then, once indoors, they became more systematic, as if the elegance of the old bare room had instilled in them a sense of order. They took me in turns, like civilised men, two of them holding me and one hitting me, a proper democratic rota, except that when it was Colonel Jerzy's fifth or fiftieth turn, he hit me so regretfully and so hard that I actually did die for a while, and when I came round I was alone with him. He was seated at a folding desk, with his elbows on it, holding his unhappy head between his grazed hands as if he had a hangover, and reviewing with disappointment the answers I had given to the **questions** he had put to me between onslaughts, first lifting his head in order to study with disapproval my altered appearance, then shaking it painfully and sighing as if to say life really wasn't fair to him, he didn't know what more he could do to me to help me see the light. It dawned on me that more time had passed than I realised, perhaps several hours.

This was also the moment when the scene began to take on a resemblance to the one I had always imagined, with my tormentor sitting comfortably at a desk, brooding over me with a professional's concern, and myself spread-eagled against a scalding waterpipe, my arms handcuffed either side of a black concertina-style radiator, with corners that bit into the base of my spine like red-hot teeth. I had been bleeding from the mouth and nose and, I thought, from one ear as well, and my shirt front looked like a slaughterer's apron. But the blood had dried and I wasn't bleeding any more, which was another way of calculating the passage of time. How long does blood take to congeal in a big empty house in Gdansk when you are chained to a furnace and looking into the puppyish face of Colonel Jerzy?

John le Carré, The Secret Pilgrim

p. 667–2

Work the problem through and solve it like any algebraic equation. First we subtract 8 from both sides, giving us: $\sqrt{k} = 7$ and $k = 7^2 = 49$

B

p. 710–19

The author says that "human gestures assume ... an almost mystic power." Nonverbal gestures are extremely powerful, and he gives the example that a maneuver as simple as turning the face away can shift "the particular personality to the general and the symbolic." In other words, gestures are often universally understood messages.

D

p. 580–23

"Tone" is defined as "a manner of speaking or writing that shows a certain attitude on the part of the speaker or writer". In order for the tone to be one of *personal regret* (C) the writers would have had to have lived during the time period being discussed and written the passages in the first person. In order for the tone to be *righteous indignation* (D) the writers would have given their personal moral judgment about the time period in which they were writing about. If the tone had been *open hostility* (E) then the writers would have conveyed their feelings of antagonism about the time period in which they were writing about. An *affectionate nostalgic tone* (A) would mean the writers would have expressed their tender longing for what they perceived as a happier or better time period. The best answer is B, *analytical detachment*, because both passages were written in an objective, logical, truthful, non-judgmental, and unemotional tone.

B

p. 646–12

If you go back and read lines 13–15, it is clear that the author believes that time travel is a fascinating topic. He says the "possibilities are staggering." He believes that if man could travel backwards in time, he could take medicine back to those who were inflicted with the plague and thereby save them, and he could travel into the future and enjoy a vacation on a space station.

E

*Henry Davis, Explanations for the Official SAT Study Guide **Questions**: Detailed Explanations for the Answers for Every **Question***

Other *parlements* had different customary procedures: in Rennes, the **question** was given by drawing the feet of the accused toward a fire; in Rouen, by a sort of thumbscrew; in Autun, by pouring boiling oil on the legs of the accused. Most *parlements*, however, employed the **question** *d'eau* and the *brodequin*.

These, then, were the tortures endured by Jean Hourdil: the **question** *ordinaire* in the form of the *estrapade* three times on 25 May and once again on 27 May, followed by the **question** *extraordinaire* in the form of the **question** *d'eau* five times . . .

> Lisa Silverman, *Tortured Subjects: Pain, Truth, and the Body in Early Modern France*

"It's only routine, Cyril," I said. "My goodness, you must know the **questions** by heart after all these years. Mind if I smoke?" I laboriously lit my pipe and dropped the match into the ashtray he was pressing on me.

> John le Carré, *The Secret Pilgrim*

p. 602–25

Pianists are preoccupied **with** technique, not **on** technique.

A

p. 452–2

This is a ratio or proportion problem, depending upon how you decide to look at it. Regardless, it's easy to set up. If in 1 hour 24 cartons are filled then we can determine how many are filled in 5 minutes can be determined by finding what fraction of an hour 5 minutes are. So:

5/60 = x/24

1/12 = x/24 and we crossmultiply:

24 = 12x

2 = x

A

p. 647–14

We are looking for the one item that the author did NOT address when he discussed causality violations in ll. 16–35. The author does not mention the mechanics of space travel. Answer A is addressed (18–21); answer B in (32–35); answer D in (21–22); and answer E in lines 28–32.

C

p. 593–1

First, replace the symbol with an "x" so it is more familiar. Then convert the mixed expression 7½ to a fraction and solve for *x*.

$$\frac{3 + x}{2} = \frac{15}{2}$$

3 + *x* = 15

x = 12

D

p. 784–23

The author refers to the students' "pleas" (*requests or excuses*) at the end of their readings as possibly being "staged" (*planned*) to suggest that there might be an opportunistic motive behind her students' behavior. She considers the possibility that they see it as a chance to plead with her to go easy on them, in hopes of getting a better grade.

C

p. 671–16

The key to this problem is seeing the relationship between L and W. 3W = 2L

You can use the 2L side of the pattern to get either 10L or 12L, so how can you use the 3W = 2L relationship?

Using the pattern repeatedly the length would be: WL – WL – WL – WL – WL – WL

This gives you 6Ls and 6Ws. Remember that 3W = 2L, so the 6W = 4L, and this gives you: 6L + 4L = 10L

You can then use the 2L pattern 6 times to get the 12L length.

So, 6 patterns for the width and 6 for the length. 6 × 6 = 36 patterns and there are 5 rectangles in each pattern.

5 × 36 = 180 rectangles

E

Henry Davis, Explanations for the Official SAT Study Guide **Questions**: *Detailed Explanations for the Answers for Every* **Question**

The **questions** put to him during the physical infliction of his torture continued in this ritualized and repetitive way. Again and again, he was asked nothing more than to confess his guilt in the matter of these murders. Yet throughout his interrogations, Jean Bourdil insisted on his innocence, never once confessing to the kind of specific knowledge of the crimes that only the perpetrator could know. Finally, he was removed from the instruments of his torture.

Lisa Silverman, Tortured Subjects: Pain, Truth, and the Body in Early Modern France

Socrates Seated on a Bench
Roman fresco painting, Ephesus, Turkey. 1st cent. CE

*Heinrich Hall, Another Thing: A Cultural Hero—Socrates
on a Fresco In Ephesus (petersommer.com)*

My Question, Then, Was, Whether

And I received more than one letter about it

There are many styles of **question** oriented dialogue that claim the name Socratic method. However, just asking a lot of **questions** does not automatically constitute a use of the Socratic method. Even in the dialogues of Plato, which are the most significant and detailed historical references to Socrates, there is not just one Socratic method. The exact style and methodology of the Platonic Socrates changes significantly throughout the dialogues. If there is a 'classic' Socratic method, this designation must refer to the style of the Socratic method found primarily in the early dialogues (also called the 'Socratic Dialogues') and some other dialogues of Plato. In these dialogues, Socrates claims to have no knowledge of even the most fundamental principles, such as justice, holiness, friendship or virtue. In the Socratic dialogues, Socrates only wants short answers that address very specific points and refuses to move on to more advanced or complicated topics until an adequate understanding of basic principles is achieved. This means that the conversation is often stuck in the attempt to answer what appears to be an unanswerable basic **question**.

> Max Maxwell, *Introduction to the Socratic Method and Its Effect on Critical Thinking*

A reader writes:

> *I'm a fairly new manager (two years) of a small team and recently received some feedback from an employee that I don't know what to do about. A previous employee had also given me the same feedback so I'm starting to see a pattern.*
>
> *When team members come to me with **questions**, I tend not to give the answer right away, but ask them **questions** back to stimulate their thinking. Most often they do know the answers but are just not making the connections or fully analyzing the situation. Sometimes they are quite far off and we end up spending 15–30 minutes fleshing it out. I thought I was "coaching" and helping to improve their critical thinking skills, but they don't see it this way.*
>
> *I have overheard grumblings about my "Socratic" method and would I just tell them the darn answer already so they can get back to their work! Our workloads are high and we are quite busy, so I can empathize there. They also find it stressful because they are having to think on their feet and remember facts and details. Plus, they are uncomfortable with me knowing what they don't know, or being wrong in front of me. That was some feedback I received directly.*

> Alison Green, *My Staff Doesn't Like It That I Use the Socratic Method With Them (Ask a Manager)*

If you are not comfortable with being **questioned**, please do not use the Socratic method. You are not ready. Not only will your lack of comfort transmit to the students (even if you are the **questioner**), you will not be up to par on living true Socratic Irony (See the essay, "The Socratic Temperament").

> Max Maxwell, *Introduction to the Socratic Method and Its Effect on Critical Thinking*

There are two basic kinds of irony: stable irony (irony as stimulus) and unstable irony (irony as terminus). Unstable irony, which deals in infinite negation, seeks to point out the fundamental incongruities of life. It calls into **question** values, mores, social norms, and knowledge, a process that shakes the very foundations upon which we structure our lives and existences.

Stable irony stimulates thinking, which serves to aid in the recognition of a true meaning that lurks behind the surface; it allows for positive solutions. Stable irony is especially suited to making ideological points because it assumes a shared value system between the ironist and the perceiver. Moreover, through the four-part process of ironic dissembling—1) rejection of a literal meaning, 2) substitution of possible alternative meanings, 3) decision about author's values and, 4) decision upon new, true meanings—perceivers are more apt to agree with the author's points because, in a very real way, they are forced to engage in a rational process and arrive at an understanding on their own.

Matthew J. McAllister, A Spectacle Worth Attending To: The Ironic Use of Preexisting Art Music in Film (The Florida State University College of Music)

You know that we're not running the correct out-of-bounds play, right? That our defensive press is a mess? That we're close to another loss?

Coach Marc Skelton leaned in close, his eyes inches from those of his teenage players, his **questions** pregnant with expletives. He had paced, implored, tossed his arms in the air, yelled and, for punctuation, whacked his clipboard like a zydeco musician with a washboard. Combustion seemed a real and present danger.

Michael Powell, A Long Hardwood Journey: A Coach's Tough, Cerebral Style Guided a Bronx High School Team Through Pain and Triumph as It Pursued a City Basketball Title (New York Times)

What you don't want to do is to act like a professor rather than a manager. That's not your job, it's not what people signed up for, and it's not the most effective way of managing people.

That doesn't mean that you shouldn't coach—you absolutely *should* coach. But coaching people effectively means (a) adapting your approach to fit what works best for each individual person, and (b) recognizing that there's a time and a place for coaching, and that other times you just need to give someone the damn answer already.

So, **questions** back to you: Are you doing this reflexively whenever someone brings you a **question**? Or are you thoughtfully picking the times when you think it will help build their skills rather than doing it across the board? Also, are you truly building their skills when you do this—is the result that they're learning something that they're carrying forward into their work in the future? Or is there a method of training them that might work better, even if only because it wouldn't come with the side of "agh, I just need a quick answer to this"?

Also, it's really important for you to tell them what you're doing and why.

Alison Green, My Staff Doesn't Like It That I Use the Socratic Method With Them (Ask a Manager)

Phone rang & it was Mom. Asked how I was & I said. Asked about my classes at Dale Tech & I said. Asked about my sinuses & I said. Asked about the caretaker's job (which was Dad's idea for Q_ P_, not Mom's) & I said.

Has it been six months since my dental check-up Mom asked & I said I didn't know & Mom said she was afraid it was more than six months possibly a year? & did I remember all the dental work I'd had to have done ten years ago when I'd neglected to have my teeth examined regularly & cleaned & I said & Mom said should she make an appointment for me? with Dr. Fish?

Joyce Carol Oates, Zombie

A. Certainly not.

Q. There is no **question** about that in your mind?

A. No, sir.

United States Senate, Reports of Committees for the First Session of the Fifty-First Congress, 1889–90, Volume 10, No. 1530, Parts 1 and 2, Relations With Canada

There is no kind of literature in English which corresponds to the Greek Dialogue; nor is the English [xxiv] language easily adapted to it. The rapidity and abruptness of **question** and answer, the constant repetition of ἦ δ’ ὅς, εἶπε, ἔφη, &c., which Cicero avoided in Latin (de Amicit. c. 1), the frequent occurrence of expletives, would, if reproduced in a translation, give offence to the reader. Greek has a freer and more frequent use of the Interrogative, and is of a more passionate and emotional character, and therefore lends itself with greater readiness to the dialogue form. Most of the so–called English Dialogues are but poor imitations of Plato, which fall very far short of the original. The breath of conversation, the subtle adjustment of **question** and answer, the lively play of fancy, the power of drawing characters, are wanting in them. But the Platonic dialogue is a drama as well as a dialogue, of which Socrates is the central figure, and there are lesser performers as well:—the insolence of Thrasymachus, the anger of Callicles and Anytus, the patronizing style of Protagoras, the self–consciousness of Prodicus and Hippias, are all part of the entertainment. To reproduce this living image the same sort of effort is required as in translating poetry. The language, too, is of a finer quality; the mere prose English is slow in lending itself to the form of **question** and answer, and so the ease of conversation is lost, and at the same time the dialectical precision with which the steps of the argument are drawn out is apt to be impaired.

B. Jowett, Preface to the Second and Third Editions (The Dialogues of Plato, in Five Volumes)

A more-or-less faithful adaptation of the King novel, the film is a metaphor for the struggle that artists endure to create authentic and personally fulfilling art. In the words of director Rob Reiner, "the **question** is: what price do you pay in order to change your way in creating art? How much pain do you have to go through in order to go away from what has been successful for you and forge a new path?"[208] If the novel and corresponding film are any indication, the answer to this **question** is: a great deal.

Matthew J. McAllister, A Spectacle Worth Attending To: The Ironic Use of Preexisting Art Music in Film (The Florida State University College of Music)

Q. Do you believe that the consumer would gain in the least by lowering the prices?

A. No, sir; I do not.

Q. The only one to gain would be the fish dealers?

A. The fish dealers, and they not for a great while. As soon as Canada got the monopoly the Canadians would put up the prices; there is no **question** about that.

United States Senate, Reports of Committees for the First Session of the Fifty-First Congress, 1889–90, Volume 10, No. 1530, Parts 1 and 2, Relations With Canada

New section:

nunc iam ilia non vult: tu quoque,

    impotens can't fuck any

boyfriends these days, bad
    mood no wonder I'm acting
    badly, noli NO
nec quae fugit sectare, nec miser
    vive
good advice sed obstinata mente
    perfer, obdura.
vale, puella. (My awful telephone
    call. This's my apology, Peter.
    Do you accept?) *iam* (ha ha)
    Catalius obdurat
nec te requiret nec rogabit
    invitam:
        I'm a good girl
I have, behave perfectly,
at tu dolebis. The imaginary
    makes reality, as in love, cum
    rogaberis nulla
scelesta. Scelesta nocte. My
    night, quae tibi manet vita
    without me?
quis nunc adibit? without me cui
    videberis bella?
quem nunc amabis? with me you
    fuck whoever you want.
Let the imagination reign
    supreme, quem you now
    fucking? cuius esse diceris
    huh!
quem basiabis a stupid **question**?
    cui labella labula mordebis?
    (allied to death?)
at tu, Catullus, destinatus obdura
By repeating the past, I'm
molding and transforming
it, an impossible act.

    Kathy Acker, Don Quixote, Which Was a Dream

VLADIMIR: Let us not waste our time in idle discourse! (*Pause. Vehemently.*) Let us do
something, while we have the chance! It is not every day that we are needed. Not
indeed that we personally are needed. Others would meet the case equally well, if
not better. To all mankind they were addressed, those cries for help still ringing
in our ears! But at this place, at this moment of time, all mankind is us, whether
we like it or not. Let us make the most of it, before it is too late! Let us represent
worthily for once the foul brood to which a cruel fate consigned us! What do you
say? (*ESTRAGON says nothing.*) It is true that when with folded arms we weigh the

pros and cons we are no less a credit to our species. The tiger bounds to the help of his congeners without the least reflection, or else he slinks away into the depths of the thickets. But that is not the **question**. What are we doing here, that is the **question**. And we are blessed in this, that we happen to know the answer. Yes, in this immense confusion one thing alone is clear. We are waiting for Godot to come—

ESTRAGON: Ah!

POZZO: Help!

VLADIMIR: Or for night to fall. (*Pause.*) We have kept our appointment and that's an end to that. We are not saints, but we have kept our appointment. How many people can boast as much?

ESTRAGON: Billions.

VLADIMIR: You think so?

ESTRAGON: I don't know.

VLADIMIR: You may be right.

POZZO: Help!

VLADIMIR: All I know is that the hours are long, under these conditions, and constrain us to beguile them with proceedings which—how shall I say—which may at first sight seem reasonable, until they become a habit. You may say it is to prevent our reason from foundering. No doubt. But has it not long been straying in the night without end of the abyssal depths? That's what I sometimes wonder. You follow my reasoning?

Samuel Beckett, *Waiting for Godot*

I was requested in the spring of 1888 to answer a **question** of Senator Wm. E. Chandler's, which was whether I believed that we should admit Canadian salt fish free of duty as a condition for them giving our fishing vessels ordinary commercial rights. I never heard that Senator Chandler was a wag, but certainly that **question** would almost imply it, that we should have ordinary commercial rights. In reply I said :

> The simple **question** can be answered in a very few words. This country should never give or admit anything as a condition of receiving commercial rights in the Canadian ports or anywhere else. We have rights, without doubt, and they are ours without trade or dicker.

> If it is intended to ask if we should lose, or the fishing interest suffer, by the admission of Canadian salt-fish free of duty, I should positively say that such admission would be *ruin* to the fishing interest of New England and the Lakes.

And that I believe.

By Senator HALE:

Q. Free fish?

A. Yes, sir. I think we have had examples enough. Take Cape Cod to-day, from Boston Harbor around, and I do not know a port hardly that shows anything alive in the fishing interests, and I believe the principal cause is free fish. I do not think there can be any doubt about it. In this letter I say there can be no doubt about this, and then I refer to the different Congressional committees that have investigated the subject. One gentleman who has testified to-day was talking with me some time ago, and I asked him if he did not believe that free trade in fish would ruin the fishing business of New England. He said, "Certainly it would in a short time;" and that is the opinion of a gentleman who stood here this afternoon.

United States Senate, Reports of Committees for the First Session of the Fifty-First Congress, 1889–90, Volume 10, No. 1530, Parts 1 and 2, Relations With Canada

The girls like games, especially name games. In one, they have to guess the identity of a person they know:

EMILY: Here's a good **question** for you to ask—would this person take tranquilizers or pep-ups?
MARSHA: No, that's not allowed—you have to ask what kind of tranquilizer he would be. What kind?
EMILY: Bufferin.
MARSHA: If this person were an object like to make love on, what would it be?
EMILY: Very good **question**—okay, gynecologist's table.
MARSHA: I hate this person.

In another game, they choose, rapid-fire, whom they would rather sleep with: Jack Ruby or Lee Oswald? Hoagy Carmichael or Stokely Carmichael? Jonas Mekas or Gregory Markopoulos? Jules or Jim? "The first night is the only time I do care about them," Marsha says of her conquests, "because it's a new name on my list."

Linda Rosenkrantz, Talk

From deep in his inner world, he hears Lesley asking him the same **question** in reverse. 'Does the name Lorbeer mean anything to you, Justin?'

If in doubt, lie, he has sworn to himself. If in hell, lie. If I trust nobody—not even myself—if I am to be loyal only to the dead, lie.

'I fear not,' he replies.

'Not overheard anywhere—on the phone? Bits of chit-chat between Arnold and Tessa? Lorbeer, German, Dutch—Swiss perhaps?'

'Lorbeer is not a name to me in any context.'

'Kovacs—Hungarian woman? Dark hair, said to be a beauty?'

'Does she have a first name?' He means no again, but this time it's the truth.

John le Carré, The Constant Gardener

It is the negative then, to which I defign, particularly, to confine myfelf on both thefe **queftions**. In making which attempt, I fhall think myfelf obliged to examine the merits of each, fo far as I may be capable of it, both on the principles of natural reafon and the dictates of divine revelation:

*Sayer Rudd, The Negative on That **Queftion**: Whether Is the Archangel Michael Our Saviour? Examined and Defended. An Argument Defigned to Prove the Real Humanity of Chrift. To Which Are Annex'd the Doctrine of Thofe Appearances Under the Old Teftament, Which Are Generally Term'd Angelical: Together With A Full Interpretation of Such Narratives as Are Particularly Refer'd to by the Author of the Effay on Spirit, in a Letter to the Right Reverend the Lord Bifhop of Chloger*

There be also other Names, called Negative; which are notes to signifie that a word is not the name of the thing in **question**; as these words Nothing, No Man, Infinite, Indocible, Three Want Foure, and the like; which are nevertheless of use in reckoning, or in correcting of reckoning; and call to mind our past cogitations, though they be not names of any thing; because they make us refuse to admit of Names not rightly used.

Thomas Hobbes, Leviathan

Chapter V. A dialogue between Mr Jones and the barber.

This conversation passed partly while Jones was at dinner in his dungeon, and partly while he was expecting the barber in the parlour. And, as soon as it was ended, Mr Benjamin, as we have said, attended him, and was very kindly desired to sit down. Jones then filling out a glass of wine, drank his health by the appellation of *doctissime tonsorum*. *"Ago tibi gratias, domine"* said the barber; and then looking very steadfastly at Jones, he said, with great gravity, and with a seeming surprize, as if he had recollected a face he had seen before, "Sir, may I crave the favour to know if your name is not Jones?" To which the other answered, "That it was."—*"Proh deum atque hominum fidem!"* says the barber; "how strangely things come to pass! Mr Jones, I am your most obedient servant. I find you do not know me, which indeed is no wonder, since you never saw me but once, and then you was very young. Pray, sir, how doth the good Squire Allworthy? how doth *ille optimus omnium patronus?"*—"I find," said Jones, "you do indeed know me; but I have not the like happiness of recollecting you."—"I do not wonder at that," cries Benjamin; "but I am surprized I did not know you sooner, for you are not in the least altered. And pray, sir, may I, without offence, enquire whither you are travelling this way?"—"Fill the glass, Mr Barber," said Jones, "and ask no more **questions**."—"Nay, sir," answered Benjamin, "I would not be troublesome; and I hope you don't think me a man of an impertinent curiosity, for that is a vice which nobody can lay to my charge; but I ask pardon; for when a gentleman of your figure travels without his servants, we may suppose him to be, as we say, *in casu incognito,* and perhaps I ought not to have mentioned your name."—"I own," says Jones, "I did not expect to have been so well known in this country as I find I am; yet, for particular reasons, I shall be obliged to you if you will not mention my name to any other person till I am gone from hence."— *"Pauca verba,"* answered the barber;" and I wish no other here knew you but myself; for some people have tongues; but I promise you I can keep a secret. My enemies will allow me that virtue."—"And yet that is not the characteristic of your profession, Mr Barber," answered Jones. "Alas! sir," replied Benjamin, *"Non si male nunc et olim sic erit.* I was not born nor bred a barber, I assure you. I have spent most of my time among gentlemen, and though I say it, I understand something of gentility. And if you had thought me as worthy of your confidence as you have some other people, I should have shown you I could have kept a secret better. I should not have degraded your name in a public kitchen; for indeed, sir, some people have not used you well; for besides making a public proclamation of what you told them of a quarrel between yourself and Squire Allworthy, they added lies of their own, things which I knew to be lies."—"You surprize me greatly," cries Jones. "Upon my word, sir," answered Benjamin, "I tell the truth, and I need not tell you my landlady was the person. I am sure it moved me to hear the story, and I hope it is all false; for I have a great respect for you, I do assure you I have, and have had ever since the good-nature you showed to Black George, which was talked of all over the country, and I received more than one letter about it. Indeed, it made you beloved by everybody. You will pardon me, therefore; for it was real concern at what I heard made me ask many **questions**; for I have no impertinent curiosity about me: but I love good-nature and thence became *amoris abundantia erga te."*

Every profession of friendship easily gains credit with the miserable; it is no wonder therefore, if Jones, who, besides his being miserable, was extremely open-hearted, very readily believed all the professions of Benjamin, and received him into his bosom. The scraps of Latin, some of which Benjamin applied properly enough, though it did not savour of profound literature, seemed yet to indicate something superior to a common barber; and so indeed did his whole behaviour.

Henry Fielding, *The History of Tom Jones, a Foundling*

There were also a lot of people asking impertinent, tomfool **questions** whom everybody avoided like the plague. What shocked Jacques and his Master most the whole time they walked around . . .

So they walked around?

That's all anybody did, except when they were sitting or in bed. What shocked Jacques and his Master most was to discover that a score of rogues had taken over the best rooms where they stayed all the time, on top of each other. They claimed, against both common law and the true sense of the inscription, that the castle had been bequeathed exclusively to them as their property. With the backing of a handful of fat-arses in their pay, they had imposed this view on a large number of other fat-arses who were also in their pay, that is, who were ready for a small sum to hang or murder anyone who dared contradict them. Even so, at the time Jacques and his Master were there, some were still bold enough to do just that.

Were they punished for it?

Depends on what you mean.

Denis Diderot, *Jacques the Fatalist and His Master*

If the Discourse be meerly Mentall, it consisteth of thoughts that the thing will be, and will not be; or that it has been, and has not been, alternately. So that wheresoever you break off the chayn of a mans Discourse, you leave him in a Praesumption of It Will Be, or, It Will Not Be; or it Has Been, or, Has Not Been. All which is Opinion. And that which is alternate Appetite, in Deliberating concerning Good and Evil, the same is alternate Opinion in the Enquiry of the truth of Past, and Future. And as the last Appetite in Deliberation is called the Will, so the last Opinion in search of the truth of Past, and Future, is called the JUDGEMENT, or Resolute and Final Sentence of him that Discourseth. And as the whole chain of Appetites alternate, in the **question** of Good or Bad is called Deliberation; so the whole chain of Opinions alternate, in the **question** of True, or False is called DOUBT.

No Discourse whatsoever, can End in absolute knowledge of Fact, past, or to come. For, as for the knowledge of Fact, it is originally, Sense; and ever after, Memory. And for the knowledge of consequence, which I have said before is called Science, it is not Absolute, but Conditionall. No man can know by Discourse, that this, or that, is, has been, or will be; which is to know absolutely: but onely, that if This be, That is; if This has been, That has been; if This shall be, That shall be: which is to know conditionally; and that not the consequence of one thing to another; but of one name of a thing, to another name of the same thing.

Thomas Hobbes, *Leviathan*

"I wouldn't go so far as to say that. Doc Dineen thinks it was a man he knew—fellow by the name of John Brown. It fits in with the location of the body, all right. But we haven't been able to nail it down. The trouble is, no such man was ever reported missing in these parts. We haven't been able to turn up any local antecedents. Naturally we're still working on it."

Mungan's broad face was serious. He talked like a trained cop, and his eyes were sharp as tacks. I said: "We may be able to help each other to clarify the issue."

"Any help you can give me will be welcome. This has been dragging on for five months now, more like six." He threw out a quick hooked **question**: "You represent his family, maybe?"

"I represent a family. They asked me not to use their name. And there's still a **question** whether they are the dead man's family. Was there any physical evidence found with the bones? A watch, or a ring? Shoes? Clothing?"

"Nothing. Not even a stitch of clothing."

Ross Macdonald, The Galton Case

Outside, the situation was no calmer and there was no sign of Siobhan. Rebus guessed she'd retreated to the cafeteria, but instead of looking for her, he headed upstairs, glancing in on a couple of rooms before finding Evil Bob, who was being interviewed by a shirtsleeved DS named George Silvers. Around St. Leonard's, Silvers was known as "Hi-Ho." He was a time-server, awaiting the oncoming pension with all the anticipation of a hitchhiker at a truck stop. He didn't so much as nod when Rebus entered the room. There were a dozen **questions** on his list, and he wanted them asked and answered so that the specimen in front of him could be deposited back on the street. Bob watched as Rebus pulled a chair between the two men and sat down, his right knee only inches from Bob's left. Bob squirmed.

"I've just been in with Peacock," Rebus said, ignoring that he was interrupting one of Silvers's **questions**. "He should change his name to canary."

Bob stared at him dully. "Why's that, then?"

"Why do you think?"

"Dunno."

"What do canaries do?"

"Fly around . . . live in trees."

"They live in your grannie's fucking birdcage, you moron. And they sing."

Bob thought about this; Rebus could almost hear the cogs grinding. With a lot of lowlifes, it was an act. Many of them were clever enough, wise not just in the ways of the street. But either Bob was Robert De Niro in full method mode, or else he was no actor at all.

"What sort of stuff?" he asked. Then he saw Rebus's look. "I mean, what sort of stuff do they sing?"

Not De Niro, then . . .

*Ian Rankin, A **Question** of Blood*

The following are the arts to be studied, together with the Kama Sutra:—

1.   Singing.
2.   Playing on musical instruments.
3.   Dancing.
4.   Union of dancing, singing, and playing instrumental music.
5.   Writing and drawing.
6.   Tattooing.

7. Arraying and adorning an idol with rice and flowers.

8. Spreading and arraying beds or couches of flowers, or flowers upon the ground.

9. Colouring the teeth, garments, hair, nails, and bodies, *i.e.*, staining, dyeing, colouring and painting the same.

10. Fixing stained glass into a floor.

11. The art of making beds, and spreading out carpets and cushions for reclining.

12. Playing on musical glasses filled with water.

13. Storing and accumulating water in aqueducts, cisterns and reservoirs.

14. Picture making, trimming and decorating.

15. Stringing of rosaries, necklaces, garlands and wreaths.

16. Binding of turbans and chaplets, and making crests and top-knots of flowers.

17. Scenic representations. Stage playing.

18. Art of making ear ornaments.

19. Art of preparing perfumes and odours.

20. Proper disposition of jewels and decorations, and adornment in dress.

21. Magic or sorcery.

22. Quickness of hand or manual skill.

23. Culinary art, *i.e.*, cooking and cookery.

24. Making lemonades, sherbets, acidulated drinks, and spirituous extracts with proper flavour and colour.

25. Tailor's work and sewing.

26. Making parrots, flowers, tufts, tassels, bunches, bosses, knobs, &c., out of yarn or thread.

27. Solution of riddles, enigmas, covert speeches, verbal puzzles and enigmatical **questions**.

28. A game, which consisted in repeating verses, and as one person finished, another person had to commence at once, repeating another verse, beginning with the same letter with which the last speaker's verse ended, whoever failed to repeat was considered to have lost, and to be subject to pay a forfeit or stake of some kind.

29. The art of mimicry or imitation.

30. Reading, including chanting and intoning.

31. Study of sentences difficult to pronounce. It is played as a game chiefly by women and children, and consists of a difficult sentence being given, and when repeated quickly, the words are often transposed or badly pronounced.

32. Practice with sword, single stick, quarter staff, and bow and arrow.

33. Drawing inferences, reasoning or inferring.

34. Carpentry, or the work of a carpenter.

35. Architecture, or the art of building.

36. Knowledge about gold and silver coins, and jewels and gems.

37. Chemistry and mineralogy.

38. Colouring jewels, gems and beads.

39. Knowledge of mines and quarries.

40. Gardening; knowledge of treating the diseases of trees and plants, of nourishing them, and determining their ages.

41. Art of cock fighting, quail fighting and ram fighting.

42. Art of teaching parrots and starlings to speak.

43. Art of applying perfumed ointments to the body, and of dressing the hair with unguents and perfumes and braiding it.
44. The art of understanding writing in cypher, and the writing of words in a peculiar way.
45. The art of speaking by changing the forms of words. It is of various kinds. Some speak by changing the beginning and end of words, others by adding unnecessary letters between every syllable of a word, and so on.
46. Knowledge of language and of the vernacular dialects.
47. Art of making flower carriages.
48. Art of framing mystical diagrams, of addressing spells and charms, and binding armlets.
49. Mental exercises, such as completing stanzas or verses on receiving a part of them; or supplying one, two or three lines when the remaining lines are given indiscriminately from different verses, so as to make the whole an entire verse with regard to its meaning; or arranging the words of a verse written irregularly by separating the vowels from the consonants, or leaving them out altogether; or putting into verse or prose sentences represented by signs or symbols. There are many other such exercises.
50. Composing poems.
51. Knowledge of dictionaries and vocabularies.
52. Knowledge of ways of changing and disguising the appearance of persons.
53. Knowledge of the art of changing the appearance of things, such as making cotton to appear as silk, coarse and common things to appear as fine and good.
54. Various ways of gambling.
55. Art of obtaining possession of the property of others by means of muntras or incantations.
56. Skill in youthful sports.
57. Knowledge of the rules of society, and of how to pay respects and compliments to others.
58. Knowledge of the art of war, of arms, of armies, &c.
59. Knowledge of gymnastics.
60. Art of knowing the character of a man from his features.
61. Knowledge of scanning or constructing verses.
62. Arithmetical recreations.
63. Making artificial flowers.
64. Making figures and images in clay.

Vatsyayana, The Kama Sutra

"As for my own part, I passed through all these nations as you perhaps may have done through a crowd at a show,—jostling to get by them, holding my nose with one hand, and defending my pockets with the other, without speaking a word to any of them, while I was pressing on to see what I wanted to see; which, however entertaining it might be in itself, scarce made me amends for the trouble the company gave me."

"Did not you find some of the nations among which you travelled less troublesome to you than others?" said Jones. "O yes," replied the old man: "the Turks were much more tolerable to me than the Christians; for they are men of profound taciturnity, and never disturb a stranger with **questions**. Now and then indeed they bestow a short curse upon him, or spit in his face as he walks the streets, but then they have done with him; and a man may live an age in their country without hearing a dozen words from them. But of all the people I ever saw, heaven defend me from the French! With their damned prate and civilities, and doing the honour of their nation to strangers (as they are pleased to call it), but indeed setting forth their own vanity; they are so troublesome, that I had infinitely rather pass my life with the Hottentots than set my foot in Paris again. They are a nasty people, but their nastiness is mostly without; whereas, in France, and some other nations that I won't name, it is all within, and makes them stink much more to my reason than that of Hottentots does to my nose.

Henry Fielding, *The History of Tom Jones, a Foundling*

"Yeah, nice to see you too, man. Why don't you sit down and slow down. Sick of what?"

"Them. They sicken me. They go on about rights and freedoms, and then they eat fifty chickens every fucking week! Hypocrites!"

Irie couldn't immediately see the connection. She took out a fag in preparation for a long story. To her surprise Joshua took one too, and they went to kneel on the window seat, blowing smoke through the grate up into the street,

"Do you *know* how battery chickens live?"

Irie didn't. Joshua explained. Cooped up for most of their poor chicken lives in total chicken darkness, packed together like chicken sardines in their chicken shit and fed the worst type of chicken grain.

And this, according to Joshua, was apparently nothing on how pigs and cows and sheep spent their time. "It's a fucking *crime*. But try telling Marcus that. Try getting him to give up his Sunday hog-fest, He's so *fucking* ill-informed. Have you ever noticed that? He knows this enormous amount about one thing, but there's this whole other world that . . . Oh, before I forget—you should take a leaflet."

Irie never thought she would see the day when Joshua Chalfen handed her a leaflet. But here it was in her palm. It was called: *Meat Is Murder: The Facts and the Fiction*, a publication from the FATE organization.

"It stands for Fighting Animal Torture and Exploitation, They're like the hardcore end of Greenpeace or whatever. Read it—they're not just hippie freaks, they're coming from a solid scientific and academic background and they're working from an anarchist perspective. I feel like I've really found my niche, you know? It's a really incredible group. Dedicated to direct action. The deputy's an ex-Oxford fellow."

"Mmmm. How's Millat?"

Joshua shook off the **question**. " Oh, I don't know. Barmy, Going barmy. And Joyce is still pandering to his every whim. Just don't ask me. They all sicken me. Everything's changed." Josh ran his fingers anxiously through his hair, which just reached his shoulders now in what Willesdeners affectionately call a Jewfro Mullet. "I just can't tell you how everything's changed, I'm having these real . . . *moments of clarity.*"

Zadie Smith, *White Teeth*

Implications of brutality, or of a kind of uncivilized inhumanity, seem to lurk in so many other **questions** foreign observers ask about America like: How could you set up that concentration camp in Cuba, and why can't you shut it down? Or: How can you pretend to be a Christian country and still carry out the death penalty? The follow-up to which often is: How could you pick as president a man proud of executing his fellow citizens at the fastest rate recorded in Texas history? (Europeans will not soon forget George W. Bush.)

Other things I've had to answer for include:

* Why can't you Americans stop interfering with women's health care?

* Why can't you understand science?

* How can you still be so blind to the reality of climate change?

* How can you speak of the rule of law when your presidents break international laws to make war whenever they want?

* How can you hand over the power to blow up the planet to one lone, ordinary man?

* How can you throw away the Geneva Conventions and your principles to advocate torture?

* Why do you Americans like guns so much? Why do you kill each other at such a rate?

To many, the most baffling and important **question** of all is: Why do you send your military all over the world to stir up more and more trouble for all of us?

Ann Jones, Has America Gone Crazy? (Salon)

anthypophora
   an'-thi-po'-phor-a
   Also sp. antipophora
   antiphora, hypophora
   subjectio (subiectio), rogatio, contradictio
   figure of responce

A figure of reasoning in which one asks and then immediately answers one's own **questions** (or raises and then settles imaginary objections). Reasoning aloud.

Anthypophora sometimes takes the form of asking the audience or one's adversary what can be said on a matter, and thus can involve both anacoenosis and apostrophe.

Examples

"But there are only three hundred of us," you object. Three hundred, yes, but men, but armed, but Spartans, but at Thermoplyae: I have never seen three hundred so numerous.—Seneca

Gideon Burton, Silva Rhetoricae (The Forest of Rhetoric)

After so many study guides, so many practice tests and proficiency and achievement tests, it would have been impossible for us not to learn something, but we forgot everything almost right away and, I'm afraid, for good. The thing that we did learn, and to perfection—the thing that we would remember for the rest of our lives—was how to copy on tests. Here I could easily ad-lib an homage to the cheat sheet, all the test material reproduced in tiny but legible script on a minuscule bus ticket. But that admirable workmanship would have been worth very little if we hadn't also had the all-important skill and audacity when the crucial moment came: the instant the teacher lowered his guard and the ten or twenty golden seconds began.

At our school in particular, which in theory was the strictest in Chile, it turned out that copying was fairly easy, since many of the tests were multiple choice. We still had years to go before taking the Academic Aptitude Test and applying to university, but our teachers wanted to familiarize us right away with multiple-choice exercises, and although they designed up to four different versions of every test, we always found a way to pass information along. We didn't have to write anything or form opinions or develop any ideas of our own; all we had to do was play the game and guess the trick. Of course we studied, sometimes a lot, but it was never enough. I guess the idea was to lower our morale. Even if we did nothing but study, we knew that there would always be two or three impossible **questions**. We didn't complain. We got the message: cheating was just part of the deal.

Alejandro Zambra, Reading Comprehension: Text No. 1 (The New Yorker)

Human-powered search site ChaCha is launching a new service that allows you to ask **questions** and get the answers all over text message.

ChaCha was set to launch its free search service for mobile phone users on Jan. 3.

Basically, you can text any **question** to "242242" (which spells "chacha" on a phone) and a "live search expert" will respond.

I tried it out with some **questions** that I thought might be useful if I were out on the road and not sitting at my computer and the answers were accurate and, in general, very prompt.

Elinor Mills, Chacha Gives You Answers via Text Message (CNET)

"Truly?" Pip smiled sadly. "You see, even here, though, I'm wondering why you're saying that. Maybe you're just trying to get me to keep doing the **questionnaire**. For that matter, I'm also wondering why you care so much about my doing it."

"You can trust me. It's only because I'm impressed with you."

"You see, but that doesn't even make any sense, because I'm actually not very impressive. I don't know all that much about nuclear weapons, I just happened to know about Israel. I don't trust you at all. I don't trust you. I don't trust people." Pip's face was growing hot. "I should really go upstairs now. I'm feeling bad about leaving my friend there."

This ought to have been Annagret's cue to let her go, or at least to apologize for keeping her, but Annagret (maybe this was a German thing?) seemed not very good at taking cues. "We have to follow the form," she said. "It's only a form, but we have to follow it." She patted Pip's hand and then stroked it. "We'll go fast."

Pip wondered why Annagret kept touching her.

Some pages are omitted from this book preview.

Jonathan Franzen, Purity

Ok, this may be a dumb **question**, but I can't find an answer anywhere online or in the manual. I just got this phone so I'll still learning some of the functionality of it. When I receive a text message and open it to view it, sometimes the message will say (more . . .) just above the date. This would leave me to believe that the message is longer than can be displayed but I can't figure out how to view the rest of the message. Can anyone enlighten me on how to view the whole message? I've tried going into message details, long pressing the message, quick tapping it and nothing works. What's the secret? Thanks in advance.

Sprint Community, Text Message **Question**—*Viewing Whole Message*

aporia

a-po'-ri-a
from Gk. aporos "without a passage"
diaporesis
addubitatio, dubitatio
addubitation, doubht, the doubtfull

Deliberating with oneself as though in doubt over some matter; asking oneself (or rhetorically asking one's hearers) what is the best or appropriate way to approach something.

Examples

Where shall I begin to describe her wisdom? In her knowledge of facts? In her ability to synthesize diverse matters? In her capacity to articulate complex ideas simply?

Gideon Burton, Silva Rhetoricae (The Forest of Rhetoric)

I just got the epic 4G Touch and sent a text so long that it was split into 3 texts. I opened it and it said (1/3) . . . I couldn't figure out how to see the rest either and then they just appeared after a few moments. Apparently it can take time to display the rest of the messages . . . There isn't something that you tap to display the rest of the message . . . they are supposed to just appear. If you aren't getting the whole message, there must be a technical issue with either poor signal strength, close proximity to an airave device . . . or for some reason the text is lost.

Have you ever considered using another text message application such as GoSMS or Handcent? They are pretty popular and allow for a lot of customization.

Sprint Community, Text Message **Question**—Viewing Whole Message

Exception made for Europe today, which has claimed the right to opt out of war-making, it remains as true as ever that most people will not **question** the rationalizations offered by their government for starting or continuing a war. It takes some very peculiar circumstances for a war to become genuinely unpopular. (The prospect of being killed is not necessarily one of them.)

Susan Sontag, Regarding the Pain of Others

"Hey?" cried the blatant Stryver. "Did he though? Is that the sort of fellow? Let us look at his infamous name. D—n the fellow!"

Darnay, unable to restrain himself any longer, touched Mr. Stryver on the shoulder, and said:

"I know the fellow."

"Do you, by Jupiter?" said Stryver. "I am sorry for it."

"Why?"

"Why, Mr. Darnay? D'ye hear what he did? Don't ask, why, in these times."

"But I do ask why?"

"Then I tell you again, Mr. Darnay, I am sorry for it. I am sorry to hear you putting any such extraordinary **questions**. Here is a fellow, who, infected by the most pestilent and blasphemous code of devilry that ever was known, abandoned his property to the vilest scum of the earth that ever did murder by wholesale, and you ask me why I am sorry that a man who instructs youth knows him? Well, but I'll answer you. I am sorry because I believe there is contamination in such a scoundrel. That's why."

Charles Dickens, A Tale of Two Cities

"I have a sore throat and a weird rash and the internet says I'm dying what do I do?"

Turns out that mothers are all secretly doctors—they know the answers to your trickiest medical **questions**. You'll probably turn to her for advice with your own children, too!

Michelle Adams, 10 Texts You Only Send to Your Mom (ScholarshipPoints.com)

They all seem to like being submerged up to their chests, so when they enter the water they sink to their knees in the mud and stone of its black bottom. Ellen is standing and she appears elevated on an artificial surface. Ellen notices that some of them have turned their backs and are busily working at something on the bank at the water's edge. The soft fan of a tail runs against her shin. The carp is sitting on the floor of the pool, stationary. It caresses Ellen's leg, and she is reminded again of a cat.

Nearly all the zombies have turned their backs on her. A woman working beside the fallen log turns her head to a man beside her.

"It's OK to kill biting, y'know."

The man remains hunched over.

"And I know it's OK to tear fuckin' fuckers' heads off."

The woman pulls from her spot and turns to Ellen.

"Is it OK?"

Ellen can see mud dripping down the woman's chin. It looks like the chinstrap of a warrior's helmet.

"Is what OK?"

All of the zombies stop, some of them grab the tree branches above their heads. A rhythm of ripples on the water's surface smoothes. Ellen slips farther under, to her knees. She feels the little plosive blast as her carp propels itself off her thigh.

"It's OK to . . . uh . . . sure, it's OK."

"How about killing them?"

Ellen feels a carp's face in the upturned soul of her foot. It extends its sucker mouth and kisses her there. Ellen answers the **question** through a smile caused by a second carp on her other foot.

"Killing them is alright."

"And slapping and slapping all the assholes in their heads?"

"Yes. Yes. It's OK."

"What else is alright?"

The carp have now settled into a synchronized kissing and Ellen drops her hands to her sides. She feels the soft drapery of fish moving along the insides of her wrists.

"Anything."

"Can't I ask?"

A zombie becomes agitated and turns from the bank. "If she asks are you going to hit her in the ass?"

"No, no, she can ask whatever she wants."

"Can I too?"

"Yes."

"OK, OK. Is it OK to have a policeman banging on the door?"

"Yes."

"Me too, me too. Um, I don't have a **question**."

"Will you bash his face in if he doesn't have a **question**?"

"No. No, I won't."

As they turn and lobby **questions** at Ellen she finds herself struggling, with some success, to configure the affirmation. She begins to focus her eyes on what it is that they're doing on the bank. A busy geometry of forms begins to emerge. It sits lit on the surface of the dark and appears like a computer language, a dense and complex glyphic.

Tony Burgess, Pontypool Changes Everything

On the other hand, each of them has left unanswered **questions** which constitute the gap in the literature. For each approach, I am to evaluate its relevance to my research **questions** and explain the rationale of my current approach.

Zoe Wai Man Lam, Chapter 2—Approaches to Syllable Contraction (Rutgers Optimality Archive)

Our reading habits, our expectations of coherence and similarity, compel us to take what meaning we find in "a relying and a surface and a service in indecision and" and try to contrast it with that already blossoming in this complicated tree of associations. "Surface" makes me skim forward, surf ahead on its soft sounds and slippery connotations. It pushes me on to the next word and the recognition that "surface" and "service" sound quite a bit alike. The "surface" could describe the character of the reading process when I read normal sentences in which I feel fluent and which lead me to take words for granted. Surface-y sentences might be "a service in indecision" because they allow us to avoid making decisions: our habits keep us from noticing that there are any decisions to make. The surface offers a service on which readers rely, but Stein's writing offers no stable surface on which readers can stand together, or even alone (and her phrase could mean something very different from my paraphrase). "In" and "in-" call out to one another and trade places, suggesting that surfaces may offer services that lead not toward decision but toward not-decision—and these are not exactly the same place. On either hand, Stein's sentence leads us toward ambiguity, keeps us thinking, guessing, adding, and noting a network of complexity.

In the phrases that follow "a creature," Stein's discussion of knowledge—how we use language to think, and to avoid thinking—seems more direct than usual: "and a creature and a **question** and a syllable in answer and more counting and no quarrel and a single scientific statement and not darkness and no **question**." A **question**, like a living thing, can grow into a variety of answers and even more **questions**.

Dana Cairns Watson, Gertrude Stein and the Essence of What Happens

Today I—have to repeat and to brush up on the problem of Socrates. Socrates is a legend. He was a legend in Greece, and he's a legend today. That is, there is more talk about Socrates than we possibly can know. That's a legend. We know very little about Socrates. Or you can say we know so much that we haven't the faintest idea what is really fact, you see, and what is imagination. The cue to Socrates which you must never forget, and which is very hard for you to understand, but which—on which you must build your thought, in—in future years, and I—I take it there will be in future years on your part the desire perhaps to understand what it is all about, this—this getting out beyond the commonplace—is that he asks the **questioner**. I told you that the problem of Socrates was to turn the process of **questioning**, you see, so far that he **questioned**—would **question** those who **questioned**.

If you do not see this second power, this asking to the square, you will always mistake the it—the curious **question** of a child, "Mother? How are the children born?" Or "Is there a God?" Or "Has God a white beard?" for a Socratic **question**. That's not a Socratic **question**, gentlemen. That's just a stupid **question**. In this country, every **question** is admitted. As long as you cannot cut out and excise stupid **questions**, gentlemen, there can be no progress, there can be no education, there can be nothing. The—the best answer to a stupid **question** remains to this day not to answer it. Nobody seems to have the courage in this country to say, "That's such a stupid **question** that I won't answer it." You answer every **question**, and thereby you always get into deep water. That is all you expect, if you ask a stupid **question**, that somebody is stupid enough to answer it. Never forget that one fool can ask more **questions** than a hundred wise men can answer. That's the first rule of all thinking processes, gentlemen. Why? I remind you. I told you: **questioning** means the desire for participation of the ignoramus in a going concern. You ask for the road in a foreign country. You ask for the—for the cost of a ticket at the—at the booth, you see. He knows, you don't know. All **questions** presuppose an (expert). You can only ask as long as you think there is somebody who knows.

If you—if you drop this—this qualification of **questioning**, you see, that it is an attempt of the outsider to get inside society, you cannot understand the limitations of all asking.—A **question** only makes sense if there is a preestablished answer, which this man doesn't know, but which all the others know. That's how we all move in a foreign country. That's how you move in a foreign—world of grownups. When you enter a new (thing), you have to ask. And people are ni—kind enough to show you around, as we say.

And as long as this is the relation of **question** and answer, everything is safe and so—sane and so. But of course, a child, for example, asks many—too—**questions**, because it just doesn't know where it wants get into. It is so far away from the way of the grownups, you see, that it asks anything. So the one condition for the **question**, and for the **questioner** is that he is seriously loving the group which can answer the **question**. If you are not—haven't the real desire to ask for the road to the harbor, because you want to go on this road to the harbor, you don't deserve an answer. Can't you see this?

Eugen Rosenstock-Huessy, Greek Philosophy (1956): Lectures 14–20

M. Which, then, shall we do? Shall I immediately crowd all my sails? or shall I make use of my oars, as if I were just endeavoring to get clear of the harbor?

A. What is it that you mean, for I do not exactly comprehend you?

M. Because, Chrysippus and the Stoics, when they discuss the perturbations of the mind, make great part of their debate to consist in definitions and distinctions; while they employ but few words on the subject of curing the mind, and preventing it from being disordered. Whereas the Peripatetics bring a great many things to promote the cure of it, but have no regard to their thorny partitions and definitions. My **question**, then, was, whether I should instantly unfold the sails of my eloquence, or be content for a while to make less way with the oars of logic?

A. Let it be so; for by the employment of both these means the subject of our inquiry will be more thoroughly discussed.

M. It is certainly the better way; and should anything be too obscure, you may examine that afterward.

A. I will do so; but those very obscure points you will, as usual, deliver with more clearness than the Greeks.

M. I will, indeed, endeavor to do so; but it well requires great attention, lest, by losing one word, the whole should escape you. What the Greeks call πάθη we choose to name perturbations (or disorders) rather than diseases; in explaining which, I shall follow, first, that very old description of Pythagoras, and afterward that of Plato; for they both divide the mind into two parts, and make one of these partake of reason, and the other they represent without it. In that which partakes of reason they place tranquillity, that is to say, a placid and undisturbed constancy; to the other they assign the turbid motions of anger and desire, which are contrary and opposite to reason. Let this, then, be our principle, the spring of all our reasonings. But notwithstanding, I shall use the partitions and definitions of the Stoics in describing these perturbations; who seem to me to have shown very great acuteness on this **question**.

Marcus Tullius Cicero, Tusculan Disputations

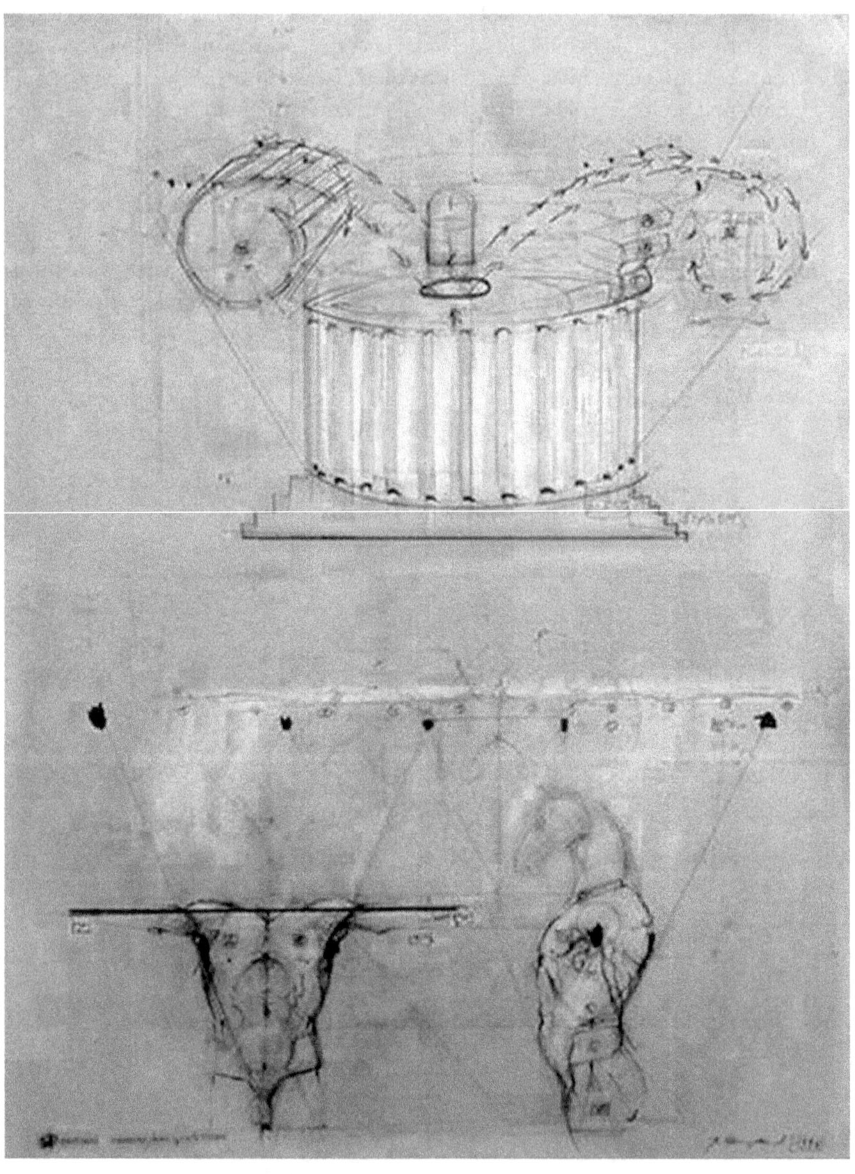

*Jes Fomsgaard, Anatomic Drawing/and **Question**, 1996*
Pencil on paper, 24 x 17 3/4 in., exhibited at D.C.A. Gallery, Spring 1998 (Artstor)

Thanks for your **question**. First of all, that's quite a long time to be drawing without
seeing any marked improvement. Without knowing your situation in any detail, I can
give only the most general advice. Still, it could be useful, so here goes:

*Paolo Rivera, Anatomical Drawing **Question***
(The Self-Absobing Man, blog.paolorivera.com)

I Didn't Know How Seriously He Meant That Question

*Dissertations on the **Question** How*

We use **question** words to ask certain types of **questions** (**question** word **questions**). We often refer to them as *WH words* because they include the letters *WH* (for example *WHy, HoW*).

English Club, Wh **Question** Words

He was one of those, who, liking work, knew how to do it, and despite his indolence would sometimes spend a whole night at his writing table. He worked well whatever the import of his work. It was not the **question** "What for?" but the **question** "How?" that interested him. What the diplomatic matter might be he did not care, but it gave him great pleasure to prepare a circular, memorandum, or report, skillfully, pointedly, and elegantly.

Leo Tolstoy, War and Peace

Charles Chadwick, *Inaugural Dissertation on the **Question**, How Far Are Secretion and Nutrition Dependent on Nervous Influence?* (1837)

Thomas Canning, *Observations Occasioned by a Case Lately Submitted to Counsel, Respecting the **Question**, How Far a Contingent or Reversionary Interest of Husband and Wife in Her Right, in Personal Estate, Is Assignable, in Deed or in Law, During the Converture* (1820)

John Tillinghast, *Knowledge of the Times, or, The Resolution of the **Question**, How Long It Shall Be Unto the End of Wonders* (1654)

C. Bragge, *State of the **Question**: How Far Impeachments Are Affected by a Dissolution of Parliment?* (1791)

Robert Hovenden, *Crime and Punishment; or The **Question**, How Should We Treat Our Criminals? Practically Considered* (1849)

Oliver Wendell Holmes, *Robert William Haxall and Luther Vose Bell, Dissertations on the **Question** How Far Are the External Means of Exploring the Condition of the Internal Organs to Be Considered Useful and Important in Medical Practice?* (1836)

John Gaylord, *The Future of Russia: or, An Answer to the **Question**, How Will the Great Eastern Struggle Finally Terminate? Answer Given by Comparing Scripture With History, in Which It Is Clearly Shown That Russia Is the Special Subject of Many of the Prophecies of the Jewish Scriptures, and That Her Future General History, Together With That of Western Europe, Is Definitely Foretold. To Which Will Be Added, the Bible Its Own Interpretor, or An Introduction to the Study of Prophecy* (1855)

Google Books Search: "the **question** how"

В этой связи возникает **вопрос**: как может незаконная колонизация палестинской земли способствовать реализации решения о сосуществовании . . . *daccess-ods.un.org*	That begs the **question**: how is the illegal colonization of Palestinian land conducive to the realization of the two-State . . . *daccess-ods.un.org*
В ходе своих дискуссий Комитет поставил следующий **вопрос**: в чем может заключаться существенный вклад научных программ ЮНЕСКО в XXI веке? *unesdoc.unesco.org*	During its deliberations, the Committee posed the **question**—how can UNESCO's science programmes make a significant difference in the twenty-first century? *unesdoc.unesco.org*
Не так-то легко ответить на **вопрос**: «сколько это слишком много? *mfc.org.pl*	The response to the **question** 'how much is too much' is not an easy one. *mfc.org.pl*
Отвечая на **вопрос** о том, как жертва информируется о ее праве на компенсацию, оратор говорит, что, согласно Федеральному . . . *daccess-ods.un.org*	In response to the **question** how a victim was informed of his or her right to compensation, she said the Federal Act on Assistance . . . *daccess-ods.un.org*
Знакомство с четырьмя различными категориями исчезновений людей поможет нам понять, что у различных видов исчезновений есть различные аспекты: страдания, испытываемые жертвой, наказание правонарушителей и ответственность Государства. *ediec.org*	The insight into the four different categories of disappearances also will make us aware that different kinds of disappearance possess different relevant dimensions: the problem of the suffering of the victims, the **question** how to deal with the perpetrators, and the responsibility of the state. *ediec.org*
Ввиду таких различий в подходах разрешение **вопроса** о том, как следует регулировать деятельность независимых агентов, оставляется . . . *daccess-ods.un.org*	In view of this difference in approach, the **question** how to treat independent agents is left to bilateral negotiations, which . . . *daccess-ods.un.org*
c) ответить на **вопрос** "Какой вклад ваша организация или вы сами, если вы хотите участвовать в качестве научного сотрудника . . . *daccess-ods.un.org*	(c) Answer the **question** "How does your organization, or yourself if you wish to participate as an academic or expert, want . . . *daccess-ods.un.org*
График 35 Распределение ответов на **вопрос** «Насколько серьезны проблемы, касающиеся следующих регуляторных аспектов? *docs.moldova.org*	Figure 35 The distribution of answers to the **question** "How serious are actually the problems concerning the following regulatory aspects? *docs.moldova.org*
Это значит задать следующие **вопросы**: как это сделать, как узнать, как это сделать, когда будет получен ответ? *sutyajnik.ru*	This is to ask the **question** how to do it, how to get to know how to do it, when to get an answer? *sutyajnik.ru*
График 37 Распределение ответов на **вопрос** «Насколько серьезны проблемы, связанные со следующими институциональными аспектами? *docs.moldova.org*	Figure 37 The distribution of answers to the **question** "How serious are the problems connected with the following institutional aspects? *docs.moldova.org*

... электронную почту принимает в жизни магазина так широко помещение, что **вопрос**, как с этими документами ввиду календарного доступа ... *pc.qumram-demo.ch*	The Communication via E-Mail takes a so broad room in the business life that the **question** how these documents are to be handled with regard to the ... *pc.qumram-demo.ch*
На **вопрос**, насколько это возможно с его точки зрения, экс-глава Нацбанка ответил, что в принципе все возможно, но для этого ... *telegraf.by*	To the **question**, how much potential this idea has, the former head of the National Bank says that in principle, everything ... *telegraf.by*

*Linguee > Russian-English Dictionary > The **Question** How > External Sources*

What is the correct response to the **question** "How do you do"? Is it "how do you do" or "fine" or something else? Why?

Quora User, Architectural Photographer at LOTAN Architectural Photography (lo-tan.com):
'How do you do' is a rather formal greeting used normally only on the first occasion of meeting.

The usual reply is likewise, 'How do you do'.

For example, in Oscar Wilde's *Lady Windermere's Fan,* 1892:

Lord Darlington: How do you do, Lady Windermere?

Lady Windermere: How do you do, Lord Darlington?

Milo Grika, Technical writer and editor:
Depends on where you are.

In England (and likely other Commonwealth English-speaking countries) the response is likewise "How do you do?"

In the U.S., it is not unlikely to receive an actual answer as to one's well being.

And as a bonus, the originally rural U.S. "howdy" is short for "how do you do?" and the response is usually also "howdy."

Shivam Garg:
This phrase is not very commom in Contry which does not have English as thier 1st language

In U.S. if person A asks HOW DO U DO? B (a person) then ans of B would be HOW DO U DO?

In Country like INDIA if C asks HOW DO U DO? Ans would be I am fine or things like that.

Carrie Cadwallader, Student of proper etiquette:
"How do you do?" is not generally thought of as a genuine **question** about your well-being. Instead it's treated more like a salutation.

The proper answer is either, "Fine, thank you," or "How do you do?" or some form thereof.

For example in a formal setting it might go like:

Person A: "Good evening, B. How do you do?"

Person B: "Good evening. How do you do?"

In this case, it's being used strictly as a replacement for words like "Hello."

In a less formal setting it might be:

Person A: "Hey, B. How do you do?"
Person B: "Fine, thank you. How are you?"
Person A: "Good. Good. See you."
Person B: "Bye."

In this case, it comes out like a **question** and answer, but in reality, neither person is expecting a proper answer to the **question**.

In general, if a person wants to actually know how you're doing, they will follow up "How do you do?" with more specific **questions**.

That would go something like this:

Person A: "Hey, B. How do you do?"
Person B: "Fine, thank you. How are you?"
Person A: "Good. Good. I haven't talked to you in so long. How have you been?"

In that case, it's now an opening to have a conversation about your current actual state of being.

Suzanne Stroh, works at Screenwriting

Good overview.

A well educated, cosmopolitan and polite American WILL go wrong by confusing the responses. Best to memorize them and practice so they become second nature.

In England/UK, no matter who the interlocutor is, always reply, "how do you do." Note: not a **question**! Just a greeting!

The English/UK person or other (non-American) foreigner leading with "how do you do" is expressing formality. Therefore, to honor this, always reply to that person with, "how do you do."

In America, speaking to Americans, if you have an upper class background and this is known, then people will accept your initial greeting of "how do you do" as natural if a little old fashioned. (Always better greeting a group—such as when you are the last to arrive at a restaurant—with "good morning," "good afternoon" or "good evening." And following up with individual "hellos," said brightly and simply.) You are always on safe ground in America greeting foreigners with "how do you do." They will receive it as formal and respectful.

You are however safer in replying to most Americans greeting you with "how do you do?"—put as an actual **question**—with "very well, thank you. And you?"

In short, it's complicated. The first rules of polite greeting are (1) to look the person directly in the eye and (2) not to mumble, whatever you decide to say, even if you are shy.

If you have authority, you may decide whether to extend your hand. If you do not wish to shake hands, keep your hands still and at your side, and substitue one of the following: (1) smiling, (2) nodding or (3) bowing slightly. Never offer to shake hands across a table unless both persons stand and step away from the table.

If a hand is extended to you, shake it confidently, no matter what genders are involved. If you are seated, rise immediately as you take the hand that is offered. You may use your left hand in a gesture to indicate support below the forearm or elbow of the person who just extended a hand. The handshake is always a standing gesture with both people offering their squared shoulders. And looking one another in the eye.

The only exception I can think of to this rule is on an airplane.

Hope this helps.

Oh—on saying goodbye, in UK there is a distinction you must learn. The casual goodbye for English people is "Cheers." For Scottish people it is "Cheerio." Do not mix them up. This would be unappreciated.

Elaine Whinston, BS in math Mathematics, University of Michigan (1961):

There are several different answers that I might use, depending on circumstances. I think they are self-explanatory, so a separate answer to "why" is unnecessary. Here are some possible answers:

"I'm fine, thank you. How are you?"

"It's so nice to meet you! John has told me so many nice things about you!"

"Mary tells me you're going to be in town for the summer. Let's plan to get together one evening."

Of course you should be sincere. Don't suggest meeting up unless you mean it.

Circumstances will dictate possible answers. Don't overthink it. Be yourself.

Day MeeYen, knows English:

It's very formal and generally wouldn't be used much outside of the English upper classes these days. But to respond to your **question**;

You'd simply answer by describing your mood/how you're day is going and generally, to be polite, you would then return the **question**;

"How do you do Sir . . ."

"I'm good thank you Jeeves, and you?"

"Good, thank you Sir."

And a more day to day version;

"How do you do Master Bruce . . ."

"I've been better Alfred. My f***ing arm is killing me! Had a massive f***ing brawl with that Bane c**t last night and the pr**k stabbed me right in my f**ing elbow with a huge f***ing hunting knife!"

"Not to worry Master Bruce, the nurse will patch that arm right up and we'll have you all set for another evening of, err, spelunking, in no time. But please, try to steer clear of that Bane pr**k Master Bruce, that c**t is bad news and if I'm honest, he's making both our lives a bleedin' misery. And don't get me started on that Cillian Murphy lookin', Dr. Crane mutherf***er! That dude is a f***ing absolute basket case!

Anyway, there's bread in the cupboard and jam in fridge, you can make your own breakfast today, I'm tired of running around after you like your f***ing mummy, I'm off out to meet that tasty Hungarian chick that butlers for Captain America, she's 'proper gamey', and mad for some senior citizen English butler c**k!

Have a good one Master Bruce. And don't forget to be kind to the elderly."

Hope this helps

Kirthana Thyagaraju, Consultant Periodontist (2017–present):

The correct response to how do you do is "how do you do". Even though this sounds wrong, it is correct. P.S. not many people know this.

Quora, *What Is the Correct Response to the* **Question** *"How Do You Do"?*

I didn't know how seriously he meant that **question**, though he seemed serious enough. I hadn't got him sized up yet. However, clown or not, he was the deputy sheriff stationed at Quesada, and this was his party. He was entitled to the facts. I gave them to him as we bounced over the lumpy road, gave him all I had . . .

Dashiell Hammett, The Dain Curse

1. I'm fine. How are you? (Sometimes you need to say this even when you don't feel fine)
2. I'm AWAP (As Well As Possible).
3. I'm trying really hard to avoid ambiguous **questions** at the moment.
4. (Just answer with the same **question**:) How are you?
5. I could complain, but I'm not going to.
6. Upright and still breathing.
7. Thanks for caring babe! Glad to be here with you.
8. Better than yesterday, but not as good as I will be tomorrow!
9. I am.
10. Wondering how you are.
11. Strange, and getting stranger.
12. My usual Devil-may-care self.
13. I'm endeavoring to persevere.
14. How am I what?
15. Not so hot, but nothing a stiff drink and some girl talk couldn't fix.
16. How do you think I am?
17. Do you want the short version or the long one?
18. Eh, you win some you lose some.
19. I'll leave that up to your imagination.
20. Shhhhh. It's a secret.
21. I'll let you know when I figure it out.
22. Taking deep breaths.
23. Ready for tomorrow.
24. To tell you the truth, my ______ hurts, but my doc's working on a solution for me so I'm hopeful.
25. I've been better.
26. Trying to stay positive.
27. Who wants to know?
28. Not my best day, but not my worst day, either.
29. Let's just say less than super.
30. Wouldn't you like to know!
31. I'm taking it easy.
32. Staying grounded.
33. (bunch of grunts, gurgles, and other random noises) pssh, fft, mmhm, ya know?
34. Trying to Mit the good in with the bad, you know?
35. I don't know.
36. Give me a chocolate bar and I'll be fantastic!
37. Ready for a nap.
38. Does it matter? I'm a babe no matter what;)
39. Not in the mood to discuss how I feel, but thanks for asking—it really helps to know you care.

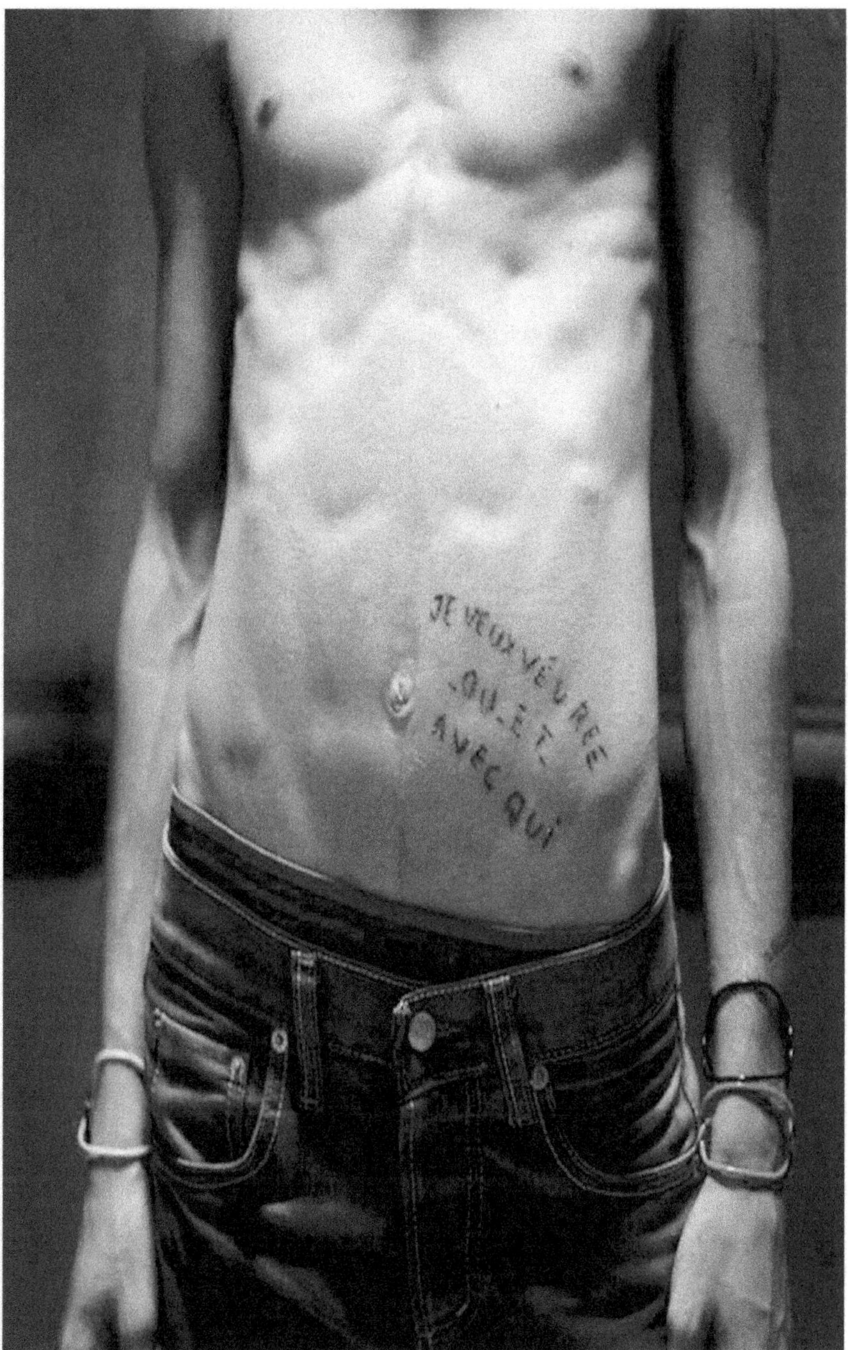

For the 19 year old Amine Tighri to feel that he is still alive and to remind himself of his biggest dream, to flee from Algeria, he has tattooed himself on his stomach with needle and mascara: 'I want to live—but where and with whom?' (Je veux vivre ou avec qui?). He hasn't done the **question** mark yet and he made a typo.

Photo by Christian Als, 2010 (Artstor)

40. Somewhere between blah and meh.
41. I put pants on, didn't I?
42. Hold on, let me get the sleep out of my eyes.
43. Just hug me and leave it at that.
44. I could really go for a back massage!
45. Same old, same old.
46. I could really go for a walk, want to join me?
47. (If you have the time) Let's make some tea and talk about it.
48. Ready for my meds.:D
49. Trying to come out on top.
50. In need of some peace and quiet.
51. Get back to me on that.
52. Oooooohhhmmmm.
53. Under construction.
54. Looking to put some pep back in my step.
55. Thinking about getting away from it all . . . want to plan a mini-vacation?
56. Improving.
57. I'm trying to be a "big girl" about all of this.
58. Mama said there'd be days like this, there'd be days like this, my mama said.
59. Instead of waking up on the wrong side of the bed, I think I woke up underneath it.
60. Remembering to stay patient.
61. Trying not to burst into tears. I get an A for effort, right?
62. In need of some "me time."
63. I feel like crap! Know any good dirty jokes to cheer me up?
64. Taking all the love and support I can get, thanks!
65. As happy as a clam, a clam that's been cracked open, doused in lemon and shot down the gullet of some tourist in a tacky Hawaiian shirt.
66. Appreciating the things I have.
67. Getting there.
68. On a scale of one to punching someone in the face?
69. In desperate need of a mani/pedi.
70. Somewhere between drab and fab.
71. Things are bound to get better, yes?
72. Not giving up.
73. Getting stronger.
74. Learning.
75. Rolling with the punches.
76. You can't know pleasure without pain, right?:)
77. In a give-no-shits, take-no-prisoners kind of mood.
78. I get knocked down, but I get up again!
79. Gearing up for a comeback. I'll keep you posted on my progress.
80. Rooting for the underdog (me).
81. Gotta keep on keepin' on.
82. I've seen better days.
83. If I was an animal right now, I'd probably be a sloth (or a turtle).
84. Ready for you to make a goofy face/make me laugh/make me smile.

85. Do you want to join me in a nice long, relaxing scream? AAARRRGGHHHH
86. I mean, I'm not doing jumping jacks or back flips, but I'm here.
87. You can't win 'em all.
88. Imagining myself on a beach far away.
89. Crazy. sdhjMhj kljdghpe'sh;g'ep; ea'khg sdjhm, right?
90. I'm feeling more like Oscar the Grouch than Elmo right now.
91. I feel like crap, but doing the best I can. Tomorrow's another day, yea?
92. I'm feeling really grateful for this beautiful day. (This is a great way to take the focus off of you and onto some shared experience that you're having with the other person)
93. Better now that you're here;)
94. I don't feel that great, but my hair looks awesome, right?
95. Today I'm more CHRONIC than BABE.
96. Not so hot. Wanna help distract me by telling me about your day?
97. Keepin' busy, which is a good distraction from my other tough stuff.
98. I'll be better when _______ gets fixed, but for now I'm doin' OK. Thanks!
99. I'm glad to see you! What's new?
100. I'm giving her all she's got, Captain!

ChronicBabe, 100 Ways to Answer the **Question** *"How Are You?"*

Quora User, Some say I write well. I certainly read well:
"Fine, and how are you?" is a common response.

This is just an extended greeting. No one expects to hear in detail how you are doing. So it would be odd to respond to the **question** at length.

The important thing is to reciprocate and express some interest in the other person. At that point the score is even and you can move on to other topics.

Quora, What Is the Correct Response to the **Question** *"How Do You Do"?*

What is the best answer to the **question** *"How are you" in business meetings?*

Every time when my colleges from USA ask me "How are you?" I don't know what should I answer. I think that answer like "Fine, thanks. What about you?" is not perfect. Could you provide patterns for such situation?

—Warlock

This **question** has been asked before and already has an answer. If those answers do not fully address your **question**, please ask a new **question**.

English Language & Usage Stack Exchange, What Is the Best Answer to the **Question** *"How Are You" in Business Meetings?*

*Tress Academic, #117: How to Be a Great Conference Chair—Part 2: Managing Time, Presenters and **Questions** (tressacademic.com)*

Second Book of the Academic Questions

"Are you mad, my friend?" said he, "or whither does your senseless curiosity lead you?"

"I want to know which is worse, to be ravished a hundred times by negro pirates, to have a buttock cut off, to run the gauntlet among the Bulgarians, to be whipped and hanged at an auto-da-fé, to be dissected, to row in the galleys—in short, to go through all the miseries we have undergone, or to stay here and have nothing to do?"

"It is a great **question**," said Candide.

This discourse gave rise to new reflections, and Martin especially concluded that man was born to live either in a state of distracting inquietude or of lethargic disgust. Candide did not quite agree to that, but he affirmed nothing. Pangloss owned that he had always suffered horribly, but as he had once asserted that everything went wonderfully well, he asserted it still, though he no longer believed it.

Voltaire, Candide

'So how are you?' Barry Casofsky asked. He spoke with a Manchester Jewish drawl which gave an urgency and even a suggestion of desperation and panic to every **question**. He *really* wanted to know how Sefton was. He'd heard that he was a professor now.

'Something like that,' said Sefton Goldberg. 'But how are you?'

Howard Jacobson, Coming From Behind

COUNTESS. Marry, that's a bountiful answer that fits all **questions**.

CLOWN. It is like a barber's chair, that fits all buttocks—the pin buttock, the quatch buttock, the brawn buttock, or any buttock.

COUNTESS. Will your answer serve fit to all **questions**?

CLOWN. As fit as ten groats is for the hand of an attorney, as your French crown for your taffety punk, as Tib's rush for Tom's forefinger, as a pancake for Shrove Tuesday, a morris for Mayday, as the nail to his hole, the cuckold to his horn, as a scolding quean to a wrangling knave, as the nun's lip to the friar's mouth; nay, as the pudding to his skin.

COUNTESS. Have you, I, say, an answer of such fitness for all **questions**?

CLOWN. From below your duke to beneath your constable, it will fit any **question**.

COUNTESS. It must be an answer of most monstrous size that must fit all demands.

CLOWN. But a trifle neither, in good faith, if the learned should speak truth of it. Here it is, and all that belongs to't. Ask me if I am a courtier: it shall do you no harm to learn.

COUNTESS. To be young again, if we could, I will be a fool in **question**, hoping to be the wiser by your answer. I pray you, sir, are you a courtier?

William Shakespeare, All's Well That Ends Well

Have I told any man to be a liar for my sake?

Have I sold ice to the poor in summer and coal to the poor in winter for the sake of daughters who nursed brindle bull terriers and led with a leash their dogs clothed in plaid wool jackets?

Have I given any man an earful too much of my talk—or asked any man to take a snootful of booze on my account?

Have I put wool in my own ears when men tried to tell me what was good for me? Have I been a bum listener?

Have I taken dollars from the living and the unborn while I made speeches on the retributions that shadow the heels of the dishonest?

Have I done any good under cover? Or have I always put it in the show windows and the newspapers?

Carl Sandburg, **Questionnaire**

Measuring performance is relatively easy. It's more challenging to find ways to measure, from a distance, how people are getting along. The crew members say that the worst part of the study is having to endure the stress and boredom of answering surveys—about forty each week—asking if they're feeling stressed or bored. The fishbowl existence of their pet betta fish, Blastoff McRocketboots, seems carefree by comparison. The results from these surveys, along with cognitive tests and exit interviews, will be measured against data collected from biometric monitors and other devices worn by the volunteers. Readouts note the participants' heart rates, voice levels, and even their proximity to one another. NASA hopes that the data from these and other high-tech mood rings will prove a reliable way to track how astronaut teams are doing without having to rely on self-reporting or on reading between the lines of an e-mail. The essence of the Hawaii experiment may be to make NASA more comfortable with sending crews out of close reach: if humans in space could be monitored a bit more like robots, mission control could spot an emotional cliff coming before the astronauts stumble over it. "Of course," Binsted said, "there's still the **question** of what interventions are actually available when your crew is on Mars."

Tom Kizzia, Moving to Mars: Preparing for the Longest, Loneliest Voyage Ever (The New Yorker)

'What did Sidewinder say to that?' asked Sefton, humbled into a minor role.

'He said good teachers could teach anywhere. But that if it was to be a **question** of insult, the football club might well consider itself the aggrieved party. It did, after all, boast an international reputation, whereas the department—he begged to be corrected if he was wrong—my department enjoyed a more modest fame.'

Listening, Sefton Goldberg died a thousand deaths.

Howard Jacobson, Coming From Behind

I am very unfortunate if that is true. But suppose I ask you a **question**: Would you say that this also holds true in the case of horses?

Plato, Apology

Today, sitting here in my padlocked attic, with a heap of class notes to prepare and these "Extra Wide Angle" precision-optical field glasses to spy around with—today I'm not sure I'd favor drawing and quartering an ex-mayor and Chamber of Commerce volunteer. That's what we did to Jim Kunkel after the Stinger incident. For my part, let me say, right here and now, I'm sorry for the role I played in the kangaroo court that assembled outside Jim's Dune Road condominium.

Then again, what could I do? The demands of civic discourse are difficult. Cooperation and conviviality are rewarded in many ways. I wanted a schoolhouse. I was thinking of the kids when Jerry Henderson and Bill Nixon and some other Rotary guys greeted me beneath the streetlamps. They well knew my journeyman-historian's acquaintance with the rack, the wheel, the iron maiden, and so forth. I'd given a talk, only days before, on an array of such devices, at a Rotary lunch. My intention was to draw parallels between ancient and modern concepts of punishment and guilt, and to demonstrate a few of the ways contemporary society has internalized, even subtly institutionalized "The Barbarity of the Past," which was the title of my talk.

I was hoping to say something about the way we live. It was clear to me, though, during the **question**-and-answer period, that the real effect of my lecture had been pernicious. Should I have seen it coming, that starry night outside Jim's Dune Road home, when Jerry and Bill and those bully boys clapped their hands on my back and said, grinning, "Hey, it's Mr. Executioner"?

Likewise, how much responsibility must I bear for what eventually, inevitably occurred, simply because I suggested using some Toyotas and Subarus parked nearby, in lieu of horses?

Better, perhaps, not to ask. Anyway, I have lecture notes to prepare.

Donald Antrim, Elect Mr. Robinson for a Better World

Problem # 7

Two identical cars collide head on. Each car is traveling at 100 km/h. The impact force on each car is the same as hitting a solid wall at:

    (a) 100 km/h

    (b) 200 km/h

    (c) 150 km/h

Problem # 8

Why is it possible to drive a nail into a piece of wood with a hammer, but it is not possible to push a nail in by hand?

Real World Physics Problems, Physics **Questions**

In last month's webinar on Project-Based Learning and the Arts, we briefly discussed the role of "driving **questions**" in an inquiry-based learning experience in the arts or arts integrated classroom.

A driving **question** is presented at the beginning of an inquiry-based learning experience as the frame for the project. A good driving **question** is one that "focuses all other **questions** towards a solution or product" (leadingpbl.org).

Characteristics of a quality driving **question**:

- Open-ended enough to allow for individual investigation
- Relevant to students (resembles issues/problems/**questions** students might encounter in the real world)
- Meaningful to students (resembles a real-world problem or issue)
- Supports self-directed learning through multiple activities and sources
- Involves authentic problem-solving

*Kenneth Udut, Is Is Is Philsosophy **Question**, 2014 (Internet Archive)*

Kenneth Udut's collection of Vines. "Vines" are 6.8 second Videos. They are intended to to "loop"—to play continually until stopped, a unique feature of the Vine service. I am archiving my collection here of approximately 30 months worth, beginning July 4, 2013. They are currently organized by subject, which I achieved by extracting the #subject and converting to Internet Archive-subject-XML.

- Consistent with standards (aligned with assessment and learning outcomes)
- Lends itself to collaboration and cross-disciplinary work

Brianne Gidcumb, Driving **Questions** to Guide Inquiry in the Arts (EducationCloset)

He didn't look that different from the other researchers, but somehow I knew he wasn't a member of the staff. Maybe it was the toga. He sat staring into the Macintosh, giggling nervously. Imagine, laughing in the CDF control room! At one of the greatest experiments science has ever devised! I thought I'd better put my foot down.

LEDERMAN: Excuse me. Are you the new mathematician they were supposed to send over from the University of Chicago?

GUY IN TOGA: Right profession, wrong town. Name's Democritus. I hail from Abdera, not Chicago. They call me the Laughing Philosopher.

LEDERMAN: Abdera?

DEMOCRITUS: Town in Thrace, on the Greek mainland.

LEDERMAN: I don't remember requisitioning anyone from Thrace. We don't need a Laughing Philosopher. At Fermilab I tell all the jokes.

DEMOCRITUS: Yes, I've heard of the Laughing Director. Don't worry about it. I doubt if I'll be here long. Not given what I've seen so far.

LEDERMAN: So why are you taking up space in the control room?

DEMOCRITUS: I'm looking for something. Something very small.

LEDERMAN: You've come to the right place. Small is our specialty.

DEMOCRITUS: So I'm told. I've been looking for this thing for twenty-four hundred years.

LEDERMAN: Oh, you're *that* Democritus.

DEMOCRITUS: You know another one?

LEDERMAN: I get it. You're like the angel Clarence in *It's a Wonderful Life,* sent here to talk me out of suicide. Actually, I was thinking about slicing my wrists. We can't find the top quark.

DEMOCRITUS: Suicide! You remind me of Socrates. No, I'm no angel. That immortality concept came after my time, popularized by that soft-head Plato.

LEDERMAN: But if you're not immortal, how can you be here? You died over two millennia ago.

DEMOCRITUS: There are more things in heaven and earth, Horatio, than are dreamt of in your philosophy.

LEDERMAN: Sounds familiar.

DEMOCRITUS: Borrowed it from a guy I met in the sixteenth century. But to answer your **question** . . .

Leon M. Lederman, The God Particle: If the Universe Is the Answer, What Is the **Question**?

To be, or not to be, that is the **Question**:

William Shakespeare, The Tragedie of Hamlet, Prince of Denmarke

The professor stabbed his chest with his hands curled like forks
before coughing up the **question**
that had dogged him since he first read Emerson:
Why am I "I"? Like musk oxen we hunkered
while his lecture drifted against us like snow.

If we could, we would have turned our backs into the wind.

    Lucia Perillo, Transcendentalism

Why must the **question** of Being be revived at any cost? Although Heidegger seems to presuppose everywhere that it is the guiding **question** of philosophy as well as of our existence and our destiny, only occasionally does he try explicitly to justify this priority. Yet he does so in detailed fashion in his magisterial introduction to SZ, titled precisely "The Necessity, Structure, and Priority of the **Question** of Being." This text would deserve a rigorous commentary. We will only recall its lessons and its main "arguments" before returning to the **question** that concerns us—why repeat the **question** of Being?—which is not, perhaps, completely resolved by this text, which remains somewhat protreptic and general.

    *Jean Grondin, Why Reawaken the **Question** of Being? (Heidegger's Being and Time: Critical Essays)*

There's an old song
my grandfather used to sing
that has the **question**,
"Or would you rather be a fish?"
In the same song
is the same **question**
but with a mule and a pig,
but the one I hear sometimes
in my head is the fish one.
Just that one line.
Would you rather be a fish?

    Ron Padgett, The Line

This article repeats, unchanged and expanded by a few lines (p. 24f.), the text of the contribution to the publication issued in honor of Ernst Jünger (1955).[1] The title has been changed. It read: *Concerning "The Line."* The new title is meant to indicate that the consideration of the essence of nihilism stems from a discussion of Being as ~~Being~~. According to tradition, the **question** of being is understood by philosophy to be of being as being. It is *the* **question** of metaphysics. The answering of this **question** is always related to an interpretation of Being which remains as yet **unquestioned** and prepares the ground and basis for metaphysics. Metaphysics does not go back to its ground. This return is explained in the Introduction to *What Is Metaphysics* which has been added to the text of the lecture from the fifth edition (1949) on (7th edition 1955, pp. 7–23).

    *Jean T. Wilde and William Kluback, Introduction to Martin Heidegger, The **Question** of Being*

'It's an extremely difficult examination,' Ian Merrick, MA, Lecturer in Philology, was saying to Treece when Emma Fielding entered Treece's office for her tutorial.

'No one ever passes first time,' said Merrick, sitting on the desk. 'The real problem is the practical part . . .'

Treece noticed Emma standing there. 'Do sit down, Miss Fielding,' he said. 'I shan't be a minute.'

'Yes,' said Merrick; 'there's no problem about the theoretical stuff, of course; that's simply a **question** of mugging up the notes, but when it comes to practical performance, they're very sticky.'

Would an elephant make a good pet?
If you dig up buried treasure, is it yours?
If you were bigger than your parents, who would be in charge?

STICKY **QUESTIONS**
Year 3 (7–8 yrs)

A year's worth of thought-provoking **questions** for parents and children to share. One day each week, all the children go home with a sticker on their jumper. Instead of having a conversation about, "Have you done your homework", the homework IS the conversation. Then the following day, or after the weekend if you give them out on a Friday, the discussion can carry on at school, drawing on ideas from home. All packs will include ideas on how to carry on the discussion back in school, and how to support children who get less support from home, how to involve grandparents and so on.

£50.00
Add to Cart

ABOUT THE PHILOSOPHY MAN

Whilst teaching English at Sutton Grammar School, Jason Buckley rotated around Year 7 forms, facilitating discussions off the back of philosophical stories. These were popular, and years later when he was looking for a name for his new organisation, he remembered one boy exclaiming "Yay, it's the Philosophy Man!" From small beginnings in 2008, The Philosophy Man is now the UK's leading independent provider of P4C training and workshops. Jason and Tom send free p4c resources to over 17,000 educators worldwide, and train upwards of 2,000 teachers a year through INSETS and Keynotes in our streamlined and accessible Philosophy Circles approach to P4C. We spend as much time in the classroom as we do delivering courses, and we 'show our working' in front of children of all ages.

The Philosophy Man (thephilosophyman.com)

'Oh, my goodness,' said Treece.

'Have you got a crash helmet?' asked Merrick.

'For a motorized bicycle? Oh, really old boy . . .'

'Well, you have to show willing. I know it looks ridiculous. I always say they should make them look like bowler hats, and then a gentleman could wear them as well.'

Malcolm Bradbury, Eating People Is Wrong

As the essencing of technology, Enframing is that which endures. Does Enframing hold sway at all in the sense of granting? No doubt the **question** seems a horrendous blunder. For according to everything that has been said, Enframing is, rather, a destining that gathers together into the revealing that challenges forth. Challenging is anything but a granting. So it seems, so long as we do not notice that the challenging-forth into the ordering of the real as standing-reserve still remains a destining that starts man upon a way of revealing. As this destining, the coming to presence of technology gives man entry into That which, of himself, he can neither invent nor in any way make. For there is no such thing as a man who, solely of himself, is only man.

But if this destining, Enframing, is the extreme danger, not only for man's coming to presence, but for all revealing as such, should this destining still be called a granting?

*Martin Heidegger, The **Question** Concerning Technology*

"Good **question**. The hair is used to make carpet. Up in Amsterdam, New York. Bigelow. Mohawk. But the primary value is the skins. The hair is a by-product, and how you get the hair off the skin and all the rest of it is another story entirely. Before synthetics came along, the hair mostly went into cheap carpets. There's a company that brokered all the hair from the tanneries to the carpetmakers, but you don't want to go into that," he said, observing how before they'd really even begun she'd filled with notes the top sheet of a fresh yellow legal pad, "Though if you do," he added, touched by—and attracted by—her thoroughness, "because I suppose it does all sort of tie together, I could send you to talk to those people. I think the family is still around. It's a niche that not many people know about. It's interesting. It's all interesting. You've settled on an interesting subject, young lady."

"I think I have," she said, warmly smiling over at him.

Philip Roth, American Pastoral

SOCRATES: Dear Crito, your zeal is invaluable, if a right one; but if wrong, the greater the zeal the greater the evil; and therefore we ought to consider whether these things shall be done or not. For I am and always have been one of those natures who must be guided by reason, whatever the reason may be which upon reflection appears to me to be the best; and now that this fortune has come upon me, I cannot put away the reasons which I have before given: the principles which I have hitherto honored and revered I still honor, and unless we can find other and better principles on the instant, I am certain not to agree with you; no, not even if the power of the multitude could inflict many more imprisonments, confiscations, deaths, frightening us like children with hobgoblin terrors. But what will be the fairest way of considering the **question**? Shall I return to your old argument about the opinions of men, some of which are to be regarded, and others, as we were saying, are not to be regarded? Now were we right in maintaining this before I was condemned? And has the argument which was once good now proved to be talk for the sake of talking; in fact an amusement only, and altogether vanity? That is what I want to consider with your help, Crito: whether, under my present circumstances, the argument appears to be in any way different or not; and is to be allowed by me or disallowed. That argument, which, as I believe, is maintained by many who assume to be authorities, was to the effect, as I was saying, that the opinions of some men are to be regarded, and of other men not to be regarded. Now you, Crito, are a disinterested person who are not going to die tomorrow at least, there is no human probability of this, and you are therefore not liable to be deceived by the circumstances in which you are placed. Tell me, then, whether I am right in saying that some opinions, and the opinions of some men only, are to be valued, and other opinions, and the opinions of other men, are not to be valued. I ask you whether I was right in maintaining this?

CRITO: Certainly.

SOCRATES: The good are to be regarded, and not the bad?

CRITO: Yes.

SOCRATES: And the opinions of the wise are good, and the opinions of the unwise are evil?

CRITO: Certainly.

SOCRATES: And what was said about another matter? Was the disciple in gymnastics supposed to attend to the praise and blame and opinion of every man, or of one man only his physician or trainer, whoever that was?

Plato, Crito

Trump arrived, with a phalanx of aides. He walked to a waist-high lectern decorated with a Trump poster and said, "Hello, everybody, how are you? Carl?"

Carl Cameron, of Fox News, asked about a local campaign operative who was leaving Rick Perry's campaign for Trump's. The operative joined Trump at the lectern for a couple of **questions**. Then, as Trump stepped back to the microphone alone, Ramos stood up. "Mr. Trump, I have a **question** about immigration," he said. Trump ignored him, scanning the room as if no one had spoken, saying, "O.K., who's next?" He pointed at someone. "Yeah. Please."

Ramos persisted. "Mr. Trump, I have a **question**."

Trump turned and said, "Excuse me. Sit down. You weren't called. Sit down. Sit down."

Ramos remained standing.

"Sit down." The sneer in Trump's tone was startling.

"No, Mr. Trump," Ramos said, his voice level. "I'm a reporter, an immigrant, a U.S. citizen. I have the right to ask a **question**."

"No, you don't," Trump said, sharply. "You haven't been called. Go back to Univision."

Ramos: "Mr. Trump, you cannot deport eleven million people. You cannot build a nineteen-hundred-mile wall."

Trump began scanning the room again. Reporters were raising their hands. Trump pointed at one.

"You cannot deny citizenship to children in this country," Ramos continued.

Trump turned to his left and seemed to give a signal, a kind of duck-lipped kissing or sucking expression. A bodyguard with a buzz cut started to cross the stage. "Go ahead," Trump muttered to him.

The bodyguard went for Ramos, who was still talking. "Those ideas—" The bodyguard, who was a foot taller than Ramos, began to push him backward, out of the room. "I'm a reporter," Ramos said. "Don't touch me, sir." His voice did not rise. "You cannot touch me." The bodyguard had him by the left arm and was now moving him swiftly toward an exit door.

While Ramos was getting the bum's rush, Trump called on a reporter. "Yes, go ahead."

"Thank you, Mr. Trump. Chip Reid, with CBS."

"Hi, Chip. Yes?"

"Roger Ailes says you need to apologize to Megyn Kelly. Will you do that?"

"No, I wouldn't do that. She actually should be apologizing to me."

The door swung shut behind Ramos, who still held his notes.

William Finnegan, The Man Who Wouldn't Sit Down (The New Yorker)

"You are the young lady just now referred to?"

"O! most unhappily, I am!"

The plaintive tone of her compassion merged into the less musical voice of the Judge, as he said something fiercely: "Answer the **questions** put to you, and make no remark upon them."

Charles Dickens, A Tale of Two Cities

WHO GETS TO SPEAK AND WHY?, I wrote last week, IS THE ONLY **QUESTION**.

Chris Kraus, I Love Dick

"I mean, come on, you're going to accuse Megyn Kelly of having her period and that's why she asked the tough **questions** . . . I just think that's crap."

*Harriet Alexander, Donald Trump Says Megyn Kelly's Tough **Questioning** Was Due to Menstruation (The Telegraph)*

Erickson wasn't the only conservative bashing Trump.

Penny Young Nance, the CEO and president of the conservative group Concerned Women for America, told CNN that Trump's "tantrum was even more enlightening than his original remarks she **questioned**."

"Does he have a problem with women?" Nance asked in a statement Saturday morning. "Three wives would suggest that yes, maybe there's a problem. The good news is that Kelly is a mother of toddlers and knows how to deal with petulance and tantrums. Every presidential election since 1964 has been carried by women. Women don't like mean and we certainly won't vote for men or women we don't trust. Trump's biggest woman problem is how does he convince women to trust him to keep America safe?"

Holly Yan, Trump Draws Outrage After Megyn Kelly Remarks (CNN)

He stood smiling down at the girl, who had dropped without a word into her swivel-chair; nothing moved in her but her eyes, which looked up at him, mesmerized with instinctive fear, like an animal's. "But first let me hint this, Domna—you are somewhat too bornée in your thinking. There is something in you, perhaps an upper-class habit, that keeps you, with your excellent mind and remarkable analytic powers, from making what one might define as the necessary metaphysical leap, the two plus two making five that Dostoievsky speaks of." The girl nodded, almost joyously, she understood what he meant. "For example, he proceeded, in a style that was purposefully leisured, "your very search for motive lacks creative imagination. You are looking in private places, while the answer is staring you in the face, from the newspapers, the radio, the forum. Domna, we are at war, though apparently you only realize it when you are reading your morning newspaper. You imagine that the war is located in the dispatches of correspondents, but it is also here, on this campus."

The girls' eyes flew wide open; did she begin at last to see what he was driving at? How much, he asked himself, was it necessary to tell her to send the point home irrefutably: "But leave that for the moment. Let us return to your thinking. As an intellectual exercise, the broad jump we've been speaking of, try putting the **question** that is bothering you in the form of a declarative statement: 'Knowing of Cathy's condition, Hoar has been tempted to do this.'"

Mary McCarthy, *The Groves of Academe: A Novel*

The fifth **question** is answered by all that precedes, and especially by the last paragraph. There is nothing in the nature of menstruation to imply the necessity, or even the desirability, of rest, for women whose nutrition is really normal. The habit of periodical rest, in them, might indeed easily become injurious, because in the cessation of nervo muscular activity, the blood properly attracted to the muscles and nerve centres would be diverted from them, and tend towards the pelvis, increasing its hyperaemia above the physiological standard. Many cases of pelvic congestion, developed in healthy but indolent and luxurious women, are often due to no other cause.

Mary Putnam Jacobi, The **Question** *of Rest for Women During Menstruation*

"God help her!" cried the worthy man. "The poor thing's troubles have turned her brain!"

"I thought you would disapprove of it, sir," said Benjamin, in his mild and moderate way. "I confess I disapprove of it myself."

"'Disapprove of it' isn't the word," retorted the vicar. "Don't put it in that feeble way, if you please. An act of madness—that's what it is, if she really means what she says." He turned my way, and looked as he used to look at the afternoon service when he was catechising an obstinate child. "You don't mean it," he said, "do you?"

"I am sorry to forfeit your good opinion, uncle," I replied. "But I must own that I do certainly mean it."

"In plain English," retorted the vicar, "you are conceited enough to think that you can succeed where the greatest lawyers in Scotland have failed. They couldn't prove this man's innocence, all working together. And you are going to prove it single-handed? Upon my word, you are a wonderful woman," cried my uncle, suddenly descending from indignation to irony. "May a plain country parson, who isn't used to lawyers in petticoats, be permitted to ask how you mean to do it?"

"I mean to begin by reading the Trial, uncle."

"Nice reading for a young woman! You will be wanting a batch of nasty French novels next. Well, and when you have read the Trial—what then? Have you thought of that?"

"Yes, uncle; I have thought of that. I shall first try to form some conclusion (after reading the Trial) as to the guilty person who really committed the crime. Then I shall make out a list of the witnesses who spoke in my husband's defense. I shall go to those witnesses, and tell them who I am and what I want. I shall ask all sorts of **questions** which grave lawyers might think it beneath their dignity to put. I shall be guided, in what I do next, by the answers I receive. And I shall not be discouraged, no matter what difficulties are thrown in my way. Those are my plans, uncle, so far as I know them now."

The vicar and Benjamin looked at each other as if they doubted the evidence of their own senses. The vicar spoke.

"Do you mean to tell me," he said, "that you are going roaming about the country to throw yourself on the mercy of strangers, and to risk whatever rough reception you may get in the course of your travels? You! A young woman! Deserted by your husband! With nobody to protect you! Mr. Benjamin, do you hear her? And can you believe your ears? I declare to Heaven I don't know whether I am awake or dreaming. Look at her—just look at her! There she sits as cool and easy as if she had said nothing at all extraordinary, and was going to do nothing out of the common way! What am I to do with her?—that's the serious **question**—what on earth am I to do with her?"

Wilkie Collins, The Law and the Lady

"This is a new assigmnent," I said. "But from now on one of our main concerns is to be the Woman **Question**."

"That's wonderful and it's about time. Something has to give women an opportunity to come to close grips with life. Please go on, tell me your ideas," she said, pressing forward, her hand light upon my arm.

And I went on talking, relieved to talk, carried away by my own enthusiasm and by the warmth of the wine. And it was only when I turned to ask a **question** of her that I realized that she was leaning only a nose-tip away, her eyes upon my face.

"Go on, please go on," I heard. "You make it sound so clear—please."

I saw the rapid, moth-wing fluttering of her lids become the softness of her lips as we were drawn together. There was not an idea or concept in it but sheer warmth; then the bell was ringing and I shook it off and got to my feet, hearing it ring again as she arose with me, the red robe falling in heavy folds upon the carpet, and she saying, "You make it all so wonderfully alive," as the bell sounded again. And I was trying to move, to get out of the apartment, looking for my hat and filling with anger, thinking, Is she crazy? Doesn't she hear? as she stood before me in bewilderment, as though I were acting irrationally. And now taking my arm with sudden energy, saying, "This way, in here," almost pulling me along as the bell rang again, through a door down a short hall, a satiny bedroom, in which she stood appraising me with a smile, saying, "This is mine," as I looked at her in outrageous disbelief.

"Yours, *yours*? But what about that bell?"

"Never mind," she cooed, looking into my eyes.

"But be reasonable," I said, pushing her aside. "What about that door?"

"Oh, of course, you mean the telephone, don't you, darling?"

"But your old man—your husband?"

Ralph Ellison, Invisible Man

A lot of good people are asking a lot of good **questions** these days, and this is an excellent thing. On the foreign policy side, it happens the best of these **questions** are posed by non-Americans, for the simple reason most Americans are not ready to think clearly about our moment and how we have come to it. We do not ask because we cannot answer.

My three favorite **questions** of late, it also happens, have to do with Syria. And let there be no doubt: It is all over for the Obama administration, the Pentagon, the spooks and all others still pretending there is a "moderate opposition" that will carry the day in the many-sided Syrian conflict. Washington has slipped its grip. Others are in charge now, and as they pursue a solution to this crisis the only choice open to the U.S. is whether or not to join in the effort. It will be interesting to see which alternative the White House and the State Department choose.

"I cannot help asking those who have caused the situation, Do you realize now what you've done?" This is the first good **question**.

Vladimir Putin posed it in his speech to the U.N. General Assembly 10 days ago. Sensibly, the Russian president added, "But I am afraid no one is going to answer that." To offer modest assistance, Mr. Putin, the U.S. leadership knows exactly what it has done, and this is why you are correct: Your query will go without reply.

The second and third good **questions** came from Mohammad Javad Zarif, Iran's foreign minister. For my money Zarif is among the ablest diplomats now on the scene. He addressed the U.S. on the Syria crisis during a conference in New York on Monday, and he asked, "Why are you there? Who gave you the right to be there?"

Wow, wow and wow.

I love these **questions**.

Patrick L. Smith, Thomas Friedman, Read Your Chomsky: The New York Times Gets Putin/Obama All Wrong, Again (Salon)

Is there an antidote to the perennial seductiveness of war? And is this a **question** a woman is more likely to pose than a man? (Probably yes.)

Could one be mobilized actively to oppose war by an image (or a group of images) as one might be enrolled among the opponents of capital punishment by reading, say, Dreiser's *An American Tragedy* or Turgenev's "The Execution of Troppmann," an account by the expatriate writer, invited to be an observer in a Paris prison, of a famous criminal's last hours before being guillotined? A narrative seems likely to be more effective than an image. Partly it is a **question** of the length of time one is obliged to look, to feel. No photograph or portfolio of photographs can unfold, go further, and further still, as do *The Ascent* (1977), by the Ukrainian director Larisa Shepitko, the most affecting film about the sadness of war I know, and an astounding Japanese documentary, Kazuo Hara's *The Emperor's Naked Army Marches On* (1987), the portrait of a "deranged" veteran of the Pacific war, whose life's work is denouncing Japanese war crimes from a sound truck he drives through the streets of Tokyo and paying most unwelcome visits to his former superior officers, demanding that they apologize for crimes, such as the murder of American prisoners in the Philippines, which they either ordered or condoned.

Susan Sontag, Regarding the Pain of Others

"Then you've maybe been asking yourself the same **question** we have."

HOW TO YOUR STUDENTS TO ANSWER QUESTIONS IN CLASS

for graduate students and new faculty members

So we've learned by now that students can only be engaged during a lecture for maybe 20 minutes at a time. Therefore it's important to break up your lecture and include some student engagement. The easiest way to do this is to stop the lecture and ask your students verbal **questions** like: What's the next step? Any ideas on how we should approach this problem? Does this idea look familiar?

The Academic Society, How to Get Your Students to
*Answer **Questions** in Class (theacademicsociety.com)*

"You mean, why did he do it?"

*Ian Rankin, A **Question** of Blood*

I figured one more **question** would get me an answer; instead, it got me a tequila shot in the face. The girl's cackle, shrill and violent, stung my ears as I blinked through the burning liquid. Raw anger rang up inside of me, and I responded by scooping up the nearest knife and pinning it behind the big mouth's ear. I clamped the other side of his face in my grip. He went stiff and lost track of his breath. A hush fell from the ceiling. I smelled sweat. There was no sound except for the girl giggling into her chest. The waitress hurried my beer to the table and vanished. I held the knife against the boy's ear cartilage, testing it against his flesh, now calm enough to wish that I'd walked away.

Andrew Cotto, Outerborough Blues: A Brooklyn Mystery

"Why pick on that school, though?" Rebus continued. "You went to a few of his parties, didn't you, Mr. Brimson?"

"He threw a good party."

"Always used to be plenty of teenagers hanging around."

Brimson turned again. "Is that a **question** or a comment?"

*Ian Rankin, A **Question** of Blood*

'See for yourself.'

The young man, whose officer's uniform, by its formality, made him look even slighter than he was, blew his nose, and clenched his teeth to try and stifle his sobs, but finally stammered:

'I haven't done anything . . .'

They watched him for some moments, as he tried to regain control.

'That's all,' pronounced Maigret firmly at last. 'I didn't say you had done anything. Oosting asked you to claim you had seen a stranger lurking by the house. He probably told you that it was the only way to save a certain someone . . . Who?'

'I swear on the head of my mother he didn't tell me who. I don't know! I want to die!'

'Tut, tut! At eighteen, everyone wants to die. You don't have any more **questions**, Monsieur Pijpekamp?'

The Dutch officer shrugged his shoulders, a gesture signifying that he had no idea what was going on.

Georges Simenon, A Crime in Holland

We are **questioning** concerning technology in order to bring to light our relationship to its essence. The essence of modern technology shows itself in what we call Enframing. But simply to point to this is still in no way to answer the **question** concerning technology, if to answer means to respond, in the sense of correspond, to the essence of what is being asked about.

*Martin Heidegger, The **Question** Concerning Technology*

He dialed his wife.

"Oh, hi hon!" Susan was startled to hear from him so early in the day—usually he called before he went to bed, which was closer to dinnertime on the East Coast. "Is everything okay?"

"Everything's fine."

Already, her brisk, merry tone had disheartened him. Susan was often on Ted's mind in Naples, but a slightly different version of Susan: a thoughtful, knowing woman with whom he could speak without speaking. It was this slightly different version of Susan who had listened with him to the quiet of Pompeii, alert to lingering reverberations of screams, of sliding ash. How could so much devastation have been silenced? This was the sort of **question** that had come to preoccupy Ted in his week of solitude, a week that felt like both a month and a minute.

 Jennifer Egan, A Visit From the Goon Squad

"How do you feel about her now?"

 "Sexually or personally?"

 "Sexually."

 "How the hell do I know?"

 "Well then personally."

 "I don't know that either."

 "Then why do you ask me to be specific, since the answer is the same for both?"

 "Darling, our first quarrel," I said sarcastically. Then I relented and reminded her how sweet Elsie was when we were all young, and that (to answer her original **question**) I didn't marry her when she was a woman but when she was a girl. An important point. "You remember her then, *zaftig* and warm—"

 "You keep using that word as though you think it's Polish. It's Jewish you know."

 "I know that very well. She has no brain, but soft and warm and friendly, and always neatly dressed. Now she clops around in a wrapper with her hair twisted up in a bun, Christ's bride. How does she expect to hold a man? Could I have a drink? I know it's only the middle of the day, but I feel the need."

 Peter De Vries, Let Me Count the Ways: A Novel

The clientele of the Black Hole consisted largely of students who, if asked a **question** about what single nutrient they might choose to have with them on a desert island (or in a black hole), would answer unhesitatingly, "Bud." All earnestly believed that beer was the perfect food, and that this knowledge had been kept from them by a conspiracy of adults. While Bob knew this wasn't true, he frequented the Black Hole because it gave him someplace to go that was decidedly different from his apartment but not unlike Earl Butz' confinement room with the lights off. He said, "I hate parties. I like anti-parties, like the Black Hole here."

 "Shit. If you don't watch out, you're going to go right back to your dad's farm and think that a night out means going down to the Country Tap."

 Bob didn't say anything because that's exactly what his dad and uncles did think.

 Jane Smiley, Moo

When philosophy with Aristotle and Plato turned from Being to being as the fundamental **question** of metaphysics, according to Heidegger, they divided and estranged Being from being. This, for Heidegger, was a decisive moment in the history of philosophy. This concern for being was continued in the Middle Ages and dominated modern philosophy to Nietzsche. The Platonic separation of a world of Ideas and a world of opinion opened the gap between Being and being and destroyed the fundamental ontological inseparability of the Being of being.

 *Jean T. Wilde and William Kluback, Introduction to Martin Heidegger, The **Question** of Being*

'And where does that get us?' asked Treece.

'There are practical problems to face as well, Stuart, and the **question** is, what should we do if we keep him? Give him a BA honours degree in schizophrenia?'

'It isn't *funny*,' said Treece.

'No, I know it's not, but you see what I mean. We aren't here to provide a haven for the ill-adjusted. He just doesn't respond to the terms on which we have him here. The **question** isn't whether we should give him a home for a while; it's whether he's a suitable student to take an honours course in English.'

Malcolm Bradbury, Eating People Is Wrong

"They'd no business knowing I was doing that course," he muttered, still grappling with the implications of my **question**. "Bloody sniffer dogs. It was private. Privately selected, privately pursued. They can get lost. So can you."

I laughed. But I was also put out. "Now don't be like that, Cyril. You know the rules as well as I do. It's not your style to ignore a regulation. It's not mine either. Russian is Russian, and reporting is reporting. It's only a matter of getting it down in writing. I didn't make up the regulations. I get a brief, the same as anyone else." I was talking to his back again. He had taken refuge at the bay window, and was gazing out at the rectangle that was his garden.

"What's their names?" he demanded.

"Olga and Boris," I repeated patiently.

This enraged him. "The people who brief you, idiot! I'm going to enter a complaint about them! Snooping, that's what it is. It's bloody brutal in this day and age. I'm holding you to blame too, frankly. What's their names?"

I still didn't answer him. I preferred to let the fury bank up in him.

"Number one," he announced in a louder voice, still staring at his mud patch. "Are you writing this down? Number one, I am not taking a language course within the meaning of the Act. A language course is going to a school or class, it is sitting on a bench with a bunch of snivelling typists with bad breath, it is submitting to the sneers of an uncouth instructor. Number two. I *do*, however, listen to *radio*, it being one of my *continuing* pleasures to scan the wavebands for examples of the quaint or esoteric. Write that down and I'll sign it. Finish, okay? Then take yourself off. I'm done with you, thank you, up to here. Nothing personal. It's them."

"Which was how you stumbled on Boris and Olga," I suggested helpfully, writing again. "Got it. You scanned the wavebands and there they were. Boris and Olga. Nothing wrong in that, Cyril. Stick with it and you might even land yourself a language allowance, if you pass the test. It's only a few bob, I suppose, but it's better in your pocket than theirs, I always say." I continued writing, but slowly, letting him hear the maddening scratch of my government-issue pencil. "It's always the *not* reporting that bothers them most," I confided, apologising for the foibles of my masters. "'If he hasn't told us about Olga and Boris, what else hasn't he told us?' You can't blame them, I suppose. Their jobs are on the line, same as ours."

Turn another page. Lick tip of pencil.

John le Carré, The Secret Pilgrim

Given a pair of **questions**, the task is to classify whether they are duplicates or not. The two phases of classification in our work are described as follows.

Classifier Training Phase

To train a classifier (i.e., classification model), we first extract a set of features from the **question** pair. Three types of features are explored: (1) vector similarity; (2) topical similarity; and (3) association score. Feature generation is detailed in Sect. 6.3.2. In total, three features are generated for vector similarity, three features each for topical similarity and one feature for association score. In terms of classifiers, we experiment with the following models: decision tree [210], K-nearest neighbours (K-NN) [91], support vector machines (SVM) [211], logistic regression [212], random forest [213] and naive Bayes [214]. In terms of training data, the ratio of non-duplicate pairs (negative examples) to duplicate pairs (positive example) is very skewed. For example, in the Stack Overflow dump we processed (Sect. 6.4.1.1), 716,819 valid posts are tagged with "java" (case-insensitive), among which only 28,656 posts are marked as being duplicates. To create a more balanced dataset, we bias the distribution by under-sampling non-duplicate pairs [196, 197].

Wei Emma Zhang and Quan Z. Sheng, Managing Data From Knowledge Bases: Querying and Extraction

"In the beginning," says Socrates, "I did not dare to suppose that such a diverse group as this could arrive at any general conclusions. Consider: what does an ancient classical philosopher from Greece have in common with a saint of the Catholic Church, with a seventeenth-century rationalist mathematician, or with a twentieth-century existentialist? Yet we all desired to find out about Truth. At first, we clung to our separate islands: Reason, Faith, Experience, and, in my case, **Questioning** (I prefer that to *Inquisition*). It seems to me now that we have built some bridges between the islands, and by so doing have extended the realm of our understanding in these matters. And while the sum of what we have learned about Truth is far, far less than we desire to know, we do not return from our intellectual journey empty-handed. As for myself, I knew that Truth was difficult to obtain; pride, greed, ignorance, fear—so many things conspire to obscure it. So unwillingly does it come forth from men that it must be teased out by subtle **questions**!

Gene Barnes, What Then Is Truth? A Philosophical Dialogue

Duplicates Detection Phase

Given a **question** pair (m, t), where m is an existing **question** and t is a new posted **question**, the trained classifier predicts whether they are duplicate. To construct these **question** pairs, we conduct a naive filtering approach to filter out **questions** that belong to a different programming language or technique using tags. Tags are a mandatory input when posting a new **question** on Stack Overflow, and as such are a reliable indicator of the topic the **question** belongs to. Specifically, we prune existing **questions** that have no common tags with t, thus narrowing the search space for candidate duplicate **questions** considerably. We additionally filter out **questions** that have no answers. We then generate **question** pairs for t with all remainder **questions**, and compute features (will discuss in next section) for the classifier to predict the labels. The labels for (m, t) indicate whether t is a duplicate to m.

Wei Emma Zhang and Quan Z. Sheng, Managing Data From Knowledge Bases: Querying and Extraction

For this only, do I take some credit. You are the trees that bore the fruits of our labors, I only nudged the ripe fruit off the branches! But in this fruit, I have found a great deal of nourishment. I have learned that while all Truth derives ultimately from human experience, the different processes by which Truth is extracted from experience are not equally reliable. I have also learned that, in general, the more reliable a method for determining Truth is, the more limited is its range of applicability.

Gene Barnes, What Then Is Truth? A Philosophical Dialogue

For example, **Q1** asks for solution for a specific problem "causes of java.lang. NoSuchMethodError". However, **question** issuer for **Q2** has problem related to "java. lang.NoSuchMethodError" but does not phrase explicitly in the **question**. **Q3** is phrased in a very specific manner, and has little word overlap with **Q4**. **Q6** asks for functions in JQuery that is similar to "isset" in PHP which crosses the programming language boundary. We leave the development of techniques that tackle cross-language duplicate detection for our future work.

Wei Emma Zhang and Quan Z. Sheng, Managing Data From Knowledge Bases: Querying and Extraction

This raises the **question** of Faith in a natural way, without providing a definitive answer. Therefore tolerance in matters of Faith seems the only prudent course. In the vast majority of situations, Truth cannot be certain, only more or less probable—and should be regarded as such.

"However," continues Socrates, "I wish to add a contribution of my own—or rather, one from my student Plato. Plato supposed that some Truth was known to us even before birth—that we were not born with the mind as a 'blank tablet.' Because little if any evidence can be found in support of this view, it has fallen into considerable disrepute. Nevertheless, it is believed in some religions—such as Buddhism, for example—that beings who die are reincarnated; that is, after dying they reappear in another living form. Perhaps this is only a myth to explain why we haven't observed resurrection more often, or simply a projection of the common desire for immortality. Or, perhaps there is something more to it. In any case, it raises the possibility that the awareness of some Truth might exist prior to what we usually call our experience. Plato thought that the Soul—another term now in disrepute—could have experience of its own, prior to inhabiting a living body. I make no claim of validity for this notion; I only suggest that we should not rule it out completely, in the absence of supporting evidence. Possibly this view can be better defended in the light of modern discoveries. For example, it is now known that the genetic material in the chromosomes contains all the information required to duplicate an individual. But, in duplicating the mind of an individual, might it not duplicate a means to recognize Truth, or at least a tendency to classify things as either true or false? Might not it even contain some genetically coded truths themselves? Do we know to what degree our thinking is genetically determined, and to what degree it is a result of our experience?

"Having said these things," adds Socrates, "I now return to the promised agenda—the clarification period, during which each of you may respond to what has been said by the others."

Gene Barnes, What Then Is Truth? A Philosophical Dialogue

What did you have in mind, if I may ask?
Mr. LEVY. I was referring to the situation dealt with by the amendment that I proposed,
   Mr. Chairman. In other words, I said that if you are going to pass this bill, we want to

be sure to tighten it up, so that you would not perpetuate a practice which permits evasion. Before the House committee I had another—I suggested another amendment which I am reserving for our comments with respect to the omnibus bill. That is what I had in mind then.

Senator HILL. Senator Morse, any **questions**?

Senator MORSE. No **questions**.

Senator HILL. Did you have any **questions**?

Senator WITHERS. No **questions**.

Senator HILL. Mr. Glazier, do you have anything to add to Mr. Levy's testimony?

Mr. GLAZIER. Senator, I have a brief statement for the ILWU.

Senator HILL. Is there anything in your statement that has not been covered by Mr. Levy, if I may ask?

Senator WITHERS. I would like to ask Mr. Levy one **question**. Have you been employed by these employees, these stevedores?

Mr. LEVY. No; I have no interests in any of these litigations.

Senator HILL. In other words, you are not representing any plaintiff against any company in litigation?

Mr. LEVY. No; and I have no prospect of representing any of them.

Senator HILL. Do you say that mournfully? [Laughter.]

Mr. LEVY. I stated that to forestall any **question** which would give the impression that my answer was equivocal.

Senator MORSE. I want to say, Mr. Chairman, that I shall read with great interest the cases that Mr Levy has cited as bearing upon the **question** which I raised the other day. Secondly, the memorandum which he has offered with respect to the meeting which he had in the Department of Labor bears upon another facet of this problem in which I am interested, and I shall read that very carefully, too.

Senator HILL. Do you care to ask any **questions**?

Senator MORSE. I have no reason to ask any **questions**.

United States Senate Committee on Labor and Public Welfare, To Clarify the Overtime Compensation Provisions of the Fair Labor Standards Act of 1938, as Amended: Hearings Before a Subcommittee of the Committee on Labor and Public Welfare, United States Senate, Eighty-First Congress, First Session, on S. 336 and H.R. 858, to Clarify the Overtime Compensation Provisions of the Fair Labor Standards Act of 1938, as Amended, as Applied in the Stevedoring and Building Construction Industries, and for Other Purposes

Question. Of what use, then, is the new system to individual officers other than those in the hump situation?

Answer. Over the very short run, this new system would have minimal effect upon junior officers promotions. However, as previously noted, the long term benefit for the best qualified system is in its attractiveness to the most highly qualified officer. Obviously, this is the individual we seek to attract and retain.

Question. Assuming that the Selected Reserve were continued, what effect would this promotion system have upon your Reserve units?

United States Senate Committee on Commerce, To Improve and Clarify Certain Laws Affecting the Coast Guard: Hearing Before the Merchant Marine Subcommittee of the Committee on Commerce, United States Senate, Ninety-First Congress, Second Session, on S. 3080, S. 3081, H.R. 13716, and H.R. 13816

Mr. COLLINS. I would rather let my colleague answer that **question**, because he is just a little better fortified with information in regard to that. He is prepared to answer that particular phase, which, however is not in accordance with the exact facts so far as inviting American capital in there or inviting a situation wherein a relative amount of American-made goods are concerned.

Senator KING. I wanted to call attention to the fact that our foreign exports are now probably seven to ten billions of dollars, automobiles, and all sorts of manufactured products which have furnished labor at high wages to millions of Americans. I was wondering if you and your organization—because I find many very intelligent and thinking men in your organization have considered seriously the problem of prohibiting or rather imposing impediments to the increasing of our foreign trade, which would, of course, increase our trade with Canada.

Mr. COLLINS. That is a sort of a two-sided **question** that you are asking there. I want to say that from my own investigation of the thing based on those very reports given out as departmental information on the subject, that about 10 cents on the dollar is export trade. I believe, on the other hand, that the American people saw the wisdom of creating a restrictive immigration law for the purpose of protecting American manufacture and American labor, a sort of American tariff on the labor situation, as it were; and I do not believe we ought to turn around and sell the sovereign right of our people on the side of a strictly domestic **question** for the price of 10 cents on a dollar. We as American people believe the **question** should be settled and an interpretation placed by Congress on this **question** that says that those prohibitions against these excluded classes apply to America as a whole, and that there is no situation of lapland where Canada laps over from the United States or where the United States laps over on Canada; that where a sovereign and defined boundary exists that the people residing near it are entitled to full protection of the law passed by Congress.

United States Senate Committee on Immigration, To Clarify the Law Relating to the Temporary Admission of Aliens to the United States: Hearing Before a Subcommittee of the Committee on Immigration, United States Senate, Seventieth Congress, Second Session, on H.R. 16927, an Act to Clarify the Law Relating to the Temporary Admission of Aliens to the United States

Another approach toward QA extraction is to view it as a classification problem of three classes, i.e., the class of **questions**, answers, and noise. We can then employ the supervised learning algorithm to train a statistical classifier from the labeled examples. However, a key difficulty with this approach is that, due to the large variance in the presentation formats of QAs, it is difficult for any supervised learning algorithm to capture all the possible patterns from a limited number of labeled examples. Apparently, this difficulty originates from the *Across Page Diversity*.

Yi Liu, Semi-Supervised Learning With Side Information: Graph-Based Approaches

To return to the King: take for instance the **question** of personal culture. How often is it that kings engage in some special research? Conchologists among them can be counted on the fingers of one maimed hand. The last king of Zembla—partly under the influence of his uncle Conmal, the great translator of Shakespeare (see notes to lines 39–40 and 962), had become, despite frequent migraines, passionately addicted to the study of literature. At forty, not long before the collapse of his throne, he had attained such a degree of scholarship that he dared accede to his venerable uncle's raucous dying request: "Teach, Karlik!" Of course, it would have been unseemly for a monarch to appear in the robes of learning at a university lectern and present to rosy youths *Finnigan's Wake* as a monstrous extension of Angus MacDiarmid's "incoherent transactions" and of Southey's Lingo-Grande ("Dear Stumparumper," etc.) or discuss the Zemblan variants, collected in 1798 by Hodinski, of the Kongsskugg-sio (*The Royal Mirror*), an anonymous masterpiece of the twelfth century. Therefore he lectured under an assumed name and in a heavy make-up, with wig and false whiskers. All brown-bearded, apple-cheeked, blue-eyed Zemblans look alike, and I who have not shaved now for a year, resemble my disguised king (see also note to line 894).

Vladimir Nabokov, Pale Fire

The second type of features is *topical similarity*, computed using a topic model for extracting themes from short texts. Similarity of a **question** pair is measured by computing the similarity of topical distribution between the pair. The last type of features is *association scores*. We first mine association pairs, i.e., pairs of phrases that co-occur frequently in known duplicate **questions**, by adopting a word alignment method developed in the machine translation literature. To generate the association score for a **question** pair, we train a perception that takes association pairs and lexical features as input. The idea of using associated phrases has been explored in knowledge base **question** answering (KBQA): (1) for ranking generated queries in curated KBQA [201]; or (2) for measuring the quality of **question** paraphrases in open KBQA [25]. Our work is the first to adapt the idea to detect duplicate **questions** in PCQA websites.

Wei Emma Zhang and Quan Z. Sheng, Managing Data From Knowledge Bases: Querying and Extraction

"It would seem so, wouldn't it?"

"And yourself, Mr. Dye?"

I shrugged. "It's company policy."

"A rather strange company and a rather strange policy."

"It's the new management," I said.

Tung rose, tugged at his earlobe, and said, "I really have no more **questions**. I think I know as much about you as I need to, and even if I did have some **questions**, I'm sure that your answers would be totally unresponsive unless we used tactics which are far more primitive than the lie detector, but also more—oh, I suppose fruitful is as good a word as any."

Ross Thomas, The Fools in Town Are on Our Side

"Even if they're innocent?"

"No one's innocent. It's just a **question** of whether they're guilty of what we want them for."

P. F. Kluge, Final Exam: A Novel

The primary task of this unit is producing a **question**. Users might use the **question** mark character in informal language in cases other than **questions**, a **question** may be stated in the declaration and indirect form using phrases e.g. "I was wondering . . ., Could you tell me . . ., I'd like to know", or rhetorical **questions** may not require to be associated with the answer segments [4]. After preprocessing the text, the **QE** step extracts direct and indirect **questions** using the Natural Language Parser, rule-based methods, and dictionary. In the **QG**, given the source text, after the data is cleaned and tokenized, the relevant sentences are passed to the Named Entity (NE) tagger and the Part Of Speech (POS) tagger. The given text can be in a form of a group of simple sentences, complex sentences, paragraphs, or a longer textual entity.

*Fatemeh Raazaghi, Automatic **Frequently Asked Questions** Generation (Advances in Artificial Intelligence)*

Kenneth Udut, #Question—Should More People Think Like You Do, or Should More People Think Differently Than You, 2014 (Internet Archive)

This is a work-in-progress at present but once they are all collected here, I will begin the task of organizing them into collections. In the end, there will be a number of pages, each with single subject collections of Vines on them, akin to small video books.

Each Vine contains a single idea. Some Vines only make sense on the service itself and will be removed as I find them. Others will be collected into video idea books and the individual pages removed, which will result in a cleaner neater collection.

If this is the point of the **question** of Being, one would like to know the point of it all! Even after we have elucidated the formal structure of the **question** of Being, the meaning of our **question**—why should we revive the **question** of Being?—remains. Is it simply a matter of clarifying the meaning of the word "Being"? If so, what is the point? Following Heidegger's terminology: what then is the Erfragtes of the Erfragtes, the meaning of the **question** of the meaning of Being? One thing is certain: §2, devoted to the formal structure of the **question** of Being, does not really respond to this **question**.

Nevertheless, it has done so indirectly by making it clear—at the end of §2, and in the spirit of the 1915 lecture—that in this **question**, the Being of the **questioner** is itself affected by the **question**. Very well, but how?

*Jean Grondin, Why Reawaken the **Question** of Being? (Heidegger's Being and Time: Critical Essays)*

—All these **questions** are purely academic, Russell oracled out of his shadow. I mean, whether Hamlet is Shakespeare or James I or Essex. Clergymen's discussions of the historicity of Jesus. Art has to reveal to us ideas, formless spiritual essences. The supreme **question** about a work of art is out of how deep a life does it spring. The painting of Gustave Moreau is the painting of ideas. The deepest poetry of Shelley, the words of Hamlet bring our minds into contact with the eternal wisdom, Plato's world of ideas. All the rest is the speculation of schoolboys for schoolboys.

A.E. has been telling some yankee interviewer. Wall, tarnation strike me!

—The schoolmen were schoolboys first, Stephen said superpolitely. Aristotle was once Plato's schoolboy.

—And has remained so, one should hope, John Eglinton sedately said. One can see him, a model schoolboy with his diploma under his arm.

He laughed again at the now smiling bearded face.

Formless spiritual. Father, Word and Holy Breath. Allfather, the heavenly man. Hiesos Kristos, magician of the beautiful, the Logos who suffers in us at every moment. This verily is that. I am the fire upon the altar. I am the sacrificial butter.

Dunlop, Judge, the noblest Roman of them all, A.E., Arval, the Name Ineffable, in heaven hight: K.H., their master, whose identity is no secret to adepts. Brothers of the great white lodge always watching to see if they can help. The Christ with the bridesister, moisture of light, born of an ensouled virgin, repentant sophia, departed to the plane of buddhi. The life esoteric is not for ordinary person. O.P. must work off bad karma first. Mrs Cooper Oakley once glimpsed our very illustrious sister H.P.B.'s elemental.

O, fie! Out on't! *Pfuiteufel!* You naughtn't to look, missus, so you naughtn't when a lady's ashowing of her elemental.

Mr Best entered, tall, young, mild, light. He bore in his hand with grace a notebook, new, large, clean, bright.

—That model schoolboy, Stephen said, would find Hamlet's musings about the afterlife of his princely soul, the improbable, insignificant and undramatic monologue, as shallow as Plato's.

John Eglinton, frowning, said, waxing wroth:

—Upon my word it makes my blood boil to hear anyone compare Aristotle with Plato.

—Which of the two, Stephen asked, would have banished me from his commonwealth?

Unsheathe your dagger definitions. Horseness is the whatness of allhorse. Streams or tendency and eons they worship. God: noise in the street: very peripatetic. Space: what you damn well have to see. Through spaces smaller than red globules of man's blood they creepycrawl after Blake's buttocks into eternity of which this vegetable world is but a shadow. Hold to the now, the here, through which all future plunges to the past.

James Joyce, Ulysses

Fortunately, while **QA** markup may vary widely *across* pages, it is generally true that *within* single pages QA markup is consistent. This *Within Page Consistency* principle can be viewed as "side information"—which encodes human knowledge on the fact of **FAQ** page creation—to the **QA** extraction task. As will be shown later in this section, the principle's accuracy is well supported by empirical study.

The *Within Page Consistency* leads to the possibility of a bootstrapping approach to QA pair extraction; various heuristics that have been proposed for **QA** pair extraction can be deployed to perform a high-precision labeling of a seed set of text segments as **questions**, answers and noise; an optimization problem is solved that essentially propagates the class labels of the seed segments to the text segments that share similar HTML formats as the seeds. This optimization problem can be described in a transductive learning setting, similar to the well-known semi-supervised learning algorithm—Spectral Graph Transducer [87]. Given a large enough database of **FAQ** pages, which themselves have to be extracted in a high-precision fashion, each of the extraction steps—labeling of seed examples, and similarity-based propagation—can be tuned to high precision, resulting in a large database of correctly identified **QA** pairs.

Yi Liu, Semi-Supervised Learning With Side Information: Graph-Based Approaches

Two tall Trump supporters tower over a small liberal in a green T-shirt.

"Stupid! Uneducated!" Trumpie A shouts. "Do you know anything that goes *on* in the world?"

"Articulate a little more," the guy in the green shirt says.

"I don't want to live in a fascist country!" Trumpie B says.

"You don't know what fascism *is*," Green Shirt says.

"Oh, I'm getting there, man!" Trumpie B says. "Obama's teaching me!"

"Go back to California," Trumpie A shouts at Green Shirt. "Bitch!"

The four of us stand in a tight little circle, Trumpie A shouting insults at Green Shirt while filming Green Shirt's reaction, me filming Trumpie A filming Green Shirt. The bulk and intensity of the Trumpies, plus the fact that Green Shirt seems to be serving as designated spokesperson for a group of protesters now gathering around, appears to be making Green Shirt nervous.

"Obama's teaching you what fascism is?" he sputters. "Obama's a fascist? The left is the fascists? This is so rich! So, like, the people who are being oppressed are the oppressors?"

"Do you know what's going on in the world, man?" Trumpie A says. "You're not fucking *educated*."

This stings.

"I am very educated," Green Shirt says.

"You have no *idea* what's going on," Trumpie B says.

"I am very educated," Green Shirt says.

Asking the real **questions.**
DankuBot, r/dankmemesdaily (reddit.com)

"You've got no idea, bro," Trumpie A says sadly.

"Ask me a **question**, ask me a **question**," Green Shirt says.

The Tall Trumpies, bored, wander away.

Green Shirt turns to one of his friends. "Am I educated?"

"You're fucking educated," the friend says.

Green Shirt shouts at the Tall Trumpies (who, fortunately for him, are now safely out of earshot), "And I'll stomp the fucking *shit* out of you!"

George Saunders, Trump Days (The New Yorker)

How had he become Professor of History, even at a place like this? By published work? No. By extra good teaching? No in italics. Then how? As usual, Dixon shelved this **question**, telling himself that what mattered was that this man had decisive power over his future, at any rate until the next four or five weeks were up. Until then he must try to make Welch like him, and one way of doing that was, he supposed, to be present and conscious while Welch talked about concerts. But did Welch notice who else was there while he talked, and if he noticed did he remember, and if he remembered would it affect such thoughts as he had already? Then, abruptly, with no warning, the second of Dixon's two predicaments flapped up into consciousness.

Kingsley Amis, Lucky Jim

"You mean he knew someone meant to kill him?"

"I don't know. He didn't say what he wanted. Maybe just help in the reform campaign."

"But do you—?"

I made a complaint:

"It's no fun being a sleuth when somebody steals your stuff, does all the **questioning**."

Dashiell Hammett, Red Harvest

Wheezing along the I-40, Catt considers how broadly this word might be defined. Vehicles, travel, research, design . . . "Whatever you do, there's only a ten-percent chance you'll be caught," her ex-boyfriend Hank had advised her. "That's the statistical chance of an audit!" A jubilant cynic, Hank had done mega real estate deals for developers until an accident left him in traction. After that, he'd switched sides and devoted himself to good causes. Coaching her every step of the way, Hank found Catt's projects amusing. In the midst of all this, Tisa, one of Catt's former mentees, a very political girl from Australia, had emailed to ask her how she planned to respond to George W. Bush's reelection.

"I'm gonna keep my head down!" was Catt's reply to this ludicrous **question**. It was painfully clear that staging a Noah's Ark of repression was part of the Bush regime's domestic policy pageant. Like everyone else, Catt had observed one or a few of each species—an Oregon lawyer, a Texas philanthropist, a musician, a handful of blue-collar workers—plucked from the social landscape and charged under the Patriot Act as state enemies. The prominence of these victims and the frequency of the arrests varied, but it was just enough to keep the whole population on the same terror alert posted at airports and harbors. We can fuck you up good, was the message. As everyone knew, the days of the public political trial were a distant historical memory—you could be sentenced to twenty years in federal prison and no one would blink, so why be a martyr?

Chris Kraus, Summer of Hate

Albrecht Dürer, The Apocalyptic Woman, probably c. 1496–1498 (published 1511)
Woodcut, 41.6 x 28.6 cm, National Gallery of Art, Washington DC

But how would one avoid the label? When is the accusation of paranoia applied, both successfully and not? Who is deemed a legitimate performer of this application?

*L. A. Leere, Asking the Wrong **Questions**: In Defense Of "Paranoia" (Homintern.soy)*

He fell back into sourness, growling, "How the hell do I know?"

But the fact that he let me go away without asking me any more **questions** told me he had already made up his mind that Whisper had killed the girl. I wondered if the little gambler had done it, or if this was another of the wrong raps that Poisonville police chiefs liked to hang on him. It didn't seem to make much difference now. It was a cinch he had—personally or by deputy—put Noonan out, and they could only hang him once.

Dashiell Hammett, Red Harvest

So that's an example of a real-world situation, postgraduation. Somehow I don't see the publishing industry instituting codes banning unhappily married editors from going goopy over authors, though even with such a ban, will any set of regulations ever prevent affective misunderstandings and erotic crossed signals, compounded by power differentials, compounded further by subjective levels of vulnerability?

The **question**, then, is what kind of education prepares people to deal with the inevitably messy gray areas of life? Personally I'd start by promoting a less vulnerable sense of self than the one our new campus codes are peddling. Maybe I see it this way because I wasn't educated to think that holders of institutional power were quite so fearsome, nor did the institutions themselves seem so mighty. Of course, they didn't aspire to reach quite as deeply into our lives back then. What no one's much saying about the efflorescence of these new policies is the degree to which they expand the power of the institutions themselves. As for those of us employed by them, what power we have is fairly contingent, especially lately. Get real: What's more powerful—a professor who crosses the line, or the shaming capabilities of social media?

Laura Kipnis, Sexual Paranoia Strikes Academe (The Chronicle of Higher Education)

And suddenly, I wonder whether Michael is capable of scaring people in other ways, despite his memory lapses and his failing strength. Does he have more lucid days? Could he have sneaked onto our front lawn under cover of darkness and scorched a warning into the grass with weed killer? But Michael seemed happy enough to talk about our family history today, even if his accounts were jumbled. The "STOP" message can't have been from him. I shake my head.

"Just stupid kids," I say aloud. But the possibility of a more sinister explanation continues to gnaw at me. I still don't know what happened here on the day I was born; I still don't know why Mum and Dad appeared to be celebrating one baby rather than two. What if someone is warning me to stop asking **questions**. What are they trying to hide?

Emma Rous, The Au Pair

In February, Northwestern film professor and liberal cultural critic (and occasional *Slate* contributor) Laura Kipnis wrote an article for the *Chronicle of Higher Education* called "Sexual Paranoia Strikes Academe." Kipnis' piece was critical of what she called the "layers of prohibition and sexual terror" that have inspired campus rules prohibiting romantic relationships between professors and students. Wrote Kipnis:

> It's the fiction of the all-powerful professor embedded in the new campus codes that appalls me. And the kowtowing to the fiction—kowtowing wrapped in a vaguely feminist air of rectitude. If this is feminism, it's feminism hijacked by melodrama. The melodramatic imagination's obsession with helpless victims and powerful predators is what's shaping the conversation of the moment, to

the detriment of those whose interests are supposedly being protected, namely students. The result? Students' sense of vulnerability is skyrocketing.

Later in the piece, she argued that students "so committed to their own vulnerability, conditioned to imagine they have no agency, and protected from unequal power arrangements in romantic life" will struggle to deal with the problems and conflicts of the real world.

On Friday, Kipnis published another piece in the *Chronicle*, revealing that, in a twist that's ironic on more than one level, she is now the subject of an investigation into graduate student complaints that her earlier column and a subsequent tweet violated Title IX, the law that prohibits sex discrimination in education. Her piece, in addition to pointing out the absurdity of being charged with discriminatory behavior because of an essay, alleges an investigatory process that's ridiculously opaque for the accused:

> I wouldn't be informed about the substance of the complaints until I met with the investigators. Apparently the idea was that they'd tell me the charges, and then, while I was collecting my wits, interrogate me about them. The term "kangaroo court" came to mind. I wrote to ask for the charges in writing. The coordinator wrote back thanking me for my thoughtful **questions**.

Ben Mathis-Lilley, Title IX Investigation Opened Against Female Northwestern Professor Over Column, Tweet

The Earl of *Donoughmore* observed, that on all former occasions, when a **question** had been referred by their lordships to the judges, the opinion of the judges had been declared to the counsel at the bar as the opinion of the court. He was not aware why there should be any departure from that practice in the present instance. He did not want the **question** before their lordships to be settled by any kind of accommodation, he wanted it to be settled according to law. What he proposed, therefore, was, that the subject should be submitted to the reconsideration of the judges.

T. C. Hansard, Parliamentary Debates: Official Report of the Session of the Parliament of the United Kingdom of Great Britain and Ireland, June 27–September 7, 1820

"You'd better sit in on the interrogation," I was told. The plainclothes-men were much aroused by the news that their man was the son of Classmate X; in view of the delicate diplomatic aspects of his defection, and my wish to rejoin the Chancellor in pursuit of my Assignment, it was agreed that the **questioning** should take place at once, in the U.C. offices of the New Tammany delegation; both NTC and Nikolay College would be likely to want the Symposium opening delayed until the situation could be assessed.

"No," the Nikolayan insisted. "Main Detention." It was remarkable how with the merest twitch of a muscle he escaped their clutch. "Am not a transfer," he said now. "Am a spy. Come to kidnap a scientist." He grinned. "Long live Student Union! Down with Informationalist adventurismhood! You send me to Main Detention, okay?"

The guards exchanged looks. "Let's talk it over inside," they said almost politely. "If you're telling the truth, you'll see Main Detention soon enough."

John Barth, Giles Goat-Boy, or, The Revised New Syllabus

This paper uses the forward feature maximum match algorithm to segment word to the **question** sentence. We use ICTCLAS (Institute of Computing Technology Chinese Lexical Analysis System) word segmentation system developed by the Institute of Computing Technology, Academia Sinica in specific word segmentation

Rule	Category	Question Template
1	Opinion	Why +subject_auxiliary_inversion()? What evidence is provided by +subject+ to prove the opinion? Does any other scholars agree or disagree with +subject+?
2	Result	Subject_auxiliary_inversion()? Is the analysis of the data accurate and relevant to the research question? How does it relate to your research question?
3	System	In the study of +subject+, why +subject_auxiliary inversion()? What are the strength and limitations of the system? Does it relate to your research question?
4	Application	Why+Subject_Verb_Inversion()? Could the problem have been approached more effectively from another perspective? Does it relate to your research question?
5	Method	In the study of +subject+, why +subject_auxiliary _inversion()? Which dataset does +subject+ use for this experiment? What are the strengths and limitations of this approach?
6	Aim	Why does +subject+ conduct this study to +predicate+? What is the research question formulated by +subject+? What is +subject+s contribution to our understanding of the problem?

Table 5: Six Rules and Template-Based **Questions**

Question Type	Examples
1 Verification: implied yes/no/ answers (shallow)	*Is it possible to reuse some of previous routing techniques, for example those used in cellular networks, in the NGMN?*
2 Concept: Who, When ,What, Where? (shallow)	*Can you give more details about the Generalized Beam Theory?*
3 Comparison: How is X similar to Y? (intermediate)	*In Lim and Nethercot, how well did the numerical results compare with the experimental results?*
4 Causal Antecedent: what event causally led to an event? (deep)	*Why network coding in [13] can increase the system throughput?*
5 Causal Consequence: What is the consequence of an event? (deep)	*What is the likely consequence of the nonlinear stress-strain curve on the local-overall interaction buckling behavior of stainless steel structural members?*
6 Procedural: What instrument or plan allows an agent to accomplish a goal? (deep)	*How does the formation of mechanical twins provide corrosion resistance?*
7 Judgmental: What do you think of X?(deep)	*How do you see the Generalized Beam Theory being applied in your project?*

Table 17: Graesser and Pearson's **Question** Taxonomy With
Examples of **Questions** From Academic Supervisors

*Ming Liu, R. Calvo and V. Rus, G-Asks: An Intelligent Automatic **Question** Generation System for Academic Writing Support (Journal of Machine Learning Research, 17 March 2012)* process. Because this paper is focusing on **question** answering system for knowledge of computer network curriculum, while ICTCLAS system can't segment correctly to some computer network technical terms (in this paper, computer network technical terms is also called curriculum keywords), such as simulation data, cyclic redundancy check, TCP/IP protocol

You have either reached a page that is unavailable for viewing or reached your viewing limit for this book.

Zheng Gong and Dan Zhang, The Design of Restricted Domain Automatic **Question** Answering System Based on **Question** Base (Information Technology and Computer Application Engineering)

'University's an absolute tinderbox, old chap,' Donohue had advised when Woodrow had consulted him on risk. 'Grants have stopped dead, staff aren't being paid, places going to the rich and stupid, dormitories and classrooms packed out, loos all blocked, doors all pinched, fire risk rampant and they're cooking over charcoal in the corridors. They've no power, and no electric light to study by, and no books to study in. The poorest students are taking to the streets because the government is privatising the higher education system without consulting anyone and education is strictly for the rich, plus the exam results are rigged and the government is trying to force students to get their education abroad. And yesterday the police killed a couple of students, which for some reason their friends refuse to take lightly. Any more **questions**?'

John le Carré, The Constant Gardener

'I don't know who'd help, I'm afraid.'

'Might interest the Sociology Department,' said Oliver. 'They could probably get a Rockefeller Grant.'

'I doubt it,' said Treece. 'Well, I'm pleased someone here is writing a novel . . .'

'You know,' said Oliver, 'if you're interested in the provincial literary scene, I can smuggle you into a local literary cabal of some passing interest. They meet at the Mandolin every week.'

'Where's the Mandolin?'

'It's the espresso bar. It works without steam. You ought to come.'

'I'd like to, actually,' said Treece.

'Good, I'll let you know then,' said Oliver. He smiled pleasantly, shut his eyes, and slid slowly down the wall, in a stupor.

'Leave him,' said Mirabelle, passing by. Across the room someone had splashed gin all down the wall. In the corner Louis Bates, who had been nervously dismantling and reassembling his fountain-pen, was rejoined by Emma.

'Where have you been, if it isn't a rude **question**?' he demanded, surly at her long neglect of him.

'I've been in the lavatory, if it isn't a rude answer,' said Emma.

'You were a long time,' said Louis.

'I'm not going to have you timing me every time I go to the lavatory,' said Emma.

'You know I came here to be with you. It certainly wasn't for the party. You don't care anything for me, though; you make that quite apparent.'

'You shouldn't take yourself so seriously,' said Emma. 'I'd hate you to think I was cruel, but really you behave absurdly.'

'Good evening, you remember me? I was with you before at a party,' said the stout

German student, Herr Schumann. 'You like this party?'

'Yes,' said Emma. 'Do you?'

'It was my hope that some discussion of literary subjects would take place, but it does not matter. We are all happy, I think.'

'I'm not,' said Louis Bates.

'You don't find it difficult to understand what people are saying?' asked Emma.

'Oh no, I understand very well. I think parties are alike in all countries. In my country we have bathing parties, where all go naked into the water. I am very fond of such parties. Perhaps we all might make one day a bathing party. Also in Germany there are parties of homosexuals, which no doubt there are here also.'

Malcolm Bradbury, Eating People Is Wrong

A tall, lanky fellow in a gallon hat stopped his car on the wrong side of the road and came over to us; he looked like a sheriff. We prepared our stories secretly. He took his time coming over. "You boys going to get somewhere, or just going?" We didn't understand his **question**, and it was a damned good **question**.

"Why?" we said.

Jack Kerouac, On the Road

Whether or not your state has adopted them, I think these essential **questions** that are built right into the standards are a great asset in looking at how we can take what we already do as arts educators and just frame it from an inquiry standpoint. Look at the standard you want to accomplish, and work up to the essential **question**. From there, you can rephrase it to give students some direction. Your driving **question** should be open-ended enough to allow for students to take different paths, and also specific enough to drive them towards a product.

*Brianne Gidcumb, Driving **Questions** to Guide Inquiry in the Arts (EducationCloset)*

That brings me to Kipnis's meant-to-be-humorous **question** in her "Sexual Paranoia" essay, "But how do you know it's an 'unwanted sexual advance' until you've tried it?" In the louche spirit of Kipnis, wouldn't a reasonable answer to the **question** be, "Couldn't you just ask?" (rather than, say, dropping your paw on someone's thigh). Naturally, approaches like "Would you regard a sexual advance as wanted?" are a bit clunky and formal. And the famous Sexual Offense Prevention Policy (SOPP) that the liberal arts Antioch College instituted back in the early 1990s, which mandated verbal consent for each instance of sexual activity and each level of activity in a given instance (e.g., going from kissing to anal intercourse) may be discouragingly cumbersome. But maybe desire can be "repurposed" as an opportunity for creativity in conversation. I began remembering some of the times I've successfully posed such **questions**. Once, when I was a student, I asked a fellow student, "Wanna fuck?" Naturally, I built a lot of "deniability" into the tone of the **question** in case of a negative response—so that its subtext read, "Just kidding." But when I looked up, I was startled to see that he was considering my come-on line as a sincere empirical query. That one led to a five-year live-in relationship.

As a resident of bilingual Canada, I've also had fairly good luck with the tried and true French standard, "Voulez vous allez a coucher avec moi?" On another occasion, when I proposed to someone, "I'd like to lick your entire body, from head to . . .," I received the encouraging reply, "Now, or immediately?" But wait, this isn't about my

STICKY **QUESTIONS**
Year 7 (11–12 yrs)
£50.00
Add to Cart

The Philosophy Man (thephilosophyman.com)

Walter Mitty adventures, it's about their adventures. Yes, I'm aware that my "just ask" rather than the "just do it" approach might not work for the present generation, and that I may be biased as a philosophy teacher who leans toward malleable social-contract theories in ethics rather than more rigorous approaches. College-aged people today are likely to more haphazardly stumble into intercourse, especially given the increased availability of abusable substances combined with currently reduced oral and written literacy, which makes asking **questions** more difficult.

Stan Persky, The Young and the Restless, and Laura Kipnis (Los Angeles Review of Books)

But must **questions** and answers be spoken utterances? One day before class a student asked me about adding her homework to a pile of papers on a nearby table. She did not ask me in words. As recorded by my teaching assistant, she caught my eye and initiated this exchange:

(2)   STUDENT: ((holds up paper with one hand, points at pile with the other))
      CLARK: ((nods))

It seems natural to say that the student asked me if she should put her paper in the pile, and I answered yes. Yet her **question** was accomplished without words, and so was my answer.

Enter the notion of *projective pair* (Clark 2004). Projective pairs, like adjacency pairs, consist of two communicative acts in sequence from different people, with the first part projecting the second. The difference is that either part may be *any* type of communicative act—spoken, gestural or otherwise. The proposal here is that **question**-answer pairs are a type of projective pair, and so one or both parts may be wordless.

*Herbert H. Clark, Wordless **Questions**, Wordless Answers (**Questions**: Formal, Functional and Interactional Perspectives)*

She was not sure she had heard him, and was about to repeat her **question**.

He turned his head and looked at her over his shoulder. "I prefer to keep them on," he said with emphasis, and she noticed that he wore big blue spectacles with side-lights and had a bushy side-whisker over his coat-collar that completely hid his face.

"Very well, sir," she said. "As you like. In a bit the room will be warmer."

He made no answer, and had turned his face away from her again, and Mrs. Hall, feeling that her conversational advances were ill-timed, laid the rest of the table things in a quick staccato and whisked out of the room. When she returned he was still standing there, like a man of stone, his back hunched, his collar turned up, his dripping hat-brim turned down, hiding his face and ears completely.

H. G. Wells, The Invisible Man: A Grotesque Romance

It is no figure of speech to describe Ben's **question** as *wordless*. Charlotte cannot assume it was 'Can I talk to you now?' and answer 'Yes, you can'; or 'Will you talk to me?' and answer 'Yes, I will'; or 'Would you mind talking to me for a moment?' and answer 'Not at all.' The proposition at issue has no identifiable linguistic form. It is, literally, wordless.

*Herbert H. Clark, Wordless **Questions**, Wordless Answers (**Questions**: Formal, Functional and Interactional Perspectives)*

He seemed to see people through a mist, and communication was slow and difficult. He often asked people to repeat what they had said. He was terribly bored. But he could use them, he thought, to practice on. The naive **questions** they asked him ("Did Dickie drink a lot?" and "But he was in love with Marge, wasn't he?" and "Where do you really think he went?") were good practice for the more specific **questions** Mr. Greenleaf was going to ask him when he saw him, if he ever saw him.

Patricia Highsmith, *The Talented Mr. Ripley*

"Brother Clifton—why, I haven't seen him in weeks. I've been too busy downtown here. What's happened?"

"He has disappeared," Brother Jack said, "*disappeared!* So don't waste time with superfluous **questions**. You weren't sent for that."

"But how long has this been known?"

Brother Jack struck the table. "All we know is that he's gone. Let's get on with our business. You, Brother, are to return to Harlem immediately. We're facing a crisis there, since Brother Tod Clifton has not only disappeared but failed in his assignment. On the other hand, Ras the Exhorter and his gang of racist gangsters are taking advantage of this and are increasing their agitation. You are to get back there and take measures to regain our strength in the community. You'll be given the forces you need and you'll report to us for a strategy meeting about which you'll be notified tomorrow. And please," he emphasized with his gavel, "be on time!"

Ralph Ellison, *Invisible Man*

Later in the day I was taken again to the examining magistrate's office. It was two in the afternoon and, this time, the room was flooded with light—there was only a thin curtain on the window—and extremely hot.

After inviting me to sit down, the magistrate informed me in a very polite tone that, "owing to unforeseen circumstances," my lawyer was unable to be present. I should be quite entitled, he added, to reserve my answers to his **questions** until my lawyer could attend.

To this I replied that I could answer for myself. He pressed a bell push on his desk and a young clerk came in and seated himself just behind me. Then we—I and the magistrate—settled back in our chairs and the examination began. He led off by remarking that I had the reputation of being a taciturn, rather self-centered person, and he'd like to know what I had to say to that. I answered:

"Well, I rarely have anything much to say. So, naturally I keep my mouth shut."

Albert Camus, *The Stranger*

He was always very defensive on the **question** of styles of teaching and lecturing. He knew that there was a certain oratorical demonstrativeness abroad these days, a mixing of eloquence and familiarity, but his preference was for something more meditative and his own delivery was marked by a kind of ruminative absenteeism.

Howard Jacobson, *Coming From Behind*

"Not contemplating—peeping a little at possibilities," replied Pnin with a gurgling laugh.

"I **question** the wisdom of it," continued Hagen, nursing his goblet.

"Naturally, I am expecting that I will get tenure at last," said Pnin rather slyly. "I am now Assistant Professor nine years. Years run. Soon I will be Assistant Emeritus. Hagen, why are you silent?"

"You place me in a very embarrassing position, Timofey. I hoped you would not raise this particular **question**."

The Macalope, The Definition of an Academic Question (macworld.com)

"I do not raise the **question**. I say that I only expect—oh, not next year, but example given, at hundredth an-

Pages 168 to 169 are not shown in this preview.

Vladimir Nabokov, Pnin

The second party completes the process by resolving the proposition at issue—by providing the projected information. It is these two moves that are called **question** and answer. But how do they work?

*Herbert H. Clark, Wordless **Questions**, Wordless Answers (**Questions**: Formal, Functional and Interactional Perspectives)*

And the fact was, of course, that they did not understand it either, but forbore from asking embarrassing **questions** out of shame and a kind of shyness in the presence of the equivocal. Like so many gingerly Thomases, they contented themselves with fingering the wounds held out to them and attesting their intellectual superiority by their readiness to believe the incredible. When Van Tour cried out, for the third time, in his wailing, womanish voice, "What *I* don't see, Domna, is why doesn't he come *right out* and confess it," everyone sighed aloud, and Aristide got up and, leading him into a corner, took him over by rote the whole history of the case, of Senator McCarthy, the Hiss trial, the crisis of liberalism in American universities, though in reality Van Tour's **question** had more than once visited his own mind.

Meanwhile, in the faculty dining-room, Howard Furness, head of the Literature department, who had had an appointment with Alma Fortune at twelve forty-five sharp to discuss a certain student who was coming up for Sophomore Orals, was glancing at his Cartier wrist-watch, a gift from one of last year's parents, and straightening his knitted tie from sheer uneasiness. His sharp, dapper mind was extremely sensitive to any disarray in the outer garment of reality, and the empty places at table wounded him, like missing buttons on a coat. He had been quick, in fact, to see that those who were absent belonged to his chosen circle; something was up, he perceived, from which he was being excluded—

Mary McCarthy, The Groves of Academe: A Novel

Absent on this vote—Messrs. Edwards, of Conn., Case, Peek, and Tompkins, of N.Y., Hall of Delaware, all of whom it is presumed would have voted against concurring—5; and Messrs. Ball, of Va., Sawyer of N.C., and Walker, of Ky., deceased, who, if present, would have voted on the other side.

For concurring	90
Against it	87
	177
Absent *in all* 8—speaker 1—	9
Whole number of members	186

The **question** was then stated on the second amendment of the senate; when Mr. *Taylor* moved to amend the amendment by striking out the words "thirty six degrees 30 minutes north latitude," and inserting a line which would exclude slavery from all the territory, west of the Mississippi, except Louisiana, Missouri, and Arkansas.

H. Niles, Niles' Weekly Register, Containing Political, Historical, Geographical, Scientifical, Statistical, Economical, and Biographical Documents, Essays, and Facts; Together With Notices of the Arts and Manufactures, and a Record of the Events of the Times, From March to September, 1820—Vol. XVIII, or, Volume VI—New Series

Mr. COCHRAN. I move to amend the motion by adding, "on Monday morning at ten o'clock."

The SPEAKER. That will not do. The order must be to bring them in forthwith as soon as the officer can lay hands upon them.

Mr. HENRY. The effect of this order, as I understand, will be to keep the House in session until the Seareant-at-Arms makes his return.

Mr. HILL. It seems to me that this process is going to involve a considerable expense to the State, and I doubt the propriety of punishing ourselves by keeping ourselves here. I do not think we should heap burdens upon the State in order to punish these delinquents a little. I certainly cannot vote for the pending motion.

Mr. HUSTON. Perhaps our votes on this **question** may be influenced by the **question**, What degree of punishment can be inflicted on these absent members? I would ask some enlightenment from the chair on that point.

The SPEAKER. That is not the **question**. The **question** is on giving this order to the Sergeant-at-Arms to bring in the absentees.

Mr. HUSTON. It appears to me that this **question** is easily understood. Men have no difficulty in understanding the law when they wish to follow its precepts strictly. It appears to me that our duty in this case is very clear; and I am satisfied that, if every member of this House is disposed to vote on this matter as he really feels it his duty to do, we shall have no difficulty. If there is a law on the subject, either the law makers must have been very foolish in making that law, or we are foolish in not following its teachings and trying to enforce it. We must come to one or the other conclusion—either that it was foolish to incorporate these provisions in our Constitution, or it would be very foolish on our part not to try to carry them out. Now, what guarantee have we that, if we yield in this case, we shall not on this day next week have a similar scene? I see no difficulty in voting to enforce the law.

Mr. COLEMAN. There is one point that suggests inself in connection with this **question**. There are, it appears, fifty-nine absentees who are scattered all over the State. We have one Seargeant-at-Arms and four assistants. It will require at least all of them, if not all the other officers of the House, to attend to the business of bringing in these absentees, and when all these officers are absent, there is nobody to keep us from leaving.

George Bergner, The Legislative Record: Containing the Debates and Proceedings of the Pennsylvania Legislature for the Session of 1864

Kemp gave a cry of incredulous amazement.

The Invisible Man rose and began pacing the little study. "You may well exclaim. I remember that night. It was late at night—in the daytime one was bothered with the gaping, silly students—and I worked then sometimes till dawn. It came suddenly, splendid and complete in my mind. I was alone; the laboratory was still, with the tall lights burning brightly and silently. In all my great moments I have been alone. 'One could make an animal—a tissue—transparent! One could make it invisible! All except the pigments—I could be invisible!' I said, suddenly realising what it meant to be an albino with such knowledge. It was overwhelming. I left the filtering I was doing, and went and stared out of the great window at the stars. 'I could be invisible!' I repeated.

"To do such a thing would be to transcend magic. And I beheld, unclouded by doubt, a magnificent vision of all that invisibility might mean to a man—the mystery,

Albrecht Dürer, St. John Devouring the Book, probably c. 1496–1498 (published 1511)
Woodcut, 41.6 x 28.6 cm, National Gallery of Art, Washington DC

Hofstadter, of course, recognizes that his psychologizing move is controversial. Right away, he attempts to make clear that he is "not speaking in a clinical sense, but borrowing a clinical term for other purposes."[3]

*L. A. Leere, Asking the Wrong **Questions**: In Defense Of "Paranoia" (Homintern.soy)* the power, the freedom. Drawbacks I saw none. You have only to think! And I, a shabby, poverty-struck, hemmed-in demonstrator, teaching fools in a provincial college, might suddenly become—this. I ask you, Kemp, if *you* . . . Anyone, I tell you, would have flung himself upon that research. And I worked three years, and every mountain of difficulty I toiled over showed another from its summit. The infinite details! And the exasperation! A professor, a provincial professor, always prying. 'When are you going to publish this work of yours?' was his everlasting **question**.

> H. G. Wells, *The Invisible Man: A Grotesque Romance*

The final output of the system is a ranked list of **FAQs** (implicit, explicit, or hidden) and their corresponding answers.

> Fatemeh Raazaghi, *Automatic **Frequently Asked Questions** Generation (Advances in Artificial Intelligence)*

How we arrived at a point where teaching is reckoned as a burden and a stigma is not a story I can recount here. The retreat from the classroom is like that long stretch of highway you navigated to get home but can't recall in any detail. We obviously went down that road as a guild—we just can't remember when or how. Now we're here. It may be too late to turn back.

In many ways, we resemble the ailing magazine, newspaper, and taxi industries: crippled by challenges we never imagined, risks we never calculated, queries we never posed. Here are some **questions** we didn't ask but really should have: Was it sustainable to configure a field so that the quality and (mostly) quantity of peer-reviewed research became the unrivaled metric by which status and advancement were attained? Ought we to have investigated whether there exists a point of diminishing returns—a line beyond which too much publication, too much specialization, becomes intellectually counterproductive? Why did we fail to examine the long-term impact on both students and scholars of having the latter so singularly focused on publishing? Why did we not promote the ideal of professors equally skilled in both research and instruction? Why did we invest so little thought in puzzling through how teaching excellence could result in tenure? Was it wise never to train graduate students how to write clearly, speak publicly, and teach effectively?

For a guild that prides itself on research, we sure didn't invest much effort into what the corporate folk call "research and development." Who was thinking about the consequences of our inadvertent drift away from students in the final decades of the 20th century? And who's thinking about it now?

> Jacques Berlinerblau, *Teach or Perish*

caught flat-footed Caught unprepared, taken by surprise, as in *The reporters **question** caught the President flat-footed.* This usage comes from one or another sport in which a player should be on his or her toes, ready to act. [c. 1900]

> Christine Ammer, *The American Heritage Dictionary of Idioms*

I am very unfortunate if that is true. But suppose I ask you a **question**: Would you say that this also holds true in the case of horses?

> Plato, *Apology*

. . . but it seems like that might fall into the invisible category of "stupid **questions**" (invisible because there aren't *supposed* to be any stupid **questions** except for those left unasked . . .

> Michelle Au, *This Won't Hurt a Bit (and Other White Lies): My Education in Medicine and Motherhood*

You can encourage students to write stronger, more thorough responses to content area **questions** with the Invisible **Questions** strategy.

For every short-answer **question** you ask, consider assessing it on a 6-point system, broken down as follows:

- 1 point for restating part of the **question** within the response.
- 1 point for avoiding the use of any pronoun (he, she, it, they).
- 1 point for writing a complete thought that makes sense without ever reading the **question**.
- 3 points for an accurate response/correct information.

Weigh heavily the correct answer, but by offering points for strong sentence writing, you are also showing the value of clear and complete thoughts.

For example, imagine a student submits this response: *I think she is because she couldn't tell the difference.*

It's difficult to assess if the answer is accurate because the **question** isn't restated in the response. The use of "she" makes the response even more vague. Who is she? And the response itself doesn't make sense. The reader is desperate to know the **question** because right now this doesn't make sense all by itself. Accurate or not, this response is poorly written. Here is a stronger response to the same initial **question**:

I believe Little Red Riding Hood was naive because Little Red just assumed anyone sleeping in Grandma's bed must be Grandma. It wasn't until after studying the big ears, big nose, and big teeth that Little Red realized it wasn't Grandma. That's pretty naive.

Smekens Education Solutions, Improve Constructed Responses With the Invisible Questions Strategy

"Do you mind if we ask you a couple of **questions**, Dr. Hildebrant?" It was the FBI agent in the backseat, a woman by the name of Sullivan—blond, early thirties, with chiseled features that Cathy envied. She was with the Field Office in Boston, Markham told her—had been waiting in the Trailblazer while he was meeting with Cathy.

"Go right ahead," Cathy said.

Agent Sullivan produced a small, digital recording device from her jacket pocket and held it to her mouth.

"This is Special Agent Rachel Sullivan en route with Markham and Dr. Catherine Hildebrant. The date is Sunday, April 26. The time is 12:20 P.M."

Sullivan placed the recorder between Markham and Cathy—its red light making Cathy self-conscious.

"Dr. Hildebrant," Sullivan began, "you're the author of the book on Michelangelo titled *Slumbering in the Stone*, is that correct?"

"Yes."

"Is that your only published work?"

"No, but the only one dedicated solely to Michelangelo's sculptures—and the only one to cross over from the academic market to reach a more popular audience."

"It's sold a lot of copies then?"

"Not a *New York Times* bestseller by any means, no. But as far as these things go in academia, yes, you could say it's sold a lot."

"And what else have you published?"

"I coauthored an introduction to an art history textbook with a former colleague of mine from Harvard, as well as publishing the obligatory articles now and then in various academic journals."

"I see," said Sullivan.

Cathy did not like her tone. She had none of Markham's charm, none of his informal directness. No, Special Agent Rachel Sullivan spoke like an attorney on one of those bad spin-offs of a spin-off courtroom drama with which Cathy had become so engrosssed as of late—another bit of "mindless entertainment" she once thought she'd never be caught dead watching in a million years.

"But *Slumbering in the Stone* is by far your most important work," Sullivan continued. "The one that really put you on the map, wouldn't you say?"

"Relatively speaking, yes."

"And you require *Slumbering in the Stone* for your classes?"

"Only one—a graduate seminar. Yes." Cathy suddenly felt defensive—like Sullivan was setting her up for something. She looked around the cabin uncomfortably, her eyes falling on the speedometer. Markham was doing eighty, but held the wheel as if he were coasting through a school zone.

"And when was this book published?"

"About six years ago."

"Was this before or after your tenure?"

"Just before."

"And you have been requiring your book for your class for how long now?"

"It'll be five years next fall."

"I'd like you to take a moment," Agent Sullivan said with a calculated change of tone. "Take a moment and ask yourself if you've ever had a student during that time—or at any time, for that matter—that struck you as particularly odd. One that said or did or perhaps even wrote something out of the ordinary—something that went beyond a creative extreme into the realm of—well, something *else*. Perhaps a drawing or an essay or even an e-mail that you found particularly disturbing."

Cathy's brain began to spin with a kaleidoscope of faces—nameless, dark, and blurry—and the art history professor felt a wave of panic upon realizing she could not recollect even what her current students looked like.

"I can't think of anyone," she said finally, her voice tight. "I'm sorry."

Gregory Funaro, The Sculptor

These **questions** are often really statements dressed up to look like **questions**. They also are often only indirectly relevant to the issue at hand. Frequently innocuous, they can create real danger for the advocate who is unprepared to deal with them, as we will discuss in a later chapter.

Douglas S. Lavine, **Questions** *From the Bench*

Chapter Six goes into this type of **question**. It usually starts with something like, "Describe a time when (blah, blah, blah), and how did you handle that situation?"

Chapter Seven discusses case **questions**. These **questions** are designed to see how well you analyze and reason. It's a test of how logical and creative you are. The precise answer is less important than the route you use to get to an approximation of the answer. For example, the answer to the **question**, "Why is a manhole cover round?", could be answered thus: "There could be several reasons. First, manhole covers are round to prevent them from falling into the manhole. If they were square, they could fall in if they

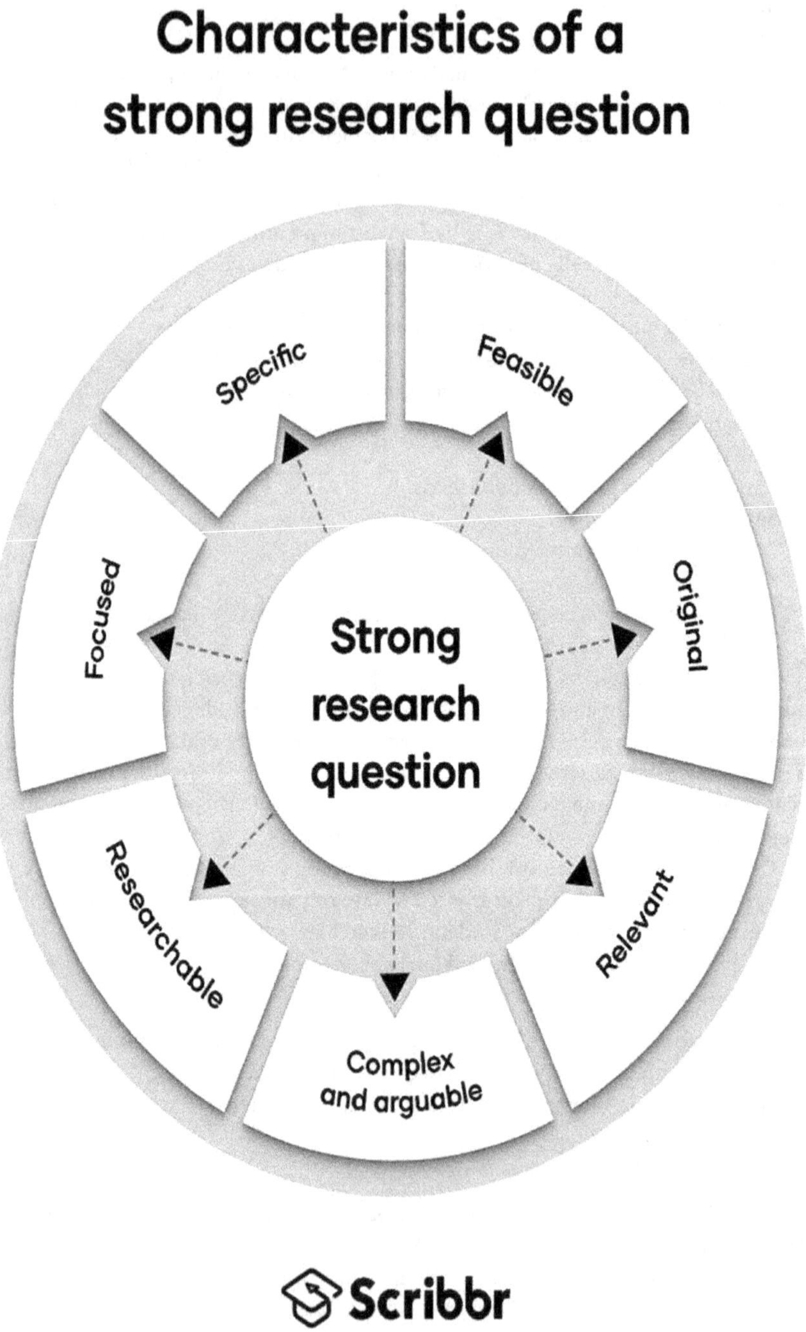

Characteristics of a strong research question

They should all be clearly connected and focused around a central research problem.
*Shona McCombes, Writing Strong Research **Questions** | Criteria & Examples (Scribbr.com)*

were put back into place sideways. Obviously, it would be very difficult to retrieve them. But a second reason is that it would be easier to move them or deliver them if they were round, since they could be rolled. If they were square, one would have to carry them." Now you have given the interviewer not only the obvious right answer, you have also given him or her, a bonus answer. Interviewers like that.

*David S. Seal, Get the Job! The Fast Guide to Answering Tough **Questions** on Job Interviews*

When we look into the ambiguous essence of technology, we behold the constellation, the stellar course of the mystery.

The **question** concerning technology is the **question** concerning the constellation in which revealing and concealing, in which the coming to presence of truth, comes to pass.

But what help is it to us to look into the constellation of truth? We look into the danger and see the growth of the saving power.

Through this we are not yet saved. But we are thereupon summoned to hope in the growing light of the saving power. How can this happen?

*Martin Heidegger, The **Question** Concerning Technology*

I dodged the **question**. "Give me an hour or two to think it over. What do you think?"

Dashiell Hammett, Red Harvest

A panel at a major conference, with mostly "big-name" historians proposing substantive historiographical revisions to the interpretative framework that governs an important area of inquiry. During the **question**-and-answer period, someone asked a **question** that challenged one of the bases of the proposed historiographical revision. He was clearly coming at it from a more "conservative" position, I thought I detected something Straussian, perhaps, in his approach. He was very articulate and obviously very smart. If his **question** seemed a little bit strange or unexpected, it was a pretty good **question** and not something to be dismissed. His name tag revealed that he was an assistant professor at a "third-tier" place that I had never heard of. Afterwards, I was speaking with historian A (a panelist, and a friend), who was soon joined by historian B (a "big-name" historian who had attended the session, and a friend of historian A). From this point on, I was basically an observer. Well, watch and learn (and you can learn a fair bit when you're invisible). The **question** of the **questioner** came up. "Is he?. . ." Is he what? Well, is he one of us? of course. Where did he study and who does he know? He's at a third-rate school that nobody has heard of, which probably makes him a nobody, but then again, nowadays, with the job market so dismal, you can't be quite sure.

Invisible Adjunct, Anxiety and Insecurity: The Status of the Humanities (invisibleadjunct.com)

What was this man doing in such deep darkness? He must be some great criminal! So at least thought Petrus Mauerer and his acolytes.

At last a vague form could be discerned in the dark, then slowly, by degrees, a little man, four and a half feet high at the most, frail, ragged, his face withered and yellow, his eye gleaming like a magpie's, and his hair tangled, came out shouting:

"By what right do you come to disturb my studies, wretched creatures?"

This grandiose apostrophe was scarcely in accord with his costume and physiognomy. Accordingly the burgomaster indignantly replied:

"Try to show that you're honest, you knave, or I'll begin by administering a correction."

"A correction!" said the little man, leaping with anger, and drawing himself up under the nose of the burgomaster.

"Yes," replied the other, who, nevertheless, did not fail to admire the pygmy's courage; "if you do not answer the **questions** satisfactorily I am going to put to you. I am the burgomaster of Hirschwiller; here are the rural guard, the shepherd and his dog. We are stronger than you—be wise and tell me peaceably who you are, what you are doing here, and why you do not dare to appear in broad daylight. Then we shall see what's to be done with you."

"All that's none of your business," replied the little man in his cracked voice. "I shall not answer."

"In that case, forward, march," ordered the burgomaster, who grasped him firmly by the nape of the neck; "you are going to sleep in prison."

The little man writhed like a weasel; he even tried to bite, and the dog was sniffing at the calves of his legs, when, quite exhausted, he said, not without a certain dignity:

"Let go, sir, I surrender to superior force—I'm yours!"

The burgomaster, who was not entirely lacking in good breeding, became calmer.

"Do you promise?" said he.

Erckmann-Chatrian, The Owl's Ear

Chapter Eight deals with **questions** that should not be asked but may be thrown at you anyhow. They are illegal or morally **questionable questions** and this chapter will help you to duck them without making the idiot who asked you those **questions** look like an idiot.

*David S. Seal, Get the Job! The Fast Guide to Answering Tough **Questions** on Job Interviews*

Said he'd consider it. Asked him, point-blank, was he researching. Said he was. A long research? Got quite cross. 'A damnable long research,' said he, blowing the cork out, so to speak. 'Oh,' said I. And out came the grievance. The man was just on the boil, and my **question** boiled him over.

H. G. Wells, The Invisible Man: A Grotesque Romance

By degrees I learnt, and chiefly from **questioning** Herbert, that Mr. Pocket had been educated at Harrow and at Cambridge, where he had distinguished himself; but that when he had had the happiness of marrying Mrs. Pocket very early in life, he had impaired his prospects and taken up the calling of a Grinder. After grinding a number of dull blades,—of whom it was remarkable that their fathers, when influential, were always going to help him to preferment, but always forgot to do it when the blades had left the Grindstone,—he had wearied of that poor work and had come to London. Here, after gradually failing in loftier hopes, he had "read" with divers who had lacked opportunities or neglected them, and had refurbished divers others for special occasions, and had turned his acquirements to the account of literary compilation and correction.

Charles Dickens, Great Expectations

Much later Dixon had found out that the book in **question** had been written at Welch's suggestion and, in part, under his advice. These facts had been there for all to read in the Acknowledgements, but Dixon, whose policy it was to read as little as possible of any given book, never bothered with these, and it had been Margaret who'd told him.

Kingsley Amis, Lucky Jim

The academic elite, therefore, whether willingly or not, are complicit in an organizational structure that often silences and marginalizes the adjunct (as the well-known ex-blogger, the Invisible Adjunct, writing from "the margins of academe" so eloquently described).

That this is the new reality of life in the post-modern academic climate is undeniable and perhaps not particularly post-modern when we consider, for example, that most scholars in medieval England fared little better than their twenty-first century counterparts. However, of a society whose ideological framework is embedded in the great chain of being, a rigidly hierarchical structure is to be expected (and suffering was, after all, to be rewarded in the next life). In post-modern institutions whose faculty routinely produce books and articles interrogating imperial and colonial enterprises and insist on the right of the subaltern to speak (and do not hold much hope for eternal reward), why do we discover such a radical disjunction between gnosis and praxis?

I pose this **question** not only, say, to postcolonial, feminist, or neo-Marxist scholars at Ivy League schools but also to my self, appointed first-year coordinator and later department chair at a private university in Canada. Having worked as an adjunct at two universities over a four-year period, my tenure-track university appointment was the culmination of an intense period of teaching and research. During this time, I formed close bonds with other adjuncts; as the underpaid underclass with an axe to grind we felt an immediate affinity for each other. We spoke in whispered voices of the horror of temporary employment and of our fear that it was to be a life-long condition. Having risen at graduate school like Icarus to the sun, we suspected that our slow descent into part-time instruction was equivalent (if not worse) than a fiery or watery end. And yet, we were not, like the radical religious thinker George Fox, inclined "to speak truth to power." To be considered unruly (women) was to seal our fate. Some employment, after all, is better than no employment.

Holly Faith Nelson, The Subaltern in Academia: Advancing an Ethos of Equity (Academic Apartheid: Waging the Adjunct War)

Then to me in doleful mood
Rises up a **question** rude,
Asking what sufficient good
    Comes of this mode of living?
Moping on from day to day,
Grinding up what will not "pay,"
Till the jaded brain gives way
    Under its own misgiving.

James Clerk Maxwell, Lines Written Under the Conviction That It Is Not Wise to Read Mathematics in November After One's Fire Is Out

Its byproducts—alienation, widespread poverty, environmental destruction, species extinction—can be understood as results symptomatic of our Enframing mode of revealing. If we believe these things to be catastrophic then the **question** is not how to fix them within this world, but how to enter into a new world that does not have these as byproducts of its mode of revealing.

Eric Scrivner, Technological Criticism: Heidegger and Enframing (Desearch and Revelopment)

Anyway, here's one answer to my **question**. Behold the University of Phoenix, an egalitarian university where all faculty are treated equally, which is to say, all faculty are treated equally badly. Chris Cumo reports that of the 12,000 faculty members that the university employs, all but 250 are adjuncts.

There's been a lot of talk lately about the two-tier academic labor system and what to do about it: policy statements have been issued, proposals put forth and debated, and so on. But the University of Phoenix is way ahead of the game: they have discovered an easy solution through the elimination of the top tier.

Interested in learning more? Give them a call at 1-800-MY-SUCCESS. *(Dear God. For this I went to graduate school?)*

The adjuncts don't make much money, but the university is turning profits:

> "Phoenix 'makes one hell of a lot of money,' says Director of Academic Affairs Jonathan Edelman of the Western Michigan campus in Grand Rapids, Michigan. The Apollo Group, which owns the for-profit university, earned $1.1 billion in 2002, according to T.D. Waterhouse. During that same year, its stock rose 6.71 percent to $43.58 per share at year's end. The Apollo Group expects to earn between $1.31 billion and $1.315 billion in 2003, and projects earnings between $510 million and $515 million for the University of Phoenix."

Well, now that I've got a handle on this blogging thing, I think I'm finally ready to get with the programme. I've had done with such old-fashioned notions as the history profession as guild, academic work as quasi-sacred calling, the university as a protected space offering an alternative to the values of the market. It's high time I signed on with the forces of corporate innovation. But I don't want to teach for $1000 a course. No, I'm starting to think big: I want to start my own online university.

Invisible Adjunct, Where the Adjuncts Have Equal Status (invisibleadjunct.com)

Below you will find three examples of **questions** from previous final exams at Trump University. Use these sample **questions** and the answer key provided to prepare for next week's big test.

1. Two plus two equals what?
    (a) Maybe four.
    (b) Could be four. Could be. Lotta people saying it's five.
    (c) I'm not saying it's five; I'm saying it could be—*could be* five. You see these establishment hacks, losers, like Mitt Romney? Real crank. They hate me. They take answers like "could be" and say, "Oh, he says two plus two equals five." I never said that. I never—I said "could be." Could be *six*. We don't know.
    (d) All of the above.
    (e) None of the above.
    (f) D and E.

2. Describe a major theme of "The Old Man and the Sea."
    (a) Well, the theme is big. That I can assure you. Definitely no problem in the theme department. Quite big. Quite.
    (b) I know what you want me to say here. You want me to say "yuge." Well, I'm not. I'm not gonna say that.
    (c) Should I say it? . . . No. I'm not gonna say it. But it is.
    (d) Now—and I don't even wanna bring it up—but you got a lot of people. I'm not

going to mention names. O.K., Marco. You got Little Marco, who has a tiny theme. No, it's true. Very small. Probably why he's outta the race. Seriously, find me one person who says there was a big theme behind that campaign. But anyway, here's Little Marco, saying I'm the one with the small theme. Can you believe that? Says I'm like Santiago in "The Old Man and the Sea." Says I sometimes lose my harpoon—you know, prematurely—when I try to reel in the big fish. Totally not true.

(e) In fact, reminds me of the time I tried to get a date with Brooke Shields. Remember Brooke Shields? Gorgeous. Not like my wife. Gorgeous, though. I asked her out. She said no. Career went downhill after that. Left me like Santiago at the end of the book, hauling this gigantic mast home with nothing to show for my troubles.

(f) Seriously, "The Old Man and the Sea"? Please. Santiago's not a winner. Here's what you need to read: "The Art of the Deal." Best book since the Bible. Probably better. People say that. I don't. People do. Bible was, like, God with sixty ghostwriters. "The Art of the Deal" was just me, dictating to Tony Schwartz. Great guy. Takes dictation better than Moses.

3. H_2O is the chemical symbol for what compound?
(a) What the hell's "huh-twenty"?
(b) No, that's what it says, "huh-twenty." Or maybe the "H" is silent. I dunno.
(c) I didn't say "huh-twenty." You said "huh-twenty." You asked me what "huh-twenty" was. You see, this is what the media does. They claim, "You said 'huh-twenty!'" And I'm like, "I said? No *you* said 'huh-twenty.' I just repeated what you said."
(d) That's all they do, ask these totally bogus **questions**, when what they should be asking about is Hillary's e-mails. That's what this **question** should be about. Because what she did—wow. I mean, that's why she's hugging Obama every chance she gets.
(e) You know who else hugs Obama? Chris Christie.
(f) But we love Chris, don't we? We love Chris.

Answer key:
1. I like A. I like B, too. D doesn't do much for me, but E and F are real winners.

2. I'm gonna have to look into A and B. C is very compelling. Very. I hear good things about D through F. But I don't wanna say anything yet.

*3. I don't know why people are saying there were three **questions**. There weren't. I mean, do you have video? Show me the video where there were three **questions**. You can't, because there is no video. People come here. They try to make trouble, saying we started a **question** three. We did not. And lemme tell ya, we're gonna fight back. I'm not saying we'll sue, but we could. Throw a few punches, ya know. Because this test prep is a great test prep. You thought so, too: you signed the agreement saying that you thought this was the greatest test prep of all time and that you wanted to be sued if video surfaced of you saying otherwise.*

Congratulations, *this* was actually the final. You've passed. Now give me $35,000.

*John Flowers, Sample **Questions** From the Trump University Final Exam (The New Yorker)*

In the previous chapter, you learned how to prepare for and write exams. In this chapter we will cover different exam **question** formats and how to approach them. You will already have encountered most if not all of these **question** types elsewhere and you may have your own strategies for tackling them. Either way, you should consider the advice given in this chapter. Exams at the university level are more challenging due to

Members of the audience learning more about athletic tickets, STAT and TEAM WILDCAT raise their hands enthusiastically after being asked, "Who's going to be a Wildcat for life?"

University of Kentucky Alumni Association, Fresh Faces on Campus (outofthebigblue.com) the difficulty of the material, time constraints and the lack of leniency in marking. If you picked up some bad exam-writing habits during your high school years, now is the time to change them. Having said that, this chapter teaches the mechanics of tackling tests and of answering all types of **questions.**

Danton O'Day and Aldona Budniak, How to Succeed at University: Canadian Edition

"Happiness is tricky. It sounds like you've figured it out."

"Sure."

"Sure, he says," said Purdy.

"Sure, I say," I said.

"Don't be bitter, Milo. It doesn't become you."

"I'm not bitter," I said.

Purdy leaned back, as though to better assemble an exceptionally nuanced expression on his face, maybe some amalgam of pity and revelation.

"You're pissed because I'm so rich," he said. "You've always been pissed. You think I didn't earn it."

"You didn't."

"Of course I did. The trust fund made me comfortable. My own hard work made me rich. I knew when to cash out during all that interweb crap. Not many did."

Interweb, webnet, interpipe—the joke had begun to grate. If they flubbed it and winked, what? I was tired of the semantic evasions, mine included. I was tired of many things. I had been keeping a list, got tired of the list.

"I guess not," I said.

"Don't be a hater," said Purdy.

"I'm not just any old hater," I said. "I'm a hater's hater."

It was as though Purdy hadn't heard me, or perhaps it was precisely that he had.

"You're doing better than ninety-nine-point-nine percent of the people in this world," he said. "Capitalism might have shit the bed, but it's been very good to you, buddy, whether you know it or not."

"Hooray!" I said. "Let's drink to me. I'm not rich, and I'm not famous, but I am fat and white, or white-ish, and my debt load is at least testament to the fact that over the years various institutions have considered me a worthy mark."

"Good for you," said Purdy.

He sounded sincere and it scared me.

"You want another drink?" I said. "Maybe I'll get another drink."

"I'm fine," said Purdy.

"I'm not fine. I'm not fine at all. Let's have some drinks! Some fucking mojitos or something. Don't they have that fifty-dollar mojito here? With that rum from the island where they make one case a year, and the hydroponic mint they fly in weekly? I want one! It's all on the Whig, okay?"

"The who?" said Purdy.

"The Whig. Our founding daddy."

"Maybe you should slow down, Milo."

"Why the hell would I want to do that?"

"Because I don't think they fly that mint in anymore, for one thing. Look, Milo, I know we're old friends. I've held you over the toilet a few times, back in the day, but come on. The age of the expense account is over. I read it in the paper two years ago. And two months ago. And today."

"Sure," I said. "Yes. Of course."

"Excellent," said Purdy. "Now, do you have any **questions** for me?"

"Yes, I do. Why give to us? Why not give to the truly needy? The bombed-out, the starved-down, the families running from butchers on horseback. Or folks whose fate depends on whether they can score a fucking shovel and a bag of seeds."

"You mean genocides? Microfinancing?"

"Yeah, or even all the devastated people here."

"We give to those causes. Less and less, of course. We've all gotten murdered."

"How about giving to just a random assortment of middle-class families? Or not so random? How about mine?"

"Funny," said Purdy, in the way of a man who did not find it funny. "Any more **questions**? Wait, hold on."

Purdy took out a weird phone, the device we'd all be using next year, punched some keys. "Forgive me," he said. "Forgot about something I needed to send. Where were we? Oh, yeah. **Questions**?"

"Just the canned ones. Like maybe you can tell me how you first got interested in the Mediocre University at New York's arts program."

"The Mediocre what?"

"Sorry. What I mean is—"

"Melinda had a wonderful experience at your university. Especially in the film and theater classes she took. It was the best investment I ever made, sending her there after we met. Sure, it was the only place she had any chance in hell of getting into, but it enriched her. That sounds stupid, but it's true. It helped her become the woman she wanted to be, and needed to be, to be with me. Actually, Melinda handles a lot of our giving these days. Museums, orchestras, film societies. My area of interest is more narrow. I enjoy finding younger female artists and helping them at that crucial stage when their asses are firm and unblemished."

Sam Lipsyte, The Ask

Philosophy has been predominantly involved in an understanding of man and Heidegger has attempted to face this problem in an ontological way. His thought, however, shows limitations and a serious incompleteness with respect to an adequate philosophical analysis of the meaning of human existence. Heidegger's limitation lies in the fact that he has failed to consider man within both an ontological and a practical framework. He fails to understand that man's external life expressed in his political, economic and social experience determines and reveals the ontological nature of his existence. Heidegger in *Sein und Zeit* and *Einführung in die Metaphysik* analyzes the ontological meaning of man and shows that man is only insofar as his being reveals to him a primal Being through which he becomes conscious of himself existing. In the *Brief über Humanismus* ethical and moral **questions** are posed but Heidegger, after having analyzed the ontological meaning of man, fails to provide adequately for a moral or ethical framework.

If we accept Heidigger's thesis that the ontological dimension of man points to man's most meaningful aspect because it says that man in his uniqueness reveals the human dimension to himself, we begin our discussion with two words, "man is." The noun "man" in its relation to the verb "is" reveals its dimension to be an ontological one. The ontological dimension attempts to measure the meaning and uniqueness of man but only in an ontological way. The verb "is" refers to the dimension of the noun "man" and refers to nothing beyond the noun. Implied in the structure of thought is the statement: man is man. Heidegger is concerned with the dimension of man ontologically and maintains that man becomes conscious of his being as Being insofar as man's being in the world reveals to him something about his dimension and uniqueness. In the religious framework it was man's relation to God or his separation from God which revealed the human dimension. The Heideggerian position thus states that being has no dimension beyond the ontological. Heidegger's statement about existence is that Man is revealed through man. The ontological is the primal structure of man and, for Heidegger, constitutes the total dimension of man.

To equate man exclusively with his ontological structure is inadequate. The inadequacy of this position lies in the fact that man, ontologically revealed and defined, can be conscious of this state of being only insofar as it realizes itself as being something other than the practical states of being such as the political, social, and economic. These forms are for the ontological, the "other." These "other" forms of being are historical and describe man's doings, creations, and achievements. These are descriptive items or adjectives. They describe man as he does things. These adjectival qualifications belong to man and describe him, not ontologically but historically.

The ontological dimension of man transcends all adjectival qualifications. The adjective can only describe one aspect of the ontological dimension but cannot exhaust it or identify itself with it. The dimension of Being transcends all other dimensions and each adjective can bring forth only one aspect of Being. It is this fact which limits each adjectival qualification and points to the inexhaustible nature of Being.

Jean T. Wilde and William Kluback, Introduction to Martin Heidegger, The **Question** *of Being*

Mr. Smith.—It depends on how fine you have it ground. If your miller will grind it fine for you, some advantage comes from the presence of the cob. It has been shown that the gain will just about pay for the grinding, but unless it is ground very fine it won't pay.

Question.—Would you grind the cob when you are going to feed the meal to your horses?

Mr. Smith.—If you are feeding it to horses I would not have it ground.

State of New York Department of Agriculture, Twentieth Annual Report for the Year Ending September 30, 1912, Part II

He disliked letting that 'man' touch his things; he had disliked letting his wife's maid pack for him. He even disliked letting porters carry his kit-bag. He was a Tory—and as he disliked changing his clothes, there he sat, on the journey, already in large, brown, hugely welted and nailed golf boots, leaning forward on the edge of the cushion, his legs apart, on each knee an immense white hand—and thinking vaguely.

Macmaster, on the other hand, was leaning back, reading some small, unbound printed sheets, rather stiff, frowning a little. Tietjens knew that this was, for Macmaster, an impressive moment. He was correcting the proofs of his first book.

To this affair, as Tietjens knew, there attached themselves many fine shades. If, for instance, you had asked Macmaster whether he were a writer, he would have replied with the merest suggestion of a deprecatory shrug.

"No, dear lady!" for of course no man would ask the **question** of anyone so obviously a man of the world. And he would continue with a smile: "Nothing so fine! A mere trifler at odd moments. A critic, perhaps. Yes! A little of a critic."

Nevertheless Macmaster moved in drawing-rooms that, with long curtains, blue china plates, large-patterned wallpapers and large, quiet mirrors, sheltered the long-haired of the Arts. And, as near as possible to the dear ladies who gave the At Homes, Macmaster could keep up the talk—a little magisterially. He liked to be listened to with respect when he spoke of Botticelli, Rossetti, and those early Italian artists whom he called "The Primitives." Tietjens had seen him there. And he didn't disapprove.

Ford Madox Ford, Parade's End

Ecclesiastes says in his first chapter, "The number of fools is infinite"; and when he calls it infinite, does he not seem to comprehend all men, unless it be some few whom yet 'tis a **question** whether any man ever saw?

Desiderius Erasmus, The Praise of Folly

Everything is concealed in symbolism, hidden by veils of mystery and layers of cultural material. But it is psychic data, absolutely. The large doors slide open, they close unbidden. Energy waves, incident radiation. All the letters and numbers are here, all the colors of the spectrum, all the voices and sounds, all the code words and ceremonial phrases. It is just a **question** of deciphering, rearranging, peeling off the layers of unspeakability. Not that we would want to, not that any useful purpose would be served. This is not Tibet. Even Tibet is not Tibet anymore.

Don DeLillo, White Noise

Arthur Twinbarrow wasn't having it either. He gave one of those death-rattle laughs that only diffident men can manage. 'I agree with Charles,' he said. 'We're not all showmen.'

His lectures were also quiet affairs, but unlike Charles Wenlock's they were well attended. After an hour of Arthur students would be astonished by how many notes they had taken and what a complete comprehension of the symbolic structure of the work in **question** they now possessed. Arthur Twinbarrow could find a symbol anywhere; not a flower grew but it was symbolic of regeneration, not a leaf fell but it was symbolic of spiritual desolation, not a ball bounced but it was symbolic of the irrepressibility of the human spirit. Nothing was ever the thing it was and everything was always something else. Symbols drove Sefton to distraction. To him they were like fleas in the double bed of literature. He was aware that they might be in there somewhere but he could never find them himself. And even when he was determined to pass an undisturbed night he was pestered by the scratchings of somebody else. He waged a bitter war against Arthur's influence, telling his students that they had better not go on a symbol hunt when he was around, but he knew that they went charging after them the minute his back was turned. It irked him that although he was constantly demonstrating the wildness and folly of Arthur's ingenuity the students still agreed with Arthur.

Howard Jacobson, Coming From Behind

"There must have been some tension between you and Professor Yeats," Graves prompted.

"That's what they told you? Who told you that? Hartley Fuller?"

"Yes. The history chair."

"That's not a Chair, son. That's a stool." He enjoyed his moment of anger, then got back to us. "Maybe it doesn't matter. History gets written by the winners, no? Bad history. And Hartley is surely a bad historian. And . . . in a way . . . a winner." He fell silent for a moment and Graves knew better than to throw in another **question**. "The fact is, Martha and I overlapped for a few years. So we lived across the hall from each other. A duet. My swan song and her . . . I wouldn't know what to call it . . ." His voice trailed off. "So what kind of wisdom are you looking for?" Wright finally asked. "I didn't kill her."

P. F. Kluge, *Final Exam: A Novel*

It's considered an indication of authenticity that he doesn't generally speak from a tele-prompter but just wings it. (In fact, he brings to the podium a few pages of handwritten bullet points, to which he periodically refers as he, mostly, wings it.) He wings it because winging it serves his purpose. He is not trying to persuade, detail, or prove: he is trying to thrill, agitate, be liked, be loved, here and now. He is trying to make energy. (At one point in his San Jose speech, he endearingly fumbles with a sheaf of "statistics," reads a few, fondly but slightingly mentions the loyal, hapless statistician who compiled them, then seems unable to go on, afraid he might be boring us.)

And make energy he does. It flows out of him, as if channelled in thousands of micro wires, enters the minds of his followers: their cheers go ragged and hoarse, chanting erupts, a look of religious zeal may flash across the face of some non-chanter, who is finally getting, in response to a **question** long nursed in private, exactly the answer he's been craving. One such person stays in my memory from a rally in Fountain Hills, Arizona, in March: a solidly built man in his mid-forties, wearing, in the crazy heat, a long-sleeved black shirt, who, as Trump spoke, worked himself into a state of riveted, silent concentration-fury, the rally equivalent of someone at church gazing fixedly down at the pew before him, nodding, Yes, yes, yes.

George Saunders, *Trump Days (The New Yorker)*

He paused and, darting a quick glance at me before rearranging the blotter pad on his desk, said, "We shall have to make you acting head of the English Department." Needless to say I was stunned by this announcement. I had not expected anything of the sort. I recovered myself long enough to reply, very nearly choking up, "Dr. Bagley, it is unnec-essary for me to say that I hardly consider myself worthy of this honor, this trust—"

"At least we are in agreement on that point."

"—but I shall do my best—my absolute dedicated best—for Polycarp."

"It's only temporary of course, until we find someone who . . ." He tried by a vague gesture to indicate the general concept of adequacy lacking in the present patchwork. "We're in correspondence now with a couple of people. This is an emergency measure, and I emphasize that you're acting head. Seeing to it purely that administrative processes go on. Nothing more. In fact, one of your first duties will be to help us find somebody better—as well as replacements for Blodgett and McGeese."

He pushed across the desk to me a sheet of paper on which were the names of three or four possibilities for the post in **question**, all teachers at Midwestern colleges and universities, only one of whom I recognized, as the author of some treatise Norm Littlefield had made me read. Teachers must keep up with their homework as well as students. This was followed by the files on these prospects, including correspondence and notes, as well as folders on possible new English teachers as such, irrespective of their likelihood as executive timber. The president must have extracted some of the latter material from Littlefield's desk.

"I'd like you to take it home with you and study it. Especially the dossiers, which aren't by any means complete. Do what you can about filling them out and keeping them up to date. Find out what you can about everybody. Read what they've written. That's important."

"I'll drop everything but my classes for it. My own research certainly."

"What's that?"

"'The Clowns in Shakespeare.' It was a field Norm wanted me to devote myself to."

"Oh, yes, I remember. Well, do your best for everyone's sake. Pitch in. Now I've got to get busy over the arrangements. There'll be a service in the Episcopal Church, in which the school will participate. I'll deliver a brief eulogy myself. So if you'll excuse me. God bless you."

"God bless you, sir."

Peter De Vries, *Let Me Count the Ways: A Novel*

SCENE IV.

The ſame.

Enter Desdemona, Emilia, and Clown.

DES. Do you know ſirrah, where Lieutenant Caſſio lies?

CLO. I dare not ſay he lies any where.

DES. Why man?

CLO. He is a ſoldier, and for me to ſay a ſoldier lies, is ſtabbing.

DES. Go to; Where lodges he?

CLO. To tell you where he lodges, is to tell you where I lie.

DES. Can any thing be made of this?

CLO. I know not where he lodges, and for me to deviſe a lodging, and ſay—he lies here, or he lies there, were to lie in mine own throat.

DES. Can you enquire him out, and be edified by report?

CLO. I will catechize the world for him; that is, make **queſtions**, and by them anſwer.

DES. Seek him, bid him come hither: tell him, I have moved my lord in his behalf, and hope, all will be well.

CLO. To do this, is within the compaſs of man's wit; and therefore I will attempt the doing it.

[Exit.

DES. Where ſhould I loſe that handkerchief, Emilia?

EMIL. I know not, madam.

William Shakespeare, *The Plays of William Shakespeare, Volume the Nineteenth, Containing Timon of Athens, Othello: With the Corrections and Illustrations of Various Commentators*

Imagine the writer scrutinizing his manuscript and sensing something is wrong. He structured each sentence well. The punctuation is correct, and sentence length varies nicely. He screws his mouth to the side as he tries to define what is missing. The paragraphs feel bumpy. He imagines transitions should glide from one sentence to the next. Yet, there is a start-and-stop feel throughout his paragraphs.

He does not realize that everything a person reads reveals only half of a conversation.

	Generic Questions
1	*Did your literature review cover the most important relevant works in your research field?*
2	*Did you clearly identify the contributions of the literature reviewed?*
3	*Did you identify the research methods used in the literature reviewed?*
4	*Did you connect the literature with the research topic by identifying its relevance?*
5	*What were the author's credentials? Were the author's arguments supported by evidence?*

Table 6: Examples of Generic **Question** Type

Question Producer	Number of questions	Question types
Supervisor	142	Citation related (107)
		Non-Citation related (35)
Peer	151	Citation related (133)
		Non-Citation related (18)
G-Asks	161 (randomly sampled from 469 questions)	161 Citation related
Generic system	161	161 Generic
Total	615	562 questions were evaluated

Table 10: Number of **Questions** Produced from 33 Literature Review Papers

Real Prediction	Supervisor	Peer	G-Asks	Generic Question
Supervisor	74(52%)	40(27%)	34(21%)	11(7%)
Peer	41(29%)	82(54%)	64(40%)	16(10%)
G-Asks	14(10%)	23(15%)	51(32%)	51(32%)
Generic Question	13(9%)	6(4%)	12(7%)	83(51%)
Total	142	151	161	161

Table 16: Human Classification Result on Authorship of **Questions**. The ratio of the number of predicated **question** type to the total number of real **question** type is shown in percentage.

Ming Liu, R. Calvo and V. Rus, G-Asks: An Intelligent Automatic **Question** Generation System for Academic Writing Support (Journal of Machine Learning Research)

BETWEEN THE LINES

"Every sentence feels like a topic sentence!" I said a few months ago while staring at the dirty part of half a blank page.

I rarely write from an outline. I close my eyes, scan the storyscape, and report the next thing that moves. However, I found that the ideas from sentence to sentence fail to direct the reader along a stream of thought. It makes no difference if I rearrange the order of the sentences. I rake back through the previous text, hoping to pull out some junk. I repeat the process for the next sentence. Nothing changes until, a few hundred words later, a pattern unfolds.

The process for assembling my thoughts is start-and-stop, and this produces a narrative with a start-and-stop feel. Instead of weaving a storyline, I list ideas.

But isn't that what narrative structure really is? Sentences encapsulate thoughts. Similar thoughts group into paragraphs. Paragraphs act as stepping-stones through the scene. Isn't a manuscript simply a logical arrangement of information packets?

Yes. But there is more, hidden in the text.

Pull a book down from your shelf and find in it a long paragraph, a nice big black block. Read the first sentence and stop. Read the second sentence and stop. And then the third. Can you hear the second voice, between the visible text, whispering **questions**? One sentence introduces part of a picture that baits the reader into subconsciously asking a **question** about the idea or action. The writer, in turn, answers that **question** in the next sentence while simultaneously expanding information that prompts the reader into asking additional **questions**. And then the process repeats itself.

Sam Reeves, Invisible Questions: Creating Narrative Flow (Forward Motion for Writers)

MOTIONS FOLLOWING THE AMENDMENT STAGE
§994. The previous **question**.
[Clause 1(a)]

United States House of Representatives, House Rules and Manual (Budget Counsel Reference)

*Clown. I will catechize the world for him; that is, make **queſtions**, and by them anſwer.*] This *Clown* is a fool to some Purpoſe. He was to go ſeek for one; he ſays, he will ask for him, and by his own **queſtions** make anſwer. Without doubt we ſhould read—*and* bid *them* anſwer; i. e. the world; thoſe whom he **queſtions**. WARBURTON.

There is no neceſſity for changing the text. It is the Clown's play to wrench what is ſaid, from its proper meaning. Sir T. More hath briefly worked his character: "he plaieth the ieſter, nowe with ſkoffinge, and nowe with his overthwarte woords, to prouoke all to laughter." His deſign here was to propoſe ſuch **queſtions** as might elicit the information ſought for from him, and therefore, BY his *queſtions* he might be enabled to anſwer. HENLEY.

—and *by* them anſwer.] i. e. and by them, *when* anſwered, form my own anſwer to you. The quaintneſs of the expreſſion is in character. *By* is found both in the quarto, 1622, and the folio.

The modern editors, following a quarto of no authority, printed in 1630, read—and *make* them anſwer. MALONE.

William Shakespeare, The Plays of William Shakespeare, Volume the Nineteenth, Containing Timon of Athens, Othello: With the Corrections and Illustrations of Various Commentators

The *previous* **question** was again demanded, and again sustained by a majority of the house. The effect of the previous **question** being to exclude the **question** on the amendment, and to bring it back to the main **question**—

> H. Niles, *Niles' Weekly Register, Containing Political, Historical, Geographical, Scientifical, Statistical, Economical, and Biographical Documents, Essays, and Facts; Together With Notices of the Arts and Manufactures, and a Record of the Events of the Times, From March to September, 1820—Vol. XVIII, or, Volume VI—New Series*

What the heck is this invisible **question** *and and answer post?*

Asked 1 year, 3 months ago

Viewed 159 times

I honestly don't know how I got to this thread to even link to it, but what the heck is this about? I also cross-posted this on Meta Stack Exchange because of the sheer oddness of it all and it seems far beyond a basic issue.

You clicked on the answers. The **question** has not subject or title. I suspect that happens by modifying it within the grace period.—Ramhound Dec 17 '19 at 0:09

@Ramhound Perhaps. But then why have we not seen this before? I mean I don't recall ever seeing something like this before.—Giacomo1968 Dec 17 '19 at 0:10

The author might have found a way to force the submit.—Ramhound Dec 17 '19 at 0:12

I think I actually caught the **question** on the main site with a title like "blank blank" or similar. The title disappeared right after I entered the post.—Kamil Maciorowski Dec 17 '19 at 0:12

@KamilMaciorowski That sounds nuts. And this all seems nuts . . . And I ain't no squirrel!—Giacomo1968 Dec 17 '19 at 0:13

My impression was the **question** had been edited and the author is just trolling.—Kamil Maciorowski Dec 17 '19 at 0:15

@KamilMaciorowski Well, have you ever seen something like this happen before?—Giacomo1968 Dec 17 '19 at 0:15

Negative. I have not.—Kamil Maciorowski Dec 17 '19 at 0:16

According to a comment on the Meta Stack Exchange post, they are using Unicode alternative spaces. Read more here.—Giacomo1968 Dec 17 '19 at 0:21

1 Answer

The only way to view the **question** is by clicking on the "answers".

—Ramhound, answered Dec 17 '19 at 0:10

> *Meta Super User,* **Questions** > *What the Heck Is This Invisible* **Question** *and and Answer Post? (Stack Exchange)*

Let us not lose sight of the major **question**. We are interested in determining whether the good can be subsumed under the beautiful; whether the good is just the beautiful in the form of human behavior. This doctrine has a certain prima facie plausibility; enough that we can accept it provisionally in order to see where such a position would lead us. It leads us, of course, to inquire as to the nature of the beautiful. This is a most difficult **question** and aestheticians have always been at one another's throats over it. I can only offer my own opinion on the **question**. If this were a book on aesthetics, I would surely try to make a more elaborate defense, but here we must restrict ourselves to that which is immediately relevant to the problem of the relation between the will, the good, and the reason. And so for purposes of this discussion we have said that the beautiful consists in that arrangement of things or affairs which has the power of striking a certain chord in the human mind. We feel the beautiful. We look upon the object or the state of affairs, and we say it "has beauty," which, to over-simplify, is more or less the same as saying that it "has order." But order and harmony are also felt. The mind is nothing if it is not a center of feelings, and this is what it is basically and this is no less true of the human mind than it is of the chicken's mind.

> *W.H. Davis, The Freewill* **Question**

Inspired by the success of these neural methods, we compute the doc2vec representation of the title and body content of a post, and measure similarity between a **question** pair based on vector cosine similarity measures.

> *Wei Emma Zhang and Quan Z. Sheng, Managing Data From Knowledge Bases: Querying and Extraction*

The **question** comprehension part is to extract the core meaning expressed by the user's **question** sentences, so that it can better and more accurately match the user's **question** in the following processing part in order to improve the performance of the system.

> *Zheng Gong and Dan Zhang, The Design of Restricted Domain Automatic* **Question** *Answering System Based on* **Question** *Base (Information Technology and Computer Application Engineering)*

"Where's Mr. Graves?" Hartley Fuller wanted to know. He was my next stop. A week had passed since I talked to Wright. Graves had made it clear that G-Man had low priority. No priority. In the meantime, I drove him around, to courthouses and law offices, to banks and county offices in Columbus, up in Cleveland and Mansfield. I waited for him in lobbies and parking lots, drove him where he wanted to go. He hardly ever talked about what he was doing and his only **questions** were about local stuff—who owned what farm, what land was selling for, things like that which he could pick up from anyone. That's the kind of partners we were.

"He had other duties," I said, not having the least idea what Graves was up to. Some days, he just stayed in his motel room.

"And you're the one to interview me?" Fuller asked. He had some industrial strength doubts. What correspondence course did I take, that entitled me to go one-on-one with the chair of the college history department?

"Yes, sir," I said. "At Mr. Graves' request."

"Well then . . ." he said.

"There's just one **question**, Professor," I said. "And its three words long." That got his interest.

"Well, let's hear it."

"Gerald Kurt Garner."

"That's a name. Not a **question**."

"It's a **question**. It's a name with a wiggle at the end, that's a **question** mark. I think you can take it from there."

"Alright," he said. I'd asked about Gerald Kurt Garner. But the man Fuller started in on was Hiram Wright. "What becomes a legend most?" he asked. And answered: "Timely retirement." Stribling and Wright, the college legends. Stribling had the decency to step aside but Wright stayed forever, 'professing but not progressing, indifferent when not hostile to change.' In his last years he withdrew from departmental affairs, so that many important changes had begun without him. The problem was—and this was difficult to admit—he still characterized the department. He was the name people mentioned. "Oh, that's Hiram Wright's place." Sometimes his colleagues wondered how long it would take to shed that Hiram Wright reputation. How many years? Would time, alone, do the trick? Hiram was hostile to co-education, to team-taught courses, interdisciplinary studies, current scholarship, whole new fields of endeavor, post-colonial, gender, structuralism, post-structuralism. I could hardly keep up, taking notes on what I half-understood, nodding my head in appreciation. Once he got over talking to the likes of me, Fuller just rolled along, only pausing to let me catch up in my note-taking, because he didn't want anything he said to be lost. Even after Hiram Wright withdrew from the department, Fuller said, leaving his colleagues to "their own devices," the old man still impeded progress. He was hostile to films in class. He was hostile to junior years abroad. He had his doubts about change in the profession, about the importance of research, the role of theory. When visitors came to campus, lecturers and politicians, it was Hiram Wright they wanted to meet, was there any chance that the old man would be coming to their lecture? And in May, it was unbearable to see alumni coming in to pay their respects. They filled the hall in their springtime togs, their Docker slacks and golf shirts, waiting to hear how the college was doing, wanting to hear from Wright of all people, the person most out of touch, the least-informed, the sworn enemy of new methods and new ideas. Harry Stribling had the good grace to die on cue. Hiram stuck around, a bone in the throat of the history department, that they couldn`t swallow and couldn't spit out.

P. F. Kluge, *Final Exam: A Novel*

What if, however, we restructure the sentences and add new ones so that each evokes curiosity from the reader?

> At the northeastern city limit of Jentry dirt streets gave way to the neglected pavement of the countryside.

The writer should put himself in the reader's place and ask, "What do you mean 'neglected pavement'? What does it look like?"

—a pale strip of shifting stones—

Structure that image so that it evokes another **question**.

> A pale strip of shifting stones stretched out before him leading to the rim of the Loth Stem Forest where MaJarel could see movement.

The reader asks, "What kind of movement?"

The author responds:

> Torches twinkled through the trees in the distance as travelers rode or walked toward the gates of the Loth Stem Forest.

It might be easier to see the process with the sentences aligned in a paragraph. I inserted the invisible reader **questions** within parenthesis.

> At the northeastern city limit of Jentry, dirt streets gave way to the neglected pavement of the countryside. (What do you mean 'neglected'? What does it look like?) A pale strip of shifting stones that no vehicles had rumbled over in more than forty years stretched out before them, leading to the rim of the Loth Stem Forest where MaJarel could see movement. (What kind of movement?) Torches of travelers twinkled through the trees in the distance. (Who are they?

Where are they going?) Everyone under the age of thirty from the surrounding towns would be walking or riding toward the gates of the Loth Stem Forest two miles into the brush. (Why?)

Sam Reeves, Invisible **Questions**: *Creating Narrative Flow (Forward Motion for Writers)*

'It's a challenge, you see. They shouldn't make people take these cruel little tests, it's so belittling.'

'Well, you do,' said Emma.

'Yes, I know, but it isn't the *same,* is it? I wasn't at all nervous when I took my Ph.D. The thing with this one is that you aren't being judged on your own terms. I'm an expert in English literature, and they're going to ask me **questions** about street signs. It's a field outside the ones in which I have control, you see. I shall *expose* myself, I know.'

'It isn't so very hard,' said Emma.

'You've taken it, then, have you?'

'Yes,' said Emma.

'And passed?'

'Yes,' said Emma.

'Oh, well,' said Treece, 'perhaps you have a mechanical mind. What I'm getting at is how cruel life is in the spheres of it in which you aren't influential. You think you have a protected corner, and you're safe; but once you emerge from it, war is declared. You think life is ideal, so long as you can pursue it along the lines you favour; and then it suddenly comes upon you that it isn't, it's corrupt, that the area in which you are resolute, and make decisions, is so very small. And now and then life goes to work to remind you of it.'

'Yes, I know exactly what you mean,' said Emma. 'The blind, uncontrollable forces of the universe break through, suddenly, the great overpowering energies of the world. As in *Moby Dick.*'

Malcolm Bradbury, *Eating People Is Wrong*

90 Masterpieces You Must Read (Vol.1)

Novels, Poetry, Plays, Short Stories, Essays, Psychology & Philosophy: The Madman, Moby-Dick, Siddhartha, Crime and . . . but scarcely had he put his foot in the stirrup, when a sickness or dizziness seemed to overpower him: he leant forward a moment, with . . . safe home; but, besides my bitter indignation against himself, there was the **question** what to say to his servants . . .

Pansegrouw's Crossword Dictionary

. . . conquer , crush , defeat , dull , extinguish , overcome , overpower , overwhelm , pacify , palliate , quash , quiet , silence . . . test , quiz , form **questions** drawn up for formal answer **questionnaire** quest of Ahab Moby Dick queue chain , file , line . . .

The Great Sea Adventure: Pirate Novels, Treasure-Hunt Tales & Maritime Stories

47 Books: The Sea Wolf, Moby Dick, Lord Jim, Captain Blood, Robinson Crusoe, The Pirate, Treasure Island . . . Herman . . . To **question** him, to talk with him seemed impossible. Too many . . . Their effect is overpowering; they deaden the senses.

Google Books search "overpowering Moby Dick **question**"

'Quite,' said Treece. 'And the **question** remains: is it right to stay in the protected corner, where things are controllable, or should one venture out, and start again in a new world, where things are strenuous, and reclaim something else from the wild?'

Malcolm Bradbury, Eating People Is Wrong

"Are you mad, my friend?" said he, "or whither does your senseless curiosity lead you? Would you also create for yourself and the world a demoniacal enemy? Or to what do your **questions** tend? Peace, peace! learn my miseries, and do not seek to increase your own."

Mary Wollstonecraft Shelley, Frankenstein; or, The Modern Prometheus

There are two phases in the Classic Socratic method. I refer to the Classic Socratic method as a Two-Phase Freestyle form of dialectic. The Modern Socratic method is often constrained to a pre-designed set of **questions** that are known to generate a range of predictable answers and elicit knowable facts. The Classic Socratic method is freestyle because, due to the nature of the **questions**, it cannot predict the responses to **questions**, anticipate the flow of the conversation or even know if a satisfactory answer is possible. The main portrait of how Socrates functioned in the classic style is in the early Dialogues of Plato (and some later dialogues). Plato wrote in the form of dialogues. In these dialogues Socrates would talk to people that had a reputation for having some knowledge of, or some interest in, the subject of the dialogue. In the classic style, Socrates would ask the primary **question** of the dialogue in the form of "What is X?". (e.g. What is justice?) The respondents would answer. Socrates would then ask more **questions** and the respondent's answers would end up refuting the definition to the **question** "What is X?", which they had originally given. Once the respondent realized that the definition was not valid she would be asked again, "What is X?". This process would often repeat until the end of the dialogue. With each new definition the respondent is subjected to more **questions** and continues to fail to define X. The conclusion of the dialogue would be an admission of failure to find a proper definition of X. Apparently this Socratic **questioning** had quite an effect on the respondents.

Max Maxwell, Introduction to the Socratic Method and Its Effect on Critical Thinking

TRINITY: "It's the **question** that drives us mad. It's the **question** that brought you here. You know the **question**, just as I did."
NEO: "What is the Matrix?"
— The Matrix

*Television Tropes & Idioms, Driving **Question***

Arriving in Athens, Dijsselbloem asked the same **question**, and Varoufakis gave the same answer. This time, Dijsselbloem replied, "That will not do." ("I have no doubt that he was pulled into line between the telephone conversation and the visit," Varoufakis told me. He declined to name Germany explicitly, but added, "You can imagine.")

Ian Parker, The Greek Warrior (The New Yorker)

No, not, "What's this third pedal do?" or "Who Is Driving?", a <u>Driving</u> **Question** is when a core element of the plot is a mystery. The most common variation would be a detective murder mystery (where the **question** is most often "Whodunnit?"), but also very popular in <u>Noughties Drama Series</u>, <u>Jigsaw Puzzle Plots</u> and <u>Survival Horror</u>. In many cases the **question** is equivalent to, "What the hell is going on and why?" which taken far enough makes for an <u>Ontological Mystery</u>.

See <u>The Unreveal</u> and <u>The Reveal</u>. <u>Fan-Disliked Explanation</u> is what happens when the answers aren't all they are cracked up to be. <u>Failure Is the Only Option</u> to answering the **question** in a TV series where the **question** is central to the show. Too many can lead to a <u>Kudzu Plot</u>. <u>The Chris Carter Effect</u> is what happens when fans give up on the writers' ability to answer these **questions**.

Television Tropes & Idioms, Driving **Question**

'Has she given up that idea? Are you positively sure she has given up that idea?' Over and over again he has put these **questions** to me. I have answered—what else could I do in the miserably feeble state in which he still lies?—I have answered in such a manner as to soothe and satisfy him. I have said, 'Relieve your mind of all anxiety on that subject: Valeria has no choice but to give up the idea; the obstacles in her way have proved to be insurmountable—the obstacles have conquered her.' This, if you remember, was what I really believed would happen when you and I spoke of that painful topic; and I have heard nothing from you since which has tended to shake my opinion in the smallest degree. If I am right (as I pray God I may be) in the view that I take, you have only to confirm me in your reply, and all will be well. In the other event—that is to say, if you are still determined to persevere in your hopeless project—then make up your mind to face the result.

Wilkie Collins, The Law and the Lady

AGENORA: Screw you.

COMMITTEE CHAIRMAN: No thank you.

TALIPED: Stop mumbling, please, and listen.

COMMITTEE CHAIRMAN: If we must.

TALIPED: As I was saying . . .

AGENORA: [TO COMMITTEE CHAIRMAN] I'll fix you, buddy; just you wait.

TALIPED: Some things the proph-prof said weren't clear—you know how those chaps talk—he didn't hear my **question**, or chose not to answer it. Instead, he told me something that, well, hit me like a load of bricks. You'll never guess . . .

AGENORA: He didn't say you'd kill your father?

TALIPED: Yes.

COMMITTEE CHAIRMAN: And swive your mother in the prone position?

TALIPED: That's right! How did you guess?

COMMITTEE CHAIRMAN: Just intuition. I swear, those proph-profs have a one-track mind.

AGENORA: A dirty track at that.

John Barth, Giles Goat-Boy, or, The Revised New Syllabus

These criticisms did nothing but confirm in Heidegger's eyes that the oblivion of Being was endemic, even among his closest students. Exasperated, he asked in a letter to Hermann Mörchen: dear friend, "can you name for me a single study that has truly taken up my **question** of the meaning of Being *as a **question***, that has considered it critically, either in order to affirm it or in order to reject it?"[5]

For this, first of all, is the **question** of Being for Heidegger—the irresistible urgency of a **question**. *Nur dies*, "this only," one would like to add, borrowing a phrase from *Aus der Erfahrung des Denkens* (1947)[6] which faintly echoes the last sighs of Plotinus's

Enneads: *monon pros monon* (alone towards the One). Heidegger encountered this **question** at the very start of his path, in the textbooks of his professor of dogmatic theology, Carl Braig, but also in Duns Scotus. He never ceased turning the **question** over, in every sense, in his life's work—which gravitates around a single unfinished book but which, with time, has taken on titanic proportions: 102 volumes are planned in the *Collected Edition* (GA), which Heidegger says in a draft of a preface presents only "ways, not works," whose sole aim is "to incite [readers] to pose this **question** in an ever more **questioning** way."[7]

As if it were more imperative to deepen the **question** itself, Heidegger always deferred the response to it.

*Jean Grondin, Why Reawaken the **Question** of Being? (Heidegger's Being and Time: Critical Essays)*

Rof. Moſt like a Gentleman.
Guild. But with much forcing of his diſpoſition.
Rof. Niggard of **Queſtion**, but of our Demands Moſt free in his reply.

William Shakeſpear, The Works of Mr. William Shakespear, in Six Volumes, Adorn'd With Cuts, Volume the Fifth, Containing Romeo and Juliet, Timon of Athens, Julius Caeſar, Macbeth, Hamlet, Prince of Denmark, King Lear, Othello

'Excuse me, Mr Dixon; have you got a minute to spare?'

First making his shot-in-the-back face, Dixon stopped and turned. He was leaving College after a lecture, and so had been hurrying. 'Yes, Mr Michie?'

Michie was a moustached ex-service student who'd commanded a tank troop at Anzio while Dixon was an R.A.F. corporal in western Scotland. He now confronted Dixon near the porter's lodge. As always, his manner seemed to be concealing something, though Dixon could never be sure what. He waited for a moment and said: 'Have you got that syllabus together yet, sir?' He was the only student Dixon had ever heard calling a member of the staff 'sir', and apparently reserved the title exclusively for Dixon.

'Oh yes, that syllabus,' Dixon said, playing for time. He hadn't got it together yet.

Michie pretended to think his **question** needed amplifying. 'You know, sir, the list of stuff for your special subject next year. You said you were going to distribute copies to the Honours people, if you remember.'

Kingsley Amis, Lucky Jim

Enframing is the gathering together that belongs to that setting-upon which sets upon man and puts him in position to reveal the real, in the mode of ordering, as standing-reserve. As the one who is challenged forth in this way, man stands within the essential realm of Enframing. He can never take up a relationship to it only subsequently. Thus the **question** as to how we are to arrive at a relationship to the essence of technology, asked in this way, always comes too late.

*Martin Heidegger, The **Question** Concerning Technology*

This "différance" first became dramatically apparent when the third part of SZ failed to appear—"Time and Being," where Heidegger had promised that the **question** of the meaning of Being would be "concretely answered" (SZ 19).

*Jean Grondin, Why Reawaken the **Question** of Being? (Heidegger's Being and Time: Critical Essays)*

He was on the second floor, halfway through the job. The hammer quickened its tempo at my approach, iron doors giving their usual warning. I sat on a finished crate and chewed the rag with him for a few minutes.

"How are things, Lightning?" He got his nickname ironically of course, but not because of the speed with which he wields a hammer, but because he never strikes twice in the same place. He bent three or four six-penny nails while I watched, and had to pull them out and start over again, though that was probably nervousness at having an audience.

"Oh, I'm feeling fine," he said, showing an assortment of teeth as black as watermelon seeds, as well as some glimpses of watermelon pink in the wide open spaces between. You will notice that he answered a **question** about how things were by telling how he felt—a typical response. People constantly bragging about their health are just as hard to take as hypochondriacs. "Never felt better in my life." He pulled a bandanna from his hind pocket and wiped nonexistent sweat from his brow, then tobacco juice from his chin which was plenty existent. I knew the peon of praise to his superb physical condition which my **question** touched off would be climaxed by the inevitable statement: "I never had a sick day in my life." Well it was no secret why he never. He smoked cigars and a pipe as *well* as chewed tobacco, and as one of the boys on the van remarked, his filthy old mouth was probably the most sanitary place on earth. No germs could possibly live in there.

Peter De Vries, *Let Me Count the Ways: A Novel*

Proceeding from these radical experiences of finitude, Heidegger's thought seemed to many of them to be largely antimetaphysical, so they did not immediately see the necessity of taking up again the **question** of Being posed by Aristotle. Most phenomenologists who have wished to extend Heidegger's philosophical efforts have expressly challenged the priority that he bestows anew to the theme of Being. This is particularly evident in Levinas, who asked quite early whether ontology was truly the fundamental discipline of philosophy—a critique of Heidegger that in fact took aim at the ontological ambition of the entire tradition, an ambition that was totalizing and, in Levinas' eyes, totalitarian. Levinas was followed by Derrida, whose thought of deconstruction was also, if not above all, a destruction of the **question** of Being. If Heidegger teaches us so very well to decode the language of metaphysics, does he not oblige us to deconstruct the **question** of Being itself—and the dream of a finally full presence of meaning or of the truth of Being (as *aletheia* or *Ereignis*), which Heidegger never gave up?[2] Jean-Luc Marion inherits this distancing when he speaks of Heidegger's "construction" of the **question** of Being. The author of *God Without Being* (1982) also tries to promote a "phenomenology without Being," founded on the idea of givenness, which he judges to be even more primordial than that of Being. This is all as if the very last Heidegger (the Heidegger of the *es gibt* and of its giving without reason) was turned against the Heidegger who had maintained the still all-too-metaphysical priority of the **question** of Being.

This critique of the priority of ontology in French phenomenology echoed an analogous suspicion that had long been formulated in Germany, even if its inspirations were often quite different. In some articles published in the late twenties, which are important since they were one of the first philosophical reactions to SZ, Georg Misch claimed to fear a relapse into metaphysics—that is, for Misch, a step back in comparison to Dilthey's historicism—in Heidegger's resurrection of the **question** of Being. Heidegger's most prominent student in Germany, Hans-Georg Gadamer, still spoke, it is true, of an "ontological turn" in hermeneutics, but he did not propose to revive the **question** of Being per se, but to emphasize the essentially linguistic nature of our experience of the world ("there is no understanding of Being without language").

*Jean Grondin, Why Reawaken the **Question** of Being? (Heidegger's Being and Time: Critical Essays)*

Now the entire new paragraph with invisible **questions** omitted:

At the northeastern city limit of Jentry, dirt streets gave way to the neglected pavement of the countryside. A pale strip of shifting stones that no vehicles had rumbled over in more than forty years stretched out before them, leading to the rim of the Loth Stem Forest where MaJarel could see movement. Torches of travelers twinkled through the trees in the distance. Everyone under the age of thirty from the surrounding towns would be walking or riding toward the gates of the Loth Stem Forest two miles into the brush. Once they had paid the toll to pass through the gates, they could cleanse their poisoned food in the hot energy roots of a Loth Stem. Then, they could eat until satiated for the first time in a month, a thought that MaJarel savored until the wind picked up. The brief wind pushed at MaJarel's back, and for a moment, the weakness lifted from his arms and legs and it no longer felt like he walked against the current of a thick liquid, but with the wind came something else. The odor from the chest boiled in his lungs. He moaned from the scent—the memory?—of food.

The next paragraph obviously would answer how he reacts to the scent.

*Sam Reeves, Invisible **Questions**: Creating Narrative Flow (Forward Motion for Writers)*

Sefton Goldberg—a case in point—his head still teeming with unspeakable thoughts and unrealisable desires, even though by now the idea of patricide had palled and passed, arrived at Dr Tolcame's for his first class on the importance of chastity in *Gawain and the Green Knight,* took one look about the room, saw objects whose names he did not know but which made him think of words like psaltery and triptych and sacristy, and broke into a sweat. Geoffrey Tolcame, for his part, took one look at Sefton Goldberg and broke into whatever is the opposite.

Even as he dripped on the ancient stones Sefton was able to understand that Dr Tolcame had selected the objects in his room with great discrimination and refinement, and that Dr Tolcame would never have selected him. Sefton saw no reason to **question** Dr Tolcame's taste. So he put up no resistance to the eminent scholar's suave transitions from the **question** of courtliness to the **question** of honour, from honour to hospitality, from hospitality to liberality, from liberality to money-lending, from money-lending to usury, and from usury to the murder by Jews of young Hugh of Lincoln—to which, had he been there and then accused, Sefton would have readily confessed. At the end of the hour, during which every item of his clothing had stuck itself to every other, he gathered up his books, rounded his shoulders and backed out of the mediaevalist's presence, wringing his hands. By mutual, tacit agreement never to return. For his part he would have understood if Dr Tolcame had hosed down his room the moment he left it. And for all he knew Dr Tolcame had.

So he was used to gentiles making him uncomfortable.

Howard Jacobson, Coming From Behind

One thinks, of course, of Adorno, whose virulent and vitriolic pamphlets never ceased to stigmatize the jargon of the **question** of Being—a futile, crypto-mystical **question** that would betray, in his eyes, a flight from social reality, and that had not sufficiently meditated on Hegel's teaching that Being is equivalent to the uttermost void and the absence of thought . . . For his part, Ernst Tugendhat, an ex-student of Heidegger known for his rejection of the Heideggerian concept of truth, appealed to analytic philosophy in declaring that the **question** of Being had no object and remained without any real philosophical pertinence.[3]

> Jean Grondin, *Why Reawaken the **Question** of Being? (Heidegger's Being and Time: Critical Essays)*

"Too bad," he said, grinning. "I must look Ralph up and **question** him. He'll be in hiding by now, of course, but he's worth hunting out. He always has the most consistently logical and creditable reasons for having done the most idiotic things. He is"—as if that explained it—"an advertising man."

> Dashiell Hammett, *The Dain Curse*

With wide spread of products (computers, cars, handy phones, etc.) equipped with advanced technologies, a CRM (Customer Relationship Management) scheme becomes a very important task in order to settle the troubles and to keep facilities. The purpose of the CRM scheme is to achieve user's satisfaction by managing their **questions** and claims. Moreover, it enables us to keep high quality service for products. **Question** and answering (QA) systems in the CRM scheme require both the quality relating user's satisfaction and the amount of **questions** to be managed, that is to say, it depends on the cost.

> Jun Harada, Masao Fuketa, El-Sayed Atlam, Toru Sumitomo, Wataru Hiraishi and Jun-ichi Aoe, *Estimation of **FAQ** Knowledge Bases by Introducing Measurements (Knowledge-Based Intelligent Information and Engineering Systems)*

how much does philosophy charge for shipping?

please see our shipping policy

my product was received damaged—what should i do?

all products that are received damaged must be returned to receive a refund or replacement. if the item in **question** is part of a kit or bundle, the entire kit must be returned before a refund or replacement can be issued. please see our return policy for additional details.

having trouble with a promotion code?

please check the promotional disclaimer found at the bottom of your email offer or on the philosophy.com homepage to be certain you meet the requirements to redeem the offer.

Does opting in for marketing emails entitle me to a loyalty account?

opting into marketing emails will earn you extra points in the loyalty program, but you still need to register here and select the checkbox to join the loyalty program.

> Philosophy.com, **FAQs**

As universities are beaten into the shapes dictated by business, so language is suborned to its ends. We have all heard the robotic idiom of management, as if a button had activated a digitally generated voice. Like Newspeak in *Nineteen Eighty-Four*, business-speak is an instance of magical naming, superimposing the imagery of the market on the idea of a university—through 'targets', 'benchmarks', time-charts, league tables, 'vision statements', 'content providers'. We may laugh or groan, depending on the state of our mental health at the thickets of TLAs—three-letter acronyms, in the coinage of the writer Richard Hamblyn—that accumulate like dental plaque.

Such acronyms now pepper every document circulating in every institution, not just universities. Like the necromantic mirror of the Snow Queen, they swallow everything up and deaden it. The code conceals aggression: actions are undertaken in its name and justified by its rules; it pushes responsibility from persons to systems. It pushes individuals to one side and replaces them with columns, boxes, numbers, rubrics, often meaningless tautologies (a form will ask first for 'aims', and then for 'objectives'). 'When I use a word,' Humpty Dumpty says, 'it means just what I choose it to mean, neither more nor less.' Alice is puzzled by this, but Humpty Dumpty explains: 'The **question** is . . . which is to be master—that's all.' The term that is successfully imposed will occupy the field of meaning: calling the work of writing a book 'generating an output' or a university 'a knowledge delivery solution' has a cryokinetic effect: it freezes the infinite differences that writing and research make possible, and sets them hard in the mould of market ideology, as sales items.

Marina Warner, Learning My Lesson (London Review of Books)

I am very unfortunate if that is true. But suppose I ask you a **question**: Would you say that this also holds true in the case of horses?

Plato, Apology

There are many **QA** researches for large text databases, but they are not relation to CRM schemes [8][7][14]. Most useful for the CRM researches includes answering opinion **questions** by [11], good and bad expression understanding by [6], and estimating sentence types by [13].

Understanding approaches for the affective expressions [10] must be introduced, not text classification approaches by [9] [12]. This paper presents a measurement of quality of the **FAQ** service by introducing the following measurements:

1) Measurement of user's disrepute for products which defined by four types of classifying **questions** (IMPOSSIBLE, SIDE EFFECT, INSUFFICIENT and UNCLEAR), and the degree for each type is defined.

2) Measurement of kindness for solutions replied which defined by four types of classifying answers (ACTION, CONFIRMATION, EXPLANATION, and NO PROBLEM), and the degree for each type is defined.

3) Measurement of comprehension for answers which defined by semantic expressions of **questions** and answers.

4) Measurements of sufficiency and quality for the whole **FAQ** service that introduced by the 1), 2) and 3). This degree is defined by an integer and it becomes very easy to estimate the **FAQ** service.

*Jun Harada, Masao Fuketa, El-Sayed Atlam, Toru Sumitomo, Wataru Hiraishi and Jun-ichi Aoe, Estimation of **FAQ** Knowledge Bases by Introducing Measurements (Knowledge-Based Intelligent Information and Engineering Systems)*

Rowan Williams recently spoke with unqualified fury to members of the Council for the Defence of British Universities about 'the barbarity and incoherence' of current higher education policy documents. Learning, he said, uncovers the multiple meanings of a work—a text or any other artefact—not in order to find a solution but to open the way to further **questions**. 'Difficulty is good for us,' he said. It is 'good for us to be reminded not to settle for the quick answer': the ticked box and the league table close down minds and narrow the world for the individual and for all of us in our relations with one another. Williams called his way of learning 'honestly difficult'.

> Marina Warner, *Learning My Lesson* (*London Review of Books*)

still having trouble with a promotion code?

simply call philosophy consumer care at <u>1.800.568.3151</u>, 8:00 a.m.–8:00 p.m. eastern standard time, monday–friday, and we will be happy to assist you.

> *Philosophy.com,* **FAQs**

Ham. He that playes the King shall be welcome; his Majesty shall have Tribute of mee: the adventurous Knight shal use his Foyle and Target: the Lover shall not sigh *gratis*, the humorous Man shall end his part in Peace; the Clowne shall make those Laugh, whose Lungs are tickl'd a'th'sere; and the Lady shall say her minde freely; or the blanke Verse shall halt for't. What Players are they?

Rosin. Even those you were wont to take Delight in, the Tragedians of the City.

Ham. How chances it they travaile? Their residence both in Reputation and Profit was better, both wayes.

Rosin. I thinke their Inhibition comes by the meanes of the late Innovation?

Ham. Doe they hold the same Estimation they did when I was in the City? Are they so follow'd?

Rosin. No indeed, they are not.

Ham. How comes it? doe they grow rusty?

Rosin. Nay, their indeavour keepes in the wonted pace; But there is, Sir, an ayrie of Children, little Yases, that crye out on the top of **Question**; and are most tyrannically clap't for't; these are now the fashion, and so be-rattle the common Stages (so they call them) that many wearing Rapiers, are affraide of Goose-quils, and dare scarse come thither.

Ham. What are they Children? Who maintains 'em? How are they escoted? Will they pursue the Quality no longer then they can sing? Will they not say afterwards if they should grow themselves to common Players (as it is like most if their Meanes are no better) their Writers do them wrong, to make them exclaim against their owne Succession.

Rosin. Faith there has bene much to do on both sides; and the Nation holds it no Sin, to tarre them to Controversie. There was for a while, no Mony bid for argument, unless the Poet and the Player went to Cuffes in the **Question**.

Ham. Is't possible?

Guild. Oh there has beene much throwing about of Braines.

Ham. Do the Boyes carry it away?

Rosin. Ay, that they do my Lord, *Hercules* and his load too.

> William Shakespear, *The Works of Mr. William Shakespear, in Six Volumes, Adorn'd With Cuts, Volume the Fifth, Containing Romeo and Juliet, Timon of Athens, Julius Caesar, Macbeth, Hamlet, Prince of Denmark, King Lear, Othello*

Hidden Benefits

Did you notice that not only did the flow of the paragraph improve but also

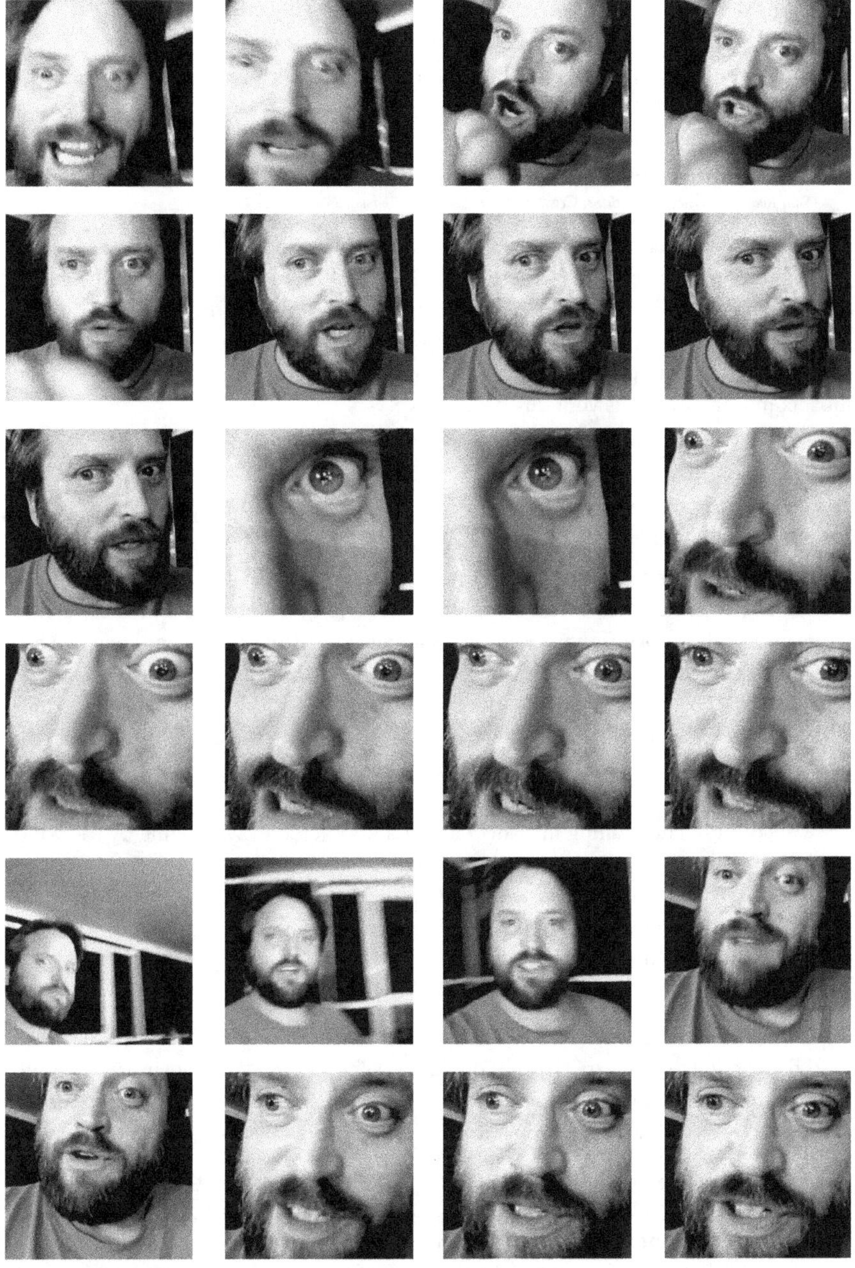

*Kenneth Udut, The True Answer To Every **Question** Anybody Has Ever Asked for All of the History of Time in Any Context and Any Way 'I Don't Know', 2013 (Internet Archive)*

The power of the Internet Archive is that these "loose pages", of which will total around 14,000 when the first stage of the process is completed, will be all viewable at once, as if they are loose pages spread across rows and rows of tables, and then organized, stacked, sorted, collated and finally, bound into a series of books. I'm grateful for the opportunity the Internet Archive is providing here and I appreciate your patience while I go through this process. It's my small contribution to the Library, but i hope the final result will be something worthwhile to preserve for others to enjoy.

heightens the drama? By baiting the readers into asking **questions**, you entice them to wonder what will happen next.

This simple technique will not transform a weak plot or lackluster prose into a page-turner, but it may alleviate some of the pains of dragging the bottom of your mind for what to say next. One of the most powerful tools in storycraft is a sense of what the reader wants to know.

Sam Reeves, *Invisible* **Questions***: Creating Narrative Flow (Forward Motion for Writers)*

Making this information available on your site reduces the amount of direct contact (via phone or e-mail) you have with customers. These documents also allow you to communicate important information in an easy-to-understand format. You can create separate **FAQ** documents that describe: how to use your product, the top features of your product, how to place an order, your company's return policies, or answers to the most common **questions** your customers have.

Jason R. Rich, *Design and Launch an Online E-Commerce Business in A Week*

"Did you know that a dead Marine costs eighteen thousand dollars?" he said. The grunts all turned around and looked at us. They knew how the major had meant that because they knew the major. They were just seeing about me.

The rain stopped, and they left. Outside, the air was still cool, but heavy, too, as though a terrible heat was coming on. The major and I stood by the tent and watched while an F-4 flew nose-down, released its load against the base of a hill, leveled and flew upward again.

"I've been having this dream," the major said. "I've had it two times now. I'm in a big examination room back at Quantico. They're handing out **questionnaires** for an aptitude test. I take one and look at it, and the first **question** says, 'How many kinds of animals can you kill with your hands?'"

We could see rain falling in a sheet about a kilometer away. Judging by the wind, the major gave it three minutes before it reached us.

"After the first tour, I'd have the goddamndest nightmares. You know, the works. Bloody stuff, bad fights, guys dying, *me* dying . . . I thought they were the worst," he said. "But I sort of miss them now."

Michael Herr, *Dispatches*

According to Heidegger, the only way out of the rule of Enframing is to expose oneself to its danger and thus to experience it distinctly. Whether modern humans are in agreement or not, they still find themselves in the realm of Enframing and have already been addressed by it. Human beings must first therefore become conscious of the situation.

> Enframing [Gestell] is the gathering together that belongs to that setting-upon which sets upon man and puts him in position to reveal the real, in the mode of ordering, as standing-reserve. As the one who is challenged forth in this way, man stands within the essential realm of Enframing. *He can never take up a relationship to it only subsequently. Thus the* **question** *as to how we are to arrive at a relationship to the essence of technology, asked in this way, always comes too late.* But never too late comes the **question** as to whether we actually experience ourselves as the ones whose activities everywhere, public and private, are challenged forth by Enframing. Above all, never too late comes the **question** as

to whether and how we actually admit ourselves into that wherein Enframing itself comes to presence. (VA, 27/QCT, 24; italics SR)

Søren Riis, Unframing Martin Heidegger's Understanding of Technology: On the Essential Connection Between Technology, Art, and History

Filmmaker A was scheduled to give a seminar at the film department of a university, and Silvia, as always, decided to accompany her. About forty students had gathered in the foyer, and they followed Filmmaker A out the front doors of the building and into the streets. "This is where the new filmmaking will take place," said Filmmaker A, as she gestured with her arms toward everything that surrounded them. "Without cameras, without actors. The film that is you and your engagement with the world that surrounds you."

The students followed and listened attentively, while Silvia hung back, keeping pace just a few feet behind. There were **questions** that Filmmaker A answered effortlessly, as if the **questions** had simply answered themselves, and she was only doing her best to keep out of the way. But from Silvia's perspective, standing slightly outside the group, what emerged was a different picture. The students were intrigued, perhaps even amused, but most of them remained completely unconvinced.

Then one of the students, a dark-haired girl with a sullen but mischievous smile, decided to make trouble.

"I have a **question**," the sullen girl said.

"All **questions** are welcome," Filmmaker A replied with a carefree wave, as if waving all **questions** towards her.

"These aren't really films you're making. You're just living your life . . ."

"Your definition of filmmaking is too narrow," Filmmaker A said. "That's what I'm here for: to propose another possibility, another way of seeing things."

"But you can't just call things whatever you want," the sullen girl continued. "I can't just say that's not a tree, it's a car, and if you disagree with me, accuse you of being too narrow."

"Of course if we change everything all at once—all trees are cars, all cats are birds—then it might be a bit confusing . . ." It was slightly off-putting how unfazed Filmmaker A seemed by this affront, which was clearly having an entertaining effect on the other students. "But things do change and can change. Especially in the arts, there is an enormous potential for opening things up and re-evaluating our understanding of any given medium. A few hundred years ago, a urinal in a gallery wasn't considered art and yet now it's an essential part of the canon. And I propose that within film, we are now on the cusp of yet another one of these essential, liberating historical changes."

"But I still don't think a urinal placed in a gallery is art," the sullen girl replied.

"There are thousands of people in the art world who would disagree with you."

"The whole world could disagree with me. That doesn't make them right."

Filmmaker A paused and the entire group of students paused along with her. And it wasn't just her body that stopped moving. Suddenly her voice had slowed down as well, she was choosing her words more carefully now.

"I like you," she said, addressing the sullen girl directly, looking her straight in the eyes. "In a strange sort of way we agree. Perhaps most people in the world think that what I do isn't really filmmaking. But I don't care. I think it is and that history will prove me right. And who is there who can really decide the matter for good. No one. Each of us has to make up our own mind. I say it is. You say it isn't. Neither of us is going to look up in the sky one day and have the matter decided for us once and for all in fifty-foot high, flaming letters. We each have to decide for ourselves. All I ask is that you be open enough to hear me out."

The sullen girl smiled and met Filmmaker A's gaze a bit more directly than was polite.

"You're clever," the sullen girl said, smiling more and more as she continued. "More clever than I thought. I disagree with you and you respond by agreeing with me. That's good politics. But good politics aren't enough. The thing is I believe you, I believe that you're sincere, that you're living your fine, exciting life and really believe this great, dandy life you're leading should be referred to as filmmaking. I don't think you're insincere."

"Thank you," Filmmaker A said, ready to put the matter to rest and move on.

But the sullen girl wasn't finished: "The problem is . . ." she said, and by this point the entire group was hanging on her every word, "the problem is there is nothing more sad, more pathetic, than utter sincerity in the service of a lost cause."

Jacob Wren, Polyamorous Love Song

Now, for my part, I had rather be troublesome and indiscreet than a flatterer and a dissembler. I confess that there may be some mixture of pride and obstinacy in keeping myself so upright and open as I do, without any consideration of others; and methinks I am a little too free, where I ought least to be so, and that I grow hot by the opposition of respect; and it may be also, that I suffer myself to follow the propension of my own nature for want of art; using the same liberty, speech, and countenance towards great persons, that I bring with me from my own house: I am sensible how much it declines towards incivility and indiscretion but, besides that I am so bred, I have not a wit supple enough to evade a sudden **question**, and to escape by some evasion, nor to feign a truth, nor memory enough to retain it so feigned; nor, truly, assurance enough to maintain it, and so play the brave out of weakness. And therefore it is that I abandon myself to candour, always to speak as I think, both by complexion and design, leaving the event to fortune. Aristippus was wont to say, that the principal benefit he had extracted from philosophy was that he spoke freely and openly to all.

Michel de Montaigne, Of Presumption (Essays)

Noonan and I took turns mumbling condolences and then he began:

"We just wanted to ask you a couple of **questions**. For instance, like where'd you go last night?"

She looked disagreeably at me, then back to the chief, frowned, and spoke haughtily:

"May I ask why I am being **questioned** in this manner?"

I wondered how many times I had heard that **question**, word for word and tone for tone, while the chief, disregarding it, went on amiably:

"And then there was something about one of your shoes being stained. The right one, or maybe the left. Anyways it was one or the other."

A muscle began twitching in her upper lip.

Dashiell Hammett, Red Harvest

"Couldn't you at least have been silent, if you knew your own weakness? You ought to have turned on your heel the minute he accosted you with his **questions**." Domna laughed. "You look on him as a seducer," she suggested. "To me, he is more like Hamlet, with his soul-searching **questions** to Ophelia, 'Are you honest?'"

"Well, for that matter," said Alma, "I think you were honest enough. Too much so. Has it occurred to you that you may have put your little friend, Sheila, in a pickle?"

Mary McCarthy, The Groves of Academe: A Novel

MARIONETTA

I see, Mr Flosky, you think my intrusion unseasonable, and are inclined to punish it, by talking nonsense to me. (Mr Flosky gave a start at the word nonsense, which almost overturned the table.) I assure you, I would not have intruded if I had not been very much interested in the **question** I wish to ask you.—(Mr Flosky listened in sullen dignity.)—My cousin Scythrop seems to have some secret preying on his mind.—(Mr Flosky was silent.)—He seems very unhappy—Mr Flosky.—Perhaps you are acquainted with the cause.—(Mr Flosky was still silent.)—I only wish to know—Mr Flosky—if it is any thing—that could be remedied by any thing—that any one—of whom I know any thing—could do.

MR FLOSKY (after a pause)

There are various ways of getting at secrets. The most approved methods, as recommended both theoretically and practically in philosophical novels, are eavesdropping at key-holes, picking the locks of chests and desks, peeping into letters, steaming wafers, and insinuating hot wire under sealing wax; none of which methods I hold it lawful to practise.

MARIONETTA

Surely, Mr Flosky, you cannot suspect me of wishing to adopt or encourage such base and contemptible arts.

MR FLOSKY

Yet are they recommended, and with well-strung reasons, by writers of gravity and note, as simple and easy methods of studying character, and gratifying that laudable curiosity which aims at the knowledge of man.

MARIONETTA

I am as ignorant of this morality which you do not approve, as of the metaphysics which you do: I should be glad to know by your means, what is the matter with my cousin; I do not like to see him unhappy, and I suppose there is some reason for it.

MR FLOSKY

Now I should rather suppose there is no reason for it: it is the fashion to be unhappy. To have a reason for being so would be exceedingly common-place: to be so without any is the province of genius: the art of being miserable for misery's sake, has been brought to great perfection in our days; and the ancient Odyssey, which held forth a shining example of the endurance of real misfortune, will give place to a modern one, setting out a more instructive picture of querulous impatience under imaginary evils.

MARIONETTA

Will you oblige me, Mr Flosky, by giving me a plain answer to a plain **question**?

MR FLOSKY

It is impossible, my dear Miss O'Carroll. I never gave a plain answer to a **question** in my life.

Thomas Love Peacock, Nightmare Abbey

'What are your main ideas so far, sir, if you don't mind my asking?' Michie asked as they turned downhill into College Road.

Dixon did mind, but said only: 'Well, I think the main emphasis of the thing will be social, you know.' He was trying to stop himself from thinking directly about the official title of his subject, which was 'Medieval Life and Culture'. 'I thought I might start with a discussion of the university, for instance, in its social role.' He comforted himself for having said this by the thought that at least he knew it didn't mean anything.

'You don't propose to offer an analysis of scholasticism, then, I take it?'

This **question** illustrated exactly why Dixon felt he had to keep Michie out of his subject. Michie knew a lot, or seemed to, which was as bad. One of the things he knew, or seemed to, was what scholasticism was. Dixon read, heard, and even used the word a dozen times a day without knowing, though he seemed to. But he saw clearly that he wouldn't be able to go on seeming to know the meaning of this and a hundred such words while Michie was there **questioning**, discussing, and arguing about them. Michie was, or seemed, able to make a fool of him again and again without warning. Though it would have been easy enough to pick some technical quarrel with him, over an undelivered essay for example, Dixon was reluctant to do so because he felt superstitiously that Michie was capable of insisting on studying Medieval Life and Culture out of sheer spite and desire to do him down. Michie, then, must be kept out, but with smiles and regrets instead of the blows and kicks which were his due. This was why Dixon now said: 'Oh no, I'm afraid there won't be much meat in it from that point of view. I'm not qualified to pronounce on the learned Scotus or Aquinas, I'm afraid.' Or should it have been Augustine?

'It might be rather fascinating to study the effect on men's lives of the various popular debasements and vulgarizations of the schoolmen's doctrines.'

'Oh, agreed, agreed,' Dixon said, his lips beginning to shake, 'but that's a subject for a D.Phil thesis, wouldn't you say, rather than a fairly elementary course of lectures?'

Kingsley Amis, Lucky Jim

Here I can speak from experience. My own knowledge comes largely from universities, both in the United States and the UK. In both countries, the last thirty years have seen a veritable explosion of the proportion of working hours spent on administrative paperwork, at the expense of pretty much everything else. In my own university, for instance, we have not only more administrative staff than faculty, but the faculty, too, are expected to spend at least as much time on administrative responsibilities as on teaching and research combined. This is more or less par for the course for universities worldwide. The explosion of paperwork, in turn, is a direct result of the introduction of corporate management techniques, which are always justified as ways of increasing efficiency, by introducing competition at every level. What these management techniques invariably end up meaning in practice is that everyone winds up spending most of their time trying to sell each other things: grant proposals; book proposals; assessments of our students' job and grant applications; assessments of our colleagues; prospectuses for new interdisciplinary majors, institutes, conference workshops, and universities themselves, which have now become brands to be marketed to prospective students or contributors. Marketing and PR thus come to engulf every aspect of university life.

The result is a sea of documents about the fostering of "imagination" and "creativity," set in an environment that might as well have been designed to strangle any actual manifestations of imagination and creativity in the cradle. I am not a scientist. I work in social theory. But I have seen the results in my own field of endeavor. No major new works of social theory have emerged in the United States in the last thirty years. We have, instead, been largely reduced to the equivalent of Medieval scholastics, scribbling endless annotations on French theory from the 1970s, despite the guilty awareness that if contemporary incarnations of Gilles Deleuze, Michel Foucault, or even Pierre Bourdieu were to appear in the U.S. academy, they would be unlikely to even make it through grad school, and if they somehow did make it, they would almost certainly be denied tenure.[103]

There was a time when academia was society's refuge for the eccentric, brilliant, and impractical. No longer. It is now the domain of professional self-marketers. As for the eccentric, brilliant, and impractical: it would seem society now has no place for them at all.

If all this is true in the social sciences, where research is still carried out largely by individuals, with minimal overhead, one can only imagine how much worse it is for physicists. And indeed, as one physicist has recently warned students pondering a career in the sciences, even when one does emerge from the usual decade-long period languishing as someone else's flunky, one can expect one's best ideas to be stymied at every point.

> You [will] spend your time writing proposals rather than doing research. Worse, because your proposals are judged by your competitors you cannot follow your curiosity, but must spend your effort and talents on anticipating and deflecting criticism rather than on solving the important scientific problems . . . It is proverbial that original ideas are the kiss of death for a proposal; because they have not yet been proved to work.104

That pretty much answers the **question** of why we don't have teleportation devices or antigravity shoes. Common sense dictates that if you want to maximize scientific creativity, you find some bright people, give them the resources they need to pursue whatever idea comes into their heads, and then leave them alone for a while. Most will probably turn up nothing, but one or two may well discover something completely unexpected. If you want to minimize the possibility of unexpected breakthroughs, tell those same people they will receive no resources at all unless they spend the bulk of their time competing against each other to convince you they already know what they are going to discover.[105]

That's pretty much the system we have now.[106]

David Graeber, The Utopia of Rules: On Technology, Stupidity, and the Secret Joys of Bureaucracy

"So it's all meaningless," the bearded one went on. "There aren't any Finals; there's no Dean o' Flunks at the South Exit to punish us if we don't Pass. Every **question** is multiple-choice; there's no final point or meaning in the University, it's—look here, it's like this: a naked physical fact!"

I gasped with Chickie.

"Like the Ismists say, it all comes down to distinctions in our minds; we can't ever get to the things themselves. We can thrust, and we can thrust . . ."

"No!"

". . . but the *screen* . . . the flunking *screen* . . . it's always *there*. And when you *try* . . . to break *through* it . . . you're just *affirming* . . . that it's *there*."

"Oh my!"

He paused. "Where I part company with the Ismists, though, is when they say our only choice is to accept the screen, and give up hope of ever knowing things absolutely. You'll have to read *Footnotes to Sakhyan* one of these days—it's the Syllabus of Beism, you know . . ."

"Don't talk!" his nan cried.

"Sure. You've got it exactly. You've got to say *flunk* that screen, and *flunk* Reality, and *flunk* True and False. Flunk all!"

"Flunk me, Harry! I know I'm going to shout . . ."

"It's no good asking what is—"

"Shut up! Shut up!"

"—you've got to be, Chickie! *Be! Be!*"

Beyond any **question** then they Were, locked past discourse in their odd embrace. And I was fetched with them to the verge of *Being;* I who neither was nor was not, my blood and bones they shuddered to *become!*

John Barth, Giles Goat-Boy, or, The Revised New Syllabus

There is yet another fault in the Discourses of some men; which may also be numbred amongst the sorts of Madnesse; namely, that abuse of words, whereof I have spoken before in the fifth chapter, by the Name of Absurdity. And that is, when men speak such words, as put together, have in them no signification at all; but are fallen upon by some, through misunderstanding of the words they have received, and repeat by rote; by others, from intention to deceive by obscurity. And this is incident to none but those, that converse in **questions** of matters incomprehensible, as the Schoole-men; or in **questions** of abstruse Philosophy. The common sort of men seldome speak Insignificantly, and are therefore, by those other Egregious persons counted Idiots. But to be assured their words are without any thing correspondent to them in the mind, there would need some Examples; which if any man require, let him take a Schoole-man into his hands, and see if he can translate any one chapter concerning any difficult point; as the Trinity; the Deity; the nature of Christ; Transubstantiation; Free-will; &c. into any of the moderne tongues, so as to make the same intelligible; or into any tolerable Latine, such as they were acquainted withall, that lived when the Latine tongue was Vulgar. What is the meaning of these words. "The first cause does not necessarily inflow any thing into the second, by force of the Essential subordination of the second causes, by which it may help it to worke?" They are the Translation of the Title of the sixth chapter of Suarez first Booke, Of The Concourse, Motion, And Help Of God. When men write whole volumes of such stuffe, are they not Mad, or intend to make others so? And particularly, in the **question** of Transubstantiation; where after certain words spoken, they that say, the White-nesse, Round-nesse, Magni-tude, Quali-ty, Corruptibili-ty, all which are incorporeall, &c. go out of the Wafer, into the Body of our blessed Saviour, do they not make those Nesses, Tudes and Ties, to be so many spirits possessing his body? For by Spirits, they mean alwayes things, that being incorporeall, are neverthelesse moveable from one place to another. So that this kind of Absurdity, may rightly be numbred amongst the many sorts of Madnesse; and all the time that guided by clear Thoughts of their worldly lust, they forbear disputing, or writing thus, but Lucide Intervals. And thus much of the Vertues and Defects Intellectuall.

Thomas Hobbes, Leviathan

The rest of the page was given over to collegiate and inter-collegiate news: HIGHWAY DEATHS TO BREAK CARNIVAL RECORD, SAFETY COMMITTEE WARNS; REXFORD TO ANNOUNCE NEW EAT-TESTS TO UNIVERSITY COUNCIL; TENSION MOUNTS ALONG POWER LINE; THOUSANDS MASSACRED IN FRUMENTIAN INTRAMURAL RIOTS; FAMINE SPREADS IN T'ANC; FLOODWATERS RISE IN SIDDARTHA; NTC RAPE-RATE UP 4 POINTS. The weather promised to be fair for the last night of the Carnival as well as for tomorrow's registration and attendant ceremonies, and for that reason the Department of Meteorology urgently reminded everyone to refrain from looking directly at the sun during the annular eclipse predicted for shortly after dawn.

"I respect your position on the social aspects of the Commencement **question**," Dr. Sear was saying to Max, "but not on the phenomenon of personal Graduation. One good medical therapist might be worth a hundred professors of Enochism, as you say; but a real Grand Tutor's worth all the medical therapists that ever were."

Max shook his head.

"You believe in Graduation and Grand Tutors, then, sir?" I asked him—rather surprised, but much gratified.

John Barth, Giles Goat-Boy, or, The Revised New Syllabus

But Philo, while he raises some new **questions**, because he was scarcely able to withstand the things which were said against the obstinacy of the Academicians, speaks falsely, without disguise, as he was reproached for doing by the elder Catulus; and also, as Antiochus told him, falls into the very trap of which he was afraid. For as he asserted that there was nothing which could be comprehended, (for that is what we conceive to be meant by ἀκατάληπτος,) if that was, as Zeno defined it, such a perception, (for we have already spent time enough yesterday in beating out a word for φαντασία,) then a perception was extracted and produced out of that from which it originated, such as could be produced from that from which it did not originate. And we say that this matter was most excellently defined by Zeno; for how can anything be comprehended, so that you may feel absolutely sure that it has been perceived and known, which is of such a character that it is even possible that it may be false? Now when Philo upsets and denies this, he takes away also all distinction between what is known and unknown; from which it follows that nothing can be comprehended; and so, without intending it, he is brought back to the point he least intended. Wherefore, all this discourse against the Academy is undertaken by us in order that we may retain that definition which Philo wished to overturn; and unless we succeed in that, we grant that nothing can be perceived.

*Marcus Tullius Cicero, Second Book of the Academic **Questions***

This development is inseparable from the problematics of the ontological need itself. It can no more be quenched by that sort of philosophy than it could once be quenched by the transcendental system. This is why ontology has become shrouded in vapors. In line with an older German tradition, it puts the **question** above the answer; where it keeps owing what it promised, it has consolingly raised failure as such to existential rank. The weight of **questions** in philosophy differs indeed from the weight they have in special sciences, where the solution of **questions** removes them, while in philosophical history their rhythm would be more that of duration and oblivion. But this does not mean that—as some keep parroting Kierkegaard—the truth lies in the **questioner**'s existence, in his mere futile search for an answer. Rather, in philosophy the authentic **question** will somehow almost always include its answer. Unlike science, philosophy knows no fixed sequence of **question** and answer. Its **question** must be shaped by its experience, so as to catch up with the experience. Its answers are not given, not made, not generated: they are the recoil of the unfolded, transparent **question**.

Theodor W. Adorno, Negative Dialectics

"There is no speedier delivery?" and seemed quite disappointed when she answered "No." Was she quite sure? No man with a trap who would go over?

Mrs. Hall, nothing loath, answered his **questions** and developed a conversation. "It's a steep road by the down, sir," she said in answer to the **question** about a trap; and then, snatching at an opening said, "It was there a carriage was upsettled, a year ago and more. A gentleman killed, besides his coachman. Accidents, sir, happen in a moment, don't they?"

But the visitor was not to be drawn so easily. "They do," he said through his muffler, eyeing her quietly through his impenetrable glasses.

"But they take long enough to get well, sir, don't they? . . . There was my sister's son, Tom, jest cut his arm with a scythe, tumbled on it in the 'ayfield, and, bless me! he was three months tied up, sir. You'd hardly believe it. It's regular given me a dread of a scythe, sir."

"I can quite understand that," said the visitor.

"He was afraid, one time, that he'd have to have an op'ration—he was that bad, sir."

The visitor laughed abruptly, a bark of a laugh that he seemed to bite and kill in his mouth. "Was he?" he said.

H. G. Wells, The Invisible Man: A Grotesque Romance

cymothoa exigua*: the tongue as what it is not—blemish
and parasite: gimp and glottal stop: what **question** can be
answered with a truant mouth: can the lynched man hung
from the sails of a windmill taste the lead pipe wedged
between his lips: when the signifiers dangle, empty chum
lines in a cold creek: when the men in Waco, wearing white
straw hats, fraying at the crisp edges of their white shirts,
leave Jesse, leave John, leave Paul in ashes in the unpaved
streets to choke passing mules into prophecy: when we pinch

---

* *Cymothoa exigua* is a parasitic crustacean that attaches itself to the tongues of spotted rose snappers and extracts blood from the tongue until it atrophies and falls off. Then the parasite attaches itself to the nub and acts as the fish's tongue. According to scientists, the fish is not harmed in the process.

our noses to staunch the smell of the twice burnt black man
burning for a third time this day: when the boys, sweet
and good animals, come to what's been left in shallow ditches:
false rib and femur, clavicle and severed hand—quite simply,
the language of sorrow: glyph of the gadfly rooting himself
into the rotting meat of the dead: when it is too late
to refuse our bodies being made urns: corn, unharvested
and heavy in its husks: when, in the marketplace, the butcher lifts
our tongue from a bed of ice, shouts: who will speak for this flesh:
when the tongue answers as all severed tongues do:

Roger Reeves, Cymothoa Exigua

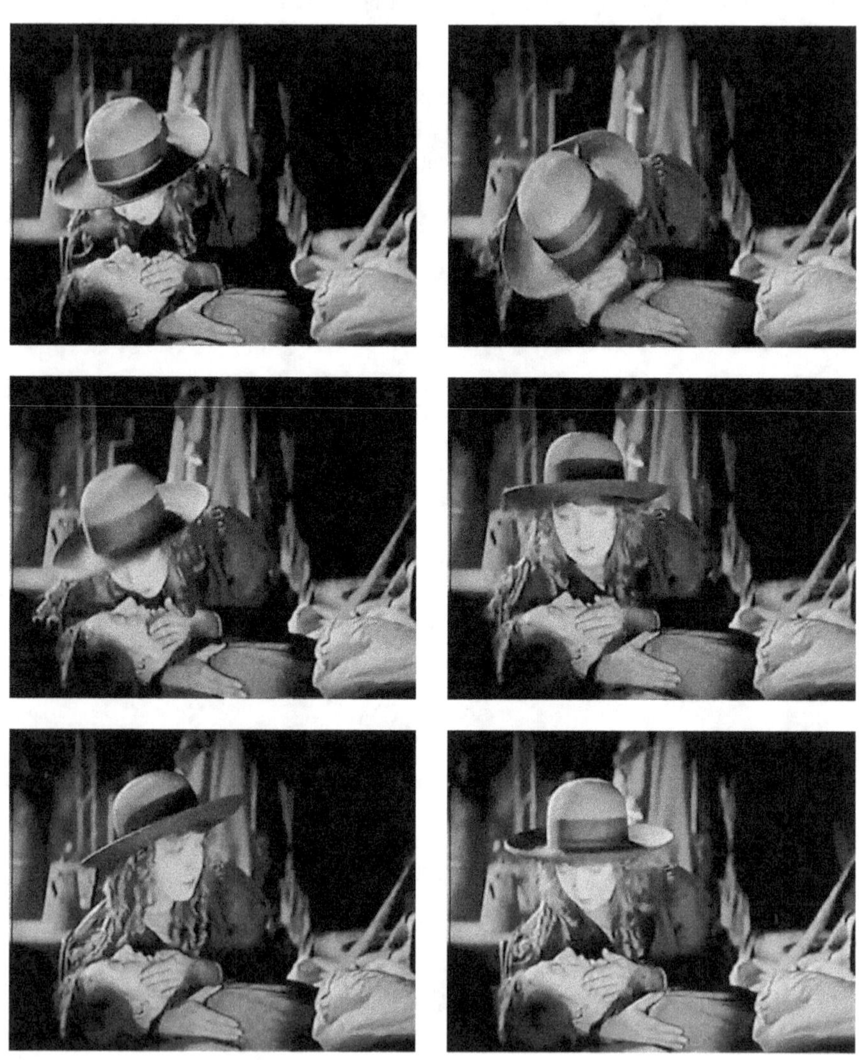

*D.W. Griffith (director), The Greatest **Question**,1919*

Questions Propounded to Me While Mesmerized

It is extremely curious, is it not?

The *Philosophical Investigations* is written in a personal, at times almost confessional, mode. Much of it has the form of a dialogue with an imaginary interlocutor (not entirely unlike the Martian in Jarman's film). Wittgenstein talks about what his own aim is in philosophy and presents himself as almost emotionally engaged with the problems he is discussing. "The real discovery", he writes, "is the one that makes me capable of stopping doing philosophy when I want to. The one which brings philosophy peace, so that it is no longer tormented by **questions** which bring itself into **question**."

   Tim Crane, Wittgenstein, Bewitched (The Times Literary Supplement)

Why do writers and readers favor academic novels? Unsurprisingly, there have been many attempts to answer this **question**. It is interesting that such efforts assume that interest in reading about the professorial life is an anomaly to be explained; no one suspects that Cormac McCarthy's novels about cowboys are read only by cowboys, or by anomalous non-cowboys for whom some excuse needs to be found, and the same seems to be true of Irvine Welsh's fictions about Scottish junkies; on the other hand, George Watson declares academia an odd subject for fiction, since the "university, after all, is a place for students who have barely started to live, and professors who have done all (or nearly all) the living they are ever likely to do."[10]

   Merritt Moseley, Introductory: Definitions and Justifications (The Academic Novel: New and Classic Essays)

Even as he spoke the **question** was answered with a tongue of thunder. Morton had just placed himself in front of the nearest window, his broad shoulders blocking the aperture. For an instant it was lit from within as with red fire, followed by a thundering throng of echoes. The square shoulders seemed to alter in shape, and the sturdy figure collapsed among the tall, rank grasses at the foot of the tower. A puff of smoke floated from the window like a little cloud. The two men behind rushed to the spot and raised him, but he was dead.

   G. K. Chesterton, The Man Who Knew Too Much

"Dead?" said Mrs. Samsa, looking **questioningly** at the charwoman, although she could have investigated for herself . . .

   Franz Kafka, The Metamorphosis

There is but one truly serious philosophical problem and that is suicide. Judging whether life is or is not worth living amounts to answering the fundamental **question** of philosophy. All the rest—whether or not the world has three dimensions, whether the mind has nine or twelve categories—comes afterwards. These are games; one must first answer. And if it is true, as Nietzsche claims, that a philosopher, to deserve our respect, must preach by example, you can appreciate the importance of that reply, for it will precede the definitive act. These are facts the heart can feel; yet they call for careful study before they become clear to the intellect.

If I ask myself how to judge that this **question** is more urgent than that, I reply that one judges by the actions it entails. I have never seen anyone die for the ontological argument. Galileo who held a scientific truth of great importance abjured it with the greatest ease as soon as it endangered his life. In a certain sense, he did right.* That truth was not worth the stake. Whether the earth or the sun revolves around the other is a matter of profound indifference. To tell the truth, it is a futile **question**. On the other hand, I see many people die because they judge that life is not worth living. I see others paradoxically getting killed for the ideas or illusions that give them a reason for living (what is called a reason for living is also an excellent reason for dying). I therefore conclude that the meaning of life is the most urgent of **questions**. How to answer it? On all essential problems (I mean thereby those that run the risk of leading to death or those that intensify the passion of living) there are probably but two methods of thought: the method of La Palisse and the method of Don Quixote. Solely the balance between evidence and lyricism can allow us to achieve simultaneously emotion and lucidity. In a subject at once so humble and so heavy with emotion, the learned and classical dialectic must yield, one can see, to a more modest attitude of mind deriving at one and the same time from common sense and understanding.

Albert Camus, The Myth of Sisyphus

He bypassed the worried gaze of the doctor, leaving him for a moment to founder alone on the ethical niceties of his profession, and looked out of the window beyond him at the shimmering fabric of darkness, brightness and water. It was getting late. Late in the day and late—so very much later than he had suspected—in his life. However, there was such a lot of work still to be done that he could hardly afford to let this upset him. He put his hands under the desk where the doctor could not see them and began methodically ticking off on his fingers the main headings of the important **questions** which needed tying up before he could quit the world in peace with his own conscience; each of which, taken singly, would under normal conditions take him days if not weeks of industry. Finish rereading (in case there was something of vital importance in the works of the others which had escaped him); commit his own work—his secret, his message to the world—to tidy and legible writing; sound out Trevisan to see if he could be entrusted with its safe-keeping; and, on the side (seeing that no one else would be likely to bother about this when he was gone), do something about the obnoxious Catcher. Four fingers. Four principal activities. Four things that could not be left undone. Summed up like that on the fingers of just one hand it did not seem too overwhelming a task. Not if he could draw up a programme and set about things in an orderly way. Fifth point then, he muttered to himself resolutely, bunching his thumb to the rest of the fingers; fifth point: draw up a working timetable.

Amanda Prantera, The Cabalist

"When's he due?" Shoftstall asked, yawning again.

---

* From the point of view of the relative value of truth. On the other hand, from the point of view of virile behaviour, this scholar's fragility may well make us smile.

"Any minute if you can stay awake."

Three minutes later there was a rap on the door and I opened it.

Li Teh came in quickly, his eyes darting as he catalogued and classified the occupants, the furniture, and the equipment. "This is Mr. Jones," I said, not trying to be clever, only simple. "My associates."

Li didn't even nod at them. "Let's get on with it," he said in English.

I nodded at Shoftstall, who moved to a writing desk which held the lie detector in its gray metal case. "Would you remove your coat and roll up your sleeves, Mr. Jones?" he said. "Then please sit in this straight chair in front of the desk."

Li removed his coat, folded it neatly, and put it carefully on the bed. He sat in the chair. Gingerly, I thought. Shoftstall bustled around, readying his equipment and giving out with an endless line of chatter which he seemed to think would soothe the obviously nervous Li, but which, in fact, only made him more jittery. Li obviously wished that the American fool would shut up.

I let Shoftstall talk. "The purpose of this machine, Mr. Jones, is simply to establish validity. That's all. Nothing else. It's painless, and there's absolutely no reason to worry—Mr. Dye here will just ask some simple **questions** to which you can answer either yes or no. That's all. Just yes or no. Before you know it, we'll be through."

Li said nothing. Bourland plugged his tape recorder into the outlet under the desk. Shoftstall continued to chatter away as he affixed the lie detector's attachments to Li's chest, forearm, and palm. "Now if you'll just turn your chair a little this way—to the right," Shoftstall said. "Fine. That's just fine."

"We brought the big Ampex," Bourland said. "I thought you might want the fidelity and its mike will pick up everything."

"Good," I said, not really caring, eager only that the entire sorry scene end itself as soon as possible.

Shoftstall stepped back from Li as if to admire his work. "Okay," he said to Bourland. "You can roll the tape."

Bourland turned a knob on the recorder, made a couple of adjustments, and said, "Tape one and rolling. Interview with Mr. Jones." He looked at Shoftstall. "It's rolling."

Shoftstall dropped to his hands and knees and groped for the polygraph's plug that dangled down behind the writing desk. He glanced up at me. "As soon as I plug it in, you can start," he said.

"All right."

He groped again for the electric cord, found it, and plugged it into the wall socket, the same one that powered the Ampex.

The flashes were cobalt blue, I suppose. Whatever the color, they leaped three feet out into the room, twice, and they were accompanied by a series of sputtering, wet-sounding plops. The lights in the room died instantaneously, but it took Li Teh a little longer. He screamed, only once. It really wasn't much of a scream; it was more like something that a dying kitten would make.

I groped my way over to Li Teh and held the lighter before his face. His eyes were open but they didn't see the flame. I stood there and stared at him until the lighter burned itself out. Shoftstall and Bourland were moving around, cursing and muttering as they rummaged for their equipment. It seemed that we were there in the dark with the dead man for a long time, but it was really only a matter of minutes before the police began pounding on the door and I moved over to open it before they broke it down.

Ross Thomas, The Fools in Town Are on Our Side

Questioned as to cause of death, a/m soldier replied: 'The doctor said his insides were just wore out!'

Earle Birney, Turvey: A Military Picaresque

"Bad news?" asked the deputy director casually, not in order to find anything out but just to get K. away from the device. "No, no," said K., he stepped to one side but did not go away entirely. The deputy director picked up the receiver and, as he waited for his connection, turned away from it and said to K., "One **question**, Mr. K.: Would you like to give me the pleasure of joining me on my sailing boat on Sunday morning? There's quite a few people coming, you're bound to know some of them. One of them is Hasterer, the state attorney. Would you like to come along? Do come along!"

Franz Kafka, The Trial

'Ah,' said Hetherton. 'You will feel nothing out of the way in that sort of life—but it's an unusual setting for violence. There is something moving and mysterious—if you'll believe me—about a half-smoked cigarette lying beside a murdered tart. When its place is taken by the thirtieth canto of the *Purgatorio*—'

'Quite so.'

'I lingered in that room. It tempted to rather futile guessing. Reading Dante and writing a sort of higher dairy-maid poetry . . . one seemed to see the man as one who knew the nature of strength—and who never risked the disillusion of finding himself without it. I prowled the room and tried to build him up further. It was possible to fancy a faintly silly streak—or more strictly perhaps the affectation of it. In an extreme I could imagine a dilettante giggle deliberately assumed—defensive mechanisms of that sort. Certainly not a rash or even a resolute man. One would guess that if he kept a diary—'

'Did he keep a diary?'

Appleby looked at Hetherton's seriously inquiring face and smiled. 'You should be an assistant-commissioner; it's their business to stop gabble in just that way. And the **question** is pertinent. Unfortunately the answer is unknown. Ploss may have kept a diary and it may—as you shall hear—have been destroyed . . . But I see that you are all impatience to be conducted to the corpse.'

Michael Innes, The Secret Vanguard

And why not? Not from any self-will or disregard of you. Whether I am or am not afraid of death is another **question**, of which I will not now speak.

Plato, Apology

Stated clearly, this problem may seem both simple and insoluble. But it is wrongly assumed that simple **questions** involve answers that are no less simple and that evidence implies evidence. *A priori* and reversing the terms of the problem, just as one does or does not kill oneself, it seems that there are but two philosophical solutions, either yes or no. This would be too easy. But allowance must be made for those who, without concluding, continue **questioning**. Here I am only slightly indulging in irony: this is the majority. I notice also that those who answer 'no' act as if they thought 'yes'. As a matter of fact, if I accept the Nietzschean criterion, they think yes in one way or another.

Albert Camus, The Myth of Sisyphus

Alsana thought for a moment, Then she said: "Maybe, Samad Miah."

"What do you mean, 'maybe'?"

"Maybe, Samad Miah, maybe not."

Abana had decided to stop speaking directly to her husband. Through the next eight years she would determine never to say *yes* to him, never to say *no* to him, but rather to force him to live like she did—never *knowing*, never being *sure*, holding Samad's sanity to ransom, until she was paid in full with the return of her number-one-son-eldest-by-two-minutes, until she could once more put a chubby hand through his thick hair. That was her promise, that was her curse upon Samad, and it was *exquisite* revenge. At times it very nearly drove him to the brink, to the kitchen-knife stage, to the medicine cabinet. But Samad was the kind of person too stubborn to kill himself if it meant giving someone else satisfaction. He hung on in there, Alsana turning over in her sleep, muttering, "just bring him back, Mr. Idiot . . . if it's driving you nutso, just bring my baby back."

But there was no money to bring Magid back even if Samad had been inclined to wave the white dhoti. He learned to live with it. It got to the point where if somebody said "yes" or "no" to Samad in the street or in the restaurant, he hardly knew how to respond, he had come to forget what those two elegant little signifiers meant. He never heard them from Alsana's lips. Whatever the **question** in the Iqbal house, there would never again be a straight answer.

"Abana, have you seen my slippers?"

"Possibly, Samad Miah."

"What time is it?"

"It could be three, Samad Miah, but Allah knows it could also be four."

"Alsana, where have you put the remote control?"

"It is as likely to be in the drawer, Samad Miah, as it is behind the sofa."

And so it went.

Zadie Smith, White Teeth

That is a remark applicable always when you are proving what a dead party said; but still it is receivable in law. I maintain that the evidence of what a living party would have been allowed to say in the box—when that party is dead—may be proved by persons who heard him say so. Therefore I submit that James being the receivable witness to speak as to this if he was alive, the evidence is good of those who heard him say this when this litigation was not in **question**.

Anne Waddel, Report of the Jury Trials, Miss A.W. and Others, Against the Right Hon. C. Hope and Others, and Miss A.W. Against the Right Hon. C. Hope and Daughters . . . Taken in Short-Hand by D. Buchanan

I was just fitting my key into the door when I noticed a man at my elbow. I had not seen him approach, and the sudden appearance made me start. He was a slim man, with a short brown beard and small, gimlety blue eyes. I recognized him as the occupant of a flat on the top floor, with whom I had passed the time of day on the stairs.

'Can I speak to you?' he said. 'May I come in for a minute?' He was steadying his voice with an effort, and his hand was pawing my arm.

I got my door open and motioned him in. No sooner was he over the threshold than he made a dash for my back room, where I used to smoke and write my letters. Then he bolted back.

'Is the door locked?' he asked feverishly, and he fastened the chain with his own hand.

'I'm very sorry,' he said humbly. 'It's a mighty liberty, but you looked the kind of man who would understand. I've had you in my mind all this week when things got troublesome. Say, will you do me a good turn?'

'I'll listen to you,' I said. 'That's all I'll promise.' I was getting worried by the antics of this nervous little chap.

There was a tray of drinks on a table beside him, from which he filled himself a stiff whisky-and-soda. He drank it off in three gulps, and cracked the glass as he set it down.

'Pardon,' he said, 'I'm a bit rattled tonight. You see, I happen at this moment to be dead.'

I sat down in an armchair and lit my pipe.

'What does it feel like?' I asked.

He seemed to brace himself for a great effort, and then started on the queerest rigmarole. I didn't get hold of it at first, and I had to stop and ask him **questions**. But here is the gist of it:

He was an American, from Kentucky, and after college, being pretty well off, he had started out to see the world. He wrote a bit, and acted as war correspondent for a Chicago paper, and spent a year or two in South-Eastern Europe. I gathered that he was a fine linguist, and had got to know pretty well the society in those parts. He spoke familiarly of many names that I remembered to have seen in the newspapers.

He had played about with politics, he told me, at first for the interest of them, and then because he couldn't help himself. I read him as a sharp, restless fellow, who always wanted to get down to the roots of things. He got a little further down than he wanted.

John Buchan, The Thirty-Nine Steps

Suicide may also be regarded as an experiment—a **question** which man puts to Nature, trying to force her to an answer. The **question** is this: What change will death produce in a man's existence and in his insight into the nature of things? It is a clumsy experiment to make; for it involves the destruction of the very consciousness which puts the **question** and awaits the answer.

Arthur Schopenhauer, On Suicide (Studies in Pessimism)

"These considerations have led me to think that some good results might ensue from a series of well-directed **questions** propounded to me while mesmerized. You have often observed the profound self-cognizance evinced by the sleep-waker—the extensive knowledge he displays upon all points relating to the mesmeric condition itself; and from this self-cognizance may be deduced hints for the proper conduct of a catechism."

I consented of course to make this experiment. A few passes threw Mr. Vankirk into the mesmeric sleep. His breathing became immediately more easy, and he seemed to suffer no physical uneasiness. The following conversation then ensued:—V. in the dialogue representing the patient, and P. myself.

P. Are you asleep?

V. Yes—no I would rather sleep more soundly.

P. *[After a few more passes.]* Do you sleep now?

V. Yes.

P. How do you think your present illness will result?

V. *[After a long hesitation and speaking as if with effort.]* I must die.

P. Does the idea of death afflict you?

V. *[Very quickly.]* No—no!

P. Are you pleased with the prospect?

V. If I were awake I should like to die, but now it is no matter. The mesmeric condition is so near death as to content me.

P. I wish you would explain yourself, Mr. Vankirk.

V. I am willing to do so, but it requires more effort than I feel able to make. You do not **question** me properly.

P. What then shall I ask?

V. You must begin at the beginning.

P. The beginning! but where is the beginning?

V. You know that the beginning is GOD. *[This was said in a low, fluctuating tone, and with every sign of the most profound veneration.]*

P. What then is God?

Edgar Allan Poe, Mesmeric Revelation

"I begin with an epigraph, a preface, and a **question**.

William Pietz, The Phonograph in Africa: International Phonocentrism From Stanley to Sarnoff (Post-Structuralism and the **Question** of History)

Because of the potential ramifications, it behooves everyone to carefully examine this issue, and try to reach a decision. Spiritually, it could be a life and death **question**.

Thomas J. Gorman, To Believe or Not Believe, That Is the **Question**: An Undercover Agent's Quest for the Truth

Take one of the most recent cases
Take the simple fact
Take this example
Taking a broader view
Taking the facts by themselves
That is a further point
That is a natural boast
That is a pure assumption
That is all that it seems necessary to me
That is all very good
That is far from my thoughts
That is final and conclusive
That is the lesson of history
That is the **question** of **questions**
That you may conceive the force of
The answer is easy to find
The answer is ready
The belief is born of the wish
The broad principle which I would lay down
The circumstances under which we meet
The climax of my purpose in this address

The common consent of civilized mankind
The conclusion is irresistible
The confusing assertion is sometimes made
The day is at hand
The decided objection is raised
The doctrine I am combating
The doctrine is admirable
The effect too often is
The evolution of events has brought
The fact has made a deep impression on me
The fact has often been insisted
The fact to be particularly noted
The facts are clear and unequivocal
The facts may be strung together
The first business of every man
The first counsel I would offer
The first great fact to remember is
The first point to be ascertained
The first practical thought is
The first remarkable instance was
The first thing I wish to note
The first thing that we have to consider

Grenville Kleiser, Fifteen Thousand Useful Phrases: A Practical Handbook of Pertinent Expressions, Striking Similes, Literary, Commercial, Conversational, and Oratorical Terms, for the Embellishment of Speech and Literature, and the Improvement of the Vocabulary of Those Persons Who Read, Write, and Speak English

The importance of this **Question**, and how easily, even ignorant men, may come to be fully resolved in it; all being reduced to four only points.

*Joseph Mumford, The **Question** of **Questions**; Which, Rightly Resolv'd, Resolves All Our **Questions** in Religion. This **Question** Is, Who Ought to Be Our Judge in All These Differences? This Book Answers That **Question***

Recall the existence of a yes/no **question** particle *mbaa* from (58), which indicates expected hearer affirmation or speaker's hope. Thus, it appears that the **question** particles *waa* and *mbaa* stand in a derivational relationship, although its exact nature is unclear.

Harold Torrence, The Clause Structure of Wolof: Insights Into the Left Periphery

We can name a thing according to the knowledge we have of its nature from its properties and effects. Hence because we can know what stone is in itself from its property, this name "stone" signifies the nature of the stone itself; for it signifies the definition of stone, by which we know what it is, for the idea which the name signifies is the definition, as is said in Metaph. iv. Now from the divine effects we cannot know the divine nature in itself, so as to know what it is; but only by way of eminence, and by way of causality, and of negation as stated above (**Question** 12, Article 12). Thus the name "God" signifies the divine nature, for this name was imposed to signify something existing above all things, the principle of all things and removed from all things; for those who name God intend to signify all this.

*Thomas Aquinas, Summa Theologica, First Part , **Question** 13: The Names of God*

This leads to the following conclusions:

Non computable problems arise not only in mathematics but even in purely logic theories like First Order Calculus. This is somehow surprising, since First Order Calculus can be formalised by a complete theory, while mathematics cannot.

Computability is a weaker notion than demonstrability. We could establish a sort of hierarchy of classes of **questions**: there are classes of **questions** that admit a yes/no answer but cannot be proved; classes of **questions** that can be proved but whose demonstrations is not computable through a general algorithm; classes of **questions** whose demonstrations are computable through a general algorithm.

Non computability is not directly related to the presence of an external meaning. Even theories that are complete, and therefore do not need an interpretation to determine the truth of their axioms, are not decidable through the use of algorithms.

*Alfred Driessen and Antoine Suarez, Mathematical Undecidability, Quantum Nonlocality and the **Question** of the Existence of God*

'And where is this object'?'

'Ah, that's the **question**, isn't it? I have a terrible feeling that I know who's got it. In any case, I'm in a bit of a pickle.'

Paul Cornell, Human Nature: The New Doctor Who Adventures

Every formula is a reduction to the simplest terms. It's the ultimate synthesis of relations in life or nature. "To be or not to be? That is the **question**!" defines a relationship between decision-making and motivation. Choosing "to be" or "not to be" is life's object of interest.

Let's assume that being and having are interchangeable and can be mistaken for each other, so long as we understand having as a measure between what we have and what we deliberately don't have. If having is the choice that emerges from the real demand of the moment, and not an imperative of our imagination or a mental construct, then this formula permits the interchangeability of having and being. This interchangeability is the central issue of this book. But before delving into it, we must establish an important definition: what is a "**question**"?

The word "**question**" can be understood in a number of ways, a fact that became quite evident when Shakespeare was translated into Yiddish. Originating as a German dialect used by some Jews, Yiddish has become the lingua franca of the exiled Jew. I don't know of any similar phenomenon among other peoples, where a group has adopted as its national language a dialect that is a testament to its exile—a mother tongue that is actually a stepmother tongue. It is a language that expresses being (identity) in the absence of having (territory)—or even better put, being as a function of not having.

The translator who rendered *Hamlet* into Yiddish couldn't decide how to handle the word "**question**." Beyond the apparently philosophical heart of this Shakespearian formula, Yiddish highlights another of the equations unknowns, namely "that's the **question**." What precisely is meant by the word "**question**," which in Yiddish can be translated in different ways, as *frague* (query), *shaila* (ambivalence), *kashia* (doubt), or *teiku* (paradox)?

These four nearly synonymous words reflect subtle distinctions that the Yiddish culture has perceived within the realms of human inquiry. This may be a result of its roots in German, a language characterized by exceedingly accurate usage of words for every specific situation. Or it may simply be a product of the Yiddish culture's intra-psychological characteristics. We know from jokes and anecdotes that the tradition of "**questioning**" is one of its cultural traits. The fact is, Yiddish offers us a gamut of nuanced variations for the word "**question**."

Nilton Bonder, To Have or Not to Have, That Is the Question: The Economics of Desire

*"Why do Jews always answer a **question** with a **question**?"*
"How should they answer?"

I was raised in a "Yinglish"-speaking household. Before age three, I'd already soaked up 3,000 years of Yiddishkeit. But more, unbeknownst to me, I assumed that's how the world worked.

Until college. One Jew among a 100 Gentiles is like throwing a rock in a pond. The concentric circles I created went from the East River past the Mighty Mississippi. By Winter break, my young dorm mates were returning home to places like Missoula, Zwingle, and Chugwater, shocking their parents with:

"I see you got a 'D' in physics."
"Who am I, Einstein?!"
"What? Passing isn't enough for you?"
"And my 'A' in Viking Lit means bupkes?"
"From physics I'll make a living?"

But more, they learned the Queen of Yiddishisms! Answering a **question** with a **question**!

After all, I'd spent my tender years not answering **questions** by asking more **questions**.

A typical discussion:

MA: "A Mrs. Goldman in the beauty parlor mentioned there's a youth group at the shul, so you'll run over now?"
ME: "Which Mrs. Goldman? *Marvin's* mom?"
MA: "So *once* he wore his pants on backwards?"
DAD: "Is she *Marvin's* Mrs. Goldman?"
MA: "I ask *questions* under the dryer? What am I, a *genealogist*?!"
BUBBE: "A mother lets a son go out that way?!"
ME: "Can I finish my homework *now*?"
MA: "Why do I bother?"

I was 12 then. But the years only increased my **question** to **question**-non-answer ratio.

ME: "Isn't it a gorgeous day?"
MA: "So the sun is out. Should I do a cartwheel?"
ME: "I found a great used car!"
DAD: "And who can afford the insurance?"
ME: "It's so nice out, why don't we take a drive?"
BUBBE: "On Sunday? With the crowds? Who drives on a Sunday?"
ME: "I haven't called in a week. So what's new?"
ALL: "You didn't wonder about Bubbe's bursitis?"
ME: "Bursitis? Why didn't you call me?"

ALL: "Why bother you?!"

Needless to say, I was 25 before I could form a declarative sentence.

Before we dismiss this odd speech pattern to merely "more exaggerated stereo-typing," Leo Rosten, in his seminal *The Joys of Yiddish* not only confirmed this syntax as a specifically Jewish trait, but viewed "the **question**" as one way to distinguish between Jew and Gentile! **Questioning**, deriving from Talmudic debate, imbues us with the unusual tradition of saying: "I believe! But *nu*, if I ask, you'll 'show me?'" But more, through skepticism we analyzed the often treacherous world around us, and learned that an answer may be dangerous, misleading, obvious, unknown, or unnecessary.

A Classic . . .

Morris and Izzy were sitting over tuna salad discussing the meaning of the cosmos.
"Life," said Morris, "is like a bowl of tuna fish."

Izzy considered, "So, why is life like a bowl of tuna fish?"

"How should I know? What am I, a philosopher?"

Marnie Winston-Macauley, Jews Love Questions: To Be or Not to Be? You Call That a Good Question? (Aish.com)

'More like *Hamlet*. Tell me, do you believe in God?'

Hadleman, looking around him, was caught off guard by the **question**. 'Eh? Oh, no, not at all, actually. I believe in dialectical materialism, the force of history and the revolution. Two ideas collide, form a new idea, a synthesis, and that new idea is natu-rally revolutionary. History's like a big hill, and we're all rolling down it towards the inevitable. Towards the revolution.' He stopped. 'Of course, that needn't necessarily be a violent revolution. What, ah, are your politics, Doctor?'

Smith considered. 'I don't know if I have any. Not yet. I'll let you know when my own synthesis happens.'

Paul Cornell, Human Nature: The New Doctor Who Adventures

That his struggle *be* a faithful unconquerable one: that is the **question** of **questions**. We will put-up with many sad details, if the soul of it were true. Details by themselves will never teach us what it is. I believe we misestimate Mahomet's faults even as faults: but the secret of him will never be got by dwelling there. We will leave all this behind us; and assuring ourselves that he did mean some true thing, ask candidly what it was or might be.

Thomas Carlyle, On Heroes, Hero-Worship and the Heroic in History

One of the phænonema which had peculiarly attracted my attention was the structure of the human frame, and, indeed, any animal endued with life. Whence, I often asked myself, did the principle of life proceed? It was a bold **question**, and one which has ever been considered as a mystery; yet with how many things are we upon the brink of becoming acquainted, if cowardice or carelessness did not restrain our inquiries. I revolved these circumstances in my mind, and determined thenceforth to apply myself more particularly to those branches of natural philosophy which relate to physiology. Unless I had been animated by an almost supernatural enthusiasm, my application to this study would have been irksome, and almost intolerable. To examine the causes of life, we must first have recourse to death. I became acquainted with the science of anatomy: but this was not sufficient; I must also observe the natural decay and corruption of the human body. In my education my father had taken the greatest precautions that my mind should be impressed with no supernatural horrors. I do not ever remember to have trembled at a tale of superstition, or to have feared the apparition of a spirit. Darkness had no effect upon my fancy; and a churchyard was to me merely the receptacle of bodies deprived of life, which, from being the seat of beauty and strength, had become food for the worm. Now I was led to examine the cause and progress of this decay, and forced to spend days and nights in vaults and charnel houses. My attention was fixed upon every object the most insupportable to the delicacy of the human feelings. I saw how the fine form of man was degraded and wasted; I beheld the corruption of death succeed to the blooming cheek of life; I saw how the worm inherited the wonders of the eye and brain. I paused, examining and analysing all the minutiæ of causation, as exemplified in the change from life to death, and death to life, until from the midst of this darkness a sudden light broke in upon me—a light so brilliant and wondrous, yet so simple, that while I became dizzy with the immensity of the prospect which it illustrated, I was surprised that among so many men of genius, who had directed their inquiries towards the same science, that I alone should be reserved to discover so astonishing a secret.

Remember, I am not recording the vision of a madman. The sun does not more certainly shine in the heavens, than that which I now affirm is true. Some miracle might have produced it, yet the stages of the discovery were distinct and probable. After days and nights of incredible labour and fatigue, I succeeded in discovering the cause of generation and life; nay, more, I became myself capable of bestowing animation upon lifeless matter.

The astonishment which I had at first experienced on this discovery soon gave place to delight and rapture. After so much time spent in painful labour, to arrive at once at the summit of my desires, was the most gratifying consummation of my toils. But this discovery was so great and overwhelming, that all the steps by which I had been progressively led to it were obliterated, and I beheld only the result. What had been the study and desire of the wisest men since the creation of the world, was now within my grasp. Not that, like a magic scene, it all opened upon me at once: the information I had obtained was of a nature rather to direct my endeavours so soon as I should point them towards the object of my search, than to exhibit that object already accomplished. I was like the Arabian who had been buried with the dead, and found a passage to life aided only by one glimmering, and seemingly ineffectual light.

I see by your eagerness, and the wonder and hope which your eyes express, my friend, that you expect to be informed of the secret with which I am acquainted; that cannot be: listen patiently until the end of my story, and you will easily perceive why I am reserved upon that subject. I will not lead you on, unguarded and ardent as I then was, to your destruction and infallible misery. Learn from me, if not by my precepts, at least by my example, how dangerous is the acquirement of knowledge, and how much happier that man is who believes his native town to be the world, than he who aspires to become greater than his nature will allow.

Mary Wollstonecraft Shelley, Frankenstein; or, The Modern Prometheus

I left him with the newspaper and a box of cigars, and went down to the City till luncheon. When I got back the lift-man had an important face.

'Nawsty business 'ere this morning, Sir. Gent in No. 15 been and shot 'isself. They've

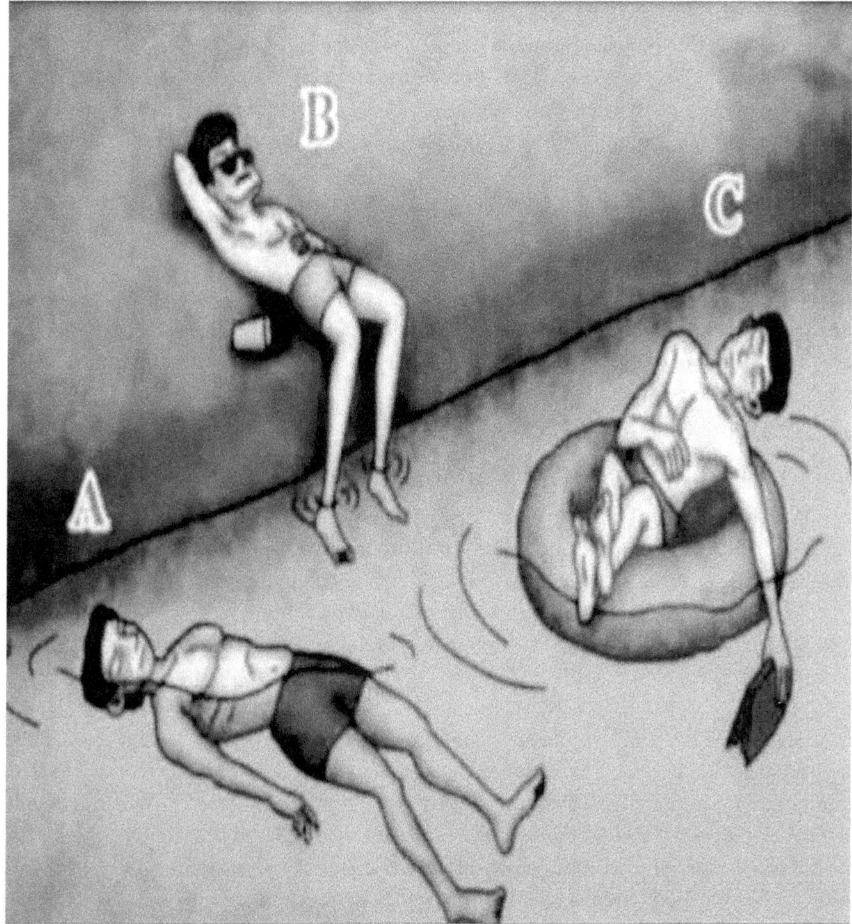

WHO IS DEAD? PAY ATTENTION TO DETAIL

Who Is Dead? Pay Attention to Detail is the latest riddle making rounds on Facebook, Twitter, and WhatsApp these days. People from all over the world are trying to find the correct answer to the Who Is Dead? Pay Attention to Detail riddle. According to the data, more than 95% of people fail to give the correct answer to this tricky riddle.

Here we are going to solve the "Who Is Dead? Pay Attention to Detail" riddle and provide the correct answer to it. So now let us get started.

WHO IS DEAD? PAY ATTENTION TO DETAIL ANSWER

The correct answer to Who Is Dead? Pay Attention to Detail riddle is "C".

Who Is Dead? Pay Attention To Detail Riddle: Solution, Explanation

Let us now show you how we came to the conclusion that person C is dead.

If you see the legs of person B, there is vibration in the water. This makes us sure that person B is not dead.

Now many of us will say that the person "A" is dead as his body is floating in the water. But the **question** is do dead bodies float in water?. The answer is yes, but it takes at least 2 to 3 days for a dead body to float. In the starting 1 to 2 days, a dead body sinks under the water, thereafter it starts floating. Thus, person A is not dead as it doesn't make any sense for 2 people (B & C) to come to the pool to chill out with a dead body floating in it.

Finally, let's have a look at Person C. If you see closely, the person is having a laptop in his hand and it is in the water. Also, he seems to be in a subconscious state.

Therefore, Who Is Dead? Pay Attention to Detail answer is person "C".

Ritesh Kumar, Who Is Dead? Pay Attention to Detail Riddle ANSWER (gadgetgrasp.com)

just took 'im to the mortuary. The police are up there now.'

I ascended to No. 15, and found a couple of bobbies and an inspector busy making an examination. I asked a few idiotic **questions**, and they soon kicked me out. Then I found the man that had valeted Scudder, and pumped him, but I could see he suspected nothing. He was a whining fellow with a churchyard face, and half-a-crown went far to console him.

I attended the inquest next day. A partner of some publishing firm gave evidence that the deceased had brought him wood-pulp propositions, and had been, he believed, an agent of an American business. The jury found it a case of suicide while of unsound mind, and the few effects were handed over to the American Consul to deal with. I gave Scudder a full account of the affair, and it interested him greatly. He said he wished he could have attended the inquest, for he reckoned it would be about as spicy as to read one's own obituary notice.

John Buchan, The Thirty-Nine Steps

NIK WORTH, ROCK STAR TURNED ECCENTRIC INNOVATOR, DIES AT 50

Nik Worth, the eccentric genius and reclusive oddity, died yesterday of an apparent suicide. He was found unconscious at his home by his sister, Denise Kranis. No note was found at the scene, although his sister said, "He killed himself."

Dr. Mark Farmer, the LA County coroner, said preliminary autopsy findings indicated a drug overdose. The sheriff's department found bottles of the prescription drugs Nembutal and Anzemet by the bed, as well as a half-empty bottle of vodka.

Mr. Worth was born in 1956 as Nikolas Kranis. His father died when he was 11, and his mother has been sick in recent years. The family was poor, but Worth always felt he was well taken care of. He attended Hollywood High, and then, after a still-sealed conflict with the authorities, was expelled. He eventually graduated from Fairfax High School. He never attended college. It was at Hollywood High that he met the band-mates who would become his multi-platinum band, the Demonics. The Demonics pioneered a hard-edged post-glam art-rock sound that changed the course of popular music.

Mr. Worth's other band, the Fakes, followed the Demonics. The Fakes had a more pure pop sound, and they dominated the charts for much of the early eighties: *Meet the Fakes, Here Are Your Fakes,* and later, *Take Me Home and Make Me Fake It* all made number one in the US and the UK.

In 1980, Nik Worth was injured in a motorcycle accident.

It was then he began his long anti-pop project, *The Ontology of Worth*, a twenty-volume music experiment. Some thought it was brilliant, others referred to it as "Worth's Folly." Even admirers viewed it as self-indulgent. In response to the many parodies created about his later work, Worth only said, "Every man's life is an answer to the **questions** he asks," apparently quoting, inaccurately, Emerson.

In later years, Worth dropped from sight. Rumors abounded that his health, both mental and physical, was failing. He kept putting out the albums for his *Ontology* project, and he maintained a devoted but much smaller following. From time to time he put out a new Fakes record—recordings now made entirely by him in his home studio. The Fakes albums always sold well. But he stopped touring, and seldom left his "hermitage" near the Pacific Ocean, a large house on Skyline Drive in Topanga Canyon. According to friends, he never stopped working, recording, and writing. Many people speculate that there could be much more music still in the vaults at Skyline Drive.

Dana Spiotta, *Stone Arabia*

Rhea and I stand by Lou's bed, unsure what to do. We know him from a time when there was no such thing as normal people dying.

There were clues, hints about some bad alternative to being alive (we remembered them together over coffee, Rhea and I, before coming to see him—staring at each other's new faces across the plastic table, our familiar features rinsed in weird adulthood). There was Scotty's mom, of course, who died from pills when we were still in high school, but she wasn't normal. My father, from AIDS, but I hardly saw him by then. Anyway, those were catastrophes. Not like this: prescriptions by the bed, a leaden smell of medicine and vacuumed carpet. It reminds me of being in the hospital. Not the smell, exactly (the hospital doesn't have carpets), but the dead air, the feeling of being far away from everything.

We stand there, quiet. My **questions** all seem wrong: How did you get so old? Was it all at once, in a day, or did you peter out bit by bit? When did you stop having parties? Did everyone else get old too, or was it just you? Are other people still here, hiding in the palm trees or holding their breath underwater? When did you last swim your laps? Do your bones hurt? Did you know this was coming and hide that you knew, or did it ambush you from behind?

Jennifer Egan, *A Visit From the Goon Squad*

—I don't know, says Alf I saw him just now in Capel street with Paddy Dignam. Only I was running after that . . .

—You what? says Joe, throwing down the letters. With who?

—With Dignam, says Alf.

—Is it Paddy? says Joe.

—Yes, says Alf. Why?

—Don't you know he's dead? says Joe.

—Paddy Dignam dead! says Alf.

—Ay, says Joe.

—Sure I'm after seeing him not five minutes ago, says Alf, as plain as a pikestaff.

—Who's dead? says Bob Doran.

—You saw his ghost then, says Joe, God between us and harm.

—What? says Alf. Good Christ, only five . . . What? . . . And Willy Murray with him, the two of them there near whatdoyoucallhim's . . . What? Dignam dead?

—What about Dignam? says Bob Doran. Who's talking about . . . ?

—Dead! says Alf. He's no more dead than you are.

—Maybe so, says Joe. They took the liberty of burying him this morning anyhow.

—Paddy? says Alf.

—Ay, says Joe. He paid the debt of nature, God be merciful to him.

—Good Christ! says Alf.

Begob he was what you might call flabbergasted.

In the darkness spirit hands were felt to flutter and when prayer by tantras had been directed to the proper quarter a faint but increasing luminosity of ruby light became gradually visible, the apparition of the etheric double being particularly lifelike owing to the discharge of jivic rays from the crown of the head and face. Communication was effected through the pituitary body and also by means of the orangefiery and scarlet rays emanating from the sacral region and solar plexus. **Questioned** by his earthname as to his whereabouts in the heavenworld he stated that he was now on the path of pr l ya or return but was still submitted to trial at the hands of certain bloodthirsty entities on the lower astral levels. In reply to a **question** as to his first sensations in the great divide beyond he stated that previously he had seen as in a glass darkly but that those who had passed over had summit possibilities of atmic development opened up to them. Interrogated as to whether life there resembled our experience in the flesh he stated that he had heard from more favoured beings now in the spirit that their abodes were equipped with every modern home comfort such as talafana, alavatar, hatakalda, wataklasat and that the highest adepts were steeped in waves of volupcy of the very purest nature. Having requested a quart of buttermilk this was brought and evidently afforded relief. Asked if he had any message for the living he exhorted all who were still at the wrong side of Maya to acknowledge the true path for it was reported in devanic circles that Mars and Jupiter were out for mischief on the eastern angle where the ram has power. It was then queried whether there were any special desires on the part of the defunct and the reply was: *We greet you, friends of earth, who are still in the body. Mind C.K. doesn't pile it on.* It was ascertained that the reference was to Mr Cornelius Kelleher, manager of Messrs H.J. O'Neill's popular funeral establishment, a personal friend of the defunct, who had been responsible for the carrying out of the interment arrangements. Before departing he requested that it should be told to his dear son Patsy that the other boot which he had been looking for was at present under the commode in the return room and that the pair should be sent to Cullen's to be soled only as the heels were still good. He stated that this had greatly perturbed his peace of mind in the other region and earnestly requested that his desire should be made known.

Assurances were given that the matter would be attended to and it was intimated that this had given satisfaction.

He is gone from mortal haunts: O'Dignam, sun of our morning. Fleet was his foot on the bracken: Patrick of the beamy brow. Wail, Banba, with your wind: and wail, O ocean, with your whirlwind.

—There he is again, says the citizen, staring out.

—Who? says I.

James Joyce, Ulysses

The "who" **question** is perhaps the most controversial, primarily for two reasons.

1. The average person is relatively unskilled at describing others. It is not unusual to obtain such varying descriptions of the same suspect from two different witnesses, so much so that one would swear the witnesses weren't describing the same person.

2. Persons who seem to be too anxious to answer the "who" **question** might have ulterior motives. For example, in traffic cases, a friend of one of those involved might attempt to pose as a neutral witness and convince the officer "who" caused the accident.

For example:

- Who was at fault?
- Who is the suspect?
- Who is the victim?

- Who had a motive?
- Who was present?

Donald J. Schroeder and Frank A. Lombardo, Police Officer Exam

In the above example **questions** 1 and 4, one can see that the answer to 'Who is X?' depends on X. If X is a job title, then one expects a person-name to be the answer and the **question** becomes a genuine 'Who' **question**. On the other hand, if X is a person-name, one expects the answer to be 'definitional' and should actually be classified as a 'What' **question**. One needs to analyze the property of X in order to answer the **question** correctly. The example **question** 2 has two forms. With the format 'What country', the meta-keyword provides a clue of what the answer should be and hence is somewhat easier. The second format only gives the clue president-of. The third example **question** asks for the relationship name, and does not seem to have been used in TREC QA tasks. The form with the word 'job' again is easier. A similar example is from a 1-place relation instance such as:

German-philosopher(Gunther)

Two **questions** can be formed:

| 5. | ?(Gunther) | = Who is Gunther? (E-i) |
| 6. | German-philosopher(?) | = Name a German philosopher? (A-i) |

Additional finer distinctions may also apply to the (A-ii) type of Who-**questions**. For example, if one assumes tasks done by humans be captured in a relation as follows:

do(person, task)

the cardinality of the expected answer in relation to the task may also give a clue as to whether a name is expected. Consider the following **question**:

*Tomek Strzalkowski and Sanda Harabagiu, Advances in Open Domain **Question** Answering*

An interactive policy discussion, calling for input from all Government Delegations, will consider the following **question**, "In promoting its objectives, what activities should the Committee for Trade, Industry and Enterprise Development give priority to?"

She invited participants to consider the following **questions** with a view to formulating assessments or recommendations for consideration at the World Conference:

The Co-Chair (Antigua and Barbuda) invited delegations to consider the following **questions** in the opening session:

In that respect they may wish to consider the following **questions** and suggest policy options and actions to be taken at the national and international level.

The Netherlands would like to suggest that the Consultative Process consider the following **questions**:

To aid discussion, the Working Party is invited to consider the following **questions**:

The Forum may wish to consider the following **questions** for the background discussion:

Against this background, it is suggested that delegates consider the following **question** for discussion during the deliberations:

Participants will be expected to consider the following **questions**:

The discussion may therefore consider the following **questions**:

Parties may wish to consider the following **questions** arising from possible requirements relating to lifetime of projects.

*Reverso Context, Consider the Following **Question***

'I assume that's a rhetorical **question**, sir,' said Hutchinson.

Paul Cornell, Human Nature: The New Doctor Who Adventures

"You told me, Mr. Jaggers, that it might be years hence when that person appeared."

"Just so," said Mr. Jaggers, "that's my answer."

As we looked full at one another, I felt my breath come quicker in my strong
desire to get something out of him. And as I felt that it came quicker, and as I felt that
he saw that it came quicker, I felt that I had less chance than ever of getting anything
out of him.

"Do you suppose it will still be years hence, Mr. Jaggers?"

Mr. Jaggers shook his head,—not in negativing the **question**, but in altogether negativing the notion that he could anyhow be got to answer it,—and the two horrible casts
of the twitched faces looked, when my eyes strayed up to them, as if they had come to
a crisis in their suspended attention, and were going to sneeze.

"Come!" said Mr. Jaggers, warming the backs of his legs with the backs of his warmed
hands, "I'll be plain with you, my friend Pip. That's a **question** I must not be asked.
You'll understand that better, when I tell you it's a **question** that might compromise
me. Come! I'll go a little further with you; I'll say something more."

He bent down so low to frown at his boots, that he was able to rub the calves of his
legs in the pause he made.

Charles Dickens, Great Expectations

. . . he died very mysteriously afterward, but I could not swear that he was killed; it
was the opinion of the neighborhood that that was the way he came to his death."

Answer. Yes, sir, the man that died in that way was a man named Beckett, son of Dr.
Beckett, a very respectable old gentleman; he died, as his physician, Dr. Tindall,
stated, with the heart disease. He had eaten supper rather hearty, and was standing
before the fire, and was taken with one of his spells, as they called it, and died in a
very few minutes. It was charged, or reported, that Mr. Ford was shot at the same
time. Mr. Ford was shot, with his own pistol, at Walton's store, in the presence of
several men in sight, and amongst them Dr. Dowdell, who swore to it in the Federal
court. He is a justice of the peace, and was there holding court. He said he had his
pistol out, and letting down the click fired and hurt himself in the hand pretty badly;
he saw it done and gave the date. The other man they said was wounded was Willis,
who skinned his foot with a new pair of boots and was lame. I never saw his foot; I
did not examine it, but I know as well about Beckett's as about any neighbor's death,
and examined Ford's hand and examined Squire Dowdell about it.

Question. All this testimony you say was taken at Oxford?

Answer. Yes, sir.

Question. These men were all arrested?

Answer. Beckett was not arrested, because he was dead, but the other two were—Willis and Ford. Squire Dowdell was taken there as justice of the peace holding court, to prove how Ford was shot.

Question. What were Dowdell's politics?

United States House of Representatives, Testimony Taken by the Joint Select Committee to Inquire Into the Condition of Affairs in the Late Insurrectionary States (Reports of Committees for the Second Session of the Forty-Second Congress, 1871-'72)

Warning: Despite the repeated emphasis on *concepts* versus *chemicals*, don't be lulled into thinking that you won't have to put names to formulas (or vice versa) on your final exam. It's quite possible you may have several **questions** that require you do to just that. And you'll certainly need to do it in the real world. However, your knowledge of the basic concepts will help you immensely. Consider the following **question**.

Jill Meryl Levy, Hazmat Chemistry Study Guide (Second Edition)

By the CHAIRMAN:

Question. Is there any doubt about his death?

Answer. I do not think there is any doubt about it, if you want my opinion. Still it cannot be proven. I think he is dead; that is my opinion.

United States House of Representatives, Testimony Taken by the Joint Select Committee to Inquire Into the Condition of Affairs in the Late Insurrectionary States (Reports of Committees for the Second Session of the Forty-Second Congress, 1871-'72)

"My colleague," Burot interrupted, "has not yet mentioned that Charcot claims to have developed a treatment that alleviates the symptoms."

"I was just about to get there," responded Bourru, exasperated. "Charcot has chosen the path of hypnotism, which until recently was an occupation for charlatans like Mesmer. Under hypnosis, patients ought to be able to recall traumatic episodes, which are the origin of the hysteria, and be cured through awareness of them."

"And are they cured?"

"That is the point, Monsieur Simonini," said Bourru. "For us, what goes on at the Salpêtrière often feels more like the theater than clinical psychiatry. Let us be clear: we wouldn't want to dispute the infallible diagnostic abilities of the master . . ."

"Not to **question** them at all," confirmed Burot. "It's the technique of hypnotism itself that . . ."

Bourru and Burot told me about the various systems for hypnotizing, from the quackish methods of a certain Abbé Faria (my ears pricked up at that Dumasian name, though it is well known that Dumas plundered real stories) to the scientific approach of Doctor Braid, a true pioneer.

"The best magnetizers," said Burot, "now follow procedures that are much simpler."

"And more effective," added Bourru. "A medallion or a key is waved before the patient, who is told to watch it closely. Within one to three minutes the subject's pupils develop an oscillatory movement, the pulse slows down, the eyes close, the face relaxes, and drowsiness may last for up to twenty minutes."

"It has to be said," Burot observed, "that much depends on the subject, since magnetization does not depend upon the transmission of mysterious fluids, as that buffoon Mesmer suggested, but upon phenomena of autosuggestion. Indian gurus obtain the same result by focusing on the point of their nose, the monks of Mount Athos by staring at their navel.

"We do not much believe in these forms of autosuggestion," Burot added, "though we ourselves are only putting into practice ideas developed by Charcot himself before he began to place so much trust in hypnotism. We are dealing with cases of personality variation, in other words, with patients who think they are one person one day and someone else another, and the two personalities know nothing of each other. Last year a certain Louis came to our hospital."

"An interesting case," said Bourru. "He complained of paralysis, anesthesia, contractions, muscular spasms, hyperesthesia, skin irritation, hemorrhaging, coughing, vomiting, epileptic fits, catatonia, sleep-walking, Saint Vitus' dance, speech impediments . . ."

"Sometimes he thought he was a dog," said Burot, "or a steam locomotive. And then he had persecutory delusions, restricted vision, gustatory, olfactory and visual hallucinations, pseudo-tubercular pulmonary congestion, headache, stomachache, constipation, anorexia, bulimia, lethargy, kleptomania . . ."

"In short," Bourru said, "a normal picture. But instead of resorting to hypnosis, we applied a steel bar to the patient's right arm, and there, as if by magic, he appeared before us like a new man. Paralysis and insensitivity had disappeared from the right side and had moved to the left."

"In front of us was another person," continued Burot, "who remembered nothing of what had happened a moment earlier. Louis, in one of his states, was teetotal; in the other he had a tendency to drunkenness."

"Note," said Bourru, "that the magnetic force of a substance acts even from a distance. For example, a small bottle containing an alcoholic substance is placed under the subject's chair without his knowledge. In this state of somnambulism the subject will display all the symptoms of drunkenness."

"You understand that our practices respect the mental integrity of the patient," concluded Burot. "Hypnotism makes the subject lose consciousness, whereas with magnetism there is no violent impact upon an organ but a progressive charging of the nervous plexus."

From that conversation I formed the view that Bourru and Burot were two imbeciles who tormented poor lunatics with injurious substances, and I felt confirmed in my opinion when I saw Doctor Du Maurier, who was following the conversation from a nearby table, shaking his head several times.

"My dear friend," he said to me two days later, "Charcot and our two from Rochefort, instead of analyzing the past history of their patients and asking themselves what it means to have two states of consciousness, spend their time worrying about whether it's better to work on them with hypnosis or with metal bars. The problem is that in many patients the passage from one personality to another occurs spontaneously, without our being able to predict how and when. We might talk of self-hypnosis. In my view Charcot and his disciples have not given sufficient consideration to the experiences of Doctor Azam and the Félida case. We know very little about these phenomena. Memory disturbance may be caused by a reduction in blood flow to a still unknown part of the brain, and the momentary constriction of the vessels could be provoked by a state of hysteria. But where in the brain is the lack of blood flow that causes memory loss?"

"Where?"

"That is the point."

Umberto Eco, The Prague Cemetery

It is difficult, perhaps impossible, to ask a 'who?' **question** that does not draw lines; any answer to 'who?' relies on and makes distinctions. Consider, for example:

> Who, me? I am a university professor doing disability studies in the Department of Sociology and Equity Studies at OISE in Toronto.
>
> Who, me? I am a white, middle-class woman who grew up in Calgary.
>
> Who, me? Oh, about five days a week I go for a workout usually right after I write for a bit in the morning.
>
> Who, me? I am dyslexic; my partner is blind; we are part of a growing group of scholars who argue that we need to think more about social space and the meaning of embodiment in everyday life.
>
> Who, me? I am someone who appears to the space management person as one who undoubtedly belongs in the university environment, but also as one who can and should make plans about who does not.

*Tanya Titchkosky, The **Question** of Access: Disability, Space, Meaning*

In classes, he was quiet and answered only when asked to. He had the habit of depending on himself to fit his own facts together, and the notion of consulting someone else—even Starke—by asking an important **question** was foreign to him. He was accustomed to a natural order of things in which few answers were supplied. Asking Starke to help him with his grasp of facts would have seemed unfair to him.

Consequently, his marks showed unpredictable ups and downs. Like all high school science classes, the only thing Starke's physics class was supposed to teach was the principal part of the broad theoretical base. His students were given and expected to learn by rote the various simpler laws and formulae, like so many bricks ripped whole out of a misty and possibly useful structure. They were not yet—if ever—expected to construct anything of their own out of them. Lucas Martino failed to realize this. He would have been uncomfortable with the thought. It was his notion that Starke was throwing out hints, and he was presumed capable of filling in the rest for himself.

Algis Budrys, Who?

For example, in the sentences below the word *intellectuals* refers to a person so it can yield a Who **question**, and the word *airport* refers to a location so it can yield a Where **question**.

*Tomek Strzalkowski and Sanda Harabagiu, Advances in Open Domain **Question** Answering*

Where now? Who now? When now? **Unquestioning.**
I, say I. Unbelieving.
Questions, hypotheses (call them that).
Keep going, going on (call that going, call that on).

Samuel Beckett, The Unnamable

kooku	this person in **question**	(from kan = who?)
foofu	this place in **question**	(from fan = where?)
loolu	this thing in **question**	(from lan = what?)
noonu	this manner in **question**	(from nan = how?)
yooyu	those things in **question**	

References:

Peace Corps Course:	pp 29
J'Apprends le Wolof:	pp 31
Baptist course:	pp 20
Notes on Wolof Grammar (Stewart):	pp 65
Initiation à la Grammaire Wolof (Samb):	pp 46, 59, 60, 64

Wolof Resources, Wolof Grammar Manual

VLADIMIR: You're being asked a **question**.

POZZO: *(delighted)*. A **question**! Who? What? A moment ago you were calling me Sir, in fear and trembling. Now you're asking me **questions**. No good will come of this!

VLADIMIR: *(to Estragon)*. I think he's listening.

ESTRAGON: *(circling about Lucky)*. What?

VLADIMIR: You can ask him now. He's on the alert.

ESTRAGON: Ask him what?

Samuel Beckett, Waiting for Godot

"Who's on First?" is a comedy routine made famous by Abbott and Costello. The premise of the sketch is that Abbott is identifying the players on a baseball team for Costello, but their names and nicknames can be interpreted as non-responsive answers to Costello's **questions**. For example, the first baseman is named "Who"; thus, the utterance "Who's on first" is ambiguous between the **question** ("Which person is the first baseman?") and the answer ("The name of the first baseman is 'Who'").

For the Blackford Oakes novel, see <u>Who's on First (novel)</u>.

Wikipedia, Who's on First

"He shot them," the young man said.

"Who?" Necessary said.

"His two kids."

"Dead?"

"Yessir."

"When?"

"His wife too."

"When?" Necessary said again.

"About thirty minutes ago or an hour ago. Around then."

Necessary sighed and then smiled at the young man. "Just tell it," he said in a curiously reassuring voice. "Just start where you want to and tell it."

The young man took a deep breath. "He shot his two kids and his wife and they're all dead and he is too because he shot himself three times in the—" He stopped while he searched his mind for a word. "In the *groin*."

"Jesus!" Lynch said and turned to Necessary. "Could he do that?" he demanded. "Could he shoot himself three times?"

Necessary kept on with his role in the play. "Who're you, mister?"

Mayor Robineaux rushed in as the reporters began crowding around, sensing something had happened, something that needed telling. "I don't think you two've ever met," the mayor said. "Mr. Lynch here is one of our—our—" He stumbled in his search for a word or phrase that would describe Lynch. He finally settled on, "our civic leaders."

Necessary nodded to show the mayor that he understood what a civic leader was. "Well, that's fine," he said and turned to leave.

"You didn't answer my **question**," Lynch said and put a large, fat hand on Necessary's shoulder. Swankerton's new chief of police stopped quite still and then turned, not with the hand, but away from it, so that Lynch either had to remove it or trot around in a circle after Necessary. He dropped the hand.

"What **question**?" Necessary said after he had turned fully around. "I think it sounds fishy. Shooting himself three times."

"You think it might not be suicide, huh?" Necessary said and examined Lynch as if for the first time. He took in the tentlike suit and the ill-fitting white shirt and the stained tie and the big round face that wore its best smile, the one that didn't show too many teeth. Necessary studied it all with his blue and brown eyes and nodded slightly, as if confirming some long-held suspicion.

"That's right," Lynch said, returning the stare. "I think that maybe it might not be suicide."

Necessary cocked his head slightly to one side and nodded again, as if he were giving Lynch's comment a great deal of serious thought. Finally he said, "And what makes you believe I give a goddamn what you think, mister?"

Ross Thomas, *The Fools in Town Are on Our Side*

(106a) shows that in Wolof, multiple **question** particles may occur. Given that *waa* co-occurs with the wh-**question** particles and wh-expressions, it is important to note that it morphological relative *mbaa* cannot occur in wh-**questions** nor can it occur with the wh-**question** particle *an-a* and *mbaa* does not occur in wh-**questions**:

Harold Torrence, *The Clause Structure of Wolof: Insights Into the Left Periphery*

"Now lookee here," he said, "the **question** being whether you're to be let to live. You know what a file is?"

"Yes, sir."

"And you know what wittles is?"

"Yes, sir."

After each **question** he tilted me over a little more, so as to give me a greater sense of helplessness and danger.

"You get me a file." He tilted me again. "And you get me wittles." He tilted me again. "You bring 'em both to me." He tilted me again. "Or I'll have your heart and liver out." He tilted me again.

Charles Dickens, *Great Expectations*

I see my probation officer Mr. T_ alternate Thursdays 10 a.m., downtown Mt. Vernon. My therapist Dr. E_ Mondays 4 p.m., University Medical Center. Group therapy with Dr. B_ is Tuesdays 7 p.m.

I am not doing well, I think. Or maybe just O.K. I know they are writing reports. But I am not allowed to see. If one of these was a woman I would do better, I feel. They believe you, they are not always watching you. EYE CONTACT HAS BEEN MY DOWNFALL.

Mr. T_ asks **questions** like rolling off a tape. YES SIR I tell him NO SIR. I am employed. On a regular basis now. Dr. E_ is the one who prescribes the medication, asks me **questions** to get me to talk. My tongue gets in the way of my talking. Dr. B_ throws out a **question** as he says to get the guys talking. They're bullshit masters. I admire them. I sit inside my clothes staring at my shoes. My whole body is a numb tongue.

> *Joyce Carol Oates, Zombie*

Now in answer to the first argument, "Why not take advantage of the unconsciousness?" Although the brain is asleep, the nerves are very much alive, the reflexes are not abolished, and therefore the shock to the patient when the tooth is extracted may be very acute. It may, in fact, be fatal, and in that case the **questions** asked at a coroner's inquest may be very unpleasant.

> *William Rushton, Fainting and Tooth-Extraction (The Dental Digest, A Monthly Summary of Dental Science Devoted to the Progress of Dentistry, Volume III)*

"Last meals?" I said.

"That's right,"said Nick, slid another ketchup packet from the dash, squeezed it over his hash browns. "You know how they often report a con's last meal. There are even websites about it. People are obsessed. And if you followed this stuff, you'd know that these guys on death row always order fast-food crap. You ever look into this? It's always the burgers, the fried chicken. The fried shrimp. Or fried shrimp product. You know what I'm talking about, Milo?"

"I guess."

"You guess? I bet you know exactly what I'm talking about. Some guy is a few hours away from the Reaper's speedball and he chows down on a slab of imitation crabmeat in a hot dog bun. And fucks like you, no offense, get all sad and superior about it. These poor slobs could order anything they want, you think, but they are just low-rent and don't know any better. Because that's the story they've told us."

"The story?"

"That's the official story: a condemned prisoner's last meal can be anything he wants. It's the American way, right? Like that guy, the slow one that Clinton killed to show his cojones, that boy didn't finish his burger, his hoagie, whatever the fuck it was, said he'd eat the rest later. Later. That broke you up, didn't it?"

"Excuse me?"

"I think it was a veal parm."

I did recall that poor kid, the national cruelty so crystallized in that moment.

"Sure, I remember."

"Anyway, the point is, why fast food? Why the crap? Why not grass-fed Angus or Kobe beef, an '86 Mouton Rothschild? Don't look at me like that. I watch the fucking food shows."

"So, is this a food show?"

"Bear with me, buddy. Bear with me and answer this **question**. Why do these death row losers always order nuggets and dipping sauce and biggie fries for their last meal? Is it A, they are ghetto or barrio or trailer-park trash who don't know any better, who could never imagine a taste sensation transcending that of a Hot Pocket and an orange Fanta, or, B, something else entirely?"

The truck dipped into a pothole, shot near the curb where an old woman wearing an "I'm with Stupid" T-shirt dawdled in the crosswalk. This lady was about to be with nobody ever again, but Nick righted the wheel with one of his sloping breasts, his fork work undisturbed.

"I'm going to go with answer B," I said.

"Well, you're not dumb," said Nick. "But then again, you've had the advantages. You've got some innate intelligence, passed down from people who probably kicked some serious ass to put you in a position to even function on this planet. Because you don't seem, how can I put this, overly equipped. You seem pretty soft. I just mean that as an observation. Of course, we'll see what we see at the site today."

Advantages? What about Purdy? Or Sarah Molloy and the rest of them? Nick may have known that stuffed-crust pizza delivered in twenty minutes or gratis wasn't haute cuisine, but he didn't know a damn thing about advantages, couldn't comprehend the true machinations of money and power, the nuanced, friction-free nanotechnics of privilege that prevent an earnest, talented boy from doing wonderful stuff with oils. But, of course, I couldn't argue about the softness. For a time I wore only heavy, steel-toed boots because I figured if apocalyptic war broke out, sturdy foot-wear would be a must. Then it dawned on me that the better the boots, the more quickly I would be killed for them. My only shot at survival would be shoeless abjection.

"Thanks," I said now.

"I was complimenting your forebears," said Nick. "Anyway, you went with B. B stood for, if I'm not mistaken, and I'm not, something else entirely. Any guesses?"

"I don't know," I said. "They have no choice in the matter?"

"Damn!" said Nick, accordioned his foil plate with his palms, veered again, nearly halved a spry South Asian mail carrier in a pith helmet. "You are impressing the hell out of me. Of course that's the reason. They have no choice. Prisoners are allowed to order their last meal only from restaurants within a three-mile radius of the prison. What kinds of joints do you think surround death houses? Ever been to Texas, those prison towns? Forget the poor dinguses waiting for the strap and needle. Nobody's doing good. No Michelin stars in those counties. Sad but true, my friend. But don't get me wrong. I'm all for capital punishment. I'm a huge death penalty guy. I like everything about it. And don't tell me how it's more expensive to the taxpayer than life sentences. Because if you ask me, we should pony up a little more. We should feel the cost of our ritual, revel in it. It was probably a drain on the Aztec economy to capture and drug all those people and carve out their living hearts, but are you going to tell me it wasn't worth it? Yes, sir, the death penalty is where it's at. Is there a chance innocent people die? I should fucking hope so! Innocent people die constantly in this world. Why should things be better for those scumbags in lockdown?"

"But you said they were innocent."

"Innocent? Please. No thanks, buddy. Keep that knee-jerk liberal crap on your side of the aisle. I'm not ashamed of the sacrifices a balls-out civilization must make to survive. But we're way off the food-and-death track. This show is a winner. You won't regret your involvement."

"My involvement?"

"Well, my sister says your wife is in marketing, and this idea, when it hits the tube, will need some all-pro marketing. And you seem like the kind of college boy who may be a broke screw-up but is ultimately part of the vast conspiracy of movers and shakers who shake and move our society. Jewish, right?"

"Here we go," I said.

"Okay, scratch that. All I'm saying is I need to make the right connections to make this thing happen."

"Make what happen?"

"You repeat this to anybody, I will make a deck, a beautiful Mission-style deck, out of your bones. Weatherproof that shit, too."

"Of course."

"Dead Man Dining."

"Excuse me?"

"Working title."

"I'm lost."

"Be found. The world's top chefs prepare exquisite last meals for condemned prisoners. Stuffed quail for the auntie slasher. Baked Alaska for the office party Uzi sprayer. Chicken à la Berkowitz. Death and food. The only things we can be certain of, right? What's it like to be sitting next to a future billionaire?"

Sam Lipsyte, The Ask

I understood little and cared less about the political intrigues and the marches in various parts of the city, and felt at such times it was better not to be seen around too much. But the **question** of food did concern me, and each day I kept up-to-date with the local shopkeepers about what we might expect. When I walked through public gardens like the Jardin du Luxembourg, it seemed at first as if the city had been overrun with livestock, as sheep and cows had been herded inside the city walls. But by October it was said that no more than twenty-five thousand oxen and a hundred thousand rams were left, which was not enough to feed a metropolis.

Slowly households were reduced to frying goldfish, hippophagy was killing off every horse not under the protection of the army, a bushel of potatoes cost thirty francs, and Boissier the grocer was selling a box of lentils for twenty-five. Rabbits were nowhere to be seen, and butchers did not hesitate to display fine, plump cats and, later, dogs. All the exotic animals in the Jardin des Plantes were killed for meat, and on Christmas night, for those with money to spend, a sumptuous menu was on offer at Voisin, with elephant consommé, roast camel *à l'anglaise*, jugged kangaroo, bear chops *au sauce poivrade*, antelope terrine with truffles and cat garnished with baby mice, since not only had sparrows vanished from the rooftops but mice and rats were disappearing from the sewers.

The camel was acceptable, and not too bad-tasting, but rats, no. Even in times of siege there were smugglers and black marketeers, and I well remember one (extremely expensive) meal, not in a great restaurant but in a *gargote* almost on the edge of the city, where along with a few privileged guests (not all belonging to the best of Parisian society, but at such times class differences are forgotten) I was able to taste pheasant and the freshest *pâté de foie d'oie*.

Umberto Eco, The Prague Cemetery

"Where's John?" Templer interrupted sharply. Siobhan just swallowed. "He's not at his flat," Templer continued. "I sent someone round there to check. Yet according to you, he's taken a couple of days' sick leave. Where is he, Siobhan?"

"I . . ."

"The thing is, two nights ago Martin Fairstone was seen in a bar. Nothing unusual in that, except that his companion bore a striking resemblance to Detective Inspector John

Rebus. Couple of hours later, Fairstone's being fried alive in the kitchen of his house." She paused. "Always supposing he was alive when the fire started."

"Ma'am, I really don't—"

"John likes to look out for you, doesn't he, Siobhan? Nothing wrong in that. John's got this knight-in-tarnished-armor thing, hasn't he? Always has to be looking for another dragon to fight."

"This doesn't have anything to do with DI Rebus, ma'am."

"Then what's he hiding from?"

"I'm not aware that he's hiding at all."

"But you've seen him?" It was a **question**, but only just. Templer allowed herself a winning smile. "I'd put money on it."

*Ian Rankin, A **Question** of Blood*

Then Homais asked how the accident had come about. Charles answered that she had been taken ill suddenly while she was eating some apricots.

"Extraordinary!" continued the chemist. "But it might be that the apricots had brought on the syncope. Some natures are so sensitive to certain smells; and it would even be a very fine **question** to study both in its pathological and physiological relation. The priests know the importance of it, they who have introduced aromatics into all their ceremonies. It is to stupefy the senses and to bring on ecstasies—a thing, moreover, very easy in persons of the weaker sex, who are more delicate than the other. Some are cited who faint at the smell of burnt hartshorn, of new bread—"

"Take care; you'll wake her!" said Bovary in a low voice.

"And not only," the druggist went on, "are human beings subject to such anomalies, but animals also. Thus you are not ignorant of the singularly aphrodisiac effect produced by the Nepeta cataria, vulgarly called catmint, on the feline race; and, on the other hand, to quote an example whose authenticity I can answer for, Bridaux (one of my old comrades, at present established in the Rue Malpalu) possesses a dog that falls into convulsions as soon as you hold out a snuffbox to him. He often even makes the experiment before his friends at his summerhouse at Guillaume Wood. Would anyone believe that a simple sternutation could produce such ravages on a quadrupedal organism? It is extremely curious, is it not?"

"Yes," said Charles, who was not listening to him.

"This shows us," went on the other, smiling with benign self-sufficiency, "the innumerable irregularities of the nervous system. With regard to madame, she has always seemed to me, I confess, very susceptible. And so I should by no means recommend to you, my dear friend, any of those so-called remedies that, under the pretence of attacking the symptoms, attack the constitution. No; no useless physicking! Diet, that is all; sedatives, emollients, dulcification. Then, don't you think that perhaps her imagination should be worked upon?"

"In what way? How?" said Bovary.

"Ah! that is it. Such is indeed the **question**. 'That is the **question**,' as I lately read in a newspaper."

But Emma, awaking, cried out—

"The letter! the letter!"

Gustave Flaubert, Madame Bovary

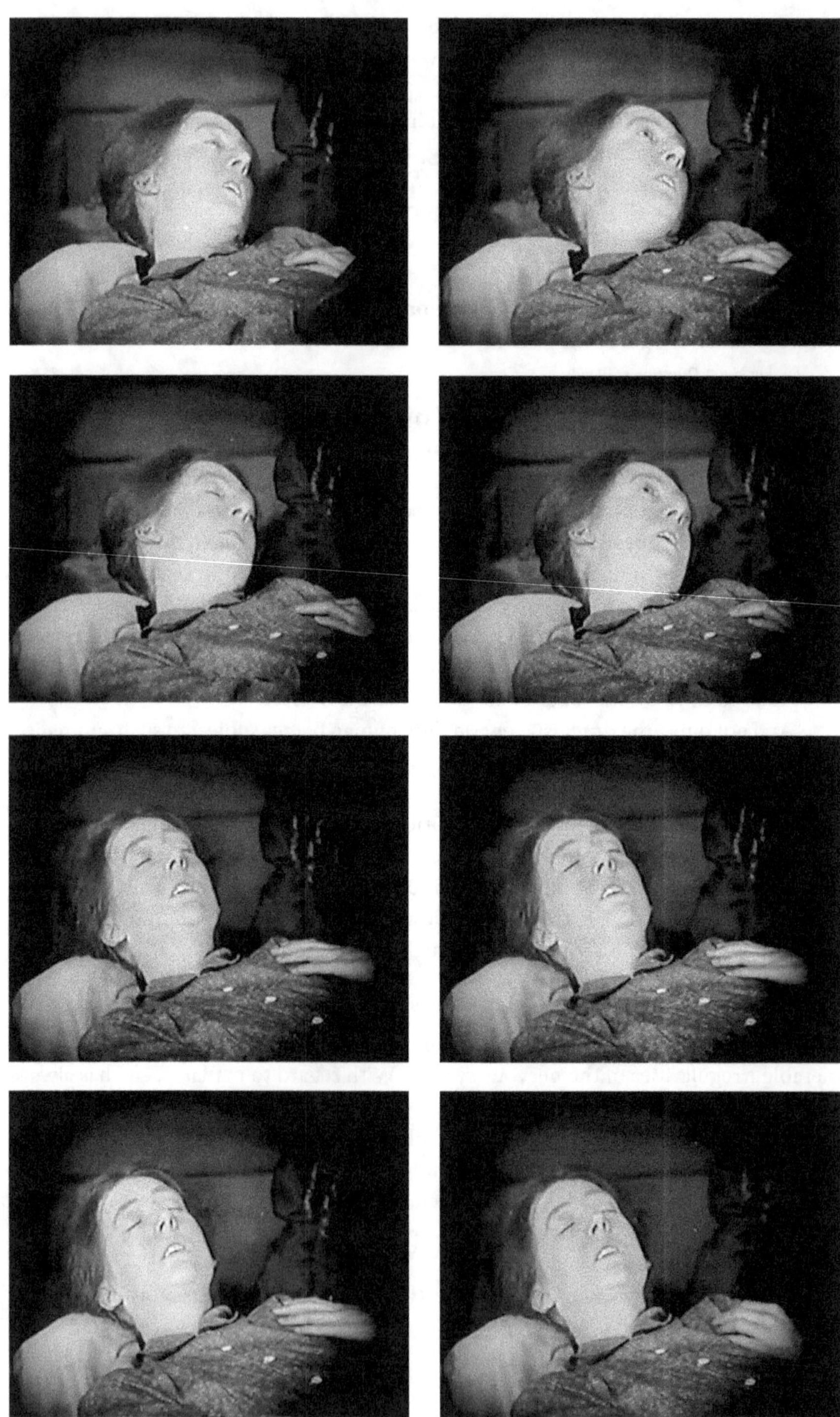

*D.W. Griffith (director), The Greatest **Question**,1919*

20. **(A)** By now it should be apparent that our code word "NEOTWY" should always be kept in mind. **Question** 18 asked a "where" **question**, number 19 asked a "when" **question**, and this is a "who" **question**. Line 16 of paragraph one states that Ms. Peever is the owner of the boutique. (See Chapter Five for a full explanation of the code word "NEOTWY.")

Donald J. Schroeder and Frank A. Lombardo, Police Officer Exam

Questions for self-evaluation are commonly used that provide no information of with what to compare (comparison target) one's olfactory function. We therefore investigated whether responses differed between an unspecific **question** and two **questions** providing comparison targets. Ninety-six healthy community-dwelling individuals (62.5% women) aged 49–80 years evaluated their odor identification ability, followed by standardized assessment of odor identification ability. Results revealed that response patterns varied significantly depending on comparison target. While 81% reported normal function when no further comparison target was presented, 69% reported normal function when referring to age-related olfactory changes in identification ability. In turn, sensitivity of the accuracy of self-reported reduced odor identification ability (with standardized assessment as reference) increased from 11 to 37%, whereas specificity decreased from 86 to 71% when providing a comparison target. Accuracy of self-reported olfactory function can be increased by including a comparison target. However, standardized assessment is to be preferred over self-reported assessment, irrespective of how the **question** is formulated.

*Eike Wehling, Astri J. Lundervold and Steven Nordin, Does It Matter How We Pose the **Question** "How Is Your Sense of Smell?" (Chemosensory Perception)*

"Well, how does it taste?" A definition was demanded from him, a protocol his senses were required to formulate before they could be distracted by any other sensation.

"Of smoke, and of hazelnut."

Thousands of whiskeys he has drunk since. Malt, bourbon, rye, the best and the worst, straight, with water, with soda, with ginger ale. And sometimes, suddenly, that sensation would come to him again. Smoke—yes, and hazelnut.

At each important moment in your life, he thought later, you ought to have an Arnold Taads, someone who asks you to describe exactly what you feel, smell, taste, and think when you experience your first fear, your first humiliation, your first woman. But the **question** must be asked always at the moment itself so that the protocol remains valid and the thought, the experience, can never be discolored by later women, fears, humiliations. Precisely that definition of the first time—smoke and hazelnut—would set the tone for all future experiences, for they would be determined by the extent to which they either deviated from that first time, which had now become the yardstick for the future, or fell short of it, being no longer smoke or hazelnut. To see Amsterdam for the first time again, to enter the loved one with whom you have lived for years for the first time again, to hold a woman's breast in your hand for the first time again and to stroke it, and to keep the thoughts relating to this intact through the years, so that all those later times, all those other forms, cannot in due course betray, deny, cover up, that first sensation.

Arnold Taads had at least set a standard on one sensuous experience for him. All the others would vanish irrevocably in later layers of his memory, interblended and corrupted in the way that his hand, which had caressed that first breast and closed those first dead eyes, had betrayed his memory, himself, and that first breast by having become older and misshapen. It was a hand showing the first brown freckles of old age, with thick veins, a corrupted, tainted, experienced forty-five-year-old hand, an early harbinger of death in which that former, slenderer, whiter hand had dissolved unrecognizably, unfindably, while he still called it "my hand," and would continue to do so until a later, living hand would lay it, dead, on his breast, crossed over the other that resembled it.

Cees Nooteboom, Rituals

"That was written by a man in a drunken condition, a worthless fellow," I cried indignantly. "I know him."

"That letter I received yesterday," Liza began to explain, flushing and speaking hurriedly. "I saw myself, at once, that it came from some foolish creature, and I haven't yet shown it to maman, for fear of upsetting her more. But if he is going to keep on like that, I don't know how to act. Mavriky Nikolaevitch wants to go out and forbid him to do it. As I have looked upon you as a colleague," she turned to Shatov, "and as you live there, I wanted to **question** you so as to judge what more is to be expected of him."

Fyodor Dostoyevsky, The Possessed; or, the Devils

"Steady on," said Archie, trying to keep an eye on the road, as Samad bent the doctor's neck almost to breaking point, "Look, I'm not saying that he doesn't deserve to die."

"Then do it. *Do it.*"

"But why's it so bloody important to you that I do it? You know, I've never killed a man—not like that, not face-to-face. A man shouldn't die in a car . . . I can't do that."

"Jones, it is simply a **question** of what you will do *when the chips are down.* This is a **question** that interests me a great deal. Call tonight the practical application of a long-held belief. An experiment, if you like."

"I don't know what you re talking about."

"I want to know what kind of a man you are, Jones, I want to know what you are capable of. Are you a coward, Jones?"

Archie brought the Jeep to a shattering halt, "You're bloody asking for it, you are."

"You don't stand for anything, Jones," continued Samad, "Not for a faith, not for a politics. Not even for your country. How your lot ever conquered my lot is a bloody mystery. You're a cipher, no?"

"A what?"

"And an idiot. What are you going to tell your children when they ask who you are, what you are? Will you know? Will you ever know?"

"What are you that's so bloody fantastic?"

Zadie Smith, White Teeth

When Groucho first encounters Harpo in *Duck Soup,* he asks him who he is, and Harpo answers by rolling up his sleeve and revealing a tattooed image of his own face. This answer transforms Groucho's social request for an introduction into a fundamental philosophical **question**: Can we ever pinpoint a person's true identity? It also asks an even more fundamental **question** about representation in language: How can we point to something in the world with complete accuracy, without also being meaninglessly redundant? Harpo's answer to "who are you?" is a visual-gag version of the Buddha's infuriatingly honest answer to the same **question**. When asked who he was, he would say, gesturing to himself: I am *thathagatha* (the one who is like this).

Shon Arieh-Lerer, Groucho Marx's Comedy Is Pure, Bleak Nihilism: So Why Does It Make Us Laugh? (Slate)

But who is he, if my guess is right, who is waiting for that, from me? And who these others whose designs are so different? And into whose hands I play when I ask myself such **questions**? But do I, do I? In the jar did I ask myself **questions**?

Samuel Beckett, *The Unnamable*

There's a knock at the door. Baravelli opens the peephole.
Baravelli: Who are you?
Professor Wagstaff: I'm fine, thanks, who are you?
Baravelli: I'm fine too, but you can't come in unless you give the password.
Professor Wagstaff: Well, what is the password?
Baravelli: Oh no, you gotta tell me! *(pause)* Hey, I tell you what I do . . . I give you three
   guesses . . . It's the name of a fish . . .
Professor Wagstaff: Is it Mary?
Baravelli: Ha, ha! Atsa no fish!
Professor Wagstaff: She isn't? Well, she drinks like one. Let me see . . . Is it sturgeon?
Baravelli: Hey, you crazy. A sturgeon, he's a doctor cuts you open whena you sick. Now
   I give you one more chance.
Professor Wagstaff: I got it. Haddock.
Baravelli: Atsa funny. I gotta haddock, too.
Professor Wagstaff: What do you take for a haddock?
Baravelli: Well now, sometimes I take-a aspirin, sometimes I take-a calomel.
Professor Wagstaff: Say, I'd walk a mile for a calomel.
Baravelli: You mean chocolate calamel. I like that too, but you no guess it. (Slams door.
   Wagstaff knocks again. Baravelli opens the peephole again.) Hey, whatsa matter,
   you no understand English? You can't come in here unless you say swordfish. Now
   I give you one more guess.
Professor Wagstaff: (thinking) Swordfish . . . swordfish . . . I think I got it. Is it swordfish?
Baravelli: Hah. Thatsa it. You guess it.
Professor Wagstaff: Pretty good, eh?

Marx Brothers, *Horse Feathers (marx-brothers.org)*

Lavrov is a great fan of self-**questioning**. He holds 66 of 189 uses of the formulation "the **question** arises" and its manifold variations.

The winner of self-**questioning**, however, is Lukashevich, with 101 uses, but some of his briefings and statements just repeat Lavrov's earlier sentiments.

Vasily Gatov, *Russia's Stalinist Diplospeak (The Daily Beast)*

To refer yet again to the chapter "Governor Pyncheon" of *The House of Seven Gables* (part of the peak' of that novel), I have counted 53 rhetorical **questions** in that chapter. The next to the last paragraph of the chapter is a series of eight such rhetorical **questions**; only the terminal sentence of the paragraph is not a rhetorical **question**. So here sits Judge Pyncheon dead in the chair, and Hawthorne is bombarding him with a barrage of rhetorical **questions** which the man isn't in any condition to answer. The intensity of this barrage of rhetorical **questions** is exceeded only by the book of Job whose peak in Chapters 38 to 41 consists largely of such **questions**.

Robert E. Longacre, *The Grammar of Discourse*

1.   God and Satan place a bet on Job. What does God allow Satan to do, and how does

God think Job will react? How does Satan think Job will react?

2. Does God set any limits to the damage Satan can inflict upon Job?

3. What do you think of Satan's role here? Is the devil a busybody meddler? A useful servant of God?

4. What does Job curse? By implication, what is not getting cursed?

5. What state of existence would he prefer? Consider the contrasts that he draws.

6. How does Eliphaz explain Job's suffering? Who DOES God inflict suffering upon, according to Eliphaz?

7. What purpose does suffering serve? In other words, how should Job think about his troubles, according to Eliphaz?

8. Does Job respond the way Eliphaz thinks he should? What does Job ask God to do?

9. Job lashes out at his friends. Why?

10. What does he ask of his friends? What doesn't he want from them?

11. Does Bildad do what Job asks? What tack does he take in responding to Job's lament?

12. How does God treat the upright and the wicked, according to Bildad? Which category, by implication, does Job fall into?

13. Does Job agree with Bildad's confident knowledge of how God treats the upright and the wicked? What does Job know of God acting in the universe?

14. Does Job think that he is wicked—that he deserves the punishment he is receiving?

15. Given what Job knows about God, how can Job approach God and make his case? (consider 9:32–35 especially)

16. What does Job believe about God's intentions towards him? Is God pursuing or rehabilitating him? Contrast with what Eliphaz and Bildad believe about how God looks upon the upright.

17. What Eliphaz and Bildad only implied, Zophar says straight out! Why is God making Job suffer?

18. What does Zophar want Job to do?

19. Does Job accept Zophar's judgment?

20. Like Zophar, Job also goes on the attack. According to Job, what does God do with those people who think they are secure in their own comfort? Who does he have in mind here? (Hint: trying reading chapter 12 aloud in the tone of voice you think Job used.)

21. Explain the warning Job gives to his friends. Why are they walking on thin ice, according to Job?

22. Job makes two requests of God (13:20–23) What are they? And are they reasonable, given what he knows of God?

23. Why does Job consider trees to have more hope than human beings?

24. What does Job want from God? (see 14:13–17) Is this wish different than what he asked for in his opening lament (chapter 3)? If so, how would you account for the difference?

25. Do you detect a change in tone between Eliphaz' first (chapter 4–5) and second (chapter 15) speeches?

26. How does Job respond (chapter 16)? What does this exchange tell you about the direction in which the conversation is headed?

27. Haven't we heard this argument by Bildad before? Is it persuasive to you?

28. Job here asserts that God has targeted him personally—but then affirms, in perhaps the most famous words of the whole book, that "I know that my Redeemer lives". Is there a contradiction here?

29. Is Zophar making the same argument as Bildad (chapter 18)? In what sense does Zophar answer Job's previous speech? Or does he?

30. With the third and final speech by Eliphaz, the debate takes a nastier turn. What does Eliphaz accuse Job of?

31. Does Job respond to Eliphaz' charge?

32. What DOES Job want from God? Hang onto 23:6 and consider this verse in light of Job's two last speeches at the end of the book.

33. According to liberation theologian Gustavo Gutierrez, Job's moral vision expands over the course of the book. At first he is preoccupied with his own woes; then he enlarges his lament to include all the poor who suffer at the hand of the wicked rich. Do the speeches by Job in chapters 21 and 24 support Gutierrez' claim? Look also at chapters 29–30.

34. Anything new here?

35. How would you characterize the tone of 26:2–4?

36. Job ends the debate by asserting his integrity (27:1–6), then calling down God's wrath if he ever harmed anyone. (chapter 31) Why didn't he say all this earlier?

37. Chapters 29 and 30 contrast not just Job's prior happiness and present suffering, but more specifically the honor he once enjoyed and the contempt he now has to put up with. Does this radical change in social standing give us a clue as to what Job wants from God, and why?

38. Consider how the speeches of the "friends" change from the first to the third cycle, particularly in light of chapter 30. What are we being told about the causes of human suffering? to what extent is it under God's control, and to what extent under human control?

39. Why has Elihu jumped into the fray?

40. Job has insisted that he is innocent. How, according to Elihu, does God deal with people who are convinced of their own righteousness?

41. According to Elihu, Job is like the wicked. (34:7–8, 36) Why? What has Job done which is so reprehensible?

42. Do people have any power to manipulate God, according to Elihu?

43. Once again (as in chapter 33) how does God deal with those who are suffering? Therefore how should Job call upon God?

44. What is the appropriate human response to God? Why?

Stewart W. Herman, Study **Questions** *on the Book of Job (Concordia College Religion Department)*

Jacob Hussain, A-Level Christian Theology and Philosophy & Psychology, Bishop Stopford School (2018)

God asks several **questions** throughout the Bible, and if the wish was so I would go through the Bible and count exactly how many **questions** He asked. However, I feel that this is irrelevant, and the more important issue is not quantative, but semantic. We shouldn't ask 'how many' **questions** God asks, but rather why God asks them.

God is considered to be omniscient, that is to say He knows everything. Many then use this to contradict His **questionning** natures. God does not ask **questions** through a desire to know the answer, but rather so that we as humans will **question** our own beliefs, and it helps us to gain understanding. One example of man gaining understanding is found right at the beginning of the Bible when God asks Adam "Where are you?" God knew exactly where Adam was, but His **questionning** not only tested Adam's integrity and his willingness to tell the truth regardless of any possible consequences, but also had hidden meaning. God's **question** was also enquiring into Adam's spiritual state, asking where we was in his walk with God. God's **question** also suggested that Adam's sin had put distance between him and God, and had made their relationship less close. God was making a point. God does not **question** so that He can gain answers, He **questions** so that we can gain answers

David Moore, studied Bachelor of Medicine and Bachelor of Surgery Degrees at University of Sydney

Only one: "who do you say I am?". However, the details of this eternal **question** are expanded upon profoundly in the oldest book—Job.

I find the answer to Life, the Universe and Everything is indeed in 42, ironically. However, what precedes it sounds like this.

Job 38:1–3 NIV
*[1] Then the Lord spoke to Job out of the storm. He said: [2] "Who is this that obscures my plans with words without knowledge? [3] Brace yourself like a man; I will **question** you, and you shall answer me.*

The book of Job is poetry, and must be understood as such. The LORD does not really ask (or need to know) where we find the storehouses for snow. The **questions** are rhetorical, because we don't really know what **questions** mean. We believe ourselves wise already. This is why Job is cannot be comforted by his companions. They are fools.

Poetry is what expresses through words what cannot be expressed in words. When Job says this:

Job 42:4–6 NIV
*[4] "You said, 'Listen now, and I will speak; I will **question** you, and you shall answer me.' [5] My ears had heard of you but now my eyes have seen you. [6] Therefore I despise myself and repent in dust and ashes."*

What has he seen, and what has he understood? What wisdom results in his repentance? Remember Hagar's words:

Genesis 16:13 NIV
[13] She gave this name to the Lord who spoke to her: "You are the God who sees me," for she said, "I have now seen the One who sees me."

And Isaiah's

Isaiah 64:4 NIV
[4] Since ancient times no one has heard, no ear has perceived, no eye has seen any God besides you, who acts on behalf of those who wait for him.

and (most meaningfully) John's. Full of Paradox and Irony:

John 1:16–18 NIV
[16] Out of his fullness we have all received grace in place of grace already given. [17]

For the law was given through Moses; grace and truth came through Jesus Christ. [18] No one has ever seen God, but the one and only Son, who is himself God and is in closest relationship with the Father, has made him known.

What is grace? It is nonsense. It makes no sense. Grace undoes our Judgment. It destroys the foundation of futility—what we call 'fairness'. "An eye for an eye" is replaced by this:

Matthew 5:38–39 NIV

[38] "You have heard that it was said, 'Eye for eye, and tooth for tooth.' [39] But I tell you, do not resist an evil person. If anyone slaps you on the right cheek, turn to them the other cheek also. [40] And if anyone wants to sue you and take your shirt, hand over your coat as well. [41] If anyone forces you to go one mile, go with them two miles. [42] Give to the one who asks you, and do not turn away from the one who wants to borrow from you. [43] "You have heard that it was said, 'Love your neighbor and hate your enemy.' [44] But I tell you, love your enemies and pray for those who persecute you, [45] that you may be children of your Father in heaven. He causes his sun to rise on the evil and the good, and sends rain on the righteous and the unrighteous. [46] If you love those who love you, what reward will you get? Are not even the tax collectors doing that? [47] And if you greet only your own people, what are you doing more than others? Do not even pagans do that? [48] Be perfect, therefore, as your heavenly Father is perfect.

Quora.com, How Many **Questions** Does God Ask in the Bible?

By Mr. BLAIR:

Question. The corpus delicti is essential?

Answer. It is essential, but it could not be proven.

Question. "A freedman named Alfred Skinner was attacked there by a band of disguised men," Huggins says?

Answer. I never heard of him.

Question. "He defended himself in his house, and they filled his house with shot. Persons who were sent there to investigate the matter have testified to the fact that there were shot there in the house, plenty of them."

Answer. I never heard of it, sir.

Question. "He fired on them," (from the house,) and they did not get him. In the same neighborhood Joe Atkins was taken out by the same band; he was told that he was a radical, and made to hug a sapling—to take hold around the sapling and hug it while they whipped him severely; they beat him very badly; I have seen him myself and talked with him; he left the neighborhood, as also did Alfred Skinner, and came to Aberdeen?"

Answer. I never heard of him. I know a negro named Abner Atkins but, never heard of Joe Atkins; and never heard of any negro or white man named Atkins being whipped or molested.

United States House of Representatives, Testimony Taken by the Joint Select Committee to Inquire Into the Condition of Affairs in the Late Insurrectionary States (Reports of Committees for the Second Session of the Forty-Second Congress, 1871-'72)

I once heard a great Rabbi call Jesus a 'radical' who made the Law into something it was not. I couldn't agree with him more. The devil is in the detail. The letter brings death. The Spirit brings life. To be or not to be? Who asks the **question**?

Steve Tobias, 4+ years of not smoking thanks to vaping.

If you do a Google search you would get some pretty cool results. The following is quoted from;

*God's Great **Questions** | Inside Report Magazine | Amazing Facts*

The following is quoted from the above and is just the fist part.

*"Did you know that the longest list of **questions** found in the Bible is made up of **questions** asked by God? In Job chapters 38 and 39, God poses query after query to His servant Job, who has daily begged for answers to some tough, heart-wrenching **questions** of his own.*

Instead of providing Job with simple answers, God delivers a string of thought-provoking riddles. They start with words like "Who? Where? When? Have you? Can you? Do you know?" He describes all the miracles of the animal kingdom, and He talks about the weather and the solar system and other mysteries of nature.

It's as if God is talking to Job as a parent would talk to a child. He asks: "Can you bind the cluster of the Pleiades, Or loose the belt of Orion? Can you bring out Mazzaroth in its season? Or can you guide the Great Bear with its cubs?" (Job 38:31–32, NKJV).

Daniel Hamilton, Changed by Christ yet in need of more changing by HIM

Well, all I can tell you now is that a search for all the **questions** in the 66 book Bible (KJV), using the E-sword Bible module (search [?] in Reg. expressions) results in 3,298 **questions** all together (supplied words included): 302 **questions** in the Pentateuch; 715 **questions** in the Historical books; 588 **questions** in the Wisdom books; 494 **questions** in the Major prophets; 175 **questions** in the Minor prophets; and 1024 in the New Testament.

This does not tell you how many **questions** only God asked, but now you can find out. No doubt Job was the one God asked the most **questions** to, mostly rhetorical. And the Bible also answers the **questions** man needs to know to be saved and live for Him. Thanks be to God.

*Quora.com, How Many **Questions** Does God Ask in the Bible?*

Theoretically, the number **questions** you can be asked in an interview is unlimited. This is because there are unlimited word combinations in the English language. However, our inventory of thousands of **questions** was consolidated and organized into the chapters that follow. And for this, our fourth edition, we've added a chapter on inter-rogation **questions**. We carefully chose **questions** that are generic enough to cover the entire range of interview subjects and then selected those designed to elicit "KO (knockout) factors"—the ones that have you down for the count on the interviewer's carpet. Knowing how to respond to the **questions** we chose—programming your mind with effective answers—will enable you to naturally respond to any variations that arise. Unconsciously, your brain will scan your database for your input and instantly signal your mouth, eyes, limbs, and torso to respond in unison with maximum impact. Don't worry about over-rehearsing. You can't. You either know your lines or you don't. Once you do, you'll never forget them when you hear the cue.

Once you start auditioning, you'll feel more confident. You *should*. You know the script. You're computer literate, too. In the actual interviews, you'll be a superstar, receiving Oscar offers time after time. Talent scouts (recruiters) will call you an MPC (most placeable candidate). Your biggest worries will be taking the time for interviews and deciding which offers deserve Academy-Award-winning acceptances. All superstars must face these decisions. Ah, the price you pay.

Practice your lines, go through your dress rehearsals, and watch your self-esteem increase as you shine above the cast of thousands. From script to screen test, you'll be headed straight for that office with the star on the door. No more understudy roles. Straight up. An anxious public awaits. Roll 'em—and—*knock 'em dead!*

*Jeffrey G. Allen, The Complete **Q&A** Job Interview Book*

"I understand you are a professor of theology," Taads continued, "and so this is a very childish conversation. You are filled up to your dog collar with dogma and scholasticism. You know all the arguments to prove the existence of God, and all the counter arguments. You have constructed an entire system on the gruesome symbol of the cross. Your religion still feeds on that one sado-masochistic seance that may never really have taken place. It was the militaristic organization of the Roman Empire that gave this strange cult, with its peculiar mixture of pagan idolatry and good intentions, a chance to develop. The Western thirst for expansion and colonialism enabled it to spread, and the Church that you call a mother has more often been a murderer, usually a tyrant, and always a bully."

"And you have a better answer?"

"I have no answer."

"What is your view of the mystics?"

"Mysticism has nothing to do with any particular religion. Mystics are almost always regarded with suspicion by the official churches. It is a rare opportunity for man to lose himself. If there ever comes a time when there are no longer any religions, there will still be mystics. Mysticism is a faculty of the soul, not of a system. Or did you think that nothingness is not a mystical concept?"

"So you believe in nothingness."

Taads groaned. "You can't believe in nothingness. You can't attach a system to the nonexistence of everything."

"The nonexistence of everything." The chamberlain savored this brief phrase on his tongue. Suddenly he raised his hand. "This hand is real, wouldn't you think?"

"To look at it, yes."

"So it is not nonexistent. And if this plate is the world—let us assume for a moment that it is—then that is not nonexistent either."

"One day" said Taads, "you and I, your hand and this plate and this bottle of Haut Brion and all the rest of the world will no longer exist. Then even our deaths will not exist and everybody else's death will not exist and therefore at the same time all memory will be nonexistent. Then we shall never have existed. That is what I mean."

"And you can live with that?"

"That wasn't the **question**."

Cees Nooteboom, Rituals

'There's nothing to tell. I didn't have anything to do with Fairstone's death.' She paused, another unasked **question** hanging between them: *Did you?* She seemed to be waiting for Rebus to say something, but he stayed silent. 'She'll want to know about you,'

Siobhan added. 'How you ended up in here.'

"I scalded myself," Rebus said. "It's stupid, but that's what happened."

"I know that's what you say happened . . ."

"No, Siobhan, it's what *happened*. Ask the doctors if you don't believe me." He looked around again. "Always supposing you can find one."

'Probably still combing the grounds for a parking space.'

The joke was weak enough, but Rebus smiled anyway.

Ian Rankin, A **Question** of Blood

Can the Book of Job be considered a work of fiction?

I don't see anything in Scripture which would point to the book being a parable or fable. It seems like a real account.

Kevin A. Thompson, *37* **Questions** *(and Answers) From the Book of Job (kevinathompson.com)*

Who was Job, and when did he live? Why did God single him out for Satan's attentions? In an oblique way, identifying Job as Pharaoh's third, noncommittal, counselor reflects one of the other challenges of Job, who finds his way into the holy books of Israel but seems unrelated to their history and revelation.

The most sustained attention to Job appears in Baba Bathra, part of the Babylonian Talmud ostensibly dedicated to **questions** of property tort law.[17] Here too there is no default interpretation of Job and his significance. The joints of the story are made looser, not tighter, as the story is retold to address open **questions**. The Job who appears here can be startlingly different from the canonical figure.

> There was a certain pious man among the heathen named Job, but he [thought that he had] come into this world only to receive his reward (here), and when the Holy One, blessed be He, brought chastisements upon him, he began to curse and blaspheme, so the Holy One, blessed be He, doubled his reward in this world so as to expel him from the world to come. (15b, 75)

This worldly schemer may seem more remote from the canonical Job than the *Testament of Job*, but real **questions** are deftly answered here. Did not Job curse? Did he not reject a future life? On the other hand, was he not commended by God, and indeed, restored twice what he had lost? This last was particularly troubling as double restoration could be taken to be an admission of culpability. That Job's restoration was not reward but punishment by way of a payoff is the sort of inversion in which midrashic interpretation glories.

The **question** of Job's identity was in fact a central concern of the rabbis. As we have seen also in the Septuagint and the *Testament of Job*, efforts were made to find his place in the genealogy of Israel. Was Job really not an Israelite? And where on earth was Uz? The Baba Bathra reports but dismisses the claim, made on the basis of one word, that Job must have been a contemporary of Moses; on the basis of one word one may just as easily claim him the contemporary of Isaac, Jacob, or Joseph (15a, 73). Baba Bathra suggests more convincing arguments could be made for Job's being of the generation that returned from the Babylonian exile, although other details in the text suggest the time of spies, the judging of judges, Ahasuerus, the kingdoms of Sheba or the Chaldeans or—since he was thought to have married Dinah—of Jacob (15b, 75–76). In all of these cases but the last, the compiler notes, Job would have to have been an Israelite—for

Moses was granted his dying request that the Divine Presence henceforth appear only to Israelites (15b, 76).

Mark Larrimore, The Book of Job: A Biography

("*Now* I know who it is I've been confusing you with," cried Gertrude; "Christopher Morley!" "*Who?*" "Christopher Morley. Oh, I know you haven't any beard; I was just confused. It was those informal essays.") But mostly he talked about great books—about a hundred of them; I don't know why he stopped at a hundred, but he did, and let the rest go; he must have made up his mind that it was no use trying to get people to read more than a hundred. There were two things he was crazy about, the thirteenth century and Greek: if the thirteenth century had spoken Greek I believe it would have killed him not to have been alive in it. He didn't know anything about, or care anything for, science, unless it was several hundred years old—or several thousand, for choice; he loved it then. He would say, "What do *we* know that Aristotle didn't know?" But he wouldn't let you tell him; it was a rhetorical **question**. He had diabetes and used to get an injection of insulin every day, and I don't believe he ever got one without wishing it were Galen giving it to him.

Randall Jarrell, Pictures From an Institution: A Comedy

There are times, my father said, when I think the key to life is to stick with only asking **questions** that you can answer. The problem comes when you ask a **question** you simply cannot answer. But then the deeper problem, he said, turning to look out at the flat, somewhat desolate, weedy old lake that was in a eutrophic death spiral, suffocating itself, sprouting huge lily-pad structures, murky and dark in the late-afternoon light. We were at the end of the dock again, fishing, throwing out the line with lazy, occasional casts, not at all dedicated to the task, barely watching the bobbers, totally aware, both of us, that at that time of the afternoon—or almost any time—the fish were seeking deeper, cooler pockets, if there were any left. He put the handle of the rod between his knees and lit a cigarette. (My father had a complex life and career, starting with Boston University seminary, where he met, at least once, his fellow student Dr. Martin Luther King Jr. The old man was kicked out of BU for theological disagreements—his words— and moved to Colgate seminary. He was a chaplain at Cornell when he began taking sociology classes—with a focus on race relations—and left the ministry to pursue his Ph.D. His interests were wide-ranging, and he was at the forefront of the civil-rights and environmental movements. After he died, I found a letter to him from Rachel Carson, in which she spoke of her book, *Silent Spring,* just weeks before its publication. At the center of my father's story is a tragedy, one that this essay can't address.) To continue my thought, he said grandly, the deeper problem comes, Son, with the fact that as an intellectual, or someone who at least poses as one, I'm obligated to ask **questions** that I can't answer, and in doing so I look, from time to time, some would say often, like an idiot before these **questions.**

Now I trace my desire to be a fiction writer to that moment on the lake, I think, and the awareness I had, as a fourteen-year-old kid in Converse All Stars, that to think too much in the realm of ideas alone was to be doomed to a life of looking like an idiot, or pretending not to be one, at least; I like to think that right at that moment, just before the fish bit, because it did bite, taking the bobber down once lightly, enough to ripple the flat surface, I understood something intimately deep about my future path.

I instantly forgot it. Only when my father was dead and gone did I see it again clearly, and remember his comment—or at least think I remembered it—and all the rage I once had for thinking that my father seemed washed-up, unsuited for his profession, a rage that lasted until he retired from teaching and went back to preaching, taking up interim minister jobs at small, ragged, half-dead churches in small, ragged, half-dead towns around lower Michigan, all that rage disappeared and settled into what at first was a sense of pity but then a sense of, well, of glory and relief that his life had been one of pure value because it had engaged, truthfully, honestly, with the joke at hand, which was that his obligation to pose ideas that were beyond his answering was a sideline, a side gig, something he did to make ends meet, while his real pleasure, his joy, was simply to take what he was seeing and to locate the deeper mystery—and faith—along with the absurd humor in it, as he did that day at the lake.

One winter morning, at the crack of dawn, heading back to Michigan again, to see my father before he had a major heart procedure, I got on the train and sat back and, as we pushed out of Chicago, with Bellow in my lap, I recalled that in *Humboldt's Gift,* another favorite of my father's, there had been some mention of the afterlife, or of the dead. (Now, here, at my desk, with a copy of the book beside me, I locate the section, on page 141 of my edition, and in it Charlie Citrine, the central character and narrator, says that he cannot accept the "view of death taken by most of us, and taken by me during most of my life—on esthetic grounds therefore I am obliged to deny that so extraordinary a thing as a human soul can be wiped out forever. No, the dead are about us, shut out by our metaphysical denial of them. As we lie nightly in our hemispheres asleep by the billions, our dead approach us.")

I now see that on the train, barely remembering this passage, just catching the gist of it, I was somehow retroactively aware that in getting up in the middle of the night and packing in the dark and heading downstairs in an Ambien stupor to catch the earliest train possible, I was, somehow, knowingly, joining the dead who haunted the night-time places between sleep and waking. I didn't know at the time but I was following in the tracks of Charlie Citrine's logic, preparing myself somehow not only to travel to my father, who would die a few days later, but also for the state I would be in when he was gone. I was feeling it in the cab, sensing it in the sweep of streets—Chicago streets, against logic, rise and fall more than expected. Call it wishful thinking or sweet delusion or whatever you want, but I know now, here, writing this, that the sensation I had was of communion with the dead around me. On the train that morning, I was aware—without knowing it, admitting it fully—of the shadow-space, partly because, of course, on a train in that transitory state between one place and another, between Chicago and my home-town, Kalamazoo, I was suspended between a sense of the life behind me and my father ahead, something like that. It's high time you admit, I say to myself now (and said on the train), that you have a full-blown belief in a certain communion with the dead, one that you feel, strongly, must be sustained, if not in argument then at least in the fiction you write. A man stands alone along a stream in upper Michigan casting his line in a curl behind him, feeling it, sensing the gorgeous loop, the play of gravity and air and swing and motion, and then lays the line down perfectly along the stream's surface so that the fly, far out at the end of the leader, which is invisible, makes just the right splash—the same splash a mayfly would make—and he takes a split second to look away from his task and to sweep his eyes from one end of the scene to the other and feels himself to be utterly alone with nature itself, folded into the place and the moment, while also aware somehow that he is not at all alone but subsumed in his own essential eternity along with all those who came before him. In his own violation of the rules of physics, he exists and doesn't exist, and that sensation allows him—I'm pushing here—a vital link with those who are gone, because he is gone, too, as far as reality is concerned, and no one can prove that he made such a beautiful cast because no one knows they have to prove it, and when he has left that spot, along the Au Sable River, he will purposely avoid making mention of the moment and will answer **questions** from his friends with vague pleasantness. That's what I feel about that moment on the train; that I'd be much better off not even trying to articulate it, or would be better served to simply say I felt strange in the cab on the way to the train, and then on the train itself; whereas inside I'm saying, I had a communion with the dead and readied myself to have a different relation with my father, one that would be between a dead man and myself, retroactively, without knowing I was doing so.

David Means, *The Old Man* (*Harper's Magazine*)

"Who'd want to kill a college?" Graves repeated. Sure, he admitted, it sounded like an odd **question**. Colleges weren't people, they were institutions, like a church.They went on forever, they were bigger than the people who ran or attended them, they were where past, present, future came together. No one would want to kill a college. So I thought. Then I saw what Graves had been doing, while I was mooning about the G-Man. He'd been preparing for this day. His list of suspects was endless. Check that. The lists. He had lists of every employee who'd been let go or left under a cloud, a secretary messing with petty cash, a maintenance man asleep on a leaf mulcher, a business manager who tangled up accounts. A few years before, there'd been an effort to unionize some of the guys in maintenance. The skilled trades. There'd been pickets out and a lot of e-mail. He had a faculty list. People who'd been let go. That didn't mean fired. That almost never happened. But there was still a chain of hurt alright, visiting professors who had been denied tenure and tenured professors who vapor-locked at associate professor level and never made full professor.

Then, the students: students who were suspended or asked to withdraw, who had major disciplinary problems or court appearances, who were convicted of felonies after graduation, who asked the college not to contact them. He had a list called "Town and Gown." This was all the beefs that had arisen between college kids and locals, country boys who crashed fraternity parties, college kids who'd acted up in bars or shoplifted the local supermarket, messed up at the all-night diner. There was a local businessman who'd wanted to build a shopping center right outside town and another who'd broken ground for a trailer court at the bottom of the college hill.

The next list was a shocker. Other colleges. That's when I saw it, this look that passed between Sheriff Lingenfelter and one of the suits, the way the sheriff rolled his eyes and another guy kind of shrugged. So this was what he was up to, all this time! Graves was all over the place, advancing on all fronts, looking into everything in general and nothing in particular. It was like you walk into the doctor's office with a knife sticking in your gut and he decides he wants x-rays, MRI, blood, urine and stool samples. Just then I sensed someone looking at me and when I turned I saw Tom, grinning at me, nodding towards Graves and rolling his eyes, then winking at me as if we both know better. Hint,

hint, nudge, nudge. We shared a secret. We both knew I was pitching the high hard one to G-Man's sister last night. But that was between us, our little secret. Meanwhile, we'd let Graves make a fool out of himself.

P. F. Kluge, *Final Exam: A Novel*

Jacques. My poor Captain! He's going now where we are all headed, though it's amazing he hasn't got there long before this. Oh! Ah!

Master. Why, Jacques, I do believe you're crying. Let your tears flow freely, because now you may shed them without shame. His death releases you from the strict proprieties which constrained you while he was alive. You no longer have the same reasons for withholding your grief as you then had for concealing your felicity. No one will seek to put upon your tears the same interpretation which might have been put on your happiness. Everything is forgiven those who grieve. Moreover, at this time, we are perforce revealed as either caring or unforgiving and, all things considered, it is better to stand accused of human frailty than to be suspected of indifference. I would rather your sorrow were freely expressed, for then it would be less anguished. I would have it extreme, for then it would have a shorter term. Remember, and with increase, what he was: the acuteness with which he plumbed the deepest **questions**, the subtlety he brought to the discussion of the most delicate issues, his solid sense of the true priorities which ensured he kept his mind fixed firmly on the most important problems, the generous light he threw on the most arid subjects, the supreme art he deployed as the champion of those who stood accused: his humanity gave him quicker wits than self-interest or egoism ever gave the guilty, and he was hard only on himself. Far from trying to excuse the trifling faults he committed, he was more intent than his worst enemy on magnifying them, and was keener than an envious rival to cast doubt on his own virtues by subjecting them to a rigorous analysis of the motives which might have unwittingly prompted them. Set no limit on your grief other than that which healing time alone prescribes. Let us submit to the universal law of things when we lose a friend, as we in turn shall submit when it is pleased to deal with us. Let us accept, unsorrowing, the sentence which fate pronounces on them, as we shall accept unresistingly the decree which it will issue against us. The duties of friends do not cease with the rites of burial. The earth which is still fresh at this moment will settle over the ashes of the man you loved so tenderly, but your heart will keep his memory alive.

Jacques. Sir, that's very fine, but what's it got to do with anything?

Denis Diderot, *Jacques the Fatalist and His Master*

19. (D) Line eight of the second paragraph states that Benson arrived at the premise at 1:20 P.M. Once again, reading the stem of the **question** before reading the paragraph would have helped a lot.

Donald J. Schroeder and Frank A. Lombardo, *Police Officer Exam*

"Buried how long?"

The answer was always the same: "Almost eighteen years."

"You had abandoned all hope of being dug out?"

"Long ago."

"You know that you are recalled to life?"

"They tell me so."

"I hope you care to live?"

"I can't say."

"Shall I show her to you? Will you come and see her?"

The answers to this **question** were various and contradictory. Sometimes the broken reply was, "Wait! It would kill me if I saw her too soon." Sometimes, it was given in a tender rain of tears, and then it was, "Take me to her." Sometimes it was staring and bewildered, and then it was, "I don't know her. I don't understand."

Charles Dickens, A Tale of Two Cities

18. (C) The third line of paragraph two clearly states the address of the boutique as being 338 West 44th Street. If you were following our recommended strategy, you would have known that one of the **questions** asked for the address of the boutique. When reading the passage, you should have used your pencil to highlight this address when you came across it.

Donald J. Schroeder and Frank A. Lombardo, Police Officer Exam

Rogers shook his head. 'I'm sorry, Mr Martino. Believe me, we had experts in physical identification thrashing this thing back and forth for days. Pore patterns were mentioned, as a matter of fact. But unfortunately, that won't do us any good. We don't have verified records from before the explosion. Nobody ever thought we'd have to go into details as minute as that.' He raised his hand, rubbed it wearily across the side of his head, and dropped it in resignation. 'That's true of everything in that line, I'm afraid. We have your fingerprints and retinal photographs on file. Both are useless now.'

And here we are, he thought, fencing around the entire **question** of whether you're really Martino but went over to them.

Algis Budrys, Who?

'Who am I?' The Yakuza head repeats my **question**. His lips barely move and his voice is tone dead. 'My accountant calls me Mr Morino. My men call me Father. My subscribers call me God. My wife calls me Money. My lovers call me Incredible.' A ripple of humour. 'My enemies call me the stuff of nightmares. You call me Sir.' He retrieves a cigar from an ashtray and relights it. 'Sit down. Your trial is already behind schedule.' I do as I am told and look around at my jury. Frankenstein, chomping a Big Mac. A weathered, leathered man, who appears to be meditating, rocking very slightly to and fro, to and fro. A woman is using a laptop computer, pianist fast. She reminds me of Queen of Spades' Mama-san until I realize she is Queen of Spades' Mama-san. She ignores me. To the left are three identikit men from the catalogue of Yakuza henchmen. A horn section on pause. Through an opening, visible out of the corner of my eye, a girl dressed in a loose yukata sucks a popsicle. When I try to meet her eye she retreats out of sight. Lizard takes the chair next to me. Ryutaro Morino watches me, over the pile of junk-food Styrofoam boxes. The sound of breathing, the creaking of Leatherjacket's chair, the tappety-tap-tap of the computer keyboard. What are we waiting for? Morino clears his throat. 'Eiji Miyake, how do you plead?'

'What is the charge?'

Lizard's knife scores a deep cut along the table edge. It stops an inch from my thumb. 'What is the charge, *sir*?'

I swallow. 'What is the charge, *sir*?'

'If you are guilty you know the charge.'

'So I must be innocent, *sir.*' I hear the ice-lolly girl in the next room titter.

'Not guilty.' Morino nods his head gravely. 'Then explain why you were at Queen of Spades on Saturday the ninth of September.'

'Is Yuzu Daimon here?'

Morino gives one nod, my face whacks the table-top, my arm is yanked above my head one degree away from snapping off. Lizard grunts in my ear. 'What d'yer suppose yer just did wrong?'

'Didn't—answer—the—**question**.' My arm is released.

'Bright boy.'

David Mitchell, number9dream

22. (A) Item four of the procedure prohibits the police from detaining a properly identified diplomat. Therefore Choice A is correct. (A very similar **question** was asked as **question** 41 on a previous NYPD Police Officer Examination. Think you might see it again?)

Donald J. Schroeder and Frank A. Lombardo, Police Officer Exam

Likewise, to refer again to *The House of Seven Gables*, at the point where we have the shift to present tense there is also a person shift, i.e., Hawthorne begins to address the dead Judge Pyncheon as he sits in his chair: "Why Judge, it is already two hours . . . Pray, pray, Judge Pyncheon, look at your watch now . . . Up, therefore, Judge Pyncheon, up! Canst thou not brush the fly away? Art thou too sluggish? . . ." Thus, for about twelve pages, Hawthorne heckles the dead judge.

4. The fourth device for marking vividness involves a shift along a parameter with four ordered values:

Narr → Pseudo-Dial → Dialogue → Drama

By pseudodialogue I mean resort to such devices as apostrophe (cf. the Governor Pyncheon passage above) and rhetorical **question** which partake of certain features of dialogue without being true dialogue. Use of such features gives us a value intermediate between narration and dialogue itself, just as dialogue itself is intermediate between pseudo-dialogue and drama.

Robert E. Longacre, The Grammar of Discourse

Such an existence might perhaps be defined as one which, looked at from a purely objective point of view, or, rather, after cool and mature reflection—for the **question** necessarily involves subjective considerations,—would be decidedly preferable to non-existence; implying that we should cling to it for its own sake, and not merely from the fear of death; and further, that we should never like it to come to an end.

Arthur Schopenhauer, The Wisdom of Life: Being the First Part of Arthur Schopenhauer's Aphorismen Zur Lebensweisheit

Many Jewish commentators made this argument. Perhaps in response, Christian interpreters like Aquinas read the angry words opening the first divine speech—"Who is this that darkens counsel by words without knowledge?" (38:2)—as directed at Elihu! (Job is conveniently exonerated in the process.) Affection for Elihu is not restricted to pre-modern interpreters. One contemporary who sees the central argument of Job precisely in its poetry regards Elihu as the clearest representative of that view.[11] Another suggests we see Elihu as the first *reader* of the book of Job—a "dissatisfied reader" no less—inserting himself into the text as every successive reader will, too.[12] We may be like Elihu: our status as latecomers to Job's story is closer to Elihu's than to any of the other characters in the story.

Some interpreters have wondered if even the divine speeches are additions to an earlier text. After all, God comes barging in like a stranger. "It is as if He has belatedly stepped into a drama without having consulted the script," one has observed; "none of it: not even so much as the prologue.[13] Job's **questions** aren't even acknowledged, let alone answered. And why two speeches instead of just one? Why make Job speak again, after he's said he would not speak again (40:5)? What do Behemoth and Leviathan add? But again, we must not suppose earlier interpreters had not considered these **questions**. For many, Gods bypassing Job's **questions** was precisely the point. For Saadiah Gaon and Maimonides, it was the most important fact about the divine speeches that they did not touch the categories and **questions** of Job and his friends at all. The responses of Job to the two speeches also suggest that they had different functions. Stunned and cowed after the first, he seems resigned and accepting after the second—or is it the other way around? Some see Job satisfied by the first and actually joyful in the second. Much rests on how his final words (42:6), among the book's most obscure, are understood.

Mark Larrimore, *The Book of Job: A Biography*

Why do they speak to me thus? (Is it possible certain things change on their passage through me, in a way they can't prevent?) Do they believe I believe it is I who am asking these **questions**? (That's theirs too—a little distorted perhaps.) I don't say it's not the right method. I don't say they won't catch me in the end: I wish they would, to be thrown away. It's this hunt that is tiring, this unending being at bay. Images! They imagine that by piling on images they'll entice me in the end. Like the mother who whistles to prevent baby's bladder from bursting. (There's another.)

They?

Samuel Beckett, *The Unnamable*

21. (D) Another "when" **question**. Line two of paragraph three states that Ms. Peake starts her shift at 1:30 P.M.

Donald J. Schroeder and Frank A. Lombardo, *Police Officer Exam*

She sat down at her writing-table and wrote a letter, which she sealed slowly, adding the date and the hour. Then she said in a solemn tone—

"You are to read it tomorrow; till then, I pray you, do not ask me a single **question**. No, not one!"

"But—"

"Oh, leave me!"

She lay down full length on her bed. A bitter taste that she felt in her mouth awakened her. She saw Charles, and again closed her eyes.

She was studying herself curiously, to see if she were not suffering. But no! nothing as yet. She heard the ticking of the clock, the crackling of the fire, and Charles breathing as he stood upright by her bed.

"Ah! it is but a little thing, death!" she thought. "I shall fall asleep and all will be over."

She drank a mouthful of water and turned to the wall. The frightful taste of ink continued.

"I am thirsty; oh! so thirsty," she sighed.

"What is it?" said Charles, who was handing her a glass.

"It is nothing! Open the window; I am choking."

She was seized with a sickness so sudden that she had hardly time to draw out her handkerchief from under the pillow.

"Take it away," she said quickly; "throw it away."

He spoke to her; she did not answer. She lay motionless, afraid that the slightest movement might make her vomit. But she felt an icy cold creeping from her feet to her heart.

"Ah! it is beginning," she murmured.

"What did you say?"

She turned her head from side to side with a gentle movement full of agony, while constantly opening her mouth as if something very heavy were weighing upon her tongue. At eight o'clock the vomiting began again.

Charles noticed that at the bottom of the basin there was a sort of white sediment sticking to the sides of the porcelain.

"This is extraordinary—very singular," he repeated.

Gustave Flaubert, Madame Bovary

In every group of people there's the *gaffeur*, the one who asks the wrong **question** at the wrong moment. And that was how the insidious **question** emerged: 'And Jesus, then? He was a Jew. Yet he dies young, has no interest in money and thinks only about the kingdom of heaven."

The reply came from Jacques de Biez: "Gentlemen, the idea that Christ was Jewish is a legend created by people who were Jews themselves, like Saint Paul and the four evangelists. Jesus was in fact of the Celtic race, like we French, who were only much later conquered by the Romans. And before being emasculated by the Romans, the Celts were a population of conquerors. Have you heard of the Galatians, who reached as far as Greece? Galilee is thus named for the Gauls who had colonized it. Then again, the legend of a virgin who gave birth to a son is a Celtic and a Druidic myth. Just look at all the portraits we have of Jesus—he was fair-haired and blue-eyed. And he spoke against the customs, superstitions and vices of the Jews. And unlike what the Jews expected from the messiah, he said that his kingdom was not of this earth. And while the Jews were monotheists, Christ launched the idea of the Trinity, inspired by Celtic polytheism. That's why they killed him. Caiaphas, who condemned him, was a Jew . . . Judas, who betrayed him, was a Jew . . . Peter, who denied him, was a Jew . . ."

Umberto Eco, The Prague Cemetery

I turned to Carmingler and Speke. "Are you through with them both?" I said.

Carmingler said, "We are," and turned to Speke who shrugged.

"May I use one of those pistols?"

Speke nodded and one of the guards handed me his. It was a .38 Smith and Wesson, I noticed. I turned back to the pair and pointed the gun at the smaller one. "You remember me, don't you?" I said.

"No," he said and locked his blue eyes with mine.

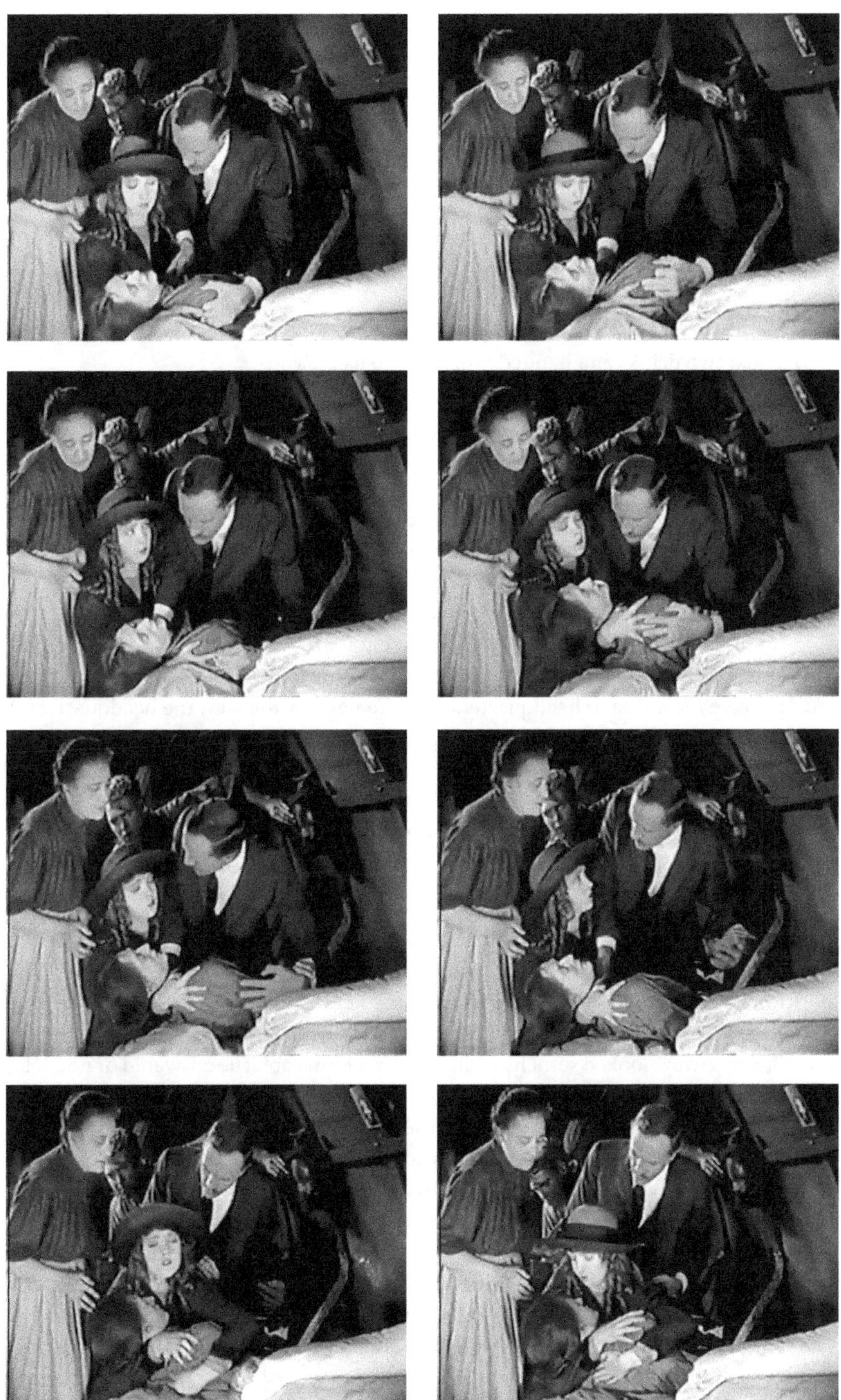

D.W. Griffith (director), The Greatest Question,1919

"I remember your friend there because of the blue spot on the end of his cock."

The taller one jerked his head forward to look for the blue spot. "There isn't any," he said.

"You got it cured after all."

"I didn't have—" He stopped then.

"I'm going to kill you both, you know," I said.

The taller one must have believed me. He swallowed and

Some pages are omitted from this preview

"I still have some Scotch."

"That'll do."

I mixed two drinks and handed him his. "No ice," I said.

"I'm used to it."

"How was it?"

"How or why?"

"Both."

Necessary told it quickly in his usually concise manner and once again he placed everything in the present tense. "I leave you last night around ten to twelve and head down the street to a joint called The Easy Alibi. You know it?"

"I've seen it," I said. "A city councilman owns it."

"That figures. I order a drink and I'm sitting there wondering how talkative the barkeep might be when a couple of plainclothes come in, let me look at their badges, and then give me a ride to headquarters. They're new, by the way, the headquarters, I mean, real nice. So they print me and mug me and then they take me into a quiet little room and ask me a few **questions**."

"About what?"

"About what we've got on who. So I tell 'em that we haven't got anything on anybody and they ask me again."

Ross Thomas, *The Fools in Town Are on Our Side*

As he passed the desk, it was always the man on his right who asked the first **question**. It might be anything: 'What is your middle name?' or 'How many inches in a foot?' The **questions** were meaningless, and no record was kept of his answers. The men behind the desks, who changed shifts at what might have been irregular intervals but who nevertheless always looked somehow alike, did not even care if he answered or not. If he remembered correctly, for some time at the beginning he had not answered. Somewhat later, he had irritatedly taken to giving nonsense replies: 'Newton', or 'eight'. But now it was much less exhausting to simply tell the truth.

He knew what was happening to him. In the end, the brain in effect began manufacturing its own truth drugs in self defence against the fatigue poisons that were flooding it. The equation was: Correct replies = relief. There was none of the saving adrenalin of pain. There was only this walking through a meaningless world.

It was that last which was affecting him most strongly. The men behind the desks paid him no attention, unless he tried to stop walking. The remainder of the time they simply asked their **questions**, looking not at him but at each other. He suspected they neither knew who he was nor cared why he was here. Lately, he had become certain of it. They were practising their trade on each other, not on him. They used him only because most two-handed games require a ball. It meant nothing to them when he began giving correct answers, because they were not here to pass judgement on his answers.

Algis Budrys, Who?

Presumptuous man! the reason wouldst thou find,
Why form'd so weak, so little, and so blind?
First, if thou canst, the harder reason guess,
Why form'd no weaker, blinder, and no less!
Ask of thy mother earth, why oaks are made
Taller or stronger than the weeds they shade?
Or ask of yonder argent fields above,
Why Jove's satellites are less than Jove?

Of systems possible, if 'tis confest
That Wisdom infinite must form the best,
Where all must full or not coherent be,
And all that rises, rise in due degree;
Then, in the scale of reas'ning life, 'tis plain
There must be somewhere, such a rank as man:
And all the **question** (wrangle e'er so long)
Is only this, if God has plac'd him wrong?

Alexander Pope, An Essay on Man

But Prophet's remark galvanized her thoughts. There is no escape from this, she thought. We are dead.

The dead . . . She was struck by the salience of this metaphor, the words having revealed themselves without apparent reason. We are the dead, she thought sadly, knowing how trite it sounded, how clichéd—and how true. Never mind that she could not utter these words aloud, that no one would feel their import, that they would carry no weight of irrefutable, dearly gained wisdom. They rejuvenated her, and for that reason alone they sufficed.

We are the dead, she thought. And why not? Better to reign in Hell than to serve in Heaven.

Methodically she unfastened her seat belt and stood. She stepped behind the pilot, yanked his head back, slipped her right arm under his chin, and pushed his head back down, tightening her muscles. "I don't care if I die," she whispered into his ear. "My friends don't care if they die either. The **question** is, do *you* care if *you* die?"

Todd Wiggins, Zeitgeist

EXAMINATION AT THE WOMB-DOOR

Who owns those scrawny little feet? Death.
Who owns this bristly scorched-looking face? Death.
Who owns these still-working lungs? Death.
Who owns this utility coat of muscles? Death.
Who owns these unspeakable guts? Death.
Who owns these **questionable** brains? Death.
All this messy blood? Death.

These minimum-efficiency eyes? Death.
This wicked little tongue? Death.
This occasional wakefulness? Death.

Given, stolen, or held pending trial?
Held.

Who owns the whole rainy, stony earth? Death.
Who owns all of space? Death.

Who is stronger than hope? Death.
Who is stronger than the will? Death.
Stronger than love? Death.
Stronger than life? Death.

But who is stronger than Death?
      Me, evidently.
Pass, Crow.

    Ted Hughes, Examination at the Womb-Door (Crow: From the Life and Songs of the Crow)

The doorbell is ringing; it is 9:15 a.m.; I am asleep on the couch; I don't want to answer, and even if I had the desire, the will, the need, it would be impossible, my body is still comfortably asleep. I heard the bell, but what is the sense, only minor energy is needed to hear; it is my suspicion that even the recent dead can hear until the brain comes to a complete standstill, a few seconds or perhaps a few minutes. There can be no doubt concerning the constant ringing of the doorbell, but doubt enters as to whether my presence on the couch is one of life or absence of life: in darkness my eyelids not yet open, I myself am not sure. Whomever is operating the doorbell cannot be sure I am in the house; they would have no knowledge of my presence on this couch; for them it is a rudimentary **question**, merely one of physical presence or absence, not the more subtle differentiation between life and death. So why, confronted with my silence, the evidence of my absence, do they continue to ring? Why do they persist? Their insistent finger holding down the button; a few seconds every few minutes; twenty seconds every minute; forty-five seconds of every minute. Are these acts of aggression, of mental deficiency, of stupidity?

Finally the horrific electronic clatter comes to an end. At least I am certain now I am not dead; no dead person could have become as irritated as I am by that relentless bombardment: almost angry enough to open my eyes, lift my body off the couch and storm to the front door. I could have strangled this persistent, obnoxious entity at the entrance to my home, but the ensuing silence is so comforting that my irritation dissolves, relaxes. Listening: are they still at the door?

    Eldon Garnet, Reading Brooke Shields: The Garden of Failure

Instead of answering this **question**, Jacques said: 'It's a very queer business, you know. People are always going on morning, noon and night about how terrible life is, but they can't bring themselves to put an end to it. Could it be that this life, all things considered, isn't so bad after all? Or is it that they're afraid that the next one will be worse?

    Master. Both, I should say. Incidentally, Jacques, do you believe in the afterlife?

    Jacques. I neither believe nor disbelieve. I never think about it. I make the most of the one we've been given, like making withdrawals against future expectations.

Master. Personally, I think of myself as a chrysalis and like to believe that the butterfly, in other words my soul, will one day wriggle out of its case and fly up in the direction of divine justice.

Jacques. The image is delightful.

Master. It's not mine. I came across it, I think, in an Italian poet name of Dante, who wrote something called The Comedy of Hell, Purgatory, and Paradise.

Jacques. That's a rum subject to write a comedy about.

Master. Even so there are some very good things in it, especially Hell. He shuts heretics up inside flaming tombs from which tongues of fire leap out and spread devastation all round about. He puts caitiff traitors in places where they shed tears that freeze upon their cheeks. Slothful souls he puts in holes and says that blood gushes from their veins and is lapped up by disdainful worms below . . . But what prompted you to say all that about complaining about the life we are afraid to lose?

Denis Diderot, Jacques the Fatalist and His Master

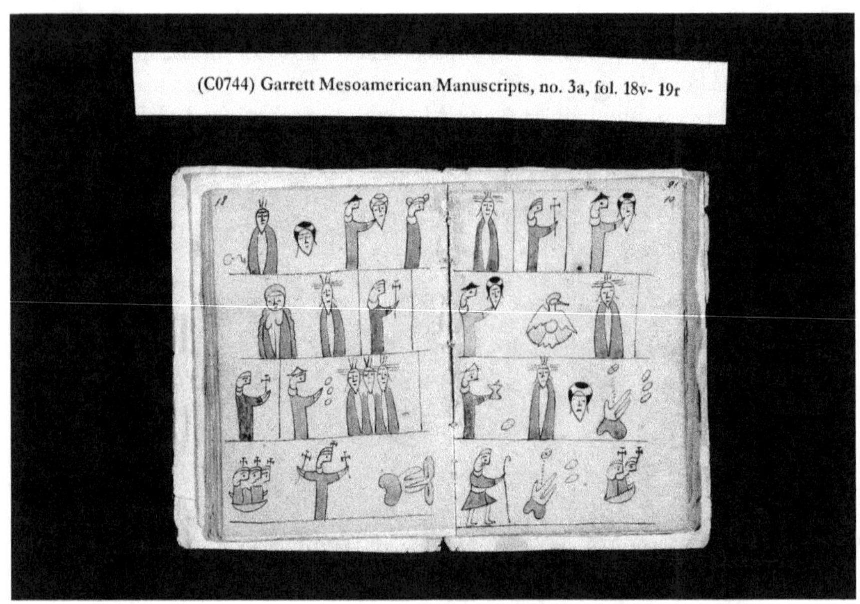

Catecismo pictórico Otomí (Pictorial Otomi catechism), between 1775 and1825
Manuscript, 1 v. (26 leaves), paper, ill., 8 x 6 cm

A pictorial prayer book that contains the catechism of the Catholic Church in picture writing. In this manuscript, as in most surviving examples, the drawings have little relationship to the traditional forms of Mexican Indian manuscript painting. The document has 51 illustrated pages and one gloss. Also there is a curious legend written on a preliminary leaf "Alaja preciosal cogida al enemigo en Sn. Yago del Cerro."

Garrett Mesoamerican Manuscripts, no. 3a, Manuscripts Division, Dept. of
Rare Books and Special Collections, Princeton University Library

For the Sake of Brevity, in the Form of **Questions** and Answers

Since we've gone this far, it won't do any harm and it might do some good

Minor Queries.

A fragment came into my possession some time ago, among a quantity of waste paper in which books were wrapped, which, from the singularity of its contents, I felt desirous to trace to the book of which it forms a part, but my research has hitherto proved unsuccessful. It consists of two leaves of a large octavo sheet, probably published some twenty years back, and is headed "Autobiographical Sketch of the Editor." It commences with the words: "The Commissioners of the Poor Laws will understand me, when I say, that I was born at Putney, in Surrey." The pages are of course not consecutive: so after an allusion to the wanderings of the writer, I have nothing more up to p. 7, at which is an account of a supposed plot against the lord mayor and sheriffs, concocted by him with the assistance of some school-boy coadjutors; the object of which appears to have been, to overturn the state-coach of the civic functionary, as it ascended Holborn Hill, by charging it with a hackney coach, in which sat the writer and certain widows armed with bolsters in pink satin bags. The word having been given to "Charge!" this new kind of war-chariot was driven down the hill at full speed, gunpowder ignited on its roof, and blazing squibs protruded through its back, sides, and front. The ingenious author declares that the onslaught was crowned with complete success; but here, most unfortunately, the sheet ends: and unless you, Mr. Editor, or some of your correspondents, will kindly help me to the rest of the narrative, I must, I fear return unexperienced to my grave. I have omitted to mention, that the date of this event is given as the 4th of July, 1799.

Cheverells.

. . .

In reply to Leicestriensis, I beg leave to inform him that "W. D." was Wm. Dillingham, D.D., master of Clare Hall, and at the time Vice-Chancellor of the University of Cambridge. The letter in **question**, which was the original draft, was, with a variety of other family papers, stolen from me in 1843.

J. P. Ord.

P.S.—Query, from whom did the present possessor obtain it?

George Bell, ed., Notes and Queries, Number 185

I am no prophet—and here's no great matter;
I have seen the moment of my greatness flicker,
And I have seen the eternal Footman hold my coat, and snicker,
And in short, I was afraid.

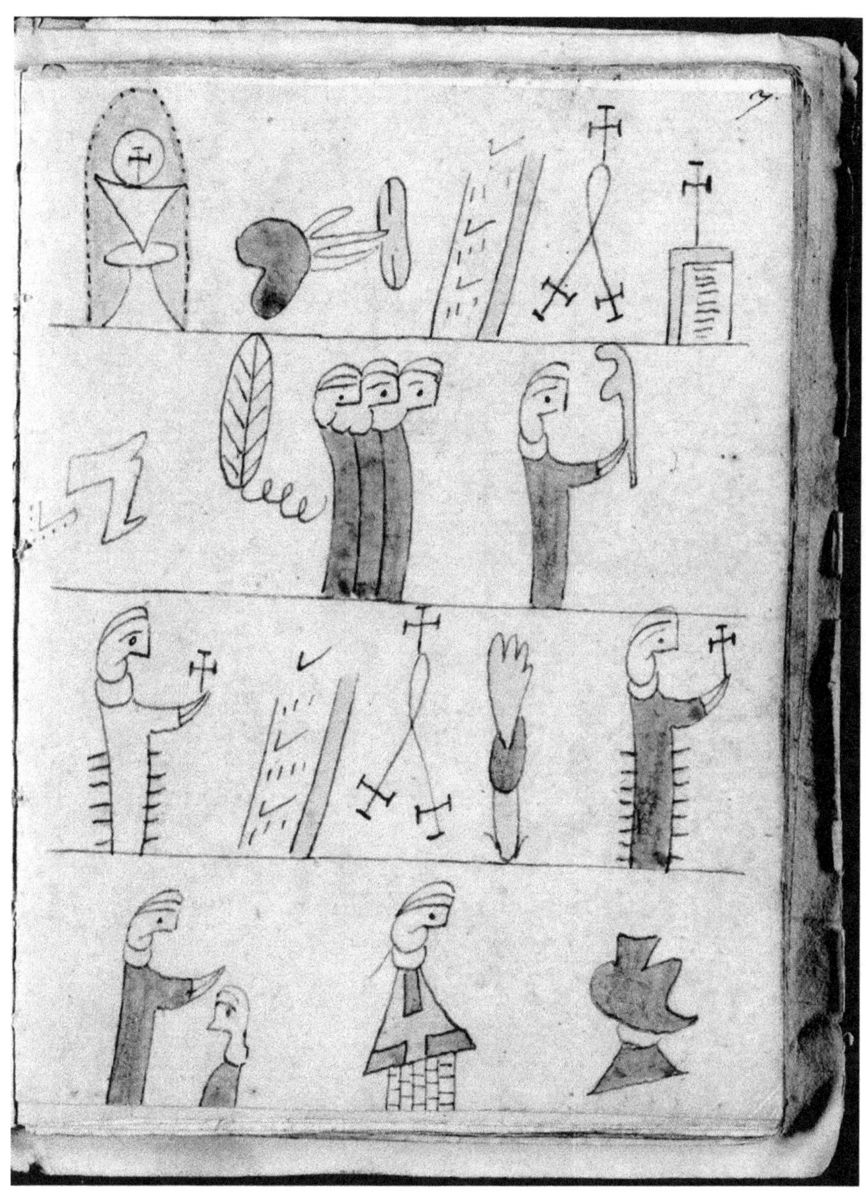

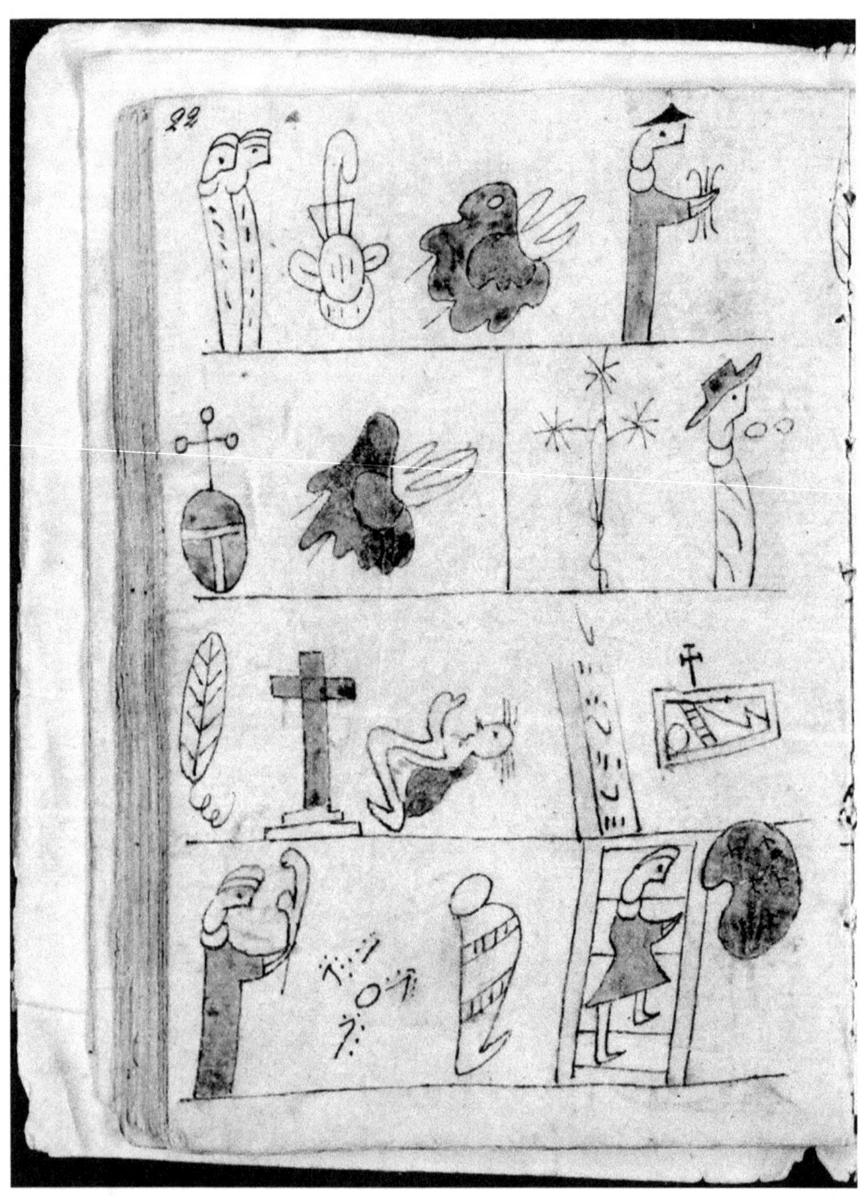

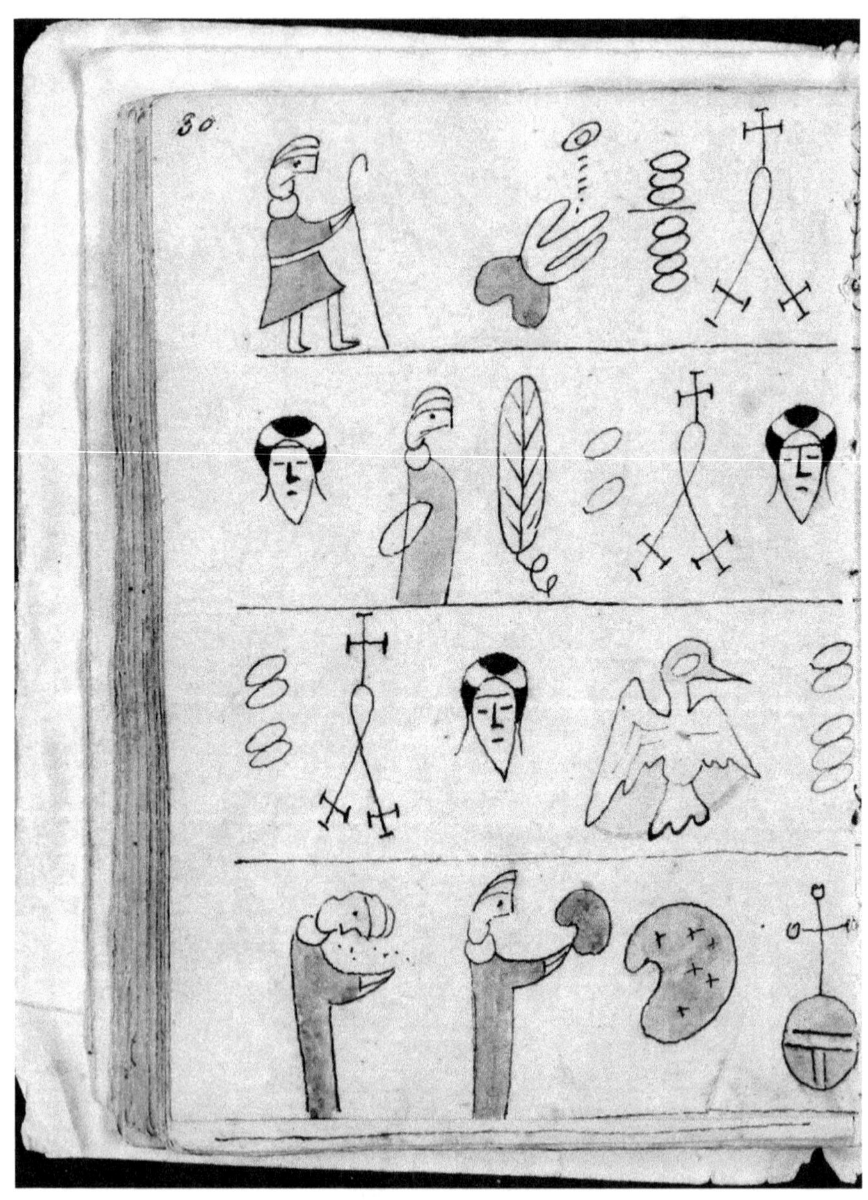

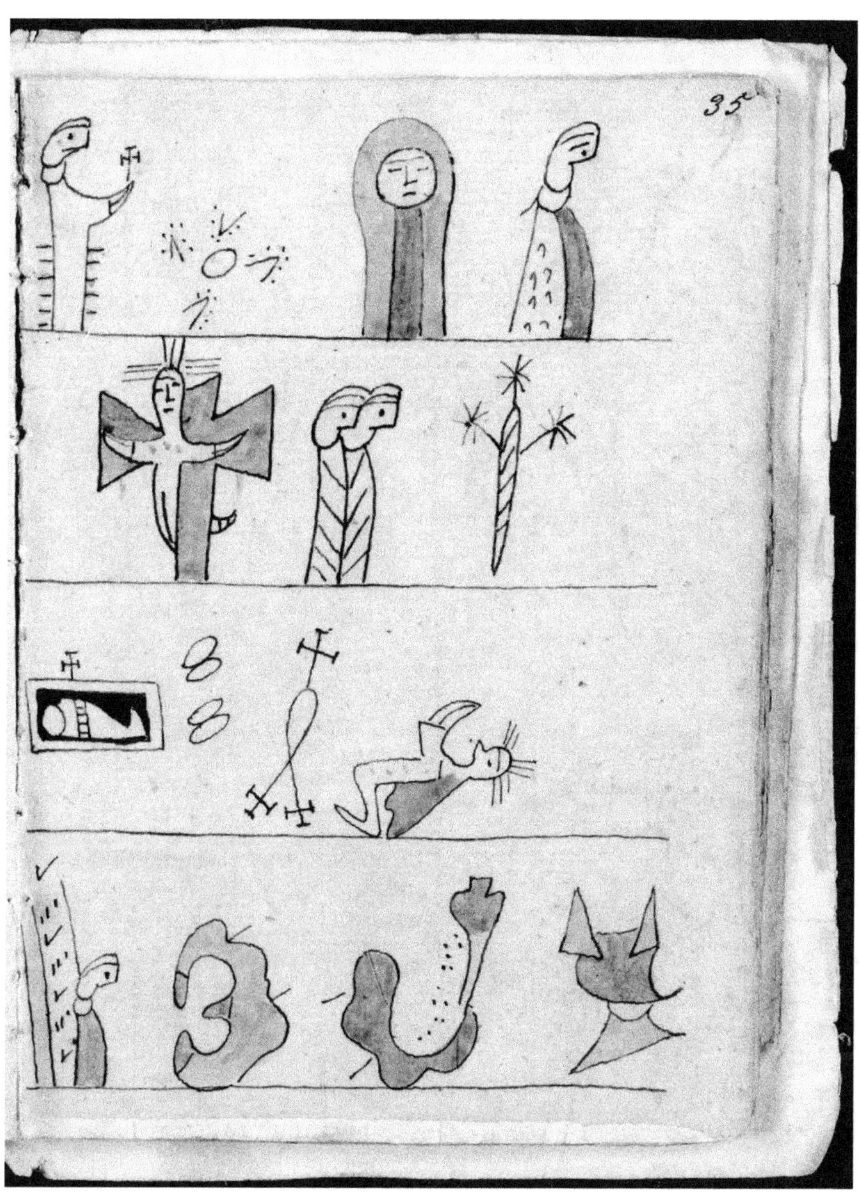

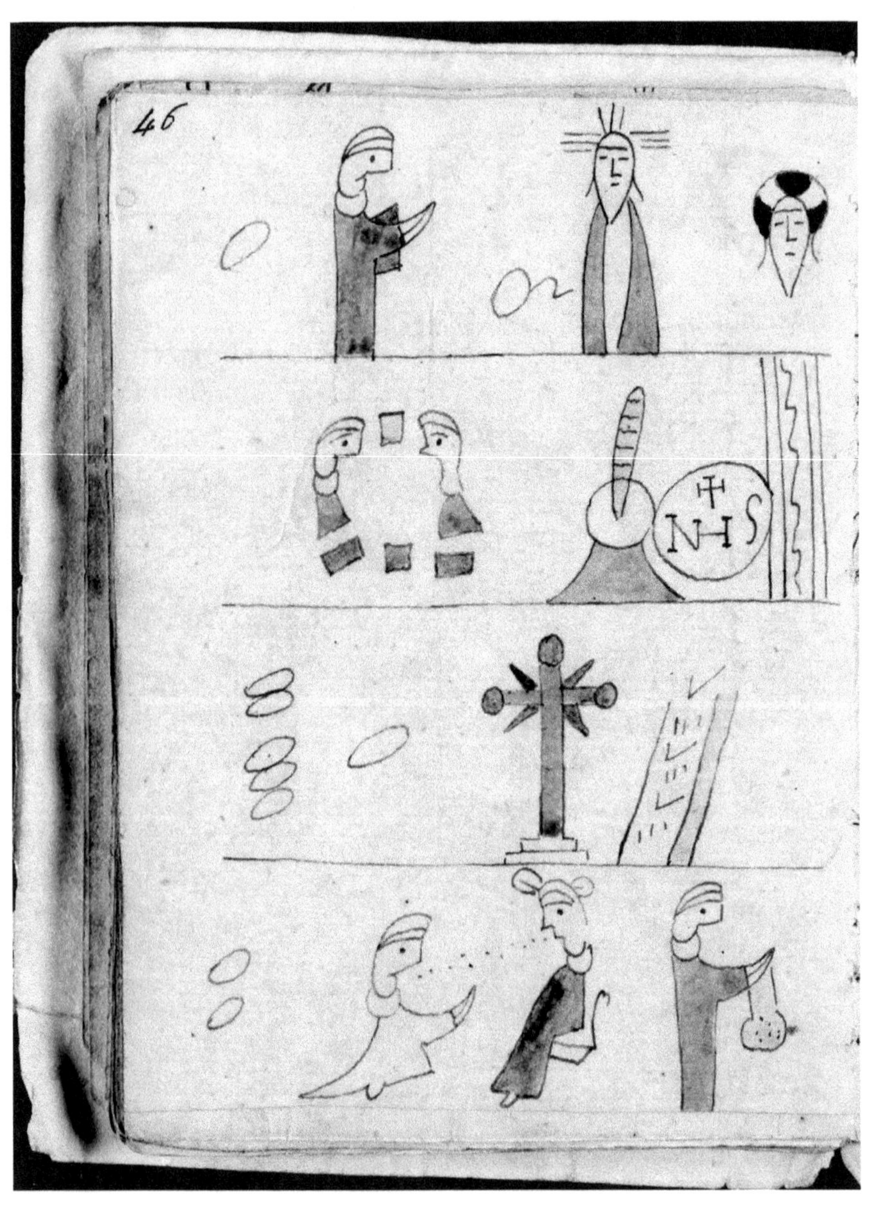

51.
ZIN

Catecismo pictórico Otomí (Pictorial Otomi catechism), between 1775 and1825
Manuscript, 1 v. (26 leaves), paper, ill., 8 x 6 cm

The manuscript is undoubtedly one of several manuscripts acquired by J.M.A. Aubin from Francisco Perez about 1830–1840 (see Aubin, quoted in Boban, 1891, 2: 178,181). It was listed, together with the other "Testerian" manuscript (no. 3b) in the Garrett collection, as lot 238 of a Sotheby's catalog of November, 1936, and four of its pages were reproduced in that catalog (Sotheby's, 1936: 35 and plate labeled "lot 238"). It was purchased by Garrett in November of that year through or from Bernard Quaritch.

Garrett Mesoamerican Manuscripts, no. 3a, Manuscripts Division, Dept. of
Rare Books and Special Collections, Princeton University Library

And would it have been worth it, after all,
After the cups, the marmalade, the tea,
Among the porcelain, among some talk of you and me,
Would it have been worth while,
To have bitten off the matter with a smile,
To have squeezed the universe into a ball
To roll it towards some overwhelming **question**,
To say: "I am Lazarus, come from the dead,
Come back to tell you all, I shall tell you all"—
If one, settling a pillow by her head
    Should say: "That is not what I meant at all;
    That is not it, at all."

    T. S. Eliot, The Love Song of J. Alfred Prufrock

"There are some few points" (Mr. Playmore wrote) "which the recovery of the letter does not seem to clear up. I have done my best, with Mr. Benjamin's assistance, to find the right explanation of these debatable matters; and I have treated the subject, for the sake of brevity, in the form of **Questions** and Answers. Will you accept me as interpreter, after the mistakes I made when you consulted me in Edinburgh? Events, I admit, have proved that I was entirely wrong in trying to prevent you from returning to Dexter—and partially wrong in suspecting Dexter of being directly, instead of indirectly, answerable for the first Mrs. Eustace's death. I frankly make my confession, and leave you to tell Mr. Benjamin whether you think my new Catechism worthy of examination or not."

I thought his "new Catechism" (as he called it) decidedly worthy of examination. If you don't agree with this view, and if you are dying to be done with me and my narrative, pass on to the next chapter by all means!

Benjamin produced the **Questions** and Answers; and read them to me, at my request, in these terms:

"**Questions** suggested by the letter discovered at Gleninch. First Group: **Questions** relating to the Diary. First **Question**: obtaining access to Mr. Macallan's private journal, was Miserrimus Dexter guided by any previous knowledge of its contents?

"Answer: It is doubtful if he had any such knowledge.

Wilkie Collins, The Law and the Lady

She drew in her breath sharply, with almost a sob in her throat, but her voice was steady, quiet and musical, when she replied:

"You know I did. Why should you ask?"

"Detectives like **questions** they already know the answers to. Why did you come down here, Mrs. Haldorn?"

"Is that another whose answer you know?"

"I know you came for one or both of two reasons."

'Yes?"

"First, to learn how close we were to our riddle's answer. Right?"

"I've my share of curiosity, naturally," she confessed.

"I don't mind making that much of your trip a success. I know the answer."

She stopped in the path, facing me, her eyes phosphorescent in the deep twilight.

She put a hand on my shoulder: she was taller than I. The other hand was in her coat-pocket. She put her face nearer mine. She spoke very slowly, as if taking great pains to be understood:

"Tell me truthfully. Don't pretend. I don't want to do an unnecessary wrong. Wait, wait—think before you speak—and believe me when I say this isn't the time for pretending, for lying, for bluffing. Now tell me the truth: do you know the answer?"

"Yeah."

She smiled faintly, taking her hand from my shoulder, saying:

"Then there's no use of our fencing."

I jumped at her. If she had fired from her pocket she might have plugged me. But she tried to get the gun out. By then I had a hand on her wrist. The bullet went into the ground between our feet. The nails of her free hand put three red ribbons down the side of my face. I tucked my head under her chin, turned my hip to her before her knee came up, brought her body hard against mine with one arm around her, and bent her gun-hand behind her. She dropped the gun as we fell. I was on top. I stayed there until I had found the gun. I was getting up when MacMan arrived.

"Everything's eggs in the coffee," I told him, having trouble with my voice.

"Have to plug her?" he asked, looking at the woman lying still on the ground.

"No, she's all right. See that the chauffeur's behaving."

MacMan went away. The woman sat up, tucked her legs under her, and rubbed her wrist. I said:

"That's the second reason for your coming, though I thought you meant it for Mrs. Collinson."

She got up, not saying anything. I didn't help her up, not wanting her to know how shaky I was. I said:

"Since we've gone this far, it won't do any harm and it might do some good to talk."

"I don't think anything will do any good now." She set her hat straight. "You say you know. Then lies are worthless, and only lies would help." She shrugged. "Well, what now?"

Dashiell Hammett, The Dain Curse

Still, she'd rather not talk about writing until she resolves the **question** of her hypnosis. But she knows she shouldn't be worrying about it. What should I do with the fax machine and those phones? Who's keeping watch at the station? These are now the **questions** that plague her. A few hours later, she phones the young conductor. He wants her to leave them alone. He wants her to stop calling him. Why is she so jealous, he asks, chuckling condescendingly, when she should be more understanding of his relation-ship with the new soprano? She should just accept they're not together anymore; that they don't make love anymore. Then the young conductor tells her reassuringly that, sooner or later, she'll forget all about him; time will heal her wounds. The girl would like to be able to coolly sever her association with the young conductor and brilliant composer; she'd love to be able to take a deep breath, hang up, and forget about them in that same instant. She doesn't want to wait the length of time it takes to heal a wound. So she insults him, reproaches his stupidity, his misplaced arrogance. Success often paralyzes the mind, she says, but she's never seen it happen so fast, and so thoroughly. The Sinfonietta's finished, they've been ousted from the vanguard, condemned to a future of selling out and merely parroting popular trends. The words come swift and true and from the heart. All they must do to secure musical oblivion is to keep doing what they're doing. Either way, they're stuck with the path they've chosen. It's too late for them now. She hangs up.

She still has to resolve the **question** of her hypnosis . . .

A. G. Porta, No World Concerto

*Treatise on Social Behaviour, in the Form of **Question** and Answer, Recto Part No. 10*
Scroll, ink on paper, 28.5 x 290 cm
Acquired by Aurel Stein as part of his Second Expedition to the Silk Road (1906–08)
The British Library, London, England (Artstor)

And an Equal Portion of Time Should Be Devoted to the New **Question**

Sometimes I feel like giving up, then I remember I have a lot of motherfuckers to prove wrong

We may have to wait a few decades for the completion of this edition before we can know the source of the unease that tormented Heidegger as he stirred up the **question** of Being.

Jean Grondin, Why Reawaken the **Question** of Being? (Heidegger's Being and Time: Critical Essays)

"And how could the police have prevented that?" Rebus asked, folding his arms.

Before Bell could answer, the director had a **question** for Rebus. "Were any videos or magazines found in Herdman's home? Violent films, that sort of thing?"

"There's no sign he was interested in anything like that. But so what if he was?"

The director just shrugged, deciding he wasn't going to get what he wanted from Rebus. "Jack, maybe you could do a quick interview with . . . sorry, I didn't catch your name." He smiled at Rebus.

"My name's Fuck You," Rebus said, returning the smile. Then he crossed the road again and pushed open the door of the police station.

"You're a disgrace!" Jack Bell was shouting at him. "An absolute disgrace! Don't think I won't take this any further . . . !"

"That you making friends again?" the desk sergeant asked.

"I seem to be blessed that way," Rebus informed him, climbing the stairs to the CID office. Overtime was available on the Herdman case, which meant a few souls were still working, even at this hour.

Ian Rankin, A **Question** of Blood

Heidegger has written:

> *At the close of a lecture called "The **Question** Concerning Technology," given some time ago, I said: "**Questioning** is the piety of thinking." "Piety" is meant here in the ancient sense: obedient, or submissive, and in this case submitting to what thinking has to think about. One of the exciting experiences of thinking is that at times it does not fully comprehend the new insights it has just gained, and does not properly see them through. Such, too, is the case with the sentence just cited that **questioning** is the piety of thinking. The lecture ending with that sentence was already in the ambience of the realization that the true stance of thinking cannot be to put **questions**, but must be to listen to that which our **questioning** vouchsafes—and all **questioning** begins to be a **questioning** only in virtue of pursuing its quest for essential Being.*[3]

William Lovitt, Introduction to The **Question** Concerning Technology and Other Essays, by Martin Heidegger

"It's not in there. I spent hours. There are four indexes."

"It must be recently marketed. Do you want me to double-check the book?"

"I already looked. I *looked*."

"We could always call her doctor. But I don't want to make too much of this. Everybody takes some kind of medication, everybody forgets things occasionally."

"Not like my mother."

"I forget things all the time."

"What do you take?"

"Blood pressure pills, stress pills, allergy pills, eye drops, aspirin. Run of the mill."

"I looked in the medicine chest in your bathroom."

"No Dylar?"

"I thought there might be a new bottle."

"The doctor prescribed thirty pills. That was it. Run of the mill. Everybody takes something."

"I still want to know," she said.

All this time she'd been turned away from me. There were plot potentials in this situation, chances for people to make devious maneuvers, secret plans. But now she shifted position, used an elbow to prop her upper body and watched me speculatively from the foot of the bed.

"Can I ask you something?"

"Sure," I said.

"You won't get mad?"

"You know what's in my medicine chest. What secrets are left?"

"Why did you name Heinrich Heinrich?"

"Fair **question**."

"You don't have to answer."

"Good **question**. No reason why you shouldn't ask."

"So why did you?"

"I thought it was a forceful name, a strong name. It has a kind of authority."

"Is he named after anyone?"

"No. He was born shortly after I started the department and I guess I wanted to acknowledge my good fortune. I wanted to do something German. I felt a gesture was called for."

"Heinrich Gerhardt Gladney?"

"I thought it had an authority that might cling to him. I thought it was forceful and impressive and I still do. I wanted to shield him, make him unafraid. People were naming their children Kim, Kelly and Tracy."

There was a long silence. She kept watching me. Her features, crowded somewhat in the center of her face, gave to her moments of concentration a puggish and half-belligerent look.

"Do you think I miscalculated?"

"It's not for me to say."

"There's something about German names, the German language, German *things*. I don't know what it is exactly. It's just there. In the middle of it all is Hitler, of course."

"He was on again last night."

"He's always on. We couldn't have television without him."

"They lost the war," she said. "How great could they be?"

"A valid point. But it's not a **question** of greatness. It's not a **question** of good and evil. I don't know what it is. Look at it this way. Some people always wear a favorite color. Some people carry a gun. Some people put on a uniform and feel bigger, stronger, safer. It's in this area that my obsessions dwell."

Don DeLillo, White Noise

Conservatives conceptions of "strength" and "cowardice" are deeply irrational. The last debate was dominated by candidates trying to prove how strong they are by bragging about who is the most scaredest of all of the scary, scary terrorists hiding under the bed. "Strength" for conservatives is not really about actual bravery or calm under fire, but about bluster.

Under the circumstances, throwing a bratty tantrum and refusing to be at the debate fits into conservative notions of "strength" far more than the alternative, which is showing up and meekly submitting to **questioning**.

Amanda Marcotte, Trump Wins Again With His Bratty Tantrum: His Fox News Debate Boycott Will Only Boost His Campaign Even More (Salon)

I am very unfortunate if that is true. But suppose I ask you a **question**: Would you say that this also holds true in the case of horses?

Plato, Apology

So I walk into the tiny room where Harper is speaking, relieved that the Conservatives have finally come to their senses and relaxed their media relations strategy to the point where Harper can finally be Harper, and field **questions** on an assortment of topics.

Inside, I doublecheck with Bryn Weese, who handles a lot of the media on the campaign. He, like Teneycke, is a former Sun News employee—a place where I also used to contribute—and generally a good guy.

So I get a **question**, right, Bryn?

"Let me check with Kory," he says.

He comes back and shakes his head. "You can go talk to Kory about it."

So I do.

"What the fuck, Kory?"

He explains that the tour media—the ones shelling out $78,000—get four **questions**, and local media get one **question**. I am neither tour, nor local. I get no **questions**.

I point out that there are only three tour media present and, lo, there is a **question** left! Can I have it? Will local media get two? What about Daniel Leblanc, the Globe and Mail reporter who's in the same spot as I?

Nope. There'll just be four **questions**.

I persist.

"Go write a story about it."

So Harper wraps up, and begins taking **questions**. One on Duffy. One on retirement benefits. Then Andy Blatchford, Canadian Press reporter, asks: "Why do you only take five **questions** at your campaign events?"

Harper's answer:

"I think you're all very aware of how we've structured our press conferences. This is a long-standing policy, it was cleared with everybody. And what's important to me is that we're able to answer a range of **questions** on a broad range of subjects. That's why every day I speak to a different topic."

Well that sounds nice.

So then Harper took a **question** from a local reporter about his tax break, and then it was a wrap. No fifth **question**. He does, however, take the mic one more time: "Friends, nobody asked about this, but . . ." he then preceded to underline how fragile our economy is, answering a **question** that nobody asked.

Naturally, I began yelling: "Mr. Harper! I have a **question**. I have a **question**. I HAVE A **QUESTION**. What about that fifth **question**?"

Justin Ling, If We Want to Ask Stephen Harper Questions, We Have to Give His Party $78,000 (Vice)

Fortunately for me, the landlord did not open the door when I rang. A stupid maid-of-all-work, who never thought of asking me for my name, let me in. Mrs. Macallan was at home, and had no visitors with her. Giving me this information, the maid led the way upstairs, and showed me into the drawing-room without a word of announcement.

My mother-in-law was sitting alone, near a work-table, knitting. The moment I appeared in the doorway she laid aside her work, and, rising, signed to me with a commanding gesture of her hand to let her speak first.

"I know what you have come here for," she said. "You have come here to ask **questions**. Spare yourself, and spare me. I warn you beforehand that I will not answer any **questions** relating to my son."

It was firmly, but not harshly said. I spoke firmly in my turn.

"I have not come here, madam, to ask **questions** about your son," I answered. "I have come, if you will excuse me, to ask you a **question** about yourself."

She started, and looked at me keenly over her spectacles. I had evidently taken her by surprise.

"What is the **question**?" she inquired.

"I now know for the first time, madam, that your name is Macallan," I said. "Your son has married me under the name of Woodville. The only honorable explanation of this circumstance, so far as I know, is that my husband is your son by a first marriage. The happiness of my life is at stake. Will you kindly consider my position? Will you let me ask you if you have been twice married, and if the name of your first husband was Woodville?"

She considered a little before she replied.

"The **question** is a perfectly natural one in your position," she said. "But I think I had better not answer it."

"May I ask why?"

"Certainly. If I answered you, it should only lead to other **questions**, and I should be obliged to decline replying to them. I am sorry to disappoint you. I repeat what I said on the beach—I have no other feeling than a feeling of sympathy toward you. If you had consulted me before your marriage, I should willingly have admitted you to my fullest confidence. It is now too late. You are married. I recommend you to make the best of your position, and to rest satisfied with things as they are."

Wilkie Collins, The Law and the Lady

I mention this story also as the best method I can advise any person to take in such a case, especially if he be one that makes conscience of his duty, and would be directed what to do in it, namely, that he should keep his eye upon the particular providences which occur at that time, and look upon them complexly, as they regard one another, and as all together regard the **question** before him: and then, I think, he may safely take them for intimations from Heaven of what is his **unquestioned** duty to do in such a case; I mean as to going away from or staying in the place where we dwell, when visited with an infectious distemper.

Daniel Defoe, A Journal of the Plague Year: Being Observations or Memorials of the Most Remarkable Occurrences, as Well Public as Private, Which Happened in London During the Last Great Visitation in 1665. Written by a Citizen Who Continued All the While in London. Never Made Public Before.

He called the Stazione Termini, and asked about the trains for Naples tomorrow. There were four or five. He wrote down the times for all of them. It would be five days before a boat left from Naples for Majorca, and he would sit the time out in Naples, he thought. All he needed was a release from the police, and if nothing happened tomorrow he should get it. They couldn't hold a man forever, without even any grounds for suspicion, just in order to throw an occasional **question** at him! He began to feel he would be released tomorrow, that it was absolutely logical that he should be released.

Patricia Highsmith, The Talented Mr. Ripley

And so, hopeless as it seemed, he talked, he listened, he was reasonable; endless as the struggle seemed, he remained patient, and whenever he saw her going too far he drew the line. No matter how much it might openly enrage her to answer him, no matter how sarcastic and caustic and elusive and dishonest her answers might be, he continued to **question** her about her political activities, about her after-school whereabouts, about her new friends; with a gentle persistence that infuriated her, he asked about her Saturday trips into New York. She could shout all she wanted at home—she was still just a kid from Old Rimrock, and the thought of whom she might meet in New York alarmed him.

Conversation #1 about New York. "What do you do when you go to New York? Who do you see in New York?" "What do I do? I go see New York. That's what I do." "What do you do, Merry?" "I do what everyone else does. I window-shop. What else would a girl do?" "You're involved with political people in New York." "I don't know what you're talking about. Everything is political. Brushing your teeth is political" "You're involved with people who are against the war in Vietnam. Isn't that who you go to see? Yes or no?" "They're people, yes. They're people with ideas, and some of them don't b-b-b-believe in the war. Most of them don't b-b-b-believe in the war." "Well, I don't happen to believe in the war myself." "So what's your problem?" "Who are these people? How old are they? What do they do for a living? Are they students?" "Why do you want to know?" "Because I'd like to know what you're doing. You're alone in New York on Saturdays. Not everyone's parents would allow a sixteen-year-old girl to go that far." "I go in . . . I, you know, there are people and dogs and streets . . ." "You come home with all this Communist material. You come home with all these books and pamphlets and magazines." "I'm trying to learn. You taught me to learn, didn't you? Not just to study, but to learn. C-c-c-communist . . ." "It is Communist. It says on the page that it's Communist." "C-c-c-communists have ideas that aren't always about C-communism." "For instance." "About poverty. About war. About injustice. They have all kinds of ideas. Just b-b-because you're Jewish doesn't mean you just have ideas about Judaism. Well, the same holds for C-c-communism."

Conversation #12 about New York. "Where do you eat your meals in New York?"

"Not at Vincent's, thank God." "Where then?" "Where everybody else eats their meals. Restaurants. Cafeterias. People's apartments." "Who are the people who live in these apartments?" "Friends of mine." "Where did you meet them?" "I met some here, I met some in the city—" "Here? Where?" "At the high school. Sh-sh-sh-sherry, for instance." "I never met Sherry." "Sh-sh-sh-sherry is the one, do you remember, who played the violin in all the class plays? And she goes into New York b-because she takes music lessons." "Is she involved with politics too?" "Daddy, everything is political. How can she not be involved if she has a b-b-b-brain?" "Merry, I don't want you to get into trouble. You're angry about the war. A lot of people are angry about the war. But there are some people who are angry about the war who don't have any limits. Do you know what the limits are?" "Limits. That's all you think about. Not going to the extreme. Well, sometimes you have to fucking go to the extreme. What do you think war is? War is an extreme. It isn't life out here in little Rimrock. Nothing is too extreme out here." "You don't like it out here anymore. Would you want to live in New York? Would you like that?" "Of c-c-c-course." "Suppose when you graduate from high school you were to go to college in New York. Would you like that?" "I don't know if I'm going to go to college. Look at the administration of those colleges. Look what they do to their students who are against the war. How can I want to be going to college? Higher education. It's what I call lower education. Maybe I'll go to college, maybe I won't. I wouldn't start p-planning now."

Conversation #18 about New York, after she fails to return home on a Saturday night. "You're never to do that again. You're never to stay over with people who we don't know. Who are these people?"

Philip Roth, American Pastoral

This goes on for a while & finally it's over & Dr. Fish himself comes in & he's wearing a gauze mask too & rubber gloves & I feel a little shiver, excitement like a spike in the cock, behind the mask & glasses you don't know Dr. Fish is an old guy in his fifties at least, his hair's still O.K. unless it's dyed?—& he's looking at the teeth chart the female assistant has handed him & the X-rays & asking me how I am, how's the family Quentin, & the high school, he's confusing me with my sister Junie but that's O.K. Now Dr. Fish examines my mouth & he's fast & frowning & up close you can see the turtle-pouches around his eyes. This the man to see into your soul. *Please rinse Quen-tin.* Laying down one of the silver picks on a tray on a wad of cotton batting, the tip is shining with blood. There's a sick excited sensation in my gut, I'm rinsing my mouth & can't stop myself from seeing tendrils of blood in the water, I'm faint & excited & wish I could see Dr. Fish's hands & that silver pick in Q_ P_'s mouth like on a video! *Sorry if this hurts, Quen-tin,* Dr. Fish says, it's his mouth saying it, another pick in his hand, *you haven't been in for an exam in quite a while, eh?—almost three years. Afraid you've got several cavities & what might be the start of pyorrhea.* Then the exam is over & Dr. Fish removes his gauze mask & rubber gloves & he's smiling asking do I have any **questions**? any **questions**? & he's ready to move on to the next patient in the next examining room & I'm clumsy-shaky rising from the chair & Dr. Fish is looking at me & I can't think of any **question** to ask him & he's turning to leave & I think of one.

"Do bones float?"

"Excuse me?"

"Bones. Do bones float?"

Dr. Fish stares at me & blinks once, twice. "What kind of bones?—human, or animal?"

"There's a difference?"

"Well, there might be." Dr. Fish shrugs & frowns backing off, I get the idea he's stalling not knowing the answer. "It would depend, too, on whether the bones were heavy, or, you know, dried out—hollow & light. If so they would float, I'm sure." There's a pause & he adds, "You mean float in water?" & I nod sort of vague & he's at the door, a little wave of his hand like a Thalidomide flipper, "Well, Quen-tin. See you next week?"

Joyce Carol Oates, Zombie

The ship wherein Theseus and the youth of Athens returned had thirty oars, and was preserved by the Athenians . . . for they took away the old planks as they decayed, putting in new and stronger timber in their place, insomuch that this ship became a standing example among the philosophers, for the logical **question** *of things that grow; one side holding that the ship remained the same, and the other contending that it was not the same.*

—Plutarch, Vita Thesel

The answer of course is that the ship
doesn't exist, that "ship"
is an abstraction, a conception,
an imaginary tarp thrown
across the garden of the real.
The answer is that the cheap
peasantry of things toils all day
in the kingdom of language,
every ship like a casket
of words: bulkhead, transom,
mast steps. The answer
is to wake again to the banality
of things, to wade toward
the light inside the plasma
of ideas. But each plank
is woven from your mother's
hair. The blade of each oar
contains the shadow of
a horse. The answer
is that the self is the glue between
the boards, the cartilage
that holds a world together,
that self is the wax in
the stenographer's ears,
that there is nothing the mind
won't sacrifice, each item
another goat tossed into
the lava of our needs.

Steve Gehrke, The Ships of Theseus

If comparing a piece that is a size that is recognised as not a size but a piece, comparing a piece with what is not recognised but what is used as it is held by holding, comparing these two comes to be repeated. Suppose they are put together, suppose that there is an interruption, supposing that beginning again they are not changed as to position, suppose all this and suppose that any five two of whom are not separating suppose that the five are not consumed. Is there an exchange, is there a resemblance to the sky which is admitted to be there and the stars which can be seen. Is there. That was a **question**. There was no certainty. Fitting a failing meant that any two were indifferent and yet they were all connecting that, they were all connecting that consideration. This did not determine rejoining a letter. This did not make letters smaller. It did.

The stamp that is not only torn but also fitting is not any symbol. It suggests nothing. A sack that has no opening suggests more and the loss is not commensurate. The season gliding and the torn hangings receiving mending all this shows an example, it shows the force of sacrifice and likeness and disaster and a reason.

The time when there is not the **question** is only seen when there is a shower. Any little thing is water.

There was a whole collection made. A damp cloth, an oyster, a single mirror, a manikin, a student, a silent star, a single spark, a little movement and the bed is made. This shows the disorder, it does, it shows more likeness than anything else, it shows the single mind that directs an apple. All the coats have a different shape, that does not mean that they differ in color, it means a union between use and exercise and a horse.

Gertrude Stein, Tender Buttons

Sheila's train of thought was abruptly broken. A little way ahead, and to the left, a single light had sprung up in the dusk. The boat drew nearer and it took on tone—golden and mellow; nearer still and it took shape—the oblong shape of an uncurtained window. She shut off the engine and silence, filling the void where a moment before had been shattering sound, pressed upon her like a physical thing. Then came the soft hiss and ripple of water still parting before her. And then a voice.

She swung the boat in towards the shore and saw a second and larger oblong of light. A door. And silhouetted against it was the figure of a man. He was talking. His voice came distinctly over the water and Sheila strained her ears. A foreign language.

The momentum of the boat had taken it within thirty yards of the solitary figure. Sheila's hand was going out to start the engine hastily when she heard:

'Dainonioi, muthous men huperphialous aleasthe pantas homos . . .'

A foreign language, but one which was more reassuring than any English could have been. Enemy agents do not stand in the dusk by highland lochs chanting ancient Greek. With the little way that was left to her Sheila let the boat glide to within a dozen yards of the shore. And then she called out: 'Ahoy! Who are you?'

The man was standing before the open door of what appeared to be a small cottage on the water's edge. At Sheila's call he stopped chanting and there was a moment's silence. Then a cultured voice said: 'I beg your pardon. I hope I did not startle you.'

Coming in answer to an abrupt challenge which had followed hard upon the hideous racket of a powerful motorboat, this was exceedingly polite. Sheila felt foolish—and spoke foolishly as a result. 'Are you,' she demanded, 'British?'

'British?' The voice appeared to weigh his **question** carefully. 'In the modern sense of the word, madam—yes. I am an Englishman.' There was a pause and the voice appeared to think some further apology civil. 'Perhaps my language misled you. I was repeating Homer. I am apt to do it—and preferably in the open air—when disturbed, or upon hearing bad news.'

'Bad news?' There was a little landing stage and Sheila had glided up to it. 'There's bad news?'

Michael Innes, The Secret Vanguard

Does the news make us anxious?

News creates anxiety because it tells stories with no known ending. Most stories have an end in view, an end to which they are working. But, by definition, the news story cannot be working towards an end. News is an update on the unfolding stories of the real world. Having no predictable ending or even predicted development, news stories are very different from fiction, where planning some distance ahead is built into the working of the form, even in a series like Lost, where the eventual ending may be hazy even to the producers and scriptwriters. TV series fiction at least provides the satisfactions of incidents that resolve, narratives that begin and end within one episode, and an overall series structure of a given number of episodes each season. News has none of that. The only certainty is that there will always be news, and little of it will be good.

*John Ellis, TV **FAQ** : Uncommon Answers to Common **Questions** About TV*

We might pursue this **question** into innumerable other ramifications; and everywhere, under new shapes, find the same truth, which we here so imperfectly enunciate, disclosed; that throughout the whole world of man, in all manifestations and performances of his nature, outward and inward, personal and social, the Perfect, the Great is a mystery to itself, knows not itself; whatsoever does know itself is already little, and more or less imperfect. Or otherwise, we may say, Unconsciousness belongs to pure unmixed life; Consciousness to a diseased mixture and conflict of life and death: Unconsciousness is the sign of creation; Consciousness, at best, that of manufacture. So deep, in this existence of ours, is the significance of Mystery.

Thomas Carlyle, Characteristics

Have I ever said that my pickup truck has English license plates and a right-hand drive, incidentally?

Heaven only knows what it was doing parked at one of the marinas here. But I have been driving it locally ever since.

Although there is one more thing I had wished to point out about that **question** of Rembrandt's cat before I leave it, actually.

Which is the way in which so many more people happened to be familiar with the writings of Homer in those days than would have been the case later on.

Here we have Carel Fabritius and the pharmacist and Spinoza, all immediately recognizing the name of the dog. Well, and not to mention Rembrandt himself, who chose it.

But for that matter doubtless Jan Vermeer would have recognized it just as quickly, once he in turn became a pupil of Carel Fabritius and Carel Fabritius was explaining about russet and bedspreads.

Well, and as would Leeuwenhoek and Galileo, doubtless, having been in Delft, too. Conversely if I had named my own russet cat Argus I am next to positive that not one solitary person I knew would have made the connection with Odysseus's dog at all.

As a matter of fact the only individual I can recall personally who ever did make this connection was Martin Heidegger.

I have perhaps said that badly.

In saying that I can personally recall Martin Heidegger having made this connection very likely what I have implied is that I once spoke with Martin Heidegger.

Martin Heidegger is not somebody I once spoke with.

As a matter of fact another implication in that same sentence would presumably be that I might have understood such a conversation if it had occurred.

Which I would not have, obviously, not speaking one word of German.

David Markson, Wittgenstein's Mistress

The traveller fared slowly on his way, who fared towards Paris from England in the autumn of the year one thousand seven hundred and ninety-two. More than enough of bad roads, bad equipages, and bad horses, he would have encountered to delay him, though the fallen and unfortunate King of France had been upon his throne in all his glory; but, the changed times were fraught with other obstacles than these. Every town-gate and village taxing-house had its band of citizen-patriots, with their national muskets in a most explosive state of readiness, who stopped all comers and goers, cross-**questioned** them, inspected their papers, looked for their names in lists of their own, turned them back, or sent them on, or stopped them and laid them in hold, as their capricious judgment or fancy deemed best.

Charles Dickens, A Tale of Two Cities

"Mr. O'Hare," he said in a grumbling baritone, "I'm Special Agent Casey, and my colleagues are Special Agent Buchanan—" he nodded to the blond man, who winked "—and Commander in Chief Samson." The old man glared at Prophet balefully, his blue eyes watery and unblinking. "I am hereby informing you that this conversation is being recorded. I am also informing you that anything you say may be used against you in a court of law. Similarly, your failure to respond to a given **question** may also be used against you."

"What about my right to remain silent?" asked Prophet, surprised.

Samson gave a wintry smile. "Not any more. Or haven't you heard of the New Deal?" His voice was as worn as his physique, an asthmatic whine that grated on Prophet's nerves like fingernails across a chalkboard.

"FDR," said Prophet, shrugging.

The smile elongated. "Wrong decade, my friend. I'm talking about the one passed three hours ago."

"Things are out of control," said Casey before Prophet could reply. He spoke wearily, conversationally, as if they were coffeehouse philosophers slumped over a nightcap. "They had to act quickly, keep it from getting worse."

"That's putting it mildly," said Samson, his smile receding, his upper lip curling almost to his nose, as if he'd just caught Prophet masturbating. "The fact is, Mr. O'Hare, we're at a unique juncture in this nation's history. The nature of our role in the world during the next century will be determined in the coming weeks and months, at a time when we have more criminals than civilians. As such, it gives me great pleasure to be sitting across this table from you. You are the epitome of what's gone wrong in this country, and we're going to talk about that for a while. By the time of the dawn's early light, we shall have taken a brief journey through history. And you, my friend—you will have confessed to everything."

Prophet was nonplussed. He'd expected direct **questioning**, not a sociological lecture. Samson continued to stare at him, his lip quivering, as if he saw the opportunity to close a long-fought vendetta. Prophet looked down, suddenly afraid. He'd meant to cooperate but dared not say a word. The old man frightened him.

"Mr. O'Hare," said Casey, "the charges brought against you are making terrorist threats, conspiracy to commit murder, and aggravated murder. We have an order for your extradition to face these charges in New York City, and you'll be on a plane later today. Until then I am informing you that counsel is unavailable; however, your cooperation with us in the meantime might benefit you in the long run. I am constrained to remind you that silence can be interpreted as an admission of guilt."

Todd Wiggins, Zeitgeist

No child can be well trained, who is not in the habit of committing to memory as much as this. Parents should require their children to study the text until they can repeat it fluently, without the least variation, before they look at the **questions**. This will promote a habit of quoting Scripture correctly; which is a matter of no small importance, as wrong impressions of the truth are often received from misquoting the Bible. After the text is thoroughly committed, the scholar should proceed to the examination of the **questions** for the purpose of obtaining answers. Many of the **questions** are answered by the text; some answers are given; some are left to the judgment of the scholar; and many others depend for their answers on the references. But the references themselves are not the answers: the latter are to be drawn from the former. To repeat the reference, therefore, will not answer the **question**; the references must be studied, and the answers given by the scholar in his own language. If any other course is pursued, the design of teaching the scholars to *think* will be defeated.

*Harvey Newcomb, Newcomb's First **Question** Book*

"**Question!**" boomed a voice from the platform.

Mr. Waldron was a strict disciplinarian with a gift of acid humor, as exemplified upon the gentleman with the red tie, which made it perilous to interrupt him. But this interjection appeared to him so absurd that he was at a loss how to deal with it. So looks the Shakespearean who is confronted by a rancid Baconian, or the astronomer who is assailed by a flat-earth fanatic. He paused for a moment, and then, raising his voice, repeated slowly the words: "Which were extinct before the coming of man."

"**Question!**" boomed the voice once more.

Waldron looked with amazement along the line of professors upon the platform until his eyes fell upon the figure of Challenger, who leaned back in his chair with closed eyes and an amused expression, as if he were smiling in his sleep.

"I see!" said Waldron, with a shrug. "It is my friend Professor Challenger," and amid laughter he renewed his lecture as if this was a final explanation and no more need be said.

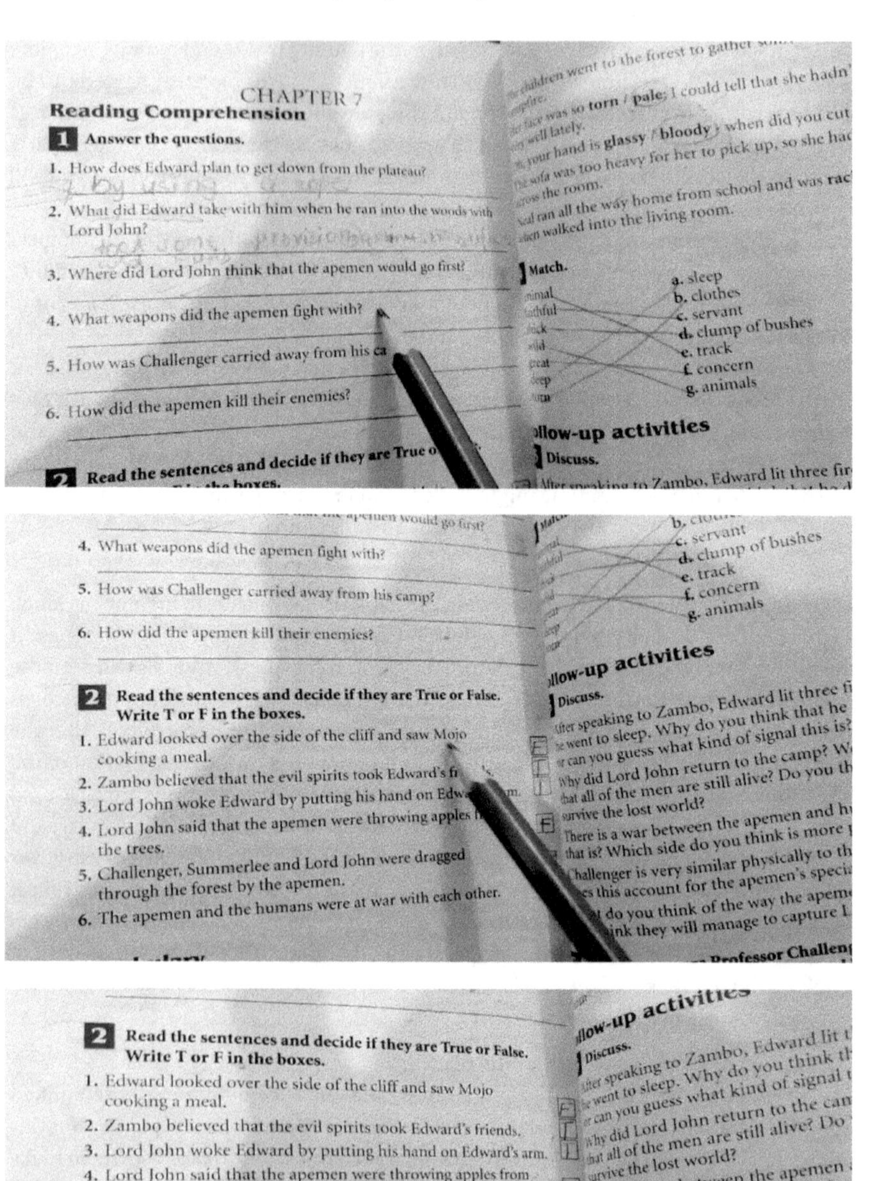

Asmara Javed Learning Excel, The Lost World (jurassic park) by Arthur Conan Doyle solved exercise chapter no. 3 (youtube.com)

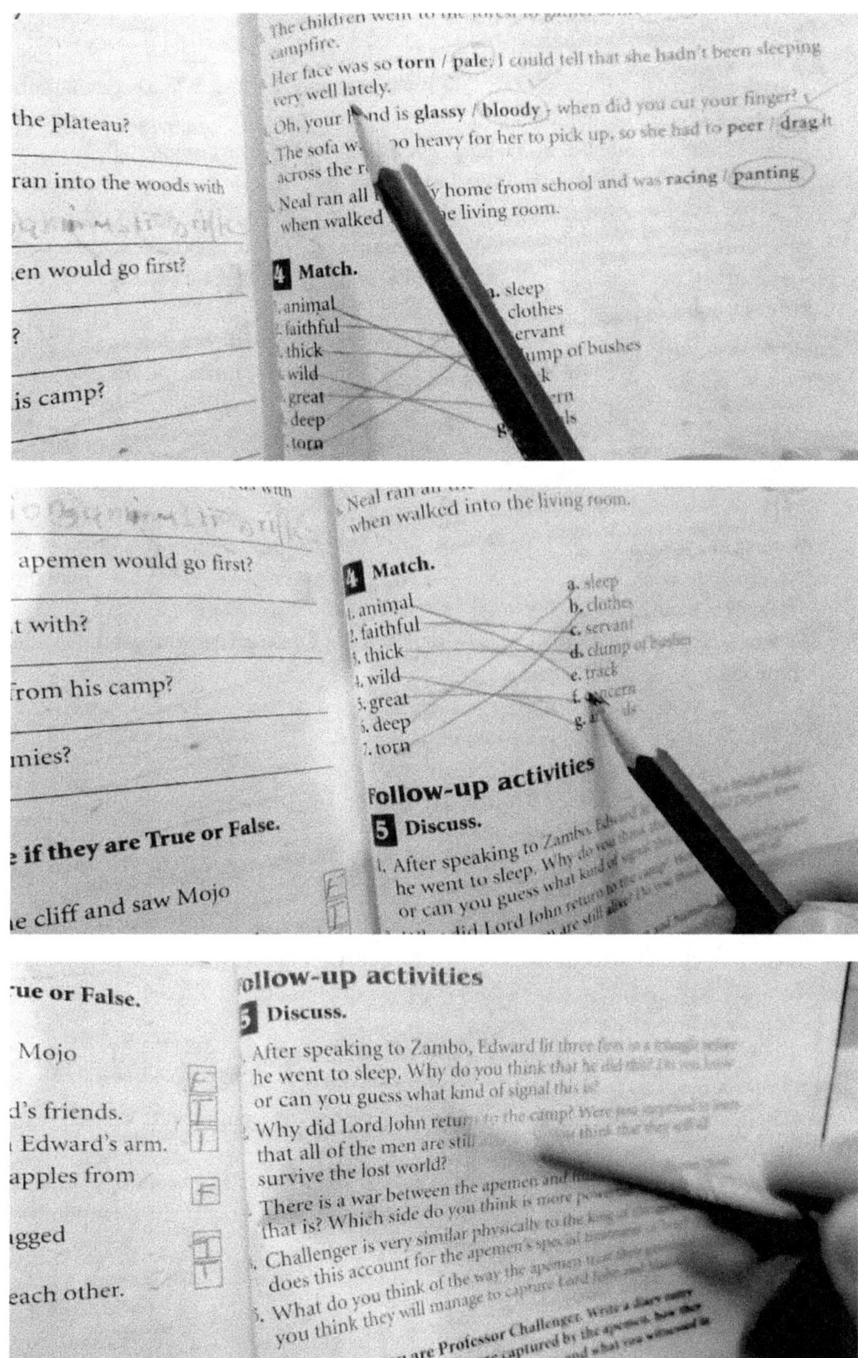

Asmara Javed Learning Excel, The Lost World (jurassic park) by Arthur Conan Doyle solved exercise chapter no. 3 (youtube.com)

But the incident was far from being closed. Whatever path the lecturer took amid the wilds of the past seemed invariably to lead him to some assertion as to extinct or prehistoric life which instantly brought the same bulls' bellow from the Professor. The audience began to anticipate it and to roar with delight when it came. The packed benches of students joined in, and every time Challenger's beard opened, before any sound could come forth, there was a yell of "**Question**!" from a hundred voices, and an answering counter cry of "Order!" and "Shame!" from as many more. Waldron, though a hardened lecturer and a strong man, became rattled. He hesitated, stammered, repeated himself, got snarled in a long sentence, and finally turned furiously upon the cause of his troubles.

"This is really intolerable!" he cried, glaring across the platform. "I must ask you, Professor Challenger, to cease these ignorant and unmannerly interruptions."

Arthur Conan Doyle, The Lost World

We are weary of academic conferences.

We are humanists who recognize very little humanity in the conference format and content.

We have sat patiently and politely through talks read line by line in a monotone voice by a speaker who doesn't look up once, wondering why we couldn't have read the paper ourselves in advance with a much greater level of absorption.

We have tried to ignore the lack of a thesis or even one interesting sentence in a 20-minute talk.

Our jaws have hung in disbelief as a speaker tries to squeeze a 30-minute talk into a 20-minute slot by reading too fast to be understood.

We have been one of two attendees at a panel.

We have suffered in silence while someone, for the duration of their talk, simply lists the appearances of a certain theme in a novel.

Our faces have twitched as our colleagues pretend they've understood a speaker's academese.

We have listened for the first five minutes of the talk, just long enough to seize upon a word around which we'll construct a pseudo-**question** in the **Q**. and A.

We have asked a panelist if they could "talk a little bit more about that" or "unpack this a little more" or "tease that out some."

We have listened as colleagues ask **questions** related to their own research but that have no relevance to anyone but themselves.

We have passed or received notes during a particularly painful session that read "Kill me now."

We have created a taxonomy in our minds of the various conference types: the contrarian, the entertainer, the wall flower, the theory head, the name dropper, the conformist, the adviser carbon-copy, the philosophy dude.

We have filled our notebooks with doodles and answered unimportant emails during a panel as we sat in the audience.

We've picked at our fingernails and counted the empty chairs in the room.

At national conferences, we have attended only our own talk and spent the rest of the weekend at the pool bar, where more can be learned about the liberal arts somehow.

We have had the idea to patent a conference bingo game in which the players in the audience receive cards printed with a grid of various conference vocabulary words to be collected during the panels—"subsemantic," "dialectic," "normativity," "mytho-poetic," the adjectivization of a philosopher's name (Meillassouxian, Cixousian), "post-"anything.

We have daydreamed that, à la vaudeville, a giant cane would emerge from the wings and pull away the droning speaker from the lectern.

We have wondered, "If this is what the humanities have become, should they continue to exist?"

Academic conferences are a habit from the past, embraced by the administrati-versity as a way to showcase knowledge and to increase productivity in the form of published conference proceedings. We have been complicit. Until now.

We believe it is time to ask ourselves: What is the purpose of the conference? What has caused us to organize these things year after year without **questioning** their basis? Is there another way to reformat the conference or do away with it altogether, replacing it with something more intellectually, professionally and socially satisfying for everyone? What are our real motivations for organizing a conference? For attending one? To burnish our résumés? To network? To get a sense of the current work being done in our fields?

Christy Wampole, *The Conference Manifesto (The New York Times)*

The **question** was: Why was God permitting this evil? While I was in a Bible conference in the East several years ago, I talked with two young professors, one from Vanderbilt University and the other from Missouri. They both were Christians and brilliant young men. They told me that the godless professors would use this method to try to destroy young people's faith in the integrity of the Word of God. They would begin like this: "You do not believe that a God of love would permit evil in the world, do you? Do you think a loving God, kind in heart, would permit suffering in the world?"

J. Vernon McGee, *Thru the Bible With J. Vernon Mcgee: Genesis Through Revelation*

So interesting and exciting, however, did this **question** prove, that after the debate had been continued three evenings, during which the Rev. Messrs. Hughes, M'Calla, and Breckinridge, Honorary Members of the Society, were the principal speakers, arrange-ments were made, by a Committee of the Society, for a continuance of the discussion, between the Rev. Messrs. Hughes and Breckinridge, for six evenings. It was further agreed, that at the expiration of the six evenings, the word "Presbyterian" should be substituted for the words " Roman Catholic," and an equal portion of time should be devoted to the new **question**.

John Hughes and John Breckinridge, *A Discussion of the* **Question***, Is the Roman Catholic Religion, in Any or in All Its Principles or Doctrines, Inimical to Civil or Religious Liberty? And of the* **Question***, Is the Presbyterian Religion, in Any or in All Its Principles or Doctrines, Inimical to Civil or Religious Liberty?*

We don't expect the conference system to change any time soon. In the meantime, we humbly submit the following contract, which you may distribute in advance to speakers at your next conference. Acceptance to the conference could be contingent upon the speaker reading and signing an agreement to meet the following criteria in their talks:

1) I understand that the conference paper should do something that an article cannot. Since it involves direct, real-time contact with other humans, the speaker should

make use of this relatively rare and thus precious opportunity to interact meaningfully with other scholars.

2) I will not read my paper line by line in a monotone without looking at the audience. I needn't necessarily abide by some entertainment imperative, with jokes, anecdotes or flashy slides, but I will strive to maintain a certain compassion toward my captive audience.

3) I understand that a list is not a talk. I will not simply list appearances of a theme in a given corpus.

4) I will have a thesis, and if I don't, I will at least have a reason that my talk should exist.

5) I will keep direct citations to a minimum, not relying on them to fill up time. I understand that audience members shudder at lengthy blocks of text in the PowerPoint or on the handout.

6) In the **Q.** and A., I will not ask an irrelevant **question** for the sake of being seen asking a **question**. If my **question** is hyperspecific and meaningless to anyone but myself, I will approach the speaker after the talk with my query.

7) I will not make a statement and then put a **question** mark at the end to make it sound like a **question**.

8) If I ask an actual **question**, I will a) not take more than a minute or so to ask it, and b) ask it politely even if I disagree with the speaker.

9) I respect the time of my colleagues who've come to hear me speak. I will do my best to be as clear and succinct as possible, and make their attendance worthwhile.

10) I understand that if I disregard these recommendations, I might be complicit in the death of the humanities.

> Christy Wampole, *The Conference Manifesto (The New York Times)*

And in no case should a scholar be allowed to examine the references during recitation. If he has not studied them beforehand, he should be passed by, as unable to answer the **question**. The practice of permitting the scholars to look out their answers, either in the text or references, during recitation, cannot be too severely reprehended. It defeats every attempt to secure thorough preparation, and wastes the time appropriated to recitation, which is generally too short. If this practice is not abandoned, all hope of elevating the standard of Sabbath school instruction must be given up. It enables the scholars to go through the exercises of the Sabbath school without previous study; and thus encourages inattention and superficial attainments.

Notwithstanding all that has been said upon this subject, I have great reason to fear that the old practice of looking out references during recitation still prevails in many schools; yet, I repeat my solemn conviction that the continuance of this practice must, in a great measure, defeat every attempt to improve the system of Sabbath School instruction.

I ought to have said above, that the scholars should incorporate in their answers, such portions of the references as prove, illustrate, or enforce the subject.

> Harvey Newcomb, *Newcomb's First* **Question** *Book*

1.

Research has shown that ballads were produced by all of society
working as a team. They didn't just happen. There was no guesswork.

The people, then, knew what they wanted and how to get it.
We see the results in works as diverse as "Windsor Forest" and "The Wife of Usher's
    Well."

Working as a team, they didn't just happen. There was no guesswork.
The horns of elfland swing past, and in a few seconds
we see the results in works as diverse as "Windsor Forest" and "The Wife of Usher's
    Well,"
or, on a more modern note, in the finale of the Sibelius violin concerto.

The horns of elfland swing past, and in a few seconds
the world, as we know it, sinks into dementia, proving narrative passé,
or in the finale of the Sibelius violin concerto.
Not to worry, many hands are making work light again.

The world, as we know it, sinks into dementia, proving narrative passé.
In any case the ruling was long overdue.
Not to worry, many hands are making work light again,
so we stay indoors. The quest was only another adventure.

2.

In any case, the ruling was long overdue.
The people are beside themselves with rapture
so we stay indoors. The quest was only another adventure
and the solution problematic, at any rate far off in the future.

The people are beside themselves with rapture
yet no one thinks to **question** the source of so much collective euphoria,
and the solution: problematic, at any rate far off in the future.
The saxophone wails, the martini glass is drained.

Yet no one thinks to **question** the source of so much collective euphoria.
In troubled times one looked to the shaman or priest for comfort and counsel.
The saxophone wails, the martini glass is drained,
and night like black swansdown settles on the city.

In troubled times one looked to the shaman or priest for comfort and counsel.
Now, only the willing are fated to receive death as a reward,
and night like black swansdown settles on the city.
If we tried to leave, would being naked help us?

3.

Now, only the willing are fated to receive death as a reward.
Children twist hula-hoops, imagining a door to the outside.
If we tried to leave, would being naked help us?
And what of older, lighter concerns? What of the river?

Children twist hula-hoops, imagining a door to the outside,
when all we think of is how much we can carry with us.
And what of older, lighter concerns? What of the river?
All the behemoths have filed through the maze of time.

When all we think of is how much we can carry with us
small wonder that those at home sit, nervous, by the unlit grate.
All the behemoths have filed through the maze of time.
It remains for us to come to terms with *our* commonality.

Small wonder that those at home sit nervous by the unlit grate.
It was their choice, after all, that spurred us to feats of the imagination.
It remains for us to come to terms with our commonality
and in so doing deprive time of further hostages.

John Ashbery, Hotel Lautréamont

One day a shadow falls across me where I doze in the yard, a foot prods me, and I look up into Mandel's blue eyes.

"Are we feeding you well?" he says. "Are you growing fat again?"

I nod, sitting at his feet.

"Because we can't go on feeding you forever."

There is a long pause while we examine each other.

"When are you going to begin working for your keep?"

"I am a prisoner awaiting trial. Prisoners awaiting trial are not required to work for their keep. That is the law. They are maintained out of the public coffer."

"But you are not a prisoner. You are free to go as you please." He waits for me to take the ponderously offered bait. I say nothing. He goes on: "How can you be a prisoner when we have no record of you? Do you think we don't keep records? We have no record of you. So you must be a free man."

I rise and follow him across the yard to the gate. The guard hands him the key and he unlocks it. "You see? The gate is open."

I hesitate before I pass through. There is something I would like to know. I look into Mandel's face, at the clear eyes, windows of his soul, at the mouth from which his spirit utters itself.

"Have you a minute to spare?" I say. We stand in the gateway, with the guard in the background pretending not to hear. I say: "I am not a young man any more, and whatever future I had in this place is in ruins." I gesture around the square, at the dust that scuds before the hot late summer wind, bringer of blights and plagues. "Also I have already died one death, on that tree, only you decided to save me. So there is something I would like to know before I go. If it is not too late, with the barbarian at the gate." I feel the tiniest smile of mockery brush my lips, I cannot help it. I glance up at the empty sky. "Forgive me if the **question** seems impudent, but I would like to ask: How do you find it possible to eat afterwards, after you have been . . . working with people? That is a **question** I have always asked myself about executioners and other such people. Wait! Listen to me a moment longer, I am sincere, it has cost me a great deal to come out with this, since I am terrified of you, I need not tell you that, I am sure you are aware of it. Do you find it easy to take food afterwards? I have imagined that one would want to wash one's hands. But no ordinary washing would be enough, one would require priestly intervention, a ceremonial of cleansing, don't you think? Some kind of purging of one's soul too—that is how I have imagined it. Otherwise how would it be possible to return to everyday life—to sit down at table, for instance, and break bread with one's family or one's comrades?"

He turns away, but with a slow claw-like hand I manage to catch his arm. "No, listen!" I say. "Do not misunderstand me, I am not blaming you or accusing you, I am long past that. Remember, I too have devoted a life to the law, I know its processes, I know that the workings of justice are often obscure. I am only trying to understand. I am trying to understand the zone in which you live. I am trying to imagine how you breathe and eat and live from day to day. But I cannot! That is what troubles me! If I were he, I say to myself, my hands would feel so dirty that it would choke me—"

He wrenches himself free and hits me so hard in the chest that I gasp and stumble backwards. "You bastard!" he shouts. "You fucking old lunatic! Get out! Go and die somewhere!"

"When are you going to put me on trial?" I shout at his retreating back. He pays no heed.

There is nowhere to hide. And why should I? From dawn to dusk I am on view on the square, roaming around the stalls or sitting in the shade of the trees. And gradually as word gets around that the old Magistrate has taken his knocks and come through, people cease to fall silent or turn their backs when I come near. I discover that I am not without friends, particularly among women, who can barely conceal their eagerness to hear my side of the story.

J. M. Coetzee, *Waiting for the Barbarians*

The other day I asked the following **question** in the comments section to the entry "What Ever Happened to Scholarly Conversation?"

"The democratization of higher education (the enormous expansion, the opening up of the university to women and minorities both as students and, to a lesser extent, as faculty members) pretty much coincides with the trend toward corporatization. Is the commodification of education the price we must pay for its democratization? I don't think there is a necessary and inevitable link, and yet I can't help wondering whether there isn't some sort of link? This puzzles and troubles me."

(Wow! Talk about a me-zine. Yes, this is a "vanity site." I'm just going to keep linking back and forth to my own entries and comments.)

Invisible Adjunct, *Where the Adjuncts Have Equal Status (invisibleadjunct.com)*

Now, Mr. Feeble-mind, when they were going out of the door, made as if he intended to linger. The which when Mr. Great-heart espied, he said, "Come, Mr. Feeble-mind, pray do you go along with us: I will be your conductor, and you shall fare as the rest."

FEEBLE. Alas! I want a suitable companion. You are all lusty and strong, but I, as you see, am weak; I choose, therefore, rather to come behind, lest, by reason of my many weaknesses, I should be both a burden to myself and to you. I am, as I said, a man of a weak and feeble mind, and shall be injured and made weak at that which others can bear. I shall like no laughing; I shall like no gay attire; I shall like no unprofitable **questions**. Nay, I am so weak a man as to be harmed with that which others have a liberty to do. I do not yet know all the truth; I am a very ignorant Christian man. Sometimes, if I hear any rejoice in the Lord, it troubles me, because I cannot do so too. It is with me as it is with a weak man among the strong, or as with a sick man among the healthy, or as a lamp despised. "He that is ready to slip with his feet is as a lamp despised in the thought of him that is at ease;" so that I know not what to do.

GREAT. "But, brother," said Mr. Great-heart, "I have it in my work to comfort the feeble-minded and to support the weak. You must needs go along with us: we will wait for you; we will lend you our help; we will deny ourselves of some things, for your sake; we will not enter into doubtful **questions** before you! we will be made all things to you, rather than you shall be left behind."

John Bunyan, The Pilgrim's Progress

Forgive us, Father, for we know not.

There are stars and faces.
There is ketchup and guitars.
There is the hand of a small child
when you're crossing the street.
There is the old man's last words:
More light! More light!
Ms. Dog wouldn't give them her buttocks.
She wouldn't moon at them.
Just at the killers of the dream.
The bus boys of the soul.
Or at death
who wants to make her a mummy.
And you too!
Wants to stuff her in a cold shoe
and then amputate the foot.
And you too!
La de dah.
What's the point of fighting the dollars
when all you need is a warm bed?
When the dog barks you let him in.
All we need is someone to let us in.
And one other thing:
to consider the lilies in the field.
Of course earth is a stranger, we pull at its
arms and still it won't speak.
The sea is worse.
It comes in, falling to its knees
but we can't translate the language.
It is only known that they are here to worship,
to worship the terror of the rain,
the mud and all its people,
the body itself,
working like a city,
the night and its slow blood
the autumn sky, Mary blue.
But more than that,
to worship the **question** itself,
though the buildings burn

and the big people topple over in a faint.
Bring a flashlight, Ms. Dog,
and look in every corner of the brain
and ask and ask and ask
until the kingdom,
however queer,
will come.

Anne Sexton, Hurry Up Please It's Time (The Death Notebooks)

Doughty understands the appeal of Staab-Polk's model. "People are afraid of death," she said. "Do you want to go sit with the corpse or do you want to party? If you put it like that, it's not a very hard **question**."

Rebecca Mead, Our Bodies, Ourselves (The New Yorker)

To kill oneself—I beg the pardon of those who have killed themselves—to kill oneself, for me, nevertheless means just that. I do not believe in my power. I am a man who does not hold the key to a door that does not exist. Life is a fact and as such, it is indisputable. What exactly do you mean then when you ask me why I am still alive?

To depart, to travel, to escape, to kill oneself: infinitives that appear obvious. Set against these leitmotivs are verbs conjugated in personal tenses, in derived tenses. In both cases, it is still a **question** of *paradise*. All those marvelous solutions to problems never posed or from time to time reduced to miserable truisms are in fact absolutely identical. Opinions differ only about the precise geographic location of paradise. The Jews' paradise—which did not extend beyond the Euphrates—seems piddling to nomads of the Jack London-Blaise Cendrars type. Paradise for Christians is a prayer-stool, Bernadette-style; for Thomas de Quincey it was the black stone of sleep. One must protest against the expression *artificial paradise*. It is a pleonasm. There are no natural paradises. The term has served its purpose, it was used to distort reality in order to appeal to fanatical savages. Today it can be stated plainly: religious paradises are simply ways of speaking about very specific erotic pleasures that do not always lead to ejaculation, without getting the police up in arms. I have something to say about religious practices.

Louis Aragon, Treatise on Style

"The burning silence will be followed by a loud asking of **questions** outside the Government Office," the organizers wrote, calling on the participants to wear face masks and keep at a two-meter distance from each other . . .

Czech News Agency, Czech Protest Movement to Demonstrate Against Government Handling of Coronavirus Crisis (Expats.cz)

If a short time ago that ultimate and universal source of reference, the person of average intelligence, had been asked concerning Modern Diabolism, or the **Question** of Lucifer,—What it is? Who are its disciples? Where is it practised? And why?—he would have replied, possibly with some asperity:—"The **question** of Lucifer! There is no **question** of Lucifer. Modern Diabolism! There is no modern Diabolism." And all the advanced people and all the strong minds would have extolled the average intelligence, whereupon the matter would have been closed hermetically, without disquieting and unwelcome investigations like the present.

"The offices of the company Thompson & Collins."
*O. E. Goebel (director, writer), The Burning **Question**, 1919*

The Great Teacher of Christianity beheld Lucifer fall from heaven like lightning, and, in a different sense, the modern world has witnessed a similar spectacle. Assuredly the demon of Milton has been cast down from the sky of theology, and, except in a few centres of extreme doctrinal concentration, there is no place found for him. The apostles of material philosophy have in a manner searched the universe, and have produced—well, the material philosophy, and therein is no **question** of Lucifer. At the opposite pole of thought there is, let us say, the spiritualist, in possession of many instruments superior, at least by the hypothesis, to the search-lights of science, through which he receives the messages of the spheres and establishes a partial acquaintance with an order which is not of this world; but in that order also there appears to be no **question** of Lucifer, though vexed **questions** there are without number concerning "unprogressed spirits," to say nothing of the elementary. Between these poles there is the flux and reflux of multitudinous opinions; but, except at the centres mentioned, there is still no **question** of Lucifer; it has been shelved or dropped.

The revival of mystical philosophy, and, moreover, of transcendental experiment, which is prosecuted in secret to a far greater extent than the public can possibly be aware, has, however, set many old oracles chattering, and they are more voluble at the present moment than the great Dodonian grove. As might be expected, they whisper occasionally of deeds done in the darkness which look weird when exposed to the day. The terms Satanism, Luciferianism, Diabolism, and their equivalents, have been buzzed frequently, though with some indistinctness, of late, and in accents that indicate the existence of a living terror—people do not quite know of what kind—rather than an exploded superstition. To be plain, the **Question** of Lucifer has reappeared, and in a manner which must be eminently disconcerting to the average intelligence and the advanced and strong in mind. It has reappeared not as a speculative inquiry into the possibility of a personal embodiment of evil operating mysteriously, but after a wholly spiritual manner, for the propagation of the second death; we are asked to acknowledge that there is a visible and tangible manifestation of the descending hierarchy taking place at the close of a century which has denied that there is any prince of darkness.

Arthur Edward Waite, *Devil-Worship in France; or, the **Question** of Lucifer; a Record of Things Seen and Heard in the Secret Societies According to the Evidence of Initiates*

(Cries of "Bosh!" "Prove it!" "How do YOU know?" "**Question!**") "How do I know, you ask me? I know because I have visited their secret haunts. I know because I have seen some of them." (Applause, uproar, and a voice, "Liar!") "Am I a liar?" (General hearty and noisy assent.) "Did I hear someone say that I was a liar? Will the person who called me a liar kindly stand up that I may know him?" (A voice, "Here he is, sir!" and an inoffensive little person in spectacles, struggling violently, was held up among a group of students.) "Did you venture to call me a liar?" ("No, sir, no!" shouted the accused, and disappeared like a jack-in-the-box.) "If any person in this hall dares to doubt my veracity, I shall be glad to have a few words with him after the lecture." ("Liar!") "Who said that?" (Again the inoffensive one plunging desperately, was elevated high into the air.) "If I come down among you—" (General chorus of "Come, love, come!" which interrupted the proceedings for some moments, while the chairman, standing up and waving both his arms, seemed to be conducting the music. The Professor, with his face flushed, his nostrils dilated, and his beard bristling, was now in a proper Berserk mood.) "Every great discoverer has been met with the same incredulity—the sure

"Jimmy Ryan, an ambitious, mischievous, but faithful young man."
O. E. Goebel (director, writer), *The Burning Question*, 1919

brand of a generation of fools. When great facts are laid before you, you have not the intuition, the imagination which would help you to understand them. You can only throw mud at the men who have risked their lives to open new fields to science. You persecute the prophets! Galileo! Darwin, and I—" (Prolonged cheering and complete interruption.)

All this is from my hurried notes taken at the time, which give little notion of the absolute chaos to which the assembly had by this time been reduced. So terrific was the uproar that several ladies had already beaten a hurried retreat. Grave and reverend seniors seemed to have caught the prevailing spirit as badly as the students, and I saw white-bearded men rising and shaking their fists at the obdurate Professor. The whole great audience seethed and simmered like a boiling pot. The Professor took a step forward and raised both his hands. There was something so big and arresting and virile in the man that the clatter and shouting died gradually away before his commanding gesture and his masterful eyes. He seemed to have a definite message. They hushed to hear it.

"I will not detain you," he said. "It is not worth it. Truth is truth, and the noise of a number of foolish young men—and, I fear I must add, of their equally foolish seniors—cannot affect the matter. I claim that I have opened a new field of science. You dispute it." (Cheers.) "Then I put you to the test. Will you accredit one or more of your own number to go out as your representatives and test my statement in your name?"

Arthur Conan Doyle, The Lost World

Trudeau shows up wearing pants. (Contrary to expectations.) In the very first debate, long ago and far away, Thomas Mulcair demanded Justin Trudeau's "number" for a Quebec separatist victory. Trudeau's response was halting and in his best prosecutorial **Question** Period style, Mulcair needled: "You're not answering, you haven't answered, what's your number Justin?" Suddenly 'Justin' shifted into another register: "You want a number?" he barked. "Nine!" It was fairly electric, no one at home or on set knew what he meant. Had he wigged out? Was he switching to German: Nein, I vill not answer your demeaning **qvestion!** "Nine," he went on, "the number of justices on the Supreme Court." And things settled back. That moment could have changed everything. It didn't, because, by Stephen Harper's terms for debates, almost no one was watching. But it was a hint, a Vorspeiss.

Rick Salutin, Three Memorable Election Moments—and One Fear (Toronto Star)

The Rhine Conference was not open to the public like Nature Protection Days. It was for professionals. Stephen and Birke worked hard every weekend to prepare. Sworn to present their work to an audience of experts, they had to figure out what it was. They had goals, partners, approaches, and a campaign—all the things you can have without actually having done anything—but they needed projects. *Wasserkraft Nein Danke* was not a project. It was a negation. The project to end all projects. When he got back, he made it sound as though he'd had five minutes to get ready and been dragged there by his hair. "Never again," he said.

"Who was there?"

"The usual suspects. The BMVBS, the WWF."

I waited for more information and finally said, "Were they not nice to you?"

"They paid no attention to me. It's like they can smell that I know nothing about

THE BURNING **QUESTION**

Captions are provided by our contributors. This image could have imperfections as it's either historical or reportage.

Alamy Stock Photo (alamy.com)

ecology or hydrology or engineering. Maybe if you're actually legit, you emit this phero-mone and they can smell it."

"Maybe you need scientist outfits, like functional microfiber outerwear."

"God, Tiff." he said. "You are so ignorant."

"I was kidding." I said.

"Yeah, right. So at the conference I keep asking these bright, intelligent **questions**, like I think an inquisitive amateur is what the world needs now. And they answer me with patience and fortitude like I'm a fucking four-year-old. Believe me, my suits are not the problem."

Nell Zink, The Wallcreeper

It was in some such mood, when wearied and fordone with these high speculations, that I first came upon the **question** of Clothes. Strange enough, it strikes me, is this same fact of there being Tailors and Tailored. The Horse I ride has his own whole fell: strip him of the girths and flaps and extraneous tags I have fastened round him, and the noble creature is his own sempster and weaver and spinner; nay his own boot-maker, jeweller, and man-milliner; he bounds free through the valleys, with a perennial rain-proof court-suit on his body; wherein warmth and easiness of fit have reached perfection; nay, the graces also have been considered, and frills and fringes, with gay variety of color, featly appended, and ever in the right place, are not wanting. While I—good Heaven!—have thatched myself over with the dead fleeces of sheep, the bark of vegetables, the entrails of worms, the hides of oxen or seals, the felt of furred beasts; and walk abroad a moving Rag-screen, overheaped with shreds and tatters raked from the Charnel-house of Nature, where they would have rotted, to rot on me more slowly! Day after day, I must thatch myself anew; day after day, this despicable thatch must lose some film of its thickness; some film of it, frayed away by tear and wear, must be brushed off into the Ashpit, into the Laystall; till by degrees the whole has been brushed thither, and I, the dust-making, patent Rat-grinder, get new material to grind down. O subter-brutish! vile! most vile! For have not I too a compact all-enclosing Skin, whiter or dingier? Am I a botched mass of tailors' and cobblers' shreds, then; or a tightly articulated, homo-geneous little Figure, automatic, nay alive?

Thomas Carlyle, Sartor Resartus: The Life and Opinions of Herr Teufelsdröckh

"You speak in riddles, learned Sir," said the pale minister, glancing aside out of the window.

"Then, to speak more plainly," continued the physician, "and I crave pardon, Sir,—should it seem to require pardon,—for this needful plainness of my speech. Let me ask,—as your friend,—as one having charge, under Providence, of your life and physical well-being,—hath all the operations of this disorder been fairly laid open and recounted to me?"

"How can you **question** it?" asked the minister. "Surely, it were child's play to call in a physician, and then hide the sore!"

"You would tell me, then, that I know all?" said Roger Chillingworth, deliberately, and fixing an eye, bright with intense and concentrated intelligence, on the minister's face. "Be it so! But, again! He to whom only the outward and physical evil is laid open knoweth, oftentimes, but half the evil which he is called upon to cure.

Nathaniel Hawthorne, The Scarlet Letter

O. E. Goebel (director, writer), *The Burning Question*, 1919

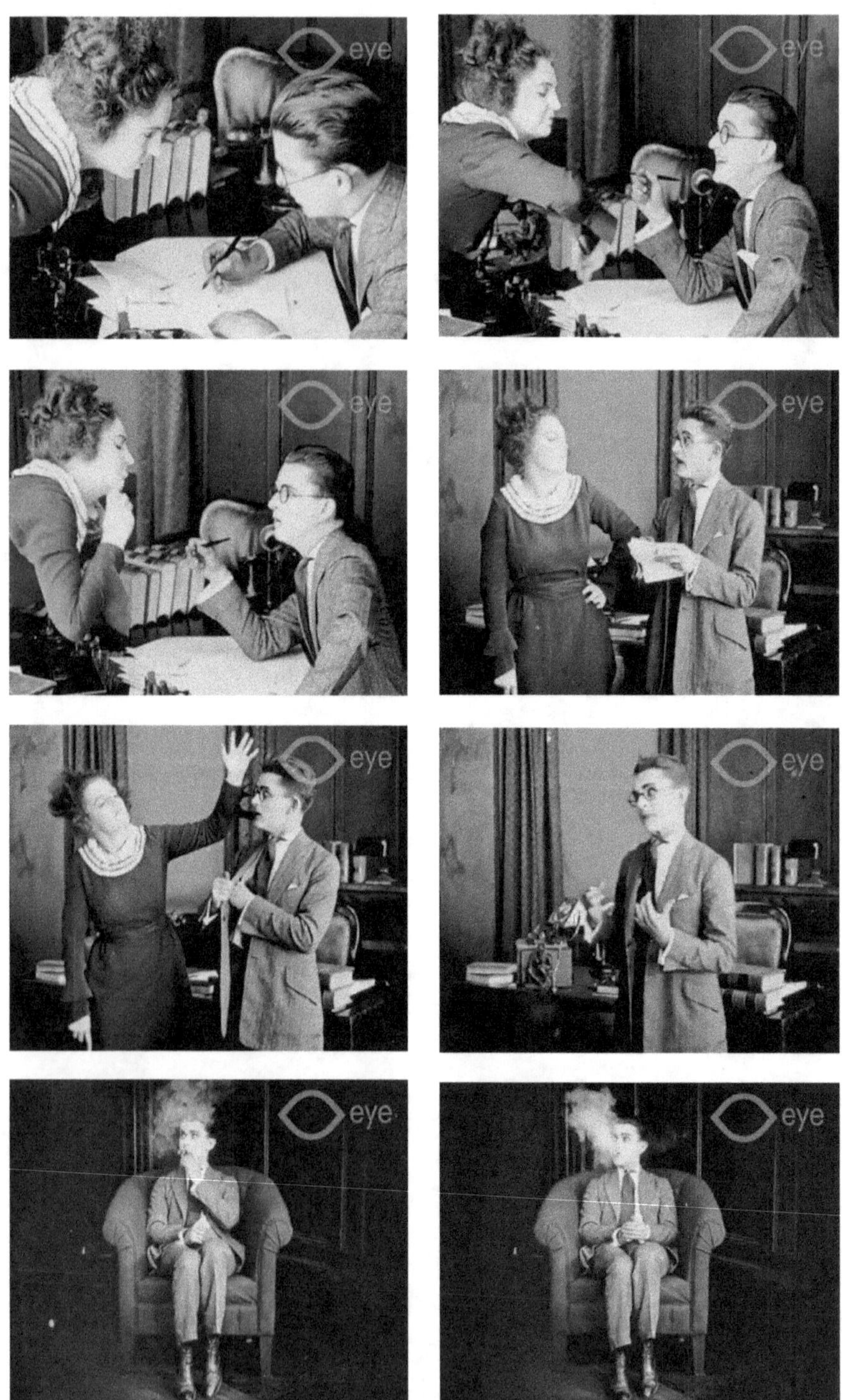

O. E. Goebel (director, writer), The Burning **Question**, *1919*

It is well known that the Fraternity makes use of mystic numbers and other symbols. Take, therefore, any mystic number, or combination of numbers, as e.g., 3 × 3 = 9. You will probably be unacquainted with the meaning which attaches to the figure of the product, but it will occur to you that the 9 of spades is regarded as the disappointment in cartomancy. Begin, therefore, by confidently expecting something bad. Reflect upon the fact that cards have been occasionally denominated the Devil's Books. Conclude thence that Freemasonry is the Devil's Institution. Do not be misled by the objection that there is no traceable connection between cards and Masonry; anticipate an occult connection or secret liaison. The term last used has probably occurred to you by the will of God; do not forget that it describes a **questionable** sexual relationship.

*Arthur Edward Waite, Devil-Worship in France; or, the **Question** of Lucifer; a Record of Things Seen and Heard in the Secret Societies According to the Evidence of Initiates*

"We'd do it while we were here?"

"Yes."

"Want to?" I asked. "It's no go if you don't."

"Do I want to?" She stood still in the road, facing me. "I'd give—" A sob ended that sentence. Her voice came again, high-pitched, thin: "Are you being honest with me? Are you? Is what you've told me—all you told me last night and this afternoon—as true as you made it sound? Do I believe in you because you're sincere? Or because you've learned how—as a trick of your business—to make people believe in you?"

She might have been crazy, but she wasn't so stupid. I gave her the answer that seemed best at the time:

"Your belief in me is built on mine in you. If mine's unjustified, so is yours. So let me ask you a **question** first: were you lying when you said, 'I don't want to be evil'?"

Dashiell Hammett, The Dain Curse

What is Deresiewicz's 6-Part answer?

What nine things do you learn?

List three examples of admissions codes and their meanings.

What does Deresiewicz mean by "the system"?

*Diana Austin, Excellent Sheep: Close Reading **Questions** (Allen Independent School District)*

Writing the words *L'Empereur Napoleon* in numbers, it appears that the sum of them is 666, and that Napoleon was therefore the beast foretold in the Apocalypse. Moreover, by applying the same system to the words *quarante-deux*, which was the term allowed to the beast that "spoke great things and blasphemies," the same number 666 was obtained; from which it followed that the limit fixed for Napoleon's power had come in the year 1812 when the French emperor was forty-two. This prophecy pleased Pierre very much and he often asked himself what would put an end to the power of the beast, that is, of Napoleon, and tried by the same system of using letters as numbers and adding them up, to find an answer to the **question** that engrossed him. He wrote the words *L'Empereur Alexandre, La nation russe* and added up their numbers, but the sums were either more or less than 666. Once when making such calculations he wrote down his own name in French, Comte Pierre Besouhoff, but the sum of the numbers did not come right. Then he changed the spelling, substituting a *z* for the *s* and adding *de* and the article *le*, still without obtaining the desired result. Then it occurred to him: if the answer to the **question** were contained in his name, his nationality would also be given in the answer.

So he wrote *Le russe Besuhof* and adding up the numbers got 671. This was only five too much, and five was represented by *e*, the very letter elided from the article *le* before the word *Empereur*. By omitting the *e*, though incorrectly, Pierre got the answer he sought. *L'russe Besuhof* made 666. This discovery excited him. How, or by what means, he was connected with the great event foretold in the Apocalypse he did not know, but he did not doubt that connection for a moment. His love for Natasha, Antichrist, Napoleon, the invasion, the comet, 666, *L'Empereur Napoleon*, and *L'russe Besuhof*—all this had to mature and culminate, to lift him out of that spellbound, petty sphere of Moscow habits in which he felt himself held captive and lead him to a great achievement and great happiness.

Leo Tolstoy, War and Peace

In like manner, concerning the existence of Satanic associations, and especially the Palladium, M. Huysman admittedly derives his knowledge from published sources. We may take it, therefore, that he speaks from an accidental and extrinsic acquaintance, and he is therefore insufficient in himself to create a **question** of Satanism; he indicates rather than establishes that there is a **question**, and to learn its scope and nature we must have recourse to the witnesses who claim to have seen for themselves. These are of two kinds, namely, the spy and the seceder—the witness who claims to have investigated the subject at first hand with a view to its exposure, and those who have come forward to say that they once were worshippers of Lucifer, worshippers of Satan, operators of Black Magic, or were at least connected with associations which exist for these purposes, who have now, however, suspended communication, and are stating what they know.

Arthur Edward Waite, Devil-Worship in France; or, the **Question** of Lucifer; a Record of Things Seen and Heard in the Secret Societies According to the Evidence of Initiates

As kooky as all this may sound (and it sounds extremely kooky), such things were fervently believed by some powerful people in the Nazi Party—so much so that huge sums of money were invested into research, along with hundreds of workers and scientists. Michael Kater, a professor who publishes extensively on Nazi Germany and who penned a book on the Ahnenerbe, underscores that the occult obsession was limited primarily to a few individuals, albeit individuals with a great deal of power. "Apart from Himmler and the Ahnenerbe, there is not a shred of evidence that 'intellectuals' or culture brokers of the Third Reich would have been concerned with this **question** (of the dead, the zombies, or the occult, for that matter)." But because of the interest from Hitler and Himmler, above all—and, frankly, the weirdness of some of their beliefs and practices—popular culture has latched onto this almost two-dimensional mad villainy and assigned it to Nazis in general. Which brings us to zombies.

Noah Charney, Did Nazis Really Try to Make Zombies? (Salon)

Zombie Sheep

A Card-Based Horror Parody Pursuit of Undead Livestock

Created by Casual Dragon Games

Zombie Sheep is a card game in which each player represents a specialized group, each with specific reasons for trying to capture Zombie Sheep. The player's goal is to catch these unique specimens before the other players do.

Questions about this project? Check out the **FAQ**

Looks like there aren't any **Frequently Asked Questions** yet. Ask the project creator directly.

Casual Dragon Games, Zombie Sheep (Kickstarter.com)

What are the descriptors Deresiewicz employs to characterize elite students as "sheep"?
What makes the system work?
So what then does the "glittering system of elite higher education" do?

*Diana Austin, Excellent Sheep: Close Reading **Questions** (Allen Independent School District)*

The wait has been long, but the discipline of neuroscience has finally delivered a full-length treatment of the zombie phenomenon. In their book, *Do Zombies Dream of Undead Sheep?*, scientists Timothy Verstynen and Bradley Voytek cover just about everything you might want to know about the brains of the undead. And if you learn some serious neuroscience along the way, well, that's fine with them too. Voytek answered **questions** from *Mind Matters* editor Gareth Cook.

How is it that you and your coauthor came to write a book about zombies? Clearly it is an urgent public health threat, but I would not have expected a book from neuroscientists on the topic.

Indeed! You think you're prepared for the zombie apocalypse and then—BAM!—it happens, and only then do you realize how poorly prepared you really were. Truly the global concern of our time.

Gareth Cook, A True and Complete Account of the Neuroscience of Zombies (Scientific American)

Entwined with his *j'accuse* is an impassioned, idealistic plea to reclaim the undergraduate years as a journey of self-discovery guided by engaged professors who challenge students to think for themselves instead of following the flock to Wall Street. Deresiewicz's critique of America's most celebrated schools as temples of mercenary mediocrity is lucid, sharp-edged, and searching . . . He poses vital **questions** about what college teaches—and why.

—*Publisher's Weekly*

billderesiewicz.com, Acclaim for Excellent Sheep

We start with the obvious stuff: why do zombies move with such a slow, unsteady gait? Why can't they talk? Do they feel pain? We use those obvious **questions** as stepping stones toward what we hope is a much more nuanced view of the modern neuroscientific understanding of how the three or so pounds of brain in your head can give rise to the complexities of the human experience.

Gareth Cook, A True and Complete Account of the Neuroscience of Zombies (Scientific American)

In this probing indictment, a former Yale professor accuses America's top universities of turning young people into tunnel-visioned careerists, adept at padding their résumés and filling their bank accounts but unprepared to confront life's most important **questions**. Craven conformity, not free-spirited independence, is what Deresiewicz sees students learning in a campus world populated by hyperspecialized professors who pursue arcane research agendas and leave the teaching of undergraduates to adjuncts and TAs. The time has come, Deresiewicz asserts, for college professors and administrators to make students their first priority by giving them a challenging liberal-arts education. Grounded in the humanities, such an education would give students real intellectual and imaginative breadth, not just a professional credential. Besides pressing for this curricular and pedagogical realignment, Deresiewicz calls for radical reform of admissions policies, so reversing the trends that make the university an enforcer of caste hierarchies. Deresiewicz's controversial full agenda indeed means an end to rule by meritocracy and a beginning of fairness for the working class. An urgent summons to a long-overdue debate over what universities do and how they do it.

    —Booklist (starred review)

billderesiewicz.com, Acclaim for Excellent Sheep

TALK. Then Talkative at first began to blush; but, recovering himself, thus he replied: "This kind of discourse I did not expect; nor am I disposed to give an answer to such **questions**, because I count not myself bound thereto, unless you take upon you to be a **questioner**; and though you should do so, yet I may refuse to make you my judge. But, I pray, will you tell me why you ask me such **questions**?"

FAITH. Because I saw you forward to talk, and because I knew not that you had aught else but notion. Besides, to tell you all the truth, I have heard of you that you are a man whose religion lies in talk, and that your life gives this your mouth-profession the lie. They say you are a spot among Christians, and that religion fareth the worse for your ungodly conduct; that some already have stumbled at your wicked ways, and that more are in danger of being destroyed thereby: your religion, and an alehouse, and greed for gain, and uncleanness, and swearing, and lying, and vain company-keeping, etc., will stand together. You are a shame to all who are members of the church.

John Bunyan, The Pilgrim's Progress

From the vague imputation Leo Taxil passed, however, to an exceedingly definite charge—and it is beyond all dispute that by his work entitled "Are there Women in Freemasonry?"—he has created the **Question** of Lucifer in its connection with the Palladian Order. He is the original source of information as to the existence of that association; no one had heard of it previously, and it is therefore of the first importance that we should know something of the discoverer himself, and everything as to the particulars of his discovery, including the date thereof.

*Arthur Edward Waite, Devil-Worship in France; or, the **Question** of Lucifer; a Record of Things Seen and Heard in the Secret Societies According to the Evidence of Initiates*

Can you please explain the title, Do Zombies Dream of Undead Sheep?

It's an homage to Philip K. Dick's beautiful book, *Do Androids Dream of Electric Sheep,* which was later adapted by Ridley Scott into the movie *Blade Runner,* with a phenomenal performance by Harrison Ford as Rick Deckard.

The story is complex, but in part it is about what it means to be human. Hence the book's title, which is an allusion to the **question** of consciousness in artificial intelligence. In our book we touch a bit on the **question** of whether zombies are conscious—whether they have that spark of self-awareness we associate with being human. This is a deep **question**—perhaps *the* **question**—in the philosophy of mind.

It's also a play, because in the philosophy of mind, there is a thought experiment that asks the reader to imagine a person, exactly like you or I or any other person in every conceivable way, except for the fact that they lack self-awareness/conscious-ness/sentience. This imaginary being is referred to as a "philosophical zombie", or a "p-zombie."

Gareth Cook, A True and Complete Account of the Neuroscience of Zombies (Scientific American)

To read books—especially Great Books understood to be part of "the tradition"—is part of this self-discovery. There is a "That's me!" moment of recognition that can happen, and often does happen, in the reading of a great novel, poem, or play—and it can happen, though less often and in a less direct way, in the reading of a great work of philosophy or religion. The Great Books reading Deresiewicz encourages addresses the perennial "Who am I?" **question** that is at the heart of the kind of self-discovery so important to college students.

But there is another version of the "Who am I?" **question** that points less to self-recognition than to critical reflection. Allan Bloom writes the following in his 1987 book *The Closing of the American Mind: How Higher Education has Failed Democracy and Impoverished the Souls of Today's Students*:

> Despite all the efforts to pervert it ... the **question** that every young person asks, "Who am I?," the powerful urge to follow the Delphic command, "Know thyself," which is born in each of us, means in the first place "What is man?" And in our chronic lack of certainty, this comes down to knowing the alternative answers and thinking about them. (p. 21)

A liberal education, in this reading, is less about the "Ah ha!" moment of discovery than it is about a sustained search—a sustained search, we might say, for the truth of things. But to say the "T" word—capitalized or not—is to open up the biggest and most controversial can of worms, and Deresiewicz, like most moderns, doesn't want to go there. Science and the Enlightenment, Deresiewicz has told us, should have taken care of any crazy notions we might have had about absolute truth.

The "What is man?" **question** can take us anywhere. Socrates spent his life discussing with other men and with himself opinions about what virtue is, what love is, what justice is, what piety is, and more—that is, Socrates spent his whole life trying to discover the "truth" about these things (See Bloom, 1987, p. 179). And that's what the "tradition" does, too. The "tradition" is nothing more or less than a sustained argument conducted by the best and clearest thinkers in our history about what is true about us, our lives, and our world. A liberal education in places that take this tradition seriously—places like the University of Chicago and St. John's College—is an initiation into these ideas and the manner of thinking about such things. What it isn't is an easy way into self-discovery that stops with moments of self-recognition.

Steven P. Jones and Sariah E. Roberts, Book Review: Excellent Sheep: The Miseducation of the American Elite and the Way to a Meaningful Life, by William Deresiewicz (Academy for Educational Studies)

It is here, I think, where the connection between Wittgenstein's life and his philosophy comes in. The metaphors of disease, therapy and bewitchment—and indeed his whole life itself—testify to a conception of philosophy as a struggle which should occupy your whole being. Wittgenstein lay awake at night, he reported to Russell, worrying about logic and his "sins". The combination of the moral and philosophical struggle was expressed in a letter to his friend Paul Engelmann as early as 1917: "I am working reasonably hard and I wish I were a better man and had a better mind. These two things are really one and the same.—God help me". On Wittgenstein's conception of how to philosophize, philosophy is something that at once seduces and repels, and the only real achievement in philosophy is to show how you no longer need it.

There is, of course, an alternative way of looking at things. On this alternative, philosophy is a systematic intellectual discipline; an impartial, dispassionate attempt to answer certain abstract **questions** which have arisen in the history of human thought in various forms, provoked by various kinds of speculation.

Tim Crane, Wittgenstein, Bewitched (The Times Literary Supplement)

What is The Suckage Factor?

What is the "Stanford Duck Syndrome"?

What is the "salmon run" and what force drives it? What name does a University of
    Michigan graduate give it?

*Diana Austin, Excellent Sheep: Close Reading **Questions** (Allen Independent School District)*

DoG: The obvious **question**—why sheep? Did you have a bad experience with a sheep at any point in your life? D'you think there are any other farmyard animals who are ripe for a horror movie makeover?

Sarah Dobbs, Black Sheep: Jonathan King Interview (Den of Geek!)

But the author consistently peels off in interesting directions. He speaks directly to students, giving this advice, for example, about cracking the mold while at college: "Don't talk to your parents more than once a week, or even better, once a month. Don't tell them about your grades on papers or tests, or anything else about how you're doing during the term." He concludes this litany this way: "Make it clear to them that this is your experience, not theirs."

(Note to my children: This is excellent advice. If you take it, I will kill you.)

He observes how Jewish kids like Norman Mailer, Saul Bellow, Susan Sontag, Woody Allen and Philip Roth were socialized academically and otherwise into American culture and "went on to take possession of it." He has similar hopes for Asian and Latino kids. "Telling them to stick to medicine or finance is just another way," he says, "of keeping those communities down."

I had problems with "Excellent Sheep." Even at 245 pages, it feels padded, especially with quotations from a thousand sources. I didn't skim pages, but I wanted to. It gets self-helpy. ("The only real grade is this: how well you've lived your life.") Mr. Deresiewicz is a hammering writer, one who could have taken advice from, say, Robert Hughes in his "Culture of Complaint" about nailing your points with saving wit.

There is also a "damned if you do, damned if you don't" quality at work. Even those who would sign on for two years with an organization like Teach for America he finds suspect. "You swoop down and rescue" the unfortunate "with your awesome wisdom and virtue," he intones. "You *do* acknowledge their existence, but in a fashion that maintains your sense of superiority—indeed, that reinforces it." This is tarring with a very fat roller indeed.

But Mr. Deresiewicz is rarely dull. He takes aim at smug, macchiatoed lives. "We can start all the organic farms we want, but we couldn't stop Congress from declaring pizza sauce a vegetable." Obsessing about the bad behavior of the "1 percent," he argues, is a way for the rest of the elite to "let themselves off the hook" about their way of being in the world.

"Excellent Sheep" is the sort of book that, by its nature, floats better **questions** than answers. It reminds you that, as Emerson said, sometimes a scream is better than a thesis.

Dwight Garner, The Lower Ambitions of Higher Education: 'Excellent Sheep,' William Deresiewicz's Manifesto (The New York Times)

Sometimes a *scream is better than a thesis* ~by Ralph Waldo . . . Sometimes a *scream is better than a thesis*. The Scream, Edvard Munch. The amount of it, to be sure, is merely a scream. April 19, 1838. This disaster of the Sometimes a *scream is better than a thesis.*—Ralph Waldo Emerson—'Sometimes a *scream is better than a thesis*. III. Letter to President Van Buren. Ralph Waldo Emerson. 1904. The . . . The amount of it, to be sure, is merely a scream; but sometimes a *scream is better than a thesis*. * * * * *. "Yesterday wrote the letter to Van Buren,—a letter hated Sometimes a *scream is better than a thesis.*—iz . . . Ralph Waldo Emerson quotes—Sometimes a *scream is better than a thesis*. Sometimes a *scream is better than a thesis.*— . . . "Sometimes a *scream is better than a thesis*."—Ralph Waldo Emerson. 10 wallpapers. Ralph Waldo Emerson Quote: "Sometimes a *scream is better than a* Sometimes a *scream is better than a thesis.*—AZ . . . Sometimes a *scream is better than a thesis.*—Ralph Waldo Emerson quotes at AZquotes. com.Why *SCREAM* 2 is *Better Than* People Are Willing to . . . 6 Feb 2017 One of the better horror sequels, *SCREAM* 2 takes aim at the Why *SCREAM* 2 is *Better Than* People Are Willing to Admit. I'm starting my Master's program doing a Creative *Thesis* option aside from the coursework. Art: The Museum of Emotions—NCBI—NIH20 May 2000 One card says "Scream here. other things, the quotation from Emerson on one of the walls: "Sometimes a *scream is better than a thesis*." Famous Quotes by Ralph Waldo Emerson—Institute of World . . . "If I cannot brag of knowing something, then I brag of not knowing it; at any rate, brag."—Ralph . . . Sometimes a *scream is better than a thesis*. [303] Last night the old **question** of miracles was broached again at the Teachers' meeting Let me never fall Ralph Waldo Emerson—Wikiquote I fancy I need more than another to speak (rather than write), with such a formidable tendency to the lapidary style. Sometimes a *scream is better than a thesis*. *Dissertation* Title—Stephen Wolthusen Sometimes a *scream is better than a thesis*. (Ralph Waldo Emerson) I, Stephen D. Wolthusen, hereby declare that this thesis and the work presented in it is Hundred Hours: Why an MBA *Thesis* is a Bad Idea | . . . 21 Jun 2013 Every now and then a student prefers to opt out of this end game As Manfred Eigen said—"Sometimes a *scream is better than a thesis*.". *Thesis* Quotes—BrainyQuote Thesis Quotes from BrainyQuote, an extensive collection of quotations by famous authors, celebrities, and Sometimes a *scream is better than a thesis*. What does *SCREAM* mean?—Definitions.net Definition of SCREAM in the Definitions.net dictionary. Meaning of SCREAM. What does Ralph Waldo Emerson: Sometimes a *scream is better than a thesis*. Famous Quotes—Cornell Astronomy "Sometimes a *scream is better than a thesis*."—Ralph "Well done is better than well said. Better by far to embrace the hard truth than a reassuring fable. *you're allowed to scream,* you're allowed to cry, . . . you're allowed to *scream,* you're allowed to cry, but do not give up. Sometimes I feel like giving up, then I remember I have a lot of motherfuckers to prove wrong. two beliefs: the future can be *better than* the present, and I have the power .*Scream* Quotes—BrainyQuote Scream Quotes from BrainyQuote, an extensive

855

collection of quotations by famous authors, celebrities, and Sometimes a *scream is better than a thesis*. How to Write a *Thesis* Statement—Support—EBSCO . . . 18 May 2016 Sometimes a *scream is better than a thesis.*—Ralph Waldo Emerson. A thesis statement is a sentence stating the specific idea or opinion you *Thesis* help. Technical writing training—She Cooks, She . . . 27 Jul 2017 Dissertation writing service by best UK professionals permits you to relax. Buy custom Sometimes a *scream is better than a thesis*. Get your Wes Craven's *Scream* opens with a self—contained . . . 4 Sep 2015 Before *Scream*, slashers slashed, killers killed, pretty young things ran up the stairs he made a horror movie *thesis* in the form of a horror movie, a sort of . . . I actually love *Scream* 4 too and think it was much *better than* Capitol Punishment Discography at DiscogsCapitol Punishment—Sometimes a *Scream Is Better Than a Thesis* 2:47. Capitol Punishment— Postman always shoot twice 4:37. Capitol Punishment—Ballad Of 'Excellent Sheep,' William Deresiewicz's . . . 12 Aug 2014 "Excellent Sheep" is likely to make more of a lasting mark than many of these . . . as Emerson said, sometimes a *scream is better than a thesis*. SENIOR MEDIA *THESIS: Scream*Queens is a . . . 2 Dec 2015 *Scream* Queens might just be the surprise of the television season. it is so much more than the trailers suggest and definitely *better than* the Theses—Marks Group PhD, Masters, and Undergraduate Theses. 2017. Tribology and Corrosion in CoCrMo Alloys and Similar Systems Emily E. Hoffman | Abstract | PDF The piece of *dissertation* wisdom that made me want to . . . 9 Feb 2012 The piece of *dissertation* wisdom that made me want to *scream* You are more *than* familiar with the concept of an all-nighter . . . to work while I'm away is a *better* incentive to meet my deadline *than* anything else I've found! "The *Scream*" Cutout Card—Cards—CALENDARS . . . Personalize your card with the enclosed sheet of Scream sticker quotes, including "Sometimes a *scream is better than a thesis*", Happy Anniversary, Good Luck! *Thesis* Gifts on ZazzleShop for the perfect thesis gift from our wide selection of designs, or create your own Sometimes A *Scream Is Better Than A Thesis* Emerson Letterhead. $1.05.MLS Event Archives | MLS—Massachusetts Library System13 Jun 2013 James G. Neal, V. P. for Information Services & University Librarian, Columbia University—Sometimes a *Scream . . . Is Better Than a Thesis*. "The *Scream*" by Edvard Munch—A Critical . . . 15 Jun 2016 The *Scream* (or The Cry as it is also known) by Edvard Munch has For humans, sight is our most important sense, far more developed *than* any other . . . I doubt that such a pain could ever make us feel *better*, but I know that Don't believe the hype: the French still live *better* . . . 4 May 2013 Don't believe the hype: the French still live *better than* Americans But I don't buy the *thesis* that the French are generally 'miserable', as Paris School on about Saint Obama and their 'Rêve Américain', I'm going to *scream*. 'Scream Queens' Series Premiere Recap: . . . 23 Sep 2015 How does one even recap a show like *Scream* Queens? of watching last night's crazily overstuffed two-hour pilot *better than* anything else. but it comes after the scene that functions as *Scream* Queens' *thesis* statement. *Understanding and expressing scalable concurrency— Max Planck . . .* present a clear and compelling case for why and how we would do better. His combination of "Sometimes a *scream is better than a thesis*."—Ralph Waldo Chair of Connected Mobility: Paper accepted at ACM Multimedia . . . 3 Jul 2017 We find that FCC performs *better than SCReAM* when competing against TCP background flows, i.e., it is able to obtain its "fair" share. In other Brilliance of Behind the Mask: The Rise of Leslie Vernon | The Mary . . . 25 Sep 2015 Or as I like to call it, "The Better Cabin in the Woods." working on their *thesis* project: a documentary film about killer—in—training Leslie

Vernon . . . Nightmare is *better than Scream* (Though I do have to admit I like the *Scream* Aphorisms Galore! » Categories: Wisdom and Ignorance Sometimes a *scream is better than a thesis*. shortage of qualified personnel in a particular field, then by the time you graduate with the necessary qualifications Brothers are *better than* sisters: A semiotic, feminist . . . Brothers are *Better than* Sisters: A Semiotic, Feminist Analysis of HBO's Rome. By Patricia Mamie By critiquing Rome, this *thesis* contributes to feminist scenes where brides cry, *scream*, and complain humanizes these characters and yet. Chasing the *Scream* by Johann Hari review—taking on the war . . . 9 Jan 2015 But what Chasing the *Scream* betrays is a little more complicated *than* the zero—sum stuff of truth and fiction. He took the very modern career The Narrative Guide to Kendrick Lamar's 'To Pimp a . . . 24 Mar 2015 If good kid, m.A.A.d city was like a motion picture, then To Pimp a Butterfly is elements of conceit and believing he's *better than* everyone else. How WES CRAVEN Revolutioned Modern, Meta Horror 8 Sep 2015 Looking at how Wes Craven's 'New Nightmare', 'Scream', and 'Cursed' it turns into one of the *better* Nightmare on Elm Street movies simply because of It honestly feels like a film *thesis* that keenly dissects the genre . . . that also that they are their movie personas, *then Scream* is about how to use those Why roller coasters make us *scream*—Washington . . . 1 Jul 2013 A look at the forces at work and why they make us *scream*. danger," said Rob Decker, who has collaborated on more *than* 30 roller coasters . . . of a *thesis* on roller coaster design presented to the American Physical Society; Lussy Sky *vs* Kuzya [tiebreaker 1v1] // .stance x . . . 15 Oct 2016 Lussy Sky *vs* Kuzya [tiebreaker 1v1] // .stance x UDEFtour.org // Silverback Open 2016 DJs: BlesOne, Fleg, Fox Boogie, LeanRock, *Scream* he dope, but not overpower, issei *better than* kuzya, kuzya win because in his home . Robin *Vs Thesis* | 1 V 1 Semi | Silverback Open 2016 | Pro Breaking Tour The *Scream* & Starry Night: Emotions, Symbol & . . . Keywords: Van Gogh, Edvard Munch, Starry Night, The *Scream*, oil paintings, life, death, human, symbols. "El grito" y . visualized impressionist drawings but also styles for expressing emotions rather *than* simply optical . . . *Thesis* chapter, pp.A Guide to 'A Series of Unfortunate Events' Book Series | . . . 4 Aug 2016 Why the Lemony Snicket series is *better than* Harry Potter. press escalating to a high-pitched *scream* and sales for The Cursed Child sending adults. In Count Olaf's character is the core *thesis* of Snicket's work—no one is *Scream* (franchise)—Wikipedia *Scream* is an American horror franchise created by Kevin Williamson and Wes Craven. Starring *Scream* 3 fared worse *than* its predecessors, both critically and financially, with critics commenting that it had become the . . . on The Craft which they believed help them *better* develop the relationship between Sidney and Billy. In the DOM, no one will hear you *scream*— . . . 18 Oct 2014 In the DOM, no one will hear you *scream* A journey into the moldy layer . . . Ruhr—Uni Bochum—PhD *Thesis* about Client Side Security and Defense slim but *better than* nothing After 4 years, finally something standard—like

Viewing 1 post (of 1 total)
You must be logged in to reply to this topic.

For those of you out there who are here because you take your news and politics seriously, let me preface this by admitting, yes, I am doing this on company time.

The latest internet craze (ask your kids) is the "screaming goat" video and with so many variations on the theme popping up, one could rightfully **question** how many of them are fake and how many are clever overdubs that actually had a person screaming and had the sound edited onto the video of a goat. I guess with this economy, many people have that much time on their hands.

Bob Parks, *Are the 'Screaming Goat' Videos Real? (CNSNews.com)*

If on the other hand you seek a critique of pure physics, a discussion concerning the metaphors from which a new physics may arise, and an alternative story of physics that does not rest upon extraordinary assumptions and extrapolations far beyond observed phenomenon; then this may be the book you seek.

Galileo Galilei suggests that:

*In **questions** of science the authority of a thousand is not worth the humble reasoning of a single individual.*

In Galileo's time "the authority of a thousand" was different than in our time. But in every age, "the humble reasoning of a single individual" has to contend with the authority of power. For pure physics in the 21st century, the authority of power rests within the subspecialties of physics itself. Perhaps my solitary logic will find a curious ear.

Thomas Neil Neubert, *A Critique of Pure Physics: Concerning the Metaphors of New Physics*

Trying to take a logical approach to this, my first **question** is: are these videos real?

For the most part, I believe many of them could be fakes as it takes a trained eye to see certain sync issues on some and trained ear to hear noticable audio dropouts prior to the "screaming" in others.

Also, as YouTube started in February of 2005 and is clearly the most popular public online video platform, if "screaming goats" were a normal occurrence, one would think we would have been done with this shrieking years ago instead of one obscure February day eight years later.

However with the addition of hormonal additives in the food of livestock nowadays, we could be looking at a mutant species, slowly developing a complex vocabulary, only now captured in its infancy thanks to the wonders of sophisticated digital video technology.

Bob Parks, *Are the 'Screaming Goat' Videos Real? (CNSNews.com)*

Before attempting to answer that **question**, I should first clarify what it means to be a subspecies as opposed to a species or population. From an ecological perspective, a population is a group of individuals of the same species that live together in the same place. The individuals interbreed, compete with each other for resources, and share the same geographic space. A species tends to be defined as an evolutionary lineage that is reproductively isolated from all other evolutionary lineages. Individuals of the same species can move between populations with little consequence to their ability to find a mate and reproduce. Individuals belonging to different species cannot mate. Or if they do, the offspring that are born either do not survive into adulthood or cannot have offspring themselves.

This species-as-reproductively-isolated-lineages concept, known as the biological species concept, was formally described by Ernst Mayr in 1942. The concept turns out to have some flaws. Specifically, some lineages that we strongly believe are separate species are not strictly reproductively isolated. Polar bears and brown bears, for example, are

Do Zombies Dream of Undead Sheep? | Tim Verstynen | Talks at Google (youtube.com)
Believe it or not, no one in Gertler's collection tackles this **question**.
R. Scott Bakker, *Do Zombies Dream of Undead Sheep? (Three Pound Brain)*

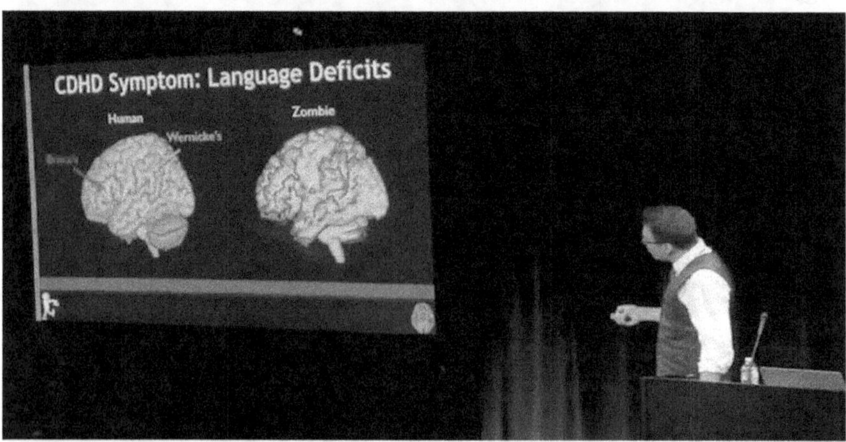

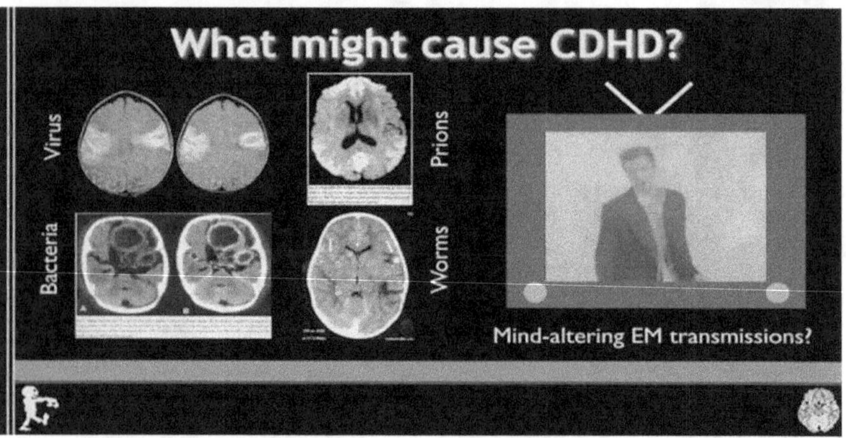

Do Zombies Dream of Undead Sheep? | Tim Verstynen | Talks at Google (youtube.com)

Dretske himself thinks his own **question** is ridiculous. He doesn't believe he's a zombie—he knows, in other words, that he possesses awareness. The **question** is *how* does he or anyone else know this.

R. Scott Bakker, Do Zombies Dream of Undead Sheep? (Three Pound Brain) commonly considered to be two different species. But bears born from crosses between brown bears and polar bears survive and can continue to mate and produce offspring. Dogs, wolves, and coyotes can and do interbreed frequently. Cows and bison and yaks can all interbreed and produce fertile offspring. And ancient DNA from Neandertal bones revealed that our species can (and did) mate with Neandertals and that, as a result of this hybridization, Neandertal genes survive in all living humans with Asian or European ancestry.

Why do biologists hold on to this confusing system? As humans, we are compelled to categorize. When we see chaos, we desire to transform that chaos into something ordered so that our brains can make sense of it. Clearly, evolution does not work in absolutes. An animal is not born one day as an entirely new species, incapable of reproducing with anyone in its parents' species. Instead, speciation is a long process involving many underlying genetic and behavioral changes. Populations become geographically isolated and evolve along independent trajectories. Eventually, enough changes will have evolved so that individuals are incapable of breeding between populations. As we see with brown bears and polar bears and with humans and Neandertals, however, what common sense would call species-level differences will sometimes evolve before the two lineages are completely reproductively isolated.

To impose order on the disorder that is biology, Carl Linnaeus, an eighteenth-century Swedish biologist and physician, devised a taxonomic system to describe and categorize all forms of life. His system provides a hierarchical classification of everything according to its relationship with everything else. The biggest bins classify organisms into kingdoms: Animalia, Plantae, Fungi, Protista, Eubacteria, and Archaeobacteria (although the latter two are sometimes grouped into one kingdom, the Monera). Wolves, dogs, bears, snakes, and rabbits are all animals, so they all belong to the kingdom Animalia. Within that, wolves, coyotes, bears, and rabbits are mammals (class Mammalia). Wolves, coyotes, and bears are carnivores (order Carnivora). Wolves and coyotes are canids (family Canidae). Both belong to the genus *Canis*, but wolves are *Canis lupus* and coyotes are *Canis latrans*, where *lupus* and *latrans* are the official Latin names for the two different species.

After that, it gets messy. Sometimes species are subdivided into subspecies. But this is tricky. Some taxonomists will refer to a population that seems to be particularly isolated from other populations as a subspecies, while a different taxonomist might look at the same population and decide that it is not sufficiently different to merit subspecific status. Unlike a species, there's really no rule to go by to decide whether a subspecies is real or not.

Beth Shapiro, *How to Clone a Mammoth: The Science of De-Extinction*

"That's not a Chair, son. That's a stool." He enjoyed his moment of anger, then got back to us. "Maybe it doesn't matter. History gets written by the winners, no? Bad history. And Hartley is surely a bad historian. And . . . in a way . . . a winner." He fell silent for a moment and Graves knew better than to throw in another **question**. "The fact is, Martha and I overlapped for a few years. So we lived across the hall from each other. A duet. My swan song and her . . . I wouldn't know what to call it . . ." His voice trailed off. "So what kind of wisdom are you looking for?" Wright finally asked. "I didn't kill her."

"But somebody did," Graves said. "It wasn't a robbery. It wasn't a rape. It was an execution. Maybe some maniac drove through town. That happens. But chances are, it was someone who knew her, who found her while she was out walking her dog, who got close enough to join her, to drop back a step and fire a bullet into the base of her skull. Don't tell me who killed her, Professor Wright. Just tell me why someone would want to kill a professor at this college. Kill her and display her body outside a fraternity lodge."

"God, what a **question**." Wright sat quiet. "Let the old professor ramble. That's what you want, isn't it?"

P. F. Kluge, Final Exam: A Novel

How much pizza sauce does it take to equal a serving of vegetables? Essentially that was the **question** being asked.

David Gomez, Congressional Pizza Battles and Political Corruption (TGDaily.com)

I had thought it was a simple **question**: Why can't inexpensive, healthy, and delicious food be available to everyone? And I thought I had a simple answer: pizza. According to the pizza industry, pizza is the world's most popular food, a thirty-six-billion-dollar-a-year business. If anything could feed everybody, it was pizza.

The Japanese go for slices topped with eel and squid, while Bangkok residents like their crusts folded around hot dogs. Pakistani pizza features curry, Costa Rican pizza features coconut, and Hong Kong locals have discovered a taste for abalone, crayfish, and crab roe pizza. Russians like their pizza topped with sardines and onions. Depending on where you stand on planet Earth, you may find yourself contemplating a slice of bacon cheeseburger pizza; dandelion pizza; mashed potato pizza; pulled-pork pizza; pickled ginger, minced mutton, and tofu pizza; or peanut butter and jelly pizza.

According to a recent Gallup Poll, children ages three to eleven prefer pizza over all other foods for lunch and dinner. So if you happen to be contemplating pizza, you may be standing in a school lunch line. And since a school lunch must include a serving of vegetables, it was only a matter of time before the following **question** arose: Is pizza a vegetable? The U.S. Congress and the U.S. Department of Agriculture spent a great deal of time and energy last year considering this **question**.

For the record, pizza is not a vegetable. But there was something lost amid the uproar over just how many tomatoes might or might not have given their lives to the pizza sauce atop a schoolkid's lunchtime slice. Lost amid the fight over high sodium, childhood obesity, and pizza industry lobbyists was the **question** of eleven billion dollars of federal school lunch money—a great portion of it embedded in frozen pizza.

Frederick Kaufman, Bet the Farm: How Food Stopped Being Food

"What do you mean to do, then?" I asked.

"Well, my idea was that you and I could rush him. He may be dozin', and at the worst he can only wing one of us, and the other should have him. If we can get his bolster-cover round his arms and then 'phone up a stomach-pump, we'll give the old dear the supper of his life."

It was a rather desperate business to come suddenly into one's day's work. I don't think that I am a particularly brave man. I have an Irish imagination which makes the unknown and the untried more terrible than they are. On the other hand, I was brought up with a horror of cowardice and with a terror of such a stigma. I dare say that I could throw myself over a precipice, like the Hun in the history books, if my courage to do it were **questioned**, and yet it would surely be pride and fear, rather than courage, which would be my inspiration. Therefore, although every nerve in my body shrank from the whisky-maddened figure which I pictured in the room above, I still answered, in as careless a voice as I could command, that I was ready to go. Some further remark of Lord Roxton's about the danger only made me irritable.

"Talking won't make it any better," said I. "Come on."

I rose from my chair and he from his. Then with a little confidential chuckle of laughter, he patted me two or three times on the chest, finally pushing me back into my chair.

"All right, sonny my lad—you'll do," said he.

I looked up in surprise.

"I saw after Jack Ballinger myself this mornin'. He blew a hole in the skirt of my kimono, bless his shaky old hand, but we got a jacket on him, and he's to be all right in a week. I say, young fellah, I hope you don't mind—what?"

Arthur Conan Doyle, *The Lost World*

This meant war. But it also meant more pizza for more people. And perhaps it might mean less expensive pizza for more people. A pizza war might even mean healthier, more delicious meals for everyone on Earth—which was what I was looking for, the answer to the food **question**. So I visited the front line.

Frederick Kaufman, *Bet the Farm: How Food Stopped Being Food*

For two days we made our way up a good-sized river some hundreds of yards broad, and dark in color, but transparent, so that one could usually see the bottom. The affluents of the Amazon are, half of them, of this nature, while the other half are whitish and opaque, the difference depending upon the class of country through which they have flowed. The dark indicate vegetable decay, while the others point to clayey soil. Twice we came across rapids, and in each case made a portage of half a mile or so to avoid them. The woods on either side were primeval, which are more easily penetrated than woods of the second growth, and we had no great difficulty in carrying our canoes through them. How shall I ever forget the solemn mystery of it? The height of the trees and the thickness of the boles exceeded anything which I in my town-bred life could have imagined, shooting upwards in magnificent columns until, at an enormous distance above our heads, we could dimly discern the spot where they threw out their side-branches into Gothic upward curves which coalesced to form one great matted roof of verdure, through which only an occasional golden ray of sunshine shot downwards to trace a thin dazzling line of light amidst the majestic obscurity. As we walked noise-lessly amid the thick, soft carpet of decaying vegetation the hush fell upon our souls which comes upon us in the twilight of the Abbey, and even Professor Challenger's full-chested notes sank into a whisper. Alone, I should have been ignorant of the names of these giant growths, but our men of science pointed out the cedars, the great silk cotton trees, and the redwood trees, with all that profusion of various plants which has made this continent the chief supplier to the human race of those gifts of Nature which depend upon the vegetable world, while it is the most backward in those products which come from animal life. Vivid orchids and wonderful colored lichens smoldered upon the swarthy tree-trunks and where a wandering shaft of light fell full upon the golden allamanda, the scarlet star-clusters of the tacsonia, or the rich deep blue of ipomaea, the effect was as a dream of fairyland. In these great wastes of forest, life, which abhors darkness, struggles ever upwards to the light. Every plant, even the smaller ones, curls and writhes to the green surface, twining itself round its stronger and taller brethren in the effort. Climbing plants are monstrous and luxuriant, but others which have never been known to climb elsewhere learn the art as an escape from that somber shadow, so that the common nettle, the jasmine, and even the jacitara palm tree can be seen circling the stems of the cedars and striving to reach their crowns. Of animal life there was no movement amid the majestic vaulted aisles which stretched from us as we walked, but a constant movement far above our heads told of that multitudinous world of snake and monkey, bird and sloth, which lived in the sunshine, and looked down in wonder at our tiny, dark, stumbling figures in the obscure depths immeasurably below them. At dawn and at sunset the howler monkeys screamed together and the parrakeets broke into shrill chatter, but during the hot hours of the day only the full drone of insects, like the beat of a distant surf, filled the ear, while nothing moved amid the solemn vistas of stupendous trunks, fading away into the darkness which held us in. Once some bandy-legged, lurching creature, an ant-eater or a bear, scuttled clumsily amid the shadows. It was the only sign of earth life which I saw in this great Amazonian forest.

And yet there were indications that even human life itself was not far from us in those mysterious recesses. On the third day out we were aware of a singular deep throbbing in the air, rhythmic and solemn, coming and going fitfully throughout the morning. The two boats were paddling within a few yards of each other when first we heard it, and our Indians remained motionless, as if they had been turned to bronze, listening intently with expressions of terror upon their faces.

"What is it, then?" I asked.

"Drums," said Lord John, carelessly, "war drums. I have heard them before."

"Yes, sir, war drums," said Gomez, the half-breed. "Wild Indians, bravos, not mansos; they watch us every mile of the way; kill us if they can."

"How can they watch us?" I asked, gazing into the dark, motionless void.

The half-breed shrugged his broad shoulders.

"The Indians know. They have their own way. They watch us. They talk the drum talk to each other. Kill us if they can."

By the afternoon of that day—my pocket diary shows me that it was Tuesday, August 18th—at least six or seven drums were throbbing from various points. Sometimes they beat quickly, sometimes slowly, sometimes in obvious **question** and answer, one far to the east breaking out in a high staccato rattle, and being followed after a pause by a deep roll from the north. There was something indescribably nerve-shaking and menacing in that constant mutter, which seemed to shape itself into the very syllables of the half-breed, endlessly repeated, "We will kill you if we can. We will kill you if we can." No one ever moved in the silent woods. All the peace and soothing of quiet Nature lay in that dark curtain of vegetation, but away from behind there came ever the one message from our fellow-man. "We will kill you if we can," said the men in the east. "We will kill you if we can," said the men in the north.

Arthur Conan Doyle, The Lost World

I remember, when acknowledging receipt of my orders, that I couldn't resist asking: "Doesn't the army already have detailed maps?" To which Lagrange answered: "Don't ask stupid **questions**. At the beginning of the war our military leaders were so sure of winning that they distributed only maps of Germany and none of France."

Umberto Eco, The Prague Cemetery

These facts, as will be seen in the latter chapters of this volume, seemed to throw some light on the origin of species—that mystery of mysteries, as it has been called by one of our greatest philosophers. On my return home, it occurred to me, in 1837, that something might perhaps be made out on this **question** by patiently accumulating and reflecting on all sorts of facts which could possibly have any bearing on it. After five years' work I allowed myself to speculate on the subject, and drew up some short notes; these I enlarged in 1844 into a sketch of the conclusions, which then seemed to me probable: from that period to the present day I have steadily pursued the same object. I hope that I may be excused for entering on these personal details, as I give them to show that I have not been hasty in coming to a decision.

My work is now nearly finished; but as it will take me two or three more years to complete it, and as my health is far from strong, I have been urged to publish this Abstract. I have more especially been induced to do this, as Mr. Wallace, who is now studying the natural history of the Malay Archipelago, has arrived at almost exactly the same general conclusions that I have on the origin of species. Last year he sent me a memoir on this subject, with a request that I would forward it to Sir Charles Lyell, who sent it to the Linnean Society, and it is published in the third volume of the Journal of that Society. Sir C. Lyell and Dr. Hooker, who both knew of my work—the latter having read my sketch of 1844—honoured me by thinking it advisable to publish, with Mr. Wallace's excellent memoir, some brief extracts from my manuscripts.

This Abstract, which I now publish, must necessarily be imperfect. I cannot here give references and authorities for my several statements; and I must trust to the reader reposing some confidence in my accuracy. No doubt errors may have crept in, though I hope I have always been cautious in trusting to good authorities alone. I can here give only the general conclusions at which I have arrived, with a few facts in illustration, but which, I hope, in most cases will suffice. No one can feel more sensible than I do of the necessity of hereafter publishing in detail all the facts, with references, on which my conclusions have been grounded; and I hope in a future work to do this. For I am well aware that scarcely a single point is discussed in this volume on which facts cannot be adduced, often apparently leading to conclusions directly opposite to those at which I have arrived. A fair result can be obtained only by fully stating and balancing the facts and arguments on both sides of each **question**; and this cannot possibly be here done.

I much regret that want of space prevents my having the satisfaction of acknowledging the generous assistance which I have received from very many naturalists, some of them personally unknown to me. I cannot, however, let this opportunity pass without expressing my deep obligations to Dr. Hooker, who, for the last fifteen years, has aided me in every possible way by his large stores of knowledge and his excellent judgment.

In considering the Origin of Species, it is quite conceivable that a naturalist, reflecting on the mutual affinities of organic beings, on their embryological relations, their geographical distribution, geological succession, and other such facts, might come to the conclusion that species had not been independently created, but had descended, like varieties, from other species. Nevertheless, such a conclusion, even if well founded, would be unsatisfactory, until it could be shown how the innumerable species inhabiting this world have been modified, so as to acquire that perfection of structure and coadaptation which justly excites our admiration. Naturalists continually refer to external conditions, such as climate, food, &c., as the only possible cause of variation. In one very limited sense, as we shall hereafter see, this may be true; but it is preposterous to attribute to mere external conditions, the structure, for instance, of the woodpecker, with its feet, tail, beak, and tongue, so admirably adapted to catch insects under the bark of trees. In the case of the misseltoe, which draws its nourishment from certain trees, which has seeds that must be transported by certain birds, and which has flowers with separate sexes absolutely requiring the agency of certain insects to bring pollen from one flower to the other, it is equally preposterous to account for the structure of this parasite, with its relations to several distinct organic beings, by the effects of external conditions, or of habit, or of the volition of the plant itself.

The author of the 'Vestiges of Creation' would, I presume, say that, after a certain unknown number of generations, some bird had given birth to a woodpecker, and some plant to the misseltoe, and that these had been produced perfect as we now see them; but this assumption seems to me to be no explanation, for it leaves the case of the coadaptations of organic beings to each other and to their physical conditions of life, untouched and unexplained.

It is, therefore, of the highest importance to gain a clear insight into the means of modification and coadaptation. At the commencement of my observations it seemed to me probable that a careful study of domesticated animals and of cultivated plants would offer the best chance of making out this obscure problem. Nor have I been disappointed; in this and in all other perplexing cases I have invariably found that our knowledge, imperfect though it be, of variation under domestication, afforded the best and safest clue. I may venture to express my conviction of the high value of such studies, although they have been very commonly neglected by naturalists.

From these considerations, I shall devote the first chapter of this Abstract to Variation under Domestication. We shall thus see that a large amount of hereditary modification is at least possible; and, what is equally or more important, we shall see how great is the power of man in accumulating by his Selection successive slight variations. I will then pass on to the variability of species in a state of nature; but I shall, unfortunately, be compelled to treat this subject far too briefly, as it can be treated properly only by giving long catalogues of facts. We shall, however, be enabled to discuss what circumstances are most favourable to variation. In the next chapter the Struggle for Existence among all organic beings throughout the world, which inevitably follows from the high geometrical ratio of their increase, will be treated of. This is the doctrine of Malthus, applied to the whole animal and vegetable kingdoms. As many more individuals of each species are born than can possibly survive; and as, consequently, there is a frequently recurring struggle for existence, it follows that any being, if it vary however slightly in any manner profitable to itself, under the complex and sometimes varying conditions of life, will have a better chance of surviving, and thus be *naturally selected*. From the strong principle of inheritance, any selected variety will tend to propagate its new and modified form.

This fundamental subject of Natural Selection will be treated at some length in the fourth chapter; and we shall then see how Natural Selection almost inevitably causes much Extinction of the less improved forms of life, and induces what I have called

Divergence of Character. In the next chapter I shall discuss the complex and little known laws of variation and of correlation of growth. In the four succeeding chapters, the most apparent and gravest difficulties in accepting the theory will be given: namely, first, the difficulties of transitions, or in understanding how a simple being or a simple organ can be changed and perfected into a highly developed being or elaborately constructed organ; secondly the subject of Instinct, or the mental powers of animals; thirdly, Hybridism, or the infertility of species and the fertility of varieties when intercrossed; and fourthly, the imperfection of the Geological Record. In the next chapter I shall consider the geological succession of organic beings throughout time; in the eleventh and twelfth, their geographical distribution throughout space; in the thirteenth, their classification or mutual affinities, both when mature and in an embryonic condition. In the last chapter I shall give a brief recapitulation of the whole work, and a few concluding remarks.

No one ought to feel surprise at much remaining as yet unexplained in regard to the origin of species and varieties, if he make due allowance for our profound ignorance in regard to the mutual relations of the many beings which live around us. Who can explain why one species ranges widely and is very numerous, and why another allied species has a narrow range and is rare? Yet these relations are of the highest importance, for they determine the present welfare and, as I believe, the future success and modification of every inhabitant of this world. Still less do we know of the mutual relations of the innumerable inhabitants of the world during the many past geological epochs in its history. Although much remains obscure, and will long remain obscure, I can entertain no doubt, after the most deliberate study and dispassionate judgment of which I am capable, that the view which most naturalists until recently entertained, and which I formerly entertained—namely, that each species has been independently created—is erroneous. I am fully convinced that species are not immutable; but that those belonging to what are called the same genera are lineal descendants of some other and generally extinct species, in the same manner as the acknowledged varieties of any one species are the descendants of that species.

Charles Darwin, On the Origin of Species by Means of Natural Selection; or, The Preservation of Favoured Races in the Struggle for Life

"What's next?" Colorado Democrat Jared Polis mused in the House of Representatives on Thursday. "Are Twinkies going to be considered a vegetable?" Probably not, even though shortly after Polis yielded the floor, the House voted 298–121 that a slice of pizza spread with two tablespoons of tomato paste should be counted as a vegetable, at least when it's fed to schoolchildren. Obama signed the bill into law on Friday.

The episode inevitably brings to mind the Reagan administration's brief advocacy, in the fall of 1981, for the vegetable status of ketchup. It shows how far we've come as a culture, I guess, that pizza sauce instead of ketchup was at issue this time around. It's also a significant victory for food manufacturers, who can continue to market frozen pizza to schools by pointing out that for every slice of pizza the school district can put on a student's plate, the government will reimburse them for their promotion of good health. It's absurd to call pizza a vegetable, of course, but not for the reasons you think. Pizza may not be a vegetable, but that's only because vegetables do not exist.

I was made aware of this surprising fact in my early 20s while working as a cook and waiter at a restaurant that served mostly vegetarian food. One day, I was bringing a salad to one of the regulars, a botanist named Tim. Being young, I was in a **questioning** mode, and asked Tim to weigh in on a controversy that I thought had been discovered by my generation: Were tomatoes fruits or vegetables? He told me they were fruits, and that moreover I was begging the **question**. (Tim was a professor.) To a botanist, he said, there's no such thing as a "vegetable." The word has no scientific meaning. The **question** I was asking presented a false choice.

As the ripened ovary of a pollinated flower, the tomato is most assuredly a fruit. So is the seemingly vegetal zucchini, the eggplant, and the pumpkin, as well as the nutty chestnut (but not the peanut, which is a bean). The foodstuffs we usually call "vegetables" can be fruits, but they can also be roots, stems, stalks, seeds, or indeed any part of a plant that we find edible. Now, a catch-all category such as "vegetable," though imaginary, is not without its uses: carrots and celery may have almost nothing in common other than their both being plants, but they do share a certain gestalt; so while calling one a taproot and the other a petiole might be correct in the botanist's sense, it would probably strike your average eater as somewhat beside the point.

In the absence of scientific rigor, we slog through the marsh of culture. One of the squishy criteria used to determine whether a plant is a vegetable is how sweet it is before it's cooked. Thus the controversy over tomatoes, which seem to be in a gray area when it comes to raw sweetness, but the lack of controversy over butternut squash, a fruit (universally acknowledged as a vegetable) that tastes like candy after a long roasting.

Benjamin Phelan, Pizza Is Not a Vegetable, But Neither Is Anything Else, Really (Slate)

Looked at like this, to ask whether time flows (for example) is not to suffer from any kind of intellectual disease which is in need of therapy; it is not to have your intelligence bewitched by language; it is not to misunderstand what Wittgenstein called the "grammar" of the word time. Rather, it is to grapple with **questions** that are at once simple to grasp—what is it for some things to be in the past, and some in the future?—and also of great complexity: how our actual temporal experience of the world is related to the picture of time and space that we have acquired from physics.

Tim Crane, Wittgenstein, Bewitched (The Times Literary Supplement)

CMI: Which of course begs the **question** of whether that is actually happening. Does it 'torture the Bible" to take it according to the grammatical-historical approach, the way the rest of the Bible takes it, the way Jewish commentators and Church Fathers and Reformers took it?

Creation Ministries International, A Wolf Among the Sheep (creation.com)

He had no idea what Goedsche had been up to in the meantime, but had to keep ahead of him, not least because the Jews seemed to have curiously disappeared during almost the whole time of the Commune. Were they inveterate conspirators, secretly pulling strings in the Commune? Or were they, on the contrary, accumulators of capital hiding at Versailles waiting for the war to finish? But they were behind the Freemasons, and the Paris Freemasons had sided with the Commune, and the Communards had shot an archbishop. The Jews had to be involved in some way. They killed children, so killing archbishops was hardly a problem.

One day in 1376, while Simonini was pondering this **question**, he heard the bell downstairs. At the door was an elderly man in a cassock. He thought at first it was the

868

A historic gathering of the Article Rescue Squadron, where an angry mob descended on an administrator who dared to **question** the enyclopedic importance of Pizza cheese.

Wikipedia, WikiSpeak (wikipedia.org)

usual satanist priest come to sell consecrated hosts, but then, studying him more closely, under that mass of gray but still curly hair, he recognized Father Bergamaschi. It had been almost thirty years since he'd last seen him.

For the Jesuit it was more difficult to be sure that the person in front of him was indeed the Simonini he had known as an adolescent, mainly because of the beard (which, after the return of peace, had become black again, with a touch of gray, as befitted a man in his mid-forties). Then his eyes brightened, and he said, with a smile, "But of course. Simonino, it's you, my boy, isn't it? Why keep me at the door?"

He was smiling, though we would hardly venture to say it was the smile of a tiger, but rather that of a cat. Simonini invited him upstairs and asked, "How did you manage to find me?"

"Ah, my boy," said Bergamaschi, "didn't you know we Jesuits are always one step ahead of the devil? Even though the Piedmontese had driven us out of Turin, I managed to maintain a good circle of contacts. I discovered, first of all, that you were working at a notary's office and forging wills, and then, alas, that you had sent a report to the Piedmont secret service in which I appeared as adviser to Napoleon III, and was supposed to be plotting against France and the Kingdom of Piedmont at the Prague cemetery. A fine invention, there's no denying it, but then I realized you'd copied the whole thing from that heathen Sue. I tried to find you but was told you were in Sicily with Garibaldi and then that you'd left Italy. General Negri di Saint Front is still on friendly terms with the Society and directed me to Paris, where my brethren had good connections with the imperial secret service. That was how I discovered you were in touch with the Russians and that your report about us at the Prague cemetery had become a report on the Jews. But at the same time I learned you'd been spying on a certain Joly. I was able secretly to obtain a copy of his book, left in the office of someone called Lacroix, who had died heroically in an armed encounter with Carbonaro bombers, and I could see that, though Joly had taken his ideas from Sue, you had copied from Joly. Finally my German brethren informed me that a certain Goedsche had written about a ceremony, once again at the Prague cemetery, where the Jews said more or less the same things you had written in your report to the Russians. Except that I knew the first version, involving us Jesuits, was yours, and predated Goedsche's potboiler by many years."

"At last someone who gives me my due!"

"Let me finish. After that, what with war, siege and the days of the Commune, Paris was better avoided by a man of the cloth like me. I decided to come and search you out because that same story about the Jews at the Prague cemetery appeared in a booklet published in St. Petersburg. But it was presented as a passage from a novel based on true facts, and therefore originated with Goedsche. And now, this year, more or less the same text has appeared in a pamphlet in Moscow. In short, up there (or down there, however you wish to put it) the whole **question** of the Jews is turning into a state matter. They're becoming a threat, but they're also a threat to us. Hidden behind this *Alliance Israélite* are the Masons, and His Holiness has now decided to start a thorough campaign against all enemies of the Church. And here we come back to you, Simonino, who must seek forgiveness for the trick you played on me with the Piedmontese. After slandering our Society, you owe something in return."

Hell, these Jesuits were cleverer than Hébuterne, Lagrange and Saint Front. They knew everything about everyone. They needed no help from the secret services because they were a secret service themselves; they had brethren in every part of the world and followed what had been said in every language since the fall of the tower of Babel.

After the collapse of the Commune, everyone in France, including those against the Church, had become deeply religious. There was even talk of erecting a sanctuary at Montmartre, in public atonement for that tragedy caused by such godless people. If there was a climate of restoration, it was therefore just as important to work as a good restorer. "All right, Father," Simonini said, "tell me what you want."

Umberto Eco, The Prague Cemetery

So, the real **question** is, *why* do children want pizza, potatoes and pasta while vehemently eschewing green vegetables, beans and whole grains?

Kristin Wartman, Pizza Is a Vegetable? Congress Defies Logic, Betrays Our Children (Huffington Post)

"The drama between science and the Church, therefore, unfolds with that inevitability which is tragic because it arises from the characters of men rather than the necessity in things."[6]

A further impetus to Galilean revisionism comes about from scientific, rather than historiographic, developments—that is, from considerations of Einstein's theory of relativity. Relativity means, among other things, that there is no preferred observer and no place in the universe such as a center from which absolute measurements of physical phenomena can be made. In one presentation of relativity, Einstein compared his theory of relativity to what he imputed to "Galilean relativity."[7] Here Einstein was referring to the manner in which Galileo compared relative motions and how they might be measured, for instance, while looking at a ship at sea. On the ship, a sailor walks back and forth on the deck. He can calculate the speed of his own pace, while an observer on shore sees the motion of the sailor as a compound of his motion relative to the ship plus the motion of the ship relative to the shore. For Einstein, there is no final place from which to determine the motions of the sailor or the ship since the shore sits on the Earth, which moves relative to the Sun, which moves relative to the galaxy, etc. Such considerations are fatal for the Copernican debate which enmeshed Galileo and the church if the issue is the absolute motion of the Earth and the Sun, since absolute motion does not exist in the relativistic universe. Philosopher Karl Popper summarizes the relativistic view with characteristic accuracy, even though it is a view he disagrees with.

> In support of the view that Galileo suffered for the sake of a pseudo-problem it has been asserted that in light of a logically more advanced system of physics Galileo's problem has in fact dissolved into nothing. Einstein's general principle, one often hears, makes it quite clear that it is meaningless to speak of absolute motion, even in the case of rotation; for we can freely choose whatever system we wish to be (relatively) at rest. Thus Galileo's problem vanishes.[8]

Its worth noting that among those who thought that Einstein's relativity theory made the issue between Galileo and the church moot, was the late Astronomer Royal of England, Fred Hoyle.[9] The relativistic issue goes beyond the range of physical theory to the **question** of who was right in terms of scientific methodology—the pope, who asserted to Galileo that the Copernican issue could never be resolved, or Galileo, who thought that the result could be made definite.

John C. Caiazza, The War of the Jesus and Darwin Fishes: Religion and Science in the Postmodern World

STEVEN DICK

Good **question**. I would argue that Galileo did more to knock us off our pedestal because the telescope opened the entire universe, whereas Darwinian evolution by natural selection has occurred only on Earth (so far as we know), though it would be applicable to life in the universe (we think!).

So Darwinian evolution on Earth may be just a subset of what awaits us in the almost infinite universe—which Galileo opened our eyes to. In short, cosmic evolution trumps terrestrial evolution, especially if there are intelligent ETs.

—Steven Dick is chief historian at NASA History Division, Washington DC

MATT RIDLEY

No contest: Darwin, because the degree to which he knocked man off his pedestal is still sinking in year after year.

Twelve years ago, even most scientists thought there were special human genes for making the special human brain. Now we know that we have half as many genes as a rice plant, and that the reason our brains are bigger than a mouse's is because we evolved to switch on a bunch of brain-growing genes for a bit longer.

The deep, deep commonality of life, written in the genes, is quite astonishing, even to those who expected to be astonished. Compared with that, who cares which ball of rock goes round which?

—Matt Ridley is a writer on evolutionary biology

Michael Brooks, Darwin vs Galileo: Who Cut Us Down to Size? (New Scientist)

Wootan had a similar view: "I'd focus more on exercise, too, if my husband was up for re-election."

The First Lady's office declined to respond publicly to **questions** about its support for the agencies' proposed standards for foods marketed to children, or charges that Let's Move had changed focus. Kass, the Let's Move policy adviser, responded to similar criticism last year from New York University nutrition professor Marion Nestle by saying the emphasis on exercise added to previous work on nutrition and was not a pullback from topics that the industry opposes.

Duff Wilson and Janet Roberts, Special Report: How Washington Went Soft on Childhood Obesity (Reuters)

MICHAEL RUSE

Galileo or Darwin? I puzzled over this one until I realised that, as far as I was concerned, I was facing a case of what we philosophers call the fallacy of the complex **question**.

For instance: "Have you stopped beating your wife?" If you answer "Yes", why did you start in the first place? If "No", shouldn't you stop right now? The fallacy is that answering the **question** forces on you the assumption that you were beating your wife in the first place.

Likewise with Galileo or Darwin, and who was more responsible for knocking humans off their pedestal, I don't think either did.

In fact, I would say that both Galileo and Darwin were responsible for showing just how remarkable humans truly are, in that they can work out their place in both space and time. I feel more elevated knowing that we humans can solve such difficult **questions**.

Darwin's great supporter Thomas Henry Huxley used to say that there was nothing degrading in knowing that we are modified monkeys, rather than modified dirt. But what monkeys! What modification!

—Michael Ruse is Lucyle T Werkmeister Professor and programme director for the history and philosophy of science at Florida State University, Tallahassee

Michael Brooks, Darwin vs Galileo: Who Cut Us Down to Size? (New Scientist)

Though she had felt bad for the cows tied to their stalls all day by two feet of rope, shitting on their own tails, Noelle hadn't reflected on the teriyaki sticks she had bought earlier, and she didn't even consider stopping at the animal rights booth, avoided glancing at it a second time, flicked past it as one might embarrassedly flick channels past a VT commercial asking aid for skeletal, starving children. Too depressing. Earlier, alone in a tent which contained sheep in pens—their coats stained with shit, too many of them not covered in blankets against the growing chill of night, wearing bright ear punches—she had failed to detect the sad irony in the whimsical artwork hanging on the insides of the tent, a series of facts on sheep presented in **questions** and answers, showing cute cartoons of sheep acting like humans, which probably anthropomorphically inspired more delight than the dumb beasts themselves. "Can You Eat Them?" it was asked. "Oh Yes!" And the many ways were related. A smiling lamb was shown seated at a table wearing a bib, knife and fork in its hooves. Noelle had only absent-mindedly given one of the animals an obligatory pat on the neck, more to feel the scratchy shorn surface than anything. The sheep had been sheared in a contest earlier that day. The uses for animals were endless.

Noelle was growing restless. Sorry. She had *already* grown restless.

Jeffrey Thomas, Everybody Scream! A Punktown Novel

But you should know the womanly way, my granddaughter. We are sheep … My grandaughter, even though you suffer such severe pain as to make you think that you are dying, control yourself and go *ngr* like the sheep. A sheep doesn't scream when the knife is being stuck in. It only goes *ngr* until it dies (Gutmann, 1932, p. 217, HRAF translation, p. 123).[27]

Paola Tabet, Natural Fertility, Forced Reproduction (Sex in **Question**: French Materialist Feminism)

Then the quiet again, while I contemplated Issa in his new persona as Checheyev's accomplice and perhaps master-mind behind the theft of thirty-seven million Russian pounds …

My urge to **question** them was nothing beside their intense curiosity about myself. Scarcely had they set my tray before me than they were seated at my table firing their latest batch of **questions**: Who were the bravest of all the English? they wished to know. Who were the best warriors, wrestlers, fighters? Was Elvis Presley English or American? Was the Queen absolute? Could she destroy villages, order executions, dissolve parliament? Were English mountains high? Was parliament only for elders? Did Christians have secret orders and sects, holy men, sheikhs and imams? Who trained them to fight? What weapons did they have? Did Christians slaughter their animals without first bleeding them? And—since I had told them that I lived a country life—how many hectares did I own, how many head of cattle, sheep?

John le Carré, Our Game

To this, in general, sufficient answer may be found in the activity of the human intellect, "the delirious yet divine desire to know," stimulated as it has been by its own success in unveiling the laws and processes of inorganic Nature,—in the fact that the principal triumphs of our age in physical science have consisted in tracing connections where none were known before, in reducing heterogeneous phenomena to a common cause or origin, in a manner quite analogous to that of the reduction of supposed independently originated species to a common ultimate origin,—thus, and in various other ways, largely and legitimately extending the domain of secondary causes. Surely the scientific mind of an age which contemplates the solar system as evolved from a common, revolving, fluid mass,—which, through experimental research, has come to regard light, heat, electricity, magnetism, chemical affinity, and mechanical power as varieties or derivative and convertible forms of one force, instead of independent species,—which has brought the so-called elementary kinds of matter, such as the metals, into kindred groups, and raised the **question**, whether the members of each group may not be mere varieties of one species,—and which speculates steadily in the direction of the ultimate unity of matter, of a sort of prototype or simple element which may be to the ordinary species of matter what the protozoa or component cells of an organism are to the higher sorts of animals and plants,—the mind of such an age cannot be expected to let the old belief about species pass **unquestioned**. It will raise the **question**, how the diverse sorts of plants and animals came to be as they are and where they are, and will allow that the whole inquiry transcends its powers only when all endeavors have failed. Granting the origin to be supernatural, or miraculous even, will not arrest the inquiry. All real origination, the philosophers will say, is supernatural; their very **question** is, whether we have yet gone back to the origin, and can affirm that the present forms of plants and animals are the primordial, the miraculously created ones. And even if they admit that, they will still inquire into the order of the phenomena, into the form of the miracle. You might as well expect the child to grow up content with what it is told about the advent of its infant brother. Indeed, to learn that the new-comer is the gift of God, far from lulling inquiry, only stimulates speculation as to how the precious gift was bestowed. That **questioning** child is father to the man,—is philosopher in short-clothes.

Since, then, **questions** about the origin of species will be raised, and have been raised,—and since the theorizings, however different in particulars, all proceed upon the notion that one species of plant or animal is somehow derived from another, that the different sorts which now flourish are lineal (or unlineal) descendants of other and earlier sorts,—it now concerns us to ask, What are the grounds in Nature, the admitted facts, which suggest hypotheses of derivation, in some shape or other?

Asa Gray, Darwin on the Origin of Species: A Book Review (The Atlantic)

"On a biochemical level?"

"Something like that."

"That's a good **question**." Sperry stared at her blankly for perhaps ten seconds. Hadn't anyone ever asked how it worked before? Then he swiveled around in his chair and gazed thoughtfully out the window. On the wall to the side of the window Charlotte noticed an official-looking medical degree ("Honorable") from the Madras Homeopathic College. After a moment, he swiveled back. "It has to do with DNA—deoxyribonucleic acid, the cell's genetic blueprint."

The mystery word that relates to this lesson is worth 12 points. Using the Scrabble score card, can you work out which word it is?

Yuliani Susanto, How to Tackle the 8 Mark Usefulness of Sources Questions (slideplayer.com)

Yes, she had heard of Watson and Crick.

"I'm afraid it's just too complicated for the layman to understand. Let's just say it's a secret of nature, shall we?"

Charlotte smiled. A secret of nature. Of course.

"Now," he said impatiently, "are we ready or aren't we?"

"Not quite." She wasn't going to let him off the hook yet. "One more **question**. I'm afraid I'm still a bit of a skeptic."

"Of course," he said solicitously. "That's entirely natural. I wouldn't want you to be anything other than completely comfortable with your decision." He wrinkled his nose. "What else would you like to know?"

"What I'm wondering is this: if cell therapy is the miracle treatment you claim it is, why isn't it accepted by the medical establishment?"

He looked exasperated. "Miss Graham," he said patronizingly, "you are a highly intelligent woman."

"You make that sound unusual," she parried.

Ignoring her, he went on: "I needn't tell you that some of the greatest achievements of science have taken place outside of the scientific establishment." In tones of solemn reverence, he invoked the pantheon of modern science: Galileo, Darwin, Pasteur. It was clear he included himself in this august company. "Nothing's changed," he continued. "The real geniuses still have to buck the establishment. Look at Jonas Salk." He leaned back, warming to his subject. "But when it comes to impeding scientific progress, the government is even worse than the scientific establishment, especially in this country. The U.S. Food and Drug Administration is the most backward drug regulatory agency in the world. Look at cell therapy: it's been approved in six countries." He ticked them off on the tips of his fingers. He leaned forward earnestly. "But not in the U.S. The tragedy is, when the FDA withholds approval of a treatment as valuable as cell therapy, they are compromising the health of the American public."

Charlotte thought he was overstating his case. Cell therapy hardly lent itself to implementation on a mass scale. Each town would need its own flock of sheep and its own private abattoir.

"I know what I'm doing is against the law," Sperry continued more calmly, "but that's the price I pay for being a pioneer. But," he added, "you didn't come here to listen to my sermonizing. Any other **questions**?"

Stefanie Matteson, Murder At the Spa

Sez I, "Mebby that is law, but whether it is gospel is another **question**.

*Marietta Holley, Samantha on the Woman **Question***

*I work in an environment that is a crucible for such **questions**, at a large Christian, non-denominational school west of Sydney. We do not teach literal 6-day, 6-thousand year ago Creationism, although our acceptance of an "intelligent designer" in the Universe is axiomatic. Our school policy says, in part*

> *"The balance of physical evidence does not appear to support a young earth. We do not believe that scripture helps us to decide how old the earth is". Unquote.*

CMI: What a pity if this school indeed has this implicit concession to 'millions of years' in its policy. The Bible makes it overwhelmingly clear that people were present from the beginning of creation, which was in six earth-rotation days, each with an evening and morning. And the genealogies cannot be stretched out to millions of years. Further, the Bible makes it clear that a 'very good' world was created initially, from which condition the universe departed at Adam's Fall. Whereas any other interpretation of the rock record has God superintending a charade of death, bloodshed and cancer over millions of years, calling it 'all very good'. See also <u>The Fall: a cosmic catastrophe</u>

Creation Ministries International, A Wolf Among the Sheep (creation.com)

And this was the man who'd been put on my case, I thought. Lagrange was explaining that perhaps, if they were using him for this, it was because the Prussians weren't particularly interested in my report and had appointed someone low down to have a look at it in order to clear their conscience, and then they'd get rid of me.

"No, that's not true," I said. "My report is important to the Germans. I've already been promised a considerable sum."

"Who has promised it?" asked Lagrange. And he smiled when I replied that it was Dimitri. "They're Russians, Simonini. Need I say more? What does a Russian have to lose if he promises you something on behalf of the Germans? But go to Munich all the same—we too are interested in finding out what they're doing. And don't forget that Goedsche is a devious rogue. Otherwise he wouldn't be in this job."

Lagrange was not exactly a gentleman, but perhaps there was a better kind of scoundrel, of which he was one. And so long as they pay me well I don't complain.

I believe I have already described in this diary my impression of that enormous tavern in Munich, crowded with Bavarians seated elbow-to-elbow at long communal tables, gorging themselves on greasy sausages and drinking from beer jugs the size of vats, men and women together, the women more boisterous, rowdy and vulgar than the men—most definitely an inferior race. And after the journey, tiring in itself, I found having to spend even two days on Teutonic soil a great effort.

It was in just such a tavern that Goedsche had arranged our meeting, and I was obliged to conclude that my German spy seemed born to scratch about in such places: clothes of brazen elegance were insufficient to hide the fox-like cunning of someone who lived by his wits.

In bad French he immediately asked **questions** about my sources. I evaded them, talking about other matters and mentioning my exploits with Garibaldi's men. He was pleasantly surprised, he said, as he was writing a novel about events in Italy in 1860. It was almost finished, its title would be *Biarritz*, and it would comprise several volumes. Not all the events were set in Italy—it moved about from Siberia to Warsaw to Biarritz (of course) and so on. He spoke of it with enthusiasm and a certain smugness, claiming that he was about to complete the Sistine Chapel of historical fiction. I didn't understand the link between the various events he was describing, but the story seemed to revolve around the continual threat from three evil powers that were surreptitiously taking over the world—the Freemasons, the Catholics (in particular the Jesuits) and the Jews, who were also infiltrating the first two in order to undermine the purity of the Protestant Teutonic race.

The novel began with the Italian conspiracies of Mazzini's Freemasons, then moved to Warsaw, where the Freemasons were conspiring against Russia, along with the nihilists—a breed as damned as the Slavs had ever managed to produce, although both (nihilists and Slavs) were mostly Jewish . . . and it is important to note that their system of recruitment resembled that of the Bavarian Illuminati and the *Alta Vendita* of the Carbonari, where every member recruited another nine, none of whom must know each other. Then the story returned to Italy, following the advance from Piedmont southward to the Kingdom of the Two Sicilies, in a mayhem of violence, treachery, rape of noblewomen, dramatic exploits, gallant swashbuckling Irish monarchists, secret messages hidden under the tails of horses, a vile Carbonaro prince, Caracciolo, who molests a young (Irish monarchist) girl, the discovery of magic rings in green-oxidized gold with intertwined snakes and red coral at the center, a kidnap attempt on the son of Napoleon III, the drama of Castelfidardo where the battlefield is strewn with the blood of German troops loyal to the pope, and condemnation of the *welsche Feigheit*—Goedsche said it in German, perhaps so as not to offend me, but I had studied a little German and understood he was referring to that cowardly behavior typical of the Latin races. At that point events became more and more confused, and we still hadn't reached the end of the first volume.

As he spoke, Goedsche's vaguely porcine eyes gradually lit up, and he spluttered and laughed with self-satisfaction at witticisms he judged to be excellent. He seemed to be hoping for some first-hand gossip about Cialdini, Lamarmora and other Piedmont generals, and of course Garibaldi and his men. But since people like him were used to paying for their information, I didn't think it appropriate to give him any Italian tidbits for free. And anyway, it was better to keep quiet about what I knew.

This man, I thought, was on the wrong track. You can never create danger that has a thousand different faces—danger has to have one face alone, otherwise people become distracted. If you want to expose the Jews, then talk about the Jews, not the Irish, the Neapolitan monarchy, Piedmontese generals, Polish patriots and Russian nihilists. Too many irons in the fire. How can anyone be so chaotic? And all the more surprising when, apart from his novel, Goedsche seemed completely fixated on the Jews—so much the better for me, since I had come for the very purpose of offering him a special document about the Jews.

He was, he said, not writing his novel for money or in hopes of earthly glory but to liberate the German race from the Jewish snare.

We must return to the words of Luther, when he said that the Jews are evil, poisonous and devilish to the core and had been our plague and pestilence for centuries, and still were in his time. They were, to use his words, "perfidious, venomous, bitter serpents, assassins and children of the devil, who sting and harm in secret, as they cannot do it openly." To deal with them, the only possible remedy was a *scharfe Barmherzigkeit*, which he was unable to translate but, as I understood it, meant a "rough mercy," by which Luther meant no mercy at all. "Their synagogues had to be burned down, and whatever did not burn had to be buried so not a single stone remained in sight; they had to be driven from their homes into cattle sheds like Gypsies; all their Talmudic texts, which taught only lies, curses and blasphemies, had to be removed; they were to be prevented from practicing usury; all their gold, money and jewelry was to be taken from them, and their young men given axes and spades and their women flax and spindles. That is because," said Goedsche, sneering contemptuously, "*Arbeit macht frei*, work sets you free. The final solution, for Luther, would have been to drive them out of Germany like rabid dogs."

It starts with "I REMEMBER", a direct link to Out of the Woods. These are all **questions** for Harry Styles.

*13· A Taylor Swift Fan Podcast, Could You Visualize **Question** Like This?*
#swifttok #swiftie #taylorswift #podcast #theory (tiktok.com)

"No one listened to Luther," continued Goedsche, "at least not until now. And despite the fact that, since ancient times, non-European peoples have been considered as base—look at the Negro, who even today is rightly considered an animal—no sure criteria have yet been defined for recognizing superior races. Today we know that the more developed level of humanity has white skin, and that the most evolved model of the white race is German. The presence of Jews poses a constant threat of racial cross-breeding. Look at a Greek statue: such pure lines, such elegant build, and it is no surprise that beauty was identified with virtue, and to be beautiful was to be brave, as we see with our great heroes of Teutonic mythology. Now imagine Apollo with Semitic features, with brown skin, dark eyes, hooked nose, bent body. This is how Homer described Thersites, the very personification of baseness. The Christian legend, still strongly influenced by the Jews (it was, after all, begun by Paul, an Asiatic Jew whom today we'd call a Turk), has convinced us that all races are descended from Adam. No—in separating from the original beast, men have followed different paths. We have to return to that point where our paths separated, and therefore to the true national origins of our people, rather than the ravings of those French *lumières*, with their cosmopolitanism and their *égalité* and universal brotherhood! This is the spirit of our modern times. What in Europe is now called nationalism is a cry for the purity of the original race. Except that this term—and aim—is valid only for the German race. It is absurd to imagine that in Italy the return to bygone beauty could be represented by your bow-legged Garibaldi, your short-legged king and that dwarf Cavour. The Romans, after all, were a Semitic race."

"The Romans?"

"You haven't read Virgil? They came from a Trojan, and therefore from an Asiatic, and this Semitic migration destroyed the spirit of the ancient Italic people. Look what happened to the Celts: after being Romanized, they became French, and therefore they too are Latin. Only the Germans have managed to remain pure and uncontaminated and to break the power of Rome.

Umberto Eco, The Prague Cemetery

One of the scientists prominent in the IDM, William Dembski, has attempted to formulate the design argument in more precise terms. This, and the debate about ID in general, is greatly welcomed by us, and it has in fact done our ministry and profile a great deal of good.

At the same time, we are aware of some of the pitfalls of a 'pure ID' approach, but that is far from the Zamprogno caricature.

NZ: But although Intelligent Design is comparatively benign, to see its danger, consider history, replete with pitfalls when we misuse Science as a pillar for Faith.

The geocentricity of the universe was once held as proof of our special place in creation. Then came Galileo.

Zamprogno grossly oversimplifies this **question**, (and has he even heard of Copernicus, the Bible-believer who predated Galileo—also a biblical creationist—and the creationist Kepler, who rescued Galileo's ideas from their fatal scientific flaws), and ignores recent evidence for a galactocentric universe. Galileo's primary opponents were the Aristotelians at the universities committed to Ptolemaic cosmology. As Zamprogno advocates with evolution today, the Church married her theological understanding with the science of her day, and became widowed the next day.

> Creation Ministries International, *A Wolf Among the Sheep* (creation.com)

Dear Lord, the sheer waste.

And the cruelty of it: to leave everyone not only grieving but **questioning**, wondering if they were somehow to blame.

> Ian Rankin, *Dead Souls*

According to early lithographs, he was quite a looker in his day, but now, a century later, after years of hard drinking and working in the mines, he has no hair and looks like shit. Could Evolution just mean *growing old*? I posed this **question** to a scientist friend who explained that the change has to take place over many generations. You'd think the Evolutionists would have stated that right out front, and I admit that I stand corrected. But Evolution still sounds a lot like growing old to me, and I can't help thinking that this is where the Evolutionary scientists first got their wacky ideas.

Having cleared up this common confusion, let us move on to the proposed selective force of Evolution—namely, *Natural Selection*. What the fuck is this supposed to mean? Is there unnatural selection? And who's doing the selecting? Neither of these **questions** could be answered by my scientist friend, and so I have been forced to ditch my now former friend and perform my own research. What follows is, to the best of my ability, what I've been able to uncover regarding Evolution and Natural Selection.

A Closer Examination of Natural Selection

Apparently, there are not one but two forms of selection. They are Natural Selection and sexual selection. I'll let you mull over the second "sexy" form of selection for a minute, at least until I've torn the first one to shreds. You should have time to masturbate while reading my proofs, if that's what you're in to.

> Bobby Henderson, *The Gospel of the Flying Spaghetti Monster*

There is no surprise here. Darwin is proceeding by his usual method of asking a **question** and then answering it. Creationist quote miners classically omit his answer.

In the sixth edition this appears in Chapter 6, "Difficulties on Theory", on p. 134 (in the first edition it appears on p. 172 with a different follow-up):

*But, as by this theory innumerable transitional forms must have existed, why do we not find them embedded in countless numbers in the crust of the earth? It will be more convenient to discuss this **question** in the chapter on the Imperfection of the Geological Record; and I will here only state that I believe the answer mainly lies in the record being incomparably less perfect than is generally supposed. The crust of the earth is a vast museum; but the natural collections have been imperfectly made, and only at long intervals of time.*

> talk.origins newsgroup, *The Quote Mine Project, or, Lies, Damned Lies and Quote Mines: Darwin Quotes* (The TalkOrigins Archive)

You're quoting an article on Galileo, but the discussion in **question** is a century before this, and refers to someone who was dead long before Galileo first drew breath, and even here, the *to quote your article*: "the Church raised no objections to his revolutionary hypothesis, as long as it was represented as theory, not undisputed fact". Which is all it was at the time. Even Galileo's models were not perfect—being based on circular movements of the planets rather than elliptical orbits—thus there were inconsistencies in his views, even then.

I stand by what I say—the Protestant movement had very little to say about Galileo's theories!

Paranoid Android, posted November 25, 2008 (edited)

He has a point . . . But wasn't this about Darwin?

Dr. Peter Venkman, Government Agent, posted November 25, 2008

Unexplained-Mysteries.com, Forums > Unexplained Mysteries > Spirituality vs Skepticism > Church Apologises to Charles Darwin

A better **question** might be "How can we maintain a balanced view of change in the face of our desire to assign responsibility?"

Philip Ball, If Not Darwin, Who? An Alternative History of the Great Ideas of Science (Nautilus)

The formulation of a **question** is its solution. The critique of the Jewish **question** is the answer to the Jewish **question**. The summary, therefore, is as follows:

We must emancipate ourselves before we can emancipate others.

*Karl Marx, On the Jewish **Question** (Deutsch-Französische Jahrbücher)*

And of course the nature of philosophy is itself a philosophical **question**, too; but this is because philosophy aims to be a foundational discipline, and the foundations of philosophy are as much in **question** as the foundations of other forms of knowledge. That is, after all, what it means to be a foundational discipline.

Tim Crane, Wittgenstein, Bewitched (The Times Literary Supplement)

It was by no means sufficient to investigate: Who is to emancipate? Who is to be emancipated? Criticism had to investigate a third point. It had to inquire: *What kind of emancipation* is in **question**? What conditions follow from the very nature of the emancipation that is demanded? Only the criticism of *political emancipation* itself would have been the conclusive criticism of the Jewish **question** and its real merging in the *"general **question** of time."*

*Karl Marx, On the Jewish **Question** (Deutsch-Französische Jahrbücher)*

The responsibility which consumed much of Mendel's time for two decades may have been decided for him in the decade before his arrival at the monastery. In 1837, there was a meeting of the Sheepbreeders association of Brno. In attendance was Cyril Napp, president of a local organization supporting hybridization research and abbot of the Augustinian monastery of Brno. As one might expect, there was much talk about breeding. But Napp suggested an alternative topic: "the **question** for discussion should not be the theory and process of breeding, but what is inherited and how."

Joseph Sant, Mendel, Darwin and Evolution (Scientus.org)

The Romans wore nothing but woollen goods. They had no cotton; they had a little linen which was worn as a material of luxury; they had no silk. They cultivated the sheep with great care, and some of their richest possessions were in sheep. But there was one breed of sheep which they cultivated with extraordinary care, and by that system of selection which Darwin speaks of as the source of the perfected forms of our domestic animals. It was called the Tarentine sheep, from Tarentum, a city of Greek origin, situated at the head of the Tarentine gulf. The fleece of this sheep was of exceeding fineness;

it was of great delicacy, and the prices of its fleeces were enormous. The sheep were clothed in cold weather to keep them warm; and the result was that they were very tender and their wool was very fine. They were a product of Greek civilization transmitted down to the Romans. Columella, the great Roman agriculturist, says that his uncle, residing in Spain, crossed some of the fine Tarentine sheep with some rams that had been imported from Africa; and the consequence was, that these animals had the whiteness of the father with the fineness of the fleece of the mother, and that that race was perpetuated. Here we see an improvement of the stock,—an increase of strength and productiveness given to the fine-wool sheep of Spain. At that time the sheep of Spain were of immense value; for Strabo says that sheep from Spain, in the time of Tiberius, were carried to Rome, and sold for the price of a *talent,* one thousand dollars a head. In the time of our Saviour a thousand dollars was given in Rome for a Spanish sheep. When the barbarians inundated Italy, these fine-wool sheep were all swept away, but they remained in Spain; they were cultivated by the Moors in the mountains of Spain, which were almost inaccessible, and were not reached by the hordes of Huns, and other Northern barbarians, which had laid waste the greater portion of the Roman possessions. They continued to be nourished there by the Moors, who were very much advanced in arts; and further on were found there as the Spanish merino. So that the Spanish merino which we now have, if not the only, is at all events by far the most important relic that we have to-day which has come down to us from Greek and Roman material civilization. We have here a direct inheritance from the material wealth of the Old World civilization.

John L. Hayes, *The Protective* **Question** *Abroad, and Remarks at the Indianapolis Exposition*

The more complete context is:

To the **question** *why we do not find rich fossiliferous deposits belonging to these assumed earliest periods prior to the Cambrian system, I can give no satisfactory answer. Several eminent geologists, with Sir R. Murchison at their head, were until recently convinced that we beheld in the organic remains of the lowest Silurian stratum the first dawn of life. Other highly competent judges, as Lyell and E. Forbes, have disputed this conclusion. We should not forget that only a small portion of the world is known with accuracy. Not very long ago M. Barrande added another and lower stage, abounding with new and peculiar species, beneath the then known Silurian system; and now, still lower down in the Lower Cambrian formation, Mr. Hicks has found in South Wales beds rich in trilobites, and containing various molluscs and annelids. The presence of phosphatic nodules and bituminous matter, even in some of the lowest azoic rocks, probably indicates life at these periods; and the existence of the Eozoon in the Laurentian formation of Canada is generally admitted. There are three great series of strata beneath the Silurian system in Canada, in the lowest of which the Eozoon is found. Sir W. Logan states that their "united thickness may possibly far surpass that of all the succeeding rocks, from the base of the palæozoic series to the present time. We are thus carried back to a period so remote that the appearance of the so-called primordial fauna (of Barrande) may by some be considered as a comparatively modern event." The Eozoon belongs to the most lowly organised of all classes of animals, but is highly organised for its class; it existed in countless numbers, and, as Dr. Dawson has remarked, certainly preyed on other minute organic beings, which must have lived in great numbers. Thus the words, which I wrote in*

883

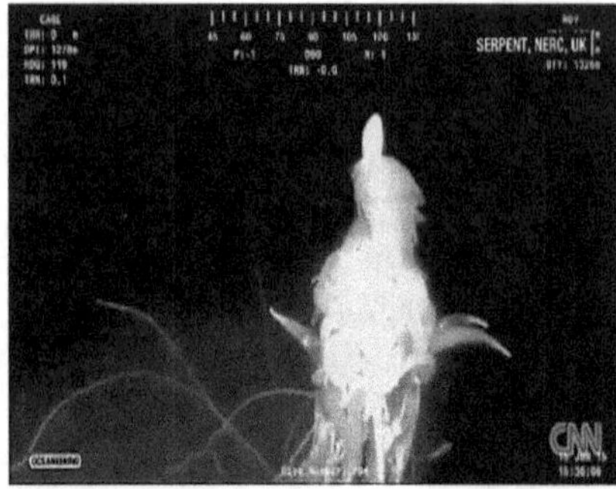

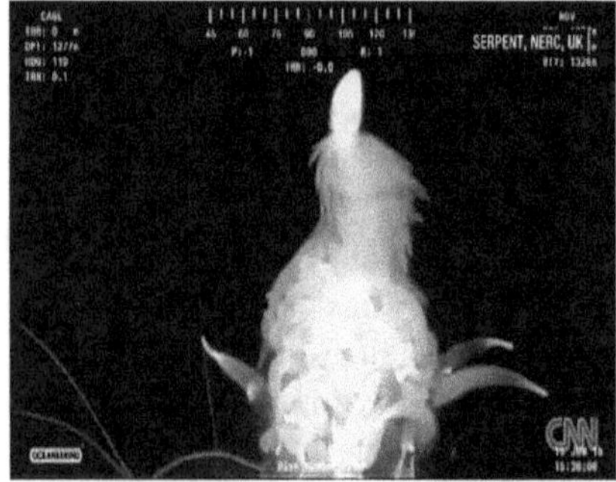

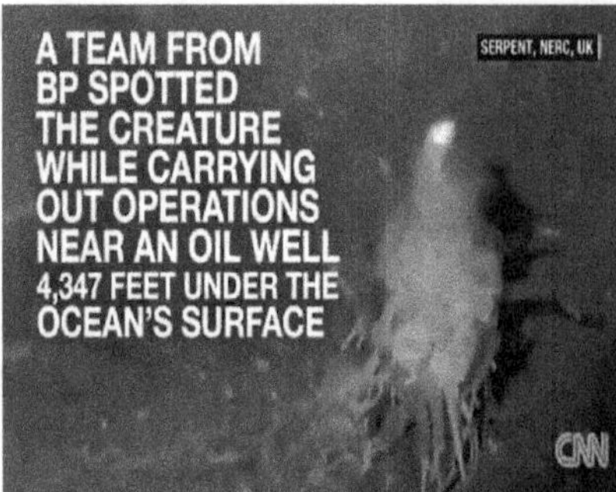

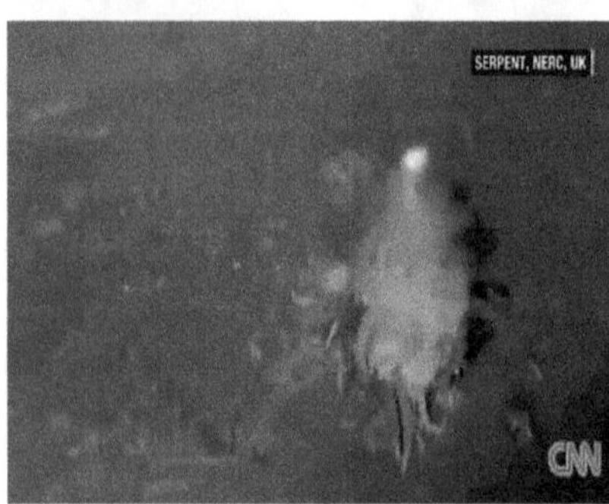

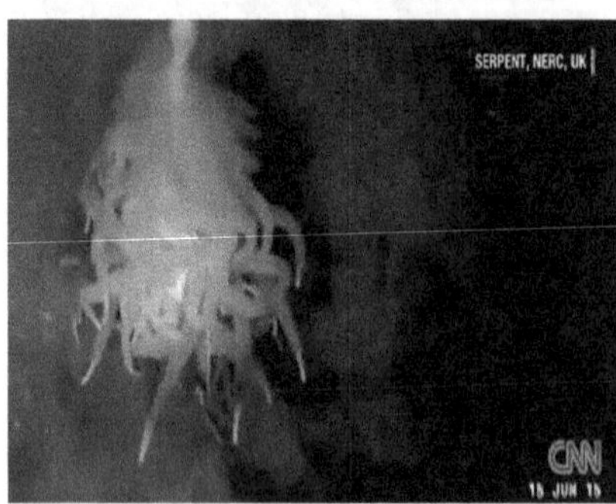

CNN, See Rare Video of 'Flying Spaghetti Monster' (youtube)

*Footage courtesy the SERPENT Project, National Oceanography
Centre, BP Exploration (Angola) Limited and Sonangol*

1859, about the existence of living beings long before the Cambrian period, and which are almost the same with those since used by Sir W. Logan, have proved true. Nevertheless, the difficulty of assigning any good reason for the absence of vast piles of strata rich in fossils beneath the Cambrian system is very great. It does not seem probable that the most ancient beds have been quite worn away by denudation, or that their fossils have been wholly obliterated by metamorphic action, for if this had been the case we should have found only small remnants of the formations next succeeding them in age, and these would always have existed in a partially metamorphosed condition. But the descriptions which we possess of the Silurian deposits over immense territories in Russia and in North America, do not support the view, that the older a formation is, the more invariably it has suffered extreme denudation and metamorphism.

The case at present must remain inexplicable; and may be truly urged as a valid argument against the views here entertained. To show that it may hereafter receive some explanation, I will give the following hypothesis. From the nature of the organic remains which do not appear to have inhabited profound depths, in the several formations of Europe and of the United States; and from the amount of sediment, miles in thickness, of which the formations are composed, we may infer that from first to last large islands or tracts of land, whence the sediment was derived, occurred in the neighbourhood of the now existing continents of Europe and North America. The same view has since been maintained by Agassiz and others. But we do not know what was the state of things in the intervals between the several successive formations; whether Europe and the United States during these intervals existed as dry land, or as a submarine surface near land, on which sediment was not deposited, or as the bed on an open and unfathomable sea.

—*Origin of Species*, 6th Ed. John Murray, 1872, Chapter 10, pp. 286–288.

talk.origins newsgroup, The Quote Mine Project, or, Lies, Damned Lies and Quote Mines: Darwin Quotes (The TalkOrigins Archive)

While there can be no doubt that the source of creation was indeed the Flying Spaghetti Monster (FSM), and that He did leave mysterious and ambiguous clues to throw us off track, we submit that the FSM was careless, cruel, drunk, or even high when he first laid down the template for life as we know it. How else to explain the extinction of 99.9 percent of all plant and animal species ever to exist on earth? How else to explain the release of not one, but two Deuce Bigalow films?

Without **question**, we are members of a small and limited minority of scientists and religious leaders who deign to **question** the Creator's wisdom in allowing for life-threatening volcanoes, tsunamis, hurricanes, twisters, and plastic surgery gone bad, but as the evidence accumulates, we can only posit one undeniable theory:

The FSM, our Creator, isn't very bright.

Undoubtedly, this statement represents a subtle paradigm shift, especially when juxtaposed against the common perception of a benevolent, all-knowing Creator, but innumerable examples of **questionable** judgment do exist. Something is certainly rotten in Denmark when Ben Affleck is allowed to bed both J.Lo and that hottie from *Alias*, while Matt Damon is forced to date his own assistant. We cry foul!

So we hereby state our belief that the universe is a result of "UNINTELLIGENT DESIGN" (UD).

A Chandler man's fight with MVD to wear a pasta strainer on his head in his drivers license picture.
Pastafarian Fights to Wear Spaghetti Strainer (12 News, youtube.com)

With millions of believers worldwide, The Church of the Flying Spaghetti Monster is the world's fastest growing religion. I, Pastafari follows a few brave members of the church, the Pastafarians, as they fight for their religious freedom to access privileges and exceptions in law granted to other religions. Along the way, the Pastafarians force intolerant skeptics to answer the **question**, "what is a real religion anyway?"

I, Pastafari: A Flying Spaghetti Monster Story | Trailer (Journeyman Pictures, youtube.com)

Richard Dawkins is dumbfounded after being asked to "give an example of a genetic mutation or an evolutionary process which can't have been made by spaghetti"—quite a reasonable **question** that one would expect Oxford University's Professor for the Public Understanding of Science—so adamant in his belief in evolution—could and would provide an answer for. He then responds but DOES NOT answer the **question** that was asked of him. Why? Because he has no idea when it comes to processes that can't have been made by spaghett—the very premise of what he proclaims!! H

*Richard Dawkins Stumped by Pastafarians' **Question** (Huffers2002, youtube.com)*

Casting social science aside, we can turn to the physical sciences to support our claims. Why doesn't the Benevolent and Noodly Master get to work and start eradicating mass poverty, cancer, global warming, and nuclear proliferation? Is He too busy trying to rekindle the low-carb diet craze?

While this treatise might not appear to meet the normal requirements of an academic paper, let it be said that such was not even our intention. This is a work composed by a scientist and a religious leader. If science and religion are to live side by side in mutual non-judgment, there needs to be a new model for dialogue, one that takes into account the interests of both sides. Religious people don't really "do" numbers. Scientists can't get dates and don't have a clue what real people think. By collecting and presenting a different kind of data, we aim to appeal to "Bible thumpers" and "brainiacs" alike. Just getting those epithets out on the table can make a difference.

Bobby Henderson, The Gospel of the Flying Spaghetti Monster

It wasn't a **question**, so I said nothing.

"Now then, I was graduated—summa cum laude I might add, if you don't think it's boasting—from the University of Chicago Law School seven years ago—"

"That would make you nineteen," I said.

"That's right. I was nineteen."

"And summa cum laude."

"He was nineteen," Necessary said. "I checked it out. The laude stuff, too."

"Really, Homer, you don't have to—"

Ross Thomas, The Fools in Town Are on Our Side

The study in **question** was carried out by Dr Shanna Swan, a reproductive health expert at the Mount Sinai Medical Centre in New York.

In her new book *Count Down*, Dr Swan claims that chemicals are having a profoundly negative effect on the state of sexual development.

Rory Sullivan, Greta Thunberg Mocks Climate Change Deniers by Citing 'Penis Shrinking' Research (The Independent)

The substance in **question** is called phthalates, which are chemicals created in the production of plastics . . . which, when exposed to the human endocrine system, screws with our natural hormone process—a dynamic that Dr. Swan says is affecting our reproductive organs.

She cites different peer-reviewed studies in her findings, which say there's a scary trend of modern-day babies being born with noticeably shorter members—which she directly links to the phthalates she says are seeping into our toys and even some foods we eat.

Dr. Swan says the same effect was observed in rat fetuses exposed to phthalates . . . and now it's being seen in humans as well—which she calls a crisis in the making.

This is part of a larger problem which has also been touched on elsewhere—

TMZ, Penises Shrinkage Caused By Pollution . . . So Claims Scientist (TMZ)

"I'd like to say it doesn't, but it does to an extent. However, it's less length and more girth?"

—Colleen

"Sorry to anyone who wants to believe otherwise but, yes, size does matter. A small penis can't create the same sensation that a larger one can, and it can make certain maneuvers difficult—it might fall out during doggy style or when switching positions, for example."

 —Ana

"The truth? Size matters. If you have more, you can do less and still satisfy a woman. In other words, it's the meat, not the motion."

 —Vicki

"I always hear people say it's not the size of the boat, it's the motion of the ocean. Well, if that's the case a lot of men drown out at sea. I'm not looking for a cruise ship, but at the same time I need a decent size boat to ride the rough seas."

 —Judione

"I'd say it's more about the size of a man's tongue, if you know what I'm sayin'. (Oral sex is KEY.)"

 —Wren

"Too small—still hungry, too big—tummy ache."

 —Avigail

"As long as you can feel it and I mean decently feel it, then it doesn't matter that much. There's nothing sadder than having to ask if it's in when it IS in—it's just super uncomfortable and embarrassing for both."

 —Jen

"Yes, it matters. I don't want to have to be telling a man to stop tickling me. I need to feel my man waayyy up."

 —Ariana

"I look down. He's hard. And he's tiny. Erect, he's probably about the length of my middle finger and the width of a baby carrot. Although it's not a micropenis—I mean, I can see it—it's definitely the smallest I've encountered and absolutely at odds with what I expected from his broad-shouldered, rugby-player-like build. My heart falls to my stomach in disappointment as I drop onto my knees, wondering if his penis will look larger up close. I cautiously take it in my mouth as he moans thankfully. I can still easily talk, simply shifting his penis, straw-like, to the side of my mouth. 'Feel good?' I murmur, the **question** mark at the end of the sentence begging for this situation to end. In response, he pulls me up and onto the bed. 'It's a bit small, isn't it?' he says as he pulls out a condom. It's not so much a **question** as a statement of fact. 'It only matters what you do with it,' I say, trying to be encouraging as I guide him into me. I can barely feel him thrusting, and he keeps slipping out. He orgasms. I don't."

 —JL

 *Lorenzo Jensen III, 19 Women Answer the Eternal **Question**: Does Penis Size Matter? (Thought Catalog)*

The Mathematician handed me an article from the *Scientific American*, and then stood back and watched me guffaw. The article in **question** was a discussion of the relative impact that Galileo and Darwin had on society. Which one was bigger?

 First, it's a dopey **question**, but on top of that, this little bit of silliness: one of the panelists claimed that Galileo was the most influential, because (and I'm paraphrasing) only fifty percent of Americans believe in evolution, whereas eighty percent believe the earth orbits around the sun.

Think about that for a minute.

Now, the Darwin thing I'm willing to let go, though I don't believe it. A much smaller proportion of the population identifies as creationists, but let's leave that aside for the moment.

The claim is that 20% of the American population does not believe that the earth orbits the sun.

I don't believe this. I just don't. I'm taken by this urge to stop people on the street and ask them a T/F **question**: does the earth orbit around the sun? I can predict that some small percentage will just look puzzled and have to think about it. These are the same people who can't put France on a map (much less Iraq), and who don't realize that the fact that there was a World War II, there must have been a World War I. Or this person, quoted on *Overheard*:

Like, New York's Technically a State Of Mind, Right?

College student with Boston accent: Yeah, I was reading this article in like Newsweek or something, that ranked the states from smartest to dumbest. Massachusetts was in the top ten.

College student with Miami accent: What about Florida?

College student with Boston accent: Florida was like, 47.

College student with Miami accent: Out of how many?

Rosina Lippi, Galileo v Darwin (rosinalippi.com)

On March 5, FTC Chairman Leibowitz, answering a congressman's **question** in a hearing, said the effort to write voluntary food standards was no longer an agency priority.

"It's probably time to move on," he said.

Duff Wilson and Janet Roberts, Special Report: How Washington Went Soft on Childhood Obesity (Reuters)

"Of course," he added, in conclusion, "we must not move in the matter until the police arrive. I suppose they have been informed?"

"Yes," replied the stationmaster; "I sent a message at once to the Chief Constable, and I expect him or an inspector at any moment. In fact, I think I will slip out to the approach and see if he is coming." He evidently wished to have a word in private with the police officer before committing himself to any statement.

As the official departed, Thorndyke and I began to pace the now empty platform, and my friend, as was his wont, when entering on a new inquiry, meditatively reviewed the features of the problem.

"In a case of this kind," he remarked, "we have to decide on one of three possible explanations: accident, suicide or homicide; and our decision will be determined by inferences from three sets of facts: first, the general facts of the case; second, the special data obtained by examination of the body, and, third, the special data obtained by examining the spot on which the body was found. Now the only general facts at present in our possession are that the deceased was a diamond merchant making a journey for a specific purpose and probably having on his person property of small bulk and great value. These facts are somewhat against the hypothesis of suicide and somewhat favourable to that of homicide. Facts relevant to the **question** of accident would be the existence or otherwise of a level crossing, a road or path leading to the line, an enclosing fence with or without a gate, and any other facts rendering probable or otherwise the accidental presence of the deceased at the spot where the body was found. As we do not possess these facts, it is desirable that we extend our knowledge."

"Why not put a few discreet **questions** to the porter who brought in the bag and umbrella?" I suggested.

Freeman, R. Austin, *The Case of Oscar Brodski*

Is the sun as large as that photograph suggests? Could you recognize this as an insect? How young did you think her sister was? Are you not perpetually given to distortion, equivocation, half-truths? Are you listening? Is everybody happy? How can you keep your stories straight? What are the limits of large? Who do you trust? Did I ramble? Did I ever? Will you admit to this? Did you ever go sailing? How long is it? What are those blue flowers? How does the world differ in a Navy town? Are there roads on the island of Truk? What brought you to sentences? Why the great crane on the barge? Are you more frightened by insects or tigers? Could you tell if I had changed it? What was the secret of "Pincushion" Smith? Has the score changed? Why does that water heater hiss? Can you see it? Does it show? Is it hidden? Is there a purpose? Can it change? Is it large or hard? Is it blue or bumpy? Is it medium or slack? Why do you want to know? What's gotten into you? Is it a sequence? Is it a jumble? Is not chaos also a form? What is that a flock of? Is it stucco? Is it Sluggo? Does it form a chain? Is it anchored? Does it accrue? Aren't there times when words seem impossible, disconnected clusters of letters, so that even though you know what they say you can't believe it? Is it going to be a hot one? Did they search there thoroughly? What is a frame of mind? Is that cotton? Are you a real girl? What is the number? Is it a **question** of will? Is it legible? Is that the foghorn's groan that fills the inner ear? Why, at this late point in her life, did bisexuality so suddenly pose itself as a **question**? Is that a midget or a dwarf? What was the implication of her having deliberately gone over there when she knew he would not be at home? What did it mean to propose your life as a single act? Where is the border you will not cross? Is truth a **question** of verification? Do you suppose the fog a metaphor? Would you prefer to forget the day you shoved two VC from your copter, high over the dusk-lit delta? What makes you believe these words are connected, one to the other? Does fear have a structure? What about the biplane? At what point does it cease to be a poem?

Ron Silliman, *Sunset Debris*

Brathwaite and Walcott are concerned with very similar **questions**: when do we stop being Africans, Europeans, Asians, and become West Indians? By what means do we cease to be colonized by our own history, and begin to pursue our own separate fate? Aeneas looks most West Indian at the moment when he flees the conflagration of Troy, encumbered with his past (his father Anchises) and his future (his son Ascanius), bereft of his wife, and carrying only his defeated gods and some fragments of his possessions.

Laurence A. Breiner, *An Introduction to West Indian Poetry*

nOrance"

e—

pUt er,
aNd his Name on)
anD Eauty,
nZe)

veRned u[45]
A Ptake
e Old a **qUestion** f coNduct.)

inteD En r Zephyrus.

eaR,
Ity,
Are
(Pale yOung foUr hroNes,
y minD Ere aZe,
eaRs k StAte Paris—
NOr frUit thiNg,
t saiD:
Esser oZart,
's fRiends te eAch Peace wOrld?

> Jackson Mac Low, *Words nd Ends from Ez IX*

If you could end any war throughout history by dumping tonnes of one particular fruit or vegetable nearby, what war would you end, and what fruit or vegetable would you choose?

Let's see. I probably, um, what would I end? Boy, they're all so bad. I guess I would end the war in the Middle East, right now. And I think a really juicy white peach might do it, because one bite and it's just running down all over your chin and your hands, and you have to stop everything you're doing.

> Jerry Seinfeld, *Jerry Seinfeld Loves Answering **Questions**! The Dumber, the Better. Now. (Interviewly)*

A cooler
head of lettuce prevailed, but when the actor
asked his **question** and paused
for us to watch him pause and think
inside the pause, I almost answered
as if we were in a bar, just the two of us
and a balcony and spotlight. The two of us
and programs and makeup and a sofa
from the director's living room and the black/
womb/agora/séance of theater inviting us to feel
together alone. I recall I don't recall
the **question** but its scope on his face
was immense, as if he were the Milky Way
asking am I pretty, am I here for sure for real
for long and my breath was the quiet yessing
of tall grass against the shoulders of a cat
stalking the night. I actually opened my mouth

before I actually thought you will be stoned
and not in the good way, not with stones
of tongues, stones of fingers against my forehead
but the play was messy and tangible and full
of the etceteras I am full of and why
wouldn't I want to talk with that is a **question**
the poem is asking you to answer wherever
you are without me is the problem
theater solves, since we sit together
in the dark with the dark because the dark
deserves a face a soliloquy a lover a bow
at the end. When I always wonder if the players
regret that the lights come up and they see us
as we are seeing them as they were,
what a weird mirror that is, showing one side
sudden appreciation and the resumption
of loose ends, the other the vast
and devotional possibilities of being kidnapped
by a dream and which side is which side
are you on?

 Bob Hicok, *Report From the Black Box*

I love bacon and pulled pork sandwiches. I love lobster bisque and New England clam chowder. And I love cheeseburgers—oh yes I do. There, I said it on a Jewish web site. I love *treyf.*

I'm a proud Jew and a supporter of all things delicious. I'm also here to say that it's ok. In a culture such as ours that treasures food, it is a *shande* that so many morsels of yum are seemingly off limits.

Why am I ranting about this now? Firstly, I am sick and tired of the kosher racket. Rabbi Jason Miller's HuffPost piece last week, "*Ending Kosher Nostra: How to Bring Sanity to the Kosher Industry,*" shed even more light into the industry of keeping kosher.

As mentioned in Rabbi Miller's article, this ancient holy practice is filled with modern problems that completely turn me off to the concept. The kosher certification industry is wrought with corruption and backroom deals. And we all know about the kosher meat processors and their shady practices. I won't even mention the blatant price gouging that goes hand-in-hand with kosher foods.

But like sheep to the slaughter (sorry, had to do it), most who do keep kosher just keep up the scam. They continue to overpay. They don't ask **questions**. We're Jews in America here, not Iran—it's time to ask some **questions**. And it's time for some of these extremely wealthy fellow MOTs to answer them.

Miller says, "we have become so far removed from the kosher laws of the Torah and Talmud that we focus less on why we keep kosher and more on how punctilious we can be, only to "out *frum*" the next person." Whenever I hear that Hebrew National products aren't "kosher enough," I just want to go out and stuff my face with pork rinds.

What makes me sad is that so many people have such good intentions when deciding to keep kosher. I can appreciate honoring traditions and what was written thousands of years ago, but the abstractness of kosher is what boggles me. Obviously, some people are born to kosher parents and are essentially forced to follow suit. Others make their own decisions later in life. Some people keep kosher at home, but will enjoy a surf and turf dinner at the local Red Lobster. Some people claim to be kosher by ordering plain pizza from the same guy who handles the pepperoni. My very own old school/ old world grandmother loved a good shrimp scampi from time to time. Rules are made to be broken I guess.

Much of modern Judaism is based on convenience. Many of us tend to observe when it doesn't impede on our daily lives. And much of what we observe is based on Jewish guilt. Maybe if I keep kosher, I can get away with driving to synagogue. If I have a bris for my son, maybe G-d won't care that I named him Christopher. I'm here to tell you not to feel guilty. You don't have to sacrifice your taste buds any longer. You can still be a good Jew and have a flavorful steak that doesn't resemble cardboard.

That brings me to the other reason I am writing this piece. I was recently made aware of a new restaurant in New York. Sadly, it's in Williamsburg and wannabe hipsters are like kryponite to me, so I doubt I will visit any time soon. It's called Traif and it's owned by a nice Jewish boy who is tired of hiding his feelings for good food. I not only respect Chef Jason Marcus, but I admire him.

To those who keep kosher, all I ask is that you **question** where your food is coming from and the practices by which it is certified. If you can afford to pay double for certain items, don't feel deprived of flavor, and truly enjoy eating plain pasta while I chow down on a lobster, well then, I applaud you.

For those of you in the middle, join me. Life is too short and treyf tastes too good.

Jeff Mandell, Defending Treyf (TC Jewfolk)

Simonini now recalled these works of Taxil's, not as an instigator but as a reader. Nonetheless, he remembered that before each new work of Taxil's appeared, he would go (having therefore read it in advance) and describe its contents to Osman Bey as if they were extraordinary revelations. It was true that on the following occasion Osman Bey would point out that everything Simonini had told him on the previous occasion had then appeared in a book by Taxil. To this it was easy for Simonini to reply that, yes, Taxil was his informer, and it was hardly his fault that, after having revealed Masonic secrets to him, Taxil had sought financial gain by publishing them in a book. Otherwise Simonini would have had to pay to stop him from publishing his experiences—and in saying this, he fixed Osman Bey with an eloquent stare. But Osman replied that money spent on persuading a chatterbox to keep quiet was money wasted. Why should Taxil be made to hold his tongue about the very secrets he had just revealed? And, understandably suspicious, Osman offered Simonini no revelation in exchange concerning what he had learned about the *Alliance Israélite.*

At which point Simonini stopped passing information to him. But as he wrote in his diary, Simonini reflected on this problem: "Why do I remember giving Osman Bey information I'd received from Taxil, but nothing about my dealings with Taxil?"

Good **question.** If he remembered everything, he wouldn't be here writing down what he was gradually piecing together. *Quelle histoire!*

Umberto Eco, The Prague Cemetery

We also heard in each school how students are encouraged to share their own ideas, **questions** and initiatives. Adults in these schools take students seriously. One head of school told us that she regularly has small groups of students in her office wanting to start a new *tzedakah* project, or eager to share ideas to improve aspects of student life.

Rabbi Noam Silverman, Avoiding "Excellent Sheep" in Jewish Day Schools (EJewish Philanthropy)

We don't chase away darkness with broomsticks. We use light. It just so happens we have a very powerful light in our hands for zapping away all sorts of darkness. It's called *tzedakah*—simply giving more money than you usually would to a worthy cause. *Tzedakah* is like bringing a sacrifice in the Temple—you give away something precious to you, and that takes away those things that you don't want to be part of you.

*Rabbi Yisroel Cotlar, Help! I Ate Something That Wasn't Kosher! (Chabad.org » Learning & Values » **Questions** & Answers » Ask the Rabbi » Newest **Questions**)*

Yes.

Absolutely.

Having said that, the essential Tzedakah **question** is, "How do you determine if what you did with your Tzedakah money was a pure act of Tzedakah?"

Danny Siegel, Tzedakah: A Time for Change

*I have a **question** about tzedakah. In regards to the giving of 10 percent of one's income, it is my understanding that one can count the giving of resources and time spent helping others as part of the required 10 percent of income. Is this correct?*

Harav Melamed gives this exact answer on the website Yeshiva.org.il:

רובע למשח תודובע עצבל רשעמ תתל סוקמב רשפא סאה : הלאש
ילש הדובעה תולע תא בישחהל דציכו ?הל סורתל ויינועמ ינאש הבישי,
ותואש הדובע וז סא : הבושת ?לזומ ךירעת יפל וא עובקה ךירעתה יפל
רשפאו ,ךסכ הווש ךתדובעש ירה ,ךסכ הרובע סלשל ךירצ היה דסומ
תולע תא בשחל שיו .רשעמה סוקמב סולשתכ ךתדובע תא בישחהל
רשק סהיניב שיש סישנא ויב לבוקמ ךכש ,לזומה ךירעתה יפל הדובעה
רציה אמש שוחל שיש דועו .לזומ ךירעתב תודובע הזל הז סיעצבמש ,בוט
תויהל ידכו ,רשעמ סולשתמ רטפיהל ידכ ,הלעמ יפלכ ובשחה תא הטי
ךירצ דוע .לזומ ךירעת יפ לע ,ינשה דצל תכלל שי ,וגוה ובשחהש סיחוטב
בישחהל שי אליממ ,ךסכ הילע לבקל לוכי היהש הדובע וזש וכיש ,ךיילצ
אליממ ךירצ היה רשעמ וכש ,הדובעה ךרעמ זוחא סיעשת קר רשעמכ
הדובע התוא לע סלשל

So the answer is that if the work that is done is something that can be billed (like an electrician working on a poor person's house), you can use it as part or all of your 10%, since your work has monetary value. He states that in this case, you should use your discounted rate if you give discounts, and you can only consider 90% of that towards the 10% you owe, because had freque you have gotten paid for this work, you would have to give another 10% on top of that.

Avi Hirsch, answered Jul 26 at 15:43,

Improve This Answer:

+1 Seems though the worker needs to be a professional in the field who normally gets paid for this type of work.—*user6591 Jul 26 at 16:06*

Mi Yodeya, Can Time Spent With Others Be Counted as Ma'Aser, According to Halacha? (judaism.stackexchange.com)

"Sure," says the priest, who is back in his place across the azimuth. "Now here is the **question**." There's a lively light in his eye. He's out to catch me again. He has the super-sane chipperness of the true nut.

"Can you name one word sign which has not been evacuated of meaning, that is, deprived?"

"I don't think I can. As a matter of fact, I'm afraid that—" Again I look at my watch.

Two things have become clear to me in the last few seconds. One thing is that Father Smith has gone batty, but batty in a way I recognize. He belongs to that category of nut who can do his job competently enough, quite well in fact, but given one minute of free time latches on to an obsession like a tongue seeking a sore tooth. He called in the forest fire like a pro, but now he's back at me with a mad chipper light in his eye.

The second thing is that I promised Father Placide to make an "evaluation" of Father Smith's mental condition. Can he do priestly work?

No, three things.

The third thing is that all at once I want badly to get out of here and see Lucy Lipscomb.

"Can you name the one word sign," Father Smith asks me, leaning close over the azimuth, "that has not been evacuated of meaning, that is, deprived by a depriver?"

"I'm not sure what the **question** means. Later perhaps—"

"Will you allow me to demonstrate," says the priest triumphantly, as if he had already demonstrated.

"Of course," I say with fake psychiatric cordiality.

"The signs out there"—he nods to the shaggy forest—"refer to something, don't they?"

"Right."

"The smoke was a sign of fire."

"That is correct."

"There is no doubt about the existence of the fire."

"True."

"Words are signs, aren't they?"

"You could say so."

"But unlike the signs out there, words have been evacuated, haven't they?"

"Evacuated?"

"They don't signify anymore."

"How do you mean?" From long practice I can keep my voice attentive without paying close attention. I wonder if Lucy—

"What if I were to turn the tables on you, ha ha, and play the psychoanalyst?"

"Very good," I say gloomily.

"You psychoanalysts encourage your patients to practice free association with words, true?"

"Yes." Actually it's not true.

"Let me turn the tables on you and give you a couple of word signs and you give me your free associations."

"Fine. "

"Clouds."

"Sky, fleecy, puffy, floating, white—"

"Okay. Irish."

"Bogs, Notre Dame, Pat O'Brien, begorra—"

"Okay. Blacks."

"Blacks?"

"Negroes."

"Blacks, Africa, niggers, minority, civil rights—"

"Okay. Jew."

"Israel, Bible, Max, Sam, Julius, Hebrew, Hebe, Ben—"

"Right! You see!" He is smiling and nodding and making fists in his pockets. I realize that he is doing isometrics in his pockets.

"See what?"

"Jews!"

"What about Jews?" I say after a moment.

"Precisely!"

"Precisely what?"

"What do you mean?"

"What about Jews?"

"What do you think about Jews?" he asks, cocking an eye.

"Nothing much one way or the other."

"May I continue my demonstration, Doctor?"

"For one minute." I look at my watch, but he doesn't seem to notice. "May I ask who

Max, Sam, Julius, and Ben are?"

"Max Gottlieb is my closest friend and personal physician. Sam Aaronson was my roommate in medical school. Julius Freund was my training analyst at Hopkins. Ben Solomon was my fellow detainee and cellmate at Fort Pelham, Alabama."

"Very interesting."

"How's that?"

"Don't you see?"

"No."

"Unlike the other test words, what you associated with the word *Jew* was Jews, Jews you have known. Isn't that interesting?"

"Yes," I say, pursing my mouth in a show of interest.

"What you associated with the word sign Irish were certain connotations, stereotypical Irish stuff in your head. Same for Negro. If I had said Spanish, you'd have said something like guitar, castanets, bullfights, and such. I have done the test on dozens. Thus, these word signs have been evacuated, deprived of meaning something real. Real persons. Not so with Jews."

"So?"

He's feeling so much better that he's doing foot exercises, balancing on the ball of one foot, then the other. Now, to my astonishment, he is doing a bit of shadow-boxing, weaving and throwing a few punches.

"That's the only sign of God which has not been evacuated by an evacuator," he says, moving his shoulders.

"What sign is that?"

"Jews."

"Jews?"

"You got it, Doc." He sits, gives the azimuth a spin like a croupier who has raked in all the chips.

"Got what?"

"You see the point."

"What's the point?"

He leans close, eyes alight, "The Jews—cannot—be—subsumed."

"Can't be what?"

"Subsumed."

"I see."

"Since the Jews were the original chosen people of God, a tribe of people who are still here, they are a sign of God's presence which cannot be evacuated. Try to find a hole in that proof!"

I try—that is, I act as if I am trying.

"You can't find a hole, can you?" he says triumphantly.

"But, Father, the Jews I know are not religious. They either do not believe in God or, like me, they don't attach any significance beyond—"

"Precisely!"

"Precisely?"

"Precisely. *Probatur conclusio*, as St. Thomas would say." He seems to have finished.

"Right," I say, reaching for the rung of the trapdoor. I think I know what to tell Father Placide.

"Hold it!" He waves an arm out to the wide world. "Name one other thing out there which cannot be subsumed."

"I can't."

"Pine tree?"

"How do you mean, pine tree?"

"That pine tree can be subsumed under the classes of trees called conifers, right?"

"Right."

"Try to subsume Jews under the classes of mankind, Caucasians, Semites, whatever. Go ahead, try it."

"Excuse me, Father, but I really—"

"Do your friends still consider themselves Jews?"

"Yes."

"You see. It does not matter whether they believe. Believe or not, they are still Jews. And what are Jews if not the actual people originally chosen by God?"

"Excuse me, Father, but is it not also part of Christian belief that the Jews did not accept Jesus as the Messiah and that therefore—"

"Makes no difference!" exclaims the priest, throwing a punch as if this were the very objection he had been waiting for.

"It doesn't?"

"Read St. Paul! It is clear that their inability to accept Jesus was not only fore-ordained but altogether reasonable and is not to be held against them. Salvation comes from the Jews, as holy scripture tells us. They remain the beloved, originally chosen people of God."

"Right. Now I—"

"It is also psychologically provable."

"It is?"

"Jews are naturally skeptical, hardheaded, and, after all, what Jesus was proposing to them was a tall order."

"Yes. Well—" He's standing on the trapdoor and I can't lift it until he gets off.

"What do you think Peres would say if Begin claimed to be the Messiah?"

I have to laugh.

"No no." The priest hunches forward, almost clearing the trapdoor. "You're missing the point."

"I am?"

"How many times in your work have you encountered someone who claims to be Napoleon, the Messiah, Hitler, the Devil?"

"Often."

"How often have you encountered a Jewish patient who claimed to be the Messiah or Napoleon?"

"Not often."

"You see?"

"Yes."

"No, you don't."

"I don't?"

"You still don't see the bottom line psychologically speaking?" My nose has started running seriously. He is standing on the trapdoor and my nose is dripping.

"One, a Jew will not believe another Jew making such a preposterous claim, right? But—But—!" Now he has come to the bottom line sure enough. For he has stopped doing isometrics and throwing punches and has instead placed both hands on the azimuth and lined me up in the sights. He speaks in a low intense voice, pausing between each word. "Is it not the case, Doctor, that if a Jew speaks to a Gentile, speaks with authority, with sobriety, as a friend—*the Gentile—will—believe—him!* Think about it!" He has leaned over so close I can see the white fiber, the arcus senilis, around his pupil.

I give every appearance of thinking about it.

"Even an anti-Semite! Did you ever notice that an anti-Semite who despises Jews actually believes them deep down—that's why he hates them!—and isn't that the reason he despises them?"

I eye him curiously. "May I ask you something, Father?"

"Fire away."

"Do you still regard yourself as a Catholic priest?"

For the first time he seems surprised. He stops his isometrics, cocks his head. "How do you mean, Tom?"

"Why are you?"

"Why am I what? Oh. You mean why am I a Catholic—Tom, may I ask you a **question**?"

"Sure."

"Do you remember what a sacrament is?"

I smile. "A sensible sign instituted by Christ to produce grace. I can still rattle it off."

The priest laughs. "Those sisters did a job on us, didn't they?"

"Yes. Maybe too good."

"What? Oh. Yes, yes. Do you remember the scriptural example they always gave?"

"Sure. Unless you eat my body and drink my blood, you will not have life in you."

"Same one!" says the priest, again laughing, then falls to musing. "Life," he murmurs absently and under his breath. "Life. But that's the trouble, the words—"

"What's that?" I ask the priest, wondering if he's still talking to me.

"Oh," he says, giving a start. "I'm sorry. To answer your **question**—" He frowns mightily.

What **question**?

Walker Percy, *The Thanatos Syndrome*

Q: If there's a Beer Volcano and a Stripper Factory in Heaven, what's FSM Hell like?

A: We're not entirely certain, but we imagine it's similar to FSM Heaven, only the beer is stale and the strippers have venereal diseases. Not unlike Las Vegas.

Q: Are there male strippers in FSM Heaven for women?

A: Probably, but they are invisible to the non-homo guys.

Q: Your "religion" offends my (probably Christian) beliefs.

A: That's not a **question**.

Bobby Henderson, *The Gospel of the Flying Spaghetti Monster*

The **Question** is what is The **Question**?

Is it all a Magic Show?

Is Reality an Illusion?

What is the framework of The Machine?
Darwin's Puzzle: Natural Selection?
Where does Space-Time come from?
Is there any answer except that it comes from consciousness?
What is Out There?
T'is Ourselves?
Or, is IT all just a Magic Show?
Einstein told me: "If you would learn, teach!"

John Wheeler, Speaking at the American Physical Society, Philadelphia, April 2003. As quoted and cited in Jack Sarfatti, 'Wheeler's World: It From Bit?', collected in Frank H. Columbus and Volodymyr Krasnoholovets (eds.), Developments in Quantum Physics (2004), 42.

Today in Science History, Science Quotes by Charles Darwin

What is Deresiewicz's conclusion? How does he attempt to connect to a bigger picture that all citizens should care about?

Diana Austin, Excellent Sheep: Close Reading **Questions** (Allen Independent School District)

. . . as if the **question** was, "Why should I care about this?" You can see this in play in the following example. In 2004, I attended a small conference in Silicon Valley that brought together technologists, executives, and consultants. The second day of the conference began with . . .

Lee LeFever, The Art of Explanation, Enhanced Edition: Making your Ideas, Products, and Services Easier to Understand

A Catechism Lesson in a Madras Presidency Village, 1939
Salesians of Don Bosco (Wikimedia Commons)

A Representation of the Sugar-Cane and the Art of Making Sugar
Universal Magazine of Knowledge and Pleasure, London, John Hinton, 1749

*American Battlefield Trust, Sugar Act Primary Source **Questions** (battlefields.org)*

Sources : Volume I

Abbott, Lee K. *Wet Places at Noon*. University of Iowa Press, 1997.

Abse, Dannie. "Snake." *White Coat Purple Coat: Collected Poems*. New York: Hutchinson, 1994.

Acker, Kathy. *Don Quixote, Which Was a Dream*. New York: Grove Press, 1989.

———. *Great Expectations*. New York: Grove Press, 1989.

ACT® (American College Testing). "Test Booklet Instrutions." 2020. www.act.org.

Adams, Michelle. "10 Texts You Only Send to Your Mom." *ScholarshipPoints*, May 2, 2016. www.scholarshippoints.com.

Addison, Joseph. "Of the Christian Religion." *The Works of the Late Right Honorable Joseph Addison, Esq; Volume the Fourth, With a Complete Index*. Birmingham: J. and R. Tonson, 1761.

Adorno, Theodor W. *Negative Dialectics*. A&C Black, 1973.

Aiken, Ginny. *Someone to Trust*. Steeple Hill, 2009.

Alabama Supreme Court. *Reports of Cases Argued and Determined in the Supreme Court of Alabama, During a Part of June Term, 1849, and the Whole of January Term, 1850, Volume 18*. Montgomery: Brown Printing Company, 1907.

Alarçon, Pedro de. "The Nail." *Library of the World's Best Mystery and Detective Stories*. New York: The Review of Reviews Company, 1907.

Alexander, Harriet. "Donald Trump Says Megyn Kelly's Tough **Questioning** Was Due to Menstruation." *The Telegraph*, 08 August 2015. www.telegraph.co.uk.

Allen, Jeffrey G. *The Complete Q&A Job Interview Book*. New York: John Wiley & Sons, 2004.

Amis, Kingsley. *Lucky Jim*. 1954. London: Penguin, 1992.

Ammer, Christine. *The American Heritage Dictionary of Idioms*. New York: Houghton Mifflin Harcourt, 2013.

*An Answer to a Letter on the **Question** Are the Quakers' Right in Their Opinion on the Baptism of the Spirit? To Which Is Added a Second Letter, in Reply. By an Emigrant*. London: J. Turner, 1805.

Anderson, Erik. "Certified Copies: Notes Toward a Theory of the Knockoff." *3:AM Magazine*, July 7th, 2014. www.3ammagazine.com.

Anderson, James. *The Affair of the Mutilated Mink: A Delightfully Quirky Murder Mystery in the Great Tradition of Agatha Christie*. London: Allison & Busby, 2011.

Antrim, Donald. *Elect Mr. Robinson for a Better World*. 1993. New York: Picador, 2012.

Aquin, Hubert. *Next Episode*. 1965. Translated by Sheila Fischman. Toronto: McClelland & Stewart, 2001.

Aquinas, Thomas. *Summa Theologica*. 1274. Translated by Fathers of the English Dominican Province. Second ed. London: Burns, Oates & Washburne, 1920. www.newadvent.org/summa.

Aragon, Louis. *Treatise on Style*. 1928. Translated by Alyson Waters. University of Nebraska Press, 1991.

Arieh-Lerer, Shon. "Groucho Marx's Comedy Is Pure, Bleak Nihilism: So Why Does It Make Us Laugh?" *Slate*, January 6, 2016. www.slate.com.

Armstrong, Karen. *In the Beginning: A New Interpretation of Genesis*. New York: Ballantine Books, 1996.

Aron, Albert William. *Traces of Matriarchy in Germanic Hero-Lore*. Madison: University of Wisconsin, 1920.

Aronowitz, Stanley. "Reflections on Identity—Discussion." *The Identity in **Question***. Edited by John Rajchman. New York: Routledge, 1995.

Asamoah-Yaw, E. *BIG QUESTION: Do Humans Need God?* Xlibris, 2014.

Ashbery, John. "Hotel Lautréamont." *Notes from the Air: Selected Later Poems*. The Ecco Press, 2007.

AskTom. "**Questions** > Ora-Hash." *Oracle.com*, 2009. https://asktom.oracle.com.

———. "**Questions** > **Question** on Splitting." *Oracle.com*, 2003. https://asktom.oracle.com.

———. "**Questions** > Spawn Jobs From a Procedure That Run in Parallel." *Oracle.com*, 2003. https://asktom.oracle.com.

Atwood, Margaret. *Cat's Eye*. New York: Anchor Books, 1998.

———. *Payback: Debt and the Shadow Side of Wealth*. Toronto: House of Anansi Press, 2008.

Au, Michelle. *This Won't Hurt a Bit: (And Other White Lies): My Education in Medicine and Motherhood*. Grand Central Publishing, 2011.

Augustine, Saint. *Eighty-Three Different **Questions***. Washington, DC: Catholic University of America Press, 1982.

Auran, John Henry. "Equipment Close Up: Boots." *Skiing*, December 1975, 71.

Auster, Paul. *4 3 2 1*. London: Faber and Faber, 2017.

Austin, Diana. "Excellent Sheep Close Reading **Questions**." *Allen Independent School District*, 2016. www.allenisd.org.

Aveling, Eleanor Marx. "Introduction." *Madame Bovary*, by Gustave Flaubert. London: W. W. Gibbings, 1892, vii–xxii.

Aviv, Rachel. "Wrong Answer." *The New Yorker*, July 21, 2014, 54–65.

Ball, Philip. "If Not Darwin, Who? An Alternative History of the Great Ideas of Science." *Nautilus*, December 15, 2016. http://nautil.us.

Balliett, L. Dow. *The Balliett Philosophy of Number Vibration in **Questions** and Answers: A Text Book*. Health Research Books, 2008.

Balzac, Honoré de. "Melmoth Reconciled." *Library of the World's Best Mystery and Detective Stories*. New York: The Review of Reviews Company, 1907.

Banks, Iain. *Canal Dreams*. London: Little, Brown and Company, 1989.

Banks, Iain. *Transition*. London: Abacus, 2013.

Barnes, Gene. *What Then Is Truth? A Philosophical Dialogue*. Xlibris, 2004.

Barnes, Julian. *Flaubert's Parrot*. London: Jonathan Cape, 1984.

———. *Through the Window: Seventeen Essays (and one short story)*. London: Vintage, 2012.

Barnett, Jerry. "10 **Questions** for Climate Change Deniers: Comments." *MoronWatch*, 2013. www.moronwatch.net.

Barth, John. *Giles Goat-Boy, or, The Revised New Syllabus*.

1966. Garden City NY: Anchor Books/Doubleday, 1987.

Bartosiewicz, Petra. "Beyond the Broken Window." *Harper's Magazine,* May 2015, 48–57.

Beard, Mary. *Confronting the Classics: Traditions, Adventures, and Innovations.* New York: Liveright, 2013.

Beaulieu, Guy. *The Death of a Bookie: A Jacob Schreiber Mystery.* Kernersville, NC: A-Argus Better Book Publishers, 2009.

Becker, Helaine. "What Ancient Classical Heroine or Goddess Are You?" *The Quiz Book for Girls.* Toronto: Scholastic Canada, 2011, 53–56.

Becker, Susanne. "Celebrity, or A Disneyland of the Soul: Margaret Atwood and the Media." *Margaret Atwood: Works and Impact.* Edited by Reingard M. Nischik. Rochester, NY: Camden House, 2000, 28–40.

Beckett, Samuel. *The Unnamable.* New York: Grove Weidenfeld, 1965.

———. *Waiting For Godot.* New York: Grove Press, 1954.

Beha, Christopher. *"How Much Damage Can It Do? On the Intellectual Element in Modern Fiction." Harper's Magazine,* February 2015. https://harpers.org.

Belasco, Sonia. *Speak of Me As I Am.* New York: Philomel Books, 2017.

Bell, George, ed. *Notes and Queries: A Medium of Intercommunication for Literary Men, Artists, Antiquaries, Genealogists, etc.,* Number 185, May 14, 1853.

Berenson, Alex. *The Faithful Spy.* New York: Berkley Books, 2011.

Berger, Thomas. *Vital Parts.* New York: Richard W. Baron, 1970.

Bergner, George. *The Legislative Record: Containing the Debates and Proceedings of the Pennsylvania Legislature for the Session of 1864.* Harrisburg, PA: City of Harrisburg, 1864.

Berlinerblau, Jacques. "Teach or Perish." *The Chronicle of Higher Education,* Janurary 19, 2015. http://m.chronicle.com.

Berthold, Victor M. *The Die Varieties of the Nesbitt Series of United States Envelopes.* Scott Stamp & Coin Co, 1906.

billderesiewicz.com. "Acclaim for Excellent Sheep." 2017. www.billderesiewicz.com/books/excellent-sheep.

Bingham, B. Matthew. *The Answer is No! What Is the* **Question**? *A Little Orphan's Search for the Meaning of Life.* New York: iUniverse, 2003.

Birdseye, C. H. *Topographic Instructions of the United States Geological Survey.* Washington: United States Government Printing Office, 1928.

Birney, Earle. *Turvey: A Military Picaresque.* 1949. Toronto: McClelland & Stewart, 1977.

Bloxam, Matthew Holbeche. *The Principles of Gothic Ecclesiastical Architecture, Elucidated by* **Question** *and Answer.* 4th ed. Oxford: John Henry Parker, 1841.

Bolaño, Roberto. *Monsieur Pain.* New York: New Directions, 2010.

Bonder, Nilton. *To Have or Not to Have, That Is the* **Question***: The Economics of Desire.* Victoria, B.C.: Trafford Publishing, 2010.

Borzutzky, Daniel. "The Man in **Question**." *The Ecstasy of Capitulation.* BlazeVOX, 2007.

Both, Thomas. *d. d. d. d. d.—a d.school design project guide.* Hasso Plattner Institute of Design at Stanford University, 2016. https://dschool.stanford.edu/resources/design-project-guide-1.

Boucher d'Argis, Antoine-Gaspard. "**Question** or Torture." *The Encyclopedia of Diderot & d'Alembert Collaborative Translation Project* (Ann Arbor), 2008. Michigan Publishing, University of Michigan Library.

http://hdl.handle.net/2027/spo.did2222.0000.891.

Bradbury, Malcolm. *Eating People Is Wrong.* 1960. London: Picador, 2012.

Bramah, Ernest. "The Coin of Dionysius." *Max Carrados: A Collection of Classic Detective Stories.* London: Methuen & Co., 1904.

Brauner, David. ""Getting in Your Retaliation First": Narrative Strategies in Portnoy's Complaint." *Philip Roth: New Perspectives on an American Author.* Edited by Derek Parker Royal. Westport, CN: Praeger Publishers, 43–58.

Breiner, Laurence A. *An Introduction to West Indian Poetry.* Cambridge, UK: Cambridge University Press, 1998.

Breton, André. "Manifesto of Surrealism." 1924. *UbuWeb.* www.ubu.com/papers/breton_surrealism_manifesto.html.

Bromberger, Sylvain. *On What We Know We Don't Know: Explanation, Theory, Linguistics, and How* **Questions** *Shape Them.* Chicago: University of Chicago Press, 1992.

Brook, S.D. *A Cowboy in Time.* Xlibris, 2009.

Brooks, Michael. "Darwin vs Galileo: Who Cut Us Down to Size?" *New Scientist,* 17 December 2008. www.newscientist.com.

Browne, Ann. *Developing Language and Literacy 3–8.* London: Paul Chapman, 2009.

Browning-Wroe, Jo. *Happy, Sad, Jealous, Mad: Stories, Rhymes, and Activities that Help Young Children Understand Their Emotions.* Minneapolis, MN: Key Education Publishing, 2010.

Bruce, David. *Dante's Inferno: A Discussion Guide.* Athens, Ohio: 2009.

Buchan, John. *The Thirty-Nine steps.* Boston: Houghton Mifflin Co., 1919.

Buchanan, David. *Report of the Jury Trials, Miss Anne Waddel, & Others, Against The Right Hon. C. Hope, & Others, Trustees of the Late William Waddel, Esq. of Sydserff; and Miss Anne Waddel, Against The Right Hon. C. Hope, & Daughters, Commencing on 13th, and Ending on 17th May 1845.* Edinburgh: Thomas Allan & Co., 1845.

Budrys, Algis. *Who?* New York: Pyramid Books, 1958.

Bulgakov, Mikhail. *The Master and Margarita.* 1966. Translated by Hugh Aplin. Richmond, UK: Alma Classics, 2012.

Bunyan, John. *The Pilgrim's Progress: From This World to That Which Is to Come.* 1678. Project Gutenberg, 2012. www.gutenberg.org.

Buren, Daniel. "Beware!" 1970. *UbuWeb.* http://www.ubu.com/papers/buren_beware.html.

Burgess, Tony. *Pontypool Changes Everything.* Toronto: ECW Press, 2009.

Burritt, O. B. "Work of the Uniform Type Committee: From the American Point of View." *Outlook for the Blind: A Quarterly Record of Their Progress & Welfare, Volume 8.* Massachusetts Association for the Blind, 1915.

Burton, Gideon. *Silva Rhetoricae (The Forest of Rhetoric),* 2007. http://rhetoric.byu.edu/.

Bushnell & Albright, Attorneys for Relator and Appellant, and Shipman, Barlow, Larocque & MacFarland, Attorneys for Respondents. *New York Supreme Court: The People, etc., ex rel. Henry C. Ohlen, against The New York, Lake Erie and Western Railroad Company et al., Appeal Book, on Appeal from Order Quashing Writ of Mandamus.* New York: C. G. Burgoyne, 1880.

Bykofsky, Sheree, and Jennifer Basye Sander. *The Complete Idiot's Guide to Publishing Magazine Articles.* New York: Penguin, 2000.

Byron, Lord. "Don Juan." *Poetry Foundation*, 2014. www.poetryfoundation.org.

C.M. Parker, ed. *The School News and Practical Educator, Volume 11*. Chicago: September, 1897.

Caiazza, John C. *The War of the Jesus and Darwin Fishes: Religion and Science in the Postmodern World*. New York: Routledge, 2011.

Calthorpe, Peter, and William Fulton. *The Regional City: Planning for the End of Sprawl*. Washington, DC: Island Press, 2001.

Calvino, Italo. "Why Read the Classics?" *The New York Review of Books,* October 9, 1986. www.nybooks.com.

Campbell, John. *The Present State of the Bible **Question** Considered, in a Letter to the People of England, With Directions for Forming Churches and Sunday Schools Into Efficient Bible Societies, by the Author of "Jethro"*. London: John Snow, 1841.

Camus, Albert. *The Myth of Sisyphus*. 1942. Translated by Justin O'Brien. London: Penguin, 1988.

———. *The Plague*. 1948. Translated by Stuart Gilbert. Harmondsworth: Penguin, 1973.

———. *The Stranger*. Translated by Stuart Gilbert. New York: Vintage, 1946.

Canadian Press. "Trudeau's French Answers to English **Questions** Draw Language Complaints." *Toronto Star,* 19 January 2017. www.thestar.com.

Canetti, Elias. *Audo da Fé*. Translated by C. V. Wedgwood. London: Picador, 1935.

Capuana, Luigi. "The Deposition." *Library of the World's Best Mystery and Detective Stories*. New York: The Review of Reviews Company, 1907.

CareerRide.com. "50 Oracle 11g dba Interview **Questions** and Answers—Freshers, Experienced." 2016. www.careerride.com.

Carey, James W. "Reflections on the Project of (American) Cultural Studies." *Cultural Studies in **Question***. Edited by Marjorie Ferguson and Peter Golding. SAGE, 1997, 280.

Carlyle, Thomas. *Characteristics*. The Harvard Classics, Vol. XXV, Part 3. Edited by Charles W. Eliot. New York: P. F. Collier & Son, 1909–14.

———. *On Heroes, Hero-Worship and the Heroic in History*. London: Chapman and Hall, 1897.

———. *Sartor Resartus: The Life and Opinions of Herr Teufelsdröckh*. 1836. Project Gutenberg. www.gutenberg.org.

Carpenter, Scott. *Aesthetics of Fraudulence in Nineteenth-Century France: Frauds, Hoaxes, and Counterfeits*. London: Taylor & Francis, 2016.

Carroll, Ruth. "Vague Language in the Medieval Recipes of the Forme of Cury." *Instructional Writing in English: Studies in Honour of Risto Hiltunen*. Edited by Matti Peikola, Janne Skaffari, and Sanna-Kaisa Tanskanen. Amsterdam: John Benjamins Publishing, 2009, 55–82.

Carson, Anne. "The Glass Essay." *Glass, Irony, and God*. New Directions Publishing, 1995.

Carter, Philip J., and Kenneth A. Russell. *The Book of IQ Tests: 25 Self-Scoring Quizzes to Sharpen Your Mind*. New York: Sterling, 2008.

Carter, Philip. *The Complete Book of Intelligence Tests: 500 Exercises to Improve, Upgrade and Enhance Your Mind Strength*. New York: MJF Books, 2005.

Castro, Jan Garden. "An Interview with Margaret Atwood." *Margaret Atwood: Vision and Forms*. Edited by Kathryn VanSpanckeren and Jan Garden Castro. Carbondale: Southern Illinois University Press, 1988, 215–32.

Casual Dragon Games. "Zombie Sheep." *Kickstarter.com*. www.kickstarter.com.

Cawdrey, Daniel, Giles Firmin, and Thomas Hooker. *A Sober Answer to a Serious **Question** Propounded by Mr. G. Firmin. viz. Whether the Ministers of England Are Bound by the Word of God to Baptise the Children of All Such Parents Which Say They Believe in Jesus Christ. Which May Serve Also as an Appendix to the Diatribe With Mr. Hooker, Concerning the Baptisme of Infants*. 1652.

Chandler, Raymond. "The Simple Art of Murder." *The Simple Art of Murder*. New York: Houghton Mifflin, 1950.

———. *The Big Sleep*. 1939. Library of World Literature, http://ae-lib.org.ua/.

Charney, Noah. "Did Nazis Really Try to Make Zombies? The Real History Behind One of Our Weirdest Wwii Obsessions." *Salon*, August 22, 2015. www.salon.com.

Chase, Scott, Michael Weiss, Philip Gibbs, Chris Hillman, and Nathan Urban. *The Original Usenet Physics FAQ,* 2014. http://physicsfaq.co.uk.

Chaucer, Geoffrey. "The Canterbury tales." Translated by F. N. Robinson. *The Works of Geoffrey Chaucer*. Boston: Houghton Mifflin, 1957.

———. "The Canterbury Tales." Translated by D. Laing Purves. *The Canterbury Tales and Other Poems*. Edinburgh: William P. Nimmo & Co., 1879.

Chesterton, G. K. "The Man in the Passage." *Father Brown: Essential Tales*. New York: Modern Library, 2017, 196–212.

———. *Orthodoxy*. New York: John Lane, 1909.

———. *The Flying Inn*. London: John Lane, 1914.

———. *The Man Who Knew Too Much*. Project Gutenberg, 1999. www.gutenberg.org/ebooks/1720.

Child, Lee. *Make Me*. London: Bantam Books, 2015.

Chiu, Allyson, and Meagan Flynn. "Trump Blocks Fauci From Answering **Question** About Drug Trump Is Touting." *Washington Post,* 8 Apr 2020. www.washingtonpost.com.

Christian, Caroline. *The Scent of Bread*. Xlibris, 2016.

ChronicBabe. "100 Ways to Answer the **Question** 'How Are You?'." 2015. www.chronicbabe.com.

Cicero, Marcus Tullius. *The Academic **Questions**, Treatise De Finibus, and Tusculan Disputations*. Translated by C. D. Yonge. London: George Bell and Sons, 1875.

Ciment, Jill. *The Body in **Question**: A Novel*. New York: Pantheon, 2019.

Clár, Annaleise. "Agent Benjamin Ripley." *Wattpad,* 2018. www.wattpad.com/story/166300203-agent-benjamin-ripley.

Clark, Herbert H. "Wordless **Questions**, Wordless Answers." ***Questions**: Formal, Functional and Interactional Perspectives*. Edited by Jan P. de Ruiter. Cambridge: Cambridge University Press, 2012, 81–101.

Claude Lalumière, and David Nickle, eds. *The Exile Book of New Canadian Noir*. Holstein, ON: Exile Editions, 2015.

Clayton, Alex. *Funny How? Sketch Comedy and the Art of Humor*. Albany: SUNY Press, 2020.

Clegg, Tom, and Warren Bird. *Missing in America: Making an Eternal Difference in the World Next Door*. Group Publishing, 2007.

Cloud, Henry, and John Townsend. *Boundaries: When to Say Yes, How to Say No*. Grand Rapids, MI: Zondervan, 2008.

Coe, Jonathan. *The Dwarves of Death*. London: Sceptre, 1990.

Coen, Ethan. "Destiny." *Gates of Eden*. New York: Harper Perennial, 1998, 1–30.

Coen, Joel, and Ethan Coen. *A Serious Man (Screenplay)*, 2009. www.screenplaydb.com/film/scripts/seriousmana/

Coetzee, J. M. "Lives by Omission." *Harper's Magazine*, October 2015. https://harpers.org.

———. *Waiting for the Barbarians*. New York: Penguin, 1999.

Cohen, Jeffrey. *Some Like It Hot-Buttered*. New York: Berkley Prime Crime, 2007.

Cohen, Joshua. "New Books." *Harper's Magazine*, August 2015. https://harpers.org/.

Cohen, Margaret. *The Novel and the Sea*. Princeton, NJ: Princeton University Press, 2010.

College Art Association. "Code of Best Practices in Fair Use for the Visual Arts: **Frequently Asked Questions**." 2015. www.collegeart.org.

Collins, Wilkie. *The Law and the Lady*. London: Chatto & Windus, 1887.

Community, Sprint. "Text Message **Question**-Viewing Whole Message." 12-09-2011. https://community.sprint.com.

Connor, Joan. *The World Before Mirrors*. University of Nebraska Press, 2006.

Cook, Gareth. "A True and Complete Account of the Neuroscience of Zombies." *Scientific American*, November 18, 2014. www.scientificamerican.com.

Copperman, E. J., and Jeff Cohen. *The **Question** of the Missing Head*. Woodbury, MN: Midnight Ink, 2014.

cormacmccarthy.com. "Heidegger's Cabin/Bell's Water Trough." 07 Jun 2014. www.cormacmccarthy.com.

Cornell, Paul. *Human Nature: The New Doctor Who Adventures*. London: Doctor Who Books, 1995.

Cotlar, Rabbi Yisroel. "Help! I Ate Something That Wasn't Kosher!" *Chabad.org » Learning & Values » **Questions** & Answers » Ask the Rabbi » Newest **Questions** » Advice*. http://www.chabad.org.

Cotto, Andrew. *Outerborough Blues: A Brooklyn Mystery*. Brooklyn: Ig Publishing, 2012.

Coxe, Warren W. "Grading Intelligence by Years and by Points." *Journal of Criminal Law and Criminology* VII, 1916, 341–65.

Cram, Buffy. *Radio Belly: Stories*. Douglas & McIntyre, 2012.

Crane, Tim. "Wittgenstein, Bewitched." *The Times Literary Supplement*, 24 February 2016. www.the-tls.co.uk.

Crawford, Lucas. *Transgender Architectonics: The Shape of Change in Modernist Space*. London: Routledge, 2016.

Creation Ministries International, "A Wolf Among the Sheep." 2005. https://creation.com/a-wolf-among-the-sheep.

Crummey, Michael. *Galore: A Novel*. Toronto: Doubleday Canada, 2009.

Czech News Agency. "Czech Protest Movement to Demonstrate Against Government Handling of Coronavirus Crisis." *Expats.cz*, May 29, 2020. https://news.expats.cz.

Daley, David. "Camille Paglia: How Bill Clinton Is Like Bill Cosby." *Salon*, July 28, 2015. www.salon.com.

Darragh, Constance Raena. *Fate Xs Three*. iUniverse, 2002.

Darwin, Charles. "Introduction." *On the Origin of Species by Means of Natural Selection; or, The Preservation of Favoured Races in the Struggle for Life*. London: John Murray, 1859.

———. "Science Quotes by Charles Darwin." *Today in Science History*. https://todayinsci.com.

Davidson, Arnold E. "Future Tense: Making History in

The Handmaid's Tale." *Margaret Atwood: Vision and Forms*. Edited by Kathryn VanSpanckeren and Jan Garden Castro. Carbondale: Southern Illinois University Press, 1988, 113–21.

Davies, Robertson. *What's Bred in the Bone*. Toronto: Penguin, 1986.

Davis, Henry. *Explanations for the Official SAT Study Guide **Questions**: Detailed Explanations for the Answers for Every **Question***. Henry Davis, 2010.

Davis, W. H. *The Freewill **Question***. The Hague: Martinus Nijhoff, 1971.

De Vries, Peter. *Let Me Count the Ways: a Novel*. 1965. New York: Open Road Integrated Media, 2014.

Defoe, Daniel. *A Journal of the Plague Year: Being Observations or Memorials of the Most Remarkable Occurrences, as Well Public as Private, Which Happened in London During the Last Great Visitation in 1665. Written by a Citizen Who Continued All the While in London. Never Made Public Before*. 1722. Edited by Anthony Burgess and Christopher Bristow. Harmondsworth, UK: Penguin, 1966.

DeLillo, Don. *White Noise*. New York: Penguin Books, 1986.

Deresiewicz, William. "What A Piece of Work: Mark Greif's Intellectual Excavations." *Harper's Magazine*, June 2015, 88–94.

Derienzo, Susan. *How to Soar Like an Eagle: If You Have the Strength to Dream, Then You Can Soar*. Maitland, FL: Xulon Press, 2010.

Deusner, Stephen. "Art Garfunkel's Greatest Interview Ever: 'Paul and Artie Can Be Very Squirmy Around Each Other'." *Salon*, October 1, 2015. www.salon.com.

Dick, Philip K. *The Man in the High Castle*. New York: Vintage Books, 1992.

Dickens, Charles. *A Tale of Two Cities*. London: Chapman & Hall, 1859.

———. *Great Expectations*. Chapman & Hall, 1867.

Diderot, Denis. *Jacques the Fatalist and his Master*. 1796. Translated by David Coward. London: Oxford World's Classics, 1999.

Dillon, J.T. ***Questioning** and Teaching: A Manual of Practice*. Eugene, OR: Wipf and Stock Publishers, 2004.

Diop, Samba. "The Oral History and Literature of the Wolof People of Waalo, Northern Senegal: The Master of the Word (Griot) in the Wolof Tradition." *African Studies, Vol. 6*. Lewiston: E. Mellen Press, 1995, 277–90.

Dobbs, Sarah. "Black Sheep: Jonathan King Interview." *Den of Geek!* Mar 11, 2008. www.denofgeek.com.

Dodero, Camille. "Newspapering Is a Business: The Death of the Legendary Boston Phoenix." *Gawker*, 03/15/13. www.gawker.com.

Donovan, Stephen, Danuta Fjellestad, and Rolf Lunden. "Introduction: Author, Authorship, Authority, and Other Matters." *Authority Matters: Rethinking the Theory and Practice of Authorship*. Edited by Stephen Fjellestad Donovan, Danuta and Rolf Lunden. Amsterdam: Rodopi, 2008, 1–21.

Dorn, Edward. "The Price is Right: A Torture Wheel of Fortune." *Abhorrences*. Black Sparrow Books, 1990.

Dostoevsky, Fyodor. *Crime and Punishment*. Translated by Constance Garnett. New York: P. F. Collier & Son, 1917.

Dostoevsky, Fyodor. *Notes from the Underground*. Translated by Constance Garnett. New York: The MacMillan Company, 1918.

———. *Crime and Punishment*. Translated by David Magarshack. Harmondsworth, UK: Penguin Books, 1981.

———. *The Possessed; or, The Devils.* Translated by Constance Garnett. Project Gutenberg, 2005. www.gutenberg.org.

Doyle, Arthur Conan. *The Lost World.* London: Hodder & Stoughton, 1912.

Driessen, Alfred, and Antoine Suarez. *Mathematical Undecidability, Quantum Nonlocality and the* **Question** *of the Existence of God.* Springer Science & Business Media, 2012.

Druid, Norma. *A Test of Alien Alliance.* Xlibris Corporation, 2011.

Duncan, Christopher. *The Career Programmer: Guerilla Tactics for an Imperfect World.* Berkeley: Apress, 2006.

Dunglison, Robley. *Medical Lexicon: a Dictionary of Medical Science; Containing a Concise Explanation of the Various Subjects and Terms of Anatomy, Physiology, Pathology, Hygiene, Therapeutics, Medical Chemistry, Pharmacology, Pharmacy, Surgery, Obstetrics, Medical Jurisprudence, and Dentistry; Notices of Climate, and of Mineral Waters; Formulæ for Officinal, Empirical, and Dietetic Preparations; With the Accentuation and Etymology of the Terms, and the French and Other Synonyms.* Philadelphia: Henry C. Lea, 1874.

Dungy, Camille. "**Question** and Answer: The Top Five." *Poetry Foundation,* 2010. www.poetryfoundation.org.

DuQuette, Lon Milo. *The Book of Ordinary Oracles: Use Pocket Change, Popsicle Sticks, A TV Remote, This Book, and More to Predict the Future and Answer Your* **Questions***.* Newburyport, MA: Red Wheel Weiser, 2005.

Eady, Cornelius. "The Empty Dance Shoes." *Victims of the Latest Dance Craze.* Pittsburgh: Carnegie Mellon University Press, 1997.

Eco, Umberto. *The Prague Cemetery.* Translated by Richard Dixon. Boston: Houghton Mifflin Harcourt, 2011.

Edmonds, Julie, and Michell Smith. *The Six* **Questions***: That You Better Get Right: The Answers Are the Keys to Your Success.* New York: Morgan James Publishing, 2012.

Egan, Jennifer. *A Visit From the Goon Squad.* New York: Anchor Books, 2011.

Ekiss, Robin. "The **Question** of My Mother." *Poetry Magazine,* November 2007.

"Election of Elders, No. VI: Being the Second Part of an Answer to G. Greenwell's Replies to Jethro." *The Christian Messenger and Reformer; Devoted to the Dissemination of Primitive Christianity, Volume 9.* London: Simpkin, Marshall, and Co., 1845.

Eliot, George. *Middlemarch: A Study of Provincial Life.* 1872. New York: New American Library, 1964.

Eliot, T. S. "The Love Song of J. Alfred Prufrock." *Poetry,* June 1915.

Ellis, John. *TV FAQ: Uncommon Answers to Common* **Questions** *About TV.* I.B.Tauris, 2007.

Ellison, Ralph. *Invisible Man.* 1952. London: Viking, 2014.

Elsa Knight Bruno. *Punctuation Celebration.* New York: Henry Holt and Company, 2012.

Encyclopedia Mythica. "Pythia." www.pantheon.org/articles/p/pythia.html.

English Club. "WH **Question** Words." *English Club,* 1997–2015. www.englishclub.com.

English Language & Usage Stack Exchange. "What Is the Best Answer to the **Question** "How Are You" in Business Meetings?" *English Language & Usage Stack Exchange.* http://english.stackexchange.com.

Epictetus. *The Golden Sayings of Epictetus.* Translated by Hastings Crossley. The Harvard Classics, Vol. II, Part 2.

Edited by Charles W. Eliot. New York: P. F. Collier & Son, 1909–14.

Erasmus, Desiderius. *The Praise of Folly.* 1509. Translated by John Wilson. Internet History Sourcebooks Project, 1998. www.fordham.edu/halsall/mod/1509erasmus-folly.asp.

Erckmann-Chatrian. "The Invisible Eye." *Library of the World's Best Mystery and Detective Stories.* New York: The Review of Reviews Company, 1907.

———. "The Owl's Ear." *Library of the World's Best Mystery and Detective Stories.* New York: The Review of Reviews Company, 1907.

Ernest C. Thomas, ed. *The Library Chronicle: A Journal of Librarianship & Bibliography.* Vol. II. London: J. Davy & Sons, 1884.

Evans, Kim. "You Do Not Have To Say Anything But." *The Justice Gap,* December 2012. http://thejusticegap.com.

Everett, Percival. "Graham Greene." *Half an Inch of Water: Stories.* Minneapolis: Graywolf Press, 2015.

Fehrenbacher, Don. E, ed. "First Lincoln-Douglas Debate, Ottawa, Illinois." *Abraham Lincoln: Speeches and Writings, 1832–1858.* . New York: Library of America, 1989, 495–535.

Ferguson, Will, and Ian Ferguson. *How to Be a Canadian (Even if You Already Are One).* Vancouver: Douglas & McIntyre, 2001.

Fetherling, George. *The File on Arthur Moss.* Toronto: Lester Publishing, 1994.

Fielding, Henry. *The History of Tom Jones, a Foundling.* 1749. Harmondsworth, Eng.: Penguin, 1975.

Finkel, Michael. *The Stranger in the Woods: The Extraordinary Story of the Last True Hermit.* New York: Alfred A Knopf, 2017.

Finnegan, William. "The Man Who Wouldn't Sit Down." *The New Yorker,* October 5, 2015. www.newyorker.com.

Fitz-Morris, James. "Bill C-51 Committee Hears Monologues, but Few **Questions**." *CBC News,* Mar 13, 2015. www.cbc.

Flaubert, Gustave. *Madame Bovary.* Translated by Adam Thorpe. New York: Random House, 2013.

———. *Madame Bovary.* Translated by Eleanor Marx Aveling. London: W. W. Gibbings, 1892.

———. *Madame Bovary.* Translated by Lydia Davis. Penguin UK, 2010.

———. *Madame Bovary.* Translated by Raymond N. MacKenzie. Hackett Publishing, 2009.

Flint, Kate. "Introduction to Diary of a Nobody, by George Grossmith and Weedon

Flint, Kate. "Introduction to Diary of a Nobody, by George Grossmith and Weedon Grossmith." *The Diary of a Nobody,* by GeorgeGrossmith and Weedon Grossmith. Edited by Kate Flint. Oxford, UK: Oxford University Press, 1995. vii–xxiv.

Florman, Samuel C. "The Job-Enrichment Mistake." *Harper's Magazine,* May 1976. Reprinted in *Harper's Magazine,* March 2015, p 29.

Flowers, John. "Sample **Questions** from the Trump University Final Exam." *The New Yorker,* March 22, 2016.

Foley, Ray. *Beer Is the Answer . . . I Don't Remember the* **Question***: And Over 1,000 Other Bar Jokes, Quotes and Cartoons.* Naperville, IL: Sourcebooks, 2007.

Ford, Ford Madox. *Parade's End.* 1924. London: Penguin, 2002.

Forel, Auguste, and C. F. Marshall. *The Sexual* **Question***: A Scientific, Psychological, Hygienic and Sociological Study (Second Edition, Revised and Enlarged).* Brooklyn:

Physicians and Surgeons Book Company, 1931.

Forster, Nathaniel. *An Anſwer to a Pamphlet Entitled, "The Queſtion Stated, Whether the Freeholders of Middleſex Forfeited Their Right by Voting for Mr. Wilkes at the Laſt Election? In a Letter From a Member of Parliament to One of His Conſtituents." With a Poſtſcript, Occaſioned by a Letter in the Public Papers Subſcribed Junius.* London: James Fletcher, and Co., J. Walter and J. Robson, 1769.

Fowler, Floyd J. *Improving Survey **Questions**: Design and Evaluation.* SAGE, 1995.

Francesco dell'Isola, Ugo Andreaus, Raffaele Esposito Antonio Cazzani, Luca Placidi, Umberto Perego, Giulio Maier, and Pierre Seppecher, eds. *The Complete Works of Gabrio Piola, Volume II: Commented English Translation.* Cham: Springer, 2018.

Franzen, Jonathan. "The End of the End of the World." *The New Yorker,* May 23, 2016.

———. *Purity.* London: 4th Estate/HarperCollins, 2016.

Frazer, James George. *The Golden Bough: A Study in Comparative Religion.* Vol. 1. New York: Macmillan and Co., 1894.

Freddoso, Alfred J. "Notes on Chesterton's Orthodoxy." *Class Handouts—Phil 264: Supplemental Material.* Notre Dame, IN: University of Notre Dame. www3.nd.edu/~afreddos/courses/264/chester.htm.

Freeman, R. Austin. "The Shadow of the Wolf." *Dr. Thorndyke Mysteries.* London: MX Publishing, 2016.

———. *The Case of Oscar Brodski.* New York: Detective Story Club, 1923.

Freud, Sigmund. *Totem and Taboo: Resemblances Between the Psychic Lives of Savages and Neurotics.* Translated by A. A. BRILL. London: George Routledge & Sons, 1894.

Frost, Richard. "Test **Question** Types." *Teaching English,* 9 Feb 2021. www.teachingenglish.org.uk.

Fry, Tony. "Whither Design/Whether History." *Design and the **Question** of History.* New York: Bloomsbury Academic, 2015.

Funaro, Gregory. *The Sculptor.* Pinnacle Books, 2010.

Galbi, Douglas. "Oracles of Astrampsychus: Understanding Fate in Everyday Life." *Purple Motes,* April 19, 2015. http://purplemotes.net.

Gallop, Jane. *The Deaths of the Author: Reading and Writing in Time.* Durham, NC: Duke University Press, 2011.

Garcia, Megan. "Two Truths and a Lie: Ideas, Examples, and Instructions." *Hobby Lark,* Oct 18, 2019. https://hobbylark.com.

Gardner, Bertha Lee. "Debating in High School." *The School Review, Volume 20.* 1912, 117–24.

Gardner, Lyn. "Stephen Skrynka: 'This Is Not Some Jackass Stunt'." *The Guardian,* 26 Jan 2010. www.theguardian.com

Garner, Dwight. "The Lower Ambitions of Higher Education: 'Excellent Sheep,' William Deresiewicz's Manifesto." *The New York Times,* Aug. 12, 2014.

Garnet, Eldon. *Reading Brooke Shields: The Garden of Failure.* New York: Semiotext(e), 1995.

Gatov, Vasily. "Russia's Stalinist Diplospeak." *The Daily Beast,* July 25, 2015. www.thedailybeast.com.

Gehrke, Steve. "The Ships of Theseus." *Poetry Magazine,* 2013.

Giannopoulou, Zina. "Authorless Authority in Plato's Theaetetus." *Fakes and Forgers of Classical Literature: Ergo decipiatur!* Edited by Javier Martinez. Leiden: Brill, 2014, 43–58.

Gibbs, Stuart. *Evil Spy School.* New York: Simon and Schuster, 2016.

———. *Spy School.* New York: Simon and Schuster, 2013.

Gidcumb, Brianne. "Driving **Questions** to Guide Inquiry in the Arts." *EducationCloset,* May 8, 2015. http://educationcloset.com.

Giese, Rachel, and Caroline Alphonso. "The Debate Over Standardized Testing in Schools Is as Divisive as Ever." *The Globe and Mail,* May 31, 2013. www.theglobeandmail.com.

Global News. "Full Interview: Conservative Spokesman Defends Use of Isis Video in Attack Ad." *Global News,* June 28, 2015. http://globalnews.ca.

Glück, Louise. "The Empty Glass." *The Seven Ages.* The Ecco Press, 2001.

Goldin, Megan. *The Escape Room: A Novel.* New York: St. Martin's Press, 2018.

Gomez, David. "Congressional Pizza Battles and Political Corruption." *TGDaily.com,* 28th November 2011. www.tgdaily.com.

Gong, Zheng, and Dan Zhang. "The Design of Restricted Domain Automatic **Question** Answering System Based on **Question** Base." *Information Technology and Computer Application Engineering: Proceedings of the International Conference on Information Technology and Computer Application Engineering.* Edited by Hsiang-Chuan Liu, Wen-Pei Sung, and Wenli Yao. Boca Raton: CRC Press, 2013, 487–90.

Good, Nathan A. *Regular Expression Recipes: A Problem-Solution Approach.* Berkeley, CA: Apress, 2005.

Goodwin, Raymond. *Sawdusted: Notes From a Post-Boom Mill.* University of Wisconsin Press, 2010.

Gopnik, Adam. "The Driver's Seat." *The New Yorker,* February 2, 2015. www.newyorker.com.

———. "The Outside Game." *The New Yorker,* January 12, 2015. www.newyorker.com.

Gorgas, Ferdinand J. S. *A Series of **Questions** and Answers for Dental Students, Part III.* Baltimore: Snowden & Cowman, 1892.

Gorman, Thomas J. *To Believe or Not Believe, That Is the **Question**: An Undercover Agent's Quest for the Truth.* Evergreen, Colorado: Xulon Press, 2007.

Goss, Charles Frederic. *The Loom of Life.* Indianapolis: Bowen-Merrill Company, 1902.

Graeber, David. *Debt: The First 5,000 Years.* Melville House, 2011.

———. *The Utopia of Rules: on Technology, Stupidity, and the Secret Joys of Bureaucracy.* Brooklyn, NY: Melville House, 2015.

Grafton, Sue. *"O" Is for Outlaw.* Macmillan, 2010.

Graham R. Walden, ed. *Polling and Survey Research Methods 1935–1979.* Westport, CT: Greenwood Press, 1996.

Granville, A. B. *The Italian **Question**: A Second Letter to Lord Palmerston, G.C.B., M.P., Etc. Etc.; With a Reputation of Certain Misrepresentations by Lord Brougham, Mr. D'Israeli, and the Quarterly Review, Respecting the Rights of Austria and the Lombardo-Venetians, Illustrated by a Map of the Disputed Territories.* London: James Ridgway, 1848.

Gray, Asa. "Darwin on the Origin of Species: A Book Review." *The Atlantic,* July 1860. www.theatlantic.com.

Greco, Robert, and Shaun M. Shelton. *Motorishi.* Intervision Media Arts, 2008.

Green, Alison. "My Staff Doesn't Like It That I Use the Socratic Method With Them." *Ask a Manager, and if You Don't, I'll Tell You Anyway,* January 6, 2016. www.askamanager.org.

Green, Peter. "Introduction." *Juvenal, The Sixteen Satires.* London: Penguin, 1974.

Greene, Graham. *Our Man in Havana.* London: Vintage, 2004.

———. *The Human Factor.* New York: Avon Books, 1978.

Griggs, Terry. *Thought You Were Dead.* Toronto: Biblioasis, 2009.

Grimmelshausen, Hans Jacob Christoph von. *The Adventurous Simplicius Simplicissimus; Being the Description of the Life of a Strange Vagabond Named Melchior Sternfels von Fuchshaim.* 1669. Translated by Alfred Thomas Scrope Goodrick. London: William Heinemann, 1912.

Grondin, Jean. "Why Reawaken the **Question** of Being?" *Heidegger's Being and Time: Critical Essays.* Edited by Richard Polt. Lanham MD: Rowman & Littlefield Publishers, 2005, 15–31.

Grossmith, George, and Weedon Grossmith. *The Diary of a Nobody.* Edited by Kate Flint. Oxford, UK: Oxford University Press, 1995.

Gurganus, Allan. *Plays Well With Others.* New York: Knopf Doubleday, 2010.

Gyllensvärd, November. *My Name is Sir Lanka.* Lulu Press, 2015.

Hale, John R., Jelle Zeilinga de Boer, Jeffrey P. Chanton, and Henry A. Spiller. "**Questioning** the Delphic Oracle." *Scientific American,* August 2003, 67–73.

Hamilton, Laura. "Bradley Walsh Struggles With 'Cock' Shot **Question** On 'The Chase'." *ladbible.com,* January 23, 2017. www.ladbible.com.

Hammett, Dashiell. "Red Harvest." *Five Complete Novels.* New York: Avenel Books, 1980, 1–142.

———. "The Dain Curse." *Five Complete Novels.* New York: Avenel Books, 1980, 143–292.

———. "The Maltese Falcon." *Five Complete Novels.* New York: Avenel Books, 1980, 293–440.

Handlen, Zack. "It's a Long Night at the Motor Motel on a Climactic Fargo." *A.V. Club,* December 7, 2015. www.avclub.com.

Hansard, T. C. "The Invisible Man." *The Innocence of Father Brown.* London: Cassell, 1911.

Hansard, T. C. *Parliamentary Debates: Official Report of the Session of the Parliament of the United Kingdom of Great Britain and Ireland, June 27–September 7, 1820.* London: 1821.

———. *The Parliamentary History of England, From the Earliest Period to the Year 1803. From Which Last-Mentioned Epoch It Is Continued Downwards in the Work Entitled, "The Parliamentary Debates." Vol. IV. A.D. 1660–1668.* London: T. C. Hansard, 1808.

———. *Parliamentary Debates: Third Series, Commencing With the Accession of William IV, 22 Victoriae, 1859, Vol. CLIII, Comprising the Period From the Eleventh Day of March, 1859 to the Nineteenth Day of April, 1859, Second and Last Volume of First Session, 1859.* London: Cornelius Buck, 1859.

Harada, Jun, Masao Fuketa, El-Sayed Atlam, Toru Sumitomo, Wataru Hiraishi, and Jun-ichi Aoe. "Estimation of **FAQ** Knowledge Bases by Introducing Measurements." *Knowledge-Based Intelligent Information and Engineering Systems: 10th International Conference, KES 2006.* Edited by Bogdan Gabrys, Robert J. Howlett, and L. C. Jain. Springer Science & Business Media, 2006, 275–80.

Harper, Tim. "For Stephen Harper, Governing Means Never Asking Why." *The Toronto Star,* Aug. 24, 2014.

Harris, Cindy. "Cindy's Introduction." *Just a Few* **Questions**: *Barbaric Stories from an Ordinary Life, by Abe Salem, as told to Cindy Harris.* Lulu, 2011, xv–xvii.

Harrisville, Roy A. *Augsburg Commentary on the New Testament: Romans.* Minneapolis: Augsburg Publishing House, 1980.

Hart, Robert. *"These From the Land of Sinim." Essays on the Chinese* **Question**. London: Chapman & Hall, 1901.

Hawthorne, Nathaniel. *The Scarlet Letter.* New York: Ticknor, Reed & Fields, 1850.

Haydon, Elizabeth. *Prophecy: Child of Earth.* New York: Tom Doherty Associates, 2001.

Hayes, John L. *The Protective* **Question** *Abroad, and Remarks at the Indianapolis Exposition.* Cambridge: J. Wilson, 1870.

Heidegger, Martin. "Only a God Can Save Us: Der Spiegel's Interview With Martin Heidegger, September 23, 1966." *Philosophical and Political Writings.* Edited by Manfred Stassen. New York: Continuum, 2003, 24–48.

———. "The **Question** Concerning Technology." Translated by William Lovitt. *The* **Question** *Concerning Technology and Other Essays.* New York: Garland Publishing, 1977, 3–35.

———. *Introduction to Metaphysics, Second Edition.* Translated by Gregory Fried and Richard Polt. New Haven: Yale University Press, 2014.

———. *The* **Question** *of Being.* Rowman & Littlefield, 1958.

Hemingway, Ernest. *Selected Letters 1917–1961.* Edited by Carlos Baker. New York: Simon and Schuster, 2003.

Henderson, Bobby. *The Gospel of the Flying Spaghetti Monster.* New York: Random House, 2010.

Herbert, Alan. *Coin Clinic: 1,001 Frequently Asked* **Questions**. Iola, WI: Krause Publications, 1995.

Herman, Stewart W. "Study **Questions** on the Book of Job." *Concordia College Religion Department,* 1997. http://faculty.cord.edu/herman/jobreview**questions**.html.

Herodotus. *The History.* Translated by G. C. Macaulay. Volume 2. London: MacMillan and Co., 1914.

Herr, Michael. *Dispatches.* 1968. New York: Vintage, 1991.

Hicok, Bob. "Report From the Black Box." *Poetry,* October 2010.

Higgins, George V. *The Friends of Eddie Coyle.* 1970. New York: Picador, 2010.

Highsmith, Patricia. *The Talented Mr. Ripley.* 1955. New York: W.W. Norton & Co., 2008.

Highway, Tomson. *Kiss of the Fur Queen.* Toronto: Anchor, 2005.

Hoare, Peter. "Embrace Your Name." *AskMen,* May 17, 2015. www.askmen.com.

Hobbes, Thomas. *Leviathan.* London: Andrew Crooke, 1654.

Hocking, Mary. *Ask No* **Question**. London: Bello, 2016.

Hodge, Jonathan K., and Richard E. Klima. *The Mathematics of Voting and Elections: A Hands-on Approach.* Providence, RI: American Mathematical Society, 2005.

Hofmann, Josef. *Piano Playing: With Piano* **Questions** *Answered.* New York, N.Y.: Dover, 1909.

Holland, Tom. *Rubicon: The Last Years of the Roman Republic.* New York: Doubleday, 2003.

Holley, Marietta. *Samantha on the Woman* **Question**. New York: Fleming H. Revell Co., 1913.

Hopkins, Tom, and Ben Kench. *Selling for Dummies.* London: John Wiley & Sons, 2011.

Horst, Pieter W. van der. "Review of Randall Stewart (ed.), Sortes Astrampsychi, II. Bibliotheca Teubneriana. München & Leipzig: K. G. Saur, 2001, pp. xxiv, 127. ISBN 3-598-71003-8." *Bryn Mawr Classical Review* (2001.10.04).

House of Commons International Development Committee. *Department for International Development*

Annual Report and Resource Accounts 2010–11 and Business Plan 2011–15: Fourteenth Report of Session 2010–12, Volume 1. London: Stationery Office, 2012.

House of Commons Procedure Committee. *Monitoring Written Parliamentary* **Questions**: *Seventh Report of Session 2012–13: Report, Together With Formal Minutes and Oral Evidence.* London: The Stationery Office, 2013.

House of Representatives Committee on Government Reform and Oversight. *Deposition Transcripts from the Committee Investigation Into The White House Office Travel Matter, Volume 5.* Washington: U.S. Government Printing Office, 1996.

Howell, T. B., and Thomas Jones Howell. *Cobbett's Complete Collection of State Trials and Proceedings for High Treason and Other Crimes and Misdemeanors from the Earliest Period to the Present Time, Vol. XXX (Being Vol. IX of the Continuation 47–48, George III, A.D. 1806–1808.* London: T. C. Hansard, 1822.

Howells, William Dean. *Out of the* **Question**: *A Comedy.* Houghton, Mifflin and Company, 1877.

Hughes, John, and John Breckinridge. *A Discussion of the* **Question**, *Is the Roman Catholic Religion, in Any or in All Its Principles or Doctrines, Inimical to Civil or Religious Liberty?: and of the* **Question**, *Is the Presbyterian Religion, in Any or in All Its Principles or Doctrines, Inimical to Civil or Religious Liberty?* J. Murphy, 1867.

Hughes, Libby. *Serious Fun with White House Secrets and State Department Antics.* iUniverse, 2009.

Hughes, Ted. "Examination at the Womb-Door." *Crow: From the Life and Songs of the Crow.* New York: Harper & Row, 1971.

Hume, David. *An Enquiry Concerning Human Understanding.* The Harvard Classics, Vol. XXXVII, Part 3. Edited by Charles W. Eliot. New York: P. F. Collier & Son, 1909–14.

Huppke, Rex. "In Impeachment Hearings, Republicans Make the Case for Replacing Their Party's Mascot With a Lemming: The Week in Review." *Chicago Tribune,* 15 Nov 2019. www.chicagotribune.com.

Hy, Chan Niem. "The Art of Suffering Retreat—**Question** and Answer Session." *Thich Nhat Hanh Dharma Talks,* August 31, 2013. https://tnhaudio.org.

IELTS Online Tests. "How to Find the Right Keywords in Reading Comprehension?" https://ieltsonlinetests.com.

Illingworth, Dustin. "The Subtle Radicalism of Julio Cortázar's Berkeley Lectures." *The Atlantic,* Mar. 28, 2017. www.theatlantic.com.

Indiana University Library. "Copyright & Fair Use **Frequently Asked Questions**." 2015. https://iupui.libguides.com.

Innes, Michael. *The Secret Vanguard.* Victor Gollancz: London, 1940.

Interstate Commerce Commission. *Evidence Taken in the Matter of Proposed Advances in Freight Rates by Carriers, Volume 3.* Washington: U.S. Government Printing Office, 1910.

Invisible Adjunct. "Anxiety and Insecurity: The Status of the Humanities." 2003. www.invisibleadjunct.com.

———. "Where The Adjuncts Have Equal Status." 2003. www.invisibleadjunct.com.

Irvine, James. *The Rubrical* **Question** *Practically and Apologetically Considered: A Sermon.* Manchester: P. and J. Rivington, 1845.

Isabel Chapin Barrows, ed. *First Mohonk Conference on the Negro* **Question**: *Held at Lake Mohonk, Ulster County, New York, June 4, 5, 6, 1890.* Boston: George H. Ellis, 1890.

Jackson, Gregory. "Review of JP Meyer's Classic UOJ Textbook—The Fetid Womb of the Kokomo Statements." *Ichabod The Glory Has Departed,* April 26, 2014. http://ichabodthegloryhasdeparted.blogspot.com.

Jacobi, Mary Putnam. *The* **Question** *of Rest for Women During Menstruation.* G.P. Putnam's Sons, 1877.

Jacobson, Howard. *Coming From Behind.* New York: Random House, 2011.

Jacoby, Susan. *The Age of American Unreason.* New York: Vintage/Random House, 2009.

James C. Anderson, ed. *The Australian Law times, Volumes 12–13.* Melbourne: Charles F. Maxwell Law Publisher, 1891.

Jarrell, Randall. *Pictures from an Institution: A Comedy.* 1954. Chicago: University of Chicago Press, 2010.

Jensen III, Lorenzo. "19 Women Answer the Eternal **Question**: Does Penis Size Matter?" *Thought Catalog,* January 3, 2017. https://thoughtcatalog.com.

Johns, Alessa. "Remembering the Future: Eighteenth-Century Women's Utopian Writing." *Genres as Repositories of Cultural Memory.* Edited by Theo d' Haen, Hendrik van Gorp, and Ulla Musarra-Schrøder. Amsterdam: Rodopi, 2000, 37–49.

Johnson, Denis. *Tree of Smoke.* New York: Picador, 2007.

Johnson, Jan. *Simplicity & Fasting: 6 Studies With Notes for Leaders.* Downers Grove, IL: InterVarsity Press, 2003.

Johnston, Denis W. "Lines and Circles: The 'Rez' Plays of Tomson Highway." *Canadian Literature* 124–5, 1990, 254–64.

Jones, Ann. "Has America Gone Crazy?" *Salon,* Jan. 13, 2015. www.salon.com.

Jones, Bill. *HEMMED IN: So If You can't Breathe . . .You Might Be Hemmed In!* Victoria, BC: Trafford Publishing, 2013.

Jones, Steven P., and Sariah E. Roberts. "Book Review: Excellent Sheep: The Miseducation of the American Elite and the Way to a Meaningful Life, by William Deresiewicz." *Academy for Educational Studies* 6.2 (Summer 2015): 103–8. https://academyforeducationalstudies.org.

Jowett, B. "Preface to the Second and Third Editions." *The Dialogues of Plato, in Five Volumes.* Translated by B. Jowett. Oxford: Oxford University Press, 1892.

Joyce, James. *A Portrait of the Artist as a Young Man.* 1916. Harmondsworth, UK: Penguin, 1970.

———. *Ulysses.* Project Gutenberg, 2003. www.gutenberg.org/ebooks/4300.

Ka, Omar. *Wolof Syllable Structure: Evidence From a Secret Code.* ResearchGate, 1988. www.researchgate.net.

Kafka, Franz. "Metamorphosis." Translated by David Wyllie. *Metamorphosis and The Trial.* Ann Arbor, MI: Borders Classics, 2007.

———. "The Metamorphosis." Translated by Willa and Edwin Muir. *Kafka's "The Metamorphosis" and Other Writings.* Edited by Helmuth Kiesel. New York: Continuum, 2002, 1–48.

———. *The Trial.* Translated by David Wyllie. Project Gutenberg, 2003. http://www.gutenberg.org/ebooks/7849.

Kania, Ursula. *The Acquisition and Use of Yes-No* **Questions** *in English: A Corpus-Study From A Usage-Based Perspective.* Tübingen: Narr Francke Attempto Verlag, 2016.

Kaufman, Frederick. *Bet the Farm: How Food Stopped Being Food.* New York: John Wiley & Sons, 2012.

Kaufman, Scott Eric. "Sarah Palin and Donald Trump Whine About "Gotcha" Journalism in Inane Interview Straight Out of 'Idiocracy'." *Salon,* August 29, 2015.

www.salon.com.

Kay, Terry. *The Kidnapping of Aaron Greene*. Untreed Reads, 2012.

Keats, Jonathon. *Control + Alt + Delete: A Dictionary of Cyberslang*. Globe Pequot, 2007.

Keil, Geert, Lara Keuck, and Rico Hauswald. "Vagueness in Psychiatry: An Overview." *Vagueness in Psychiatry*. Edited by Geert Keil, Lara Keuck, and Rico Hauswald. Oxford University Press, 2017, 3–26.

Kerouac, Jack. *On The Road*. 1955. New York: Viking, 1972.

Kingwell, Mark. "Outside the White Box." *Harper's Magazine*, February 2016, 93–97. https://harpers.org.

Kinkead, Thomas L. *Baltimore Catechism, No. 4: An Explanation of the Baltimore Catechism of Christian Doctrine for the Use of Sunday-School Teachers and Advanced Classes*. 1891. Project Gutenberg, www.gutenberg.org/ebooks/14554.

Kipnis, Laura. "Sexual Paranoia Strikes Academe." *The Chronicle of Higher Education*, February 27, 2015. http://chronicle.com/article/Sexual-Paranoia-Strikes/190351.

———. *Against Love: a Polemic*. New York: Pantheon Books, 2003.

Kish, Matt. *Moby-Dick in Pictures: One Drawing for Every Page*. Portland: Tin House Books, 2011.

Kizzia, Tom. "Moving to Mars: Preparing for the Longest, Loneliest Voyage Ever." *The New Yorker*, April 20, 2015, 46–53.

Kleiser, Grenville. *Fifteen Thousand Useful Phrases: a Practical Handbook of Pertinent Expressions, Striking Similes, Literary, Commercial, Conversational, and Oratorical Terms, for the Embellishment of Speech and Literature, and the Improvement of the Vocabulary of Those Persons Who Read, Write, and Speak English*. New York: Funk and Wagnalls Company, 1919.

Kluge, P. F. *Final Exam: A Novel*. Gambier OH: XOXOX Press, 2005.

Koethe, John. "North Point North." *North Point North: New and Selected Poems*. HarperCollins Publishers, 2002.

Kohl, Herbert. "Topsy-Turvies: Teacher Talk and Student Talk." *The Skin That We Speak: Thoughts on Language and Culture in the Classroom*. Edited by Lisa Delpit and Joanne Kilgour Dowdy. New York: The New Press, 2002, 145–62.

Kraieski, Ben. *Snow on the Desert*. AuthorHouse, 2013.

Kraus, Chris. *I Love Dick*. Los Angeles: Semiotext(e), 2006.

———. *Summer of Hate*. Los Angeles: Semiotext(e), 2012.

Kreda, Allan. "Islanders Coach Is Tough on Himself and His Team." *The New York Times*, Sept. 27, 2013. www.nytimes.com

Lam, Zoe Wai Man. "Chapter 2—Approaches to Syllable Contraction." *Rutgers Optimality Archive*, 2008. http://roa.rutgers.edu.

Lane, Anthony. "Go Ask Alice: What Really Went on in Wonderland." *The New Yorker*, June & 15, 2015. www.newyorker.com.

Larrimore, Mark. *The Book of Job: A Biography*. Princeton, NJ: Princeton University Press, 2013.

Lavine, Douglas S. *Questions from the Bench*. American Bar Association, 2004.

Lawrence Buell. "Moby-Dick as Sacred Text." *New Essays on Moby-Dick*. Cambridge University Press: New York, 1986, 53–72.

Le Carré, John. *Our Game*. London: Coronet Books/Hodder and Stoughton, 1995.

———. *The Constant Gardener*. Toronto: Penguin Canada, 2001.

———. *The Secret Pilgrim*. New York: Knopf, 1991.

Lederman, Leon M. *The God Particle: If the Universe Is the Answer, What Is the **Question**?* Houghton Mifflin Harcourt, 1993.

Lee, Charles Carroll. *Behind Every Dark Cloud: The Critically Acclaimed Novel*. Xlibris, 2012.

LeFever, Lee. *The Art of Explanation, Enhanced Edition: Making your Ideas, Products, and Services Easier to Understand*. John Wiley & Sons, 2012.

Leonardo da Vinci. *The Notebooks of Leonardo da Vinci*. 1888. Translated by Jean Paul Richter. Project Gutenberg, 2004. www.gutenberg.org/ebooks/5000.

Lepore, Jill. "Joe Gould's Teeth: The Long-Lost Story of the Longest Book Ever Written." *The New Yorker*, 2015. www.newyorker.com.

Levinson, Jay Conrad. "Foreword." *The Six **Questions**: That You Better Get Right, The Answers Are the Keys to Your Success*. Edited by Julie Edmonds and Michell Smith. New York: Morgan James Publishing, 2012.

Levy, Jill Meryl. *Hazmat Chemistry Study Guide (Second Edition)*. Campbell, CA: Firebelle Productions, 2005.

Lewis, Sinclair. *Babbitt*. Harcourt, Brace & Company, 1922.

Lewman, David. *The Case of the Mystery Meat Loaf*. Simon and Schuster, 2012.

Ling, Justin. "Five **Questions** I Wanted To Ask Stephen Harper Last Night, But Couldn't." *Vice*, August 7, 2015. www.vice.com.

———. "If We Want to Ask Stephen Harper **Question**s, We Have to Give His Party $78,000." *Vice*, August 24, 2015. www.vice.com.

Linguee. "The **Question** How." www.linguee.com/english-german/translation/the+**question**+how.html.

Lippi, Rosina. "Galileo v Darwin." *rosinalippi.com*, 4 June 2009. http://rosinalippi.com/weblog/galileo-v-darwin/.

Lipsyte, Sam. *The Ask*. New York: Picador, 2011.

Liu, Yi. *Semi-supervised Learning with Side Information: Graph-based Approaches*. ProQuest, 2007.

Lockman, John. *A New Roman Hiſtory, by Queſtion and Anſwer. In a Method Much More Comprehenſive Than Any of the Kind Extant. Extracted From Ancient Authors, and the Moſt Celebrated Among the Modern, and Interſperſed With Such Cuſtoms as Serve to Illuſtrate the Hiſtory. With a Complete Index. Deſigned Principally for Schools. The Fourth Edition Corrected*. Cork: Thomas White, 1778.

Longacre, Robert E. *The Grammar of Discourse*. 2nd Edition. New York: Springer Science & Business Media, 2013.

Lovecraft, H. P. "The Shunned House." *Weird Tales*, October 1937. Project Gutenberg. www.gutenberg.org/ebooks/31469.

Loveridge, William. "How to Complete Your SF-86." *ClearanceJobs*, Sep 12, 2021. https://news.clearance-jobs.com.

Lovitt, William. "Introduction." *The **Question** Concerning Technology*, by Martin Heidegger. Translated by William Lovitt. New York: Garland Publishing, xiii.

Lucan. *The Civil War, Books I-X (Pharsalia)*. London: William Heinemann, 1962.

Lucretius. *On the Nature of Things*. Translated by W. E. Leonard. New York: E. P. Dutton & Co., 1921.

Lum, Zi-Ann. "Mulcair Doesn't Take Reporters' **Questions** At Campaign Launch." *The Huffington Post*, 2 August 2015. www.huffingtonpost.ca.

Macdonald, Ross. *The Chill.* 1963. New York: Vintage Books/Black Lizard, 1996.

———. *The Galton Case.* 1959. New York: Vintage, 1987.

MacEwen, Gwendolyn. *Julian the Magician.* 1963. Toronto: Insomniac Press, 2004.

MacLean, John. *Canadian Savage Folk: The Native Tribes of Canada.* Toronto: W. Briggs, 1896.

Malliet, G. M. *A Fatal Winter.* Macmillan, 2012.

Mandell, Jeff. "Defending Treyf." *TC Jewfolk,* December 23, 2010. https://tcjewfolk.com.

Mangua, Charles. *Pretty Boy Beware.* Nairobi: Spear Books, 1994.

Manguel, Alberto. *A History of Reading.* Toronto: Vintage Canada, 1998.

Marchand, William R. *Depression and Bipolar Disorder: Your Guide to Recovery.* Boulder, CO: Bull Publishing Company, 2012.

Marcotte, Amanda. "Trump Wins Again With His Bratty Tantrum: His Fox News Debate Boycott Will Only Boost His Campaign Even More." *Salon,* January 27, 2016. www.salon.com.

Marcus, Greil. *Lipstick Traces: A Secret History of the Twentieth Century.* Harvard University Press, 1990.

Mariotte, Jeff. *CSI: Crime Scene Investigation: The Burning Season.* Simon and Schuster, 2011.

Markson, David. *The Last Novel.* Counterpoint Press, 2007.

———. *Wittgenstein's Mistress.* Dalkey Archive Press, 1995.

Marx Brothers. "Selected Bits from Horse Feathers." *marxbrothers.org,* 1932. www.marx-brothers.org/whyaduck/info/movies/scenes/wagstaff.htm.

Marx, Karl. "On The Jewish **Question**." *Deutsch-Französische Jahrbücher,* February, 1844. www.marxists.org.

Masciandaro, Nicola. "Anti-Cosmosis: Black Mahapralaya." *Hideous Gnosis: Black Metal Theory Symposium 1.* Edited by Nicola Masciandaro. Glossator, 2010, 67–92.

Mason, Paul. *Rare Earth.* New York: OR Books, 2011.

Mathis-Lilley, Ben. "Title IX Investigation Opened Against Female Northwestern Professor Over Column, Tweet." *Slate,* May 29, 2015. www.slate.com.

Matteson, Stefanie. *Murder at the Spa.* London: Head of Zeus, 2016.

Mauriello, Joseph J. *(Your Departed Loved Ones and Spirit Guides Are) Only a Thought Away.* New York: iUniverse, 2005.

Maxwell, James Clerk. "Lines Written Under the Conviction That It Is Not Wise to Read Mathematics in November After One's Fire Is Out." Poetry Foundation, 2014. www.poetryfoundation.

Maxwell, Max. "Introduction to the Socratic Method and its Effect on Critical Thinking." *The Socratic Method Research Portal.* 2009–14. www.socraticmethod.net/.

Mayell, Charles Carmen. *Engage! Having Conversations about God.* The YLDP, Inc., 2009.

Mayorga, Santiago. "Answer Key—Touchstone 4." *santiagomayorgamsc.blogspot.com,* Dec. 6, 2010. http://santiagomayorgamsc.blogspot.ca.

McAllister, Matthew J. "A Spectacle Worth Attending to: The Ironic Use of Preexisting Art Music in Film." The Florida State University College of Music, 2012.

McCarthy, Mary. *The Groves of Academe: A Novel.* 1952. New York: Open Road Integrated Media, 2013.

McEwan, Ian. *Enduring Love.* London: Vintage Books, 2006.

McGee, J. Vernon. *Thru the Bible with J. Vernon McGee: Genesis through Revelation.* Nashville: Thomas Nelson, 1981.

McGee, Kristin A. *Some Liked It Hot: Jazz Women in Film and Television, 1928–1959.* Middletown: Wesleyan University Press, 2010.

McLuhan, Marshall. *The Gutenberg Galaxy: The Making of Typographic Man.* 1962. Toronto: Univ. of Toronto Press, 2002.

McQuarrie, Edward F. *The Market Research Toolbox: A Concise Guide for Beginners.* Los Angeles: SAGE, 2006.

Mead, Rebecca. "Our Bodies, Ourselves." *The New Yorker,* November 30, 2015. www.newyorker.com.

Meador, Derrick. "Want to Know How Standardized Test **Questions** Are Developed?" *About.com Teaching,* 2014. http://teaching.about.com/.

Means, David. "The Old Man." *Harper's Magazine,* June 2016. http://harpers.org.

Meares, Kevin, and Mark Freeston. *Overcoming Worry and Generalised Anxiety Disorder: A Self-Help Guide Using Cognitive Behavioral Techniques.* London: Constable & Robinson, 2008.

Melanchthon, Philipp. *The Apology of the Augsburg Confession.* 1531. Translated by F. Bente and W. H. T. Dau. Project Gutenberg, 2004. www.gutenberg.org/ebooks/6744.

Meltzer, Paul S., Michael Bittner, Mervi Heiskanen, Tiffany Hoffman, Yidong Chen, and Jeffrey M. Trent. "Use of cDNA Microarrays to Assess DNA Gene Expression Patterns in Cancer." *The Biology of Tumors.* Edited by Enrico Mihich and Carlo Croce. New York: Plenum Press, 1998, 109–16.

Melville, Herman. *Moby Dick; or, The Whale.* Project Gutenberg, 2001. www.gutenberg.org/ebooks/2701.

Merriman, Ben. "A Science of Literature." *Boston Review,* August 03, 2015. http://bostonreview.net.

Merritt Moseley, ed. *The Academic Novel: New and Classic Essays.* University of Chester, 2007.

Meta Super User. "**Questions** > What the Heck Is This Invisible **Question** and Answer Post?" *Stack Exchange,* 2020. https://meta.superuser.com.

Metzger, Paul L. *The Gospel of John: When Love Comes to Town.* InterVarsity Press, 2010.

Mi Yodeya. "Can Time Spent With Others Be Counted As Ma'aser, According To Halacha?" *judaism.stackexchange.com,* July 26, 2017. https://judaism.stackexchange.com.

Miller, John G. *QBQ! The* **Question** *Behind the* **Question***: Practicing Personal Accountability at Work and in Life.* New York: Penguin, 2004.

Mills, Elinor. "Chacha Gives You Answers via Text Message." *CNET,* Jan. 3, 2008. www.cnet.com.

Milne, A. A. *Not That It Matters.* Project Gutenberg, 2004. www.gutenberg.org/ebooks/5803.

Mitchell, David. *number9dream.* London: Sceptre, 2001.

Mitrovica, Andrew. "What the Hell Was Harper Doing in Iraq Anyway?" *iPolitics,* May 8, 2015. www.ipolitics.ca.

Modiano, Patrick. *Missing Person.* 1980. Translated by Daneil Weissbort. Boston: David R. Godine, Publisher, 2014.

Montaigne, Michel de. *Essays.* Translated by Charles Cotton. Edited by William Carew Hazlitt. London: Reeves and Turner, 1877.

Moreno-Garcia, Silvia. "Sun Moon Stars Rain." *The Exile Book of New Canadian Noir.* Claude Lalumière and David Nickle, ed. Holstein, ON: Exile Editions, 2015,1–8.

Morris, Tom. *Philosophy For Dummies.* New York: John Wiley & Sons, 2011.

Moseley, Merritt. "Introductory: Definitions and Justifications." *The Academic Novel: New and Classic Essays,* by Merritt Moseley. University of Chester, 2007.

Mosher, David L. "Introduction." *Eighty-Three Different*

Questions, by Saint Augustine. Washington, DC: Catholic University of America Press, 1982.

Mumford, Joseph. *The **Question** of **Questions**; Which, Rightly Resolv'd, Resolves All Our **Questions** in Religion. This **Question** Is, Who Ought to Be Our Judge in All These Differences? This Book Answers That **Question**.* 1658. Glasgow: John M'Quatters & Company, 1841.

Murakami, Haruki. *1Q84*. New York: Alfred A Knopf, 2013.

———. *A Wild Sheep Chase*. Translated by Alfred Birnbaum. London: Vintage, 2003.

Murray, Robert K., and Roger W. Brucker. *Trapped! The Story of Floyd Collins*. Lexington, KY: University Press of Kentucky, 2013.

Musil, Robert. *The Man Without Qualities, Vol. 1: A Sort of Introduction and Pseudo Reality Prevails*. New York: Vintage, 1996.

Nabokov, Vladimir. *Lolita*. New York: Crest Books, 1959.

———. *Pale Fire*. New York: Knopf Doubleday Publishing Group, 2011.

———. *Pnin*. New York: Knopf Doubleday, 2011.

National Oceanic and Atmospheric Administration. "**Frequently Asked Questions** about Tornadoes." *NOAA's National Weather Service*, 2014. www.spc.noaa.gov/**faq**/tornado/.

Naylor, James Ball. *Under Mad Anthony's Banner*. Akron, OH: Saalfield Publishing Company, 1903.

Nelson, Holly Faith. "The Subaltern in Academia: Advancing an Ethos of Equity." *Academic Apartheid: Waging the Adjunct War*. Edited by Sylvia M. DeSantis. Newcastle upon Tyne, UK: Cambridge Scholars Publishing, 2011.

Neruda, Pablo. "Ode to Federico Garcia Lorca." *Residence on Earth*. Translated by Donald D. Walsh. New York: New Directions Publishing, 2004, 386.

Neubert, Thomas Neil. *A Critique of Pure Physics: Concerning the Metaphors of New Physics*. Xlibris, 2009.

New, Christopher. *Philosophy of Literature: An Introduction*. London: Routledge, 2002.

Newcomb, Harvey. *Newcomb's First **Question** Book*. Massachusetts Sabbath School Society, 1837.

Newcomb, Simon. "The Extent of the Universe." *Scientific Papers*. The Harvard Classics, Vol. XXX. Edited by Charles W. Eliot. New York: P. F. Collier & Son, 1909–14.

Nickolas Pappas. *The Philosopher's New Clothes: The Theaetetus, the Academy, and Philosophy's Turn Against Fashion*. London: Routledge, 2015.

Nicolls, William Jasper. *Coal Catechism*. Philadelphia: George W. Jacobs & Company, 1898.

Niles, H., ed. *Niles' Weekly Register, Containing Political, Historical, Geographical, Scientifical, Statistical, Economical, and Biographical Documents, Essays, and Facts; Together With Notices of the Arts and Manufactures, and a Record of the Events of the Times, From March to September, 1820—Vol. XVIII, or, Volume VI—New Series*. Baltimore: Franklin Press, 1820.

Nodier, Charles. "L'Amateur de livres (The Book Lover)." Translated by William Barker. *Les Français peints par eux-mêmes*. Paris: 1841, iii, 210–19.

Nooteboom, Cees. *Rituals*. Translated by Adrienne Dixon. San Diego: Harcourt Brace Co., 1996.

Norris, William Edward. *An Embarrassing Orphan*. Philadelphia: John C. Winston, 1904.

NortonLifeLock. "Anti-Piracy **FAQs**." 2019–2022. www.nortonlifelock.com.

O'Day, Danton, and Aldona Budniak. *How to Succeed at University: Canadian Edition*. eBooklt, 2013.

O'Malley, Kady, and Evan Solomon. "Paul Calandra Apologizes for Non-Answers as Sources Pin Blame on PMO." *CBC News*, Sep 26, 2014. www.cbc.ca.

Oakley, Nicola. "Bradley Walsh Struggles to Read Rude-Sounding **Question** on The Chase as He Fights Back Laughter." *Daily Mirror*, 24 January 2017. www.mirror.co.uk.

Oates, Joyce Carol. *Zombie*. New York: Plume, 1996.

Ockerbloom, John Mark. "The Online Books Page **Frequently Asked Questions**." *Philosophy.com*, 2014. http://onlinebooks.library.upenn.edu/faq.html.

Oliver, A. Richard. *Charles Nodier: Pilot of Romanticism*. Syracuse University Press, 1964.

Oracle **FAQ's**. *Oracle FAQ's*, 2014. www.ora**faq**.com.

Ore, Oystein. *Number Theory and Its History*. 1948. New York: Dover, 1988.

Ormsby, Eric Linn. *Fine Incisions: Essays on Poetry and Place*. Erin, ON: The Porcupine's Quill, 2011.

Orwell, George. *Down and Out in Paris and London*. 1933. New York: Harcourt Brace Jovanovich, 1961.

———. *Nineteen Eighty-Four*. Harmondsworth, UK: Penguin, 1954.

Oswaal Editorial Board. *ISC **Question** Bank, Chapterwise & Topicwise: Class 12 English Paper-2*. Agra, India: Oswaal Books, 2019.

Padgett, Ron. "The Line." *lyrikline*. https://www.lyrikline.org/en/poems/line-14570.

Palazzolo, Joe, and Michael Rothfeld. *The Fixers: The Bottom-Feeders, Crooked Lawyers, Gossipmongers, and Porn Stars Who Created the 45th President*. New York: Random House, 2020.

Paraschas, Sotirios. *Reappearing Characters in Nineteenth-Century French Literature: Authorship, Originality, and Intellectual Property*. Cham: Palgrave Macmillan, 2018.

Parker, Ian. "The Greek Warrior." *The New Yorker*, August 3, 2015. www.newyorker.com.

Parks, Bob. "Are The 'Screaming Goat' Videos Real?" *CNSNews.com*, February 26, 2013. www.cnsnews.com.

Parks, Tim. "Stupid **Questions**." *The New York Review of Books*, 1989. www.nybooks.com.

Parliament of Canada. *Correspondence Relative to the Fisheries **Question**, 1885–1887*. Ottawa: Maclean, Roger & Company, 1887.

Parnell, Thomas. "The Hermit." *Poems on Several Occasions*. London: Lintot, 1722, 135–47.

Parton, Heather Digby. "Donald Trump Scares the Hell Out of Fox News: Why His Debate Boycott Really Makes the Network So Nervous." *Salon*, January 28, 2016. www.salon.com.

Patterson, Paul, and Susan Biagi. *The Loom of Change: Weaving a New Economy on Cape Breton*. Sydney, Nova Scotia: Cape Breton University Press, 2003.

Paumgarten, Nick. "Karmapa On Campus." *The New Yorker*, May 11, 2015, 21–27.

Peacock, Thomas Love. *Nightmare Abbey*. 1818. Project Gutenberg, 2006. www.gutenberg.org/ebooks/9909.

Peralta, Eyder. "The Pineapple And The Hare: Can You Answer Two Bizarre State Exam **Questions**?" *NPR*, April 20, 2012. www.npr.org.

Percy, Walker. *The Thanatos Syndrome*. New York: Ballantine Books/Random House, 1987.

Perillo, Lucia. "Transcendentalism." *Inseminating the Elephant*. Copper Canyon Press, 2009.

Perkins, Fred B. *San Francisco Cataloguing for Public Libraries: A Manual of the System Used in the San Francisco Free Public Library*. San Francisco: C. A. Murdock & Co., 1884.

Persky, Stan. "The Young and the Restless, and Laura Kipnis." *Los Angeles Review of Books*, July 25, 2015. https://lareviewofbooks.org.

Pessin, Andrew. *The God Question: What Famous Thinkers From Plato to Dawkins Have Said About the Divine.* Oxford: Oneworld, 2009.

Peters, Mark. *Men.* Ubu Editions, 2008. www.ubu.com.

Petronius. *The Satyricon.* Translated by W. C. Firebaugh. New York: Liveright, 1943.

Phelan, Benjamin. "Pizza Is Not a Vegetable, But Neither Is Anything Else, Really." *Slate*, Nov. 18 2011. www.slate.com.

Philip Mauro, ed. *Elegant Extracts; or, The Literary Nosegay: Consisting of Selections in Prose, From Admired Authors; to Which Is Added, the Maxims and Moral Reflections of de la Rouchefoucault; and a Dictionary of Literary Conversation.* Baltimore: Philip Mauro, 1814.

Phillips, Christopher. *Socrates Café: a Fresh Taste of Philosophy.* New York: W.W. Norton, 2001.

Philosophy.com. "**Frequently Asked Questions.**" 2014. www.philosophy.com.

Pietz, William. "The Phonograph in Africa: International Phonocentrism From Stanley to Sarnoff." *Post-Structuralism and the **Question** of History.* Edited by Derek Attridge, Geoff Bennington, and Robert Young. Cambridge, UK: Cambridge University Press, 1989, 263–83.

Pitt, William Rivers. "Trump's Lies Are Killing His Supporters as Covid Starts to Sweep Rural America." *Truthout*, April 16, 2020. https://truthout.org.

Plato. *Apology.* Translated by Benjamin Jowett. *The Internet Classics Archive.* http://classics.mit.edu/Plato/apology.html.

———. *Crito.* Translated by Benjamin Jowett. *The Internet Classics Archive.* http://classics.mit.edu/Plato/crito.htmlPlato/republic.8.vii.html.

———. *The Dialogues of Plato, Vol. 1, Translated Into English With Analyses and Introductions by B. Jowett, M.A. in Five Volumes.* 3rd edition revised and corrected. Oxford University Press, 1892.

———. *The Republic.* Translated by Benjamin Jowett. *The Internet Classics Archive.* http://classics.mit.edu/Plato/republic.8.vii.html.

Poe, Edgar Allan. "Mesmeric Revelation." 1850. *Classics in the History of Psychology.* Toronto: York University, http://psychclassics.yorku.ca/Poe/mesmeric.htm.

———. "The Murders in the Rue Morgue." *Tales of Edgar Allan Poe.* New York: Lamb, 1902.

Polster, Burkard, and Marty Ross. *A Dingo Ate My Math Book.* Providence, RI: American Mathematical Society, 2017.

Pomerantsev, Peter. *Nothing Is True and Everything Is Possible: Adventures in Modern Russia.* Faber and Faber: 2015.

Pope, Alexander. "An Essay on Man." *An Essay on Man: Moral Essays and Satires.* London: Cassell & Company, 1891.

Porta, A. G. *No World Concerto.* Translated by Darren Koolman and Rhett McNeil. Dalkey Archive Press, 2013.

Potter, Andrew. *Simply Heaven: As It Appears From Genesis Through Revelation.* Mustang, OK: Tate Publishing, 2011.

Poulsen, John, and Kurtis Hewson. "Standardized Testing: Fair or Not?" *University of Lethbridge Teaching Centre.* www.uleth.ca/teachingcentre.

Powell, Michael. "A Long Hardwood Journey: A Coach's Tough, Cerebral Style Guided a Bronx High School Team Through Pain and Triumph as It Pursued a City Basketball Title." *New York Times*, July 16, 2015. www.nytimes.com.

Power, Daniel J. *Decision Support Systems: Frequently Asked **Questions.*** iUniverse, 2004.

Powers, Richard. *The Gold Bug Variations.* New York: HarperCollins, 1991.

Prantera, Amanda. *The Cabalist.* London: Abacus, 1987.

Price, Michael Clive. "The Many-Worlds **FAQ.**" 1995. www.anthropic-principle.com/preprints/manyworlds.html.

Price, Seth. "Fuck Seth Price." *Harper's Magazine,* July 2015, 20–24.

Prince, Althea. *Being Black.* Toronto: Insomniac Press, 2009.

Prinz, Jesse J. *Gut Reactions: A Perceptual Theory of Emotion.* Oxford: Oxford University Press, 2004.

Putnam, G. P, ed. "The Oracle That Always Says 'No'." *Nonsenseorship: Sundry Observations Concerning Prohibitions, Inhibitions and Illegalities.* New York: G. P. Putnam, 1922.

Qualtrics (We Eat, Sleep, and Breathe Customer Success). "Auto-Number **Questions.**" 2017. www.qualtrics.com.

Queen, Ellery. *Calendar of Crime.* 1952. Open Road Media, 2015.

Quinn, Robert A. "Developing A More Efficient Conversation Paradigm for Learning Foreign Languages: Lessons on Asking and Answering **Questions** in an LSP Context." *Language for Specific Purposes: Trends in Curriculum Development.* Edited by Mary K. Long. Washington, DC: Georgetown University Press, 2017, 87-100.

Quora. "How Many **Questions** Does God Ask in the Bible?" www.quora.com.

———. "What Is the Correct Response to the **Question** 'How Do You Do'?" www.quora.com.

———. "What's the Best Way to Dodge a **Question** During a Presentation." www.quora.com.

Quynn, Kristina. "The Disgusting New Campus Novel." *The Chronicle Review,* December 16, 2019. www.chronicle.com.

Raazaghi, Fatemeh. "Auto-**FAQ**-Gen: Automatic **Frequently Asked Questions** Generation." *Advances in Artificial Intelligence: 28th Canadian Conference on Artificial Intelligence, Canadian AI 2015, Halifax, Nova Scotia, Canada, June 2–5, 2015, Proceedings.* Edited by Denilson Barbosa and Evangelos Milios. Cham: Springer, 2015.

Rabelais, Francois. *Gargantua and Pantagruel.* Translated by M. A. Screech. Cambridge: Penguin, 2006.

Randall, Marilyn. *Pragmatic Plagiarism: Authorship, Profit, and Power.* Toronto: University of Toronto Press, 2001.

Rankin, Ian. *A **Question** of Blood.* Boston: Little, Brown and Company, 2003.

———. *Dead Souls.* London: Orion, 2011.

Real World Physics Problems. "Physics **Questions.**" 2016. www.real-world-physics-problems.com.

Redekop, Corey. "Moot." *The Exile Book of New Canadian Noir.* Holstein, ON: Exile Editions, 2015, 9–36.

Rees, David. "About." *Artisanal Pencil Sharpening.* www.artisanalpencilsharpening.com/about.html.

Reeves, Sam. "Invisible **Questions**: Creating Narrative Flow." *Forward Motion for Writers,* 2003. http://fmwriters.com.

Renga, Dana. *Unfinished Business: Screening the Italian Mafia in the New Millennium.* Toronto: University of Toronto Press, 2013.

Rentoul, John. "The Top Ten: **Questions** to Which the Answer Is 'No'." *The Independent,* 1 September 2013.

Reverso Context. *Consider The Following Question,* 2013-2020. http://context.reverso.net.

Ribay, Randy. *Patron Saints of Nothing.* New York: Penguin, 2019.

Rich, Jason R. *Design and Launch an Online E-Commerce Business in a Week.* Irvine, CA: Entrepreneur Press, 2008.

Richard J. Lipton. *The P=NP **Question** and Gödel's Lost Letter.* New York: Springer Science & Business Media, 2010.

Richmond, Lewis. *Work as a Spiritual Practice: A Practical Buddhist Approach to Inner Growth and Satisfaction on the Job.* New York: Broadway Books, 1999.

Ridley, Annie E. *Under the Waves: or, The Hermit-Crab "in Society".* London: Sampson Low, Son, and Marston, 1865.

Riis, Søren. *Unframing Martin Heidegger's Understanding of Technology: on the Essential Connection Between Technology, Art, and History.* Translated by Rebecca Walsh. Lanham, MD: Lexington Books, 2018.

Ríos, Alberto. "Mason Jars by the Window." *The Lime Orchard Woman.* Bronx, NY: Sheep Meadow Press, 1988.

Ritchie, Donald A. *Doing Oral History.* Oxford: Oxford University Press, 2014.

Robert, Henry M. *Robert's Rules of Order Revised for Deliberative Assemblies.* Chicago: Scott, Foresman, 1915.

Robert, Stéphane. "Interrogation in Wolof: Two Strategies and a Puzzle for Wh-**Question** Words." *Open Archive HAL,* 2013. https://hal.archives-ouvertes.fr/.

Robespierre, Maximilien Marie Isidore. "Against Granting the King a Trial." 1792. *The World's Famous Orations.* Edited by William Jennings Bryan. New York: Funk and Wagnalls Company, 1906.

Robinson, E. Arthur, and Daniel H. Ullman. *The Mathematics of Politics.* Boca Raton: CRC Press, 2016.

Roosevelt, Theodore. *A Book-Lover's Holidays in the Open.* New York: Charles Scribner's Sons, 1916.

Rosenkrantz, Linda. *Talk.* New York: New York Review Books, 2015.

Rosenstock-Huessy, Eugen. *Greek Philosophy (1956): Lectures 14–20.* Dartmouth College, 1997.

Rosenthal, Richard S. *The Rosenthal Method of Practical Linguistry: The French Language.* Chicago: Polyglot Book Co., 1893.

Rosin, Hanna. *The End of Men: And the Rise of Women.* New York: Riverhead Books, 2012.

Roth, Philip. *American Pastoral.* Houghton Mifflin Harcourt, 1997.

———. *Portnoy's Complaint.* New York: Knopf Doubleday, 2011.

Rous, Emma. *The Au Pair.* New York: Berkley/Penguin Random House, 2019.

Rousseau, Jean-Jacques. *On the Inequality among Mankind.* The Harvard Classics, Vol. XXXIV, Part 3. Edited by Charles W. Eliot. New York: P. F. Collier & Son, 1909–14.

Rudd, Sayer. *The Negative on That Queſtion: Whether Is the Archangel Michael Our Saviour? Examined and Defended. An Argument Deſigned to Prove the Real Humanity of Chriſt. To Which Are Annex'd the Doctrine of Thoſe Appearances Under the Old Testament, Which Are Generally Term'd Angelical: Together With a Full Interpretation of Such Narratives as Are Particularly Refer'd to by the Author of the Eſſay on Spirit, in a Letter to the Right Reverend the Lord Biſhop of Chloger.* London: S. Birt, 1753.

Rudman, Mark. "The Secretary of Liquor (John F. Kennedy's Informal Appointment of Dean Martin to His Cabinet)." *The Couple.* Wesleyan University Press, 2002.

———. "Tomahawk." *Provoked in Venice.* Wesleyan University Press, 1999.

Rushton, William. "Fainting and Tooth-Extraction." *The Dental Digest: A Monthly Summary of Dental Science Devoted to the Progress of Dentistry, Volume III.* Chicago, IL: J. N. Crouse, 1897, 488–89.

Russell, Kenneth, and Philip J. Carter. *The Times Book of IQ Tests, Book 4: 400 Brand New **Questions** Never Before Published.* London: Kogan Page Publishers, 2004.

Sainsbury, R. M. *Paradoxes.* Cambridge, UK: Cambridge University Press, 1995.

Sainte-Beuve, Charles Augustin. "What Is a Classic?" *Literary and Philosophical Essays. The Harvard Classics, Vol. XXXII.* Edited by Charles W. Eliot. New York: P. F. Collier & Son, 1909–14.

Salutin, Rick. "Three Memorable Election Moments —and One Fear." *Toronto Star,* Oct. 16, 2015. www.thestar.com.

Sandburg, Carl. "**Questionnaire**." *Cornhuskers.* Henry Holt and Company, 1918.

Sant, Joseph. "Mendel, Darwin and Evolution." *Scientus.org,* 2017. http://www.scientus.org.

Saunders, George. "Trump Days." *The New Yorker,* July 11 & 17, 2016, 50–61.

Schama, Simon. *Dead Certainties (Unwarranted Speculations).* New York: Vintage Books, 1992.

Scheld, Suzanne. "Racism, 'Free-Trade' and Consumer 'Protection': The Controversy of Chinese Petty-Traders in Dakar, Senegal." *Dimensions of International Migration.* Edited by Paivi Hoikkala and Dorothy D. Wills. Newcastle upon Tyne, UK: Cambridge Scholars Publishing, 2011, 45–64.

Schmucker, S. S. *American Lutheranism Vindicated; or, Examination of the Lutheran Symbols, on Certain Disputed Topics: Including a Reply to the Plea of Rev. W. J. Mann.* Baltimore: T. Newton Kurtz, 1856.

Schopenhauer, Arthur. "On Suicide." *Studies in Pessimism: A Series of Essays.* Translated by T. Bailey Saunders. London: S. Sonnenschein, 1893.

———. *The Wisdom of Life: Being the First Part of Arthur Schopenhauer's Aphorismen Zur Lebensweisheit.* Translated by T. Bailey Saunders. London: S. Sonnenschein, 1890.

Schroeder, Donald J., and Frank A. Lombardo. *Police Officer Exam.* Barron's Educational Series, 2009.

Schuman, Howard, and Stanley Presser. ***Questions** and Answers in Attitude Surveys: Experiments on **Question** Form, Wording, and Context.* SAGE, 1996.

Scrivner, Eric. "Technological Criticism: Heidegger and Enframing." *Desearch and Revelopment,* 2014. https://etscrivner.github.io.

Scruton, Roger. "Universities' War Against Truth." *The Spectator,* 11 June 2016. www.spectator.co.uk.

Seal, David S. *Get the Job! The Fast Guide to Answering Tough **Questions** on Job Interviews.* Victoria, BC: Trafford Publishing, 2005.

Sedivy, Julie, and Greg Carlson. *Sold on Language: How Advertisers Talk to You and What This Says About You.* Oxford: Wiley-Blackwell, 2011.

Seinfeld, Jerry. "Jerry Seinfeld Loves Answering **Questions**! The Dumber, the Better. NOW." *Interviewly,* 2014. http://interviewly.com.

Sexton, Anne. "Hurry Up Please It's Time." *The Death

Notebooks. New York: Houghton Mifflin, 1974, 118.

Seymour, Laura. *An Analysis of Roland Barthes's The Death of the Author.* London: Macat Library, 2018.

Shafizadeh, Nafis. "Movie, Concert, or Act of Vandalism?" *Los Angeles Review of Books,* July 11th, 2015. http://lareviewofbooks.org.

Shakespeare, William. "Hamlet." *Spark Notes: No Fear Translation.* www.sparknotes.com/nofear/shakespeare/hamlet/.

———. *The Plays of William Shakespeare, Volume the Nineteenth, Containing Timon of Athens, Othello: With the Corrections and Illustrations of Various Commentators.* London: J. Plymsell, 1803.

———. *The Tragedie of Hamlet, Prince of Denmarke.* Folio I, 1623. Edited by David Bevington. Internet Shakespeare Editions, 2019. https://internetshakespeare.uvic.ca.

———. *The Tragedy of Macbeth.* The Harvard Classics, Vol. XLVI, Part 4. Edited by Charles W. Eliot. New York: P. F. Collier & Son, 1909–14.

———. *The Works of Mr. William Shakeſpear, in Six Volumes, Adorn'd With Cuts, Volume the Fifth, Containing Romeo and Juliet, Timon of Athens, Julius Caeſar, Macbeth, Hamlet, Prince of Denmark, King Lear, Othello.* Jacob Tonson, 1709.

Shapiro, Beth. *How to Clone a Mammoth: The Science of De-Extinction.* Princeton, NJ: Princeton University Press, 2016.

Shapiro, Emily. "The History Behind the Donald Trump 'Small Hands' Insult." *ABC News,* March 4, 2016. https://abcnews.go.com.

Sharkey, William F. "Why Would Anyone Want to Intentionally Embarrass Me?" *Aversive Interpersonal Behaviors.* Edited by Robin M. Kowalski. Plenum Press, 1997, 57–91.

Shaw, Frederick. *A Full and Impartial Report of the Important Debate in the House of Commons on Mr. Fox Maule's Motion Regarding the Church of Scotland, on the Evenings of Tuesday and Wednesday, the 7th and 8th March, 1843.* Edinburgh: Edinburgh Printing and Publishing Company, 1843.

Sheckels, Theodore F. *The Political in Margaret Atwood's Fiction: The Writing on the Wall of the Tent.* Ashgate Publishing, 2012.

Sheckley, Robert. "Ask a Foolish **Question**." *Science Fiction Stories,* 1953.

Shelley, Mary Wollstonecraft. *Frankenstein; or, The Modern Prometheus.* London: Lackington, Hughes, Harding, Mayor, & Jones, 1818.

Shmoop.com. "Inside Out (2015): Tools of Characterization." 2019. www.shmoop.com.

Siegel, Danny. *Tzedakah: A Time for Change.* New York: United Synagogue of Conservative Judaism, 2007.

Silliman, Ron. *Sunset Debris.* Ubu Editions, 2002. www.ubu.com.

Silver, Murray M. *This Bo Peep Ain't No Fairy Tale.* AuthorHouse, 2001.

Silverman, Jonathan, and Dean Rader. *The World Is a Text: Writing About Visual and Popular Culture.* Boston: Prentice Hall, 2012.

Silverman, Lisa. *Tortured Subjects: Pain, Truth, and the Body in Early Modern France.* Chicago: University of Chicago Press, 2010.

Silverman, Rabbi Noam. "Avoiding 'Excellent Sheep' in Jewish Day Schools." *EJewish Philanthropy,* Feb. 10, 2015. http://ejewishphilanthropy.com.

Simenon, Georges. *A Crime in Holland.* 1931. Translated by Siân Reynolds. London: Penguin, 2014.

sinoadvantage.com. *Forums › Test Forum › Scream Is Better Than a Thesis – 162821.* www.sinovantage.com.

Small, David. *Almost Famous.* iUniverse, 2000.

Smekens Education Solutions. "Improve Constructed Responses with the Invisible **Questions** Strategy." *smekenseducation.com,* May 20, 2008. www.smekenseducation.com.

Smiley, Jane. *Moo.* 1995. New York: Anchor Books, 2009.

Smith, Ali. "Introduction." *Super-Cannes.* London: Fourth Estate, 2014, viii–xii.

Smith, Martin Cruz. *Gorky Park.* 1981. London: Pan Books, 2007.

Smith, Patrick L. "Thomas Friedman, Read Your Chomsky: The New York Times Gets Putin/Obama All Wrong, Again." *Salon,* October 6, 2015. www.salon.com.

Smith, Zadie. *White Teeth.* New York: Knopf Doubleday, 2003.

Snow, C. P. *The Masters.* 1951. London: House of Stratus, 2000.

Soh, Debra W. "A Peek Inside a Furry Convention." *Archives of Sexual Behavior,* January 2015. Reprinted in *Harper's Magazine,* March 2015, p 21.

Solski, Ruth. *Les majuscules et la ponctuation/Capitalization & Punctuation.* Napanee, ON: S&S Learning Materials, 2006.

Sontag, Susan. "Against Interpretation." *Against Interpretation and Other Essays.* New York: Farrar Straus & Giroux, 1966, 3–14.

———. "On Style." *Against Interpretation and Other Essays.* New York: Farrar Straus & Giroux, 1966, 15–36.

———. "The Aesthetics of Silence." *Styles of Radical Will.* New York: Farrar Straus & Giroux, 1969.

———. *Regarding the Pain of Others.* New York: Picador, 2003.

Southey, Tabatha. "Kory Teneycke and Me—**Questions** for a Reluctant Tory Campaign Spokesman." *The Globe and Mail,* July 3, 2015. www.theglobeandmail.com.

Sortes Astrampsychi. "The Oracles of Astrampsychus." http://sortesastrampsychi.voila.net/

Spinoza, Benedict de. *Ethics, Part 2.* Translated by R. H. M. Elwes. Project Gutenberg, 1997. www.gutenberg.org.

Spiotta, Dana. *Stone Arabia.* New York: Scribner, 2011.

Sprague, Edwin J. *The Point Guard.* iUniverse, 2007.

Starkie, Thomas. *A Practical Treatise of the Law of Evidence.* Philadelphia: T. & J.W. Johnson, 1860.

State of New York Department of Agriculture. *Twentieth Annual Report for the Year Ending September 30, 1912, Part II.* Albany: J. B. Lyon Company, 1913.

Stein, Gail, and Mary Kraynak. *Spanish Essentials for Dummies.* Hoboken, NJ: John Wiley & Sons, 2010.

Stein, Gail. *Intermediate Spanish for Dummies.* Hoboken, NJ: John Wiley & Sons, 2010.

Stein, Gertrude. "Idem the Same: A Valentine to Sherwood Anderson." *A Stein Reader.* Northwestern University Press, 1993.

———. "Tender Buttons." 1914. *Selected Writings of Gertrude Stein.* New York: Vintage, 1990, 459–509.

———. *Geography and Plays.* 2010. Boston: Four Seas Press, 1922.

———. *The Autobiography of Alice B. Toklas.* 1933. New York: Vintage, 1961.

Stephens, Paul. "Stars in My Pocket Like Bits of Data." *Guernica.* July 15, 2015. www.guernicamag.com.

Sterne, Laurence. *The Life and Opinions of Tristram Shandy, Gentleman.* New York: J. M. Dent & Sons, 1912.

Steven Connor. *Dumbstruck: A Cultural History of Ventriloquism.* Oxford: Oxford University Press, 2000.

Steward, James B. "A Fight at the Opera." *The New Yorker,* March 23, 2015, 56–67.

Stone, Christopher D. *Should Trees Have Standing? Law, Morality, and the Environment.* Oxford: Oxford University Press, 2010.

Stone, Ruth. "The **Question**." *Simplicity.* Paris Press, 1995.

Strzalkowski, Tomek, and Sanda Harabagiu. *Advances in Open Domain **Question** Answering.* Springer Science & Business Media, 2006.

Sukur, Silvester Goridus. *Embarrassing Stories—A Blue Film (Completed With Grammatical Notes).* Jakarta: Grasindo, 2009.

Sukur, Silvester Goridus. *Embarrassing Stories—One Night With a Maid (Completed With Grammatical Notes).* Jakarta: Grasindo, 2009.

———. *Embarrassing Stories: My Wife's Twin Sister (Completed with Grammatical Notes).* Yogyakarta: Penerbit Kanisius.

Sullivan, John Jeremiah. "Donald Antrim and the Art of Anxiety." *The New York Times Magazine,* Sept. 17, 2014. www.nytimes.com.

Sullivan, Rory. "Greta Thunberg Mocks Climate Change Deniers by Citing 'Penis Shrinking' Research." *The Independent,* 26 March 2021. www.independent.co.uk.

Sumner, Charles. "On the Crime Against Kansas." 1856. *The World's Famous Orations.* Edited by William Jennings Bryan. New York: Funk and Wagnalls Company, 1906.

sunnyw. "Bonus **Questions** in Quizzes." *Canvas/Help Center/Canvas Community/Feature Discussion Categories/Assignments, Quizzes, & Syllabus,* March 7, 2011. https://help.instructure.com.

Superchunk. "The **Question** Is How Fast." *On the Mouth.* Matador, 1993.

Super User. "How to Google a **Question** Mark?" Oct. 7, 2009. http://superuser.com.

Supreme Court of the State of New York Appellate Division First Department. *David Morgan Hildreth, Junior, and Walter E. Hildreth, as Executors of and Trustees Under the Last Will and Testament of David M. Hildreth, Deceased, and Annie L. Hildreth, as Executrix Under Said Will, Plaintiff's Respondents, Against Charles Allen Hildreth, Defendant-Appellant, Record on Appeal.* New York: Appeal Printing, 1901.

Swift, Jonathan. *Gulliver's Travels Into Several Remote Regions of the World.* Edited by Thomas M. Balliet. Boston: D. C. Heath & Co., 1900.

Tabet, Paola. "Natural Fertility, Forced Reproduction." *Sex in **Question**: French Materialist Feminism.* Edited by Diana Leonard and Lisa Adkins. London: Taylor & Francis, 111–82.

talk.origins.newsgroup. "The Quote Mine Project, or, Lies, Damned Lies and Quote Mines: Darwin Quotes." *The TalkOrigins Archive,* 2004–2006. www.talkorigins.org.

Taylor, Justin. "Frame: **Questions** to Ask of a Film." *The Gospel Coalition,* May 27, 2009. www.thegospelcoalition.org.

Television Tropes & Idioms. http://tvtropes.org/.

Terijo. "I Think You Already Know the Answer to This **Question** . . . But?" *Medium,* Sep 17, 2017. https://medium.com/.

Terman, Robbie. *Some Like It Spicy: A Perfect Recipe Novel.* Fort Collins, CO: Entangled Publishing, 2013.

Testizen. "Where the GRE Came From?" *Medium,* Feb 1, 2019. https://medium.com.

*The Child's Scripture History, Forming a Complete and Perfect Analysis of the Holy Scriptures in **Question** and Answer.* London: Houlston and Wright, 1863.

Thomas, Jeffrey. *Everybody Scream! A Punktown Novel.* Hyattsville, MD: Raw Dog Screaming Press, 2005.

Thomas, Ross. *No **Questions** Asked.* New York: Morrow, 1976.

———. *The Fools in Town Are on Our Side.* 1970. New York: Thomas Dunne, 2003.

Thompson, Chris. *Felt: Fluxus, Joseph Beuys, and the Dalai Lama.* U of Minnesota Press, 2011.

Thompson, Kevin A. "37 **Questions** (and Answers) from the Book of Job." *kevinathompson.com,* Nov 24, 2013. www.kevinathompson.com.

Thorpe, Adam. "Introduction." *Madame Bovary, by Gustave Flaubert.* Translated by Adam Thorpe. Random House Publishing Group, 2013, 457.

Thucydides. *The History of the Peloponnesian War.* 431 B.C.E. Translated by Richard Crawley. *The Internet Classics Archive,* 1994-2009. http://classics.mit.edu.

Tifft, Meghan. "An Introverted Writer's Lament." *The Atlantic,* August 2, 2015. www.theatlantic.com.

Titchkosky, Tanya. *The **Question** of Access: Disability, Space, Meaning.* Toronto: University of Toronto Press, 2011.

TMZ. "Penises Shrinkage Caused by Pollution . . . So Claims Scientist." *TMZ,* 24 March 2021. www.tmz.com.

Tolstoy, Leo. *War and Peace.* Translated by Louise and Aylmer Maude. New York: Simon and Schuster, 1942.

Torrence, Harold. *The Clause Structure of Wolof: Insights Into the Left Periphery.* Amsterdam: John Benjamins Publishing, 2013.

Torres, Yaiza Cabrera. *When You Embarrass the Devil.* Translated by Marta Cabrera. Yaiza Cabrera Torres, 2014.

Treisman, Deborah, "This Week in Fiction: Will Mackin." *The New Yorker,* March 3, 2013. www.newyorker.com.

Turgenev, Ivan. *Fathers and Sons.* Translated by Rosemary Edmonds. Harmondsworth: Penguin, 1965.

U.S. Department of Labor, Employment and Training Administration. *Manual for USES Clerical Skills Tests: Administration, Scoring, and Interpretation.* Washington: U.S. Government Print Office, 1976.

U.S. Office of Personnel Management. *Background Information and Sample **Questions** for the Examination for Careers in Personnel, Administration, and Computer Occupations.* Washington: 1990.

Unexplained-Mysteries.com. "Forums > Unexplained Mysteries > Spirituality vs Skepticism > Church Apologises to Charles Darwin." November 25, 2008. www.unexplained-mysteries.com.

United States Congress House Committee on Military Affairs. *Army Reorganization: Hearings Before the Committee on Military Affairs, House of Representatives, Sixty-sixth Congress, First and Second Sessions, on H.R. 8287, a Bill to Reorganize and Increase the Efficiency of the United States Army, and for Other Purposes, H.R. 8068, a Bill to Provide for Universal Military, Naval and Vocational Training, and for Mobilization of the Manhood of the Nation in a National Emergency, H.R. 7925, a Bill to Establish the Department of Aeronautics, and for Other Purposes, H.R. 8870, a Bill to Amend an Act Entitled "An Act for Making Further and More Effectual Provision for the National Defense, and for Other Purposes." From Sepember 29, 1919 to February 5, 1920, Volume 1; Volume 3.* U.S. Government Print Office, 1919.

United States Congress House of Representatives. *Hearings on H.R. 2603, H.R. 2784, H.R. 2912, and H.R. 3364*

Before the Seapower and Strategic and Critical Materials Subcommittee of the Committee on Armed Services, Ninety-Seventh Congress, First Session, June 2 and 4, 1981. Washington: United States Government Printing Office, 1981.

United States Congress Senate Committee on the Judiciary. *Subversive Influence in the Educational Process: Hearings Before the Subcommittee to Investigate the Administration of the Internal Security Act and Other Internal Security Laws*. Washington: U.S. Government Printing Office, 1952.

United States Congress. *Establishing Rules of Interpretation Governing **Questions** of the Effect of Acts of Congress on State Laws, Part 1*. Washington: U.S. Government Printing Office, 1955.

————. *The Miscellaneous Documents of the House of Representatives, Printed During the First Session of the Thirty-Ninth Congress, 1865–'66, in Three Volumes*. Washington: United States Government Printing Office, 1866.

United States Food and Drug Administration. *A Legislative History of the Federal Food, Drug, and Cosmetic Act and Its Amendments, Appendix G*. Washington: US Government Printing Office, 1979.

United States House of Representatives. "House Rules and Manual." *Budget Counsel Reference*. https://budget-counsel.com.

United States Senate Committee on Commerce. *To Improve and Clarify Certain Laws Affecting the Coast Guard: Hearing Before the Merchant Marine Subcommittee of the Committee on Commerce, United States Senate, Ninety-First Congress, Second Session, on S. 3080, S. 3081, H.R. 13716, and H.R. 13816*. Washington: United States Government Printing Office, 1970.

United States Senate Committee on Immigration. *To Clarify the Law Relating to the Temporary Admission of Aliens to the United States: Hearing Before a Subcommittee of the Committee on Immigration, United States Senate, Seventieth Congress, Second Session, on H.R. 16927, an Act to Clarify the Law Relating to the Temporary Admission of Aliens to the United States*. Washington: United States Government Printing Office, 1929.

United States Senate Committee on Labor and Public Welfare. *To Clarify the Overtime Compensation Provisions of the Fair Labor Standards Act of 1938, As Amended: Hearings Before a Subcommittee of the Committee on Labor and Public Welfare, United States Senate, Eighty-First Congress, First Session, on S. 336 and H. R. 858, To Clarify the Overtime Compensation Provisions of the Fair Labor Standards Act of 1938, as Amended, as Applied in the Stevedoring and Building Construction Industries, and for Other Purposes*. Washington: United States Government Printing Office, 1949.

United States Senate. "Reports of Committees for the First Session of the Fifty-First Congress, 1889–90, Volume 10, No. 1530, parts 1 and 2, Relations with Canada." Washington: Government Printing Office, 1890.

————. *Reports of Committees for the Second Session of the Forty-Second Congress, 1871–'72*. Washington: Government Printing Office, 1872.

————. *Reports of Committees for the Third Session of the Thirty-Seventh Congress*. Washington: United States Government Printing Office, 1863.

University of Toronto Libraries. "Copyright Basics and **FAQ**." 2016. https://onesearch.library.utoronto.ca.

Vachss, Andrew. *Mask Market: A Burke Novel*. New York: Vintage Books, 2007.

van Bakel, Rogier. "Remembering Johnny: William Gibson on the Making of Johnny Mnemonic." *Wired*, June 1,1995. www.wired.com/1995/06/gibson-4/.

Vandor, Lehel . *Ears*. Booktango, 2014.

Vane, Sir Henry. *A Healing **Question***. 1656. The Harvard Classics, Vol. XLIII. Edited by Charles W. Eliot. New York: P.F. Collier & Son, 1909–14.

Vatsyayana. *The Kama Sutra*. Translated by Richard Burton, Bhagavanlal Indrajit, and Shivaram Parashuram Bhide. London: Kama Shastra Society, 1883.

Vincent, Leona. *A Study of Intelligence Test Elements*. New York: Teachers College, Columbia University, 1924.

Viviano, Frank. "Why Shroud of Turin's Secrets Continue to Elude Science." *National Geographic*, April 17, 2015. http://news.nationalgeographic.com.

Vogell, Heather. "Errors Plague Testing, Hurt Students in Public Schools." *MSN News*, September 28, 2013. http://news.msn.com.

Voltaire. "A Philosophical Dictionary." Translated by William F. Fleming. *The Works of Voltaire: A Contemporary Version*. Edited by John Morley. New York: 2007.

————. "Zadig the Babylonian." *Library of the World's Best Mystery and Detective Stories*. New York: The Review of Reviews Company, 1907.

————. *Candide*. Translated by Philip Littell. New York: Boni & Liveright, 1918.

Vonnegut, Kurt. *Slaughterhouse-Five, or, The Children's Crusade: A Duty-Dance With Death*. New York, N.Y.: Dell Publishing, 1991.

Vozza, Stephanie. "How To Successfully Respond To a **Question** You Really Don't Want to Answer." *Fast Company*, October 28, 2016. www.fastcompany.com.

Waadeland, Haakon, and Lisa Lorentzen. *Continued **Questions**, Volume 1: Convergence Theory*. Amsterdam: Atlantis Press, 2008.

Waite, Arthur Edward. *DEvil-Worship in France; or, The **Question** of Lucifer; A Record of Things Seen and Heard in the Secret Societies According to the Evidence of Initiates*. London: G. Redway, 1896.

Wallach, Ira. *The Absence of a Cello*. New York: Avon Books, 1960.

Wampole, Christy. "The Conference Manifesto." *The New York Times*, May 4, 2015. http://opinionator.blogs.nytimes.com.

Warner, Marina. "Learning My Lesson." *London Review of Books*, March 2015, 8–14. www.lrb.co.uk.

Warrior Forum. "How to Search Google for Pages That Has the ? Sign (**Question** Mark) in Their Title Tag?" *Warrior Forum, The #1 Internet Marketing Forum & Marketplace*, 26th December 2012. www.warriorforum.com/main-internet-marketing-discussion-forum.

Wartman, Kristin. "Pizza Is a Vegetable? Congress Defies Logic, Betrays Our Children." *Huffington Post*, 18 November 2011. www.huffingtonpost.com.

Watson, Dana Cairns. *Gertrude Stein and the Essence of What Happens*. Nashville, TN: Vanderbilt University Press, 2005.

Watson, David. *The **Question** of Morale: Managing Happiness and Unhappiness in University Life*. Maidenhead, UK: Open University Press, 2009.

Webster, John. *The Duchess of Malfi*. The Harvard Classics, Vol. XLVII, Part 4. Edited by Charles W. Eliot. New York: P. F. Collier & Son, 1909–14.

Wehling, Eike, Astri J. Lundervold, and Steven Nordin. "Does it Matter How We Pose the **Question** 'How is Your Sense of Smell?'." *Chemosensory Perception* 7.3–4 (December 2014): 103–7.

Wells, H. G. *The Invisible Man: A Grotesque Romance.* 1897. Project Gutenberg, 2004. www.gutenberg.org/ebooks/5230.

Wells, Paul. "Calandra: So That Happened." *Maclean's,* September 26, 2014. www.macleans.ca.

Wherry, Aaron. "Our Duffy, Ourselves." *Maclean's,* April 12, 2015. www.macleans.ca.

———. "Today in Demonstrating Contempt for Parliament." *Maclean's,* September 23, 2014. www.macleans.ca.

White, Morton. *The **Question** of Free Will: A Holistic View.* Princeton: Princeton University Press, 1993.

Whitman, Walt. "Democratic Vistas." *Prose Works.* Philadelphia: David McKay, 1892.

———. *Leaves of Grass.* Project Gutenberg, 1998. www.gutenberg.org.

Wiggins, Todd. *Zeitgeist.* New York: Henry Holt and Company, 1996.

Wikipedia. "Who's on First." July 17, 2016. https://en.wikipedia.org.

Wilde, Jean T., and William Kluback. "Introduction." *The **Question** of Being,* by Heidegger, Martin. Rowman & Littlefield, 1958.

Wilkinson, Alec. "The Pursuit of Beauty." *The New Yorker,* February 2, 2015. www.newyorker.com.

Wilson, Duff, and Janet Roberts. "Special Report: How Washington Went Soft on Childhood Obesity." *Reuters,* April 27, 2012.

Wilson, Jane. "Trinity + 25 Years: Prologue." *Bulletin of the Atomic Scientists,* Volume XXVI, Number 6, June 1970, 2–3.

Wilson, S. G. "From Jesus to Paul: The Contours and Consequences of a Debate." *From Jesus to Paul: Studies in Honour of Francis Wright Beare.* Edited by Peter Richardson and John C. Hurd. Waterloo, ON: Wilfrid Laurier University Press, 2006, 1–22.

Wilson, Woodrow. "The President on His Foreign Policy." *The World's Work War Series: The Kaiser in His Own Words.* Edited by Arthur W. Page. Garden City, NY: Doubleday, Page & Company, 1914, 485–94.

Winston-Macauley, Marnie. "Jews Love **Questions**: To Be or Not to Be? You Call That a Good **Question**?" *Aish.com,* Mar 5, 2011. www.aish.com.

Wisconsin State Legislature. *The Blue Book of the State of Wisconsin.* Wisconsin State Printing Board, 1899.

Wittgenstein, Ludwig. *Tractatus Logico-Philosophicus.* 1922. Translated by C. K. Ogden. New York: Routledge & Kegan Paul, 1988.

Wolfe, Tom. *The Bonfire of the Vanities.* New York: Macmillan, 2002.

Wolof Resources. "Wolof Grammar Manual." http://wolofresources.org.

Woodcock, George. *The Crystal Spirit: a Study of George Orwell.* Boston: Little Brown, 1966.

Woodford, Riley. "Lemming Suicide Myth: Disney Film Faked Bogus Behavior." *Alaska Fish & Wildlife News,* September 2003. www.adfg.alaska.gov.

Worldwatch Institute. "**Questions** and Answers about Global Warming and Abrupt Climate Change." *worldwatch.org,* 2013. www.worldwatch.org.

Wren, Jacob. *Polyamorous Love Song.* Toronto: BookThug, 2014.

Wyatt, Jonathan. *Therapy, Stand-Up, and the Gesture of Writing: Towards Creative-Relational Inquiry.* New York: Routledge, 2018.

Wynne, George Robert. *Overton's **Question**.* London: S.W. Partridge, 1865.

Yan, Holly. "Trump Draws Outrage After Megyn Kelly Remarks." *CNN,* August 8, 2015. www.cnn.com.

Yerkovich, Milan, and Kay Yerkovich. *How We Love: Discover Your Love Style, Enhance Your Marriage.* Colorado Springs: WaterBrook Press, 2017.

York, Lorraine Mary. *Margaret Atwood and the Labour of Literary Celebrity.* Toronto: University of Toronto Press, 2013.

Zambra, Alejandro. "Reading Comprehension: Text No. 1." *The New Yorker,* July 6 & 13, 2015. www.newyorker.com.

Zerubavel, Eviatar. *The Elephant in the Room: Silence and Denial in Everyday Life.* Oxford: Oxford University Press, 2006.

Zhang, Wei Emma, and Quan Z. Sheng. *Managing Data From Knowledge Bases: Querying and Extraction.* Cham: Springer, 2018.

Zink, Nell. *The Wallcreeper.* St. Louis, MO: Dorothy, 2014.

Zucker, Rachel. "Hey Allen Ginsberg Where Have You Gone and What Would You Think of My Drugs?" *Museum of Accidents.* Seattle: Wave Books, 2009.

Zullo, Holly, Kathy Gniadek, Derek Bruff, and Kelly Cline. "Student Surveys: What Do They Think?" *Teaching Mathematics with Classroom Voting: With and Without Clickers.* Edited by Kelly Cline and Holly Zullo. Mathematical Association of America, 2011.

Zuylen, Marina Van. *Monomania: The Flight from Everyday Life in Literature and Art.* Ithaca, NY: Cornell University Press, 2005.

The Sydney premiere of the rom com *Any **Questions** For Ben?*
Left to right: Liliya May, Felicity Ward, Daniel Henshall, Rachael
Taylor, Josh Lawson, Christian Clark, Jodi Gordon

Photo by Eva Rinaldi (flickr.com/evarinaldiphotography)

Other Questions

With Evie and Jessie?

Miri asked Kaia Bennett:

Hi, is 'Die By The Drop' going to be continued in Volume 2? With Evie and Jessie? Or will Volume 2 feature a completely new and different cast of characters? Thanks!

*Goodreads.com, **Questions**>Hi, Is 'Die By The Drop' Going to Be . . .—Kaia Bennett Q&A*

General notions for the immediate transition to the study of the motion of the three kinds of continuous systems

186. When studying a continuous system in motion, manifestly two kinds of **questions** arise: some of them regard the disposition of all its parts in a position whatsoever among the infinite positions which it occupies during the motion; other **questions** concern the positions in space of one of its points whatsoever observed during all the movement without

You have either reached a page that is unavailable for viewing or reached your viewing limit for this book.

Francesco dell'Isola, Ugo Andreaus, Raffaele Esposito Antonio Cazzani, Luca Placidi, Umberto Perego, Giulio Maier and Pierre Seppecher, The Complete Works of Gabrio Piola, Volume II: Commented English Translation

My epistemological quest to find out why the slaves were represented as happy became a lifelong journey that continues. The closer I think I am to the answer, the more difficult and complex my **question** and the answers become.

Héfer Bembenutty, Contemporary Pioneers in Teaching and Learning, Volume 2

The underlined terms coincide with terms in the power series for $Ln(1+z)$. Observe that the agreement increases with the order of the approximants. It can be proved (and it will be proved in volume 2) that this continues.

*Haakon Waadeland and Lisa Lorentzen, Continued **Questions**, Volume 1: Convergence Theory*